The Harriet Beecher Stowe Collection

By

Harriet Beecher Stowe

Cover Photograph: Erik Söderström

ISBN: 978-1-78139-529-5

Contents

UNCLE TOM'S CABIN

VOLUME I

VOLUME II

THE KEY TO UNCLE TOM'S CABIN

PART I

PART II

THE MINISTER'S WOOING.

THE PEARL OF ORR'S ISLAND

UNCLE TOM'S CABIN

OR

LIFE AMONG THE LOWLY

VOLUME I

CHAPTER I

IN WHICH THE READER IS INTRODUCED TO A MAN OF HUMANITY

Late in the afternoon of a chilly day in February, two gentlemen were sitting alone over their wine, in a well-furnished dining parlor, in the town of P——, in Kentucky. There were no servants present, and the gentlemen, with chairs closely approaching, seemed to be discussing some subject with great earnestness.

For convenience sake, we have said, hitherto, two *gentlemen*. One of the parties, however, when critically examined, did not seem, strictly speaking, to come under the species. He was a short, thick-set man, with coarse, commonplace features, and that swaggering air of pretension which marks a low man who is trying to elbow his way upward in the world. He was much over-dressed, in a gaudy vest of many colors, a blue neckerchief, bedropped gayly with yellow spots, and arranged with a flaunting tie, quite in keeping with the general air of the man. His hands, large and coarse, were plentifully bedecked with rings; and he wore a heavy gold watch-chain, with a bundle of seals of portentous size, and a great variety of colors, attached to it,—which, in the ardor of conversation, he was in the habit of flourishing and jingling with evident satisfaction. His conversation was in free and easy defiance of Murray's Grammar,[1] and was garnished at convenient intervals with various profane expressions, which not even the desire to be graphic in our account shall induce us to transcribe.

His companion, Mr. Shelby, had the appearance of a gentleman; and the arrangements of the house, and the general air of the housekeeping, indicated easy, and even opulent circumstances. As we before stated, the two were in the midst of an earnest conversation.

"That is the way I should arrange the matter," said Mr. Shelby.

"I can't make trade that way—I positively can't, Mr. Shelby," said the other, holding up a glass of wine between his eye and the light.

---

[1] English Grammar (1795), by Lindley Murray (1745-1826), the most authoritative American grammarian of his day.

"Why, the fact is, Haley, Tom is an uncommon fellow; he is certainly worth that sum anywhere,—steady, honest, capable, manages my whole farm like a clock."

"You mean honest, as niggers go," said Haley, helping himself to a glass of brandy.

"No; I mean, really, Tom is a good, steady, sensible, pious fellow. He got religion at a camp-meeting, four years ago; and I believe he really *did* get it. I've trusted him, since then, with everything I have,—money, house, horses,—and let him come and go round the country; and I always found him true and square in everything."

"Some folks don't believe there is pious niggers Shelby," said Haley, with a candid flourish of his hand, "but *I do*. I had a fellow, now, in this yer last lot I took to Orleans—'t was as good as a meetin, now, really, to hear that critter pray; and he was quite gentle and quiet like. He fetched me a good sum, too, for I bought him cheap of a man that was 'bliged to sell out; so I realized six hundred on him. Yes, I consider religion a valeyable thing in a nigger, when it's the genuine article, and no mistake."

"Well, Tom's got the real article, if ever a fellow had," rejoined the other. "Why, last fall, I let him go to Cincinnati alone, to do business for me, and bring home five hundred dollars. 'Tom,' says I to him, 'I trust you, because I think you're a Christian—I know you wouldn't cheat.' Tom comes back, sure enough; I knew he would. Some low fellows, they say, said to him—Tom, why don't you make tracks for Canada?' 'Ah, master trusted me, and I couldn't,'—they told me about it. I am sorry to part with Tom, I must say. You ought to let him cover the whole balance of the debt; and you would, Haley, if you had any conscience."

"Well, I've got just as much conscience as any man in business can afford to keep,—just a little, you know, to swear by, as 't were," said the trader, jocularly; "and, then, I'm ready to do anything in reason to 'blige friends; but this yer, you see, is a leetle too hard on a fellow—a leetle too hard." The trader sighed contemplatively, and poured out some more brandy.

"Well, then, Haley, how will you trade?" said Mr. Shelby, after an uneasy interval of silence.

"Well, haven't you a boy or gal that you could throw in with Tom?"

"Hum!—none that I could well spare; to tell the truth, it's only hard necessity makes me willing to sell at all. I don't like parting with any of my hands, that's a fact."

Here the door opened, and a small quadroon boy, between four and five years of age, entered the room. There was something in his appearance remarkably beautiful and engaging. His black hair, fine as floss silk, hung in glossy curls about his round, dimpled face, while a pair of large dark eyes, full of fire and softness, looked out from beneath the rich, long lashes, as he peered curiously into the apartment. A gay robe of scarlet and yellow plaid, carefully made and neatly fitted, set off to advantage the dark and rich style of his beauty; and a certain comic air of assurance, blended with bashfulness, showed that he had been not unused to being petted and noticed by his master.

"Hulloa, Jim Crow!" said Mr. Shelby, whistling, and snapping a bunch of raisins towards him, "pick that up, now!"

The child scampered, with all his little strength, after the prize, while his master laughed.

"Come here, Jim Crow," said he. The child came up, and the master patted the curly head, and chucked him under the chin.

"Now, Jim, show this gentleman how you can dance and sing." The boy commenced one of those wild, grotesque songs common among the negroes, in a rich, clear voice, accompanying his singing with many comic evolutions of the hands, feet, and whole body, all in perfect time to the music.

"Bravo!" said Haley, throwing him a quarter of an orange.

"Now, Jim, walk like old Uncle Cudjoe, when he has the rheumatism," said his master.

Instantly the flexible limbs of the child assumed the appearance of deformity and distortion, as, with his back humped up, and his master's stick in his hand, he hobbled about the room, his childish face drawn into a doleful pucker, and spitting from right to left, in imitation of an old man.

Both gentlemen laughed uproariously.

"Now, Jim," said his master, "show us how old Elder Robbins leads the psalm." The boy drew his chubby face down to a formidable length, and commenced toning a psalm tune through his nose, with imperturbable gravity.

"Hurrah! bravo! what a young 'un!" said Haley; "that chap's a case, I'll promise. Tell you what," said he, suddenly clapping his hand on Mr. Shelby's shoulder, "fling in that chap, and I'll settle the business—I will. Come, now, if that ain't doing the thing up about the rightest!"

At this moment, the door was pushed gently open, and a young quadroon woman, apparently about twenty-five, entered the room.

There needed only a glance from the child to her, to identify her as its mother. There was the same rich, full, dark eye, with its long lashes; the same ripples of silky black hair. The brown of her complexion gave way on the cheek to a perceptible flush, which deepened as she saw the gaze of the strange man fixed upon her in bold and undisguised admiration. Her dress was of the neatest possible fit, and set off to advantage her finely moulded shape;—a delicately formed hand and a trim foot and ankle were items of appearance that did not escape the quick eye of the trader, well used to run up at a glance the points of a fine female article.

"Well, Eliza?" said her master, as she stopped and looked hesitatingly at him.

"I was looking for Harry, please, sir;" and the boy bounded toward her, showing his spoils, which he had gathered in the skirt of his robe.

"Well, take him away then," said Mr. Shelby; and hastily she withdrew, carrying the child on her arm.

"By Jupiter," said the trader, turning to him in admiration, "there's an article, now! You might make your fortune on that ar gal in Orleans, any day. I've seen over a thousand, in my day, paid down for gals not a bit handsomer."

"I don't want to make my fortune on her," said Mr. Shelby, dryly; and, seeking to turn the conversation, he uncorked a bottle of fresh wine, and asked his companion's opinion of it.

"Capital, sir,—first chop!" said the trader; then turning, and slapping his hand familiarly on Shelby's shoulder, he added—

"Come, how will you trade about the gal?—what shall I say for her—what'll you take?"

"Mr. Haley, she is not to be sold," said Shelby. "My wife would not part with her for her weight in gold."

"Ay, ay! women always say such things, cause they ha'nt no sort of calculation. Just show 'em how many watches, feathers, and trinkets, one's weight in gold would buy, and that alters the case, *I* reckon."

"I tell you, Haley, this must not be spoken of; I say no, and I mean no," said Shelby, decidedly.

"Well, you'll let me have the boy, though," said the trader; "you must own I've come down pretty handsomely for him."

"What on earth can you want with the child?" said Shelby.

"Why, I've got a friend that's going into this yer branch of the business—wants to buy up handsome boys to raise for the market. Fancy articles entirely—sell for waiters, and so on, to rich 'uns, that can pay for handsome 'uns. It sets off one of yer great places—a real handsome boy to open door, wait, and tend. They fetch a good sum; and this little devil is such a comical, musical concern, he's just the article!'

"I would rather not sell him," said Mr. Shelby, thoughtfully; "the fact is, sir, I'm a humane man, and I hate to take the boy from his mother, sir."

"O, you do?—La! yes—something of that ar natur. I understand, perfectly. It is mighty onpleasant getting on with women, sometimes, I al'ays hates these yer screechin,' screamin' times. They are *mighty* onpleasant; but, as I manages business, I generally avoids 'em, sir. Now, what if you get the girl off for a day, or a week, or so; then the thing's done quietly,—all over before she comes home. Your wife might get her some ear-rings, or a new gown, or some such truck, to make up with her."

"I'm afraid not."

"Lor bless ye, yes! These critters ain't like white folks, you know; they gets over things, only manage right. Now, they say," said Haley, assuming a candid and confidential air, "that this kind o' trade is hardening to the feelings; but I never found it so. Fact is, I never could do things up the way some fellers manage the business. I've seen 'em as would pull a woman's child out of her arms, and set him up to sell, and she screechin' like mad all the time;—very bad policy—damages the article—makes 'em quite unfit for service sometimes. I knew a real handsome gal once, in Orleans, as was entirely ruined by this sort o' handling. The fellow that was trading for her didn't want her baby; and she was one of your real high sort, when her blood was up. I tell you, she squeezed up her child in her arms, and talked, and went on real awful. It kinder makes my blood run cold to think of 't; and when they carried off the child, and locked her up, she jest went ravin' mad, and died in a week. Clear waste, sir, of a thousand dollars, just for want of management,—there's where 't is. It's always best to do the humane thing, sir; that's been *my* experience." And the trader leaned back in his chair, and folded his arm, with an air of virtuous decision, apparently considering himself a second Wilberforce.

The subject appeared to interest the gentleman deeply; for while Mr. Shelby was thoughtfully peeling an orange, Haley broke out afresh, with becoming diffidence, but as if actually driven by the force of truth to say a few words more.

"It don't look well, now, for a feller to be praisin' himself; but I say it jest because it's the truth. I believe I'm reckoned to bring in about the finest droves of niggers that is brought in,—at least, I've been told so; if I have once, I reckon I have a hundred times,—all in good case,—fat and likely, and I lose as few as any man in the business. And I lays it all to my management, sir; and humanity, sir, I may say, is the great pillar of *my* management."

Mr. Shelby did not know what to say, and so he said, "Indeed!"

"Now, I've been laughed at for my notions, sir, and I've been talked to. They an't pop'lar, and they an't common; but I stuck to 'em, sir; I've stuck to 'em, and realized well on 'em; yes, sir, they have paid their passage, I may say," and the trader laughed at his joke.

There was something so piquant and original in these elucidations of humanity, that Mr. Shelby could not help laughing in company. Perhaps you laugh too, dear reader; but you know humanity comes out in a variety of strange forms now-a-days, and there is no end to the odd things that humane people will say and do.

Mr. Shelby's laugh encouraged the trader to proceed.

"It's strange, now, but I never could beat this into people's heads. Now, there was Tom Loker, my old partner, down in Natchez; he was a clever fellow, Tom was, only the very devil with niggers,—on principle 't was, you see, for a better hearted feller never broke bread; 't was his *system*, sir. I used to talk to Tom. 'Why, Tom,' I used to say, 'when your gals takes on and cry, what's the use o' crackin on' em over the head, and knockin' on 'em round? It's ridiculous,' says I, 'and don't do no sort o' good. Why, I don't see no harm in their cryin',' says I; 'it's natur,' says I, 'and if natur can't blow off one way, it will another. Besides, Tom,' says I, 'it jest spiles your gals; they get sickly, and down in the mouth; and sometimes they gets ugly,—particular yallow gals do,—and it's the devil and all gettin' on 'em broke in. Now,' says I, 'why can't you kinder coax 'em up, and speak 'em fair? Depend on it, Tom, a little humanity, thrown in along, goes a heap further than all your jawin' and crackin'; and it pays better,' says I, 'depend on 't.' But Tom couldn't get the hang on 't; and he spiled so many for me, that I had to break off with him, though he was a good-hearted fellow, and as fair a business hand as is goin'."

"And do you find your ways of managing do the business better than Tom's?" said Mr. Shelby.

"Why, yes, sir, I may say so. You see, when I any ways can, I takes a leetle care about the onpleasant parts, like selling young uns and that,—get the gals out of the way—out of sight, out of mind, you know,—and when it's clean done, and can't be helped, they naturally gets used to it. 'Tan't, you know, as if it was white folks, that's brought up in the way of 'spectin' to keep their children and wives, and all that. Niggers, you know, that's fetched up properly, ha'n't no kind of 'spectations of no kind; so all these things comes easier."

"I'm afraid mine are not properly brought up, then," said Mr. Shelby.

"S'pose not; you Kentucky folks spile your niggers. You mean well by 'em, but 'tan't no real kindness, arter all. Now, a nigger, you see, what's got to be hacked and tumbled round the world, and sold to Tom, and Dick, and the Lord knows who, 'tan't no kindness to be givin' on him notions and expectations, and bringin' on him up too well, for the rough and tumble comes all the harder on him arter. Now, I venture to say, your niggers would be quite chop-fallen in a place where some of your plantation niggers would be singing and whooping like all possessed. Every man, you know, Mr. Shelby, naturally thinks well of his own ways; and I think I treat niggers just about as well as it's ever worth while to treat 'em."

"It's a happy thing to be satisfied," said Mr. Shelby, with a slight shrug, and some perceptible feelings of a disagreeable nature.

"Well," said Haley, after they had both silently picked their nuts for a season, "what do you say?"

"I'll think the matter over, and talk with my wife," said Mr. Shelby. "Meantime, Haley, if you want the matter carried on in the quiet way you speak of, you'd best not let your business in this neighborhood be known. It will get out among my boys, and it will not be a particularly quiet business getting away any of my fellows, if they know it, I'll promise you."

"O! certainly, by all means, mum! of course. But I'll tell you. I'm in a devil of a hurry, and shall want to know, as soon as possible, what I may depend on," said he, rising and putting on his overcoat.

"Well, call up this evening, between six and seven, and you shall have my answer," said Mr. Shelby, and the trader bowed himself out of the apartment.

"I'd like to have been able to kick the fellow down the steps," said he to himself, as he saw the door fairly closed, "with his impudent assurance; but he knows how much he has me at advantage. If anybody had ever said to me that I should sell Tom down south to one of those rascally traders, I should have said, 'Is thy servant a dog, that he should do this thing?' And now it must come, for aught I see. And Eliza's child, too! I know that I shall have some fuss with wife about that; and, for that matter, about Tom, too. So much for being in debt,—heigho! The fellow sees his advantage, and means to push it."

Perhaps the mildest form of the system of slavery is to be seen in the State of Kentucky. The general prevalence of agricultural pursuits of a quiet and gradual nature, not requiring those periodic seasons of hurry and pressure that are called for in the business of more southern districts, makes the task of the negro a more healthful and reasonable one; while the master, content with a more gradual style of acquisition, has not those temptations to hardheartedness which always overcome frail human nature when the prospect of sudden and rapid gain is weighed in the balance, with no heavier counterpoise than the interests of the helpless and unprotected.

Whoever visits some estates there, and witnesses the good-humored indulgence of some masters and mistresses, and the affectionate loyalty of some slaves, might be tempted to dream the oft-fabled poetic legend of a patriarchal institution, and all that; but over and above the scene there broods a portentous shadow—the shadow of *law*. So long as the law considers all these human beings, with beating hearts and living affections, only as so many *things* belonging to a master,—so long as the failure, or misfortune, or imprudence, or death of the kindest owner, may cause them any day to exchange a life of kind protection and indulgence for one of hopeless misery and toil,—so long it is impossible to make anything beautiful or desirable in the best regulated administration of slavery.

Mr. Shelby was a fair average kind of man, good-natured and kindly, and disposed to easy indulgence of those around him, and there had never been a lack of anything which might contribute to the physical comfort of the negroes on his estate. He had, however, speculated largely and quite loosely; had involved himself deeply, and his notes to a large amount had come into the hands of Haley; and this small piece of information is the key to the preceding conversation.

Now, it had so happened that, in approaching the door, Eliza had caught enough of the conversation to know that a trader was making offers to her master for somebody.

She would gladly have stopped at the door to listen, as she came out; but her mistress just then calling, she was obliged to hasten away.

Still she thought she heard the trader make an offer for her boy;—could she be mistaken? Her heart swelled and throbbed, and she involuntarily strained him so tight that the little fellow looked up into her face in astonishment.

"Eliza, girl, what ails you today?" said her mistress, when Eliza had upset the wash-pitcher, knocked down the workstand, and finally was abstractedly offering her mistress a long nightgown in place of the silk dress she had ordered her to bring from the wardrobe.

Eliza started. "O, missis!" she said, raising her eyes; then, bursting into tears, she sat down in a chair, and began sobbing.

"Why, Eliza child, what ails you?" said her mistress.

"O! missis, missis," said Eliza, "there's been a trader talking with master in the parlor! I heard him."

"Well, silly child, suppose there has."

"O, missis, *do* you suppose mas'r would sell my Harry?" And the poor creature threw herself into a chair, and sobbed convulsively.

"Sell him! No, you foolish girl! You know your master never deals with those southern traders, and never means to sell any of his servants, as long as they behave well. Why, you silly child, who do you think would want to buy your Harry? Do you think all the world are set on him as you are, you goosie? Come, cheer up, and hook my dress. There now, put my back hair up in that pretty braid you learnt the other day, and don't go listening at doors any more."

"Well, but, missis, *you* never would give your consent—to—to—"

"Nonsense, child! to be sure, I shouldn't. What do you talk so for? I would as soon have one of my own children sold. But really, Eliza, you are getting altogether too proud of that little fellow. A man can't put his nose into the door, but you think he must be coming to buy him."

Reassured by her mistress' confident tone, Eliza proceeded nimbly and adroitly with her toilet, laughing at her own fears, as she proceeded.

Mrs. Shelby was a woman of high class, both intellectually and morally. To that natural magnanimity and generosity of mind which one often marks as characteristic of the women of Kentucky, she added high moral and religious sensibility and principle, carried out with great energy and ability into practical results. Her husband, who made no professions to any particular religious character, nevertheless reverenced and respected the consistency of hers, and stood, perhaps, a little in awe of her opinion. Certain it was that he gave her unlimited scope in all her benevolent efforts for the comfort, instruction, and improvement of her servants, though he never took any decided part in them himself. In fact, if not exactly a believer in the doctrine of the efficiency of the extra good works of saints, he really seemed somehow or other to fancy that his wife had piety and benevolence enough for two—to indulge a shadowy expectation of getting into heaven through her superabundance of qualities to which he made no particular pretension.

The heaviest load on his mind, after his conversation with the trader, lay in the foreseen necessity of breaking to his wife the arrangement contemplated,—meeting the importunities and opposition which he knew he should have reason to encounter.

Mrs. Shelby, being entirely ignorant of her husband's embarrassments, and knowing only the general kindliness of his temper, had been quite sincere in the entire incredulity with which she had met Eliza's suspicions. In fact, she dismissed the matter from her mind, without a second thought; and being occupied in preparations for an evening visit, it passed out of her thoughts entirely.

CHAPTER II

THE MOTHER

Eliza had been brought up by her mistress, from girlhood, as a petted and indulged favorite.

The traveller in the south must often have remarked that peculiar air of refinement, that softness of voice and manner, which seems in many cases to be a particular gift to the quadroon and mulatto women. These natural graces in the quadroon are often united with beauty of the most dazzling kind, and in almost every case with a personal appearance prepossessing and agreeable. Eliza, such as we have described her, is not a fancy sketch, but taken from remembrance, as we saw her, years ago, in Kentucky. Safe under the protecting care of her mistress, Eliza had reached maturity without those temptations which make beauty so fatal an inheritance to a slave. She had been married to a bright and talented young mulatto man, who was a slave on a neighboring estate, and bore the name of George Harris.

This young man had been hired out by his master to work in a bagging factory, where his adroitness and ingenuity caused him to be considered the first hand in the place. He had invented a machine for the cleaning of the hemp, which, considering the education and circumstances of the inventor, displayed quite as much mechanical genius as Whitney's cotton-gin.[1]

He was possessed of a handsome person and pleasing manners, and was a general favorite in the factory. Nevertheless, as this young man was in the eye of the law not a man, but a thing, all these superior qualifications were subject to the control of a vulgar, narrow-minded, tyrannical master. This same gentleman, having heard of the fame of George's invention, took a ride over to the factory, to see what this intelligent chattel had been about. He was received with great enthusiasm by the employer, who congratulated him on possessing so valuable a slave.

He was waited upon over the factory, shown the machinery by George, who, in high spirits, talked so fluently, held himself so erect, looked so handsome and

---

[1] A machine of this description was really the invention of a young colored man in Kentucky. [Mrs. Stowe's note.]

manly, that his master began to feel an uneasy consciousness of inferiority. What business had his slave to be marching round the country, inventing machines, and holding up his head among gentlemen? He'd soon put a stop to it. He'd take him back, and put him to hoeing and digging, and "see if he'd step about so smart." Accordingly, the manufacturer and all hands concerned were astounded when he suddenly demanded George's wages, and announced his intention of taking him home.

"But, Mr. Harris," remonstrated the manufacturer, "isn't this rather sudden?"

"What if it is?—isn't the man *mine*?"

"We would be willing, sir, to increase the rate of compensation."

"No object at all, sir. I don't need to hire any of my hands out, unless I've a mind to."

"But, sir, he seems peculiarly adapted to this business."

"Dare say he may be; never was much adapted to anything that I set him about, I'll be bound."

"But only think of his inventing this machine," interposed one of the workmen, rather unluckily.

"O yes! a machine for saving work, is it? He'd invent that, I'll be bound; let a nigger alone for that, any time. They are all labor-saving machines themselves, every one of 'em. No, he shall tramp!"

George had stood like one transfixed, at hearing his doom thus suddenly pronounced by a power that he knew was irresistible. He folded his arms, tightly pressed in his lips, but a whole volcano of bitter feelings burned in his bosom, and sent streams of fire through his veins. He breathed short, and his large dark eyes flashed like live coals; and he might have broken out into some dangerous ebullition, had not the kindly manufacturer touched him on the arm, and said, in a low tone,

"Give way, George; go with him for the present. We'll try to help you, yet."

The tyrant observed the whisper, and conjectured its import, though he could not hear what was said; and he inwardly strengthened himself in his determination to keep the power he possessed over his victim.

George was taken home, and put to the meanest drudgery of the farm. He had been able to repress every disrespectful word; but the flashing eye, the gloomy and troubled brow, were part of a natural language that could not be repressed,—indubitable signs, which showed too plainly that the man could not become a thing.

It was during the happy period of his employment in the factory that George had seen and married his wife. During that period,—being much trusted and favored by his employer,—he had free liberty to come and go at discretion. The marriage was highly approved of by Mrs. Shelby, who, with a little womanly complacency in match-making, felt pleased to unite her handsome favorite with one of her own class who seemed in every way suited to her; and so they were married in her mistress' great parlor, and her mistress herself adorned the bride's beautiful hair with orange-blossoms, and threw over it the bridal veil, which certainly could scarce have rested on a fairer head; and there was no lack of white gloves, and cake and wine,—of admiring guests to praise the bride's beauty, and her mistress' indulgence and liberality. For a year or two Eliza saw her husband frequently, and there was nothing to interrupt their happiness, except the loss of two infant children, to whom she was passionately attached, and whom she mourned with a grief so intense as to call for gentle remonstrance from her mistress, who sought, with maternal anxiety, to direct her naturally passionate feelings within the bounds of reason and religion.

After the birth of little Harry, however, she had gradually become tranquillized and settled; and every bleeding tie and throbbing nerve, once more entwined with that little life, seemed to become sound and healthful, and Eliza was a happy woman up to the time that her husband was rudely torn from his kind employer, and brought under the iron sway of his legal owner.

The manufacturer, true to his word, visited Mr. Harris a week or two after George had been taken away, when, as he hoped, the heat of the occasion had passed away, and tried every possible inducement to lead him to restore him to his former employment.

"You needn't trouble yourself to talk any longer," said he, doggedly; "I know my own business, sir."

"I did not presume to interfere with it, sir. I only thought that you might think it for your interest to let your man to us on the terms proposed."

"O, I understand the matter well enough. I saw your winking and whispering, the day I took him out of the factory; but you don't come it over me that way. It's a free country, sir; the man's *mine*, and I do what I please with him,—that's it!"

And so fell George's last hope;—nothing before him but a life of toil and drudgery, rendered more bitter by every little smarting vexation and indignity which tyrannical ingenuity could devise.

A very humane jurist once said, The worst use you can put a man to is to hang him. No; there is another use that a man can be put to that is WORSE!

CHAPTER III

THE HUSBAND AND FATHER

Mrs. Shelby had gone on her visit, and Eliza stood in the verandah, rather dejectedly looking after the retreating carriage, when a hand was laid on her shoulder. She turned, and a bright smile lighted up her fine eyes.

"George, is it you? How you frightened me! Well; I am so glad you 's come! Missis is gone to spend the afternoon; so come into my little room, and we'll have the time all to ourselves."

Saying this, she drew him into a neat little apartment opening on the verandah, where she generally sat at her sewing, within call of her mistress.

"How glad I am!—why don't you smile?—and look at Harry—how he grows." The boy stood shyly regarding his father through his curls, holding close to the skirts of his mother's dress. "Isn't he beautiful?" said Eliza, lifting his long curls and kissing him.

"I wish he'd never been born!" said George, bitterly. "I wish I'd never been born myself!"

Surprised and frightened, Eliza sat down, leaned her head on her husband's shoulder, and burst into tears.

"There now, Eliza, it's too bad for me to make you feel so, poor girl!" said he, fondly; "it's too bad: O, how I wish you never had seen me—you might have been happy!"

"George! George! how can you talk so? What dreadful thing has happened, or is going to happen? I'm sure we've been very happy, till lately."

"So we have, dear," said George. Then drawing his child on his knee, he gazed intently on his glorious dark eyes, and passed his hands through his long curls.

"Just like you, Eliza; and you are the handsomest woman I ever saw, and the best one I ever wish to see; but, oh, I wish I'd never seen you, nor you me!"

"O, George, how can you!"

"Yes, Eliza, it's all misery, misery, misery! My life is bitter as wormwood; the very life is burning out of me. I'm a poor, miserable, forlorn drudge; I shall only drag you down with me, that's all. What's the use of our trying to do anything, trying to know anything, trying to be anything? What's the use of living? I wish I was dead!"

"O, now, dear George, that is really wicked! I know how you feel about losing your place in the factory, and you have a hard master; but pray be patient, and perhaps something—"

"Patient!" said he, interrupting her; "haven't I been patient? Did I say a word when he came and took me away, for no earthly reason, from the place where everybody was kind to me? I'd paid him truly every cent of my earnings,—and they all say I worked well."

"Well, it *is* dreadful," said Eliza; "but, after all, he is your master, you know."

"My master! and who made him my master? That's what I think of—what right has he to me? I'm a man as much as he is. I'm a better man than he is. I know more about business than he does; I am a better manager than he is; I can read better than he can; I can write a better hand,—and I've learned it all myself, and no thanks to him,—I've learned it in spite of him; and now what right has he to make a dray-horse of me?—to take me from things I can do, and do better than he can, and put me to work that any horse can do? He tries to do it; he says he'll bring me down and humble me, and he puts me to just the hardest, meanest and dirtiest work, on purpose!"

"O, George! George! you frighten me! Why, I never heard you talk so; I'm afraid you'll do something dreadful. I don't wonder at your feelings, at all; but oh, do be careful—do, do—for my sake—for Harry's!"

"I have been careful, and I have been patient, but it's growing worse and worse; flesh and blood can't bear it any longer;—every chance he can get to insult and torment me, he takes. I thought I could do my work well, and keep on quiet, and have some time to read and learn out of work hours; but the more he sees I can do, the more he loads on. He says that though I don't say anything, he sees I've got the devil in me, and he means to bring it out; and one of these days it will come out in a way that he won't like, or I'm mistaken!"

"O dear! what shall we do?" said Eliza, mournfully.

"It was only yesterday," said George, "as I was busy loading stones into a cart, that young Mas'r Tom stood there, slashing his whip so near the horse that the creature was frightened. I asked him to stop, as pleasant as I could,—he just kept right on. I begged him again, and then he turned on me, and began striking me. I held his hand, and then he screamed and kicked and ran to his father, and told him that I was fighting him. He came in a rage, and said he'd teach me who was my master; and he tied me to a tree, and cut switches for young master, and told him that he might whip me till he was tired;—and he did do it! If I don't make him remember it, some time!" and the brow of the young man grew dark, and his eyes burned with an expression that made his young wife tremble. "Who made this man my master? That's what I want to know!" he said.

"Well," said Eliza, mournfully, "I always thought that I must obey my master and mistress, or I couldn't be a Christian."

"There is some sense in it, in your case; they have brought you up like a child, fed you, clothed you, indulged you, and taught you, so that you have a good education; that is some reason why they should claim you. But I have been kicked and cuffed and sworn at, and at the best only let alone; and what do I owe? I've paid for all my keeping a hundred times over. I *won't* bear it. No, I *won't*!" he said, clenching his hand with a fierce frown.

Eliza trembled, and was silent. She had never seen her husband in this mood before; and her gentle system of ethics seemed to bend like a reed in the surges of such passions.

"You know poor little Carlo, that you gave me," added George; "the creature has been about all the comfort that I've had. He has slept with me nights, and followed me around days, and kind o' looked at me as if he understood how I felt. Well, the other day I was just feeding him with a few old scraps I picked up by the kitchen door, and Mas'r came along, and said I was feeding him up at his expense, and that he couldn't afford to have every nigger keeping his dog, and ordered me to tie a stone to his neck and throw him in the pond."

"O, George, you didn't do it!"

"Do it? not I!—but he did. Mas'r and Tom pelted the poor drowning creature with stones. Poor thing! he looked at me so mournful, as if he wondered why I didn't save him. I had to take a flogging because I wouldn't do it myself. I don't care. Mas'r will find out that I'm one that whipping won't tame. My day will come yet, if he don't look out."

"What are you going to do? O, George, don't do anything wicked; if you only trust in God, and try to do right, he'll deliver you."

"I an't a Christian like you, Eliza; my heart's full of bitterness; I can't trust in God. Why does he let things be so?"

"O, George, we must have faith. Mistress says that when all things go wrong to us, we must believe that God is doing the very best."

"That's easy to say for people that are sitting on their sofas and riding in their carriages; but let 'em be where I am, I guess it would come some harder. I wish I could be good; but my heart burns, and can't be reconciled, anyhow. You couldn't in my place,—you can't now, if I tell you all I've got to say. You don't know the whole yet."

"What can be coming now?"

"Well, lately Mas'r has been saying that he was a fool to let me marry off the place; that he hates Mr. Shelby and all his tribe, because they are proud, and hold their heads up above him, and that I've got proud notions from you; and he says he won't let me come here any more, and that I shall take a wife and settle down on his place. At first he only scolded and grumbled these things; but yesterday he told me that I should take Mina for a wife, and settle down in a cabin with her, or he would sell me down river."

"Why—but you were married to *me*, by the minister, as much as if you'd been a white man!" said Eliza, simply.

CHAPTER III

"Don't you know a slave can't be married? There is no law in this country for that; I can't hold you for my wife, if he chooses to part us. That's why I wish I'd never seen you,—why I wish I'd never been born; it would have been better for us both,—it would have been better for this poor child if he had never been born. All this may happen to him yet!"

"O, but master is so kind!"

"Yes, but who knows?—he may die—and then he may be sold to nobody knows who. What pleasure is it that he is handsome, and smart, and bright? I tell you, Eliza, that a sword will pierce through your soul for every good and pleasant thing your child is or has; it will make him worth too much for you to keep."

The words smote heavily on Eliza's heart; the vision of the trader came before her eyes, and, as if some one had struck her a deadly blow, she turned pale and gasped for breath. She looked nervously out on the verandah, where the boy, tired of the grave conversation, had retired, and where he was riding triumphantly up and down on Mr. Shelby's walking-stick. She would have spoken to tell her husband her fears, but checked herself.

"No, no,—he has enough to bear, poor fellow!" she thought. "No, I won't tell him; besides, it an't true; Missis never deceives us."

"So, Eliza, my girl," said the husband, mournfully, "bear up, now; and good-by, for I'm going."

"Going, George! Going where?"

"To Canada," said he, straightening himself up; "and when I'm there, I'll buy you; that's all the hope that's left us. You have a kind master, that won't refuse to sell you. I'll buy you and the boy;—God helping me, I will!"

"O, dreadful! if you should be taken?"

"I won't be taken, Eliza; I'll *die* first! I'll be free, or I'll die!"

"You won't kill yourself!"

"No need of that. They will kill me, fast enough; they never will get me down the river alive!"

"O, George, for my sake, do be careful! Don't do anything wicked; don't lay hands on yourself, or anybody else! You are tempted too much—too much; but don't—go you must—but go carefully, prudently; pray God to help you."

"Well, then, Eliza, hear my plan. Mas'r took it into his head to send me right by here, with a note to Mr. Symmes, that lives a mile past. I believe he expected I should come here to tell you what I have. It would please him, if he thought it would aggravate 'Shelby's folks,' as he calls 'em. I'm going home quite resigned, you understand, as if all was over. I've got some preparations made,—and there are those that will help me; and, in the course of a week or so, I shall be among the missing, some day. Pray for me, Eliza; perhaps the good Lord will hear *you*."

"O, pray yourself, George, and go trusting in him; then you won't do anything wicked."

"Well, now, *good-by*," said George, holding Eliza's hands, and gazing into her eyes, without moving. They stood silent; then there were last words, and sobs, and bitter weeping,—such parting as those may make whose hope to meet again is as the spider's web,—and the husband and wife were parted.

CHAPTER IV

AN EVENING IN UNCLE TOM'S CABIN

The cabin of Uncle Tom was a small log building, close adjoining to "the house," as the negro *par excellence* designates his master's dwelling. In front it had a neat garden-patch, where, every summer, strawberries, raspberries, and a variety of fruits and vegetables, flourished under careful tending. The whole front of it was covered by a large scarlet bignonia and a native multiflora rose, which, entwisting and interlacing, left scarce a vestige of the rough logs to be seen. Here, also, in summer, various brilliant annuals, such as marigolds, petunias, four-o'clocks, found an indulgent corner in which to unfold their splendors, and were the delight and pride of Aunt Chloe's heart.

Let us enter the dwelling. The evening meal at the house is over, and Aunt Chloe, who presided over its preparation as head cook, has left to inferior officers in the kitchen the business of clearing away and washing dishes, and come out into her own snug territories, to "get her ole man's supper"; therefore, doubt not that it is her you see by the fire, presiding with anxious interest over certain frizzling items in a stew-pan, and anon with grave consideration lifting the cover of a bake-kettle, from whence steam forth indubitable intimations of "something good." A round, black, shining face is hers, so glossy as to suggest the idea that she might have been washed over with white of eggs, like one of her own tea rusks. Her whole plump countenance beams with satisfaction and contentment from under her well-starched checked turban, bearing on it, however, if we must confess it, a little of that tinge of self-consciousness which becomes the first cook of the neighborhood, as Aunt Chloe was universally held and acknowledged to be.

A cook she certainly was, in the very bone and centre of her soul. Not a chicken or turkey or duck in the barn-yard but looked grave when they saw her approaching, and seemed evidently to be reflecting on their latter end; and certain it was that she was always meditating on trussing, stuffing and roasting, to a degree that was calculated to inspire terror in any reflecting fowl living. Her corn-cake, in all its varieties of hoe-cake, dodgers, muffins, and other species too numerous to mention, was a sublime mystery to all less practised compounders; and she would shake her fat sides with honest pride and merriment, as she would narrate the fruitless efforts that one and another of her compeers had made to attain to her elevation.

The arrival of company at the house, the arranging of dinners and suppers "in style," awoke all the energies of her soul; and no sight was more welcome to her than a pile of travelling trunks launched on the verandah, for then she foresaw fresh efforts and fresh triumphs.

Just at present, however, Aunt Chloe is looking into the bake-pan; in which congenial operation we shall leave her till we finish our picture of the cottage.

In one corner of it stood a bed, covered neatly with a snowy spread; and by the side of it was a piece of carpeting, of some considerable size. On this piece of carpeting Aunt Chloe took her stand, as being decidedly in the upper walks of life; and it and the bed by which it lay, and the whole corner, in fact, were treated with distinguished consideration, and made, so far as possible, sacred from the marauding inroads and desecrations of little folks. In fact, that corner was the *drawing-room* of the establishment. In the other corner was a bed of much humbler pretensions, and evidently designed for *use*. The wall over the fireplace was adorned with some very brilliant scriptural prints, and a portrait of General Washington, drawn and colored in a manner which would certainly have astonished that hero, if ever he happened to meet with its like.

On a rough bench in the corner, a couple of woolly-headed boys, with glistening black eyes and fat shining cheeks, were busy in superintending the first walking operations of the baby, which, as is usually the case, consisted in getting up on its feet, balancing a moment, and then tumbling down,—each successive failure being violently cheered, as something decidedly clever.

A table, somewhat rheumatic in its limbs, was drawn out in front of the fire, and covered with a cloth, displaying cups and saucers of a decidedly brilliant pattern, with other symptoms of an approaching meal. At this table was seated Uncle Tom, Mr. Shelby's best hand, who, as he is to be the hero of our story, we must daguerreotype for our readers. He was a large, broad-chested, powerfully-made man, of a full glossy black, and a face whose truly African features were characterized by an expression of grave and steady good sense, united with much kindliness and benevolence. There was something about his whole air self-respecting and dignified, yet united with a confiding and humble simplicity.

He was very busily intent at this moment on a slate lying before him, on which he was carefully and slowly endeavoring to accomplish a copy of some letters, in which operation he was overlooked by young Mas'r George, a smart, bright boy of thirteen, who appeared fully to realize the dignity of his position as instructor.

"Not that way, Uncle Tom,—not that way," said he, briskly, as Uncle Tom laboriously brought up the tail of his *g* the wrong side out; "that makes a *q*, you see."

"La sakes, now, does it?" said Uncle Tom, looking with a respectful, admiring air, as his young teacher flourishingly scrawled *q*'s and *g*'s innumerable for his edification; and then, taking the pencil in his big, heavy fingers, he patiently recommenced.

"How easy white folks al'us does things!" said Aunt Chloe, pausing while she was greasing a griddle with a scrap of bacon on her fork, and regarding young Master George with pride. "The way he can write, now! and read, too! and then to come out here evenings and read his lessons to us,—it's mighty interestin'!"

"But, Aunt Chloe, I'm getting mighty hungry," said George. "Isn't that cake in the skillet almost done?"

"Mose done, Mas'r George," said Aunt Chloe, lifting the lid and peeping in,—"browning beautiful—a real lovely brown. Ah! let me alone for dat. Missis let Sally try to make some cake, t' other day, jes to *larn* her, she said. 'O, go way, Missis,' said I; 'it really hurts my feelin's, now, to see good vittles spilt dat ar way! Cake ris all to one side—no shape at all; no more than my shoe; go way!"

And with this final expression of contempt for Sally's greenness, Aunt Chloe whipped the cover off the bake-kettle, and disclosed to view a neatly-baked pound-cake, of which no city confectioner need to have been ashamed. This being evidently the central point of the entertainment, Aunt Chloe began now to bustle about earnestly in the supper department.

"Here you, Mose and Pete! get out de way, you niggers! Get away, Polly, honey,—mammy'll give her baby some fin, by and by. Now, Mas'r George, you jest take off dem books, and set down now with my old man, and I'll take up de sausages, and have de first griddle full of cakes on your plates in less dan no time."

"They wanted me to come to supper in the house," said George; "but I knew what was what too well for that, Aunt Chloe."

"So you did—so you did, honey," said Aunt Chloe, heaping the smoking batter-cakes on his plate; "you know'd your old aunty'd keep the best for you. O, let you alone for dat! Go way!" And, with that, aunty gave George a nudge with her finger, designed to be immensely facetious, and turned again to her griddle with great briskness.

"Now for the cake," said Mas'r George, when the activity of the griddle department had somewhat subsided; and, with that, the youngster flourished a large knife over the article in question.

"La bless you, Mas'r George!" said Aunt Chloe, with earnestness, catching his arm, "you wouldn't be for cuttin' it wid dat ar great heavy knife! Smash all down—spile all de pretty rise of it. Here, I've got a thin old knife, I keeps sharp a purpose. Dar now, see! comes apart light as a feather! Now eat away—you won't get anything to beat dat ar."

"Tom Lincon says," said George, speaking with his mouth full, "that their Jinny is a better cook than you."

"Dem Lincons an't much count, no way!" said Aunt Chloe, contemptuously; "I mean, set along side *our* folks. They 's 'spectable folks enough in a kinder plain way; but, as to gettin' up anything in style, they don't begin to have a notion on 't. Set Mas'r Lincon, now, alongside Mas'r Shelby! Good Lor! and Missis Lincon,—can she kinder sweep it into a room like my missis,—so kinder splendid, yer know! O, go way! don't tell me nothin' of dem Lincons!"—and Aunt Chloe tossed her head as one who hoped she did know something of the world.

"Well, though, I've heard you say," said George, "that Jinny was a pretty fair cook."

"So I did," said Aunt Chloe,—"I may say dat. Good, plain, common cookin', Jinny'll do;—make a good pone o' bread,—bile her taters *far*,—her corn cakes isn't extra, not extra now, Jinny's corn cakes isn't, but then they's far,—but, Lor, come to de higher branches, and what *can* she do? Why, she makes pies—sartin she does; but what kinder crust? Can she make your real flecky paste, as melts in your mouth, and lies all up like a puff? Now, I went over thar when Miss Mary was gwine to be married, and Jinny she jest showed me de weddin' pies. Jinny and I is good friends, ye know. I never said nothin'; but go 'long, Mas'r George! Why, I shouldn't sleep a wink for a week, if I had a batch of pies like dem ar. Why, dey wan't no 'count 't all."

"I suppose Jinny thought they were ever so nice," said George.

"Thought so!—didn't she? Thar she was, showing em, as innocent—ye see, it's jest here, Jinny *don't know*. Lor, the family an't nothing! She can't be spected to know! 'Ta'nt no fault o' hem. Ah, Mas'r George, you doesn't know half 'your privileges in yer family and bringin' up!" Here Aunt Chloe sighed, and rolled up her eyes with emotion.

"I'm sure, Aunt Chloe, I understand my pie and pudding privileges," said George. "Ask Tom Lincon if I don't crow over him, every time I meet him."

Aunt Chloe sat back in her chair, and indulged in a hearty guffaw of laughter, at this witticism of young Mas'r's, laughing till the tears rolled down her black, shining cheeks, and varying the exercise with playfully slapping and poking Mas'r Georgey, and telling him to go way, and that he was a case—that he was fit to kill her, and that he sartin would kill her, one of these days; and, between each of these sanguinary predictions, going off into a laugh, each longer and stronger than the other, till George really began to think that he was a very dangerously witty fellow, and that it became him to be careful how he talked "as funny as he could."

"And so ye telled Tom, did ye? O, Lor! what young uns will be up ter! Ye crowed over Tom? O, Lor! Mas'r George, if ye wouldn't make a hornbug laugh!"

"Yes," said George, "I says to him, 'Tom, you ought to see some of Aunt Chloe's pies; they're the right sort,' says I."

"Pity, now, Tom couldn't," said Aunt Chloe, on whose benevolent heart the idea of Tom's benighted condition seemed to make a strong impression. "Ye oughter just ask him here to dinner, some o' these times, Mas'r George," she added; "it would look quite pretty of ye. Ye know, Mas'r George, ye oughtenter feel 'bove nobody, on 'count yer privileges, 'cause all our privileges is gi'n to us; we ought al'ays to 'member that," said Aunt Chloe, looking quite serious.

"Well, I mean to ask Tom here, some day next week," said George; "and you do your prettiest, Aunt Chloe, and we'll make him stare. Won't we make him eat so he won't get over it for a fortnight?"

CHAPTER IV

"Yes, yes—sartin," said Aunt Chloe, delighted; "you'll see. Lor! to think of some of our dinners! Yer mind dat ar great chicken pie I made when we guv de dinner to General Knox? I and Missis, we come pretty near quarrelling about dat ar crust. What does get into ladies sometimes, I don't know; but, sometimes, when a body has de heaviest kind o' 'sponsibility on 'em, as ye may say, and is all kinder *'seris'* and taken up, dey takes dat ar time to be hangin' round and kinder interferin'! Now, Missis, she wanted me to do dis way, and she wanted me to do dat way; and, finally, I got kinder sarcy, and, says I, 'Now, Missis, do jist look at dem beautiful white hands o' yourn with long fingers, and all a sparkling with rings, like my white lilies when de dew 's on 'em; and look at my great black stumpin hands. Now, don't ye think dat de Lord must have meant *me* to make de pie-crust, and you to stay in de parlor? Dar! I was jist so sarcy, Mas'r George."

"And what did mother say?" said George.

"Say?—why, she kinder larfed in her eyes—dem great handsome eyes o' hern; and, says she, 'Well, Aunt Chloe, I think you are about in the right on 't,' says she; and she went off in de parlor. She oughter cracked me over de head for bein' so sarcy; but dar's whar 't is—I can't do nothin' with ladies in de kitchen!"

"Well, you made out well with that dinner,—I remember everybody said so," said George.

"Didn't I? And wan't I behind de dinin'-room door dat bery day? and didn't I see de General pass his plate three times for some more dat bery pie?—and, says he, 'You must have an uncommon cook, Mrs. Shelby.' Lor! I was fit to split myself.

"And de Gineral, he knows what cookin' is," said Aunt Chloe, drawing herself up with an air. "Bery nice man, de Gineral! He comes of one of de bery *fustest* families in Old Virginny! He knows what's what, now, as well as I do—de Gineral. Ye see, there's *pints* in all pies, Mas'r George; but tan't everybody knows what they is, or as orter be. But the Gineral, he knows; I knew by his 'marks he made. Yes, he knows what de pints is!"

By this time, Master George had arrived at that pass to which even a boy can come (under uncommon circumstances, when he really could not eat another morsel), and, therefore, he was at leisure to notice the pile of woolly heads and glistening eyes which were regarding their operations hungrily from the opposite corner.

"Here, you Mose, Pete," he said, breaking off liberal bits, and throwing it at them; "you want some, don't you? Come, Aunt Chloe, bake them some cakes."

And George and Tom moved to a comfortable seat in the chimney-corner, while Aunte Chloe, after baking a goodly pile of cakes, took her baby on her lap, and began alternately filling its mouth and her own, and distributing to Mose and Pete, who seemed rather to prefer eating theirs as they rolled about on the floor under the table, tickling each other, and occasionally pulling the baby's toes.

"O! go long, will ye?" said the mother, giving now and then a kick, in a kind of general way, under the table, when the movement became too obstreperous. "Can't ye be decent when white folks comes to see ye? Stop dat ar, now, will ye?

Better mind yerselves, or I'll take ye down a button-hole lower, when Mas'r George is gone!"

What meaning was couched under this terrible threat, it is difficult to say; but certain it is that its awful indistinctness seemed to produce very little impression on the young sinners addressed.

"La, now!" said Uncle Tom, "they are so full of tickle all the while, they can't behave theirselves."

Here the boys emerged from under the table, and, with hands and faces well plastered with molasses, began a vigorous kissing of the baby.

"Get along wid ye!" said the mother, pushing away their woolly heads. "Ye'll all stick together, and never get clar, if ye do dat fashion. Go long to de spring and wash yerselves!" she said, seconding her exhortations by a slap, which resounded very formidably, but which seemed only to knock out so much more laugh from the young ones, as they tumbled precipitately over each other out of doors, where they fairly screamed with merriment.

"Did ye ever see such aggravating young uns?" said Aunt Chloe, rather complacently, as, producing an old towel, kept for such emergencies, she poured a little water out of the cracked tea-pot on it, and began rubbing off the molasses from the baby's face and hands; and, having polished her till she shone, she set her down in Tom's lap, while she busied herself in clearing away supper. The baby employed the intervals in pulling Tom's nose, scratching his face, and burying her fat hands in his woolly hair, which last operation seemed to afford her special content.

"Aint she a peart young un?" said Tom, holding her from him to take a full-length view; then, getting up, he set her on his broad shoulder, and began capering and dancing with her, while Mas'r George snapped at her with his pocket-handkerchief, and Mose and Pete, now returned again, roared after her like bears, till Aunt Chloe declared that they "fairly took her head off" with their noise. As, according to her own statement, this surgical operation was a matter of daily occurrence in the cabin, the declaration no whit abated the merriment, till every one had roared and tumbled and danced themselves down to a state of composure.

"Well, now, I hopes you're done," said Aunt Chloe, who had been busy in pulling out a rude box of a trundle-bed; "and now, you Mose and you Pete, get into thar; for we's goin' to have the meetin'."

"O mother, we don't wanter. We wants to sit up to meetin',—meetin's is so curis. We likes 'em."

"La, Aunt Chloe, shove it under, and let 'em sit up," said Mas'r George, decisively, giving a push to the rude machine.

Aunt Chloe, having thus saved appearances, seemed highly delighted to push the thing under, saying, as she did so, "Well, mebbe 't will do 'em some good."

The house now resolved itself into a committee of the whole, to consider the accommodations and arrangements for the meeting.

"What we's to do for cheers, now, *I* declar I don't know," said Aunt Chloe. As the meeting had been held at Uncle Tom's weekly, for an indefinite length of time, without any more "cheers," there seemed some encouragement to hope that a way would be discovered at present.

"Old Uncle Peter sung both de legs out of dat oldest cheer, last week," suggested Mose.

"You go long! I'll boun' you pulled 'em out; some o' your shines," said Aunt Chloe.

"Well, it'll stand, if it only keeps jam up agin de wall!" said Mose.

"Den Uncle Peter mus'n't sit in it, cause he al'ays hitches when he gets a singing. He hitched pretty nigh across de room, t' other night," said Pete.

"Good Lor! get him in it, then," said Mose, "and den he'd begin, 'Come saints—and sinners, hear me tell,' and den down he'd go,"—and Mose imitated precisely the nasal tones of the old man, tumbling on the floor, to illustrate the supposed catastrophe.

"Come now, be decent, can't ye?" said Aunt Chloe; "an't yer shamed?"

Mas'r George, however, joined the offender in the laugh, and declared decidedly that Mose was a "buster." So the maternal admonition seemed rather to fail of effect.

"Well, ole man," said Aunt Chloe, "you'll have to tote in them ar bar'ls."

"Mother's bar'ls is like dat ar widder's, Mas'r George was reading 'bout, in de good book,—dey never fails," said Mose, aside to Peter.

"I'm sure one on 'em caved in last week," said Pete, "and let 'em all down in de middle of de singin'; dat ar was failin', warnt it?"

During this aside between Mose and Pete, two empty casks had been rolled into the cabin, and being secured from rolling, by stones on each side, boards were laid across them, which arrangement, together with the turning down of certain tubs and pails, and the disposing of the rickety chairs, at last completed the preparation.

"Mas'r George is such a beautiful reader, now, I know he'll stay to read for us," said Aunt Chloe; "'pears like 't will be so much more interestin'."

George very readily consented, for your boy is always ready for anything that makes him of importance.

The room was soon filled with a motley assemblage, from the old gray-headed patriarch of eighty, to the young girl and lad of fifteen. A little harmless gossip ensued on various themes, such as where old Aunt Sally got her new red headkerchief, and how "Missis was a going to give Lizzy that spotted muslin gown, when she'd got her new berage made up;" and how Mas'r Shelby was thinking of buying a new sorrel colt, that was going to prove an addition to the glories of the place. A few of the worshippers belonged to families hard by, who had got permission to attend, and who brought in various choice scraps of information, about the sayings and doings at the house and on the place, which circulated as freely as the same sort of small change does in higher circles.

After a while the singing commenced, to the evident delight of all present. Not even all the disadvantage of nasal intonation could prevent the effect of the naturally fine voices, in airs at once wild and spirited. The words were sometimes the well-known and common hymns sung in the churches about, and sometimes of a wilder, more indefinite character, picked up at camp-meetings.

The chorus of one of them, which ran as follows, was sung with great energy and unction:

"Die on the field of battle, Die on the field of battle, Glory in my soul."

Another special favorite had oft repeated the words—

"O, I'm going to glory,—won't you come along with me? Don't you see the angels beck'ning, and a calling me away? Don't you see the golden city and the everlasting day?"

There were others, which made incessant mention of "Jordan's banks," and "Canaan's fields," and the "New Jerusalem;" for the negro mind, impassioned and imaginative, always attaches itself to hymns and expressions of a vivid and pictorial nature; and, as they sung, some laughed, and some cried, and some clapped hands, or shook hands rejoicingly with each other, as if they had fairly gained the other side of the river.

Various exhortations, or relations of experience, followed, and intermingled with the singing. One old gray-headed woman, long past work, but much revered as a sort of chronicle of the past, rose, and leaning on her staff, said—"Well, chil'en! Well, I'm mighty glad to hear ye all and see ye all once more, 'cause I don't know when I'll be gone to glory; but I've done got ready, chil'en; 'pears like I'd got my little bundle all tied up, and my bonnet on, jest a waitin' for the stage to come along and take me home; sometimes, in the night, I think I hear the wheels a rattlin', and I'm lookin' out all the time; now, you jest be ready too, for I tell ye all, chil'en," she said striking her staff hard on the floor, "dat ar *glory* is a mighty thing! It's a mighty thing, chil'en,—you don'no nothing about it,—it's *wonderful*." And the old creature sat down, with streaming tears, as wholly overcome, while the whole circle struck up—

"O Canaan, bright Canaan I'm bound for the land of Canaan."

Mas'r George, by request, read the last chapters of Revelation, often interrupted by such exclamations as "The *sakes* now!" "Only hear that!" "Jest think on 't!" "Is all that a comin' sure enough?"

George, who was a bright boy, and well trained in religious things by his mother, finding himself an object of general admiration, threw in expositions of his own, from time to time, with a commendable seriousness and gravity, for which he was admired by the young and blessed by the old; and it was agreed, on all hands, that "a minister couldn't lay it off better than he did; that 't was reely 'mazin'!"

Uncle Tom was a sort of patriarch in religious matters, in the neighborhood. Having, naturally, an organization in which the *morale* was strongly predominant, together with a greater breadth and cultivation of mind than obtained among his companions, he was looked up to with great respect, as a sort of minister among them; and the simple, hearty, sincere style of his exhortations might have edified even better educated persons. But it was in prayer that he especially excelled. Nothing could exceed the touching simplicity, the childlike earnestness, of his prayer, enriched with the language of Scripture, which seemed so entirely to have wrought itself into his being, as to have become a part of himself, and to drop from his lips unconsciously; in the language of a pious old negro, he "prayed right up." And so much did his prayer always work on the devotional feelings of his audiences, that there seemed often a danger that it would be lost altogether in the abundance of the responses which broke out everywhere around him.

While this scene was passing in the cabin of the man, one quite otherwise passed in the halls of the master.

The trader and Mr. Shelby were seated together in the dining room aforenamed, at a table covered with papers and writing utensils.

Mr. Shelby was busy in counting some bundles of bills, which, as they were counted, he pushed over to the trader, who counted them likewise.

"All fair," said the trader; "and now for signing these yer."

Mr. Shelby hastily drew the bills of sale towards him, and signed them, like a man that hurries over some disagreeable business, and then pushed them over with the money. Haley produced, from a well-worn valise, a parchment, which, after looking over it a moment, he handed to Mr. Shelby, who took it with a gesture of suppressed eagerness.

"Wal, now, the thing's *done*!" said the trader, getting up.

"It's *done*!" said Mr. Shelby, in a musing tone; and, fetching a long breath, he repeated, *"It's done!"*

"Yer don't seem to feel much pleased with it, 'pears to me," said the trader.

"Haley," said Mr. Shelby, "I hope you'll remember that you promised, on your honor, you wouldn't sell Tom, without knowing what sort of hands he's going into."

"Why, you've just done it sir," said the trader.

"Circumstances, you well know, *obliged* me," said Shelby, haughtily.

"Wal, you know, they may 'blige *me*, too," said the trader. "Howsomever, I'll do the very best I can in gettin' Tom a good berth; as to my treatin' on him bad, you needn't be a grain afeard. If there's anything that I thank the Lord for, it is that I'm never noways cruel."

After the expositions which the trader had previously given of his humane principles, Mr. Shelby did not feel particularly reassured by these declarations; but, as they were the best comfort the case admitted of, he allowed the trader to depart in silence, and betook himself to a solitary cigar.

CHAPTER V

SHOWING THE FEELINGS OF LIVING PROPERTY ON CHANGING OWNERS

Mr. and Mrs. Shelby had retired to their apartment for the night. He was lounging in a large easy-chair, looking over some letters that had come in the afternoon mail, and she was standing before her mirror, brushing out the complicated braids and curls in which Eliza had arranged her hair; for, noticing her pale cheeks and haggard eyes, she had excused her attendance that night, and ordered her to bed. The employment, naturally enough, suggested her conversation with the girl in the morning; and turning to her husband, she said, carelessly,

"By the by, Arthur, who was that low-bred fellow that you lugged in to our dinner-table today?"

"Haley is his name," said Shelby, turning himself rather uneasily in his chair, and continuing with his eyes fixed on a letter.

"Haley! Who is he, and what may be his business here, pray?"

"Well, he's a man that I transacted some business with, last time I was at Natchez," said Mr. Shelby.

"And he presumed on it to make himself quite at home, and call and dine here, ay?"

"Why, I invited him; I had some accounts with him," said Shelby.

"Is he a negro-trader?" said Mrs. Shelby, noticing a certain embarrassment in her husband's manner.

"Why, my dear, what put that into your head?" said Shelby, looking up.

"Nothing,—only Eliza came in here, after dinner, in a great worry, crying and taking on, and said you were talking with a trader, and that she heard him make an offer for her boy—the ridiculous little goose!"

"She did, hey?" said Mr. Shelby, returning to his paper, which he seemed for a few moments quite intent upon, not perceiving that he was holding it bottom upwards.

"It will have to come out," said he, mentally; "as well now as ever."

"I told Eliza," said Mrs. Shelby, as she continued brushing her hair, "that she was a little fool for her pains, and that you never had anything to do with that sort of persons. Of course, I knew you never meant to sell any of our people,—least of all, to such a fellow."

"Well, Emily," said her husband, "so I have always felt and said; but the fact is that my business lies so that I cannot get on without. I shall have to sell some of my hands."

"To that creature? Impossible! Mr. Shelby, you cannot be serious."

"I'm sorry to say that I am," said Mr. Shelby. "I've agreed to sell Tom."

"What! our Tom?—that good, faithful creature!—been your faithful servant from a boy! O, Mr. Shelby!—and you have promised him his freedom, too,—you and I have spoken to him a hundred times of it. Well, I can believe anything now,—I can believe *now* that you could sell little Harry, poor Eliza's only child!" said Mrs. Shelby, in a tone between grief and indignation.

"Well, since you must know all, it is so. I have agreed to sell Tom and Harry both; and I don't know why I am to be rated, as if I were a monster, for doing what every one does every day."

"But why, of all others, choose these?" said Mrs. Shelby. "Why sell them, of all on the place, if you must sell at all?"

"Because they will bring the highest sum of any,—that's why. I could choose another, if you say so. The fellow made me a high bid on Eliza, if that would suit you any better," said Mr. Shelby.

"The wretch!" said Mrs. Shelby, vehemently.

"Well, I didn't listen to it, a moment,—out of regard to your feelings, I wouldn't;—so give me some credit."

"My dear," said Mrs. Shelby, recollecting herself, "forgive me. I have been hasty. I was surprised, and entirely unprepared for this;—but surely you will allow me to intercede for these poor creatures. Tom is a noble-hearted, faithful fellow, if he is black. I do believe, Mr. Shelby, that if he were put to it, he would lay down his life for you."

"I know it,—I dare say;—but what's the use of all this?—I can't help myself."

"Why not make a pecuniary sacrifice? I'm willing to bear my part of the inconvenience. O, Mr. Shelby, I have tried—tried most faithfully, as a Christian woman should—to do my duty to these poor, simple, dependent creatures. I have cared for them, instructed them, watched over them, and know all their little cares and joys, for years; and how can I ever hold up my head again among them, if, for the sake of a little paltry gain, we sell such a faithful, excellent, confiding creature as poor Tom, and tear from him in a moment all we have taught him to love and value? I have taught them the duties of the family, of parent and child, and husband and wife; and how can I bear to have this open acknowledgment that we care for no tie, no duty, no relation, however sacred, compared with money? I have talked with Eliza about her boy—her duty to him as a Christian mother, to watch over him, pray for him, and bring him up in a Christian way; and now what can I say, if you tear him away, and sell him, soul and body, to a profane, unprincipled man, just to save a little money? I have told her that one soul is worth more than all the money in the world; and how will she believe me when she sees us turn round and sell her child?—sell him, perhaps, to certain ruin of body and soul!"

"I'm sorry you feel so about it,—indeed I am," said Mr. Shelby; "and I respect your feelings, too, though I don't pretend to share them to their full extent; but I tell you now, solemnly, it's of no use—I can't help myself. I didn't mean to tell you this Emily; but, in plain words, there is no choice between selling these two and selling everything. Either they must go, or *all* must. Haley has come into possession of a mortgage, which, if I don't clear off with him directly, will take everything before it. I've raked, and scraped, and borrowed, and all but begged,—and the price of these two was needed to make up the balance, and I had to give them up. Haley fancied the child; he agreed to settle the matter that way, and no other. I was in his power, and *had* to do it. If you feel so to have them sold, would it be any better to have *all* sold?"

Mrs. Shelby stood like one stricken. Finally, turning to her toilet, she rested her face in her hands, and gave a sort of groan.

"This is God's curse on slavery!—a bitter, bitter, most accursed thing!—a curse to the master and a curse to the slave! I was a fool to think I could make anything good out of such a deadly evil. It is a sin to hold a slave under laws like ours,—I always felt it was,—I always thought so when I was a girl,—I thought so still more after I joined the church; but I thought I could gild it over,—I thought, by kindness, and care, and instruction, I could make the condition of mine better than freedom—fool that I was!"

"Why, wife, you are getting to be an abolitionist, quite."

"Abolitionist! if they knew all I know about slavery, they *might* talk! We don't need them to tell us; you know I never thought that slavery was right—never felt willing to own slaves."

"Well, therein you differ from many wise and pious men," said Mr. Shelby. "You remember Mr. B.'s sermon, the other Sunday?"

"I don't want to hear such sermons; I never wish to hear Mr. B. in our church again. Ministers can't help the evil, perhaps,—can't cure it, any more than we can,—but defend it!—it always went against my common sense. And I think you didn't think much of that sermon, either."

"Well," said Shelby, "I must say these ministers sometimes carry matters further than we poor sinners would exactly dare to do. We men of the world must wink pretty hard at various things, and get used to a deal that isn't the exact thing. But we don't quite fancy, when women and ministers come out broad and square, and go beyond us in matters of either modesty or morals, that's a fact. But now, my dear, I trust you see the necessity of the thing, and you see that I have done the very best that circumstances would allow."

"O yes, yes!" said Mrs. Shelby, hurriedly and abstractedly fingering her gold watch,—"I haven't any jewelry of any amount," she added, thoughtfully; "but would not this watch do something?—it was an expensive one, when it was bought. If I could only at least save Eliza's child, I would sacrifice anything I have."

CHAPTER V

"I'm sorry, very sorry, Emily," said Mr. Shelby, "I'm sorry this takes hold of you so; but it will do no good. The fact is, Emily, the thing's done; the bills of sale are already signed, and in Haley's hands; and you must be thankful it is no worse. That man has had it in his power to ruin us all,—and now he is fairly off. If you knew the man as I do, you'd think that we had had a narrow escape."

"Is he so hard, then?"

"Why, not a cruel man, exactly, but a man of leather,—a man alive to nothing but trade and profit,—cool, and unhesitating, and unrelenting, as death and the grave. He'd sell his own mother at a good percentage—not wishing the old woman any harm, either."

"And this wretch owns that good, faithful Tom, and Eliza's child!"

"Well, my dear, the fact is that this goes rather hard with me; it's a thing I hate to think of. Haley wants to drive matters, and take possession tomorrow. I'm going to get out my horse bright and early, and be off. I can't see Tom, that's a fact; and you had better arrange a drive somewhere, and carry Eliza off. Let the thing be done when she is out of sight."

"No, no," said Mrs. Shelby; "I'll be in no sense accomplice or help in this cruel business. I'll go and see poor old Tom, God help him, in his distress! They shall see, at any rate, that their mistress can feel for and with them. As to Eliza, I dare not think about it. The Lord forgive us! What have we done, that this cruel necessity should come on us?"

There was one listener to this conversation whom Mr. and Mrs. Shelby little suspected.

Communicating with their apartment was a large closet, opening by a door into the outer passage. When Mrs. Shelby had dismissed Eliza for the night, her feverish and excited mind had suggested the idea of this closet; and she had hidden herself there, and, with her ear pressed close against the crack of the door, had lost not a word of the conversation.

When the voices died into silence, she rose and crept stealthily away. Pale, shivering, with rigid features and compressed lips, she looked an entirely altered being from the soft and timid creature she had been hitherto. She moved cautiously along the entry, paused one moment at her mistress' door, and raised her hands in mute appeal to Heaven, and then turned and glided into her own room. It was a quiet, neat apartment, on the same floor with her mistress. There was a pleasant sunny window, where she had often sat singing at her sewing; there a little case of books, and various little fancy articles, ranged by them, the gifts of Christmas holidays; there was her simple wardrobe in the closet and in the drawers:—here was, in short, her home; and, on the whole, a happy one it had been to her. But there, on the bed, lay her slumbering boy, his long curls falling negligently around his unconscious face, his rosy mouth half open, his little fat hands thrown out over the bedclothes, and a smile spread like a sunbeam over his whole face.

"Poor boy! poor fellow!" said Eliza; "they have sold you! but your mother will save you yet!"

No tear dropped over that pillow; in such straits as these, the heart has no tears to give,—it drops only blood, bleeding itself away in silence. She took a piece of paper and a pencil, and wrote, hastily,

"O, Missis! dear Missis! don't think me ungrateful,—don't think hard of me, any way,—I heard all you and master said tonight. I am going to try to save my boy—you will not blame me! God bless and reward you for all your kindness!"

Hastily folding and directing this, she went to a drawer and made up a little package of clothing for her boy, which she tied with a handkerchief firmly round her waist; and, so fond is a mother's remembrance, that, even in the terrors of that hour, she did not forget to put in the little package one or two of his favorite toys, reserving a gayly painted parrot to amuse him, when she should be called on to awaken him. It was some trouble to arouse the little sleeper; but, after some effort, he sat up, and was playing with his bird, while his mother was putting on her bonnet and shawl.

"Where are you going, mother?" said he, as she drew near the bed, with his little coat and cap.

His mother drew near, and looked so earnestly into his eyes, that he at once divined that something unusual was the matter.

"Hush, Harry," she said; "mustn't speak loud, or they will hear us. A wicked man was coming to take little Harry away from his mother, and carry him 'way off in the dark; but mother won't let him—she's going to put on her little boy's cap and coat, and run off with him, so the ugly man can't catch him."

Saying these words, she had tied and buttoned on the child's simple outfit, and, taking him in her arms, she whispered to him to be very still; and, opening a door in her room which led into the outer verandah, she glided noiselessly out.

It was a sparkling, frosty, starlight night, and the mother wrapped the shawl close round her child, as, perfectly quiet with vague terror, he clung round her neck.

Old Bruno, a great Newfoundland, who slept at the end of the porch, rose, with a low growl, as she came near. She gently spoke his name, and the animal, an old pet and playmate of hers, instantly, wagging his tail, prepared to follow her, though apparently revolving much, in this simple dog's head, what such an indiscreet midnight promenade might mean. Some dim ideas of imprudence or impropriety in the measure seemed to embarrass him considerably; for he often stopped, as Eliza glided forward, and looked wistfully, first at her and then at the house, and then, as if reassured by reflection, he pattered along after her again. A few minutes brought them to the window of Uncle Tom's cottage, and Eliza stopping, tapped lightly on the window-pane.

The prayer-meeting at Uncle Tom's had, in the order of hymn-singing, been protracted to a very late hour; and, as Uncle Tom had indulged himself in a few lengthy solos afterwards, the consequence was, that, although it was now between twelve and one o'clock, he and his worthy helpmeet were not yet asleep.

CHAPTER V

"Good Lord! what's that?" said Aunt Chloe, starting up and hastily drawing the curtain. "My sakes alive, if it an't Lizy! Get on your clothes, old man, quick!—there's old Bruno, too, a pawin round; what on airth! I'm gwine to open the door."

And suiting the action to the word, the door flew open, and the light of the tallow candle, which Tom had hastily lighted, fell on the haggard face and dark, wild eyes of the fugitive.

"Lord bless you!—I'm skeered to look at ye, Lizy! Are ye tuck sick, or what's come over ye?"

"I'm running away—Uncle Tom and Aunt Chloe—carrying off my child—Master sold him!"

"Sold him?" echoed both, lifting up their hands in dismay.

"Yes, sold him!" said Eliza, firmly; "I crept into the closet by Mistress' door tonight, and I heard Master tell Missis that he had sold my Harry, and you, Uncle Tom, both, to a trader; and that he was going off this morning on his horse, and that the man was to take possession today."

Tom had stood, during this speech, with his hands raised, and his eyes dilated, like a man in a dream. Slowly and gradually, as its meaning came over him, he collapsed, rather than seated himself, on his old chair, and sunk his head down upon his knees.

"The good Lord have pity on us!" said Aunt Chloe. "O! it don't seem as if it was true! What has he done, that Mas'r should sell *him*?"

"He hasn't done anything,—it isn't for that. Master don't want to sell, and Missis she's always good. I heard her plead and beg for us; but he told her 't was no use; that he was in this man's debt, and that this man had got the power over him; and that if he didn't pay him off clear, it would end in his having to sell the place and all the people, and move off. Yes, I heard him say there was no choice between selling these two and selling all, the man was driving him so hard. Master said he was sorry; but oh, Missis—you ought to have heard her talk! If she an't a Christian and an angel, there never was one. I'm a wicked girl to leave her so; but, then, I can't help it. She said, herself, one soul was worth more than the world; and this boy has a soul, and if I let him be carried off, who knows what'll become of it? It must be right: but, if it an't right, the Lord forgive me, for I can't help doing it!"

"Well, old man!" said Aunt Chloe, "why don't you go, too? Will you wait to be toted down river, where they kill niggers with hard work and starving? I'd a heap rather die than go there, any day! There's time for ye,—be off with Lizy,—you've got a pass to come and go any time. Come, bustle up, and I'll get your things together."

Tom slowly raised his head, and looked sorrowfully but quietly around, and said,

"No, no—I an't going. Let Eliza go—it's her right! I wouldn't be the one to say no—'tan't in *natur* for her to stay; but you heard what she said! If I must be sold, or all the people on the place, and everything go to rack, why, let me be sold. I s'pose I can bar it as well as any on 'em," he added, while something like a sob and a sigh shook his broad, rough chest convulsively. "Mas'r always found me on the spot—he always will. I never have broke trust, nor used my pass no ways contrary to my word, and I never will. It's better for me alone to go, than to break up the place and sell all. Mas'r an't to blame, Chloe, and he'll take care of you and the poor—"

Here he turned to the rough trundle bed full of little woolly heads, and broke fairly down. He leaned over the back of the chair, and covered his face with his large hands. Sobs, heavy, hoarse and loud, shook the chair, and great tears fell through his fingers on the floor; just such tears, sir, as you dropped into the coffin where lay your first-born son; such tears, woman, as you shed when you heard the cries of your dying babe. For, sir, he was a man,—and you are but another man. And, woman, though dressed in silk and jewels, you are but a woman, and, in life's great straits and mighty griefs, ye feel but one sorrow!

"And now," said Eliza, as she stood in the door, "I saw my husband only this afternoon, and I little knew then what was to come. They have pushed him to the very last standing place, and he told me, today, that he was going to run away. Do try, if you can, to get word to him. Tell him how I went, and why I went; and tell him I'm going to try and find Canada. You must give my love to him, and tell him, if I never see him again," she turned away, and stood with her back to them for a moment, and then added, in a husky voice, "tell him to be as good as he can, and try and meet me in the kingdom of heaven."

"Call Bruno in there," she added. "Shut the door on him, poor beast! He mustn't go with me!"

A few last words and tears, a few simple adieus and blessings, and clasping her wondering and affrighted child in her arms, she glided noiselessly away.

CHAPTER VI

DISCOVERY

Mr. and Mrs. Shelby, after their protracted discussion of the night before, did not readily sink to repose, and, in consequence, slept somewhat later than usual, the ensuing morning.

"I wonder what keeps Eliza," said Mrs. Shelby, after giving her bell repeated pulls, to no purpose.

Mr. Shelby was standing before his dressing-glass, sharpening his razor; and just then the door opened, and a colored boy entered, with his shaving-water.

"Andy," said his mistress, "step to Eliza's door, and tell her I have rung for her three times. Poor thing!" she added, to herself, with a sigh.

Andy soon returned, with eyes very wide in astonishment.

"Lor, Missis! Lizy's drawers is all open, and her things all lying every which way; and I believe she's just done clared out!"

The truth flashed upon Mr. Shelby and his wife at the same moment. He exclaimed,

"Then she suspected it, and she's off!"

"The Lord be thanked!" said Mrs. Shelby. "I trust she is."

"Wife, you talk like a fool! Really, it will be something pretty awkward for me, if she is. Haley saw that I hesitated about selling this child, and he'll think I connived at it, to get him out of the way. It touches my honor!" And Mr. Shelby left the room hastily.

There was great running and ejaculating, and opening and shutting of doors, and appearance of faces in all shades of color in different places, for about a quarter of an hour. One person only, who might have shed some light on the matter, was entirely silent, and that was the head cook, Aunt Chloe. Silently, and with a heavy cloud settled down over her once joyous face, she proceeded making out her breakfast biscuits, as if she heard and saw nothing of the excitement around her.

Very soon, about a dozen young imps were roosting, like so many crows, on the verandah railings, each one determined to be the first one to apprize the strange Mas'r of his ill luck.

"He'll be rael mad, I'll be bound," said Andy.

"*Won't* he swar!" said little black Jake.

"Yes, for he *does* swar," said woolly-headed Mandy. "I hearn him yesterday, at dinner. I hearn all about it then, 'cause I got into the closet where Missis keeps the great jugs, and I hearn every word." And Mandy, who had never in her life thought of the meaning of a word she had heard, more than a black cat, now took airs of superior wisdom, and strutted about, forgetting to state that, though actually coiled up among the jugs at the time specified, she had been fast asleep all the time.

When, at last, Haley appeared, booted and spurred, he was saluted with the bad tidings on every hand. The young imps on the verandah were not disappointed in their hope of hearing him "swar," which he did with a fluency and fervency which delighted them all amazingly, as they ducked and dodged hither and thither, to be out of the reach of his riding-whip; and, all whooping off together, they tumbled, in a pile of immeasurable giggle, on the withered turf under the verandah, where they kicked up their heels and shouted to their full satisfaction.

"If I had the little devils!" muttered Haley, between his teeth.

"But you ha'nt got 'em, though!" said Andy, with a triumphant flourish, and making a string of indescribable mouths at the unfortunate trader's back, when he was fairly beyond hearing.

"I say now, Shelby, this yer 's a most extro'rnary business!" said Haley, as he abruptly entered the parlor. "It seems that gal 's off, with her young un."

"Mr. Haley, Mrs. Shelby is present," said Mr. Shelby.

"I beg pardon, ma'am," said Haley, bowing slightly, with a still lowering brow; "but still I say, as I said before, this yer's a sing'lar report. Is it true, sir?"

"Sir," said Mr. Shelby, "if you wish to communicate with me, you must observe something of the decorum of a gentleman. Andy, take Mr. Haley's hat and riding-whip. Take a seat, sir. Yes, sir; I regret to say that the young woman, excited by overhearing, or having reported to her, something of this business, has taken her child in the night, and made off."

"I did expect fair dealing in this matter, I confess," said Haley.

"Well, sir," said Mr. Shelby, turning sharply round upon him, "what am I to understand by that remark? If any man calls my honor in question, I have but one answer for him."

The trader cowered at this, and in a somewhat lower tone said that "it was plaguy hard on a fellow, that had made a fair bargain, to be gulled that way."

"Mr. Haley," said Mr. Shelby, "if I did not think you had some cause for disappointment, I should not have borne from you the rude and unceremonious style of your entrance into my parlor this morning. I say thus much, however, since appearances call for it, that I shall allow of no insinuations cast upon me, as if I were at all partner to any unfairness in this matter. Moreover, I shall feel bound to give you every assistance, in the use of horses, servants, &c., in the recovery of your property. So, in short, Haley," said he, suddenly dropping from the tone of dignified coolness to his ordinary one of easy frankness, "the best way for you is to keep good-natured and eat some breakfast, and we will then see what is to be done."

Mrs. Shelby now rose, and said her engagements would prevent her being at the breakfast-table that morning; and, deputing a very respectable mulatto woman to attend to the gentlemen's coffee at the side-board, she left the room.

"Old lady don't like your humble servant, over and above," said Haley, with an uneasy effort to be very familiar.

"I am not accustomed to hear my wife spoken of with such freedom," said Mr. Shelby, dryly.

"Beg pardon; of course, only a joke, you know," said Haley, forcing a laugh.

"Some jokes are less agreeable than others," rejoined Shelby.

"Devilish free, now I've signed those papers, cuss him!" muttered Haley to himself; "quite grand, since yesterday!"

Never did fall of any prime minister at court occasion wider surges of sensation than the report of Tom's fate among his compeers on the place. It was the topic in every mouth, everywhere; and nothing was done in the house or in the field, but to discuss its probable results. Eliza's flight—an unprecedented event on the place—was also a great accessory in stimulating the general excitement.

Black Sam, as he was commonly called, from his being about three shades blacker than any other son of ebony on the place, was revolving the matter profoundly in all its phases and bearings, with a comprehensiveness of vision and a strict lookout to his own personal well-being, that would have done credit to any white patriot in Washington.

"It's an ill wind dat blow nowhar,—dat ar a fact," said Sam, sententiously, giving an additional hoist to his pantaloons, and adroitly substituting a long nail in place of a missing suspender-button, with which effort of mechanical genius he seemed highly delighted.

"Yes, it's an ill wind blows nowhar," he repeated. "Now, dar, Tom's down—wal, course der's room for some nigger to be up—and why not dis nigger?—dat's de idee. Tom, a ridin' round de country—boots blacked—pass in his pocket—all grand as Cuffee—but who he? Now, why shouldn't Sam?—dat's what I want to know."

"Halloo, Sam—O Sam! Mas'r wants you to cotch Bill and Jerry," said Andy, cutting short Sam's soliloquy.

"High! what's afoot now, young un?"

"Why, you don't know, I s'pose, that Lizy's cut stick, and clared out, with her young un?"

"You teach your granny!" said Sam, with infinite contempt; "knowed it a heap sight sooner than you did; this nigger an't so green, now!"

"Well, anyhow, Mas'r wants Bill and Jerry geared right up; and you and I 's to go with Mas'r Haley, to look arter her."

"Good, now! dat's de time o' day!" said Sam. "It's Sam dat's called for in dese yer times. He's de nigger. See if I don't cotch her, now; Mas'r'll see what Sam can do!"

"Ah! but, Sam," said Andy, "you'd better think twice; for Missis don't want her cotched, and she'll be in yer wool."

"High!" said Sam, opening his eyes. "How you know dat?"

"Heard her say so, my own self, dis blessed mornin', when I bring in Mas'r's shaving-water. She sent me to see why Lizy didn't come to dress her; and when I telled her she was off, she jest ris up, and ses she, 'The Lord be praised;' and Mas'r, he seemed rael mad, and ses he, 'Wife, you talk like a fool.' But Lor! she'll bring him to! I knows well enough how that'll be,—it's allers best to stand Missis' side the fence, now I tell yer."

Black Sam, upon this, scratched his woolly pate, which, if it did not contain very profound wisdom, still contained a great deal of a particular species much in demand among politicians of all complexions and countries, and vulgarly denominated "knowing which side the bread is buttered;" so, stopping with grave consideration, he again gave a hitch to his pantaloons, which was his regularly organized method of assisting his mental perplexities.

"Der an't no saying'—never—'bout no kind o' thing in *dis* yer world," he said, at last. Sam spoke like a philosopher, emphasizing *this*—as if he had had a large experience in different sorts of worlds, and therefore had come to his conclusions advisedly.

"Now, sartin I'd a said that Missis would a scoured the varsal world after Lizy," added Sam, thoughtfully.

"So she would," said Andy; "but can't ye see through a ladder, ye black nigger? Missis don't want dis yer Mas'r Haley to get Lizy's boy; dat's de go!"

"High!" said Sam, with an indescribable intonation, known only to those who have heard it among the negroes.

"And I'll tell yer more 'n all," said Andy; "I specs you'd better be making tracks for dem hosses,—mighty sudden, too,—-for I hearn Missis 'quirin' arter yer,—so you've stood foolin' long enough."

Sam, upon this, began to bestir himself in real earnest, and after a while appeared, bearing down gloriously towards the house, with Bill and Jerry in a full canter, and adroitly throwing himself off before they had any idea of stopping, he brought them up alongside of the horse-post like a tornado. Haley's horse, which was a skittish young colt, winced, and bounced, and pulled hard at his halter.

"Ho, ho!" said Sam, "skeery, ar ye?" and his black visage lighted up with a curious, mischievous gleam. "I'll fix ye now!" said he.

There was a large beech-tree overshadowing the place, and the small, sharp, triangular beech-nuts lay scattered thickly on the ground. With one of these in his fingers, Sam approached the colt, stroked and patted, and seemed apparently busy in soothing his agitation. On pretence of adjusting the saddle, he adroitly slipped under it the sharp little nut, in such a manner that the least weight brought upon the saddle would annoy the nervous sensibilities of the animal, without leaving any perceptible graze or wound.

"Dar!" he said, rolling his eyes with an approving grin; "me fix 'em!"

CHAPTER VI

At this moment Mrs. Shelby appeared on the balcony, beckoning to him. Sam approached with as good a determination to pay court as did ever suitor after a vacant place at St. James' or Washington.

"Why have you been loitering so, Sam? I sent Andy to tell you to hurry."

"Lord bless you, Missis!" said Sam, "horses won't be cotched all in a minit; they'd done clared out way down to the south pasture, and the Lord knows whar!"

"Sam, how often must I tell you not to say 'Lord bless you, and the Lord knows,' and such things? It's wicked."

"O, Lord bless my soul! I done forgot, Missis! I won't say nothing of de sort no more."

"Why, Sam, you just *have* said it again."

"Did I? O, Lord! I mean—I didn't go fur to say it."

"You must be *careful*, Sam."

"Just let me get my breath, Missis, and I'll start fair. I'll be bery careful."

"Well, Sam, you are to go with Mr. Haley, to show him the road, and help him. Be careful of the horses, Sam; you know Jerry was a little lame last week; *don't ride them too fast*."

Mrs. Shelby spoke the last words with a low voice, and strong emphasis.

"Let dis child alone for dat!" said Sam, rolling up his eyes with a volume of meaning. "Lord knows! High! Didn't say dat!" said he, suddenly catching his breath, with a ludicrous flourish of apprehension, which made his mistress laugh, spite of herself. "Yes, Missis, I'll look out for de hosses!"

"Now, Andy," said Sam, returning to his stand under the beech-trees, "you see I wouldn't be 't all surprised if dat ar gen'lman's crittur should gib a fling, by and by, when he comes to be a gettin' up. You know, Andy, critturs *will* do such things;" and therewith Sam poked Andy in the side, in a highly suggestive manner.

"High!" said Andy, with an air of instant appreciation.

"Yes, you see, Andy, Missis wants to make time,—dat ar's clar to der most or'nary 'bserver. I jis make a little for her. Now, you see, get all dese yer hosses loose, caperin' permiscus round dis yer lot and down to de wood dar, and I spec Mas'r won't be off in a hurry."

Andy grinned.

"Yer see," said Sam, "yer see, Andy, if any such thing should happen as that Mas'r Haley's horse *should* begin to act contrary, and cut up, you and I jist lets go of our'n to help him, and *we'll help him*—oh yes!" And Sam and Andy laid their heads back on their shoulders, and broke into a low, immoderate laugh, snapping their fingers and flourishing their heels with exquisite delight.

At this instant, Haley appeared on the verandah. Somewhat mollified by certain cups of very good coffee, he came out smiling and talking, in tolerably restored humor. Sam and Andy, clawing for certain fragmentary palm-leaves, which they were in the habit of considering as hats, flew to the horseposts, to be ready to "help Mas'r."

Sam's palm-leaf had been ingeniously disentangled from all pretensions to braid, as respects its brim; and the slivers starting apart, and standing upright, gave it a blazing air of freedom and defiance, quite equal to that of any Fejee chief; while the whole brim of Andy's being departed bodily, he rapped the crown on his head with a dexterous thump, and looked about well pleased, as if to say, "Who says I haven't got a hat?"

"Well, boys," said Haley, "look alive now; we must lose no time."

"Not a bit of him, Mas'r!" said Sam, putting Haley's rein in his hand, and holding his stirrup, while Andy was untying the other two horses.

The instant Haley touched the saddle, the mettlesome creature bounded from the earth with a sudden spring, that threw his master sprawling, some feet off, on the soft, dry turf. Sam, with frantic ejaculations, made a dive at the reins, but only succeeded in brushing the blazing palm-leaf afore-named into the horse's eyes, which by no means tended to allay the confusion of his nerves. So, with great vehemence, he overturned Sam, and, giving two or three contemptuous snorts, flourished his heels vigorously in the air, and was soon prancing away towards the lower end of the lawn, followed by Bill and Jerry, whom Andy had not failed to let loose, according to contract, speeding them off with various direful ejaculations. And now ensued a miscellaneous scene of confusion. Sam and Andy ran and shouted,—dogs barked here and there,—and Mike, Mose, Mandy, Fanny, and all the smaller specimens on the place, both male and female, raced, clapped hands, whooped, and shouted, with outrageous officiousness and untiring zeal.

Haley's horse, which was a white one, and very fleet and spirited, appeared to enter into the spirit of the scene with great gusto; and having for his coursing ground a lawn of nearly half a mile in extent, gently sloping down on every side into indefinite woodland, he appeared to take infinite delight in seeing how near he could allow his pursuers to approach him, and then, when within a hand's breadth, whisk off with a start and a snort, like a mischievous beast as he was and career far down into some alley of the wood-lot. Nothing was further from Sam's mind than to have any one of the troop taken until such season as should seem to him most befitting,—and the exertions that he made were certainly most heroic. Like the sword of Coeur De Lion, which always blazed in the front and thickest of the battle, Sam's palm-leaf was to be seen everywhere when there was the least danger that a horse could be caught; there he would bear down full tilt, shouting, "Now for it! cotch him! cotch him!" in a way that would set everything to indiscriminate rout in a moment.

Haley ran up and down, and cursed and swore and stamped miscellaneously. Mr. Shelby in vain tried to shout directions from the balcony, and Mrs. Shelby from her chamber window alternately laughed and wondered,—not without some inkling of what lay at the bottom of all this confusion.

At last, about twelve o'clock, Sam appeared triumphant, mounted on Jerry, with Haley's horse by his side, reeking with sweat, but with flashing eyes and dilated nostrils, showing that the spirit of freedom had not yet entirely subsided.

"He's cotched!" he exclaimed, triumphantly. "If 't hadn't been for me, they might a bust themselves, all on 'em; but I cotched him!"

"You!" growled Haley, in no amiable mood. "If it hadn't been for you, this never would have happened."

"Lord bless us, Mas'r," said Sam, in a tone of the deepest concern, "and me that has been racin' and chasin' till the sweat jest pours off me!"

"Well, well!" said Haley, "you've lost me near three hours, with your cursed nonsense. Now let's be off, and have no more fooling."

"Why, Mas'r," said Sam, in a deprecating tone, "I believe you mean to kill us all clar, horses and all. Here we are all just ready to drop down, and the critters all in a reek of sweat. Why, Mas'r won't think of startin' on now till arter dinner. Mas'r's hoss wants rubben down; see how he splashed hisself; and Jerry limps too; don't think Missis would be willin' to have us start dis yer way, no how. Lord bless you, Mas'r, we can ketch up, if we do stop. Lizy never was no great of a walker."

Mrs. Shelby, who, greatly to her amusement, had overheard this conversation from the verandah, now resolved to do her part. She came forward, and, courteously expressing her concern for Haley's accident, pressed him to stay to dinner, saying that the cook should bring it on the table immediately.

Thus, all things considered, Haley, with rather an equivocal grace, proceeded to the parlor, while Sam, rolling his eyes after him with unutterable meaning, proceeded gravely with the horses to the stable-yard.

"Did yer see him, Andy? *did* yer see him?" said Sam, when he had got fairly beyond the shelter of the barn, and fastened the horse to a post. "O, Lor, if it warn't as good as a meetin', now, to see him a dancin' and kickin' and swarin' at us. Didn't I hear him? Swar away, ole fellow (says I to myself); will yer have yer hoss now, or wait till you cotch him? (says I). Lor, Andy, I think I can see him now." And Sam and Andy leaned up against the barn and laughed to their hearts' content.

"Yer oughter seen how mad he looked, when I brought the hoss up. Lord, he'd a killed me, if he durs' to; and there I was a standin' as innercent and as humble."

"Lor, I seed you," said Andy; "an't you an old hoss, Sam?"

"Rather specks I am," said Sam; "did yer see Missis up stars at the winder? I seed her laughin'."

"I'm sure, I was racin' so, I didn't see nothing," said Andy.

"Well, yer see," said Sam, proceeding gravely to wash down Haley's pony, "I 'se 'quired what yer may call a habit *o' bobservation*, Andy. It's a very 'portant habit, Andy; and I 'commend yer to be cultivatin' it, now yer young. Hist up that hind foot, Andy. Yer see, Andy, it's *bobservation* makes all de difference in niggers. Didn't I see which way the wind blew dis yer mornin'? Didn't I see what Missis wanted, though she never let on? Dat ar's bobservation, Andy. I 'spects it's what you may call a faculty. Faculties is different in different peoples, but cultivation of 'em goes a great way."

"I guess if I hadn't helped your bobservation dis mornin', yer wouldn't have seen your way so smart," said Andy.

"Andy," said Sam, "you's a promisin' child, der an't no manner o' doubt. I thinks lots of yer, Andy; and I don't feel no ways ashamed to take idees from you. We oughtenter overlook nobody, Andy, cause the smartest on us gets tripped up sometimes. And so, Andy, let's go up to the house now. I'll be boun' Missis'll give us an uncommon good bite, dis yer time."

CHAPTER VII

THE MOTHER'S STRUGGLE

It is impossible to conceive of a human creature more wholly desolate and forlorn than Eliza, when she turned her footsteps from Uncle Tom's cabin.

Her husband's suffering and dangers, and the danger of her child, all blended in her mind, with a confused and stunning sense of the risk she was running, in leaving the only home she had ever known, and cutting loose from the protection of a friend whom she loved and revered. Then there was the parting from every familiar object,—the place where she had grown up, the trees under which she had played, the groves where she had walked many an evening in happier days, by the side of her young husband,—everything, as it lay in the clear, frosty starlight, seemed to speak reproachfully to her, and ask her whither could she go from a home like that?

But stronger than all was maternal love, wrought into a paroxysm of frenzy by the near approach of a fearful danger. Her boy was old enough to have walked by her side, and, in an indifferent case, she would only have led him by the hand; but now the bare thought of putting him out of her arms made her shudder, and she strained him to her bosom with a convulsive grasp, as she went rapidly forward.

The frosty ground creaked beneath her feet, and she trembled at the sound; every quaking leaf and fluttering shadow sent the blood backward to her heart, and quickened her footsteps. She wondered within herself at the strength that seemed to be come upon her; for she felt the weight of her boy as if it had been a feather, and every flutter of fear seemed to increase the supernatural power that bore her on, while from her pale lips burst forth, in frequent ejaculations, the prayer to a Friend above—"Lord, help! Lord, save me!"

If it were *your* Harry, mother, or your Willie, that were going to be torn from you by a brutal trader, tomorrow morning,—if you had seen the man, and heard that the papers were signed and delivered, and you had only from twelve o'clock till morning to make good your escape,—how fast could *you* walk? How many miles could you make in those few brief hours, with the darling at your bosom,—the little sleepy head on your shoulder,—the small, soft arms trustingly holding on to your neck?

For the child slept. At first, the novelty and alarm kept him waking; but his mother so hurriedly repressed every breath or sound, and so assured him that if he were only still she would certainly save him, that he clung quietly round her neck, only asking, as he found himself sinking to sleep,

"Mother, I don't need to keep awake, do I?"

"No, my darling; sleep, if you want to."

"But, mother, if I do get asleep, you won't let him get me?"

"No! so may God help me!" said his mother, with a paler cheek, and a brighter light in her large dark eyes.

"You're *sure*, an't you, mother?"

"Yes, *sure*!" said the mother, in a voice that startled herself; for it seemed to her to come from a spirit within, that was no part of her; and the boy dropped his little weary head on her shoulder, and was soon asleep. How the touch of those warm arms, the gentle breathings that came in her neck, seemed to add fire and spirit to her movements! It seemed to her as if strength poured into her in electric streams, from every gentle touch and movement of the sleeping, confiding child. Sublime is the dominion of the mind over the body, that, for a time, can make flesh and nerve impregnable, and string the sinews like steel, so that the weak become so mighty.

The boundaries of the farm, the grove, the wood-lot, passed by her dizzily, as she walked on; and still she went, leaving one familiar object after another, slacking not, pausing not, till reddening daylight found her many a long mile from all traces of any familiar objects upon the open highway.

She had often been, with her mistress, to visit some connections, in the little village of T——, not far from the Ohio river, and knew the road well. To go thither, to escape across the Ohio river, were the first hurried outlines of her plan of escape; beyond that, she could only hope in God.

When horses and vehicles began to move along the highway, with that alert perception peculiar to a state of excitement, and which seems to be a sort of inspiration, she became aware that her headlong pace and distracted air might bring on her remark and suspicion. She therefore put the boy on the ground, and, adjusting her dress and bonnet, she walked on at as rapid a pace as she thought consistent with the preservation of appearances. In her little bundle she had provided a store of cakes and apples, which she used as expedients for quickening the speed of the child, rolling the apple some yards before them, when the boy would run with all his might after it; and this ruse, often repeated, carried them over many a half-mile.

After a while, they came to a thick patch of woodland, through which murmured a clear brook. As the child complained of hunger and thirst, she climbed over the fence with him; and, sitting down behind a large rock which concealed them from the road, she gave him a breakfast out of her little package. The boy wondered and grieved that she could not eat; and when, putting his arms round her neck, he tried to wedge some of his cake into her mouth, it seemed to her that the rising in her throat would choke her.

CHAPTER VII

"No, no, Harry darling! mother can't eat till you are safe! We must go on—on—till we come to the river!" And she hurried again into the road, and again constrained herself to walk regularly and composedly forward.

She was many miles past any neighborhood where she was personally known. If she should chance to meet any who knew her, she reflected that the well-known kindness of the family would be of itself a blind to suspicion, as making it an unlikely supposition that she could be a fugitive. As she was also so white as not to be known as of colored lineage, without a critical survey, and her child was white also, it was much easier for her to pass on unsuspected.

On this presumption, she stopped at noon at a neat farmhouse, to rest herself, and buy some dinner for her child and self; for, as the danger decreased with the distance, the supernatural tension of the nervous system lessened, and she found herself both weary and hungry.

The good woman, kindly and gossipping, seemed rather pleased than otherwise with having somebody come in to talk with; and accepted, without examination, Eliza's statement, that she "was going on a little piece, to spend a week with her friends,"—all which she hoped in her heart might prove strictly true.

An hour before sunset, she entered the village of T——, by the Ohio river, weary and foot-sore, but still strong in heart. Her first glance was at the river, which lay, like Jordan, between her and the Canaan of liberty on the other side.

It was now early spring, and the river was swollen and turbulent; great cakes of floating ice were swinging heavily to and fro in the turbid waters. Owing to the peculiar form of the shore on the Kentucky side, the land bending far out into the water, the ice had been lodged and detained in great quantities, and the narrow channel which swept round the bend was full of ice, piled one cake over another, thus forming a temporary barrier to the descending ice, which lodged, and formed a great, undulating raft, filling up the whole river, and extending almost to the Kentucky shore.

Eliza stood, for a moment, contemplating this unfavorable aspect of things, which she saw at once must prevent the usual ferry-boat from running, and then turned into a small public house on the bank, to make a few inquiries.

The hostess, who was busy in various fizzing and stewing operations over the fire, preparatory to the evening meal, stopped, with a fork in her hand, as Eliza's sweet and plaintive voice arrested her.

"What is it?" she said.

"Isn't there any ferry or boat, that takes people over to B——, now?" she said.

"No, indeed!" said the woman; "the boats has stopped running."

Eliza's look of dismay and disappointment struck the woman, and she said, inquiringly,

"May be you're wanting to get over?—anybody sick? Ye seem mighty anxious?"

"I've got a child that's very dangerous," said Eliza. "I never heard of it till last night, and I've walked quite a piece today, in hopes to get to the ferry."

"Well, now, that's onlucky," said the woman, whose motherly sympathies were much aroused; "I'm re'lly consarned for ye. Solomon!" she called, from the window, towards a small back building. A man, in leather apron and very dirty hands, appeared at the door.

"I say, Sol," said the woman, "is that ar man going to tote them bar'ls over tonight?"

"He said he should try, if 't was any way prudent," said the man.

"There's a man a piece down here, that's going over with some truck this evening, if he durs' to; he'll be in here to supper tonight, so you'd better set down and wait. That's a sweet little fellow," added the woman, offering him a cake.

But the child, wholly exhausted, cried with weariness.

"Poor fellow! he isn't used to walking, and I've hurried him on so," said Eliza.

"Well, take him into this room," said the woman, opening into a small bedroom, where stood a comfortable bed. Eliza laid the weary boy upon it, and held his hands in hers till he was fast asleep. For her there was no rest. As a fire in her bones, the thought of the pursuer urged her on; and she gazed with longing eyes on the sullen, surging waters that lay between her and liberty.

Here we must take our leave of her for the present, to follow the course of her pursuers.

Though Mrs. Shelby had promised that the dinner should be hurried on table, yet it was soon seen, as the thing has often been seen before, that it required more than one to make a bargain. So, although the order was fairly given out in Haley's hearing, and carried to Aunt Chloe by at least half a dozen juvenile messengers, that dignitary only gave certain very gruff snorts, and tosses of her head, and went on with every operation in an unusually leisurely and circumstantial manner.

For some singular reason, an impression seemed to reign among the servants generally that Missis would not be particularly disobliged by delay; and it was wonderful what a number of counter accidents occurred constantly, to retard the course of things. One luckless wight contrived to upset the gravy; and then gravy had to be got up *de novo*, with due care and formality, Aunt Chloe watching and stirring with dogged precision, answering shortly, to all suggestions of haste, that she "warn't a going to have raw gravy on the table, to help nobody's catchings." One tumbled down with the water, and had to go to the spring for more; and another precipitated the butter into the path of events; and there was from time to time giggling news brought into the kitchen that "Mas'r Haley was mighty oneasy, and that he couldn't sit in his cheer no ways, but was a walkin' and stalkin' to the winders and through the porch."

"Sarves him right!" said Aunt Chloe, indignantly. "He'll get wus nor oneasy, one of these days, if he don't mend his ways. *His* master'll be sending for him, and then see how he'll look!"

"He'll go to torment, and no mistake," said little Jake.

"He desarves it!" said Aunt Chloe, grimly; "he's broke a many, many, many hearts,—I tell ye all!" she said, stopping, with a fork uplifted in her hands; "it's like what Mas'r George reads in Ravelations,—souls a callin' under the altar! and a callin' on the Lord for vengeance on sich!—and by and by the Lord he'll hear 'em—so he will!"

Aunt Chloe, who was much revered in the kitchen, was listened to with open mouth; and, the dinner being now fairly sent in, the whole kitchen was at leisure to gossip with her, and to listen to her remarks.

"Sich'll be burnt up forever, and no mistake; won't ther?" said Andy.

"I'd be glad to see it, I'll be boun'," said little Jake.

"Chil'en!" said a voice, that made them all start. It was Uncle Tom, who had come in, and stood listening to the conversation at the door.

"Chil'en!" he said, "I'm afeard you don't know what ye're sayin'. Forever is a *dre'ful* word, chil'en; it's awful to think on 't. You oughtenter wish that ar to any human crittur."

"We wouldn't to anybody but the soul-drivers," said Andy; "nobody can help wishing it to them, they 's so awful wicked."

"Don't natur herself kinder cry out on 'em?" said Aunt Chloe. "Don't dey tear der suckin' baby right off his mother's breast, and sell him, and der little children as is crying and holding on by her clothes,—don't dey pull 'em off and sells 'em? Don't dey tear wife and husband apart?" said Aunt Chloe, beginning to cry, "when it's jest takin' the very life on 'em?—and all the while does they feel one bit, don't dey drink and smoke, and take it oncommon easy? Lor, if the devil don't get them, what's he good for?" And Aunt Chloe covered her face with her checked apron, and began to sob in good earnest.

"Pray for them that 'spitefully use you, the good book says," says Tom.

"Pray for 'em!" said Aunt Chloe; "Lor, it's too tough! I can't pray for 'em."

"It's natur, Chloe, and natur 's strong," said Tom, "but the Lord's grace is stronger; besides, you oughter think what an awful state a poor crittur's soul 's in that'll do them ar things,—you oughter thank God that you an't *like* him, Chloe. I'm sure I'd rather be sold, ten thousand times over, than to have all that ar poor crittur's got to answer for."

"So 'd I, a heap," said Jake. "Lor, *shouldn't* we cotch it, Andy?"

Andy shrugged his shoulders, and gave an acquiescent whistle.

"I'm glad Mas'r didn't go off this morning, as he looked to," said Tom; "that ar hurt me more than sellin', it did. Mebbe it might have been natural for him, but 't would have come desp't hard on me, as has known him from a baby; but I've seen Mas'r, and I begin ter feel sort o' reconciled to the Lord's will now. Mas'r couldn't help hisself; he did right, but I'm feared things will be kinder goin' to rack, when I'm gone Mas'r can't be spected to be a pryin' round everywhar, as I've done, a keepin' up all the ends. The boys all means well, but they 's powerful car'less. That ar troubles me."

The bell here rang, and Tom was summoned to the parlor.

"Tom," said his master, kindly, "I want you to notice that I give this gentleman bonds to forfeit a thousand dollars if you are not on the spot when he wants you; he's going today to look after his other business, and you can have the day to yourself. Go anywhere you like, boy."

"Thank you, Mas'r," said Tom.

"And mind yourself," said the trader, "and don't come it over your master with any o' yer nigger tricks; for I'll take every cent out of him, if you an't thar. If he'd hear to me, he wouldn't trust any on ye—slippery as eels!"

"Mas'r," said Tom,—and he stood very straight,—"I was jist eight years old when ole Missis put you into my arms, and you wasn't a year old. 'Thar,' says she, 'Tom, that's to be *your* young Mas'r; take good care on him,' says she. And now I jist ask you, Mas'r, have I ever broke word to you, or gone contrary to you, 'specially since I was a Christian?"

Mr. Shelby was fairly overcome, and the tears rose to his eyes.

"My good boy," said he, "the Lord knows you say but the truth; and if I was able to help it, all the world shouldn't buy you."

"And sure as I am a Christian woman," said Mrs. Shelby, "you shall be redeemed as soon as I can any way bring together means. Sir," she said to Haley, "take good account of who you sell him to, and let me know."

"Lor, yes, for that matter," said the trader, "I may bring him up in a year, not much the wuss for wear, and trade him back."

"I'll trade with you then, and make it for your advantage," said Mrs. Shelby.

"Of course," said the trader, "all 's equal with me; li'ves trade 'em up as down, so I does a good business. All I want is a livin', you know, ma'am; that's all any on us wants, I, s'pose."

Mr. and Mrs. Shelby both felt annoyed and degraded by the familiar impudence of the trader, and yet both saw the absolute necessity of putting a constraint on their feelings. The more hopelessly sordid and insensible he appeared, the greater became Mrs. Shelby's dread of his succeeding in recapturing Eliza and her child, and of course the greater her motive for detaining him by every female artifice. She therefore graciously smiled, assented, chatted familiarly, and did all she could to make time pass imperceptibly.

At two o'clock Sam and Andy brought the horses up to the posts, apparently greatly refreshed and invigorated by the scamper of the morning.

Sam was there new oiled from dinner, with an abundance of zealous and ready officiousness. As Haley approached, he was boasting, in flourishing style, to Andy, of the evident and eminent success of the operation, now that he had "farly come to it."

"Your master, I s'pose, don't keep no dogs," said Haley, thoughtfully, as he prepared to mount.

"Heaps on 'em," said Sam, triumphantly; "thar's Bruno—he's a roarer! and, besides that, 'bout every nigger of us keeps a pup of some natur or uther."

"Poh!" said Haley,—and he said something else, too, with regard to the said dogs, at which Sam muttered,

"I don't see no use cussin' on 'em, no way."

"But your master don't keep no dogs (I pretty much know he don't) for trackin' out niggers."

Sam knew exactly what he meant, but he kept on a look of earnest and desperate simplicity.

"Our dogs all smells round considable sharp. I spect they's the kind, though they han't never had no practice. They 's *far* dogs, though, at most anything, if you'd get 'em started. Here, Bruno," he called, whistling to the lumbering Newfoundland, who came pitching tumultuously toward them.

"You go hang!" said Haley, getting up. "Come, tumble up now."

Sam tumbled up accordingly, dexterously contriving to tickle Andy as he did so, which occasioned Andy to split out into a laugh, greatly to Haley's indignation, who made a cut at him with his riding-whip.

"I 's 'stonished at yer, Andy," said Sam, with awful gravity. "This yer's a seris bisness, Andy. Yer mustn't be a makin' game. This yer an't no way to help Mas'r."

"I shall take the straight road to the river," said Haley, decidedly, after they had come to the boundaries of the estate. "I know the way of all of 'em,—they makes tracks for the underground."

"Sartin," said Sam, "dat's de idee. Mas'r Haley hits de thing right in de middle. Now, der's two roads to de river,—de dirt road and der pike,—which Mas'r mean to take?"

Andy looked up innocently at Sam, surprised at hearing this new geographical fact, but instantly confirmed what he said, by a vehement reiteration.

"Cause," said Sam, "I'd rather be 'clined to 'magine that Lizy 'd take de dirt road, bein' it's the least travelled."

Haley, notwithstanding that he was a very old bird, and naturally inclined to be suspicious of chaff, was rather brought up by this view of the case.

"If yer warn't both on yer such cussed liars, now!" he said, contemplatively as he pondered a moment.

The pensive, reflective tone in which this was spoken appeared to amuse Andy prodigiously, and he drew a little behind, and shook so as apparently to run a great risk of failing off his horse, while Sam's face was immovably composed into the most doleful gravity.

"Course," said Sam, "Mas'r can do as he'd ruther, go de straight road, if Mas'r thinks best,—it's all one to us. Now, when I study 'pon it, I think de straight road de best, *deridedly*."

"She would naturally go a lonesome way," said Haley, thinking aloud, and not minding Sam's remark.

"Dar an't no sayin'," said Sam; "gals is pecular; they never does nothin' ye thinks they will; mose gen'lly the contrary. Gals is nat'lly made contrary; and so, if you thinks they've gone one road, it is sartin you'd better go t' other, and then you'll be sure to find 'em. Now, my private 'pinion is, Lizy took der road; so I think we'd better take de straight one."

This profound generic view of the female sex did not seem to dispose Haley particularly to the straight road, and he announced decidedly that he should go the other, and asked Sam when they should come to it.

"A little piece ahead," said Sam, giving a wink to Andy with the eye which was on Andy's side of the head; and he added, gravely, "but I've studded on de matter, and I'm quite clar we ought not to go dat ar way. I nebber been over it no way. It's despit lonesome, and we might lose our way,—whar we'd come to, de Lord only knows."

"Nevertheless," said Haley, "I shall go that way."

"Now I think on 't, I think I hearn 'em tell that dat ar road was all fenced up and down by der creek, and thar, an't it, Andy?"

Andy wasn't certain; he'd only "hearn tell" about that road, but never been over it. In short, he was strictly noncommittal.

Haley, accustomed to strike the balance of probabilities between lies of greater or lesser magnitude, thought that it lay in favor of the dirt road aforesaid. The mention of the thing he thought he perceived was involuntary on Sam's part at first, and his confused attempts to dissuade him he set down to a desperate lying on second thoughts, as being unwilling to implicate Liza.

When, therefore, Sam indicated the road, Haley plunged briskly into it, followed by Sam and Andy.

Now, the road, in fact, was an old one, that had formerly been a thoroughfare to the river, but abandoned for many years after the laying of the new pike. It was open for about an hour's ride, and after that it was cut across by various farms and fences. Sam knew this fact perfectly well,—indeed, the road had been so long closed up, that Andy had never heard of it. He therefore rode along with an air of dutiful submission, only groaning and vociferating occasionally that 't was "desp't rough, and bad for Jerry's foot."

"Now, I jest give yer warning," said Haley, "I know yer; yer won't get me to turn off this road, with all yer fussin'—so you shet up!"

"Mas'r will go his own way!" said Sam, with rueful submission, at the same time winking most portentously to Andy, whose delight was now very near the explosive point.

Sam was in wonderful spirits,—professed to keep a very brisk lookout,—at one time exclaiming that he saw "a gal's bonnet" on the top of some distant eminence, or calling to Andy "if that thar wasn't 'Lizy' down in the hollow;" always making these exclamations in some rough or craggy part of the road, where the sudden quickening of speed was a special inconvenience to all parties concerned, and thus keeping Haley in a state of constant commotion.

After riding about an hour in this way, the whole party made a precipitate and tumultuous descent into a barn-yard belonging to a large farming establishment. Not a soul was in sight, all the hands being employed in the fields; but, as the barn stood conspicuously and plainly square across the road, it was evident that their journey in that direction had reached a decided finale.

"Wan't dat ar what I telled Mas'r?" said Sam, with an air of injured innocence. "How does strange gentleman spect to know more about a country dan de natives born and raised?"

"You rascal!" said Haley, "you knew all about this."

CHAPTER VII

"Didn't I tell yer I *knowd*, and yer wouldn't believe me? I telled Mas'r 't was all shet up, and fenced up, and I didn't spect we could get through,—Andy heard me."

It was all too true to be disputed, and the unlucky man had to pocket his wrath with the best grace he was able, and all three faced to the right about, and took up their line of march for the highway.

In consequence of all the various delays, it was about three-quarters of an hour after Eliza had laid her child to sleep in the village tavern that the party came riding into the same place. Eliza was standing by the window, looking out in another direction, when Sam's quick eye caught a glimpse of her. Haley and Andy were two yards behind. At this crisis, Sam contrived to have his hat blown off, and uttered a loud and characteristic ejaculation, which startled her at once; she drew suddenly back; the whole train swept by the window, round to the front door.

A thousand lives seemed to be concentrated in that one moment to Eliza. Her room opened by a side door to the river. She caught her child, and sprang down the steps towards it. The trader caught a full glimpse of her just as she was disappearing down the bank; and throwing himself from his horse, and calling loudly on Sam and Andy, he was after her like a hound after a deer. In that dizzy moment her feet to her scarce seemed to touch the ground, and a moment brought her to the water's edge. Right on behind they came; and, nerved with strength such as God gives only to the desperate, with one wild cry and flying leap, she vaulted sheer over the turbid current by the shore, on to the raft of ice beyond. It was a desperate leap—impossible to anything but madness and despair; and Haley, Sam, and Andy, instinctively cried out, and lifted up their hands, as she did it.

The huge green fragment of ice on which she alighted pitched and creaked as her weight came on it, but she staid there not a moment. With wild cries and desperate energy she leaped to another and still another cake; stumbling—leaping—slipping—springing upwards again! Her shoes are gone—her stockings cut from her feet—while blood marked every step; but she saw nothing, felt nothing, till dimly, as in a dream, she saw the Ohio side, and a man helping her up the bank.

"Yer a brave gal, now, whoever ye ar!" said the man, with an oath.

Eliza recognized the voice and face for a man who owned a farm not far from her old home.

"O, Mr. Symmes!—save me—do save me—do hide me!" said Elia.

"Why, what's this?" said the man. "Why, if 'tan't Shelby's gal!"

"My child!—this boy!—he'd sold him! There is his Mas'r," said she, pointing to the Kentucky shore. "O, Mr. Symmes, you've got a little boy!"

"So I have," said the man, as he roughly, but kindly, drew her up the steep bank. "Besides, you're a right brave gal. I like grit, wherever I see it."

When they had gained the top of the bank, the man paused.

"I'd be glad to do something for ye," said he; "but then there's nowhar I could take ye. The best I can do is to tell ye to go *thar*," said he, pointing to a large white house which stood by itself, off the main street of the village. "Go thar;

they're kind folks. Thar's no kind o' danger but they'll help you,—they're up to all that sort o' thing."

"The Lord bless you!" said Eliza, earnestly.

"No 'casion, no 'casion in the world," said the man. "What I've done's of no 'count."

"And, oh, surely, sir, you won't tell any one!"

"Go to thunder, gal! What do you take a feller for? In course not," said the man. "Come, now, go along like a likely, sensible gal, as you are. You've arnt your liberty, and you shall have it, for all me."

The woman folded her child to her bosom, and walked firmly and swiftly away. The man stood and looked after her.

"Shelby, now, mebbe won't think this yer the most neighborly thing in the world; but what's a feller to do? If he catches one of my gals in the same fix, he's welcome to pay back. Somehow I never could see no kind o' critter a strivin' and pantin', and trying to clar theirselves, with the dogs arter 'em and go agin 'em. Besides, I don't see no kind of 'casion for me to be hunter and catcher for other folks, neither."

So spoke this poor, heathenish Kentuckian, who had not been instructed in his constitutional relations, and consequently was betrayed into acting in a sort of Christianized manner, which, if he had been better situated and more enlightened, he would not have been left to do.

Haley had stood a perfectly amazed spectator of the scene, till Eliza had disappeared up the bank, when he turned a blank, inquiring look on Sam and Andy.

"That ar was a tolable fair stroke of business," said Sam.

"The gal 's got seven devils in her, I believe!" said Haley. "How like a wildcat she jumped!"

"Wal, now," said Sam, scratching his head, "I hope Mas'r'll 'scuse us trying dat ar road. Don't think I feel spry enough for dat ar, no way!" and Sam gave a hoarse chuckle.

"*You* laugh!" said the trader, with a growl.

"Lord bless you, Mas'r, I couldn't help it now," said Sam, giving way to the long pent-up delight of his soul. "She looked so curi's, a leapin' and springin'—ice a crackin'—and only to hear her,—plump! ker chunk! ker splash! Spring! Lord! how she goes it!" and Sam and Andy laughed till the tears rolled down their cheeks.

"I'll make ye laugh t' other side yer mouths!" said the trader, laying about their heads with his riding-whip.

Both ducked, and ran shouting up the bank, and were on their horses before he was up.

"Good-evening, Mas'r!" said Sam, with much gravity. "I berry much spect Missis be anxious 'bout Jerry. Mas'r Haley won't want us no longer. Missis wouldn't hear of our ridin' the critters over Lizy's bridge tonight;" and, with a facetious poke into Andy's ribs, he started off, followed by the latter, at full speed,—their shouts of laughter coming faintly on the wind.

CHAPTER VIII

ELIZA'S ESCAPE

Eliza made her desperate retreat across the river just in the dusk of twilight. The gray mist of evening, rising slowly from the river, enveloped her as she disappeared up the bank, and the swollen current and floundering masses of ice presented a hopeless barrier between her and her pursuer. Haley therefore slowly and discontentedly returned to the little tavern, to ponder further what was to be done. The woman opened to him the door of a little parlor, covered with a rag carpet, where stood a table with a very shining black oil-cloth, sundry lank, high-backed wood chairs, with some plaster images in resplendent colors on the mantel-shelf, above a very dimly-smoking grate; a long hard-wood settle extended its uneasy length by the chimney, and here Haley sat him down to meditate on the instability of human hopes and happiness in general.

"What did I want with the little cuss, now," he said to himself, "that I should have got myself treed like a coon, as I am, this yer way?" and Haley relieved himself by repeating over a not very select litany of imprecations on himself, which, though there was the best possible reason to consider them as true, we shall, as a matter of taste, omit.

He was startled by the loud and dissonant voice of a man who was apparently dismounting at the door. He hurried to the window.

"By the land! if this yer an't the nearest, now, to what I've heard folks call Providence," said Haley. "I do b'lieve that ar's Tom Loker."

Haley hastened out. Standing by the bar, in the corner of the room, was a brawny, muscular man, full six feet in height, and broad in proportion. He was dressed in a coat of buffalo-skin, made with the hair outward, which gave him a shaggy and fierce appearance, perfectly in keeping with the whole air of his physiognomy. In the head and face every organ and lineament expressive of brutal and unhesitating violence was in a state of the highest possible development. Indeed, could our readers fancy a bull-dog come unto man's estate, and walking about in a hat and coat, they would have no unapt idea of the general style and effect of his physique. He was accompanied by a travelling companion, in many respects an exact contrast to himself. He was short and slender, lithe and catlike in his motions, and had a peering, mousing expression about his keen black eyes, with which every feature of his face seemed sharpened into sympathy; his thin, long nose, ran out as if it was eager to bore into the nature of things in general; his sleek, thin, black hair was stuck eagerly forward, and all his motions and evolutions expressed a dry, cautious acuteness. The great man poured out a big tumbler half full of raw spirits, and gulped it down without a word. The little man stood tiptoe, and putting his head first to one side and then the other, and snuffing considerately in the directions of the various bottles, ordered at last a mint julep, in a thin and quivering voice, and with an air of great circumspection. When poured out, he took it and looked at it with a sharp, complacent air, like a man who thinks he has done about the right thing, and hit the nail on the head, and proceeded to dispose of it in short and well-advised sips.

"Wal, now, who'd a thought this yer luck 'ad come to me? Why, Loker, how are ye?" said Haley, coming forward, and extending his hand to the big man.

"The devil!" was the civil reply. "What brought you here, Haley?"

The mousing man, who bore the name of Marks, instantly stopped his sipping, and, poking his head forward, looked shrewdly on the new acquaintance, as a cat sometimes looks at a moving dry leaf, or some other possible object of pursuit.

"I say, Tom, this yer's the luckiest thing in the world. I'm in a devil of a hobble, and you must help me out."

"Ugh? aw! like enough!" grunted his complacent acquaintance. "A body may be pretty sure of that, when *you're* glad to see 'em; something to be made off of 'em. What's the blow now?"

"You've got a friend here?" said Haley, looking doubtfully at Marks; "partner, perhaps?"

"Yes, I have. Here, Marks! here's that ar feller that I was in with in Natchez."

"Shall be pleased with his acquaintance," said Marks, thrusting out a long, thin hand, like a raven's claw. "Mr. Haley, I believe?"

"The same, sir," said Haley. "And now, gentlemen, seein' as we've met so happily, I think I'll stand up to a small matter of a treat in this here parlor. So, now, old coon," said he to the man at the bar, "get us hot water, and sugar, and cigars, and plenty of the *real stuff* and we'll have a blow-out."

Behold, then, the candles lighted, the fire stimulated to the burning point in the grate, and our three worthies seated round a table, well spread with all the accessories to good fellowship enumerated before.

Haley began a pathetic recital of his peculiar troubles. Loker shut up his mouth, and listened to him with gruff and surly attention. Marks, who was anxiously and with much fidgeting compounding a tumbler of punch to his own peculiar taste, occasionally looked up from his employment, and, poking his sharp nose and chin almost into Haley's face, gave the most earnest heed to the whole narrative. The conclusion of it appeared to amuse him extremely, for he shook his shoulders and sides in silence, and perked up his thin lips with an air of great internal enjoyment.

CHAPTER VIII

"So, then, ye'r fairly sewed up, an't ye?" he said; "he! he! he! It's neatly done, too."

"This yer young-un business makes lots of trouble in the trade," said Haley, dolefully.

"If we could get a breed of gals that didn't care, now, for their young uns," said Marks; "tell ye, I think 't would be 'bout the greatest mod'rn improvement I knows on,"—and Marks patronized his joke by a quiet introductory sniggle.

"Jes so," said Haley; "I never couldn't see into it; young uns is heaps of trouble to 'em; one would think, now, they'd be glad to get clar on 'em; but they arn't. And the more trouble a young un is, and the more good for nothing, as a gen'l thing, the tighter they sticks to 'em."

"Wal, Mr. Haley," said Marks, "'est pass the hot water. Yes, sir, you say 'est what I feel and all'us have. Now, I bought a gal once, when I was in the trade,—a tight, likely wench she was, too, and quite considerable smart,—and she had a young un that was mis'able sickly; it had a crooked back, or something or other; and I jest gin 't away to a man that thought he'd take his chance raising on 't, being it didn't cost nothin';—never thought, yer know, of the gal's takin' on about it,—but, Lord, yer oughter seen how she went on. Why, re'lly, she did seem to me to valley the child more 'cause *'t was* sickly and cross, and plagued her; and she warn't making b'lieve, neither,—cried about it, she did, and lopped round, as if she'd lost every friend she had. It re'lly was droll to think on 't. Lord, there ain't no end to women's notions."

"Wal, jest so with me," said Haley. "Last summer, down on Red River, I got a gal traded off on me, with a likely lookin' child enough, and his eyes looked as bright as yourn; but, come to look, I found him stone blind. Fact—he was stone blind. Wal, ye see, I thought there warn't no harm in my jest passing him along, and not sayin' nothin'; and I'd got him nicely swapped off for a keg o' whiskey; but come to get him away from the gal, she was jest like a tiger. So 't was before we started, and I hadn't got my gang chained up; so what should she do but ups on a cotton-bale, like a cat, ketches a knife from one of the deck hands, and, I tell ye, she made all fly for a minit, till she saw 't wan't no use; and she jest turns round, and pitches head first, young un and all, into the river,—went down plump, and never ris."

"Bah!" said Tom Loker, who had listened to these stories with ill-repressed disgust,—"shif'less, both on ye! *my* gals don't cut up no such shines, I tell ye!"

"Indeed! how do you help it?" said Marks, briskly.

"Help it? why, I buys a gal, and if she's got a young un to be sold, I jest walks up and puts my fist to her face, and says, 'Look here, now, if you give me one word out of your head, I'll smash yer face in. I won't hear one word—not the beginning of a word.' I says to 'em, 'This yer young un's mine, and not yourn, and you've no kind o' business with it. I'm going to sell it, first chance; mind, you don't cut up none o' yer shines about it, or I'll make ye wish ye'd never been born.' I tell ye, they sees it an't no play, when I gets hold. I makes 'em as whist as fishes;

and if one on 'em begins and gives a yelp, why,—" and Mr. Loker brought down his fist with a thump that fully explained the hiatus.

"That ar's what ye may call *emphasis*," said Marks, poking Haley in the side, and going into another small giggle. "An't Tom peculiar? he! he! I say, Tom, I s'pect you make 'em *understand*, for all niggers' heads is woolly. They don't never have no doubt o' your meaning, Tom. If you an't the devil, Tom, you 's his twin brother, I'll say that for ye!"

Tom received the compliment with becoming modesty, and began to look as affable as was consistent, as John Bunyan says, "with his doggish nature."

Haley, who had been imbibing very freely of the staple of the evening, began to feel a sensible elevation and enlargement of his moral faculties,—a phenomenon not unusual with gentlemen of a serious and reflective turn, under similar circumstances.

"Wal, now, Tom," he said, "ye re'lly is too bad, as I al'ays have told ye; ye know, Tom, you and I used to talk over these yer matters down in Natchez, and I used to prove to ye that we made full as much, and was as well off for this yer world, by treatin' on 'em well, besides keepin' a better chance for comin' in the kingdom at last, when wust comes to wust, and thar an't nothing else left to get, ye know."

"Boh!" said Tom, "*don't* I know?—don't make me too sick with any yer stuff,—my stomach is a leetle riled now;" and Tom drank half a glass of raw brandy.

"I say," said Haley, and leaning back in his chair and gesturing impressively, "I'll say this now, I al'ays meant to drive my trade so as to make money on 't *fust and foremost*, as much as any man; but, then, trade an't everything, and money an't everything, 'cause we 's all got souls. I don't care, now, who hears me say it,—and I think a cussed sight on it,—so I may as well come out with it. I b'lieve in religion, and one of these days, when I've got matters tight and snug, I calculates to tend to my soul and them ar matters; and so what's the use of doin' any more wickedness than 's re'lly necessary?—it don't seem to me it's 't all prudent."

"Tend to yer soul!" repeated Tom, contemptuously; "take a bright lookout to find a soul in you,—save yourself any care on that score. If the devil sifts you through a hair sieve, he won't find one."

"Why, Tom, you're cross," said Haley; "why can't ye take it pleasant, now, when a feller's talking for your good?"

"Stop that ar jaw o' yourn, there," said Tom, gruffly. "I can stand most any talk o' yourn but your pious talk,—that kills me right up. After all, what's the odds between me and you? 'Tan't that you care one bit more, or have a bit more feelin'—it's clean, sheer, dog meanness, wanting to cheat the devil and save your own skin; don't I see through it? And your 'gettin' religion,' as you call it, arter all, is too p'isin mean for any crittur;—run up a bill with the devil all your life, and then sneak out when pay time comes! Bob!"

"Come, come, gentlemen, I say; this isn't business," said Marks. "There's different ways, you know, of looking at all subjects. Mr. Haley is a very nice man, no doubt, and has his own conscience; and, Tom, you have your ways, and very good ones, too, Tom; but quarrelling, you know, won't answer no kind of purpose. Let's go to business. Now, Mr. Haley, what is it?—you want us to undertake to catch this yer gal?"

"The gal's no matter of mine,—she's Shelby's; it's only the boy. I was a fool for buying the monkey!"

"You're generally a fool!" said Tom, gruffly.

"Come, now, Loker, none of your huffs," said Marks, licking his lips; "you see, Mr. Haley 's a puttin' us in a way of a good job, I reckon; just hold still—these yer arrangements is my forte. This yer gal, Mr. Haley, how is she? what is she?"

"Wal! white and handsome—well brought up. I'd a gin Shelby eight hundred or a thousand, and then made well on her."

"White and handsome—well brought up!" said Marks, his sharp eyes, nose and mouth, all alive with enterprise. "Look here, now, Loker, a beautiful opening. We'll do a business here on our own account;—we does the catchin'; the boy, of course, goes to Mr. Haley,—we takes the gal to Orleans to speculate on. An't it beautiful?"

Tom, whose great heavy mouth had stood ajar during this communication, now suddenly snapped it together, as a big dog closes on a piece of meat, and seemed to be digesting the idea at his leisure.

"Ye see," said Marks to Haley, stirring his punch as he did so, "ye see, we has justices convenient at all p'ints along shore, that does up any little jobs in our line quite reasonable. Tom, he does the knockin' down and that ar; and I come in all dressed up—shining boots—everything first chop, when the swearin' 's to be done. You oughter see, now," said Marks, in a glow of professional pride, "how I can tone it off. One day, I'm Mr. Twickem, from New Orleans; 'nother day, I'm just come from my plantation on Pearl River, where I works seven hundred niggers; then, again, I come out a distant relation of Henry Clay, or some old cock in Kentuck. Talents is different, you know. Now, Tom's roarer when there's any thumping or fighting to be done; but at lying he an't good, Tom an't,—ye see it don't come natural to him; but, Lord, if thar's a feller in the country that can swear to anything and everything, and put in all the circumstances and flourishes with a long face, and carry 't through better 'n I can, why, I'd like to see him, that's all! I b'lieve my heart, I could get along and snake through, even if justices were more particular than they is. Sometimes I rather wish they was more particular; 't would be a heap more relishin' if they was,—more fun, yer know."

Tom Loker, who, as we have made it appear, was a man of slow thoughts and movements, here interrupted Marks by bringing his heavy fist down on the table, so as to make all ring again, *"It'll do!"* he said.

"Lord bless ye, Tom, ye needn't break all the glasses!" said Marks; "save your fist for time o' need."

"But, gentlemen, an't I to come in for a share of the profits?" said Haley.

"An't it enough we catch the boy for ye?" said Loker. "What do ye want?"

"Wal," said Haley, "if I gives you the job, it's worth something,—say ten per cent. on the profits, expenses paid."

"Now," said Loker, with a tremendous oath, and striking the table with his heavy fist, "don't I know *you*, Dan Haley? Don't you think to come it over me! Suppose Marks and I have taken up the catchin' trade, jest to 'commodate gentlemen like you, and get nothin' for ourselves?—Not by a long chalk! we'll have the gal out and out, and you keep quiet, or, ye see, we'll have both,—what's to hinder? Han't you show'd us the game? It's as free to us as you, I hope. If you or Shelby wants to chase us, look where the partridges was last year; if you find them or us, you're quite welcome."

"O, wal, certainly, jest let it go at that," said Haley, alarmed; "you catch the boy for the job;—you allers did trade *far* with me, Tom, and was up to yer word."

"Ye know that," said Tom; "I don't pretend none of your snivelling ways, but I won't lie in my 'counts with the devil himself. What I ses I'll do, I will do,—you know *that*, Dan Haley."

"Jes so, jes so,—I said so, Tom," said Haley; "and if you'd only promise to have the boy for me in a week, at any point you'll name, that's all I want."

"But it an't all I want, by a long jump," said Tom. "Ye don't think I did business with you, down in Natchez, for nothing, Haley; I've learned to hold an eel, when I catch him. You've got to fork over fifty dollars, flat down, or this child don't start a peg. I know yer."

"Why, when you have a job in hand that may bring a clean profit of somewhere about a thousand or sixteen hundred, why, Tom, you're onreasonable," said Haley.

"Yes, and hasn't we business booked for five weeks to come,—all we can do? And suppose we leaves all, and goes to bush-whacking round arter yer young uns, and finally doesn't catch the gal,—and gals allers is the devil *to* catch,—what's then? would you pay us a cent—would you? I think I see you a doin' it—ugh! No, no; flap down your fifty. If we get the job, and it pays, I'll hand it back; if we don't, it's for our trouble,—that's *far*, an't it, Marks?"

"Certainly, certainly," said Marks, with a conciliatory tone; "it's only a retaining fee, you see,—he! he! he!—we lawyers, you know. Wal, we must all keep good-natured,—keep easy, yer know. Tom'll have the boy for yer, anywhere ye'll name; won't ye, Tom?"

"If I find the young un, I'll bring him on to Cincinnati, and leave him at Granny Belcher's, on the landing," said Loker.

Marks had got from his pocket a greasy pocket-book, and taking a long paper from thence, he sat down, and fixing his keen black eyes on it, began mumbling over its contents: "Barnes—Shelby County—boy Jim, three hundred dollars for him, dead or alive.

"Edwards—Dick and Lucy—man and wife, six hundred dollars; wench Polly and two children—six hundred for her or her head.

CHAPTER VIII

"I'm jest a runnin' over our business, to see if we can take up this yer handily. Loker," he said, after a pause, "we must set Adams and Springer on the track of these yer; they've been booked some time."

"They'll charge too much," said Tom.

"I'll manage that ar; they 's young in the business, and must spect to work cheap," said Marks, as he continued to read. "Ther's three on 'em easy cases, 'cause all you've got to do is to shoot 'em, or swear they is shot; they couldn't, of course, charge much for that. Them other cases," he said, folding the paper, "will bear puttin' off a spell. So now let's come to the particulars. Now, Mr. Haley, you saw this yer gal when she landed?"

"To be sure,—plain as I see you."

"And a man helpin' on her up the bank?" said Loker.

"To be sure, I did."

"Most likely," said Marks, "she's took in somewhere; but where, 's a question. Tom, what do you say?"

"We must cross the river tonight, no mistake," said Tom.

"But there's no boat about," said Marks. "The ice is running awfully, Tom; an't it dangerous?"

"Don'no nothing 'bout that,—only it's got to be done," said Tom, decidedly.

"Dear me," said Marks, fidgeting, "it'll be—I say," he said, walking to the window, "it's dark as a wolf's mouth, and, Tom—"

"The long and short is, you're scared, Marks; but I can't help that,—you've got to go. Suppose you want to lie by a day or two, till the gal 's been carried on the underground line up to Sandusky or so, before you start."

"O, no; I an't a grain afraid," said Marks, "only—"

"Only what?" said Tom.

"Well, about the boat. Yer see there an't any boat."

"I heard the woman say there was one coming along this evening, and that a man was going to cross over in it. Neck or nothing, we must go with him," said Tom.

"I s'pose you've got good dogs," said Haley.

"First rate," said Marks. "But what's the use? you han't got nothin' o' hers to smell on."

"Yes, I have," said Haley, triumphantly. "Here's her shawl she left on the bed in her hurry; she left her bonnet, too."

"That ar's lucky," said Loker; "fork over."

"Though the dogs might damage the gal, if they come on her unawars," said Haley.

"That ar's a consideration," said Marks. "Our dogs tore a feller half to pieces, once, down in Mobile, 'fore we could get 'em off."

"Well, ye see, for this sort that's to be sold for their looks, that ar won't answer, ye see," said Haley.

"I do see," said Marks. "Besides, if she's got took in, 'tan't no go, neither. Dogs is no 'count in these yer up states where these critters gets carried; of course, ye can't get on their track. They only does down in plantations, where niggers, when they runs, has to do their own running, and don't get no help."

"Well," said Loker, who had just stepped out to the bar to make some inquiries, "they say the man's come with the boat; so, Marks—"

That worthy cast a rueful look at the comfortable quarters he was leaving, but slowly rose to obey. After exchanging a few words of further arrangement, Haley, with visible reluctance, handed over the fifty dollars to Tom, and the worthy trio separated for the night.

If any of our refined and Christian readers object to the society into which this scene introduces them, let us beg them to begin and conquer their prejudices in time. The catching business, we beg to remind them, is rising to the dignity of a lawful and patriotic profession. If all the broad land between the Mississippi and the Pacific becomes one great market for bodies and souls, and human property retains the locomotive tendencies of this nineteenth century, the trader and catcher may yet be among our aristocracy.

While this scene was going on at the tavern, Sam and Andy, in a state of high felicitation, pursued their way home.

Sam was in the highest possible feather, and expressed his exultation by all sorts of supernatural howls and ejaculations, by divers odd motions and contortions of his whole system. Sometimes he would sit backward, with his face to the horse's tail and sides, and then, with a whoop and a somerset, come right side up in his place again, and, drawing on a grave face, begin to lecture Andy in high-sounding tones for laughing and playing the fool. Anon, slapping his sides with his arms, he would burst forth in peals of laughter, that made the old woods ring as they passed. With all these evolutions, he contrived to keep the horses up to the top of their speed, until, between ten and eleven, their heels resounded on the gravel at the end of the balcony. Mrs. Shelby flew to the railings.

"Is that you, Sam? Where are they?"

"Mas'r Haley 's a-restin' at the tavern; he's drefful fatigued, Missis."

"And Eliza, Sam?"

"Wal, she's clar 'cross Jordan. As a body may say, in the land o' Canaan."

"Why, Sam, what *do* you mean?" said Mrs. Shelby, breathless, and almost faint, as the possible meaning of these words came over her.

"Wal, Missis, de Lord he persarves his own. Lizy's done gone over the river into 'Hio, as 'markably as if de Lord took her over in a charrit of fire and two hosses."

Sam's vein of piety was always uncommonly fervent in his mistress' presence; and he made great capital of scriptural figures and images.

"Come up here, Sam," said Mr. Shelby, who had followed on to the verandah, "and tell your mistress what she wants. Come, come, Emily," said he, passing his arm round her, "you are cold and all in a shiver; you allow yourself to feel too much."

"Feel too much! Am not I a woman,—a mother? Are we not both responsible to God for this poor girl? My God! lay not this sin to our charge."

"What sin, Emily? You see yourself that we have only done what we were obliged to."

"There's an awful feeling of guilt about it, though," said Mrs. Shelby. "I can't reason it away."

"Here, Andy, you nigger, be alive!" called Sam, under the verandah; "take these yer hosses to der barn; don't ye hear Mas'r a callin'?" and Sam soon appeared, palm-leaf in hand, at the parlor door.

"Now, Sam, tell us distinctly how the matter was," said Mr. Shelby. "Where is Eliza, if you know?"

"Wal, Mas'r, I saw her, with my own eyes, a crossin' on the floatin' ice. She crossed most 'markably; it wasn't no less nor a miracle; and I saw a man help her up the 'Hio side, and then she was lost in the dusk."

"Sam, I think this rather apocryphal,—this miracle. Crossing on floating ice isn't so easily done," said Mr. Shelby.

"Easy! couldn't nobody a done it, without de Lord. Why, now," said Sam, "'t was jist dis yer way. Mas'r Haley, and me, and Andy, we comes up to de little tavern by the river, and I rides a leetle ahead,—(I's so zealous to be a cotchin' Lizy, that I couldn't hold in, no way),—and when I comes by the tavern winder, sure enough there she was, right in plain sight, and dey diggin' on behind. Wal, I loses off my hat, and sings out nuff to raise the dead. Course Lizy she hars, and she dodges back, when Mas'r Haley he goes past the door; and then, I tell ye, she clared out de side door; she went down de river bank;—Mas'r Haley he seed her, and yelled out, and him, and me, and Andy, we took arter. Down she come to the river, and thar was the current running ten feet wide by the shore, and over t' other side ice a sawin' and a jiggling up and down, kinder as 't were a great island. We come right behind her, and I thought my soul he'd got her sure enough,—when she gin sich a screech as I never hearn, and thar she was, clar over t' other side of the current, on the ice, and then on she went, a screeching and a jumpin',—the ice went crack! c'wallop! cracking! chunk! and she a boundin' like a buck! Lord, the spring that ar gal's got in her an't common, I'm o' 'pinion."

Mrs. Shelby sat perfectly silent, pale with excitement, while Sam told his story.

"God be praised, she isn't dead!" she said; "but where is the poor child now?"

"De Lord will pervide," said Sam, rolling up his eyes piously. "As I've been a sayin', dis yer 's a providence and no mistake, as Missis has allers been a instructin' on us. Thar's allers instruments ris up to do de Lord's will. Now, if 't hadn't been for me today, she'd a been took a dozen times. Warn't it I started off de hosses, dis yer mornin' and kept 'em chasin' till nigh dinner time? And didn't I car Mas'r Haley night five miles out of de road, dis evening, or else he'd a come up with Lizy as easy as a dog arter a coon. These yer 's all providences."

"They are a kind of providences that you'll have to be pretty sparing of, Master Sam. I allow no such practices with gentlemen on my place," said Mr. Shelby, with as much sternness as he could command, under the circumstances.

Now, there is no more use in making believe be angry with a negro than with a child; both instinctively see the true state of the case, through all attempts to affect the contrary; and Sam was in no wise disheartened by this rebuke, though he assumed an air of doleful gravity, and stood with the corners of his mouth lowered in most penitential style.

"Mas'r quite right,—quite; it was ugly on me,—there's no disputin' that ar; and of course Mas'r and Missis wouldn't encourage no such works. I'm sensible of dat ar; but a poor nigger like me 's 'mazin' tempted to act ugly sometimes, when fellers will cut up such shines as dat ar Mas'r Haley; he an't no gen'l'man no way; anybody's been raised as I've been can't help a seein' dat ar."

"Well, Sam," said Mrs. Shelby, "as you appear to have a proper sense of your errors, you may go now and tell Aunt Chloe she may get you some of that cold ham that was left of dinner today. You and Andy must be hungry."

"Missis is a heap too good for us," said Sam, making his bow with alacrity, and departing.

It will be perceived, as has been before intimated, that Master Sam had a native talent that might, undoubtedly, have raised him to eminence in political life,—a talent of making capital out of everything that turned up, to be invested for his own especial praise and glory; and having done up his piety and humility, as he trusted, to the satisfaction of the parlor, he clapped his palm-leaf on his head, with a sort of rakish, free-and-easy air, and proceeded to the dominions of Aunt Chloe, with the intention of flourishing largely in the kitchen.

"I'll speechify these yer niggers," said Sam to himself, "now I've got a chance. Lord, I'll reel it off to make 'em stare!"

It must be observed that one of Sam's especial delights had been to ride in attendance on his master to all kinds of political gatherings, where, roosted on some rail fence, or perched aloft in some tree, he would sit watching the orators, with the greatest apparent gusto, and then, descending among the various brethren of his own color, assembled on the same errand, he would edify and delight them with the most ludicrous burlesques and imitations, all delivered with the most imperturbable earnestness and solemnity; and though the auditors immediately about him were generally of his own color, it not infrequently happened that they were fringed pretty deeply with those of a fairer complexion, who listened, laughing and winking, to Sam's great self-congratulation. In fact, Sam considered oratory as his vocation, and never let slip an opportunity of magnifying his office.

Now, between Sam and Aunt Chloe there had existed, from ancient times, a sort of chronic feud, or rather a decided coolness; but, as Sam was meditating something in the provision department, as the necessary and obvious foundation of his operations, he determined, on the present occasion, to be eminently conciliatory; for he well knew that although "Missis' orders" would undoubtedly be followed to the letter, yet he should gain a considerable deal by enlisting the spirit also. He therefore appeared before Aunt Chloe with a touchingly subdued, resigned expression, like one who has suffered immeasurable hardships in behalf of a persecuted fellow-creature,—enlarged upon the fact that Missis had directed him to come to Aunt Chloe for whatever might be wanting to make up the balance in his solids and fluids,—and thus unequivocally acknowledged her right and supremacy in the cooking department, and all thereto pertaining.

The thing took accordingly. No poor, simple, virtuous body was ever cajoled by the attentions of an electioneering politician with more ease than Aunt Chloe was won over by Master Sam's suavities; and if he had been the prodigal son himself, he could not have been overwhelmed with more maternal bountifulness; and he soon found himself seated, happy and glorious, over a large tin pan, containing a sort of *olla podrida* of all that had appeared on the table for two or three days past. Savory morsels of ham, golden blocks of corn-cake, fragments of pie of every conceivable mathematical figure, chicken wings, gizzards, and drumsticks, all appeared in picturesque confusion; and Sam, as monarch of all he surveyed, sat with his palm-leaf cocked rejoicingly to one side, and patronizing Andy at his right hand.

The kitchen was full of all his compeers, who had hurried and crowded in, from the various cabins, to hear the termination of the day's exploits. Now was Sam's hour of glory. The story of the day was rehearsed, with all kinds of ornament and varnishing which might be necessary to heighten its effect; for Sam, like some of our fashionable dilettanti, never allowed a story to lose any of its gilding by passing through his hands. Roars of laughter attended the narration, and were taken up and prolonged by all the smaller fry, who were lying, in any quantity, about on the floor, or perched in every corner. In the height of the uproar and laughter, Sam, however, preserved an immovable gravity, only from time to time rolling his eyes up, and giving his auditors divers inexpressibly droll glances, without departing from the sententious elevation of his oratory.

"Yer see, fellow-countrymen," said Sam, elevating a turkey's leg, with energy, "yer see, now what dis yer chile 's up ter, for fendin' yer all,—yes, all on yer. For him as tries to get one o' our people is as good as tryin' to get all; yer see the principle 's de same,—dat ar's clar. And any one o' these yer drivers that comes smelling round arter any our people, why, he's got *me* in his way; *I'm* the feller he's got to set in with,—I'm the feller for yer all to come to, bredren,—I'll stand up for yer rights,—I'll fend 'em to the last breath!"

"Why, but Sam, yer telled me, only this mornin', that you'd help this yer Mas'r to cotch Lizy; seems to me yer talk don't hang together," said Andy.

"I tell you now, Andy," said Sam, with awful superiority, "don't yer be a talkin' 'bout what yer don't know nothin' on; boys like you, Andy, means well, but they can't be spected to collusitate the great principles of action."

Andy looked rebuked, particularly by the hard word collusitate, which most of the youngerly members of the company seemed to consider as a settler in the case, while Sam proceeded.

"Dat ar was *conscience*, Andy; when I thought of gwine arter Lizy, I railly spected Mas'r was sot dat way. When I found Missis was sot the contrar, dat ar was conscience *more yet*,—cause fellers allers gets more by stickin' to Missis' side,—so yer see I 's persistent either way, and sticks up to conscience, and holds on to principles. Yes, *principles*," said Sam, giving an enthusiastic toss to a chicken's neck,—"what's principles good for, if we isn't persistent, I wanter know? Thar, Andy, you may have dat ar bone,—tan't picked quite clean."

Sam's audience hanging on his words with open mouth, he could not but proceed.

"Dis yer matter 'bout persistence, feller-niggers," said Sam, with the air of one entering into an abstruse subject, "dis yer 'sistency 's a thing what an't seed into very clar, by most anybody. Now, yer see, when a feller stands up for a thing one day and night, de contrar de next, folks ses (and nat'rally enough dey ses), why he an't persistent,—hand me dat ar bit o' corn-cake, Andy. But let's look inter it. I hope the gen'lmen and der fair sex will scuse my usin' an or'nary sort o' 'parison. Here! I'm a trying to get top o' der hay. Wal, I puts up my larder dis yer side; 'tan't no go;—den, cause I don't try dere no more, but puts my larder right de contrar side, an't I persistent? I'm persistent in wantin' to get up which ary side my larder is; don't you see, all on yer?"

"It's the only thing ye ever was persistent in, Lord knows!" muttered Aunt Chloe, who was getting rather restive; the merriment of the evening being to her somewhat after the Scripture comparison,—like "vinegar upon nitre."

"Yes, indeed!" said Sam, rising, full of supper and glory, for a closing effort. "Yes, my feller-citizens and ladies of de other sex in general, I has principles,—I'm proud to 'oon 'em,—they 's perquisite to dese yer times, and ter *all* times. I has principles, and I sticks to 'em like forty,—jest anything that I thinks is principle, I goes in to 't;—I wouldn't mind if dey burnt me 'live,—I'd walk right up to de stake, I would, and say, here I comes to shed my last blood fur my principles, fur my country, fur de gen'l interests of society."

"Well," said Aunt Chloe, "one o' yer principles will have to be to get to bed some time tonight, and not be a keepin' everybody up till mornin'; now, every one of you young uns that don't want to be cracked, had better be scase, mighty sudden."

"Niggers! all on yer," said Sam, waving his palm-leaf with benignity, "I give yer my blessin'; go to bed now, and be good boys."

And, with this pathetic benediction, the assembly dispersed.

CHAPTER IX

IN WHICH IT APPEARS THAT A SENATOR IS BUT A MAN

The light of the cheerful fire shone on the rug and carpet of a cosey parlor, and glittered on the sides of the tea-cups and well-brightened tea-pot, as Senator Bird was drawing off his boots, preparatory to inserting his feet in a pair of new handsome slippers, which his wife had been working for him while away on his senatorial tour. Mrs. Bird, looking the very picture of delight, was superintending the arrangements of the table, ever and anon mingling admonitory remarks to a number of frolicsome juveniles, who were effervescing in all those modes of untold gambol and mischief that have astonished mothers ever since the flood.

"Tom, let the door-knob alone,—there's a man! Mary! Mary! don't pull the cat's tail,—poor pussy! Jim, you mustn't climb on that table,—no, no!—You don't know, my dear, what a surprise it is to us all, to see you here tonight!" said she, at last, when she found a space to say something to her husband.

"Yes, yes, I thought I'd just make a run down, spend the night, and have a little comfort at home. I'm tired to death, and my head aches!"

Mrs. Bird cast a glance at a camphor-bottle, which stood in the half-open closet, and appeared to meditate an approach to it, but her husband interposed.

"No, no, Mary, no doctoring! a cup of your good hot tea, and some of our good home living, is what I want. It's a tiresome business, this legislating!"

And the senator smiled, as if he rather liked the idea of considering himself a sacrifice to his country.

"Well," said his wife, after the business of the tea-table was getting rather slack, "and what have they been doing in the Senate?"

Now, it was a very unusual thing for gentle little Mrs. Bird ever to trouble her head with what was going on in the house of the state, very wisely considering that she had enough to do to mind her own. Mr. Bird, therefore, opened his eyes in surprise, and said,

"Not very much of importance."

"Well; but is it true that they have been passing a law forbidding people to give meat and drink to those poor colored folks that come along? I heard they were talking of some such law, but I didn't think any Christian legislature would pass it!"

"Why, Mary, you are getting to be a politician, all at once."

"No, nonsense! I wouldn't give a fig for all your politics, generally, but I think this is something downright cruel and unchristian. I hope, my dear, no such law has been passed."

"There has been a law passed forbidding people to help off the slaves that come over from Kentucky, my dear; so much of that thing has been done by these reckless Abolitionists, that our brethren in Kentucky are very strongly excited, and it seems necessary, and no more than Christian and kind, that something should be done by our state to quiet the excitement."

"And what is the law? It don't forbid us to shelter those poor creatures a night, does it, and to give 'em something comfortable to eat, and a few old clothes, and send them quietly about their business?"

"Why, yes, my dear; that would be aiding and abetting, you know."

Mrs. Bird was a timid, blushing little woman, of about four feet in height, and with mild blue eyes, and a peach-blow complexion, and the gentlest, sweetest voice in the world;—as for courage, a moderate-sized cock-turkey had been known to put her to rout at the very first gobble, and a stout house-dog, of moderate capacity, would bring her into subjection merely by a show of his teeth. Her husband and children were her entire world, and in these she ruled more by entreaty and persuasion than by command or argument. There was only one thing that was capable of arousing her, and that provocation came in on the side of her unusually gentle and sympathetic nature;—anything in the shape of cruelty would throw her into a passion, which was the more alarming and inexplicable in proportion to the general softness of her nature. Generally the most indulgent and easy to be entreated of all mothers, still her boys had a very reverent remembrance of a most vehement chastisement she once bestowed on them, because she found them leagued with several graceless boys of the neighborhood, stoning a defenceless kitten.

"I'll tell you what," Master Bill used to say, "I was scared that time. Mother came at me so that I thought she was crazy, and I was whipped and tumbled off to bed, without any supper, before I could get over wondering what had come about; and, after that, I heard mother crying outside the door, which made me feel worse than all the rest. I'll tell you what," he'd say, "we boys never stoned another kitten!"

On the present occasion, Mrs. Bird rose quickly, with very red cheeks, which quite improved her general appearance, and walked up to her husband, with quite a resolute air, and said, in a determined tone,

"Now, John, I want to know if you think such a law as that is right and Christian?"

"You won't shoot me, now, Mary, if I say I do!"

"I never could have thought it of you, John; you didn't vote for it?"

"Even so, my fair politician."

CHAPTER IX

"You ought to be ashamed, John! Poor, homeless, houseless creatures! It's a shameful, wicked, abominable law, and I'll break it, for one, the first time I get a chance; and I hope I *shall* have a chance, I do! Things have got to a pretty pass, if a woman can't give a warm supper and a bed to poor, starving creatures, just because they are slaves, and have been abused and oppressed all their lives, poor things!"

"But, Mary, just listen to me. Your feelings are all quite right, dear, and interesting, and I love you for them; but, then, dear, we mustn't suffer our feelings to run away with our judgment; you must consider it's a matter of private feeling,—there are great public interests involved,—there is such a state of public agitation rising, that we must put aside our private feelings."

"Now, John, I don't know anything about politics, but I can read my Bible; and there I see that I must feed the hungry, clothe the naked, and comfort the desolate; and that Bible I mean to follow."

"But in cases where your doing so would involve a great public evil—"

"Obeying God never brings on public evils. I know it can't. It's always safest, all round, to *do as He* bids us.

"Now, listen to me, Mary, and I can state to you a very clear argument, to show—"

"O, nonsense, John! you can talk all night, but you wouldn't do it. I put it to you, John,—would *you* now turn away a poor, shivering, hungry creature from your door, because he was a runaway? *Would* you, now?"

Now, if the truth must be told, our senator had the misfortune to be a man who had a particularly humane and accessible nature, and turning away anybody that was in trouble never had been his forte; and what was worse for him in this particular pinch of the argument was, that his wife knew it, and, of course was making an assault on rather an indefensible point. So he had recourse to the usual means of gaining time for such cases made and provided; he said "ahem," and coughed several times, took out his pocket-handkerchief, and began to wipe his glasses. Mrs. Bird, seeing the defenceless condition of the enemy's territory, had no more conscience than to push her advantage.

"I should like to see you doing that, John—I really should! Turning a woman out of doors in a snowstorm, for instance; or may be you'd take her up and put her in jail, wouldn't you? You would make a great hand at that!"

"Of course, it would be a very painful duty," began Mr. Bird, in a moderate tone.

"Duty, John! don't use that word! You know it isn't a duty—it can't be a duty! If folks want to keep their slaves from running away, let 'em treat 'em well,—that's my doctrine. If I had slaves (as I hope I never shall have), I'd risk their wanting to run away from me, or you either, John. I tell you folks don't run away when they are happy; and when they do run, poor creatures! they suffer enough with cold and hunger and fear, without everybody's turning against them; and, law or no law, I never will, so help me God!"

"Mary! Mary! My dear, let me reason with you."

"I hate reasoning, John,—especially reasoning on such subjects. There's a way you political folks have of coming round and round a plain right thing; and you don't believe in it yourselves, when it comes to practice. I know *you* well enough, John. You don't believe it's right any more than I do; and you wouldn't do it any sooner than I."

At this critical juncture, old Cudjoe, the black man-of-all-work, put his head in at the door, and wished "Missis would come into the kitchen;" and our senator, tolerably relieved, looked after his little wife with a whimsical mixture of amusement and vexation, and, seating himself in the arm-chair, began to read the papers.

After a moment, his wife's voice was heard at the door, in a quick, earnest tone,—"John! John! I do wish you'd come here, a moment."

He laid down his paper, and went into the kitchen, and started, quite amazed at the sight that presented itself:—A young and slender woman, with garments torn and frozen, with one shoe gone, and the stocking torn away from the cut and bleeding foot, was laid back in a deadly swoon upon two chairs. There was the impress of the despised race on her face, yet none could help feeling its mournful and pathetic beauty, while its stony sharpness, its cold, fixed, deathly aspect, struck a solemn chill over him. He drew his breath short, and stood in silence. His wife, and their only colored domestic, old Aunt Dinah, were busily engaged in restorative measures; while old Cudjoe had got the boy on his knee, and was busy pulling off his shoes and stockings, and chafing his little cold feet.

"Sure, now, if she an't a sight to behold!" said old Dinah, compassionately; "'pears like 't was the heat that made her faint. She was tol'able peart when she cum in, and asked if she couldn't warm herself here a spell; and I was just a-askin' her where she cum from, and she fainted right down. Never done much hard work, guess, by the looks of her hands."

"Poor creature!" said Mrs. Bird, compassionately, as the woman slowly unclosed her large, dark eyes, and looked vacantly at her. Suddenly an expression of agony crossed her face, and she sprang up, saying, "O, my Harry! Have they got him?"

The boy, at this, jumped from Cudjoe's knee, and running to her side put up his arms. "O, he's here! he's here!" she exclaimed.

"O, ma'am!" said she, wildly, to Mrs. Bird, "do protect us! don't let them get him!"

"Nobody shall hurt you here, poor woman," said Mrs. Bird, encouragingly. "You are safe; don't be afraid."

"God bless you!" said the woman, covering her face and sobbing; while the little boy, seeing her crying, tried to get into her lap.

With many gentle and womanly offices, which none knew better how to render than Mrs. Bird, the poor woman was, in time, rendered more calm. A temporary bed was provided for her on the settle, near the fire; and, after a short time, she fell into a heavy slumber, with the child, who seemed no less weary, soundly sleeping on her arm; for the mother resisted, with nervous anxiety, the kindest attempts to take him from her; and, even in sleep, her arm encircled him with an unrelaxing clasp, as if she could not even then be beguiled of her vigilant hold.

Mr. and Mrs. Bird had gone back to the parlor, where, strange as it may appear, no reference was made, on either side, to the preceding conversation; but Mrs. Bird busied herself with her knitting-work, and Mr. Bird pretended to be reading the paper.

"I wonder who and what she is!" said Mr. Bird, at last, as he laid it down.

"When she wakes up and feels a little rested, we will see," said Mrs. Bird.

"I say, wife!" said Mr. Bird after musing in silence over his newspaper.

"Well, dear!"

"She couldn't wear one of your gowns, could she, by any letting down, or such matter? She seems to be rather larger than you are."

A quite perceptible smile glimmered on Mrs. Bird's face, as she answered, "We'll see."

Another pause, and Mr. Bird again broke out,

"I say, wife!"

"Well! What now?"

"Why, there's that old bombazin cloak, that you keep on purpose to put over me when I take my afternoon's nap; you might as well give her that,—she needs clothes."

At this instant, Dinah looked in to say that the woman was awake, and wanted to see Missis.

Mr. and Mrs. Bird went into the kitchen, followed by the two eldest boys, the smaller fry having, by this time, been safely disposed of in bed.

The woman was now sitting up on the settle, by the fire. She was looking steadily into the blaze, with a calm, heart-broken expression, very different from her former agitated wildness.

"Did you want me?" said Mrs. Bird, in gentle tones. "I hope you feel better now, poor woman!"

A long-drawn, shivering sigh was the only answer; but she lifted her dark eyes, and fixed them on her with such a forlorn and imploring expression, that the tears came into the little woman's eyes.

"You needn't be afraid of anything; we are friends here, poor woman! Tell me where you came from, and what you want," said she.

"I came from Kentucky," said the woman.

"When?" said Mr. Bird, taking up the interogatory.

"Tonight."

"How did you come?"

"I crossed on the ice."

"Crossed on the ice!" said every one present.

"Yes," said the woman, slowly, "I did. God helping me, I crossed on the ice; for they were behind me—right behind—and there was no other way!"

"Law, Missis," said Cudjoe, "the ice is all in broken-up blocks, a swinging and a tetering up and down in the water!"

"I know it was—I know it!" said she, wildly; "but I did it! I wouldn't have thought I could,—I didn't think I should get over, but I didn't care! I could but die, if I didn't. The Lord helped me; nobody knows how much the Lord can help 'em, till they try," said the woman, with a flashing eye.

"Were you a slave?" said Mr. Bird.

"Yes, sir; I belonged to a man in Kentucky."

"Was he unkind to you?"

"No, sir; he was a good master."

"And was your mistress unkind to you?"

"No, sir—no! my mistress was always good to me."

"What could induce you to leave a good home, then, and run away, and go through such dangers?"

The woman looked up at Mrs. Bird, with a keen, scrutinizing glance, and it did not escape her that she was dressed in deep mourning.

"Ma'am," she said, suddenly, "have you ever lost a child?"

The question was unexpected, and it was thrust on a new wound; for it was only a month since a darling child of the family had been laid in the grave.

Mr. Bird turned around and walked to the window, and Mrs. Bird burst into tears; but, recovering her voice, she said,

"Why do you ask that? I have lost a little one."

"Then you will feel for me. I have lost two, one after another,—left 'em buried there when I came away; and I had only this one left. I never slept a night without him; he was all I had. He was my comfort and pride, day and night; and, ma'am, they were going to take him away from me,—to *sell* him,—sell him down south, ma'am, to go all alone,—a baby that had never been away from his mother in his life! I couldn't stand it, ma'am. I knew I never should be good for anything, if they did; and when I knew the papers the papers were signed, and he was sold, I took him and came off in the night; and they chased me,—the man that bought him, and some of Mas'r's folks,—and they were coming down right behind me, and I heard 'em. I jumped right on to the ice; and how I got across, I don't know,—but, first I knew, a man was helping me up the bank."

The woman did not sob nor weep. She had gone to a place where tears are dry; but every one around her was, in some way characteristic of themselves, showing signs of hearty sympathy.

The two little boys, after a desperate rummaging in their pockets, in search of those pocket-handkerchiefs which mothers know are never to be found there, had thrown themselves disconsolately into the skirts of their mother's gown, where they were sobbing, and wiping their eyes and noses, to their hearts' content;—Mrs. Bird had her face fairly hidden in her pocket-handkerchief; and old Dinah, with tears streaming down her black, honest face, was ejaculating, "Lord have mercy on us!" with all the fervor of a camp-meeting;—while old Cudjoe, rubbing his eyes very hard with his cuffs, and making a most uncommon variety of wry faces, occasionally responded in the same key, with great fervor. Our senator was a statesman, and of course could not be expected to cry, like other mortals; and so he turned his back to the company, and looked out of the window, and seemed particularly busy in clearing his throat and wiping his spectacle-glasses, occasionally blowing his nose in a manner that was calculated to excite suspicion, had any one been in a state to observe critically.

"How came you to tell me you had a kind master?" he suddenly exclaimed, gulping down very resolutely some kind of rising in his throat, and turning suddenly round upon the woman.

"Because he *was* a kind master; I'll say that of him, any way;—and my mistress was kind; but they couldn't help themselves. They were owing money; and there was some way, I can't tell how, that a man had a hold on them, and they were obliged to give him his will. I listened, and heard him telling mistress that, and she begging and pleading for me,—and he told her he couldn't help himself, and that the papers were all drawn;—and then it was I took him and left my home, and came away. I knew 't was no use of my trying to live, if they did it; for 't 'pears like this child is all I have."

"Have you no husband?"

"Yes, but he belongs to another man. His master is real hard to him, and won't let him come to see me, hardly ever; and he's grown harder and harder upon us, and he threatens to sell him down south;—it's like I'll never see *him* again!"

The quiet tone in which the woman pronounced these words might have led a superficial observer to think that she was entirely apathetic; but there was a calm, settled depth of anguish in her large, dark eye, that spoke of something far otherwise.

"And where do you mean to go, my poor woman?" said Mrs. Bird.

"To Canada, if I only knew where that was. Is it very far off, is Canada?" said she, looking up, with a simple, confiding air, to Mrs. Bird's face.

"Poor thing!" said Mrs. Bird, involuntarily.

"Is 't a very great way off, think?" said the woman, earnestly.

"Much further than you think, poor child!" said Mrs. Bird; "but we will try to think what can be done for you. Here, Dinah, make her up a bed in your own room, close by the kitchen, and I'll think what to do for her in the morning. Meanwhile, never fear, poor woman; put your trust in God; he will protect you."

Mrs. Bird and her husband reentered the parlor. She sat down in her little rocking-chair before the fire, swaying thoughtfully to and fro. Mr. Bird strode up and down the room, grumbling to himself, "Pish! pshaw! confounded awkward business!" At length, striding up to his wife, he said,

"I say, wife, she'll have to get away from here, this very night. That fellow will be down on the scent bright and early tomorrow morning: if 't was only the woman, she could lie quiet till it was over; but that little chap can't be kept still by a troop of horse and foot, I'll warrant me; he'll bring it all out, popping his head out of some window or door. A pretty kettle of fish it would be for me, too, to be caught with them both here, just now! No; they'll have to be got off tonight."

"Tonight! How is it possible?—where to?"

"Well, I know pretty well where to," said the senator, beginning to put on his boots, with a reflective air; and, stopping when his leg was half in, he embraced his knee with both hands, and seemed to go off in deep meditation.

"It's a confounded awkward, ugly business," said he, at last, beginning to tug at his boot-straps again, "and that's a fact!" After one boot was fairly on, the senator sat with the other in his hand, profoundly studying the figure of the carpet. "It will have to be done, though, for aught I see,—hang it all!" and he drew the other boot anxiously on, and looked out of the window.

Now, little Mrs. Bird was a discreet woman,—a woman who never in her life said, "I told you so!" and, on the present occasion, though pretty well aware of the shape her husband's meditations were taking, she very prudently forbore to meddle with them, only sat very quietly in her chair, and looked quite ready to hear her liege lord's intentions, when he should think proper to utter them.

"You see," he said, "there's my old client, Van Trompe, has come over from Kentucky, and set all his slaves free; and he has bought a place seven miles up the creek, here, back in the woods, where nobody goes, unless they go on purpose; and it's a place that isn't found in a hurry. There she'd be safe enough; but the plague of the thing is, nobody could drive a carriage there tonight, but *me*."

"Why not? Cudjoe is an excellent driver."

"Ay, ay, but here it is. The creek has to be crossed twice; and the second crossing is quite dangerous, unless one knows it as I do. I have crossed it a hundred times on horseback, and know exactly the turns to take. And so, you see, there's no help for it. Cudjoe must put in the horses, as quietly as may be, about twelve o'clock, and I'll take her over; and then, to give color to the matter, he must carry me on to the next tavern to take the stage for Columbus, that comes by about three or four, and so it will look as if I had had the carriage only for that. I shall get into business bright and early in the morning. But I'm thinking I shall feel rather cheap there, after all that's been said and done; but, hang it, I can't help it!"

"Your heart is better than your head, in this case, John," said the wife, laying her little white hand on his. "Could I ever have loved you, had I not known you better than you know yourself?" And the little woman looked so handsome, with the tears sparkling in her eyes, that the senator thought he must be a decidedly clever fellow, to get such a pretty creature into such a passionate admiration of him; and so, what could he do but walk off soberly, to see about the carriage. At the door, however, he stopped a moment, and then coming back, he said, with some hesitation.

"Mary, I don't know how you'd feel about it, but there's that drawer full of things—of—of—poor little Henry's." So saying, he turned quickly on his heel, and shut the door after him.

His wife opened the little bed-room door adjoining her room and, taking the candle, set it down on the top of a bureau there; then from a small recess she took a key, and put it thoughtfully in the lock of a drawer, and made a sudden pause, while two boys, who, boy like, had followed close on her heels, stood looking, with silent, significant glances, at their mother. And oh! mother that reads this, has there never been in your house a drawer, or a closet, the opening of which has been to you like the opening again of a little grave? Ah! happy mother that you are, if it has not been so.

Mrs. Bird slowly opened the drawer. There were little coats of many a form and pattern, piles of aprons, and rows of small stockings; and even a pair of little shoes, worn and rubbed at the toes, were peeping from the folds of a paper. There was a toy horse and wagon, a top, a ball,—memorials gathered with many a tear and many a heart-break! She sat down by the drawer, and, leaning her head on her hands over it, wept till the tears fell through her fingers into the drawer; then suddenly raising her head, she began, with nervous haste, selecting the plainest and most substantial articles, and gathering them into a bundle.

"Mamma," said one of the boys, gently touching her arm, "you going to give away *those* things?"

"My dear boys," she said, softly and earnestly, "if our dear, loving little Henry looks down from heaven, he would be glad to have us do this. I could not find it in my heart to give them away to any common person—to anybody that was happy; but I give them to a mother more heart-broken and sorrowful than I am; and I hope God will send his blessings with them!"

There are in this world blessed souls, whose sorrows all spring up into joys for others; whose earthly hopes, laid in the grave with many tears, are the seed from which spring healing flowers and balm for the desolate and the distressed. Among such was the delicate woman who sits there by the lamp, dropping slow tears, while she prepares the memorials of her own lost one for the outcast wanderer.

After a while, Mrs. Bird opened a wardrobe, and, taking from thence a plain, serviceable dress or two, she sat down busily to her work-table, and, with needle, scissors, and thimble, at hand, quietly commenced the "letting down" process which her husband had recommended, and continued busily at it till the old clock in the corner struck twelve, and she heard the low rattling of wheels at the door.

"Mary," said her husband, coming in, with his overcoat in his hand, "you must wake her up now; we must be off."

Mrs. Bird hastily deposited the various articles she had collected in a small plain trunk, and locking it, desired her husband to see it in the carriage, and then proceeded to call the woman. Soon, arrayed in a cloak, bonnet, and shawl, that had belonged to her benefactress, she appeared at the door with her child in her arms. Mr. Bird hurried her into the carriage, and Mrs. Bird pressed on after her to the carriage steps. Eliza leaned out of the carriage, and put out her hand,—a hand as soft and beautiful as was given in return. She fixed her large, dark eyes, full of earnest meaning, on Mrs. Bird's face, and seemed going to speak. Her lips moved,—she tried once or twice, but there was no sound,—and pointing upward, with a look never to be forgotten, she fell back in the seat, and covered her face. The door was shut, and the carriage drove on.

What a situation, now, for a patriotic senator, that had been all the week before spurring up the legislature of his native state to pass more stringent resolutions against escaping fugitives, their harborers and abettors!

Our good senator in his native state had not been exceeded by any of his brethren at Washington, in the sort of eloquence which has won for them immortal renown! How sublimely he had sat with his hands in his pockets, and scouted all sentimental weakness of those who would put the welfare of a few miserable fugitives before great state interests!

He was as bold as a lion about it, and "mightily convinced" not only himself, but everybody that heard him;—but then his idea of a fugitive was only an idea of the letters that spell the word,—or at the most, the image of a little newspaper picture of a man with a stick and bundle with "Ran away from the subscriber" under it. The magic of the real presence of distress,—the imploring human eye, the frail, trembling human hand, the despairing appeal of helpless agony,—these he had never tried. He had never thought that a fugitive might be a hapless mother, a defenceless child,—like that one which was now wearing his lost boy's little well-known cap; and so, as our poor senator was not stone or steel,—as he was a man, and a downright noble-hearted one, too,—he was, as everybody must see, in a sad case for his patriotism. And you need not exult over him, good brother of the Southern States; for we have some inklings that many of you, under similar circumstances, would not do much better. We have reason to know, in Kentucky, as in Mississippi, are noble and generous hearts, to whom never was tale of suffering told in vain. Ah, good brother! is it fair for you to expect of us services which your own brave, honorable heart would not allow you to render, were you in our place?

Be that as it may, if our good senator was a political sinner, he was in a fair way to expiate it by his night's penance. There had been a long continuous period of rainy weather, and the soft, rich earth of Ohio, as every one knows, is admirably suited to the manufacture of mud—and the road was an Ohio railroad of the good old times.

"And pray, what sort of a road may that be?" says some eastern traveller, who has been accustomed to connect no ideas with a railroad, but those of smoothness or speed.

Know, then, innocent eastern friend, that in benighted regions of the west, where the mud is of unfathomable and sublime depth, roads are made of round rough logs, arranged transversely side by side, and coated over in their pristine freshness with earth, turf, and whatsoever may come to hand, and then the rejoicing native calleth it a road, and straightway essayeth to ride thereupon. In process of time, the rains wash off all the turf and grass aforesaid, move the logs hither and thither, in picturesque positions, up, down and crosswise, with divers chasms and ruts of black mud intervening.

Over such a road as this our senator went stumbling along, making moral reflections as continuously as under the circumstances could be expected,—the carriage proceeding along much as follows,—bump! bump! bump! slush! down in the mud!—the senator, woman and child, reversing their positions so suddenly as to come, without any very accurate adjustment, against the windows of the downhill side. Carriage sticks fast, while Cudjoe on the outside is heard making a great muster among the horses. After various ineffectual pullings and twitchings, just as the senator is losing all patience, the carriage suddenly rights itself with a bounce,—two front wheels go down into another abyss, and senator, woman, and child, all tumble promiscuously on to the front seat,—senator's hat is jammed over his eyes and nose quite unceremoniously, and he considers himself fairly extinguished;—child cries, and Cudjoe on the outside delivers animated addresses to the horses, who are kicking, and floundering, and straining under repeated cracks of the whip. Carriage springs up, with another bounce,—down go the hind wheels,—senator, woman, and child, fly over on to the back seat, his elbows encountering her bonnet, and both her feet being jammed into his hat, which flies off in the concussion. After a few moments the "slough" is passed, and the horses stop, panting;—the senator finds his hat, the woman straightens her bonnet and hushes her child, and they brace themselves for what is yet to come.

For a while only the continuous bump! bump! intermingled, just by way of variety, with divers side plunges and compound shakes; and they begin to flatter themselves that they are not so badly off, after all. At last, with a square plunge, which puts all on to their feet and then down into their seats with incredible quickness, the carriage stops,—and, after much outside commotion, Cudjoe appears at the door.

"Please, sir, it's powerful bad spot, this' yer. I don't know how we's to get clar out. I'm a thinkin' we'll have to be a gettin' rails."

The senator despairingly steps out, picking gingerly for some firm foothold; down goes one foot an immeasurable depth,—he tries to pull it up, loses his balance, and tumbles over into the mud, and is fished out, in a very despairing condition, by Cudjoe.

But we forbear, out of sympathy to our readers' bones. Western travellers, who have beguiled the midnight hour in the interesting process of pulling down rail fences, to pry their carriages out of mud holes, will have a respectful and mournful sympathy with our unfortunate hero. We beg them to drop a silent tear, and pass on.

It was full late in the night when the carriage emerged, dripping and bespattered, out of the creek, and stood at the door of a large farmhouse.

It took no inconsiderable perseverance to arouse the inmates; but at last the respectable proprietor appeared, and undid the door. He was a great, tall, bristling Orson of a fellow, full six feet and some inches in his stockings, and arrayed in a red flannel hunting-shirt. A very heavy mat of sandy hair, in a decidedly tousled condition, and a beard of some days' growth, gave the worthy man an appearance, to say the least, not particularly prepossessing. He stood for a few minutes holding the candle aloft, and blinking on our travellers with a dismal and mystified expression that was truly ludicrous. It cost some effort of our senator to induce him to comprehend the case fully; and while he is doing his best at that, we shall give him a little introduction to our readers.

Honest old John Van Trompe was once quite a considerable land-owner and slave-owner in the State of Kentucky. Having "nothing of the bear about him but the skin," and being gifted by nature with a great, honest, just heart, quite equal to his gigantic frame, he had been for some years witnessing with repressed uneasiness the workings of a system equally bad for oppressor and oppressed. At last, one day, John's great heart had swelled altogether too big to wear his bonds any longer; so he just took his pocket-book out of his desk, and went over into Ohio, and bought a quarter of a township of good, rich land, made out free papers for all his people,—men, women, and children,—packed them up in wagons, and sent them off to settle down; and then honest John turned his face up the creek, and sat quietly down on a snug, retired farm, to enjoy his conscience and his reflections.

"Are you the man that will shelter a poor woman and child from slave-catchers?" said the senator, explicitly.

"I rather think I am," said honest John, with some considerable emphasis.

"I thought so," said the senator.

"If there's anybody comes," said the good man, stretching his tall, muscular form upward, "why here I'm ready for him: and I've got seven sons, each six foot high, and they'll be ready for 'em. Give our respects to 'em," said John; "tell 'em it's no matter how soon they call,—make no kinder difference to us," said John, running his fingers through the shock of hair that thatched his head, and bursting out into a great laugh.

Weary, jaded, and spiritless, Eliza dragged herself up to the door, with her child lying in a heavy sleep on her arm. The rough man held the candle to her face, and uttering a kind of compassionate grunt, opened the door of a small bed-room adjoining to the large kitchen where they were standing, and motioned her to go in. He took down a candle, and lighting it, set it upon the table, and then addressed himself to Eliza.

"Now, I say, gal, you needn't be a bit afeard, let who will come here. I'm up to all that sort o' thing," said he, pointing to two or three goodly rifles over the mantel-piece; "and most people that know me know that 't wouldn't be healthy to try to get anybody out o' my house when I'm agin it. So *now* you jist go to sleep now, as quiet as if yer mother was a rockin' ye," said he, as he shut the door.

"Why, this is an uncommon handsome un," he said to the senator. "Ah, well; handsome uns has the greatest cause to run, sometimes, if they has any kind o' feelin, such as decent women should. I know all about that."

The senator, in a few words, briefly explained Eliza's history.

"O! ou! aw! now, I want to know?" said the good man, pitifully; "sho! now sho! That's natur now, poor crittur! hunted down now like a deer,—hunted down, jest for havin' natural feelin's, and doin' what no kind o' mother could help a doin'! I tell ye what, these yer things make me come the nighest to swearin', now, o' most anything," said honest John, as he wiped his eyes with the back of a great, freckled, yellow hand. "I tell yer what, stranger, it was years and years before I'd jine the church, 'cause the ministers round in our parts used to preach that the Bible went in for these ere cuttings up,—and I couldn't be up to 'em with their Greek and Hebrew, and so I took up agin 'em, Bible and all. I never jined the church till I found a minister that was up to 'em all in Greek and all that, and he said right the contrary; and then I took right hold, and jined the church,—I did now, fact," said John, who had been all this time uncorking some very frisky bottled cider, which at this juncture he presented.

"Ye'd better jest put up here, now, till daylight," said he, heartily, "and I'll call up the old woman, and have a bed got ready for you in no time."

"Thank you, my good friend," said the senator, "I must be along, to take the night stage for Columbus."

"Ah! well, then, if you must, I'll go a piece with you, and show you a cross road that will take you there better than the road you came on. That road's mighty bad."

John equipped himself, and, with a lantern in hand, was soon seen guiding the senator's carriage towards a road that ran down in a hollow, back of his dwelling. When they parted, the senator put into his hand a ten-dollar bill.

"It's for her," he said, briefly.

"Ay, ay," said John, with equal conciseness.

They shook hands, and parted.

CHAPTER X

THE PROPERTY IS CARRIED OFF

The February morning looked gray and drizzling through the window of Uncle Tom's cabin. It looked on downcast faces, the images of mournful hearts. The little table stood out before the fire, covered with an ironing-cloth; a coarse but clean shirt or two, fresh from the iron, hung on the back of a chair by the fire, and Aunt Chloe had another spread out before her on the table. Carefully she rubbed and ironed every fold and every hem, with the most scrupulous exactness, every now and then raising her hand to her face to wipe off the tears that were coursing down her cheeks.

Tom sat by, with his Testament open on his knee, and his head leaning upon his hand;—but neither spoke. It was yet early, and the children lay all asleep together in their little rude trundle-bed.

Tom, who had, to the full, the gentle, domestic heart, which woe for them! has been a peculiar characteristic of his unhappy race, got up and walked silently to look at his children.

"It's the last time," he said.

Aunt Chloe did not answer, only rubbed away over and over on the coarse shirt, already as smooth as hands could make it; and finally setting her iron suddenly down with a despairing plunge, she sat down to the table, and "lifted up her voice and wept."

"S'pose we must be resigned; but oh Lord! how ken I? If I know'd anything whar you 's goin', or how they'd sarve you! Missis says she'll try and 'deem ye, in a year or two; but Lor! nobody never comes up that goes down thar! They kills 'em! I've hearn 'em tell how dey works 'em up on dem ar plantations."

"There'll be the same God there, Chloe, that there is here."

"Well," said Aunt Chloe, "s'pose dere will; but de Lord lets drefful things happen, sometimes. I don't seem to get no comfort dat way."

"I'm in the Lord's hands," said Tom; "nothin' can go no furder than he lets it;—and thar's *one* thing I can thank him for. It's *me* that's sold and going down, and not you nur the chil'en. Here you're safe;—what comes will come only on me; and the Lord, he'll help me,—I know he will."

CHAPTER X

Ah, brave, manly heart,—smothering thine own sorrow, to comfort thy beloved ones! Tom spoke with a thick utterance, and with a bitter choking in his throat,—but he spoke brave and strong.

"Let's think on our marcies!" he added, tremulously, as if he was quite sure he needed to think on them very hard indeed.

"Marcies!" said Aunt Chloe; "don't see no marcy in 't! 'tan't right! tan't right it should be so! Mas'r never ought ter left it so that ye *could* be took for his debts. Ye've arnt him all he gets for ye, twice over. He owed ye yer freedom, and ought ter gin 't to yer years ago. Mebbe he can't help himself now, but I feel it's wrong. Nothing can't beat that ar out o' me. Sich a faithful crittur as ye've been,—and allers sot his business 'fore yer own every way,—and reckoned on him more than yer own wife and chil'en! Them as sells heart's love and heart's blood, to get out thar scrapes, de Lord'll be up to 'em!"

"Chloe! now, if ye love me, ye won't talk so, when perhaps jest the last time we'll ever have together! And I'll tell ye, Chloe, it goes agin me to hear one word agin Mas'r. Wan't he put in my arms a baby?—it's natur I should think a heap of him. And he couldn't be spected to think so much of poor Tom. Mas'rs is used to havin' all these yer things done for 'em, and nat'lly they don't think so much on 't. They can't be spected to, no way. Set him 'longside of other Mas'rs—who's had the treatment and livin' I've had? And he never would have let this yer come on me, if he could have seed it aforehand. I know he wouldn't."

"Wal, any way, thar's wrong about it *somewhar*," said Aunt Chloe, in whom a stubborn sense of justice was a predominant trait; "I can't jest make out whar 't is, but thar's wrong somewhar, I'm *clar* o' that."

"Yer ought ter look up to the Lord above—he's above all—thar don't a sparrow fall without him."

"It don't seem to comfort me, but I spect it orter," said Aunt Chloe. "But dar's no use talkin'; I'll jes wet up de corn-cake, and get ye one good breakfast, 'cause nobody knows when you'll get another."

In order to appreciate the sufferings of the negroes sold south, it must be remembered that all the instinctive affections of that race are peculiarly strong. Their local attachments are very abiding. They are not naturally daring and enterprising, but home-loving and affectionate. Add to this all the terrors with which ignorance invests the unknown, and add to this, again, that selling to the south is set before the negro from childhood as the last severity of punishment. The threat that terrifies more than whipping or torture of any kind is the threat of being sent down river. We have ourselves heard this feeling expressed by them, and seen the unaffected horror with which they will sit in their gossipping hours, and tell frightful stories of that "down river," which to them is

"That undiscovered country, from whose bourn No traveller returns."[1]

A missionary figure among the fugitives in Canada told us that many of the fugitives confessed themselves to have escaped from comparatively kind masters,

---

[1] A slightly inaccurate quotation from Hamlet, Act III, scene I, lines 369-370.

and that they were induced to brave the perils of escape, in almost every case, by the desperate horror with which they regarded being sold south,—a doom which was hanging either over themselves or their husbands, their wives or children. This nerves the African, naturally patient, timid and unenterprising, with heroic courage, and leads him to suffer hunger, cold, pain, the perils of the wilderness, and the more dread penalties of recapture.

The simple morning meal now smoked on the table, for Mrs. Shelby had excused Aunt Chloe's attendance at the great house that morning. The poor soul had expended all her little energies on this farewell feast,—had killed and dressed her choicest chicken, and prepared her corn-cake with scrupulous exactness, just to her husband's taste, and brought out certain mysterious jars on the mantel-piece, some preserves that were never produced except on extreme occasions.

"Lor, Pete," said Mose, triumphantly, "han't we got a buster of a breakfast!" at the same time catching at a fragment of the chicken.

Aunt Chloe gave him a sudden box on the ear. "Thar now! crowing over the last breakfast yer poor daddy's gwine to have to home!"

"O, Chloe!" said Tom, gently.

"Wal, I can't help it," said Aunt Chloe, hiding her face in her apron; "I 's so tossed about it, it makes me act ugly."

The boys stood quite still, looking first at their father and then at their mother, while the baby, climbing up her clothes, began an imperious, commanding cry.

"Thar!" said Aunt Chloe, wiping her eyes and taking up the baby; "now I's done, I hope,—now do eat something. This yer's my nicest chicken. Thar, boys, ye shall have some, poor critturs! Yer mammy's been cross to yer."

The boys needed no second invitation, and went in with great zeal for the eatables; and it was well they did so, as otherwise there would have been very little performed to any purpose by the party.

"Now," said Aunt Chloe, bustling about after breakfast, "I must put up yer clothes. Jest like as not, he'll take 'em all away. I know thar ways—mean as dirt, they is! Wal, now, yer flannels for rhumatis is in this corner; so be careful, 'cause there won't nobody make ye no more. Then here's yer old shirts, and these yer is new ones. I toed off these yer stockings last night, and put de ball in 'em to mend with. But Lor! who'll ever mend for ye?" and Aunt Chloe, again overcome, laid her head on the box side, and sobbed. "To think on 't! no crittur to do for ye, sick or well! I don't railly think I ought ter be good now!"

The boys, having eaten everything there was on the breakfast-table, began now to take some thought of the case; and, seeing their mother crying, and their father looking very sad, began to whimper and put their hands to their eyes. Uncle Tom had the baby on his knee, and was letting her enjoy herself to the utmost extent, scratching his face and pulling his hair, and occasionally breaking out into clamorous explosions of delight, evidently arising out of her own internal reflections.

"Ay, crow away, poor crittur!" said Aunt Chloe; "ye'll have to come to it, too! ye'll live to see yer husband sold, or mebbe be sold yerself; and these yer boys, they's to be sold, I s'pose, too, jest like as not, when dey gets good for somethin'; an't no use in niggers havin' nothin'!"

Here one of the boys called out, "Thar's Missis a-comin' in!"

"She can't do no good; what's she coming for?" said Aunt Chloe.

Mrs. Shelby entered. Aunt Chloe set a chair for her in a manner decidedly gruff and crusty. She did not seem to notice either the action or the manner. She looked pale and anxious.

"Tom," she said, "I come to—" and stopping suddenly, and regarding the silent group, she sat down in the chair, and, covering her face with her handkerchief, began to sob.

"Lor, now, Missis, don't—don't!" said Aunt Chloe, bursting out in her turn; and for a few moments they all wept in company. And in those tears they all shed together, the high and the lowly, melted away all the heart-burnings and anger of the oppressed. O, ye who visit the distressed, do ye know that everything your money can buy, given with a cold, averted face, is not worth one honest tear shed in real sympathy?

"My good fellow," said Mrs. Shelby, "I can't give you anything to do you any good. If I give you money, it will only be taken from you. But I tell you solemnly, and before God, that I will keep trace of you, and bring you back as soon as I can command the money;—and, till then, trust in God!"

Here the boys called out that Mas'r Haley was coming, and then an unceremonious kick pushed open the door. Haley stood there in very ill humor, having ridden hard the night before, and being not at all pacified by his ill success in recapturing his prey.

"Come," said he, "ye nigger, ye'r ready? Servant, ma'am!" said he, taking off his hat, as he saw Mrs. Shelby.

Aunt Chloe shut and corded the box, and, getting up, looked gruffly on the trader, her tears seeming suddenly turned to sparks of fire.

Tom rose up meekly, to follow his new master, and raised up his heavy box on his shoulder. His wife took the baby in her arms to go with him to the wagon, and the children, still crying, trailed on behind.

Mrs. Shelby, walking up to the trader, detained him for a few moments, talking with him in an earnest manner; and while she was thus talking, the whole family party proceeded to a wagon, that stood ready harnessed at the door. A crowd of all the old and young hands on the place stood gathered around it, to bid farewell to their old associate. Tom had been looked up to, both as a head servant and a Christian teacher, by all the place, and there was much honest sympathy and grief about him, particularly among the women.

"Why, Chloe, you bar it better 'n we do!" said one of the women, who had been weeping freely, noticing the gloomy calmness with which Aunt Chloe stood by the wagon.

"I's done *my* tears!" she said, looking grimly at the trader, who was coming up. "I does not feel to cry 'fore dat ar old limb, no how!"

"Get in!" said Haley to Tom, as he strode through the crowd of servants, who looked at him with lowering brows.

Tom got in, and Haley, drawing out from under the wagon seat a heavy pair of shackles, made them fast around each ankle.

A smothered groan of indignation ran through the whole circle, and Mrs. Shelby spoke from the verandah,—"Mr. Haley, I assure you that precaution is entirely unnecessary."

"Don' know, ma'am; I've lost one five hundred dollars from this yer place, and I can't afford to run no more risks."

"What else could she spect on him?" said Aunt Chloe, indignantly, while the two boys, who now seemed to comprehend at once their father's destiny, clung to her gown, sobbing and groaning vehemently.

"I'm sorry," said Tom, "that Mas'r George happened to be away."

George had gone to spend two or three days with a companion on a neighboring estate, and having departed early in the morning, before Tom's misfortune had been made public, had left without hearing of it.

"Give my love to Mas'r George," he said, earnestly.

Haley whipped up the horse, and, with a steady, mournful look, fixed to the last on the old place, Tom was whirled away.

Mr. Shelby at this time was not at home. He had sold Tom under the spur of a driving necessity, to get out of the power of a man whom he dreaded,—and his first feeling, after the consummation of the bargain, had been that of relief. But his wife's expostulations awoke his half-slumbering regrets; and Tom's manly disinterestedness increased the unpleasantness of his feelings. It was in vain that he said to himself that he had a *right* to do it,—that everybody did it,—and that some did it without even the excuse of necessity;—he could not satisfy his own feelings; and that he might not witness the unpleasant scenes of the consummation, he had gone on a short business tour up the country, hoping that all would be over before he returned.

Tom and Haley rattled on along the dusty road, whirling past every old familiar spot, until the bounds of the estate were fairly passed, and they found themselves out on the open pike. After they had ridden about a mile, Haley suddenly drew up at the door of a blacksmith's shop, when, taking out with him a pair of handcuffs, he stepped into the shop, to have a little alteration in them.

"These yer 's a little too small for his build," said Haley, showing the fetters, and pointing out to Tom.

"Lor! now, if thar an't Shelby's Tom. He han't sold him, now?" said the smith.

"Yes, he has," said Haley.

"Now, ye don't! well, reely," said the smith, "who'd a thought it! Why, ye needn't go to fetterin' him up this yer way. He's the faithfullest, best crittur—"

"Yes, yes," said Haley; "but your good fellers are just the critturs to want ter run off. Them stupid ones, as doesn't care whar they go, and shifless, drunken ones, as don't care for nothin', they'll stick by, and like as not be rather pleased to be toted round; but these yer prime fellers, they hates it like sin. No way but to fetter 'em; got legs,—they'll use 'em,—no mistake."

"Well," said the smith, feeling among his tools, "them plantations down thar, stranger, an't jest the place a Kentuck nigger wants to go to; they dies thar tol'able fast, don't they?"

"Wal, yes, tol'able fast, ther dying is; what with the 'climating and one thing and another, they dies so as to keep the market up pretty brisk," said Haley.

"Wal, now, a feller can't help thinkin' it's a mighty pity to have a nice, quiet, likely feller, as good un as Tom is, go down to be fairly ground up on one of them ar sugar plantations."

"Wal, he's got a fa'r chance. I promised to do well by him. I'll get him in house-servant in some good old family, and then, if he stands the fever and 'climating, he'll have a berth good as any nigger ought ter ask for."

"He leaves his wife and chil'en up here, s'pose?"

"Yes; but he'll get another thar. Lord, thar's women enough everywhar," said Haley.

Tom was sitting very mournfully on the outside of the shop while this conversation was going on. Suddenly he heard the quick, short click of a horse's hoof behind him; and, before he could fairly awake from his surprise, young Master George sprang into the wagon, threw his arms tumultuously round his neck, and was sobbing and scolding with energy.

"I declare, it's real mean! I don't care what they say, any of 'em! It's a nasty, mean shame! If I was a man, they shouldn't do it,—they should not, *so*!" said George, with a kind of subdued howl.

"O! Mas'r George! this does me good!" said Tom. "I couldn't bar to go off without seein' ye! It does me real good, ye can't tell!" Here Tom made some movement of his feet, and George's eye fell on the fetters.

"What a shame!" he exclaimed, lifting his hands. "I'll knock that old fellow down—I will!"

"No you won't, Mas'r George; and you must not talk so loud. It won't help me any, to anger him."

"Well, I won't, then, for your sake; but only to think of it—isn't it a shame? They never sent for me, nor sent me any word, and, if it hadn't been for Tom Lincon, I shouldn't have heard it. I tell you, I blew 'em up well, all of 'em, at home!"

"That ar wasn't right, I'm 'feard, Mas'r George."

"Can't help it! I say it's a shame! Look here, Uncle Tom," said he, turning his back to the shop, and speaking in a mysterious tone, *"I've brought you my dollar!"*

"O! I couldn't think o' takin' on 't, Mas'r George, no ways in the world!" said Tom, quite moved.

"But you *shall* take it!" said George; "look here—I told Aunt Chloe I'd do it, and she advised me just to make a hole in it, and put a string through, so you could hang it round your neck, and keep it out of sight; else this mean scamp would take it away. I tell ye, Tom, I want to blow him up! it would do me good!"

"No, don't Mas'r George, for it won't do *me* any good."

"Well, I won't, for your sake," said George, busily tying his dollar round Tom's neck; "but there, now, button your coat tight over it, and keep it, and remember, every time you see it, that I'll come down after you, and bring you back. Aunt Chloe and I have been talking about it. I told her not to fear; I'll see to it, and I'll tease father's life out, if he don't do it."

"O! Mas'r George, ye mustn't talk so 'bout yer father!"

"Lor, Uncle Tom, I don't mean anything bad."

"And now, Mas'r George," said Tom, "ye must be a good boy; 'member how many hearts is sot on ye. Al'ays keep close to yer mother. Don't be gettin' into any of them foolish ways boys has of gettin' too big to mind their mothers. Tell ye what, Mas'r George, the Lord gives good many things twice over; but he don't give ye a mother but once. Ye'll never see sich another woman, Mas'r George, if ye live to be a hundred years old. So, now, you hold on to her, and grow up, and be a comfort to her, thar's my own good boy,—you will now, won't ye?"

"Yes, I will, Uncle Tom," said George seriously.

"And be careful of yer speaking, Mas'r George. Young boys, when they comes to your age, is wilful, sometimes—it is natur they should be. But real gentlemen, such as I hopes you'll be, never lets fall on words that isn't 'spectful to thar parents. Ye an't 'fended, Mas'r George?"

"No, indeed, Uncle Tom; you always did give me good advice."

"I's older, ye know," said Tom, stroking the boy's fine, curly head with his large, strong hand, but speaking in a voice as tender as a woman's, "and I sees all that's bound up in you. O, Mas'r George, you has everything,—l'arnin', privileges, readin', writin',—and you'll grow up to be a great, learned, good man and all the people on the place and your mother and father'll be so proud on ye! Be a good Mas'r, like yer father; and be a Christian, like yer mother. 'Member yer Creator in the days o' yer youth, Mas'r George."

"I'll be *real* good, Uncle Tom, I tell you," said George. "I'm going to be a *first-rater*; and don't you be discouraged. I'll have you back to the place, yet. As I told Aunt Chloe this morning, I'll build our house all over, and you shall have a room for a parlor with a carpet on it, when I'm a man. O, you'll have good times yet!"

Haley now came to the door, with the handcuffs in his hands.

"Look here, now, Mister," said George, with an air of great superiority, as he got out, "I shall let father and mother know how you treat Uncle Tom!"

"You're welcome," said the trader.

"I should think you'd be ashamed to spend all your life buying men and women, and chaining them, like cattle! I should think you'd feel mean!" said George.

"So long as your grand folks wants to buy men and women, I'm as good as they is," said Haley; "'tan't any meaner sellin' on 'em, that 't is buyin'!"

"I'll never do either, when I'm a man," said George; "I'm ashamed, this day, that I'm a Kentuckian. I always was proud of it before;" and George sat very straight on his horse, and looked round with an air, as if he expected the state would be impressed with his opinion.

"Well, good-by, Uncle Tom; keep a stiff upper lip," said George.

CHAPTER X

"Good-by, Mas'r George," said Tom, looking fondly and admiringly at him. "God Almighty bless you! Ah! Kentucky han't got many like you!" he said, in the fulness of his heart, as the frank, boyish face was lost to his view. Away he went, and Tom looked, till the clatter of his horse's heels died away, the last sound or sight of his home. But over his heart there seemed to be a warm spot, where those young hands had placed that precious dollar. Tom put up his hand, and held it close to his heart.

"Now, I tell ye what, Tom," said Haley, as he came up to the wagon, and threw in the handcuffs, "I mean to start fa'r with ye, as I gen'ally do with my niggers; and I'll tell ye now, to begin with, you treat me fa'r, and I'll treat you fa'r; I an't never hard on my niggers. Calculates to do the best for 'em I can. Now, ye see, you'd better jest settle down comfortable, and not be tryin' no tricks; because nigger's tricks of all sorts I'm up to, and it's no use. If niggers is quiet, and don't try to get off, they has good times with me; and if they don't, why, it's thar fault, and not mine."

Tom assured Haley that he had no present intentions of running off. In fact, the exhortation seemed rather a superfluous one to a man with a great pair of iron fetters on his feet. But Mr. Haley had got in the habit of commencing his relations with his stock with little exhortations of this nature, calculated, as he deemed, to inspire cheerfulness and confidence, and prevent the necessity of any unpleasant scenes.

And here, for the present, we take our leave of Tom, to pursue the fortunes of other characters in our story.

CHAPTER XI

IN WHICH PROPERTY GETS INTO AN IMPROPER STATE OF MIND

It was late in a drizzly afternoon that a traveler alighted at the door of a small country hotel, in the village of N——, in Kentucky. In the barroom he found assembled quite a miscellaneous company, whom stress of weather had driven to harbor, and the place presented the usual scenery of such reunions. Great, tall, raw-boned Kentuckians, attired in hunting-shirts, and trailing their loose joints over a vast extent of territory, with the easy lounge peculiar to the race,—rifles stacked away in the corner, shot-pouches, game-bags, hunting-dogs, and little negroes, all rolled together in the corners,—were the characteristic features in the picture. At each end of the fireplace sat a long-legged gentleman, with his chair tipped back, his hat on his head, and the heels of his muddy boots reposing sublimely on the mantel-piece,—a position, we will inform our readers, decidedly favorable to the turn of reflection incident to western taverns, where travellers exhibit a decided preference for this particular mode of elevating their understandings.

Mine host, who stood behind the bar, like most of his country men, was great of stature, good-natured and loose-jointed, with an enormous shock of hair on his head, and a great tall hat on the top of that.

In fact, everybody in the room bore on his head this characteristic emblem of man's sovereignty; whether it were felt hat, palm-leaf, greasy beaver, or fine new chapeau, there it reposed with true republican independence. In truth, it appeared to be the characteristic mark of every individual. Some wore them tipped rakishly to one side—these were your men of humor, jolly, free-and-easy dogs; some had them jammed independently down over their noses—these were your hard characters, thorough men, who, when they wore their hats, *wanted* to wear them, and to wear them just as they had a mind to; there were those who had them set far over back—wide-awake men, who wanted a clear prospect; while careless men, who did not know, or care, how their hats sat, had them shaking about in all directions. The various hats, in fact, were quite a Shakespearean study.

CHAPTER XI

Divers negroes, in very free-and-easy pantaloons, and with no redundancy in the shirt line, were scuttling about, hither and thither, without bringing to pass any very particular results, except expressing a generic willingness to turn over everything in creation generally for the benefit of Mas'r and his guests. Add to this picture a jolly, crackling, rollicking fire, going rejoicingly up a great wide chimney,—the outer door and every window being set wide open, and the calico window-curtain flopping and snapping in a good stiff breeze of damp raw air,—and you have an idea of the jollities of a Kentucky tavern.

Your Kentuckian of the present day is a good illustration of the doctrine of transmitted instincts and peculiarities. His fathers were mighty hunters,—men who lived in the woods, and slept under the free, open heavens, with the stars to hold their candles; and their descendant to this day always acts as if the house were his camp,—wears his hat at all hours, tumbles himself about, and puts his heels on the tops of chairs or mantelpieces, just as his father rolled on the green sward, and put his upon trees and logs,—keeps all the windows and doors open, winter and summer, that he may get air enough for his great lungs,—calls everybody "stranger," with nonchalant *bonhommie*, and is altogether the frankest, easiest, most jovial creature living.

Into such an assembly of the free and easy our traveller entered. He was a short, thick-set man, carefully dressed, with a round, good-natured countenance, and something rather fussy and particular in his appearance. He was very careful of his valise and umbrella, bringing them in with his own hands, and resisting, pertinaciously, all offers from the various servants to relieve him of them. He looked round the barroom with rather an anxious air, and, retreating with his valuables to the warmest corner, disposed them under his chair, sat down, and looked rather apprehensively up at the worthy whose heels illustrated the end of the mantel-piece, who was spitting from right to left, with a courage and energy rather alarming to gentlemen of weak nerves and particular habits.

"I say, stranger, how are ye?" said the aforesaid gentleman, firing an honorary salute of tobacco-juice in the direction of the new arrival.

"Well, I reckon," was the reply of the other, as he dodged, with some alarm, the threatening honor.

"Any news?" said the respondent, taking out a strip of tobacco and a large hunting-knife from his pocket.

"Not that I know of," said the man.

"Chaw?" said the first speaker, handing the old gentleman a bit of his tobacco, with a decidedly brotherly air.

"No, thank ye—it don't agree with me," said the little man, edging off.

"Don't, eh?" said the other, easily, and stowing away the morsel in his own mouth, in order to keep up the supply of tobacco-juice, for the general benefit of society.

The old gentleman uniformly gave a little start whenever his long-sided brother fired in his direction; and this being observed by his companion, he very good-naturedly turned his artillery to another quarter, and proceeded to storm one of the fire-irons with a degree of military talent fully sufficient to take a city.

"What's that?" said the old gentleman, observing some of the company formed in a group around a large handbill.

"Nigger advertised!" said one of the company, briefly.

Mr. Wilson, for that was the old gentleman's name, rose up, and, after carefully adjusting his valise and umbrella, proceeded deliberately to take out his spectacles and fix them on his nose; and, this operation being performed, read as follows:

"Ran away from the subscriber, my mulatto boy, George. Said George six feet in height, a very light mulatto, brown curly hair; is very intelligent, speaks handsomely, can read and write, will probably try to pass for a white man, is deeply scarred on his back and shoulders, has been branded in his right hand with the letter H. "I will give four hundred dollars for him alive, and the same sum for satisfactory proof that he has been *killed."*

The old gentleman read this advertisement from end to end in a low voice, as if he were studying it.

The long-legged veteran, who had been besieging the fire-iron, as before related, now took down his cumbrous length, and rearing aloft his tall form, walked up to the advertisement and very deliberately spit a full discharge of tobacco-juice on it.

"There's my mind upon that!" said he, briefly, and sat down again.

"Why, now, stranger, what's that for?" said mine host.

"I'd do it all the same to the writer of that ar paper, if he was here," said the long man, coolly resuming his old employment of cutting tobacco. "Any man that owns a boy like that, and can't find any better way o' treating on him, *deserves* to lose him. Such papers as these is a shame to Kentucky; that's my mind right out, if anybody wants to know!"

"Well, now, that's a fact," said mine host, as he made an entry in his book.

"I've got a gang of boys, sir," said the long man, resuming his attack on the fire-irons, "and I jest tells 'em—'Boys,' says I,—'*run* now! dig! put! jest when ye want to! I never shall come to look after you!' That's the way I keep mine. Let 'em know they are free to run any time, and it jest breaks up their wanting to. More 'n all, I've got free papers for 'em all recorded, in case I gets keeled up any o' these times, and they know it; and I tell ye, stranger, there an't a fellow in our parts gets more out of his niggers than I do. Why, my boys have been to Cincinnati, with five hundred dollars' worth of colts, and brought me back the money, all straight, time and agin. It stands to reason they should. Treat 'em like dogs, and you'll have dogs' works and dogs' actions. Treat 'em like men, and you'll have men's works." And the honest drover, in his warmth, endorsed this moral sentiment by firing a perfect *feu de joi* at the fireplace.

"I think you're altogether right, friend," said Mr. Wilson; "and this boy described here *is* a fine fellow—no mistake about that. He worked for me some half-dozen years in my bagging factory, and he was my best hand, sir. He is an ingenious fellow, too: he invented a machine for the cleaning of hemp—a really valuable affair; it's gone into use in several factories. His master holds the patent of it."

"I'll warrant ye," said the drover, "holds it and makes money out of it, and then turns round and brands the boy in his right hand. If I had a fair chance, I'd mark him, I reckon so that he'd carry it *one* while."

"These yer knowin' boys is allers aggravatin' and sarcy," said a coarse-looking fellow, from the other side of the room; "that's why they gets cut up and marked so. If they behaved themselves, they wouldn't."

"That is to say, the Lord made 'em men, and it's a hard squeeze gettin 'em down into beasts," said the drover, dryly.

"Bright niggers isn't no kind of 'vantage to their masters," continued the other, well entrenched, in a coarse, unconscious obtuseness, from the contempt of his opponent; "what's the use o' talents and them things, if you can't get the use on 'em yourself? Why, all the use they make on 't is to get round you. I've had one or two of these fellers, and I jest sold 'em down river. I knew I'd got to lose 'em, first or last, if I didn't."

"Better send orders up to the Lord, to make you a set, and leave out their souls entirely," said the drover.

Here the conversation was interrupted by the approach of a small one-horse buggy to the inn. It had a genteel appearance, and a well-dressed, gentlemanly man sat on the seat, with a colored servant driving.

The whole party examined the new comer with the interest with which a set of loafers in a rainy day usually examine every newcomer. He was very tall, with a dark, Spanish complexion, fine, expressive black eyes, and close-curling hair, also of a glossy blackness. His well-formed aquiline nose, straight thin lips, and the admirable contour of his finely-formed limbs, impressed the whole company instantly with the idea of something uncommon. He walked easily in among the company, and with a nod indicated to his waiter where to place his trunk, bowed to the company, and, with his hat in his hand, walked up leisurely to the bar, and gave in his name as Henry Butter, Oaklands, Shelby County. Turning, with an indifferent air, he sauntered up to the advertisement, and read it over.

"Jim," he said to his man, "seems to me we met a boy something like this, up at Beman's, didn't we?"

"Yes, Mas'r," said Jim, "only I an't sure about the hand."

"Well, I didn't look, of course," said the stranger with a careless yawn. Then walking up to the landlord, he desired him to furnish him with a private apartment, as he had some writing to do immediately.

The landlord was all obsequious, and a relay of about seven negroes, old and young, male and female, little and big, were soon whizzing about, like a covey of partridges, bustling, hurrying, treading on each other's toes, and tumbling over each other, in their zeal to get Mas'r's room ready, while he seated himself easily on a chair in the middle of the room, and entered into conversation with the man who sat next to him.

The manufacturer, Mr. Wilson, from the time of the entrance of the stranger, had regarded him with an air of disturbed and uneasy curiosity. He seemed to himself to have met and been acquainted with him somewhere, but he could not recollect. Every few moments, when the man spoke, or moved, or smiled, he would start and fix his eyes on him, and then suddenly withdraw them, as the bright, dark eyes met his with such unconcerned coolness. At last, a sudden recollection seemed to flash upon him, for he stared at the stranger with such an air of blank amazement and alarm, that he walked up to him.

"Mr. Wilson, I think," said he, in a tone of recognition, and extending his hand. "I beg your pardon, I didn't recollect you before. I see you remember me,—Mr. Butler, of Oaklands, Shelby County."

"Ye—yes—yes, sir," said Mr. Wilson, like one speaking in a dream.

Just then a negro boy entered, and announced that Mas'r's room was ready.

"Jim, see to the trunks," said the gentleman, negligently; then addressing himself to Mr. Wilson, he added—"I should like to have a few moments' conversation with you on business, in my room, if you please."

Mr. Wilson followed him, as one who walks in his sleep; and they proceeded to a large upper chamber, where a new-made fire was crackling, and various servants flying about, putting finishing touches to the arrangements.

When all was done, and the servants departed, the young man deliberately locked the door, and putting the key in his pocket, faced about, and folding his arms on his bosom, looked Mr. Wilson full in the face.

"George!" said Mr. Wilson.

"Yes, George," said the young man.

"I couldn't have thought it!"

"I am pretty well disguised, I fancy," said the young man, with a smile. "A little walnut bark has made my yellow skin a genteel brown, and I've dyed my hair black; so you see I don't answer to the advertisement at all."

"O, George! but this is a dangerous game you are playing. I could not have advised you to it."

"I can do it on my own responsibility," said George, with the same proud smile.

We remark, *en passant*, that George was, by his father's side, of white descent. His mother was one of those unfortunates of her race, marked out by personal beauty to be the slave of the passions of her possessor, and the mother of children who may never know a father. From one of the proudest families in Kentucky he had inherited a set of fine European features, and a high, indomitable spirit. From his mother he had received only a slight mulatto tinge, amply compensated by its accompanying rich, dark eye. A slight change in the tint of the skin and the color of his hair had metamorphosed him into the Spanish-looking fellow he then appeared; and as gracefulness of movement and gentlemanly manners had always been perfectly natural to him, he found no difficulty in playing the bold part he had adopted—that of a gentleman travelling with his domestic.

CHAPTER XI

Mr. Wilson, a good-natured but extremely fidgety and cautious old gentleman, ambled up and down the room, appearing, as John Bunyan hath it, "much tumbled up and down in his mind," and divided between his wish to help George, and a certain confused notion of maintaining law and order: so, as he shambled about, he delivered himself as follows:

"Well, George, I s'pose you're running away—leaving your lawful master, George—(I don't wonder at it)—at the same time, I'm sorry, George,—yes, decidedly—I think I must say that, George—it's my duty to tell you so."

"Why are you sorry, sir?" said George, calmly.

"Why, to see you, as it were, setting yourself in opposition to the laws of your country."

"*My* country!" said George, with a strong and bitter emphasis; "what country have I, but the grave,—and I wish to God that I was laid there!"

"Why, George, no—no—it won't do; this way of talking is wicked—unscriptural. George, you've got a hard master—in fact, he is—well he conducts himself reprehensibly—I can't pretend to defend him. But you know how the angel commanded Hagar to return to her mistress, and submit herself under the hand;[1] and the apostle sent back Onesimus to his master."[2]

"Don't quote Bible at me that way, Mr. Wilson," said George, with a flashing eye, "don't! for my wife is a Christian, and I mean to be, if ever I get to where I can; but to quote Bible to a fellow in my circumstances, is enough to make him give it up altogether. I appeal to God Almighty;—I'm willing to go with the case to Him, and ask Him if I do wrong to seek my freedom."

"These feelings are quite natural, George," said the good-natured man, blowing his nose. "Yes, they're natural, but it is my duty not to encourage 'em in you. Yes, my boy, I'm sorry for you, now; it's a bad case—very bad; but the apostle says, 'Let everyone abide in the condition in which he is called.' We must all submit to the indications of Providence, George,—don't you see?"

George stood with his head drawn back, his arms folded tightly over his broad breast, and a bitter smile curling his lips.

"I wonder, Mr. Wilson, if the Indians should come and take you a prisoner away from your wife and children, and want to keep you all your life hoeing corn for them, if you'd think it your duty to abide in the condition in which you were called. I rather think that you'd think the first stray horse you could find an indication of Providence—shouldn't you?"

The little old gentleman stared with both eyes at this illustration of the case; but, though not much of a reasoner, he had the sense in which some logicians on this particular subject do not excel,—that of saying nothing, where nothing could

---

[1] Gen. 16. The angel bade the pregnant Hagar return to her mistress Sarai, even though Sarai had dealt harshly with her.

[2] Phil. 1:10. Onesimus went back to his master to become no longer a servant but a "brother beloved."

be said. So, as he stood carefully stroking his umbrella, and folding and patting down all the creases in it, he proceeded on with his exhortations in a general way.

"You see, George, you know, now, I always have stood your friend; and whatever I've said, I've said for your good. Now, here, it seems to me, you're running an awful risk. You can't hope to carry it out. If you're taken, it will be worse with you than ever; they'll only abuse you, and half kill you, and sell you down the river."

"Mr. Wilson, I know all this," said George. "I *do* run a risk, but—" he threw open his overcoat, and showed two pistols and a bowie-knife. "There!" he said, "I'm ready for 'em! Down south I never *will* go. No! if it comes to that, I can earn myself at least six feet of free soil,—the first and last I shall ever own in Kentucky!"

"Why, George, this state of mind is awful; it's getting really desperate George. I'm concerned. Going to break the laws of your country!"

"My country again! Mr. Wilson, *you* have a country; but what country have *I*, or any one like me, born of slave mothers? What laws are there for us? We don't make them,—we don't consent to them,—we have nothing to do with them; all they do for us is to crush us, and keep us down. Haven't I heard your Fourth-of-July speeches? Don't you tell us all, once a year, that governments derive their just power from the consent of the governed? Can't a fellow *think*, that hears such things? Can't he put this and that together, and see what it comes to?"

Mr. Wilson's mind was one of those that may not unaptly be represented by a bale of cotton,—downy, soft, benevolently fuzzy and confused. He really pitied George with all his heart, and had a sort of dim and cloudy perception of the style of feeling that agitated him; but he deemed it his duty to go on talking *good* to him, with infinite pertinacity.

"George, this is bad. I must tell you, you know, as a friend, you'd better not be meddling with such notions; they are bad, George, very bad, for boys in your condition,—very;" and Mr. Wilson sat down to a table, and began nervously chewing the handle of his umbrella.

"See here, now, Mr. Wilson," said George, coming up and sitting himself determinately down in front of him; "look at me, now. Don't I sit before you, every way, just as much a man as you are? Look at my face,—look at my hands,—look at my body," and the young man drew himself up proudly; "why am I *not* a man, as much as anybody? Well, Mr. Wilson, hear what I can tell you. I had a father—one of your Kentucky gentlemen—who didn't think enough of me to keep me from being sold with his dogs and horses, to satisfy the estate, when he died. I saw my mother put up at sheriff's sale, with her seven children. They were sold before her eyes, one by one, all to different masters; and I was the youngest. She came and kneeled down before old Mas'r, and begged him to buy her with me, that she might have at least one child with her; and he kicked her away with his heavy boot. I saw him do it; and the last that I heard was her moans and screams, when I was tied to his horse's neck, to be carried off to his place."

"Well, then?"

CHAPTER XI

"My master traded with one of the men, and bought my oldest sister. She was a pious, good girl,—a member of the Baptist church,—and as handsome as my poor mother had been. She was well brought up, and had good manners. At first, I was glad she was bought, for I had one friend near me. I was soon sorry for it. Sir, I have stood at the door and heard her whipped, when it seemed as if every blow cut into my naked heart, and I couldn't do anything to help her; and she was whipped, sir, for wanting to live a decent Christian life, such as your laws give no slave girl a right to live; and at last I saw her chained with a trader's gang, to be sent to market in Orleans,—sent there for nothing else but that,—and that's the last I know of her. Well, I grew up,—long years and years,—no father, no mother, no sister, not a living soul that cared for me more than a dog; nothing but whipping, scolding, starving. Why, sir, I've been so hungry that I have been glad to take the bones they threw to their dogs; and yet, when I was a little fellow, and laid awake whole nights and cried, it wasn't the hunger, it wasn't the whipping, I cried for. No, sir, it was for *my mother* and *my sisters*,—it was because I hadn't a friend to love me on earth. I never knew what peace or comfort was. I never had a kind word spoken to me till I came to work in your factory. Mr. Wilson, you treated me well; you encouraged me to do well, and to learn to read and write, and to try to make something of myself; and God knows how grateful I am for it. Then, sir, I found my wife; you've seen her,—you know how beautiful she is. When I found she loved me, when I married her, I scarcely could believe I was alive, I was so happy; and, sir, she is as good as she is beautiful. But now what? Why, now comes my master, takes me right away from my work, and my friends, and all I like, and grinds me down into the very dirt! And why? Because, he says, I forgot who I was; he says, to teach me that I am only a nigger! After all, and last of all, he comes between me and my wife, and says I shall give her up, and live with another woman. And all this your laws give him power to do, in spite of God or man. Mr. Wilson, look at it! There isn't *one* of all these things, that have broken the hearts of my mother and my sister, and my wife and myself, but your laws allow, and give every man power to do, in Kentucky, and none can say to him nay! Do you call these the laws of *my* country? Sir, I haven't any country, anymore than I have any father. But I'm going to have one. I don't want anything of *your* country, except to be let alone,—to go peaceably out of it; and when I get to Canada, where the laws will own me and protect me, *that* shall be my country, and its laws I will obey. But if any man tries to stop me, let him take care, for I am desperate. I'll fight for my liberty to the last breath I breathe. You say your fathers did it; if it was right for them, it is right for me!"

This speech, delivered partly while sitting at the table, and partly walking up and down the room,—delivered with tears, and flashing eyes, and despairing gestures,—was altogether too much for the good-natured old body to whom it was addressed, who had pulled out a great yellow silk pocket-handkerchief, and was mopping up his face with great energy.

"Blast 'em all!" he suddenly broke out. "Haven't I always said so—the infernal old cusses! I hope I an't swearing, now. Well! go ahead, George, go ahead; but be careful, my boy; don't shoot anybody, George, unless—well—you'd *better* not shoot, I reckon; at least, I wouldn't *hit* anybody, you know. Where is your wife, George?" he added, as he nervously rose, and began walking the room.

"Gone, sir gone, with her child in her arms, the Lord only knows where;—gone after the north star; and when we ever meet, or whether we meet at all in this world, no creature can tell."

"Is it possible! astonishing! from such a kind family?"

"Kind families get in debt, and the laws of *our* country allow them to sell the child out of its mother's bosom to pay its master's debts," said George, bitterly.

"Well, well," said the honest old man, fumbling in his pocket: "I s'pose, perhaps, I an't following my judgment,—hang it, I *won't* follow my judgment!" he added, suddenly; "so here, George," and, taking out a roll of bills from his pocket-book, he offered them to George.

"No, my kind, good sir!" said George, "you've done a great deal for me, and this might get you into trouble. I have money enough, I hope, to take me as far as I need it."

"No; but you must, George. Money is a great help everywhere;—can't have too much, if you get it honestly. Take it,—*do* take it, *now*,—do, my boy!"

"On condition, sir, that I may repay it at some future time, I will," said George, taking up the money.

"And now, George, how long are you going to travel in this way?—not long or far, I hope. It's well carried on, but too bold. And this black fellow,—who is he?"

"A true fellow, who went to Canada more than a year ago. He heard, after he got there, that his master was so angry at him for going off that he had whipped his poor old mother; and he has come all the way back to comfort her, and get a chance to get her away."

"Has he got her?"

"Not yet; he has been hanging about the place, and found no chance yet. Meanwhile, he is going with me as far as Ohio, to put me among friends that helped him, and then he will come back after her.

"Dangerous, very dangerous!" said the old man.

George drew himself up, and smiled disdainfully.

The old gentleman eyed him from head to foot, with a sort of innocent wonder.

"George, something has brought you out wonderfully. You hold up your head, and speak and move like another man," said Mr. Wilson.

"Because I'm a *freeman*!" said George, proudly. "Yes, sir; I've said Mas'r for the last time to any man. *I'm free!"*

"Take care! You are not sure,—you may be taken."

"All men are free and equal *in the grave*, if it comes to that, Mr. Wilson," said George.

"I'm perfectly dumb-founded with your boldness!" said Mr. Wilson,—"to come right here to the nearest tavern!"

"Mr. Wilson, it is *so* bold, and this tavern is so near, that they will never think of it; they will look for me on ahead, and you yourself wouldn't know me. Jim's master don't live in this county; he isn't known in these parts. Besides, he is given up; nobody is looking after him, and nobody will take me up from the advertisement, I think."

"But the mark in your hand?"

George drew off his glove, and showed a newly-healed scar in his hand.

"That is a parting proof of Mr. Harris' regard," he said, scornfully. "A fortnight ago, he took it into his head to give it to me, because he said he believed I should try to get away one of these days. Looks interesting, doesn't it?" he said, drawing his glove on again.

"I declare, my very blood runs cold when I think of it,—your condition and your risks!" said Mr. Wilson.

"Mine has run cold a good many years, Mr. Wilson; at present, it's about up to the boiling point," said George.

"Well, my good sir," continued George, after a few moments' silence, "I saw you knew me; I thought I'd just have this talk with you, lest your surprised looks should bring me out. I leave early tomorrow morning, before daylight; by tomorrow night I hope to sleep safe in Ohio. I shall travel by daylight, stop at the best hotels, go to the dinner-tables with the lords of the land. So, good-by, sir; if you hear that I'm taken, you may know that I'm dead!"

George stood up like a rock, and put out his hand with the air of a prince. The friendly little old man shook it heartily, and after a little shower of caution, he took his umbrella, and fumbled his way out of the room.

George stood thoughtfully looking at the door, as the old man closed it. A thought seemed to flash across his mind. He hastily stepped to it, and opening it, said,

"Mr. Wilson, one word more."

The old gentleman entered again, and George, as before, locked the door, and then stood for a few moments looking on the floor, irresolutely. At last, raising his head with a sudden effort—"Mr. Wilson, you have shown yourself a Christian in your treatment of me,—I want to ask one last deed of Christian kindness of you."

"Well, George."

"Well, sir,—what you said was true. I *am* running a dreadful risk. There isn't, on earth, a living soul to care if I die," he added, drawing his breath hard, and speaking with a great effort,—"I shall be kicked out and buried like a dog, and nobody'll think of it a day after,—*only my poor wife!* Poor soul! she'll mourn and grieve; and if you'd only contrive, Mr. Wilson, to send this little pin to her. She gave it to me for a Christmas present, poor child! Give it to her, and tell her I loved her to the last. Will you? *Will* you?" he added, earnestly.

"Yes, certainly—poor fellow!" said the old gentleman, taking the pin, with watery eyes, and a melancholy quiver in his voice.

"Tell her one thing," said George; "it's my last wish, if she *can* get to Canada, to go there. No matter how kind her mistress is,—no matter how much she loves her home; beg her not to go back,—for slavery always ends in misery. Tell her to bring up our boy a free man, and then he won't suffer as I have. Tell her this, Mr. Wilson, will you?"

"Yes, George. I'll tell her; but I trust you won't die; take heart,—you're a brave fellow. Trust in the Lord, George. I wish in my heart you were safe through, though,—that's what I do."

"*Is* there a God to trust in?" said George, in such a tone of bitter despair as arrested the old gentleman's words. "O, I've seen things all my life that have made me feel that there can't be a God. You Christians don't know how these things look to us. There's a God for you, but is there any for us?"

"O, now, don't—don't, my boy!" said the old man, almost sobbing as he spoke; "don't feel so! There is—there is; clouds and darkness are around about him, but righteousness and judgment are the habitation of his throne. There's a *God*, George,—believe it; trust in Him, and I'm sure He'll help you. Everything will be set right,—if not in this life, in another."

The real piety and benevolence of the simple old man invested him with a temporary dignity and authority, as he spoke. George stopped his distracted walk up and down the room, stood thoughtfully a moment, and then said, quietly,

"Thank you for saying that, my good friend; I'll *think of that*."

CHAPTER XII

SELECT INCIDENT OF LAWFUL TRADE

"In Ramah there was a voice heard,—weeping, and lamentation, and great mourning; Rachel weeping for her children, and would not be comforted."[1]

Mr. Haley and Tom jogged onward in their wagon, each, for a time, absorbed in his own reflections. Now, the reflections of two men sitting side by side are a curious thing,—seated on the same seat, having the same eyes, ears, hands and organs of all sorts, and having pass before their eyes the same objects,—it is wonderful what a variety we shall find in these same reflections!

As, for example, Mr. Haley: he thought first of Tom's length, and breadth, and height, and what he would sell for, if he was kept fat and in good case till he got him into market. He thought of how he should make out his gang; he thought of the respective market value of certain supposititious men and women and children who were to compose it, and other kindred topics of the business; then he thought of himself, and how humane he was, that whereas other men chained their "niggers" hand and foot both, he only put fetters on the feet, and left Tom the use of his hands, as long as he behaved well; and he sighed to think how ungrateful human nature was, so that there was even room to doubt whether Tom appreciated his mercies. He had been taken in so by "niggers" whom he had favored; but still he was astonished to consider how good-natured he yet remained!

As to Tom, he was thinking over some words of an unfashionable old book, which kept running through his head, again and again, as follows: "We have here no continuing city, but we seek one to come; wherefore God himself is not ashamed to be called our God; for he hath prepared for us a city." These words of an ancient volume, got up principally by "ignorant and unlearned men," have, through all time, kept up, somehow, a strange sort of power over the minds of poor, simple fellows, like Tom. They stir up the soul from its depths, and rouse, as with trumpet call, courage, energy, and enthusiasm, where before was only the blackness of despair.

---

[1] Jer. 31:15.

Mr. Haley pulled out of his pocket sundry newspapers, and began looking over their advertisements, with absorbed interest. He was not a remarkably fluent reader, and was in the habit of reading in a sort of recitative half-aloud, by way of calling in his ears to verify the deductions of his eyes. In this tone he slowly recited the following paragraph:

"EXECUTOR'S SALE,—NEGROES!—Agreeably to order of court, will be sold, on Tuesday, February 20, before the Court-house door, in the town of Washington, Kentucky, the following negroes: Hagar, aged 60; John, aged 30; Ben, aged 21; Saul, aged 25; Albert, aged 14. Sold for the benefit of the creditors and heirs of the estate of Jesse Blutchford,

"SAMUEL MORRIS, THOMAS FLINT, *Executors*."

"This yer I must look at," said he to Tom, for want of somebody else to talk to.

"Ye see, I'm going to get up a prime gang to take down with ye, Tom; it'll make it sociable and pleasant like,—good company will, ye know. We must drive right to Washington first and foremost, and then I'll clap you into jail, while I does the business."

Tom received this agreeable intelligence quite meekly; simply wondering, in his own heart, how many of these doomed men had wives and children, and whether they would feel as he did about leaving them. It is to be confessed, too, that the naive, off-hand information that he was to be thrown into jail by no means produced an agreeable impression on a poor fellow who had always prided himself on a strictly honest and upright course of life. Yes, Tom, we must confess it, was rather proud of his honesty, poor fellow,—not having very much else to be proud of;—if he had belonged to some of the higher walks of society, he, perhaps, would never have been reduced to such straits. However, the day wore on, and the evening saw Haley and Tom comfortably accommodated in Washington,—the one in a tavern, and the other in a jail.

About eleven o'clock the next day, a mixed throng was gathered around the court-house steps,—smoking, chewing, spitting, swearing, and conversing, according to their respective tastes and turns,—waiting for the auction to commence. The men and women to be sold sat in a group apart, talking in a low tone to each other. The woman who had been advertised by the name of Hagar was a regular African in feature and figure. She might have been sixty, but was older than that by hard work and disease, was partially blind, and somewhat crippled with rheumatism. By her side stood her only remaining son, Albert, a bright-looking little fellow of fourteen years. The boy was the only survivor of a large family, who had been successively sold away from her to a southern market. The mother held on to him with both her shaking hands, and eyed with intense trepidation every one who walked up to examine him.

"Don't be feard, Aunt Hagar," said the oldest of the men, "I spoke to Mas'r Thomas 'bout it, and he thought he might manage to sell you in a lot both together."

"Dey needn't call me worn out yet," said she, lifting her shaking hands. "I can cook yet, and scrub, and scour,—I'm wuth a buying, if I do come cheap;—tell em dat ar,—you *tell* em," she added, earnestly.

Haley here forced his way into the group, walked up to the old man, pulled his mouth open and looked in, felt of his teeth, made him stand and straighten himself, bend his back, and perform various evolutions to show his muscles; and then passed on to the next, and put him through the same trial. Walking up last to the boy, he felt of his arms, straightened his hands, and looked at his fingers, and made him jump, to show his agility.

"He an't gwine to be sold widout me!" said the old woman, with passionate eagerness; "he and I goes in a lot together; I 's rail strong yet, Mas'r and can do heaps o' work,—heaps on it, Mas'r."

"On plantation?" said Haley, with a contemptuous glance. "Likely story!" and, as if satisfied with his examination, he walked out and looked, and stood with his hands in his pocket, his cigar in his mouth, and his hat cocked on one side, ready for action.

"What think of 'em?" said a man who had been following Haley's examination, as if to make up his own mind from it.

"Wal," said Haley, spitting, "I shall put in, I think, for the youngerly ones and the boy."

"They want to sell the boy and the old woman together," said the man.

"Find it a tight pull;—why, she's an old rack o' bones,—not worth her salt."

"You wouldn't then?" said the man.

"Anybody 'd be a fool 't would. She's half blind, crooked with rheumatis, and foolish to boot."

"Some buys up these yer old critturs, and ses there's a sight more wear in 'em than a body 'd think," said the man, reflectively.

"No go, 't all," said Haley; "wouldn't take her for a present,—fact,—I've *seen*, now."

"Wal, 't is kinder pity, now, not to buy her with her son,—her heart seems so sot on him,—s'pose they fling her in cheap."

"Them that's got money to spend that ar way, it's all well enough. I shall bid off on that ar boy for a plantation-hand;—wouldn't be bothered with her, no way, not if they'd give her to me," said Haley.

"She'll take on desp't," said the man.

"Nat'lly, she will," said the trader, coolly.

The conversation was here interrupted by a busy hum in the audience; and the auctioneer, a short, bustling, important fellow, elbowed his way into the crowd. The old woman drew in her breath, and caught instinctively at her son.

"Keep close to yer mammy, Albert,—close,—dey'll put us up togedder," she said.

"O, mammy, I'm feard they won't," said the boy.

"Dey must, child; I can't live, no ways, if they don't" said the old creature, vehemently.

The stentorian tones of the auctioneer, calling out to clear the way, now announced that the sale was about to commence. A place was cleared, and the bidding began. The different men on the list were soon knocked off at prices which showed a pretty brisk demand in the market; two of them fell to Haley.

"Come, now, young un," said the auctioneer, giving the boy a touch with his hammer, "be up and show your springs, now."

"Put us two up togedder, togedder,—do please, Mas'r," said the old woman, holding fast to her boy.

"Be off," said the man, gruffly, pushing her hands away; "you come last. Now, darkey, spring;" and, with the word, he pushed the boy toward the block, while a deep, heavy groan rose behind him. The boy paused, and looked back; but there was no time to stay, and, dashing the tears from his large, bright eyes, he was up in a moment.

His fine figure, alert limbs, and bright face, raised an instant competition, and half a dozen bids simultaneously met the ear of the auctioneer. Anxious, half-frightened, he looked from side to side, as he heard the clatter of contending bids,—now here, now there,—till the hammer fell. Haley had got him. He was pushed from the block toward his new master, but stopped one moment, and looked back, when his poor old mother, trembling in every limb, held out her shaking hands toward him.

"Buy me too, Mas'r, for de dear Lord's sake!—buy me,—I shall die if you don't!"

"You'll die if I do, that's the kink of it," said Haley,—"no!" And he turned on his heel.

The bidding for the poor old creature was summary. The man who had addressed Haley, and who seemed not destitute of compassion, bought her for a trifle, and the spectators began to disperse.

The poor victims of the sale, who had been brought up in one place together for years, gathered round the despairing old mother, whose agony was pitiful to see.

"Couldn't dey leave me one? Mas'r allers said I should have one,—he did," she repeated over and over, in heart-broken tones.

"Trust in the Lord, Aunt Hagar," said the oldest of the men, sorrowfully.

"What good will it do?" said she, sobbing passionately.

"Mother, mother,—don't! don't!" said the boy. "They say you 's got a good master."

"I don't care,—I don't care. O, Albert! oh, my boy! you 's my last baby. Lord, how ken I?"

"Come, take her off, can't some of ye?" said Haley, dryly; "don't do no good for her to go on that ar way."

The old men of the company, partly by persuasion and partly by force, loosed the poor creature's last despairing hold, and, as they led her off to her new master's wagon, strove to comfort her.

CHAPTER XII

"Now!" said Haley, pushing his three purchases together, and producing a bundle of handcuffs, which he proceeded to put on their wrists; and fastening each handcuff to a long chain, he drove them before him to the jail.

A few days saw Haley, with his possessions, safely deposited on one of the Ohio boats. It was the commencement of his gang, to be augmented, as the boat moved on, by various other merchandise of the same kind, which he, or his agent, had stored for him in various points along shore.

The La Belle Riviere, as brave and beautiful a boat as ever walked the waters of her namesake river, was floating gayly down the stream, under a brilliant sky, the stripes and stars of free America waving and fluttering over head; the guards crowded with well-dressed ladies and gentlemen walking and enjoying the delightful day. All was full of life, buoyant and rejoicing;—all but Haley's gang, who were stored, with other freight, on the lower deck, and who, somehow, did not seem to appreciate their various privileges, as they sat in a knot, talking to each other in low tones.

"Boys," said Haley, coming up, briskly, "I hope you keep up good heart, and are cheerful. Now, no sulks, ye see; keep stiff upper lip, boys; do well by me, and I'll do well by you."

The boys addressed responded the invariable "Yes, Mas'r," for ages the watchword of poor Africa; but it's to be owned they did not look particularly cheerful; they had their various little prejudices in favor of wives, mothers, sisters, and children, seen for the last time,—and though "they that wasted them required of them mirth," it was not instantly forthcoming.

"I've got a wife," spoke out the article enumerated as "John, aged thirty," and he laid his chained hand on Tom's knee,—"and she don't know a word about this, poor girl!"

"Where does she live?" said Tom.

"In a tavern a piece down here," said John; "I wish, now, I *could* see her once more in this world," he added.

Poor John! It *was* rather natural; and the tears that fell, as he spoke, came as naturally as if he had been a white man. Tom drew a long breath from a sore heart, and tried, in his poor way, to comfort him.

And over head, in the cabin, sat fathers and mothers, husbands and wives; and merry, dancing children moved round among them, like so many little butterflies, and everything was going on quite easy and comfortable.

"O, mamma," said a boy, who had just come up from below, "there's a negro trader on board, and he's brought four or five slaves down there."

"Poor creatures!" said the mother, in a tone between grief and indignation.

"What's that?" said another lady.

"Some poor slaves below," said the mother.

"And they've got chains on," said the boy.

"What a shame to our country that such sights are to be seen!" said another lady.

"O, there's a great deal to be said on both sides of the subject," said a genteel woman, who sat at her state-room door sewing, while her little girl and boy were playing round her. "I've been south, and I must say I think the negroes are better off than they would be to be free."

"In some respects, some of them are well off, I grant," said the lady to whose remark she had answered. "The most dreadful part of slavery, to my mind, is its outrages on the feelings and affections,—the separating of families, for example."

"That *is* a bad thing, certainly," said the other lady, holding up a baby's dress she had just completed, and looking intently on its trimmings; "but then, I fancy, it don't occur often."

"O, it does," said the first lady, eagerly; "I've lived many years in Kentucky and Virginia both, and I've seen enough to make any one's heart sick. Suppose, ma'am, your two children, there, should be taken from you, and sold?"

"We can't reason from our feelings to those of this class of persons," said the other lady, sorting out some worsteds on her lap.

"Indeed, ma'am, you can know nothing of them, if you say so," answered the first lady, warmly. "I was born and brought up among them. I know they *do* feel, just as keenly,—even more so, perhaps,—as we do."

The lady said "Indeed!" yawned, and looked out the cabin window, and finally repeated, for a finale, the remark with which she had begun,—"After all, I think they are better off than they would be to be free."

"It's undoubtedly the intention of Providence that the African race should be servants,—kept in a low condition," said a grave-looking gentleman in black, a clergyman, seated by the cabin door. "'Cursed be Canaan; a servant of servants shall he be,' the scripture says."[1]

"I say, stranger, is that ar what that text means?" said a tall man, standing by.

"Undoubtedly. It pleased Providence, for some inscrutable reason, to doom the race to bondage, ages ago; and we must not set up our opinion against that."

"Well, then, we'll all go ahead and buy up niggers," said the man, "if that's the way of Providence,—won't we, Squire?" said he, turning to Haley, who had been standing, with his hands in his pockets, by the stove and intently listening to the conversation.

"Yes," continued the tall man, "we must all be resigned to the decrees of Providence. Niggers must be sold, and trucked round, and kept under; it's what they's made for. 'Pears like this yer view 's quite refreshing, an't it, stranger?" said he to Haley.

"I never thought on 't," said Haley, "I couldn't have said as much, myself; I ha'nt no larning. I took up the trade just to make a living; if 'tan't right, I calculated to 'pent on 't in time, ye know."

"And now you'll save yerself the trouble, won't ye?" said the tall man. "See what 't is, now, to know scripture. If ye'd only studied yer Bible, like this yer good

---

[1] Gen. 9:25. This is what Noah says when he wakes out of drunkenness and realizes that his youngest son, Ham, father of Canaan, has seen him naked.

man, ye might have know'd it before, and saved ye a heap o' trouble. Ye could jist have said, 'Cussed be'—what's his name?—'and 't would all have come right.'" And the stranger, who was no other than the honest drover whom we introduced to our readers in the Kentucky tavern, sat down, and began smoking, with a curious smile on his long, dry face.

A tall, slender young man, with a face expressive of great feeling and intelligence, here broke in, and repeated the words, "'All things whatsoever ye would that men should do unto you, do ye even so unto them.' I suppose," he added, "*that* is scripture, as much as 'Cursed be Canaan.'"

"Wal, it seems quite *as* plain a text, stranger," said John the drover, "to poor fellows like us, now;" and John smoked on like a volcano.

The young man paused, looked as if he was going to say more, when suddenly the boat stopped, and the company made the usual steamboat rush, to see where they were landing.

"Both them ar chaps parsons?" said John to one of the men, as they were going out.

The man nodded.

As the boat stopped, a black woman came running wildly up the plank, darted into the crowd, flew up to where the slave gang sat, and threw her arms round that unfortunate piece of merchandise before enumerate—"John, aged thirty," and with sobs and tears bemoaned him as her husband.

But what needs tell the story, told too oft,—every day told,—of heart-strings rent and broken,—the weak broken and torn for the profit and convenience of the strong! It needs not to be told;—every day is telling it,—telling it, too, in the ear of One who is not deaf, though he be long silent.

The young man who had spoken for the cause of humanity and God before stood with folded arms, looking on this scene. He turned, and Haley was standing at his side. "My friend," he said, speaking with thick utterance, "how can you, how dare you, carry on a trade like this? Look at those poor creatures! Here I am, rejoicing in my heart that I am going home to my wife and child; and the same bell which is a signal to carry me onward towards them will part this poor man and his wife forever. Depend upon it, God will bring you into judgment for this."

The trader turned away in silence.

"I say, now," said the drover, touching his elbow, "there's differences in parsons, an't there? 'Cussed be Canaan' don't seem to go down with this 'un, does it?"

Haley gave an uneasy growl.

"And that ar an't the worst on 't," said John; "mabbee it won't go down with the Lord, neither, when ye come to settle with Him, one o' these days, as all on us must, I reckon."

Haley walked reflectively to the other end of the boat.

"If I make pretty handsomely on one or two next gangs," he thought, "I reckon I'll stop off this yer; it's really getting dangerous." And he took out his pocket-book, and began adding over his accounts,—a process which many gentlemen besides Mr. Haley have found a specific for an uneasy conscience.

The boat swept proudly away from the shore, and all went on merrily, as before. Men talked, and loafed, and read, and smoked. Women sewed, and children played, and the boat passed on her way.

One day, when she lay to for a while at a small town in Kentucky, Haley went up into the place on a little matter of business.

Tom, whose fetters did not prevent his taking a moderate circuit, had drawn near the side of the boat, and stood listlessly gazing over the railing. After a time, he saw the trader returning, with an alert step, in company with a colored woman, bearing in her arms a young child. She was dressed quite respectably, and a colored man followed her, bringing along a small trunk. The woman came cheerfully onward, talking, as she came, with the man who bore her trunk, and so passed up the plank into the boat. The bell rung, the steamer whizzed, the engine groaned and coughed, and away swept the boat down the river.

The woman walked forward among the boxes and bales of the lower deck, and, sitting down, busied herself with chirruping to her baby.

Haley made a turn or two about the boat, and then, coming up, seated himself near her, and began saying something to her in an indifferent undertone.

Tom soon noticed a heavy cloud passing over the woman's brow; and that she answered rapidly, and with great vehemence.

"I don't believe it,—I won't believe it!" he heard her say. "You're jist a foolin' with me."

"If you won't believe it, look here!" said the man, drawing out a paper; "this yer's the bill of sale, and there's your master's name to it; and I paid down good solid cash for it, too, I can tell you,—so, now!"

"I don't believe Mas'r would cheat me so; it can't be true!" said the woman, with increasing agitation.

"You can ask any of these men here, that can read writing. Here!" he said, to a man that was passing by, "jist read this yer, won't you! This yer gal won't believe me, when I tell her what 't is."

"Why, it's a bill of sale, signed by John Fosdick," said the man, "making over to you the girl Lucy and her child. It's all straight enough, for aught I see."

The woman's passionate exclamations collected a crowd around her, and the trader briefly explained to them the cause of the agitation.

"He told me that I was going down to Louisville, to hire out as cook to the same tavern where my husband works,—that's what Mas'r told me, his own self; and I can't believe he'd lie to me," said the woman.

"But he has sold you, my poor woman, there's no doubt about it," said a good-natured looking man, who had been examining the papers; "he has done it, and no mistake."

"Then it's no account talking," said the woman, suddenly growing quite calm; and, clasping her child tighter in her arms, she sat down on her box, turned her back round, and gazed listlessly into the river.

"Going to take it easy, after all!" said the trader. "Gal's got grit, I see."

CHAPTER XII

The woman looked calm, as the boat went on; and a beautiful soft summer breeze passed like a compassionate spirit over her head,—the gentle breeze, that never inquires whether the brow is dusky or fair that it fans. And she saw sunshine sparkling on the water, in golden ripples, and heard gay voices, full of ease and pleasure, talking around her everywhere; but her heart lay as if a great stone had fallen on it. Her baby raised himself up against her, and stroked her cheeks with his little hands; and, springing up and down, crowing and chatting, seemed determined to arouse her. She strained him suddenly and tightly in her arms, and slowly one tear after another fell on his wondering, unconscious face; and gradually she seemed, and little by little, to grow calmer, and busied herself with tending and nursing him.

The child, a boy of ten months, was uncommonly large and strong of his age, and very vigorous in his limbs. Never, for a moment, still, he kept his mother constantly busy in holding him, and guarding his springing activity.

"That's a fine chap!" said a man, suddenly stopping opposite to him, with his hands in his pockets. "How old is he?"

"Ten months and a half," said the mother.

The man whistled to the boy, and offered him part of a stick of candy, which he eagerly grabbed at, and very soon had it in a baby's general depository, to wit, his mouth.

"Rum fellow!" said the man "Knows what's what!" and he whistled, and walked on. When he had got to the other side of the boat, he came across Haley, who was smoking on top of a pile of boxes.

The stranger produced a match, and lighted a cigar, saying, as he did so,

"Decentish kind o' wench you've got round there, stranger."

"Why, I reckon she *is* tol'able fair," said Haley, blowing the smoke out of his mouth.

"Taking her down south?" said the man.

Haley nodded, and smoked on.

"Plantation hand?" said the man.

"Wal," said Haley, "I'm fillin' out an order for a plantation, and I think I shall put her in. They telled me she was a good cook; and they can use her for that, or set her at the cotton-picking. She's got the right fingers for that; I looked at 'em. Sell well, either way;" and Haley resumed his cigar.

"They won't want the young 'un on the plantation," said the man.

"I shall sell him, first chance I find," said Haley, lighting another cigar.

"S'pose you'd be selling him tol'able cheap," said the stranger, mounting the pile of boxes, and sitting down comfortably.

"Don't know 'bout that," said Haley; "he's a pretty smart young 'un, straight, fat, strong; flesh as hard as a brick!"

"Very true, but then there's the bother and expense of raisin'."

"Nonsense!" said Haley; "they is raised as easy as any kind of critter there is going; they an't a bit more trouble than pups. This yer chap will be running all around, in a month."

"I've got a good place for raisin', and I thought of takin' in a little more stock," said the man. "One cook lost a young 'un last week,—got drownded in a washtub, while she was a hangin' out the clothes,—and I reckon it would be well enough to set her to raisin' this yer."

Haley and the stranger smoked a while in silence, neither seeming willing to broach the test question of the interview. At last the man resumed:

"You wouldn't think of wantin' more than ten dollars for that ar chap, seeing you *must* get him off yer hand, any how?"

Haley shook his head, and spit impressively.

"That won't do, no ways," he said, and began his smoking again.

"Well, stranger, what will you take?"

"Well, now," said Haley, "I *could* raise that ar chap myself, or get him raised; he's oncommon likely and healthy, and he'd fetch a hundred dollars, six months hence; and, in a year or two, he'd bring two hundred, if I had him in the right spot; I shan't take a cent less nor fifty for him now."

"O, stranger! that's rediculous, altogether," said the man.

"Fact!" said Haley, with a decisive nod of his head.

"I'll give thirty for him," said the stranger, "but not a cent more."

"Now, I'll tell ye what I will do," said Haley, spitting again, with renewed decision. "I'll split the difference, and say forty-five; and that's the most I will do."

"Well, agreed!" said the man, after an interval.

"Done!" said Haley. "Where do you land?"

"At Louisville," said the man.

"Louisville," said Haley. "Very fair, we get there about dusk. Chap will be asleep,—all fair,—get him off quietly, and no screaming,—happens beautiful,—I like to do everything quietly,—I hates all kind of agitation and fluster." And so, after a transfer of certain bills had passed from the man's pocket-book to the trader's, he resumed his cigar.

It was a bright, tranquil evening when the boat stopped at the wharf at Louisville. The woman had been sitting with her baby in her arms, now wrapped in a heavy sleep. When she heard the name of the place called out, she hastily laid the child down in a little cradle formed by the hollow among the boxes, first carefully spreading under it her cloak; and then she sprung to the side of the boat, in hopes that, among the various hotel-waiters who thronged the wharf, she might see her husband. In this hope, she pressed forward to the front rails, and, stretching far over them, strained her eyes intently on the moving heads on the shore, and the crowd pressed in between her and the child.

"Now's your time," said Haley, taking the sleeping child up, and handing him to the stranger. "Don't wake him up, and set him to crying, now; it would make a devil of a fuss with the gal." The man took the bundle carefully, and was soon lost in the crowd that went up the wharf.

When the boat, creaking, and groaning, and puffing, had loosed from the wharf, and was beginning slowly to strain herself along, the woman returned to her old seat. The trader was sitting there,—the child was gone!

CHAPTER XII

"Why, why,—where?" she began, in bewildered surprise.

"Lucy," said the trader, "your child's gone; you may as well know it first as last. You see, I know'd you couldn't take him down south; and I got a chance to sell him to a first-rate family, that'll raise him better than you can."

The trader had arrived at that stage of Christian and political perfection which has been recommended by some preachers and politicians of the north, lately, in which he had completely overcome every humane weakness and prejudice. His heart was exactly where yours, sir, and mine could be brought, with proper effort and cultivation. The wild look of anguish and utter despair that the woman cast on him might have disturbed one less practised; but he was used to it. He had seen that same look hundreds of times. You can get used to such things, too, my friend; and it is the great object of recent efforts to make our whole northern community used to them, for the glory of the Union. So the trader only regarded the mortal anguish which he saw working in those dark features, those clenched hands, and suffocating breathings, as necessary incidents of the trade, and merely calculated whether she was going to scream, and get up a commotion on the boat; for, like other supporters of our peculiar institution, he decidedly disliked agitation.

But the woman did not scream. The shot had passed too straight and direct through the heart, for cry or tear.

Dizzily she sat down. Her slack hands fell lifeless by her side. Her eyes looked straight forward, but she saw nothing. All the noise and hum of the boat, the groaning of the machinery, mingled dreamily to her bewildered ear; and the poor, dumb-stricken heart had neither cry not tear to show for its utter misery. She was quite calm.

The trader, who, considering his advantages, was almost as humane as some of our politicians, seemed to feel called on to administer such consolation as the case admitted of.

"I know this yer comes kinder hard, at first, Lucy," said he; "but such a smart, sensible gal as you are, won't give way to it. You see it's *necessary*, and can't be helped!"

"O! don't, Mas'r, don't!" said the woman, with a voice like one that is smothering.

"You're a smart wench, Lucy," he persisted; "I mean to do well by ye, and get ye a nice place down river; and you'll soon get another husband,—such a likely gal as you—"

"O! Mas'r, if you *only* won't talk to me now," said the woman, in a voice of such quick and living anguish that the trader felt that there was something at present in the case beyond his style of operation. He got up, and the woman turned away, and buried her head in her cloak.

The trader walked up and down for a time, and occasionally stopped and looked at her.

"Takes it hard, rather," he soliloquized, "but quiet, tho';—let her sweat a while; she'll come right, by and by!"

Tom had watched the whole transaction from first to last, and had a perfect understanding of its results. To him, it looked like something unutterably horrible and cruel, because, poor, ignorant black soul! he had not learned to generalize, and to take enlarged views. If he had only been instructed by certain ministers of Christianity, he might have thought better of it, and seen in it an every-day incident of a lawful trade; a trade which is the vital support of an institution which an American divine[1] tells us has *"no evils but such as are inseparable from any other relations in social and domestic life."* But Tom, as we see, being a poor, ignorant fellow, whose reading had been confined entirely to the New Testament, could not comfort and solace himself with views like these. His very soul bled within him for what seemed to him the *wrongs* of the poor suffering thing that lay like a crushed reed on the boxes; the feeling, living, bleeding, yet immortal *thing*, which American state law coolly classes with the bundles, and bales, and boxes, among which she is lying.

Tom drew near, and tried to say something; but she only groaned. Honestly, and with tears running down his own cheeks, he spoke of a heart of love in the skies, of a pitying Jesus, and an eternal home; but the ear was deaf with anguish, and the palsied heart could not feel.

Night came on,—night calm, unmoved, and glorious, shining down with her innumerable and solemn angel eyes, twinkling, beautiful, but silent. There was no speech nor language, no pitying voice or helping hand, from that distant sky. One after another, the voices of business or pleasure died away; all on the boat were sleeping, and the ripples at the prow were plainly heard. Tom stretched himself out on a box, and there, as he lay, he heard, ever and anon, a smothered sob or cry from the prostrate creature,—"O! what shall I do? O Lord! O good Lord, do help me!" and so, ever and anon, until the murmur died away in silence.

At midnight, Tom waked, with a sudden start. Something black passed quickly by him to the side of the boat, and he heard a splash in the water. No one else saw or heard anything. He raised his head,—the woman's place was vacant! He got up, and sought about him in vain. The poor bleeding heart was still, at last, and the river rippled and dimpled just as brightly as if it had not closed above it.

Patience! patience! ye whose hearts swell indignant at wrongs like these. Not one throb of anguish, not one tear of the oppressed, is forgotten by the Man of Sorrows, the Lord of Glory. In his patient, generous bosom he bears the anguish of a world. Bear thou, like him, in patience, and labor in love; for sure as he is God, "the year of his redeemed *shall* come."

The trader waked up bright and early, and came out to see to his live stock. It was now his turn to look about in perplexity.

"Where alive is that gal?" he said to Tom.

---

[1] Dr. Joel Parker of Philadelphia. [Mrs. Stowe's note.] Presbyterian clergyman (1799-1873), a friend of the Beecher family. Mrs. Stowe attempted unsuccessfully to have this identifying note removed from the stereotype-plate of the first edition.

CHAPTER XII

Tom, who had learned the wisdom of keeping counsel, did not feel called upon to state his observations and suspicions, but said he did not know.

"She surely couldn't have got off in the night at any of the landings, for I was awake, and on the lookout, whenever the boat stopped. I never trust these yer things to other folks."

This speech was addressed to Tom quite confidentially, as if it was something that would be specially interesting to him. Tom made no answer.

The trader searched the boat from stem to stern, among boxes, bales and barrels, around the machinery, by the chimneys, in vain.

"Now, I say, Tom, be fair about this yer," he said, when, after a fruitless search, he came where Tom was standing. "You know something about it, now. Don't tell me,—I know you do. I saw the gal stretched out here about ten o'clock, and ag'in at twelve, and ag'in between one and two; and then at four she was gone, and you was a sleeping right there all the time. Now, you know something,—you can't help it."

"Well, Mas'r," said Tom, "towards morning something brushed by me, and I kinder half woke; and then I hearn a great splash, and then I clare woke up, and the gal was gone. That's all I know on 't."

The trader was not shocked nor amazed; because, as we said before, he was used to a great many things that you are not used to. Even the awful presence of Death struck no solemn chill upon him. He had seen Death many times,—met him in the way of trade, and got acquainted with him,—and he only thought of him as a hard customer, that embarrassed his property operations very unfairly; and so he only swore that the gal was a baggage, and that he was devilish unlucky, and that, if things went on in this way, he should not make a cent on the trip. In short, he seemed to consider himself an ill-used man, decidedly; but there was no help for it, as the woman had escaped into a state which *never will* give up a fugitive,—not even at the demand of the whole glorious Union. The trader, therefore, sat discontentedly down, with his little account-book, and put down the missing body and soul under the head of *losses!*

"He's a shocking creature, isn't he,—this trader? so unfeeling! It's dreadful, really!"

"O, but nobody thinks anything of these traders! They are universally despised,—never received into any decent society."

But who, sir, makes the trader? Who is most to blame? The enlightened, cultivated, intelligent man, who supports the system of which the trader is the inevitable result, or the poor trader himself? You make the public statement that calls for his trade, that debauches and depraves him, till he feels no shame in it; and in what are you better than he?

Are you educated and he ignorant, you high and he low, you refined and he coarse, you talented and he simple?

In the day of a future judgment, these very considerations may make it more tolerable for him than for you.

In concluding these little incidents of lawful trade, we must beg the world not to think that American legislators are entirely destitute of humanity, as might, perhaps, be unfairly inferred from the great efforts made in our national body to protect and perpetuate this species of traffic.

Who does not know how our great men are outdoing themselves, in declaiming against the *foreign* slave-trade. There are a perfect host of Clarksons and Wilberforces[1] risen up among us on that subject, most edifying to hear and behold. Trading negroes from Africa, dear reader, is so horrid! It is not to be thought of! But trading them from Kentucky,—that's quite another thing!

[1] Thomas Clarkson (1760-1846) and William Wilberforce (1759-1833), English philanthropists and anti-slavery agitators who helped to secure passage of the Emancipation Bill by Parliament in 1833.

CHAPTER XIII

THE QUAKER SETTLEMENT

A quiet scene now rises before us. A large, roomy, neatly-painted kitchen, its yellow floor glossy and smooth, and without a particle of dust; a neat, well-blacked cooking-stove; rows of shining tin, suggestive of unmentionable good things to the appetite; glossy green wood chairs, old and firm; a small flag-bottomed rocking-chair, with a patch-work cushion in it, neatly contrived out of small pieces of different colored woollen goods, and a larger sized one, motherly and old, whose wide arms breathed hospitable invitation, seconded by the solicitation of its feather cushions,—a real comfortable, persuasive old chair, and worth, in the way of honest, homely enjoyment, a dozen of your plush or *brochetelle* drawing-room gentry; and in the chair, gently swaying back and forward, her eyes bent on some fine sewing, sat our fine old friend Eliza. Yes, there she is, paler and thinner than in her Kentucky home, with a world of quiet sorrow lying under the shadow of her long eyelashes, and marking the outline of her gentle mouth! It was plain to see how old and firm the girlish heart was grown under the discipline of heavy sorrow; and when, anon, her large dark eye was raised to follow the gambols of her little Harry, who was sporting, like some tropical butterfly, hither and thither over the floor, she showed a depth of firmness and steady resolve that was never there in her earlier and happier days.

By her side sat a woman with a bright tin pan in her lap, into which she was carefully sorting some dried peaches. She might be fifty-five or sixty; but hers was one of those faces that time seems to touch only to brighten and adorn. The snowy lisse crape cap, made after the strait Quaker pattern,—the plain white muslin handkerchief, lying in placid folds across her bosom,—the drab shawl and dress,—showed at once the community to which she belonged. Her face was round and rosy, with a healthful downy softness, suggestive of a ripe peach. Her hair, partially silvered by age, was parted smoothly back from a high placid forehead, on which time had written no inscription, except peace on earth, good will to men, and beneath shone a large pair of clear, honest, loving brown eyes; you only needed to look straight into them, to feel that you saw to the bottom of a heart as good and true as ever throbbed in woman's bosom. So much has been said and sung of beautiful young girls, why don't somebody wake up to the beauty of old women? If any want to get up an inspiration under this head, we refer them to our good friend Rachel Halliday, just as she sits there in her little rocking-chair. It had a turn for quacking and squeaking,—that chair had,—either from having taken cold in early life, or from some asthmatic affection, or perhaps from nervous derangement; but, as she gently swung backward and forward, the chair kept up a kind of subdued "creechy crawchy," that would have been intolerable in any other chair. But old Simeon Halliday often declared it was as good as any music to him, and the children all avowed that they wouldn't miss of hearing mother's chair for anything in the world. For why? for twenty years or more, nothing but loving words, and gentle moralities, and motherly loving kindness, had come from that chair;—head-aches and heart-aches innumerable had been cured there,—difficulties spiritual and temporal solved there,—all by one good, loving woman, God bless her!

"And so thee still thinks of going to Canada, Eliza?" she said, as she was quietly looking over her peaches.

"Yes, ma'am," said Eliza, firmly. "I must go onward. I dare not stop."

"And what'll thee do, when thee gets there? Thee must think about that, my daughter."

"My daughter" came naturally from the lips of Rachel Halliday; for hers was just the face and form that made "mother" seem the most natural word in the world.

Eliza's hands trembled, and some tears fell on her fine work; but she answered, firmly,

"I shall do—anything I can find. I hope I can find something."

"Thee knows thee can stay here, as long as thee pleases," said Rachel.

"O, thank you," said Eliza, "but"—she pointed to Harry—"I can't sleep nights; I can't rest. Last night I dreamed I saw that man coming into the yard," she said, shuddering.

"Poor child!" said Rachel, wiping her eyes; "but thee mustn't feel so. The Lord hath ordered it so that never hath a fugitive been stolen from our village. I trust thine will not be the first."

The door here opened, and a little short, round, pin-cushiony woman stood at the door, with a cheery, blooming face, like a ripe apple. She was dressed, like Rachel, in sober gray, with the muslin folded neatly across her round, plump little chest.

"Ruth Stedman," said Rachel, coming joyfully forward; "how is thee, Ruth? she said, heartily taking both her hands.

"Nicely," said Ruth, taking off her little drab bonnet, and dusting it with her handkerchief, displaying, as she did so, a round little head, on which the Quaker cap sat with a sort of jaunty air, despite all the stroking and patting of the small fat hands, which were busily applied to arranging it. Certain stray locks of decidedly curly hair, too, had escaped here and there, and had to be coaxed and cajoled into their place again; and then the new comer, who might have been five-and-twenty, turned from the small looking-glass, before which she had been making these arrangements, and looked well pleased,—as most people who looked at her might have been,—for she was decidedly a wholesome, whole-hearted, chirruping little woman, as ever gladdened man's heart withal.

"Ruth, this friend is Eliza Harris; and this is the little boy I told thee of."

"I am glad to see thee, Eliza,—very," said Ruth, shaking hands, as if Eliza were an old friend she had long been expecting; "and this is thy dear boy,—I brought a cake for him," she said, holding out a little heart to the boy, who came up, gazing through his curls, and accepted it shyly.

"Where's thy baby, Ruth?" said Rachel.

"O, he's coming; but thy Mary caught him as I came in, and ran off with him to the barn, to show him to the children."

At this moment, the door opened, and Mary, an honest, rosy-looking girl, with large brown eyes, like her mother's, came in with the baby.

"Ah! ha!" said Rachel, coming up, and taking the great, white, fat fellow in her arms, "how good he looks, and how he does grow!"

"To be sure, he does," said little bustling Ruth, as she took the child, and began taking off a little blue silk hood, and various layers and wrappers of outer garments; and having given a twitch here, and a pull there, and variously adjusted and arranged him, and kissed him heartily, she set him on the floor to collect his thoughts. Baby seemed quite used to this mode of proceeding, for he put his thumb in his mouth (as if it were quite a thing of course), and seemed soon absorbed in his own reflections, while the mother seated herself, and taking out a long stocking of mixed blue and white yarn, began to knit with briskness.

"Mary, thee'd better fill the kettle, hadn't thee?" gently suggested the mother.

Mary took the kettle to the well, and soon reappearing, placed it over the stove, where it was soon purring and steaming, a sort of censer of hospitality and good cheer. The peaches, moreover, in obedience to a few gentle whispers from Rachel, were soon deposited, by the same hand, in a stew-pan over the fire.

Rachel now took down a snowy moulding-board, and, tying on an apron, proceeded quietly to making up some biscuits, first saying to Mary,—"Mary, hadn't thee better tell John to get a chicken ready?" and Mary disappeared accordingly.

"And how is Abigail Peters?" said Rachel, as she went on with her biscuits.

"O, she's better," said Ruth; "I was in, this morning; made the bed, tidied up the house. Leah Hills went in, this afternoon, and baked bread and pies enough to last some days; and I engaged to go back to get her up, this evening."

"I will go in tomorrow, and do any cleaning there may be, and look over the mending," said Rachel.

"Ah! that is well," said Ruth. "I've heard," she added, "that Hannah Stanwood is sick. John was up there, last night,—I must go there tomorrow."

"John can come in here to his meals, if thee needs to stay all day," suggested Rachel.

"Thank thee, Rachel; will see, tomorrow; but, here comes Simeon."

Simeon Halliday, a tall, straight, muscular man, in drab coat and pantaloons, and broad-brimmed hat, now entered.

"How is thee, Ruth?" he said, warmly, as he spread his broad open hand for her little fat palm; "and how is John?"

"O! John is well, and all the rest of our folks," said Ruth, cheerily.

"Any news, father?" said Rachel, as she was putting her biscuits into the oven.

"Peter Stebbins told me that they should be along tonight, with *friends*," said Simeon, significantly, as he was washing his hands at a neat sink, in a little back porch.

"Indeed!" said Rachel, looking thoughtfully, and glancing at Eliza.

"Did thee say thy name was Harris?" said Simeon to Eliza, as he reentered.

Rachel glanced quickly at her husband, as Eliza tremulously answered "yes;" her fears, ever uppermost, suggesting that possibly there might be advertisements out for her.

"Mother!" said Simeon, standing in the porch, and calling Rachel out.

"What does thee want, father?" said Rachel, rubbing her floury hands, as she went into the porch.

"This child's husband is in the settlement, and will be here tonight," said Simeon.

"Now, thee doesn't say that, father?" said Rachel, all her face radiant with joy.

"It's really true. Peter was down yesterday, with the wagon, to the other stand, and there he found an old woman and two men; and one said his name was George Harris; and from what he told of his history, I am certain who he is. He is a bright, likely fellow, too."

"Shall we tell her now?" said Simeon.

"Let's tell Ruth," said Rachel. "Here, Ruth,—come here."

Ruth laid down her knitting-work, and was in the back porch in a moment.

"Ruth, what does thee think?" said Rachel. "Father says Eliza's husband is in the last company, and will be here tonight."

A burst of joy from the little Quakeress interrupted the speech. She gave such a bound from the floor, as she clapped her little hands, that two stray curls fell from under her Quaker cap, and lay brightly on her white neckerchief.

"Hush thee, dear!" said Rachel, gently; "hush, Ruth! Tell us, shall we tell her now?"

"Now! to be sure,—this very minute. Why, now, suppose 't was my John, how should I feel? Do tell her, right off."

"Thee uses thyself only to learn how to love thy neighbor, Ruth," said Simeon, looking, with a beaming face, on Ruth.

"To be sure. Isn't it what we are made for? If I didn't love John and the baby, I should not know how to feel for her. Come, now do tell her,—do!" and she laid her hands persuasively on Rachel's arm. "Take her into thy bed-room, there, and let me fry the chicken while thee does it."

CHAPTER XIII

Rachel came out into the kitchen, where Eliza was sewing, and opening the door of a small bed-room, said, gently, "Come in here with me, my daughter; I have news to tell thee."

The blood flushed in Eliza's pale face; she rose, trembling with nervous anxiety, and looked towards her boy.

"No, no," said little Ruth, darting up, and seizing her hands. "Never thee fear; it's good news, Eliza,—go in, go in!" And she gently pushed her to the door which closed after her; and then, turning round, she caught little Harry in her arms, and began kissing him.

"Thee'll see thy father, little one. Does thee know it? Thy father is coming," she said, over and over again, as the boy looked wonderingly at her.

Meanwhile, within the door, another scene was going on. Rachel Halliday drew Eliza toward her, and said, "The Lord hath had mercy on thee, daughter; thy husband hath escaped from the house of bondage."

The blood flushed to Eliza's cheek in a sudden glow, and went back to her heart with as sudden a rush. She sat down, pale and faint.

"Have courage, child," said Rachel, laying her hand on her head. "He is among friends, who will bring him here tonight."

"Tonight!" Eliza repeated, "tonight!" The words lost all meaning to her; her head was dreamy and confused; all was mist for a moment.

When she awoke, she found herself snugly tucked up on the bed, with a blanket over her, and little Ruth rubbing her hands with camphor. She opened her eyes in a state of dreamy, delicious languor, such as one who has long been bearing a heavy load, and now feels it gone, and would rest. The tension of the nerves, which had never ceased a moment since the first hour of her flight, had given way, and a strange feeling of security and rest came over her; and as she lay, with her large, dark eyes open, she followed, as in a quiet dream, the motions of those about her. She saw the door open into the other room; saw the supper-table, with its snowy cloth; heard the dreamy murmur of the singing tea-kettle; saw Ruth tripping backward and forward, with plates of cake and saucers of preserves, and ever and anon stopping to put a cake into Harry's hand, or pat his head, or twine his long curls round her snowy fingers. She saw the ample, motherly form of Rachel, as she ever and anon came to the bedside, and smoothed and arranged something about the bedclothes, and gave a tuck here and there, by way of expressing her good-will; and was conscious of a kind of sunshine beaming down upon her from her large, clear, brown eyes. She saw Ruth's husband come in,—saw her fly up to him, and commence whispering very earnestly, ever and anon, with impressive gesture, pointing her little finger toward the room. She saw her, with the baby in her arms, sitting down to tea; she saw them all at table, and little Harry in a high chair, under the shadow of Rachel's ample wing; there were low murmurs of talk, gentle tinkling of tea-spoons, and musical clatter of cups and saucers, and all mingled in a delightful dream of rest; and Eliza slept, as she had not slept before, since the fearful midnight hour when she had taken her child and fled through the frosty starlight.

She dreamed of a beautiful country,—a land, it seemed to her, of rest,—green shores, pleasant islands, and beautifully glittering water; and there, in a house which kind voices told her was a home, she saw her boy playing, free and happy child. She heard her husband's footsteps; she felt him coming nearer; his arms were around her, his tears falling on her face, and she awoke! It was no dream. The daylight had long faded; her child lay calmly sleeping by her side; a candle was burning dimly on the stand, and her husband was sobbing by her pillow.

The next morning was a cheerful one at the Quaker house. "Mother" was up betimes, and surrounded by busy girls and boys, whom we had scarce time to introduce to our readers yesterday, and who all moved obediently to Rachel's gentle "Thee had better," or more gentle "Hadn't thee better?" in the work of getting breakfast; for a breakfast in the luxurious valleys of Indiana is a thing complicated and multiform, and, like picking up the rose-leaves and trimming the bushes in Paradise, asking other hands than those of the original mother. While, therefore, John ran to the spring for fresh water, and Simeon the second sifted meal for corn-cakes, and Mary ground coffee, Rachel moved gently, and quietly about, making biscuits, cutting up chicken, and diffusing a sort of sunny radiance over the whole proceeding generally. If there was any danger of friction or collision from the ill-regulated zeal of so many young operators, her gentle "Come! come!" or "I wouldn't, now," was quite sufficient to allay the difficulty. Bards have written of the cestus of Venus, that turned the heads of all the world in successive generations. We had rather, for our part, have the cestus of Rachel Halliday, that kept heads from being turned, and made everything go on harmoniously. We think it is more suited to our modern days, decidedly.

While all other preparations were going on, Simeon the elder stood in his shirt-sleeves before a little looking-glass in the corner, engaged in the anti-patriarchal operation of shaving. Everything went on so sociably, so quietly, so harmoniously, in the great kitchen,—it seemed so pleasant to every one to do just what they were doing, there was such an atmosphere of mutual confidence and good fellowship everywhere,—even the knives and forks had a social clatter as they went on to the table; and the chicken and ham had a cheerful and joyous fizzle in the pan, as if they rather enjoyed being cooked than otherwise;—and when George and Eliza and little Harry came out, they met such a hearty, rejoicing welcome, no wonder it seemed to them like a dream.

At last, they were all seated at breakfast, while Mary stood at the stove, baking griddle-cakes, which, as they gained the true exact golden-brown tint of perfection, were transferred quite handily to the table.

Rachel never looked so truly and benignly happy as at the head of her table. There was so much motherliness and full-heartedness even in the way she passed a plate of cakes or poured a cup of coffee, that it seemed to put a spirit into the food and drink she offered.

It was the first time that ever George had sat down on equal terms at any white man's table; and he sat down, at first, with some constraint and awkwardness; but they all exhaled and went off like fog, in the genial morning rays of this simple, overflowing kindness.

This, indeed, was a home,—*home,*—a word that George had never yet known a meaning for; and a belief in God, and trust in his providence, began to encircle his heart, as, with a golden cloud of protection and confidence, dark, misanthropic, pining atheistic doubts, and fierce despair, melted away before the light of a living Gospel, breathed in living faces, preached by a thousand unconscious acts of love and good will, which, like the cup of cold water given in the name of a disciple, shall never lose their reward.

"Father, what if thee should get found out again?" said Simeon second, as he buttered his cake.

"I should pay my fine," said Simeon, quietly.

"But what if they put thee in prison?"

"Couldn't thee and mother manage the farm?" said Simeon, smiling.

"Mother can do almost everything," said the boy. "But isn't it a shame to make such laws?"

"Thee mustn't speak evil of thy rulers, Simeon," said his father, gravely. "The Lord only gives us our worldly goods that we may do justice and mercy; if our rulers require a price of us for it, we must deliver it up.

"Well, I hate those old slaveholders!" said the boy, who felt as unchristian as became any modern reformer.

"I am surprised at thee, son," said Simeon; "thy mother never taught thee so. I would do even the same for the slaveholder as for the slave, if the Lord brought him to my door in affliction."

Simeon second blushed scarlet; but his mother only smiled, and said, "Simeon is my good boy; he will grow older, by and by, and then he will be like his father."

"I hope, my good sir, that you are not exposed to any difficulty on our account," said George, anxiously.

"Fear nothing, George, for therefore are we sent into the world. If we would not meet trouble for a good cause, we were not worthy of our name."

"But, for *me*," said George, "I could not bear it."

"Fear not, then, friend George; it is not for thee, but for God and man, we do it," said Simeon. "And now thou must lie by quietly this day, and tonight, at ten o'clock, Phineas Fletcher will carry thee onward to the next stand,—thee and the rest of thy company. The pursuers are hard after thee; we must not delay."

"If that is the case, why wait till evening?" said George.

"Thou art safe here by daylight, for every one in the settlement is a Friend, and all are watching. It has been found safer to travel by night."

CHAPTER XIV

EVANGELINE

"A young star! which shone O'er life—too sweet an image, for such glass! A lovely being, scarcely formed or moulded; A rose with all its sweetest leaves yet folded."

The Mississippi! How, as by an enchanted wand, have its scenes been changed, since Chateaubriand wrote his prose-poetic description of it,[1] as a river of mighty, unbroken solitudes, rolling amid undreamed wonders of vegetable and animal existence.

But as in an hour, this river of dreams and wild romance has emerged to a reality scarcely less visionary and splendid. What other river of the world bears on its bosom to the ocean the wealth and enterprise of such another country?—a country whose products embrace all between the tropics and the poles! Those turbid waters, hurrying, foaming, tearing along, an apt resemblance of that headlong tide of business which is poured along its wave by a race more vehement and energetic than any the old world ever saw. Ah! would that they did not also bear along a more fearful freight,—the tears of the oppressed, the sighs of the helpless, the bitter prayers of poor, ignorant hearts to an unknown God—unknown, unseen and silent, but who will yet "come out of his place to save all the poor of the earth!"

The slanting light of the setting sun quivers on the sea-like expanse of the river; the shivery canes, and the tall, dark cypress, hung with wreaths of dark, funereal moss, glow in the golden ray, as the heavily-laden steamboat marches onward.

Piled with cotton-bales, from many a plantation, up over deck and sides, till she seems in the distance a square, massive block of gray, she moves heavily onward to the nearing mart. We must look some time among its crowded decks before we shall find again our humble friend Tom. High on the upper deck, in a little nook among the everywhere predominant cotton-bales, at last we may find him.

---

[1] In Atala; or the Love and Constantcy of Two Savages in the Desert (1801) by Francois Auguste Rene, Vicomte de Chateaubriand (1768-1848).

CHAPTER XIV

Partly from confidence inspired by Mr. Shelby's representations, and partly from the remarkably inoffensive and quiet character of the man, Tom had insensibly won his way far into the confidence even of such a man as Haley.

At first he had watched him narrowly through the day, and never allowed him to sleep at night unfettered; but the uncomplaining patience and apparent contentment of Tom's manner led him gradually to discontinue these restraints, and for some time Tom had enjoyed a sort of parole of honor, being permitted to come and go freely where he pleased on the boat.

Ever quiet and obliging, and more than ready to lend a hand in every emergency which occurred among the workmen below, he had won the good opinion of all the hands, and spent many hours in helping them with as hearty a good will as ever he worked on a Kentucky farm.

When there seemed to be nothing for him to do, he would climb to a nook among the cotton-bales of the upper deck, and busy himself in studying over his Bible,—and it is there we see him now.

For a hundred or more miles above New Orleans, the river is higher than the surrounding country, and rolls its tremendous volume between massive levees twenty feet in height. The traveller from the deck of the steamer, as from some floating castle top, overlooks the whole country for miles and miles around. Tom, therefore, had spread out full before him, in plantation after plantation, a map of the life to which he was approaching.

He saw the distant slaves at their toil; he saw afar their villages of huts gleaming out in long rows on many a plantation, distant from the stately mansions and pleasure-grounds of the master;—and as the moving picture passed on, his poor, foolish heart would be turning backward to the Kentucky farm, with its old shadowy beeches,—to the master's house, with its wide, cool halls, and, near by, the little cabin overgrown with the multiflora and bignonia. There he seemed to see familiar faces of comrades who had grown up with him from infancy; he saw his busy wife, bustling in her preparations for his evening meals; he heard the merry laugh of his boys at their play, and the chirrup of the baby at his knee; and then, with a start, all faded, and he saw again the canebrakes and cypresses and gliding plantations, and heard again the creaking and groaning of the machinery, all telling him too plainly that all that phase of life had gone by forever.

In such a case, you write to your wife, and send messages to your children; but Tom could not write,—the mail for him had no existence, and the gulf of separation was unbridged by even a friendly word or signal.

Is it strange, then, that some tears fall on the pages of his Bible, as he lays it on the cotton-bale, and, with patient finger, threading his slow way from word to word, traces out its promises? Having learned late in life, Tom was but a slow reader, and passed on laboriously from verse to verse. Fortunate for him was it that the book he was intent on was one which slow reading cannot injure,—nay, one whose words, like ingots of gold, seem often to need to be weighed separately, that the mind may take in their priceless value. Let us follow him a moment, as, pointing to each word, and pronouncing each half aloud, he reads,

"Let—not—your—heart—be—troubled. In—my —Father's—house—are—many—mansions. I—go—to—prepare—a—place—for—you."

Cicero, when he buried his darling and only daughter, had a heart as full of honest grief as poor Tom's,—perhaps no fuller, for both were only men;—but Cicero could pause over no such sublime words of hope, and look to no such future reunion; and if he *had* seen them, ten to one he would not have believed,—he must fill his head first with a thousand questions of authenticity of manuscript, and correctness of translation. But, to poor Tom, there it lay, just what he needed, so evidently true and divine that the possibility of a question never entered his simple head. It must be true; for, if not true, how could he live?

As for Tom's Bible, though it had no annotations and helps in margin from learned commentators, still it had been embellished with certain way-marks and guide-boards of Tom's own invention, and which helped him more than the most learned expositions could have done. It had been his custom to get the Bible read to him by his master's children, in particular by young Master George; and, as they read, he would designate, by bold, strong marks and dashes, with pen and ink, the passages which more particularly gratified his ear or affected his heart. His Bible was thus marked through, from one end to the other, with a variety of styles and designations; so he could in a moment seize upon his favorite passages, without the labor of spelling out what lay between them;—and while it lay there before him, every passage breathing of some old home scene, and recalling some past enjoyment, his Bible seemed to him all of this life that remained, as well as the promise of a future one.

Among the passengers on the boat was a young gentleman of fortune and family, resident in New Orleans, who bore the name of St. Clare. He had with him a daughter between five and six years of age, together with a lady who seemed to claim relationship to both, and to have the little one especially under her charge.

Tom had often caught glimpses of this little girl,—for she was one of those busy, tripping creatures, that can be no more contained in one place than a sunbeam or a summer breeze,—nor was she one that, once seen, could be easily forgotten.

Her form was the perfection of childish beauty, without its usual chubbiness and squareness of outline. There was about it an undulating and aerial grace, such as one might dream of for some mythic and allegorical being. Her face was remarkable less for its perfect beauty of feature than for a singular and dreamy earnestness of expression, which made the ideal start when they looked at her, and by which the dullest and most literal were impressed, without exactly knowing why. The shape of her head and the turn of her neck and bust was peculiarly noble, and the long golden-brown hair that floated like a cloud around it, the deep spiritual gravity of her violet blue eyes, shaded by heavy fringes of golden brown,—all marked her out from other children, and made every one turn and look after her, as she glided hither and thither on the boat. Nevertheless, the little one was not what you would have called either a grave child or a sad one. On the contrary, an airy and innocent playfulness seemed to flicker like the shadow of summer leaves over her childish face, and around her buoyant figure. She was always in motion, always with a half smile on her rosy mouth, flying hither and thither, with an undulating and cloud-like tread, singing to herself as she moved as in a happy dream. Her father and female guardian were incessantly busy in pursuit of her,—but, when caught, she melted from them again like a summer cloud; and as no word of chiding or reproof ever fell on her ear for whatever she chose to do, she pursued her own way all over the boat. Always dressed in white, she seemed to move like a shadow through all sorts of places, without contracting spot or stain; and there was not a corner or nook, above or below, where those fairy footsteps had not glided, and that visionary golden head, with its deep blue eyes, fleeted along.

The fireman, as he looked up from his sweaty toil, sometimes found those eyes looking wonderingly into the raging depths of the furnace, and fearfully and pityingly at him, as if she thought him in some dreadful danger. Anon the steersman at the wheel paused and smiled, as the picture-like head gleamed through the window of the round house, and in a moment was gone again. A thousand times a day rough voices blessed her, and smiles of unwonted softness stole over hard faces, as she passed; and when she tripped fearlessly over dangerous places, rough, sooty hands were stretched involuntarily out to save her, and smooth her path.

Tom, who had the soft, impressible nature of his kindly race, ever yearning toward the simple and childlike, watched the little creature with daily increasing interest. To him she seemed something almost divine; and whenever her golden head and deep blue eyes peered out upon him from behind some dusky cotton-bale, or looked down upon him over some ridge of packages, he half believed that he saw one of the angels stepped out of his New Testament.

Often and often she walked mournfully round the place where Haley's gang of men and women sat in their chains. She would glide in among them, and look at them with an air of perplexed and sorrowful earnestness; and sometimes she would lift their chains with her slender hands, and then sigh wofully, as she glided away. Several times she appeared suddenly among them, with her hands full of candy, nuts, and oranges, which she would distribute joyfully to them, and then be gone again.

Tom watched the little lady a great deal, before he ventured on any overtures towards acquaintanceship. He knew an abundance of simple acts to propitiate and invite the approaches of the little people, and he resolved to play his part right skilfully. He could cut cunning little baskets out of cherry-stones, could make grotesque faces on hickory-nuts, or odd-jumping figures out of elder-pith, and he was a very Pan in the manufacture of whistles of all sizes and sorts. His pockets were full of miscellaneous articles of attraction, which he had hoarded in days of old for his master's children, and which he now produced, with commendable prudence and economy, one by one, as overtures for acquaintance and friendship.

The little one was shy, for all her busy interest in everything going on, and it was not easy to tame her. For a while, she would perch like a canary-bird on some box or package near Tom, while busy in the little arts afore-named, and take from him, with a kind of grave bashfulness, the little articles he offered. But at last they got on quite confidential terms.

"What's little missy's name?" said Tom, at last, when he thought matters were ripe to push such an inquiry.

"Evangeline St. Clare," said the little one, "though papa and everybody else call me Eva. Now, what's your name?"

"My name's Tom; the little chil'en used to call me Uncle Tom, way back thar in Kentuck."

"Then I mean to call you Uncle Tom, because, you see, I like you," said Eva. "So, Uncle Tom, where are you going?"

"I don't know, Miss Eva."

"Don't know?" said Eva.

"No, I am going to be sold to somebody. I don't know who."

"My papa can buy you," said Eva, quickly; "and if he buys you, you will have good times. I mean to ask him, this very day."

"Thank you, my little lady," said Tom.

The boat here stopped at a small landing to take in wood, and Eva, hearing her father's voice, bounded nimbly away. Tom rose up, and went forward to offer his service in wooding, and soon was busy among the hands.

Eva and her father were standing together by the railings to see the boat start from the landing-place, the wheel had made two or three revolutions in the water, when, by some sudden movement, the little one suddenly lost her balance and fell sheer over the side of the boat into the water. Her father, scarce knowing what he did, was plunging in after her, but was held back by some behind him, who saw that more efficient aid had followed his child.

Tom was standing just under her on the lower deck, as she fell. He saw her strike the water, and sink, and was after her in a moment. A broad-chested, strong-armed fellow, it was nothing for him to keep afloat in the water, till, in a moment or two the child rose to the surface, and he caught her in his arms, and, swimming with her to the boat-side, handed her up, all dripping, to the grasp of hundreds of hands, which, as if they had all belonged to one man, were stretched eagerly out to receive her. A few moments more, and her father bore her, dripping and senseless, to the ladies' cabin, where, as is usual in cases of the kind, there ensued a very well-meaning and kind-hearted strife among the female occupants generally, as to who should do the most things to make a disturbance, and to hinder her recovery in every way possible.

It was a sultry, close day, the next day, as the steamer drew near to New Orleans. A general bustle of expectation and preparation was spread through the boat; in the cabin, one and another were gathering their things together, and arranging them, preparatory to going ashore. The steward and chambermaid, and all, were busily engaged in cleaning, furbishing, and arranging the splendid boat, preparatory to a grand entree.

CHAPTER XIV

On the lower deck sat our friend Tom, with his arms folded, and anxiously, from time to time, turning his eyes towards a group on the other side of the boat.

There stood the fair Evangeline, a little paler than the day before, but otherwise exhibiting no traces of the accident which had befallen her. A graceful, elegantly-formed young man stood by her, carelessly leaning one elbow on a bale of cotton while a large pocket-book lay open before him. It was quite evident, at a glance, that the gentleman was Eva's father. There was the same noble cast of head, the same large blue eyes, the same golden-brown hair; yet the expression was wholly different. In the large, clear blue eyes, though in form and color exactly similar, there was wanting that misty, dreamy depth of expression; all was clear, bold, and bright, but with a light wholly of this world: the beautifully cut mouth had a proud and somewhat sarcastic expression, while an air of free-and-easy superiority sat not ungracefully in every turn and movement of his fine form. He was listening, with a good-humored, negligent air, half comic, half contemptuous, to Haley, who was very volubly expatiating on the quality of the article for which they were bargaining.

"All the moral and Christian virtues bound in black Morocco, complete!" he said, when Haley had finished. "Well, now, my good fellow, what's the damage, as they say in Kentucky; in short, what's to be paid out for this business? How much are you going to cheat me, now? Out with it!"

"Wal," said Haley, "if I should say thirteen hundred dollars for that ar fellow, I shouldn't but just save myself; I shouldn't, now, re'ly."

"Poor fellow!" said the young man, fixing his keen, mocking blue eye on him; "but I suppose you'd let me have him for that, out of a particular regard for me."

"Well, the young lady here seems to be sot on him, and nat'lly enough."

"O! certainly, there's a call on your benevolence, my friend. Now, as a matter of Christian charity, how cheap could you afford to let him go, to oblige a young lady that's particular sot on him?"

"Wal, now, just think on 't," said the trader; "just look at them limbs,—broad-chested, strong as a horse. Look at his head; them high forrads allays shows calculatin niggers, that'll do any kind o' thing. I've, marked that ar. Now, a nigger of that ar heft and build is worth considerable, just as you may say, for his body, supposin he's stupid; but come to put in his calculatin faculties, and them which I can show he has oncommon, why, of course, it makes him come higher. Why, that ar fellow managed his master's whole farm. He has a strornary talent for business."

"Bad, bad, very bad; knows altogether too much!" said the young man, with the same mocking smile playing about his mouth. "Never will do, in the world. Your smart fellows are always running off, stealing horses, and raising the devil generally. I think you'll have to take off a couple of hundred for his smartness."

"Wal, there might be something in that ar, if it warnt for his character; but I can show recommends from his master and others, to prove he is one of your real pious,—the most humble, prayin, pious crittur ye ever did see. Why, he's been called a preacher in them parts he came from."

"And I might use him for a family chaplain, possibly," added the young man, dryly. "That's quite an idea. Religion is a remarkably scarce article at our house."

"You're joking, now."

"How do you know I am? Didn't you just warrant him for a preacher? Has he been examined by any synod or council? Come, hand over your papers."

If the trader had not been sure, by a certain good-humored twinkle in the large eye, that all this banter was sure, in the long run, to turn out a cash concern, he might have been somewhat out of patience; as it was, he laid down a greasy pocket-book on the cotton-bales, and began anxiously studying over certain papers in it, the young man standing by, the while, looking down on him with an air of careless, easy drollery.

"Papa, do buy him! it's no matter what you pay," whispered Eva, softly, getting up on a package, and putting her arm around her father's neck. "You have money enough, I know. I want him."

"What for, pussy? Are you going to use him for a rattle-box, or a rocking-horse, or what?

"I want to make him happy."

"An original reason, certainly."

Here the trader handed up a certificate, signed by Mr. Shelby, which the young man took with the tips of his long fingers, and glanced over carelessly.

"A gentlemanly hand," he said, "and well spelt, too. Well, now, but I'm not sure, after all, about this religion," said he, the old wicked expression returning to his eye; "the country is almost ruined with pious white people; such pious politicians as we have just before elections,—such pious goings on in all departments of church and state, that a fellow does not know who'll cheat him next. I don't know, either, about religion's being up in the market, just now. I have not looked in the papers lately, to see how it sells. How many hundred dollars, now, do you put on for this religion?"

"You like to be jokin, now," said the trader; "but, then, there's *sense* under all that ar. I know there's differences in religion. Some kinds is mis'rable: there's your meetin pious; there's your singin, roarin pious; them ar an't no account, in black or white;—but these rayly is; and I've seen it in niggers as often as any, your rail softly, quiet, stiddy, honest, pious, that the hull world couldn't tempt 'em to do nothing that they thinks is wrong; and ye see in this letter what Tom's old master says about him."

"Now," said the young man, stooping gravely over his book of bills, "if you can assure me that I really can buy *this* kind of pious, and that it will be set down to my account in the book up above, as something belonging to me, I wouldn't care if I did go a little extra for it. How d'ye say?"

"Wal, raily, I can't do that," said the trader. "I'm a thinkin that every man'll have to hang on his own hook, in them ar quarters."

"Rather hard on a fellow that pays extra on religion, and can't trade with it in the state where he wants it most, an't it, now?" said the young man, who had been making out a roll of bills while he was speaking. "There, count your money, old boy!" he added, as he handed the roll to the trader.

"All right," said Haley, his face beaming with delight; and pulling out an old inkhorn, he proceeded to fill out a bill of sale, which, in a few moments, he handed to the young man.

"I wonder, now, if I was divided up and inventoried," said the latter as he ran over the paper, "how much I might bring. Say so much for the shape of my head, so much for a high forehead, so much for arms, and hands, and legs, and then so much for education, learning, talent, honesty, religion! Bless me! there would be small charge on that last, I'm thinking. But come, Eva," he said; and taking the hand of his daughter, he stepped across the boat, and carelessly putting the tip of his finger under Tom's chin, said, good-humoredly, "Look-up, Tom, and see how you like your new master."

Tom looked up. It was not in nature to look into that gay, young, handsome face, without a feeling of pleasure; and Tom felt the tears start in his eyes as he said, heartily, "God bless you, Mas'r!"

"Well, I hope he will. What's your name? Tom? Quite as likely to do it for your asking as mine, from all accounts. Can you drive horses, Tom?"

"I've been allays used to horses," said Tom. "Mas'r Shelby raised heaps of 'em."

"Well, I think I shall put you in coachy, on condition that you won't be drunk more than once a week, unless in cases of emergency, Tom."

Tom looked surprised, and rather hurt, and said, "I never drink, Mas'r."

"I've heard that story before, Tom; but then we'll see. It will be a special accommodation to all concerned, if you don't. Never mind, my boy," he added, good-humoredly, seeing Tom still looked grave; "I don't doubt you mean to do well."

"I sartin do, Mas'r," said Tom.

"And you shall have good times," said Eva. "Papa is very good to everybody, only he always will laugh at them."

"Papa is much obliged to you for his recommendation," said St. Clare, laughing, as he turned on his heel and walked away.

CHAPTER XV

OF TOM'S NEW MASTER, AND VARIOUS OTHER MATTERS

Since the thread of our humble hero's life has now become interwoven with that of higher ones, it is necessary to give some brief introduction to them.

Augustine St. Clare was the son of a wealthy planter of Louisiana. The family had its origin in Canada. Of two brothers, very similar in temperament and character, one had settled on a flourishing farm in Vermont, and the other became an opulent planter in Louisiana. The mother of Augustine was a Huguenot French lady, whose family had emigrated to Louisiana during the days of its early settlement. Augustine and another brother were the only children of their parents. Having inherited from his mother an exceeding delicacy of constitution, he was, at the instance of physicians, during many years of his boyhood, sent to the care of his uncle in Vermont, in order that his constitution might be strengthened by the cold of a more bracing climate.

In childhood, he was remarkable for an extreme and marked sensitiveness of character, more akin to the softness of woman than the ordinary hardness of his own sex. Time, however, overgrew this softness with the rough bark of manhood, and but few knew how living and fresh it still lay at the core. His talents were of the very first order, although his mind showed a preference always for the ideal and the æsthetic, and there was about him that repugnance to the actual business of life which is the common result of this balance of the faculties. Soon after the completion of his college course, his whole nature was kindled into one intense and passionate effervescence of romantic passion. His hour came,—the hour that comes only once; his star rose in the horizon,—that star that rises so often in vain, to be remembered only as a thing of dreams; and it rose for him in vain. To drop the figure,—he saw and won the love of a high-minded and beautiful woman, in one of the northern states, and they were affianced. He returned south to make arrangements for their marriage, when, most unexpectedly, his letters were returned to him by mail, with a short note from her guardian, stating to him that ere this reached him the lady would be the wife of another. Stung to madness, he vainly hoped, as many another has done, to fling the whole thing from his heart by one desperate effort. Too proud to supplicate or seek explanation, he threw himself at once into a whirl of fashionable society, and in a fortnight from the time of the fatal letter was the accepted lover of the reigning belle of the season; and as soon as arrangements could be made, he became the husband of a fine figure, a pair of bright dark eyes, and a hundred thousand dollars; and, of course, everybody thought him a happy fellow.

The married couple were enjoying their honeymoon, and entertaining a brilliant circle of friends in their splendid villa, near Lake Pontchartrain, when, one day, a letter was brought to him in *that* well-remembered writing. It was handed to him while he was in full tide of gay and successful conversation, in a whole room-full of company. He turned deadly pale when he saw the writing, but still preserved his composure, and finished the playful warfare of badinage which he was at the moment carrying on with a lady opposite; and, a short time after, was missed from the circle. In his room, alone, he opened and read the letter, now worse than idle and useless to be read. It was from her, giving a long account of a persecution to which she had been exposed by her guardian's family, to lead her to unite herself with their son: and she related how, for a long time, his letters had ceased to arrive; how she had written time and again, till she became weary and doubtful; how her health had failed under her anxieties, and how, at last, she had discovered the whole fraud which had been practised on them both. The letter ended with expressions of hope and thankfulness, and professions of undying affection, which were more bitter than death to the unhappy young man. He wrote to her immediately:

"I have received yours,—but too late. I believed all I heard. I was desperate. *I am married*, and all is over. Only forget,—it is all that remains for either of us."

And thus ended the whole romance and ideal of life for Augustine St. Clare. But the *real* remained,—the *real*, like the flat, bare, oozy tide-mud, when the blue sparkling wave, with all its company of gliding boats and white-winged ships, its music of oars and chiming waters, has gone down, and there it lies, flat, slimy, bare,—exceedingly real.

Of course, in a novel, people's hearts break, and they die, and that is the end of it; and in a story this is very convenient. But in real life we do not die when all that makes life bright dies to us. There is a most busy and important round of eating, drinking, dressing, walking, visiting, buying, selling, talking, reading, and all that makes up what is commonly called *living*, yet to be gone through; and this yet remained to Augustine. Had his wife been a whole woman, she might yet have done something—as woman can—to mend the broken threads of life, and weave again into a tissue of brightness. But Marie St. Clare could not even see that they had been broken. As before stated, she consisted of a fine figure, a pair of splendid eyes, and a hundred thousand dollars; and none of these items were precisely the ones to minister to a mind diseased.

When Augustine, pale as death, was found lying on the sofa, and pleaded sudden sick-headache as the cause of his distress, she recommended to him to smell of hartshorn; and when the paleness and headache came on week after week, she only said that she never thought Mr. St. Clare was sickly; but it seems he was very liable to sick-headaches, and that it was a very unfortunate thing for her, because he didn't enjoy going into company with her, and it seemed odd to go so much alone, when they were just married. Augustine was glad in his heart that he had married so undiscerning a woman; but as the glosses and civilities of the honeymoon wore away, he discovered that a beautiful young woman, who has lived all her life to be caressed and waited on, might prove quite a hard mistress in domestic life. Marie never had possessed much capability of affection, or much sensibility, and the little that she had, had been merged into a most intense and unconscious selfishness; a selfishness the more hopeless, from its quiet obtuseness, its utter ignorance of any claims but her own. From her infancy, she had been surrounded with servants, who lived only to study her caprices; the idea that they had either feelings or rights had never dawned upon her, even in distant perspective. Her father, whose only child she had been, had never denied her anything that lay within the compass of human possibility; and when she entered life, beautiful, accomplished, and an heiress, she had, of course, all the eligibles and non-eligibles of the other sex sighing at her feet, and she had no doubt that Augustine was a most fortunate man in having obtained her. It is a great mistake to suppose that a woman with no heart will be an easy creditor in the exchange of affection. There is not on earth a more merciless exactor of love from others than a thoroughly selfish woman; and the more unlovely she grows, the more jealously and scrupulously she exacts love, to the uttermost farthing. When, therefore, St. Clare began to drop off those gallantries and small attentions which flowed at first through the habitude of courtship, he found his sultana no way ready to resign her slave; there were abundance of tears, poutings, and small tempests, there were discontents, pinings, upbraidings. St. Clare was good-natured and self-indulgent, and sought to buy off with presents and flatteries; and when Marie became mother to a beautiful daughter, he really felt awakened, for a time, to something like tenderness.

St. Clare's mother had been a woman of uncommon elevation and purity of character, and he gave to his child his mother's name, fondly fancying that she would prove a reproduction of her image. The thing had been remarked with petulant jealousy by his wife, and she regarded her husband's absorbing devotion to the child with suspicion and dislike; all that was given to her seemed so much taken from herself. From the time of the birth of this child, her health gradually sunk. A life of constant inaction, bodily and mental,—the friction of ceaseless ennui and discontent, united to the ordinary weakness which attended the period of maternity,—in course of a few years changed the blooming young belle into a yellow faded, sickly woman, whose time was divided among a variety of fanciful diseases, and who considered herself, in every sense, the most ill-used and suffering person in existence.

There was no end of her various complaints; but her principal forte appeared to lie in sick-headache, which sometimes would confine her to her room three days out of six. As, of course, all family arrangements fell into the hands of servants,

CHAPTER XV

St. Clare found his menage anything but comfortable. His only daughter was exceedingly delicate, and he feared that, with no one to look after her and attend to her, her health and life might yet fall a sacrifice to her mother's inefficiency. He had taken her with him on a tour to Vermont, and had persuaded his cousin, Miss Ophelia St. Clare, to return with him to his southern residence; and they are now returning on this boat, where we have introduced them to our readers.

And now, while the distant domes and spires of New Orleans rise to our view, there is yet time for an introduction to Miss Ophelia.

Whoever has travelled in the New England States will remember, in some cool village, the large farmhouse, with its clean-swept grassy yard, shaded by the dense and massive foliage of the sugar maple; and remember the air of order and stillness, of perpetuity and unchanging repose, that seemed to breathe over the whole place. Nothing lost, or out of order; not a picket loose in the fence, not a particle of litter in the turfy yard, with its clumps of lilac bushes growing up under the windows. Within, he will remember wide, clean rooms, where nothing ever seems to be doing or going to be done, where everything is once and forever rigidly in place, and where all household arrangements move with the punctual exactness of the old clock in the corner. In the family "keeping-room," as it is termed, he will remember the staid, respectable old book-case, with its glass doors, where Rollin's History,[1] Milton's Paradise Lost, Bunyan's Pilgrim's Progress, and Scott's Family Bible,[2] stand side by side in decorous order, with multitudes of other books, equally solemn and respectable. There are no servants in the house, but the lady in the snowy cap, with the spectacles, who sits sewing every afternoon among her daughters, as if nothing ever had been done, or were to be done,—she and her girls, in some long-forgotten fore part of the day, "*did up the work*," and for the rest of the time, probably, at all hours when you would see them, it is "*done up*." The old kitchen floor never seems stained or spotted; the tables, the chairs, and the various cooking utensils, never seem deranged or disordered; though three and sometimes four meals a day are got there, though the family washing and ironing is there performed, and though pounds of butter and cheese are in some silent and mysterious manner there brought into existence.

On such a farm, in such a house and family, Miss Ophelia had spent a quiet existence of some forty-five years, when her cousin invited her to visit his southern mansion. The eldest of a large family, she was still considered by her father and mother as one of "the children," and the proposal that she should go to *Orleans* was a most momentous one to the family circle. The old gray-headed father

---

[1] The Ancient History, ten volumes (1730-1738), by the French historian Charles Rollin (1661-1741).

[2] Scott's Family Bible (1788-1792), edited with notes by the English Biblical commentator, Thomas Scott (1747-1821).

took down Morse's Atlas[1] out of the book-case, and looked out the exact latitude and longitude; and read Flint's Travels in the South and West,[2] to make up his own mind as to the nature of the country.

The good mother inquired, anxiously, "if Orleans wasn't an awful wicked place," saying, "that it seemed to her most equal to going to the Sandwich Islands, or anywhere among the heathen."

It was known at the minister's and at the doctor's, and at Miss Peabody's milliner shop, that Ophelia St. Clare was "talking about" going away down to Orleans with her cousin; and of course the whole village could do no less than help this very important process of *talking about* the matter. The minister, who inclined strongly to abolitionist views, was quite doubtful whether such a step might not tend somewhat to encourage the southerners in holding on to their slaves; while the doctor, who was a stanch colonizationist, inclined to the opinion that Miss Ophelia ought to go, to show the Orleans people that we don't think hardly of them, after all. He was of opinion, in fact, that southern people needed encouraging. When however, the fact that she had resolved to go was fully before the public mind, she was solemnly invited out to tea by all her friends and neighbors for the space of a fortnight, and her prospects and plans duly canvassed and inquired into. Miss Moseley, who came into the house to help to do the dressmaking, acquired daily accessions of importance from the developments with regard to Miss Ophelia's wardrobe which she had been enabled to make. It was credibly ascertained that Squire Sinclare, as his name was commonly contracted in the neighborhood, had counted out fifty dollars, and given them to Miss Ophelia, and told her to buy any clothes she thought best; and that two new silk dresses, and a bonnet, had been sent for from Boston. As to the propriety of this extraordinary outlay, the public mind was divided,—some affirming that it was well enough, all things considered, for once in one's life, and others stoutly affirming that the money had better have been sent to the missionaries; but all parties agreed that there had been no such parasol seen in those parts as had been sent on from New York, and that she had one silk dress that might fairly be trusted to stand alone, whatever might be said of its mistress. There were credible rumors, also, of a hemstitched pocket-handkerchief; and report even went so far as to state that Miss Ophelia had one pocket-handkerchief with lace all around it,—it was even added that it was worked in the corners; but this latter point was never satisfactorily ascertained, and remains, in fact, unsettled to this day.

Miss Ophelia, as you now behold her, stands before you, in a very shining brown linen travelling-dress, tall, square-formed, and angular. Her face was thin, and rather sharp in its outlines; the lips compressed, like those of a person who is

---

[1] The Cerographic Atlas of the United States (1842-1845), by Sidney Edwards Morse (1794-1871), son of the geographer, Jedidiah Morse, and brother of the painter-inventor, Samuel F. B. Morse.

[2] Recollections of the Last Ten Years (1826) by Timothy Flint (1780-1840), missionary of Presbyterianism to the trans-Allegheny West.

in the habit of making up her mind definitely on all subjects; while the keen, dark eyes had a peculiarly searching, advised movement, and travelled over everything, as if they were looking for something to take care of.

All her movements were sharp, decided, and energetic; and, though she was never much of a talker, her words were remarkably direct, and to the purpose, when she did speak.

In her habits, she was a living impersonation of order, method, and exactness. In punctuality, she was as inevitable as a clock, and as inexorable as a railroad engine; and she held in most decided contempt and abomination anything of a contrary character.

The great sin of sins, in her eyes,—the sum of all evils,—was expressed by one very common and important word in her vocabulary—"shiftlessness." Her finale and ultimatum of contempt consisted in a very emphatic pronunciation of the word "shiftless;" and by this she characterized all modes of procedure which had not a direct and inevitable relation to accomplishment of some purpose then definitely had in mind. People who did nothing, or who did not know exactly what they were going to do, or who did not take the most direct way to accomplish what they set their hands to, were objects of her entire contempt,—a contempt shown less frequently by anything she said, than by a kind of stony grimness, as if she scorned to say anything about the matter.

As to mental cultivation,—she had a clear, strong, active mind, was well and thoroughly read in history and the older English classics, and thought with great strength within certain narrow limits. Her theological tenets were all made up, labelled in most positive and distinct forms, and put by, like the bundles in her patch trunk; there were just so many of them, and there were never to be any more. So, also, were her ideas with regard to most matters of practical life,—such as housekeeping in all its branches, and the various political relations of her native village. And, underlying all, deeper than anything else, higher and broader, lay the strongest principle of her being—conscientiousness. Nowhere is conscience so dominant and all-absorbing as with New England women. It is the granite formation, which lies deepest, and rises out, even to the tops of the highest mountains.

Miss Ophelia was the absolute bond-slave of the "*ought*." Once make her certain that the "path of duty," as she commonly phrased it, lay in any given direction, and fire and water could not keep her from it. She would walk straight down into a well, or up to a loaded cannon's mouth, if she were only quite sure that there the path lay. Her standard of right was so high, so all-embracing, so minute, and making so few concessions to human frailty, that, though she strove with heroic ardor to reach it, she never actually did so, and of course was burdened with a constant and often harassing sense of deficiency;—this gave a severe and somewhat gloomy cast to her religious character.

But, how in the world can Miss Ophelia get along with Augustine St. Clare,—gay, easy, unpunctual, unpractical, sceptical,—in short,—walking with impudent and nonchalant freedom over every one of her most cherished habits and opinions?

To tell the truth, then, Miss Ophelia loved him. When a boy, it had been hers to teach him his catechism, mend his clothes, comb his hair, and bring him up generally in the way he should go; and her heart having a warm side to it, Augustine had, as he usually did with most people, monopolized a large share of it for himself, and therefore it was that he succeeded very easily in persuading her that the "path of duty" lay in the direction of New Orleans, and that she must go with him to take care of Eva, and keep everything from going to wreck and ruin during the frequent illnesses of his wife. The idea of a house without anybody to take care of it went to her heart; then she loved the lovely little girl, as few could help doing; and though she regarded Augustine as very much of a heathen, yet she loved him, laughed at his jokes, and forbore with his failings, to an extent which those who knew him thought perfectly incredible. But what more or other is to be known of Miss Ophelia our reader must discover by a personal acquaintance.

There she is, sitting now in her state-room, surrounded by a mixed multitude of little and big carpet-bags, boxes, baskets, each containing some separate responsibility which she is tying, binding up, packing, or fastening, with a face of great earnestness.

"Now, Eva, have you kept count of your things? Of course you haven't,—children never do: there's the spotted carpet-bag and the little blue band-box with your best bonnet,—that's two; then the India rubber satchel is three; and my tape and needle box is four; and my band-box, five; and my collar-box; and that little hair trunk, seven. What have you done with your sunshade? Give it to me, and let me put a paper round it, and tie it to my umbrella with my shade;—there, now."

"Why, aunty, we are only going up home;—what is the use?"

"To keep it nice, child; people must take care of their things, if they ever mean to have anything; and now, Eva, is your thimble put up?"

"Really, aunty, I don't know."

"Well, never mind; I'll look your box over,—thimble, wax, two spools, scissors, knife, tape-needle; all right,—put it in here. What did you ever do, child, when you were coming on with only your papa. I should have thought you'd a lost everything you had."

"Well, aunty, I did lose a great many; and then, when we stopped anywhere, papa would buy some more of whatever it was."

"Mercy on us, child,—what a way!"

"It was a very easy way, aunty," said Eva.

"It's a dreadful shiftless one," said aunty.

"Why, aunty, what'll you do now?" said Eva; "that trunk is too full to be shut down."

"It *must* shut down," said aunty, with the air of a general, as she squeezed the things in, and sprung upon the lid;—still a little gap remained about the mouth of the trunk.

CHAPTER XV

"Get up here, Eva!" said Miss Ophelia, courageously; "what has been done can be done again. This trunk has *got to be* shut and locked—there are no two ways about it."

And the trunk, intimidated, doubtless, by this resolute statement, gave in. The hasp snapped sharply in its hole, and Miss Ophelia turned the key, and pocketed it in triumph.

"Now we're ready. Where's your papa? I think it time this baggage was set out. Do look out, Eva, and see if you see your papa."

"O, yes, he's down the other end of the gentlemen's cabin, eating an orange."

"He can't know how near we are coming," said aunty; "hadn't you better run and speak to him?"

"Papa never is in a hurry about anything," said Eva, "and we haven't come to the landing. Do step on the guards, aunty. Look! there's our house, up that street!"

The boat now began, with heavy groans, like some vast, tired monster, to prepare to push up among the multiplied steamers at the levee. Eva joyously pointed out the various spires, domes, and way-marks, by which she recognized her native city.

"Yes, yes, dear; very fine," said Miss Ophelia. "But mercy on us! the boat has stopped! where is your father?"

And now ensued the usual turmoil of landing—waiters running twenty ways at once—men tugging trunks, carpet-bags, boxes—women anxiously calling to their children, and everybody crowding in a dense mass to the plank towards the landing.

Miss Ophelia seated herself resolutely on the lately vanquished trunk, and marshalling all her goods and chattels in fine military order, seemed resolved to defend them to the last.

"Shall I take your trunk, ma'am?" "Shall I take your baggage?" "Let me 'tend to your baggage, Missis?" "Shan't I carry out these yer, Missis?" rained down upon her unheeded. She sat with grim determination, upright as a darning-needle stuck in a board, holding on her bundle of umbrella and parasols, and replying with a determination that was enough to strike dismay even into a hackman, wondering to Eva, in each interval, "what upon earth her papa could be thinking of; he couldn't have fallen over, now,—but something must have happened;"—and just as she had begun to work herself into a real distress, he came up, with his usually careless motion, and giving Eva a quarter of the orange he was eating, said,

"Well, Cousin Vermont, I suppose you are all ready."

"I've been ready, waiting, nearly an hour," said Miss Ophelia; "I began to be really concerned about you.

"That's a clever fellow, now," said he. "Well, the carriage is waiting, and the crowd are now off, so that one can walk out in a decent and Christian manner, and not be pushed and shoved. Here," he added to a driver who stood behind him, "take these things."

"I'll go and see to his putting them in," said Miss Ophelia.

"O, pshaw, cousin, what's the use?" said St. Clare.

"Well, at any rate, I'll carry this, and this, and this," said Miss Ophelia, singling out three boxes and a small carpet-bag.

"My dear Miss Vermont, positively you mustn't come the Green Mountains over us that way. You must adopt at least a piece of a southern principle, and not walk out under all that load. They'll take you for a waiting-maid; give them to this fellow; he'll put them down as if they were eggs, now."

Miss Ophelia looked despairingly as her cousin took all her treasures from her, and rejoiced to find herself once more in the carriage with them, in a state of preservation.

"Where's Tom?" said Eva.

"O, he's on the outside, Pussy. I'm going to take Tom up to mother for a peace-offering, to make up for that drunken fellow that upset the carriage."

"O, Tom will make a splendid driver, I know," said Eva; "he'll never get drunk."

The carriage stopped in front of an ancient mansion, built in that odd mixture of Spanish and French style, of which there are specimens in some parts of New Orleans. It was built in the Moorish fashion,—a square building enclosing a court-yard, into which the carriage drove through an arched gateway. The court, in the inside, had evidently been arranged to gratify a picturesque and voluptuous ideality. Wide galleries ran all around the four sides, whose Moorish arches, slender pillars, and arabesque ornaments, carried the mind back, as in a dream, to the reign of oriental romance in Spain. In the middle of the court, a fountain threw high its silvery water, falling in a never-ceasing spray into a marble basin, fringed with a deep border of fragrant violets. The water in the fountain, pellucid as crystal, was alive with myriads of gold and silver fishes, twinkling and darting through it like so many living jewels. Around the fountain ran a walk, paved with a mosaic of pebbles, laid in various fanciful patterns; and this, again, was surrounded by turf, smooth as green velvet, while a carriage-drive enclosed the whole. Two large orange-trees, now fragrant with blossoms, threw a delicious shade; and, ranged in a circle round upon the turf, were marble vases of arabesque sculpture, containing the choicest flowering plants of the tropics. Huge pomegranate trees, with their glossy leaves and flame-colored flowers, dark-leaved Arabian jessamines, with their silvery stars, geraniums, luxuriant roses bending beneath their heavy abundance of flowers, golden jessamines, lemon-scented verbenum, all united their bloom and fragrance, while here and there a mystic old aloe, with its strange, massive leaves, sat looking like some old enchanter, sitting in weird grandeur among the more perishable bloom and fragrance around it.

The galleries that surrounded the court were festooned with a curtain of some kind of Moorish stuff, and could be drawn down at pleasure, to exclude the beams of the sun. On the whole, the appearance of the place was luxurious and romantic.

As the carriage drove in, Eva seemed like a bird ready to burst from a cage, with the wild eagerness of her delight.

"O, isn't it beautiful, lovely! my own dear, darling home!" she said to Miss Ophelia. "Isn't it beautiful?"

CHAPTER XV

"'T is a pretty place," said Miss Ophelia, as she alighted; "though it looks rather old and heathenish to me."

Tom got down from the carriage, and looked about with an air of calm, still enjoyment. The negro, it must be remembered, is an exotic of the most gorgeous and superb countries of the world, and he has, deep in his heart, a passion for all that is splendid, rich, and fanciful; a passion which, rudely indulged by an untrained taste, draws on them the ridicule of the colder and more correct white race.

St. Clare, who was in heart a poetical voluptuary, smiled as Miss Ophelia made her remark on his premises, and, turning to Tom, who was standing looking round, his beaming black face perfectly radiant with admiration, he said,

"Tom, my boy, this seems to suit you."

"Yes, Mas'r, it looks about the right thing," said Tom.

All this passed in a moment, while trunks were being hustled off, hackman paid, and while a crowd, of all ages and sizes,—men, women, and children,—came running through the galleries, both above and below to see Mas'r come in. Foremost among them was a highly-dressed young mulatto man, evidently a very *distingue* personage, attired in the ultra extreme of the mode, and gracefully waving a scented cambric handkerchief in his hand.

This personage had been exerting himself, with great alacrity, in driving all the flock of domestics to the other end of the verandah.

"Back! all of you. I am ashamed of you," he said, in a tone of authority. "Would you intrude on Master's domestic relations, in the first hour of his return?"

All looked abashed at this elegant speech, delivered with quite an air, and stood huddled together at a respectful distance, except two stout porters, who came up and began conveying away the baggage.

Owing to Mr. Adolph's systematic arrangements, when St. Clare turned round from paying the hackman, there was nobody in view but Mr. Adolph himself, conspicuous in satin vest, gold guard-chain, and white pants, and bowing with inexpressible grace and suavity.

"Ah, Adolph, is it you?" said his master, offering his hand to him; "how are you, boy?" while Adolph poured forth, with great fluency, an extemporary speech, which he had been preparing, with great care, for a fortnight before.

"Well, well," said St. Clare, passing on, with his usual air of negligent drollery, "that's very well got up, Adolph. See that the baggage is well bestowed. I'll come to the people in a minute;" and, so saying, he led Miss Ophelia to a large parlor that opened on the verandah.

While this had been passing, Eva had flown like a bird, through the porch and parlor, to a little boudoir opening likewise on the verandah.

A tall, dark-eyed, sallow woman, half rose from a couch on which she was reclining.

"Mamma!" said Eva, in a sort of a rapture, throwing herself on her neck, and embracing her over and over again.

"That'll do,—take care, child,—don't, you make my head ache," said the mother, after she had languidly kissed her.

St. Clare came in, embraced his wife in true, orthodox, husbandly fashion, and then presented to her his cousin. Marie lifted her large eyes on her cousin with an air of some curiosity, and received her with languid politeness. A crowd of servants now pressed to the entry door, and among them a middle-aged mulatto woman, of very respectable appearance, stood foremost, in a tremor of expectation and joy, at the door.

"O, there's Mammy!" said Eva, as she flew across the room; and, throwing herself into her arms, she kissed her repeatedly.

This woman did not tell her that she made her head ache, but, on the contrary, she hugged her, and laughed, and cried, till her sanity was a thing to be doubted of; and when released from her, Eva flew from one to another, shaking hands and kissing, in a way that Miss Ophelia afterwards declared fairly turned her stomach.

"Well!" said Miss Ophelia, "you southern children can do something that *I* couldn't."

"What, now, pray?" said St. Clare.

"Well, I want to be kind to everybody, and I wouldn't have anything hurt; but as to kissing—"

"Niggers," said St. Clare, "that you're not up to,—hey?"

"Yes, that's it. How can she?"

St. Clare laughed, as he went into the passage. "Halloa, here, what's to pay out here? Here, you all—Mammy, Jimmy, Polly, Sukey—glad to see Mas'r?" he said, as he went shaking hands from one to another. "Look out for the babies!" he added, as he stumbled over a sooty little urchin, who was crawling upon all fours. "If I step upon anybody, let 'em mention it."

There was an abundance of laughing and blessing Mas'r, as St. Clare distributed small pieces of change among them.

"Come, now, take yourselves off, like good boys and girls," he said; and the whole assemblage, dark and light, disappeared through a door into a large verandah, followed by Eva, who carried a large satchel, which she had been filling with apples, nuts, candy, ribbons, laces, and toys of every description, during her whole homeward journey.

As St. Clare turned to go back his eye fell upon Tom, who was standing uneasily, shifting from one foot to the other, while Adolph stood negligently leaning against the banisters, examining Tom through an opera-glass, with an air that would have done credit to any dandy living.

"Puh! you puppy," said his master, striking down the opera glass; "is that the way you treat your company? Seems to me, Dolph," he added, laying his finger on the elegant figured satin vest that Adolph was sporting, "seems to me that's *my* vest."

"O! Master, this vest all stained with wine; of course, a gentleman in Master's standing never wears a vest like this. I understood I was to take it. It does for a poor nigger-fellow, like me."

And Adolph tossed his head, and passed his fingers through his scented hair, with a grace.

"So, that's it, is it?" said St. Clare, carelessly. "Well, here, I'm going to show this Tom to his mistress, and then you take him to the kitchen; and mind you don't put on any of your airs to him. He's worth two such puppies as you."

"Master always will have his joke," said Adolph, laughing. "I'm delighted to see Master in such spirits."

"Here, Tom," said St. Clare, beckoning.

Tom entered the room. He looked wistfully on the velvet carpets, and the before unimagined splendors of mirrors, pictures, statues, and curtains, and, like the Queen of Sheba before Solomon, there was no more spirit in him. He looked afraid even to set his feet down.

"See here, Marie," said St. Clare to his wife, "I've bought you a coachman, at last, to order. I tell you, he's a regular hearse for blackness and sobriety, and will drive you like a funeral, if you want. Open your eyes, now, and look at him. Now, don't say I never think about you when I'm gone."

Marie opened her eyes, and fixed them on Tom, without rising.

"I know he'll get drunk," she said.

"No, he's warranted a pious and sober article."

"Well, I hope he may turn out well," said the lady; "it's more than I expect, though."

"Dolph," said St. Clare, "show Tom down stairs; and, mind yourself," he added; "remember what I told you."

Adolph tripped gracefully forward, and Tom, with lumbering tread, went after.

"He's a perfect behemoth!" said Marie.

"Come, now, Marie," said St. Clare, seating himself on a stool beside her sofa, "be gracious, and say something pretty to a fellow."

"You've been gone a fortnight beyond the time," said the lady, pouting.

"Well, you know I wrote you the reason."

"Such a short, cold letter!" said the lady.

"Dear me! the mail was just going, and it had to be that or nothing."

"That's just the way, always," said the lady; "always something to make your journeys long, and letters short."

"See here, now," he added, drawing an elegant velvet case out of his pocket, and opening it, "here's a present I got for you in New York."

It was a daguerreotype, clear and soft as an engraving, representing Eva and her father sitting hand in hand.

Marie looked at it with a dissatisfied air.

"What made you sit in such an awkward position?" she said.

"Well, the position may be a matter of opinion; but what do you think of the likeness?"

"If you don't think anything of my opinion in one case, I suppose you wouldn't in another," said the lady, shutting the daguerreotype.

"Hang the woman!" said St. Clare, mentally; but aloud he added, "Come, now, Marie, what do you think of the likeness? Don't be nonsensical, now."

"It's very inconsiderate of you, St. Clare," said the lady, "to insist on my talking and looking at things. You know I've been lying all day with the sick-headache; and there's been such a tumult made ever since you came, I'm half dead."

"You're subject to the sick-headache, ma'am!" said Miss Ophelia, suddenly rising from the depths of the large arm-chair, where she had sat quietly, taking an inventory of the furniture, and calculating its expense.

"Yes, I'm a perfect martyr to it," said the lady.

"Juniper-berry tea is good for sick-headache," said Miss Ophelia; "at least, Auguste, Deacon Abraham Perry's wife, used to say so; and she was a great nurse."

"I'll have the first juniper-berries that get ripe in our garden by the lake brought in for that special purpose," said St. Clare, gravely pulling the bell as he did so; "meanwhile, cousin, you must be wanting to retire to your apartment, and refresh yourself a little, after your journey. Dolph," he added, "tell Mammy to come here." The decent mulatto woman whom Eva had caressed so rapturously soon entered; she was dressed neatly, with a high red and yellow turban on her head, the recent gift of Eva, and which the child had been arranging on her head. "Mammy," said St. Clare, "I put this lady under your care; she is tired, and wants rest; take her to her chamber, and be sure she is made comfortable," and Miss Ophelia disappeared in the rear of Mammy.

CHAPTER XVI

TOM'S MISTRESS AND HER OPINIONS

"And now, Marie," said St. Clare, "your golden days are dawning. Here is our practical, business-like New England cousin, who will take the whole budget of cares off your shoulders, and give you time to refresh yourself, and grow young and handsome. The ceremony of delivering the keys had better come off forthwith."

This remark was made at the breakfast-table, a few mornings after Miss Ophelia had arrived.

"I'm sure she's welcome," said Marie, leaning her head languidly on her hand. "I think she'll find one thing, if she does, and that is, that it's we mistresses that are the slaves, down here."

"O, certainly, she will discover that, and a world of wholesome truths besides, no doubt," said St. Clare.

"Talk about our keeping slaves, as if we did it for our *convenience*," said Marie. "I'm sure, if we consulted *that*, we might let them all go at once."

Evangeline fixed her large, serious eyes on her mother's face, with an earnest and perplexed expression, and said, simply, "What do you keep them for, mamma?"

"I don't know, I'm sure, except for a plague; they are the plague of my life. I believe that more of my ill health is caused by them than by any one thing; and ours, I know, are the very worst that ever anybody was plagued with."

"O, come, Marie, you've got the blues, this morning," said St. Clare. "You know 't isn't so. There's Mammy, the best creature living,—what could you do without her?"

"Mammy is the best I ever knew," said Marie; "and yet Mammy, now, is selfish—dreadfully selfish; it's the fault of the whole race."

"Selfishness *is* a dreadful fault," said St. Clare, gravely.

"Well, now, there's Mammy," said Marie, "I think it's selfish of her to sleep so sound nights; she knows I need little attentions almost every hour, when my worst turns are on, and yet she's so hard to wake. I absolutely am worse, this very morning, for the efforts I had to make to wake her last night."

"Hasn't she sat up with you a good many nights, lately, mamma?" said Eva.

"How should you know that?" said Marie, sharply; "she's been complaining, I suppose."

"She didn't complain; she only told me what bad nights you'd had,—so many in succession."

"Why don't you let Jane or Rosa take her place, a night or two," said St. Clare, "and let her rest?"

"How can you propose it?" said Marie. "St. Clare, you really are inconsiderate. So nervous as I am, the least breath disturbs me; and a strange hand about me would drive me absolutely frantic. If Mammy felt the interest in me she ought to, she'd wake easier,—of course, she would. I've heard of people who had such devoted servants, but it never was *my* luck;" and Marie sighed.

Miss Ophelia had listened to this conversation with an air of shrewd, observant gravity; and she still kept her lips tightly compressed, as if determined fully to ascertain her longitude and position, before she committed herself.

"Now, Mammy has a *sort* of goodness," said Marie; "she's smooth and respectful, but she's selfish at heart. Now, she never will be done fidgeting and worrying about that husband of hers. You see, when I was married and came to live here, of course, I had to bring her with me, and her husband my father couldn't spare. He was a blacksmith, and, of course, very necessary; and I thought and said, at the time, that Mammy and he had better give each other up, as it wasn't likely to be convenient for them ever to live together again. I wish, now, I'd insisted on it, and married Mammy to somebody else; but I was foolish and indulgent, and didn't want to insist. I told Mammy, at the time, that she mustn't ever expect to see him more than once or twice in her life again, for the air of father's place doesn't agree with my health, and I can't go there; and I advised her to take up with somebody else; but no—she wouldn't. Mammy has a kind of obstinacy about her, in spots, that everybody don't see as I do."

"Has she children?" said Miss Ophelia.

"Yes; she has two."

"I suppose she feels the separation from them?"

"Well, of course, I couldn't bring them. They were little dirty things—I couldn't have them about; and, besides, they took up too much of her time; but I believe that Mammy has always kept up a sort of sulkiness about this. She won't marry anybody else; and I do believe, now, though she knows how necessary she is to me, and how feeble my health is, she would go back to her husband tomorrow, if she only could. I *do*, indeed," said Marie; "they are just so selfish, now, the best of them."

"It's distressing to reflect upon," said St. Clare, dryly.

Miss Ophelia looked keenly at him, and saw the flush of mortification and repressed vexation, and the sarcastic curl of the lip, as he spoke.

"Now, Mammy has always been a pet with me," said Marie. "I wish some of your northern servants could look at her closets of dresses,—silks and muslins, and one real linen cambric, she has hanging there. I've worked sometimes whole afternoons, trimming her caps, and getting her ready to go to a party. As to abuse, she don't know what it is. She never was whipped more than once or twice in her whole life. She has her strong coffee or her tea every day, with white sugar in it. It's abominable, to be sure; but St. Clare will have high life below-stairs, and they every one of them live just as they please. The fact is, our servants are over-indulged. I suppose it is partly our fault that they are selfish, and act like spoiled children; but I've talked to St. Clare till I am tired."

"And I, too," said St. Clare, taking up the morning paper.

Eva, the beautiful Eva, had stood listening to her mother, with that expression of deep and mystic earnestness which was peculiar to her. She walked softly round to her mother's chair, and put her arms round her neck.

"Well, Eva, what now?" said Marie.

"Mamma, couldn't I take care of you one night—just one? I know I shouldn't make you nervous, and I shouldn't sleep. I often lie awake nights, thinking—"

"O, nonsense, child—nonsense!" said Marie; "you are such a strange child!"

"But may I, mamma? I think," she said, timidly, "that Mammy isn't well. She told me her head ached all the time, lately."

"O, that's just one of Mammy's fidgets! Mammy is just like all the rest of them—makes such a fuss about every little headache or finger-ache; it'll never do to encourage it—never! I'm principled about this matter," said she, turning to Miss Ophelia; "you'll find the necessity of it. If you encourage servants in giving way to every little disagreeable feeling, and complaining of every little ailment, you'll have your hands full. I never complain myself—nobody knows what I endure. I feel it a duty to bear it quietly, and I do."

Miss Ophelia's round eyes expressed an undisguised amazement at this peroration, which struck St. Clare as so supremely ludicrous, that he burst into a loud laugh.

"St. Clare always laughs when I make the least allusion to my ill health," said Marie, with the voice of a suffering martyr. "I only hope the day won't come when he'll remember it!" and Marie put her handkerchief to her eyes.

Of course, there was rather a foolish silence. Finally, St. Clare got up, looked at his watch, and said he had an engagement down street. Eva tripped away after him, and Miss Ophelia and Marie remained at the table alone.

"Now, that's just like St. Clare!" said the latter, withdrawing her handkerchief with somewhat of a spirited flourish when the criminal to be affected by it was no longer in sight. "He never realizes, never can, never will, what I suffer, and have, for years. If I was one of the complaining sort, or ever made any fuss about my ailments, there would be some reason for it. Men do get tired, naturally, of a complaining wife. But I've kept things to myself, and borne, and borne, till St. Clare has got in the way of thinking I can bear anything."

Miss Ophelia did not exactly know what she was expected to answer to this.

While she was thinking what to say, Marie gradually wiped away her tears, and smoothed her plumage in a general sort of way, as a dove might be supposed to make toilet after a shower, and began a housewifely chat with Miss Ophelia, concerning cupboards, closets, linen-presses, store-rooms, and other matters, of which the latter was, by common understanding, to assume the direction,—giving her so many cautious directions and charges, that a head less systematic and business-like than Miss Ophelia's would have been utterly dizzied and confounded.

"And now," said Marie, "I believe I've told you everything; so that, when my next sick turn comes on, you'll be able to go forward entirely, without consulting me;—only about Eva,—she requires watching."

"She seems to be a good child, very," said Miss Ophelia; "I never saw a better child."

"Eva's peculiar," said her mother, "very. There are things about her so singular; she isn't like me, now, a particle;" and Marie sighed, as if this was a truly melancholy consideration.

Miss Ophelia in her own heart said, "I hope she isn't," but had prudence enough to keep it down.

"Eva always was disposed to be with servants; and I think that well enough with some children. Now, I always played with father's little negroes—it never did me any harm. But Eva somehow always seems to put herself on an equality with every creature that comes near her. It's a strange thing about the child. I never have been able to break her of it. St. Clare, I believe, encourages her in it. The fact is, St. Clare indulges every creature under this roof but his own wife."

Again Miss Ophelia sat in blank silence.

"Now, there's no way with servants," said Marie, "but to *put them down*, and keep them down. It was always natural to me, from a child. Eva is enough to spoil a whole house-full. What she will do when she comes to keep house herself, I'm sure I don't know. I hold to being *kind* to servants—I always am; but you must make 'em *know their place*. Eva never does; there's no getting into the child's head the first beginning of an idea what a servant's place is! You heard her offering to take care of me nights, to let Mammy sleep! That's just a specimen of the way the child would be doing all the time, if she was left to herself."

"Why," said Miss Ophelia, bluntly, "I suppose you think your servants are human creatures, and ought to have some rest when they are tired."

"Certainly, of course. I'm very particular in letting them have everything that comes convenient,—anything that doesn't put one at all out of the way, you know. Mammy can make up her sleep, some time or other; there's no difficulty about that. She's the sleepiest concern that ever I saw; sewing, standing, or sitting, that creature will go to sleep, and sleep anywhere and everywhere. No danger but Mammy gets sleep enough. But this treating servants as if they were exotic flowers, or china vases, is really ridiculous," said Marie, as she plunged languidly into the depths of a voluminous and pillowy lounge, and drew towards her an elegant cut-glass vinaigrette.

"You see," she continued, in a faint and lady-like voice, like the last dying breath of an Arabian jessamine, or something equally ethereal, "you see, Cousin Ophelia, I don't often speak of myself. It isn't my *habit*; 't isn't agreeable to me. In fact, I haven't strength to do it. But there are points where St. Clare and I differ.

St. Clare never understood me, never appreciated me. I think it lies at the root of all my ill health. St. Clare means well, I am bound to believe; but men are constitutionally selfish and inconsiderate to woman. That, at least, is my impression."

Miss Ophelia, who had not a small share of the genuine New England caution, and a very particular horror of being drawn into family difficulties, now began to foresee something of this kind impending; so, composing her face into a grim neutrality, and drawing out of her pocket about a yard and a quarter of stocking, which she kept as a specific against what Dr. Watts asserts to be a personal habit of Satan when people have idle hands, she proceeded to knit most energetically, shutting her lips together in a way that said, as plain as words could, "You needn't try to make me speak. I don't want anything to do with your affairs,"—in fact, she looked about as sympathizing as a stone lion. But Marie didn't care for that. She had got somebody to talk to, and she felt it her duty to talk, and that was enough; and reinforcing herself by smelling again at her vinaigrette, she went on.

"You see, I brought my own property and servants into the connection, when I married St. Clare, and I am legally entitled to manage them my own way. St. Clare had his fortune and his servants, and I'm well enough content he should manage them his way; but St. Clare will be interfering. He has wild, extravagant notions about things, particularly about the treatment of servants. He really does act as if he set his servants before me, and before himself, too; for he lets them make him all sorts of trouble, and never lifts a finger. Now, about some things, St. Clare is really frightful—he frightens me—good-natured as he looks, in general. Now, he has set down his foot that, come what will, there shall not be a blow struck in this house, except what he or I strike; and he does it in a way that I really dare not cross him. Well, you may see what that leads to; for St. Clare wouldn't raise his hand, if every one of them walked over him, and I—you see how cruel it would be to require me to make the exertion. Now, you know these servants are nothing but grown-up children."

"I don't know anything about it, and I thank the Lord that I don't!" said Miss Ophelia, shortly.

"Well, but you will have to know something, and know it to your cost, if you stay here. You don't know what a provoking, stupid, careless, unreasonable, childish, ungrateful set of wretches they are."

Marie seemed wonderfully supported, always, when she got upon this topic; and she now opened her eyes, and seemed quite to forget her languor.

"You don't know, and you can't, the daily, hourly trials that beset a housekeeper from them, everywhere and every way. But it's no use to complain to St. Clare. He talks the strangest stuff. He says we have made them what they are, and ought to bear with them. He says their faults are all owing to us, and that it would be cruel to make the fault and punish it too. He says we shouldn't do any better, in their place; just as if one could reason from them to us, you know."

"Don't you believe that the Lord made them of one blood with us?" said Miss Ophelia, shortly.

"No, indeed not I! A pretty story, truly! They are a degraded race."

"Don't you think they've got immortal souls?" said Miss Ophelia, with increasing indignation.

"O, well," said Marie, yawning, "that, of course—nobody doubts that. But as to putting them on any sort of equality with us, you know, as if we could be compared, why, it's impossible! Now, St. Clare really has talked to me as if keeping Mammy from her husband was like keeping me from mine. There's no comparing in this way. Mammy couldn't have the feelings that I should. It's a different thing altogether,—of course, it is,—and yet St. Clare pretends not to see it. And just as if Mammy could love her little dirty babies as I love Eva! Yet St. Clare once really and soberly tried to persuade me that it was my duty, with my weak health, and all I suffer, to let Mammy go back, and take somebody else in her place. That was a little too much even for *me* to bear. I don't often show my feelings, I make it a principle to endure everything in silence; it's a wife's hard lot, and I bear it. But I did break out, that time; so that he has never alluded to the subject since. But I know by his looks, and little things that he says, that he thinks so as much as ever; and it's so trying, so provoking!"

Miss Ophelia looked very much as if she was afraid she should say something; but she rattled away with her needles in a way that had volumes of meaning in it, if Marie could only have understood it.

"So, you just see," she continued, "what you've got to manage. A household without any rule; where servants have it all their own way, do what they please, and have what they please, except so far as I, with my feeble health, have kept up government. I keep my cowhide about, and sometimes I do lay it on; but the exertion is always too much for me. If St. Clare would only have this thing done as others do—"

"And how's that?"

"Why, send them to the calaboose, or some of the other places to be flogged. That's the only way. If I wasn't such a poor, feeble piece, I believe I should manage with twice the energy that St. Clare does."

"And how does St. Clare contrive to manage?" said Miss Ophelia. "You say he never strikes a blow."

"Well, men have a more commanding way, you know; it is easier for them; besides, if you ever looked full in his eye, it's peculiar,—that eye,—and if he speaks decidedly, there's a kind of flash. I'm afraid of it, myself; and the servants know they must mind. I couldn't do as much by a regular storm and scolding as St. Clare can by one turn of his eye, if once he is in earnest. O, there's no trouble about St. Clare; that's the reason he's no more feeling for me. But you'll find, when you come to manage, that there's no getting along without severity,—they are so bad, so deceitful, so lazy."

"The old tune," said St. Clare, sauntering in. "What an awful account these wicked creatures will have to settle, at last, especially for being lazy! You see, cousin," said he, as he stretched himself at full length on a lounge opposite to Marie, "it's wholly inexcusable in them, in the light of the example that Marie and I set them,—this laziness."

CHAPTER XVI

"Come, now, St. Clare, you are too bad!" said Marie.

"Am I, now? Why, I thought I was talking good, quite remarkably for me. I try to enforce your remarks, Marie, always."

"You know you meant no such thing, St. Clare," said Marie.

"O, I must have been mistaken, then. Thank you, my dear, for setting me right."

"You do really try to be provoking," said Marie.

"O, come, Marie, the day is growing warm, and I have just had a long quarrel with Dolph, which has fatigued me excessively; so, pray be agreeable, now, and let a fellow repose in the light of your smile."

"What's the matter about Dolph?" said Marie. "That fellow's impudence has been growing to a point that is perfectly intolerable to me. I only wish I had the undisputed management of him a while. I'd bring him down!"

"What you say, my dear, is marked with your usual acuteness and good sense," said St. Clare. "As to Dolph, the case is this: that he has so long been engaged in imitating my graces and perfections, that he has, at last, really mistaken himself for his master; and I have been obliged to give him a little insight into his mistake."

"How?" said Marie.

"Why, I was obliged to let him understand explicitly that I preferred to keep *some* of my clothes for my own personal wearing; also, I put his magnificence upon an allowance of cologne-water, and actually was so cruel as to restrict him to one dozen of my cambric handkerchiefs. Dolph was particularly huffy about it, and I had to talk to him like a father, to bring him round."

"O! St. Clare, when will you learn how to treat your servants? It's abominable, the way you indulge them!" said Marie.

"Why, after all, what's the harm of the poor dog's wanting to be like his master; and if I haven't brought him up any better than to find his chief good in cologne and cambric handkerchiefs, why shouldn't I give them to him?"

"And why haven't you brought him up better?" said Miss Ophelia, with blunt determination.

"Too much trouble,—laziness, cousin, laziness,—which ruins more souls than you can shake a stick at. If it weren't for laziness, I should have been a perfect angel, myself. I'm inclined to think that laziness is what your old Dr. Botherem, up in Vermont, used to call the 'essence of moral evil.' It's an awful consideration, certainly."

"I think you slaveholders have an awful responsibility upon you," said Miss Ophelia. "I wouldn't have it, for a thousand worlds. You ought to educate your slaves, and treat them like reasonable creatures,—like immortal creatures, that you've got to stand before the bar of God with. That's my mind," said the good lady, breaking suddenly out with a tide of zeal that had been gaining strength in her mind all the morning.

"O! come, come," said St. Clare, getting up quickly; "what do you know about us?" And he sat down to the piano, and rattled a lively piece of music. St. Clare had a decided genius for music. His touch was brilliant and firm, and his fingers flew over the keys with a rapid and bird-like motion, airy, and yet decided. He played piece after piece, like a man who is trying to play himself into a good humor. After pushing the music aside, he rose up, and said, gayly, "Well, now, cousin, you've given us a good talk and done your duty; on the whole, I think the better of you for it. I make no manner of doubt that you threw a very diamond of truth at me, though you see it hit me so directly in the face that it wasn't exactly appreciated, at first."

"For my part, I don't see any use in such sort of talk," said Marie. "I'm sure, if anybody does more for servants than we do, I'd like to know who; and it don't do 'em a bit good,—not a particle,—they get worse and worse. As to talking to them, or anything like that, I'm sure I have talked till I was tired and hoarse, telling them their duty, and all that; and I'm sure they can go to church when they like, though they don't understand a word of the sermon, more than so many pigs,—so it isn't of any great use for them to go, as I see; but they do go, and so they have every chance; but, as I said before, they are a degraded race, and always will be, and there isn't any help for them; you can't make anything of them, if you try. You see, Cousin Ophelia, I've tried, and you haven't; I was born and bred among them, and I know."

Miss Ophelia thought she had said enough, and therefore sat silent. St. Clare whistled a tune.

"St. Clare, I wish you wouldn't whistle," said Marie; "it makes my head worse."

"I won't," said St. Clare. "Is there anything else you wouldn't wish me to do?"

"I wish you *would* have some kind of sympathy for my trials; you never have any feeling for me."

"My dear accusing angel!" said St. Clare.

"It's provoking to be talked to in that way."

"Then, how will you be talked to? I'll talk to order,—any way you'll mention,—only to give satisfaction."

A gay laugh from the court rang through the silken curtains of the verandah. St. Clare stepped out, and lifting up the curtain, laughed too.

"What is it?" said Miss Ophelia, coming to the railing.

There sat Tom, on a little mossy seat in the court, every one of his button-holes stuck full of cape jessamines, and Eva, gayly laughing, was hanging a wreath of roses round his neck; and then she sat down on his knee, like a chip-sparrow, still laughing.

"O, Tom, you look so funny!"

Tom had a sober, benevolent smile, and seemed, in his quiet way, to be enjoying the fun quite as much as his little mistress. He lifted his eyes, when he saw his master, with a half-deprecating, apologetic air.

"How can you let her?" said Miss Ophelia.

"Why not?" said St. Clare.

"Why, I don't know, it seems so dreadful!"

CHAPTER XVI

"You would think no harm in a child's caressing a large dog, even if he was black; but a creature that can think, and reason, and feel, and is immortal, you shudder at; confess it, cousin. I know the feeling among some of you northerners well enough. Not that there is a particle of virtue in our not having it; but custom with us does what Christianity ought to do,—obliterates the feeling of personal prejudice. I have often noticed, in my travels north, how much stronger this was with you than with us. You loathe them as you would a snake or a toad, yet you are indignant at their wrongs. You would not have them abused; but you don't want to have anything to do with them yourselves. You would send them to Africa, out of your sight and smell, and then send a missionary or two to do up all the self-denial of elevating them compendiously. Isn't that it?"

"Well, cousin," said Miss Ophelia, thoughtfully, "there may be some truth in this."

"What would the poor and lowly do, without children?" said St. Clare, leaning on the railing, and watching Eva, as she tripped off, leading Tom with her. "Your little child is your only true democrat. Tom, now is a hero to Eva; his stories are wonders in her eyes, his songs and Methodist hymns are better than an opera, and the traps and little bits of trash in his pocket a mine of jewels, and he the most wonderful Tom that ever wore a black skin. This is one of the roses of Eden that the Lord has dropped down expressly for the poor and lowly, who get few enough of any other kind."

"It's strange, cousin," said Miss Ophelia, "one might almost think you were a *professor*, to hear you talk."

"A professor?" said St. Clare.

"Yes; a professor of religion."

"Not at all; not a professor, as your town-folks have it; and, what is worse, I'm afraid, not a *practiser*, either."

"What makes you talk so, then?"

"Nothing is easier than talking," said St. Clare. "I believe Shakespeare makes somebody say, 'I could sooner show twenty what were good to be done, than be one of the twenty to follow my own showing.'[1] Nothing like division of labor. My forte lies in talking, and yours, cousin, lies in doing."

In Tom's external situation, at this time, there was, as the world says, nothing to complain of Little Eva's fancy for him—the instinctive gratitude and loveliness of a noble nature—had led her to petition her father that he might be her especial attendant, whenever she needed the escort of a servant, in her walks or rides; and Tom had general orders to let everything else go, and attend to Miss Eva whenever she wanted him,—orders which our readers may fancy were far from disagreeable to him. He was kept well dressed, for St. Clare was fastidiously particular on this point. His stable services were merely a sinecure, and consisted simply in a daily care and inspection, and directing an under-servant in his duties; for Marie St. Clare declared that she could not have any smell of the horses about

---

[1] The Merchant of Venice, Act 1, scene 2, lines 17-18.

him when he came near her, and that he must positively not be put to any service that would make him unpleasant to her, as her nervous system was entirely inadequate to any trial of that nature; one snuff of anything disagreeable being, according to her account, quite sufficient to close the scene, and put an end to all her earthly trials at once. Tom, therefore, in his well-brushed broadcloth suit, smooth beaver, glossy boots, faultless wristbands and collar, with his grave, good-natured black face, looked respectable enough to be a Bishop of Carthage, as men of his color were, in other ages.

Then, too, he was in a beautiful place, a consideration to which his sensitive race was never indifferent; and he did enjoy with a quiet joy the birds, the flowers, the fountains, the perfume, and light and beauty of the court, the silken hangings, and pictures, and lustres, and statuettes, and gilding, that made the parlors within a kind of Aladdin's palace to him.

If ever Africa shall show an elevated and cultivated race,—and come it must, some time, her turn to figure in the great drama of human improvement.—life will awake there with a gorgeousness and splendor of which our cold western tribes faintly have conceived. In that far-off mystic land of gold, and gems, and spices, and waving palms, and wondrous flowers, and miraculous fertility, will awake new forms of art, new styles of splendor; and the negro race, no longer despised and trodden down, will, perhaps, show forth some of the latest and most magnificent revelations of human life. Certainly they will, in their gentleness, their lowly docility of heart, their aptitude to repose on a superior mind and rest on a higher power, their childlike simplicity of affection, and facility of forgiveness. In all these they will exhibit the highest form of the peculiarly *Christian life*, and, perhaps, as God chasteneth whom he loveth, he hath chosen poor Africa in the furnace of affliction, to make her the highest and noblest in that kingdom which he will set up, when every other kingdom has been tried, and failed; for the first shall be last, and the last first.

Was this what Marie St. Clare was thinking of, as she stood, gorgeously dressed, on the verandah, on Sunday morning, clasping a diamond bracelet on her slender wrist? Most likely it was. Or, if it wasn't that, it was something else; for Marie patronized good things, and she was going now, in full force,—diamonds, silk, and lace, and jewels, and all,—to a fashionable church, to be very religious. Marie always made a point to be very pious on Sundays. There she stood, so slender, so elegant, so airy and undulating in all her motions, her lace scarf enveloping her like a mist. She looked a graceful creature, and she felt very good and very elegant indeed. Miss Ophelia stood at her side, a perfect contrast. It was not that she had not as handsome a silk dress and shawl, and as fine a pocket-handkerchief; but stiffness and squareness, and bolt-uprightness, enveloped her with as indefinite yet appreciable a presence as did grace her elegant neighbor; not the grace of God, however,—that is quite another thing!

"Where's Eva?" said Marie.

"The child stopped on the stairs, to say something to Mammy."

CHAPTER XVI

And what was Eva saying to Mammy on the stairs? Listen, reader, and you will hear, though Marie does not.

"Dear Mammy, I know your head is aching dreadfully."

"Lord bless you, Miss Eva! my head allers aches lately. You don't need to worry."

"Well, I'm glad you're going out; and here,"—and the little girl threw her arms around her,—"Mammy, you shall take my vinaigrette."

"What! your beautiful gold thing, thar, with them diamonds! Lor, Miss, 't wouldn't be proper, no ways."

"Why not? You need it, and I don't. Mamma always uses it for headache, and it'll make you feel better. No, you shall take it, to please me, now."

"Do hear the darlin talk!" said Mammy, as Eva thrust it into her bosom, and kissing her, ran down stairs to her mother.

"What were you stopping for?"

"I was just stopping to give Mammy my vinaigrette, to take to church with her."

"Eva" said Marie, stamping impatiently,—"your gold vinaigrette to *Mammy!* When will you learn what's *proper*? Go right and take it back this moment!"

Eva looked downcast and aggrieved, and turned slowly.

"I say, Marie, let the child alone; she shall do as she pleases," said St. Clare.

"St. Clare, how will she ever get along in the world?" said Marie.

"The Lord knows," said St. Clare, "but she'll get along in heaven better than you or I."

"O, papa, don't," said Eva, softly touching his elbow; "it troubles mother."

"Well, cousin, are you ready to go to meeting?" said Miss Ophelia, turning square about on St. Clare.

"I'm not going, thank you."

"I do wish St. Clare ever would go to church," said Marie; "but he hasn't a particle of religion about him. It really isn't respectable."

"I know it," said St. Clare. "You ladies go to church to learn how to get along in the world, I suppose, and your piety sheds respectability on us. If I did go at all, I would go where Mammy goes; there's something to keep a fellow awake there, at least."

"What! those shouting Methodists? Horrible!" said Marie.

"Anything but the dead sea of your respectable churches, Marie. Positively, it's too much to ask of a man. Eva, do you like to go? Come, stay at home and play with me."

"Thank you, papa; but I'd rather go to church."

"Isn't it dreadful tiresome?" said St. Clare.

"I think it is tiresome, some," said Eva, "and I am sleepy, too, but I try to keep awake."

"What do you go for, then?"

"Why, you know, papa," she said, in a whisper, "cousin told me that God wants to have us; and he gives us everything, you know; and it isn't much to do it, if he wants us to. It isn't so very tiresome after all."

"You sweet, little obliging soul!" said St. Clare, kissing her; "go along, that's a good girl, and pray for me."

"Certainly, I always do," said the child, as she sprang after her mother into the carriage.

St. Clare stood on the steps and kissed his hand to her, as the carriage drove away; large tears were in his eyes.

"O, Evangeline! rightly named," he said; "hath not God made thee an evangel to me?"

So he felt a moment; and then he smoked a cigar, and read the Picayune, and forgot his little gospel. Was he much unlike other folks?

"You see, Evangeline," said her mother, "it's always right and proper to be kind to servants, but it isn't proper to treat them *just* as we would our relations, or people in our own class of life. Now, if Mammy was sick, you wouldn't want to put her in your own bed."

"I should feel just like it, mamma," said Eva, "because then it would be handier to take care of her, and because, you know, my bed is better than hers."

Marie was in utter despair at the entire want of moral perception evinced in this reply.

"What can I do to make this child understand me?" she said.

"Nothing," said Miss Ophelia, significantly.

Eva looked sorry and disconcerted for a moment; but children, luckily, do not keep to one impression long, and in a few moments she was merrily laughing at various things which she saw from the coach-windows, as it rattled along.

"Well, ladies," said St. Clare, as they were comfortably seated at the dinner-table, "and what was the bill of fare at church today?"

"O, Dr. G—— preached a splendid sermon," said Marie. "It was just such a sermon as you ought to hear; it expressed all my views exactly."

"It must have been very improving," said St. Clare. "The subject must have been an extensive one."

"Well, I mean all my views about society, and such things," said Marie. "The text was, 'He hath made everything beautiful in its season;' and he showed how all the orders and distinctions in society came from God; and that it was so appropriate, you know, and beautiful, that some should be high and some low, and that some were born to rule and some to serve, and all that, you know; and he applied it so well to all this ridiculous fuss that is made about slavery, and he proved distinctly that the Bible was on our side, and supported all our institutions so convincingly. I only wish you'd heard him."

"O, I didn't need it," said St. Clare. "I can learn what does me as much good as that from the Picayune, any time, and smoke a cigar besides; which I can't do, you know, in a church."

"Why," said Miss Ophelia, "don't you believe in these views?"

"Who,—I? You know I'm such a graceless dog that these religious aspects of such subjects don't edify me much. If I was to say anything on this slavery matter, I would say out, fair and square, 'We're in for it; we've got 'em, and mean to keep 'em,—it's for our convenience and our interest;' for that's the long and short of it,—that's just the whole of what all this sanctified stuff amounts to, after all; and I think that it will be intelligible to everybody, everywhere."

"I do think, Augustine, you are so irreverent!" said Marie. "I think it's shocking to hear you talk."

"Shocking! it's the truth. This religious talk on such matters,—why don't they carry it a little further, and show the beauty, in its season, of a fellow's taking a glass too much, and sitting a little too late over his cards, and various providential arrangements of that sort, which are pretty frequent among us young men;—we'd like to hear that those are right and godly, too."

"Well," said Miss Ophelia, "do you think slavery right or wrong?"

"I'm not going to have any of your horrid New England directness, cousin," said St. Clare, gayly. "If I answer that question, I know you'll be at me with half a dozen others, each one harder than the last; and I'm not a going to define my position. I am one of the sort that lives by throwing stones at other people's glass houses, but I never mean to put up one for them to stone."

"That's just the way he's always talking," said Marie; "you can't get any satisfaction out of him. I believe it's just because he don't like religion, that he's always running out in this way he's been doing."

"Religion!" said St. Clare, in a tone that made both ladies look at him. "Religion! Is what you hear at church, religion? Is that which can bend and turn, and descend and ascend, to fit every crooked phase of selfish, worldly society, religion? Is that religion which is less scrupulous, less generous, less just, less considerate for man, than even my own ungodly, worldly, blinded nature? No! When I look for a religion, I must look for something above me, and not something beneath."

"Then you don't believe that the Bible justifies slavery," said Miss Ophelia.

"The Bible was my *mother's* book," said St. Clare. "By it she lived and died, and I would be very sorry to think it did. I'd as soon desire to have it proved that my mother could drink brandy, chew tobacco, and swear, by way of satisfying me that I did right in doing the same. It wouldn't make me at all more satisfied with these things in myself, and it would take from me the comfort of respecting her; and it really is a comfort, in this world, to have anything one can respect. In short, you see," said he, suddenly resuming his gay tone, "all I want is that different things be kept in different boxes. The whole frame-work of society, both in Europe and America, is made up of various things which will not stand the scrutiny of any very ideal standard of morality. It's pretty generally understood that men don't aspire after the absolute right, but only to do about as well as the rest of the world. Now, when any one speaks up, like a man, and says slavery is necessary to us, we can't get along without it, we should be beggared if we give it up, and, of course, we mean to hold on to it,—this is strong, clear, well-defined language; it has the respectability of truth to it; and, if we may judge by their practice, the majority of the world will bear us out in it. But when he begins to put on a long face, and snuffle, and quote Scripture, I incline to think he isn't much better than he should be."

"You are very uncharitable," said Marie.

"Well," said St. Clare, "suppose that something should bring down the price of cotton once and forever, and make the whole slave property a drug in the market, don't you think we should soon have another version of the Scripture doctrine? What a flood of light would pour into the church, all at once, and how immediately it would be discovered that everything in the Bible and reason went the other way!"

"Well, at any rate," said Marie, as she reclined herself on a lounge, "I'm thankful I'm born where slavery exists; and I believe it's right,—indeed, I feel it must be; and, at any rate, I'm sure I couldn't get along without it."

"I say, what do you think, Pussy?" said her father to Eva, who came in at this moment, with a flower in her hand.

"What about, papa?"

"Why, which do you like the best,—to live as they do at your uncle's, up in Vermont, or to have a house-full of servants, as we do?"

"O, of course, our way is the pleasantest," said Eva.

"Why so?" said St. Clare, stroking her head.

"Why, it makes so many more round you to love, you know," said Eva, looking up earnestly.

"Now, that's just like Eva," said Marie; "just one of her odd speeches."

"Is it an odd speech, papa?" said Eva, whisperingly, as she got upon his knee.

"Rather, as this world goes, Pussy," said St. Clare. "But where has my little Eva been, all dinner-time?"

"O, I've been up in Tom's room, hearing him sing, and Aunt Dinah gave me my dinner."

"Hearing Tom sing, hey?"

"O, yes! he sings such beautiful things about the New Jerusalem, and bright angels, and the land of Canaan."

"I dare say; it's better than the opera, isn't it?"

"Yes, and he's going to teach them to me."

"Singing lessons, hey?—you *are* coming on."

"Yes, he sings for me, and I read to him in my Bible; and he explains what it means, you know."

"On my word," said Marie, laughing, "that is the latest joke of the season."

"Tom isn't a bad hand, now, at explaining Scripture, I'll dare swear," said St. Clare. "Tom has a natural genius for religion. I wanted the horses out early, this morning, and I stole up to Tom's cubiculum there, over the stables, and there I heard him holding a meeting by himself; and, in fact, I haven't heard anything quite so savory as Tom's prayer, this some time. He put in for me, with a zeal that was quite apostolic."

"Perhaps he guessed you were listening. I've heard of that trick before."

"If he did, he wasn't very polite; for he gave the Lord his opinion of me, pretty freely. Tom seemed to think there was decidedly room for improvement in me, and seemed very earnest that I should be converted."

"I hope you'll lay it to heart," said Miss Ophelia.

"I suppose you are much of the same opinion," said St. Clare. "Well, we shall see,—shan't we, Eva?"

CHAPTER XVII

THE FREEMAN'S DEFENCE

There was a gentle bustle at the Quaker house, as the afternoon drew to a close. Rachel Halliday moved quietly to and fro, collecting from her household stores such needments as could be arranged in the smallest compass, for the wanderers who were to go forth that night. The afternoon shadows stretched eastward, and the round red sun stood thoughtfully on the horizon, and his beams shone yellow and calm into the little bed-room where George and his wife were sitting. He was sitting with his child on his knee, and his wife's hand in his. Both looked thoughtful and serious and traces of tears were on their cheeks.

"Yes, Eliza," said George, "I know all you say is true. You are a good child,—a great deal better than I am; and I will try to do as you say. I'll try to act worthy of a free man. I'll try to feel like a Christian. God Almighty knows that I've meant to do well,—tried hard to do well,—when everything has been against me; and now I'll forget all the past, and put away every hard and bitter feeling, and read my Bible, and learn to be a good man."

"And when we get to Canada," said Eliza, "I can help you. I can do dress-making very well; and I understand fine washing and ironing; and between us we can find something to live on."

"Yes, Eliza, so long as we have each other and our boy. O! Eliza, if these people only knew what a blessing it is for a man to feel that his wife and child belong to *him*! I've often wondered to see men that could call their wives and children *their own* fretting and worrying about anything else. Why, I feel rich and strong, though we have nothing but our bare hands. I feel as if I could scarcely ask God for any more. Yes, though I've worked hard every day, till I am twenty-five years old, and have not a cent of money, nor a roof to cover me, nor a spot of land to call my own, yet, if they will only let me alone now, I will be satisfied,—thankful; I will work, and send back the money for you and my boy. As to my old master, he has been paid five times over for all he ever spent for me. I don't owe him anything."

"But yet we are not quite out of danger," said Eliza; "we are not yet in Canada."

"True," said George, "but it seems as if I smelt the free air, and it makes me strong."

At this moment, voices were heard in the outer apartment, in earnest conversation, and very soon a rap was heard on the door. Eliza started and opened it.

Simeon Halliday was there, and with him a Quaker brother, whom he introduced as Phineas Fletcher. Phineas was tall and lathy, red-haired, with an expression of great acuteness and shrewdness in his face. He had not the placid, quiet, unworldly air of Simeon Halliday; on the contrary, a particularly wide-awake and *au fait* appearance, like a man who rather prides himself on knowing what he is about, and keeping a bright lookout ahead; peculiarities which sorted rather oddly with his broad brim and formal phraseology.

"Our friend Phineas hath discovered something of importance to the interests of thee and thy party, George," said Simeon; "it were well for thee to hear it."

"That I have," said Phineas, "and it shows the use of a man's always sleeping with one ear open, in certain places, as I've always said. Last night I stopped at a little lone tavern, back on the road. Thee remembers the place, Simeon, where we sold some apples, last year, to that fat woman, with the great ear-rings. Well, I was tired with hard driving; and, after my supper I stretched myself down on a pile of bags in the corner, and pulled a buffalo over me, to wait till my bed was ready; and what does I do, but get fast asleep."

"With one ear open, Phineas?" said Simeon, quietly.

"No; I slept, ears and all, for an hour or two, for I was pretty well tired; but when I came to myself a little, I found that there were some men in the room, sitting round a table, drinking and talking; and I thought, before I made much muster, I'd just see what they were up to, especially as I heard them say something about the Quakers. 'So,' says one, 'they are up in the Quaker settlement, no doubt,' says he. Then I listened with both ears, and I found that they were talking about this very party. So I lay and heard them lay off all their plans. This young man, they said, was to be sent back to Kentucky, to his master, who was going to make an example of him, to keep all niggers from running away; and his wife two of them were going to run down to New Orleans to sell, on their own account, and they calculated to get sixteen or eighteen hundred dollars for her; and the child, they said, was going to a trader, who had bought him; and then there was the boy, Jim, and his mother, they were to go back to their masters in Kentucky. They said that there were two constables, in a town a little piece ahead, who would go in with 'em to get 'em taken up, and the young woman was to be taken before a judge; and one of the fellows, who is small and smooth-spoken, was to swear to her for his property, and get her delivered over to him to take south. They've got a right notion of the track we are going tonight; and they'll be down after us, six or eight strong. So now, what's to be done?"

The group that stood in various attitudes, after this communication, were worthy of a painter. Rachel Halliday, who had taken her hands out of a batch of biscuit, to hear the news, stood with them upraised and floury, and with a face of the deepest concern. Simeon looked profoundly thoughtful; Eliza had thrown her arms around her husband, and was looking up to him. George stood with clenched hands and glowing eyes, and looking as any other man might look, whose wife was to be sold at auction, and son sent to a trader, all under the shelter of a Christian nation's laws.

"What *shall* we do, George?" said Eliza faintly.

"I know what *I* shall do," said George, as he stepped into the little room, and began examining pistols.

"Ay, ay," said Phineas, nodding his head to Simeon; "thou seest, Simeon, how it will work."

"I see," said Simeon, sighing; "I pray it come not to that."

"I don't want to involve any one with or for me," said George. "If you will lend me your vehicle and direct me, I will drive alone to the next stand. Jim is a giant in strength, and brave as death and despair, and so am I."

"Ah, well, friend," said Phineas, "but thee'll need a driver, for all that. Thee's quite welcome to do all the fighting, thee knows; but I know a thing or two about the road, that thee doesn't."

"But I don't want to involve you," said George.

"Involve," said Phineas, with a curious and keen expression of face, "When thee does involve me, please to let me know."

"Phineas is a wise and skilful man," said Simeon. "Thee does well, George, to abide by his judgment; and," he added, laying his hand kindly on George's shoulder, and pointing to the pistols, "be not over hasty with these,—young blood is hot."

"I will attack no man," said George. "All I ask of this country is to be let alone, and I will go out peaceably; but,"—he paused, and his brow darkened and his face worked,—"I've had a sister sold in that New Orleans market. I know what they are sold for; and am I going to stand by and see them take my wife and sell her, when God has given me a pair of strong arms to defend her? No; God help me! I'll fight to the last breath, before they shall take my wife and son. Can you blame me?"

"Mortal man cannot blame thee, George. Flesh and blood could not do otherwise," said Simeon. "Woe unto the world because of offences, but woe unto them through whom the offence cometh."

"Would not even you, sir, do the same, in my place?"

"I pray that I be not tried," said Simeon; "the flesh is weak."

"I think my flesh would be pretty tolerable strong, in such a case," said Phineas, stretching out a pair of arms like the sails of a windmill. "I an't sure, friend George, that I shouldn't hold a fellow for thee, if thee had any accounts to settle with him."

"If man should *ever* resist evil," said Simeon, "then George should feel free to do it now: but the leaders of our people taught a more excellent way; for the wrath of man worketh not the righteousness of God; but it goes sorely against the corrupt will of man, and none can receive it save they to whom it is given. Let us pray the Lord that we be not tempted."

"And so *I* do," said Phineas; "but if we are tempted too much—why, let them look out, that's all."

"It's quite plain thee wasn't born a Friend," said Simeon, smiling. "The old nature hath its way in thee pretty strong as yet."

To tell the truth, Phineas had been a hearty, two-fisted backwoodsman, a vigorous hunter, and a dead shot at a buck; but, having wooed a pretty Quakeress, had been moved by the power of her charms to join the society in his neighborhood; and though he was an honest, sober, and efficient member, and nothing particular could be alleged against him, yet the more spiritual among them could not but discern an exceeding lack of savor in his developments.

"Friend Phineas will ever have ways of his own," said Rachel Halliday, smiling; "but we all think that his heart is in the right place, after all."

"Well," said George, "isn't it best that we hasten our flight?"

"I got up at four o'clock, and came on with all speed, full two or three hours ahead of them, if they start at the time they planned. It isn't safe to start till dark, at any rate; for there are some evil persons in the villages ahead, that might be disposed to meddle with us, if they saw our wagon, and that would delay us more than the waiting; but in two hours I think we may venture. I will go over to Michael Cross, and engage him to come behind on his swift nag, and keep a bright lookout on the road, and warn us if any company of men come on. Michael keeps a horse that can soon get ahead of most other horses; and he could shoot ahead and let us know, if there were any danger. I am going out now to warn Jim and the old woman to be in readiness, and to see about the horse. We have a pretty fair start, and stand a good chance to get to the stand before they can come up with us. So, have good courage, friend George; this isn't the first ugly scrape that I've been in with thy people," said Phineas, as he closed the door.

"Phineas is pretty shrewd," said Simeon. "He will do the best that can be done for thee, George."

"All I am sorry for," said George, "is the risk to you."

"Thee'll much oblige us, friend George, to say no more about that. What we do we are conscience bound to do; we can do no other way. And now, mother," said he, turning to Rachel, "hurry thy preparations for these friends, for we must not send them away fasting."

And while Rachel and her children were busy making corn-cake, and cooking ham and chicken, and hurrying on the *et ceteras* of the evening meal, George and his wife sat in their little room, with their arms folded about each other, in such talk as husband and wife have when they know that a few hours may part them forever.

"Eliza," said George, "people that have friends, and houses, and lands, and money, and all those things *can't* love as we do, who have nothing but each other. Till I knew you, Eliza, no creature had loved me, but my poor, heart-broken mother and sister. I saw poor Emily that morning the trader carried her off. She came to the corner where I was lying asleep, and said, 'Poor George, your last friend is going. What will become of you, poor boy?' And I got up and threw my arms round her, and cried and sobbed, and she cried too; and those were the last kind words I got for ten long years; and my heart all withered up, and felt as dry as ashes, till I met you. And your loving me,—why, it was almost like raising one from the dead! I've been a new man ever since! And now, Eliza, I'll give my last drop of blood, but they *shall not* take you from me. Whoever gets you must walk over my dead body."

"O, Lord, have mercy!" said Eliza, sobbing. "If he will only let us get out of this country together, that is all we ask."

"Is God on their side?" said George, speaking less to his wife than pouring out his own bitter thoughts. "Does he see all they do? Why does he let such things happen? And they tell us that the Bible is on their side; certainly all the power is. They are rich, and healthy, and happy; they are members of churches, expecting to go to heaven; and they get along so easy in the world, and have it all their own way; and poor, honest, faithful Christians,—Christians as good or better than they,—are lying in the very dust under their feet. They buy 'em and sell 'em, and make trade of their heart's blood, and groans and tears,—and God *lets* them."

"Friend George," said Simeon, from the kitchen, "listen to this Psalm; it may do thee good."

George drew his seat near the door, and Eliza, wiping her tears, came forward also to listen, while Simeon read as follows:

"But as for me, my feet were almost gone; my steps had well-nigh slipped. For I was envious of the foolish, when I saw the prosperity of the wicked. They are not in trouble like other men, neither are they plagued like other men. Therefore, pride compasseth them as a chain; violence covereth them as a garment. Their eyes stand out with fatness; they have more than heart could wish. They are corrupt, and speak wickedly concerning oppression; they speak loftily. Therefore his people return, and the waters of a full cup are wrung out to them, and they say, How doth God know? and is there knowledge in the Most High?"

"Is not that the way thee feels, George?"

"It is so indeed," said George,—"as well as I could have written it myself."

"Then, hear," said Simeon: "When I thought to know this, it was too painful for me until I went unto the sanctuary of God. Then understood I their end. Surely thou didst set them in slippery places, thou castedst them down to destruction. As a dream when one awaketh, so, oh Lord, when thou awakest, thou shalt despise their image. Nevertheless I am continually with thee; thou hast holden me by my right hand. Thou shalt guide me by thy counsel, and afterwards receive me to glory. It is good for me to draw near unto God. I have put my trust in the Lord God."[1]

The words of holy trust, breathed by the friendly old man, stole like sacred music over the harassed and chafed spirit of George; and after he ceased, he sat with a gentle and subdued expression on his fine features.

"If this world were all, George," said Simeon, "thee might, indeed, ask where is the Lord? But it is often those who have least of all in this life whom he

[1] Ps. 73, "The End of the Wicked contrasted with that of the Righteous."

chooseth for the kingdom. Put thy trust in him and, no matter what befalls thee here, he will make all right hereafter."

If these words had been spoken by some easy, self-indulgent exhorter, from whose mouth they might have come merely as pious and rhetorical flourish, proper to be used to people in distress, perhaps they might not have had much effect; but coming from one who daily and calmly risked fine and imprisonment for the cause of God and man, they had a weight that could not but be felt, and both the poor, desolate fugitives found calmness and strength breathing into them from it.

And now Rachel took Eliza's hand kindly, and led the way to the supper-table. As they were sitting down, a light tap sounded at the door, and Ruth entered.

"I just ran in," she said, "with these little stockings for the boy,—three pair, nice, warm woollen ones. It will be so cold, thee knows, in Canada. Does thee keep up good courage, Eliza?" she added, tripping round to Eliza's side of the table, and shaking her warmly by the hand, and slipping a seed-cake into Harry's hand. "I brought a little parcel of these for him," she said, tugging at her pocket to get out the package. "Children, thee knows, will always be eating."

"O, thank you; you are too kind," said Eliza.

"Come, Ruth, sit down to supper," said Rachel.

"I couldn't, any way. I left John with the baby, and some biscuits in the oven; and I can't stay a moment, else John will burn up all the biscuits, and give the baby all the sugar in the bowl. That's the way he does," said the little Quakeress, laughing. "So, good-by, Eliza; good-by, George; the Lord grant thee a safe journey;" and, with a few tripping steps, Ruth was out of the apartment.

A little while after supper, a large covered-wagon drew up before the door; the night was clear starlight; and Phineas jumped briskly down from his seat to arrange his passengers. George walked out of the door, with his child on one arm and his wife on the other. His step was firm, his face settled and resolute. Rachel and Simeon came out after them.

"You get out, a moment," said Phineas to those inside, "and let me fix the back of the wagon, there, for the women-folks and the boy."

"Here are the two buffaloes," said Rachel. "Make the seats as comfortable as may be; it's hard riding all night."

Jim came out first, and carefully assisted out his old mother, who clung to his arm, and looked anxiously about, as if she expected the pursuer every moment.

"Jim, are your pistols all in order?" said George, in a low, firm voice.

"Yes, indeed," said Jim.

"And you've no doubt what you shall do, if they come?"

"I rather think I haven't," said Jim, throwing open his broad chest, and taking a deep breath. "Do you think I'll let them get mother again?"

During this brief colloquy, Eliza had been taking her leave of her kind friend, Rachel, and was handed into the carriage by Simeon, and, creeping into the back part with her boy, sat down among the buffalo-skins. The old woman was next handed in and seated and George and Jim placed on a rough board seat front of them, and Phineas mounted in front.

"Farewell, my friends," said Simeon, from without.

"God bless you!" answered all from within.

And the wagon drove off, rattling and jolting over the frozen road.

There was no opportunity for conversation, on account of the roughness of the way and the noise of the wheels. The vehicle, therefore, rumbled on, through long, dark stretches of woodland,—over wide dreary plains,—up hills, and down valleys,—and on, on, on they jogged, hour after hour. The child soon fell asleep, and lay heavily in his mother's lap. The poor, frightened old woman at last forgot her fears; and, even Eliza, as the night waned, found all her anxieties insufficient to keep her eyes from closing. Phineas seemed, on the whole, the briskest of the company, and beguiled his long drive with whistling certain very unquaker-like songs, as he went on.

But about three o'clock George's ear caught the hasty and decided click of a horse's hoof coming behind them at some distance and jogged Phineas by the elbow. Phineas pulled up his horses, and listened.

"That must be Michael," he said; "I think I know the sound of his gallop;" and he rose up and stretched his head anxiously back over the road.

A man riding in hot haste was now dimly descried at the top of a distant hill.

"There he is, I do believe!" said Phineas. George and Jim both sprang out of the wagon before they knew what they were doing. All stood intensely silent, with their faces turned towards the expected messenger. On he came. Now he went down into a valley, where they could not see him; but they heard the sharp, hasty tramp, rising nearer and nearer; at last they saw him emerge on the top of an eminence, within hail.

"Yes, that's Michael!" said Phineas; and, raising his voice, "Halloa, there, Michael!"

"Phineas! is that thee?"

"Yes; what news—they coming?"

"Right on behind, eight or ten of them, hot with brandy, swearing and foaming like so many wolves."

And, just as he spoke, a breeze brought the faint sound of galloping horsemen towards them.

"In with you,—quick, boys, *in!*" said Phineas. "If you must fight, wait till I get you a piece ahead." And, with the word, both jumped in, and Phineas lashed the horses to a run, the horseman keeping close beside them. The wagon rattled, jumped, almost flew, over the frozen ground; but plainer, and still plainer, came the noise of pursuing horsemen behind. The women heard it, and, looking anxiously out, saw, far in the rear, on the brow of a distant hill, a party of men looming up against the red-streaked sky of early dawn. Another hill, and their pursuers had evidently caught sight of their wagon, whose white cloth-covered top made it conspicuous at some distance, and a loud yell of brutal triumph came forward on the wind. Eliza sickened, and strained her child closer to her bosom; the old woman prayed and groaned, and George and Jim clenched their pistols with the grasp of despair. The pursuers gained on them fast; the carriage made a sudden turn, and brought them near a ledge of a steep overhanging rock, that rose in an isolated ridge or clump in a large lot, which was, all around it, quite clear and smooth. This isolated pile, or range of rocks, rose up black and heavy against the brightening sky, and seemed to promise shelter and concealment. It was a place well known to Phineas, who had been familiar with the spot in his hunting days; and it was to gain this point he had been racing his horses.

"Now for it!" said he, suddenly checking his horses, and springing from his seat to the ground. "Out with you, in a twinkling, every one, and up into these rocks with me. Michael, thee tie thy horse to the wagon, and drive ahead to Amariah's and get him and his boys to come back and talk to these fellows."

In a twinkling they were all out of the carriage.

"There," said Phineas, catching up Harry, "you, each of you, see to the women; and run, *now* if you ever *did* run!"

They needed no exhortation. Quicker than we can say it, the whole party were over the fence, making with all speed for the rocks, while Michael, throwing himself from his horse, and fastening the bridle to the wagon, began driving it rapidly away.

"Come ahead," said Phineas, as they reached the rocks, and saw in the mingled starlight and dawn, the traces of a rude but plainly marked foot-path leading up among them; "this is one of our old hunting-dens. Come up!"

Phineas went before, springing up the rocks like a goat, with the boy in his arms. Jim came second, bearing his trembling old mother over his shoulder, and George and Eliza brought up the rear. The party of horsemen came up to the fence, and, with mingled shouts and oaths, were dismounting, to prepare to follow them. A few moments' scrambling brought them to the top of the ledge; the path then passed between a narrow defile, where only one could walk at a time, till suddenly they came to a rift or chasm more than a yard in breadth, and beyond which lay a pile of rocks, separate from the rest of the ledge, standing full thirty feet high, with its sides steep and perpendicular as those of a castle. Phineas easily leaped the chasm, and sat down the boy on a smooth, flat platform of crisp white moss, that covered the top of the rock.

"Over with you!" he called; "spring, now, once, for your lives!" said he, as one after another sprang across. Several fragments of loose stone formed a kind of breast-work, which sheltered their position from the observation of those below.

"Well, here we all are," said Phineas, peeping over the stone breast-work to watch the assailants, who were coming tumultuously up under the rocks. "Let 'em get us, if they can. Whoever comes here has to walk single file between those two rocks, in fair range of your pistols, boys, d'ye see?"

"I do see," said George! "and now, as this matter is ours, let us take all the risk, and do all the fighting."

"Thee's quite welcome to do the fighting, George," said Phineas, chewing some checkerberry-leaves as he spoke; "but I may have the fun of looking on, I suppose. But see, these fellows are kinder debating down there, and looking up, like hens when they are going to fly up on to the roost. Hadn't thee better give 'em a word of advice, before they come up, just to tell 'em handsomely they'll be shot if they do?"

The party beneath, now more apparent in the light of the dawn, consisted of our old acquaintances, Tom Loker and Marks, with two constables, and a posse consisting of such rowdies at the last tavern as could be engaged by a little brandy to go and help the fun of trapping a set of niggers.

"Well, Tom, yer coons are farly treed," said one.

"Yes, I see 'em go up right here," said Tom; "and here's a path. I'm for going right up. They can't jump down in a hurry, and it won't take long to ferret 'em out."

"But, Tom, they might fire at us from behind the rocks," said Marks. "That would be ugly, you know."

"Ugh!" said Tom, with a sneer. "Always for saving your skin, Marks! No danger! niggers are too plaguy scared!"

"I don't know why I *shouldn't* save my skin," said Marks. "It's the best I've got; and niggers *do* fight like the devil, sometimes."

At this moment, George appeared on the top of a rock above them, and, speaking in a calm, clear voice, said,

"Gentlemen, who are you, down there, and what do you want?"

"We want a party of runaway niggers," said Tom Loker. "One George Harris, and Eliza Harris, and their son, and Jim Selden, and an old woman. We've got the officers, here, and a warrant to take 'em; and we're going to have 'em, too. D'ye hear? An't you George Harris, that belongs to Mr. Harris, of Shelby county, Kentucky?"

"I am George Harris. A Mr. Harris, of Kentucky, did call me his property. But now I'm a free man, standing on God's free soil; and my wife and my child I claim as mine. Jim and his mother are here. We have arms to defend ourselves, and we mean to do it. You can come up, if you like; but the first one of you that comes within the range of our bullets is a dead man, and the next, and the next; and so on till the last."

"O, come! come!" said a short, puffy man, stepping forward, and blowing his nose as he did so. "Young man, this an't no kind of talk at all for you. You see, we're officers of justice. We've got the law on our side, and the power, and so forth; so you'd better give up peaceably, you see; for you'll certainly have to give up, at last."

"I know very well that you've got the law on your side, and the power," said George, bitterly. "You mean to take my wife to sell in New Orleans, and put my boy like a calf in a trader's pen, and send Jim's old mother to the brute that whipped and abused her before, because he couldn't abuse her son. You want to send Jim and me back to be whipped and tortured, and ground down under the heels of them that you call masters; and your laws *will* bear you out in it,—more shame for you and them! But you haven't got us. We don't own your laws; we don't own your country; we stand here as free, under God's sky, as you are; and, by the great God that made us, we'll fight for our liberty till we die."

CHAPTER XVII

George stood out in fair sight, on the top of the rock, as he made his declaration of independence; the glow of dawn gave a flush to his swarthy cheek, and bitter indignation and despair gave fire to his dark eye; and, as if appealing from man to the justice of God, he raised his hand to heaven as he spoke.

If it had been only a Hungarian youth, now bravely defending in some mountain fastness the retreat of fugitives escaping from Austria into America, this would have been sublime heroism; but as it was a youth of African descent, defending the retreat of fugitives through America into Canada, of course we are too well instructed and patriotic to see any heroism in it; and if any of our readers do, they must do it on their own private responsibility. When despairing Hungarian fugitives make their way, against all the search-warrants and authorities of their lawful government, to America, press and political cabinet ring with applause and welcome. When despairing African fugitives do the same thing,—it is—what *is* it?

Be it as it may, it is certain that the attitude, eye, voice, manner, of the speaker for a moment struck the party below to silence. There is something in boldness and determination that for a time hushes even the rudest nature. Marks was the only one who remained wholly untouched. He was deliberately cocking his pistol, and, in the momentary silence that followed George's speech, he fired at him.

"Ye see ye get jist as much for him dead as alive in Kentucky," he said coolly, as he wiped his pistol on his coat-sleeve.

George sprang backward,—Eliza uttered a shriek,—the ball had passed close to his hair, had nearly grazed the cheek of his wife, and struck in the tree above.

"It's nothing, Eliza," said George, quickly.

"Thee'd better keep out of sight, with thy speechifying," said Phineas; "they're mean scamps."

"Now, Jim," said George, "look that your pistols are all right, and watch that pass with me. The first man that shows himself I fire at; you take the second, and so on. It won't do, you know, to waste two shots on one."

"But what if you don't hit?"

"I *shall* hit," said George, coolly.

"Good! now, there's stuff in that fellow," muttered Phineas, between his teeth.

The party below, after Marks had fired, stood, for a moment, rather undecided.

"I think you must have hit some on 'em," said one of the men. "I heard a squeal!"

"I'm going right up for one," said Tom. "I never was afraid of niggers, and I an't going to be now. Who goes after?" he said, springing up the rocks.

George heard the words distinctly. He drew up his pistol, examined it, pointed it towards that point in the defile where the first man would appear.

One of the most courageous of the party followed Tom, and, the way being thus made, the whole party began pushing up the rock,—the hindermost pushing the front ones faster than they would have gone of themselves. On they came, and in a moment the burly form of Tom appeared in sight, almost at the verge of the chasm.

George fired,—the shot entered his side,—but, though wounded, he would not retreat, but, with a yell like that of a mad bull, he was leaping right across the chasm into the party.

"Friend," said Phineas, suddenly stepping to the front, and meeting him with a push from his long arms, "thee isn't wanted here."

Down he fell into the chasm, crackling down among trees, bushes, logs, loose stones, till he lay bruised and groaning thirty feet below. The fall might have killed him, had it not been broken and moderated by his clothes catching in the branches of a large tree; but he came down with some force, however,—more than was at all agreeable or convenient.

"Lord help us, they are perfect devils!" said Marks, heading the retreat down the rocks with much more of a will than he had joined the ascent, while all the party came tumbling precipitately after him,—the fat constable, in particular, blowing and puffing in a very energetic manner.

"I say, fellers," said Marks, "you jist go round and pick up Tom, there, while I run and get on to my horse to go back for help,—that's you;" and, without minding the hootings and jeers of his company, Marks was as good as his word, and was soon seen galloping away.

"Was ever such a sneaking varmint?" said one of the men; "to come on his business, and he clear out and leave us this yer way!"

"Well, we must pick up that feller," said another. "Cuss me if I much care whether he is dead or alive."

The men, led by the groans of Tom, scrambled and crackled through stumps, logs and bushes, to where that hero lay groaning and swearing with alternate vehemence.

"Ye keep it agoing pretty loud, Tom," said one. "Ye much hurt?"

"Don't know. Get me up, can't ye? Blast that infernal Quaker! If it hadn't been for him, I'd a pitched some on 'em down here, to see how they liked it."

With much labor and groaning, the fallen hero was assisted to rise; and, with one holding him up under each shoulder, they got him as far as the horses.

"If you could only get me a mile back to that ar tavern. Give me a handkerchief or something, to stuff into this place, and stop this infernal bleeding."

George looked over the rocks, and saw them trying to lift the burly form of Tom into the saddle. After two or three ineffectual attempts, he reeled, and fell heavily to the ground.

"O, I hope he isn't killed!" said Eliza, who, with all the party, stood watching the proceeding.

"Why not?" said Phineas; "serves him right."

"Because after death comes the judgment," said Eliza.

"Yes," said the old woman, who had been groaning and praying, in her Methodist fashion, during all the encounter, "it's an awful case for the poor crittur's soul."

"On my word, they're leaving him, I do believe," said Phineas.

CHAPTER XVII

It was true; for after some appearance of irresolution and consultation, the whole party got on their horses and rode away. When they were quite out of sight, Phineas began to bestir himself.

"Well, we must go down and walk a piece," he said. "I told Michael to go forward and bring help, and be along back here with the wagon; but we shall have to walk a piece along the road, I reckon, to meet them. The Lord grant he be along soon! It's early in the day; there won't be much travel afoot yet a while; we an't much more than two miles from our stopping-place. If the road hadn't been so rough last night, we could have outrun 'em entirely."

As the party neared the fence, they discovered in the distance, along the road, their own wagon coming back, accompanied by some men on horseback.

"Well, now, there's Michael, and Stephen and Amariah," exclaimed Phineas, joyfully. "Now we *are* made—as safe as if we'd got there."

"Well, do stop, then," said Eliza, "and do something for that poor man; he's groaning dreadfully."

"It would be no more than Christian," said George; "let's take him up and carry him on."

"And doctor him up among the Quakers!" said Phineas; "pretty well, that! Well, I don't care if we do. Here, let's have a look at him;" and Phineas, who in the course of his hunting and backwoods life had acquired some rude experience of surgery, kneeled down by the wounded man, and began a careful examination of his condition.

"Marks," said Tom, feebly, "is that you, Marks?"

"No; I reckon 'tan't friend," said Phineas. "Much Marks cares for thee, if his own skin's safe. He's off, long ago."

"I believe I'm done for," said Tom. "The cussed sneaking dog, to leave me to die alone! My poor old mother always told me 't would be so."

"La sakes! jist hear the poor crittur. He's got a mammy, now," said the old negress. "I can't help kinder pityin' on him."

"Softly, softly; don't thee snap and snarl, friend," said Phineas, as Tom winced and pushed his hand away. "Thee has no chance, unless I stop the bleeding." And Phineas busied himself with making some off-hand surgical arrangements with his own pocket-handkerchief, and such as could be mustered in the company.

"You pushed me down there," said Tom, faintly.

"Well if I hadn't thee would have pushed us down, thee sees," said Phineas, as he stooped to apply his bandage. "There, there,—let me fix this bandage. We mean well to thee; we bear no malice. Thee shall be taken to a house where they'll nurse thee first rate, well as thy own mother could."

Tom groaned, and shut his eyes. In men of his class, vigor and resolution are entirely a physical matter, and ooze out with the flowing of the blood; and the gigantic fellow really looked piteous in his helplessness.

The other party now came up. The seats were taken out of the wagon. The buffalo-skins, doubled in fours, were spread all along one side, and four men, with great difficulty, lifted the heavy form of Tom into it. Before he was gotten in, he fainted entirely. The old negress, in the abundance of her compassion, sat down on the bottom, and took his head in her lap. Eliza, George and Jim, bestowed themselves, as well as they could, in the remaining space and the whole party set forward.

"What do you think of him?" said George, who sat by Phineas in front.

"Well it's only a pretty deep flesh-wound; but, then, tumbling and scratching down that place didn't help him much. It has bled pretty freely,—pretty much drained him out, courage and all,—but he'll get over it, and may be learn a thing or two by it."

"I'm glad to hear you say so," said George. "It would always be a heavy thought to me, if I'd caused his death, even in a just cause."

"Yes," said Phineas, "killing is an ugly operation, any way they'll fix it,—man or beast. I've seen a buck that was shot down and a dying, look that way on a feller with his eye, that it reely most made a feller feel wicked for killing on him; and human creatures is a more serious consideration yet, bein', as thy wife says, that the judgment comes to 'em after death. So I don't know as our people's notions on these matters is too strict; and, considerin' how I was raised, I fell in with them pretty considerably."

"What shall you do with this poor fellow?" said George.

"O, carry him along to Amariah's. There's old Grandmam Stephens there,—Dorcas, they call her,—she's most an amazin' nurse. She takes to nursing real natural, and an't never better suited than when she gets a sick body to tend. We may reckon on turning him over to her for a fortnight or so."

A ride of about an hour more brought the party to a neat farmhouse, where the weary travellers were received to an abundant breakfast. Tom Loker was soon carefully deposited in a much cleaner and softer bed than he had ever been in the habit of occupying. His wound was carefully dressed and bandaged, and he lay languidly opening and shutting his eyes on the white window-curtains and gently-gliding figures of his sick room, like a weary child. And here, for the present, we shall take our leave of one party.

CHAPTER XVIII

MISS OPHELIA'S EXPERIENCES AND OPINIONS

Our friend Tom, in his own simple musings, often compared his more fortunate lot, in the bondage into which he was cast, with that of Joseph in Egypt; and, in fact, as time went on, and he developed more and more under the eye of his master, the strength of the parallel increased.

St. Clare was indolent and careless of money. Hitherto the providing and marketing had been principally done by Adolph, who was, to the full, as careless and extravagant as his master; and, between them both, they had carried on the dispersing process with great alacrity. Accustomed, for many years, to regard his master's property as his own care, Tom saw, with an uneasiness he could scarcely repress, the wasteful expenditure of the establishment; and, in the quiet, indirect way which his class often acquire, would sometimes make his own suggestions.

St. Clare at first employed him occasionally; but, struck with his soundness of mind and good business capacity, he confided in him more and more, till gradually all the marketing and providing for the family were intrusted to him.

"No, no, Adolph," he said, one day, as Adolph was deprecating the passing of power out of his hands; "let Tom alone. You only understand what you want; Tom understands cost and come to; and there may be some end to money, bye and bye if we don't let somebody do that."

Trusted to an unlimited extent by a careless master, who handed him a bill without looking at it, and pocketed the change without counting it, Tom had every facility and temptation to dishonesty; and nothing but an impregnable simplicity of nature, strengthened by Christian faith, could have kept him from it. But, to that nature, the very unbounded trust reposed in him was bond and seal for the most scrupulous accuracy.

With Adolph the case had been different. Thoughtless and self-indulgent, and unrestrained by a master who found it easier to indulge than to regulate, he had fallen into an absolute confusion as to *meum tuum* with regard to himself and his master, which sometimes troubled even St. Clare. His own good sense taught him that such a training of his servants was unjust and dangerous. A sort of chronic remorse went with him everywhere, although not strong enough to make any decided change in his course; and this very remorse reacted again into indulgence. He passed lightly over the most serious faults, because he told himself that, if he had done his part, his dependents had not fallen into them.

Tom regarded his gay, airy, handsome young master with an odd mixture of fealty, reverence, and fatherly solicitude. That he never read the Bible; never went to church; that he jested and made free with any and every thing that came in the way of his wit; that he spent his Sunday evenings at the opera or theatre; that he went to wine parties, and clubs, and suppers, oftener than was at all expedient,—were all things that Tom could see as plainly as anybody, and on which he based a conviction that "Mas'r wasn't a Christian;"—a conviction, however, which he would have been very slow to express to any one else, but on which he founded many prayers, in his own simple fashion, when he was by himself in his little dormitory. Not that Tom had not his own way of speaking his mind occasionally, with something of the tact often observable in his class; as, for example, the very day after the Sabbath we have described, St. Clare was invited out to a convivial party of choice spirits, and was helped home, between one and two o'clock at night, in a condition when the physical had decidedly attained the upper hand of the intellectual. Tom and Adolph assisted to get him composed for the night, the latter in high spirits, evidently regarding the matter as a good joke, and laughing heartily at the rusticity of Tom's horror, who really was simple enough to lie awake most of the rest of the night, praying for his young master.

"Well, Tom, what are you waiting for?" said St. Clare, the next day, as he sat in his library, in dressing-gown and slippers. St. Clare had just been entrusting Tom with some money, and various commissions. "Isn't all right there, Tom?" he added, as Tom still stood waiting.

"I'm 'fraid not, Mas'r," said Tom, with a grave face.

St. Clare laid down his paper, and set down his coffee-cup, and looked at Tom.

"Why Tom, what's the case? You look as solemn as a coffin."

"I feel very bad, Mas'r. I allays have thought that Mas'r would be good to everybody."

"Well, Tom, haven't I been? Come, now, what do you want? There's something you haven't got, I suppose, and this is the preface."

"Mas'r allays been good to me. I haven't nothing to complain of on that head. But there is one that Mas'r isn't good to."

"Why, Tom, what's got into you? Speak out; what do you mean?"

"Last night, between one and two, I thought so. I studied upon the matter then. Mas'r isn't good to *himself*."

Tom said this with his back to his master, and his hand on the door-knob. St. Clare felt his face flush crimson, but he laughed.

"O, that's all, is it?" he said, gayly.

"All!" said Tom, turning suddenly round and falling on his knees. "O, my dear young Mas'r; I'm 'fraid it will be *loss of all—all*—body and soul. The good Book says, 'it biteth like a serpent and stingeth like an adder!' my dear Mas'r!"

Tom's voice choked, and the tears ran down his cheeks.

"You poor, silly fool!" said St. Clare, with tears in his own eyes. "Get up, Tom. I'm not worth crying over."

But Tom wouldn't rise, and looked imploring.

"Well, I won't go to any more of their cursed nonsense, Tom," said St. Clare; "on my honor, I won't. I don't know why I haven't stopped long ago. I've always despised *it*, and myself for it,—so now, Tom, wipe up your eyes, and go about your errands. Come, come," he added, "no blessings. I'm not so wonderfully good, now," he said, as he gently pushed Tom to the door. "There, I'll pledge my honor to you, Tom, you don't see me so again," he said; and Tom went off, wiping his eyes, with great satisfaction.

"I'll keep my faith with him, too," said St. Clare, as he closed the door.

And St. Clare did so,—for gross sensualism, in any form, was not the peculiar temptation of his nature.

But, all this time, who shall detail the tribulations manifold of our friend Miss Ophelia, who had begun the labors of a Southern housekeeper?

There is all the difference in the world in the servants of Southern establishments, according to the character and capacity of the mistresses who have brought them up.

South as well as north, there are women who have an extraordinary talent for command, and tact in educating. Such are enabled, with apparent ease, and without severity, to subject to their will, and bring into harmonious and systematic order, the various members of their small estate,—to regulate their peculiarities, and so balance and compensate the deficiencies of one by the excess of another, as to produce a harmonious and orderly system.

Such a housekeeper was Mrs. Shelby, whom we have already described; and such our readers may remember to have met with. If they are not common at the South, it is because they are not common in the world. They are to be found there as often as anywhere; and, when existing, find in that peculiar state of society a brilliant opportunity to exhibit their domestic talent.

Such a housekeeper Marie St. Clare was not, nor her mother before her. Indolent and childish, unsystematic and improvident, it was not to be expected that servants trained under her care should not be so likewise; and she had very justly described to Miss Ophelia the state of confusion she would find in the family, though she had not ascribed it to the proper cause.

The first morning of her regency, Miss Ophelia was up at four o'clock; and having attended to all the adjustments of her own chamber, as she had done ever since she came there, to the great amazement of the chambermaid, she prepared for a vigorous onslaught on the cupboards and closets of the establishment of which she had the keys.

The store-room, the linen-presses, the china-closet, the kitchen and cellar, that day, all went under an awful review. Hidden things of darkness were brought to light to an extent that alarmed all the principalities and powers of kitchen and chamber, and caused many wonderings and murmurings about "dese yer northern ladies" from the domestic cabinet.

Old Dinah, the head cook, and principal of all rule and authority in the kitchen department, was filled with wrath at what she considered an invasion of privilege. No feudal baron in *Magna Charta* times could have more thoroughly resented some incursion of the crown.

Dinah was a character in her own way, and it would be injustice to her memory not to give the reader a little idea of her. She was a native and essential cook, as much as Aunt Chloe,—cooking being an indigenous talent of the African race; but Chloe was a trained and methodical one, who moved in an orderly domestic harness, while Dinah was a self-taught genius, and, like geniuses in general, was positive, opinionated and erratic, to the last degree.

Like a certain class of modern philosophers, Dinah perfectly scorned logic and reason in every shape, and always took refuge in intuitive certainty; and here she was perfectly impregnable. No possible amount of talent, or authority, or explanation, could ever make her believe that any other way was better than her own, or that the course she had pursued in the smallest matter could be in the least modified. This had been a conceded point with her old mistress, Marie's mother; and "Miss Marie," as Dinah always called her young mistress, even after her marriage, found it easier to submit than contend; and so Dinah had ruled supreme. This was the easier, in that she was perfect mistress of that diplomatic art which unites the utmost subservience of manner with the utmost inflexibility as to measure.

Dinah was mistress of the whole art and mystery of excuse-making, in all its branches. Indeed, it was an axiom with her that the cook can do no wrong; and a cook in a Southern kitchen finds abundance of heads and shoulders on which to lay off every sin and frailty, so as to maintain her own immaculateness entire. If any part of the dinner was a failure, there were fifty indisputably good reasons for it; and it was the fault undeniably of fifty other people, whom Dinah berated with unsparing zeal.

But it was very seldom that there was any failure in Dinah's last results. Though her mode of doing everything was peculiarly meandering and circuitous, and without any sort of calculation as to time and place,—though her kitchen generally looked as if it had been arranged by a hurricane blowing through it, and she had about as many places for each cooking utensil as there were days in the year,—yet, if one would have patience to wait her own good time, up would come her dinner in perfect order, and in a style of preparation with which an epicure could find no fault.

It was now the season of incipient preparation for dinner. Dinah, who required large intervals of reflection and repose, and was studious of ease in all her arrangements, was seated on the kitchen floor, smoking a short, stumpy pipe, to which she was much addicted, and which she always kindled up, as a sort of censer, whenever she felt the need of an inspiration in her arrangements. It was Dinah's mode of invoking the domestic Muses.

Seated around her were various members of that rising race with which a Southern household abounds, engaged in shelling peas, peeling potatoes, picking pin-feathers out of fowls, and other preparatory arrangements,—Dinah every once in a while interrupting her meditations to give a poke, or a rap on the head, to some of the young operators, with the pudding-stick that lay by her side. In fact, Dinah ruled over the woolly heads of the younger members with a rod of iron, and seemed to consider them born for no earthly purpose but to "save her steps," as she phrased it. It was the spirit of the system under which she had grown up, and she carried it out to its full extent.

Miss Ophelia, after passing on her reformatory tour through all the other parts of the establishment, now entered the kitchen. Dinah had heard, from various sources, what was going on, and resolved to stand on defensive and conservative ground,—mentally determined to oppose and ignore every new measure, without any actual observable contest.

The kitchen was a large brick-floored apartment, with a great old-fashioned fireplace stretching along one side of it,—an arrangement which St. Clare had vainly tried to persuade Dinah to exchange for the convenience of a modern cook-stove. Not she. No Puseyite,[1] or conservative of any school, was ever more inflexibly attached to time-honored inconveniences than Dinah.

When St. Clare had first returned from the north, impressed with the system and order of his uncle's kitchen arrangements, he had largely provided his own with an array of cupboards, drawers, and various apparatus, to induce systematic regulation, under the sanguine illusion that it would be of any possible assistance to Dinah in her arrangements. He might as well have provided them for a squirrel or a magpie. The more drawers and closets there were, the more hiding-holes could Dinah make for the accommodation of old rags, hair-combs, old shoes, ribbons, cast-off artificial flowers, and other articles of *vertu*, wherein her soul delighted.

When Miss Ophelia entered the kitchen Dinah did not rise, but smoked on in sublime tranquillity, regarding her movements obliquely out of the corner of her eye, but apparently intent only on the operations around her.

Miss Ophelia commenced opening a set of drawers.

"What is this drawer for, Dinah?" she said.

"It's handy for most anything, Missis," said Dinah. So it appeared to be. From the variety it contained, Miss Ophelia pulled out first a fine damask table-cloth stained with blood, having evidently been used to envelop some raw meat.

"What's this, Dinah? You don't wrap up meat in your mistress' best table-cloths?"

"O Lor, Missis, no; the towels was all a missin'—so I jest did it. I laid out to wash that a,—that's why I put it thar."

"Shif less!" said Miss Ophelia to herself, proceeding to tumble over the drawer, where she found a nutmeg-grater and two or three nutmegs, a Methodist hymn-book, a couple of soiled Madras handkerchiefs, some yarn and knitting-

---

[1] Edward Bouverie Pusey (1800-1882), champion of the orthodoxy of revealed religion, defender of the Oxford movement, and Regius professor of Hebrew and Canon of Christ Church, Oxford.

work, a paper of tobacco and a pipe, a few crackers, one or two gilded china-saucers with some pomade in them, one or two thin old shoes, a piece of flannel carefully pinned up enclosing some small white onions, several damask table-napkins, some coarse crash towels, some twine and darning-needles, and several broken papers, from which sundry sweet herbs were sifting into the drawer.

"Where do you keep your nutmegs, Dinah?" said Miss Ophelia, with the air of one who prayed for patience.

"Most anywhar, Missis; there's some in that cracked tea-cup, up there, and there's some over in that ar cupboard."

"Here are some in the grater," said Miss Ophelia, holding them up.

"Laws, yes, I put 'em there this morning,—I likes to keep my things handy," said Dinah. "You, Jake! what are you stopping for! You'll cotch it! Be still, thar!" she added, with a dive of her stick at the criminal.

"What's this?" said Miss Ophelia, holding up the saucer of pomade.

"Laws, it's my har *grease*;—I put it thar to have it handy."

"Do you use your mistress' best saucers for that?"

"Law! it was cause I was driv, and in sich a hurry;—I was gwine to change it this very day."

"Here are two damask table-napkins."

"Them table-napkins I put thar, to get 'em washed out, some day."

"Don't you have some place here on purpose for things to be washed?"

"Well, Mas'r St. Clare got dat ar chest, he said, for dat; but I likes to mix up biscuit and hev my things on it some days, and then it an't handy a liftin' up the lid."

"Why don't you mix your biscuits on the pastry-table, there?"

"Law, Missis, it gets sot so full of dishes, and one thing and another, der an't no room, noway—"

"But you should *wash* your dishes, and clear them away."

"Wash my dishes!" said Dinah, in a high key, as her wrath began to rise over her habitual respect of manner; "what does ladies know 'bout work, I want to know? When 'd Mas'r ever get his dinner, if I vas to spend all my time a washin' and a puttin' up dishes? Miss Marie never telled me so, nohow."

"Well, here are these onions."

"Laws, yes!" said Dinah; "thar *is* whar I put 'em, now. I couldn't 'member. Them 's particular onions I was a savin' for dis yer very stew. I'd forgot they was in dat ar old flannel."

Miss Ophelia lifted out the sifting papers of sweet herbs.

"I wish Missis wouldn't touch dem ar. I likes to keep my things where I knows whar to go to 'em," said Dinah, rather decidedly.

"But you don't want these holes in the papers."

"Them 's handy for siftin' on 't out," said Dinah.

"But you see it spills all over the drawer."

"Laws, yes! if Missis will go a tumblin' things all up so, it will. Missis has spilt lots dat ar way," said Dinah, coming uneasily to the drawers. "If Missis only will go up stars till my clarin' up time comes, I'll have everything right; but I can't do nothin' when ladies is round, a henderin'. You, Sam, don't you gib the baby dat ar sugar-bowl! I'll crack ye over, if ye don't mind!"

"I'm going through the kitchen, and going to put everything in order, *once*, Dinah; and then I'll expect you to *keep* it so."

"Lor, now! Miss Phelia; dat ar an't no way for ladies to do. I never did see ladies doin' no sich; my old Missis nor Miss Marie never did, and I don't see no kinder need on 't;" and Dinah stalked indignantly about, while Miss Ophelia piled and sorted dishes, emptied dozens of scattering bowls of sugar into one receptacle, sorted napkins, table-cloths, and towels, for washing; washing, wiping, and arranging with her own hands, and with a speed and alacrity which perfectly amazed Dinah.

"Lor now! if dat ar de way dem northern ladies do, dey an't ladies, nohow," she said to some of her satellites, when at a safe hearing distance. "I has things as straight as anybody, when my clarin' up times comes; but I don't want ladies round, a henderin', and getting my things all where I can't find 'em."

To do Dinah justice, she had, at irregular periods, paroxyms of reformation and arrangement, which she called "clarin' up times," when she would begin with great zeal, and turn every drawer and closet wrong side outward, on to the floor or tables, and make the ordinary confusion seven-fold more confounded. Then she would light her pipe, and leisurely go over her arrangements, looking things over, and discoursing upon them; making all the young fry scour most vigorously on the tin things, and keeping up for several hours a most energetic state of confusion, which she would explain to the satisfaction of all inquirers, by the remark that she was a "clarin' up." "She couldn't hev things a gwine on so as they had been, and she was gwine to make these yer young ones keep better order;" for Dinah herself, somehow, indulged the illusion that she, herself, was the soul of order, and it was only the *young uns*, and the everybody else in the house, that were the cause of anything that fell short of perfection in this respect. When all the tins were scoured, and the tables scrubbed snowy white, and everything that could offend tucked out of sight in holes and corners, Dinah would dress herself up in a smart dress, clean apron, and high, brilliant Madras turban, and tell all marauding "young uns" to keep out of the kitchen, for she was gwine to have things kept nice. Indeed, these periodic seasons were often an inconvenience to the whole household; for Dinah would contract such an immoderate attachment to her scoured tin, as to insist upon it that it shouldn't be used again for any possible purpose,—at least, till the ardor of the "clarin' up" period abated.

Miss Ophelia, in a few days, thoroughly reformed every department of the house to a systematic pattern; but her labors in all departments that depended on the cooperation of servants were like those of Sisyphus or the Danaides. In despair, she one day appealed to St. Clare.

"There is no such thing as getting anything like a system in this family!"

"To be sure, there isn't," said St. Clare.

"Such shiftless management, such waste, such confusion, I never saw!"

"I dare say you didn't."

"You would not take it so coolly, if you were housekeeper."

"My dear cousin, you may as well understand, once for all, that we masters are divided into two classes, oppressors and oppressed. We who are good-natured and hate severity make up our minds to a good deal of inconvenience. If we *will keep* a shambling, loose, untaught set in the community, for our convenience, why, we must take the consequence. Some rare cases I have seen, of persons, who, by a peculiar tact, can produce order and system without severity; but I'm not one of them,—and so I made up my mind, long ago, to let things go just as they do. I will not have the poor devils thrashed and cut to pieces, and they know it,—and, of course, they know the staff is in their own hands."

"But to have no time, no place, no order,—all going on in this shiftless way!"

"My dear Vermont, you natives up by the North Pole set an extravagant value on time! What on earth is the use of time to a fellow who has twice as much of it as he knows what to do with? As to order and system, where there is nothing to be done but to lounge on the sofa and read, an hour sooner or later in breakfast or dinner isn't of much account. Now, there's Dinah gets you a capital dinner,—soup, ragout, roast fowl, dessert, ice-creams and all,—and she creates it all out of chaos and old night down there, in that kitchen. I think it really sublime, the way she manages. But, Heaven bless us! if we are to go down there, and view all the smoking and squatting about, and hurryscurryation of the preparatory process, we should never eat more! My good cousin, absolve yourself from that! It's more than a Catholic penance, and does no more good. You'll only lose your own temper, and utterly confound Dinah. Let her go her own way."

"But, Augustine, you don't know how I found things."

"Don't I? Don't I know that the rolling-pin is under her bed, and the nutmeg-grater in her pocket with her tobacco,—that there are sixty-five different sugar-bowls, one in every hole in the house,—that she washes dishes with a dinner-napkin one day, and with a fragment of an old petticoat the next? But the upshot is, she gets up glorious dinners, makes superb coffee; and you must judge her as warriors and statesmen are judged, *by her success*."

"But the waste,—the expense!"

"O, well! Lock everything you can, and keep the key. Give out by driblets, and never inquire for odds and ends,—it isn't best."

"That troubles me, Augustine. I can't help feeling as if these servants were not *strictly honest*. Are you sure they can be relied on?"

Augustine laughed immoderately at the grave and anxious face with which Miss Ophelia propounded the question.

"O, cousin, that's too good,—*honest!*—as if that's a thing to be expected! Honest!—why, of course, they arn't. Why should they be? What upon earth is to make them so?"

"Why don't you instruct?"

"Instruct! O, fiddlestick! What instructing do you think I should do? I look like it! As to Marie, she has spirit enough, to be sure, to kill off a whole plantation, if I'd let her manage; but she wouldn't get the cheatery out of them."

"Are there no honest ones?"

"Well, now and then one, whom Nature makes so impracticably simple, truthful and faithful, that the worst possible influence can't destroy it. But, you see, from the mother's breast the colored child feels and sees that there are none but underhand ways open to it. It can get along no other way with its parents, its mistress, its young master and missie play-fellows. Cunning and deception become necessary, inevitable habits. It isn't fair to expect anything else of him. He ought not to be punished for it. As to honesty, the slave is kept in that dependent, semi-childish state, that there is no making him realize the rights of property, or feel that his master's goods are not his own, if he can get them. For my part, I don't see how they *can* be honest. Such a fellow as Tom, here, is,—is a moral miracle!"

"And what becomes of their souls?" said Miss Ophelia.

"That isn't my affair, as I know of," said St. Clare; "I am only dealing in facts of the present life. The fact is, that the whole race are pretty generally understood to be turned over to the devil, for our benefit, in this world, however it may turn out in another!"

"This is perfectly horrible!" said Miss Ophelia; "you ought to be ashamed of yourselves!"

"I don't know as I am. We are in pretty good company, for all that," said St. Clare, "as people in the broad road generally are. Look at the high and the low, all the world over, and it's the same story,—the lower class used up, body, soul and spirit, for the good of the upper. It is so in England; it is so everywhere; and yet all Christendom stands aghast, with virtuous indignation, because we do the thing in a little different shape from what they do it."

"It isn't so in Vermont."

"Ah, well, in New England, and in the free States, you have the better of us, I grant. But there's the bell; so, Cousin, let us for a while lay aside our sectional prejudices, and come out to dinner."

As Miss Ophelia was in the kitchen in the latter part of the afternoon, some of the sable children called out, "La, sakes! thar's Prue a coming, grunting along like she allers does."

A tall, bony colored woman now entered the kitchen, bearing on her head a basket of rusks and hot rolls.

"Ho, Prue! you've come," said Dinah.

Prue had a peculiar scowling expression of countenance, and a sullen, grumbling voice. She set down her basket, squatted herself down, and resting her elbows on her knees said,

"O Lord! I wish't I 's dead!"

"Why do you wish you were dead?" said Miss Ophelia.

"I'd be out o' my misery," said the woman, gruffly, without taking her eyes from the floor.

"What need you getting drunk, then, and cutting up, Prue?" said a spruce quadroon chambermaid, dangling, as she spoke, a pair of coral ear-drops.

The woman looked at her with a sour surly glance.

"Maybe you'll come to it, one of these yer days. I'd be glad to see you, I would; then you'll be glad of a drop, like me, to forget your misery."

"Come, Prue," said Dinah, "let's look at your rusks. Here's Missis will pay for them."

Miss Ophelia took out a couple of dozen.

"Thar's some tickets in that ar old cracked jug on the top shelf," said Dinah. "You, Jake, climb up and get it down."

"Tickets,—what are they for?" said Miss Ophelia.

"We buy tickets of her Mas'r, and she gives us bread for 'em."

"And they counts my money and tickets, when I gets home, to see if I 's got the change; and if I han't, they half kills me."

"And serves you right," said Jane, the pert chambermaid, "if you will take their money to get drunk on. That's what she does, Missis."

"And that's what I *will* do,—I can't live no other ways,—drink and forget my misery."

"You are very wicked and very foolish," said Miss Ophelia, "to steal your master's money to make yourself a brute with."

"It's mighty likely, Missis; but I will do it,—yes, I will. O Lord! I wish I 's dead, I do,—I wish I 's dead, and out of my misery!" and slowly and stiffly the old creature rose, and got her basket on her head again; but before she went out, she looked at the quadroon girl, who still stood playing with her ear-drops.

"Ye think ye're mighty fine with them ar, a frolickin' and a tossin' your head, and a lookin' down on everybody. Well, never mind,—you may live to be a poor, old, cut-up crittur, like me. Hope to the Lord ye will, I do; then see if ye won't drink,—drink,—drink,—yerself into torment; and sarve ye right, too—ugh!" and, with a malignant howl, the woman left the room.

"Disgusting old beast!" said Adolph, who was getting his master's shaving-water. "If I was her master, I'd cut her up worse than she is."

"Ye couldn't do that ar, no ways," said Dinah. "Her back's a far sight now,—she can't never get a dress together over it."

"I think such low creatures ought not to be allowed to go round to genteel families," said Miss Jane. "What do you think, Mr. St. Clare?" she said, coquettishly tossing her head at Adolph.

It must be observed that, among other appropriations from his master's stock, Adolph was in the habit of adopting his name and address; and that the style under which he moved, among the colored circles of New Orleans, was that of *Mr. St. Clare*.

"I'm certainly of your opinion, Miss Benoir," said Adolph.

Benoir was the name of Marie St. Clare's family, and Jane was one of her servants.

"Pray, Miss Benoir, may I be allowed to ask if those drops are for the ball, to-morrow night? They are certainly bewitching!"

"I wonder, now, Mr. St. Clare, what the impudence of you men will come to!" said Jane, tossing her pretty head 'til the ear-drops twinkled again. "I shan't dance with you for a whole evening, if you go to asking me any more questions."

"O, you couldn't be so cruel, now! I was just dying to know whether you would appear in your pink tarletane," said Adolph.

"What is it?" said Rosa, a bright, piquant little quadroon who came skipping down stairs at this moment.

"Why, Mr. St. Clare's so impudent!"

"On my honor," said Adolph, "I'll leave it to Miss Rosa now."

"I know he's always a saucy creature," said Rosa, poising herself on one of her little feet, and looking maliciously at Adolph. "He's always getting me so angry with him."

"O! ladies, ladies, you will certainly break my heart, between you," said Adolph. "I shall be found dead in my bed, some morning, and you'll have it to answer for."

"Do hear the horrid creature talk!" said both ladies, laughing immoderately.

"Come,—clar out, you! I can't have you cluttering up the kitchen," said Dinah; "in my way, foolin' round here."

"Aunt Dinah's glum, because she can't go to the ball," said Rosa.

"Don't want none o' your light-colored balls," said Dinah; "cuttin' round, makin' b'lieve you's white folks. Arter all, you's niggers, much as I am."

"Aunt Dinah greases her wool stiff, every day, to make it lie straight," said Jane.

"And it will be wool, after all," said Rosa, maliciously shaking down her long, silky curls.

"Well, in the Lord's sight, an't wool as good as har, any time?" said Dinah. "I'd like to have Missis say which is worth the most,—a couple such as you, or one like me. Get out wid ye, ye trumpery,—I won't have ye round!"

Here the conversation was interrupted in a two-fold manner. St. Clare's voice was heard at the head of the stairs, asking Adolph if he meant to stay all night with his shaving-water; and Miss Ophelia, coming out of the dining-room, said,

"Jane and Rosa, what are you wasting your time for, here? Go in and attend to your muslins."

Our friend Tom, who had been in the kitchen during the conversation with the old rusk-woman, had followed her out into the street. He saw her go on, giving every once in a while a suppressed groan. At last she set her basket down on a doorstep, and began arranging the old, faded shawl which covered her shoulders.

"I'll carry your basket a piece," said Tom, compassionately.

"Why should ye?" said the woman. "I don't want no help."

"You seem to be sick, or in trouble, or somethin'," said Tom.

"I an't sick," said the woman, shortly.

"I wish," said Tom, looking at her earnestly,—"I wish I could persuade you to leave off drinking. Don't you know it will be the ruin of ye, body and soul?"

"I knows I'm gwine to torment," said the woman, sullenly. "Ye don't need to tell me that ar. I 's ugly, I 's wicked,—I 's gwine straight to torment. O, Lord! I wish I 's thar!"

Tom shuddered at these frightful words, spoken with a sullen, impassioned earnestness.

"O, Lord have mercy on ye! poor crittur. Han't ye never heard of Jesus Christ?"

"Jesus Christ,—who's he?"

"Why, he's *the Lord*," said Tom.

"I think I've hearn tell o' the Lord, and the judgment and torment. I've heard o' that."

"But didn't anybody ever tell you of the Lord Jesus, that loved us poor sinners, and died for us?"

"Don't know nothin' 'bout that," said the woman; "nobody han't never loved me, since my old man died."

"Where was you raised?" said Tom.

"Up in Kentuck. A man kept me to breed chil'en for market, and sold 'em as fast as they got big enough; last of all, he sold me to a speculator, and my Mas'r got me o' him."

"What set you into this bad way of drinkin'?"

"To get shet o' my misery. I had one child after I come here; and I thought then I'd have one to raise, cause Mas'r wasn't a speculator. It was de peartest little thing! and Missis she seemed to think a heap on 't, at first; it never cried,—it was likely and fat. But Missis tuck sick, and I tended her; and I tuck the fever, and my milk all left me, and the child it pined to skin and bone, and Missis wouldn't buy milk for it. She wouldn't hear to me, when I telled her I hadn't milk. She said she knowed I could feed it on what other folks eat; and the child kinder pined, and cried, and cried, and cried, day and night, and got all gone to skin and bones, and Missis got sot agin it and she said 't wan't nothin' but crossness. She wished it was dead, she said; and she wouldn't let me have it o' nights, cause, she said, it kept me awake, and made me good for nothing. She made me sleep in her room; and I had to put it away off in a little kind o' garret, and thar it cried itself to death, one night. It did; and I tuck to drinkin', to keep its crying out of my ears! I did,—and I will drink! I will, if I do go to torment for it! Mas'r says I shall go to torment, and I tell him I've got thar now!"

"O, ye poor crittur!" said Tom, "han't nobody never telled ye how the Lord Jesus loved ye, and died for ye? Han't they telled ye that he'll help ye, and ye can go to heaven, and have rest, at last?"

"I looks like gwine to heaven," said the woman; "an't thar where white folks is gwine? S'pose they'd have me thar? I'd rather go to torment, and get away from Mas'r and Missis. I had *so*," she said, as with her usual groan, she got her basket on her head, and walked sullenly away.

CHAPTER XVIII

Tom turned, and walked sorrowfully back to the house. In the court he met little Eva,—a crown of tuberoses on her head, and her eyes radiant with delight.

"O, Tom! here you are. I'm glad I've found you. Papa says you may get out the ponies, and take me in my little new carriage," she said, catching his hand. "But what's the matter Tom?—you look sober."

"I feel bad, Miss Eva," said Tom, sorrowfully. "But I'll get the horses for you."

"But do tell me, Tom, what is the matter. I saw you talking to cross old Prue."

Tom, in simple, earnest phrase, told Eva the woman's history. She did not exclaim or wonder, or weep, as other children do. Her cheeks grew pale, and a deep, earnest shadow passed over her eyes. She laid both hands on her bosom, and sighed heavily.

VOLUME II

CHAPTER XIX

MISS OPHELIA'S EXPERIENCES AND OPINIONS CONTINUED

"Tom, you needn't get me the horses. I don't want to go," she said.

"Why not, Miss Eva?"

"These things sink into my heart, Tom," said Eva,—"they sink into my heart," she repeated, earnestly. "I don't want to go;" and she turned from Tom, and went into the house.

A few days after, another woman came, in old Prue's place, to bring the rusks; Miss Ophelia was in the kitchen.

"Lor!" said Dinah, "what's got Prue?"

"Prue isn't coming any more," said the woman, mysteriously.

"Why not?" said Dinah, "she an't dead, is she?"

"We doesn't exactly know. She's down cellar," said the woman, glancing at Miss Ophelia.

After Miss Ophelia had taken the rusks, Dinah followed the woman to the door.

"What *has* got Prue, any how?" she said.

The woman seemed desirous, yet reluctant, to speak, and answered, in low, mysterious tone.

"Well, you mustn't tell nobody, Prue, she got drunk agin,—and they had her down cellar,—and thar they left her all day,—and I hearn 'em saying that the *flies had got to her*,—and *she's dead*!"

Dinah held up her hands, and, turning, saw close by her side the spirit-like form of Evangeline, her large, mystic eyes dilated with horror, and every drop of blood driven from her lips and cheeks.

"Lor bless us! Miss Eva's gwine to faint away! What go us all, to let her har such talk? Her pa'll be rail mad."

"I shan't faint, Dinah," said the child, firmly; "and why shouldn't I hear it? It an't so much for me to hear it, as for poor Prue to suffer it."

"*Lor sakes*! it isn't for sweet, delicate young ladies, like you,—these yer stories isn't; it's enough to kill 'em!"

Eva sighed again, and walked up stairs with a slow and melancholy step.

Miss Ophelia anxiously inquired the woman's story. Dinah gave a very garrulous version of it, to which Tom added the particulars which he had drawn from her that morning.

"An abominable business,—perfectly horrible!" she exclaimed, as she entered the room where St. Clare lay reading his paper.

"Pray, what iniquity has turned up now?" said he.

"What now? why, those folks have whipped Prue to death!" said Miss Ophelia, going on, with great strength of detail, into the story, and enlarging on its most shocking particulars.

"I thought it would come to that, some time," said St. Clare, going on with his paper.

"Thought so!—an't you going to *do* anything about it?" said Miss Ophelia. "Haven't you got any *selectmen*, or anybody, to interfere and look after such matters?"

"It's commonly supposed that the *property* interest is a sufficient guard in these cases. If people choose to ruin their own possessions, I don't know what's to be done. It seems the poor creature was a thief and a drunkard; and so there won't be much hope to get up sympathy for her."

"It is perfectly outrageous,—it is horrid, Augustine! It will certainly bring down vengeance upon you."

"My dear cousin, I didn't do it, and I can't help it; I would, if I could. If low-minded, brutal people will act like themselves, what am I to do? they have absolute control; they are irresponsible despots. There would be no use in interfering; there is no law that amounts to anything practically, for such a case. The best we can do is to shut our eyes and ears, and let it alone. It's the only resource left us."

"How can you shut your eyes and ears? How can you let such things alone?"

"My dear child, what do you expect? Here is a whole class,—debased, uneducated, indolent, provoking,—put, without any sort of terms or conditions, entirely into the hands of such people as the majority in our world are; people who have neither consideration nor self-control, who haven't even an enlightened regard to their own interest,—for that's the case with the largest half of mankind. Of course, in a community so organized, what can a man of honorable and humane feelings do, but shut his eyes all he can, and harden his heart? I can't buy every poor wretch I see. I can't turn knight-errant, and undertake to redress every individual case of wrong in such a city as this. The most I can do is to try and keep out of the way of it."

St. Clare's fine countenance was for a moment overcast; he said,

"Come, cousin, don't stand there looking like one of the Fates; you've only seen a peep through the curtain,—a specimen of what is going on, the world over, in some shape or other. If we are to be prying and spying into all the dismals of life, we should have no heart to anything. 'T is like looking too close into the details of Dinah's kitchen;" and St. Clare lay back on the sofa, and busied himself with his paper.

CHAPTER XIX

Miss Ophelia sat down, and pulled out her knitting-work, and sat there grim with indignation. She knit and knit, but while she mused the fire burned; at last she broke out—"I tell you, Augustine, I can't get over things so, if you can. It's a perfect abomination for you to defend such a system,—that's *my* mind!"

"What now?" said St. Clare, looking up. "At it again, hey?"

"I say it's perfectly abominable for you to defend such a system!" said Miss Ophelia, with increasing warmth.

"*I* defend it, my dear lady? Who ever said I did defend it?" said St. Clare.

"Of course, you defend it,—you all do,—all you Southerners. What do you have slaves for, if you don't?"

"Are you such a sweet innocent as to suppose nobody in this world ever does what they don't think is right? Don't you, or didn't you ever, do anything that you did not think quite right?"

"If I do, I repent of it, I hope," said Miss Ophelia, rattling her needles with energy.

"So do I," said St. Clare, peeling his orange; "I'm repenting of it all the time."

"What do you keep on doing it for?"

"Didn't you ever keep on doing wrong, after you'd repented, my good cousin?"

"Well, only when I've been very much tempted," said Miss Ophelia.

"Well, I'm very much tempted," said St. Clare; "that's just my difficulty."

"But I always resolve I won't and I try to break off."

"Well, I have been resolving I won't, off and on, these ten years," said St. Clare; "but I haven't, some how, got clear. Have you got clear of all your sins, cousin?"

"Cousin Augustine," said Miss Ophelia, seriously, and laying down her knitting-work, "I suppose I deserve that you should reprove my short-comings. I know all you say is true enough; nobody else feels them more than I do; but it does seem to me, after all, there is some difference between me and you. It seems to me I would cut off my right hand sooner than keep on, from day to day, doing what I thought was wrong. But, then, my conduct is so inconsistent with my profession, I don't wonder you reprove me."

"O, now, cousin," said Augustine, sitting down on the floor, and laying his head back in her lap, "don't take on so awfully serious! You know what a good-for-nothing, saucy boy I always was. I love to poke you up,—that's all,—just to see you get earnest. I do think you are desperately, distressingly good; it tires me to death to think of it."

"But this is a serious subject, my boy, Auguste," said Miss Ophelia, laying her hand on his forehead.

"Dismally so," said he; "and I—well, I never want to talk seriously in hot weather. What with mosquitos and all, a fellow can't get himself up to any very sublime moral flights; and I believe," said St. Clare, suddenly rousing himself up, "there's a theory, now! I understand now why northern nations are always more virtuous than southern ones,—I see into that whole subject."

"O, Augustine, you are a sad rattle-brain!"

"Am I? Well, so I am, I suppose; but for once I will be serious, now; but you must hand me that basket of oranges;—you see, you'll have to 'stay me with flagons and comfort me with apples,' if I'm going to make this effort. Now," said Augustine, drawing the basket up, "I'll begin: When, in the course of human events, it becomes necessary for a fellow to hold two or three dozen of his fellow-worms in captivity, a decent regard to the opinions of society requires—"

"I don't see that you are growing more serious," said Miss Ophelia.

"Wait,—I'm coming on,—you'll hear. The short of the matter is, cousin," said he, his handsome face suddenly settling into an earnest and serious expression, "on this abstract question of slavery there can, as I think, be but one opinion. Planters, who have money to make by it,—clergymen, who have planters to please,—politicians, who want to rule by it,—may warp and bend language and ethics to a degree that shall astonish the world at their ingenuity; they can press nature and the Bible, and nobody knows what else, into the service; but, after all, neither they nor the world believe in it one particle the more. It comes from the devil, that's the short of it;—and, to my mind, it's a pretty respectable specimen of what he can do in his own line."

Miss Ophelia stopped her knitting, and looked surprised, and St. Clare, apparently enjoying her astonishment, went on.

"You seem to wonder; but if you will get me fairly at it, I'll make a clean breast of it. This cursed business, accursed of God and man, what is it? Strip it of all its ornament, run it down to the root and nucleus of the whole, and what is it? Why, because my brother Quashy is ignorant and weak, and I am intelligent and strong,—because I know how, and *can* do it,—therefore, I may steal all he has, keep it, and give him only such and so much as suits my fancy. Whatever is too hard, too dirty, too disagreeable, for me, I may set Quashy to doing. Because I don't like work, Quashy shall work. Because the sun burns me, Quashy shall stay in the sun. Quashy shall earn the money, and I will spend it. Quashy shall lie down in every puddle, that I may walk over dry-shod. Quashy shall do my will, and not his, all the days of his mortal life, and have such chance of getting to heaven, at last, as I find convenient. This I take to be about what slavery *is*. I defy anybody on earth to read our slave-code, as it stands in our law-books, and make anything else of it. Talk of the *abuses* of slavery! Humbug! The *thing itself* is the essence of all abuse! And the only reason why the land don't sink under it, like Sodom and Gomorrah, is because it is *used* in a way infinitely better than it is. For pity's sake, for shame's sake, because we are men born of women, and not savage beasts, many of us do not, and dare not,—we would *scorn* to use the full power which our savage laws put into our hands. And he who goes the furthest, and does the worst, only uses within limits the power that the law gives him."

St. Clare had started up, and, as his manner was when excited, was walking, with hurried steps, up and down the floor. His fine face, classic as that of a Greek statue, seemed actually to burn with the fervor of his feelings. His large blue eyes flashed, and he gestured with an unconscious eagerness. Miss Ophelia had never seen him in this mood before, and she sat perfectly silent.

"I declare to you," said he, suddenly stopping before his cousin "(It's no sort of use to talk or to feel on this subject), but I declare to you, there have been times when I have thought, if the whole country would sink, and hide all this injustice and misery from the light, I would willingly sink with it. When I have been travelling up and down on our boats, or about on my collecting tours, and reflected that every brutal, disgusting, mean, low-lived fellow I met, was allowed by our laws to become absolute despot of as many men, women and children, as he could cheat, steal, or gamble money enough to buy,—when I have seen such men in actual ownership of helpless children, of young girls and women,—I have been ready to curse my country, to curse the human race!"

"Augustine! Augustine!" said Miss Ophelia, "I'm sure you've said enough. I never, in my life, heard anything like this, even at the North."

"At the North!" said St. Clare, with a sudden change of expression, and resuming something of his habitual careless tone. "Pooh! your northern folks are cold-blooded; you are cool in everything! You can't begin to curse up hill and down as we can, when we get fairly at it."

"Well, but the question is," said Miss Ophelia.

"O, yes, to be sure, the *question is*,—and a deuce of a question it is! How came *you* in this state of sin and misery? Well, I shall answer in the good old words you used to teach me, Sundays. I came so by ordinary generation. My servants were my father's, and, what is more, my mother's; and now they are mine, they and their increase, which bids fair to be a pretty considerable item. My father, you know, came first from New England; and he was just such another man as your father,—a regular old Roman,—upright, energetic, noble-minded, with an iron will. Your father settled down in New England, to rule over rocks and stones, and to force an existence out of Nature; and mine settled in Louisiana, to rule over men and women, and force existence out of them. My mother," said St. Clare, getting up and walking to a picture at the end of the room, and gazing upward with a face fervent with veneration, "*she was divine!* Don't look at me so!—you know what I mean! She probably was of mortal birth; but, as far as ever I could observe, there was no trace of any human weakness or error about her; and everybody that lives to remember her, whether bond or free, servant, acquaintance, relation, all say the same. Why, cousin, that mother has been all that has stood between me and utter unbelief for years. She was a direct embodiment and personification of the New Testament,—a living fact, to be accounted for, and to be accounted for in no other way than by its truth. O, mother! mother!" said St. Clare, clasping his hands, in a sort of transport; and then suddenly checking himself, he came back, and seating himself on an ottoman, he went on:

"My brother and I were twins; and they say, you know, that twins ought to resemble each other; but we were in all points a contrast. He had black, fiery eyes, coal-black hair, a strong, fine Roman profile, and a rich brown complexion. I had blue eyes, golden hair, a Greek outline, and fair complexion. He was active and observing, I dreamy and inactive. He was generous to his friends and equals, but proud, dominant, overbearing, to inferiors, and utterly unmerciful to whatever set itself up against him. Truthful we both were; he from pride and courage, I from a sort of abstract ideality. We loved each other about as boys generally do,—off and on, and in general;—he was my father's pet, and I my mother's.

"There was a morbid sensitiveness and acuteness of feeling in me on all possible subjects, of which he and my father had no kind of understanding, and with which they could have no possible sympathy. But mother did; and so, when I had quarreled with Alfred, and father looked sternly on me, I used to go off to mother's room, and sit by her. I remember just how she used to look, with her pale cheeks, her deep, soft, serious eyes, her white dress,—she always wore white; and I used to think of her whenever I read in Revelations about the saints that were arrayed in fine linen, clean and white. She had a great deal of genius of one sort and another, particularly in music; and she used to sit at her organ, playing fine old majestic music of the Catholic church, and singing with a voice more like an angel than a mortal woman; and I would lay my head down on her lap, and cry, and dream, and feel,—oh, immeasurably!—things that I had no language to say!

"In those days, this matter of slavery had never been canvassed as it has now; nobody dreamed of any harm in it.

"My father was a born aristocrat. I think, in some preexistent state, he must have been in the higher circles of spirits, and brought all his old court pride along with him; for it was ingrain, bred in the bone, though he was originally of poor and not in any way of noble family. My brother was begotten in his image.

"Now, an aristocrat, you know, the world over, has no human sympathies, beyond a certain line in society. In England the line is in one place, in Burmah in another, and in America in another; but the aristocrat of all these countries never goes over it. What would be hardship and distress and injustice in his own class, is a cool matter of course in another one. My father's dividing line was that of color. *Among his equals*, never was a man more just and generous; but he considered the negro, through all possible gradations of color, as an intermediate link between man and animals, and graded all his ideas of justice or generosity on this hypothesis. I suppose, to be sure, if anybody had asked him, plump and fair, whether they had human immortal souls, he might have hemmed and hawed, and said yes. But my father was not a man much troubled with spiritualism; religious sentiment he had none, beyond a veneration for God, as decidedly the head of the upper classes.

"Well, my father worked some five hundred negroes; he was an inflexible, driving, punctilious business man; everything was to move by system,—to be sustained with unfailing accuracy and precision. Now, if you take into account that all this was to be worked out by a set of lazy, twaddling, shiftless laborers, who had grown up, all their lives, in the absence of every possible motive to learn how to do anything but 'shirk,' as you Vermonters say, and you'll see that there might naturally be, on his plantation, a great many things that looked horrible and distressing to a sensitive child, like me.

"Besides all, he had an overseer,—great, tall, slab-sided, two-fisted renegade son of Vermont—(begging your pardon),—who had gone through a regular apprenticeship in hardness and brutality and taken his degree to be admitted to practice. My mother never could endure him, nor I; but he obtained an entire ascendency over my father; and this man was the absolute despot of the estate.

"I was a little fellow then, but I had the same love that I have now for all kinds of human things,—a kind of passion for the study of humanity, come in what shape it would. I was found in the cabins and among the field-hands a great deal, and, of course, was a great favorite; and all sorts of complaints and grievances were breathed in my ear; and I told them to mother, and we, between us, formed a sort of committee for a redress of grievances. We hindered and repressed a great deal of cruelty, and congratulated ourselves on doing a vast deal of good, till, as often happens, my zeal overacted. Stubbs complained to my father that he couldn't manage the hands, and must resign his position. Father was a fond, indulgent husband, but a man that never flinched from anything that he thought necessary; and so he put down his foot, like a rock, between us and the field-hands. He told my mother, in language perfectly respectful and deferential, but quite explicit, that over the house-servants she should be entire mistress, but that with the field-hands he could allow no interference. He revered and respected her above all living beings; but he would have said it all the same to the virgin Mary herself, if she had come in the way of his system.

"I used sometimes to hear my mother reasoning cases with him,—endeavoring to excite his sympathies. He would listen to the most pathetic appeals with the most discouraging politeness and equanimity. 'It all resolves itself into this,' he would say; 'must I part with Stubbs, or keep him? Stubbs is the soul of punctuality, honesty, and efficiency,—a thorough business hand, and as humane as the general run. We can't have perfection; and if I keep him, I must sustain his administration as a *whole*, even if there are, now and then, things that are exceptionable. All government includes some necessary hardness. General rules will bear hard on particular cases.' This last maxim my father seemed to consider a settler in most alleged cases of cruelty. After he had said *that*, he commonly drew up his feet on the sofa, like a man that has disposed of a business, and betook himself to a nap, or the newspaper, as the case might be.

"The fact is my father showed the exact sort of talent for a statesman. He could have divided Poland as easily as an orange, or trod on Ireland as quietly and systematically as any man living. At last my mother gave up, in despair. It never will be known, till the last account, what noble and sensitive natures like hers have felt, cast, utterly helpless, into what seems to them an abyss of injustice and cruelty, and which seems so to nobody about them. It has been an age of long sorrow of such natures, in such a hell-begotten sort of world as ours. What remained for her, but to train her children in her own views and sentiments? Well, after all you say about training, children will grow up substantially what they *are* by nature, and only that. From the cradle, Alfred was an aristocrat; and as he grew up, instinctively, all his sympathies and all his reasonings were in that line, and all mother's exhortations went to the winds. As to me, they sunk deep into me. She never contradicted, in form, anything my father said, or seemed directly to differ from him; but she impressed, burnt into my very soul, with all the force of her deep, earnest nature, an idea of the dignity and worth of the meanest human soul. I have looked in her face with solemn awe, when she would point up to the stars in the evening, and say to me, 'See there, Auguste! the poorest, meanest soul on our place will be living, when all these stars are gone forever,—will live as long as God lives!'

"She had some fine old paintings; one, in particular, of Jesus healing a blind man. They were very fine, and used to impress me strongly. 'See there, Auguste,' she would say; 'the blind man was a beggar, poor and loathsome; therefore, he would not heal him *afar off!* He called him to him, and put *his hands on him!* Remember this, my boy.' If I had lived to grow up under her care, she might have stimulated me to I know not what of enthusiasm. I might have been a saint, reformer, martyr,—but, alas! alas! I went from her when I was only thirteen, and I never saw her again!"

St. Clare rested his head on his hands, and did not speak for some minutes. After a while, he looked up, and went on:

"What poor, mean trash this whole business of human virtue is! A mere matter, for the most part, of latitude and longitude, and geographical position, acting with natural temperament. The greater part is nothing but an accident! Your father, for example, settles in Vermont, in a town where all are, in fact, free and equal; becomes a regular church member and deacon, and in due time joins an Abolition society, and thinks us all little better than heathens. Yet he is, for all the world, in constitution and habit, a duplicate of my father. I can see it leaking out in fifty different ways,—just the same strong, overbearing, dominant spirit. You know very well how impossible it is to persuade some of the folks in your village that Squire Sinclair does not feel above them. The fact is, though he has fallen on democratic times, and embraced a democratic theory, he is to the heart an aristocrat, as much as my father, who ruled over five or six hundred slaves."

Miss Ophelia felt rather disposed to cavil at this picture, and was laying down her knitting to begin, but St. Clare stopped her.

"Now, I know every word you are going to say. I do not say they *were* alike, in fact. One fell into a condition where everything acted against the natural tendency, and the other where everything acted for it; and so one turned out a pretty wilful, stout, overbearing old democrat, and the other a wilful, stout old despot. If both had owned plantations in Louisiana, they would have been as like as two old bullets cast in the same mould."

"What an undutiful boy you are!" said Miss Ophelia.

"I don't mean them any disrespect," said St. Clare. "You know reverence is not my forte. But, to go back to my history:

"When father died, he left the whole property to us twin boys, to be divided as we should agree. There does not breathe on God's earth a nobler-souled, more generous fellow, than Alfred, in all that concerns his equals; and we got on admirably with this property question, without a single unbrotherly word or feeling. We undertook to work the plantation together; and Alfred, whose outward life and capabilities had double the strength of mine, became an enthusiastic planter, and a wonderfully successful one.

"But two years' trial satisfied me that I could not be a partner in that matter. To have a great gang of seven hundred, whom I could not know personally, or feel any individual interest in, bought and driven, housed, fed, worked like so many horned cattle, strained up to military precision,—the question of how little of life's commonest enjoyments would keep them in working order being a constantly recurring problem,—the necessity of drivers and overseers,—the ever-necessary whip, first, last, and only argument,—the whole thing was insufferably disgusting and loathsome to me; and when I thought of my mother's estimate of one poor human soul, it became even frightful!

"It's all nonsense to talk to me about slaves *enjoying* all this! To this day, I have no patience with the unutterable trash that some of your patronizing Northerners have made up, as in their zeal to apologize for our sins. We all know better. Tell me that any man living wants to work all his days, from day-dawn till dark, under the constant eye of a master, without the power of putting forth one irresponsible volition, on the same dreary, monotonous, unchanging toil, and all for two pairs of pantaloons and a pair of shoes a year, with enough food and shelter to keep him in working order! Any man who thinks that human beings can, as a general thing, be made about as comfortable that way as any other, I wish he might try it. I'd buy the dog, and work him, with a clear conscience!"

"I always have supposed," said Miss Ophelia, "that you, all of you, approved of these things, and thought them *right*—according to Scripture."

"Humbug! We are not quite reduced to that yet. Alfred who is as determined a despot as ever walked, does not pretend to this kind of defence;—no, he stands, high and haughty, on that good old respectable ground, *the right of the strongest*; and he says, and I think quite sensibly, that the American planter is 'only doing, in another form, what the English aristocracy and capitalists are doing by the lower classes;' that is, I take it, *appropriating* them, body and bone, soul and spirit, to their use and convenience. He defends both,—and I think, at least, *consistently*. He says that there can be no high civilization without enslavement of the masses, either nominal or real. There must, he says, be a lower class, given up to physical toil and confined to an animal nature; and a higher one thereby acquires leisure and wealth for a more expanded intelligence and improvement, and becomes the directing soul of the lower. So he reasons, because, as I said, he is born an aristocrat;—so I don't believe, because I was born a democrat."

"How in the world can the two things be compared?" said Miss Ophelia. "The English laborer is not sold, traded, parted from his family, whipped."

"He is as much at the will of his employer as if he were sold to him. The slave-owner can whip his refractory slave to death,—the capitalist can starve him to death. As to family security, it is hard to say which is the worst,—to have one's children sold, or see them starve to death at home."

"But it's no kind of apology for slavery, to prove that it isn't worse than some other bad thing."

"I didn't give it for one,—nay, I'll say, besides, that ours is the more bold and palpable infringement of human rights; actually buying a man up, like a horse,—looking at his teeth, cracking his joints, and trying his paces and then paying down for him,—having speculators, breeders, traders, and brokers in human bodies and souls,—sets the thing before the eyes of the civilized world in a more tangible form, though the thing done be, after all, in its nature, the same; that is, appropriating one set of human beings to the use and improvement of another without any regard to their own."

"I never thought of the matter in this light," said Miss Ophelia.

"Well, I've travelled in England some, and I've looked over a good many documents as to the state of their lower classes; and I really think there is no denying Alfred, when he says that his slaves are better off than a large class of the population of England. You see, you must not infer, from what I have told you, that Alfred is what is called a hard master; for he isn't. He is despotic, and unmerciful to insubordination; he would shoot a fellow down with as little remorse as he would shoot a buck, if he opposed him. But, in general, he takes a sort of pride in having his slaves comfortably fed and accommodated.

"When I was with him, I insisted that he should do something for their instruction; and, to please me, he did get a chaplain, and used to have them catechized Sunday, though, I believe, in his heart, that he thought it would do about as much good to set a chaplain over his dogs and horses. And the fact is, that a mind stupefied and animalized by every bad influence from the hour of birth, spending the whole of every week-day in unreflecting toil, cannot be done much with by a few hours on Sunday. The teachers of Sunday-schools among the manufacturing population of England, and among plantation-hands in our country, could perhaps testify to the same result, *there and here*. Yet some striking exceptions there are among us, from the fact that the negro is naturally more impressible to religious sentiment than the white."

"Well," said Miss Ophelia, "how came you to give up your plantation life?"

"Well, we jogged on together some time, till Alfred saw plainly that I was no planter. He thought it absurd, after he had reformed, and altered, and improved everywhere, to suit my notions, that I still remained unsatisfied. The fact was, it was, after all, the THING that I hated—the using these men and women, the perpetuation of all this ignorance, brutality and vice,—just to make money for me!

"Besides, I was always interfering in the details. Being myself one of the laziest of mortals, I had altogether too much fellow-feeling for the lazy; and when poor, shiftless dogs put stones at the bottom of their cotton-baskets to make them weigh heavier, or filled their sacks with dirt, with cotton at the top, it seemed so exactly like what I should do if I were they, I couldn't and wouldn't have them flogged for it. Well, of course, there was an end of plantation discipline; and Alf and I came to about the same point that I and my respected father did, years before. So he told me that I was a womanish sentimentalist, and would never do for business life; and advised me to take the bank-stock and the New Orleans family mansion, and go to writing poetry, and let him manage the plantation. So we parted, and I came here."

"But why didn't you free your slaves?"

"Well, I wasn't up to that. To hold them as tools for money-making, I could not;—have them to help spend money, you know, didn't look quite so ugly to me. Some of them were old house-servants, to whom I was much attached; and the younger ones were children to the old. All were well satisfied to be as they were." He paused, and walked reflectively up and down the room.

"There was," said St. Clare, "a time in my life when I had plans and hopes of doing something in this world, more than to float and drift. I had vague, indistinct yearnings to be a sort of emancipator,—to free my native land from this spot and stain. All young men have had such fever-fits, I suppose, some time,—but then—"

"Why didn't you?" said Miss Ophelia;—"you ought not to put your hand to the plough, and look back."

"O, well, things didn't go with me as I expected, and I got the despair of living that Solomon did. I suppose it was a necessary incident to wisdom in us both; but, some how or other, instead of being actor and regenerator in society, I became a piece of driftwood, and have been floating and eddying about, ever since. Alfred scolds me, every time we meet; and he has the better of me, I grant,—for he really does something; his life is a logical result of his opinions and mine is a contemptible *non sequitur*."

"My dear cousin, can you be satisfied with such a way of spending your probation?"

"Satisfied! Was I not just telling you I despised it? But, then, to come back to this point,—we were on this liberation business. I don't think my feelings about slavery are peculiar. I find many men who, in their hearts, think of it just as I do. The land groans under it; and, bad as it is for the slave, it is worse, if anything, for the master. It takes no spectacles to see that a great class of vicious, improvident, degraded people, among us, are an evil to us, as well as to themselves. The capitalist and aristocrat of England cannot feel that as we do, because they do not mingle with the class they degrade as we do. They are in our homes; they are the associates of our children, and they form their minds faster than we can; for they are a race that children always will cling to and assimilate with. If Eva, now, was not more angel than ordinary, she would be ruined. We might as well allow the small-pox to run among them, and think our children would not take it, as to let them be uninstructed and vicious, and think our children will not be affected by that. Yet our laws positively and utterly forbid any efficient general educational system, and they do it wisely, too; for, just begin and thoroughly educate one generation, and the whole thing would be blown sky high. If we did not give them liberty, they would take it."

"And what do you think will be the end of this?" said Miss Ophelia.

"I don't know. One thing is certain,—that there is a mustering among the masses, the world over; and there is a *dies iræ* coming on, sooner or later. The same thing is working in Europe, in England, and in this country. My mother used to tell me of a millennium that was coming, when Christ should reign, and all men should be free and happy. And she taught me, when I was a boy, to pray, 'thy kingdom come.' Sometimes I think all this sighing, and groaning, and stirring among the dry bones foretells what she used to tell me was coming. But who may abide the day of His appearing?"

"Augustine, sometimes I think you are not far from the kingdom," said Miss Ophelia, laying down her knitting, and looking anxiously at her cousin.

"Thank you for your good opinion, but it's up and down with me,—up to heaven's gate in theory, down in earth's dust in practice. But there's the teabell,—do let's go,—and don't say, now, I haven't had one downright serious talk, for once in my life."

At table, Marie alluded to the incident of Prue. "I suppose you'll think, cousin," she said, "that we are all barbarians."

"I think that's a barbarous thing," said Miss Ophelia, "but I don't think you are all barbarians."

"Well, now," said Marie, "I know it's impossible to get along with some of these creatures. They are so bad they ought not to live. I don't feel a particle of sympathy for such cases. If they'd only behave themselves, it would not happen."

"But, mamma," said Eva, "the poor creature was unhappy; that's what made her drink."

"O, fiddlestick! as if that were any excuse! I'm unhappy, very often. I presume," she said, pensively, "that I've had greater trials than ever she had. It's just because they are so bad. There's some of them that you cannot break in by any kind of severity. I remember father had a man that was so lazy he would run away just to get rid of work, and lie round in the swamps, stealing and doing all sorts of horrid things. That man was caught and whipped, time and again, and it never did him any good; and the last time he crawled off, though he couldn't but just go, and died in the swamp. There was no sort of reason for it, for father's hands were always treated kindly."

"I broke a fellow in, once," said St. Clare, "that all the overseers and masters had tried their hands on in vain."

"You!" said Marie; "well, I'd be glad to know when *you* ever did anything of the sort."

"Well, he was a powerful, gigantic fellow,—a native-born African; and he appeared to have the rude instinct of freedom in him to an uncommon degree. He was a regular African lion. They called him Scipio. Nobody could do anything with him; and he was sold round from overseer to overseer, till at last Alfred bought him, because he thought he could manage him. Well, one day he knocked down the overseer, and was fairly off into the swamps. I was on a visit to Alf's plantation, for it was after we had dissolved partnership. Alfred was greatly exasperated; but I told him that it was his own fault, and laid him any wager that I could break the man; and finally it was agreed that, if I caught him, I should have him to experiment on. So they mustered out a party of some six or seven, with guns and dogs, for the hunt. People, you know, can get up as much enthusiasm in hunting a man as a deer, if it is only customary; in fact, I got a little excited myself, though I had only put in as a sort of mediator, in case he was caught.

"Well, the dogs bayed and howled, and we rode and scampered, and finally we started him. He ran and bounded like a buck, and kept us well in the rear for some time; but at last he got caught in an impenetrable thicket of cane; then he turned to bay, and I tell you he fought the dogs right gallantly. He dashed them to right and left, and actually killed three of them with only his naked fists, when a shot from a gun brought him down, and he fell, wounded and bleeding, almost at my feet. The poor fellow looked up at me with manhood and despair both in his eye. I kept back the dogs and the party, as they came pressing up, and claimed him as my prisoner. It was all I could do to keep them from shooting him, in the flush of success; but I persisted in my bargain, and Alfred sold him to me. Well, I took him in hand, and in one fortnight I had him tamed down as submissive and tractable as heart could desire."

"What in the world did you do to him?" said Marie.

"Well, it was quite a simple process. I took him to my own room, had a good bed made for him, dressed his wounds, and tended him myself, until he got fairly on his feet again. And, in process of time, I had free papers made out for him, and told him he might go where he liked."

"And did he go?" said Miss Ophelia.

"No. The foolish fellow tore the paper in two, and absolutely refused to leave me. I never had a braver, better fellow,—trusty and true as steel. He embraced Christianity afterwards, and became as gentle as a child. He used to oversee my place on the lake, and did it capitally, too. I lost him the first cholera season. In fact, he laid down his life for me. For I was sick, almost to death; and when, through the panic, everybody else fled, Scipio worked for me like a giant, and actually brought me back into life again. But, poor fellow! he was taken, right after, and there was no saving him. I never felt anybody's loss more."

Eva had come gradually nearer and nearer to her father, as he told the story,—her small lips apart, her eyes wide and earnest with absorbing interest.

As he finished, she suddenly threw her arms around his neck, burst into tears, and sobbed convulsively.

"Eva, dear child! what is the matter?" said St. Clare, as the child's small frame trembled and shook with the violence of her feelings. "This child," he added, "ought not to hear any of this kind of thing,—she's nervous."

"No, papa, I'm not nervous," said Eva, controlling herself, suddenly, with a strength of resolution singular in such a child. "I'm not nervous, but these things *sink into my heart*."

"What do you mean, Eva?"

"I can't tell you, papa, I think a great many thoughts. Perhaps some day I shall tell you."

"Well, think away, dear,—only don't cry and worry your papa," said St. Clare, "Look here,—see what a beautiful peach I have got for you."

Eva took it and smiled, though there was still a nervous twiching about the corners of her mouth.

"Come, look at the gold-fish," said St. Clare, taking her hand and stepping on to the verandah. A few moments, and merry laughs were heard through the silken curtains, as Eva and St. Clare were pelting each other with roses, and chasing each other among the alleys of the court.

There is danger that our humble friend Tom be neglected amid the adventures of the higher born; but, if our readers will accompany us up to a little loft over the stable, they may, perhaps, learn a little of his affairs. It was a decent room, containing a bed, a chair, and a small, rough stand, where lay Tom's Bible and hymn-book; and where he sits, at present, with his slate before him, intent on something that seems to cost him a great deal of anxious thought.

The fact was, that Tom's home-yearnings had become so strong that he had begged a sheet of writing-paper of Eva, and, mustering up all his small stock of literary attainment acquired by Mas'r George's instructions, he conceived the bold idea of writing a letter; and he was busy now, on his slate, getting out his first draft. Tom was in a good deal of trouble, for the forms of some of the letters he had forgotten entirely; and of what he did remember, he did not know exactly which to use. And while he was working, and breathing very hard, in his earnestness, Eva alighted, like a bird, on the round of his chair behind him, and peeped over his shoulder.

"O, Uncle Tom! what funny things you *are* making, there!"

"I'm trying to write to my poor old woman, Miss Eva, and my little chil'en," said Tom, drawing the back of his hand over his eyes; "but, some how, I'm feard I shan't make it out."

"I wish I could help you, Tom! I've learnt to write some. Last year I could make all the letters, but I'm afraid I've forgotten."

So Eva put her golden head close to his, and the two commenced a grave and anxious discussion, each one equally earnest, and about equally ignorant; and, with a deal of consulting and advising over every word, the composition began, as they both felt very sanguine, to look quite like writing.

"Yes, Uncle Tom, it really begins to look beautiful," said Eva, gazing delightedly on it. "How pleased your wife'll be, and the poor little children! O, it's a shame you ever had to go away from them! I mean to ask papa to let you go back, some time."

"Missis said that she would send down money for me, as soon as they could get it together," said Tom. "I'm 'spectin, she will. Young Mas'r George, he said he'd come for me; and he gave me this yer dollar as a sign;" and Tom drew from under his clothes the precious dollar.

"O, he'll certainly come, then!" said Eva. "I'm so glad!"

"And I wanted to send a letter, you know, to let 'em know whar I was, and tell poor Chloe that I was well off,—cause she felt so drefful, poor soul!"

"I say Tom!" said St. Clare's voice, coming in the door at this moment.

Tom and Eva both started.

"What's here?" said St. Clare, coming up and looking at the slate.

"O, it's Tom's letter. I'm helping him to write it," said Eva; "isn't it nice?"

"I wouldn't discourage either of you," said St. Clare, "but I rather think, Tom, you'd better get me to write your letter for you. I'll do it, when I come home from my ride."

"It's very important he should write," said Eva, "because his mistress is going to send down money to redeem him, you know, papa; he told me they told him so."

St. Clare thought, in his heart, that this was probably only one of those things which good-natured owners say to their servants, to alleviate their horror of being sold, without any intention of fulfilling the expectation thus excited. But he did not make any audible comment upon it,—only ordered Tom to get the horses out for a ride.

Tom's letter was written in due form for him that evening, and safely lodged in the post-office.

Miss Ophelia still persevered in her labors in the housekeeping line. It was universally agreed, among all the household, from Dinah down to the youngest urchin, that Miss Ophelia was decidedly "curis,"—a term by which a southern servant implies that his or her betters don't exactly suit them.

The higher circle in the family—to wit, Adolph, Jane and Rosa—agreed that she was no lady; ladies never keep working about as she did,—that she had no *air* at all; and they were surprised that she should be any relation of the St. Clares. Even Marie declared that it was absolutely fatiguing to see Cousin Ophelia always so busy. And, in fact, Miss Ophelia's industry was so incessant as to lay some foundation for the complaint. She sewed and stitched away, from daylight till dark, with the energy of one who is pressed on by some immediate urgency; and then, when the light faded, and the work was folded away, with one turn out came the ever-ready knitting-work, and there she was again, going on as briskly as ever. It really was a labor to see her.

CHAPTER XX

TOPSY

One morning, while Miss Ophelia was busy in some of her domestic cares, St. Clare's voice was heard, calling her at the foot of the stairs.

"Come down here, Cousin, I've something to show you."

"What is it?" said Miss Ophelia, coming down, with her sewing in her hand.

"I've made a purchase for your department,—see here," said St. Clare; and, with the word, he pulled along a little negro girl, about eight or nine years of age.

She was one of the blackest of her race; and her round shining eyes, glittering as glass beads, moved with quick and restless glances over everything in the room. Her mouth, half open with astonishment at the wonders of the new Mas'r's parlor, displayed a white and brilliant set of teeth. Her woolly hair was braided in sundry little tails, which stuck out in every direction. The expression of her face was an odd mixture of shrewdness and cunning, over which was oddly drawn, like a kind of veil, an expression of the most doleful gravity and solemnity. She was dressed in a single filthy, ragged garment, made of bagging; and stood with her hands demurely folded before her. Altogether, there was something odd and goblin-like about her appearance,—something, as Miss Ophelia afterwards said, "so heathenish," as to inspire that good lady with utter dismay; and turning to St. Clare, she said,

"Augustine, what in the world have you brought that thing here for?"

"For you to educate, to be sure, and train in the way she should go. I thought she was rather a funny specimen in the Jim Crow line. Here, Topsy," he added, giving a whistle, as a man would to call the attention of a dog, "give us a song, now, and show us some of your dancing."

The black, glassy eyes glittered with a kind of wicked drollery, and the thing struck up, in a clear shrill voice, an odd negro melody, to which she kept time with her hands and feet, spinning round, clapping her hands, knocking her knees together, in a wild, fantastic sort of time, and producing in her throat all those odd guttural sounds which distinguish the native music of her race; and finally, turning a summerset or two, and giving a prolonged closing note, as odd and unearthly as that of a steam-whistle, she came suddenly down on the carpet, and stood with her hands folded, and a most sanctimonious expression of meekness and solemnity over her face, only broken by the cunning glances which she shot askance from the corners of her eyes.

Miss Ophelia stood silent, perfectly paralyzed with amazement. St. Clare, like a mischievous fellow as he was, appeared to enjoy her astonishment; and, addressing the child again, said,

"Topsy, this is your new mistress. I'm going to give you up to her; see now that you behave yourself."

"Yes, Mas'r," said Topsy, with sanctimonious gravity, her wicked eyes twinkling as she spoke.

"You're going to be good, Topsy, you understand," said St. Clare.

"O yes, Mas'r," said Topsy, with another twinkle, her hands still devoutly folded.

"Now, Augustine, what upon earth is this for?" said Miss Ophelia. "Your house is so full of these little plagues, now, that a body can't set down their foot without treading on 'em. I get up in the morning, and find one asleep behind the door, and see one black head poking out from under the table, one lying on the door-mat,—and they are mopping and mowing and grinning between all the railings, and tumbling over the kitchen floor! What on earth did you want to bring this one for?"

"For you to educate—didn't I tell you? You're always preaching about educating. I thought I would make you a present of a fresh-caught specimen, and let you try your hand on her, and bring her up in the way she should go."

"*I* don't want her, I am sure;—I have more to do with 'em now than I want to."

"That's you Christians, all over!—you'll get up a society, and get some poor missionary to spend all his days among just such heathen. But let me see one of you that would take one into your house with you, and take the labor of their conversion on yourselves! No; when it comes to that, they are dirty and disagreeable, and it's too much care, and so on."

"Augustine, you know I didn't think of it in that light," said Miss Ophelia, evidently softening. "Well, it might be a real missionary work," said she, looking rather more favorably on the child.

St. Clare had touched the right string. Miss Ophelia's conscientiousness was ever on the alert. "But," she added, "I really didn't see the need of buying this one;—there are enough now, in your house, to take all my time and skill."

"Well, then, Cousin," said St. Clare, drawing her aside, "I ought to beg your pardon for my good-for-nothing speeches. You are so good, after all, that there's no sense in them. Why, the fact is, this concern belonged to a couple of drunken creatures that keep a low restaurant that I have to pass by every day, and I was tired of hearing her screaming, and them beating and swearing at her. She looked bright and funny, too, as if something might be made of her;—so I bought her, and I'll give her to you. Try, now, and give her a good orthodox New England bringing up, and see what it'll make of her. You know I haven't any gift that way; but I'd like you to try."

"Well, I'll do what I can," said Miss Ophelia; and she approached her new subject very much as a person might be supposed to approach a black spider, supposing them to have benevolent designs toward it.

"She's dreadfully dirty, and half naked," she said.

"Well, take her down stairs, and make some of them clean and clothe her up."

Miss Ophelia carried her to the kitchen regions.

"Don't see what Mas'r St. Clare wants of 'nother nigger!" said Dinah, surveying the new arrival with no friendly air. "Won't have her around under *my* feet, *I* know!"

"Pah!" said Rosa and Jane, with supreme disgust; "let her keep out of our way! What in the world Mas'r wanted another of these low niggers for, I can't see!"

"You go long! No more nigger dan you be, Miss Rosa," said Dinah, who felt this last remark a reflection on herself. "You seem to tink yourself white folks. You an't nerry one, black *nor* white, I'd like to be one or turrer."

Miss Ophelia saw that there was nobody in the camp that would undertake to oversee the cleansing and dressing of the new arrival; and so she was forced to do it herself, with some very ungracious and reluctant assistance from Jane.

It is not for ears polite to hear the particulars of the first toilet of a neglected, abused child. In fact, in this world, multitudes must live and die in a state that it would be too great a shock to the nerves of their fellow-mortals even to hear described. Miss Ophelia had a good, strong, practical deal of resolution; and she went through all the disgusting details with heroic thoroughness, though, it must be confessed, with no very gracious air,—for endurance was the utmost to which her principles could bring her. When she saw, on the back and shoulders of the child, great welts and calloused spots, ineffaceable marks of the system under which she had grown up thus far, her heart became pitiful within her.

"See there!" said Jane, pointing to the marks, "don't that show she's a limb? We'll have fine works with her, I reckon. I hate these nigger young uns! so disgusting! I wonder that Mas'r would buy her!"

The "young un" alluded to heard all these comments with the subdued and doleful air which seemed habitual to her, only scanning, with a keen and furtive glance of her flickering eyes, the ornaments which Jane wore in her ears. When arrayed at last in a suit of decent and whole clothing, her hair cropped short to her head, Miss Ophelia, with some satisfaction, said she looked more Christian-like than she did, and in her own mind began to mature some plans for her instruction.

Sitting down before her, she began to question her.

"How old are you, Topsy?"

"Dun no, Missis," said the image, with a grin that showed all her teeth.

"Don't know how old you are? Didn't anybody ever tell you? Who was your mother?"

"Never had none!" said the child, with another grin.

"Never had any mother? What do you mean? Where were you born?"

"Never was born!" persisted Topsy, with another grin, that looked so goblin-like, that, if Miss Ophelia had been at all nervous, she might have fancied that she had got hold of some sooty gnome from the land of Diablerie; but Miss Ophelia was not nervous, but plain and business-like, and she said, with some sternness,

"You mustn't answer me in that way, child; I'm not playing with you. Tell me where you were born, and who your father and mother were."

"Never was born," reiterated the creature, more emphatically; "never had no father nor mother, nor nothin'. I was raised by a speculator, with lots of others. Old Aunt Sue used to take car on us."

The child was evidently sincere, and Jane, breaking into a short laugh, said,

"Laws, Missis, there's heaps of 'em. Speculators buys 'em up cheap, when they's little, and gets 'em raised for market."

"How long have you lived with your master and mistress?"

"Dun no, Missis."

"Is it a year, or more, or less?"

"Dun no, Missis."

"Laws, Missis, those low negroes,—they can't tell; they don't know anything about time," said Jane; "they don't know what a year is; they don't know their own ages.

"Have you ever heard anything about God, Topsy?"

The child looked bewildered, but grinned as usual.

"Do you know who made you?"

"Nobody, as I knows on," said the child, with a short laugh.

The idea appeared to amuse her considerably; for her eyes twinkled, and she added,

"I spect I grow'd. Don't think nobody never made me."

"Do you know how to sew?" said Miss Ophelia, who thought she would turn her inquiries to something more tangible.

"No, Missis."

"What can you do?—what did you do for your master and mistress?"

"Fetch water, and wash dishes, and rub knives, and wait on folks."

"Were they good to you?"

"Spect they was," said the child, scanning Miss Ophelia cunningly.

Miss Ophelia rose from this encouraging colloquy; St. Clare was leaning over the back of her chair.

"You find virgin soil there, Cousin; put in your own ideas,—you won't find many to pull up."

Miss Ophelia's ideas of education, like all her other ideas, were very set and definite; and of the kind that prevailed in New England a century ago, and which are still preserved in some very retired and unsophisticated parts, where there are no railroads. As nearly as could be expressed, they could be comprised in very few words: to teach them to mind when they were spoken to; to teach them the catechism, sewing, and reading; and to whip them if they told lies. And though, of course, in the flood of light that is now poured on education, these are left far away in the rear, yet it is an undisputed fact that our grandmothers raised some tolerably fair men and women under this regime, as many of us can remember and testify. At all events, Miss Ophelia knew of nothing else to do; and, therefore, applied her mind to her heathen with the best diligence she could command.

The child was announced and considered in the family as Miss Ophelia's girl; and, as she was looked upon with no gracious eye in the kitchen, Miss Ophelia resolved to confine her sphere of operation and instruction chiefly to her own chamber. With a self-sacrifice which some of our readers will appreciate, she resolved, instead of comfortably making her own bed, sweeping and dusting her own chamber,—which she had hitherto done, in utter scorn of all offers of help from the chambermaid of the establishment,—to condemn herself to the martyrdom of instructing Topsy to perform these operations,—ah, woe the day! Did any of our readers ever do the same, they will appreciate the amount of her self-sacrifice.

Miss Ophelia began with Topsy by taking her into her chamber, the first morning, and solemnly commencing a course of instruction in the art and mystery of bed-making.

Behold, then, Topsy, washed and shorn of all the little braided tails wherein her heart had delighted, arrayed in a clean gown, with well-starched apron, standing reverently before Miss Ophelia, with an expression of solemnity well befitting a funeral.

"Now, Topsy, I'm going to show you just how my bed is to be made. I am very particular about my bed. You must learn exactly how to do it."

"Yes, ma'am," says Topsy, with a deep sigh, and a face of woful earnestness.

"Now, Topsy, look here;—this is the hem of the sheet,—this is the right side of the sheet, and this is the wrong;—will you remember?"

"Yes, ma'am," says Topsy, with another sigh.

"Well, now, the under sheet you must bring over the bolster,—so—and tuck it clear down under the mattress nice and smooth,—so,—do you see?"

"Yes, ma'am," said Topsy, with profound attention.

"But the upper sheet," said Miss Ophelia, "must be brought down in this way, and tucked under firm and smooth at the foot,—so,—the narrow hem at the foot."

"Yes, ma'am," said Topsy, as before;—but we will add, what Miss Ophelia did not see, that, during the time when the good lady's back was turned in the zeal of her manipulations, the young disciple had contrived to snatch a pair of gloves and a ribbon, which she had adroitly slipped into her sleeves, and stood with her hands dutifully folded, as before.

"Now, Topsy, let's see *you* do this," said Miss Ophelia, pulling off the clothes, and seating herself.

Topsy, with great gravity and adroitness, went through the exercise completely to Miss Ophelia's satisfaction; smoothing the sheets, patting out every wrinkle, and exhibiting, through the whole process, a gravity and seriousness with which her instructress was greatly edified. By an unlucky slip, however, a fluttering fragment of the ribbon hung out of one of her sleeves, just as she was finishing, and caught Miss Ophelia's attention. Instantly, she pounced upon it. "What's this? You naughty, wicked child,—you've been stealing this!"

The ribbon was pulled out of Topsy's own sleeve, yet was she not in the least disconcerted; she only looked at it with an air of the most surprised and unconscious innocence.

"Laws! why, that ar's Miss Feely's ribbon, an't it? How could it a got caught in my sleeve?

"Topsy, you naughty girl, don't you tell me a lie,—you stole that ribbon!"

"Missis, I declar for 't, I didn't;—never seed it till dis yer blessed minnit."

"Topsy," said Miss Ophelia, "don't you know it's wicked to tell lies?"

"I never tell no lies, Miss Feely," said Topsy, with virtuous gravity; "it's jist the truth I've been a tellin now, and an't nothin else."

"Topsy, I shall have to whip you, if you tell lies so."

"Laws, Missis, if you's to whip all day, couldn't say no other way," said Topsy, beginning to blubber. "I never seed dat ar,—it must a got caught in my sleeve. Miss Feeley must have left it on the bed, and it got caught in the clothes, and so got in my sleeve."

Miss Ophelia was so indignant at the barefaced lie, that she caught the child and shook her.

"Don't you tell me that again!"

The shake brought the glove on to the floor, from the other sleeve.

"There, you!" said Miss Ophelia, "will you tell me now, you didn't steal the ribbon?"

Topsy now confessed to the gloves, but still persisted in denying the ribbon.

"Now, Topsy," said Miss Ophelia, "if you'll confess all about it, I won't whip you this time." Thus adjured, Topsy confessed to the ribbon and gloves, with woful protestations of penitence.

"Well, now, tell me. I know you must have taken other things since you have been in the house, for I let you run about all day yesterday. Now, tell me if you took anything, and I shan't whip you."

"Laws, Missis! I took Miss Eva's red thing she wars on her neck."

"You did, you naughty child!—Well, what else?"

"I took Rosa's yer-rings,—them red ones."

"Go bring them to me this minute, both of 'em."

"Laws, Missis! I can't,—they 's burnt up!"

"Burnt up!—what a story! Go get 'em, or I'll whip you."

Topsy, with loud protestations, and tears, and groans, declared that she *could* not. "They 's burnt up,—they was."

"What did you burn 'em for?" said Miss Ophelia.

"Cause I 's wicked,—I is. I 's mighty wicked, any how. I can't help it."

Just at this moment, Eva came innocently into the room, with the identical coral necklace on her neck.

"Why, Eva, where did you get your necklace?" said Miss Ophelia.

"Get it? Why, I've had it on all day," said Eva.

"Did you have it on yesterday?"

"Yes; and what is funny, Aunty, I had it on all night. I forgot to take it off when I went to bed."

Miss Ophelia looked perfectly bewildered; the more so, as Rosa, at that instant, came into the room, with a basket of newly-ironed linen poised on her head, and the coral ear-drops shaking in her ears!

"I'm sure I can't tell anything what to do with such a child!" she said, in despair. "What in the world did you tell me you took those things for, Topsy?"

"Why, Missis said I must 'fess; and I couldn't think of nothin' else to 'fess," said Topsy, rubbing her eyes.

"But, of course, I didn't want you to confess things you didn't do," said Miss Ophelia; "that's telling a lie, just as much as the other."

"Laws, now, is it?" said Topsy, with an air of innocent wonder.

"La, there an't any such thing as truth in that limb," said Rosa, looking indignantly at Topsy. "If I was Mas'r St. Clare, I'd whip her till the blood run. I would,—I'd let her catch it!"

"No, no Rosa," said Eva, with an air of command, which the child could assume at times; "you mustn't talk so, Rosa. I can't bear to hear it."

"La sakes! Miss Eva, you 's so good, you don't know nothing how to get along with niggers. There's no way but to cut 'em well up, I tell ye."

"Rosa!" said Eva, "hush! Don't you say another word of that sort!" and the eye of the child flashed, and her cheek deepened its color.

Rosa was cowed in a moment.

"Miss Eva has got the St. Clare blood in her, that's plain. She can speak, for all the world, just like her papa," she said, as she passed out of the room.

Eva stood looking at Topsy.

There stood the two children representatives of the two extremes of society. The fair, high-bred child, with her golden head, her deep eyes, her spiritual, noble brow, and prince-like movements; and her black, keen, subtle, cringing, yet acute neighbor. They stood the representatives of their races. The Saxon, born of ages of cultivation, command, education, physical and moral eminence; the Afric, born of ages of oppression, submission, ignorance, toil and vice!

Something, perhaps, of such thoughts struggled through Eva's mind. But a child's thoughts are rather dim, undefined instincts; and in Eva's noble nature many such were yearning and working, for which she had no power of utterance. When Miss Ophelia expatiated on Topsy's naughty, wicked conduct, the child looked perplexed and sorrowful, but said, sweetly.

"Poor Topsy, why need you steal? You're going to be taken good care of now. I'm sure I'd rather give you anything of mine, than have you steal it."

It was the first word of kindness the child had ever heard in her life; and the sweet tone and manner struck strangely on the wild, rude heart, and a sparkle of something like a tear shone in the keen, round, glittering eye; but it was followed by the short laugh and habitual grin. No! the ear that has never heard anything but abuse is strangely incredulous of anything so heavenly as kindness; and Topsy only thought Eva's speech something funny and inexplicable,—she did not believe it.

But what was to be done with Topsy? Miss Ophelia found the case a puzzler; her rules for bringing up didn't seem to apply. She thought she would take time to think of it; and, by the way of gaining time, and in hopes of some indefinite moral virtues supposed to be inherent in dark closets, Miss Ophelia shut Topsy up in one till she had arranged her ideas further on the subject.

"I don't see," said Miss Ophelia to St. Clare, "how I'm going to manage that child, without whipping her."

"Well, whip her, then, to your heart's content; I'll give you full power to do what you like."

"Children always have to be whipped," said Miss Ophelia; "I never heard of bringing them up without."

"O, well, certainly," said St. Clare; "do as you think best. Only I'll make one suggestion: I've seen this child whipped with a poker, knocked down with the shovel or tongs, whichever came handiest, &c.; and, seeing that she is used to that style of operation, I think your whippings will have to be pretty energetic, to make much impression."

"What is to be done with her, then?" said Miss Ophelia.

"You have started a serious question," said St. Clare; "I wish you'd answer it. What is to be done with a human being that can be governed only by the lash,—*that* fails,—it's a very common state of things down here!"

"I'm sure I don't know; I never saw such a child as this."

"Such children are very common among us, and such men and women, too. How are they to be governed?" said St. Clare.

"I'm sure it's more than I can say," said Miss Ophelia.

"Or I either," said St. Clare. "The horrid cruelties and outrages that once and a while find their way into the papers,—such cases as Prue's, for example,—what do they come from? In many cases, it is a gradual hardening process on both sides,—the owner growing more and more cruel, as the servant more and more callous. Whipping and abuse are like laudanum; you have to double the dose as the sensibilities decline. I saw this very early when I became an owner; and I resolved never to begin, because I did not know when I should stop,—and I resolved, at least, to protect my own moral nature. The consequence is, that my servants act like spoiled children; but I think that better than for us both to be brutalized together. You have talked a great deal about our responsibilities in educating, Cousin. I really wanted you to *try* with one child, who is a specimen of thousands among us."

"It is your system makes such children," said Miss Ophelia.

"I know it; but they are *made*,—they exist,—and what *is* to be done with them?"

"Well, I can't say I thank you for the experiment. But, then, as it appears to be a duty, I shall persevere and try, and do the best I can," said Miss Ophelia; and Miss Ophelia, after this, did labor, with a commendable degree of zeal and energy, on her new subject. She instituted regular hours and employments for her, and undertook to teach her to read and sew.

In the former art, the child was quick enough. She learned her letters as if by magic, and was very soon able to read plain reading; but the sewing was a more difficult matter. The creature was as lithe as a cat, and as active as a monkey, and the confinement of sewing was her abomination; so she broke her needles, threw them slyly out of the window, or down in chinks of the walls; she tangled, broke, and dirtied her thread, or, with a sly movement, would throw a spool away altogether. Her motions were almost as quick as those of a practised conjurer, and her command of her face quite as great; and though Miss Ophelia could not help feeling that so many accidents could not possibly happen in succession, yet she could not, without a watchfulness which would leave her no time for anything else, detect her.

Topsy was soon a noted character in the establishment. Her talent for every species of drollery, grimace, and mimicry,—for dancing, tumbling, climbing, singing, whistling, imitating every sound that hit her fancy,—seemed inexhaustible. In her play-hours, she invariably had every child in the establishment at her heels, open-mouthed with admiration and wonder,—not excepting Miss Eva, who appeared to be fascinated by her wild diablerie, as a dove is sometimes charmed by a glittering serpent. Miss Ophelia was uneasy that Eva should fancy Topsy's society so much, and implored St. Clare to forbid it.

"Poh! let the child alone," said St. Clare. "Topsy will do her good."

"But so depraved a child,—are you not afraid she will teach her some mischief?"

"She can't teach her mischief; she might teach it to some children, but evil rolls off Eva's mind like dew off a cabbage-leaf,—not a drop sinks in."

"Don't be too sure," said Miss Ophelia. "I know I'd never let a child of mine play with Topsy."

"Well, your children needn't," said St. Clare, "but mine may; if Eva could have been spoiled, it would have been done years ago."

Topsy was at first despised and contemned by the upper servants. They soon found reason to alter their opinion. It was very soon discovered that whoever cast an indignity on Topsy was sure to meet with some inconvenient accident shortly after;—either a pair of ear-rings or some cherished trinket would be missing, or an article of dress would be suddenly found utterly ruined, or the person would stumble accidently into a pail of hot water, or a libation of dirty slop would unaccountably deluge them from above when in full gala dress;-and on all these occasions, when investigation was made, there was nobody found to stand sponsor for the indignity. Topsy was cited, and had up before all the domestic judicatories, time and again; but always sustained her examinations with most edifying innocence and gravity of appearance. Nobody in the world ever doubted who did the things; but not a scrap of any direct evidence could be found to establish the suppositions, and Miss Ophelia was too just to feel at liberty to proceed to any length without it.

The mischiefs done were always so nicely timed, also, as further to shelter the aggressor. Thus, the times for revenge on Rosa and Jane, the two chamber maids, were always chosen in those seasons when (as not unfrequently happened) they were in disgrace with their mistress, when any complaint from them would of course meet with no sympathy. In short, Topsy soon made the household understand the propriety of letting her alone; and she was let alone, accordingly.

Topsy was smart and energetic in all manual operations, learning everything that was taught her with surprising quickness. With a few lessons, she had learned to do the proprieties of Miss Ophelia's chamber in a way with which even that particular lady could find no fault. Mortal hands could not lay spread smoother, adjust pillows more accurately, sweep and dust and arrange more perfectly, than Topsy, when she chose,—but she didn't very often choose. If Miss Ophelia, after three or four days of careful patient supervision, was so sanguine as to suppose that Topsy had at last fallen into her way, could do without over-looking, and so go off and busy herself about something else, Topsy would hold a perfect carnival of confusion, for some one or two hours. Instead of making the bed, she would amuse herself with pulling off the pillowcases, butting her woolly head among the pillows, till it would sometimes be grotesquely ornamented with feathers sticking out in various directions; she would climb the posts, and hang head downward from the tops; flourish the sheets and spreads all over the apartment; dress the bolster up in Miss Ophelia's night-clothes, and enact various performances with that,—singing and whistling, and making grimaces at herself in the looking-glass; in short, as Miss Ophelia phrased it, "raising Cain" generally.

On one occasion, Miss Ophelia found Topsy with her very best scarlet India Canton crape shawl wound round her head for a turban, going on with her rehearsals before the glass in great style,—Miss Ophelia having, with carelessness most unheard-of in her, left the key for once in her drawer.

"Topsy!" she would say, when at the end of all patience, "what does make you act so?"

"Dunno, Missis,—I spects cause I 's so wicked!"

"I don't know anything what I shall do with you, Topsy."

"Law, Missis, you must whip me; my old Missis allers whipped me. I an't used to workin' unless I gets whipped."

"Why, Topsy, I don't want to whip you. You can do well, if you've a mind to; what is the reason you won't?"

"Laws, Missis, I 's used to whippin'; I spects it's good for me."

Miss Ophelia tried the recipe, and Topsy invariably made a terrible commotion, screaming, groaning and imploring, though half an hour afterwards, when roosted on some projection of the balcony, and surrounded by a flock of admiring "young uns," she would express the utmost contempt of the whole affair.

"Law, Miss Feely whip!—wouldn't kill a skeeter, her whippins. Oughter see how old Mas'r made the flesh fly; old Mas'r know'd how!"

Topsy always made great capital of her own sins and enormities, evidently considering them as something peculiarly distinguishing.

"Law, you niggers," she would say to some of her auditors, "does you know you 's all sinners? Well, you is—everybody is. White folks is sinners too,—Miss Feely says so; but I spects niggers is the biggest ones; but lor! ye an't any on ye up to me. I 's so awful wicked there can't nobody do nothin' with me. I used to keep old Missis a swarin' at me half de time. I spects I 's the wickedest critter in the world;" and Topsy would cut a summerset, and come up brisk and shining on to a higher perch, and evidently plume herself on the distinction.

Miss Ophelia busied herself very earnestly on Sundays, teaching Topsy the catechism. Topsy had an uncommon verbal memory, and committed with a fluency that greatly encouraged her instructress.

"What good do you expect it is going to do her?" said St. Clare.

"Why, it always has done children good. It's what children always have to learn, you know," said Miss Ophelia.

"Understand it or not," said St. Clare.

"O, children never understand it at the time; but, after they are grown up, it'll come to them."

"Mine hasn't come to me yet," said St. Clare, "though I'll bear testimony that you put it into me pretty thoroughly when I was a boy.'"

"Ah, you were always good at learning, Augustine. I used to have great hopes of you," said Miss Ophelia.

"Well, haven't you now?" said St. Clare.

"I wish you were as good as you were when you were a boy, Augustine."

"So do I, that's a fact, Cousin," said St. Clare. "Well, go ahead and catechize Topsy; may be you'll make out something yet."

Topsy, who had stood like a black statue during this discussion, with hands decently folded, now, at a signal from Miss Ophelia, went on:

"Our first parents, being left to the freedom of their own will, fell from the state wherein they were created."

Topsy's eyes twinkled, and she looked inquiringly.

"What is it, Topsy?" said Miss Ophelia.

"Please, Missis, was dat ar state Kintuck?"

"What state, Topsy?"

"Dat state dey fell out of. I used to hear Mas'r tell how we came down from Kintuck."

St. Clare laughed.

"You'll have to give her a meaning, or she'll make one," said he. "There seems to be a theory of emigration suggested there."

"O! Augustine, be still," said Miss Ophelia; "how can I do anything, if you will be laughing?"

"Well, I won't disturb the exercises again, on my honor;" and St. Clare took his paper into the parlor, and sat down, till Topsy had finished her recitations. They were all very well, only that now and then she would oddly transpose some important words, and persist in the mistake, in spite of every effort to the contrary; and St. Clare, after all his promises of goodness, took a wicked pleasure in these mistakes, calling Topsy to him whenever he had a mind to amuse himself, and getting her to repeat the offending passages, in spite of Miss Ophelia's remonstrances.

"How do you think I can do anything with the child, if you will go on so, Augustine?" she would say.

"Well, it is too bad,—I won't again; but I do like to hear the droll little image stumble over those big words!"

"But you confirm her in the wrong way."

"What's the odds? One word is as good as another to her."

"You wanted me to bring her up right; and you ought to remember she is a reasonable creature, and be careful of your influence over her."

"O, dismal! so I ought; but, as Topsy herself says, 'I 's so wicked!'"

In very much this way Topsy's training proceeded, for a year or two,—Miss Ophelia worrying herself, from day to day, with her, as a kind of chronic plague, to whose inflictions she became, in time, as accustomed, as persons sometimes do to the neuralgia or sick headache.

St. Clare took the same kind of amusement in the child that a man might in the tricks of a parrot or a pointer. Topsy, whenever her sins brought her into disgrace in other quarters, always took refuge behind his chair; and St. Clare, in one way or other, would make peace for her. From him she got many a stray picayune, which she laid out in nuts and candies, and distributed, with careless generosity, to all the children in the family; for Topsy, to do her justice, was good-natured and liberal, and only spiteful in self-defence. She is fairly introduced into our *corps de ballet*, and will figure, from time to time, in her turn, with other performers.

CHAPTER XXI

KENTUCK

Our readers may not be unwilling to glance back, for a brief interval, at Uncle Tom's Cabin, on the Kentucky farm, and see what has been transpiring among those whom he had left behind.

It was late in the summer afternoon, and the doors and windows of the large parlor all stood open, to invite any stray breeze, that might feel in a good humor, to enter. Mr. Shelby sat in a large hall opening into the room, and running through the whole length of the house, to a balcony on either end. Leisurely tipped back on one chair, with his heels in another, he was enjoying his after-dinner cigar. Mrs. Shelby sat in the door, busy about some fine sewing; she seemed like one who had something on her mind, which she was seeking an opportunity to introduce.

"Do you know," she said, "that Chloe has had a letter from Tom?"

"Ah! has she? Tom 's got some friend there, it seems. How is the old boy?"

"He has been bought by a very fine family, I should think," said Mrs. Shelby,—"is kindly treated, and has not much to do."

"Ah! well, I'm glad of it,—very glad," said Mr. Shelby, heartily. "Tom, I suppose, will get reconciled to a Southern residence;—hardly want to come up here again."

"On the contrary he inquires very anxiously," said Mrs. Shelby, "when the money for his redemption is to be raised."

"I'm sure *I* don't know," said Mr. Shelby. "Once get business running wrong, there does seem to be no end to it. It's like jumping from one bog to another, all through a swamp; borrow of one to pay another, and then borrow of another to pay one,—and these confounded notes falling due before a man has time to smoke a cigar and turn round,—dunning letters and dunning messages,—all scamper and hurry-scurry."

"It does seem to me, my dear, that something might be done to straighten matters. Suppose we sell off all the horses, and sell one of your farms, and pay up square?"

CHAPTER XXI

"O, ridiculous, Emily! You are the finest woman in Kentucky; but still you haven't sense to know that you don't understand business;—women never do, and never can.

"But, at least," said Mrs. Shelby, "could not you give me some little insight into yours; a list of all your debts, at least, and of all that is owed to you, and let me try and see if I can't help you to economize."

"O, bother! don't plague me, Emily!—I can't tell exactly. I know somewhere about what things are likely to be; but there's no trimming and squaring my affairs, as Chloe trims crust off her pies. You don't know anything about business, I tell you."

And Mr. Shelby, not knowing any other way of enforcing his ideas, raised his voice,—a mode of arguing very convenient and convincing, when a gentleman is discussing matters of business with his wife.

Mrs. Shelby ceased talking, with something of a sigh. The fact was, that though her husband had stated she was a woman, she had a clear, energetic, practical mind, and a force of character every way superior to that of her husband; so that it would not have been so very absurd a supposition, to have allowed her capable of managing, as Mr. Shelby supposed. Her heart was set on performing her promise to Tom and Aunt Chloe, and she sighed as discouragements thickened around her.

"Don't you think we might in some way contrive to raise that money? Poor Aunt Chloe! her heart is so set on it!"

"I'm sorry, if it is. I think I was premature in promising. I'm not sure, now, but it's the best way to tell Chloe, and let her make up her mind to it. Tom'll have another wife, in a year or two; and she had better take up with somebody else."

"Mr. Shelby, I have taught my people that their marriages are as sacred as ours. I never could think of giving Chloe such advice."

"It's a pity, wife, that you have burdened them with a morality above their condition and prospects. I always thought so."

"It's only the morality of the Bible, Mr. Shelby."

"Well, well, Emily, I don't pretend to interfere with your religious notions; only they seem extremely unfitted for people in that condition."

"They are, indeed," said Mrs. Shelby, "and that is why, from my soul, I hate the whole thing. I tell you, my dear, *I* cannot absolve myself from the promises I make to these helpless creatures. If I can get the money no other way I will take music-scholars;—I could get enough, I know, and earn the money myself."

"You wouldn't degrade yourself that way, Emily? I never could consent to it."

"Degrade! would it degrade me as much as to break my faith with the helpless? No, indeed!"

"Well, you are always heroic and transcendental," said Mr. Shelby, "but I think you had better think before you undertake such a piece of Quixotism."

Here the conversation was interrupted by the appearance of Aunt Chloe, at the end of the verandah.

"If you please, Missis," said she.

"Well, Chloe, what is it?" said her mistress, rising, and going to the end of the balcony.

"If Missis would come and look at dis yer lot o' poetry."

Chloe had a particular fancy for calling poultry poetry,—an application of language in which she always persisted, notwithstanding frequent corrections and advisings from the young members of the family.

"La sakes!" she would say, "I can't see; one jis good as turry,—poetry suthin good, any how;" and so poetry Chloe continued to call it.

Mrs. Shelby smiled as she saw a prostrate lot of chickens and ducks, over which Chloe stood, with a very grave face of consideration.

"I'm a thinkin whether Missis would be a havin a chicken pie o' dese yer."

"Really, Aunt Chloe, I don't much care;—serve them any way you like."

Chloe stood handling them over abstractedly; it was quite evident that the chickens were not what she was thinking of. At last, with the short laugh with which her tribe often introduce a doubtful proposal, she said,

"Laws me, Missis! what should Mas'r and Missis be a troublin theirselves 'bout de money, and not a usin what's right in der hands?" and Chloe laughed again.

"I don't understand you, Chloe," said Mrs. Shelby, nothing doubting, from her knowledge of Chloe's manner, that she had heard every word of the conversation that had passed between her and her husband.

"Why, laws me, Missis!" said Chloe, laughing again, "other folks hires out der niggers and makes money on 'em! Don't keep sich a tribe eatin 'em out of house and home."

"Well, Chloe, who do you propose that we should hire out?"

"Laws! I an't a proposin nothin; only Sam he said der was one of dese yer *perfectioners*, dey calls 'em, in Louisville, said he wanted a good hand at cake and pastry; and said he'd give four dollars a week to one, he did."

"Well, Chloe."

"Well, laws, I 's a thinkin, Missis, it's time Sally was put along to be doin' something. Sally 's been under my care, now, dis some time, and she does most as well as me, considerin; and if Missis would only let me go, I would help fetch up de money. I an't afraid to put my cake, nor pies nother, 'long side no *perfectioner's*.

"Confectioner's, Chloe."

"Law sakes, Missis! 'tan't no odds;—words is so curis, can't never get 'em right!"

"But, Chloe, do you want to leave your children?"

"Laws, Missis! de boys is big enough to do day's works; dey does well enough; and Sally, she'll take de baby,—she's such a peart young un, she won't take no lookin arter."

"Louisville is a good way off."

"Law sakes! who's afeard?—it's down river, somer near my old man, perhaps?" said Chloe, speaking the last in the tone of a question, and looking at Mrs. Shelby.

"No, Chloe; it's many a hundred miles off," said Mrs. Shelby.

Chloe's countenance fell.

"Never mind; your going there shall bring you nearer, Chloe. Yes, you may go; and your wages shall every cent of them be laid aside for your husband's redemption."

As when a bright sunbeam turns a dark cloud to silver, so Chloe's dark face brightened immediately,—it really shone.

"Laws! if Missis isn't too good! I was thinking of dat ar very thing; cause I shouldn't need no clothes, nor shoes, nor nothin,—I could save every cent. How many weeks is der in a year, Missis?"

"Fifty-two," said Mrs. Shelby.

"Laws! now, dere is? and four dollars for each on em. Why, how much 'd dat ar be?"

"Two hundred and eight dollars," said Mrs. Shelby.

"Why-e!" said Chloe, with an accent of surprise and delight; "and how long would it take me to work it out, Missis?"

"Some four or five years, Chloe; but, then, you needn't do it all,—I shall add something to it."

"I wouldn't hear to Missis' givin lessons nor nothin. Mas'r's quite right in dat ar;—'t wouldn't do, no ways. I hope none our family ever be brought to dat ar, while I 's got hands."

"Don't fear, Chloe; I'll take care of the honor of the family," said Mrs. Shelby, smiling. "But when do you expect to go?"

"Well, I want spectin nothin; only Sam, he's a gwine to de river with some colts, and he said I could go 'long with him; so I jes put my things together. If Missis was willin, I'd go with Sam tomorrow morning, if Missis would write my pass, and write me a commendation."

"Well, Chloe, I'll attend to it, if Mr. Shelby has no objections. I must speak to him."

Mrs. Shelby went up stairs, and Aunt Chloe, delighted, went out to her cabin, to make her preparation.

"Law sakes, Mas'r George! ye didn't know I 's a gwine to Louisville tomorrow!" she said to George, as entering her cabin, he found her busy in sorting over her baby's clothes. "I thought I'd jis look over sis's things, and get 'em straightened up. But I'm gwine, Mas'r George,—gwine to have four dollars a week; and Missis is gwine to lay it all up, to buy back my old man agin!"

"Whew!" said George, "here's a stroke of business, to be sure! How are you going?"

"Tomorrow, wid Sam. And now, Mas'r George, I knows you'll jis sit down and write to my old man, and tell him all about it,—won't ye?"

"To be sure," said George; "Uncle Tom'll be right glad to hear from us. I'll go right in the house, for paper and ink; and then, you know, Aunt Chloe, I can tell about the new colts and all."

"Sartin, sartin, Mas'r George; you go 'long, and I'll get ye up a bit o' chicken, or some sich; ye won't have many more suppers wid yer poor old aunty."

CHAPTER XXII

"THE GRASS WITHERETH—THE FLOWER FADETH"

Life passes, with us all, a day at a time; so it passed with our friend Tom, till two years were gone. Though parted from all his soul held dear, and though often yearning for what lay beyond, still was he never positively and consciously miserable; for, so well is the harp of human feeling strung, that nothing but a crash that breaks every string can wholly mar its harmony; and, on looking back to seasons which in review appear to us as those of deprivation and trial, we can remember that each hour, as it glided, brought its diversions and alleviations, so that, though not happy wholly, we were not, either, wholly miserable.

Tom read, in his only literary cabinet, of one who had "learned in whatsoever state he was, therewith to be content." It seemed to him good and reasonable doctrine, and accorded well with the settled and thoughtful habit which he had acquired from the reading of that same book.

His letter homeward, as we related in the last chapter, was in due time answered by Master George, in a good, round, school-boy hand, that Tom said might be read "most acrost the room." It contained various refreshing items of home intelligence, with which our reader is fully acquainted: stated how Aunt Chloe had been hired out to a confectioner in Louisville, where her skill in the pastry line was gaining wonderful sums of money, all of which, Tom was informed, was to be laid up to go to make up the sum of his redemption money; Mose and Pete were thriving, and the baby was trotting all about the house, under the care of Sally and the family generally.

Tom's cabin was shut up for the present; but George expatiated brilliantly on ornaments and additions to be made to it when Tom came back.

The rest of this letter gave a list of George's school studies, each one headed by a flourishing capital; and also told the names of four new colts that appeared on the premises since Tom left; and stated, in the same connection, that father and mother were well. The style of the letter was decidedly concise and terse; but Tom thought it the most wonderful specimen of composition that had appeared in modern times. He was never tired of looking at it, and even held a council with Eva on the expediency of getting it framed, to hang up in his room. Nothing but the difficulty of arranging it so that both sides of the page would show at once stood in the way of this undertaking.

The friendship between Tom and Eva had grown with the child's growth. It would be hard to say what place she held in the soft, impressible heart of her faithful attendant. He loved her as something frail and earthly, yet almost worshipped her as something heavenly and divine. He gazed on her as the Italian sailor gazes on his image of the child Jesus,—with a mixture of reverence and tenderness; and to humor her graceful fancies, and meet those thousand simple wants which invest childhood like a many-colored rainbow, was Tom's chief delight. In the market, at morning, his eyes were always on the flower-stalls for rare bouquets for her, and the choicest peach or orange was slipped into his pocket to give to her when he came back; and the sight that pleased him most was her sunny head looking out the gate for his distant approach, and her childish questions,—"Well, Uncle Tom, what have you got for me today?"

Nor was Eva less zealous in kind offices, in return. Though a child, she was a beautiful reader;—a fine musical ear, a quick poetic fancy, and an instinctive sympathy with what's grand and noble, made her such a reader of the Bible as Tom had never before heard. At first, she read to please her humble friend; but soon her own earnest nature threw out its tendrils, and wound itself around the majestic book; and Eva loved it, because it woke in her strange yearnings, and strong, dim emotions, such as impassioned, imaginative children love to feel.

The parts that pleased her most were the Revelations and the Prophecies,—parts whose dim and wondrous imagery, and fervent language, impressed her the more, that she questioned vainly of their meaning;—and she and her simple friend, the old child and the young one, felt just alike about it. All that they knew was, that they spoke of a glory to be revealed,—a wondrous something yet to come, wherein their soul rejoiced, yet knew not why; and though it be not so in the physical, yet in moral science that which cannot be understood is not always profitless. For the soul awakes, a trembling stranger, between two dim eternities,—the eternal past, the eternal future. The light shines only on a small space around her; therefore, she needs must yearn towards the unknown; and the voices and shadowy movings which come to her from out the cloudy pillar of inspiration have each one echoes and answers in her own expecting nature. Its mystic imagery are so many talismans and gems inscribed with unknown hieroglyphics; she folds them in her bosom, and expects to read them when she passes beyond the veil.

At this time in our story, the whole St. Clare establishment is, for the time being, removed to their villa on Lake Pontchartrain. The heats of summer had driven all who were able to leave the sultry and unhealthy city, to seek the shores of the lake, and its cool sea-breezes.

St. Clare's villa was an East Indian cottage, surrounded by light verandahs of bamboo-work, and opening on all sides into gardens and pleasure-grounds. The common sitting-room opened on to a large garden, fragrant with every picturesque plant and flower of the tropics, where winding paths ran down to the very shores of the lake, whose silvery sheet of water lay there, rising and falling in the sunbeams,—a picture never for an hour the same, yet every hour more beautiful.

It is now one of those intensely golden sunsets which kindles the whole horizon into one blaze of glory, and makes the water another sky. The lake lay in rosy or golden streaks, save where white-winged vessels glided hither and thither, like so many spirits, and little golden stars twinkled through the glow, and looked down at themselves as they trembled in the water.

Tom and Eva were seated on a little mossy seat, in an arbor, at the foot of the garden. It was Sunday evening, and Eva's Bible lay open on her knee. She read,— "And I saw a sea of glass, mingled with fire."

"Tom," said Eva, suddenly stopping, and pointing to the lake, "there 't is."

"What, Miss Eva?"

"Don't you see,—there?" said the child, pointing to the glassy water, which, as it rose and fell, reflected the golden glow of the sky. "There's a 'sea of glass, mingled with fire.'"

"True enough, Miss Eva," said Tom; and Tom sang—

"O, had I the wings of the morning, I'd fly away to Canaan's shore; Bright angels should convey me home, To the new Jerusalem."

"Where do you suppose new Jerusalem is, Uncle Tom?" said Eva.

"O, up in the clouds, Miss Eva."

"Then I think I see it," said Eva. "Look in those clouds!—they look like great gates of pearl; and you can see beyond them—far, far off—it's all gold. Tom, sing about 'spirits bright.'"

Tom sung the words of a well-known Methodist hymn,

"I see a band of spirits bright, That taste the glories there; They all are robed in spotless white, And conquering palms they bear."

"Uncle Tom, I've seen *them*," said Eva.

Tom had no doubt of it at all; it did not surprise him in the least. If Eva had told him she had been to heaven, he would have thought it entirely probable.

"They come to me sometimes in my sleep, those spirits;" and Eva's eyes grew dreamy, and she hummed, in a low voice,

"They are all robed in spotless white, And conquering palms they bear."

"Uncle Tom," said Eva, "I'm going there."

"Where, Miss Eva?"

The child rose, and pointed her little hand to the sky; the glow of evening lit her golden hair and flushed cheek with a kind of unearthly radiance, and her eyes were bent earnestly on the skies.

"I'm going *there*," she said, "to the spirits bright, Tom; *I'm going, before long*."

The faithful old heart felt a sudden thrust; and Tom thought how often he had noticed, within six months, that Eva's little hands had grown thinner, and her skin more transparent, and her breath shorter; and how, when she ran or played in the garden, as she once could for hours, she became soon so tired and languid. He had heard Miss Ophelia speak often of a cough, that all her medicaments could not cure; and even now that fervent cheek and little hand were burning with hectic fever; and yet the thought that Eva's words suggested had never come to him till now.

Has there ever been a child like Eva? Yes, there have been; but their names are always on grave-stones, and their sweet smiles, their heavenly eyes, their singular words and ways, are among the buried treasures of yearning hearts. In how many families do you hear the legend that all the goodness and graces of the living are nothing to the peculiar charms of one who *is not*. It is as if heaven had an especial band of angels, whose office it was to sojourn for a season here, and endear to them the wayward human heart, that they might bear it upward with them in their homeward flight. When you see that deep, spiritual light in the eye,—when the little soul reveals itself in words sweeter and wiser than the ordinary words of children,—hope not to retain that child; for the seal of heaven is on it, and the light of immortality looks out from its eyes.

Even so, beloved Eva! fair star of thy dwelling! Thou art passing away; but they that love thee dearest know it not.

The colloquy between Tom and Eva was interrupted by a hasty call from Miss Ophelia.

"Eva—Eva!—why, child, the dew is falling; you mustn't be out there!"

Eva and Tom hastened in.

Miss Ophelia was old, and skilled in the tactics of nursing. She was from New England, and knew well the first guileful footsteps of that soft, insidious disease, which sweeps away so many of the fairest and loveliest, and, before one fibre of life seems broken, seals them irrevocably for death.

She had noted the slight, dry cough, the daily brightening cheek; nor could the lustre of the eye, and the airy buoyancy born of fever, deceive her.

She tried to communicate her fears to St. Clare; but he threw back her suggestions with a restless petulance, unlike his usual careless good-humor.

"Don't be croaking, Cousin,—I hate it!" he would say; "don't you see that the child is only growing. Children always lose strength when they grow fast."

"But she has that cough!"

"O! nonsense of that cough!—it is not anything. She has taken a little cold, perhaps."

"Well, that was just the way Eliza Jane was taken, and Ellen and Maria Sanders."

"O! stop these hobgoblin' nurse legends. You old hands got so wise, that a child cannot cough, or sneeze, but you see desperation and ruin at hand. Only take care of the child, keep her from the night air, and don't let her play too hard, and she'll do well enough."

So St. Clare said; but he grew nervous and restless. He watched Eva feverishly day by day, as might be told by the frequency with which he repeated over that "the child was quite well"—that there wasn't anything in that cough,—it was only some little stomach affection, such as children often had. But he kept by her more than before, took her oftener to ride with him, brought home every few days some receipt or strengthening mixture,—"not," he said, "that the child *needed* it, but then it would not do her any harm."

If it must be told, the thing that struck a deeper pang to his heart than anything else was the daily increasing maturity of the child's mind and feelings. While still retaining all a child's fanciful graces, yet she often dropped, unconsciously, words of such a reach of thought, and strange unworldly wisdom, that they seemed to be an inspiration. At such times, St. Clare would feel a sudden thrill, and clasp her in his arms, as if that fond clasp could save her; and his heart rose up with wild determination to keep her, never to let her go.

The child's whole heart and soul seemed absorbed in works of love and kindness. Impulsively generous she had always been; but there was a touching and womanly thoughtfulness about her now, that every one noticed. She still loved to play with Topsy, and the various colored children; but she now seemed rather a spectator than an actor of their plays, and she would sit for half an hour at a time, laughing at the odd tricks of Topsy,—and then a shadow would seem to pass across her face, her eyes grew misty, and her thoughts were afar.

"Mamma," she said, suddenly, to her mother, one day, "why don't we teach our servants to read?"

"What a question child! People never do."

"Why don't they?" said Eva.

"Because it is no use for them to read. It don't help them to work any better, and they are not made for anything else."

"But they ought to read the Bible, mamma, to learn God's will."

"O! they can get that read to them all *they* need."

"It seems to me, mamma, the Bible is for every one to read themselves. They need it a great many times when there is nobody to read it."

"Eva, you are an odd child," said her mother.

"Miss Ophelia has taught Topsy to read," continued Eva.

"Yes, and you see how much good it does. Topsy is the worst creature I ever saw!"

"Here's poor Mammy!" said Eva. "She does love the Bible so much, and wishes so she could read! And what will she do when I can't read to her?"

Marie was busy, turning over the contents of a drawer, as she answered,

"Well, of course, by and by, Eva, you will have other things to think of besides reading the Bible round to servants. Not but that is very proper; I've done it myself, when I had health. But when you come to be dressing and going into company, you won't have time. See here!" she added, "these jewels I'm going to give you when you come out. I wore them to my first ball. I can tell you, Eva, I made a sensation."

Eva took the jewel-case, and lifted from it a diamond necklace. Her large, thoughtful eyes rested on them, but it was plain her thoughts were elsewhere.

"How sober you look child!" said Marie.

"Are these worth a great deal of money, mamma?"

"To be sure, they are. Father sent to France for them. They are worth a small fortune."

"I wish I had them," said Eva, "to do what I pleased with!"

"What would you do with them?"

"I'd sell them, and buy a place in the free states, and take all our people there, and hire teachers, to teach them to read and write."

Eva was cut short by her mother's laughing.

"Set up a boarding-school! Wouldn't you teach them to play on the piano, and paint on velvet?"

"I'd teach them to read their own Bible, and write their own letters, and read letters that are written to them," said Eva, steadily. "I know, mamma, it does come very hard on them that they can't do these things. Tom feels it—Mammy does,—a great many of them do. I think it's wrong."

"Come, come, Eva; you are only a child! You don't know anything about these things," said Marie; "besides, your talking makes my head ache."

Marie always had a headache on hand for any conversation that did not exactly suit her.

Eva stole away; but after that, she assiduously gave Mammy reading lessons.

CHAPTER XXIII

HENRIQUE

About this time, St. Clare's brother Alfred, with his eldest son, a boy of twelve, spent a day or two with the family at the lake.

No sight could be more singular and beautiful than that of these twin brothers. Nature, instead of instituting resemblances between them, had made them opposites on every point; yet a mysterious tie seemed to unite them in a closer friendship than ordinary.

They used to saunter, arm in arm, up and down the alleys and walks of the garden. Augustine, with his blue eyes and golden hair, his ethereally flexible form and vivacious features; and Alfred, dark-eyed, with haughty Roman profile, firmly-knit limbs, and decided bearing. They were always abusing each other's opinions and practices, and yet never a whit the less absorbed in each other's society; in fact, the very contrariety seemed to unite them, like the attraction between opposite poles of the magnet.

Henrique, the eldest son of Alfred, was a noble, dark-eyed, princely boy, full of vivacity and spirit; and, from the first moment of introduction, seemed to be perfectly fascinated by the spirituelle graces of his cousin Evangeline.

Eva had a little pet pony, of a snowy whiteness. It was easy as a cradle, and as gentle as its little mistress; and this pony was now brought up to the back verandah by Tom, while a little mulatto boy of about thirteen led along a small black Arabian, which had just been imported, at a great expense, for Henrique.

Henrique had a boy's pride in his new possession; and, as he advanced and took the reins out of the hands of his little groom, he looked carefully over him, and his brow darkened.

"What's this, Dodo, you little lazy dog! you haven't rubbed my horse down, this morning."

"Yes, Mas'r," said Dodo, submissively; "he got that dust on his own self."

"You rascal, shut your mouth!" said Henrique, violently raising his riding-whip. "How dare you speak?"

The boy was a handsome, bright-eyed mulatto, of just Henrique's size, and his curling hair hung round a high, bold forehead. He had white blood in his veins, as could be seen by the quick flush in his cheek, and the sparkle of his eye, as he eagerly tried to speak.

"Mas'r Henrique!—" he began.

Henrique struck him across the face with his riding-whip, and, seizing one of his arms, forced him on to his knees, and beat him till he was out of breath.

"There, you impudent dog! Now will you learn not to answer back when I speak to you? Take the horse back, and clean him properly. I'll teach you your place!"

"Young Mas'r," said Tom, "I specs what he was gwine to say was, that the horse would roll when he was bringing him up from the stable; he's so full of spirits,—that's the way he got that dirt on him; I looked to his cleaning."

"You hold your tongue till you're asked to speak!" said Henrique, turning on his heel, and walking up the steps to speak to Eva, who stood in her riding-dress.

"Dear Cousin, I'm sorry this stupid fellow has kept you waiting," he said. "Let's sit down here, on this seat till they come. What's the matter, Cousin?—you look sober."

"How could you be so cruel and wicked to poor Dodo?" asked Eva.

"Cruel,—wicked!" said the boy, with unaffected surprise. "What do you mean, dear Eva?"

"I don't want you to call me dear Eva, when you do so," said Eva.

"Dear Cousin, you don't know Dodo; it's the only way to manage him, he's so full of lies and excuses. The only way is to put him down at once,—not let him open his mouth; that's the way papa manages."

"But Uncle Tom said it was an accident, and he never tells what isn't true."

"He's an uncommon old nigger, then!" said Henrique. "Dodo will lie as fast as he can speak."

"You frighten him into deceiving, if you treat him so."

"Why, Eva, you've really taken such a fancy to Dodo, that I shall be jealous."

"But you beat him,—and he didn't deserve it."

"O, well, it may go for some time when he does, and don't get it. A few cuts never come amiss with Dodo,—he's a regular spirit, I can tell you; but I won't beat him again before you, if it troubles you."

Eva was not satisfied, but found it in vain to try to make her handsome cousin understand her feelings.

Dodo soon appeared, with the horses.

"Well, Dodo, you've done pretty well, this time," said his young master, with a more gracious air. "Come, now, and hold Miss Eva's horse while I put her on to the saddle."

Dodo came and stood by Eva's pony. His face was troubled; his eyes looked as if he had been crying.

Henrique, who valued himself on his gentlemanly adroitness in all matters of gallantry, soon had his fair cousin in the saddle, and, gathering the reins, placed them in her hands.

But Eva bent to the other side of the horse, where Dodo was standing, and said, as he relinquished the reins,—"That's a good boy, Dodo;—thank you!"

Dodo looked up in amazement into the sweet young face; the blood rushed to his cheeks, and the tears to his eyes.

"Here, Dodo," said his master, imperiously.

Dodo sprang and held the horse, while his master mounted.

"There's a picayune for you to buy candy with, Dodo," said Henrique; "go get some."

And Henrique cantered down the walk after Eva. Dodo stood looking after the two children. One had given him money; and one had given him what he wanted far more,—a kind word, kindly spoken. Dodo had been only a few months away from his mother. His master had bought him at a slave warehouse, for his handsome face, to be a match to the handsome pony; and he was now getting his breaking in, at the hands of his young master.

The scene of the beating had been witnessed by the two brothers St. Clare, from another part of the garden.

Augustine's cheek flushed; but he only observed, with his usual sarcastic carelessness.

"I suppose that's what we may call republican education, Alfred?"

"Henrique is a devil of a fellow, when his blood's up," said Alfred, carelessly.

"I suppose you consider this an instructive practice for him," said Augustine, drily.

"I couldn't help it, if I didn't. Henrique is a regular little tempest;—his mother and I have given him up, long ago. But, then, that Dodo is a perfect sprite,—no amount of whipping can hurt him."

"And this by way of teaching Henrique the first verse of a republican's catechism, 'All men are born free and equal!'"

"Poh!" said Alfred; "one of Tom Jefferson's pieces of French sentiment and humbug. It's perfectly ridiculous to have that going the rounds among us, to this day."

"I think it is," said St. Clare, significantly.

"Because," said Alfred, "we can see plainly enough that all men are *not* born free, nor born equal; they are born anything else. For my part, I think half this republican talk sheer humbug. It is the educated, the intelligent, the wealthy, the refined, who ought to have equal rights and not the canaille."

"If you can keep the canaille of that opinion," said Augustine. "They took *their* turn once, in France."

"Of course, they must be *kept down*, consistently, steadily, as I *should*," said Alfred, setting his foot hard down as if he were standing on somebody.

"It makes a terrible slip when they get up," said Augustine,—"in St. Domingo, for instance."

"Poh!" said Alfred, "we'll take care of that, in this country. We must set our face against all this educating, elevating talk, that is getting about now; the lower class must not be educated."

"That is past praying for," said Augustine; "educated they will be, and we have only to say how. Our system is educating them in barbarism and brutality. We are breaking all humanizing ties, and making them brute beasts; and, if they get the upper hand, such we shall find them."

"They shall never get the upper hand!" said Alfred.

"That's right," said St. Clare; "put on the steam, fasten down the escape-valve, and sit on it, and see where you'll land."

"Well," said Alfred, "we *will* see. I'm not afraid to sit on the escape-valve, as long as the boilers are strong, and the machinery works well."

"The nobles in Louis XVI.'s time thought just so; and Austria and Pius IX. think so now; and, some pleasant morning, you may all be caught up to meet each other in the air, *when the boilers burst*."

"*Dies declarabit*," said Alfred, laughing.

"I tell you," said Augustine, "if there is anything that is revealed with the strength of a divine law in our times, it is that the masses are to rise, and the under class become the upper one."

"That's one of your red republican humbugs, Augustine! Why didn't you ever take to the stump;—you'd make a famous stump orator! Well, I hope I shall be dead before this millennium of your greasy masses comes on."

"Greasy or not greasy, they will govern *you*, when their time comes," said Augustine; "and they will be just such rulers as you make them. The French noblesse chose to have the people '*sans culottes*,' and they had '*sans culotte*' governors to their hearts' content. The people of Hayti—"

"O, come, Augustine! as if we hadn't had enough of that abominable, contemptible Hayti![1] The Haytiens were not Anglo Saxons; if they had been there would have been another story. The Anglo Saxon is the dominant race of the world, and *is to be so*."

"Well, there is a pretty fair infusion of Anglo Saxon blood among our slaves, now," said Augustine. "There are plenty among them who have only enough of the African to give a sort of tropical warmth and fervor to our calculating firmness and foresight. If ever the San Domingo hour comes, Anglo Saxon blood will lead on the day. Sons of white fathers, with all our haughty feelings burning in their veins, will not always be bought and sold and traded. They will rise, and raise with them their mother's race."

"Stuff!—nonsense!"

---

[1] In August 1791, as a consequence of the French Revolution, the black slaves and mulattoes on Haiti rose in revolt against the whites, and in the period of turmoil that followed enormous cruelties were practised by both sides. The "Emperor" Dessalines, come to power in 1804, massacred all the whites on the island. Haitian bloodshed became an argument to show the barbarous nature of the Negro, a doctrine Wendell Phillips sought to combat in his celebrated lecture on Toussaint L'Ouverture.

CHAPTER XXIII

"Well," said Augustine, "there goes an old saying to this effect, 'As it was in the days of Noah so shall it be;—they ate, they drank, they planted, they builded, and knew not till the flood came and took them.'"

"On the whole, Augustine, I think your talents might do for a circuit rider," said Alfred, laughing. "Never you fear for us; possession is our nine points. We've got the power. This subject race," said he, stamping firmly, "is down and shall *stay* down! We have energy enough to manage our own powder."

"Sons trained like your Henrique will be grand guardians of your powder-magazines," said Augustine,—"so cool and self-possessed! The proverb says, 'They that cannot govern themselves cannot govern others.'"

"There is a trouble there" said Alfred, thoughtfully; "there's no doubt that our system is a difficult one to train children under. It gives too free scope to the passions, altogether, which, in our climate, are hot enough. I find trouble with Henrique. The boy is generous and warm-hearted, but a perfect fire-cracker when excited. I believe I shall send him North for his education, where obedience is more fashionable, and where he will associate more with equals, and less with dependents."

"Since training children is the staple work of the human race," said Augustine, "I should think it something of a consideration that our system does not work well there."

"It does not for some things," said Alfred; "for others, again, it does. It makes boys manly and courageous; and the very vices of an abject race tend to strengthen in them the opposite virtues. I think Henrique, now, has a keener sense of the beauty of truth, from seeing lying and deception the universal badge of slavery."

"A Christian-like view of the subject, certainly!" said Augustine.

"It's true, Christian-like or not; and is about as Christian-like as most other things in the world," said Alfred.

"That may be," said St. Clare.

"Well, there's no use in talking, Augustine. I believe we've been round and round this old track five hundred times, more or less. What do you say to a game of backgammon?"

The two brothers ran up the verandah steps, and were soon seated at a light bamboo stand, with the backgammon-board between them. As they were setting their men, Alfred said,

"I tell you, Augustine, if I thought as you do, I should do something."

"I dare say you would,—you are one of the doing sort,—but what?"

"Why, elevate your own servants, for a specimen," said Alfred, with a half-scornful smile.

"You might as well set Mount Ætna on them flat, and tell them to stand up under it, as tell me to elevate my servants under all the superincumbent mass of society upon them. One man can do nothing, against the whole action of a community. Education, to do anything, must be a state education; or there must be enough agreed in it to make a current."

"You take the first throw," said Alfred; and the brothers were soon lost in the game, and heard no more till the scraping of horses' feet was heard under the verandah.

"There come the children," said Augustine, rising. "Look here, Alf! Did you ever see anything so beautiful?" And, in truth, it *was* a beautiful sight. Henrique, with his bold brow, and dark, glossy curls, and glowing cheek, was laughing gayly as he bent towards his fair cousin, as they came on. She was dressed in a blue riding dress, with a cap of the same color. Exercise had given a brilliant hue to her cheeks, and heightened the effect of her singularly transparent skin, and golden hair.

"Good heavens! what perfectly dazzling beauty!" said Alfred. "I tell you, Auguste, won't she make some hearts ache, one of these days?"

"She will, too truly,—God knows I'm afraid so!" said St. Clare, in a tone of sudden bitterness, as he hurried down to take her off her horse.

"Eva darling! you're not much tired?" he said, as he clasped her in his arms.

"No, papa," said the child; but her short, hard breathing alarmed her father.

"How could you ride so fast, dear?—you know it's bad for you."

"I felt so well, papa, and liked it so much, I forgot."

St. Clare carried her in his arms into the parlor, and laid her on the sofa.

"Henrique, you must be careful of Eva," said he; "you mustn't ride fast with her."

"I'll take her under my care," said Henrique, seating himself by the sofa, and taking Eva's hand.

Eva soon found herself much better. Her father and uncle resumed their game, and the children were left together.

"Do you know, Eva, I'm sorry papa is only going to stay two days here, and then I shan't see you again for ever so long! If I stay with you, I'd try to be good, and not be cross to Dodo, and so on. I don't mean to treat Dodo ill; but, you know, I've got such a quick temper. I'm not really bad to him, though. I give him a picayune, now and then; and you see he dresses well. I think, on the whole, Dodo 's pretty well off."

"Would you think you were well off, if there were not one creature in the world near you to love you?"

"I?—Well, of course not."

"And you have taken Dodo away from all the friends he ever had, and now he has not a creature to love him;—nobody can be good that way."

"Well, I can't help it, as I know of. I can't get his mother and I can't love him myself, nor anybody else, as I know of."

"Why can't you?" said Eva.

"*Love* Dodo! Why, Eva, you wouldn't have me! I may *like* him well enough; but you don't *love* your servants."

"I do, indeed."

"How odd!"

"Don't the Bible say we must love everybody?"

"O, the Bible! To be sure, it says a great many such things; but, then, nobody ever thinks of doing them,—you know, Eva, nobody does."

Eva did not speak; her eyes were fixed and thoughtful for a few moments.

"At any rate," she said, "dear Cousin, do love poor Dodo, and be kind to him, for my sake!"

"I could love anything, for your sake, dear Cousin; for I really think you are the loveliest creature that I ever saw!" And Henrique spoke with an earnestness that flushed his handsome face. Eva received it with perfect simplicity, without even a change of feature; merely saying, "I'm glad you feel so, dear Henrique! I hope you will remember."

The dinner-bell put an end to the interview.

CHAPTER XXIV

FORESHADOWINGS

Two days after this, Alfred St. Clare and Augustine parted; and Eva, who had been stimulated, by the society of her young cousin, to exertions beyond her strength, began to fail rapidly. St. Clare was at last willing to call in medical advice,—a thing from which he had always shrunk, because it was the admission of an unwelcome truth.

But, for a day or two, Eva was so unwell as to be confined to the house; and the doctor was called.

Marie St. Clare had taken no notice of the child's gradually decaying health and strength, because she was completely absorbed in studying out two or three new forms of disease to which she believed she herself was a victim. It was the first principle of Marie's belief that nobody ever was or could be so great a sufferer as *herself*; and, therefore, she always repelled quite indignantly any suggestion that any one around her could be sick. She was always sure, in such a case, that it was nothing but laziness, or want of energy; and that, if they had had the suffering *she* had, they would soon know the difference.

Miss Ophelia had several times tried to awaken her maternal fears about Eva; but to no avail.

"I don't see as anything ails the child," she would say; "she runs about, and plays."

"But she has a cough."

"Cough! you don't need to tell *me* about a cough. I've always been subject to a cough, all my days. When I was of Eva's age, they thought I was in a consumption. Night after night, Mammy used to sit up with me. O! Eva's cough is not anything."

"But she gets weak, and is short-breathed."

"Law! I've had that, years and years; it's only a nervous affection."

"But she sweats so, nights!"

"Well, I have, these ten years. Very often, night after night, my clothes will be wringing wet. There won't be a dry thread in my night-clothes and the sheets will be so that Mammy has to hang them up to dry! Eva doesn't sweat anything like that!"

Miss Ophelia shut her mouth for a season. But, now that Eva was fairly and visibly prostrated, and a doctor called, Marie, all on a sudden, took a new turn.

"She knew it," she said; "she always felt it, that she was destined to be the most miserable of mothers. Here she was, with her wretched health, and her only darling child going down to the grave before her eyes;"—and Marie routed up Mammy nights, and rumpussed and scolded, with more energy than ever, all day, on the strength of this new misery.

"My dear Marie, don't talk so!" said St. Clare. "You ought not to give up the case so, at once."

"You have not a mother's feelings, St. Clare! You never could understand me!—you don't now."

"But don't talk so, as if it were a gone case!"

"I can't take it as indifferently as you can, St. Clare. If *you* don't feel when your only child is in this alarming state, I do. It's a blow too much for me, with all I was bearing before."

"It's true," said St. Clare, "that Eva is very delicate, *that* I always knew; and that she has grown so rapidly as to exhaust her strength; and that her situation is critical. But just now she is only prostrated by the heat of the weather, and by the excitement of her cousin's visit, and the exertions she made. The physician says there is room for hope."

"Well, of course, if you can look on the bright side, pray do; it's a mercy if people haven't sensitive feelings, in this world. I am sure I wish I didn't feel as I do; it only makes me completely wretched! I wish I *could* be as easy as the rest of you!"

And the "rest of them" had good reason to breathe the same prayer, for Marie paraded her new misery as the reason and apology for all sorts of inflictions on every one about her. Every word that was spoken by anybody, everything that was done or was not done everywhere, was only a new proof that she was surrounded by hard-hearted, insensible beings, who were unmindful of her peculiar sorrows. Poor Eva heard some of these speeches; and nearly cried her little eyes out, in pity for her mamma, and in sorrow that she should make her so much distress.

In a week or two, there was a great improvement of symptoms,—one of those deceitful lulls, by which her inexorable disease so often beguiles the anxious heart, even on the verge of the grave. Eva's step was again in the garden,—in the balconies; she played and laughed again,—and her father, in a transport, declared that they should soon have her as hearty as anybody. Miss Ophelia and the physician alone felt no encouragement from this illusive truce. There was one other heart, too, that felt the same certainty, and that was the little heart of Eva. What is it that sometimes speaks in the soul so calmly, so clearly, that its earthly time is short? Is it the secret instinct of decaying nature, or the soul's impulsive throb, as immortality draws on? Be it what it may, it rested in the heart of Eva, a calm, sweet, prophetic certainty that Heaven was near; calm as the light of sunset, sweet as the bright stillness of autumn, there her little heart reposed, only troubled by sorrow for those who loved her so dearly.

For the child, though nursed so tenderly, and though life was unfolding before her with every brightness that love and wealth could give, had no regret for herself in dying.

In that book which she and her simple old friend had read so much together, she had seen and taken to her young heart the image of one who loved the little child; and, as she gazed and mused, He had ceased to be an image and a picture of the distant past, and come to be a living, all-surrounding reality. His love enfolded her childish heart with more than mortal tenderness; and it was to Him, she said, she was going, and to his home.

But her heart yearned with sad tenderness for all that she was to leave behind. Her father most,—for Eva, though she never distinctly thought so, had an instinctive perception that she was more in his heart than any other. She loved her mother because she was so loving a creature, and all the selfishness that she had seen in her only saddened and perplexed her; for she had a child's implicit trust that her mother could not do wrong. There was something about her that Eva never could make out; and she always smoothed it over with thinking that, after all, it was mamma, and she loved her very dearly indeed.

She felt, too, for those fond, faithful servants, to whom she was as daylight and sunshine. Children do not usually generalize; but Eva was an uncommonly mature child, and the things that she had witnessed of the evils of the system under which they were living had fallen, one by one, into the depths of her thoughtful, pondering heart. She had vague longings to do something for them,—to bless and save not only them, but all in their condition,—longings that contrasted sadly with the feebleness of her little frame.

"Uncle Tom," she said, one day, when she was reading to her friend, "I can understand why Jesus *wanted* to die for us."

"Why, Miss Eva?"

"Because I've felt so, too."

"What is it Miss Eva?—I don't understand."

"I can't tell you; but, when I saw those poor creatures on the boat, you know, when you came up and I,—some had lost their mothers, and some their husbands, and some mothers cried for their little children—and when I heard about poor Prue,—oh, wasn't that dreadful!—and a great many other times, I've felt that I would be glad to die, if my dying could stop all this misery. *I would* die for them, Tom, if I could," said the child, earnestly, laying her little thin hand on his.

Tom looked at the child with awe; and when she, hearing her father's voice, glided away, he wiped his eyes many times, as he looked after her.

"It's jest no use tryin' to keep Miss Eva here," he said to Mammy, whom he met a moment after. "She's got the Lord's mark in her forehead."

"Ah, yes, yes," said Mammy, raising her hands; "I've allers said so. She wasn't never like a child that's to live—there was allers something deep in her eyes. I've told Missis so, many the time; it's a comin' true,—we all sees it,—dear, little, blessed lamb!"

Eva came tripping up the verandah steps to her father. It was late in the afternoon, and the rays of the sun formed a kind of glory behind her, as she came forward in her white dress, with her golden hair and glowing cheeks, her eyes unnaturally bright with the slow fever that burned in her veins.

St. Clare had called her to show a statuette that he had been buying for her; but her appearance, as she came on, impressed him suddenly and painfully. There is a kind of beauty so intense, yet so fragile, that we cannot bear to look at it. Her father folded her suddenly in his arms, and almost forgot what he was going to tell her.

"Eva, dear, you are better now-a-days,—are you not?"

"Papa," said Eva, with sudden firmness "I've had things I wanted to say to you, a great while. I want to say them now, before I get weaker."

St. Clare trembled as Eva seated herself in his lap. She laid her head on his bosom, and said,

"It's all no use, papa, to keep it to myself any longer. The time is coming that I am going to leave you. I am going, and never to come back!" and Eva sobbed.

"O, now, my dear little Eva!" said St. Clare, trembling as he spoke, but speaking cheerfully, "you've got nervous and low-spirited; you mustn't indulge such gloomy thoughts. See here, I've bought a statuette for you!"

"No, papa," said Eva, putting it gently away, "don't deceive yourself!—I am *not* any better, I know it perfectly well,—and I am going, before long. I am not nervous,—I am not low-spirited. If it were not for you, papa, and my friends, I should be perfectly happy. I want to go,—I long to go!"

"Why, dear child, what has made your poor little heart so sad? You have had everything, to make you happy, that could be given you."

"I had rather be in heaven; though, only for my friends' sake, I would be willing to live. There are a great many things here that make me sad, that seem dreadful to me; I had rather be there; but I don't want to leave you,—it almost breaks my heart!"

"What makes you sad, and seems dreadful, Eva?"

"O, things that are done, and done all the time. I feel sad for our poor people; they love me dearly, and they are all good and kind to me. I wish, papa, they were all *free*."

"Why, Eva, child, don't you think they are well enough off now?"

"O, but, papa, if anything should happen to you, what would become of them? There are very few men like you, papa. Uncle Alfred isn't like you, and mamma isn't; and then, think of poor old Prue's owners! What horrid things people do, and can do!" and Eva shuddered.

"My dear child, you are too sensitive. I'm sorry I ever let you hear such stories."

"O, that's what troubles me, papa. You want me to live so happy, and never to have any pain,—never suffer anything,—not even hear a sad story, when other poor creatures have nothing but pain and sorrow, all their lives;—it seems selfish. I ought to know such things, I ought to feel about them! Such things always sunk into my heart; they went down deep; I've thought and thought about them. Papa, isn't there any way to have all slaves made free?"

"That's a difficult question, dearest. There's no doubt that this way is a very bad one; a great many people think so; I do myself I heartily wish that there were not a slave in the land; but, then, I don't know what is to be done about it!"

"Papa, you are such a good man, and so noble, and kind, and you always have a way of saying things that is so pleasant, couldn't you go all round and try to persuade people to do right about this? When I am dead, papa, then you will think of me, and do it for my sake. I would do it, if I could."

"When you are dead, Eva," said St. Clare, passionately. "O, child, don't talk to me so! You are all I have on earth."

"Poor old Prue's child was all that she had,—and yet she had to hear it crying, and she couldn't help it! Papa, these poor creatures love their children as much as you do me. O! do something for them! There's poor Mammy loves her children; I've seen her cry when she talked about them. And Tom loves his children; and it's dreadful, papa, that such things are happening, all the time!"

"There, there, darling," said St. Clare, soothingly; "only don't distress yourself, don't talk of dying, and I will do anything you wish."

"And promise me, dear father, that Tom shall have his freedom as soon as"—she stopped, and said, in a hesitating tone—"I am gone!"

"Yes, dear, I will do anything in the world,—anything you could ask me to."

"Dear papa," said the child, laying her burning cheek against his, "how I wish we could go together!"

"Where, dearest?" said St. Clare.

"To our Saviour's home; it's so sweet and peaceful there—it is all so loving there!" The child spoke unconsciously, as of a place where she had often been. "Don't you want to go, papa?" she said.

St. Clare drew her closer to him, but was silent.

"You will come to me," said the child, speaking in a voice of calm certainty which she often used unconsciously.

"I shall come after you. I shall not forget you."

The shadows of the solemn evening closed round them deeper and deeper, as St. Clare sat silently holding the little frail form to his bosom. He saw no more the deep eyes, but the voice came over him as a spirit voice, and, as in a sort of judgment vision, his whole past life rose in a moment before his eyes: his mother's prayers and hymns; his own early yearnings and aspirings for good; and, between them and this hour, years of worldliness and scepticism, and what man calls respectable living. We can think *much*, very much, in a moment. St. Clare saw and felt many things, but spoke nothing; and, as it grew darker, he took his child to her bed-room; and, when she was prepared for rest; he sent away the attendants, and rocked her in his arms, and sung to her till she was asleep.

CHAPTER XXV

THE LITTLE EVANGELIST

It was Sunday afternoon. St. Clare was stretched on a bamboo lounge in the verandah, solacing himself with a cigar. Marie lay reclined on a sofa, opposite the window opening on the verandah, closely secluded, under an awning of transparent gauze, from the outrages of the mosquitos, and languidly holding in her hand an elegantly bound prayer-book. She was holding it because it was Sunday, and she imagined she had been reading it,—though, in fact, she had been only taking a succession of short naps, with it open in her hand.

Miss Ophelia, who, after some rummaging, had hunted up a small Methodist meeting within riding distance, had gone out, with Tom as driver, to attend it; and Eva had accompanied them.

"I say, Augustine," said Marie after dozing a while, "I must send to the city after my old Doctor Posey; I'm sure I've got the complaint of the heart."

"Well; why need you send for him? This doctor that attends Eva seems skilful."

"I would not trust him in a critical case," said Marie; "and I think I may say mine is becoming so! I've been thinking of it, these two or three nights past; I have such distressing pains, and such strange feelings."

"O, Marie, you are blue; I don't believe it's heart complaint."

"I dare say *you* don't," said Marie; "I was prepared to expect *that*. You can be alarmed enough, if Eva coughs, or has the least thing the matter with her; but you never think of me."

"If it's particularly agreeable to you to have heart disease, why, I'll try and maintain you have it," said St. Clare; "I didn't know it was."

"Well, I only hope you won't be sorry for this, when it's too late!" said Marie; "but, believe it or not, my distress about Eva, and the exertions I have made with that dear child, have developed what I have long suspected."

What the *exertions* were which Marie referred to, it would have been difficult to state. St. Clare quietly made this commentary to himself, and went on smoking, like a hard-hearted wretch of a man as he was, till a carriage drove up before the verandah, and Eva and Miss Ophelia alighted.

Miss Ophelia marched straight to her own chamber, to put away her bonnet and shawl, as was always her manner, before she spoke a word on any subject; while Eva came, at St. Clare's call, and was sitting on his knee, giving him an account of the services they had heard.

They soon heard loud exclamations from Miss Ophelia's room, which, like the one in which they were sitting, opened on to the verandah and violent reproof addressed to somebody.

"What new witchcraft has Tops been brewing?" asked St. Clare. "That commotion is of her raising, I'll be bound!"

And, in a moment after, Miss Ophelia, in high indignation, came dragging the culprit along.

"Come out here, now!" she said. "I *will* tell your master!"

"What's the case now?" asked Augustine.

"The case is, that I cannot be plagued with this child, any longer! It's past all bearing; flesh and blood cannot endure it! Here, I locked her up, and gave her a hymn to study; and what does she do, but spy out where I put my key, and has gone to my bureau, and got a bonnet-trimming, and cut it all to pieces to make dolls' jackets! I never saw anything like it, in my life!"

"I told you, Cousin," said Marie, "that you'd find out that these creatures can't be brought up without severity. If I had *my* way, now," she said, looking reproachfully at St. Clare, "I'd send that child out, and have her thoroughly whipped; I'd have her whipped till she couldn't stand!"

"I don't doubt it," said St. Clare. "Tell me of the lovely rule of woman! I never saw above a dozen women that wouldn't half kill a horse, or a servant, either, if they had their own way with them!—let alone a man."

"There is no use in this shilly-shally way of yours, St. Clare!" said Marie. "Cousin is a woman of sense, and she sees it now, as plain as I do."

Miss Ophelia had just the capability of indignation that belongs to the thorough-paced housekeeper, and this had been pretty actively roused by the artifice and wastefulness of the child; in fact, many of my lady readers must own that they should have felt just so in her circumstances; but Marie's words went beyond her, and she felt less heat.

"I wouldn't have the child treated so, for the world," she said; "but, I am sure, Augustine, I don't know what to do. I've taught and taught; I've talked till I'm tired; I've whipped her; I've punished her in every way I can think of, and she's just what she was at first."

"Come here, Tops, you monkey!" said St. Clare, calling the child up to him.

Topsy came up; her round, hard eyes glittering and blinking with a mixture of apprehensiveness and their usual odd drollery.

"What makes you behave so?" said St. Clare, who could not help being amused with the child's expression.

"Spects it's my wicked heart," said Topsy, demurely; "Miss Feely says so."

"Don't you see how much Miss Ophelia has done for you? She says she has done everything she can think of."

"Lor, yes, Mas'r! old Missis used to say so, too. She whipped me a heap harder, and used to pull my har, and knock my head agin the door; but it didn't do me no good! I spects, if they 's to pull every spire o' har out o' my head, it wouldn't do no good, neither,—I 's so wicked! Laws! I 's nothin but a nigger, no ways!"

"Well, I shall have to give her up," said Miss Ophelia; "I can't have that trouble any longer."

"Well, I'd just like to ask one question," said St. Clare.

"What is it?"

"Why, if your Gospel is not strong enough to save one heathen child, that you can have at home here, all to yourself, what's the use of sending one or two poor missionaries off with it among thousands of just such? I suppose this child is about a fair sample of what thousands of your heathen are."

Miss Ophelia did not make an immediate answer; and Eva, who had stood a silent spectator of the scene thus far, made a silent sign to Topsy to follow her. There was a little glass-room at the corner of the verandah, which St. Clare used as a sort of reading-room; and Eva and Topsy disappeared into this place.

"What's Eva going about, now?" said St. Clare; "I mean to see."

And, advancing on tiptoe, he lifted up a curtain that covered the glass-door, and looked in. In a moment, laying his finger on his lips, he made a silent gesture to Miss Ophelia to come and look. There sat the two children on the floor, with their side faces towards them. Topsy, with her usual air of careless drollery and unconcern; but, opposite to her, Eva, her whole face fervent with feeling, and tears in her large eyes.

"What does make you so bad, Topsy? Why won't you try and be good? Don't you love *anybody*, Topsy?"

"Donno nothing 'bout love; I loves candy and sich, that's all," said Topsy.

"But you love your father and mother?"

"Never had none, ye know. I telled ye that, Miss Eva."

"O, I know," said Eva, sadly; "but hadn't you any brother, or sister, or aunt, or—"

"No, none on 'em,—never had nothing nor nobody."

"But, Topsy, if you'd only try to be good, you might—"

"Couldn't never be nothin' but a nigger, if I was ever so good," said Topsy. "If I could be skinned, and come white, I'd try then."

"But people can love you, if you are black, Topsy. Miss Ophelia would love you, if you were good."

Topsy gave the short, blunt laugh that was her common mode of expressing incredulity.

"Don't you think so?" said Eva.

"No; she can't bar me, 'cause I'm a nigger!—she'd 's soon have a toad touch her! There can't nobody love niggers, and niggers can't do nothin'! *I* don't care," said Topsy, beginning to whistle.

"O, Topsy, poor child, *I* love you!" said Eva, with a sudden burst of feeling, and laying her little thin, white hand on Topsy's shoulder; "I love you, because you haven't had any father, or mother, or friends;—because you've been a poor, abused child! I love you, and I want you to be good. I am very unwell, Topsy, and I think I shan't live a great while; and it really grieves me, to have you be so naughty. I wish you would try to be good, for my sake;—it's only a little while I shall be with you."

The round, keen eyes of the black child were overcast with tears;—large, bright drops rolled heavily down, one by one, and fell on the little white hand. Yes, in that moment, a ray of real belief, a ray of heavenly love, had penetrated the darkness of her heathen soul! She laid her head down between her knees, and wept and sobbed,—while the beautiful child, bending over her, looked like the picture of some bright angel stooping to reclaim a sinner.

"Poor Topsy!" said Eva, "don't you know that Jesus loves all alike? He is just as willing to love you, as me. He loves you just as I do,—only more, because he is better. He will help you to be good; and you can go to Heaven at last, and be an angel forever, just as much as if you were white. Only think of it, Topsy!—*you* can be one of those spirits bright, Uncle Tom sings about."

"O, dear Miss Eva, dear Miss Eva!" said the child; "I will try, I will try; I never did care nothin' about it before."

St. Clare, at this instant, dropped the curtain. "It puts me in mind of mother," he said to Miss Ophelia. "It is true what she told me; if we want to give sight to the blind, we must be willing to do as Christ did,—call them to us, and *put our hands on them*."

"I've always had a prejudice against negroes," said Miss Ophelia, "and it's a fact, I never could bear to have that child touch me; but, I don't think she knew it."

"Trust any child to find that out," said St. Clare; "there's no keeping it from them. But I believe that all the trying in the world to benefit a child, and all the substantial favors you can do them, will never excite one emotion of gratitude, while that feeling of repugnance remains in the heart;—it's a queer kind of a fact,—but so it is."

"I don't know how I can help it," said Miss Ophelia; "they *are* disagreeable to me,—this child in particular,—how can I help feeling so?"

"Eva does, it seems."

"Well, she's so loving! After all, though, she's no more than Christ-like," said Miss Ophelia; "I wish I were like her. She might teach me a lesson."

"It wouldn't be the first time a little child had been used to instruct an old disciple, if it *were* so," said St. Clare.

CHAPTER XXVI

DEATH

Weep not for those whom the veil of the tomb, In life's early morning, hath hid from our eyes.[1]

Eva's bed-room was a spacious apartment, which, like all the other rooms in the house, opened on to the broad verandah. The room communicated, on one side, with her father and mother's apartment; on the other, with that appropriated to Miss Ophelia. St. Clare had gratified his own eye and taste, in furnishing this room in a style that had a peculiar keeping with the character of her for whom it was intended. The windows were hung with curtains of rose-colored and white muslin, the floor was spread with a matting which had been ordered in Paris, to a pattern of his own device, having round it a border of rose-buds and leaves, and a centre-piece with full-flown roses. The bedstead, chairs, and lounges, were of bamboo, wrought in peculiarly graceful and fanciful patterns. Over the head of the bed was an alabaster bracket, on which a beautiful sculptured angel stood, with drooping wings, holding out a crown of myrtle-leaves. From this depended, over the bed, light curtains of rose-colored gauze, striped with silver, supplying that protection from mosquitos which is an indispensable addition to all sleeping accommodation in that climate. The graceful bamboo lounges were amply supplied with cushions of rose-colored damask, while over them, depending from the hands of sculptured figures, were gauze curtains similar to those of the bed. A light, fanciful bamboo table stood in the middle of the room, where a Parian vase, wrought in the shape of a white lily, with its buds, stood, ever filled with flowers. On this table lay Eva's books and little trinkets, with an elegantly wrought alabaster writing-stand, which her father had supplied to her when he saw her trying to improve herself in writing. There was a fireplace in the room, and on the marble mantle above stood a beautifully wrought statuette of Jesus receiving little children, and on either side marble vases, for which it was Tom's pride and delight to offer bouquets every morning. Two or three exquisite paintings of children, in

---

[1] "Weep Not for Those," a poem by Thomas Moore (1779-1852).

various attitudes, embellished the wall. In short, the eye could turn nowhere without meeting images of childhood, of beauty, and of peace. Those little eyes never opened, in the morning light, without falling on something which suggested to the heart soothing and beautiful thoughts.

The deceitful strength which had buoyed Eva up for a little while was fast passing away; seldom and more seldom her light footstep was heard in the verandah, and oftener and oftener she was found reclined on a little lounge by the open window, her large, deep eyes fixed on the rising and falling waters of the lake.

It was towards the middle of the afternoon, as she was so reclining,—her Bible half open, her little transparent fingers lying listlessly between the leaves,—suddenly she heard her mother's voice, in sharp tones, in the verandah.

"What now, you baggage!—what new piece of mischief! You've been picking the flowers, hey?" and Eva heard the sound of a smart slap.

"Law, Missis! they 's for Miss Eva," she heard a voice say, which she knew belonged to Topsy.

"Miss Eva! A pretty excuse!—you suppose she wants *your* flowers, you good-for-nothing nigger! Get along off with you!"

In a moment, Eva was off from her lounge, and in the verandah.

"O, don't, mother! I should like the flowers; do give them to me; I want them!"

"Why, Eva, your room is full now."

"I can't have too many," said Eva. "Topsy, do bring them here."

Topsy, who had stood sullenly, holding down her head, now came up and offered her flowers. She did it with a look of hesitation and bashfulness, quite unlike the eldrich boldness and brightness which was usual with her.

"It's a beautiful bouquet!" said Eva, looking at it.

It was rather a singular one,—a brilliant scarlet geranium, and one single white japonica, with its glossy leaves. It was tied up with an evident eye to the contrast of color, and the arrangement of every leaf had carefully been studied.

Topsy looked pleased, as Eva said,—"Topsy, you arrange flowers very prettily. Here," she said, "is this vase I haven't any flowers for. I wish you'd arrange something every day for it."

"Well, that's odd!" said Marie. "What in the world do you want that for?"

"Never mind, mamma; you'd as lief as not Topsy should do it,—had you not?"

"Of course, anything you please, dear! Topsy, you hear your young mistress;—see that you mind."

Topsy made a short courtesy, and looked down; and, as she turned away, Eva saw a tear roll down her dark cheek.

"You see, mamma, I knew poor Topsy wanted to do something for me," said Eva to her mother.

"O, nonsense! it's only because she likes to do mischief. She knows she mustn't pick flowers,—so she does it; that's all there is to it. But, if you fancy to have her pluck them, so be it."

"Mamma, I think Topsy is different from what she used to be; she's trying to be a good girl."

"She'll have to try a good while before *she* gets to be good," said Marie, with a careless laugh.

"Well, you know, mamma, poor Topsy! everything has always been against her."

"Not since she's been here, I'm sure. If she hasn't been talked to, and preached to, and every earthly thing done that anybody could do;—and she's just so ugly, and always will be; you can't make anything of the creature!"

"But, mamma, it's so different to be brought up as I've been, with so many friends, so many things to make me good and happy; and to be brought up as she's been, all the time, till she came here!"

"Most likely," said Marie, yawning,—"dear me, how hot it is!"

"Mamma, you believe, don't you, that Topsy could become an angel, as well as any of us, if she were a Christian?"

"Topsy! what a ridiculous idea! Nobody but you would ever think of it. I suppose she could, though."

"But, mamma, isn't God her father, as much as ours? Isn't Jesus her Saviour?"

"Well, that may be. I suppose God made everybody," said Marie. "Where is my smelling-bottle?"

"It's such a pity,—oh! *such* a pity!" said Eva, looking out on the distant lake, and speaking half to herself.

"What's a pity?" said Marie.

"Why, that any one, who could be a bright angel, and live with angels, should go all down, down down, and nobody help them!—oh dear!"

"Well, we can't help it; it's no use worrying, Eva! I don't know what's to be done; we ought to be thankful for our own advantages."

"I hardly can be," said Eva, "I'm so sorry to think of poor folks that haven't any."

"That's odd enough," said Marie;—"I'm sure my religion makes me thankful for my advantages."

"Mamma," said Eva, "I want to have some of my hair cut off,—a good deal of it."

"What for?" said Marie.

"Mamma, I want to give some away to my friends, while I am able to give it to them myself. Won't you ask aunty to come and cut it for me?"

Marie raised her voice, and called Miss Ophelia, from the other room.

The child half rose from her pillow as she came in, and, shaking down her long golden-brown curls, said, rather playfully, "Come aunty, shear the sheep!"

"What's that?" said St. Clare, who just then entered with some fruit he had been out to get for her.

"Papa, I just want aunty to cut off some of my hair;—there's too much of it, and it makes my head hot. Besides, I want to give some of it away."

Miss Ophelia came, with her scissors.

"Take care,—don't spoil the looks of it!" said her father; "cut underneath, where it won't show. Eva's curls are my pride."

"O, papa!" said Eva, sadly.

"Yes, and I want them kept handsome against the time I take you up to your uncle's plantation, to see Cousin Henrique," said St. Clare, in a gay tone.

"I shall never go there, papa;—I am going to a better country. O, do believe me! Don't you see, papa, that I get weaker, every day?"

"Why do you insist that I shall believe such a cruel thing, Eva?" said her father.

"Only because it is *true*, papa: and, if you will believe it now, perhaps you will get to feel about it as I do."

St. Clare closed his lips, and stood gloomily eying the long, beautiful curls, which, as they were separated from the child's head, were laid, one by one, in her lap. She raised them up, looked earnestly at them, twined them around her thin fingers, and looked from time to time, anxiously at her father.

"It's just what I've been foreboding!" said Marie; "it's just what has been preying on my health, from day to day, bringing me downward to the grave, though nobody regards it. I have seen this, long. St. Clare, you will see, after a while, that I was right."

"Which will afford you great consolation, no doubt!" said St. Clare, in a dry, bitter tone.

Marie lay back on a lounge, and covered her face with her cambric handkerchief.

Eva's clear blue eye looked earnestly from one to the other. It was the calm, comprehending gaze of a soul half loosed from its earthly bonds; it was evident she saw, felt, and appreciated, the difference between the two.

She beckoned with her hand to her father. He came and sat down by her.

"Papa, my strength fades away every day, and I know I must go. There are some things I want to say and do,—that I ought to do; and you are so unwilling to have me speak a word on this subject. But it must come; there's no putting it off. Do be willing I should speak now!"

"My child, I *am* willing!" said St. Clare, covering his eyes with one hand, and holding up Eva's hand with the other.

"Then, I want to see all our people together. I have some things I *must* say to them," said Eva.

"*Well*," said St. Clare, in a tone of dry endurance.

Miss Ophelia despatched a messenger, and soon the whole of the servants were convened in the room.

Eva lay back on her pillows; her hair hanging loosely about her face, her crimson cheeks contrasting painfully with the intense whiteness of her complexion and the thin contour of her limbs and features, and her large, soul-like eyes fixed earnestly on every one.

The servants were struck with a sudden emotion. The spiritual face, the long locks of hair cut off and lying by her, her father's averted face, and Marie's sobs, struck at once upon the feelings of a sensitive and impressible race; and, as they came in, they looked one on another, sighed, and shook their heads. There was a deep silence, like that of a funeral.

Eva raised herself, and looked long and earnestly round at every one. All looked sad and apprehensive. Many of the women hid their faces in their aprons.

"I sent for you all, my dear friends," said Eva, "because I love you. I love you all; and I have something to say to you, which I want you always to remember. . . . I am going to leave you. In a few more weeks you will see me no more—"

Here the child was interrupted by bursts of groans, sobs, and lamentations, which broke from all present, and in which her slender voice was lost entirely. She waited a moment, and then, speaking in a tone that checked the sobs of all, she said,

"If you love me, you must not interrupt me so. Listen to what I say. I want to speak to you about your souls. . . . Many of you, I am afraid, are very careless. You are thinking only about this world. I want you to remember that there is a beautiful world, where Jesus is. I am going there, and you can go there. It is for you, as much as me. But, if you want to go there, you must not live idle, careless, thoughtless lives. You must be Christians. You must remember that each one of you can become angels, and be angels forever. . . . If you want to be Christians, Jesus will help you. You must pray to him; you must read—"

The child checked herself, looked piteously at them, and said, sorrowfully,

"O dear! you *can't* read—poor souls!" and she hid her face in the pillow and sobbed, while many a smothered sob from those she was addressing, who were kneeling on the floor, aroused her.

"Never mind," she said, raising her face and smiling brightly through her tears, "I have prayed for you; and I know Jesus will help you, even if you can't read. Try all to do the best you can; pray every day; ask Him to help you, and get the Bible read to you whenever you can; and I think I shall see you all in heaven."

"Amen," was the murmured response from the lips of Tom and Mammy, and some of the elder ones, who belonged to the Methodist church. The younger and more thoughtless ones, for the time completely overcome, were sobbing, with their heads bowed upon their knees.

"I know," said Eva, "you all love me."

"Yes; oh, yes! indeed we do! Lord bless her!" was the involuntary answer of all.

"Yes, I know you do! There isn't one of you that hasn't always been very kind to me; and I want to give you something that, when you look at, you shall always remember me, I'm going to give all of you a curl of my hair; and, when you look at it, think that I loved you and am gone to heaven, and that I want to see you all there."

It is impossible to describe the scene, as, with tears and sobs, they gathered round the little creature, and took from her hands what seemed to them a last mark of her love. They fell on their knees; they sobbed, and prayed, and kissed the hem of her garment; and the elder ones poured forth words of endearment, mingled in prayers and blessings, after the manner of their susceptible race.

As each one took their gift, Miss Ophelia, who was apprehensive for the effect of all this excitement on her little patient, signed to each one to pass out of the apartment.

At last, all were gone but Tom and Mammy.

"Here, Uncle Tom," said Eva, "is a beautiful one for you. O, I am so happy, Uncle Tom, to think I shall see you in heaven,—for I'm sure I shall; and Mammy,—dear, good, kind Mammy!" she said, fondly throwing her arms round her old nurse,—"I know you'll be there, too."

"O, Miss Eva, don't see how I can live without ye, no how!" said the faithful creature. "'Pears like it's just taking everything off the place to oncet!" and Mammy gave way to a passion of grief.

Miss Ophelia pushed her and Tom gently from the apartment, and thought they were all gone; but, as she turned, Topsy was standing there.

"Where did you start up from?" she said, suddenly.

"I was here," said Topsy, wiping the tears from her eyes. "O, Miss Eva, I've been a bad girl; but won't you give *me* one, too?"

"Yes, poor Topsy! to be sure, I will. There—every time you look at that, think that I love you, and wanted you to be a good girl!"

"O, Miss Eva, I *is* tryin!" said Topsy, earnestly; "but, Lor, it's so hard to be good! 'Pears like I an't used to it, no ways!"

"Jesus knows it, Topsy; he is sorry for you; he will help you."

Topsy, with her eyes hid in her apron, was silently passed from the apartment by Miss Ophelia; but, as she went, she hid the precious curl in her bosom.

All being gone, Miss Ophelia shut the door. That worthy lady had wiped away many tears of her own, during the scene; but concern for the consequence of such an excitement to her young charge was uppermost in her mind.

St. Clare had been sitting, during the whole time, with his hand shading his eyes, in the same attitude.

When they were all gone, he sat so still.

"Papa!" said Eva, gently, laying her hand on his.

He gave a sudden start and shiver; but made no answer.

"Dear papa!" said Eva.

"*I cannot*," said St. Clare, rising, "I *cannot* have it so! The Almighty hath dealt *very bitterly* with me!" and St. Clare pronounced these words with a bitter emphasis, indeed.

"Augustine! has not God a right to do what he will with his own?" said Miss Ophelia.

"Perhaps so; but that doesn't make it any easier to bear," said he, with a dry, hard, tearless manner, as he turned away.

"Papa, you break my heart!" said Eva, rising and throwing herself into his arms; "you must not feel so!" and the child sobbed and wept with a violence which alarmed them all, and turned her father's thoughts at once to another channel.

"There, Eva,—there, dearest! Hush! hush! I was wrong; I was wicked. I will feel any way, do any way,—only don't distress yourself; don't sob so. I will be resigned; I was wicked to speak as I did."

Eva soon lay like a wearied dove in her father's arms; and he, bending over her, soothed her by every tender word he could think of.

Marie rose and threw herself out of the apartment into her own, when she fell into violent hysterics.

"You didn't give me a curl, Eva," said her father, smiling sadly.

"They are all yours, papa," said she, smiling—"yours and mamma's; and you must give dear aunty as many as she wants. I only gave them to our poor people myself, because you know, papa, they might be forgotten when I am gone, and because I hoped it might help them remember. . . . You are a Christian, are you not, papa?" said Eva, doubtfully.

"Why do you ask me?"

"I don't know. You are so good, I don't see how you can help it."

"What is being a Christian, Eva?"

"Loving Christ most of all," said Eva.

"Do you, Eva?"

"Certainly I do."

"You never saw him," said St. Clare.

"That makes no difference," said Eva. "I believe him, and in a few days I shall *see* him;" and the young face grew fervent, radiant with joy.

St. Clare said no more. It was a feeling which he had seen before in his mother; but no chord within vibrated to it.

Eva, after this, declined rapidly; there was no more any doubt of the event; the fondest hope could not be blinded. Her beautiful room was avowedly a sick room; and Miss Ophelia day and night performed the duties of a nurse,—and never did her friends appreciate her value more than in that capacity. With so well-trained a hand and eye, such perfect adroitness and practice in every art which could promote neatness and comfort, and keep out of sight every disagreeable incident of sickness,—with such a perfect sense of time, such a clear, untroubled head, such exact accuracy in remembering every prescription and direction of the doctors,—she was everything to him. They who had shrugged their shoulders at her little peculiarities and setnesses, so unlike the careless freedom of southern manners, acknowledged that now she was the exact person that was wanted.

Uncle Tom was much in Eva's room. The child suffered much from nervous restlessness, and it was a relief to her to be carried; and it was Tom's greatest delight to carry her little frail form in his arms, resting on a pillow, now up and down her room, now out into the verandah; and when the fresh sea-breezes blew from the lake,—and the child felt freshest in the morning,—he would sometimes walk with her under the orange-trees in the garden, or, sitting down in some of their old seats, sing to her their favorite old hymns.

Her father often did the same thing; but his frame was slighter, and when he was weary, Eva would say to him,

"O, papa, let Tom take me. Poor fellow! it pleases him; and you know it's all he can do now, and he wants to do something!"

"So do I, Eva!" said her father.

"Well, papa, you can do everything, and are everything to me. You read to me,—you sit up nights,—and Tom has only this one thing, and his singing; and I know, too, he does it easier than you can. He carries me so strong!"

The desire to do something was not confined to Tom. Every servant in the establishment showed the same feeling, and in their way did what they could.

Poor Mammy's heart yearned towards her darling; but she found no opportunity, night or day, as Marie declared that the state of her mind was such, it was impossible for her to rest; and, of course, it was against her principles to let any one else rest. Twenty times in a night, Mammy would be roused to rub her feet, to bathe her head, to find her pocket-handkerchief, to see what the noise was in Eva's room, to let down a curtain because it was too light, or to put it up because it was too dark; and, in the daytime, when she longed to have some share in the nursing of her pet, Marie seemed unusually ingenious in keeping her busy anywhere and everywhere all over the house, or about her own person; so that stolen interviews and momentary glimpses were all she could obtain.

"I feel it my duty to be particularly careful of myself, now," she would say, "feeble as I am, and with the whole care and nursing of that dear child upon me."

"Indeed, my dear," said St. Clare, "I thought our cousin relieved you of that."

"You talk like a man, St. Clare,—just as if a mother *could* be relieved of the care of a child in that state; but, then, it's all alike,—no one ever knows what I feel! I can't throw things off, as you do."

St. Clare smiled. You must excuse him, he couldn't help it,—for St. Clare could smile yet. For so bright and placid was the farewell voyage of the little spirit,—by such sweet and fragrant breezes was the small bark borne towards the heavenly shores,—that it was impossible to realize that it was death that was approaching. The child felt no pain,—only a tranquil, soft weakness, daily and almost insensibly increasing; and she was so beautiful, so loving, so trustful, so happy, that one could not resist the soothing influence of that air of innocence and peace which seemed to breathe around her. St. Clare found a strange calm coming over him. It was not hope,—that was impossible; it was not resignation; it was only a calm resting in the present, which seemed so beautiful that he wished to think of no future. It was like that hush of spirit which we feel amid the bright, mild woods of autumn, when the bright hectic flush is on the trees, and the last lingering flowers by the brook; and we joy in it all the more, because we know that soon it will all pass away.

The friend who knew most of Eva's own imaginings and foreshadowings was her faithful bearer, Tom. To him she said what she would not disturb her father by saying. To him she imparted those mysterious intimations which the soul feels, as the cords begin to unbind, ere it leaves its clay forever.

Tom, at last, would not sleep in his room, but lay all night in the outer verandah, ready to rouse at every call.

CHAPTER XXVI

"Uncle Tom, what alive have you taken to sleeping anywhere and everywhere, like a dog, for?" said Miss Ophelia. "I thought you was one of the orderly sort, that liked to lie in bed in a Christian way."

"I do, Miss Feely," said Tom, mysteriously. "I do, but now—"

"Well, what now?"

"We mustn't speak loud; Mas'r St. Clare won't hear on 't; but Miss Feely, you know there must be somebody watchin' for the bridegroom."

"What do you mean, Tom?"

"You know it says in Scripture, 'At midnight there was a great cry made. Behold, the bridegroom cometh.' That's what I'm spectin now, every night, Miss Feely,—and I couldn't sleep out o' hearin, no ways."

"Why, Uncle Tom, what makes you think so?"

"Miss Eva, she talks to me. The Lord, he sends his messenger in the soul. I must be thar, Miss Feely; for when that ar blessed child goes into the kingdom, they'll open the door so wide, we'll all get a look in at the glory, Miss Feely."

"Uncle Tom, did Miss Eva say she felt more unwell than usual tonight?"

"No; but she telled me, this morning, she was coming nearer,—thar's them that tells it to the child, Miss Feely. It's the angels,—'it's the trumpet sound afore the break o' day,'" said Tom, quoting from a favorite hymn.

This dialogue passed between Miss Ophelia and Tom, between ten and eleven, one evening, after her arrangements had all been made for the night, when, on going to bolt her outer door, she found Tom stretched along by it, in the outer verandah.

She was not nervous or impressible; but the solemn, heart-felt manner struck her. Eva had been unusually bright and cheerful, that afternoon, and had sat raised in her bed, and looked over all her little trinkets and precious things, and designated the friends to whom she would have them given; and her manner was more animated, and her voice more natural, than they had known it for weeks. Her father had been in, in the evening, and had said that Eva appeared more like her former self than ever she had done since her sickness; and when he kissed her for the night, he said to Miss Ophelia,—"Cousin, we may keep her with us, after all; she is certainly better;" and he had retired with a lighter heart in his bosom than he had had there for weeks.

But at midnight,—strange, mystic hour!—when the veil between the frail present and the eternal future grows thin,—then came the messenger!

There was a sound in that chamber, first of one who stepped quickly. It was Miss Ophelia, who had resolved to sit up all night with her little charge, and who, at the turn of the night, had discerned what experienced nurses significantly call "a change." The outer door was quickly opened, and Tom, who was watching outside, was on the alert, in a moment.

"Go for the doctor, Tom! lose not a moment," said Miss Ophelia; and, stepping across the room, she rapped at St. Clare's door.

"Cousin," she said, "I wish you would come."

Those words fell on his heart like clods upon a coffin. Why did they? He was up and in the room in an instant, and bending over Eva, who still slept.

What was it he saw that made his heart stand still? Why was no word spoken between the two? Thou canst say, who hast seen that same expression on the face dearest to thee;—that look indescribable, hopeless, unmistakable, that says to thee that thy beloved is no longer thine.

On the face of the child, however, there was no ghastly imprint,—only a high and almost sublime expression,—the overshadowing presence of spiritual natures, the dawning of immortal life in that childish soul.

They stood there so still, gazing upon her, that even the ticking of the watch seemed too loud. In a few moments, Tom returned, with the doctor. He entered, gave one look, and stood silent as the rest.

"When did this change take place?" said he, in a low whisper, to Miss Ophelia.

"About the turn of the night," was the reply.

Marie, roused by the entrance of the doctor, appeared, hurriedly, from the next room.

"Augustine! Cousin!—O!—what!" she hurriedly began.

"Hush!" said St. Clare, hoarsely; *"she is dying!"*

Mammy heard the words, and flew to awaken the servants. The house was soon roused,—lights were seen, footsteps heard, anxious faces thronged the verandah, and looked tearfully through the glass doors; but St. Clare heard and said nothing,—he saw only *that look* on the face of the little sleeper.

"O, if she would only wake, and speak once more!" he said; and, stooping over her, he spoke in her ear,—"Eva, darling!"

The large blue eyes unclosed—a smile passed over her face;—she tried to raise her head, and to speak.

"Do you know me, Eva?"

"Dear papa," said the child, with a last effort, throwing her arms about his neck. In a moment they dropped again; and, as St. Clare raised his head, he saw a spasm of mortal agony pass over the face,—she struggled for breath, and threw up her little hands.

"O, God, this is dreadful!" he said, turning away in agony, and wringing Tom's hand, scarce conscious what he was doing. "O, Tom, my boy, it is killing me!"

Tom had his master's hands between his own; and, with tears streaming down his dark cheeks, looked up for help where he had always been used to look.

"Pray that this may be cut short!" said St. Clare,—"this wrings my heart."

"O, bless the Lord! it's over,—it's over, dear Master!" said Tom; "look at her."

The child lay panting on her pillows, as one exhausted,—the large clear eyes rolled up and fixed. Ah, what said those eyes, that spoke so much of heaven! Earth was past,—and earthly pain; but so solemn, so mysterious, was the triumphant brightness of that face, that it checked even the sobs of sorrow. They pressed around her, in breathless stillness.

"Eva," said St. Clare, gently.

She did not hear.

CHAPTER XXVI

"O, Eva, tell us what you see! What is it?" said her father.

A bright, a glorious smile passed over her face, and she said, brokenly,—"O! love,—joy,—peace!" gave one sigh and passed from death unto life!

"Farewell, beloved child! the bright, eternal doors have closed after thee; we shall see thy sweet face no more. O, woe for them who watched thy entrance into heaven, when they shall wake and find only the cold gray sky of daily life, and thou gone forever!"

CHAPTER XXVII

"THIS IS THE LAST OF EARTH"

The statuettes and pictures in Eva's room were shrouded in white napkins, and only hushed breathings and muffled footfalls were heard there, and the light stole in solemnly through windows partially darkened by closed blinds.

The bed was draped in white; and there, beneath the drooping angel-figure, lay a little sleeping form,—sleeping never to waken!

There she lay, robed in one of the simple white dresses she had been wont to wear when living; the rose-colored light through the curtains cast over the icy coldness of death a warm glow. The heavy eyelashes drooped softly on the pure cheek; the head was turned a little to one side, as if in natural sleep, but there was diffused over every lineament of the face that high celestial expression, that mingling of rapture and repose, which showed it was no earthly or temporary sleep, but the long, sacred rest which "He giveth to his beloved."

There is no death to such as thou, dear Eva! neither darkness nor shadow of death; only such a bright fading as when the morning star fades in the golden dawn. Thine is the victory without the battle,—the crown without the conflict.

So did St. Clare think, as, with folded arms, he stood there gazing. Ah! who shall say what he did think? for, from the hour that voices had said, in the dying chamber, "she is gone," it had been all a dreary mist, a heavy "dimness of anguish." He had heard voices around him; he had had questions asked, and answered them; they had asked him when he would have the funeral, and where they should lay her; and he had answered, impatiently, that he cared not.

Adolph and Rosa had arranged the chamber; volatile, fickle and childish, as they generally were, they were soft-hearted and full of feeling; and, while Miss Ophelia presided over the general details of order and neatness, it was their hands that added those soft, poetic touches to the arrangements, that took from the death-room the grim and ghastly air which too often marks a New England funeral.

There were still flowers on the shelves,—all white, delicate and fragrant, with graceful, drooping leaves. Eva's little table, covered with white, bore on it her favorite vase, with a single white moss rose-bud in it. The folds of the drapery, the fall of the curtains, had been arranged and rearranged, by Adolph and Rosa, with that nicety of eye which characterizes their race. Even now, while St. Clare stood there thinking, little Rosa tripped softly into the chamber with a basket of white flowers. She stepped back when she saw St. Clare, and stopped respectfully; but, seeing that he did not observe her, she came forward to place them around the dead. St. Clare saw her as in a dream, while she placed in the small hands a fair cape jessamine, and, with admirable taste, disposed other flowers around the couch.

The door opened again, and Topsy, her eyes swelled with crying, appeared, holding something under her apron. Rosa made a quick forbidding gesture; but she took a step into the room.

"You must go out," said Rosa, in a sharp, positive whisper; "*you* haven't any business here!"

"O, do let me! I brought a flower,—such a pretty one!" said Topsy, holding up a half-blown tea rose-bud. "Do let me put just one there."

"Get along!" said Rosa, more decidedly.

"Let her stay!" said St. Clare, suddenly stamping his foot. "She shall come."

Rosa suddenly retreated, and Topsy came forward and laid her offering at the feet of the corpse; then suddenly, with a wild and bitter cry, she threw herself on the floor alongside the bed, and wept, and moaned aloud.

Miss Ophelia hastened into the room, and tried to raise and silence her; but in vain.

"O, Miss Eva! oh, Miss Eva! I wish I 's dead, too,—I do!"

There was a piercing wildness in the cry; the blood flushed into St. Clare's white, marble-like face, and the first tears he had shed since Eva died stood in his eyes.

"Get up, child," said Miss Ophelia, in a softened voice; "don't cry so. Miss Eva is gone to heaven; she is an angel."

"But I can't see her!" said Topsy. "I never shall see her!" and she sobbed again.

They all stood a moment in silence.

"*She* said she *loved* me," said Topsy,—"she did! O, dear! oh, dear! there an't *nobody* left now,—there an't!"

"That's true enough" said St. Clare; "but do," he said to Miss Ophelia, "see if you can't comfort the poor creature."

"I jist wish I hadn't never been born," said Topsy. "I didn't want to be born, no ways; and I don't see no use on 't."

Miss Ophelia raised her gently, but firmly, and took her from the room; but, as she did so, some tears fell from her eyes.

"Topsy, you poor child," she said, as she led her into her room, "don't give up! *I* can love you, though I am not like that dear little child. I hope I've learnt something of the love of Christ from her. I can love you; I do, and I'll try to help you to grow up a good Christian girl."

Miss Ophelia's voice was more than her words, and more than that were the honest tears that fell down her face. From that hour, she acquired an influence over the mind of the destitute child that she never lost.

"O, my Eva, whose little hour on earth did so much of good," thought St. Clare, "what account have I to give for my long years?"

There were, for a while, soft whisperings and footfalls in the chamber, as one after another stole in, to look at the dead; and then came the little coffin; and then there was a funeral, and carriages drove to the door, and strangers came and were seated; and there were white scarfs and ribbons, and crape bands, and mourners dressed in black crape; and there were words read from the Bible, and prayers offered; and St. Clare lived, and walked, and moved, as one who has shed every tear;—to the last he saw only one thing, that golden head in the coffin; but then he saw the cloth spread over it, the lid of the coffin closed; and he walked, when he was put beside the others, down to a little place at the bottom of the garden, and there, by the mossy seat where she and Tom had talked, and sung, and read so often, was the little grave. St. Clare stood beside it,—looked vacantly down; he saw them lower the little coffin; he heard, dimly, the solemn words, "I am the resurrection and the Life; he that believeth in me, though he were dead, yet shall he live;" and, as the earth was cast in and filled up the little grave, he could not realize that it was his Eva that they were hiding from his sight.

Nor was it!—not Eva, but only the frail seed of that bright, immortal form with which she shall yet come forth, in the day of the Lord Jesus!

And then all were gone, and the mourners went back to the place which should know her no more; and Marie's room was darkened, and she lay on the bed, sobbing and moaning in uncontrollable grief, and calling every moment for the attentions of all her servants. Of course, they had no time to cry,—why should they? the grief was *her* grief, and she was fully convinced that nobody on earth did, could, or would feel it as she did.

"St. Clare did not shed a tear," she said; "he didn't sympathize with her; it was perfectly wonderful to think how hard-hearted and unfeeling he was, when he must know how she suffered."

So much are people the slave of their eye and ear, that many of the servants really thought that Missis was the principal sufferer in the case, especially as Marie began to have hysterical spasms, and sent for the doctor, and at last declared herself dying; and, in the running and scampering, and bringing up hot bottles, and heating of flannels, and chafing, and fussing, that ensued, there was quite a diversion.

Tom, however, had a feeling at his own heart, that drew him to his master. He followed him wherever he walked, wistfully and sadly; and when he saw him sitting, so pale and quiet, in Eva's room, holding before his eyes her little open Bible, though seeing no letter or word of what was in it, there was more sorrow to Tom in that still, fixed, tearless eye, than in all Marie's moans and lamentations.

In a few days the St. Clare family were back again in the city; Augustine, with the restlessness of grief, longing for another scene, to change the current of his thoughts. So they left the house and garden, with its little grave, and came back to New Orleans; and St. Clare walked the streets busily, and strove to fill up the chasm in his heart with hurry and bustle, and change of place; and people who saw him in the street, or met him at the cafe, knew of his loss only by the weed on his hat; for there he was, smiling and talking, and reading the newspaper, and speculating on politics, and attending to business matters; and who could see that all this smiling outside was but a hollowed shell over a heart that was a dark and silent sepulchre?

"Mr. St. Clare is a singular man," said Marie to Miss Ophelia, in a complaining tone. "I used to think, if there was anything in the world he did love, it was our dear little Eva; but he seems to be forgetting her very easily. I cannot ever get him to talk about her. I really did think he would show more feeling!"

"Still waters run deepest, they used to tell me," said Miss Ophelia, oracularly.

"O, I don't believe in such things; it's all talk. If people have feeling, they will show it,—they can't help it; but, then, it's a great misfortune to have feeling. I'd rather have been made like St. Clare. My feelings prey upon me so!"

"Sure, Missis, Mas'r St. Clare is gettin' thin as a shader. They say, he don't never eat nothin'," said Mammy. "I know he don't forget Miss Eva; I know there couldn't nobody,—dear, little, blessed cretur!" she added, wiping her eyes.

"Well, at all events, he has no consideration for me," said Marie; "he hasn't spoken one word of sympathy, and he must know how much more a mother feels than any man can."

"The heart knoweth its own bitterness," said Miss Ophelia, gravely.

"That's just what I think. I know just what I feel,—nobody else seems to. Eva used to, but she is gone!" and Marie lay back on her lounge, and began to sob disconsolately.

Marie was one of those unfortunately constituted mortals, in whose eyes whatever is lost and gone assumes a value which it never had in possession. Whatever she had, she seemed to survey only to pick flaws in it; but, once fairly away, there was no end to her valuation of it.

While this conversation was taking place in the parlor another was going on in St. Clare's library.

Tom, who was always uneasily following his master about, had seen him go to his library, some hours before; and, after vainly waiting for him to come out, determined, at last, to make an errand in. He entered softly. St. Clare lay on his lounge, at the further end of the room. He was lying on his face, with Eva's Bible open before him, at a little distance. Tom walked up, and stood by the sofa. He hesitated; and, while he was hesitating, St. Clare suddenly raised himself up. The honest face, so full of grief, and with such an imploring expression of affection and sympathy, struck his master. He laid his hand on Tom's, and bowed down his forehead on it.

"O, Tom, my boy, the whole world is as empty as an egg-shell."

"I know it, Mas'r,—I know it," said Tom; "but, oh, if Mas'r could only look up,—up where our dear Miss Eva is,—up to the dear Lord Jesus!"

"Ah, Tom! I do look up; but the trouble is, I don't see anything, when I do, I wish I could."

Tom sighed heavily.

"It seems to be given to children, and poor, honest fellows, like you, to see what we can't," said St. Clare. "How comes it?"

"Thou has 'hid from the wise and prudent, and revealed unto babes,'" murmured Tom; "'even so, Father, for so it seemed good in thy sight.'"

"Tom, I don't believe,—I can't believe,—I've got the habit of doubting," said St. Clare. "I want to believe this Bible,—and I can't."

"Dear Mas'r, pray to the good Lord,—'Lord, I believe; help thou my unbelief.'"

"Who knows anything about anything?" said St. Clare, his eyes wandering dreamily, and speaking to himself. "Was all that beautiful love and faith only one of the ever-shifting phases of human feeling, having nothing real to rest on, passing away with the little breath? And is there no more Eva,—no heaven,—no Christ,—nothing?"

"O, dear Mas'r, there is! I know it; I'm sure of it," said Tom, falling on his knees. "Do, do, dear Mas'r, believe it!"

"How do you know there's any Christ, Tom! You never saw the Lord."

"Felt Him in my soul, Mas'r,—feel Him now! O, Mas'r, when I was sold away from my old woman and the children, I was jest a'most broke up. I felt as if there warn't nothin' left; and then the good Lord, he stood by me, and he says, 'Fear not, Tom;' and he brings light and joy in a poor feller's soul,—makes all peace; and I 's so happy, and loves everybody, and feels willin' jest to be the Lord's, and have the Lord's will done, and be put jest where the Lord wants to put me. I know it couldn't come from me, cause I 's a poor, complainin' cretur; it comes from the Lord; and I know He's willin' to do for Mas'r."

Tom spoke with fast-running tears and choking voice. St. Clare leaned his head on his shoulder, and wrung the hard, faithful, black hand.

"Tom, you love me," he said.

"I 's willin' to lay down my life, this blessed day, to see Mas'r a Christian."

"Poor, foolish boy!" said St. Clare, half-raising himself. "I'm not worth the love of one good, honest heart, like yours."

"O, Mas'r, dere's more than me loves you,—the blessed Lord Jesus loves you."

"How do you know that Tom?" said St. Clare.

"Feels it in my soul. O, Mas'r! 'the love of Christ, that passeth knowledge.'"

"Singular!" said St. Clare, turning away, "that the story of a man that lived and died eighteen hundred years ago can affect people so yet. But he was no man," he added, suddenly. "No man ever had such long and living power! O, that I could believe what my mother taught me, and pray as I did when I was a boy!"

"If Mas'r pleases," said Tom, "Miss Eva used to read this so beautifully. I wish Mas'r'd be so good as read it. Don't get no readin', hardly, now Miss Eva's gone."

The chapter was the eleventh of John,—the touching account of the raising of Lazarus, St. Clare read it aloud, often pausing to wrestle down feelings which were roused by the pathos of the story. Tom knelt before him, with clasped hands, and with an absorbed expression of love, trust, adoration, on his quiet face.

"Tom," said his Master, "this is all *real* to you!"

"I can jest fairly *see* it Mas'r," said Tom.

"I wish I had your eyes, Tom."

"I wish, to the dear Lord, Mas'r had!"

"But, Tom, you know that I have a great deal more knowledge than you; what if I should tell you that I don't believe this Bible?"

"O, Mas'r!" said Tom, holding up his hands, with a deprecating gesture.

"Wouldn't it shake your faith some, Tom?"

"Not a grain," said Tom.

"Why, Tom, you must know I know the most."

"O, Mas'r, haven't you jest read how he hides from the wise and prudent, and reveals unto babes? But Mas'r wasn't in earnest, for sartin, now?" said Tom, anxiously.

"No, Tom, I was not. I don't disbelieve, and I think there is reason to believe; and still I don't. It's a troublesome bad habit I've got, Tom."

"If Mas'r would only pray!"

"How do you know I don't, Tom?"

"Does Mas'r?"

"I would, Tom, if there was anybody there when I pray; but it's all speaking unto nothing, when I do. But come, Tom, you pray now, and show me how."

Tom's heart was full; he poured it out in prayer, like waters that have been long suppressed. One thing was plain enough; Tom thought there was somebody to hear, whether there were or not. In fact, St. Clare felt himself borne, on the tide of his faith and feeling, almost to the gates of that heaven he seemed so vividly to conceive. It seemed to bring him nearer to Eva.

"Thank you, my boy," said St. Clare, when Tom rose. "I like to hear you, Tom; but go, now, and leave me alone; some other time, I'll talk more."

Tom silently left the room.

CHAPTER XXVIII

REUNION

Week after week glided away in the St. Clare mansion, and the waves of life settled back to their usual flow, where that little bark had gone down. For how imperiously, how coolly, in disregard of all one's feeling, does the hard, cold, uninteresting course of daily realities move on! Still must we eat, and drink, and sleep, and wake again,—still bargain, buy, sell, ask and answer questions,—pursue, in short, a thousand shadows, though all interest in them be over; the cold mechanical habit of living remaining, after all vital interest in it has fled.

All the interests and hopes of St. Clare's life had unconsciously wound themselves around this child. It was for Eva that he had managed his property; it was for Eva that he had planned the disposal of his time; and, to do this and that for Eva,—to buy, improve, alter, and arrange, or dispose something for her,—had been so long his habit, that now she was gone, there seemed nothing to be thought of, and nothing to be done.

True, there was another life,—a life which, once believed in, stands as a solemn, significant figure before the otherwise unmeaning ciphers of time, changing them to orders of mysterious, untold value. St. Clare knew this well; and often, in many a weary hour, he heard that slender, childish voice calling him to the skies, and saw that little hand pointing to him the way of life; but a heavy lethargy of sorrow lay on him,—he could not arise. He had one of those natures which could better and more clearly conceive of religious things from its own perceptions and instincts, than many a matter-of-fact and practical Christian. The gift to appreciate and the sense to feel the finer shades and relations of moral things, often seems an attribute of those whose whole life shows a careless disregard of them. Hence Moore, Byron, Goethe, often speak words more wisely descriptive of the true religious sentiment, than another man, whose whole life is governed by it. In such minds, disregard of religion is a more fearful treason,—a more deadly sin.

St. Clare had never pretended to govern himself by any religious obligation; and a certain fineness of nature gave him such an instinctive view of the extent of the requirements of Christianity, that he shrank, by anticipation, from what he felt would be the exactions of his own conscience, if he once did resolve to assume them. For, so inconsistent is human nature, especially in the ideal, that not to undertake a thing at all seems better than to undertake and come short.

Still St. Clare was, in many respects, another man. He read his little Eva's Bible seriously and honestly; he thought more soberly and practically of his relations to his servants,—enough to make him extremely dissatisfied with both his past and present course; and one thing he did, soon after his return to New Orleans, and that was to commence the legal steps necessary to Tom's emancipation, which was to be perfected as soon as he could get through the necessary formalities. Meantime, he attached himself to Tom more and more, every day. In all the wide world, there was nothing that seemed to remind him so much of Eva; and he would insist on keeping him constantly about him, and, fastidious and unapproachable as he was with regard to his deeper feelings, he almost thought aloud to Tom. Nor would any one have wondered at it, who had seen the expression of affection and devotion with which Tom continually followed his young master.

"Well, Tom," said St. Clare, the day after he had commenced the legal formalities for his enfranchisement, "I'm going to make a free man of you;—so have your trunk packed, and get ready to set out for Kentuck."

The sudden light of joy that shone in Tom's face as he raised his hands to heaven, his emphatic "Bless the Lord!" rather discomposed St. Clare; he did not like it that Tom should be so ready to leave him.

"You haven't had such very bad times here, that you need be in such a rapture, Tom," he said drily.

"No, no, Mas'r! 'tan't that,—it's bein' a *freeman!* that's what I'm joyin' for."

"Why, Tom, don't you think, for your own part, you've been better off than to be free?"

"*No, indeed*, Mas'r St. Clare," said Tom, with a flash of energy. "No, indeed!"

"Why, Tom, you couldn't possibly have earned, by your work, such clothes and such living as I have given you."

"Knows all that, Mas'r St. Clare; Mas'r's been too good; but, Mas'r, I'd rather have poor clothes, poor house, poor everything, and have 'em *mine*, than have the best, and have 'em any man's else,—I had *so*, Mas'r; I think it's natur, Mas'r."

"I suppose so, Tom, and you'll be going off and leaving me, in a month or so," he added, rather discontentedly. "Though why you shouldn't, no mortal knows," he said, in a gayer tone; and, getting up, he began to walk the floor.

"Not while Mas'r is in trouble," said Tom. "I'll stay with Mas'r as long as he wants me,—so as I can be any use."

"Not while I'm in trouble, Tom?" said St. Clare, looking sadly out of the window. . . . "And when will *my* trouble be over?"

"When Mas'r St. Clare's a Christian," said Tom.

"And you really mean to stay by till that day comes?" said St. Clare, half smiling, as he turned from the window, and laid his hand on Tom's shoulder. "Ah, Tom, you soft, silly boy! I won't keep you till that day. Go home to your wife and children, and give my love to all."

"I 's faith to believe that day will come," said Tom, earnestly, and with tears in his eyes; "the Lord has a work for Mas'r."

"A work, hey?" said St. Clare, "well, now, Tom, give me your views on what sort of a work it is;—let's hear."

"Why, even a poor fellow like me has a work from the Lord; and Mas'r St. Clare, that has larnin, and riches, and friends,—how much he might do for the Lord!"

"Tom, you seem to think the Lord needs a great deal done for him," said St. Clare, smiling.

"We does for the Lord when we does for his critturs," said Tom.

"Good theology, Tom; better than Dr. B. preaches, I dare swear," said St. Clare.

The conversation was here interrupted by the announcement of some visitors.

Marie St. Clare felt the loss of Eva as deeply as she could feel anything; and, as she was a woman that had a great faculty of making everybody unhappy when she was, her immediate attendants had still stronger reason to regret the loss of their young mistress, whose winning ways and gentle intercessions had so often been a shield to them from the tyrannical and selfish exactions of her mother. Poor old Mammy, in particular, whose heart, severed from all natural domestic ties, had consoled itself with this one beautiful being, was almost heart-broken. She cried day and night, and was, from excess of sorrow, less skilful and alert in her ministrations of her mistress than usual, which drew down a constant storm of invectives on her defenceless head.

Miss Ophelia felt the loss; but, in her good and honest heart, it bore fruit unto everlasting life. She was more softened, more gentle; and, though equally assiduous in every duty, it was with a chastened and quiet air, as one who communed with her own heart not in vain. She was more diligent in teaching Topsy,—taught her mainly from the Bible,—did not any longer shrink from her touch, or manifest an ill-repressed disgust, because she felt none. She viewed her now through the softened medium that Eva's hand had first held before her eyes, and saw in her only an immortal creature, whom God had sent to be led by her to glory and virtue. Topsy did not become at once a saint; but the life and death of Eva did work a marked change in her. The callous indifference was gone; there was now sensibility, hope, desire, and the striving for good,—a strife irregular, interrupted, suspended oft, but yet renewed again.

One day, when Topsy had been sent for by Miss Ophelia, she came, hastily thrusting something into her bosom.

"What are you doing there, you limb? You've been stealing something, I'll be bound," said the imperious little Rosa, who had been sent to call her, seizing her, at the same time, roughly by the arm.

"You go 'long, Miss Rosa!" said Topsy, pulling from her; "'tan't none o' your business!"

"None o' your sa'ce!" said Rosa, "I saw you hiding something,—I know yer tricks," and Rosa seized her arm, and tried to force her hand into her bosom, while

Topsy, enraged, kicked and fought valiantly for what she considered her rights. The clamor and confusion of the battle drew Miss Ophelia and St. Clare both to the spot.

"She's been stealing!" said Rosa.

"I han't, neither!" vociferated Topsy, sobbing with passion.

"Give me that, whatever it is!" said Miss Ophelia, firmly.

Topsy hesitated; but, on a second order, pulled out of her bosom a little parcel done up in the foot of one of her own old stockings.

Miss Ophelia turned it out. There was a small book, which had been given to Topsy by Eva, containing a single verse of Scripture, arranged for every day in the year, and in a paper the curl of hair that she had given her on that memorable day when she had taken her last farewell.

St. Clare was a good deal affected at the sight of it; the little book had been rolled in a long strip of black crape, torn from the funeral weeds.

"What did you wrap *this* round the book for?" said St. Clare, holding up the crape.

"Cause,—cause,—cause 't was Miss Eva. O, don't take 'em away, please!" she said; and, sitting flat down on the floor, and putting her apron over her head, she began to sob vehemently.

It was a curious mixture of the pathetic and the ludicrous,—the little old stockings,—black crape,—text-book,—fair, soft curl,—and Topsy's utter distress.

St. Clare smiled; but there were tears in his eyes, as he said,

"Come, come,—don't cry; you shall have them!" and, putting them together, he threw them into her lap, and drew Miss Ophelia with him into the parlor.

"I really think you can make something of that concern," he said, pointing with his thumb backward over his shoulder. "Any mind that is capable of a *real sorrow* is capable of good. You must try and do something with her."

"The child has improved greatly," said Miss Ophelia. "I have great hopes of her; but, Augustine," she said, laying her hand on his arm, "one thing I want to ask; whose is this child to be?—yours or mine?"

"Why, I gave her to you," said Augustine.

"But not legally;—I want her to be mine legally," said Miss Ophelia.

"Whew! cousin," said Augustine. "What will the Abolition Society think? They'll have a day of fasting appointed for this backsliding, if you become a slaveholder!"

"O, nonsense! I want her mine, that I may have a right to take her to the free States, and give her her liberty, that all I am trying to do be not undone."

"O, cousin, what an awful 'doing evil that good may come'! I can't encourage it."

"I don't want you to joke, but to reason," said Miss Ophelia. "There is no use in my trying to make this child a Christian child, unless I save her from all the chances and reverses of slavery; and, if you really are willing I should have her, I want you to give me a deed of gift, or some legal paper."

"Well, well," said St. Clare, "I will;" and he sat down, and unfolded a newspaper to read.

"But I want it done now," said Miss Ophelia.

"What's your hurry?"

"Because now is the only time there ever is to do a thing in," said Miss Ophelia. "Come, now, here's paper, pen, and ink; just write a paper."

St. Clare, like most men of his class of mind, cordially hated the present tense of action, generally; and, therefore, he was considerably annoyed by Miss Ophelia's downrightness.

"Why, what's the matter?" said he. "Can't you take my word? One would think you had taken lessons of the Jews, coming at a fellow so!"

"I want to make sure of it," said Miss Ophelia. "You may die, or fail, and then Topsy be hustled off to auction, spite of all I can do."

"Really, you are quite provident. Well, seeing I'm in the hands of a Yankee, there is nothing for it but to concede;" and St. Clare rapidly wrote off a deed of gift, which, as he was well versed in the forms of law, he could easily do, and signed his name to it in sprawling capitals, concluding by a tremendous flourish.

"There, isn't that black and white, now, Miss Vermont?" he said, as he handed it to her.

"Good boy," said Miss Ophelia, smiling. "But must it not be witnessed?"

"O, bother!—yes. Here," he said, opening the door into Marie's apartment, "Marie, Cousin wants your autograph; just put your name down here."

"What's this?" said Marie, as she ran over the paper. "Ridiculous! I thought Cousin was too pious for such horrid things," she added, as she carelessly wrote her name; "but, if she has a fancy for that article, I am sure she's welcome."

"There, now, she's yours, body and soul," said St. Clare, handing the paper.

"No more mine now than she was before," Miss Ophelia. "Nobody but God has a right to give her to me; but I can protect her now."

"Well, she's yours by a fiction of law, then," said St. Clare, as he turned back into the parlor, and sat down to his paper.

Miss Ophelia, who seldom sat much in Marie's company, followed him into the parlor, having first carefully laid away the paper.

"Augustine," she said, suddenly, as she sat knitting, "have you ever made any provision for your servants, in case of your death?"

"No," said St. Clare, as he read on.

"Then all your indulgence to them may prove a great cruelty, by and by."

St. Clare had often thought the same thing himself; but he answered, negligently.

"Well, I mean to make a provision, by and by."

"When?" said Miss Ophelia.

"O, one of these days."

"What if you should die first?"

CHAPTER XXVIII

"Cousin, what's the matter?" said St. Clare, laying down his paper and looking at her. "Do you think I show symptoms of yellow fever or cholera, that you are making post mortem arrangements with such zeal?"

"'In the midst of life we are in death,'" said Miss Ophelia.

St. Clare rose up, and laying the paper down, carelessly, walked to the door that stood open on the verandah, to put an end to a conversation that was not agreeable to him. Mechanically, he repeated the last word again,—*"Death!"*— and, as he leaned against the railings, and watched the sparkling water as it rose and fell in the fountain; and, as in a dim and dizzy haze, saw flowers and trees and vases of the courts, he repeated, again the mystic word so common in every mouth, yet of such fearful power,—"DEATH!" "Strange that there should be such a word," he said, "and such a thing, and we ever forget it; that one should be living, warm and beautiful, full of hopes, desires and wants, one day, and the next be gone, utterly gone, and forever!"

It was a warm, golden evening; and, as he walked to the other end of the verandah, he saw Tom busily intent on his Bible, pointing, as he did so, with his finger to each successive word, and whispering them to himself with an earnest air.

"Want me to read to you, Tom?" said St. Clare, seating himself carelessly by him.

"If Mas'r pleases," said Tom, gratefully, "Mas'r makes it so much plainer."

St. Clare took the book and glanced at the place, and began reading one of the passages which Tom had designated by the heavy marks around it. It ran as follows:

"When the Son of man shall come in his glory, and all his holy angels with him, then shall he sit upon the throne of his glory: and before him shall be gathered all nations; and he shall separate them one from another, as a shepherd divideth his sheep from the goats." St. Clare read on in an animated voice, till he came to the last of the verses.

"Then shall the king say unto him on his left hand, Depart from me, ye cursed, into everlasting fire: for I was an hungered, and ye gave me no meat: I was thirsty, and ye gave me no drink: I was a stranger, and ye took me not in: naked, and ye clothed me not: I was sick, and in prison, and ye visited me not. Then shall they answer unto Him, Lord when saw we thee an hungered, or athirst, or a stranger, or naked, or sick, or in prison, and did not minister unto thee? Then shall he say unto them, Inasmuch as ye did it not to one of the least of these my brethren, ye did it not to me."

St. Clare seemed struck with this last passage, for he read it twice,—the second time slowly, and as if he were revolving the words in his mind.

"Tom," he said, "these folks that get such hard measure seem to have been doing just what I have,—living good, easy, respectable lives; and not troubling themselves to inquire how many of their brethren were hungry or athirst, or sick, or in prison."

Tom did not answer.

St. Clare rose up and walked thoughtfully up and down the verandah, seeming to forget everything in his own thoughts; so absorbed was he, that Tom had to remind him twice that the teabell had rung, before he could get his attention.

St. Clare was absent and thoughtful, all tea-time. After tea, he and Marie and Miss Ophelia took possession of the parlor almost in silence.

Marie disposed herself on a lounge, under a silken mosquito curtain, and was soon sound asleep. Miss Ophelia silently busied herself with her knitting. St. Clare sat down to the piano, and began playing a soft and melancholy movement with the Æolian accompaniment. He seemed in a deep reverie, and to be soliloquizing to himself by music. After a little, he opened one of the drawers, took out an old music-book whose leaves were yellow with age, and began turning it over.

"There," he said to Miss Ophelia, "this was one of my mother's books,—and here is her handwriting,—come and look at it. She copied and arranged this from Mozart's Requiem." Miss Ophelia came accordingly.

"It was something she used to sing often," said St. Clare. "I think I can hear her now."

He struck a few majestic chords, and began singing that grand old Latin piece, the "Dies Iræ."

Tom, who was listening in the outer verandah, was drawn by the sound to the very door, where he stood earnestly. He did not understand the words, of course; but the music and manner of singing appeared to affect him strongly, especially when St. Clare sang the more pathetic parts. Tom would have sympathized more heartily, if he had known the meaning of the beautiful words:—

"Recordare Jesu pie Quod sum causa tuær viæ Ne me perdas, illa die Quærens me sedisti lassus Redemisti crucem passus Tantus labor non sit cassus."[1]

St. Clare threw a deep and pathetic expression into the words; for the shadowy veil of years seemed drawn away, and he seemed to hear his mother's voice leading his. Voice and instrument seemed both living, and threw out with vivid sympathy those strains which the ethereal Mozart first conceived as his own dying requiem.

When St. Clare had done singing, he sat leaning his head upon his hand a few moments, and then began walking up and down the floor.

"What a sublime conception is that of a last judgment!" said he,—"a righting of all the wrongs of ages!—a solving of all moral problems, by an unanswerable wisdom! It is, indeed, a wonderful image."

"It is a fearful one to us," said Miss Ophelia.

"It ought to be to me, I suppose," said St. Clare stopping, thoughtfully. "I was reading to Tom, this afternoon, that chapter in Matthew that gives an account of it, and I have been quite struck with it. One should have expected some terrible

---

[1] These lines have been thus rather inadequately translated: "Think, O Jesus, for what reason Thou endured'st earth's spite and treason, Nor me lose, in that dread season; Seeking me, thy worn feet hasted, On the cross thy soul death tasted, Let not all these toils be wasted." [Mrs. Stowe's note.]

enormities charged to those who are excluded from Heaven, as the reason; but no,—they are condemned for *not* doing positive good, as if that included every possible harm."

"Perhaps," said Miss Ophelia, "it is impossible for a person who does no good not to do harm."

"And what," said St. Clare, speaking abstractedly, but with deep feeling, "what shall be said of one whose own heart, whose education, and the wants of society, have called in vain to some noble purpose; who has floated on, a dreamy, neutral spectator of the struggles, agonies, and wrongs of man, when he should have been a worker?"

"I should say," said Miss Ophelia, "that he ought to repent, and begin now."

"Always practical and to the point!" said St. Clare, his face breaking out into a smile. "You never leave me any time for general reflections, Cousin; you always bring me short up against the actual present; you have a kind of eternal *now*, always in your mind."

"*Now* is all the time I have anything to do with," said Miss Ophelia.

"Dear little Eva,—poor child!" said St. Clare, "she had set her little simple soul on a good work for me."

It was the first time since Eva's death that he had ever said as many words as these to her, and he spoke now evidently repressing very strong feeling.

"My view of Christianity is such," he added, "that I think no man can consistently profess it without throwing the whole weight of his being against this monstrous system of injustice that lies at the foundation of all our society; and, if need be, sacrificing himself in the battle. That is, I mean that *I* could not be a Christian otherwise, though I have certainly had intercourse with a great many enlightened and Christian people who did no such thing; and I confess that the apathy of religious people on this subject, their want of perception of wrongs that filled me with horror, have engendered in me more scepticism than any other thing."

"If you knew all this," said Miss Ophelia, "why didn't you do it?"

"O, because I have had only that kind of benevolence which consists in lying on a sofa, and cursing the church and clergy for not being martyrs and confessors. One can see, you know, very easily, how others ought to be martyrs."

"Well, are you going to do differently now?" said Miss Ophelia.

"God only knows the future," said St. Clare. "I am braver than I was, because I have lost all; and he who has nothing to lose can afford all risks."

"And what are you going to do?"

"My duty, I hope, to the poor and lowly, as fast as I find it out," said St. Clare, "beginning with my own servants, for whom I have yet done nothing; and, perhaps, at some future day, it may appear that I can do something for a whole class; something to save my country from the disgrace of that false position in which she now stands before all civilized nations."

"Do you suppose it possible that a nation ever will voluntarily emancipate?" said Miss Ophelia.

"I don't know," said St. Clare. "This is a day of great deeds. Heroism and disinterestedness are rising up, here and there, in the earth. The Hungarian nobles set free millions of serfs, at an immense pecuniary loss; and, perhaps, among us may be found generous spirits, who do not estimate honor and justice by dollars and cents."

"I hardly think so," said Miss Ophelia.

"But, suppose we should rise up tomorrow and emancipate, who would educate these millions, and teach them how to use their freedom? They never would rise to do much among us. The fact is, we are too lazy and unpractical, ourselves, ever to give them much of an idea of that industry and energy which is necessary to form them into men. They will have to go north, where labor is the fashion,—the universal custom; and tell me, now, is there enough Christian philanthropy, among your northern states, to bear with the process of their education and elevation? You send thousands of dollars to foreign missions; but could you endure to have the heathen sent into your towns and villages, and give your time, and thoughts, and money, to raise them to the Christian standard? That's what I want to know. If we emancipate, are you willing to educate? How many families, in your town, would take a negro man and woman, teach them, bear with them, and seek to make them Christians? How many merchants would take Adolph, if I wanted to make him a clerk; or mechanics, if I wanted him taught a trade? If I wanted to put Jane and Rosa to a school, how many schools are there in the northern states that would take them in? how many families that would board them? and yet they are as white as many a woman, north or south. You see, Cousin, I want justice done us. We are in a bad position. We are the more *obvious* oppressors of the negro; but the unchristian prejudice of the north is an oppressor almost equally severe."

"Well, Cousin, I know it is so," said Miss Ophelia,—"I know it was so with me, till I saw that it was my duty to overcome it; but, I trust I have overcome it; and I know there are many good people at the north, who in this matter need only to be *taught* what their duty is, to do it. It would certainly be a greater self-denial to receive heathen among us, than to send missionaries to them; but I think we would do it."

"*You* would, I know," said St. Clare. "I'd like to see anything you wouldn't do, if you thought it your duty!"

"Well, I'm not uncommonly good," said Miss Ophelia. "Others would, if they saw things as I do. I intend to take Topsy home, when I go. I suppose our folks will wonder, at first; but I think they will be brought to see as I do. Besides, I know there are many people at the north who do exactly what you said."

"Yes, but they are a minority; and, if we should begin to emancipate to any extent, we should soon hear from you."

Miss Ophelia did not reply. There was a pause of some moments; and St. Clare's countenance was overcast by a sad, dreamy expression.

"I don't know what makes me think of my mother so much, tonight," he said. "I have a strange kind of feeling, as if she were near me. I keep thinking of things she used to say. Strange, what brings these past things so vividly back to us, sometimes!"

St. Clare walked up and down the room for some minutes more, and then said,

"I believe I'll go down street, a few moments, and hear the news, tonight."

He took his hat, and passed out.

Tom followed him to the passage, out of the court, and asked if he should attend him.

"No, my boy," said St. Clare. "I shall be back in an hour."

Tom sat down in the verandah. It was a beautiful moonlight evening, and he sat watching the rising and falling spray of the fountain, and listening to its murmur. Tom thought of his home, and that he should soon be a free man, and able to return to it at will. He thought how he should work to buy his wife and boys. He felt the muscles of his brawny arms with a sort of joy, as he thought they would soon belong to himself, and how much they could do to work out the freedom of his family. Then he thought of his noble young master, and, ever second to that, came the habitual prayer that he had always offered for him; and then his thoughts passed on to the beautiful Eva, whom he now thought of among the angels; and he thought till he almost fancied that that bright face and golden hair were looking upon him, out of the spray of the fountain. And, so musing, he fell asleep, and dreamed he saw her coming bounding towards him, just as she used to come, with a wreath of jessamine in her hair, her cheeks bright, and her eyes radiant with delight; but, as he looked, she seemed to rise from the ground; her cheeks wore a paler hue,—her eyes had a deep, divine radiance, a golden halo seemed around her head,—and she vanished from his sight; and Tom was awakened by a loud knocking, and a sound of many voices at the gate.

He hastened to undo it; and, with smothered voices and heavy tread, came several men, bringing a body, wrapped in a cloak, and lying on a shutter. The light of the lamp fell full on the face; and Tom gave a wild cry of amazement and despair, that rung through all the galleries, as the men advanced, with their burden, to the open parlor door, where Miss Ophelia still sat knitting.

St. Clare had turned into a cafe, to look over an evening paper. As he was reading, an affray arose between two gentlemen in the room, who were both partially intoxicated. St. Clare and one or two others made an effort to separate them, and St. Clare received a fatal stab in the side with a bowie-knife, which he was attempting to wrest from one of them.

The house was full of cries and lamentations, shrieks and screams, servants frantically tearing their hair, throwing themselves on the ground, or running distractedly about, lamenting. Tom and Miss Ophelia alone seemed to have any presence of mind; for Marie was in strong hysteric convulsions. At Miss Ophelia's direction, one of the lounges in the parlor was hastily prepared, and the bleeding form laid upon it. St. Clare had fainted, through pain and loss of blood; but, as Miss Ophelia applied restoratives, he revived, opened his eyes, looked fixedly on them, looked earnestly around the room, his eyes travelling wistfully over every object, and finally they rested on his mother's picture.

The physician now arrived, and made his examination. It was evident, from the expression of his face, that there was no hope; but he applied himself to dressing the wound, and he and Miss Ophelia and Tom proceeded composedly with this work, amid the lamentations and sobs and cries of the affrighted servants, who had clustered about the doors and windows of the verandah.

"Now," said the physician, "we must turn all these creatures out; all depends on his being kept quiet."

St. Clare opened his eyes, and looked fixedly on the distressed beings, whom Miss Ophelia and the doctor were trying to urge from the apartment. "Poor creatures!" he said, and an expression of bitter self-reproach passed over his face. Adolph absolutely refused to go. Terror had deprived him of all presence of mind; he threw himself along the floor, and nothing could persuade him to rise. The rest yielded to Miss Ophelia's urgent representations, that their master's safety depended on their stillness and obedience.

St. Clare could say but little; he lay with his eyes shut, but it was evident that he wrestled with bitter thoughts. After a while, he laid his hand on Tom's, who was kneeling beside him, and said, "Tom! poor fellow!"

"What, Mas'r?" said Tom, earnestly.

"I am dying!" said St. Clare, pressing his hand; "pray!"

"If you would like a clergyman—" said the physician.

St. Clare hastily shook his head, and said again to Tom, more earnestly, "Pray!"

And Tom did pray, with all his mind and strength, for the soul that was passing,—the soul that seemed looking so steadily and mournfully from those large, melancholy blue eyes. It was literally prayer offered with strong crying and tears.

When Tom ceased to speak, St. Clare reached out and took his hand, looking earnestly at him, but saying nothing. He closed his eyes, but still retained his hold; for, in the gates of eternity, the black hand and the white hold each other with an equal clasp. He murmured softly to himself, at broken intervals,

"Recordare Jesu pie—

* * * *

Ne me perdas—illa die Quærens me—sedisti lassus."

It was evident that the words he had been singing that evening were passing through his mind,—words of entreaty addressed to Infinite Pity. His lips moved at intervals, as parts of the hymn fell brokenly from them.

"His mind is wandering," said the doctor.

"No! it is coming HOME, at last!" said St. Clare, energetically; "at last! at last!"

The effort of speaking exhausted him. The sinking paleness of death fell on him; but with it there fell, as if shed from the wings of some pitying spirit, a beautiful expression of peace, like that of a wearied child who sleeps.

So he lay for a few moments. They saw that the mighty hand was on him. Just before the spirit parted, he opened his eyes, with a sudden light, as of joy and recognition, and said *"Mother!"* and then he was gone!

CHAPTER XXIX

THE UNPROTECTED

We hear often of the distress of the negro servants, on the loss of a kind master; and with good reason, for no creature on God's earth is left more utterly unprotected and desolate than the slave in these circumstances.

The child who has lost a father has still the protection of friends, and of the law; he is something, and can do something,—has acknowledged rights and position; the slave has none. The law regards him, in every respect, as devoid of rights as a bale of merchandise. The only possible acknowledgment of any of the longings and wants of a human and immortal creature, which are given to him, comes to him through the sovereign and irresponsible will of his master; and when that master is stricken down, nothing remains.

The number of those men who know how to use wholly irresponsible power humanely and generously is small. Everybody knows this, and the slave knows it best of all; so that he feels that there are ten chances of his finding an abusive and tyrannical master, to one of his finding a considerate and kind one. Therefore is it that the wail over a kind master is loud and long, as well it may be.

When St. Clare breathed his last, terror and consternation took hold of all his household. He had been stricken down so in a moment, in the flower and strength of his youth! Every room and gallery of the house resounded with sobs and shrieks of despair.

Marie, whose nervous system had been enervated by a constant course of self-indulgence, had nothing to support the terror of the shock, and, at the time her husband breathed his last, was passing from one fainting fit to another; and he to whom she had been joined in the mysterious tie of marriage passed from her forever, without the possibility of even a parting word.

Miss Ophelia, with characteristic strength and self-control, had remained with her kinsman to the last,—all eye, all ear, all attention; doing everything of the little that could be done, and joining with her whole soul in the tender and impassioned prayers which the poor slave had poured forth for the soul of his dying master.

When they were arranging him for his last rest, they found upon his bosom a small, plain miniature case, opening with a spring. It was the miniature of a noble and beautiful female face; and on the reverse, under a crystal, a lock of dark hair. They laid them back on the lifeless breast,—dust to dust,—poor mournful relics of early dreams, which once made that cold heart beat so warmly!

Tom's whole soul was filled with thoughts of eternity; and while he ministered around the lifeless clay, he did not once think that the sudden stroke had left him in hopeless slavery. He felt at peace about his master; for in that hour, when he had poured forth his prayer into the bosom of his Father, he had found an answer of quietness and assurance springing up within himself. In the depths of his own affectionate nature, he felt able to perceive something of the fulness of Divine love; for an old oracle hath thus written,—"He that dwelleth in love dwelleth in God, and God in him." Tom hoped and trusted, and was at peace.

But the funeral passed, with all its pageant of black crape, and prayers, and solemn faces; and back rolled the cool, muddy waves of every-day life; and up came the everlasting hard inquiry of "What is to be done next?"

It rose to the mind of Marie, as, dressed in loose morning-robes, and surrounded by anxious servants, she sat up in a great easy-chair, and inspected samples of crape and bombazine. It rose to Miss Ophelia, who began to turn her thoughts towards her northern home. It rose, in silent terrors, to the minds of the servants, who well knew the unfeeling, tyrannical character of the mistress in whose hands they were left. All knew, very well, that the indulgences which had been accorded to them were not from their mistress, but from their master; and that, now he was gone, there would be no screen between them and every tyrannous infliction which a temper soured by affliction might devise.

It was about a fortnight after the funeral, that Miss Ophelia, busied one day in her apartment, heard a gentle tap at the door. She opened it, and there stood Rosa, the pretty young quadroon, whom we have before often noticed, her hair in disorder, and her eyes swelled with crying.

"O, Miss Feeley," she said, falling on her knees, and catching the skirt of her dress, "*do, do go* to Miss Marie for me! do plead for me! She's goin' to send me out to be whipped—look there!" And she handed to Miss Ophelia a paper.

It was an order, written in Marie's delicate Italian hand, to the master of a whipping-establishment to give the bearer fifteen lashes.

"What have you been doing?" said Miss Ophelia.

"You know, Miss Feely, I've got such a bad temper; it's very bad of me. I was trying on Miss Marie's dress, and she slapped my face; and I spoke out before I thought, and was saucy; and she said that she'd bring me down, and have me know, once for all, that I wasn't going to be so topping as I had been; and she wrote this, and says I shall carry it. I'd rather she'd kill me, right out."

Miss Ophelia stood considering, with the paper in her hand.

"You see, Miss Feely," said Rosa, "I don't mind the whipping so much, if Miss Marie or you was to do it; but, to be sent to a *man!* and such a horrid man,—the shame of it, Miss Feely!"

CHAPTER XXIX

Miss Ophelia well knew that it was the universal custom to send women and young girls to whipping-houses, to the hands of the lowest of men,—men vile enough to make this their profession,—there to be subjected to brutal exposure and shameful correction. She had *known* it before; but hitherto she had never realized it, till she saw the slender form of Rosa almost convulsed with distress. All the honest blood of womanhood, the strong New England blood of liberty, flushed to her cheeks, and throbbed bitterly in her indignant heart; but, with habitual prudence and self-control, she mastered herself, and, crushing the paper firmly in her hand, she merely said to Rosa,

"Sit down, child, while I go to your mistress."

"Shameful! monstrous! outrageous!" she said to herself, as she was crossing the parlor.

She found Marie sitting up in her easy-chair, with Mammy standing by her, combing her hair; Jane sat on the ground before her, busy in chafing her feet.

"How do you find yourself, today?" said Miss Ophelia.

A deep sigh, and a closing of the eyes, was the only reply, for a moment; and then Marie answered, "O, I don't know, Cousin; I suppose I'm as well as I ever shall be!" and Marie wiped her eyes with a cambric handkerchief, bordered with an inch deep of black.

"I came," said Miss Ophelia, with a short, dry cough, such as commonly introduces a difficult subject,—"I came to speak with you about poor Rosa."

Marie's eyes were open wide enough now, and a flush rose to her sallow cheeks, as she answered, sharply,

"Well, what about her?"

"She is very sorry for her fault."

"She is, is she? She'll be sorrier, before I've done with her! I've endured that child's impudence long enough; and now I'll bring her down,—I'll make her lie in the dust!"

"But could not you punish her some other way,—some way that would be less shameful?"

"I mean to shame her; that's just what I want. She has all her life presumed on her delicacy, and her good looks, and her lady-like airs, till she forgets who she is;—and I'll give her one lesson that will bring her down, I fancy!"

"But, Cousin, consider that, if you destroy delicacy and a sense of shame in a young girl, you deprave her very fast."

"Delicacy!" said Marie, with a scornful laugh,—"a fine word for such as she! I'll teach her, with all her airs, that she's no better than the raggedest black wench that walks the streets! She'll take no more airs with me!"

"You will answer to God for such cruelty!" said Miss Ophelia, with energy.

"Cruelty,—I'd like to know what the cruelty is! I wrote orders for only fifteen lashes, and told him to put them on lightly. I'm sure there's no cruelty there!"

"No cruelty!" said Miss Ophelia. "I'm sure any girl might rather be killed outright!"

"It might seem so to anybody with your feeling; but all these creatures get used to it; it's the only way they can be kept in order. Once let them feel that they are to take any airs about delicacy, and all that, and they'll run all over you, just as my servants always have. I've begun now to bring them under; and I'll have them all to know that I'll send one out to be whipped, as soon as another, if they don't mind themselves!" said Marie, looking around her decidedly.

Jane hung her head and cowered at this, for she felt as if it was particularly directed to her. Miss Ophelia sat for a moment, as if she had swallowed some explosive mixture, and were ready to burst. Then, recollecting the utter uselessness of contention with such a nature, she shut her lips resolutely, gathered herself up, and walked out of the room.

It was hard to go back and tell Rosa that she could do nothing for her; and, shortly after, one of the man-servants came to say that her mistress had ordered him to take Rosa with him to the whipping-house, whither she was hurried, in spite of her tears and entreaties.

A few days after, Tom was standing musing by the balconies, when he was joined by Adolph, who, since the death of his master, had been entirely crestfallen and disconsolate. Adolph knew that he had always been an object of dislike to Marie; but while his master lived he had paid but little attention to it. Now that he was gone, he had moved about in daily dread and trembling, not knowing what might befall him next. Marie had held several consultations with her lawyer; after communicating with St. Clare's brother, it was determined to sell the place, and all the servants, except her own personal property, and these she intended to take with her, and go back to her father's plantation.

"Do ye know, Tom, that we've all got to be sold?" said Adolph.

"How did you hear that?" said Tom.

"I hid myself behind the curtains when Missis was talking with the lawyer. In a few days we shall be sent off to auction, Tom."

"The Lord's will be done!" said Tom, folding his arms and sighing heavily.

"We'll never get another such a master," said Adolph, apprehensively; "but I'd rather be sold than take my chance under Missis."

Tom turned away; his heart was full. The hope of liberty, the thought of distant wife and children, rose up before his patient soul, as to the mariner shipwrecked almost in port rises the vision of the church-spire and loving roofs of his native village, seen over the top of some black wave only for one last farewell. He drew his arms tightly over his bosom, and choked back the bitter tears, and tried to pray. The poor old soul had such a singular, unaccountable prejudice in favor of liberty, that it was a hard wrench for him; and the more he said, "Thy will be done," the worse he felt.

He sought Miss Ophelia, who, ever since Eva's death, had treated him with marked and respectful kindness.

"Miss Feely," he said, "Mas'r St. Clare promised me my freedom. He told me that he had begun to take it out for me; and now, perhaps, if Miss Feely would be good enough to speak bout it to Missis, she would feel like goin' on with it, was it as Mas'r St. Clare's wish."

"I'll speak for you, Tom, and do my best," said Miss Ophelia; "but, if it depends on Mrs. St. Clare, I can't hope much for you;—nevertheless, I will try."

This incident occurred a few days after that of Rosa, while Miss Ophelia was busied in preparations to return north.

Seriously reflecting within herself, she considered that perhaps she had shown too hasty a warmth of language in her former interview with Marie; and she resolved that she would now endeavor to moderate her zeal, and to be as conciliatory as possible. So the good soul gathered herself up, and, taking her knitting, resolved to go into Marie's room, be as agreeable as possible, and negotiate Tom's case with all the diplomatic skill of which she was mistress.

She found Marie reclining at length upon a lounge, supporting herself on one elbow by pillows, while Jane, who had been out shopping, was displaying before her certain samples of thin black stuffs.

"That will do," said Marie, selecting one; "only I'm not sure about its being properly mourning."

"Laws, Missis," said Jane, volubly, "Mrs. General Derbennon wore just this very thing, after the General died, last summer; it makes up lovely!"

"What do you think?" said Marie to Miss Ophelia.

"It's a matter of custom, I suppose," said Miss Ophelia. "You can judge about it better than I."

"The fact is," said Marie, "that I haven't a dress in the world that I can wear; and, as I am going to break up the establishment, and go off, next week, I must decide upon something."

"Are you going so soon?"

"Yes. St. Clare's brother has written, and he and the lawyer think that the servants and furniture had better be put up at auction, and the place left with our lawyer."

"There's one thing I wanted to speak with you about," said Miss Ophelia. "Augustine promised Tom his liberty, and began the legal forms necessary to it. I hope you will use your influence to have it perfected."

"Indeed, I shall do no such thing!" said Marie, sharply. "Tom is one of the most valuable servants on the place,—it couldn't be afforded, any way. Besides, what does he want of liberty? He's a great deal better off as he is."

"But he does desire it, very earnestly, and his master promised it," said Miss Ophelia.

"I dare say he does want it," said Marie; "they all want it, just because they are a discontented set,—always wanting what they haven't got. Now, I'm principled against emancipating, in any case. Keep a negro under the care of a master, and he does well enough, and is respectable; but set them free, and they get lazy, and won't work, and take to drinking, and go all down to be mean, worthless fellows, I've seen it tried, hundreds of times. It's no favor to set them free."

"But Tom is so steady, industrious, and pious."

"O, you needn't tell me! I've see a hundred like him. He'll do very well, as long as he's taken care of,—that's all."

"But, then, consider," said Miss Ophelia, "when you set him up for sale, the chances of his getting a bad master."

"O, that's all humbug!" said Marie; "it isn't one time in a hundred that a good fellow gets a bad master; most masters are good, for all the talk that is made. I've lived and grown up here, in the South, and I never yet was acquainted with a master that didn't treat his servants well,—quite as well as is worth while. I don't feel any fears on that head."

"Well," said Miss Ophelia, energetically, "I know it was one of the last wishes of your husband that Tom should have his liberty; it was one of the promises that he made to dear little Eva on her death-bed, and I should not think you would feel at liberty to disregard it."

Marie had her face covered with her handkerchief at this appeal, and began sobbing and using her smelling-bottle, with great vehemence.

"Everybody goes against me!" she said. "Everybody is so inconsiderate! I shouldn't have expected that *you* would bring up all these remembrances of my troubles to me,—it's so inconsiderate! But nobody ever does consider,—my trials are so peculiar! It's so hard, that when I had only one daughter, she should have been taken!—and when I had a husband that just exactly suited me,—and I'm so hard to be suited!—he should be taken! And you seem to have so little feeling for me, and keep bringing it up to me so carelessly,—when you know how it overcomes me! I suppose you mean well; but it is very inconsiderate,—very!" And Marie sobbed, and gasped for breath, and called Mammy to open the window, and to bring her the camphor-bottle, and to bathe her head, and unhook her dress. And, in the general confusion that ensued, Miss Ophelia made her escape to her apartment.

She saw, at once, that it would do no good to say anything more; for Marie had an indefinite capacity for hysteric fits; and, after this, whenever her husband's or Eva's wishes with regard to the servants were alluded to, she always found it convenient to set one in operation. Miss Ophelia, therefore, did the next best thing she could for Tom,—she wrote a letter to Mrs. Shelby for him, stating his troubles, and urging them to send to his relief.

The next day, Tom and Adolph, and some half a dozen other servants, were marched down to a slave-warehouse, to await the convenience of the trader, who was going to make up a lot for auction.

CHAPTER XXX

THE SLAVE WAREHOUSE

A slave warehouse! Perhaps some of my readers conjure up horrible visions of such a place. They fancy some foul, obscure den, some horrible *Tartarus "informis, ingens, cui lumen ademptum."* But no, innocent friend; in these days men have learned the art of sinning expertly and genteelly, so as not to shock the eyes and senses of respectable society. Human property is high in the market; and is, therefore, well fed, well cleaned, tended, and looked after, that it may come to sale sleek, and strong, and shining. A slave-warehouse in New Orleans is a house externally not much unlike many others, kept with neatness; and where every day you may see arranged, under a sort of shed along the outside, rows of men and women, who stand there as a sign of the property sold within.

Then you shall be courteously entreated to call and examine, and shall find an abundance of husbands, wives, brothers, sisters, fathers, mothers, and young children, to be "sold separately, or in lots to suit the convenience of the purchaser;" and that soul immortal, once bought with blood and anguish by the Son of God, when the earth shook, and the rocks rent, and the graves were opened, can be sold, leased, mortgaged, exchanged for groceries or dry goods, to suit the phases of trade, or the fancy of the purchaser.

It was a day or two after the conversation between Marie and Miss Ophelia, that Tom, Adolph, and about half a dozen others of the St. Clare estate, were turned over to the loving kindness of Mr. Skeggs, the keeper of a depot on —— street, to await the auction, next day.

Tom had with him quite a sizable trunk full of clothing, as had most others of them. They were ushered, for the night, into a long room, where many other men, of all ages, sizes, and shades of complexion, were assembled, and from which roars of laughter and unthinking merriment were proceeding.

"Ah, ha! that's right. Go it, boys,—go it!" said Mr. Skeggs, the keeper. "My people are always so merry! Sambo, I see!" he said, speaking approvingly to a burly negro who was performing tricks of low buffoonery, which occasioned the shouts which Tom had heard.

As might be imagined, Tom was in no humor to join these proceedings; and, therefore, setting his trunk as far as possible from the noisy group, he sat down on it, and leaned his face against the wall.

The dealers in the human article make scrupulous and systematic efforts to promote noisy mirth among them, as a means of drowning reflection, and rendering them insensible to their condition. The whole object of the training to which the negro is put, from the time he is sold in the northern market till he arrives south, is systematically directed towards making him callous, unthinking, and brutal. The slave-dealer collects his gang in Virginia or Kentucky, and drives them to some convenient, healthy place,—often a watering place,—to be fattened. Here they are fed full daily; and, because some incline to pine, a fiddle is kept commonly going among them, and they are made to dance daily; and he who refuses to be merry—in whose soul thoughts of wife, or child, or home, are too strong for him to be gay—is marked as sullen and dangerous, and subjected to all the evils which the ill will of an utterly irresponsible and hardened man can inflict upon him. Briskness, alertness, and cheerfulness of appearance, especially before observers, are constantly enforced upon them, both by the hope of thereby getting a good master, and the fear of all that the driver may bring upon them if they prove unsalable.

"What dat ar nigger doin here?" said Sambo, coming up to Tom, after Mr. Skeggs had left the room. Sambo was a full black, of great size, very lively, voluble, and full of trick and grimace.

"What you doin here?" said Sambo, coming up to Tom, and poking him facetiously in the side. "Meditatin', eh?"

"I am to be sold at the auction tomorrow!" said Tom, quietly.

"Sold at auction,—haw! haw! boys, an't this yer fun? I wish't I was gwine that ar way!—tell ye, wouldn't I make em laugh? But how is it,—dis yer whole lot gwine tomorrow?" said Sambo, laying his hand freely on Adolph's shoulder.

"Please to let me alone!" said Adolph, fiercely, straightening himself up, with extreme disgust.

"Law, now, boys! dis yer's one o' yer white niggers,—kind o' cream color, ye know, scented!" said he, coming up to Adolph and snuffing. "O Lor! he'd do for a tobaccer-shop; they could keep him to scent snuff! Lor, he'd keep a whole shope agwine,—he would!"

"I say, keep off, can't you?" said Adolph, enraged.

"Lor, now, how touchy we is,—we white niggers! Look at us now!" and Sambo gave a ludicrous imitation of Adolph's manner; "here's de airs and graces. We's been in a good family, I specs."

"Yes," said Adolph; "I had a master that could have bought you all for old truck!"

"Laws, now, only think," said Sambo, "the gentlemens that we is!"

"I belonged to the St. Clare family," said Adolph, proudly.

"Lor, you did! Be hanged if they ar'n't lucky to get shet of ye. Spects they's gwine to trade ye off with a lot o' cracked tea-pots and sich like!" said Sambo, with a provoking grin.

Adolph, enraged at this taunt, flew furiously at his adversary, swearing and striking on every side of him. The rest laughed and shouted, and the uproar brought the keeper to the door.

"What now, boys? Order,—order!" he said, coming in and flourishing a large whip.

All fled in different directions, except Sambo, who, presuming on the favor which the keeper had to him as a licensed wag, stood his ground, ducking his head with a facetious grin, whenever the master made a dive at him.

"Lor, Mas'r, 'tan't us,—we 's reglar stiddy,—it's these yer new hands; they 's real aggravatin',—kinder pickin' at us, all time!"

The keeper, at this, turned upon Tom and Adolph, and distributing a few kicks and cuffs without much inquiry, and leaving general orders for all to be good boys and go to sleep, left the apartment.

While this scene was going on in the men's sleeping-room, the reader may be curious to take a peep at the corresponding apartment allotted to the women. Stretched out in various attitudes over the floor, he may see numberless sleeping forms of every shade of complexion, from the purest ebony to white, and of all years, from childhood to old age, lying now asleep. Here is a fine bright girl, of ten years, whose mother was sold out yesterday, and who tonight cried herself to sleep when nobody was looking at her. Here, a worn old negress, whose thin arms and callous fingers tell of hard toil, waiting to be sold tomorrow, as a cast-off article, for what can be got for her; and some forty or fifty others, with heads variously enveloped in blankets or articles of clothing, lie stretched around them. But, in a corner, sitting apart from the rest, are two females of a more interesting appearance than common. One of these is a respectably-dressed mulatto woman between forty and fifty, with soft eyes and a gentle and pleasing physiognomy. She has on her head a high-raised turban, made of a gay red Madras handkerchief, of the first quality, her dress is neatly fitted, and of good material, showing that she has been provided for with a careful hand. By her side, and nestling closely to her, is a young girl of fifteen,—her daughter. She is a quadroon, as may be seen from her fairer complexion, though her likeness to her mother is quite discernible. She has the same soft, dark eye, with longer lashes, and her curling hair is of a luxuriant brown. She also is dressed with great neatness, and her white, delicate hands betray very little acquaintance with servile toil. These two are to be sold tomorrow, in the same lot with the St. Clare servants; and the gentleman to whom they belong, and to whom the money for their sale is to be transmitted, is a member of a Christian church in New York, who will receive the money, and go thereafter to the sacrament of his Lord and theirs, and think no more of it.

These two, whom we shall call Susan and Emmeline, had been the personal attendants of an amiable and pious lady of New Orleans, by whom they had been carefully and piously instructed and trained. They had been taught to read and write, diligently instructed in the truths of religion, and their lot had been as happy an one as in their condition it was possible to be. But the only son of their protectress had the management of her property; and, by carelessness and extravagance involved it to a large amount, and at last failed. One of the largest creditors was the respectable firm of B. & Co., in New York. B. & Co. wrote to their lawyer in New Orleans, who attached the real estate (these two articles and a lot of plantation hands formed the most valuable part of it), and wrote word to that effect to New York. Brother B., being, as we have said, a Christian man, and a resident in a free State, felt some uneasiness on the subject. He didn't like trading in slaves and souls of men,—of course, he didn't; but, then, there were thirty thousand dollars in the case, and that was rather too much money to be lost for a principle; and so, after much considering, and asking advice from those that he knew would advise to suit him, Brother B. wrote to his lawyer to dispose of the business in the way that seemed to him the most suitable, and remit the proceeds.

The day after the letter arrived in New Orleans, Susan and Emmeline were attached, and sent to the depot to await a general auction on the following morning; and as they glimmer faintly upon us in the moonlight which steals through the grated window, we may listen to their conversation. Both are weeping, but each quietly, that the other may not hear.

"Mother, just lay your head on my lap, and see if you can't sleep a little," says the girl, trying to appear calm.

"I haven't any heart to sleep, Em; I can't; it's the last night we may be together!"

"O, mother, don't say so! perhaps we shall get sold together,—who knows?"

"If 't was anybody's else case, I should say so, too, Em," said the woman; "but I'm so feard of losin' you that I don't see anything but the danger."

"Why, mother, the man said we were both likely, and would sell well."

Susan remembered the man's looks and words. With a deadly sickness at her heart, she remembered how he had looked at Emmeline's hands, and lifted up her curly hair, and pronounced her a first-rate article. Susan had been trained as a Christian, brought up in the daily reading of the Bible, and had the same horror of her child's being sold to a life of shame that any other Christian mother might have; but she had no hope,—no protection.

"Mother, I think we might do first rate, if you could get a place as cook, and I as chambermaid or seamstress, in some family. I dare say we shall. Let's both look as bright and lively as we can, and tell all we can do, and perhaps we shall," said Emmeline.

"I want you to brush your hair all back straight, tomorrow," said Susan.

"What for, mother? I don't look near so well, that way."

"Yes, but you'll sell better so."

"I don't see why!" said the child.

"Respectable families would be more apt to buy you, if they saw you looked plain and decent, as if you wasn't trying to look handsome. I know their ways better 'n you do," said Susan.

"Well, mother, then I will."

"And, Emmeline, if we shouldn't ever see each other again, after tomorrow,—if I'm sold way up on a plantation somewhere, and you somewhere else,—always remember how you've been brought up, and all Missis has told you; take your Bible with you, and your hymn-book; and if you're faithful to the Lord, he'll be faithful to you."

So speaks the poor soul, in sore discouragement; for she knows that tomorrow any man, however vile and brutal, however godless and merciless, if he only has money to pay for her, may become owner of her daughter, body and soul; and then, how is the child to be faithful? She thinks of all this, as she holds her daughter in her arms, and wishes that she were not handsome and attractive. It seems almost an aggravation to her to remember how purely and piously, how much above the ordinary lot, she has been brought up. But she has no resort but to *pray*; and many such prayers to God have gone up from those same trim, neatly-arranged, respectable slave-prisons,—prayers which God has not forgotten, as a coming day shall show; for it is written, "Who causeth one of these little ones to offend, it were better for him that a millstone were hanged about his neck, and that he were drowned in the depths of the sea."

The soft, earnest, quiet moonbeam looks in fixedly, marking the bars of the grated windows on the prostrate, sleeping forms. The mother and daughter are singing together a wild and melancholy dirge, common as a funeral hymn among the slaves:

"O, where is weeping Mary? O, where is weeping Mary? 'Rived in the goodly land. She is dead and gone to Heaven; She is dead and gone to Heaven; 'Rived in the goodly land."

These words, sung by voices of a peculiar and melancholy sweetness, in an air which seemed like the sighing of earthy despair after heavenly hope, floated through the dark prison rooms with a pathetic cadence, as verse after verse was breathed out:

"O, where are Paul and Silas? O, where are Paul and Silas? Gone to the goodly land. They are dead and gone to Heaven; They are dead and gone to Heaven; 'Rived in the goodly land."

Sing on poor souls! The night is short, and the morning will part you forever!

But now it is morning, and everybody is astir; and the worthy Mr. Skeggs is busy and bright, for a lot of goods is to be fitted out for auction. There is a brisk lookout on the toilet; injunctions passed around to every one to put on their best face and be spry; and now all are arranged in a circle for a last review, before they are marched up to the Bourse.

Mr. Skeggs, with his palmetto on and his cigar in his mouth, walks around to put farewell touches on his wares.

"How's this?" he said, stepping in front of Susan and Emmeline. "Where's your curls, gal?"

The girl looked timidly at her mother, who, with the smooth adroitness common among her class, answers,

"I was telling her, last night, to put up her hair smooth and neat, and not havin' it flying about in curls; looks more respectable so."

"Bother!" said the man, peremptorily, turning to the girl; "you go right along, and curl yourself real smart!" He added, giving a crack to a rattan he held in his hand, "And be back in quick time, too!"

"You go and help her," he added, to the mother. "Them curls may make a hundred dollars difference in the sale of her."

Beneath a splendid dome were men of all nations, moving to and fro, over the marble pave. On every side of the circular area were little tribunes, or stations, for the use of speakers and auctioneers. Two of these, on opposite sides of the area, were now occupied by brilliant and talented gentlemen, enthusiastically forcing up, in English and French commingled, the bids of connoisseurs in their various wares. A third one, on the other side, still unoccupied, was surrounded by a group, waiting the moment of sale to begin. And here we may recognize the St. Clare servants,—Tom, Adolph, and others; and there, too, Susan and Emmeline, awaiting their turn with anxious and dejected faces. Various spectators, intending to purchase, or not intending, examining, and commenting on their various points and faces with the same freedom that a set of jockeys discuss the merits of a horse.

"Hulloa, Alf! what brings you here?" said a young exquisite, slapping the shoulder of a sprucely-dressed young man, who was examining Adolph through an eye-glass.

"Well! I was wanting a valet, and I heard that St. Clare's lot was going. I thought I'd just look at his—"

"Catch me ever buying any of St. Clare's people! Spoilt niggers, every one. Impudent as the devil!" said the other.

"Never fear that!" said the first. "If I get 'em, I'll soon have their airs out of them; they'll soon find that they've another kind of master to deal with than Monsieur St. Clare. 'Pon my word, I'll buy that fellow. I like the shape of him."

"You'll find it'll take all you've got to keep him. He's deucedly extravagant!"

"Yes, but my lord will find that he *can't* be extravagant with *me*. Just let him be sent to the calaboose a few times, and thoroughly dressed down! I'll tell you if it don't bring him to a sense of his ways! O, I'll reform him, up hill and down,—you'll see. I buy him, that's flat!"

Tom had been standing wistfully examining the multitude of faces thronging around him, for one whom he would wish to call master. And if you should ever be under the necessity, sir, of selecting, out of two hundred men, one who was to become your absolute owner and disposer, you would, perhaps, realize, just as Tom did, how few there were that you would feel at all comfortable in being made over to. Tom saw abundance of men,—great, burly, gruff men; little, chirping, dried men; long-favored, lank, hard men; and every variety of stubbed-looking, commonplace men, who pick up their fellow-men as one picks up chips, putting them into the fire or a basket with equal unconcern, according to their convenience; but he saw no St. Clare.

CHAPTER XXX

A little before the sale commenced, a short, broad, muscular man, in a checked shirt considerably open at the bosom, and pantaloons much the worse for dirt and wear, elbowed his way through the crowd, like one who is going actively into a business; and, coming up to the group, began to examine them systematically. From the moment that Tom saw him approaching, he felt an immediate and revolting horror at him, that increased as he came near. He was evidently, though short, of gigantic strength. His round, bullet head, large, light-gray eyes, with their shaggy, sandy eyebrows, and stiff, wiry, sun-burned hair, were rather unprepossessing items, it is to be confessed; his large, coarse mouth was distended with tobacco, the juice of which, from time to time, he ejected from him with great decision and explosive force; his hands were immensely large, hairy, sun-burned, freckled, and very dirty, and garnished with long nails, in a very foul condition. This man proceeded to a very free personal examination of the lot. He seized Tom by the jaw, and pulled open his mouth to inspect his teeth; made him strip up his sleeve, to show his muscle; turned him round, made him jump and spring, to show his paces.

"Where was you raised?" he added, briefly, to these investigations.

"In Kintuck, Mas'r," said Tom, looking about, as if for deliverance.

"What have you done?"

"Had care of Mas'r's farm," said Tom.

"Likely story!" said the other, shortly, as he passed on. He paused a moment before Dolph; then spitting a discharge of tobacco-juice on his well-blacked boots, and giving a contemptuous umph, he walked on. Again he stopped before Susan and Emmeline. He put out his heavy, dirty hand, and drew the girl towards him; passed it over her neck and bust, felt her arms, looked at her teeth, and then pushed her back against her mother, whose patient face showed the suffering she had been going through at every motion of the hideous stranger.

The girl was frightened, and began to cry.

"Stop that, you minx!" said the salesman; "no whimpering here,—the sale is going to begin." And accordingly the sale begun.

Adolph was knocked off, at a good sum, to the young gentlemen who had previously stated his intention of buying him; and the other servants of the St. Clare lot went to various bidders.

"Now, up with you, boy! d'ye hear?" said the auctioneer to Tom.

Tom stepped upon the block, gave a few anxious looks round; all seemed mingled in a common, indistinct noise,—the clatter of the salesman crying off his qualifications in French and English, the quick fire of French and English bids; and almost in a moment came the final thump of the hammer, and the clear ring on the last syllable of the word *"dollars,"* as the auctioneer announced his price, and Tom was made over.—He had a master!

He was pushed from the block;—the short, bullet-headed man seizing him roughly by the shoulder, pushed him to one side, saying, in a harsh voice, "Stand there, *you!*"

Tom hardly realized anything; but still the bidding went on,—ratting, clattering, now French, now English. Down goes the hammer again,—Susan is sold! She goes down from the block, stops, looks wistfully back,—her daughter stretches her hands towards her. She looks with agony in the face of the man who has bought her,—a respectable middle-aged man, of benevolent countenance.

"O, Mas'r, please do buy my daughter!"

"I'd like to, but I'm afraid I can't afford it!" said the gentleman, looking, with painful interest, as the young girl mounted the block, and looked around her with a frightened and timid glance.

The blood flushes painfully in her otherwise colorless cheek, her eye has a feverish fire, and her mother groans to see that she looks more beautiful than she ever saw her before. The auctioneer sees his advantage, and expatiates volubly in mingled French and English, and bids rise in rapid succession.

"I'll do anything in reason," said the benevolent-looking gentleman, pressing in and joining with the bids. In a few moments they have run beyond his purse. He is silent; the auctioneer grows warmer; but bids gradually drop off. It lies now between an aristocratic old citizen and our bullet-headed acquaintance. The citizen bids for a few turns, contemptuously measuring his opponent; but the bullet-head has the advantage over him, both in obstinacy and concealed length of purse, and the controversy lasts but a moment; the hammer falls,—he has got the girl, body and soul, unless God help her!

Her master is Mr. Legree, who owns a cotton plantation on the Red River. She is pushed along into the same lot with Tom and two other men, and goes off, weeping as she goes.

The benevolent gentleman is sorry; but, then, the thing happens every day! One sees girls and mothers crying, at these sales, *always!* it can't be helped, &c.; and he walks off, with his acquisition, in another direction.

Two days after, the lawyer of the Christian firm of B. & Co., New York, send on their money to them. On the reverse of that draft, so obtained, let them write these words of the great Paymaster, to whom they shall make up their account in a future day: *"When he maketh inquisition for blood, he forgetteth not the cry of the humble!"*

CHAPTER XXXI

THE MIDDLE PASSAGE

"Thou art of purer eyes than to behold evil, and canst not look upon iniquity: wherefore lookest thou upon them that deal treacherously, and holdest thy tongue when the wicked devoureth the man that is more righteous than he?"—HAB. 1: 13.

On the lower part of a small, mean boat, on the Red River, Tom sat,—chains on his wrists, chains on his feet, and a weight heavier than chains lay on his heart. All had faded from his sky,—moon and star; all had passed by him, as the trees and banks were now passing, to return no more. Kentucky home, with wife and children, and indulgent owners; St. Clare home, with all its refinements and splendors; the golden head of Eva, with its saint-like eyes; the proud, gay, handsome, seemingly careless, yet ever-kind St. Clare; hours of ease and indulgent leisure,—all gone! and in place thereof, *what* remains?

It is one of the bitterest apportionments of a lot of slavery, that the negro, sympathetic and assimilative, after acquiring, in a refined family, the tastes and feelings which form the atmosphere of such a place, is not the less liable to become the bond-slave of the coarsest and most brutal,—just as a chair or table, which once decorated the superb saloon, comes, at last, battered and defaced, to the barroom of some filthy tavern, or some low haunt of vulgar debauchery. The great difference is, that the table and chair cannot feel, and the *man* can; for even a legal enactment that he shall be "taken, reputed, adjudged in law, to be a chattel personal," cannot blot out his soul, with its own private little world of memories, hopes, loves, fears, and desires.

Mr. Simon Legree, Tom's master, had purchased slaves at one place and another, in New Orleans, to the number of eight, and driven them, handcuffed, in couples of two and two, down to the good steamer Pirate, which lay at the levee, ready for a trip up the Red River.

Having got them fairly on board, and the boat being off, he came round, with that air of efficiency which ever characterized him, to take a review of them. Stopping opposite to Tom, who had been attired for sale in his best broadcloth suit, with well-starched linen and shining boots, he briefly expressed himself as follows:

"Stand up."

Tom stood up.

"Take off that stock!" and, as Tom, encumbered by his fetters, proceeded to do it, he assisted him, by pulling it, with no gentle hand, from his neck, and putting it in his pocket.

Legree now turned to Tom's trunk, which, previous to this, he had been ransacking, and, taking from it a pair of old pantaloons and dilapidated coat, which Tom had been wont to put on about his stable-work, he said, liberating Tom's hands from the handcuffs, and pointing to a recess in among the boxes,

"You go there, and put these on."

Tom obeyed, and in a few moments returned.

"Take off your boots," said Mr. Legree.

Tom did so.

"There," said the former, throwing him a pair of coarse, stout shoes, such as were common among the slaves, "put these on."

In Tom's hurried exchange, he had not forgotten to transfer his cherished Bible to his pocket. It was well he did so; for Mr. Legree, having refitted Tom's handcuffs, proceeded deliberately to investigate the contents of his pockets. He drew out a silk handkerchief, and put it into his own pocket. Several little trifles, which Tom had treasured, chiefly because they had amused Eva, he looked upon with a contemptuous grunt, and tossed them over his shoulder into the river.

Tom's Methodist hymn-book, which, in his hurry, he had forgotten, he now held up and turned over.

Humph! pious, to be sure. So, what's yer name,—you belong to the church, eh?"

"Yes, Mas'r," said Tom, firmly.

"Well, I'll soon have *that* out of you. I have none o' yer bawling, praying, singing niggers on my place; so remember. Now, mind yourself," he said, with a stamp and a fierce glance of his gray eye, directed at Tom, "*I'm* your church now! You understand,—you've got to be as *I* say."

Something within the silent black man answered *No!* and, as if repeated by an invisible voice, came the words of an old prophetic scroll, as Eva had often read them to him,—"Fear not! for I have redeemed thee. I have called thee by name. Thou art MINE!"

But Simon Legree heard no voice. That voice is one he never shall hear. He only glared for a moment on the downcast face of Tom, and walked off. He took Tom's trunk, which contained a very neat and abundant wardrobe, to the forecastle, where it was soon surrounded by various hands of the boat. With much laughing, at the expense of niggers who tried to be gentlemen, the articles very readily were sold to one and another, and the empty trunk finally put up at auction. It was a good joke, they all thought, especially to see how Tom looked after his things, as they were going this way and that; and then the auction of the trunk, that was funnier than all, and occasioned abundant witticisms.

This little affair being over, Simon sauntered up again to his property.

"Now, Tom, I've relieved you of any extra baggage, you see. Take mighty good care of them clothes. It'll be long enough 'fore you get more. I go in for making niggers careful; one suit has to do for one year, on my place."

Simon next walked up to the place where Emmeline was sitting, chained to another woman.

"Well, my dear," he said, chucking her under the chin, "keep up your spirits."

The involuntary look of horror, fright and aversion, with which the girl regarded him, did not escape his eye. He frowned fiercely.

"None o' your shines, gal! you's got to keep a pleasant face, when I speak to ye,—d'ye hear? And you, you old yellow poco moonshine!" he said, giving a shove to the mulatto woman to whom Emmeline was chained, "don't you carry that sort of face! You's got to look chipper, I tell ye!"

"I say, all on ye," he said retreating a pace or two back, "look at me,—look at me,—look me right in the eye,—*straight*, now!" said he, stamping his foot at every pause.

As by a fascination, every eye was now directed to the glaring greenish-gray eye of Simon.

"Now," said he, doubling his great, heavy fist into something resembling a blacksmith's hammer, "d'ye see this fist? Heft it!" he said, bringing it down on Tom's hand. "Look at these yer bones! Well, I tell ye this yer fist has got as hard as iron *knocking down niggers*. I never see the nigger, yet, I couldn't bring down with one crack," said he, bringing his fist down so near to the face of Tom that he winked and drew back. "I don't keep none o' yer cussed overseers; I does my own overseeing; and I tell you things *is* seen to. You's every one on ye got to toe the mark, I tell ye; quick,—straight,—the moment I speak. That's the way to keep in with me. Ye won't find no soft spot in me, nowhere. So, now, mind yerselves; for I don't show no mercy!"

The women involuntarily drew in their breath, and the whole gang sat with downcast, dejected faces. Meanwhile, Simon turned on his heel, and marched up to the bar of the boat for a dram.

"That's the way I begin with my niggers," he said, to a gentlemanly man, who had stood by him during his speech. "It's my system to begin strong,—just let 'em know what to expect."

"Indeed!" said the stranger, looking upon him with the curiosity of a naturalist studying some out-of-the-way specimen.

"Yes, indeed. I'm none o' yer gentlemen planters, with lily fingers, to slop round and be cheated by some old cuss of an overseer! Just feel of my knuckles, now; look at my fist. Tell ye, sir, the flesh on 't has come jest like a stone, practising on nigger—feel on it."

The stranger applied his fingers to the implement in question, and simply said,

"'T is hard enough; and, I suppose," he added, "practice has made your heart just like it."

"Why, yes, I may say so," said Simon, with a hearty laugh. "I reckon there's as little soft in me as in any one going. Tell you, nobody comes it over me! Niggers never gets round me, neither with squalling nor soft soap,—that's a fact."

"You have a fine lot there."

"Real," said Simon. "There's that Tom, they telled me he was suthin' uncommon. I paid a little high for him, tendin' him for a driver and a managing chap; only get the notions out that he's larnt by bein' treated as niggers never ought to be, he'll do prime! The yellow woman I got took in on. I rayther think she's sickly, but I shall put her through for what she's worth; she may last a year or two. I don't go for savin' niggers. Use up, and buy more, 's my way;-makes you less trouble, and I'm quite sure it comes cheaper in the end;" and Simon sipped his glass.

"And how long do they generally last?" said the stranger.

"Well, donno; 'cordin' as their constitution is. Stout fellers last six or seven years; trashy ones gets worked up in two or three. I used to, when I fust begun, have considerable trouble fussin' with 'em and trying to make 'em hold out,—doctorin' on 'em up when they's sick, and givin' on 'em clothes and blankets, and what not, tryin' to keep 'em all sort o' decent and comfortable. Law, 't wasn't no sort o' use; I lost money on 'em, and 't was heaps o' trouble. Now, you see, I just put 'em straight through, sick or well. When one nigger's dead, I buy another; and I find it comes cheaper and easier, every way."

The stranger turned away, and seated himself beside a gentleman, who had been listening to the conversation with repressed uneasiness.

"You must not take that fellow to be any specimen of Southern planters," said he.

"I should hope not," said the young gentleman, with emphasis.

"He is a mean, low, brutal fellow!" said the other.

"And yet your laws allow him to hold any number of human beings subject to his absolute will, without even a shadow of protection; and, low as he is, you cannot say that there are not many such."

"Well," said the other, "there are also many considerate and humane men among planters."

"Granted," said the young man; "but, in my opinion, it is you considerate, humane men, that are responsible for all the brutality and outrage wrought by these wretches; because, if it were not for your sanction and influence, the whole system could not keep foothold for an hour. If there were no planters except such as that one," said he, pointing with his finger to Legree, who stood with his back to them, "the whole thing would go down like a millstone. It is your respectability and humanity that licenses and protects his brutality."

"You certainly have a high opinion of my good nature," said the planter, smiling, "but I advise you not to talk quite so loud, as there are people on board the boat who might not be quite so tolerant to opinion as I am. You had better wait till I get up to my plantation, and there you may abuse us all, quite at your leisure."

The young gentleman colored and smiled, and the two were soon busy in a game of backgammon. Meanwhile, another conversation was going on in the lower part of the boat, between Emmeline and the mulatto woman with whom she was confined. As was natural, they were exchanging with each other some particulars of their history.

"Who did you belong to?" said Emmeline.

"Well, my Mas'r was Mr. Ellis,—lived on Levee-street. P'raps you've seen the house."

"Was he good to you?" said Emmeline.

"Mostly, till he tuk sick. He's lain sick, off and on, more than six months, and been orful oneasy. 'Pears like he warnt willin' to have nobody rest, day or night; and got so curous, there couldn't nobody suit him. 'Pears like he just grew crosser, every day; kep me up nights till I got farly beat out, and couldn't keep awake no longer; and cause I got to sleep, one night, Lors, he talk so orful to me, and he tell me he'd sell me to just the hardest master he could find; and he'd promised me my freedom, too, when he died."

"Had you any friends?" said Emmeline.

"Yes, my husband,—he's a blacksmith. Mas'r gen'ly hired him out. They took me off so quick, I didn't even have time to see him; and I's got four children. O, dear me!" said the woman, covering her face with her hands.

It is a natural impulse, in every one, when they hear a tale of distress, to think of something to say by way of consolation. Emmeline wanted to say something, but she could not think of anything to say. What was there to be said? As by a common consent, they both avoided, with fear and dread, all mention of the horrible man who was now their master.

True, there is religious trust for even the darkest hour. The mulatto woman was a member of the Methodist church, and had an unenlightened but very sincere spirit of piety. Emmeline had been educated much more intelligently,—taught to read and write, and diligently instructed in the Bible, by the care of a faithful and pious mistress; yet, would it not try the faith of the firmest Christian, to find themselves abandoned, apparently, of God, in the grasp of ruthless violence? How much more must it shake the faith of Christ's poor little ones, weak in knowledge and tender in years!

The boat moved on,—freighted with its weight of sorrow,—up the red, muddy, turbid current, through the abrupt tortuous windings of the Red river; and sad eyes gazed wearily on the steep red-clay banks, as they glided by in dreary sameness. At last the boat stopped at a small town, and Legree, with his party, disembarked.

CHAPTER XXXII

DARK PLACES

"The dark places of the earth are full of the habitations of cruelty."[1]

Trailing wearily behind a rude wagon, and over a ruder road, Tom and his associates faced onward.

In the wagon was seated Simon Legree and the two women, still fettered together, were stowed away with some baggage in the back part of it, and the whole company were seeking Legree's plantation, which lay a good distance off.

It was a wild, forsaken road, now winding through dreary pine barrens, where the wind whispered mournfully, and now over log causeways, through long cypress swamps, the doleful trees rising out of the slimy, spongy ground, hung with long wreaths of funeral black moss, while ever and anon the loathsome form of the mocassin snake might be seen sliding among broken stumps and shattered branches that lay here and there, rotting in the water.

It is disconsolate enough, this riding, to the stranger, who, with well-filled pocket and well-appointed horse, threads the lonely way on some errand of business; but wilder, drearier, to the man enthralled, whom every weary step bears further from all that man loves and prays for.

So one should have thought, that witnessed the sunken and dejected expression on those dark faces; the wistful, patient weariness with which those sad eyes rested on object after object that passed them in their sad journey.

Simon rode on, however, apparently well pleased, occasionally pulling away at a flask of spirit, which he kept in his pocket.

"I say, *you!*" he said, as he turned back and caught a glance at the dispirited faces behind him. "Strike up a song, boys,—come!"

The men looked at each other, and the "*come*" was repeated, with a smart crack of the whip which the driver carried in his hands. Tom began a Methodist hymn.

---

[1] Ps. 74:20.

"Jerusalem, my happy home, Name ever dear to me! When shall my sorrows have an end, Thy joys when shall—"[1]

"Shut up, you black cuss!" roared Legree; "did ye think I wanted any o' yer infernal old Methodism? I say, tune up, now, something real rowdy,—quick!"

One of the other men struck up one of those unmeaning songs, common among the slaves.

"Mas'r see'd me cotch a coon, High boys, high! He laughed to split,—d'ye see the moon, Ho! ho! ho! boys, ho! Ho! yo! hi—e! *oh!"*

The singer appeared to make up the song to his own pleasure, generally hitting on rhyme, without much attempt at reason; and the party took up the chorus, at intervals,

"Ho! ho! ho! boys, ho! High—e—oh! high—e—oh!"

It was sung very boisterouly, and with a forced attempt at merriment; but no wail of despair, no words of impassioned prayer, could have had such a depth of woe in them as the wild notes of the chorus. As if the poor, dumb heart, threatened,—prisoned,—took refuge in that inarticulate sanctuary of music, and found there a language in which to breathe its prayer to God! There was a prayer in it, which Simon could not hear. He only heard the boys singing noisily, and was well pleased; he was making them "keep up their spirits."

"Well, my little dear," said he, turning to Emmeline, and laying his hand on her shoulder, "we're almost home!"

When Legree scolded and stormed, Emmeline was terrified; but when he laid his hand on her, and spoke as he now did, she felt as if she had rather he would strike her. The expression of his eyes made her soul sick, and her flesh creep. Involuntarily she clung closer to the mulatto woman by her side, as if she were her mother.

"You didn't ever wear ear-rings," he said, taking hold of her small ear with his coarse fingers.

"No, Mas'r!" said Emmeline, trembling and looking down.

"Well, I'll give you a pair, when we get home, if you're a good girl. You needn't be so frightened; I don't mean to make you work very hard. You'll have fine times with me, and live like a lady,—only be a good girl."

Legree had been drinking to that degree that he was inclining to be very gracious; and it was about this time that the enclosures of the plantation rose to view. The estate had formerly belonged to a gentleman of opulence and taste, who had bestowed some considerable attention to the adornment of his grounds. Having died insolvent, it had been purchased, at a bargain, by Legree, who used it, as he did everything else, merely as an implement for money-making. The place had that ragged, forlorn appearance, which is always produced by the evidence that the care of the former owner has been left to go to utter decay.

---

[1] "Jerusalem, my happy home," anonymous hymn dating from the latter part of the sixteenth century, sung to the tune of "St. Stephen." Words derive from St. Augustine's Meditations.

What was once a smooth-shaven lawn before the house, dotted here and there with ornamental shrubs, was now covered with frowsy tangled grass, with horse-posts set up, here and there, in it, where the turf was stamped away, and the ground littered with broken pails, cobs of corn, and other slovenly remains. Here and there, a mildewed jessamine or honeysuckle hung raggedly from some ornamental support, which had been pushed to one side by being used as a horse-post. What once was a large garden was now all grown over with weeds, through which, here and there, some solitary exotic reared its forsaken head. What had been a conservatory had now no window-shades, and on the mouldering shelves stood some dry, forsaken flower-pots, with sticks in them, whose dried leaves showed they had once been plants.

The wagon rolled up a weedy gravel walk, under a noble avenue of China trees, whose graceful forms and ever-springing foliage seemed to be the only things there that neglect could not daunt or alter,—like noble spirits, so deeply rooted in goodness, as to flourish and grow stronger amid discouragement and decay.

The house had been large and handsome. It was built in a manner common at the South; a wide verandah of two stories running round every part of the house, into which every outer door opened, the lower tier being supported by brick pillars.

But the place looked desolate and uncomfortable; some windows stopped up with boards, some with shattered panes, and shutters hanging by a single hinge,—all telling of coarse neglect and discomfort.

Bits of board, straw, old decayed barrels and boxes, garnished the ground in all directions; and three or four ferocious-looking dogs, roused by the sound of the wagon-wheels, came tearing out, and were with difficulty restrained from laying hold of Tom and his companions, by the effort of the ragged servants who came after them.

"Ye see what ye'd get!" said Legree, caressing the dogs with grim satisfaction, and turning to Tom and his companions. "Ye see what ye'd get, if ye try to run off. These yer dogs has been raised to track niggers; and they'd jest as soon chaw one on ye up as eat their supper. So, mind yerself! How now, Sambo!" he said, to a ragged fellow, without any brim to his hat, who was officious in his attentions. "How have things been going?"

"Fust rate, Mas'r."

"Quimbo," said Legree to another, who was making zealous demonstrations to attract his attention, "ye minded what I telled ye?"

"Guess I did, didn't I?"

These two colored men were the two principal hands on the plantation. Legree had trained them in savageness and brutality as systematically as he had his bull-dogs; and, by long practice in hardness and cruelty, brought their whole nature to about the same range of capacities. It is a common remark, and one that is thought to militate strongly against the character of the race, that the negro overseer is always more tyrannical and cruel than the white one. This is simply saying that the negro mind has been more crushed and debased than the white. It is no more true of this race than of every oppressed race, the world over. The slave is always a tyrant, if he can get a chance to be one.

Legree, like some potentates we read of in history, governed his plantation by a sort of resolution of forces. Sambo and Quimbo cordially hated each other; the plantation hands, one and all, cordially hated them; and, by playing off one against another, he was pretty sure, through one or the other of the three parties, to get informed of whatever was on foot in the place.

Nobody can live entirely without social intercourse; and Legree encouraged his two black satellites to a kind of coarse familiarity with him,—a familiarity, however, at any moment liable to get one or the other of them into trouble; for, on the slightest provocation, one of them always stood ready, at a nod, to be a minister of his vengeance on the other.

As they stood there now by Legree, they seemed an apt illustration of the fact that brutal men are lower even than animals. Their coarse, dark, heavy features; their great eyes, rolling enviously on each other; their barbarous, guttural, half-brute intonation; their dilapidated garments fluttering in the wind,—were all in admirable keeping with the vile and unwholesome character of everything about the place.

"Here, you Sambo," said Legree, "take these yer boys down to the quarters; and here's a gal I've got for *you*," said he, as he separated the mulatto woman from Emmeline, and pushed her towards him;—"I promised to bring you one, you know."

The woman gave a start, and drawing back, said, suddenly,

"O, Mas'r! I left my old man in New Orleans."

"What of that, you—; won't you want one here? None o' your words,—go long!" said Legree, raising his whip.

"Come, mistress," he said to Emmeline, "you go in here with me."

A dark, wild face was seen, for a moment, to glance at the window of the house; and, as Legree opened the door, a female voice said something, in a quick, imperative tone. Tom, who was looking, with anxious interest, after Emmeline, as she went in, noticed this, and heard Legree answer, angrily, "You may hold your tongue! I'll do as I please, for all you!"

Tom heard no more; for he was soon following Sambo to the quarters. The quarters was a little sort of street of rude shanties, in a row, in a part of the plantation, far off from the house. They had a forlorn, brutal, forsaken air. Tom's heart sunk when he saw them. He had been comforting himself with the thought of a cottage, rude, indeed, but one which he might make neat and quiet, and where he might have a shelf for his Bible, and a place to be alone out of his laboring hours. He looked into several; they were mere rude shells, destitute of any species of furniture, except a heap of straw, foul with dirt, spread confusedly over the floor, which was merely the bare ground, trodden hard by the tramping of innumerable feet.

"Which of these will be mine?" said he, to Sambo, submissively.

"Dunno; ken turn in here, I spose," said Sambo; "spects thar's room for another thar; thar's a pretty smart heap o' niggers to each on 'em, now; sure, I dunno what I 's to do with more."

It was late in the evening when the weary occupants of the shanties came flocking home,—men and women, in soiled and tattered garments, surly and uncomfortable, and in no mood to look pleasantly on new-comers. The small village was alive with no inviting sounds; hoarse, guttural voices contending at the hand-mills where their morsel of hard corn was yet to be ground into meal, to fit it for the cake that was to constitute their only supper. From the earliest dawn of the day, they had been in the fields, pressed to work under the driving lash of the overseers; for it was now in the very heat and hurry of the season, and no means was left untried to press every one up to the top of their capabilities. "True," says the negligent lounger; "picking cotton isn't hard work." Isn't it? And it isn't much inconvenience, either, to have one drop of water fall on your head; yet the worst torture of the inquisition is produced by drop after drop, drop after drop, falling moment after moment, with monotonous succession, on the same spot; and work, in itself not hard, becomes so, by being pressed, hour after hour, with unvarying, unrelenting sameness, with not even the consciousness of free-will to take from its tediousness. Tom looked in vain among the gang, as they poured along, for companionable faces. He saw only sullen, scowling, imbruted men, and feeble, discouraged women, or women that were not women,—the strong pushing away the weak,—the gross, unrestricted animal selfishness of human beings, of whom nothing good was expected and desired; and who, treated in every way like brutes, had sunk as nearly to their level as it was possible for human beings to do. To a late hour in the night the sound of the grinding was protracted; for the mills were few in number compared with the grinders, and the weary and feeble ones were driven back by the strong, and came on last in their turn.

"Ho yo!" said Sambo, coming to the mulatto woman, and throwing down a bag of corn before her; "what a cuss yo name?"

"Lucy," said the woman.

"Wal, Lucy, yo my woman now. Yo grind dis yer corn, and get *my* supper baked, ye har?"

"I an't your woman, and I won't be!" said the woman, with the sharp, sudden courage of despair; "you go long!"

"I'll kick yo, then!" said Sambo, raising his foot threateningly.

"Ye may kill me, if ye choose,—the sooner the better! Wish't I was dead!" said she.

"I say, Sambo, you go to spilin' the hands, I'll tell Mas'r o' you," said Quimbo, who was busy at the mill, from which he had viciously driven two or three tired women, who were waiting to grind their corn.

"And, I'll tell him ye won't let the women come to the mills, yo old nigger!" said Sambo. "Yo jes keep to yo own row."

Tom was hungry with his day's journey, and almost faint for want of food.

CHAPTER XXXII

"Thar, yo!" said Quimbo, throwing down a coarse bag, which contained a peck of corn; "thar, nigger, grab, take car on 't,—yo won't get no more, *dis* yer week."

Tom waited till a late hour, to get a place at the mills; and then, moved by the utter weariness of two women, whom he saw trying to grind their corn there, he ground for them, put together the decaying brands of the fire, where many had baked cakes before them, and then went about getting his own supper. It was a new kind of work there,—a deed of charity, small as it was; but it woke an answering touch in their hearts,—an expression of womanly kindness came over their hard faces; they mixed his cake for him, and tended its baking; and Tom sat down by the light of the fire, and drew out his Bible,—for he had need for comfort.

"What's that?" said one of the woman.

"A Bible," said Tom.

"Good Lord! han't seen un since I was in Kentuck."

"Was you raised in Kentuck?" said Tom, with interest.

"Yes, and well raised, too; never 'spected to come to dis yer!" said the woman, sighing.

"What's dat ar book, any way?" said the other woman.

"Why, the Bible."

"Laws a me! what's dat?" said the woman.

"Do tell! you never hearn on 't?" said the other woman. "I used to har Missis a readin' on 't, sometimes, in Kentuck; but, laws o' me! we don't har nothin' here but crackin' and swarin'."

"Read a piece, anyways!" said the first woman, curiously, seeing Tom attentively poring over it.

Tom read,—"Come unto Me, all ye that labor and are heavy laden, and I will give you rest."

"Them's good words, enough," said the woman; "who says 'em?"

"The Lord," said Tom.

"I jest wish I know'd whar to find Him," said the woman. "I would go; 'pears like I never should get rested again. My flesh is fairly sore, and I tremble all over, every day, and Sambo's allers a jawin' at me, 'cause I doesn't pick faster; and nights it's most midnight 'fore I can get my supper; and den 'pears like I don't turn over and shut my eyes, 'fore I hear de horn blow to get up, and at it agin in de mornin'. If I knew whar de Lor was, I'd tell him."

"He's here, he's everywhere," said Tom.

"Lor, you an't gwine to make me believe dat ar! I know de Lord an't here," said the woman; "'tan't no use talking, though. I's jest gwine to camp down, and sleep while I ken."

The women went off to their cabins, and Tom sat alone, by the smouldering fire, that flickered up redly in his face.

The silver, fair-browed moon rose in the purple sky, and looked down, calm and silent, as God looks on the scene of misery and oppression,—looked calmly on the lone black man, as he sat, with his arms folded, and his Bible on his knee.

"Is God HERE?" Ah, how is it possible for the untaught heart to keep its faith, unswerving, in the face of dire misrule, and palpable, unrebuked injustice? In that simple heart waged a fierce conflict; the crushing sense of wrong, the foreshadowing, of a whole life of future misery, the wreck of all past hopes, mournfully tossing in the soul's sight, like dead corpses of wife, and child, and friend, rising from the dark wave, and surging in the face of the half-drowned mariner! Ah, was it easy *here* to believe and hold fast the great password of Christian faith, that "God IS, and is the REWARDER of them that diligently seek Him"?

Tom rose, disconsolate, and stumbled into the cabin that had been allotted to him. The floor was already strewn with weary sleepers, and the foul air of the place almost repelled him; but the heavy night-dews were chill, and his limbs weary, and, wrapping about him a tattered blanket, which formed his only bed-clothing, he stretched himself in the straw and fell asleep.

In dreams, a gentle voice came over his ear; he was sitting on the mossy seat in the garden by Lake Pontchartrain, and Eva, with her serious eyes bent downward, was reading to him from the Bible; and he heard her read.

"When thou passest through the waters, I will be with thee, and the rivers they shall not overflow thee; when thou walkest through the fire, thou shalt not be burned, neither shall the flame kindle upon thee; for I am the Lord thy God, the Holy One of Israel, thy Saviour."

Gradually the words seemed to melt and fade, as in a divine music; the child raised her deep eyes, and fixed them lovingly on him, and rays of warmth and comfort seemed to go from them to his heart; and, as if wafted on the music, she seemed to rise on shining wings, from which flakes and spangles of gold fell off like stars, and she was gone.

Tom woke. Was it a dream? Let it pass for one. But who shall say that that sweet young spirit, which in life so yearned to comfort and console the distressed, was forbidden of God to assume this ministry after death?

It is a beautiful belief, That ever round our head Are hovering, on angel wings, The spirits of the dead.

CHAPTER XXXIII

CASSY

"And behold, the tears of such as were oppressed, and they had no comforter; and on the side of their oppressors there was power, but they had no comforter."—ECCL. 4:1

It took but a short time to familiarize Tom with all that was to be hoped or feared in his new way of life. He was an expert and efficient workman in whatever he undertook; and was, both from habit and principle, prompt and faithful. Quiet and peaceable in his disposition, he hoped, by unremitting diligence, to avert from himself at least a portion of the evils of his condition. He saw enough of abuse and misery to make him sick and weary; but he determined to toil on, with religious patience, committing himself to Him that judgeth righteously, not without hope that some way of escape might yet be opened to him.

Legree took a silent note of Tom's availability. He rated him as a first-class hand; and yet he felt a secret dislike to him,—the native antipathy of bad to good. He saw, plainly, that when, as was often the case, his violence and brutality fell on the helpless, Tom took notice of it; for, so subtle is the atmosphere of opinion, that it will make itself felt, without words; and the opinion even of a slave may annoy a master. Tom in various ways manifested a tenderness of feeling, a commiseration for his fellow-sufferers, strange and new to them, which was watched with a jealous eye by Legree. He had purchased Tom with a view of eventually making him a sort of overseer, with whom he might, at times, intrust his affairs, in short absences; and, in his view, the first, second, and third requisite for that place, was *hardness*. Legree made up his mind, that, as Tom was not hard to his hand, he would harden him forthwith; and some few weeks after Tom had been on the place, he determined to commence the process.

One morning, when the hands were mustered for the field, Tom noticed, with surprise, a new comer among them, whose appearance excited his attention. It was a woman, tall and slenderly formed, with remarkably delicate hands and feet, and dressed in neat and respectable garments. By the appearance of her face, she might have been between thirty-five and forty; and it was a face that, once seen, could never be forgotten,—one of those that, at a glance, seem to convey to us an idea of a wild, painful, and romantic history. Her forehead was high, and her eyebrows marked with beautiful clearness. Her straight, well-formed nose, her finely-cut mouth, and the graceful contour of her head and neck, showed that she must once have been beautiful; but her face was deeply wrinkled with lines of pain, and of proud and bitter endurance. Her complexion was sallow and unhealthy, her cheeks thin, her features sharp, and her whole form emaciated. But her eye was the most remarkable feature,—so large, so heavily black, overshadowed by long lashes of equal darkness, and so wildly, mournfully despairing. There was a fierce pride and defiance in every line of her face, in every curve of the flexible lip, in every motion of her body; but in her eye was a deep, settled night of anguish,—an expression so hopeless and unchanging as to contrast fearfully with the scorn and pride expressed by her whole demeanor.

Where she came from, or who she was, Tom did not know. The first he did know, she was walking by his side, erect and proud, in the dim gray of the dawn. To the gang, however, she was known; for there was much looking and turning of heads, and a smothered yet apparent exultation among the miserable, ragged, half-starved creatures by whom she was surrounded.

"Got to come to it, at last,—glad of it!" said one.

"He! he! he!" said another; "you'll know how good it is, Misse!"

"We'll see her work!"

"Wonder if she'll get a cutting up, at night, like the rest of us!"

"I'd be glad to see her down for a flogging, I'll bound!" said another.

The woman took no notice of these taunts, but walked on, with the same expression of angry scorn, as if she heard nothing. Tom had always lived among refined, and cultivated people, and he felt intuitively, from her air and bearing, that she belonged to that class; but how or why she could be fallen to those degrading circumstances, he could not tell. The women neither looked at him nor spoke to him, though, all the way to the field, she kept close at his side.

Tom was soon busy at his work; but, as the woman was at no great distance from him, he often glanced an eye to her, at her work. He saw, at a glance, that a native adroitness and handiness made the task to her an easier one than it proved to many. She picked very fast and very clean, and with an air of scorn, as if she despised both the work and the disgrace and humiliation of the circumstances in which she was placed.

In the course of the day, Tom was working near the mulatto woman who had been bought in the same lot with himself. She was evidently in a condition of great suffering, and Tom often heard her praying, as she wavered and trembled, and seemed about to fall down. Tom silently as he came near to her, transferred several handfuls of cotton from his own sack to hers.

"O, don't, don't!" said the woman, looking surprised; "it'll get you into trouble."

Just then Sambo came up. He seemed to have a special spite against this woman; and, flourishing his whip, said, in brutal, guttural tones, "What dis yer,

Luce,—foolin' a'" and, with the word, kicking the woman with his heavy cowhide shoe, he struck Tom across the face with his whip.

Tom silently resumed his task; but the woman, before at the last point of exhaustion, fainted.

"I'll bring her to!" said the driver, with a brutal grin. "I'll give her something better than camphire!" and, taking a pin from his coat-sleeve, he buried it to the head in her flesh. The woman groaned, and half rose. "Get up, you beast, and work, will yer, or I'll show yer a trick more!"

The woman seemed stimulated, for a few moments, to an unnatural strength, and worked with desperate eagerness.

"See that you keep to dat ar," said the man, "or yer'll wish yer's dead tonight, I reckin!"

"That I do now!" Tom heard her say; and again he heard her say, "O, Lord, how long! O, Lord, why don't you help us?"

At the risk of all that he might suffer, Tom came forward again, and put all the cotton in his sack into the woman's.

"O, you mustn't! you donno what they'll do to ye!" said the woman.

"I can bar it!" said Tom, "better 'n you;" and he was at his place again. It passed in a moment.

Suddenly, the stranger woman whom we have described, and who had, in the course of her work, come near enough to hear Tom's last words, raised her heavy black eyes, and fixed them, for a second, on him; then, taking a quantity of cotton from her basket, she placed it in his.

"You know nothing about this place," she said, "or you wouldn't have done that. When you've been here a month, you'll be done helping anybody; you'll find it hard enough to take care of your own skin!"

"The Lord forbid, Missis!" said Tom, using instinctively to his field companion the respectful form proper to the high bred with whom he had lived.

"The Lord never visits these parts," said the woman, bitterly, as she went nimbly forward with her work; and again the scornful smile curled her lips.

But the action of the woman had been seen by the driver, across the field; and, flourishing his whip, he came up to her.

"What! what!" he said to the woman, with an air of triumph, "You a foolin'? Go along! yer under me now,—mind yourself, or yer'll cotch it!"

A glance like sheet-lightning suddenly flashed from those black eyes; and, facing about, with quivering lip and dilated nostrils, she drew herself up, and fixed a glance, blazing with rage and scorn, on the driver.

"Dog!" she said, "touch *me*, if you dare! I've power enough, yet, to have you torn by the dogs, burnt alive, cut to inches! I've only to say the word!"

"What de devil you here for, den?" said the man, evidently cowed, and sullenly retreating a step or two. "Didn't mean no harm, Misse Cassy!"

"Keep your distance, then!" said the woman. And, in truth, the man seemed greatly inclined to attend to something at the other end of the field, and started off in quick time.

The woman suddenly turned to her work, and labored with a despatch that was perfectly astonishing to Tom. She seemed to work by magic. Before the day was through, her basket was filled, crowded down, and piled, and she had several times put largely into Tom's. Long after dusk, the whole weary train, with their baskets on their heads, defiled up to the building appropriated to the storing and weighing the cotton. Legree was there, busily conversing with the two drivers.

"Dat ar Tom's gwine to make a powerful deal o' trouble; kept a puttin' into Lucy's basket.—One o' these yer dat will get all der niggers to feelin' 'bused, if Masir don't watch him!" said Sambo.

"Hey-dey! The black cuss!" said Legree. "He'll have to get a breakin' in, won't he, boys?"

Both negroes grinned a horrid grin, at this intimation.

"Ay, ay! Let Mas'r Legree alone, for breakin' in! De debil heself couldn't beat Mas'r at dat!" said Quimbo.

"Wal, boys, the best way is to give him the flogging to do, till he gets over his notions. Break him in!"

"Lord, Mas'r'll have hard work to get dat out o' him!"

"It'll have to come out of him, though!" said Legree, as he rolled his tobacco in his mouth.

"Now, dar's Lucy,—de aggravatinest, ugliest wench on de place!" pursued Sambo.

"Take care, Sam; I shall begin to think what's the reason for your spite agin Lucy."

"Well, Mas'r knows she sot herself up agin Mas'r, and wouldn't have me, when he telled her to."

"I'd a flogged her into 't," said Legree, spitting, "only there's such a press o' work, it don't seem wuth a while to upset her jist now. She's slender; but these yer slender gals will bear half killin' to get their own way!"

"Wal, Lucy was real aggravatin' and lazy, sulkin' round; wouldn't do nothin,—and Tom he stuck up for her."

"He did, eh! Wal, then, Tom shall have the pleasure of flogging her. It'll be a good practice for him, and he won't put it on to the gal like you devils, neither."

"Ho, ho! haw! haw! haw!" laughed both the sooty wretches; and the diabolical sounds seemed, in truth, a not unapt expression of the fiendish character which Legree gave them.

"Wal, but, Mas'r, Tom and Misse Cassy, and dey among 'em, filled Lucy's basket. I ruther guess der weight 's in it, Mas'r!"

"*I do the weighing!*" said Legree, emphatically.

Both the drivers again laughed their diabolical laugh.

"So!" he added, "Misse Cassy did her day's work."

"She picks like de debil and all his angels!"

"She's got 'em all in her, I believe!" said Legree; and, growling a brutal oath, he proceeded to the weighing-room.

CHAPTER XXXIII

Slowly the weary, dispirited creatures, wound their way into the room, and, with crouching reluctance, presented their baskets to be weighed.

Legree noted on a slate, on the side of which was pasted a list of names, the amount.

Tom's basket was weighed and approved; and he looked, with an anxious glance, for the success of the woman he had befriended.

Tottering with weakness, she came forward, and delivered her basket. It was of full weight, as Legree well perceived; but, affecting anger, he said,

"What, you lazy beast! short again! stand aside, you'll catch it, pretty soon!"

The woman gave a groan of utter despair, and sat down on a board.

The person who had been called Misse Cassy now came forward, and, with a haughty, negligent air, delivered her basket. As she delivered it, Legree looked in her eyes with a sneering yet inquiring glance.

She fixed her black eyes steadily on him, her lips moved slightly, and she said something in French. What it was, no one knew; but Legree's face became perfectly demoniacal in its expression, as she spoke; he half raised his hand, as if to strike,—a gesture which she regarded with fierce disdain, as she turned and walked away.

"And now," said Legree, "come here, you Tom. You see, I telled ye I didn't buy ye jest for the common work; I mean to promote ye, and make a driver of ye; and tonight ye may jest as well begin to get yer hand in. Now, ye jest take this yer gal and flog her; ye've seen enough on't to know how."

"I beg Mas'r's pardon," said Tom; "hopes Mas'r won't set me at that. It's what I an't used to,—never did,—and can't do, no way possible."

"Ye'll larn a pretty smart chance of things ye never did know, before I've done with ye!" said Legree, taking up a cowhide, and striking Tom a heavy blow cross the cheek, and following up the infliction by a shower of blows.

"There!" he said, as he stopped to rest; "now, will ye tell me ye can't do it?"

"Yes, Mas'r," said Tom, putting up his hand, to wipe the blood, that trickled down his face. "I'm willin' to work, night and day, and work while there's life and breath in me; but this yer thing I can't feel it right to do;—and, Mas'r, I *never* shall do it,—*never*!"

Tom had a remarkably smooth, soft voice, and a habitually respectful manner, that had given Legree an idea that he would be cowardly, and easily subdued. When he spoke these last words, a thrill of amazement went through every one; the poor woman clasped her hands, and said, "O Lord!" and every one involuntarily looked at each other and drew in their breath, as if to prepare for the storm that was about to burst.

Legree looked stupefied and confounded; but at last burst forth,—"What! ye blasted black beast! tell *me* ye don't think it *right* to do what I tell ye! What have any of you cussed cattle to do with thinking what's right? I'll put a stop to it! Why, what do ye think ye are? May be ye think ye'r a gentleman master, Tom, to be a telling your master what's right, and what ain't! So you pretend it's wrong to flog the gal!"

"I think so, Mas'r," said Tom; "the poor crittur's sick and feeble; 't would be downright cruel, and it's what I never will do, nor begin to. Mas'r, if you mean to kill me, kill me; but, as to my raising my hand agin any one here, I never shall,—I'll die first!"

Tom spoke in a mild voice, but with a decision that could not be mistaken. Legree shook with anger; his greenish eyes glared fiercely, and his very whiskers seemed to curl with passion; but, like some ferocious beast, that plays with its victim before he devours it, he kept back his strong impulse to proceed to immediate violence, and broke out into bitter raillery.

"Well, here's a pious dog, at last, let down among us sinners!—a saint, a gentleman, and no less, to talk to us sinners about our sins! Powerful holy critter, he must be! Here, you rascal, you make believe to be so pious,—didn't you never hear, out of yer Bible, 'Servants, obey yer masters'? An't I yer master? Didn't I pay down twelve hundred dollars, cash, for all there is inside yer old cussed black shell? An't yer mine, now, body and soul?" he said, giving Tom a violent kick with his heavy boot; "tell me!"

In the very depth of physical suffering, bowed by brutal oppression, this question shot a gleam of joy and triumph through Tom's soul. He suddenly stretched himself up, and, looking earnestly to heaven, while the tears and blood that flowed down his face mingled, he exclaimed,

"No! no! no! my soul an't yours, Mas'r! You haven't bought it,—ye can't buy it! It's been bought and paid for, by one that is able to keep it;—no matter, no matter, you can't harm me!"

"I can't!" said Legree, with a sneer; "we'll see,—we'll see! Here, Sambo, Quimbo, give this dog such a breakin' in as he won't get over, this month!"

The two gigantic negroes that now laid hold of Tom, with fiendish exultation in their faces, might have formed no unapt personification of powers of darkness. The poor woman screamed with apprehension, and all rose, as by a general impulse, while they dragged him unresisting from the place.

CHAPTER XXXIV

THE QUADROON'S STORY

And behold the tears of such as are oppressed; and on the side of their oppressors there was power. Wherefore I praised the dead that are already dead more than the living that are yet alive.—ECCL. 4:1.

It was late at night, and Tom lay groaning and bleeding alone, in an old forsaken room of the gin-house, among pieces of broken machinery, piles of damaged cotton, and other rubbish which had there accumulated.

The night was damp and close, and the thick air swarmed with myriads of mosquitos, which increased the restless torture of his wounds; whilst a burning thirst—a torture beyond all others—filled up the uttermost measure of physical anguish.

"O, good Lord! *Do* look down,—give me the victory!—give me the victory over all!" prayed poor Tom, in his anguish.

A footstep entered the room, behind him, and the light of a lantern flashed on his eyes.

"Who's there? O, for the Lord's massy, please give me some water!"

The woman Cassy—for it was she,—set down her lantern, and, pouring water from a bottle, raised his head, and gave him drink. Another and another cup were drained, with feverish eagerness.

"Drink all ye want," she said; "I knew how it would be. It isn't the first time I've been out in the night, carrying water to such as you."

"Thank you, Missis," said Tom, when he had done drinking.

"Don't call me Missis! I'm a miserable slave, like yourself,—a lower one than you can ever be!" said she, bitterly; "but now," said she, going to the door, and dragging in a small pallaise, over which she had spread linen cloths wet with cold water, "try, my poor fellow, to roll yourself on to this."

Stiff with wounds and bruises, Tom was a long time in accomplishing this movement; but, when done, he felt a sensible relief from the cooling application to his wounds.

The woman, whom long practice with the victims of brutality had made familiar with many healing arts, went on to make many applications to Tom's wounds, by means of which he was soon somewhat relieved.

"Now," said the woman, when she had raised his head on a roll of damaged cotton, which served for a pillow, "there's the best I can do for you."

Tom thanked her; and the woman, sitting down on the floor, drew up her knees, and embracing them with her arms, looked fixedly before her, with a bitter and painful expression of countenance. Her bonnet fell back, and long wavy streams of black hair fell around her singular and melancholy-face.

"It's no use, my poor fellow!" she broke out, at last, "it's of no use, this you've been trying to do. You were a brave fellow,—you had the right on your side; but it's all in vain, and out of the question, for you to struggle. You are in the devil's hands;—he is the strongest, and you must give up!"

Give up! and, had not human weakness and physical agony whispered that, before? Tom started; for the bitter woman, with her wild eyes and melancholy voice, seemed to him an embodiment of the temptation with which he had been wrestling.

"O Lord! O Lord!" he groaned, "how can I give up?"

"There's no use calling on the Lord,—he never hears," said the woman, steadily; "there isn't any God, I believe; or, if there is, he's taken sides against us. All goes against us, heaven and earth. Everything is pushing us into hell. Why shouldn't we go?"

Tom closed his eyes, and shuddered at the dark, atheistic words.

"You see," said the woman, "*you* don't know anything about it—I do. I've been on this place five years, body and soul, under this man's foot; and I hate him as I do the devil! Here you are, on a lone plantation, ten miles from any other, in the swamps; not a white person here, who could testify, if you were burned alive,—if you were scalded, cut into inch-pieces, set up for the dogs to tear, or hung up and whipped to death. There's no law here, of God or man, that can do you, or any one of us, the least good; and, this man! there's no earthly thing that he's too good to do. I could make any one's hair rise, and their teeth chatter, if I should only tell what I've seen and been knowing to, here,—and it's no use resisting! Did I *want* to live with him? Wasn't I a woman delicately bred; and he,—God in heaven! what was he, and is he? And yet, I've lived with him, these five years, and cursed every moment of my life,—night and day! And now, he's got a new one,—a young thing, only fifteen, and she brought up, she says, piously. Her good mistress taught her to read the Bible; and she's brought her Bible here—to hell with her!"—and the woman laughed a wild and doleful laugh, that rung, with a strange, supernatural sound, through the old ruined shed.

Tom folded his hands; all was darkness and horror.

"O Jesus! Lord Jesus! have you quite forgot us poor critturs?" burst forth, at last;—"help, Lord, I perish!"

The woman sternly continued:

"And what are these miserable low dogs you work with, that you should suffer on their account? Every one of them would turn against you, the first time they got a chance. They are all of 'em as low and cruel to each other as they can be; there's no use in your suffering to keep from hurting them."

"Poor critturs!" said Tom,—"what made 'em cruel?—and, if I give out, I shall get used to 't, and grow, little by little, just like 'em! No, no, Missis! I've lost everything,—wife, and children, and home, and a kind Mas'r,—and he would have set me free, if he'd only lived a week longer; I've lost everything in *this* world, and it's clean gone, forever,—and now I *can't* lose Heaven, too; no, I can't get to be wicked, besides all!"

"But it can't be that the Lord will lay sin to our account," said the woman; "he won't charge it to us, when we're forced to it; he'll charge it to them that drove us to it."

"Yes," said Tom; "but that won't keep us from growing wicked. If I get to be as hard-hearted as that ar' Sambo, and as wicked, it won't make much odds to me how I come so; it's the bein' so,—that ar's what I'm a dreadin'."

The woman fixed a wild and startled look on Tom, as if a new thought had struck her; and then, heavily groaning, said,

"O God a' mercy! you speak the truth! O—O—O!"—and, with groans, she fell on the floor, like one crushed and writhing under the extremity of mental anguish.

There was a silence, a while, in which the breathing of both parties could be heard, when Tom faintly said, "O, please, Missis!"

The woman suddenly rose up, with her face composed to its usual stern, melancholy expression.

"Please, Missis, I saw 'em throw my coat in that ar' corner, and in my coat-pocket is my Bible;—if Missis would please get it for me."

Cassy went and got it. Tom opened, at once, to a heavily marked passage, much worn, of the last scenes in the life of Him by whose stripes we are healed.

"If Missis would only be so good as read that ar',—it's better than water."

Cassy took the book, with a dry, proud air, and looked over the passage. She then read aloud, in a soft voice, and with a beauty of intonation that was peculiar, that touching account of anguish and of glory. Often, as she read, her voice faltered, and sometimes failed her altogether, when she would stop, with an air of frigid composure, till she had mastered herself. When she came to the touching words, "Father forgive them, for they know not what they do," she threw down the book, and, burying her face in the heavy masses of her hair, she sobbed aloud, with a convulsive violence.

Tom was weeping, also, and occasionally uttering a smothered ejaculation.

"If we only could keep up to that ar'!" said Tom;—"it seemed to come so natural to him, and we have to fight so hard for 't! O Lord, help us! O blessed Lord Jesus, do help us!"

"Missis," said Tom, after a while, "I can see that, some how, you're quite 'bove me in everything; but there's one thing Missis might learn even from poor Tom. Ye said the Lord took sides against us, because he lets us be 'bused and knocked round; but ye see what come on his own Son,—the blessed Lord of Glory,—wan't he allays poor? and have we, any on us, yet come so low as he come? The Lord han't forgot us,—I'm sartin' o' that ar'. If we suffer with him, we shall also reign, Scripture says; but, if we deny Him, he also will deny us. Didn't they all suffer?—the Lord and all his? It tells how they was stoned and sawn asunder, and wandered about in sheep-skins and goat-skins, and was destitute, afflicted, tormented. Sufferin' an't no reason to make us think the Lord's turned agin us; but jest the contrary, if only we hold on to him, and doesn't give up to sin."

"But why does he put us where we can't help but sin?" said the woman.

"I think we *can* help it," said Tom.

"You'll see," said Cassy; "what'll you do? Tomorrow they'll be at you again. I know 'em; I've seen all their doings; I can't bear to think of all they'll bring you to;—and they'll make you give out, at last!"

"Lord Jesus!" said Tom, "you *will* take care of my soul? O Lord, do!—don't let me give out!"

"O dear!" said Cassy; "I've heard all this crying and praying before; and yet, they've been broken down, and brought under. There's Emmeline, she's trying to hold on, and you're trying,—but what use? You must give up, or be killed by inches."

"Well, then, I *will* die!" said Tom. "Spin it out as long as they can, they can't help my dying, some time!—and, after that, they can't do no more. I'm clar, I'm set! I *know* the Lord'll help me, and bring me through."

The woman did not answer; she sat with her black eyes intently fixed on the floor.

"May be it's the way," she murmured to herself; "but those that *have* given up, there's no hope for them!—none! We live in filth, and grow loathsome, till we loathe ourselves! And we long to die, and we don't dare to kill ourselves!—No hope! no hope! no hope?—this girl now,—just as old as I was!

"You see me now," she said, speaking to Tom very rapidly; "see what I am! Well, I was brought up in luxury; the first I remember is, playing about, when I was a child, in splendid parlors,—when I was kept dressed up like a doll, and company and visitors used to praise me. There was a garden opening from the saloon windows; and there I used to play hide-and-go-seek, under the orange-trees, with my brothers and sisters. I went to a convent, and there I learned music, French and embroidery, and what not; and when I was fourteen, I came out to my father's funeral. He died very suddenly, and when the property came to be settled, they found that there was scarcely enough to cover the debts; and when the creditors took an inventory of the property, I was set down in it. My mother was a slave woman, and my father had always meant to set me free; but he had not done it, and so I was set down in the list. I'd always known who I was, but never thought much about it. Nobody ever expects that a strong, healthy man is going to die. My father was a well man only four hours before he died;—it was one of the first cholera cases in New Orleans. The day after the funeral, my father's wife took her children, and went up to her father's plantation. I thought they treated me strangely, but didn't know. There was a young lawyer who they left to settle the business; and he came every day, and was about the house, and spoke very politely to me. He brought with him, one day, a young man, whom I thought the handsomest I had ever seen. I shall never forget that evening. I walked with him in the garden. I was lonesome and full of sorrow, and he was so kind and gentle to me; and he told me that he had seen me before I went to the convent, and that he had loved me a great while, and that he would be my friend and protector;—in short, though he didn't tell me, he had paid two thousand dollars for me, and I was his property,—I became his willingly, for I loved him. Loved!" said the woman, stopping. "O, how I *did* love that man! How I love him now,—and always shall, while I breathe! He was so beautiful, so high, so noble! He put me into a beautiful house, with servants, horses, and carriages, and furniture, and dresses. Everything that money could buy, he gave me; but I didn't set any value on all that,—I only cared for him. I loved him better than my God and my own soul, and, if I tried, I couldn't do any other way from what he wanted me to.

"I wanted only one thing—I did want him to *marry* me. I thought, if he loved me as he said he did, and if I was what he seemed to think I was, he would be willing to marry me and set me free. But he convinced me that it would be impossible; and he told me that, if we were only faithful to each other, it was marriage before God. If that is true, wasn't I that man's wife? Wasn't I faithful? For seven years, didn't I study every look and motion, and only live and breathe to please him? He had the yellow fever, and for twenty days and nights I watched with him. I alone,—and gave him all his medicine, and did everything for him; and then he called me his good angel, and said I'd saved his life. We had two beautiful children. The first was a boy, and we called him Henry. He was the image of his father,—he had such beautiful eyes, such a forehead, and his hair hung all in curls around it; and he had all his father's spirit, and his talent, too. Little Elise, he said, looked like me. He used to tell me that I was the most beautiful woman in Louisiana, he was so proud of me and the children. He used to love to have me dress them up, and take them and me about in an open carriage, and hear the remarks that people would make on us; and he used to fill my ears constantly with the fine things that were said in praise of me and the children. O, those were happy days! I thought I was as happy as any one could be; but then there came evil times. He had a cousin come to New Orleans, who was his particular friend,—he thought all the world of him;—but, from the first time I saw him, I couldn't tell why, I dreaded him; for I felt sure he was going to bring misery on us. He got Henry to going out with him, and often he would not come home nights till two or three o'clock. I did not dare say a word; for Henry was so high spirited, I was afraid to. He got him to the gaming-houses; and he was one of the sort that, when he once got a going there, there was no holding back. And then he introduced him to another lady, and I saw soon that his heart was gone from me. He never told me, but I saw it,—I knew it, day after day,—I felt my heart breaking, but I could not say a word! At this, the wretch offered to buy me and the children of Henry, to clear off his gambling debts, which stood in the way of his marrying as he wished;—and *he sold us*. He told me, one day, that he had business in the country, and should be gone two or three weeks. He spoke kinder than usual, and said he should come back; but it didn't deceive me. I knew that the time had come; I was just like one turned into stone; I couldn't speak, nor shed a tear. He kissed me and kissed the children, a good many times, and went out. I saw him get on his horse, and I watched him till he was quite out of sight; and then I fell down, and fainted.

"Then *he* came, the cursed wretch! he came to take possession. He told me that he had bought me and my children; and showed me the papers. I cursed him before God, and told him I'd die sooner than live with him."

"'Just as you please,' said he; 'but, if you don't behave reasonably, I'll sell both the children, where you shall never see them again.' He told me that he always had meant to have me, from the first time he saw me; and that he had drawn Henry on, and got him in debt, on purpose to make him willing to sell me. That he got him in love with another woman; and that I might know, after all that, that he should not give up for a few airs and tears, and things of that sort.

"I gave up, for my hands were tied. He had my children;—whenever I resisted his will anywhere, he would talk about selling them, and he made me as submissive as he desired. O, what a life it was! to live with my heart breaking, every day,—to keep on, on, on, loving, when it was only misery; and to be bound, body and soul, to one I hated. I used to love to read to Henry, to play to him, to waltz with him, and sing to him; but everything I did for this one was a perfect drag,—yet I was afraid to refuse anything. He was very imperious, and harsh to the children. Elise was a timid little thing; but Henry was bold and high-spirited, like his father, and he had never been brought under, in the least, by any one. He was always finding fault, and quarrelling with him; and I used to live in daily fear and dread. I tried to make the child respectful;—I tried to keep them apart, for I held on to those children like death; but it did no good. *He sold both those children.* He took me to ride, one day, and when I came home, they were nowhere to be found! He told me he had sold them; he showed me the money, the price of their blood. Then it seemed as if all good forsook me. I raved and cursed,—cursed God and man; and, for a while, I believe, he really was afraid of me. But he didn't give up so. He told me that my children were sold, but whether I ever saw their faces again, depended on him; and that, if I wasn't quiet, they should smart for it. Well, you can do anything with a woman, when you've got her children. He made me submit; he made me be peaceable; he flattered me with hopes that, perhaps, he would buy them back; and so things went on, a week or two. One day, I was out walking, and passed by the calaboose; I saw a crowd about the gate, and heard a child's voice,—and suddenly my Henry broke away from two or three men who were holding him, and ran, screaming, and caught my dress. They came up to him, swearing dreadfully; and one man, whose face I shall never forget, told him that he wouldn't get away so; that he was going with him into the calaboose, and he'd get a lesson there he'd never forget. I tried to beg and plead,—they only laughed; the poor boy screamed and looked into my face, and held on to me, until, in tearing him off, they tore the skirt of my dress half away; and they carried him in, screaming 'Mother! mother! mother!' There was one man stood there seemed to pity me. I offered him all the money I had, if he'd only interfere. He shook his head, and said that the boy had been impudent and disobedient, ever since he bought him; that he was going to break him in, once for all. I turned and ran; and every step of the way, I thought that I heard him scream. I got into the house; ran, all out of breath, to the parlor, where I found Butler. I told him, and begged him to go and interfere. He only laughed, and told me the boy had got his deserts. He'd got to be broken in,—the sooner the better; 'what did I expect?' he asked.

"It seemed to me something in my head snapped, at that moment. I felt dizzy and furious. I remember seeing a great sharp bowie-knife on the table; I remember something about catching it, and flying upon him; and then all grew dark, and I didn't know any more,—not for days and days.

"When I came to myself, I was in a nice room,—but not mine. An old black woman tended me; and a doctor came to see me, and there was a great deal of care taken of me. After a while, I found that he had gone away, and left me at this house to be sold; and that's why they took such pains with me.

"I didn't mean to get well, and hoped I shouldn't; but, in spite of me the fever went off and I grew healthy, and finally got up. Then, they made me dress up, every day; and gentlemen used to come in and stand and smoke their cigars, and look at me, and ask questions, and debate my price. I was so gloomy and silent, that none of them wanted me. They threatened to whip me, if I wasn't gayer, and didn't take some pains to make myself agreeable. At length, one day, came a gentleman named Stuart. He seemed to have some feeling for me; he saw that something dreadful was on my heart, and he came to see me alone, a great many times, and finally persuaded me to tell him. He bought me, at last, and promised to do all he could to find and buy back my children. He went to the hotel where my Henry was; they told him he had been sold to a planter up on Pearl River; that was the last that I ever heard. Then he found where my daughter was; an old woman was keeping her. He offered an immense sum for her, but they would not sell her. Butler found out that it was for me he wanted her; and he sent me word that I should never have her. Captain Stuart was very kind to me; he had a splendid plantation, and took me to it. In the course of a year, I had a son born. O, that child!—how I loved it! How just like my poor Henry the little thing looked! But I had made up my mind,—yes, I had. I would never again let a child live to grow up! I took the little fellow in my arms, when he was two weeks old, and kissed him, and cried over him; and then I gave him laudanum, and held him close to my bosom, while he slept to death. How I mourned and cried over it! and who ever dreamed that it was anything but a mistake, that had made me give it the laudanum? but it's one of the few things that I'm glad of, now. I am not sorry, to this day; he, at least, is out of pain. What better than death could I give him, poor child! After a while, the cholera came, and Captain Stuart died; everybody died that wanted to live,—and I,—I, though I went down to death's door,—*I lived!* Then I was sold, and passed from hand to hand, till I grew faded and wrinkled, and I had a fever; and then this wretch bought me, and brought me here,—and here I am!"

The woman stopped. She had hurried on through her story, with a wild, passionate utterance; sometimes seeming to address it to Tom, and sometimes speaking as in a soliloquy. So vehement and overpowering was the force with which she spoke, that, for a season, Tom was beguiled even from the pain of his wounds, and, raising himself on one elbow, watched her as she paced restlessly up and down, her long black hair swaying heavily about her, as she moved.

"You tell me," she said, after a pause, "that there is a God,—a God that looks down and sees all these things. May be it's so. The sisters in the convent used to tell me of a day of judgment, when everything is coming to light;—won't there be vengeance, then!

"They think it's nothing, what we suffer,—nothing, what our children suffer! It's all a small matter; yet I've walked the streets when it seemed as if I had misery enough in my one heart to sink the city. I've wished the houses would fall on me, or the stones sink under me. Yes! and, in the judgment day, I will stand up before God, a witness against those that have ruined me and my children, body and soul!

"When I was a girl, I thought I was religious; I used to love God and prayer. Now, I'm a lost soul, pursued by devils that torment me day and night; they keep pushing me on and on—and I'll do it, too, some of these days!" she said, clenching her hand, while an insane light glanced in her heavy black eyes. "I'll send him where he belongs,—a short way, too,—one of these nights, if they burn me alive for it!" A wild, long laugh rang through the deserted room, and ended in a hysteric sob; she threw herself on the floor, in convulsive sobbing and struggles.

In a few moments, the frenzy fit seemed to pass off; she rose slowly, and seemed to collect herself.

"Can I do anything more for you, my poor fellow?" she said, approaching where Tom lay; "shall I give you some more water?"

There was a graceful and compassionate sweetness in her voice and manner, as she said this, that formed a strange contrast with the former wildness.

Tom drank the water, and looked earnestly and pitifully into her face.

"O, Missis, I wish you'd go to him that can give you living waters!"

"Go to him! Where is he? Who is he?" said Cassy.

"Him that you read of to me,—the Lord."

"I used to see the picture of him, over the altar, when I was a girl," said Cassy, her dark eyes fixing themselves in an expression of mournful reverie; "but, *he isn't here!* there's nothing here, but sin and long, long, long despair! O!" She laid her hand on her breast and drew in her breath, as if to lift a heavy weight.

Tom looked as if he would speak again; but she cut him short, with a decided gesture.

"Don't talk, my poor fellow. Try to sleep, if you can." And, placing water in his reach, and making whatever little arrangements for his comforts she could, Cassy left the shed.

CHAPTER XXXV

THE TOKENS

"And slight, withal, may be the things that bring Back on the heart the weight which it would fling Aside forever; it may be a sound, A flower, the wind, the ocean, which shall wound,— Striking the electric chain wherewith we're darkly bound." CHILDE HAROLD'S PILGRIMAGE, CAN. 4.

The sitting-room of Legree's establishment was a large, long room, with a wide, ample fireplace. It had once been hung with a showy and expensive paper, which now hung mouldering, torn and discolored, from the damp walls. The place had that peculiar sickening, unwholesome smell, compounded of mingled damp, dirt and decay, which one often notices in close old houses. The wall-paper was defaced, in spots, by slops of beer and wine; or garnished with chalk memorandums, and long sums footed up, as if somebody had been practising arithmetic there. In the fireplace stood a brazier full of burning charcoal; for, though the weather was not cold, the evenings always seemed damp and chilly in that great room; and Legree, moreover, wanted a place to light his cigars, and heat his water for punch. The ruddy glare of the charcoal displayed the confused and unpromising aspect of the room,—saddles, bridles, several sorts of harness, riding-whips, overcoats, and various articles of clothing, scattered up and down the room in confused variety; and the dogs, of whom we have before spoken, had encamped themselves among them, to suit their own taste and convenience.

Legree was just mixing himself a tumbler of punch, pouring his hot water from a cracked and broken-nosed pitcher, grumbling, as he did so,

"Plague on that Sambo, to kick up this yer row between me and the new hands! The fellow won't be fit to work for a week, now,—right in the press of the season!"

"Yes, just like you," said a voice, behind his chair. It was the woman Cassy, who had stolen upon his soliloquy.

"Hah! you she-devil! you've come back, have you?"

"Yes, I have," she said, coolly; "come to have my own way, too!"

"You lie, you jade! I'll be up to my word. Either behave yourself, or stay down to the quarters, and fare and work with the rest."

"I'd rather, ten thousand times," said the woman, "live in the dirtiest hole at the quarters, than be under your hoof!"

"But you *are* under my hoof, for all that," said he, turning upon her, with a savage grin; "that's one comfort. So, sit down here on my knee, my dear, and hear to reason," said he, laying hold on her wrist.

"Simon Legree, take care!" said the woman, with a sharp flash of her eye, a glance so wild and insane in its light as to be almost appalling. "You're afraid of me, Simon," she said, deliberately; "and you've reason to be! But be careful, for I've got the devil in me!"

The last words she whispered in a hissing tone, close to his ear.

"Get out! I believe, to my soul, you have!" said Legree, pushing her from him, and looking uncomfortably at her. "After all, Cassy," he said, "why can't you be friends with me, as you used to?"

"Used to!" said she, bitterly. She stopped short,—a word of choking feelings, rising in her heart, kept her silent.

Cassy had always kept over Legree the kind of influence that a strong, impassioned woman can ever keep over the most brutal man; but, of late, she had grown more and more irritable and restless, under the hideous yoke of her servitude, and her irritability, at times, broke out into raving insanity; and this liability made her a sort of object of dread to Legree, who had that superstitious horror of insane persons which is common to coarse and uninstructed minds. When Legree brought Emmeline to the house, all the smouldering embers of womanly feeling flashed up in the worn heart of Cassy, and she took part with the girl; and a fierce quarrel ensued between her and Legree. Legree, in a fury, swore she should be put to field service, if she would not be peaceable. Cassy, with proud scorn, declared she *would* go to the field. And she worked there one day, as we have described, to show how perfectly she scorned the threat.

Legree was secretly uneasy, all day; for Cassy had an influence over him from which he could not free himself. When she presented her basket at the scales, he had hoped for some concession, and addressed her in a sort of half conciliatory, half scornful tone; and she had answered with the bitterest contempt.

The outrageous treatment of poor Tom had roused her still more; and she had followed Legree to the house, with no particular intention, but to upbraid him for his brutality.

"I wish, Cassy," said Legree, "you'd behave yourself decently."

"*You* talk about behaving decently! And what have you been doing?—you, who haven't even sense enough to keep from spoiling one of your best hands, right in the most pressing season, just for your devilish temper!"

"I was a fool, it's a fact, to let any such brangle come up," said Legree; "but, when the boy set up his will, he had to be broke in."

"I reckon you won't break *him* in!"

"Won't I?" said Legree, rising, passionately. "I'd like to know if I won't? He'll be the first nigger that ever came it round me! I'll break every bone in his body, but he *shall* give up!"

Just then the door opened, and Sambo entered. He came forward, bowing, and holding out something in a paper.

"What's that, you dog?" said Legree.

"It's a witch thing, Mas'r!"

"A what?"

"Something that niggers gets from witches. Keeps 'em from feelin' when they 's flogged. He had it tied round his neck, with a black string."

Legree, like most godless and cruel men, was superstitious. He took the paper, and opened it uneasily.

There dropped out of it a silver dollar, and a long, shining curl of fair hair,—hair which, like a living thing, twined itself round Legree's fingers.

"Damnation!" he screamed, in sudden passion, stamping on the floor, and pulling furiously at the hair, as if it burned him. "Where did this come from? Take it off!—burn it up!—burn it up!" he screamed, tearing it off, and throwing it into the charcoal. "What did you bring it to me for?"

Sambo stood, with his heavy mouth wide open, and aghast with wonder; and Cassy, who was preparing to leave the apartment, stopped, and looked at him in perfect amazement.

"Don't you bring me any more of your devilish things!" said he, shaking his fist at Sambo, who retreated hastily towards the door; and, picking up the silver dollar, he sent it smashing through the window-pane, out into the darkness.

Sambo was glad to make his escape. When he was gone, Legree seemed a little ashamed of his fit of alarm. He sat doggedly down in his chair, and began sullenly sipping his tumbler of punch.

Cassy prepared herself for going out, unobserved by him; and slipped away to minister to poor Tom, as we have already related.

And what was the matter with Legree? and what was there in a simple curl of fair hair to appall that brutal man, familiar with every form of cruelty? To answer this, we must carry the reader backward in his history. Hard and reprobate as the godless man seemed now, there had been a time when he had been rocked on the bosom of a mother,—cradled with prayers and pious hymns,—his now seared brow bedewed with the waters of holy baptism. In early childhood, a fair-haired woman had led him, at the sound of Sabbath bell, to worship and to pray. Far in New England that mother had trained her only son, with long, unwearied love, and patient prayers. Born of a hard-tempered sire, on whom that gentle woman had wasted a world of unvalued love, Legree had followed in the steps of his father. Boisterous, unruly, and tyrannical, he despised all her counsel, and would none of her reproof; and, at an early age, broke from her, to seek his fortunes at sea. He never came home but once, after; and then, his mother, with the yearning of a heart that must love something, and has nothing else to love, clung to him, and sought, with passionate prayers and entreaties, to win him from a life of sin, to his soul's eternal good.

That was Legree's day of grace; then good angels called him; then he was almost persuaded, and mercy held him by the hand. His heart inly relented,—there was a conflict,—but sin got the victory, and he set all the force of his rough nature against the conviction of his conscience. He drank and swore,—was wilder and more brutal than ever. And, one night, when his mother, in the last agony of her despair, knelt at his feet, he spurned her from him,—threw her senseless on the floor, and, with brutal curses, fled to his ship. The next Legree heard of his mother was, when, one night, as he was carousing among drunken companions, a letter was put into his hand. He opened it, and a lock of long, curling hair fell from it, and twined about his fingers. The letter told him his mother was dead, and that, dying, she blest and forgave him.

There is a dread, unhallowed necromancy of evil, that turns things sweetest and holiest to phantoms of horror and affright. That pale, loving mother,—her dying prayers, her forgiving love,—wrought in that demoniac heart of sin only as a damning sentence, bringing with it a fearful looking for of judgment and fiery indignation. Legree burned the hair, and burned the letter; and when he saw them hissing and crackling in the flame, inly shuddered as he thought of everlasting fires. He tried to drink, and revel, and swear away the memory; but often, in the deep night, whose solemn stillness arraigns the bad soul in forced communion with herself, he had seen that pale mother rising by his bedside, and felt the soft twining of that hair around his fingers, till the cold sweat would roll down his face, and he would spring from his bed in horror. Ye who have wondered to hear, in the same evangel, that God is love, and that God is a consuming fire, see ye not how, to the soul resolved in evil, perfect love is the most fearful torture, the seal and sentence of the direst despair?

"Blast it!" said Legree to himself, as he sipped his liquor; "where did he get that? If it didn't look just like—whoo! I thought I'd forgot that. Curse me, if I think there's any such thing as forgetting anything, any how,—hang it! I'm lonesome! I mean to call Em. She hates me—the monkey! I don't care,—I'll *make* her come!"

Legree stepped out into a large entry, which went up stairs, by what had formerly been a superb winding staircase; but the passage-way was dirty and dreary, encumbered with boxes and unsightly litter. The stairs, uncarpeted, seemed winding up, in the gloom, to nobody knew where! The pale moonlight streamed through a shattered fanlight over the door; the air was unwholesome and chilly, like that of a vault.

Legree stopped at the foot of the stairs, and heard a voice singing. It seemed strange and ghostlike in that dreary old house, perhaps because of the already tremulous state of his nerves. Hark! what is it?

A wild, pathetic voice, chants a hymn common among the slaves:

"O there'll be mourning, mourning, mourning, O there'll be mourning, at the judgment-seat of Christ!"

"Blast the girl!" said Legree. "I'll choke her.—Em! Em!" he called, harshly; but only a mocking echo from the walls answered him. The sweet voice still sung on:

"Parents and children there shall part! Parents and children there shall part! Shall part to meet no more!"

And clear and loud swelled through the empty halls the refrain,

"O there'll be mourning, mourning, mourning, O there'll be mourning, at the judgment-seat of Christ!"

Legree stopped. He would have been ashamed to tell of it, but large drops of sweat stood on his forehead, his heart beat heavy and thick with fear; he even thought he saw something white rising and glimmering in the gloom before him, and shuddered to think what if the form of his dead mother should suddenly appear to him.

"I know one thing," he said to himself, as he stumbled back in the sitting-room, and sat down; "I'll let that fellow alone, after this! What did I want of his cussed paper? I b'lieve I am bewitched, sure enough! I've been shivering and sweating, ever since! Where did he get that hair? It couldn't have been *that!* I burnt *that* up, I know I did! It would be a joke, if hair could rise from the dead!"

Ah, Legree! that golden tress *was* charmed; each hair had in it a spell of terror and remorse for thee, and was used by a mightier power to bind thy cruel hands from inflicting uttermost evil on the helpless!

"I say," said Legree, stamping and whistling to the dogs, "wake up, some of you, and keep me company!" but the dogs only opened one eye at him, sleepily, and closed it again.

"I'll have Sambo and Quimbo up here, to sing and dance one of their hell dances, and keep off these horrid notions," said Legree; and, putting on his hat, he went on to the verandah, and blew a horn, with which he commonly summoned his two sable drivers.

Legree was often wont, when in a gracious humor, to get these two worthies into his sitting-room, and, after warming them up with whiskey, amuse himself by setting them to singing, dancing or fighting, as the humor took him.

It was between one and two o'clock at night, as Cassy was returning from her ministrations to poor Tom, that she heard the sound of wild shrieking, whooping, halloing, and singing, from the sitting-room, mingled with the barking of dogs, and other symptoms of general uproar.

She came up on the verandah steps, and looked in. Legree and both the drivers, in a state of furious intoxication, were singing, whooping, upsetting chairs, and making all manner of ludicrous and horrid grimaces at each other.

She rested her small, slender hand on the window-blind, and looked fixedly at them;—there was a world of anguish, scorn, and fierce bitterness, in her black eyes, as she did so. "Would it be a sin to rid the world of such a wretch?" she said to herself.

She turned hurriedly away, and, passing round to a back door, glided up stairs, and tapped at Emmeline's door.

CHAPTER XXXVI

EMMELINE AND CASSY

Cassy entered the room, and found Emmeline sitting, pale with fear, in the furthest corner of it. As she came in, the girl started up nervously; but, on seeing who it was, rushed forward, and catching her arm, said, "O Cassy, is it you? I'm so glad you've come! I was afraid it was—. O, you don't know what a horrid noise there has been, down stairs, all this evening!"

"I ought to know," said Cassy, dryly. "I've heard it often enough."

"O Cassy! do tell me,—couldn't we get away from this place? I don't care where,—into the swamp among the snakes,—anywhere! *Couldn't* we get *somewhere* away from here?"

"Nowhere, but into our graves," said Cassy.

"Did you ever try?"

"I've seen enough of trying and what comes of it," said Cassy.

"I'd be willing to live in the swamps, and gnaw the bark from trees. I an't afraid of snakes! I'd rather have one near me than him," said Emmeline, eagerly.

"There have been a good many here of your opinion," said Cassy; "but you couldn't stay in the swamps,—you'd be tracked by the dogs, and brought back, and then—then—"

"What would he do?" said the girl, looking, with breathless interest, into her face.

"What *wouldn't* he do, you'd better ask," said Cassy. "He's learned his trade well, among the pirates in the West Indies. You wouldn't sleep much, if I should tell you things I've seen,—things that he tells of, sometimes, for good jokes. I've heard screams here that I haven't been able to get out of my head for weeks and weeks. There's a place way out down by the quarters, where you can see a black, blasted tree, and the ground all covered with black ashes. Ask anyone what was done there, and see if they will dare to tell you."

"O! what do you mean?"

"I won't tell you. I hate to think of it. And I tell you, the Lord only knows what we may see tomorrow, if that poor fellow holds out as he's begun."

"Horrid!" said Emmeline, every drop of blood receding from her cheeks. "O, Cassy, do tell me what I shall do!"

"What I've done. Do the best you can,—do what you must,—and make it up in hating and cursing."

"He wanted to make me drink some of his hateful brandy," said Emmeline; "and I hate it so—"

"You'd better drink," said Cassy. "I hated it, too; and now I can't live without it. One must have something;—things don't look so dreadful, when you take that."

"Mother used to tell me never to touch any such thing," said Emmeline.

"*Mother* told you!" said Cassy, with a thrilling and bitter emphasis on the word mother. "What use is it for mothers to say anything? You are all to be bought and paid for, and your souls belong to whoever gets you. That's the way it goes. I say, *drink* brandy; drink all you can, and it'll make things come easier."

"O, Cassy! do pity me!"

"Pity you!—don't I? Haven't I a daughter,—Lord knows where she is, and whose she is, now,—going the way her mother went, before her, I suppose, and that her children must go, after her! There's no end to the curse—forever!"

"I wish I'd never been born!" said Emmeline, wringing her hands.

"That's an old wish with me," said Cassy. "I've got used to wishing that. I'd die, if I dared to," she said, looking out into the darkness, with that still, fixed despair which was the habitual expression of her face when at rest.

"It would be wicked to kill one's self," said Emmeline.

"I don't know why,—no wickeder than things we live and do, day after day. But the sisters told me things, when I was in the convent, that make me afraid to die. If it would only be the end of us, why, then—"

Emmeline turned away, and hid her face in her hands.

While this conversation was passing in the chamber, Legree, overcome with his carouse, had sunk to sleep in the room below. Legree was not an habitual drunkard. His coarse, strong nature craved, and could endure, a continual stimulation, that would have utterly wrecked and crazed a finer one. But a deep, underlying spirit of cautiousness prevented his often yielding to appetite in such measure as to lose control of himself.

This night, however, in his feverish efforts to banish from his mind those fearful elements of woe and remorse which woke within him, he had indulged more than common; so that, when he had discharged his sable attendants, he fell heavily on a settle in the room, and was sound asleep.

O! how dares the bad soul to enter the shadowy world of sleep?—that land whose dim outlines lie so fearfully near to the mystic scene of retribution! Legree dreamed. In his heavy and feverish sleep, a veiled form stood beside him, and laid a cold, soft hand upon him. He thought he knew who it was; and shuddered, with creeping horror, though the face was veiled. Then he thought he felt *that hair* twining round his fingers; and then, that it slid smoothly round his neck, and tightened and tightened, and he could not draw his breath; and then he thought voices *whispered* to him,—whispers that chilled him with horror. Then it seemed to him he was on the edge of a frightful abyss, holding on and struggling in mortal fear, while dark hands stretched up, and were pulling him over; and Cassy came behind him laughing, and pushed him. And then rose up that solemn veiled figure, and drew aside the veil. It was his mother; and she turned away from him, and he fell down, down, down, amid a confused noise of shrieks, and groans, and shouts of demon laughter,—and Legree awoke.

Calmly the rosy hue of dawn was stealing into the room. The morning star stood, with its solemn, holy eye of light, looking down on the man of sin, from out the brightening sky. O, with what freshness, what solemnity and beauty, is each new day born; as if to say to insensate man, "Behold! thou hast one more chance! *Strive* for immortal glory!" There is no speech nor language where this voice is not heard; but the bold, bad man heard it not. He woke with an oath and a curse. What to him was the gold and purple, the daily miracle of morning! What to him the sanctity of the star which the Son of God has hallowed as his own emblem? Brute-like, he saw without perceiving; and, stumbling forward, poured out a tumbler of brandy, and drank half of it.

"I've had a h—l of a night!" he said to Cassy, who just then entered from an opposite door.

"You'll get plenty of the same sort, by and by," said she, dryly.

"What do you mean, you minx?"

"You'll find out, one of these days," returned Cassy, in the same tone. "Now Simon, I've one piece of advice to give you."

"The devil, you have!"

"My advice is," said Cassy, steadily, as she began adjusting some things about the room, "that you let Tom alone."

"What business is 't of yours?"

"What? To be sure, I don't know what it should be. If you want to pay twelve hundred for a fellow, and use him right up in the press of the season, just to serve your own spite, it's no business of mine, I've done what I could for him."

"You have? What business have you meddling in my matters?"

"None, to be sure. I've saved you some thousands of dollars, at different times, by taking care of your hands,—that's all the thanks I get. If your crop comes shorter into market than any of theirs, you won't lose your bet, I suppose? Tompkins won't lord it over you, I suppose,—and you'll pay down your money like a lady, won't you? I think I see you doing it!"

Legree, like many other planters, had but one form of ambition,—to have in the heaviest crop of the season,—and he had several bets on this very present season pending in the next town. Cassy, therefore, with woman's tact, touched the only string that could be made to vibrate.

"Well, I'll let him off at what he's got," said Legree; "but he shall beg my pardon, and promise better fashions."

"That he won't do," said Cassy.

"Won't,—eh?"

"No, he won't," said Cassy.

"I'd like to know *why*, Mistress," said Legree, in the extreme of scorn.

"Because he's done right, and he knows it, and won't say he's done wrong."

"Who a cuss cares what he knows? The nigger shall say what I please, or—"

"Or, you'll lose your bet on the cotton crop, by keeping him out of the field, just at this very press."

"But he *will* give up,—course, he will; don't I know what niggers is? He'll beg like a dog, this morning."

"He won't, Simon; you don't know this kind. You may kill him by inches,—you won't get the first word of confession out of him."

"We'll see,—where is he?" said Legree, going out.

"In the waste-room of the gin-house," said Cassy.

Legree, though he talked so stoutly to Cassy, still sallied forth from the house with a degree of misgiving which was not common with him. His dreams of the past night, mingled with Cassy's prudential suggestions, considerably affected his mind. He resolved that nobody should be witness of his encounter with Tom; and determined, if he could not subdue him by bullying, to defer his vengeance, to be wreaked in a more convenient season.

The solemn light of dawn—the angelic glory of the morning-star—had looked in through the rude window of the shed where Tom was lying; and, as if descending on that star-beam, came the solemn words, "I am the root and offspring of David, and the bright and morning star." The mysterious warnings and intimations of Cassy, so far from discouraging his soul, in the end had roused it as with a heavenly call. He did not know but that the day of his death was dawning in the sky; and his heart throbbed with solemn throes of joy and desire, as he thought that the wondrous *all*, of which he had often pondered,—the great white throne, with its ever radiant rainbow; the white-robed multitude, with voices as many waters; the crowns, the palms, the harps,—might all break upon his vision before that sun should set again. And, therefore, without shuddering or trembling, he heard the voice of his persecutor, as he drew near.

"Well, my boy," said Legree, with a contemptuous kick, "how do you find yourself? Didn't I tell yer I could larn yer a thing or two? How do yer like it—eh? How did yer whaling agree with yer, Tom? An't quite so crank as ye was last night. Ye couldn't treat a poor sinner, now, to a bit of sermon, could ye,—eh?"

Tom answered nothing.

"Get up, you beast!" said Legree, kicking him again.

This was a difficult matter for one so bruised and faint; and, as Tom made efforts to do so, Legree laughed brutally.

"What makes ye so spry, this morning, Tom? Cotched cold, may be, last night."

Tom by this time had gained his feet, and was confronting his master with a steady, unmoved front.

"The devil, you can!" said Legree, looking him over. "I believe you haven't got enough yet. Now, Tom, get right down on yer knees and beg my pardon, for yer shines last night."

Tom did not move.

"Down, you dog!" said Legree, striking him with his riding-whip.

"Mas'r Legree," said Tom, "I can't do it. I did only what I thought was right. I shall do just so again, if ever the time comes. I never will do a cruel thing, come what may."

"Yes, but ye don't know what may come, Master Tom. Ye think what you've got is something. I tell you 'tan't anything,—nothing 't all. How would ye like to be tied to a tree, and have a slow fire lit up around ye;—wouldn't that be pleasant,—eh, Tom?"

"Mas'r," said Tom, "I know ye can do dreadful things; but,"—he stretched himself upward and clasped his hands,—"but, after ye've killed the body, there an't no more ye can do. And O, there's all ETERNITY to come, after that!"

ETERNITY,—the word thrilled through the black man's soul with light and power, as he spoke; it thrilled through the sinner's soul, too, like the bite of a scorpion. Legree gnashed on him with his teeth, but rage kept him silent; and Tom, like a man disenthralled, spoke, in a clear and cheerful voice,

"Mas'r Legree, as ye bought me, I'll be a true and faithful servant to ye. I'll give ye all the work of my hands, all my time, all my strength; but my soul I won't give up to mortal man. I will hold on to the Lord, and put his commands before all,—die or live; you may be sure on 't. Mas'r Legree, I ain't a grain afeard to die. I'd as soon die as not. Ye may whip me, starve me, burn me,—it'll only send me sooner where I want to go."

"I'll make ye give out, though, 'fore I've done!" said Legree, in a rage.

"I shall have *help*," said Tom; "you'll never do it."

"Who the devil's going to help you?" said Legree, scornfully.

"The Lord Almighty," said Tom.

"D—n you!" said Legree, as with one blow of his fist he felled Tom to the earth.

A cold soft hand fell on Legree's at this moment. He turned,—it was Cassy's; but the cold soft touch recalled his dream of the night before, and, flashing through the chambers of his brain, came all the fearful images of the night-watches, with a portion of the horror that accompanied them.

"Will you be a fool?" said Cassy, in French. "Let him go! Let me alone to get him fit to be in the field again. Isn't it just as I told you?"

They say the alligator, the rhinoceros, though enclosed in bullet-proof mail, have each a spot where they are vulnerable; and fierce, reckless, unbelieving reprobates, have commonly this point in superstitious dread.

Legree turned away, determined to let the point go for the time.

"Well, have it your own way," he said, doggedly, to Cassy.

"Hark, ye!" he said to Tom; "I won't deal with ye now, because the business is pressing, and I want all my hands; but I *never* forget. I'll score it against ye, and sometime I'll have my pay out o' yer old black hide,—mind ye!"

Legree turned, and went out.

"There you go," said Cassy, looking darkly after him; "your reckoning's to come, yet!—My poor fellow, how are you?"

"The Lord God hath sent his angel, and shut the lion's mouth, for this time," said Tom.

"For this time, to be sure," said Cassy; "but now you've got his ill will upon you, to follow you day in, day out, hanging like a dog on your throat,—sucking your blood, bleeding away your life, drop by drop. I know the man."

CHAPTER XXXVII

LIBERTY

"No matter with what solemnities he may have been devoted upon the altar of slavery, the moment he touches the sacred soil of Britain, the altar and the God sink together in the dust, and he stands redeemed, regenerated, and disenthralled, by the irresistible genius of universal emancipation." CURRAN.[1]

A while we must leave Tom in the hands of his persecutors, while we turn to pursue the fortunes of George and his wife, whom we left in friendly hands, in a farmhouse on the road-side.

Tom Loker we left groaning and touzling in a most immaculately clean Quaker bed, under the motherly supervision of Aunt Dorcas, who found him to the full as tractable a patient as a sick bison.

Imagine a tall, dignified, spiritual woman, whose clear muslin cap shades waves of silvery hair, parted on a broad, clear forehead, which overarches thoughtful gray eyes. A snowy handkerchief of lisse crape is folded neatly across her bosom; her glossy brown silk dress rustles peacefully, as she glides up and down the chamber.

"The devil!" says Tom Loker, giving a great throw to the bedclothes.

"I must request thee, Thomas, not to use such language," says Aunt Dorcas, as she quietly rearranged the bed.

"Well, I won't, granny, if I can help it," says Tom; "but it is enough to make a fellow swear,—so cursedly hot!"

Dorcas removed a comforter from the bed, straightened the clothes again, and tucked them in till Tom looked something like a chrysalis; remarking, as she did so,

"I wish, friend, thee would leave off cursing and swearing, and think upon thy ways."

---

[1] John Philpot Curran (1750-1817), Irish orator and judge who worked for Catholic emancipation.

"What the devil," said Tom, "should I think of *them* for? Last thing ever *I* want to think of—hang it all!" And Tom flounced over, untucking and disarranging everything, in a manner frightful to behold.

"That fellow and gal are here, I s'pose," said he, sullenly, after a pause.

"They are so," said Dorcas.

"They'd better be off up to the lake," said Tom; "the quicker the better."

"Probably they will do so," said Aunt Dorcas, knitting peacefully.

"And hark ye," said Tom; "we've got correspondents in Sandusky, that watch the boats for us. I don't care if I tell, now. I hope they *will* get away, just to spite Marks,—the cursed puppy!—d—n him!"

"Thomas!" said Dorcas.

"I tell you, granny, if you bottle a fellow up too tight, I shall split," said Tom. "But about the gal,—tell 'em to dress her up some way, so's to alter her. Her description's out in Sandusky."

"We will attend to that matter," said Dorcas, with characteristic composure.

As we at this place take leave of Tom Loker, we may as well say, that, having lain three weeks at the Quaker dwelling, sick with a rheumatic fever, which set in, in company with his other afflictions, Tom arose from his bed a somewhat sadder and wiser man; and, in place of slave-catching, betook himself to life in one of the new settlements, where his talents developed themselves more happily in trapping bears, wolves, and other inhabitants of the forest, in which he made himself quite a name in the land. Tom always spoke reverently of the Quakers. "Nice people," he would say; "wanted to convert me, but couldn't come it, exactly. But, tell ye what, stranger, they do fix up a sick fellow first rate,—no mistake. Make jist the tallest kind o' broth and knicknacks."

As Tom had informed them that their party would be looked for in Sandusky, it was thought prudent to divide them. Jim, with his old mother, was forwarded separately; and a night or two after, George and Eliza, with their child, were driven privately into Sandusky, and lodged beneath a hospital roof, preparatory to taking their last passage on the lake.

Their night was now far spent, and the morning star of liberty rose fair before them!—electric word! What is it? Is there anything more in it than a name—a rhetorical flourish? Why, men and women of America, does your heart's blood thrill at that word, for which your fathers bled, and your braver mothers were willing that their noblest and best should die?

Is there anything in it glorious and dear for a nation, that is not also glorious and dear for a man? What is freedom to a nation, but freedom to the individuals in it? What is freedom to that young man, who sits there, with his arms folded over his broad chest, the tint of African blood in his cheek, its dark fires in his eyes,—what is freedom to George Harris? To your fathers, freedom was the right of a nation to be a nation. To him, it is the right of a man to be a man, and not a brute; the right to call the wife of his bosom his wife, and to protect her from lawless violence; the right to protect and educate his child; the right to have a home of his own, a religion of his own, a character of his own, unsubject to the will of another. All these thoughts were rolling and seething in George's breast, as he was pensively leaning his head on his hand, watching his wife, as she was adapting to her slender and pretty form the articles of man's attire, in which it was deemed safest she should make her escape.

"Now for it," said she, as she stood before the glass, and shook down her silky abundance of black curly hair. "I say, George, it's almost a pity, isn't it," she said, as she held up some of it, playfully,—"pity it's all got to come off?"

George smiled sadly, and made no answer.

Eliza turned to the glass, and the scissors glittered as one long lock after another was detached from her head.

"There, now, that'll do," she said, taking up a hair-brush; "now for a few fancy touches."

"There, an't I a pretty young fellow?" she said, turning around to her husband, laughing and blushing at the same time.

"You always will be pretty, do what you will," said George.

"What does make you so sober?" said Eliza, kneeling on one knee, and laying her hand on his. "We are only within twenty-four hours of Canada, they say. Only a day and a night on the lake, and then—oh, then!—"

"O, Eliza!" said George, drawing her towards him; "that is it! Now my fate is all narrowing down to a point. To come so near, to be almost in sight, and then lose all. I should never live under it, Eliza."

"Don't fear," said his wife, hopefully. "The good Lord would not have brought us so far, if he didn't mean to carry us through. I seem to feel him with us, George."

"You are a blessed woman, Eliza!" said George, clasping her with a convulsive grasp. "But,—oh, tell me! can this great mercy be for us? Will these years and years of misery come to an end?—shall we be free?

"I am sure of it, George," said Eliza, looking upward, while tears of hope and enthusiasm shone on her long, dark lashes. "I feel it in me, that God is going to bring us out of bondage, this very day."

"I will believe you, Eliza," said George, rising suddenly up, "I will believe,—come let's be off. Well, indeed," said he, holding her off at arm's length, and looking admiringly at her, "you *are* a pretty little fellow. That crop of little, short curls, is quite becoming. Put on your cap. So—a little to one side. I never saw you look quite so pretty. But, it's almost time for the carriage;—I wonder if Mrs. Smyth has got Harry rigged?"

The door opened, and a respectable, middle-aged woman entered, leading little Harry, dressed in girl's clothes.

"What a pretty girl he makes," said Eliza, turning him round. "We call him Harriet, you see;—don't the name come nicely?"

The child stood gravely regarding his mother in her new and strange attire, observing a profound silence, and occasionally drawing deep sighs, and peeping at her from under his dark curls.

"Does Harry know mamma?" said Eliza, stretching her hands toward him.

CHAPTER XXXVII

The child clung shyly to the woman.

"Come Eliza, why do you try to coax him, when you know that he has got to be kept away from you?"

"I know it's foolish," said Eliza; "yet, I can't bear to have him turn away from me. But come,—where's my cloak? Here,—how is it men put on cloaks, George?"

"You must wear it so," said her husband, throwing it over his shoulders.

"So, then," said Eliza, imitating the motion,—"and I must stamp, and take long steps, and try to look saucy."

"Don't exert yourself," said George. "There is, now and then, a modest young man; and I think it would be easier for you to act that character."

"And these gloves! mercy upon us!" said Eliza; "why, my hands are lost in them."

"I advise you to keep them on pretty strictly," said George. "Your slender paw might bring us all out. Now, Mrs. Smyth, you are to go under our charge, and be our aunty,—you mind."

"I've heard," said Mrs. Smyth, "that there have been men down, warning all the packet captains against a man and woman, with a little boy."

"They have!" said George. "Well, if we see any such people, we can tell them."

A hack now drove to the door, and the friendly family who had received the fugitives crowded around them with farewell greetings.

The disguises the party had assumed were in accordance with the hints of Tom Loker. Mrs. Smyth, a respectable woman from the settlement in Canada, whither they were fleeing, being fortunately about crossing the lake to return thither, had consented to appear as the aunt of little Harry; and, in order to attach him to her, he had been allowed to remain, the two last days, under her sole charge; and an extra amount of petting, jointed to an indefinite amount of seed-cakes and candy, had cemented a very close attachment on the part of the young gentleman.

The hack drove to the wharf. The two young men, as they appeared, walked up the plank into the boat, Eliza gallantly giving her arm to Mrs. Smyth, and George attending to their baggage.

George was standing at the captain's office, settling for his party, when he overheard two men talking by his side.

"I've watched every one that came on board," said one, "and I know they're not on this boat."

The voice was that of the clerk of the boat. The speaker whom he addressed was our sometime friend Marks, who, with that valuable perseverance which characterized him, had come on to Sandusky, seeking whom he might devour.

"You would scarcely know the woman from a white one," said Marks. "The man is a very light mulatto; he has a brand in one of his hands."

The hand with which George was taking the tickets and change trembled a little; but he turned coolly around, fixed an unconcerned glance on the face of the speaker, and walked leisurely toward another part of the boat, where Eliza stood waiting for him.

Mrs. Smyth, with little Harry, sought the seclusion of the ladies' cabin, where the dark beauty of the supposed little girl drew many flattering comments from the passengers.

George had the satisfaction, as the bell rang out its farewell peal, to see Marks walk down the plank to the shore; and drew a long sigh of relief, when the boat had put a returnless distance between them.

It was a superb day. The blue waves of Lake Erie danced, rippling and sparkling, in the sun-light. A fresh breeze blew from the shore, and the lordly boat ploughed her way right gallantly onward.

O, what an untold world there is in one human heart! Who thought, as George walked calmly up and down the deck of the steamer, with his shy companion at his side, of all that was burning in his bosom? The mighty good that seemed approaching seemed too good, too fair, even to be a reality; and he felt a jealous dread, every moment of the day, that something would rise to snatch it from him.

But the boat swept on. Hours fleeted, and, at last, clear and full rose the blessed English shores; shores charmed by a mighty spell,—with one touch to dissolve every incantation of slavery, no matter in what language pronounced, or by what national power confirmed.

George and his wife stood arm in arm, as the boat neared the small town of Amherstberg, in Canada. His breath grew thick and short; a mist gathered before his eyes; he silently pressed the little hand that lay trembling on his arm. The bell rang; the boat stopped. Scarcely seeing what he did, he looked out his baggage, and gathered his little party. The little company were landed on the shore. They stood still till the boat had cleared; and then, with tears and embracings, the husband and wife, with their wondering child in their arms, knelt down and lifted up their hearts to God!

"'T was something like the burst from death to life; From the grave's cerements to the robes of heaven; From sin's dominion, and from passion's strife, To the pure freedom of a soul forgiven; Where all the bonds of death and hell are riven, And mortal puts on immortality, When Mercy's hand hath turned the golden key, And Mercy's voice hath said, *Rejoice, thy soul is free."*

The little party were soon guided, by Mrs. Smyth, to the hospitable abode of a good missionary, whom Christian charity has placed here as a shepherd to the outcast and wandering, who are constantly finding an asylum on this shore.

Who can speak the blessedness of that first day of freedom? Is not the *sense* of liberty a higher and a finer one than any of the five? To move, speak and breathe,—go out and come in unwatched, and free from danger! Who can speak the blessings of that rest which comes down on the free man's pillow, under laws which insure to him the rights that God has given to man? How fair and precious to that mother was that sleeping child's face, endeared by the memory of a thousand dangers! How impossible was it to sleep, in the exuberant possession of such blessedness! And yet, these two had not one acre of ground,—not a roof that they could call their own,—they had spent their all, to the last dollar. They had nothing more than the birds of the air, or the flowers of the field,—yet they could not sleep for joy. "O, ye who take freedom from man, with what words shall ye answer it to God?"

CHAPTER XXXVIII

THE VICTORY

"Thanks be unto God, who giveth us the victory."[1]

Have not many of us, in the weary way of life, felt, in some hours, how far easier it were to die than to live?

The martyr, when faced even by a death of bodily anguish and horror, finds in the very terror of his doom a strong stimulant and tonic. There is a vivid excitement, a thrill and fervor, which may carry through any crisis of suffering that is the birth-hour of eternal glory and rest.

But to live,—to wear on, day after day, of mean, bitter, low, harassing servitude, every nerve dampened and depressed, every power of feeling gradually smothered,—this long and wasting heart-martyrdom, this slow, daily bleeding away of the inward life, drop by drop, hour after hour,—this is the true searching test of what there may be in man or woman.

When Tom stood face to face with his persecutor, and heard his threats, and thought in his very soul that his hour was come, his heart swelled bravely in him, and he thought he could bear torture and fire, bear anything, with the vision of Jesus and heaven but just a step beyond; but, when he was gone, and the present excitement passed off, came back the pain of his bruised and weary limbs,—came back the sense of his utterly degraded, hopeless, forlorn estate; and the day passed wearily enough.

Long before his wounds were healed, Legree insisted that he should be put to the regular field-work; and then came day after day of pain and weariness, aggravated by every kind of injustice and indignity that the ill-will of a mean and malicious mind could devise. Whoever, in *our* circumstances, has made trial of pain, even with all the alleviations which, for us, usually attend it, must know the irritation that comes with it. Tom no longer wondered at the habitual surliness of his associates; nay, he found the placid, sunny temper, which had been the habitude of his life, broken in on, and sorely strained, by the inroads of the same

---

[1] I Cor. 15:57.

thing. He had flattered himself on leisure to read his Bible; but there was no such thing as leisure there. In the height of the season, Legree did not hesitate to press all his hands through, Sundays and week-days alike. Why shouldn't he?—he made more cotton by it, and gained his wager; and if it wore out a few more hands, he could buy better ones. At first, Tom used to read a verse or two of his Bible, by the flicker of the fire, after he had returned from his daily toil; but, after the cruel treatment he received, he used to come home so exhausted, that his head swam and his eyes failed when he tried to read; and he was fain to stretch himself down, with the others, in utter exhaustion.

Is it strange that the religious peace and trust, which had upborne him hitherto, should give way to tossings of soul and despondent darkness? The gloomiest problem of this mysterious life was constantly before his eyes,—souls crushed and ruined, evil triumphant, and God silent. It was weeks and months that Tom wrestled, in his own soul, in darkness and sorrow. He thought of Miss Ophelia's letter to his Kentucky friends, and would pray earnestly that God would send him deliverance. And then he would watch, day after day, in the vague hope of seeing somebody sent to redeem him; and, when nobody came, he would crush back to his soul bitter thoughts,—that it was vain to serve God, that God had forgotten him. He sometimes saw Cassy; and sometimes, when summoned to the house, caught a glimpse of the dejected form of Emmeline, but held very little communion with either; in fact, there was no time for him to commune with anybody.

One evening, he was sitting, in utter dejection and prostration, by a few decaying brands, where his coarse supper was baking. He put a few bits of brushwood on the fire, and strove to raise the light, and then drew his worn Bible from his pocket. There were all the marked passages, which had thrilled his soul so often,—words of patriarchs and seers, poets and sages, who from early time had spoken courage to man,—voices from the great cloud of witnesses who ever surround us in the race of life. Had the word lost its power, or could the failing eye and weary sense no longer answer to the touch of that mighty inspiration? Heavily sighing, he put it in his pocket. A coarse laugh roused him; he looked up,—Legree was standing opposite to him.

"Well, old boy," he said, "you find your religion don't work, it seems! I thought I should get that through your wool, at last!"

The cruel taunt was more than hunger and cold and nakedness. Tom was silent.

"You were a fool," said Legree; "for I meant to do well by you, when I bought you. You might have been better off than Sambo, or Quimbo either, and had easy times; and, instead of getting cut up and thrashed, every day or two, ye might have had liberty to lord it round, and cut up the other niggers; and ye might have had, now and then, a good warming of whiskey punch. Come, Tom, don't you think you'd better be reasonable?—heave that ar old pack of trash in the fire, and join my church!"

"The Lord forbid!" said Tom, fervently.

"You see the Lord an't going to help you; if he had been, he wouldn't have let *me* get you! This yer religion is all a mess of lying trumpery, Tom. I know all about it. Ye'd better hold to me; I'm somebody, and can do something!"

"No, Mas'r," said Tom; "I'll hold on. The Lord may help me, or not help; but I'll hold to him, and believe him to the last!"

"The more fool you!" said Legree, spitting scornfully at him, and spurning him with his foot. "Never mind; I'll chase you down, yet, and bring you under,—you'll see!" and Legree turned away.

When a heavy weight presses the soul to the lowest level at which endurance is possible, there is an instant and desperate effort of every physical and moral nerve to throw off the weight; and hence the heaviest anguish often precedes a return tide of joy and courage. So was it now with Tom. The atheistic taunts of his cruel master sunk his before dejected soul to the lowest ebb; and, though the hand of faith still held to the eternal rock, it was a numb, despairing grasp. Tom sat, like one stunned, at the fire. Suddenly everything around him seemed to fade, and a vision rose before him of one crowned with thorns, buffeted and bleeding. Tom gazed, in awe and wonder, at the majestic patience of the face; the deep, pathetic eyes thrilled him to his inmost heart; his soul woke, as, with floods of emotion, he stretched out his hands and fell upon his knees,—when, gradually, the vision changed: the sharp thorns became rays of glory; and, in splendor inconceivable, he saw that same face bending compassionately towards him, and a voice said, "He that overcometh shall sit down with me on my throne, even as I also overcome, and am set down with my Father on his throne."

How long Tom lay there, he knew not. When he came to himself, the fire was gone out, his clothes were wet with the chill and drenching dews; but the dread soul-crisis was past, and, in the joy that filled him, he no longer felt hunger, cold, degradation, disappointment, wretchedness. From his deepest soul, he that hour loosed and parted from every hope in life that now is, and offered his own will an unquestioning sacrifice to the Infinite. Tom looked up to the silent, ever-living stars,—types of the angelic hosts who ever look down on man; and the solitude of the night rung with the triumphant words of a hymn, which he had sung often in happier days, but never with such feeling as now:

"The earth shall be dissolved like snow, The sun shall cease to shine; But God, who called me here below, Shall be forever mine. "And when this mortal life shall fail, And flesh and sense shall cease, I shall possess within the veil A life of joy and peace. "When we've been there ten thousand years, Bright shining like the sun, We've no less days to sing God's praise Than when we first begun."

Those who have been familiar with the religious histories of the slave population know that relations like what we have narrated are very common among them. We have heard some from their own lips, of a very touching and affecting character. The psychologist tells us of a state, in which the affections and images of the mind become so dominant and overpowering, that they press into their service the outward imagining. Who shall measure what an all-pervading Spirit may do with these capabilities of our mortality, or the ways in which He may encourage the desponding souls of the desolate? If the poor forgotten slave believes that Jesus hath appeared and spoken to him, who shall contradict him? Did He not say that his mission, in all ages, was to bind up the broken-hearted, and set at liberty them that are bruised?

When the dim gray of dawn woke the slumberers to go forth to the field, there was among those tattered and shivering wretches one who walked with an exultant tread; for firmer than the ground he trod on was his strong faith in Almighty, eternal love. Ah, Legree, try all your forces now! Utmost agony, woe, degradation, want, and loss of all things, shall only hasten on the process by which he shall be made a king and a priest unto God!

From this time, an inviolable sphere of peace encompassed the lowly heart of the oppressed one,—an ever-present Saviour hallowed it as a temple. Past now the bleeding of earthly regrets; past its fluctuations of hope, and fear, and desire; the human will, bent, and bleeding, and struggling long, was now entirely merged in the Divine. So short now seemed the remaining voyage of life,—so near, so vivid, seemed eternal blessedness,—that life's uttermost woes fell from him unharming.

All noticed the change in his appearance. Cheerfulness and alertness seemed to return to him, and a quietness which no insult or injury could ruffle seemed to possess him.

"What the devil's got into Tom?" Legree said to Sambo. "A while ago he was all down in the mouth, and now he's peart as a cricket."

"Dunno, Mas'r; gwine to run off, mebbe."

"Like to see him try that," said Legree, with a savage grin, "wouldn't we, Sambo?"

"Guess we would! Haw! haw! ho!" said the sooty gnome, laughing obsequiously. "Lord, de fun! To see him stickin' in de mud,—chasin' and tarin' through de bushes, dogs a holdin' on to him! Lord, I laughed fit to split, dat ar time we cotched Molly. I thought they'd a had her all stripped up afore I could get 'em off. She car's de marks o' dat ar spree yet."

"I reckon she will, to her grave," said Legree. "But now, Sambo, you look sharp. If the nigger's got anything of this sort going, trip him up."

"Mas'r, let me lone for dat," said Sambo, "I'll tree de coon. Ho, ho, ho!"

This was spoken as Legree was getting on his horse, to go to the neighboring town. That night, as he was returning, he thought he would turn his horse and ride round the quarters, and see if all was safe.

It was a superb moonlight night, and the shadows of the graceful China trees lay minutely pencilled on the turf below, and there was that transparent stillness in the air which it seems almost unholy to disturb. Legree was a little distance from the quarters, when he heard the voice of some one singing. It was not a usual sound there, and he paused to listen. A musical tenor voice sang,

"When I can read my title clear To mansions in the skies, I'll bid farewell to every fear, And wipe my weeping eyes "Should earth against my soul engage, And hellish darts be hurled, Then I can smile at Satan's rage, And face a frowning world. "Let cares like a wild deluge come, And storms of sorrow fall, May I but safely reach my home, My God, my Heaven, my All."[1]

"So ho!" said Legree to himself, "he thinks so, does he? How I hate these cursed Methodist hymns! Here, you nigger," said he, coming suddenly out upon Tom, and raising his riding-whip, "how dare you be gettin' up this yer row, when you ought to be in bed? Shut yer old black gash, and get along in with you!"

"Yes, Mas'r," said Tom, with ready cheerfulness, as he rose to go in.

Legree was provoked beyond measure by Tom's evident happiness; and riding up to him, belabored him over his head and shoulders.

"There, you dog," he said, "see if you'll feel so comfortable, after that!"

But the blows fell now only on the outer man, and not, as before, on the heart. Tom stood perfectly submissive; and yet Legree could not hide from himself that his power over his bond thrall was somehow gone. And, as Tom disappeared in his cabin, and he wheeled his horse suddenly round, there passed through his mind one of those vivid flashes that often send the lightning of conscience across the dark and wicked soul. He understood full well that it was GOD who was standing between him and his victim, and he blasphemed him. That submissive and silent man, whom taunts, nor threats, nor stripes, nor cruelties, could disturb, roused a voice within him, such as of old his Master roused in the demoniac soul, saying, "What have we to do with thee, thou Jesus of Nazareth?—art thou come to torment us before the time?"

Tom's whole soul overflowed with compassion and sympathy for the poor wretches by whom he was surrounded. To him it seemed as if his life-sorrows were now over, and as if, out of that strange treasury of peace and joy, with which he had been endowed from above, he longed to pour out something for the relief of their woes. It is true, opportunities were scanty; but, on the way to the fields, and back again, and during the hours of labor, chances fell in his way of extending a helping-hand to the weary, the disheartened and discouraged. The poor, worn-down, brutalized creatures, at first, could scarce comprehend this; but, when it was continued week after week, and month after month, it began to awaken long-silent chords in their benumbed hearts. Gradually and imperceptibly the strange, silent, patient man, who was ready to bear every one's burden, and sought help from none,—who stood aside for all, and came last, and took least, yet was foremost to share his little all with any who needed,—the man who, in cold nights, would give up his tattered blanket to add to the comfort of some woman who shivered with sickness, and who filled the baskets of the weaker ones in the field, at the terrible risk of coming short in his own measure,—and who, though pursued with unrelenting cruelty by their common tyrant, never joined in uttering a word of reviling or cursing,—this man, at last, began to have a strange power over them; and, when the more pressing season was past, and they were allowed again their Sundays for their own use, many would gather together to hear from

---

[1] "On My Journey Home," hymn by Isaac Watts, found in many of the southern country songbooks of the ante bellum period.

him of Jesus. They would gladly have met to hear, and pray, and sing, in some place, together; but Legree would not permit it, and more than once broke up such attempts, with oaths and brutal execrations,—so that the blessed news had to circulate from individual to individual. Yet who can speak the simple joy with which some of those poor outcasts, to whom life was a joyless journey to a dark unknown, heard of a compassionate Redeemer and a heavenly home? It is the statement of missionaries, that, of all races of the earth, none have received the Gospel with such eager docility as the African. The principle of reliance and unquestioning faith, which is its foundation, is more a native element in this race than any other; and it has often been found among them, that a stray seed of truth, borne on some breeze of accident into hearts the most ignorant, has sprung up into fruit, whose abundance has shamed that of higher and more skilful culture.

The poor mulatto woman, whose simple faith had been well-nigh crushed and overwhelmed, by the avalanche of cruelty and wrong which had fallen upon her, felt her soul raised up by the hymns and passages of Holy Writ, which this lowly missionary breathed into her ear in intervals, as they were going to and returning from work; and even the half-crazed and wandering mind of Cassy was soothed and calmed by his simple and unobtrusive influences.

Stung to madness and despair by the crushing agonies of a life, Cassy had often resolved in her soul an hour of retribution, when her hand should avenge on her oppressor all the injustice and cruelty to which she had been witness, or which *she* had in her own person suffered.

One night, after all in Tom's cabin were sunk in sleep, he was suddenly aroused by seeing her face at the hole between the logs, that served for a window. She made a silent gesture for him to come out.

Tom came out the door. It was between one and two o'clock at night,—broad, calm, still moonlight. Tom remarked, as the light of the moon fell upon Cassy's large, black eyes, that there was a wild and peculiar glare in them, unlike their wonted fixed despair.

"Come here, Father Tom," she said, laying her small hand on his wrist, and drawing him forward with a force as if the hand were of steel; "come here,—I've news for you."

"What, Misse Cassy?" said Tom, anxiously.

"Tom, wouldn't you like your liberty?"

"I shall have it, Misse, in God's time," said Tom. "Ay, but you may have it tonight," said Cassy, with a flash of sudden energy. "Come on."

Tom hesitated.

"Come!" said she, in a whisper, fixing her black eyes on him. "Come along! He's asleep—sound. I put enough into his brandy to keep him so. I wish I'd had more,—I shouldn't have wanted you. But come, the back door is unlocked; there's an axe there, I put it there,—his room door is open; I'll show you the way. I'd a done it myself, only my arms are so weak. Come along!"

"Not for ten thousand worlds, Misse!" said Tom, firmly, stopping and holding her back, as she was pressing forward.

"But think of all these poor creatures," said Cassy. "We might set them all free, and go somewhere in the swamps, and find an island, and live by ourselves; I've heard of its being done. Any life is better than this."

"No!" said Tom, firmly. "No! good never comes of wickedness. I'd sooner chop my right hand off!"

"Then *I* shall do it," said Cassy, turning.

"O, Misse Cassy!" said Tom, throwing himself before her, "for the dear Lord's sake that died for ye, don't sell your precious soul to the devil, that way! Nothing but evil will come of it. The Lord hasn't called us to wrath. We must suffer, and wait his time."

"Wait!" said Cassy. "Haven't I waited?—waited till my head is dizzy and my heart sick? What has he made me suffer? What has he made hundreds of poor creatures suffer? Isn't he wringing the life-blood out of you? I'm called on; they call me! His time's come, and I'll have his heart's blood!"

"No, no, no!" said Tom, holding her small hands, which were clenched with spasmodic violence. "No, ye poor, lost soul, that ye mustn't do. The dear, blessed Lord never shed no blood but his own, and that he poured out for us when we was enemies. Lord, help us to follow his steps, and love our enemies."

"Love!" said Cassy, with a fierce glare; "love *such* enemies! It isn't in flesh and blood."

"No, Misse, it isn't," said Tom, looking up; "but *He* gives it to us, and that's the victory. When we can love and pray over all and through all, the battle's past, and the victory's come,—glory be to God!" And, with streaming eyes and choking voice, the black man looked up to heaven.

And this, oh Africa! latest called of nations,—called to the crown of thorns, the scourge, the bloody sweat, the cross of agony,—this is to be *thy* victory; by this shalt thou reign with Christ when his kingdom shall come on earth.

The deep fervor of Tom's feelings, the softness of his voice, his tears, fell like dew on the wild, unsettled spirit of the poor woman. A softness gathered over the lurid fires of her eye; she looked down, and Tom could feel the relaxing muscles of her hands, as she said,

"Didn't I tell you that evil spirits followed me? O! Father Tom, I can't pray,—I wish I could. I never have prayed since my children were sold! What you say must be right, I know it must; but when I try to pray, I can only hate and curse. I can't pray!"

"Poor soul!" said Tom, compassionately. "Satan desires to have ye, and sift ye as wheat. I pray the Lord for ye. O! Misse Cassy, turn to the dear Lord Jesus. He came to bind up the broken-hearted, and comfort all that mourn."

Cassy stood silent, while large, heavy tears dropped from her downcast eyes.

"Misse Cassy," said Tom, in a hesitating tone, after surveying her in silence, "if ye only could get away from here,—if the thing was possible,—I'd 'vise ye and Emmeline to do it; that is, if ye could go without blood-guiltiness,—not otherwise."

"Would you try it with us, Father Tom?"

"No," said Tom; "time was when I would; but the Lord's given me a work among these yer poor souls, and I'll stay with 'em and bear my cross with 'em till the end. It's different with you; it's a snare to you,—it's more'n you can stand,—and you'd better go, if you can."

"I know no way but through the grave," said Cassy. "There's no beast or bird but can find a home some where; even the snakes and the alligators have their places to lie down and be quiet; but there's no place for us. Down in the darkest swamps, their dogs will hunt us out, and find us. Everybody and everything is against us; even the very beasts side against us,—and where shall we go?"

Tom stood silent; at length he said,

"Him that saved Daniel in the den of lions,—that saved the children in the fiery furnace,—Him that walked on the sea, and bade the winds be still,—He's alive yet; and I've faith to believe he can deliver you. Try it, and I'll pray, with all my might, for you."

By what strange law of mind is it that an idea long overlooked, and trodden under foot as a useless stone, suddenly sparkles out in new light, as a discovered diamond?

Cassy had often revolved, for hours, all possible or probable schemes of escape, and dismissed them all, as hopeless and impracticable; but at this moment there flashed through her mind a plan, so simple and feasible in all its details, as to awaken an instant hope.

"Father Tom, I'll try it!" she said, suddenly.

"Amen!" said Tom; "the Lord help ye!"

CHAPTER XXXIX

THE STRATAGEM

"The way of the wicked is as darkness; he knoweth not at what he stumbleth."[1]

The garret of the house that Legree occupied, like most other garrets, was a great, desolate space, dusty, hung with cobwebs, and littered with cast-off lumber. The opulent family that had inhabited the house in the days of its splendor had imported a great deal of splendid furniture, some of which they had taken away with them, while some remained standing desolate in mouldering, unoccupied rooms, or stored away in this place. One or two immense packing-boxes, in which this furniture was brought, stood against the sides of the garret. There was a small window there, which let in, through its dingy, dusty panes, a scanty, uncertain light on the tall, high-backed chairs and dusty tables, that had once seen better days. Altogether, it was a weird and ghostly place; but, ghostly as it was, it wanted not in legends among the superstitious negroes, to increase its terrors. Some few years before, a negro woman, who had incurred Legree's displeasure, was confined there for several weeks. What passed there, we do not say; the negroes used to whisper darkly to each other; but it was known that the body of the unfortunate creature was one day taken down from there, and buried; and, after that, it was said that oaths and cursings, and the sound of violent blows, used to ring through that old garret, and mingled with wailings and groans of despair. Once, when Legree chanced to overhear something of this kind, he flew into a violent passion, and swore that the next one that told stories about that garret should have an opportunity of knowing what was there, for he would chain them up there for a week. This hint was enough to repress talking, though, of course, it did not disturb the credit of the story in the least.

Gradually, the staircase that led to the garret, and even the passage-way to the staircase, were avoided by every one in the house, from every one fearing to speak of it, and the legend was gradually falling into desuetude. It had suddenly

---

[1] Prov. 4:19.

occurred to Cassy to make use of the superstitious excitability, which was so great in Legree, for the purpose of her liberation, and that of her fellow-sufferer.

The sleeping-room of Cassy was directly under the garret. One day, without consulting Legree, she suddenly took it upon her, with some considerable ostentation, to change all the furniture and appurtenances of the room to one at some considerable distance. The under-servants, who were called on to effect this movement, were running and bustling about with great zeal and confusion, when Legree returned from a ride.

"Hallo! you Cass!" said Legree, "what's in the wind now?"

"Nothing; only I choose to have another room," said Cassy, doggedly.

"And what for, pray?" said Legree.

"I choose to," said Cassy.

"The devil you do! and what for?"

"I'd like to get some sleep, now and then."

"Sleep! well, what hinders your sleeping?"

"I could tell, I suppose, if you want to hear," said Cassy, dryly.

"Speak out, you minx!" said Legree.

"O! nothing. I suppose it wouldn't disturb *you!* Only groans, and people scuffing, and rolling round on the garret floor, half the night, from twelve to morning!"

"People up garret!" said Legree, uneasily, but forcing a laugh; "who are they, Cassy?"

Cassy raised her sharp, black eyes, and looked in the face of Legree, with an expression that went through his bones, as she said, "To be sure, Simon, who are they? I'd like to have *you* tell me. You don't know, I suppose!"

With an oath, Legree struck at her with his riding-whip; but she glided to one side, and passed through the door, and looking back, said, "If you'll sleep in that room, you'll know all about it. Perhaps you'd better try it!" and then immediately she shut and locked the door.

Legree blustered and swore, and threatened to break down the door; but apparently thought better of it, and walked uneasily into the sitting-room. Cassy perceived that her shaft had struck home; and, from that hour, with the most exquisite address, she never ceased to continue the train of influences she had begun.

In a knot-hole of the garret, that had opened, she had inserted the neck of an old bottle, in such a manner that when there was the least wind, most doleful and lugubrious wailing sounds proceeded from it, which, in a high wind, increased to a perfect shriek, such as to credulous and superstitious ears might easily seem to be that of horror and despair.

These sounds were, from time to time, heard by the servants, and revived in full force the memory of the old ghost legend. A superstitious creeping horror seemed to fill the house; and though no one dared to breathe it to Legree, he found himself encompassed by it, as by an atmosphere.

No one is so thoroughly superstitious as the godless man. The Christian is composed by the belief of a wise, all-ruling Father, whose presence fills the void unknown with light and order; but to the man who has dethroned God, the spirit-land is, indeed, in the words of the Hebrew poet, "a land of darkness and the shadow of death," without any order, where the light is as darkness. Life and death to him are haunted grounds, filled with goblin forms of vague and shadowy dread.

Legree had had the slumbering moral elements in him roused by his encounters with Tom,—roused, only to be resisted by the determinate force of evil; but still there was a thrill and commotion of the dark, inner world, produced by every word, or prayer, or hymn, that reacted in superstitious dread.

The influence of Cassy over him was of a strange and singular kind. He was her owner, her tyrant and tormentor. She was, as he knew, wholly, and without any possibility of help or redress, in his hands; and yet so it is, that the most brutal man cannot live in constant association with a strong female influence, and not be greatly controlled by it. When he first bought her, she was, as she said, a woman delicately bred; and then he crushed her, without scruple, beneath the foot of his brutality. But, as time, and debasing influences, and despair, hardened womanhood within her, and waked the fires of fiercer passions, she had become in a measure his mistress, and he alternately tyrannized over and dreaded her.

This influence had become more harassing and decided, since partial insanity had given a strange, weird, unsettled cast to all her words and language.

A night or two after this, Legree was sitting in the old sitting-room, by the side of a flickering wood fire, that threw uncertain glances round the room. It was a stormy, windy night, such as raises whole squadrons of nondescript noises in rickety old houses. Windows were rattling, shutters flapping, and wind carousing, rumbling, and tumbling down the chimney, and, every once in a while, puffing out smoke and ashes, as if a legion of spirits were coming after them. Legree had been casting up accounts and reading newspapers for some hours, while Cassy sat in the corner; sullenly looking into the fire. Legree laid down his paper, and seeing an old book lying on the table, which he had noticed Cassy reading, the first part of the evening, took it up, and began to turn it over. It was one of those collections of stories of bloody murders, ghostly legends, and supernatural visitations, which, coarsely got up and illustrated, have a strange fascination for one who once begins to read them.

Legree poohed and pished, but read, turning page after page, till, finally, after reading some way, he threw down the book, with an oath.

"You don't believe in ghosts, do you, Cass?" said he, taking the tongs and settling the fire. "I thought you'd more sense than to let noises scare *you*."

"No matter what I believe," said Cassy, sullenly.

"Fellows used to try to frighten me with their yarns at sea," said Legree. "Never come it round me that way. I'm too tough for any such trash, tell ye."

Cassy sat looking intensely at him in the shadow of the corner. There was that strange light in her eyes that always impressed Legree with uneasiness.

CHAPTER XXXIX

"Them noises was nothing but rats and the wind," said Legree. "Rats will make a devil of a noise. I used to hear 'em sometimes down in the hold of the ship; and wind,—Lord's sake! ye can make anything out o' wind."

Cassy knew Legree was uneasy under her eyes, and, therefore, she made no answer, but sat fixing them on him, with that strange, unearthly expression, as before.

"Come, speak out, woman,—don't you think so?" said Legree.

"Can rats walk down stairs, and come walking through the entry, and open a door when you've locked it and set a chair against it?" said Cassy; "and come walk, walk, walking right up to your bed, and put out their hand, so?"

Cassy kept her glittering eyes fixed on Legree, as she spoke, and he stared at her like a man in the nightmare, till, when she finished by laying her hand, icy cold, on his, he sprung back, with an oath.

"Woman! what do you mean? Nobody did?"

"O, no,—of course not,—did I say they did?" said Cassy, with a smile of chilling derision.

"But—did—have you really seen?—Come, Cass, what is it, now,—speak out!"

"You may sleep there, yourself," said Cassy, "if you want to know."

"Did it come from the garret, Cassy?"

"*It*,—what?" said Cassy.

"Why, what you told of—"

"I didn't tell you anything," said Cassy, with dogged sullenness.

Legree walked up and down the room, uneasily.

"I'll have this yer thing examined. I'll look into it, this very night. I'll take my pistols—"

"Do," said Cassy; "sleep in that room. I'd like to see you doing it. Fire your pistols,—do!"

Legree stamped his foot, and swore violently.

"Don't swear," said Cassy; "nobody knows who may be hearing you. Hark! What was that?"

"What?" said Legree, starting.

A heavy old Dutch clock, that stood in the corner of the room, began, and slowly struck twelve.

For some reason or other, Legree neither spoke nor moved; a vague horror fell on him; while Cassy, with a keen, sneering glitter in her eyes, stood looking at him, counting the strokes.

"Twelve o'clock; well *now* we'll see," said she, turning, and opening the door into the passage-way, and standing as if listening.

"Hark! What's that?" said she, raising her finger.

"It's only the wind," said Legree. "Don't you hear how cursedly it blows?"

"Simon, come here," said Cassy, in a whisper, laying her hand on his, and leading him to the foot of the stairs: "do you know what *that* is? Hark!"

A wild shriek came pealing down the stairway. It came from the garret. Legree's knees knocked together; his face grew white with fear.

"Hadn't you better get your pistols?" said Cassy, with a sneer that froze Legree's blood. "It's time this thing was looked into, you know. I'd like to have you go up now; *they're at it.*"

"I won't go!" said Legree, with an oath.

"Why not? There an't any such thing as ghosts, you know! Come!" and Cassy flitted up the winding stairway, laughing, and looking back after him. "Come on."

"I believe you *are* the devil!" said Legree. "Come back you hag,—come back, Cass! You shan't go!"

But Cassy laughed wildly, and fled on. He heard her open the entry doors that led to the garret. A wild gust of wind swept down, extinguishing the candle he held in his hand, and with it the fearful, unearthly screams; they seemed to be shrieked in his very ear.

Legree fled frantically into the parlor, whither, in a few moments, he was followed by Cassy, pale, calm, cold as an avenging spirit, and with that same fearful light in her eye.

"I hope you are satisfied," said she.

"Blast you, Cass!" said Legree.

"What for?" said Cassy. "I only went up and shut the doors. *What's the matter with that garret*, Simon, do you suppose?" said she.

"None of your business!" said Legree.

"O, it an't? Well," said Cassy, "at any rate, I'm glad *I* don't sleep under it."

Anticipating the rising of the wind, that very evening, Cassy had been up and opened the garret window. Of course, the moment the doors were opened, the wind had drafted down, and extinguished the light.

This may serve as a specimen of the game that Cassy played with Legree, until he would sooner have put his head into a lion's mouth than to have explored that garret. Meanwhile, in the night, when everybody else was asleep, Cassy slowly and carefully accumulated there a stock of provisions sufficient to afford subsistence for some time; she transferred, article by article, a greater part of her own and Emmeline's wardrobe. All things being arranged, they only waited a fitting opportunity to put their plan in execution.

By cajoling Legree, and taking advantage of a good-natured interval, Cassy had got him to take her with him to the neighboring town, which was situated directly on the Red River. With a memory sharpened to almost preternatural clearness, she remarked every turn in the road, and formed a mental estimate of the time to be occupied in traversing it.

At the time when all was matured for action, our readers may, perhaps, like to look behind the scenes, and see the final *coup d'etat.*

It was now near evening, Legree had been absent, on a ride to a neighboring farm. For many days Cassy had been unusually gracious and accommodating in her humors; and Legree and she had been, apparently, on the best of terms. At present, we may behold her and Emmeline in the room of the latter, busy in sorting and arranging two small bundles.

"There, these will be large enough," said Cassy. "Now put on your bonnet, and let's start; it's just about the right time."

"Why, they can see us yet," said Emmeline.

"I mean they shall," said Cassy, coolly. "Don't you know that they must have their chase after us, at any rate? The way of the thing is to be just this:—We will steal out of the back door, and run down by the quarters. Sambo or Quimbo will be sure to see us. They will give chase, and we will get into the swamp; then, they can't follow us any further till they go up and give the alarm, and turn out the dogs, and so on; and, while they are blundering round, and tumbling over each other, as they always do, you and I will slip along to the creek, that runs back of the house, and wade along in it, till we get opposite the back door. That will put the dogs all at fault; for scent won't lie in the water. Every one will run out of the house to look after us, and then we'll whip in at the back door, and up into the garret, where I've got a nice bed made up in one of the great boxes. We must stay in that garret a good while, for, I tell you, he will raise heaven and earth after us. He'll muster some of those old overseers on the other plantations, and have a great hunt; and they'll go over every inch of ground in that swamp. He makes it his boast that nobody ever got away from him. So let him hunt at his leisure."

"Cassy, how well you have planned it!" said Emmeline. "Who ever would have thought of it, but you?"

There was neither pleasure nor exultation in Cassy's eyes,—only a despairing firmness.

"Come," she said, reaching her hand to Emmeline.

The two fugitives glided noiselessly from the house, and flitted, through the gathering shadows of evening, along by the quarters. The crescent moon, set like a silver signet in the western sky, delayed a little the approach of night. As Cassy expected, when quite near the verge of the swamps that encircled the plantation, they heard a voice calling to them to stop. It was not Sambo, however, but Legree, who was pursuing them with violent execrations. At the sound, the feebler spirit of Emmeline gave way; and, laying hold of Cassy's arm, she said, "O, Cassy, I'm going to faint!"

"If you do, I'll kill you!" said Cassy, drawing a small, glittering stiletto, and flashing it before the eyes of the girl.

The diversion accomplished the purpose. Emmeline did not faint, and succeeded in plunging, with Cassy, into a part of the labyrinth of swamp, so deep and dark that it was perfectly hopeless for Legree to think of following them, without assistance.

"Well," said he, chuckling brutally; "at any rate, they've got themselves into a trap now—the baggage! They're safe enough. They shall sweat for it!"

"Hulloa, there! Sambo! Quimbo! All hands!" called Legree, coming to the quarters, when the men and women were just returning from work. "There's two runaways in the swamps. I'll give five dollars to any nigger as catches 'em. Turn out the dogs! Turn out Tiger, and Fury, and the rest!"

The sensation produced by this news was immediate. Many of the men sprang forward, officiously, to offer their services, either from the hope of the reward, or from that cringing subserviency which is one of the most baleful effects of slavery. Some ran one way, and some another. Some were for getting flambeaux of pine-knots. Some were uncoupling the dogs, whose hoarse, savage bay added not a little to the animation of the scene.

"Mas'r, shall we shoot 'em, if can't cotch 'em?" said Sambo, to whom his master brought out a rifle.

"You may fire on Cass, if you like; it's time she was gone to the devil, where she belongs; but the gal, not," said Legree. "And now, boys, be spry and smart. Five dollars for him that gets 'em; and a glass of spirits to every one of you, anyhow."

The whole band, with the glare of blazing torches, and whoop, and shout, and savage yell, of man and beast, proceeded down to the swamp, followed, at some distance, by every servant in the house. The establishment was, of a consequence, wholly deserted, when Cassy and Emmeline glided into it the back way. The whooping and shouts of their pursuers were still filling the air; and, looking from the sitting-room windows, Cassy and Emmeline could see the troop, with their flambeaux, just dispersing themselves along the edge of the swamp.

"See there!" said Emmeline, pointing to Cassy; "the hunt is begun! Look how those lights dance about! Hark! the dogs! Don't you hear? If we were only *there*, our chances wouldn't be worth a picayune. O, for pity's sake, do let's hide ourselves. Quick!"

"There's no occasion for hurry," said Cassy, coolly; "they are all out after the hunt,—that's the amusement of the evening! We'll go up stairs, by and by. Meanwhile," said she, deliberately taking a key from the pocket of a coat that Legree had thrown down in his hurry, "meanwhile I shall take something to pay our passage."

She unlocked the desk, took from it a roll of bills, which she counted over rapidly.

"O, don't let's do that!" said Emmeline.

"Don't!" said Cassy; "why not? Would you have us starve in the swamps, or have that that will pay our way to the free states. Money will do anything, girl." And, as she spoke, she put the money in her bosom.

"It would be stealing," said Emmeline, in a distressed whisper.

"Stealing!" said Cassy, with a scornful laugh. "They who steal body and soul needn't talk to us. Every one of these bills is stolen,—stolen from poor, starving, sweating creatures, who must go to the devil at last, for his profit. Let *him* talk about stealing! But come, we may as well go up garret; I've got a stock of candles there, and some books to pass away the time. You may be pretty sure they won't come *there* to inquire after us. If they do, I'll play ghost for them."

CHAPTER XXXIX

When Emmeline reached the garret, she found an immense box, in which some heavy pieces of furniture had once been brought, turned on its side, so that the opening faced the wall, or rather the eaves. Cassy lit a small lamp, and creeping round under the eaves, they established themselves in it. It was spread with a couple of small mattresses and some pillows; a box near by was plentifully stored with candles, provisions, and all the clothing necessary to their journey, which Cassy had arranged into bundles of an astonishingly small compass.

"There," said Cassy, as she fixed the lamp into a small hook, which she had driven into the side of the box for that purpose; "this is to be our home for the present. How do you like it?"

"Are you sure they won't come and search the garret?"

"I'd like to see Simon Legree doing that," said Cassy. "No, indeed; he will be too glad to keep away. As to the servants, they would any of them stand and be shot, sooner than show their faces here."

Somewhat reassured, Emmeline settled herself back on her pillow.

"What did you mean, Cassy, by saying you would kill me?" she said, simply.

"I meant to stop your fainting," said Cassy, "and I did do it. And now I tell you, Emmeline, you must make up your mind *not* to faint, let what will come; there's no sort of need of it. If I had not stopped you, that wretch might have had his hands on you now."

Emmeline shuddered.

The two remained some time in silence. Cassy busied herself with a French book; Emmeline, overcome with the exhaustion, fell into a doze, and slept some time. She was awakened by loud shouts and outcries, the tramp of horses' feet, and the baying of dogs. She started up, with a faint shriek.

"Only the hunt coming back," said Cassy, coolly; "never fear. Look out of this knot-hole. Don't you see 'em all down there? Simon has to give up, for this night. Look, how muddy his horse is, flouncing about in the swamp; the dogs, too, look rather crestfallen. Ah, my good sir, you'll have to try the race again and again,— the game isn't there."

"O, don't speak a word!" said Emmeline; "what if they should hear you?"

"If they do hear anything, it will make them very particular to keep away," said Cassy. "No danger; we may make any noise we please, and it will only add to the effect."

At length the stillness of midnight settled down over the house. Legree, cursing his ill luck, and vowing dire vengeance on the morrow, went to bed.

CHAPTER XL

THE MARTYR

"Deem not the just by Heaven forgot! Though life its common gifts deny,—Though, with a crushed and bleeding heart, And spurned of man, he goes to die! For God hath marked each sorrowing day, And numbered every bitter tear, And heaven's long years of bliss shall pay For all his children suffer here." BRYANT.[1]

The longest way must have its close,—the gloomiest night will wear on to a morning. An eternal, inexorable lapse of moments is ever hurrying the day of the evil to an eternal night, and the night of the just to an eternal day. We have walked with our humble friend thus far in the valley of slavery; first through flowery fields of ease and indulgence, then through heart-breaking separations from all that man holds dear. Again, we have waited with him in a sunny island, where generous hands concealed his chains with flowers; and, lastly, we have followed him when the last ray of earthly hope went out in night, and seen how, in the blackness of earthly darkness, the firmament of the unseen has blazed with stars of new and significant lustre.

The morning-star now stands over the tops of the mountains, and gales and breezes, not of earth, show that the gates of day are unclosing.

The escape of Cassy and Emmeline irritated the before surly temper of Legree to the last degree; and his fury, as was to be expected, fell upon the defenceless head of Tom. When he hurriedly announced the tidings among his hands, there was a sudden light in Tom's eye, a sudden upraising of his hands, that did not escape him. He saw that he did not join the muster of the pursuers. He thought of forcing him to do it; but, having had, of old, experience of his inflexibility when commanded to take part in any deed of inhumanity, he would not, in his hurry, stop to enter into any conflict with him.

Tom, therefore, remained behind, with a few who had learned of him to pray, and offered up prayers for the escape of the fugitives.

---

[1] This poem does not appear in the collected works of William Cullen Bryant, nor in the collected poems of his brother, John Howard Bryant. It was probably copied from a newspaper or magazine.

CHAPTER XL

When Legree returned, baffled and disappointed, all the long-working hatred of his soul towards his slave began to gather in a deadly and desperate form. Had not this man braved him,—steadily, powerfully, resistlessly,—ever since he bought him? Was there not a spirit in him which, silent as it was, burned on him like the fires of perdition?

"I *hate* him!" said Legree, that night, as he sat up in his bed; "I *hate* him! And isn't he MINE? Can't I do what I like with him? Who's to hinder, I wonder?" And Legree clenched his fist, and shook it, as if he had something in his hands that he could rend in pieces.

But, then, Tom was a faithful, valuable servant; and, although Legree hated him the more for that, yet the consideration was still somewhat of a restraint to him.

The next morning, he determined to say nothing, as yet; to assemble a party, from some neighboring plantations, with dogs and guns; to surround the swamp, and go about the hunt systematically. If it succeeded, well and good; if not, he would summon Tom before him, and—his teeth clenched and his blood boiled—*then* he would break the fellow down, or—there was a dire inward whisper, to which his soul assented.

Ye say that the *interest* of the master is a sufficient safeguard for the slave. In the fury of man's mad will, he will wittingly, and with open eye, sell his own soul to the devil to gain his ends; and will he be more careful of his neighbor's body?

"Well," said Cassy, the next day, from the garret, as she reconnoitred through the knot-hole, "the hunt's going to begin again, today!"

Three or four mounted horsemen were curvetting about, on the space in front of the house; and one or two leashes of strange dogs were struggling with the negroes who held them, baying and barking at each other.

The men are, two of them, overseers of plantations in the vicinity; and others were some of Legree's associates at the tavern-bar of a neighboring city, who had come for the interest of the sport. A more hard-favored set, perhaps, could not be imagined. Legree was serving brandy, profusely, round among them, as also among the negroes, who had been detailed from the various plantations for this service; for it was an object to make every service of this kind, among the negroes, as much of a holiday as possible.

Cassy placed her ear at the knot-hole; and, as the morning air blew directly towards the house, she could overhear a good deal of the conversation. A grave sneer overcast the dark, severe gravity of her face, as she listened, and heard them divide out the ground, discuss the rival merits of the dogs, give orders about firing, and the treatment of each, in case of capture.

Cassy drew back; and, clasping her hands, looked upward, and said, "O, great Almighty God! we are *all* sinners; but what have *we* done, more than all the rest of the world, that we should be treated so?"

There was a terrible earnestness in her face and voice, as she spoke.

"If it wasn't for *you*, child," she said, looking at Emmeline, "I'd *go* out to them; and I'd thank any one of them that *would* shoot me down; for what use will freedom be to me? Can it give me back my children, or make me what I used to be?"

Emmeline, in her child-like simplicity, was half afraid of the dark moods of Cassy. She looked perplexed, but made no answer. She only took her hand, with a gentle, caressing movement.

"Don't!" said Cassy, trying to draw it away; "you'll get me to loving you; and I never mean to love anything, again!"

"Poor Cassy!" said Emmeline, "don't feel so! If the Lord gives us liberty, perhaps he'll give you back your daughter; at any rate, I'll be like a daughter to you. I know I'll never see my poor old mother again! I shall love you, Cassy, whether you love me or not!"

The gentle, child-like spirit conquered. Cassy sat down by her, put her arm round her neck, stroked her soft, brown hair; and Emmeline then wondered at the beauty of her magnificent eyes, now soft with tears.

"O, Em!" said Cassy, "I've hungered for my children, and thirsted for them, and my eyes fail with longing for them! Here! here!" she said, striking her breast, "it's all desolate, all empty! If God would give me back my children, then I could pray."

"You must trust him, Cassy," said Emmeline; "he is our Father!"

"His wrath is upon us," said Cassy; "he has turned away in anger."

"No, Cassy! He will be good to us! Let us hope in Him," said Emmeline,—"I always have had hope."

The hunt was long, animated, and thorough, but unsuccessful; and, with grave, ironic exultation, Cassy looked down on Legree, as, weary and dispirited, he alighted from his horse.

"Now, Quimbo," said Legree, as he stretched himself down in the sitting-room, "you jest go and walk that Tom up here, right away! The old cuss is at the bottom of this yer whole matter; and I'll have it out of his old black hide, or I'll know the reason why!"

Sambo and Quimbo, both, though hating each other, were joined in one mind by a no less cordial hatred of Tom. Legree had told them, at first, that he had bought him for a general overseer, in his absence; and this had begun an ill will, on their part, which had increased, in their debased and servile natures, as they saw him becoming obnoxious to their master's displeasure. Quimbo, therefore, departed, with a will, to execute his orders.

Tom heard the message with a forewarning heart; for he knew all the plan of the fugitives' escape, and the place of their present concealment;—he knew the deadly character of the man he had to deal with, and his despotic power. But he felt strong in God to meet death, rather than betray the helpless.

He sat his basket down by the row, and, looking up, said, "Into thy hands I commend my spirit! Thou hast redeemed me, oh Lord God of truth!" and then quietly yielded himself to the rough, brutal grasp with which Quimbo seized him.

"Ay, ay!" said the giant, as he dragged him along; "ye'll cotch it, now! I'll boun' Mas'r's back 's up *high!* No sneaking out, now! Tell ye, ye'll get it, and no mistake! See how ye'll look, now, helpin' Mas'r's niggers to run away! See what ye'll get!"

The savage words none of them reached that ear!—a higher voice there was saying, "Fear not them that kill the body, and, after that, have no more that they can do." Nerve and bone of that poor man's body vibrated to those words, as if touched by the finger of God; and he felt the strength of a thousand souls in one. As he passed along, the trees and bushes, the huts of his servitude, the whole scene of his degradation, seemed to whirl by him as the landscape by the rushing ear. His soul throbbed,—his home was in sight,—and the hour of release seemed at hand.

"Well, Tom!" said Legree, walking up, and seizing him grimly by the collar of his coat, and speaking through his teeth, in a paroxysm of determined rage, "do you know I've made up my mind to KILL YOU?"

"It's very likely, Mas'r," said Tom, calmly.

"I *have*," said Legree, with a grim, terrible calmness, "*done—just—that—thing*, Tom, unless you'll tell me what you know about these yer gals!"

Tom stood silent.

"D'ye hear?" said Legree, stamping, with a roar like that of an incensed lion. "Speak!"

"*I han't got nothing to tell, Mas'r*," said Tom, with a slow, firm, deliberate utterance.

"Do you dare to tell me, ye old black Christian, ye don't *know*?" said Legree.

Tom was silent.

"Speak!" thundered Legree, striking him furiously. "Do you know anything?"

"I know, Mas'r; but I can't tell anything. *I can die!*"

Legree drew in a long breath; and, suppressing his rage, took Tom by the arm, and, approaching his face almost to his, said, in a terrible voice, "Hark 'e, Tom!—ye think, 'cause I've let you off before, I don't mean what I say; but, this time, *I've made up my mind*, and counted the cost. You've always stood it out again' me: now, *I'll conquer ye, or kill ye!*—one or t' other. I'll count every drop of blood there is in you, and take 'em, one by one, till ye give up!"

Tom looked up to his master, and answered, "Mas'r, if you was sick, or in trouble, or dying, and I could save ye, I'd *give* ye my heart's blood; and, if taking every drop of blood in this poor old body would save your precious soul, I'd give 'em freely, as the Lord gave his for me. O, Mas'r! don't bring this great sin on your soul! It will hurt you more than 't will me! Do the worst you can, my troubles'll be over soon; but, if ye don't repent, yours won't *never* end!"

Like a strange snatch of heavenly music, heard in the lull of a tempest, this burst of feeling made a moment's blank pause. Legree stood aghast, and looked at Tom; and there was such a silence, that the tick of the old clock could be heard, measuring, with silent touch, the last moments of mercy and probation to that hardened heart.

It was but a moment. There was one hesitating pause,—one irresolute, relenting thrill,—and the spirit of evil came back, with seven-fold vehemence; and Legree, foaming with rage, smote his victim to the ground.

Scenes of blood and cruelty are shocking to our ear and heart. What man has nerve to do, man has not nerve to hear. What brother-man and brother-Christian must suffer, cannot be told us, even in our secret chamber, it so harrows the soul! And yet, oh my country! these things are done under the shadow of thy laws! O, Christ! thy church sees them, almost in silence!

But, of old, there was One whose suffering changed an instrument of torture, degradation and shame, into a symbol of glory, honor, and immortal life; and, where His spirit is, neither degrading stripes, nor blood, nor insults, can make the Christian's last struggle less than glorious.

Was he alone, that long night, whose brave, loving spirit was bearing up, in that old shed, against buffeting and brutal stripes?

Nay! There stood by him ONE,—seen by him alone,—"like unto the Son of God."

The tempter stood by him, too,—blinded by furious, despotic will,—every moment pressing him to shun that agony by the betrayal of the innocent. But the brave, true heart was firm on the Eternal Rock. Like his Master, he knew that, if he saved others, himself he could not save; nor could utmost extremity wring from him words, save of prayers and holy trust.

"He's most gone, Mas'r," said Sambo, touched, in spite of himself, by the patience of his victim.

"Pay away, till he gives up! Give it to him!—give it to him!" shouted Legree. "I'll take every drop of blood he has, unless he confesses!"

Tom opened his eyes, and looked upon his master. "Ye poor miserable critter!" he said, "there ain't no more ye can do! I forgive ye, with all my soul!" and he fainted entirely away.

"I b'lieve, my soul, he's done for, finally," said Legree, stepping forward, to look at him. "Yes, he is! Well, his mouth's shut up, at last,—that's one comfort!"

Yes, Legree; but who shall shut up that voice in thy soul? that soul, past repentance, past prayer, past hope, in whom the fire that never shall be quenched is already burning!

Yet Tom was not quite gone. His wondrous words and pious prayers had struck upon the hearts of the imbruted blacks, who had been the instruments of cruelty upon him; and, the instant Legree withdrew, they took him down, and, in their ignorance, sought to call him back to life,—as if *that* were any favor to him.

"Sartin, we 's been doin' a drefful wicked thing!" said Sambo; "hopes Mas'r'll have to 'count for it, and not we."

They washed his wounds,—they provided a rude bed, of some refuse cotton, for him to lie down on; and one of them, stealing up to the house, begged a drink of brandy of Legree, pretending that he was tired, and wanted it for himself. He brought it back, and poured it down Tom's throat.

"O, Tom!" said Quimbo, "we's been awful wicked to ye!"

"I forgive ye, with all my heart!" said Tom, faintly.

"O, Tom! do tell us who is *Jesus*, anyhow?" said Sambo;—"Jesus, that's been a standin' by you so, all this night!—Who is he?"

The word roused the failing, fainting spirit. He poured forth a few energetic sentences of that wondrous One,—his life, his death, his everlasting presence, and power to save.

They wept,—both the two savage men.

"Why didn't I never hear this before?" said Sambo; "but I do believe!—I can't help it! Lord Jesus, have mercy on us!"

"Poor critters!" said Tom, "I'd be willing to bar all I have, if it'll only bring ye to Christ! O, Lord! give me these two more souls, I pray!"

That prayer was answered!

CHAPTER XLI

THE YOUNG MASTER

Two days after, a young man drove a light wagon up through the avenue of China trees, and, throwing the reins hastily on the horse's neck, sprang out and inquired for the owner of the place.

It was George Shelby; and, to show how he came to be there, we must go back in our story.

The letter of Miss Ophelia to Mrs. Shelby had, by some unfortunate accident, been detained, for a month or two, at some remote post-office, before it reached its destination; and, of course, before it was received, Tom was already lost to view among the distant swamps of the Red River.

Mrs. Shelby read the intelligence with the deepest concern; but any immediate action upon it was an impossibility. She was then in attendance on the sick-bed of her husband, who lay delirious in the crisis of a fever. Master George Shelby, who, in the interval, had changed from a boy to a tall young man, was her constant and faithful assistant, and her only reliance in superintending his father's affairs. Miss Ophelia had taken the precaution to send them the name of the lawyer who did business for the St. Clares; and the most that, in the emergency, could be done, was to address a letter of inquiry to him. The sudden death of Mr. Shelby, a few days after, brought, of course, an absorbing pressure of other interests, for a season.

Mr. Shelby showed his confidence in his wife's ability, by appointing her sole executrix upon his estates; and thus immediately a large and complicated amount of business was brought upon her hands.

Mrs. Shelby, with characteristic energy, applied herself to the work of straightening the entangled web of affairs; and she and George were for some time occupied with collecting and examining accounts, selling property and settling debts; for Mrs. Shelby was determined that everything should be brought into tangible and recognizable shape, let the consequences to her prove what they might. In the mean time, they received a letter from the lawyer to whom Miss Ophelia had referred them, saying that he knew nothing of the matter; that the man was sold at a public auction, and that, beyond receiving the money, he knew nothing of the affair.

Neither George nor Mrs. Shelby could be easy at this result; and, accordingly, some six months after, the latter, having business for his mother, down the river, resolved to visit New Orleans, in person, and push his inquiries, in hopes of discovering Tom's whereabouts, and restoring him.

After some months of unsuccessful search, by the merest accident, George fell in with a man, in New Orleans, who happened to be possessed of the desired information; and with his money in his pocket, our hero took steamboat for Red River, resolving to find out and re-purchase his old friend.

He was soon introduced into the house, where he found Legree in the sitting-room.

Legree received the stranger with a kind of surly hospitality,

"I understand," said the young man, "that you bought, in New Orleans, a boy, named Tom. He used to be on my father's place, and I came to see if I couldn't buy him back."

Legree's brow grew dark, and he broke out, passionately: "Yes, I did buy such a fellow,—and a h—l of a bargain I had of it, too! The most rebellious, saucy, impudent dog! Set up my niggers to run away; got off two gals, worth eight hundred or a thousand apiece. He owned to that, and, when I bid him tell me where they was, he up and said he knew, but he wouldn't tell; and stood to it, though I gave him the cussedest flogging I ever gave nigger yet. I b'lieve he's trying to die; but I don't know as he'll make it out."

"Where is he?" said George, impetuously. "Let me see him." The cheeks of the young man were crimson, and his eyes flashed fire; but he prudently said nothing, as yet.

"He's in dat ar shed," said a little fellow, who stood holding George's horse.

Legree kicked the boy, and swore at him; but George, without saying another word, turned and strode to the spot.

Tom had been lying two days since the fatal night, not suffering, for every nerve of suffering was blunted and destroyed. He lay, for the most part, in a quiet stupor; for the laws of a powerful and well-knit frame would not at once release the imprisoned spirit. By stealth, there had been there, in the darkness of the night, poor desolated creatures, who stole from their scanty hours' rest, that they might repay to him some of those ministrations of love in which he had always been so abundant. Truly, those poor disciples had little to give,—only the cup of cold water; but it was given with full hearts.

Tears had fallen on that honest, insensible face,—tears of late repentance in the poor, ignorant heathen, whom his dying love and patience had awakened to repentance, and bitter prayers, breathed over him to a late-found Saviour, of whom they scarce knew more than the name, but whom the yearning ignorant heart of man never implores in vain.

Cassy, who had glided out of her place of concealment, and, by overhearing, learned the sacrifice that had been made for her and Emmeline, had been there, the night before, defying the danger of detection; and, moved by the last few words which the affectionate soul had yet strength to breathe, the long winter of despair, the ice of years, had given way, and the dark, despairing woman had wept and prayed.

When George entered the shed, he felt his head giddy and his heart sick.

"Is it possible,—is it possible?" said he, kneeling down by him. "Uncle Tom, my poor, poor old friend!"

Something in the voice penetrated to the ear of the dying. He moved his head gently, smiled, and said,

"Jesus can make a dying-bed Feel soft as down pillows are."

Tears which did honor to his manly heart fell from the young man's eyes, as he bent over his poor friend.

"O, dear Uncle Tom! do wake,—do speak once more! Look up! Here's Mas'r George,—your own little Mas'r George. Don't you know me?"

"Mas'r George!" said Tom, opening his eyes, and speaking in a feeble voice; "Mas'r George!" He looked bewildered.

Slowly the idea seemed to fill his soul; and the vacant eye became fixed and brightened, the whole face lighted up, the hard hands clasped, and tears ran down the cheeks.

"Bless the Lord! it is,—it is,—it's all I wanted! They haven't forgot me. It warms my soul; it does my heart good! Now I shall die content! Bless the Lord, on my soul!"

"You shan't die! you *mustn't* die, nor think of it! I've come to buy you, and take you home," said George, with impetuous vehemence.

"O, Mas'r George, ye're too late. The Lord's bought me, and is going to take me home,—and I long to go. Heaven is better than Kintuck."

"O, don't die! It'll kill me!—it'll break my heart to think what you've suffered,—and lying in this old shed, here! Poor, poor fellow!"

"Don't call me poor fellow!" said Tom, solemnly, "I *have* been poor fellow; but that's all past and gone, now. I'm right in the door, going into glory! O, Mas'r George! *Heaven has come!* I've got the victory!—the Lord Jesus has given it to me! Glory be to His name!"

George was awe-struck at the force, the vehemence, the power, with which these broken sentences were uttered. He sat gazing in silence.

Tom grasped his hand, and continued,—"Ye mustn't, now, tell Chloe, poor soul! how ye found me;—'t would be so drefful to her. Only tell her ye found me going into glory; and that I couldn't stay for no one. And tell her the Lord's stood by me everywhere and al'ays, and made everything light and easy. And oh, the poor chil'en, and the baby;—my old heart's been most broke for 'em, time and agin! Tell 'em all to follow me—follow me! Give my love to Mas'r, and dear good Missis, and everybody in the place! Ye don't know! 'Pears like I loves 'em all! I loves every creature everywhar!—it's nothing *but* love! O, Mas'r George! what a thing 't is to be a Christian!"

At this moment, Legree sauntered up to the door of the shed, looked in, with a dogged air of affected carelessness, and turned away.

"The old Satan!" said George, in his indignation. "It's a comfort to think the devil will pay *him* for this, some of these days!"

"O, don't!—oh, ye mustn't!" said Tom, grasping his hand; "he's a poor mis'able critter! it's awful to think on 't! Oh, if he only could repent, the Lord would forgive him now; but I'm 'feared he never will!"

"I hope he won't!" said George; "I never want to see *him* in heaven!"

"Hush, Mas'r George!—it worries me! Don't feel so! He an't done me no real harm,—only opened the gate of the kingdom for me; that's all!"

At this moment, the sudden flush of strength which the joy of meeting his young master had infused into the dying man gave way. A sudden sinking fell upon him; he closed his eyes; and that mysterious and sublime change passed over his face, that told the approach of other worlds.

He began to draw his breath with long, deep inspirations; and his broad chest rose and fell, heavily. The expression of his face was that of a conqueror.

"Who,—who,—who shall separate us from the love of Christ?" he said, in a voice that contended with mortal weakness; and, with a smile, he fell asleep.

George sat fixed with solemn awe. It seemed to him that the place was holy; and, as he closed the lifeless eyes, and rose up from the dead, only one thought possessed him,—that expressed by his simple old friend,—"What a thing it is to be a Christian!"

He turned: Legree was standing, sullenly, behind him.

Something in that dying scene had checked the natural fierceness of youthful passion. The presence of the man was simply loathsome to George; and he felt only an impulse to get away from him, with as few words as possible.

Fixing his keen dark eyes on Legree, he simply said, pointing to the dead, "You have got all you ever can of him. What shall I pay you for the body? I will take it away, and bury it decently."

"I don't sell dead niggers," said Legree, doggedly. "You are welcome to bury him where and when you like."

"Boys," said George, in an authoritative tone, to two or three negroes, who were looking at the body, "help me lift him up, and carry him to my wagon; and get me a spade."

One of them ran for a spade; the other two assisted George to carry the body to the wagon.

George neither spoke to nor looked at Legree, who did not countermand his orders, but stood, whistling, with an air of forced unconcern. He sulkily followed them to where the wagon stood at the door.

George spread his cloak in the wagon, and had the body carefully disposed of in it,—moving the seat, so as to give it room. Then he turned, fixed his eyes on Legree, and said, with forced composure,

"I have not, as yet, said to you what I think of this most atrocious affair;—this is not the time and place. But, sir, this innocent blood shall have justice. I will proclaim this murder. I will go to the very first magistrate, and expose you."

"Do!" said Legree, snapping his fingers, scornfully. "I'd like to see you doing it. Where you going to get witnesses?—how you going to prove it?—Come, now!"

George saw, at once, the force of this defiance. There was not a white person on the place; and, in all southern courts, the testimony of colored blood is nothing. He felt, at that moment, as if he could have rent the heavens with his heart's indignant cry for justice; but in vain.

"After all, what a fuss, for a dead nigger!" said Legree.

The word was as a spark to a powder magazine. Prudence was never a cardinal virtue of the Kentucky boy. George turned, and, with one indignant blow, knocked Legree flat upon his face; and, as he stood over him, blazing with wrath and defiance, he would have formed no bad personification of his great namesake triumphing over the dragon.

Some men, however, are decidedly bettered by being knocked down. If a man lays them fairly flat in the dust, they seem immediately to conceive a respect for him; and Legree was one of this sort. As he rose, therefore, and brushed the dust from his clothes, he eyed the slowly-retreating wagon with some evident consideration; nor did he open his mouth till it was out of sight.

Beyond the boundaries of the plantation, George had noticed a dry, sandy knoll, shaded by a few trees; there they made the grave.

"Shall we take off the cloak, Mas'r?" said the negroes, when the grave was ready.

"No, no,—bury it with him! It's all I can give you, now, poor Tom, and you shall have it."

They laid him in; and the men shovelled away, silently. They banked it up, and laid green turf over it.

"You may go, boys," said George, slipping a quarter into the hand of each. They lingered about, however.

"If young Mas'r would please buy us—" said one.

"We'd serve him so faithful!" said the other.

"Hard times here, Mas'r!" said the first. "Do, Mas'r, buy us, please!"

"I can't!—I can't!" said George, with difficulty, motioning them off; "it's impossible!"

The poor fellows looked dejected, and walked off in silence.

"Witness, eternal God!" said George, kneeling on the grave of his poor friend; "oh, witness, that, from this hour, I will do *what one man can* to drive out this curse of slavery from my land!"

There is no monument to mark the last resting-place of our friend. He needs none! His Lord knows where he lies, and will raise him up, immortal, to appear with him when he shall appear in his glory.

CHAPTER XLI

Pity him not! Such a life and death is not for pity! Not in the riches of omnipotence is the chief glory of God; but in self-denying, suffering love! And blessed are the men whom he calls to fellowship with him, bearing their cross after him with patience. Of such it is written, "Blessed are they that mourn, for they shall be comforted."

CHAPTER XLII

AN AUTHENTIC GHOST STORY

For some remarkable reason, ghostly legends were uncommonly rife, about this time, among the servants on Legree's place.

It was whisperingly asserted that footsteps, in the dead of night, had been heard descending the garret stairs, and patrolling the house. In vain the doors of the upper entry had been locked; the ghost either carried a duplicate key in its pocket, or availed itself of a ghost's immemorial privilege of coming through the keyhole, and promenaded as before, with a freedom that was alarming.

Authorities were somewhat divided, as to the outward form of the spirit, owing to a custom quite prevalent among negroes,—and, for aught we know, among whites, too,—of invariably shutting the eyes, and covering up heads under blankets, petticoats, or whatever else might come in use for a shelter, on these occasions. Of course, as everybody knows, when the bodily eyes are thus out of the lists, the spiritual eyes are uncommonly vivacious and perspicuous; and, therefore, there were abundance of full-length portraits of the ghost, abundantly sworn and testified to, which, as is often the case with portraits, agreed with each other in no particular, except the common family peculiarity of the ghost tribe,—the wearing of a *white sheet.* The poor souls were not versed in ancient history, and did not know that Shakspeare had authenticated this costume, by telling how

"The sheeted dead Did squeak and gibber in the streets of Rome."[1]

And, therefore, their all hitting upon this is a striking fact in pneumatology, which we recommend to the attention of spiritual media generally.

Be it as it may, we have private reasons for knowing that a tall figure in a white sheet did walk, at the most approved ghostly hours, around the Legree premises,—pass out the doors, glide about the house,—disappear at intervals, and, reappearing, pass up the silent stairway, into that fatal garret; and that, in the morning, the entry doors were all found shut and locked as firm as ever.

---

[1] Hamlet, Act I, scene 1, lines 115-116

CHAPTER XLII

Legree could not help overhearing this whispering; and it was all the more exciting to him, from the pains that were taken to conceal it from him. He drank more brandy than usual; held up his head briskly, and swore louder than ever in the daytime; but he had bad dreams, and the visions of his head on his bed were anything but agreeable. The night after Tom's body had been carried away, he rode to the next town for a carouse, and had a high one. Got home late and tired; locked his door, took out the key, and went to bed.

After all, let a man take what pains he may to hush it down, a human soul is an awful ghostly, unquiet possession, for a bad man to have. Who knows the metes and bounds of it? Who knows all its awful perhapses,—those shudderings and tremblings, which it can no more live down than it can outlive its own eternity! What a fool is he who locks his door to keep out spirits, who has in his own bosom a spirit he dares not meet alone,—whose voice, smothered far down, and piled over with mountains of earthliness, is yet like the forewarning trumpet of doom!

But Legree locked his door and set a chair against it; he set a night-lamp at the head of his bed; and put his pistols there. He examined the catches and fastenings of the windows, and then swore he "didn't care for the devil and all his angels," and went to sleep.

Well, he slept, for he was tired,—slept soundly. But, finally, there came over his sleep a shadow, a horror, an apprehension of something dreadful hanging over him. It was his mother's shroud, he thought; but Cassy had it, holding it up, and showing it to him. He heard a confused noise of screams and groanings; and, with it all, he knew he was asleep, and he struggled to wake himself. He was half awake. He was sure something was coming into his room. He knew the door was opening, but he could not stir hand or foot. At last he turned, with a start; the door *was* open, and he saw a hand putting out his light.

It was a cloudy, misty moonlight, and there he saw it!—something white, gliding in! He heard the still rustle of its ghostly garments. It stood still by his bed;—a cold hand touched his; a voice said, three times, in a low, fearful whisper, "Come! come! come!" And, while he lay sweating with terror, he knew not when or how, the thing was gone. He sprang out of bed, and pulled at the door. It was shut and locked, and the man fell down in a swoon.

After this, Legree became a harder drinker than ever before. He no longer drank cautiously, prudently, but imprudently and recklessly.

There were reports around the country, soon after that he was sick and dying. Excess had brought on that frightful disease that seems to throw the lurid shadows of a coming retribution back into the present life. None could bear the horrors of that sick room, when he raved and screamed, and spoke of sights which almost stopped the blood of those who heard him; and, at his dying bed, stood a stern, white, inexorable figure, saying, "Come! come! come!"

By a singular coincidence, on the very night that this vision appeared to Legree, the house-door was found open in the morning, and some of the negroes had seen two white figures gliding down the avenue towards the high-road.

It was near sunrise when Cassy and Emmeline paused, for a moment, in a little knot of trees near the town.

Cassy was dressed after the manner of the Creole Spanish ladies,—wholly in black. A small black bonnet on her head, covered by a veil thick with embroidery, concealed her face. It had been agreed that, in their escape, she was to personate the character of a Creole lady, and Emmeline that of her servant.

Brought up, from early life, in connection with the highest society, the language, movements and air of Cassy, were all in agreement with this idea; and she had still enough remaining with her, of a once splendid wardrobe, and sets of jewels, to enable her to personate the thing to advantage.

She stopped in the outskirts of the town, where she had noticed trunks for sale, and purchased a handsome one. This she requested the man to send along with her. And, accordingly, thus escorted by a boy wheeling her trunk, and Emmeline behind her, carrying her carpet-bag and sundry bundles, she made her appearance at the small tavern, like a lady of consideration.

The first person that struck her, after her arrival, was George Shelby, who was staying there, awaiting the next boat.

Cassy had remarked the young man from her loophole in the garret, and seen him bear away the body of Tom, and observed with secret exultation, his rencontre with Legree. Subsequently she had gathered, from the conversations she had overheard among the negroes, as she glided about in her ghostly disguise, after nightfall, who he was, and in what relation he stood to Tom. She, therefore, felt an immediate accession of confidence, when she found that he was, like herself, awaiting the next boat.

Cassy's air and manner, address, and evident command of money, prevented any rising disposition to suspicion in the hotel. People never inquire too closely into those who are fair on the main point, of paying well,—a thing which Cassy had foreseen when she provided herself with money.

In the edge of the evening, a boat was heard coming along, and George Shelby handed Cassy aboard, with the politeness which comes naturally to every Kentuckian, and exerted himself to provide her with a good state-room.

Cassy kept her room and bed, on pretext of illness, during the whole time they were on Red River; and was waited on, with obsequious devotion, by her attendant.

When they arrived at the Mississippi river, George, having learned that the course of the strange lady was upward, like his own, proposed to take a state-room for her on the same boat with himself,—good-naturedly compassionating her feeble health, and desirous to do what he could to assist her.

Behold, therefore, the whole party safely transferred to the good steamer Cincinnati, and sweeping up the river under a powerful head of steam.

Cassy's health was much better. She sat upon the guards, came to the table, and was remarked upon in the boat as a lady that must have been very handsome.

From the moment that George got the first glimpse of her face, he was troubled with one of those fleeting and indefinite likenesses, which almost every body can remember, and has been, at times, perplexed with. He could not keep himself from looking at her, and watching her perpetually. At table, or sitting at her state-room door, still she would encounter the young man's eyes fixed on her, and politely withdrawn, when she showed, by her countenance, that she was sensible to the observation.

Cassy became uneasy. She began to think that he suspected something; and finally resolved to throw herself entirely on his generosity, and intrusted him with her whole history.

George was heartily disposed to sympathize with any one who had escaped from Legree's plantation,—a place that he could not remember or speak of with patience,—and, with the courageous disregard of consequences which is characteristic of his age and state, he assured her that he would do all in his power to protect and bring them through.

The next state-room to Cassy's was occupied by a French lady, named De Thoux, who was accompanied by a fine little daughter, a child of some twelve summers.

This lady, having gathered, from George's conversation, that he was from Kentucky, seemed evidently disposed to cultivate his acquaintance; in which design she was seconded by the graces of her little girl, who was about as pretty a plaything as ever diverted the weariness of a fortnight's trip on a steamboat.

George's chair was often placed at her state-room door; and Cassy, as she sat upon the guards, could hear their conversation.

Madame de Thoux was very minute in her inquiries as to Kentucky, where she said she had resided in a former period of her life. George discovered, to his surprise, that her former residence must have been in his own vicinity; and her inquiries showed a knowledge of people and things in his vicinity, that was perfectly surprising to him.

"Do you know," said Madame de Thoux to him, one day, "of any man, in your neighborhood, of the name of Harris?"

"There is an old fellow, of that name, lives not far from my father's place," said George. "We never have had much intercourse with him, though."

"He is a large slave-owner, I believe," said Madame de Thoux, with a manner which seemed to betray more interest than she was exactly willing to show.

"He is," said George, looking rather surprised at her manner.

"Did you ever know of his having—perhaps, you may have heard of his having a mulatto boy, named George?"

"O, certainly,—George Harris,—I know him well; he married a servant of my mother's, but has escaped, now, to Canada."

"He has?" said Madame de Thoux, quickly. "Thank God!"

George looked a surprised inquiry, but said nothing.

Madame de Thoux leaned her head on her hand, and burst into tears.

"He is my brother," she said.

"Madame!" said George, with a strong accent of surprise.

"Yes," said Madame de Thoux, lifting her head, proudly, and wiping her tears, "Mr. Shelby, George Harris is my brother!"

"I am perfectly astonished," said George, pushing back his chair a pace or two, and looking at Madame de Thoux.

"I was sold to the South when he was a boy," said she. "I was bought by a good and generous man. He took me with him to the West Indies, set me free, and married me. It is but lately that he died; and I was going up to Kentucky, to see if I could find and redeem my brother."

"I heard him speak of a sister Emily, that was sold South," said George.

"Yes, indeed! I am the one," said Madame de Thoux;—"tell me what sort of a—"

"A very fine young man," said George, "notwithstanding the curse of slavery that lay on him. He sustained a first rate character, both for intelligence and principle. I know, you see," he said; "because he married in our family."

"What sort of a girl?" said Madame de Thoux, eagerly.

"A treasure," said George; "a beautiful, intelligent, amiable girl. Very pious. My mother had brought her up, and trained her as carefully, almost, as a daughter. She could read and write, embroider and sew, beautifully; and was a beautiful singer."

"Was she born in your house?" said Madame de Thoux.

"No. Father bought her once, in one of his trips to New Orleans, and brought her up as a present to mother. She was about eight or nine years old, then. Father would never tell mother what he gave for her; but, the other day, in looking over his old papers, we came across the bill of sale. He paid an extravagant sum for her, to be sure. I suppose, on account of her extraordinary beauty."

George sat with his back to Cassy, and did not see the absorbed expression of her countenance, as he was giving these details.

At this point in the story, she touched his arm, and, with a face perfectly white with interest, said, "Do you know the names of the people he bought her of?"

"A man of the name of Simmons, I think, was the principal in the transaction. At least, I think that was the name on the bill of sale."

"O, my God!" said Cassy, and fell insensible on the floor of the cabin.

George was wide awake now, and so was Madame de Thoux. Though neither of them could conjecture what was the cause of Cassy's fainting, still they made all the tumult which is proper in such cases;—George upsetting a wash-pitcher, and breaking two tumblers, in the warmth of his humanity; and various ladies in the cabin, hearing that somebody had fainted, crowded the state-room door, and kept out all the air they possibly could, so that, on the whole, everything was done that could be expected.

Poor Cassy! when she recovered, turned her face to the wall, and wept and sobbed like a child,—perhaps, mother, you can tell what she was thinking of! Perhaps you cannot,—but she felt as sure, in that hour, that God had had mercy on her, and that she should see her daughter,—as she did, months afterwards,—when—but we anticipate.

CHAPTER XLIII

RESULTS

The rest of our story is soon told. George Shelby, interested, as any other young man might be, by the romance of the incident, no less than by feelings of humanity, was at the pains to send to Cassy the bill of sale of Eliza; whose date and name all corresponded with her own knowledge of facts, and felt no doubt upon her mind as to the identity of her child. It remained now only for her to trace out the path of the fugitives.

Madame de Thoux and she, thus drawn together by the singular coincidence of their fortunes, proceeded immediately to Canada, and began a tour of inquiry among the stations, where the numerous fugitives from slavery are located. At Amherstberg they found the missionary with whom George and Eliza had taken shelter, on their first arrival in Canada; and through him were enabled to trace the family to Montreal.

George and Eliza had now been five years free. George had found constant occupation in the shop of a worthy machinist, where he had been earning a competent support for his family, which, in the mean time, had been increased by the addition of another daughter.

Little Harry—a fine bright boy—had been put to a good school, and was making rapid proficiency in knowledge.

The worthy pastor of the station, in Amherstberg, where George had first landed, was so much interested in the statements of Madame de Thoux and Cassy, that he yielded to the solicitations of the former, to accompany them to Montreal, in their search,—she bearing all the expense of the expedition.

The scene now changes to a small, neat tenement, in the outskirts of Montreal; the time, evening. A cheerful fire blazes on the hearth; a tea-table, covered with a snowy cloth, stands prepared for the evening meal. In one corner of the room was a table covered with a green cloth, where was an open writing-desk, pens, paper, and over it a shelf of well-selected books.

This was George's study. The same zeal for self-improvement, which led him to steal the much coveted arts of reading and writing, amid all the toil and discouragements of his early life, still led him to devote all his leisure time to self-cultivation.

At this present time, he is seated at the table, making notes from a volume of the family library he has been reading.

"Come, George," says Eliza, "you've been gone all day. Do put down that book, and let's talk, while I'm getting tea,—do."

And little Eliza seconds the effort, by toddling up to her father, and trying to pull the book out of his hand, and install herself on his knee as a substitute.

"O, you little witch!" says George, yielding, as, in such circumstances, man always must.

"That's right," says Eliza, as she begins to cut a loaf of bread. A little older she looks; her form a little fuller; her air more matronly than of yore; but evidently contented and happy as woman need be.

"Harry, my boy, how did you come on in that sum, today?" says George, as he laid his hand on his son's head.

Harry has lost his long curls; but he can never lose those eyes and eyelashes, and that fine, bold brow, that flushes with triumph, as he answers, "I did it, every bit of it, *myself*, father; and *nobody* helped me!"

"That's right," says his father; "depend on yourself, my son. You have a better chance than ever your poor father had."

At this moment, there is a rap at the door; and Eliza goes and opens it. The delighted—"Why! this you?"—calls up her husband; and the good pastor of Amherstberg is welcomed. There are two more women with him, and Eliza asks them to sit down.

Now, if the truth must be told, the honest pastor had arranged a little programme, according to which this affair was to develop itself; and, on the way up, all had very cautiously and prudently exhorted each other not to let things out, except according to previous arrangement.

What was the good man's consternation, therefore, just as he had motioned to the ladies to be seated, and was taking out his pocket-handkerchief to wipe his mouth, so as to proceed to his introductory speech in good order, when Madame de Thoux upset the whole plan, by throwing her arms around George's neck, and letting all out at once, by saying, "O, George! don't you know me? I'm your sister Emily."

Cassy had seated herself more composedly, and would have carried on her part very well, had not little Eliza suddenly appeared before her in exact shape and form, every outline and curl, just as her daughter was when she saw her last. The little thing peered up in her face; and Cassy caught her up in her arms, pressed her to her bosom, saying, what, at the moment she really believed, "Darling, I'm your mother!"

In fact, it was a troublesome matter to do up exactly in proper order; but the good pastor, at last, succeeded in getting everybody quiet, and delivering the speech with which he had intended to open the exercises; and in which, at last, he succeeded so well, that his whole audience were sobbing about him in a manner that ought to satisfy any orator, ancient or modern.

They knelt together, and the good man prayed,—for there are some feelings so agitated and tumultuous, that they can find rest only by being poured into the bosom of Almighty love,—and then, rising up, the new-found family embraced each other, with a holy trust in Him, who from such peril and dangers, and by such unknown ways, had brought them together.

The note-book of a missionary, among the Canadian fugitives, contains truth stranger than fiction. How can it be otherwise, when a system prevails which whirls families and scatters their members, as the wind whirls and scatters the leaves of autumn? These shores of refuge, like the eternal shore, often unite again, in glad communion, hearts that for long years have mourned each other as lost. And affecting beyond expression is the earnestness with which every new arrival among them is met, if, perchance, it may bring tidings of mother, sister, child or wife, still lost to view in the shadows of slavery.

Deeds of heroism are wrought here more than those of romance, when defying torture, and braving death itself, the fugitive voluntarily threads his way back to the terrors and perils of that dark land, that he may bring out his sister, or mother, or wife.

One young man, of whom a missionary has told us, twice re-captured, and suffering shameful stripes for his heroism, had escaped again; and, in a letter which we heard read, tells his friends that he is going back a third time, that he may, at last, bring away his sister. My good sir, is this man a hero, or a criminal? Would not you do as much for your sister? And can you blame him?

But, to return to our friends, whom we left wiping their eyes, and recovering themselves from too great and sudden a joy. They are now seated around the social board, and are getting decidedly companionable; only that Cassy, who keeps little Eliza on her lap, occasionally squeezes the little thing, in a manner that rather astonishes her, and obstinately refuses to have her mouth stuffed with cake to the extent the little one desires,—alleging, what the child rather wonders at, that she has got something better than cake, and doesn't want it.

And, indeed, in two or three days, such a change has passed over Cassy, that our readers would scarcely know her. The despairing, haggard expression of her face had given way to one of gentle trust. She seemed to sink, at once, into the bosom of the family, and take the little ones into her heart, as something for which it long had waited. Indeed, her love seemed to flow more naturally to the little Eliza than to her own daughter; for she was the exact image and body of the child whom she had lost. The little one was a flowery bond between mother and daughter, through whom grew up acquaintanceship and affection. Eliza's steady, consistent piety, regulated by the constant reading of the sacred word, made her a proper guide for the shattered and wearied mind of her mother. Cassy yielded at once, and with her whole soul, to every good influence, and became a devout and tender Christian.

After a day or two, Madame de Thoux told her brother more particularly of her affairs. The death of her husband had left her an ample fortune, which she generously offered to share with the family. When she asked George what way she could best apply it for him, he answered, "Give me an education, Emily; that has always been my heart's desire. Then, I can do all the rest."

On mature deliberation, it was decided that the whole family should go, for some years, to France; whither they sailed, carrying Emmeline with them.

The good looks of the latter won the affection of the first mate of the vessel; and, shortly after entering the port, she became his wife.

George remained four years at a French university, and, applying himself with an unintermitted zeal, obtained a very thorough education.

Political troubles in France, at last, led the family again to seek an asylum in this country.

George's feelings and views, as an educated man, may be best expressed in a letter to one of his friends.

"I feel somewhat at a loss, as to my future course. True, as you have said to me, I might mingle in the circles of the whites, in this country, my shade of color is so slight, and that of my wife and family scarce perceptible. Well, perhaps, on sufferance, I might. But, to tell you the truth, I have no wish to.

"My sympathies are not for my father's race, but for my mother's. To him I was no more than a fine dog or horse: to my poor heart-broken mother I was a *child*; and, though I never saw her, after the cruel sale that separated us, till she died, yet I *know* she always loved me dearly. I know it by my own heart. When I think of all she suffered, of my own early sufferings, of the distresses and struggles of my heroic wife, of my sister, sold in the New Orleans slave-market,—though I hope to have no unchristian sentiments, yet I may be excused for saying, I have no wish to pass for an American, or to identify myself with them.

"It is with the oppressed, enslaved African race that I cast in my lot; and, if I wished anything, I would wish myself two shades darker, rather than one lighter.

"The desire and yearning of my soul is for an African *nationality*. I want a people that shall have a tangible, separate existence of its own; and where am I to look for it? Not in Hayti; for in Hayti they had nothing to start with. A stream cannot rise above its fountain. The race that formed the character of the Haytiens was a worn-out, effeminate one; and, of course, the subject race will be centuries in rising to anything.

"Where, then, shall I look? On the shores of Africa I see a republic,—a republic formed of picked men, who, by energy and self-educating force, have, in many cases, individually, raised themselves above a condition of slavery. Having gone through a preparatory stage of feebleness, this republic has, at last, become an acknowledged nation on the face of the earth,—acknowledged by both France and England. There it is my wish to go, and find myself a people.

"I am aware, now, that I shall have you all against me; but, before you strike, hear me. During my stay in France, I have followed up, with intense interest, the history of my people in America. I have noted the struggle between abolitionist and colonizationist, and have received some impressions, as a distant spectator, which could never have occurred to me as a participator.

"I grant that this Liberia may have subserved all sorts of purposes, by being played off, in the hands of our oppressors, against us. Doubtless the scheme may have been used, in unjustifiable ways, as a means of retarding our emancipation. But the question to me is, Is there not a God above all man's schemes? May He not have over-ruled their designs, and founded for us a nation by them?

"In these days, a nation is born in a day. A nation starts, now, with all the great problems of republican life and civilization wrought out to its hand;—it has not to discover, but only to apply. Let us, then, all take hold together, with all our might, and see what we can do with this new enterprise, and the whole splendid continent of Africa opens before us and our children. *Our nation* shall roll the tide of civilization and Christianity along its shores, and plant there mighty republics, that, growing with the rapidity of tropical vegetation, shall be for all coming ages.

"Do you say that I am deserting my enslaved brethren? I think not. If I forget them one hour, one moment of my life, so may God forget me! But, what can I do for them, here? Can I break their chains? No, not as an individual; but, let me go and form part of a nation, which shall have a voice in the councils of nations, and then we can speak. A nation has a right to argue, remonstrate, implore, and present the cause of its race,—which an individual has not.

"If Europe ever becomes a grand council of free nations,—as I trust in God it will,—if, there, serfdom, and all unjust and oppressive social inequalities, are done away; and if they, as France and England have done, acknowledge our position,—then, in the great congress of nations, we will make our appeal, and present the cause of our enslaved and suffering race; and it cannot be that free, enlightened America will not then desire to wipe from her escutcheon that bar sinister which disgraces her among nations, and is as truly a curse to her as to the enslaved.

"But, you will tell me, our race have equal rights to mingle in the American republic as the Irishman, the German, the Swede. Granted, they have. We *ought* to be free to meet and mingle,—to rise by our individual worth, without any consideration of caste or color; and they who deny us this right are false to their own professed principles of human equality. We ought, in particular, to be allowed *here*. We have *more* than the rights of common men;—we have the claim of an injured race for reparation. But, then, *I do not want it*; I want a country, a nation, of my own. I think that the African race has peculiarities, yet to be unfolded in the light of civilization and Christianity, which, if not the same with those of the Anglo-Saxon, may prove to be, morally, of even a higher type.

"To the Anglo-Saxon race has been intrusted the destinies of the world, during its pioneer period of struggle and conflict. To that mission its stern, inflexible, energetic elements, were well adapted; but, as a Christian, I look for another era to arise. On its borders I trust we stand; and the throes that now convulse the nations are, to my hope, but the birth-pangs of an hour of universal peace and brotherhood.

"I trust that the development of Africa is to be essentially a Christian one. If not a dominant and commanding race, they are, at least, an affectionate, magnanimous, and forgiving one. Having been called in the furnace of injustice and oppression, they have need to bind closer to their hearts that sublime doctrine of love and forgiveness, through which alone they are to conquer, which it is to be their mission to spread over the continent of Africa.

"In myself, I confess, I am feeble for this,—full half the blood in my veins is the hot and hasty Saxon; but I have an eloquent preacher of the Gospel ever by my side, in the person of my beautiful wife. When I wander, her gentler spirit ever restores me, and keeps before my eyes the Christian calling and mission of our race. As a Christian patriot, as a teacher of Christianity, I go to *my country*,—my chosen, my glorious Africa!—and to her, in my heart, I sometimes apply those splendid words of prophecy: 'Whereas thou hast been forsaken and hated, so that no man went through thee; *I* will make thee an eternal excellence, a joy of many generations!'

"You will call me an enthusiast: you will tell me that I have not well considered what I am undertaking. But I have considered, and counted the cost. I go to *Liberia*, not as an Elysium of romance, but as to *a field of work*. I expect to work with both hands,—to work *hard*; to work against all sorts of difficulties and discouragements; and to work till I die. This is what I go for; and in this I am quite sure I shall not be disappointed.

"Whatever you may think of my determination, do not divorce me from your confidence; and think that, in whatever I do, I act with a heart wholly given to my people.

"GEORGE HARRIS."

George, with his wife, children, sister and mother, embarked for Africa, some few weeks after. If we are not mistaken, the world will yet hear from him there.

Of our other characters we have nothing very particular to write, except a word relating to Miss Ophelia and Topsy, and a farewell chapter, which we shall dedicate to George Shelby.

Miss Ophelia took Topsy home to Vermont with her, much to the surprise of the grave deliberative body whom a New Englander recognizes under the term "*Our folks*." "Our folks," at first, thought it an odd and unnecessary addition to their well-trained domestic establishment; but, so thoroughly efficient was Miss Ophelia in her conscientious endeavor to do her duty by her *élève*, that the child rapidly grew in grace and in favor with the family and neighborhood. At the age of womanhood, she was, by her own request, baptized, and became a member of the Christian church in the place; and showed so much intelligence, activity and zeal, and desire to do good in the world, that she was at last recommended, and approved as a missionary to one of the stations in Africa; and we have heard that the same activity and ingenuity which, when a child, made her so multiform and restless in her developments, is now employed, in a safer and wholesomer manner, in teaching the children of her own country.

P.S.—It will be a satisfaction to some mother, also, to state, that some inquiries, which were set on foot by Madame de Thoux, have resulted recently in the discovery of Cassy's son. Being a young man of energy, he had escaped, some years before his mother, and been received and educated by friends of the oppressed in the north. He will soon follow his family to Africa.

CHAPTER XLIV

THE LIBERATOR

George Shelby had written to his mother merely a line, stating the day that she might expect him home. Of the death scene of his old friend he had not the heart to write. He had tried several times, and only succeeded in half choking himself; and invariably finished by tearing up the paper, wiping his eyes, and rushing somewhere to get quiet.

There was a pleased bustle all though the Shelby mansion, that day, in expectation of the arrival of young Mas'r George.

Mrs. Shelby was seated in her comfortable parlor, where a cheerful hickory fire was dispelling the chill of the late autumn evening. A supper-table, glittering with plate and cut glass, was set out, on whose arrangements our former friend, old Chloe, was presiding.

Arrayed in a new calico dress, with clean, white apron, and high, well-starched turban, her black polished face glowing with satisfaction, she lingered, with needless punctiliousness, around the arrangements of the table, merely as an excuse for talking a little to her mistress.

"Laws, now! won't it look natural to him?" she said. "Thar,—I set his plate just whar he likes it round by the fire. Mas'r George allers wants de warm seat. O, go way!—why didn't Sally get out de *best* tea-pot,—de little new one, Mas'r George got for Missis, Christmas? I'll have it out! And Missis has heard from Mas'r George?" she said, inquiringly.

"Yes, Chloe; but only a line, just to say he would be home tonight, if he could,—that's all."

"Didn't say nothin' 'bout my old man, s'pose?" said Chloe, still fidgeting with the tea-cups.

"No, he didn't. He did not speak of anything, Chloe. He said he would tell all, when he got home."

"Jes like Mas'r George,—he's allers so ferce for tellin' everything hisself. I allers minded dat ar in Mas'r George. Don't see, for my part, how white people gen'lly can bar to hev to write things much as they do, writin' 's such slow, oneasy kind o' work."

Mrs. Shelby smiled.

"I'm a thinkin' my old man won't know de boys and de baby. Lor'! she's de biggest gal, now,—good she is, too, and peart, Polly is. She's out to the house, now, watchin' de hoe-cake. I 's got jist de very pattern my old man liked so much, a bakin'. Jist sich as I gin him the mornin' he was took off. Lord bless us! how I felt, dat ar morning!"

Mrs. Shelby sighed, and felt a heavy weight on her heart, at this allusion. She had felt uneasy, ever since she received her son's letter, lest something should prove to be hidden behind the veil of silence which he had drawn.

"Missis has got dem bills?" said Chloe, anxiously.

"Yes, Chloe."

"'Cause I wants to show my old man dem very bills de *perfectioner* gave me. 'And,' say he, 'Chloe, I wish you'd stay longer.' 'Thank you, Mas'r,' says I, 'I would, only my old man's coming home, and Missis,—she can't do without me no longer.' There's jist what I telled him. Berry nice man, dat Mas'r Jones was."

Chloe had pertinaciously insisted that the very bills in which her wages had been paid should be preserved, to show her husband, in memorial of her capability. And Mrs. Shelby had readily consented to humor her in the request.

"He won't know Polly,—my old man won't. Laws, it's five year since they tuck him! She was a baby den,—couldn't but jist stand. Remember how tickled he used to be, cause she would keep a fallin' over, when she sot out to walk. Laws a me!"

The rattling of wheels now was heard.

"Mas'r George!" said Aunt Chloe, starting to the window.

Mrs. Shelby ran to the entry door, and was folded in the arms of her son. Aunt Chloe stood anxiously straining her eyes out into the darkness.

"O, *poor* Aunt Chloe!" said George, stopping compassionately, and taking her hard, black hand between both his; "I'd have given all my fortune to have brought him with me, but he's gone to a better country."

There was a passionate exclamation from Mrs. Shelby, but Aunt Chloe said nothing.

The party entered the supper-room. The money, of which Chloe was so proud, was still lying on the table.

"Thar," said she, gathering it up, and holding it, with a trembling hand, to her mistress, "don't never want to see nor hear on 't again. Jist as I knew 't would be,—sold, and murdered on dem ar' old plantations!"

Chloe turned, and was walking proudly out of the room. Mrs. Shelby followed her softly, and took one of her hands, drew her down into a chair, and sat down by her.

"My poor, good Chloe!" said she.

Chloe leaned her head on her mistress' shoulder, and sobbed out, "O Missis! 'scuse me, my heart's broke,—dat's all!"

"I know it is," said Mrs. Shelby, as her tears fell fast; "and *I* cannot heal it, but Jesus can. He healeth the broken hearted, and bindeth up their wounds."

There was a silence for some time, and all wept together. At last, George, sitting down beside the mourner, took her hand, and, with simple pathos, repeated the triumphant scene of her husband's death, and his last messages of love.

About a month after this, one morning, all the servants of the Shelby estate were convened together in the great hall that ran through the house, to hear a few words from their young master.

To the surprise of all, he appeared among them with a bundle of papers in his hand, containing a certificate of freedom to every one on the place, which he read successively, and presented, amid the sobs and tears and shouts of all present.

Many, however, pressed around him, earnestly begging him not to send them away; and, with anxious faces, tendering back their free papers.

"We don't want to be no freer than we are. We's allers had all we wanted. We don't want to leave de ole place, and Mas'r and Missis, and de rest!"

"My good friends," said George, as soon as he could get a silence, "there'll be no need for you to leave me. The place wants as many hands to work it as it did before. We need the same about the house that we did before. But, you are now free men and free women. I shall pay you wages for your work, such as we shall agree on. The advantage is, that in case of my getting in debt, or dying,—things that might happen,—you cannot now be taken up and sold. I expect to carry on the estate, and to teach you what, perhaps, it will take you some time to learn,—how to use the rights I give you as free men and women. I expect you to be good, and willing to learn; and I trust in God that I shall be faithful, and willing to teach. And now, my friends, look up, and thank God for the blessing of freedom."

An aged, partriarchal negro, who had grown gray and blind on the estate, now rose, and, lifting his trembling hand said, "Let us give thanks unto the Lord!" As all kneeled by one consent, a more touching and hearty *Te Deum* never ascended to heaven, though borne on the peal of organ, bell and cannon, than came from that honest old heart.

On rising, another struck up a Methodist hymn, of which the burden was,

"The year of Jubilee is come,— Return, ye ransomed sinners, home."

"One thing more," said George, as he stopped the congratulations of the throng; "you all remember our good old Uncle Tom?"

George here gave a short narration of the scene of his death, and of his loving farewell to all on the place, and added,

"It was on his grave, my friends, that I resolved, before God, that I would never own another slave, while it was possible to free him; that nobody, through me, should ever run the risk of being parted from home and friends, and dying on a lonely plantation, as he died. So, when you rejoice in your freedom, think that you owe it to that good old soul, and pay it back in kindness to his wife and children. Think of your freedom, every time you see UNCLE TOM'S CABIN; and let it be a memorial to put you all in mind to follow in his steps, and be honest and faithful and Christian as he was."

CHAPTER XLV

CONCLUDING REMARKS

The writer has often been inquired of, by correspondents from different parts of the country, whether this narrative is a true one; and to these inquiries she will give one general answer.

The separate incidents that compose the narrative are, to a very great extent, authentic, occurring, many of them, either under her own observation, or that of her personal friends. She or her friends have observed characters the counterpart of almost all that are here introduced; and many of the sayings are word for word as heard herself, or reported to her.

The personal appearance of Eliza, the character ascribed to her, are sketches drawn from life. The incorruptible fidelity, piety and honesty, of Uncle Tom, had more than one development, to her personal knowledge. Some of the most deeply tragic and romantic, some of the most terrible incidents, have also their parallels in reality. The incident of the mother's crossing the Ohio river on the ice is a well-known fact. The story of "old Prue," in the second volume, was an incident that fell under the personal observation of a brother of the writer, then collecting-clerk to a large mercantile house, in New Orleans. From the same source was derived the character of the planter Legree. Of him her brother thus wrote, speaking of visiting his plantation, on a collecting tour; "He actually made me feel of his fist, which was like a blacksmith's hammer, or a nodule of iron, telling me that it was 'calloused with knocking down niggers.' When I left the plantation, I drew a long breath, and felt as if I had escaped from an ogre's den."

That the tragical fate of Tom, also, has too many times had its parallel, there are living witnesses, all over our land, to testify. Let it be remembered that in all southern states it is a principle of jurisprudence that no person of colored lineage can testify in a suit against a white, and it will be easy to see that such a case may occur, wherever there is a man whose passions outweigh his interests, and a slave who has manhood or principle enough to resist his will. There is, actually, nothing to protect the slave's life, but the *character* of the master. Facts too shocking to be contemplated occasionally force their way to the public ear, and the comment that one often hears made on them is more shocking than the thing itself. It is said,

"Very likely such cases may now and then occur, but they are no sample of general practice." If the laws of New England were so arranged that a master could *now and then* torture an apprentice to death, would it be received with equal composure? Would it be said, "These cases are rare, and no samples of general practice"? This injustice is an *inherent* one in the slave system,—it cannot exist without it.

The public and shameless sale of beautiful mulatto and quadroon girls has acquired a notoriety, from the incidents following the capture of the Pearl. We extract the following from the speech of Hon. Horace Mann, one of the legal counsel for the defendants in that case. He says: "In that company of seventy-six persons, who attempted, in 1848, to escape from the District of Columbia in the schooner Pearl, and whose officers I assisted in defending, there were several young and healthy girls, who had those peculiar attractions of form and feature which connoisseurs prize so highly. Elizabeth Russel was one of them. She immediately fell into the slave-trader's fangs, and was doomed for the New Orleans market. The hearts of those that saw her were touched with pity for her fate. They offered eighteen hundred dollars to redeem her; and some there were who offered to give, that would not have much left after the gift; but the fiend of a slave-trader was inexorable. She was despatched to New Orleans; but, when about half way there, God had mercy on her, and smote her with death. There were two girls named Edmundson in the same company. When about to be sent to the same market, an older sister went to the shambles, to plead with the wretch who owned them, for the love of God, to spare his victims. He bantered her, telling what fine dresses and fine furniture they would have. 'Yes,' she said, 'that may do very well in this life, but what will become of them in the next?' They too were sent to New Orleans; but were afterwards redeemed, at an enormous ransom, and brought back." Is it not plain, from this, that the histories of Emmeline and Cassy may have many counterparts?

Justice, too, obliges the author to state that the fairness of mind and generosity attributed to St. Clare are not without a parallel, as the following anecdote will show. A few years since, a young southern gentleman was in Cincinnati, with a favorite servant, who had been his personal attendant from a boy. The young man took advantage of this opportunity to secure his own freedom, and fled to the protection of a Quaker, who was quite noted in affairs of this kind. The owner was exceedingly indignant. He had always treated the slave with such indulgence, and his confidence in his affection was such, that he believed he must have been practised upon to induce him to revolt from him. He visited the Quaker, in high anger; but, being possessed of uncommon candor and fairness, was soon quieted by his arguments and representations. It was a side of the subject which he never had heard,—never had thought on; and he immediately told the Quaker that, if his slave would, to his own face, say that it was his desire to be free, he would liberate him. An interview was forthwith procured, and Nathan was asked by his young master whether he had ever had any reason to complain of his treatment, in any respect.

"No, Mas'r," said Nathan; "you've always been good to me."

"Well, then, why do you want to leave me?"

"Mas'r may die, and then who get me?—I'd rather be a free man."

After some deliberation, the young master replied, "Nathan, in your place, I think I should feel very much so, myself. You are free."

He immediately made him out free papers; deposited a sum of money in the hands of the Quaker, to be judiciously used in assisting him to start in life, and left a very sensible and kind letter of advice to the young man. That letter was for some time in the writer's hands.

The author hopes she has done justice to that nobility, generosity, and humanity, which in many cases characterize individuals at the South. Such instances save us from utter despair of our kind. But, she asks any person, who knows the world, are such characters *common*, anywhere?

For many years of her life, the author avoided all reading upon or allusion to the subject of slavery, considering it as too painful to be inquired into, and one which advancing light and civilization would certainly live down. But, since the legislative act of 1850, when she heard, with perfect surprise and consternation, Christian and humane people actually recommending the remanding escaped fugitives into slavery, as a duty binding on good citizens,—when she heard, on all hands, from kind, compassionate and estimable people, in the free states of the North, deliberations and discussions as to what Christian duty could be on this head,—she could only think, These men and Christians cannot know what slavery is; if they did, such a question could never be open for discussion. And from this arose a desire to exhibit it in a *living dramatic reality*. She has endeavored to show it fairly, in its best and its worst phases. In its *best* aspect, she has, perhaps, been successful; but, oh! who shall say what yet remains untold in that valley and shadow of death, that lies the other side?

To you, generous, noble-minded men and women, of the South,—you, whose virtue, and magnanimity and purity of character, are the greater for the severer trial it has encountered,—to you is her appeal. Have you not, in your own secret souls, in your own private conversings, felt that there are woes and evils, in this accursed system, far beyond what are here shadowed, or can be shadowed? Can it be otherwise? Is *man* ever a creature to be trusted with wholly irresponsible power? And does not the slave system, by denying the slave all legal right of testimony, make every individual owner an irresponsible despot? Can anybody fail to make the inference what the practical result will be? If there is, as we admit, a public sentiment among you, men of honor, justice and humanity, is there not also another kind of public sentiment among the ruffian, the brutal and debased? And cannot the ruffian, the brutal, the debased, by slave law, own just as many slaves as the best and purest? Are the honorable, the just, the high-minded and compassionate, the majority anywhere in this world?

The slave-trade is now, by American law, considered as piracy. But a slave-trade, as systematic as ever was carried on on the coast of Africa, is an inevitable attendant and result of American slavery. And its heart-break and its horrors, can they be told?

The writer has given only a faint shadow, a dim picture, of the anguish and despair that are, at this very moment, riving thousands of hearts, shattering thousands of families, and driving a helpless and sensitive race to frenzy and despair. There are those living who know the mothers whom this accursed traffic has driven to the murder of their children; and themselves seeking in death a shelter from woes more dreaded than death. Nothing of tragedy can be written, can be spoken, can be conceived, that equals the frightful reality of scenes daily and hourly acting on our shores, beneath the shadow of American law, and the shadow of the cross of Christ.

And now, men and women of America, is this a thing to be trifled with, apologized for, and passed over in silence? Farmers of Massachusetts, of New Hampshire, of Vermont, of Connecticut, who read this book by the blaze of your winter-evening fire,—strong-hearted, generous sailors and ship-owners of Maine,—is this a thing for you to countenance and encourage? Brave and generous men of New York, farmers of rich and joyous Ohio, and ye of the wide prairie states,—answer, is this a thing for you to protect and countenance? And you, mothers of America,—you who have learned, by the cradles of your own children, to love and feel for all mankind,—by the sacred love you bear your child; by your joy in his beautiful, spotless infancy; by the motherly pity and tenderness with which you guide his growing years; by the anxieties of his education; by the prayers you breathe for his soul's eternal good;—I beseech you, pity the mother who has all your affections, and not one legal right to protect, guide, or educate, the child of her bosom! By the sick hour of your child; by those dying eyes, which you can never forget; by those last cries, that wrung your heart when you could neither help nor save; by the desolation of that empty cradle, that silent nursery,—I beseech you, pity those mothers that are constantly made childless by the American slave-trade! And say, mothers of America, is this a thing to be defended, sympathized with, passed over in silence?

Do you say that the people of the free state have nothing to do with it, and can do nothing? Would to God this were true! But it is not true. The people of the free states have defended, encouraged, and participated; and are more guilty for it, before God, than the South, in that they have not the apology of education or custom.

If the mothers of the free states had all felt as they should, in times past, the sons of the free states would not have been the holders, and, proverbially, the hardest masters of slaves; the sons of the free states would not have connived at the extension of slavery, in our national body; the sons of the free states would not, as they do, trade the souls and bodies of men as an equivalent to money, in their mercantile dealings. There are multitudes of slaves temporarily owned, and sold again, by merchants in northern cities; and shall the whole guilt or obloquy of slavery fall only on the South?

Northern men, northern mothers, northern Christians, have something more to do than denounce their brethren at the South; they have to look to the evil among themselves.

But, what can any individual do? Of that, every individual can judge. There is one thing that every individual can do,—they can see to it that *they feel right*. An atmosphere of sympathetic influence encircles every human being; and the man or woman who *feels* strongly, healthily and justly, on the great interests of humanity, is a constant benefactor to the human race. See, then, to your sympathies in this matter! Are they in harmony with the sympathies of Christ? or are they swayed and perverted by the sophistries of worldly policy?

Christian men and women of the North! still further,—you have another power; you can *pray!* Do you believe in prayer? or has it become an indistinct apostolic tradition? You pray for the heathen abroad; pray also for the heathen at home. And pray for those distressed Christians whose whole chance of religious improvement is an accident of trade and sale; from whom any adherence to the morals of Christianity is, in many cases, an impossibility, unless they have given them, from above, the courage and grace of martyrdom.

But, still more. On the shores of our free states are emerging the poor, shattered, broken remnants of families,—men and women, escaped, by miraculous providences from the surges of slavery,—feeble in knowledge, and, in many cases, infirm in moral constitution, from a system which confounds and confuses every principle of Christianity and morality. They come to seek a refuge among you; they come to seek education, knowledge, Christianity.

What do you owe to these poor unfortunates, oh Christians? Does not every American Christian owe to the African race some effort at reparation for the wrongs that the American nation has brought upon them? Shall the doors of churches and school-houses be shut upon them? Shall states arise and shake them out? Shall the church of Christ hear in silence the taunt that is thrown at them, and shrink away from the helpless hand that they stretch out; and, by her silence, encourage the cruelty that would chase them from our borders? If it must be so, it will be a mournful spectacle. If it must be so, the country will have reason to tremble, when it remembers that the fate of nations is in the hands of One who is very pitiful, and of tender compassion.

Do you say, "We don't want them here; let them go to Africa"?

That the providence of God has provided a refuge in Africa, is, indeed, a great and noticeable fact; but that is no reason why the church of Christ should throw off that responsibility to this outcast race which her profession demands of her.

To fill up Liberia with an ignorant, inexperienced, half-barbarized race, just escaped from the chains of slavery, would be only to prolong, for ages, the period of struggle and conflict which attends the inception of new enterprises. Let the church of the north receive these poor sufferers in the spirit of Christ; receive them to the educating advantages of Christian republican society and schools, until they have attained to somewhat of a moral and intellectual maturity, and then assist them in their passage to those shores, where they may put in practice the lessons they have learned in America.

There is a body of men at the north, comparatively small, who have been doing this; and, as the result, this country has already seen examples of men, formerly slaves, who have rapidly acquired property, reputation, and education. Talent has been developed, which, considering the circumstances, is certainly remarkable; and, for moral traits of honesty, kindness, tenderness of feeling,—for heroic efforts and self-denials, endured for the ransom of brethren and friends yet in slavery,—they have been remarkable to a degree that, considering the influence under which they were born, is surprising.

The writer has lived, for many years, on the frontier-line of slave states, and has had great opportunities of observation among those who formerly were slaves. They have been in her family as servants; and, in default of any other school to receive them, she has, in many cases, had them instructed in a family school, with her own children. She has also the testimony of missionaries, among the fugitives in Canada, in coincidence with her own experience; and her deductions, with regard to the capabilities of the race, are encouraging in the highest degree.

The first desire of the emancipated slave, generally, is for *education.* There is nothing that they are not willing to give or do to have their children instructed, and, so far as the writer has observed herself, or taken the testimony of teachers among them, they are remarkably intelligent and quick to learn. The results of schools, founded for them by benevolent individuals in Cincinnati, fully establish this.

The author gives the following statement of facts, on the authority of Professor C. E. Stowe, then of Lane Seminary, Ohio, with regard to emancipated slaves, now resident in Cincinnati; given to show the capability of the race, even without any very particular assistance or encouragement.

The initial letters alone are given. They are all residents of Cincinnati.

"B——. Furniture maker; twenty years in the city; worth ten thousand dollars, all his own earnings; a Baptist.

"C——. Full black; stolen from Africa; sold in New Orleans; been free fifteen years; paid for himself six hundred dollars; a farmer; owns several farms in Indiana; Presbyterian; probably worth fifteen or twenty thousand dollars, all earned by himself.

"K——. Full black; dealer in real estate; worth thirty thousand dollars; about forty years old; free six years; paid eighteen hundred dollars for his family; member of the Baptist church; received a legacy from his master, which he has taken good care of, and increased.

"G——. Full black; coal dealer; about thirty years old; worth eighteen thousand dollars; paid for himself twice, being once defrauded to the amount of sixteen hundred dollars; made all his money by his own efforts—much of it while a slave, hiring his time of his master, and doing business for himself; a fine, gentlemanly fellow.

"W——. Three-fourths black; barber and waiter; from Kentucky; nineteen years free; paid for self and family over three thousand dollars; deacon in the Baptist church.

"G. D——. Three-fourths black; white-washer; from Kentucky; nine years free; paid fifteen hundred dollars for self and family; recently died, aged sixty; worth six thousand dollars."

Professor Stowe says, "With all these, except G——, I have been, for some years, personally acquainted, and make my statements from my own knowledge."

The writer well remembers an aged colored woman, who was employed as a washerwoman in her father's family. The daughter of this woman married a slave. She was a remarkably active and capable young woman, and, by her industry and thrift, and the most persevering self-denial, raised nine hundred dollars for her husband's freedom, which she paid, as she raised it, into the hands of his master. She yet wanted a hundred dollars of the price, when he died. She never recovered any of the money.

These are but few facts, among multitudes which might be adduced, to show the self-denial, energy, patience, and honesty, which the slave has exhibited in a state of freedom.

And let it be remembered that these individuals have thus bravely succeeded in conquering for themselves comparative wealth and social position, in the face of every disadvantage and discouragement. The colored man, by the law of Ohio, cannot be a voter, and, till within a few years, was even denied the right of testimony in legal suits with the white. Nor are these instances confined to the State of Ohio. In all states of the Union we see men, but yesterday burst from the shackles of slavery, who, by a self-educating force, which cannot be too much admired, have risen to highly respectable stations in society. Pennington, among clergymen, Douglas and Ward, among editors, are well known instances.

If this persecuted race, with every discouragement and disadvantage, have done thus much, how much more they might do if the Christian church would act towards them in the spirit of her Lord!

This is an age of the world when nations are trembling and convulsed. A mighty influence is abroad, surging and heaving the world, as with an earthquake. And is America safe? Every nation that carries in its bosom great and unredressed injustice has in it the elements of this last convulsion.

For what is this mighty influence thus rousing in all nations and languages those groanings that cannot be uttered, for man's freedom and equality?

O, Church of Christ, read the signs of the times! Is not this power the spirit of Him whose kingdom is yet to come, and whose will to be done on earth as it is in heaven?

But who may abide the day of his appearing? "for that day shall burn as an oven: and he shall appear as a swift witness against those that oppress the hireling in his wages, the widow and the fatherless, and that *turn aside the stranger in his right*: and he shall break in pieces the oppressor."

Are not these dread words for a nation bearing in her bosom so mighty an injustice? Christians! every time that you pray that the kingdom of Christ may come, can you forget that prophecy associates, in dread fellowship, the *day of vengeance* with the year of his redeemed?

A day of grace is yet held out to us. Both North and South have been guilty before God; and the *Christian church* has a heavy account to answer. Not by combining together, to protect injustice and cruelty, and making a common capital of sin, is this Union to be saved,—but by repentance, justice and mercy; for, not surer is the eternal law by which the millstone sinks in the ocean, than that stronger law, by which injustice and cruelty shall bring on nations the wrath of Almighty God!

THE KEY TO UNCLE TOM'S CABIN

PART I

Stowe wrote this book to defend her novel against one of the most wide-spread complaints that pro-slavery critics lodged against it -- that as an account of slavery *Uncle Tom's Cabin* was wholly false, or at least wildly exaggerated. Thus *The Key* is organized around that defensive project, taking up her major characters one at a time, for example, to cite real life equivalents to them. At the same time, defending her novel led her to mount a more aggressive attack on slavery in the South than the novel itself had. In the novel she works hard to be sympathetic to white southerners as well as black slaves; here, her prose seems much angrier, both morally and rhetorically more contemptuous. One explanation for this sharper tone could be the novel's reception in the South, where no one seems to have appreciated her attempt to be fair. Stowe was probably unprepared for the South's shrill rejection of the book.

The Key is prickly, dense book, with none of the readability of *Uncle Tom's Cabin*. When it first came out, it was also a best seller, though it's likely many bought it without understanding its nature. It's also a kind of fiction. Although it claims to be about the sources Stowe consulted while writing the novel, for example, she read many of the works cited here only after the novel was published.

CHAPTER I.

AT different times, doubt has been expressed whether the scenes and characters pourtrayed in "Uncle Tom's Cabin" convey a fair representation of slavery as it at present exists. This work, more, perhaps, than any other work of fiction that ever was written, has been a collection and arrangement of real incidents, of actions really performed, of words and expressions really uttered, grouped together with reference to a general result, in the same manner that the mosaic artist groups his fragments of various stones into one general picture. His is a mosaic of gems—this is a mosaic of facts.

Artistically considered, it might not be best to point out in which quarry and from which region each fragment of the mosaic picture had its origin; and it is equally unartistic to disentangle the glittering web of fiction, and show out of what real warp and woof it is woven, and with what real colouring dyed. But the book had a purpose entirely transcending the artistic one, and accordingly encounters at the hands of the public demands not usually made on fictitious works. It is *treated* as a reality—sifted, tried, and tested, as a reality; and therefore as a reality it may be proper that it should be defended.

The writer acknowledges that the book is a very inadequate representation of slavery; and it is so, necessarily, for this reason—that slavery, in some of its workings, is too dreadful for the purposes of art. A work which should represent it strictly as it is would be a work which could not be read; and all works which ever mean to give pleasure must draw a veil somewhere, or they cannot succeed.

The author will now proceed along the course of the story, from the first page, and develop, as far as possible, the incidents by which different parts were suggested.

CHAPTER II.

MR. HALEY.

IN the very first chapter of the book we encounter the character of the negro-trader, Mr. Haley. His name stands at the head of this chapter as the representative of all the different characters introduced in the work which exhibit the trader, the kidnapper, the negro-catcher, the negro-whipper, and all the other inevitable auxiliaries and indispensable appendages of what is often called the "divinely-instituted relation" of slavery. The author's first personal observation of this class of beings was somewhat as follows:

Several years ago, while one morning employed in the duties of the nursery, a coloured woman was announced. She was ushered into the nursery, and the author thought, on first survey, that a more surly, unpromising face she had never seen. The woman was thoroughly black, thickset, firmly built, and with strongly-marked African features. Those who have been accustomed to read the expressions of the African face know what a peculiar effect is produced by a lowering, desponding expression upon its dark features. It is like the shadow of a thunder-cloud. Unlike her race generally, the woman did not smile when smiled upon, nor utter any pleasant remark in reply to such as were addressed to her. The youngest pet of the nursery, a boy about three years old, walked up, and laid his little hand on her knee, and seemed astonished not to meet the quick smile which the negro almost always has in reserve for the little child. The writer thought her very cross and disagreeable, and, after a few moments' silence, asked, with perhaps a little impatience, "Do you want anything of me to-day?"

"Here are some papers," said the woman, pushing them towards her; "perhaps you would read them."

The first paper opened was a letter from a negro-trader in Kentucky, stating concisely that he had waited about as long as he could for her child; that he wanted to start for the South, and must get it off his hands; that, if she would send him two hundred dollars before the end of the week, she should have it; if not, that he would set it up at auction, at the court-house door on Saturday. He added, also, that he might have got more than that for the child, but that he was willing to let her have it cheap.

CHAPTER II.

"What sort of man is this?" said the author to the woman, when she had done reading the letter.

"Dunno, ma'am; great Christian I know—member of the Methodist church, anyhow."

The expression of sullen irony with which this was said was a thing to be remembered.

"And how old is this child?" said the author to her.

The woman looked at the little boy who had been standing at her knee with an expressive glance, and said, "She will be three years old this summer."

On further inquiry into the history of the woman, it appeared that she had been set free by the will of her owners; that the child was legally entitled to freedom, but had been seized on by the heirs of the estate. She was poor and friendless, without money to maintain a suit, and the heirs, of course, threw the child into the hands of the trader. The necessary sum, it may be added, was all raised in the small neighbourhood which then surrounded the Lane Theological Seminary, and the child was redeemed.

If the public would like a specimen of the correspondence which passes between these worthies, who are the principal reliance of the community for supporting and extending the institution of slavery, the following may be interesting as a matter of literary curiosity. It was forwarded by Mr. M. J. Thomas, of Philadelphia, to the *National Era,* and stated by him to be "a copy taken verbatim from the original, found among the papers of the person to whom it was addressed, at the time of his arrest and conviction, for passing a variety of counterfeit banknotes:"—

> *Poolsville, Montgomery Co., Md., March 24, 1831.*
>
> DEAR SIR,—I arrived home in safety with Louisa, John having been rescued from me, out of a two-storey window, at twelve o'clock at night. I offered a reward of fifty dollars, and have him here safe in jail. The persons who took him, brought him to Fredericktown jail. I wish you to write to no person in this State but myself. Kephart and myself are determined to go the whole hog for any negro you can find, and you must give me the earliest information, as soon as you do find any. Enclosed you will receive a handbill, and I can make a good bargain if you can find them. I will, in all cases, as soon as a negro runs off, send you a handbill immediately, so that you may be on the look-out. Please tell the constable to go on with the sale of John's property; and, when the money is made, I will send on an order to you for it. Please attend to this for me; likewise write to me, and inform me of any negro you think has run away—no matter where you think he has come from, nor how far—and I will try to find out his master. Let me know where you think he is from, with all particular marks, and if I don't find his master, Joe's dead!
>
> Write to me about the crooked-fingered negro, and let me know which hand and which finger, colour, &c.; likewise any mark the fel-

> low has who says he got away from the negro-buyer, with his height and colour, or any other you think has run off.
>
> Give my respects to your partner, and be sure you write to no person but myself. If any person writes to you, you can inform me of it, and I will try to buy from them. I think we can make money, if we do business together; for I have plenty of money, if you can find plenty of negroes. Let we know if Daniel is still where he was, and if you have heard anything of Francis since I left you. Accept for myself my regard and esteem. REUBEN B. CARLLEY. *John C. Saunders.*

This letter strikingly illustrates the character of these fellow-patriots with whom the great men of our land have been acting in conjunction, in carrying out the beneficent provisions of the Fugitive Slave Law.

With regard to the *Kephart* named in this letter, the community of Boston may have a special interest to know further particulars, as he was one of the dignitaries sent from the South to assist the good citizens of that place in the religious and patriotic enterprise of 1851, at the time that Shadrach was unfortunately rescued. It, therefore, may be well to introduce somewhat particularly JOHN KEPHART, as sketched by RICHARD H. DANA, Jun., one of the lawyers employed in the defence of the perpetrators of the rescue:—

> I shall never forget John Caphart. I have been eleven years at the bar, and in that time have seen many developments of vice and hardness, but I never met with anything so cold-blooded as the testimony of that man. John Caphart is a tall, sallow man, of about fifty, with jet-black hair, a restless, dark eye, and an anxious, care-worn look, which, had there been enough of moral element in the expression, might be called melancholy. His frame was strong, and in youth he had evidently been powerful, but he was not robust. Yet there was a calm, cruel look, a power of will and a quickness of muscular action, which still render him a terror in his vocation.
>
> In the manner of giving in his testimony, there was no bluster or outward show of insolence. His contempt for the humane feelings of the audience and community about him was too true to require any assumption of that kind. He neither paraded nor attempted to conceal the worst features of his calling. He treated it as a matter of business, which he knew the community shuddered at, but the moral nature of which he was utterly indifferent to, beyond a certain secret pleasure in thus indirectly inflicting a little torture on his hearers.
>
> I am not, however, altogether clear, to do John Caphart justice, that he is entirely conscience-proof. There was something in his anxious look which leaves one not without hope.
>
> At the first trial we did not know of his pursuits, and he passed merely as a policeman of Norfolk, Virginia. But, at the second trial, some one in the room gave me a hint of the occupations many of these policemen take to, which led to my cross-examination.

CHAPTER II.

From the Examination of John Caphart, in the "Rescue Trials," at Boston, in June and November, 1851, *and October,* 1852.

Question. Is it a part of your duty, as a policeman, to take up coloured persons who are out after hours in the streets?

Answer. Yes, sir.

Q. What is done with them?

A. We put them in the lock-up, and in the morning they are brought into court and ordered to be punished—those that are to be punished.

Q. What punishment do they get?

A. Not exceeding thirty-nine lashes.

Q. Who gives them these lashes?

A. Any of the officers. I do sometimes.

Q. Are you paid extra for this? How much?

A. Fifty cents a head. It used to be sixty-two cents. Now it is fifty. Fifty cents for each one we arrest, and fifty more for each one we flog.

Q. Are these persons you flog men and boys only, or are they women and girls also?

A. Men, women, boys, and girls, just as it happens.

[The government interfered, and tried to prevent any further examination; and said, among other things, that he only performed his duty as police-officer under the law. After a discussion, Judge Curtis allowed it to proceed.]

Q. Is your flogging confined to these cases? Do you not flog slaves at the request of their masters?

A. Sometimes I do. Certainly, when I am called upon.

Q. In these cases of private flogging, are the negroes sent to you? Have you a place for flogging?

A. No. I go round, as I am sent for.

Q. Is this part of your duty as an officer?

A. No, sir.

Q. In these cases of private flogging, do you inquire into the circumstances, to see what the fault has been, or if there is any?

A. That's none of my business. I do as I am requested. The master is responsible.

Q. In these cases, too, I suppose you flog women and girls, as well as men?

A. Women and men.

Q. Mr. Caphart, how long have you been engaged in this business?

A. Ever since 1836.

Q. How many negroes do you suppose you have flogged, in all, women and children included?

A. [Looking calmly round the room.] I don't know how many niggers you have got here in Massachusetts, but I should think I had flogged as many as you've got in the State.

[The same man testified that he was often employed to pursue fugitive slaves. His reply to the question was, "I never refuse a good job in that line."]

Q. Don't they sometimes turn out bad jobs?

A. Never, if I can help it.

Q. Are they not sometimes discharged after you get them?

A. Not often. I don't know that they ever are, except those Portuguese the counsel read about.

[I had found, in a Virginia report, a case of some two hundred Portuguese negroes, whom this John Caphart had seized from a vessel, and endeavoured to get condemned as slaves, but whom the Court discharged.]

Hon. John P. Hale, associated with Mr. Dana as counsel for the defence in the Rescue Trials, said of him in his closing argument:—

> Why, gentlemen, he sells agony! Torture is his stock-in-trade! He is a walking scourge! He hawks, peddles, retails, groans and tears about the streets of Norfolk!

See also the following correspondence between the two traders, one in North Carolina, the other in New Orleans: with a word of comment by Bishop Wilberforce, of Oxford:—

Halifax, N. C., Nov. 16, 1839.

DEAR SIR,—I have shipped in the brig Addison—prices are below:

No.;		Dollars.
1.	Caroline Ennis	650.00
2.	Silvy Holland	625.00
3.	Silvy Booth	487.50
4.	Maria Pollock	475.00
5.	Emeline Pollock	475.00
6.	Delia Averit	475.00

The two girls that cost 650 dollars, and 625 dollars, were bought before I shipped my first. I have a great many negroes offered to me, but I will not pay the prices they ask, for I know they will come down. I have no opposition in market. I will wait until I hear from you before I buy, and then I can judge what I must pay. Goodwin will send you the bill of lading for my negroes, as he shipped them with his own. Write often, as the times are critical, and it depends on the prices you get to govern me in buying. Yours, &c.*Mr. Theophilus Freeman, New Orleans.* G. W. BARNES.

The above was a small but choice invoice of wives and mothers. Nine days before, namely, 7th November, Mr. Barnes advised Mr. Freeman of having shipped a lot, of forty-three men and women. Mr. Freeman, informing one of his correspondents of the state of the market, writes (*Sunday,* 21st Sept., 1839), "I bought a boy yesterday, sixteen years old, and likely, *weighing* one hundred and ten pounds, at 700 dollars. I sold a likely girl, twelve years old, at 500 dollars. I bought a man yesterday, twenty years old, six feet high at 820 dollars; one *to-day,* twenty-four years old, at 850 dollars, black and sleek as a mole."

The writer has drawn in this work only one class of the negro-traders. There are all varieties of them, up to the great wholesale purchasers, who keep their large trading-houses; who are gentlemanly in manners and courteous in address; who, in many respects, often perform actions of real generosity; who consider slavery a very great evil, and hope the country will at some time be delivered from it, but who think that so long as clergyman and layman, saint and sinner, are all agreed in the propriety and necessity of slave-holding, it is better that the necessary trade in the article be conducted by men of humanity and decency, than by swearing, brutal men, of the Tom Loker school. These men are exceedingly sensitive with regard to what they consider the injustice of the world, in excluding them from good society, simply because they undertake to supply a demand in the community, which the bar, the press, and the pulpit, all pronounce to be a proper one. In this respect, society certainly imitates the unreasonableness of the ancient Egyptians, who employed a certain class of men to prepare dead bodies for embalming, but flew at them with sticks and stones the moment the operation was over, on account of the sacrilegious liberty which they had taken. If there is an ill-used class of men in the world, it is certainly the slave-traders; for, if there is no harm in the institution of slavery—if it is a divinely-appointed and honourable one, like civil government and the family state, and like other species of property relation—then there is no earthly reason why a man may not as innocently be a slave trader as any other kind of trader.

CHAPTER III.

MR. AND MRS. SHELBY.

IT was the design of the writer, in delineating the domestic arrangements of Mr. and Mrs. Shelby, to show a picture of the fairest side of slave-life, where easy indulgence and good-natured forbearance are tempered by just discipline and religious instruction, skilfully and judiciously imparted.

The writer did not come to her task without reading much upon both sides of the question, and making a particular effort to collect all the most favourable representations of slavery which she could obtain. And, as the reader may have a curiosity to examine some of the documents, the writer will present them quite at large. There is no kind of danger to the world in letting the very fairest side of slavery be seen; in fact, the horrors and barbarities which are necessarily inherent in it are so terrible that one stands absolutely in need of all the comfort which can be gained from incidents like the subjoined, to save them from utter despair of human nature. The first account is from Mr. J. K. Paulding's Letters on Slavery; and is a letter from a Virginia planter, whom we should judge, from his style, to be a very amiable, agreeable man, and who probably describes very fairly the state of things on his own domain.

DEAR SIR,—As regards the first query, which relates to the "rights and duties of the slave," I do not know how extensive a view of this branch of the subject is contemplated. In its simplest aspect, as understood and acted on in Virginia, I should say that the slave is entitled to an abundance of good plain food; to coarse but comfortable apparel; to a warm but humble dwelling; to protection when well, and to succour when sick; and, in return, that it is his duty to render to his master all the service he can consistently with perfect health, and to behave submissively and honestly. Other remarks suggest themselves, but they will be more appropriately introduced under different heads.

2nd. *The domestic relations of master and slave.*—These relations are much misunderstood by many persons at the North, who regard the terms as synonymous with oppressor and oppressed. Nothing can be further from the fact. The condition of the negroes in this State has been greatly ameliorated. The proprietors were formerly fewer and richer than at present. Distant quarters were often kept up to support the aristocratic mansion. They were rarely visited by their owners; and heartless overseers, frequently changed, were employed to manage them for a share of the crop. These men scourged the land, and sometimes the slaves. Their tenure was but for a year, and of course they made the most of their brief authority. Owing to the influence of our institutions, property has become subdivided, and most persons live on or near their estates. There are exceptions to be sure, and particularly among wealthy gentlemen in the towns; but these last are almost all enlightened and humane, and alike liberal to the soil and to the slave who cultivates it. I could point out some noble instances of patriotic and spirited improvement among them. But, to return to the resident proprietors: most of them have been raised on the estates; from the older negroes they have received in infancy numberless acts of kindness; the younger ones have not unfrequently been their playmates (not the most suitable, I admit), and much good-will is thus generated on both sides. In addition to this, most men feel attached to their property; and this attachment is stronger in the case of persons than of things. I know it, and feel it. It is true there are harsh masters; but there are also bad husbands and bad fathers. They are all exceptions to the rule, not the rule itself. Shall we therefore condemn in the gross those relations, and the rights and authority they imply, from their occasional abuse? I could mention many instances of strong attachment on the part of the slave, but will only adduce one or two, of which I have been the object. It became a question whether a faithful servant, bred up with me from boyhood, should give up his master, or his wife and children, to whom he was affectionately attached, and most attentive and kind. The trial was a severe one, but he determined to break those tender ties, and remain with me. I left it entirely to his discretion, though I would not, from considerations of interest, have taken for him quadruple the price I should probably have obtained. Fortunately, in the sequel, I was enabled to purchase his family, with the exception of a daughter, happily situated; and nothing but death shall henceforth part them. Were it put to the test, I am convinced that many masters would receive this striking proof of devotion. A gentleman but a day or two since informed me of a similar, and even stronger case, afforded by one of his slaves. As the reward of assiduous and delicate attention to a venerated parent, in her last illness, I proposed to purchase and liberate a healthy and intelligent woman, about thirty years of age, the best nurse, and, in all respects, one of the best servants in the State, of which I was only part owner; but she declined to leave the family, and has been since rather better than free. I shall be excused for stating a ludicrous case I heard of some time ago. A favourite and indulged servant requested his master to sell him to another gentleman. His master refused to do so, but told him he was at perfect liberty to go to the North, if he were not already free enough. After a while he repeated the request; and, on being urged to give an explanation of his singular conduct, told his master that he considered himself consumptive, and would soon die; and he thought Mr. B— was better able to bear the loss than his master. He was sent to a medicinal spring, and recovered his health, if, indeed, he had ever lost it, of which his master had been unapprised. It may not be amiss to describe my deportment towards my servants, whom I endeavour to render happy while I make them profitable. I never turn a deaf ear, but listen patiently to their communications. I chat familiarly with those who have passed service, or have not begun to render it. With the others I observe a more prudent reserve, but I encourage all to approach me without awe. I hardly ever go to town without having commissions to execute for some of them; and think they prefer to employ me, from a belief that, if their money should not quite hold out, I would add a little to it; and I not unfrequently do, in order to get a better article. The relation between myself and my slaves is decidedly friendly. I keep up pretty exact discipline, mingled with kindness, and hardly ever lose property by thievish, or labour by runaway slaves. I never lock the outer doors of my house. It is done, but done by the servants; and I rarely bestow a thought on the matter. I leave home periodically for two months, and commit the dwelling-house, plate, and other valuables, to the servants, without even an enumeration of the articles.

3rd. *The duration of the labour of the slave.*—The day is usually considered long enough. Employment at night is not exacted by me, except to shell corn once a week for their own consumption, and on a few other extraordinary occasions. *The people,* as we generally call them, are required to leave their houses at daybreak, and to work until dark, with the intermission of half an hour to an hour at breakfast, and one to two hours at dinner, according to the season and sort of work. In this respect I suppose our negroes will bear a favourable comparison with any labourers whatever.

4th. *The liberty usually allowed the slave—his holidays and amusements, and the way in which they usually spend their evenings and holidays.*—They are prohibited from going off the estate without first obtaining leave; though they often transgress, and with impunity, except in flagrant cases. Those who have wives on other plantations visit them on certain specified nights, and have an allowance of time for going and returning, proportioned to the distance. My negroes are permitted, and indeed, encouraged, to raise as many ducks and chickens as they can; to cultivate vegetables for their own use, and a patch of corn for sale; to exercise their trades, when they possess one, which many do; to catch muskrats and other animals for the fur or the flesh; to raise bees; and, in fine, to earn an honest penny in any way which chance or their own ingenuity may offer. The modes specified are, however, those most commonly resorted to, and enable provident servants to make from five to thirty dollars a-piece. The corn is a different sort from that which I cultivate, and is all bought by me. A great many fowls are raised; I have this year known ten dollars' worth sold by one man at one time. One of the chief sources of profit is the fur of the muskrat; for the purpose of catching which the marshes on the estate have been parcelled out and appropriated from time immemorial, and held by a tenure little short of fee-simple. The negroes are indebted to Nat Turner and Tappan for a curtailment of some of their privileges. As a sincere friend to the blacks, I have much regretted the reckless interference of these persons, on account of the restrictions it has become, or been thought, necessary to impose. Since the exploit of the former hero, they have been forbidden to preach, except to their fellow slaves, the property of the same owner; to have public funerals, unless a white person officiates; or to be taught to read and write. Their funerals formerly gave them great satisfaction, and it was customary here to furnish the relations of the deceased with bacon, spirit, flour, sugar, and butter, with which a grand entertainment, in their way, was got up. We were once much amused by a hearty fellow requesting his mistress to let him have his funeral during his lifetime, when it would do him some good. The waggish request was granted; and I venture to say there never was a funeral the subject of which enjoyed it so much. When permitted, some of our negroes preached with great fluency. I was present a few years since, when an Episcopal minister addressed the people, by appointment. On the conclusion of an excellent sermon, a negro preacher rose and thanked the gentleman kindly for his discourse, but frankly told him the congregation "did not understand his *lingo*." He then proceeded himself, with great vehemence and volubility, coining words where they had not been made to his hand, or rather his tongue, and impressing his hearers, doubtless, with a decided opinion of his superiority over his white co-labourer in the field of grace. My brother and I, who own contiguous estates, have lately erected a chapel on the line between them, and have employed an acceptable minister of the Baptist persuasion, to which the negroes almost exclusively belong, to afford them religious instruction. Except as a preparatory step to emancipation, I consider it exceedingly impolitic, even as regards the slaves themselves, to permit them to read and write: "Where ignorance is bliss, `tis folly to be wise." And it is certainly impolitic as regards their masters, on the principle that "knowledge is power." My servants have not as long holidays as those of most other persons. I allow three days at Christmas, and at each of three other periods, besides a little time to work their patches; or, if very busy, I sometimes prefer to work them myself. Most of the ancient pastimes have been lost in this neighbourhood, and religion, mock or real, has succeeded them. The banjo, their national instrument, is known but in name or in a few of the tunes which have survived. Some of the younger negroes sing and dance, but the evenings and holidays are usually occupied in working, in visiting, and in praying and singing hymns. The primitive customs and sports are, I believe, better preserved further south, where slaves were brought from Africa long after they ceased to come here.

6th. *The provision usually made for their food and clothing, for those who are too young or too old to labour.*—My men receive twelve quarts of Indian meal (the abundant and universal allowance in this State), seven salted herrings, and two pounds of smoked bacon or three pounds of pork, a-week; the other hands proportionally less. But, generally speaking, their food is issued daily, with the exception of meal, and consists of fish or bacon for breakfast, and meat, fresh or salted, with vegetables whenever we can provide them, for dinner; or for a month or two in the spring, fresh fish cooked with a little bacon. This mode is rather more expensive to me than that of weekly rations, but more comfortable to the servants. Superannuated or invalid slaves draw their provisions regularly once a-week; and the moment a child ceases to be nourished by its mother, it receives eight quarts of meal (more than it can consume) and one half-pound of lard. Besides the food furnished by me, nearly all the servants are able to make some addition from their private stores; and there is among the adults hardly an instance of one so improvident as not to do it. He must be an unthrifty fellow, indeed, who cannot realise the wish of the famous Henry IV. in regard to the French peasantry, and enjoy his fowl on Sunday. I always keep on hand, for the use of the negroes, sugar, molasses, &c., which, though not regularly issued, are applied for on the slightest pretexts, and frequently no pretext at all, and are never refused except in cases of misconduct. In regard to clothing: the men and boys receive a winter coat and trousers of strong cloth, three shirts, a stout pair of shoes and socks, and a pair of summer pantaloons, every year; a hat about every second year, and a great-coat and blanket every third year. Instead of great-coats and hats, the women have large capes to protect the bust in bad weather, and handkerchiefs for the head. The articles furnished are good and serviceable; and, with their own acquisitions, make their appearance decent and respectable. On Sunday these are even fine. The aged and invalid are clad as regularly as the rest, but less substantially. Mothers receive a little raw cotton, in proportion to the number of children, with the privilege of having the yarn, when spun, woven at my expense. I provide them with blankets. Orphans are put with careful women, and treated with tenderness. I am attached to the little slaves, and encourage familiarity among them. Sometimes, when I ride near the quarters, they come running after me with the most whimsical requests, and are rendered happy by the distribution of some little donation. The clothing described is that which is given to the crop hands. Home-servants, a numerous class in Virginia, are of course clad in a different and very superior manner. I neglected to mention, in the proper place, that there are on each of my plantations a kitchen, an oven, and one or more cooks; and that each hand is furnished with a tin bucket for his food, which is carried into the field by little negroes, who also supply the labourers with water.

6th. Their treatment when sick.—My negroes go, or are carried, as soon as they are attacked, to a spacious and well-ventilated hospital, near the mansion-house. They are there received by an attentive nurse, who has an assortment of medicine, additional bed-clothing, and the command of as much light food as she may require, either from the table or the store-room of the proprietor. Wine, sago, rice, and other little comforts appertaining to such an establishment, are always kept on hand. The condition of the sick is much better than that of the poor whites or free coloured people in the neighbourhood.

7th. Their rewards and punishments.—I occasionally bestow little gratuities for good conduct, and particularly after harvest; and hardly ever refuse a favour asked by those who faithfully perform their duty. Vicious and idle servants are punished with stripes, moderately inflicted; to which, in the case of theft, is added privation of meat, a severe punishment to those who are never suffered to be without it on any other account. From my limited observation, I think that servants to the North work much harder than our slaves. I was educated at a college in one of the free States, and, on my return to Virginia, was struck with the contrast.

CHAPTER III.

I was astonished at the number of idle domestics, and actually worried my mother, much to my contrition since, to reduce the establishment: I say to my contrition, because, after eighteen years' residence in the good Old Dominion, I find myself surrounded by a troop of servants about as numerous as that against which I formerly so loudly exclaimed. While on this subject it may not be amiss to state a case of manumission which occurred about three years since. My nearest neighbour, a man of immense wealth, owned a favourite servant, a fine fellow, with polished manners and excellent disposition, who reads and writes, and is thoroughly versed in the duties of a butler and housekeeper, in the performance of which he was trusted without limit. This man was, on the death of his master, emancipated with a legacy of 6,000 dollars, besides about 2,000 dollars more which he had been permitted to accumulate, and had deposited with his master, who had given him credit for it. The use that this man, apparently so well qualified for freedom, and who has had an opportunity of travelling and of judging for himself, makes of his money and his time, is somewhat remarkable. In consequence of his exemplary conduct, he has been permitted to reside in the State, and for very moderate wages occupies the same situation he did in the old establishment, and will probably continue to occupy it as long as he lives. He has no children of his own, but has put a little girl, a relation of his, to school. Except in this instance, and in the purchase of a few plain articles of furniture, his freedom and his money seem not much to have benefited him. A servant of mine who is intimate with him, thinks he is not as happy as he was before his liberation. Several other servants were freed at the same time, with smaller legacies, but I do not know what has become of them.

I do not regard negro slavery, however mitigated, as a Utopian system, and have not intended so to delineate it. But it exists, and the difficulty of removing it is felt and acknowledged by all, save the fanatics, who, like "fools, rush in where angels dare not tread." It is pleasing to know that its burdens are not too heavy to be borne. That the treatment of slaves in this State is humane, and even indulgent, may be inferred from the fact of their rapid increase and great longevity. I believe that, constituted as they are, morally and physically, they are as happy as any peasantry in the world; and I venture to affirm, as the result of my reading and inquiry, that in no country are the labourers so liberally and invariably supplied with bread and meat as are the negro slaves of the United States. However great the dearth of provisions, famine never reaches them.

P.S. It might have been stated above that on this estate there are about one hundred and sixty blacks. With the exception of infants, there has been, in eighteen months, but one death, that I remember—that of a man fully sixty-five years of age. The bill for medical attendance, from the second day of last November, comprising upwards of a year, is less than forty dollars.

The following accounts are taken from "Ingraham's Travels in the Southwest," a work which seems to have been written as much to show the beauties of slavery as anything else. Speaking of the state of things on some Southern plantations, he gives the following pictures, which are presented without note or comment:

The little candidates for "field honours" are useless articles on a plantation during the first five or six years of their existence. They are then to take their first lesson in the elementary part of their education. When they have learned their manual alphabet tolerably well, they are placed in the field to take a spell at cotton-picking. The first day in the field is their proudest day. The young negroes look forward to it with as much restlessness and impatience as school-boys to a vacation. Black children are not put to work so young as many children of poor parents in the North. It is often the case that the children of the domestic servants become pets in the house and the playmates of the white children of the family. No scene can be livelier or more interesting to a Northerner, than that which the negro quarters of a well-regulated plantation present on a Sabbath morning, just before church hours. In every cabin the men are shaving and dressing; the women, arrayed in their gay muslins, are arranging their frizzly hair—in which they take no little pride—or investigating the condition of their children; the old people, neatly clothed, are quietly conversing or smoking about the doors; and those of the younger portion who are not undergoing the infliction of the wash-tub are enjoying themselves in the shade of the trees, or around some little pond, with as much zest as though slavery and freedom were synonymous terms. When all are dressed, and the hour arrives for worship, they lock up their cabins, and the whole population of the little village proceeds to chapel, where divine service is performed, sometimes by an officiating clergyman, and often by the planter himself, if a church member. The whole plantation is also frequently formed into a Sabbath class, which is instructed by the planter, or some member of his family; and often, such is the anxiety of the master that they should perfectly understand what they are taught—a hard matter in the present state of their intellect—that no means calculated to advance their progress are left untried. I was not long since shown a manuscript catechism, drawn up with great care and judgment by a distinguished planter, on a plan admirably adapted to the comprehension of the negroes.

It is now popular to treat slaves with kindness; and those planters who are known to be inhumanly rigorous to their slaves are scarcely countenanced by the more intelligent and humane portion of the community. Such instances, however, are very rare; but there are unprincipled men everywhere, who will give vent to their ill-feelings and bad passions, not with less good-will upon the back of an indented apprentice than upon that of a purchased slave. Private chapels are now introduced upon most of the plantations of the more wealthy, which are far from any church; Sabbath-schools are instituted for the black children, and Bible-classes for the parents, which are superintended by the planter, a chaplain, or some of the female members of the family.

Nor are planters indifferent to the comfort of their grey-headed slaves. I have been much affected at beholding many exhibitions of their kindly feeling towards them. They always address them in a mild and pleasant manner, as "Uncle," or

"Aunty," titles as peculiar to the old negro and negress as "boy" and "girl" to all under forty years of age. Some old Africans are allowed to spend their last years in their houses, without doing any kind of labour; these, if not too infirm, cultivate little patches of ground, on which they raise a few vegetables—for vegetables grow nearly all the year round in this climate—and make a little money to purchase a few extra comforts. They are also always receiving presents from their masters and mistresses, and the negroes on the estate, the latter of whom are extremely desirous of seeing the old people comfortable. A relation of the extra comforts which some planters allow their slaves would hardly obtain credit at the North. But you must recollect that Southern planters are men, and men of feeling, generous and high-minded, and possessing as much of the "milk of human kindness" as the sons of colder climes—although they may have been educated to regard that as right which a different education has led Northerners to consider wrong.

With regard to the character of Mrs. Shelby, the writer must say a few words. While travelling in Kentucky, a few years since, some pious ladies expressed to her the same sentiments with regard to slavery which the reader has heard expressed by Mrs. Shelby.

There are many whose natural sense of justice cannot be made to tolerate the enormities of the system, even though they hear it defended by clergymen from the pulpit, and see it countenanced by all that is most honourable in rank and wealth.

A pious lady said to the author, with regard to instructing her slaves, "I am ashamed to teach them what is right; I know that they know as well as I do that it is wrong to hold them as slaves, and I am ashamed to look them in the face." Pointing to an intelligent mulatto woman who passed through the room, she continued, "Now, there's B—: she is as intelligent and capable as any white woman I ever knew, and as well able to have her liberty and take care of herself; and she knows it isn't right to keep her as we do, and I know it too; and yet I cannot get my husband to think as I do, or I should be glad to set them free."

A venerable friend of the writer, a lady born and educated a slaveholder, used to the writer the very words attributed to Mrs. Shelby: "I never thought it was right to hold slaves. I always thought it was wrong when I was a girl, and I thought so still more when I came to join the church." An incident related by this friend of her examination for the church, shows in a striking manner what a difference may often exist between theoretical and practical benevolence.

A certain class of theologians in New England have advocated the doctrine of disinterested benevolence with such zeal, as to make it an imperative article of belief, that every individual ought to be willing to endure everlasting misery, if by doing so they could, on the whole, produce a greater amount of general good in the universe; and the inquiry was sometimes made of candidates for church-membership, whether they could bring themselves to this point as a test of their sincerity. The clergyman who was to examine this lady, was particularly interested in these speculations. When he came to inquire of her with regard to her views as to the obligations of Christianity, she informed him decidedly that she had brought her mind to the point of emancipating all her slaves, of whom she had a large number. The clergyman seemed rather to consider this as an excess of zeal, and recommended that she should take time to reflect upon it. He was, however, very urgent to know whether, if it should appear for the greatest good of the universe, she would be willing to be damned. Entirely unaccustomed to theological speculations, the good woman answered, with some vehemence, that "she was sure she was not;" adding, naturally enough, that if that had been her purpose, she need not have come to join the church. The good lady, however, was admitted, and proved her devotion to the general good by the more tangible method of setting all her slaves at liberty, and carefully watching over their education and interests after they were liberated.

Mrs. Shelby is a fair type of the very best class of Southern women; and while the evils of the institution are felt and deplored, and while the world looks with just indignation on the national support and patronage which is given to it, and on the men who, knowing its nature, deliberately make efforts to perpetuate and extend it, it is but justice that it should bear in mind the virtues of such persons.

Many of them, surrounded by circumstances over which they can have no control, perplexed by domestic cares, of which women in free States can have very little conception, loaded down by duties and responsibilities which wear upon the very springs of life, still go on bravely and patiently from day to day, doing all they can to alleviate what they cannot prevent, and, as far as the sphere of their own immediate power extends, rescuing those who are dependent upon them from the evils of the system.

We read of Him who shall at last come to judgment, that "His fan is in his hand, and he will thoroughly purge his floor, and gather his wheat into the garner." Out of the great abyss of national sin he will rescue every grain of good and honest purpose and intention. His eyes, which are as a flame of fire, penetrate at once those intricate mazes where human judgment is lost, and will save and honour at last the truly good and sincere, however they may have been involved with the evil; and such souls as have resisted the greatest temptations, and persisted in good under the most perplexing circumstances, are those of whom he has written, "And they shall be mine, saith the Lord of Hosts, in that day when I make up my jewels; and I will spare them as a man spareth his own son that serveth him."

CHAPTER IV.

GEORGE HARRIS.

THE character of George Harris has been represented as overdrawn, both as respects personal qualities and general intelligence. It has been said, too, that so many afflictive incidents happening to a slave are improbable, and present a distorted view of the institution.

In regard to person, it must be remembered that the half-breeds often inherit, to a great degree, the traits of their white ancestors. For this there is abundant evidence in the advertisements of the papers. Witness the following from the *Chattanooga* (Tenn.) *Gazette,* October 5th, 1852.

500 DOLLARS REWARD.

Run away from the subscriber, on the 25th May, a VERY BRIGHT MULATTO BOY, about 20 or 22 years old, named WASH. Said boy, without close observation, might pass himself for a white man, as he is very bright—has sandy hair, blue eyes, and a fine set of teeth. He is an excellent bricklayer; but I have no idea that he will pursue his trade, for fear of detection. Although he is like a white man in appearance, he has the disposition of a negro, and delights in comic songs and witty expressions. He is an excellent house servant, very handy about a hotel—tall, slender, and has rather a down look, especially when spoken to, and is sometimes inclined to be sulky. I have no doubt that he has been decoyed off by some scoundrel, and I will give the above reward for the apprehension of the boy and thief, if delivered at Chattanooga. Or, I will give 200 dollars for the boy alone; or 100 dollars if confined in any jail in the United States, so that I can get him.

GEORGE O. RAGLAND.

Chattanooga, June 15, 1852.

From the *Capitolian Vis-à-vis,* West Baton Rouge, Louisiana, November 1, 1852:

150 DOLLARS REWARD.

Run away about the 15th of August last, *Joe,* a yellow man; small, about 5 feet 8 or 9 inches high, and about twenty years of age. *Has a Roman nose,* was raised in New Orleans, and *speaks French and English.* He was bought last winter of Mr. Digges, Banks Arcade, New Orleans.

In regard to general intelligence, the reader will recollect that the writer stated it as a fact which she learned while on a journey through Kentucky, that a young coloured man invented a machine for cleaning hemp, like that alluded to in her story.

Advertisements, also, occasionally propose for sale artisans of different descriptions. Slaves are often employed as pilots for vessels, and highly valued for their skill and knowledge. The following are advertisements from recent newspapers.

From the *South Carolinian* (Columbia), December 4th, 1852.

VALUABLE NEGROES AT AUCTION.

BY J. AND L. T. LEVIN.

WILL be Sold, on MONDAY, the 6th Day of December, the following valuable NEGROES:—

Andrew, 24 years of age, a bricklayer and plasterer, and thorough workman.

George, 22 years of age, one of the best barbers in the State.

James, 19 years of age, an excellent painter.

These boys were raised in Columbia, and are exceptions to most of boys, and are sold for no fault whatever.

The terms of sale are one-half cash, the balance on a credit of six months, with interest, for notes payable at bank, with two or more approved endorsers.

Purchasers to pay for necessary papers.

WILLIAM DOUGLASS.

November 27, 36.

From the same paper of November 18th, 1852.

Will be sold at private sale, a LIKELY MAN, boat hand, and good pilot; is well acquainted with all the inlets between here and Savannah and Georgetown.

With regard to the incidents of George Harris's life, that he may not be supposed a purely exceptional case, we propose to offer some parallel facts from the lives of slaves of our personal acquaintance.

Lewis Clark is an acquaintance of the writer. Soon after his escape from slavery, he was received into the family of a sister-in-law of the author, and there educated. His conduct during this time was such as to win for him uncommon affection and respect, and the author has frequently heard him spoken of in the highest terms by all who knew him.

The gentleman in whose family he so long resided, says of him, in a recent letter to the writer, "I would trust him, as the saying is, with untold gold."

Lewis is a quadroon, a fine-looking man, with European features, hair slightly wavy, and with an intelligent, agreeable expression of countenance.

CHAPTER IV.

The reader is now desired to compare the following incidents of his life, part of which he related personally to the author, with the incidents of the life of George Harris.

His mother was a handsome quadroon woman, the daughter of her master, and given by him in marriage to a free white man, a Scotchman, with the express understanding that she and her children were to be free. This engagement, if made sincerely at all, was never complied with. His mother had nine children, and on the death of her husband, came back, with all these children, as slaves in her father's house.

A married daughter of the family, who was the dread of the whole household, on account of the violence of her temper, had taken from the family, upon her marriage, a young girl. By the violence of her abuse she soon reduced the child to a state of idiocy, and then came imperiously back to her father's establishment, declaring that the child was good for nothing, and that she would have another, and, as poor Lewis' evil star would have it, fixed her eye upon him.

To avoid one of her terrible outbreaks of temper, the family offered up this boy as a pacificatory sacrifice. The incident is thus described by Lewis, in a published narrative:—

Every boy was ordered in, to pass before this female sorceress, that she might select a victim for her unprovoked malice, on whom to pour the vials of her wrath for years. I was that unlucky fellow. Mr. Campbell, my grandfather, objected, because it would divide a family, and offered her Moses; but objections and claims of every kind were swept away by the wild passion and shrill-toned voice of Mrs. B. Me she would have, and none else. Mr. Campbell went out to hunt, and drive away bad thoughts; the old lady became quiet, for she was sure none of her blood ran in my veins, and if there was any of her husband's there, it was no fault of hers. Slave-holding women are always revengeful toward the children of slaves that have any of the blood of their husbands in them. I was too young—only seven years of age—to understand what was going on. But my poor and affectionate mother understood and appreciated it all. When she left the kitchen of the mansion-house, where she was employed as cook, and came home to her own little cottage, the tear of anguish was in her eye, and the image of sorrow upon every feature of her face. She knew the female Nero whose rod was now to be over me. That night sleep departed from her eyes. With the youngest child clasped firmly to her bosom, she spent the night in walking the floor, coming ever and anon to lift up the clothes and look at me and my poor brother, who lay sleeping together. *Sleeping,* I said. Brother slept, but not I. I saw my mother when she first came to me, and I could not sleep. The vision of that night—its deep, ineffaceable impression—is now before my mind with all the distinctness of yesterday. In the morning I was put into the carriage with Mrs. B. and her children, and my weary pilgrimage of suffering was fairly begun.

Mrs. Banton is a character that can only exist where the laws of the land clothe with absolute power the coarsest, most brutal and violent-tempered, equally with the most generous and humane.

If irresponsible power is a trial to the virtue of the most watchful and careful, how fast must it develop cruelty in those who are naturally violent and brutal!

This woman was united to a drunken husband, of a temper equally ferocious. A recital of all the physical torture which this pair contrived to inflict on a hapless child, some of which have left ineffaceable marks on his person, would be too trying to humanity, and we gladly draw a veil over it.

Some incidents, however, are presented in the following extracts:—

A very trivial offence was sufficient to call forth a great burst of indignation from this woman of ungoverned passions. In my simplicity, I put my lips to the same vessel, and drank out of it, from which her children were accustomed to drink. She expressed her utter abhorrence of such an act by throwing my head violently back, and dashing into my face two dippers of water. The shower of water was followed by a heavier shower of *kicks;* but the words, bitter and cutting, that followed, were like a storm of hail upon my young heart. "She would teach me better manners than that; she would let me know I was to be brought up to her hand; she would have *one* slave that knew his place; if I wanted water, go to the spring, and not drink there in the house." This was new times for me; for some days I was completely benumbed with my sorrow.

* * * * *

If there be one so lost to all feeling as even to say that the slaves do not suffer when *families* are separated, let such a one go to the ragged quilt which was my couch and pillow, and stand there night after night, for long, weary hours, and see the bitter tears streaming down the face of that more than orphan boy, while with half-suppressed sighs and sobs he calls again and again upon his absent mother.

> "Say, wast thou conscious of the tears I shed?
> Hovered thy spirit o'er thy sorrowing son?
> Wretch even *then!* life's journey just begun."

He was employed till late at night in spinning flax or rocking the baby, and called at a very early hour in the morning; and if he did not start at the first summons, a cruel chastisement was sure to follow. He says:—

Such horror has seized me, lest I might not hear the first shrill call, that I have often in dreams fancied I heard that unwelcome voice, and have leaped from my couch and walked through the house and out of it before I awoke. I have gone and called the other slaves, in my sleep, and asked them if they did not hear master call. Never, while I live, will the remembrance of those long bitter nights of fear pass from my mind.

He adds to these words which should be deeply pondered by those who lay the flattering unction to their souls that the oppressed do not feel the sundering of family ties.

But all my severe labour, and bitter and cruel punishments, for these ten years of captivity with this worse than Arab family, all these were as nothing to the sufferings I experienced by being separated from my mother, brothers, and sisters;

the same things, with them near to sympathise with me, to hear my story of sorrow, would have been comparatively tolerable.

They were distant only about thirty miles, and yet, in ten long lonely years of childhood, I was only permitted to see them three times.

My mother occasionally found an opportunity to send me some token of remembrance and affection—a sugar-plum or an apple; but I scarcely ever ate them; they were laid up, and handled, and wept over, till they wasted away in my hand.

My thoughts continually by day, and my dreams by night, were of mother and home; and the horror experienced in the morning, when I awoke and behold it was a dream, is beyond the power of language to describe.

Lewis had a beautiful sister by the name of Delia, who, on the death of her grandfather, was sold, with all the other children of his mother, for the purpose of dividing the estate. She was a pious girl, a member of the Baptist church. She fell into the hands of a brutal, drunken man, who wished to make her his mistress. Milton Clark, a brother of Lewis, in the narrative of his life, describes the scene where he, with his mother, stood at the door while this girl was brutally whipped before it for wishing to conform to the principles of her Christian profession. As her resolution was unconquerable, she was placed in a coffle and sent down to the New Orleans market. Here she was sold to a Frenchman named Coval; he took her to Mexico, emancipated and married her. After residing some time in France and the West Indies with him, he died, leaving her a fortune of twenty or thirty thousand dollars. At her death she endeavoured to leave this by will to purchase the freedom of her brothers; but, as a slave cannot take property, or even have it left in trust for him, they never received any of it.

The incidents of the recovery of Lewis' freedom are thus told:—

I had long thought and dreamed of LIBERTY; I was now determined to make an effort to gain it. No tongue can tell the doubt, the perplexities, the anxiety, which a slave feels when making up his mind upon this subject. If he makes an effort and is not successful, he must be laughed at by his fellows, he will be beaten unmercifully by the master, and then watched and used the harder for it all his life.

And then, if he gets away, *who, what* will he find? He is ignorant of the world. All the white part of mankind that he has ever seen are enemies to him and all his kindred. How can he venture where none but white faces shall greet him? The master tells him that abolitionists *decoy* slaves off into the free States to catch them and sell them to Louisiana or Mississippi; and, if he goes to Canada, the British will put him in a *mine under ground, with both eyes put out, for life*. How does he know what or whom to believe? A horror of great darkness comes upon him, as he thinks over what may befall him. Long, very long time did I think of escaping before I made the effort.

At length the report was started that I was to be sold for Louisiana. Then I thought it was time to act. My mind was made up.

* * * * * * * * *

What my feelings were when I reached the free shore can be better imagined than described. I trembled all over with deep emotion, and I could feel my hair rise up on my head. I was on what was called a *free* soil, among a people who had no slaves. I saw white men at work, and no slave smarting beneath the lash. Everything was indeed *new* and wonderful. Not knowing where to find a friend, and being ignorant of the country, unwilling to inquire lest I should betray my ignorance, it was a whole week before I reached Cincinnati. At one place where I put up, I had a great many more questions put to me than I wished to answer. At another place I was very much annoyed by the officiousness of the landlord, who made it a point to supply every guest with newspapers. I took the copy handed me, and turned it over in a somewhat awkward manner, I suppose. He came to me to point out a veto, or some other very important news. I thought it best to decline his assistance, and gave up the paper, saying my eyes were not in a fit condition to read much.

At another place, the neighbours, on learning that a Kentuckian was at the tavern, came in great earnestness to find out what my business was. Kentuckians sometimes came there to kidnap their citizens. They were in the habit of watching them close. I at length satisfied them by assuring them that I was not, nor my father before me, any slaveholder at all; but, lest their suspicions should be excited in another direction, I added my grandfather was a slaveholder.

* * * * * * * * *

At daylight we were in Canada. When I stepped ashore here, I said, Sure enough I AM FREE. Good Heavens! what a sensation, when it first visits the bosoms of a full-grown man; one *born* to bondage; one who had been taught from early infancy that this was his inevitable lot for life! Not till *then* did I dare to cherish for a moment the feeling that *one* of the limbs of my body was my own. The slaves often say, when cut in the hand or foot, "Plague on the old foot," or "the old hand! It is master's, let him take care of it; nigger don't care if he never get well." My hands, my feet were now my own.

It will be recollected that George, in conversing with Eliza, gives an account of a scene in which he was violently beaten by his master's young son. This incident was suggested by the following letter from John M. Nelson to Mr. Theodore Weld, given in *Slavery As It Is,* p. 51.

Mr. Nelson removed from Virginia to Highland County, Ohio, many years since, where he is extensively known and respected. The letter is dated January 3rd, 1839.

I was born and raised in Augusta County, Virginia; my father was an elder in the Presbyterian church, and was "owner" of about twenty slaves; he was what was generally termed a "good master." His slaves were generally tolerably well fed and clothed, and not over-worked; they were sometimes permitted to attend church, and called in to family worship; few of them, however, availed themselves of these privileges. On some occasions I have seen him whip them severely, particularly for the crime of trying to obtain their liberty, or for what was called "running away." For *this* they were scourged more severely than for anything else. After they have been retaken, I have seen them stripped naked and suspended by the hands, sometimes to a tree, sometimes to a post, until their toes barely touched the ground, and whipped with a cowhide until the blood dripped from their backs. A boy named Jack, particularly, I have seen served in this way more than once. When I was quite a child, I recollect it grieved me very much to see one *tied up* to be whipped, and I used to intercede with tears in their behalf, and mingle my cries with theirs, and feel almost willing to take part of the punishment; I have been severely rebuked by my father for this kind of sympathy. Yet, such is the hardening nature of such scenes, that from this kind of commiseration for the suffering slave I became so blunted that I could not only witness their stripes with composure, but *myself* inflict them, and that without remorse. One case I have often looked back to with sorrow and contrition, particularly since I have been convinced that “negroes are men.” When I was perhaps fourteen or fifteen years of age, I undertook to correct a young fellow named Ned, for some supposed offence, I think it was leaving a bridle out of its proper place; he, being larger and stronger than myself, took hold of my arms and held me, in order to prevent my striking him. This I considered the height of insolence, and cried for help, when my father and mother both came running to my rescue. My father stripped and tied him, and took him into the orchard, where switches were plenty, and directed me to whip him; when one switch wore out, he supplied me with others. After I had whipped him a while, he fell on his knees to implore forgiveness, and I kicked him in the face; my father said, “Don't kick him, but whip him;” this I did until his back was literally covered with *welts*. I know I have repented, and trust I have obtained pardon for these things.

My father owned a woman we used to call Aunt Grace; she was purchased in Old Virginia. She has told me that her old master, in his *will,* gave her her freedom, but at his death his sons had sold her to my father. When he bought her she manifested some unwillingness to go with him; when she was put in irons and taken by force. This was before I was born; but I remember to have seen the irons, and was told that was what they had been used for. Aunt Grace is still living, and must be between seventy and eighty years of age; she has, for the last forty years, been an exemplary Christian. When I was a youth, I took some pains to learn her to read; this is now a great consolation to her. Since age and infirmity have rendered her of little value to her “owners,” she is permitted to read as much as she pleases; this she can do, with the aid of glasses, in the old family Bible, which is almost the only book she has ever looked into. This, with some little mending for the black children, is all she does; she is still held as a slave. I well remember what *a heart-rending scene* there was in the family when *my father sold her husband;* this was, I suppose, thirty-five years ago. And yet my father was considered one of the best of masters. I know of few who were better, but of *many* who were worse.

With regard to the intelligence of George, and his teaching himself to read and write, there is a most interesting and affecting parallel to it in the “Life of Frederick Douglass”—a book which can be recommended to anyone who has a curiosity to trace the workings of an intelligent and active mind through all the squalid misery, degradation and oppression, of slavery. A few incidents will be given.

Like Clark, Douglass was the son of a white man. He was a plantation slave in a proud old family; his situation, probably, may be considered as an average one; that is to say, he led a life of dirt, degradation, discomfort of various kinds, made tolerable as a matter of daily habit, and considered as enviable in comparison with the lot of those who suffer worse abuse. An incident which Douglass relates of his mother is touching; he states that it is customary at an early age to separate mothers from their children, for the purpose of blunting and deadening natural affection. When he was three years old his mother was sent to work on a plantation eight or ten miles distant, and after that he never saw her except in the night. After her day's toil she would occasionally walk over to her child, lie down with him in her arms, hush him to sleep in her bosom, then rise up and walk back again to be ready for her field-work by daylight. Now, we ask the highest-born lady in England or America, who is a mother, whether this does not show that this poor field-labourer had in her bosom, beneath her dirt and rags, a true mother's heart?

The last and bitterest indignity which had been heaped on the head of the unhappy slaves has been the denial to them of those holy affections which God gives alike to all. We are told, in fine phrase, by languid ladies of fashion, that "it is not to be supposed that those creatures have the same feelings that we have," when, perhaps, the very speaker could not endure one tithe of the fatigue and suffering which the slave-mother often bears for her child. Every mother who has a mother's heart within her ought to know that this is blasphemy against nature, and, standing between the cradle of her living and the grave of her dead child, should indignantly reject such a slander on all motherhood.

Douglass thus relates the account of his learning to read, after he had been removed to the situation of house-servant in Baltimore.

It seems that his mistress, newly-married and unaccustomed to the management of slaves, was very kind to him, and, amongst other acts of kindness, commenced teaching him to read. His master, discovering what was going on, he says,

At once forbade Mrs. Auld to instruct me further, telling her, among other things, that it was unlawful, as well as unsafe, to teach a slave to read. To use his own words, further, he said, "If you give a nigger an inch he will take an ell. A nigger should know nothing but to obey his master—to do as he is told to do. Learning would *spoil* the best nigger in the world. Now," said he, "if you teach that nigger (speaking of myself) how to read, there would be no keeping him. It would for ever unfit him to be a slave. He would at once become unmanageable, and of no value to his master. As to himself, it could do him no good, but a great deal of harm. It would make him discontented and unhappy." These words sank deep into my heart, stirred up sentiments within that lay slumbering, and called into existence an entirely new train of thought. It was a new and special revelation, explaining dark and mysterious things, with which my youthful understanding had struggled, but struggled in vain. I now understood what had been to me a most perplexing difficulty—to wit, the white man's power to enslave the black man. It was a grand achievement, and I prized it highly. From that moment I understood the pathway from slavery to freedom.

After this, his mistress was as watchful to prevent his learning to read as she had before been to instruct him. His course after this he thus describes:—

From this time I was most narrowly watched. If I was in a separate room any considerable length of time, I was sure to be suspected of having a book, and was at once called to give an account of myself; all this, however, was too late—the first step had been taken. Mistress, in teaching me the alphabet, had given me the *inch,* and no precaution could prevent me from taking the *ell.*

The plan which I adopted, and the one by which I was most successful, was that of making friends of all the little white boys whom I met in the street. As many of these as I could I converted into teachers. With their kindly aid, obtained at different times and in different places, I finally succeeded in learning to read. When I was sent of errands I always took my book with me, and by going one part of my errand quickly, I found time to get a lesson before my return. I used also to carry bread with me, enough of which was always in the house, and to which I was always welcome, for I was much better off in this regard than many of the poor white children in our neighbourhood. This bread I used to bestow upon the poor hungry little urchins, who, in return, would give me that more valuable bread of knowledge. I am strongly tempted to give the names of two or three of those little boys, as a testimonial of the gratitude and affection I bear them, but prudence forbids; not that it would injure me, but it might embarrass them, for it is almost an unpardonable offence to teach slaves to read in this Christian country. It is enough to say of the dear little fellows, that they lived in Philpot-street, very near Durgin and Bailey's ship-yard. I used to talk this matter of slavery over with them. I would sometimes say to them, I wished I could be free as they would be when they got to be men. "You will be free as soon as you are twenty-one, *but I am a slave for life!* Have not I as good a right to be free as you have?" These words used to trouble them; they would express for me the liveliest sympathy, and console me with the hope that something would occur by which I might be free.

I was now about twelve years old, and the thought of being a slave for life began to bear heavily upon my heart. Just about this time I got hold of a book entitled the "Columbian Orator." Every opportunity I got I used to read this book. Among much of other interesting matter, I found in it a dialogue between a master and his slave. The slave was represented as having run away from his master three times. The dialogue represented the conversation which took place between them when the slave was retaken the third time. In this dialogue the whole argument in behalf of slavery was brought forward by the master, all of which was disposed of by the slave. The slave was made to say some very smart as well as impressive things in reply to his master— things which had the desired though unexpected effect; for the conversation resulted in the voluntary emancipation of the slave on the part of the master.

In the same book I met with one of Sheridan's mighty speeches on and in behalf of Catholic emancipation. These were choice documents to me. I read them over and over again, with unabated interest. They gave tongue to interesting thoughts of my own soul, which had frequently flashed through my mind, and died away for want of utterance. The moral which I gained from the dialogue was the power of truth over the conscience of even a slaveholder. What I got from Sheridan was a bold denunciation of slavery, and a powerful vindication of human rights. The reading of these documents enabled me to utter my thoughts, and to meet the arguments brought forward to sustain slavery; but while they relieved me of one difficulty, they brought on another still more painful than the one of which I was relieved. The more I read, the more I was led to abhor and detest my enslavers. I could regard them in no other light than a band of successful robbers, who had left their homes and gone to Africa and stolen us from our homes, and in a strange land reduced us to slavery. I loathed them as being the meanest as well as the most wicked of men. As I read and contemplated the subject, behold! that very discontentment which Master Hugh had predicted would follow my learning to read had already come, to torment and sting my soul to unutterable anguish. As I writhed under it, I would at times feel that learning to read had been a curse rather than a blessing. It had given me a view of my wretched condition without the remedy. It opened my eyes to the horrible pit, but to no ladder upon which to get out. In moments of agony I envied my fellow slaves for their stupidity. I have often wished myself a beast. I preferred the condition of the meanest reptile to my own: anything, no matter what, to get rid of thinking! It was this everlasting thinking of my condition that tormented me: there was no getting rid of it. It was pressed upon me by every object within sight or hearing, animate or inanimate. The silver trump of freedom had roused my soul to eternal wakefulness. Freedom now appeared, to disappear no more for ever. It was heard in every sound and seen in every thing. It was ever present to torment me with a sense of my wretched condition. I saw nothing without seeing it, I heard nothing without hearing it, and felt nothing without feeling it. It looked from every star, it smiled in every calm, breathed in every wind, and moved in every storm.

I often found myself regretting my own existence, and wishing myself dead; and but for the hope of being free, I have no doubt but that I should have killed myself, or done something for which I should have been killed. While in this state of mind I was eager to hear any one speak of slavery. I was a ready listener. Every little while I could hear something about the abolitionists. It was some time before I found what the word meant. It was always used in such connexions as to make it an interesting word to me. If a slave ran away and succeeded in getting clear, or if a slave killed his master, set fire to a barn, or did anything very wrong in the mind of a slave-holder, it was spoken of as the fruit of *abolition.* Hearing the word in this connexion very often, I set about learning what it meant. The dictionary afforded me little or no help. I found it was "the act of abolishing;" but then I did not know what was to be abolished. Here I was perplexed. I did not care to ask anyone about its meaning, for I was satisfied that it was something they wanted me to know very little about. After a patient waiting, I got one of our city papers, containing an account of the number of petitions from the North praying for the abolition of slavery in the District of Columbia, and of the slave-trade between the States. From this time I understood the words *abolition* and *abolitionist,* and always drew near when that word was spoken, expecting to hear something of importance to myself and fellow-slaves. The light broke in upon me by degrees. I went one day down on the wharf of Mr. Waters, and seeing two Irishmen unloading a scow of stone, I went, unasked, and helped them. When we had finished, one of them came to me and asked me if I was a slave. I told him that I was. He asked, "Are ye a slave for life?" I told him that I was. The good Irishman seemed to be deeply affected by the statement. He said to the other that it was a pity so fine a little fellow as myself should be a slave for life. He said it was a shame to hold me. They both advised me to run away to the North; that I should find friends there, and that I should be free. I pretended not to be interested in what they said, and treated them as if I did not understand them; for I feared they might be treacherous. White men have been known to encourage slaves to escape, and then, to get the reward, catch them and return them to their masters. I was afraid that these seemingly good men might use me so; but I nevertheless remembered their advice, and from that time I resolved to run away. I looked forward to a time at which it would be safe for me to escape. I was too young to think of doing so immediately; besides, I wished to learn how to write, as I might have occasion to write my own pass. I consoled myself with the hope that I should one day find a good chance. Meanwhile I would learn to write.

The idea as to how I might learn to write was suggested to me by being in Durgin and Bailey's ship-yard, and frequently seeing the ship-carpenters, after hewing and getting a piece of timber ready for use, write on the timber the name of that part of the ship for which it was intended. When a piece of timber was intended for the larboard-side it would be marked thus—"L." When a piece for the starboard-side it would be marked thus—"S." A piece for the larboard-side forward would be marked thus—"L. F." When a piece was for starboard-side forward it would be marked thus—"S. F." For larboard-aft it would be marked thus—"L. A." For starboard-aft it would be marked thus—"S. A." I soon learned the names of these letters, and for what they were intended when placed upon a piece of timber in the ship-yard. I immediately commenced copying them, and in a short time was able to make the four letters named. After that, when I met with any boy who I knew could write, I would tell him I could write as well as he. The next word would be, "I don't believe you. Let me see you try it." I would then make the letters which I had been so fortunate as to learn, and ask him to beat that. In this way I got a good many lessons in writing, which it was quite possible I should never have gotten in any other way. During this time my copy-book was the board fence, brick wall, and pavement; my pen and ink was a lump of chalk. With this I learned mainly how to write. I then commenced and continued copying the Italics in Webster's Spelling-Book, until I could make them all without looking on the book. By this time my little master Thomas had gone to school and learned how to write, and had written over a number of copy-books. These had been brought home, and shown to some of our neighbours, and then laid aside. My mistress used to go to class-meeting at the Wilk-street meeting-house every Monday afternoon, and leave me to take care of the house. When left thus I used to spend the time in writing in the spaces left in Master Thomas's copying-book, copying what he had written. I continued to do this until I could write a hand very similar to that of Master Thomas. Thus, after a long, tedious effort for years, I finally succeeded in learning how to write.

These few quoted incidents will show that the case of George Harris is by no means so uncommon as might be supposed.

Let the reader peruse the account which George Harris gives of the sale of his mother and her children, and then read the following account given by the venerable Josiah Henson, now pastor of the missionary settlement at Dawn, in Canada.

After the death of his master, he says, the slaves of the plantation were all put up at auction, and sold to the highest bidder.

My brothers and sisters were bid off one by one, while my mother, holding my hand, looked on in an agony of grief, the cause of which I but ill understood at first, but which dawned on my mind with dreadful clearness as the sale proceeded. My mother was then separated from me and put up in her turn. She was bought by a man named Isaac R., residing in Montgomery County [Maryland], and then I was offered to the assembled purchasers. My mother, half distracted with the parting for ever from all her children, pushed through the crowd, while the bidding for me was going on, to the spot where R. was standing. She fell at his feet, and clung to his knees, entreating him, in tones that a mother only could command, to buy her *baby* as well as herself, and spare to her one of her little ones at least. Will it, can it be believed, that this man, thus appealed to, was capable, not merely of turning a deaf ear to her supplication, but of disengaging himself from her with such violent blows and kicks as to reduce her to the necessity of creeping out of his reach, and mingling the groan of bodily suffering with the sob of a breaking heart?

Now all these incidents that have been given are *real* incidents of slavery, related by those who know slavery by the best of all tests—experience; and they are given by men who have earned a good character in freedom, which makes their word as good as the word of any man living.

The case of Lewis Clark might be called a harder one than common. The case of Douglass is probably a very fair average specimen.

The writer had conversed, in her time, with a very considerable number of liberated slaves, many of whom stated that their own individual lot had been comparatively a mild one; but she never talked with one who did not let fall, first or last, some incident which he had observed, some scene which he had witnessed, which went to show some most horrible abuse of the system; and what was most affecting about it, the narrator often evidently considered it so much a matter of course as to mention it incidentally, without any particular emotion.

CHAPTER IV.

It is supposed by many that the great outcry among those who are opposed to slavery comes from a morbid reading of unauthenticated accounts got up in abolition papers, &c. This idea is a very mistaken one. The accounts which tell against the slave-system are derived from the continual living testimony of the poor slave himself; often from that of the fugitives from slavery who are continually passing through our Northern cities.

As a specimen of some of the incidents, thus developed, is given the following fact of recent occurrence, related to the author by a lady in Boston. This lady, who was much in the habit of visiting the poor, was sent for, a month or two since, to see a mulatto woman, who had just arrived at a coloured boarding-house near by, and who appeared to be in much dejection of mind. A little conversation showed her to be a fugitive. Her history was as follows: She, with her brother, were, as is often the case, both the children and slaves of their master. At his death, they were left to his legitimate daughter as her servants, and treated with as much consideration as very common kind of people might be expected to show those who were entirely and in every respect at their disposal.

The wife of her brother ran away to Canada; and as there was some talk of selling her and her child, in consequence of some embarrassment in the family affairs, her brother, a fine-spirited young man, determined to effect her escape, also, to a land of liberty. He concealed her for some time in the back part of an obscure dwelling in the city, till he could find an opportunity to send her off. While she was in this retreat, he was indefatigable in his attentions to her, frequently bringing her fruit and flowers, and doing everything he could to beguile the weariness of her imprisonment.

At length, the steward of a vessel, whom he had obliged, offered to conceal him on board the ship, and give him a chance to escape. The noble-hearted fellow, though tempted by an offer which would enable him immediately to join his wife, to whom he was tenderly attached, preferred to give this offer to his sister, and during the absence of the captain of the vessel she and her child were brought on board and secreted.

The captain, when he returned and discovered what had been done, was very angry, as the thing, if detected, would have involved him in very serious difficulties. He declared at first, that he would send the woman up into town to jail; but, by her entreaties and those of the steward, was induced to wait till evening, and send word to her brother to come and take her back. After dark the brother came on board, and, instead of taking his sister away, began to appeal to the humanity of the captain in the most moving terms. He told his sister's history and his own, and pleaded eloquently his desire for her liberty. The captain had determined to be obdurate, but, alas! he was only a man. Perhaps he had himself a wife and child—perhaps he felt that, were he in the young man's case, he would do just so for his sister. Be it as it may, he was at last overcome. He said to the young man, "I must send you away from my ship; I'll put off a boat and see you get into it, and you must row off, and never let me see your faces again; and if, after all, you should come back and get on board, it will be your fault and not mine."

So, in the rain and darkness, the young man and his sister and child were lowered over the side of the vessel, and rowed away. After a while the ship weighed anchor, but before she reached Boston it was discovered that the woman and child were on board.

The lady to whom this story was related, was requested to write a letter, in certain terms, to a person in the city whence the fugitive had come, to let the brother know of her safe arrival.

The fugitive was furnished with work, by which she could support herself and child, and the lady carefully attended to her wants for a few weeks.

One morning she came in, with a good deal of agitation, exclaiming, "O ma'am, he's come! George is come!" And in a few minutes the young man was introduced.

The lady who gave this relation belongs to the first circles of Boston society; she says that she never was more impressed by the personal manners of any gentleman than by those of this fugitive brother. So much did he have the air of a perfect, finished gentleman, that she felt she could not question him with regard to his escape with the familiarity with which persons of his condition are commonly approached; and it was not till he requested her to write a letter for him, because he could not write himself, that she could realize that this fine specimen of manhood had been all his life a slave.

The remainder of the history is no less romantic. The lady had a friend in Montreal, whither George's wife had gone; and, after furnishing money to pay their expenses, she presented them with a letter to this gentleman, requesting the latter to assist the young man in finding his wife. When they landed at Montreal, George stepped on shore and presented this letter to the first man he met, asking him if he knew to whom it was directed. The gentleman proved to be the very person to whom the letter was addressed. He knew George's wife, brought him to her without delay, so that, by return mail, the lady had the satisfaction of learning the happy termination of the adventure.

This is but a specimen of histories which are continually transpiring; so that those who speak of slavery can say, "We speak that which we do know, and testify that we have seen."

But we shall be told the slaves are all a lying race, and that these are lies which they tell us. There are some things, however, about these slaves, which cannot lie. Those deep lines of patient sorrow upon the face; that attitude of crouching and humble subjection; that sad, habitual expression of hope deferred in the eye, would tell their story if the slave never spoke.

It is not long since the writer has seen faces such as might haunt one's dreams for weeks.

Suppose a poor, worn-out mother, sickly, feeble, and old— her hands worn to the bone with hard, unpaid toil, whose nine children have been sold to the slave trader, and whose tenth soon is to be sold, unless by her labour as a washerwoman she can raise nine hundred dollars! Such are the kind of cases constantly coming to one's knowledge, such are the witnesses which will not let us sleep.

CHAPTER IV.

Doubt has been expressed whether such a thing as an advertisement for a man "*dead or alive,*" like the advertisement for George Harris, was ever published in the Southern States. The scene of the story in which that occurs is supposed to be laid a few years back, at the time when the black laws of Ohio were passed. That at this time such advertisements were common in the newspapers, there is abundant evidence. That they are less common now, is a matter of hope and gratulation.

In the year 1839, Mr. Theodore D. Weld made a systematic attempt to collect and arrange the statistics of slavery. A mass of facts and statistics was gathered, which was authenticated with the most unquestionable accuracy. Some of the "one thousand" witnesses, whom he brings upon the stand, were ministers, lawyers, merchants, and men of various other callings, who were either natives of the slave States, or had been residents there for many years of their life. Many of these were slaveholders. Others of the witnesses were, or had been, slave-drivers, or officers of coasting-vessels engaged in the slave-trade.

Another part of his evidence was gathered from public speeches in Congress, in the State legislatures, and elsewhere. But the majority of it was taken from recent newspapers.

The papers from which these facts were copied were preserved and put on file in a public place, where they remained for some years for the information of the curious. After Mr. Weld's book was completed, a copy of it was sent, through the mail, to every editor from whose paper such advertisements had been taken, and to every individual of whom any facts had been narrated, with the passage concerning them marked.

It is quite possible that this may have had some influence in rendering such advertisements less common. Men of sense often go on doing a thing which is very absurd, or even inhuman, simply because it has always been done before them, and they follow general custom, without much reflection. When their attention, however, is called to it by a stranger who sees the thing from another point of view, they become immediately sensible of the impropriety of the practice, and discontinue it. The reader will, however, be pained to notice, when he comes to the legal part of the book, that, even in some of the largest cities of our slave States, this barbarity had not been entirely discontinued in the year 1850.

The list of advertisements in Mr. Weld's book is here inserted, not to weary the reader with its painful details, but that, by running his eye over the dates of the papers quoted, and the places of their publication, he may form a fair estimate of the extent to which this atrocity was *publicly* practised.

The *Wilmington* (North Carolina) *Advertiser,* of July 13, 1838, contains the following advertisement:

"100 dollars will be paid to any person who may apprehend, and safely confine in any jail in this State, a certain negro man, named ALFRED. And the same reward will be paid if satisfactory evidence is given of *his having been* KILLED. He has one or more scars on one of his hands, caused by his having been shot.

"THE CITIZENS OF ONSLOW.

"*Richlands, Onslow Co. May* 16, 1838."

In the same column with the above, and directly under it, is the following.

"RAN AWAY, my negro man RICHARD. A reward of 25 dollars will be paid for his apprehension, DEAD or ALIVE. Satisfactory proof will only be required of his being KILLED. He has with him, in all probability, his wife ELIZA, who ran away from Col. Thompson, now a resident of Alabama, about the time he commenced his journey to that State.

"DURANT H. RHODES."

In the *Macon* (Georgia) *Telegraph,* May 28, is the following.

"About the first of March last the negro man RANSON left me without the least provocation whatever; I will give a reward of twenty dollars for said negro if taken, DEAD OR ALIVE; and if killed in any attempt, an advance of five dollars will be paid.

"BRYANT JOHNSON.

"*Crawford Co., Georgia.*"

See the *Newbern* (North Carolina) *Spectator,* Jan. 5, 1838, for the following.

"RAN AWAY from the subscriber, a negro man, named SAMPSON. Fifty dollars reward will be given for the delivery of him to me, or his confinement in any jail, so that I get him; and should he resist in being taken, so that violence is necessary to arrest him, I will not hold any person liable to damages should the slave be killed.

"ENOCH FOY,

"*Jones Co., N. C.*"

From the *Charleston* (South Carolina) *Courier,* Feb. 20, 1836.

"300 DOLLARS REWARD. Ran away from the subscriber, in November last, his two negro men, named BILLY and POMPEY.

"Billy is 25 years old, and is known as the patroon of my boat for many years. In all probability he may resist; in that event, 50 dollars will be paid for his HEAD."

CHAPTER V.

ELIZA.

THE writer stated in her book that Eliza was a portrait drawn from life. The incident which brought the original to her notice may be simply narrated.

While the writer was travelling in Kentucky, many years ago, she attended church in a small country town. While there, her attention was called to a beautiful quadroon girl, who sat in one of the slips of the church, and appeared to have charge of some young children. The description of Eliza may suffice for a description of her. When the author returned from the church, she inquired about the girl, and was told that she was as good and amiable as she was beautiful; that she was a pious girl, and a member of the Church; and, finally, that she was *owned* by Mr. So-and-so. The idea that this girl was a slave struck a chill to her heart, and she said earnestly, “Oh, I hope they treat her kindly.”

“Oh, certainly,” was the reply; “they think as much of her as of their own children.”

“I hope they will never sell her,” said a person in the company.

“Certainly they will not; a Southern gentleman, not long ago, offered her master a thousand dollars for her; but he told him that she was too good to be his wife, and he certainly should not have her for a mistress.”

That is all the writer knows of that girl.

With regard to the incident of Eliza's crossing the river on the ice—as the possibility of the thing has been disputed—the writer gives the following circumstance in confirmation.

Last spring, while the author was in New York, a Presbyterian clergyman of Ohio came to her, and said, “I understand they dispute that fact about the woman's crossing the river. Now, I know all about that, for I got the story from the very man that helped her up the bank. I know it is true, for she is now living in Canada.”

It has been objected that the representation of the scene in which the plan for kidnapping Eliza is concocted by Haley, Marks, and Loker, at the tavern, is a gross caricature on the state of things in Ohio.

What knowledge the author has had of the facilities which some justices of the peace, under the old fugitive law of Ohio, were in the habit of giving to kidnapping, may be inferred by comparing the statement in her book with some in her personal knowledge.

"Ye see," said Marks to Haley, stirring his punch as he did so, "ye see, we has justices convenient at all p'ints along shore, that does up any little jobs in our line quite reasonable. Tom, he does the knockin' down, and that ar; and I come in all dressed up—shining boots—everything first chop—when the swearin's to be done. You oughter see me, now!" said Marks, in a glow of professional pride, "how I can tone it off. One day I'm Mr. Twickem, from New Orleans; 'nother day, I'm just come from my plantation on Pearl river, where I works seven hundred niggers; then, again, I come out a distant relation to Henry Clay, or some old cock in Kentuck. Talents is different, you know. Now, Tom's a roarer when there's any thumping or fighting to be done; but at lying he an't good, Tom an't; ye see it don't come natural to him; but, Lord! if thar's a feller in the country that can swear to anything and everything, and put in all the circumstances and flourishes with a longer face, and carry't through better'n I can, why, I'd like to see him, that's all! I b'lieve, my heart, I could get along, and snake through, even if justices were more particular than they is. Sometimes I rather wish they was more particular; 'twould be a heap more relishin' if they was—more fun, yer know."

In the year 1839, the writer received into her family, as a servant, a girl from Kentucky. She had been the slave of one of the lowest and most brutal families, with whom she had been brought up, in a log-cabin, in a state of half-barbarism. In proceeding to give her religious instruction, the author heard, for the first time in her life, an inquiry which she had not supposed possible to be made in America—"Who is Jesus Christ, now, anyhow?"

When the author told her the history of the love and life and death of Christ, the girl seemed wholly overcome; tears streamed down her cheeks, and she exclaimed piteously, "Why didn't nobody never tell me this before?"

"But," said the writer to her, "haven't you ever seen the Bible?"

"Yes, I have seen Missus a-readin' on't sometimes; but, law sakes! she's just a readin' on't 'cause she could; don't s'pose it did her no good, no way."

She said she had been to one or two camp-meetings in her life, but "didn't notice very particular."

At all events, the story certainly made great impression on her, and had such an effect in improving her conduct, that the writer had great hopes of her.

On inquiring into her history, it was discovered that, by the laws of Ohio, she was legally entitled to her freedom, from the fact of her having been brought into the State, and left there, temporarily, by the consent of her mistress. These facts being properly authenticated before the proper authorities, papers attesting her freedom were drawn up, and it was now supposed that all danger of pursuit was over. After she had remained in the family for some months, word was sent, from various sources, to Professor Stowe, that the girl's young master was over, looking for her, and that, if care were not taken, she would be conveyed back into slavery.

CHAPTER V.

Professor Stowe called on the magistrate who had authenticated her papers, and inquired whether they were not sufficient to protect her. The reply was, Certainly they are, in law, if she could have a fair hearing; but they will come to your house in the night, with an officer and a warrant; they will take her before Justice D—, and swear to her. He's the man that does all this kind of business, and he'll deliver her up, and there'll be an end of it.

Mr. Stowe then inquired what could be done; and was recommended to carry her to some place of security till the inquiry for her was over. Accordingly, that night, a brother of the author, with Professor Stowe, performed for the fugitive that office which the senator is represented as performing for Eliza. They drove about ten miles on a solitary road, crossed the creek at a very dangerous fording, and presented themselves, at mid-night, at the house of John Van Zandt, a noble-minded Kentuckian, who had performed the good deed which the author, in her story, ascribes to Van Tromp.

After some rapping at the door, the worthy owner of the mansion appeared, candle in hand, as has been narrated.

"Are you the man that would save a poor coloured girl from kidnappers?" was the first question.

"Guess I am," was the prompt response; "where is she?"

"Why, she's here."

"But how did you come?"

"I crossed the creek."

"Why, the Lord helped you!" said he; "I shouldn't dare cross it myself in the night. A man and his wife, and five children were drowned there, a little while ago."

The reader may be interested to know that the poor girl was never re-taken: that she married well in Cincinnati, is a very respectable woman, and the mother of a large family of children.

CHAPTER VI.

UNCLE TOM.

THE character of Uncle Tom has been objected to as improbable; and yet the writer has received more confirmations of that character, and from a great variety of sources, than of any other in the book.

Many people have said to her, "I knew an Uncle Tom in such-and-such a Southern State." All the histories of this kind which have thus been related to her would of themselves, if collected, make a small volume. The author will relate a few of them.

While visiting in an obscure town in Maine, in the family of a friend, the conversation happened to turn upon this subject, and the gentleman with whose family she was staying related the following. He said, that when on a visit to his brother in New Orleans, some years before, he found in his possession a most valuable negro man, of such remarkable probity and honesty that his brother literally trusted him with all he had. He had frequently seen him take out a handful of bills, without looking at them, and hand them to this servant, bidding him go and provide what was necessary for the family, and bring him the change. He remonstrated with his brother on this imprudence; but the latter replied that he had had such proofs of this servant's impregnable conscientiousness that he felt it safe to trust him to any extent.

The history of the servant was this. He had belonged to a man in Baltimore, who, having a general prejudice against all the religious exercises of slaves, did all that he could to prevent his having any time for devotional duties, and strictly forbade him to read the Bible and pray, either by himself or with the other servants; and because, like a certain man of old, named Daniel, he constantly disobeyed this unchristian edict, his master inflicted upon him that punishment which a master always has in his power to inflict—he sold him into perpetual exile from his wife and children, down to New Orleans.

The gentleman who gave the writer this information says that, although not a religious man at the time, he was so struck with the man's piety, that he said to his brother, "I hope you will never do anything to deprive this man of his religious privileges, for I think a judgment will come upon you if you do." To this his brother replied that he should be very foolish to do it, since he had made up his mind that the man's religion was the root of his extraordinary excellences.

Some time since there was sent to the writer from the South, through the mail, a little book, entitled "Sketches of Old Virginia Family Servants," with a preface by Bishop Meade. The book contains an account of the following servants: African Bella, Old Milly, Blind Lucy, Aunt Betty, Springsfield Bob, Mammy Chris, Diana Washington, Aunt Margaret, Rachel Parker, Nelly Jackson, My Own Mammy, Aunt Beck.

The following extract from Bishop Meade's preface may not be uninteresting:—

The following sketches were placed in my hands with a request that I would examine them with a view to publication.

After reading them, I could not but think that they would be both pleasing and edifying.

Very many such examples of fidelity and piety might be added from the old Virginia families. These will suffice as specimens, and will serve to show how interesting the relation between master and servant often is.

Many will doubtless be surprised to find that there was so much intelligence as well as piety in some of the old servants of Virginia, and that they had learned to read the Sacred Scriptures, so as to be useful in this way among their fellow-servants. It is, and always has been true, in regard to the servants of the Southern States, that although public schools may have been prohibited, yet no interference has been attempted, where the owners have chosen to teach their servants, or permit them to learn in a private way how to read God's word. Accordingly, there always have been some who were thus taught. In the more Southern States the number of these has most abounded. Of this fact I became well assured about thirty years since, when visiting the Atlantic States, with a view to the formation of auxiliary colonization societies, and the selection of the first colonists for Africa. In the city of Charleston, South Carolina, I found more intelligence and character among the free coloured population than anywhere else. The same was true of some of those in bondage. A respectable number might be seen in certain parts of the Episcopal churches which I attended, using their prayer-books, and joining in the responses of the church.

Many purposes of convenience and hospitality were subserved by this encouragement of cultivation in some of the servants, on the part of the owners.

When travelling many years since with a sick wife, and two female relatives, from Charleston to Virginia, at a period of the year when many of the families from the country resort to the town for health, we were kindly urged to call at the seat of one of the first families in South Carolina; and a letter from the mistress, then in the city, was given us, to her servant, who had charge of the house in the absence of the family. On reaching there, and delivering the letter to a most respectable-looking female servant, who immediately read it, we were kindly welcomed and entertained, during a part of two days, as sumptuously as though the owner had been present. We understood that it was no uncommon thing in

South Carolina for travellers to be thus entertained by the servants in the absence of the owners, on receiving letters from the same.

Instances of confidential and affectionate relationship between servants and their masters and mistresses, such as are set forth in the following sketches, are still to be found in all the slave-holding States. I mention one, which has come under my own observation. The late Judge Upshur, of Virginia, had a faithful house-servant (by his will now set free), with whom he used to correspond on matters of business when he was absent on his circuit. I was dining at his house, some years since, with a number of persons, himself being absent, when the conversation turned on the subject of the presidential election, then going on through the United States, and about which there was an intense interest; when his servant informed us that he had that day received a letter from his master, then on the western shore, in which he stated that the friends of General Harrison might be relieved from all uneasiness, as the returns already received made his election quite certain.

Of course it is not to be supposed that we design to convey the impression that such instances are numerous, the nature of the relationship forbidding it; but we do mean emphatically to affirm that there is far more of kindly and Christian intercourse than many at a distance are apt to believe. That there is a great and sad want of Christian instruction, notwithstanding the more recent efforts put forth to impart it, we most sorrowfully acknowledge.

Bishop Meade adds that these sketches are published with the hope that they might have the effect of turning the attention of ministers and heads of families more seriously to the duty of caring for the souls of their servants.

With regard to the servant of Judge Upshur, spoken of in this communication of Bishop Meade, his master has left, in his last will, the following remarkable tribute to his worth and excellence of character:—

I emancipate and set free my servant, David Rice, and direct my executors to give him *one hundred dollars*. I recommend him in the strongest manner to the respect, esteem, and confidence of any community in which he may happen to live. He has been my slave for twenty-four years, during all which time he has been trusted to every extent, and in every respect; my confidence in him has been unbounded; his relation to myself and family has always been such as to afford him daily opportunities to deceive and injure us; yet he has never been detected in any serious fault, nor even in an unintentional breach of decorum of his station. His intelligence is of a high order, his integrity above all suspicion, and his sense of right and propriety correct, and even refined. I feel that he is justly entitled to carry this certificate from me in the new relations which he must now form; it is due to his long and most faithful services, and to the sincere and steady friendship which I bear to him. In the uninterrupted confidential intercourse of twenty-four years, I have never given him, nor had occasion to give him, one unpleasant word. I know no man who has fewer faults or more excellences than he.

CHAPTER VI.

In the free States there have been a few instances of such extraordinary piety among negroes, that their biography and sayings have been collected in religious tracts, and published for the instruction of the community.

One of these was, before his conversion, a convict in a State-prison in New York, and there received what was, perhaps, the first religious instruction that had ever been imparted to him. He became so eminent an example of humility, faith, and, above all, fervent love, that his presence in the neighbourhood was esteemed a blessing to the church. A lady has described to the writer the manner in which he would stand up and exhort in the church-meetings for prayer, when, with streaming eyes and the deepest abasement, humbly addressing them as his masters and misses, he would nevertheless pour forth religious exhortations which were edifying to the most cultivated and refined.

In the town of Brunswick, Maine, where the writer lived when writing "Uncle Tom's Cabin," may now be seen the grave of an aged coloured woman, named Phebe, who was so eminent for her piety and loveliness of character, that the writer has never heard her name mentioned except with that degree of awe and respect which one would imagine due to a saint. The small cottage where she resided is still visited and looked upon as a sort of shrine, as the spot where old Phebe lived and prayed. Her prayers and pious exhortations were supposed to have been the cause of the conversion of many young people in the place. Notwithstanding that the unchristian feeling of caste prevails as strongly in Maine as anywhere else in New England, and the negro, commonly speaking, is an object of aversion and contempt, yet, so great was the influence of her piety and loveliness of character, that she was uniformly treated with the utmost respect and attention by all classes of people. The most cultivated and intelligent ladies of the place esteemed it a privilege to visit her cottage; and when she was old and helpless, her wants were most tenderly provided for. When the news of her death was spread abroad in the place, it excited a general and very tender sensation of regret. "We have lost Phebe's prayers," was the remark frequently made afterwards by members of the church, as they met one another. At her funeral, the ex-governor of the State and the professors of the college officiated as pall-bearers, and a sermon was preached, in which the many excellences of her Christian character were held up as an example to the community. A small religious tract, containing an account of her life, was published by the American Tract Society, prepared by a lady of Brunswick. The writer recollects that on reading the tract, when she first went to Brunswick, a doubt arose in her mind whether it was not somewhat exaggerated. Some time afterwards she overheard some young persons conversing together about the tract, and saying that they did not think it gave exactly the right idea of Phebe. "Why, is it too highly coloured?" was the inquiry of the author. "Oh, no, no, indeed!" was the earnest response; "it doesn't begin to give an idea of how good she was."

Such instances as these serve to illustrate the words of the Apostle, "God hath chosen the foolish things of the world to confound the wise; and God hath chosen the weak things of the world to confound the things which are mighty."

John Bunyan says, that although the valley of humiliation be unattractive in the eyes of the men of this world, yet the very sweetest flowers grow there. So it is with the condition of the lowly and poor in this world. God has often, indeed always, shown a particular regard for it, in selecting from that class the recipients of his grace. It is to be remembered that Jesus Christ, when he came to found the Christian dispensation, did not choose his apostles from the chief priests and the scribes, learned in the law and high in the church; nor did he choose them from philosophers and poets, whose educated and comprehensive minds might be supposed best able to appreciate his great designs; but he chose twelve plain, poor fishermen, who were ignorant, and felt that they were ignorant, and who, therefore, were willing to give themselves up with all simplicity to his guidance. What God asks of the soul more than anything else is faith and simplicity, the affection and reliance of the little child. Even these twelve fancied too much that they were wise, and Jesus was obliged to set a little child in the midst of them, as a more perfect teacher.

The negro race is confessedly more simple, docile, childlike, and affectionate, than other races; and hence the divine graces of love and faith, when in-breathed by the Holy Spirit, find in their natural temperament a more congenial atmosphere.

A last instance parallel with that of Uncle Tom is to be found in the published memoirs of the venerable Josiah Henson, now, as we have said, a clergyman in Canada. He was “raised” in the State of Maryland. His first recollections were of seeing his father mutilated and covered with blood, suffering the penalty of the law for the crime of raising his hand against a white man—that white man being the overseer, who had attempted a brutal assault upon his mother. This punishment made his father surly and dangerous, and he was subsequently sold South, and thus parted for ever from his wife and children. Henson grew up in a state of heathenism, without any religious instruction, till, in a camp-meeting, he first heard of Jesus Christ, and was electrified by the great and thrilling news that He had tasted death for every man, the bond as well as the free. This story produced an immediate conversion, such as we read of in the Acts of the Apostles, where the Ethiopian eunuch, from one interview, hearing the story of the cross, at once believes and is baptized. Henson forthwith not only became a Christian, but began to declare the news to those about him; and, being a man of great natural force of mind and strength of character, his earnest endeavours to enlighten his fellow-heathen were so successful, that he was gradually led to assume the station of a negro preacher; and though he could not read a word of the Bible or hymn-book, his labours in this line were much prospered. He became immediately a very valuable slave to his master, and was intrusted by the latter with the oversight of his whole estate, which he managed with great judgment and prudence. His master appears to have been a very ordinary man in every respect,—to have been entirely incapable of estimating him in any other light than as exceedingly valuable property, and to have had no other feeling excited by his extraordinary faithfulness than the desire to make the most of him. When his affairs became embarrassed, he formed the design of removing all his negroes into Kentucky, and intrusted the operation entirely to his overseer. Henson was to take them alone, without any other attendant, from Maryland to Kentucky, a distance of some thousands of miles, giving only his promise as a Christian that he would faithfully perform this undertaking. On the way thither they passed through a portion of Ohio, and there Henson was informed that he could now secure his own freedom and that of all his fellows, and he was strongly urged to do it. He was exceedingly tempted and tried, but his Christian principle was invulnerable. No inducements could lead him to feel that it was right for a Christian to violate a pledge solemnly given, and his influence over the whole band was so great that he took them all with him into Kentucky. Those causists among us who lately seem to think and teach that it is right for us to violate the plain commands of God, whenever some great national good can be secured by it, would do well to contemplate the inflexible principle of this poor slave, who, without being able to read a letter of the Bible, was yet enabled to perform this most sublime act of self-renunciation in obedience to its commands. Subsequently to this, his master, in a relenting moment, was induced by a friend to sell him his freedom for four hundred dollars; but, when the excitement of the importunity had passed off, he regretted that he had suffered so valuable a piece of property to leave his hands for so slight a remuneration. By an unworthy artifice, therefore, he got possession of his servant's free papers, and condemned him still to hopeless slavery. Subsequently, his affairs becoming still more involved, he sent his son down the river with a flat boat loaded with cattle and produce for the New Orleans market, directing him to take Henson along, and sell him after they had sold the cattle and the boat. All the depths of the negro's soul were torn up and thrown into convulsion by this horrible piece of ingratitude, cruelty and injustice; and, while outwardly calm, he was struggling with most bitter temptations from within, which, as he could not read the Bible, he could repel only by a recollection of its sacred truths, and by earnest prayer. As he neared the New Orleans market, he says that these convulsions of soul increased, especially when he met some of his old companions from Kentucky, whose despairing countenances and emaciated forms told of hard work and insufficient food, and confirmed all his worst fears of the lower country. In the transports of his despair, the temptation was more urgently presented to him to murder his young master and the other hand on the flat boat in their sleep, to seize upon the boat, and make his escape. He thus relates the scene where he was almost brought to the perpetration of this deed:—

One dark, rainy night, within a few days of New Orleans, my hour seemed to have come. I was alone on the deck; Mr. Amos and the hands were all asleep below, and I crept down noiselessly, got hold of an axe, entered the cabin, and looking by the aid of the dim light there for my victims, my eye fell upon Master Amos, who was nearest to me; my hand slid along the axe-handle, I raised it to strike the fatal blow, when suddenly the thought came to me, "What! commit *murder!* and you a Christian?" I had not called it murder before. It was self-defence—it was preventing others from murdering me—it was justifiable, it was even praiseworthy. But now, all at once, the truth burst upon me that it was a crime. I was going to kill a young man, who had done nothing to injure me, but obey commands which he could not resist; I was about to lose the fruit of all my efforts at self-improvement, the character I had acquired, and the peace of mind which had never deserted me. All this came upon me instantly, and with a distinctness which made me almost think I heard it whispered in my ear; and I believe I even turned my head to listen. I shrunk back, laid down the axe, crept up on deck again, and thanked God, as I have done every day since, that I had not committed murder.

My feelings were still agitated, but they were changed. I was filled with shame and remorse for the design I had entertained, and with the fear that my companions would detect it in my face, or that a careless word would betray my guilty thoughts. I remained on deck all night, instead of rousing one of the men to relieve me; and nothing brought composure to my mind, but the solemn resolution I then made to resign myself to the will of God, and take with thankfulness, if I could, but with submission, at all events, whatever he might decide should be my lot. I reflected that if my life were reduced to a brief term, I should have less to suffer, and that it was better to die with a Christian's hope, and a quiet conscience, than to live with the incessant recollection of a crime that would destroy the value of life, and under the weight of a secret that would crush out the satisfaction that might be expected from freedom, and every other blessing.

Subsequently to this, his young master was taken violently down with the river fever, and became as helpless as a child. He passionately entreated Henson not to desert him, but to attend to the selling of the boat and produce, and put him on board the steamboat, and not to leave him, dead or alive, till he had carried him back to his father.

The young master was borne in the arms of his faithful servant to the steamboat, and there nursed by him with unremitting attention during the journey up the river; nor did he leave him till he had placed him in his father's arms.

Our love for human nature would lead us to add, with sorrow, that all this disinterestedness and kindness was rewarded only by empty praises, such as would be bestowed upon a very fine dog; and Henson indignantly resolved no longer to submit to the injustice. With a degree of prudence, courage, and address, which can scarcely find a parallel in any history, he managed, with his wife and two children, to escape into Canada. Here he learned to read, and by his superior talent and capacity for management, laid the foundation of the fugitive settlement of Dawn, which is understood to be one of the most flourishing in Canada.

It would be well for the most cultivated of us to ask, whether our ten talents in the way of religious knowledge have enabled us to bring forth as much fruit to the glory of God, to withstand temptation as patiently, to return good for evil as disinterestedly, as this poor ignorant slave. A writer in England has sneeringly remarked that such a man as Uncle Tom might be imported as a missionary to teach the most cultivated in England or America the true nature of religion. These instances show that what has been said with a sneer is in truth a sober verity; and it should never be forgotten that out of this race whom man despiseth have often been chosen of God true messengers of his grace, and temples for the indwelling of his Spirit.

"*For thus saith the high and lofty One that inhabiteth eternity, whose name is holy, I dwell in the high and holy place, with him also that is of a contrite and humble spirit, to revive the spirit of the humble, and to revive the heart of the contrite ones.*"

The vision attributed to Uncle Tom introduces quite a curious chapter of psychology with regard to the negro race, and indicates a peculiarity which goes far to show how very different they are from the white race. They are possessed of a nervous organisation peculiarly susceptible and impressible. Their sensations and impressions are very vivid, and their fancy and imagination lively. In this respect the race has an Oriental character, and betrays its tropical origin. Like the Hebrews of old and the Oriental nations of the present, they give vent to their emotions with the utmost vivacity of expression, and their whole bodily system sympathises with the movements of their minds. When in distress, they actually lift up their voices to weep, and "cry with an exceeding bitter cry." When alarmed, they are often paralysed, and rendered entirely helpless. Their religious exercises are all coloured by this sensitive and exceedingly vivacious temperament. Like Oriental nations, they incline much to outward expressions, violent gesticulations, and agitating movements of the body. Sometimes in their religious meetings they will spring from the floor many times in succession, with a violence and rapidity which is perfectly astonishing. They will laugh, weep, and embrace each other convulsively, and sometimes become entirely paralysed and cataleptic. A clergyman from the North once remonstrated with a Southern clergyman for permitting such extravagances among his flock. The reply of the Southern minister was, in effect, this: "Sir, I am satisfied that the races are so essentially different that they cannot be regulated by the same rules. I at first felt as you do; and though I saw that genuine conversions did take place, with all this outward manifestation, I was still so much annoyed by it as to forbid it among my negroes, till I was satisfied that the repression of it was a serious hindrance to real religious feeling; and then I became certain that all men cannot be regulated in their religious exercises by one model. I am assured that conversions produced with these accessories are quite as apt to be genuine, and to be as influential over the heart and life, as those produced in any other way." The fact is, that the Anglo-Saxon race—cool, logical, and practical—have yet to learn the doctrine of toleration for the peculiarities of other races; and perhaps it was with a foresight of their peculiar character and dominant position in the earth, that God gave the Bible to them in the fervent language and with the glowing imagery of the more susceptible and passionate Oriental races.

Mesmerists have found that the negroes are singularly susceptible to all that class of influences which produce catalepsy, mesmeric sleep, and partial clairvoyant phenomena.

The African race, in their own climate, are believers in spells, in "fetish and obi," in "the evil eye," and other singular influences, for which probably there is an origin in this peculiarity of constitution. The magicians in scriptural history were Africans; and the so-called magical arts are still practised in Egypt, and other parts of Africa, with a degree of skill and success which can only be accounted for by supposing peculiarities of nervous constitution quite different from those of the whites. Considering those distinctive traits of the race, it is no matter of surprise to find in their religious histories, when acted upon by the powerful stimulant of the Christian religion, very peculiar features. We are not surprised to find almost constantly, in the narrations of their religious histories, accounts of visions, of heavenly voices, of mysterious sympathies and transmissions of knowledge from heart to heart without the intervention of the senses, or what the Quakers call being "baptized into the spirit" of those who are distant.

Cases of this kind are constantly recurring in their histories. The young man whose story was related to the Boston lady, and introduced above in the chapter on George Harris, stated this incident concerning the recovery of his liberty: That after the departure of his wife and sister, he for a long time, and very earnestly, sought some opportunity of escape, but that every avenue appeared to be closed to him. At length, in despair, he retreated to his room, and threw himself upon his bed, resolving to give up the undertaking, when just as he was sinking to sleep, he was roused by a voice saying in his ear, "Why do you sleep now? Rise up, if you ever mean to be free!" He sprang up, went immediately out, and in the course of two hours discovered the means of escape which he used.

A lady whose history is known to the writer resided for some time on a Southern plantation, and was in the habit of imparting religious instruction to the slaves. One day a woman from a distant plantation called at her residence, and inquired for her. The lady asked in surprise, "How did you know about me?" The old woman's reply was, that she had long been distressed about her soul; but that, several nights before, some one had appeared to her in a dream, told her to go to this plantation and inquire for the strange lady there, and that she would teach her the way to heaven.

Another specimen of the same kind was related to the writer, by a slave-woman who had been through the whole painful experience of a slave's life. She was originally a young girl of pleasing exterior and gentle nature, carefully reared as a seamstress and nurse to the children of a family in Virginia, and attached with all the warmth of her susceptible nature to these children. Although one of the tenderest of mothers when the writer knew her, yet she assured the writer that she had never loved a child of her own as she loved the dear little young mistress who was her particular charge. Owing, probably, to some pecuniary difficulty in the family, this girl, whom we call Louisa, was sold to go on to a Southern plantation. She has often described the scene when she was forced into a carriage, and saw her dear young mistress leaning from the window, stretching her arms towards her, screaming and calling her name with all the vehemence of childish grief. She was carried in a coffle, and sold as cook on a Southern plantation. With the utmost earnestness of language she has described to the writer her utter loneliness, and the distress and despair of her heart, in this situation, parted for ever from all she held dear on earth, without even the possibility of writing letters or sending messages, surrounded by those who felt no kind of interest in her, and forced to a toil for which her more delicate education had entirely unfitted her. Under these circumstances, she began to believe that it was for some dreadful sin she had thus been afflicted. The course of her mind after this may be best told in her own simple words:—

"After that, I began to feel awful wicked—oh, so wicked, you've no idea! I felt so wicked that my sins seemed like a load on me, and I went so heavy all the day! I felt so wicked that I didn't feel worthy to pray in the house, and I used to go way off in the lot and pray. At last one day, when I was praying, the Lord he came and spoke to me."

"The Lord spoke to you? What do you mean, Louisa?"

With a face of the utmost earnestness she answered, "Why, ma'am, the Lord Jesus he came and spoke to me, you know; and I never, till the last day of my life, shall forget what he said to me."

"What was it?" said the writer.

"He said, `Fear not, my little one; thy sins are forgiven thee;'" and she added to this some verses, which the writer recognized as those of a Methodist hymn.

Being curious to examine more closely this phenomenon, the author said,

"You mean that you dreamed this, Louisa?"

With an air of wounded feeling, and much earnestness, she answered,

"O no, Mrs. Stowe; that never was a dream; you'll never make me believe that."

The thought at once arose in the writer's mind, If the Lord Jesus is indeed everywhere present, and if he is as tender-hearted and compassionate as he was on earth—and we know he is— must he not sometimes long to speak to the poor desolate slave, when he knows that no voice but His can carry comfort and healing to his soul?

This instance of Louisa is so exactly parallel to another case, which the author received from an authentic source, that she is tempted to place the two side by side.

Among the slaves who were brought into the New England States, at the time when slavery was prevalent, was one woman, who immediately on being told the history of the love of Jesus Christ, exclaimed, "He is the one; this is what I wanted!"

This language causing surprise, her history was inquired into. It was briefly this:—While living in her simple hut in Africa, the kidnappers one day rushed upon her family, and carried her husband and children off to the slave-ship, she escaping into the woods. On returning to her desolate home, she mourned with the bitterness of "Rachel weeping for her children." For many days her heart was oppressed with a heavy weight of sorrow; and, refusing all sustenance, she wandered up and down the desolate forest.

At last, she says, a strong impulse came over her to kneel down and pour out her sorrows into the ear of some unknown Being whom she fancied to be above her, in the sky.

She did so; and to her surprise, found an inexpressible sensation of relief. After this, it was her custom daily to go out to this same spot, and supplicate this unknown Friend. Subsequently, she was herself taken and brought over to America; and when the story of Jesus and his love was related to her, she immediately felt in her soul that this Jesus was the very friend who had spoken comfort to her yearning spirit in the distant forest of Africa.

Compare now these experiences with the earnest and beautiful language of Paul: "He hath made of one blood all nations of men, for to dwell on all the face of the earth; and hath determined the times before appointed *and the bounds* of their habitation, *that* THEY SHOULD *seek the Lord, if haply they might* FEEL AFTER HIM AND FIND HIM, *though he be not far from every one of us*."

Is not this truly "*feeling after God and finding Him?*" And may we not hope that the yearning, troubled, helpless heart of man, pressed by the insufferable anguish of this short life, or wearied by its utter vanity, never extends its ignorant pleading hand to God in vain? Is not the veil which divides us from an almighty and most merciful Father much thinner than we, in the pride of our philosophy, are apt to imagine? and is it not the most worthy conception of Him to suppose that the more utterly helpless and ignorant the human being is that seeks His aid, the more tender and the more condescending will be His communication with that soul?

If a mother has among her children one whom sickness has made blind, or deaf, or dumb, incapable of acquiring knowledge through the usual channels of communication, does she not seek to reach its darkened mind by modes of communication tenderer and more intimate than those which she uses with the stronger and more favoured ones? But can the love of any mother be compared with the infinite love of Jesus? Has He not described himself as that good Shepherd who leaves the whole flock of secure and well-instructed ones, to follow over the mountains of sin and ignorance the one lost sheep; and when He hath found it, rejoicing more over that one than over the ninety and nine that went not astray? Has He not told us that each of these little ones has a guardian angel that doth always behold the face of his Father which is in heaven? And is it not comforting to us to think that His love and care will be in proportion to the ignorance and the wants of His chosen ones?

* * * * *

Since the above was prepared for the press the author has received the following extract from a letter written by a gentleman in Missouri to the editor of the *Oberlin* (Ohio) *Evangelist:*—

I really thought, while reading "Uncle Tom's Cabin," that the authoress, when describing the character of Tom, had in her mind's eye a slave whose acquaintance I made some years since, in the State of Mississippi, called "Uncle Jacob." I was staying a day or two with a planter, and in the evening, when out in the yard,

CHAPTER VI.

I heard a well-known hymn and tune sung in one of the "quarters," and then the voice of prayer; and oh, *such* a prayer! what fervour! what unction! nay, the man "prayed right up;" and when I read of Uncle Tom, how "nothing could exceed the touching simplicity, the child-like earnestness, of his prayer, enriched with the language of Scripture, which seemed so entirely to have wrought itself into his being as to have become a part of himself," the recollections of that evening prayer were strangely vivid. On entering the house, and referring to what I had heard, his master replied, "Ah, sir, if I covet anything in this world, it is Uncle Jacob's religion. If there is a good man on earth, he certainly is one." He said Uncle Jacob was a regulator on the plantation; that a *word* or a *look* from him, addressed to younger slaves, had more efficiency than a *blow* from the overseer.

The next morning Uncle Jacob informed me he was from Kentucky, opposite Cincinnati; that his opportunities for attending religious worship had been frequent; that at about the age of forty he was sold South, was set to picking cotton; could not, when doing his best, pick the task assigned him; was whipped and whipped, he could not possibly tell how often; was of opinion that the overseer came to the conclusion that whipping could not bring one more pound out of him, for he set him to driving a team. At this and other work he could "make a *hand;*" had changed owners three or four times. He expressed himself as well pleased with his present situation as he expected to be in the South, but was yearning to return to his former associations in Kentucky.

CHAPTER VII.

MISS OPHELIA.

MISS OPHELIA stands as the representative of a numerous class of the very best of Northern people; to whom perhaps, if our Lord should again address his churches a letter, as he did those of old time, he would use the same words as then: "I know thy works, and thy labour, and thy patience, and how thou canst not bear them which are evil; and thou hast tried them which are apostles and are not, and hast found them liars; and hast borne, and hast patience, and for my name's sake hast laboured and hast not fainted. Nevertheless, I have somewhat against thee, because thou hast left thy first love."

There are in this class of people, activity, zeal, unflinching conscientiousness, clear intellectual discriminations between truth and error, and great logical and doctrinal correctness; but there is a want of that spirit of love, without which, in the eye of Christ, the most perfect character is as deficient as a wax flower — wanting in life and perfume.

Yet this blessed principle is not dead in their hearts, but only sleepeth; and so great is the real and genuine goodness, that when the true magnet of divine love is applied, they always answer to its touch.

So when the gentle Eva, who is an impersonation in childish form of the love of Christ, solves at once, by a blessed instinct, the problem which Ophelia has long been unable to solve by dint of utmost hammering and vehement effort, she at once, with a good and honest heart, perceives and acknowledges her mistake, and is willing to learn even of a little child.

Miss Ophelia, again, represents one great sin, of which, unconsciously, American Christians have allowed themselves to be guilty. Unconsciously it must be, for nowhere is conscience so predominant as among this class, and nowhere is there a more honest strife to bring every thought into captivity to the obedience of Christ.

One of the first and most declared objects of the gospel has been to break down all those irrational barriers and prejudices which separate the human brotherhood into diverse and contending clans. Paul says, "In Christ Jesus there is neither Jew nor Greek, barbarian, Scythian, bond nor free." The Jews at that time were separated from the Gentiles by an insuperable wall of prejudice. They could not eat and drink together, nor pray together. But the apostles most earnestly laboured to show them the sin of this prejudice. St. Paul says to the Ephesians, speaking of this former division, "He is our peace, who hath made both one, and hath broken down the middle wall of partition between us.

It is very easy to see that, although slavery has been abolished in the New England States, it has left behind it the most baneful feature of the system—that which makes American worse than Roman slavery—the prejudice of caste and colour. In the New England States the negro has been treated as belonging to an inferior race of beings; forced to sit apart by himself in the place of worship; his children excluded from the schools; himself excluded from the railroad-car and the omnibus, and the peculiarities of his race made the subject of bitter contempt and ridicule.

This course of conduct has been justified by saying that they are a degraded race. But how came they degraded? Take any class of men, and shut them from the means of education, deprive them of hope and self-respect, close to them all avenues of honourable ambition, and you will make just such a race of them as the negroes have been among us.

So singular and so melancholy is the dominion of prejudice over the human mind, that professors of Christianity in our New England States have often, with very serious self-denial to themselves, sent the gospel to heathen as dark-complexioned as the Africans, when in their very neighbourhood were persons of dark complexion, who, on that account, were forbidden to send their children to the schools and discouraged from entering the churches. The effect of this has been directly to degrade and depress the race; and then this very degradation and depression has been pleaded as the reason for continuing this course.

Not long since the writer called upon a benevolent lady, and during the course of the call the conversation turned upon the incidents of a fire which had occurred the night before in the neighbourhood. A deserted house had been burned to the ground. The lady said it was supposed it had been set on fire. "What could be any one's motive for setting it on fire?" said the writer.

"Well," replied the lady, "it was supposed that a coloured family was about to move into it, and it was thought that the neighbourhood wouldn't consent to that. So it was supposed that was the reason."

This was said with an air of innocence and much unconcern.

The writer inquired, "Was it a family of bad character?"

"No, not particularly, that I know of," said the lady; "but then they are negroes, you know."

Now, this lady is a very pious lady. She probably would deny herself to send the gospel to the heathen; and if she had ever thought of considering this family a heathen family, would have felt the deepest interest in their welfare, because on the subject of duty to the heathen she had been frequently instructed from the pulpit, and had all her religious and conscientious sensibilities awake. Probably she had never listened from the pulpit to a sermon which should exhibit the great truth, that "in Christ Jesus there is neither Jew nor Greek, barbarian, Scythian, bond nor free."

Supposing our Lord was now on earth, as he was once, what course is it probable that he would pursue with regard to this unchristian prejudice of colour?

There was a class of men in those days as much despised by the Jews as the negroes are by us; and it was a complaint made of Christ that he was a friend of publicans and sinners. And if Christ should enter, on some communion season, into a place of worship, and see the coloured man sitting afar off by himself, would it not be just in his spirit to go there and sit with him, rather than to take the seats of his richer and more prosperous brethren?

It is, however, but just to our Northern Christians to say that this sin has been committed ignorantly and in unbelief, and that within a few years signs of a much better spirit have begun to manifest themselves. In some places, recently, the doors of school-houses have been thrown open to the children, and many a good Miss Ophelia has opened her eyes in astonishment to find that, while she has been devouring the *Missionary Herald,* and going without butter on her bread and sugar in her tea to send the gospel to the Sandwich Islands, there is a very thriving colony of heathen in her own neighbourhood at home; and, true to her own good and honest heart, she has resolved *not* to give up her prayers and efforts for the heathen abroad, but to add thereunto labours for the heathen at home.

Our safety and hope in this matter is this: that there are multitudes in all our churches who do most truly and sincerely love Christ above all things, and who, just so soon as a little reflection shall have made them sensible of their duty in this respect, will most earnestly perform it.

It is true that, if they do so, they may be called Abolitionists; but the true Miss Ophelia is not afraid of a hard name in a good cause, and has rather learned to consider "the reproach of Christ a greater treasure than the riches of Egypt."

That there is much already for Christians to do in enlightening the moral sense of the community on this subject, will appear if we consider that even so well-educated and gentlemanly a man as Frederick Douglass was recently obliged to pass the night on the deck of a steamer, when in delicate health, because this senseless prejudice deprived him of a place in the cabin; and that that very laborious and useful minister, Dr. Pennington, of New York, has, during the last season, been often obliged seriously to endanger his health, by walking to his pastoral labours, over his very extended parish, under a burning sun, because he could not be allowed the common privilege of the omnibus, which conveys every class of white men, from the most refined to the lowest and most disgusting.

Let us consider now the number of professors of the religion of Christ in New York; and consider also that, by the very fact of their profession, they consider Dr. Pennington the brother of their Lord, and a member with them of the body of Christ.

Now, these Christians are influential, rich and powerful; they can control public sentiment on any subject that they think of any particular importance; and they profess, by their religion, that "if one member suffers, all the members suffer with it."

It is a serious question, whether such a marked indignity offered to Christ and his ministry, in the person of a coloured brother, without any remonstrance on their parts, will not lead to a general feeling that all that the Bible says about the union of Christians is a mere hollow sound, and means nothing.

Those who are anxious to do something directly to improve the condition of the slave can do it in no way so directly as by elevating the condition of the free coloured people around them, and taking every pains to give them equal rights and privileges.

This unchristian prejudice has doubtless stood in the way of the emancipation of hundreds of slaves. The slaveholder, feeling and acknowledging the evils of slavery, has come to the North, and seen evidences of this unkindly and unchristian state of feeling towards the slave, and has thus reflected within himself:—

"If I keep my slave at the South, he is, it is true, under the dominion of a very severe law; but then he enjoys the advantage of my friendship and assistance, and derives, through his connexion with me and my family, some kind of a position in the community. As my servant, he is allowed a seat in the car, and a place at the table. But if I emancipate and send him North, he will encounter substantially all the disadvantages of slavery, with no master to protect him."

This mode of reasoning has proved an apology to many a man for keeping his slaves in a position which he confesses to be a bad one; and it will be at once perceived that, should the position of the negro be conspicuously reversed in our Northern States, the effect upon the emancipation of the slave would be very great. They, then, who keep up this prejudice may be said to be, in a certain sense, slaveholders.

It is not meant by this that all distinctions of society should be broken over, and that people should be obliged to choose their intimate associates from a class unfitted by education and habits to sympathise with them.

The negro should not be lifted out of his sphere of life because he is a negro; but he should be treated with Christian courtesy *in* his sphere. In the railroad-car, in the omnibus and steam-boat, all ranks and degrees of white persons move with unquestioned freedom side by side; and Christianity requires that the negro have the same privilege.

That the dirtiest and most uneducated foreigner or American, with breath redolent of whisky, and clothes foul and disordered, should have an unquestioned right to take a seat next to any person in a railroad-car or steam-boat, and that the respectable, decent, and gentlemanly negro, should be excluded simply because he is a negro, cannot be considered otherwise than as an irrational and unchristian thing; and any Christian who allows such things done in his presence without remonstrance and the use of his Christian influence, will certainly be made deeply sensible of his error when he comes at last to direct and personal interview with his Lord.

There is no hope for this matter if the love of Christ is not strong enough, and if it cannot be said, with regard to the two races, “He is our peace who hath made both one, and hath broken down the middle wall of partition between us.”

The time is coming rapidly when the upper classes in society must learn that their education, wealth, and refinement, are not their own; that they have no right to use them for their own selfish benefit; but that they should hold them rather, as Fenelon expresses it, as “a ministry,” a stewardship, which they hold in trust for the benefit of their poorer brethren.

In some of the very highest circles in England and America, we begin to see illustrious examples of the commencement of such a condition of things.

One of the merchant princes of Boston, whose funeral has lately been celebrated in our city, afforded in his life a beautiful example of this truth. His wealth was the wealth of thousands. He was the steward of the widow and the orphan. His funds were a savings' bank, wherein were laid up the resources of the poor; and the mourners at his funeral were the scholars of the schools which he had founded, the officers of literary institutions which his munificence had endowed, the widows and orphans whom he had counselled and supported, and the men, in all ranks and conditions of life, who had been made by his benevolence to feel that his wealth was their wealth. May God raise up many men in Boston to enter into the spirit and labours of Amos Lawrence!

This is the *true* socialism, which comes from the spirit of Christ, and, without breaking down existing orders of society, *by love* makes the property and possessions of the higher class the property of the lower.

Men are always seeking to begin their reforms with the *outward* and *physical*. Christ begins his reforms in the heart. Men would break up all ranks of society, and throw all property into a common stock; but Christ would inspire the higher class with that Divine Spirit by which all the wealth, and means, and advantages of their position are used for the good of the lower.

We see, also, in the highest aristocracy of England instances of the same tendency.

Among her oldest nobility there begin to arise lecturers to mechanics and patrons of ragged-schools; and it is said that even on the throne of England is a woman who weekly instructs her class of Sunday-school scholars from the children in the vicinity of her country residence.

In this way, and not by an outward and physical division of property, shall all things be had in common. And when the white race shall regard their superiority over the coloured one only as a talent intrusted for the advantage of their weaker brother, *then* will the prejudice of caste melt away in the light of Christianity.

CHAPTER VIII.

MARIE ST. CLARE.

MARIE ST. CLARE is the type of a class of women not peculiar to any latitude, nor any condition of society. She may be found in England or in America. In the northern free States we have many Marie St. Clares, more or less fully developed.

When found in a northern latitude, she is for ever in trouble about her domestic relations. Her servants never do anything right. Strange to tell, they are not perfect, and she thinks it a very great shame. She is fully convinced that she ought to have every moral and Christian virtue in her kitchen for a little less than the ordinary wages; and when her cook leaves her, because she finds she can get better wages and less work in a neighbouring family, she thinks it shockingly selfish, unprincipled conduct. She is of opinion that servants ought to be perfectly disinterested; that they ought to be willing to take up with the worst rooms in the house, with very moderate wages, and very indifferent food, when they can get much better elsewhere, purely for the sake of pleasing her. She likes to get hold of foreign servants, who have not yet learned our ways, who are used to working for low wages, and who will be satisfied with almost anything; but she is often heard to lament that they soon get spoiled, and want as many privileges as anybody else—which is perfectly shocking. Marie often wishes that she could be a slaveholder, or could live somewhere where the lower class are kept down, and made to know their place. She is always hunting for cheap seamstresses, and will tell you, in an under-tone, that she has discovered a woman who will make linen shirts beautifully, stitch the collars and wristbands twice, all for thirty-seven cents, when many seamstresses get a dollar for it; says she does it because she's poor, and has no friends; thinks you had better be careful in your conversation, and not let her know what prices are, or else she will get spoiled, and go to raising her price—these sewing-women are so selfish. When Marie St. Clare has the misfortune to live in a free State, there is no end to her troubles. Her cook is always going off for better wages and more comfortable quarters; her chambermaid, strangely enough, won't agree to be chambermaid and seamstress both for half wages, and so she deserts. Marie's kitchen-cabinet, therefore, is always in a state of revolution; and she often declares, with affected earnestness, that servants are the torment of her life. If her husband endeavour to remonstrate, or suggest another mode of treatment, he is a hard-hearted, unfeeling man; "he doesn't love her, and she always knew he didn't;" and so he is disposed of.

But when Marie comes under a system of laws which gives her absolute control over her dependants, which enables her to separate them, at her pleasure, from their dearest family connexions, or to inflict upon them the most disgraceful and violent punishments, without even the restraint which seeing the execution might possibly produce—then it is that the character arrives at full maturity. Human nature is no worse at the South than at the North; but law at the South distinctly provides for and protects the worst abuses to which that nature is liable.

It is often supposed that domestic servitude in slave-states is a kind of paradise; that house-servants are invariably pets; that young mistresses are always fond of their "mammies," and young masters always handsome, good-natured, and indulgent.

Let anyone in Old England or New England look about among their immediate acquaintances, and ask how many there are who would use absolute despotic power amiably in a family, especially over a class degraded by servitude, ignorant, indolent, deceitful, provoking, as slaves almost necessarily are, and always must be.

Let them look into their own hearts, and ask themselves if they would dare to be trusted with such a power. Do they not find in themselves temptations to be unjust to those who are inferiors and dependants? Do they not find themselves tempted to be irritable and provoked, when the service of their families is negligently performed? And if they had the power to inflict cruel punishments, or to have them inflicted by sending the servant out to some place of correction, would they not be tempted to use that liberty?

With regard to those degrading punishments to which females are subjected, by being sent to professional whippers, or by having such functionaries sent for to the house—as John Caphart testifies that he has often been in Baltimore—what can be said of their influence both on the superior and on the inferior class? It is very painful indeed to contemplate this subject. The mind instinctively shrinks from it; but still it is a very serious question whether it be not our duty to encounter this pain, that our sympathies may be quickened into more active exercise. For this reason we give here the testimony of a gentleman whose accuracy will not be doubted, and who subjected himself to the pain of being an eye-witness to a scene of this kind in the calaboose in New Orleans. As the reader will perceive from the account, it was a scene of such every-day occurrence as not to excite any particular remark, or any expression of sympathy from those of the same condition and colour with the sufferer.

When our missionaries first went to India, it was esteemed a duty among Christian nations to make themselves acquainted with the cruelties and atrocities of idolatrous worship, as a means of quickening our zeal to send them the gospel.

CHAPTER VIII.

If it be said that we in the free States have no such interest in slavery, as we do not support it, and have no power to prevent it, it is replied that slavery does exist in the district of Columbia, which belongs to the whole United States; and that the free States are, before God, guilty of the crime of continuing it there, unless they will honestly do what in them lies for its extermination.

The subjoined account was written by the benevolent Dr. Howe, whose labours in behalf of the blind have rendered his name dear to humanity, and was sent in a letter to the Hon. Charles Summer. If anyone think it too painful to be perused, let him ask himself if God will hold those guiltless who suffer a system to continue, the details of which they cannot even read. That this describes a common scene in the calaboose we shall by and by produce other witnesses to show.

I have passed ten days in New Orleans, not unprofitably, I trust, in examining the public institutions—the schools, asylums, hospitals, prisons, &c. With the exception of the first, there is little hope of amelioration. I know not how much merit there may be in their system; but I do know that, in the administration of the penal code, there are abominations which should bring down the fate of Sodom upon the city. If Howard or Mrs. Fry ever discovered so ill-administered a den of thieves as the New Orleans prison, they never described it. In the negroes' apartment I saw much which made me blush that I was a white man, and which, for a moment, stirred up an evil spirit in my animal nature. Entering a large paved court-yard, around which ran galleries filled with slaves of all ages, sexes, and colours, I heard the snap of a whip, every stroke of which sounded like the sharp crack of a pistol. I turned my head, and beheld a sight which absolutely chilled me to the marrow of my bones, and gave me, for the first time in my life, the sensation of my hair stiffening at the roots. There lay a black girl flat upon her face, on a board, her two thumbs tied, and fastened to one end, her feet tied and drawn tightly to the other end, while a strap passed over the small of her back, and, fastened around the board, compressed her closely to it. Below the strap she was entirely naked. By her side, and six feet off, stood a huge negro, with a long whip, which he applied with dreadful power and wonderful precision. Every stroke brought away a strip of skin, which clung to the lash, or fell quivering on the pavement, while the blood followed after it. The poor creature writhed and shrieked, and, in a voice which showed alike her fear of death and her dreadful agony, screamed to her master who stood at her head, “Oh, spare my life! don't cut my soul out!” But still fell the horrid lash; till strip after strip peeled off from the skin; gash after gash was cut in her living flesh, until it became a livid and bloody mass of raw and quivering muscle. It was with the greatest difficulty I refrained from springing upon the torturer, and arresting his lash; but, alas! what could I do, but turn aside to hide my tears for the sufferer, and my blushes for humanity? This was in a public and regularly-organised prison; the punishment was one recognised and authorised by the law. But think you the poor wretch had committed a heinous offence, and had been convicted thereof, and sentenced to the lash? Not at all. She was brought by her master to be whipped by the common executioner, without trial, judge or jury, just at his beck or nod, for some real or supposed offence, or to gratify his own whim or malice. And he may bring her day after day, without cause assigned, and inflict any number of lashes he pleases, short of twenty-five, provided only he pays the fee. Or, if he choose, he may have a private whipping-board on his own premises, and brutalise himself there. A shocking part of this horrid punishment was its publicity, as I have said; it was in a court-yard surrounded by galleries, which were filled with coloured persons of all sexes—runaways, slaves committed for some crime, or slaves up for sale. You would naturally suppose they crowded forward, and gazed, horror-stricken, at the brutal spectacle below; but they did not; many of them hardly noticed it, and many were entirely indifferent to it. They went on in their childish pursuits, and some were laughing outright in the distant parts of the galleries; so low can man, created in God's image, be sunk in brutality.

CHAPTER IX.

ST. CLARE.

IT is with pleasure that we turn from the dark picture just presented, to the character of the generous and noble-hearted St. Clare, wherein the fairest picture of our Southern brother is presented.

It has been the writer's object to separate carefully, as far as possible, the system from the men. It is her sincere belief that, while the irresponsible power of slavery is such that no human being ought ever to possess it, probably that power was never exercised more leniently than in many cases in the Southern States. She has been astonished to see how, under all the disadvantages which attend the early possession of arbitrary power, all the temptations which every reflecting mind must see will arise from the possession of this power in various forms, there are often developed such fine and interesting traits of character. To say that these cases are common, alas! is not in our power. Men know human nature too well to believe us if we should. But the more dreadful the evil to be assailed, the more careful should we be to be just in our apprehensions, and to balance the horror which certain abuses must necessarily excite, by a consideration of those excellent and redeeming traits which are often found in individuals connected with the system.

The twin brothers, Alfred and Augustine St. Clare, represent two classes of men which are to be found in all countries. They are the radically aristocratic and democratic men. The aristocrat by position is not always the aristocrat by nature, and *vice versâ;* but the aristocrat by nature, whether he be in a higher or lower position in society, is he who, though he may be just, generous, and humane, to those whom he considers his equals, is entirely insensible to the wants and sufferings, and common humanity of those whom he considers the lower orders. The sufferings of a countess would make him weep, the sufferings of a seamstress are quite another matter.

On the other hand, the democrat is often found in the highest position of life. To this man, superiority to his brother is a thing which he can never boldly and nakedly assert without a secret pain. In the lowest and humblest walk of life, he acknowledges the sacredness of a common humanity; and however degraded by the opinions and institutions of society any particular class may be, there is an instinctive feeling in his soul which teaches him that they are *men* of like passions with himself. Such men have a penetration which at once sees through all the false shows of outward custom which make one man so dissimilar to another, to those great generic capabilities, sorrows, wants, and weaknesses, wherein all men and women are alike; and there is no such thing as making them realize that one order of human beings have any prescriptive right over another order, or that the tears and sufferings of one are not just as good as those of another order.

That such men are to be found at the South in the relation of slave-masters, that when so found they cannot and will not be deluded by any of the shams and sophistry wherewith slavery has been defended, that they look upon it as a relic of a barbarous age, and utterly scorn and contemn all its apologists, we can abundantly show. Many of the most illustrious Southern men of the Revolution were of this class, and many men of distinguished position of later day have entertained the same sentiments.

Witness the following letter of Patrick Henry, the sentiments of which are so much an echo of those of St. Clare that the reader might suppose one to be a copy of the other:—

LETTER OF PATRICK HENRY.

Hanover, January 18*th,* 1773.

DEAR SIR,—I take this opportunity to acknowledge the receipt of Anthony Benezet's book against the slave-trade; I thank you for it. Is it not a little surprising that the professors of Christianity, whose chief excellence consists in softening the human heart, in cherishing and improving its finer feelings, should encourage a practice so totally repugnant to the first impressions of right and wrong? What adds to the wonder is, that this abominable practice has been introduced in the most enlightened ages. Times that seem to have pretensions to boast of high improvements in the arts and sciences, and refined morality, have brought into general use, and guarded by many laws, a species of violence and tyranny which our more rude and barbarous but more honest ancestors detested. Is it not amazing that at a time when the rights of humanity are defined and understood with precision, in a country above all others fond of liberty—that in such an age and in such a country we find men professing a religion the most mild, humane, gentle, and generous, adopting such a principle, as repugnant to humanity as it is inconsistent with the Bible, and destructive to liberty? Every thinking, honest man rejects it in speculation. How free in practice from conscientious motives!

Would anyone believe that I am master of slaves of my own purchase? I am drawn along by the general inconvenience of living here without them. I will not, I cannot justify it. However culpable my conduct, I will so far pay my devoir to Virtue as to own the excellence and rectitude of her precepts, and lament my want of conformity to them.

I believe a time will come when an opportunity will be offered to abolish this lamentable evil. Everything we can do is to improve it, if it happens in our day; if not, let us transmit to our descendants, together with our slaves, a pity for their unhappy lot, and an abhorrence for slavery. If we cannot reduce this wished-for reformation to practice, let us treat the unhappy victims with lenity. It is the furthest advance we can make towards justice. It is a debt we owe to the purity of our religion, to show that it is at variance with that law which warrants slavery.

I know not when to stop. I could say many things on the subject, a serious view of which gives *a gloomy prospect to future times!*

What a sorrowful thing it is that such men live an inglorious life, drawn along by the general current of society, when they ought to be its regenerators! Has God endowed them with such nobleness of soul, such clearness of perception, for nothing? Should they, to whom he has given superior powers of insight and feeling, live as all the world live?

Southern men of this class have often risen up to reprove the men of the North, when they are drawn in to apologize for the system of slavery. Thus, on one occasion, a representative from one of the Northern States, a gentleman now occupying the very highest rank of distinction and official station, used in Congress the following language:—

The great relation of servitude, in some form or other, with greater or less departure from the theoretic equality of men, is inseparable from our nature. Domestic slavery is not, in my judgment, to be set down as an immoral or irreligious relation. The slaves of this country are better clothed and fed than the peasantry of some of the most prosperous states of Europe.

He was answered by Mr. Mitchell, of Tennessee, in these words:—

Sir, I do not go the length of the gentleman from Massachusetts, and hold that the existence of slavery in this country is almost a blessing. On the contrary, I am firmly settled in the opinion that it is a great curse—one of the greatest that could have been interwoven in our system. I, Mr. Chairman, am one of those whom these poor wretches call masters. I do not task them; I feed and clothe them well; but yet, alas! they are slaves, and slavery is a curse in any shape. It is no doubt true that there are persons in Europe far more degraded than our slaves—worse fed, worse clothed, &c.; but, sir, this is far from proving that negroes ought to be slaves.

The celebrated John Randolph, of Roanoke, said in Congress, on one occasion:—

Sir, I envy neither the heart nor the head of that man from the North who rises here to defend slavery on principle.

The following lines from the will of this eccentric man show that this clear sense of justice, which is a gift of superior natures, at last produced some appropriate fruits in practice:—

I give to my slaves their freedom, to which my conscience tells me they are justly entitled. It has a long time been a matter of the deepest regret to me, that the circumstances under which I inherited them, and the obstacles thrown in the way by the laws of the land, have prevented my emancipating them in my lifetime, which it is my full intention to do in case I can accomplish it.

The influence on such minds as these of that kind of theological teaching which prevails in the majority of the pulpits at the South, and which justifies slavery directly from the Bible, cannot be sufficiently regretted. Such men are shocked to find their spiritual teachers less conscientious than themselves; and if the Biblical argument succeeds in bewildering them, it produces scepticism with regard to the Bible itself. Professor Stowe states that, during his residence in Ohio, he visited at the house of a gentleman who had once been a Virginian planter, and during the first years of his life was an avowed sceptic. He stated that his scepticism was entirely referable to this one cause —that his minister had constructed a scriptural argument in defence of slavery which he was unable to answer, and that his moral sense was so shocked by the idea that the Bible defended such an atrocious system, that he became an entire unbeliever, and so continued until he came under the ministration of a clergyman in Ohio, who succeeded in presenting to him the true scriptural view of the subject. He immediately threw aside his scepticism and became a member of a Christian church.

So we hear the *Baltimore Sun,* a paper in a slave State, and no way suspected of leaning towards abolitionism, thus scornfully disposing of the scriptural argument:—

Messrs. Burgess, Taylor, and Co., Sun Iron Building, send us a copy of a work of imposing exterior, a handsome work of nearly six hundred pages, from the pen of the Rev. Josiah Priest, A.M., and published by Rev. W. S. Brown, M.D., at Glasgow, Kentucky, the copy before us conveying the assurance that it is the "fifth edition, stereotyped." And we have no doubt it is; and the *fiftieth* edition may be published, but it will amount to nothing, for there is nothing in it. The book comprises the usually quoted facts associated with the history of slavery, as recorded in the Scriptures, accompanied by the opinions and arguments of *another* man in relation thereto. And this sort of thing may go on to the end of time. It can accomplish nothing towards the perpetuation of slavery. The book is called "Bible Defence of Slavery; and Origin, Fortunes, and History of the Negro Race." Bible defence of slavery! There is no such thing as a Bible defence of slavery at the present day. Slavery in the United States is a social institution, originating in the convenience and cupidity of our ancestors, existing by State laws, and recognised to a certain extent—for the recovery of slave property—by the constitution. And nobody would pretend that, if it were inexpedient and unprofitable for any man or any State to continue to hold slaves, they would be bound to do so on the ground of a "Bible defence" of it. Slavery is recorded in the Bible, and approved, with many degrading characteristics. War is recorded in the Bible, and approved, under what seems to us the extreme of cruelty. But are slavery and war to *endure* for ever because we find them in the Bible? or are they to *cease* at once and for ever because the Bible inculcates peace and brotherhood?

The book before us exhibits great research, but is obnoxious to severe criticism, on account of its gratuitous assumptions. The writer is constantly assuming this, that, and the other. In a work of this sort a "doubtless" this, and "no doubt" the other, and "such is our belief," with respect to important premises, will not be acceptable to the intelligent reader. Many of the positions assumed are ludicrous; and the fancy of the writer runs to exuberance in putting words and speeches into the mouths of the ancients, predicated upon the brief record of Scripture history. The argument from the *curse of Ham* is not worth the paper it is written upon. It is just equivalent to that of *Blackwood's Magazine,* we remember examining some years since, in reference to the admission of Rothschild to Parliament. The writer maintained the religious obligation of the *Christian* public to perpetuate the political disabilities of the Jews because it would be resisting the Divine will to remove them, in view of the "curse" which the aforesaid Christian Pharisee understood to be levelled against the sons of Abraham. Admitting that God has cursed both the Jewish race and the descendants of Ham, He is able to fulfil His purpose, though the "rest of mankind" should in all things act up to the benevolent precepts of the "Divine law." *Man* may very safely cultivate the highest principles of the Christian dispensation, and leave God to work out the fulfilment of His *curse.*

According to the same book and the same logic, all mankind being under a "curse," none of us ought to work out any alleviation for ourselves, and we are sinning heinously in harnessing steam to the performance of manual labour, cutting wheat by McCormick's *diablerie,* and laying hold of the lightning to carry our messages for us, instead of footing it ourselves, as our father Adam did. With a little more common sense, and much less of the uncommon sort, we should better understand Scripture, the institutions under which we live, the several rights of our fellow-citizens in all sections of the country, and the good, sound, practical, social relations which ought to contribute infinitely more than they do to the happiness of mankind.

If the reader wishes to know what kind of preaching it is that St. Clare alludes to, when he says he can learn what is quite as much to the purpose from the *Picayune,* and that such scriptural expositions of their peculiar relations don't edify him much, he is referred to the following extract from a sermon preached in New Orleans, by the Rev. Theophilus Clapp. Let our reader now imagine that he sees St. Clare seated in the front slip, waggishly taking notes of the following specimen of ethics and humanity:—

Let all Christian teachers show our servants the importance of being submissive, obedient, industrious, honest, and faithful to the interests of their masters. Let their minds be filled with sweet anticipations of rest eternal beyond the grave. Let them be trained to direct their views to that fascinating and glorious futurity where the sins, sorrows, and troubles of earth will be contemplated under the aspect of means indispensable to our everlasting progress in knowledge, virtue, and happiness. I would say to every slave in the United States, "You should realise that a wise, kind, and merciful Providence has appointed for you your condition in life; and, all things considered, you could not be more eligibly situated. The burden of your care, toils, and responsibilities is much lighter than that which God has imposed on your master. The most enlightened philanthropists, with unlimited resources, could not place you in a situation more favourable to your present and everlasting welfare than that which you now occupy. You have your troubles; so have all. Remember how evanescent are the pleasures and joys of human life.

But, as Mr. Clapp will not, perhaps, be accepted as a representation of orthodoxy, let him be supposed to listen to the following declarations of the Rev. James Smylie, a clergyman of great influence in the Presbyterian Church, in a tract upon slavery, which he states in the introduction to have been written with particular reference to removing the conscientious scruples of religious people in Mississippi and Louisiana with regard to its propriety.

If I believed, or was of opinion, that it was the legitimate tendency of the gospel to abolish slavery, how would I approach a man, possessing as many slaves as Abraham had, and tell him I wished to obtain his permission to preach to his slaves?

Suppose the man to be ignorant of the gospel, and that he would inquire of me what was my object; I would tell him candidly (and every minister ought to be candid) that I wished to preach the gospel, because its legitimate tendency is to make his slaves honest, trusty, and faithful; not serving "with eye-service, as men-pleasers," "not purloining, but showing all good fidelity." "And is this," he would ask, "really the tendency of the gospel?" I would answer, "Yes." Then I might expect that a man who had a thousand slaves, if he believed me, would not only permit me to preach to his slaves, but would do more. He would be willing to build me a house, furnish me a garden, and ample provision for a support; because he would conclude, *verily that this preacher would be worth more to him than a dozen overseers*. But suppose, them, he would tell me that he understood the tendency of the gospel was to abolish slavery, and inquire of me if that was the fact. Ah! this is the rub. He has now cornered me. What shall I say? Shall I, like a dishonest man, twist and dodge, and shift and turn, to evade an answer? No; I must, Kentuckian like, come out *broad, flat-footed,* and tell him that *abolition is the tendency of the gospel*. What am I now to calculate upon? I have told the man that it is the tendency of the gospel to make him so poor as to oblige him to take hold of the maul and wedge himself; he must catch, curry, and saddle his own horse; he must black his own *brogans* (for he will not be able to buy boots). His wife must go herself to the wash-tub, take hold of the scrubbing-broom, wash the pots, and cook all that she and her railmauler will eat.

Query.—Is it to be expected that a master, ignorant heretofore of the tendency of the gospel, would fall so desperately in love with it, from knowledge of its tendency, that he would encourage the preaching of it among his slaves? Verily, NO.

But suppose, when he put the last question to me as to its tendency, I *could* and *would,* without a twist or quibble, tell him *plainly* and *candidly* that it was a slander on the gospel to say that emancipation or abolition was its legitimate tendency. I would tell him that the commandments of *some* men, and not the commandments of God, made slavery a sin.—*Smylie on Slavery,* p. 71.

One can imagine the expression of countenance and tone of voice with which St. Clare would receive such expositions of the gospel. It is to be remarked that this tract does not contain the opinions of one man only, but that it has in its appendix a letter from two ecclesiastical bodies of the Presbyterian Church, substantially endorsing its sentiments.

Can any one wonder that a man like St. Clare should put such questions as these?

"Is what you hear at church religion? Is that which can bend and turn, and descend and ascend, to fit every crooked phase of selfish, worldly society, religion? Is *that* religion which is less scrupulous, less generous, less just, less considerate for man, than even my own ungodly, worldly, blinded nature? No! When I look for a religion, I must look for something above me, and not something beneath."

The character of St. Clare was drawn by the writer with enthusiasm and with hope. Will this hope never be realised? Will those men at the South, to whom God has given the power to perceive and the heart to feel the unutterable wrong and injustice of slavery, always remain silent and inactive? What nobler ambition to a Southern man than to deliver his country from this disgrace? From the South must the deliverer arise. How long shall he delay? There is a crown brighter than any earthly ambition has ever worn—there is a laurel which will not fade: it is prepared and waiting for that hero who shall rise up for liberty at the South, and free that noble and beautiful country from the burden and disgrace of slavery.

CHAPTER X.

LEGREE.

AS St. Clare and the Shelbys are the representatives of one class of masters, so Legree is the representative of another; and, as all good masters are not as enlightened, as generous, and as considerate, as St. Clare and Mr. Shelby, or as careful and successful in religious training as Mrs. Shelby, so all bad masters do not unite the personal ugliness, the coarseness and profaneness, of Legree.

Legree is introduced not for the sake of vilifying masters as a class, but for the sake of bringing to the minds of honourable Southern men, who are masters, a very important feature in the system of slavery, upon which, perhaps, they have never reflected. It is this: that *no Southern law requires any test of* CHARACTER *from the man to whom the absolute power of master is granted.*

In the second part of this book it will be shown that the legal power of the master amounts to an absolute despotism over body and soul, and that there is no protection for the slave's life or limb, his family relations, his conscience, nay, more, his eternal interests, but the CHARACTER of the master.

Rev. Charles C. Jones, of Georgia, in addressing masters, tells them that they have the power to open the kingdom of heaven, or to shut it, to their slaves (*Religious Instruction of the Negroes,* p. 158); and a South Carolinian, in a recent article in *Frazer's Magazine,* apparently in a very serious spirit, thus acknowledges the fact of this awful power: "Yes, we would have the whole South to feel that the *soul* of the slave is in some sense in the master's keeping, and to be charged against him hereafter."

Now, it is respectfully submitted to men of this high class, who are the law-makers, whether this awful power to bind and to loose, to open and to shut the kingdom of heaven, ought to be intrusted to every man in the community, without any other qualification than that of property to buy. Let this gentleman of South Carolina cast his eyes around the world. Let him travel for one week through any district of country either in the South or the North, and ask himself how many of the men whom he meets are fit to be trusted with this power,— how many are fit to be trusted with their own souls, much less with those of others?

CHAPTER X.

Now, in all the theory of government as it is managed in our country, just in proportion to the extent of power is the strictness with which qualification for the proper exercise of it is demanded. The physician may not meddle with the body, to prescribe for its ailments, without a certificate that he is properly qualified. The judge may not decide on the laws which relate to property, without a long course of training, and most abundant preparation. It is only this office of MASTER, which contains the power to bind and to loose, and to open and shut the kingdom of heaven, and involves responsibility for the soul as well as the body, that is thrown out to every hand, and committed without inquiry to any man of any character. A man may have made all his property by piracy upon the high seas, as we have represented in the case of Legree, and there is no law whatever to prevent his investing that property in acquiring this absolute control over the souls and bodies of his fellow-beings. To the half-maniac drunkard, to the man notorious for hardness and cruelty, to the man sunk entirely below public opinion, to the bitter infidel and blasphemer, the law confides this power, just as freely as to the most honourable and religious man on earth. And yet, men who make and uphold these laws think they are guiltless before God, because, individually, they do not perpetrate the wrongs which they allow others to perpetrate!

To the Pirate Legree the law gives a power which no man of woman born, save One, ever was good enough to exercise.

Are there such men as Legree? Let any one go into the low districts and dens of New York, let them go into some of the lanes and alleys of London, and will they not there see many Legrees? Nay, take the purest district of New England, and let people cast about in their memory and see if there have not been men there, hard, coarse, unfeeling, brutal, who, if they had possessed the absolute power of Legree, would have used it in the same way; and that there should be Legrees in the Southern States, is only saying that human nature is the same there that it is everywhere. The only difference is this—that in free States Legree is chained and restrained by law; in the slave States, the law makes him an absolute, irresponsible despot.

It is a shocking task to confirm by fact this part of the writer's story. One may well approach it in fear and trembling. It is so mournful to think that man, made in the image of God, and by his human birth a brother of Jesus Christ, can sink so low, can do such things as the very soul shudders to contemplate—and to think that the very man who thus sinks is our brother—is capable, like us, of the renewal by the Spirit of grace, by which he might be created in the image of Christ and be made equal unto the angels. They who uphold the laws which grant this awful power, have another heavy responsibility, of which they little dream. How many souls of masters have been ruined through it! How has this absolute authority provoked and developed wickedness which otherwise might have been suppressed! How many have stumbled into everlasting perdition over this stumbling-stone of IRRESPONSIBLE POWER!

What facts do the judicial trials of slave-holding States occasionally develope! What horrible records defile the pages of the law-book, describing unheard-of scenes of torture and agony, perpetrated in this nineteenth century of the Christian era, by the irresponsible despot who owns the body and soul! Let any one read, if they can, the ninety-third page of Weld's *Slavery As It Is,* where the Rev. Mr. Dickey gives an account of a trial in Kentucky for a deed of butchery and blood too repulsive to humanity to be here described. The culprit was convicted, and *sentenced* to death. Mr. Dickey's account of the finale is thus:—

The Court sat—Isham was judged to be guilty of a capital crime in the affair of George. He was to be hanged at Salem. The day was set. My good old father visited him in the prison—two or three times talked and prayed with him; I visited him once myself. We fondly hoped that he was a sincere penitent. Before the day of execution came, by some means, I never knew what, Isham was *missing*. About two years after, we learned that he had gone down to Natchez, and had married a lady of some refinement and piety. I saw her letters to his sisters, who were worthy members of the church of which I was pastor. The last letter told of his death. He was in Jackson's army, and fell in the famous battle of New Orleans.

I am, sir, your friend, WM. DICKEY.

But the reader will have too much reason to know of the possibility of the existence of such men as Legree, when he comes to read the records of the trials and judicial decisions in Part II.

Let not the Southern country be taunted as the only country in the world which produces such men; let us in sorrow and in humility concede that such men are found everywhere; but let not the Southern country deny the awful charge that she invests such men with absolute, irresponsible power over both the body and the soul.

With regard to that atrocious system of working up the human being in a given time on which Legree is represented as conducting his plantation, there is unfortunately too much reason to know that it has been practised and is still practised.

In Mr. Weld's book, *Slavery As It Is,* under the head of Labour, p. 39, are given several extracts from various documents, to show that this system has been pursued on some plantations to such an extent as to shorten life, and to prevent the increase of the slave population, so that, unless annually renewed, it would of itself die out. Of these documents we quote the following:—

The Agricultural Society of Baton Rouge, La., in its report published in 1829, furnishes a laboured estimate of the amount of expenditure necessarily incurred in conducting "a well-regulated sugar estate." In this estimate, the annual net loss of slaves, over and above the supply by propagation, is set down at TWO AND A HALF PER CENT.! The late Hon. Josiah S. Johnson, a member of Congress from Louisiana, addressed a letter to the Secretary of the United States Treasury in 1830, containing a similar estimate, apparently made with great care, and going into minute details. Many items in this estimate differ from the preceding; but the estimate of the annual *decrease* of the slaves on a plantation was the same—TWO AND A HALF PER CENT.!

In September, 1834, the writer of this had an interview with James G. Birney, Esq., who then resided at Kentucky, having removed with his family from Alabama the year before. A few hours before that interview, and on the morning of the same day, Mr. B. had spent a couple of hours with Hon. Henry Clay, at his residence, near Lexington. Mr. Birney remarked that Mr. Clay had just told him he had lately been led to mistrust certain estimates as to the increase of the slave population in the far South-west—estimates which he had presented, I think, in a speech before the Colonization Society. He now believed that the births among the slaves in that quarter were *not equal to the deaths;* and that, of course, the slave population, independent of immigration from the slave-selling States, was *not sustaining itself.*

Among other facts stated by Mr. Clay was the following, which we copy *verbatim* from the original memorandum made at the time by Mr. Birney, with which he has kindly furnished us.

"*Sept.* 16, 1834.—Hon. H. Clay, in a conversation at his own house on the subject of slavery, informed me that Hon. Outerbridge Horsey—formerly a senator in Congress from the State of Delaware, and the owner of a sugar plantation in Louisiana—declared to him that his overseer worked his hands so closely that one of the women brought forth a child whilst engaged in the labours of the field.

"Also that, a few years since, he was at a brick-yard in the environs of New Orleans, in which a hundred hands were employed; among them were from *twenty to thirty young women,* in the prime of life. He was told by the proprietor that there had *not been a child born among them for the last two or three years, although they all had husbands.*"

The late Mr. Samuel Blackwell, a highly respectable citizen of Jersey City, opposite the city of New York, and a member of the Presbyterian church, visited many of the sugar plantations in Louisiana a few years since; and having, for many years, been the owner of an extensive sugar refinery in England, and subsequently in this country, he had not only every facility afforded him by the planters for personal inspection of all parts of the process of sugar-making, but received from them the most unreserved communications as to their management of their slaves. Mr. B—, after his return, frequently made the following statement to gentlemen of his acquaintance:—"That the planters generally declared to him that they were *obliged* so to overwork their slaves, during the sugar-making season (from eight to ten weeks), as to *use them up* in seven or eight years. For, said they, after the process is commenced, it must be pushed, without cessation, night and day; and we cannot afford to keep a sufficient number of slaves to do the *extra* work at the time of sugar-making, as we could not profitably employ them the rest of the year."

Dr. Demming, a gentleman of high respectability, residing in Ashland, Richland County, Ohio, stated to Professor Wright, of New York city—"That, during a recent tour at the South, while ascending the Ohio river on the steam-boat `Fame,' he had an opportunity of conversing with a Mr. Dickinson, a resident of Pittsburg, in company with a number of cotton-planters and slave-dealers from Louisiana, Alabama, and Mississippi. Mr. Dickinson stated as a fact, that the sugar-planters upon the sugar-coast in Louisiana had ascertained that, as it was usually necessary to employ about *twice* the amount of labour during the boiling season that was required during the season of raising, they could, by excessive driving, day and night, during the boiling season, accomplish the whole labour *with one set of hands*. By pursuing this plan, they could afford *to sacrifice a set of hands once in seven years!* He further stated that this horrible system was now practised to a considerable extent! The correctness of this statement was substantially admitted by the slave-holders then on board."

The following testimony of the Rev. Dr. Channing, of Boston, who resided some time in Virginia, shows that the over-working of slaves, to such an extent as to abridge life, and cause a decrease of population, is not confined to the far South and South-west:—

"I heard of an estate managed by an individual who was considered as singularly successful, and who was able to govern the slaves without the use of the whip. I was anxious to see him, and trusted that some discovery had been made favourable to humanity. I asked him how he was able to dispense with corporal punishment. He replied to me, with a very determined look, 'The slaves know that the work *must* be done, and that it is better to do it without punishment than with it.' In other words, the certainty and dread of chastisement were so impressed on them that they never incurred it.

"I then found that the slaves on this well-managed estate *decreased* in number. I asked the cause. He replied, with perfect frankness and ease, 'The gang is not large enough for the estate.' In other words, they were not equal to the work of the plantation, and yet were *made to do it,* though with the certainty of abridging life.

"On this plantation the huts were uncommonly convenient. There was an unusual air of neatness. A superficial observer would have called the slaves, happy. Yet they were living under a severe, subduing discipline, and were *over-worked* to a degree that *shortened life*."

— *Channing on Slavery,* p. 162, first edition. A friend of the writer—the Rev. Mr. Barrows, now officiating as teacher of Hebrew in Andover Theological Seminary—stated as following, in conversation with her:—That, while at New Orleans, some time since, he was invited by a planter to visit his estate, as he considered it to be a model one. He found good dwellings for the slaves, abundant provision distributed to them, all cruel punishments superseded by rational and reasonable ones, and half a day, every week, allowed to the negroes to cultivate their own grounds. Provision was also made for their moral and religious instruction. Mr. Barrows then asked the planter,

"Do you consider your estate a fair specimen?" The gentleman replied, "There are two systems pursued among us. One is, to make all we can out of a negro in a few years, and then supply his place with another; and the other is, to treat him as I do. My neighbour on the next plantation pursues the opposite system. His boys are hard worked and scantily fed; and I have had them come to me, and get down on their knees to beg me to buy them."

Mr. Barrows says he subsequently passed by this plantation, and that the woe-struck, dejected aspect of its labourers fully confirmed the account. He also says that the gentleman who managed so benevolently told him, “I do not make much money out of my slaves.”

It will be easy to show that such is the nature of slavery, and the temptations of masters, that such well-regulated plantations are, and must be, infinitely in the minority, and exceptional cases.

The Rev. Charles C. Jones, a man of the finest feelings of humanity, and for many years an assiduous labourer for the benefit of the slave, himself the owner of a plantation, and qualified, therefore, to judge, both by experience and observation, says, after speaking of the great improvidence of the negroes, engendered by slavery:—

And, indeed, once for all, I will here say that the wastes of the system are so great, as well as the fluctuation in prices of the staple articles for market, that it is *difficult, nay, impossible,* to indulge in large expenditures on plantations, and make them savingly profitable.

— *Religious Instruction,* p. 116. If even the religious and benevolent master feels the difficulty of uniting any great consideration for the comfort of the slave with prudence and economy, how readily must the moral question be solved by minds of the coarse style of thought which we have supposed in Legree!

“I used to, when I fust begun, have considerable trouble fussin' with 'em, and trying to make 'em hold out—doctorin' on 'em up when they's sick, and givin' on 'em clothes, and blankets, and what not, trying to keep 'em all sort o' decent and comfortable. Law, 't want no sort o' use; I lost money on 'em, and 't was heaps o' trouble. Now, you see, I just put'm straight through, sick or well. When one nigger's dead, I buy another; and I find it comes cheaper and easier every way.”

Added to this, the peculiar mode of labour on the sugar plantation is such that the master, at a certain season of the year, must over-work his slaves, unless he is willing to incur great pecuniary loss. In that very gracefully written apology for slavery, Professor Ingraham's “Travels in the South-west,” the following description of sugar-making is given. We quote from him in preference to anyone else, because he speaks as an apologist, and describes the thing with the grace of a Mr. Skimpole.

When the grinding has once commenced, there is no cessation of labour till it is completed. From beginning to end a busy and cheerful scene continues. The negroes,

“—Whose sore task
Does not divide the Sunday from the week,”

work from eighteen to twenty hours,

“And make the night joint labourer with the day;”

though, to lighten the burden as much as possible, the gang is divided into two watches, one taking the first and the other the last part of the night; and, notwithstanding this continued labour, the negroes improve in appearance, and appear fat and flourishing. They drink freely of cane-juice, and the sickly among them revive, and become robust and healthy.

After the grinding is finished, the negroes have several holidays, when they are quite at liberty to dance and frolic as much as they please; and the cane-song—which is improvised by one of the gang, the rest all joining in a prolonged and unintelligible chorus—now breaks, night and day, upon the ear, in notes "most musical, most melancholy."

The above is inserted as a specimen of the facility with which the most horrible facts may be told in the genteelest phrase. In a work entitled "Travels in Louisiana in 1802" is the following extract (see Weld's *Slavery As It Is,* p. 134), from which it appears that this *cheerful* process of labouring night and day lasts *three months!*

"At the rolling of sugars, *an interval of from two to three months,* they (the slaves in Louisiana) work *both night and day*. Abridged of their sleep, they scarcely retire to rest during the whole period."—P. 81.

Now, let any one learn the private history of seven hundred blacks—men and women—compelled to work day and night under the lash of a driver, for a period of three months!

Possibly, if the gentleman who wrote the account were employed, with his wife and family, in this "cheerful scene" of labour—if he saw the woman that he loved, the daughter who was dear to him as his own soul, forced on in the general gang, in this toil which

> "Does not divide the Sabbath from the week,
> And makes the night joint labourer with the day,'

—possibly, if he saw all this, he might have another opinion of its cheerfulness; and it might be an eminently salutary thing if every apologist for slavery were to enjoy some such privilege for a season, particularly as Mr. Ingraham is careful to tell us that its effect upon the general health is so excellent that the negroes improve in appearance, and appear fat and flourishing, and that the sickly among them revive, and become robust and healthy. One would think it a surprising fact, if working slaves night and day, and giving them cane-juice to drink, really produces such salutary results, that the practice should not be continued the whole year round; though, perhaps, in this case, the negroes would become so fat as to be unable to labour. Possibly, it is because this healthful process is not longer continued that the agricultural societies of Louisiana are obliged to set down an annual loss of slaves on sugar plantations to the amount of two and a half per cent. This ought to be looked into by philanthropists. Perhaps working them all night for six months, instead of three, might remedy the evil.

But this periodical pressure is not confined to the making of sugar. There is also a press in the cotton season, as any one can observe by reading the Southern newspapers. At a certain season of the year, the whole interest of the community is engaged in gathering in the cotton crop. Concerning this Mr. Weld says (*Slavery as It is,* p. 34):—

In the cotton and sugar region there is a fearful amount of desperate gambling, in which, though money is the ostensible stake and forfeit, *human life* is the real one. The length to which this rivalry is carried at the South and South-west, the multitude of planters who engage in it, and the recklessness of human life exhibited in driving the murderous game to its issue, cannot well be imagined by one who has not lived in the midst of it. Desire of gain is only one of the motives that stimulates them; the *éclat* of having made the largest crop with a given number of hands is also a powerful stimulant; the Southern newspapers, at the crop season, chronicle carefully the "cotton brag," and the "crack cotton-picking," and unparalleled driving,&c. Even the editors of professedly religious papers cheer on the *mêlée,* and sing the triumphs of the victor. Among these we recollect the celebrated Rev. J. N. Maffit, recently editor of a religious paper at Natchez, Mississippi, in which he took care to assign a prominent place and capitals to "THE COTTON BRAG."

As a specimen, of recent date, of this kind of affair, we subjoin the following from the *Fairfield Herald,* Winsboro, S. C., November 4, 1852:—

COTTON-PICKING.

We find in many of our southern and western exchanges notices of the amount of cotton picked by hands, and the quantity by each hand; and, as we have received a similar account, which we have not seen excelled, so far as regards the quantity picked by one hand, we with pleasure furnish the statement, with the remark that it is from a citizen of this district, overseeing for Major H. W. Parr.

Broad River, October 12, 1852.

"MESSRS. EDITORS,—By way of contributing something to your variety (provided it meets your approbation), I send you the return of a day's picking of cotton, not by picked hands, but the fag-end of a set of hands on one plantation, the able-bodied hands having been drawn out for other purposes. Now for the result of a day's picking, from sun-up until sun-down, by twenty-two hands—women, boys, and two men:—4,880 lbs. of clean-picked cotton from the stalk.

"The highest, 350 lbs., by several; the lowest, 115 lbs. One of the number has picked in the last seven and a-half days (Sunday excepted), eleven hours each day, 1,900 lbs. clean cotton. When any of my agricultural friends beat this, in the same time, and during sunshine, I will try again.

"JAMES STEWARD."

It seems that this agriculturist professes to have accomplished all these extraordinary results with what he very elegantly terms the "fag-end" of a set of hands; and, the more to exalt his glory in the matter, he distinctly informs the public that there were no "able-bodied" hands employed; that this whole triumphant result was worked out of women and children, and two disabled men; in other words, he boasts that out of women and children, and the feeble and sickly, *he* has extracted 4,880 pounds of clean-picked cotton in a day; and that one of these same hands has been made to pick 1,900 pounds of clean cotton in a week! and adds, complacently, that, when any of his agricultural friends beat this, in the same time, and during sunshine, he "will try again."

Will any of our readers now consider the forcing up of the hands on Legree's plantation an exaggeration? Yet see how complacently this account is quoted by the editor, as a most praiseworthy and laudable thing!

"BEHOLD THE HIRE OF THE LABOURERS WHO HAVE REAPED YOUR FIELDS, WHICH IS OF YOU KEPT BACK BY FRAUD, CRIETH! AND THE CRIES OF THEM WHICH HAVE REAPED ARE ENTERED INTO THE EARS OF THE LORD OF SABOATH."

That the representations of the style of dwelling-house, modes of housekeeping, and, in short, the features of life generally, as described on Legree's plantation, are not wild and fabulous drafts on the imagination, or exaggerated pictures of exceptional cases, there is the most abundant testimony before the world, and has been for a long number of years. Let the reader weigh the following testimony with regard to the dwellings of the negroes, which has been for some years before the world, in the work of Mr. Weld. It shows the state of things in this respect, at least up to the year 1838.

Mr. Stephen E. Maltby, Inspector of Provisions, Skaneateles, New York, who has lived in Alabama.—"The huts where the slaves slept generally contained but *one* apartment, and that *without floor*."

Mr. George A. Avery, elder of the 4th Presbyterian Church, Rochester, New York, who lived four years in Virginia.—"Amongst all the negro cabins which I saw in Virginia, *I cannot call to mind one* in which there was any other floor than the *earth;* anything that a Northern labourer, or mechanic, white or coloured, would call a *bed,* nor a solitary *partition* to separate the sexes."

William Ladd, Esq., Minot, Maine, President of the American Peace Society, formerly a slaveholder in Florida.—"The dwellings of the slaves were palmetto huts, built by themselves of stakes and poles, thatched with the palmetto-leaf. The door, when they had any, was generally of the same materials, sometimes boards found on the beach. They had *no floors,* no separate apartments; except the Guinea negroes had sometimes a small enclosure for their `god houses.' These huts the slaves built themselves after task and on Sundays."

Rev. Joseph M. Sadd, Pastor of Presbyterian Church, Castile, Greene County, New York, who lived in Missouri five years previous to 1837.—"The slaves live *generally* in *miserable huts,* which are *without floors;* and have a single apartment only, where both sexes are herded promiscuously together."

Mr. George W. Westgate, member of the Congregational Church in Quincy, Illinois, who has spent a number of years in slave States.—"On old plantations the negro quarters are of frame and clapboards, seldom affording a comfortable shelter from wind or rain; their size varies from eight by ten, to ten by twelve feet, and six or eight feet high; sometimes there is a hole cut for a window, but I never saw a sash, or glass, in any. In the new country, and in the woods, the quarters are generally built of logs, of similar dimensions."

Mr. Cornelius Johnson, a member of a Christian Church in Farmington, Ohio. Mr. J. lived in Mississippi in 1837-38.—"Their houses were commonly built of logs; sometimes they were framed, often they had no floor; some of them have two apartments, commonly but one; each of those apartments contained a family. Sometimes these families consisted of a man and his wife and children, while in other instances persons of both sexes were thrown together, without any regard to family relationship."

The *Western Medical Reformer,* in an article on the Cachexia Africana, by a Kentucky physician, thus speaks of the huts of the slaves: "They are *crowded* together in a *small hut,* and sometimes having an imperfect, and sometimes no floor, and seldom raised from the ground, ill-ventilated, and surrounded with filth."

Mr. William Leftwich, a native of Virginia, but has resided most of his life in Madison County, Alabama.—"The dwellings of the slaves are log huts, from ten to twelve feet square, often without windows, doors, or floors; they have neither chairs, table, nor bedstead."

Reuben L. Macy, of Hudson, New York, a member of the Religious Society of Friends. He lived in South Carolina in 1818-19.—"The houses for the field-slaves were about fourteen feet square, built in the coarsest manner, with one room, *without any chimney or flooring, with a hole in the roof to let the smoke out.*"

Mr. Lemuel Sapington, of Lancaster, Pennsylvania, a native of Maryland, formerly a slave-holder.—"The descriptions generally given of negro quarters are correct; the quarters are *without floors, and not sufficient to keep off the inclemency of the weather;* they are uncomfortable both in summer and winter."

Rev. John Rankin, a native of Tennessee.—"When they return to their miserable huts at night, they find not there the means of comfortable rest; but *on the cold ground they must lie without covering, and shiver while they slumber.*"

Philemon Bliss, Esq., Elyria, Ohio, who lived in Florida in 1835.—"The dwellings of the slaves are usually small *open* log huts, with but one apartment, and very generally *without floors.*"

— *Slavery as It is,* p. 43. The Rev. C. C. Jones, to whom we have already alluded, when taking a survey of the condition of the negroes considered as a field for missionary effort, takes into account all the conditions of their external life. He speaks of a part of Georgia where as much attention had been paid to the comfort of the negro as in any part of the United States. He gives the following picture:—

Their *general mode of living* is coarse and vulgar. Many negro-houses are small, low to the ground, blackened with smoke, often with dirt floors, and the furniture of the plainest kind. On some estates the houses are framed, weather-boarded, neatly whitewashed, and made sufficiently large and comfortable in every respect. The improvement in the size, material, and finish of negro-houses is extending. Occasionally they may be found constructed of tabby or brick.

— *Religious Instruction of the Negroes,* p. 116. Now, admitting what Mr. Jones says, to wit, that improvements with regard to the accommodation of the negroes are continually making among enlightened and Christian people, still, if we take into account how many people there are who are neither enlightened nor Christian, how unproductive of any benefit to the master all these improvements are, and how entirely, therefore, they must be the result either of native generosity or of Christian sentiment, the reader may fairly conclude that such improvements are the exception, rather than the rule.

A friend of the writer, travelling in Georgia during the last month, thus writes:—

Upon the long line of rice and cotton plantations extending along the railroad from Savannah to this city, the negro quarters contain scarcely a single hut which a Northern farmer would deem fit shelter for his cattle. They are all built of poles, with the ends so slightly notched that they are almost as open as children's cob-houses (which they very much resemble), without a single glazed window, and with only one mud chimney to each cluster of from four to eight cabins. And yet our fellow-travellers were quietly expatiating upon the negro's strange inability to endure cold weather.

Let this modern picture be compared with the account given by the Rev. Horace Moulton, who spent five years in Georgia between 1817 and 1824, and it will be seen, in that State at least, there is some resemblance between the more remote and more recent practice:—

The huts of the slaves are mostly of the poorest kind. They are not as good as those temporary shanties which are thrown up beside railroads. They are erected with posts and crotchets, with but little or no frame-work about them. They have no stoves or chimneys; some of them have something like a fire-place at one end, and a board or two off at that side, or on the roof, to let off the smoke. Others have nothing like a fire-place in them; in these the fire is sometimes made in the middle of the hut. These buildings have but one apartment in them; the places where they pass in and out serve both for doors and windows; the sides and roofs are covered with coarse, and in many instances with refuse, boards. In warm weather, especially in the spring, the slaves keep up a smoke, or fire and smoke, all night, to drive away the gnats and mosquitoes, which are very troublesome in all the low country of the South; so much so, that the whites sleep under frames with nets over them, knit so fine that the mosquitoes cannot fly through them.

— *Slavery As It Is,* p. 19. The same Mr. Moulton gives the following account of the food of the slaves, and the mode of procedure on the plantation on which he was engaged. It may be here mentioned that at the time he was at the South he was engaged in certain business relations which caused him frequently to visit different plantations, and to have under his control many of the slaves. His opportunities for observation, therefore, were quite intimate. There is a homely matter-of-fact distinctness in the style that forbids the idea of its being a fancy sketch:—

It was a general custom, wherever I have been, for the master to give each of his slaves, male and female, *one peck of corn per week* for their food. This, at fifty cents per bushel, which was all that it was worth when I was there, would amount to twelve and a half cents per week for board per head.

It cost me, upon an average, when at the South, one dollar per day for board—the price of fourteen bushels of corn per week. This would make my board equal in amount to the board of *forty-six slaves!* This is all that good or bad masters allow their slaves, round about Savannah, on the plantations. One peck of gourd-seed corn is to be measured out to each slave once every week. One man with whom I laboured, however, being desirous to get all the work out of his hands he could, before I left (about fifty in number), bought for them every week, or twice a week, a beef's head from market. With this they made a soup in a large iron kettle, around which the hands came at meal-time, and dipping out the soup, would mix it with their hominy, and eat it as though it were a feast. This man permitted his slaves to eat twice a day while I was doing a job for him. He promised me a beaver hat, and as good a suit of clothes as could be bought in the city, if I would accomplish so much for him before I returned to the North; giving me the entire control over his slaves. Thus you may see the temptations overseers sometimes have, to get all the work they can out of the poor slaves. The above is an exception to the general rule of feeding. For, in all other places where I worked and visited, the slaves had *nothing from the masters but the corn,* or its equivalent in potatoes or rice; and to this they were not permitted to come but *once a day*. The custom was to blow the horn early in the morning, as a signal for the hands to rise and go to work. When commenced, they continue work until about eleven o'clock A.M., when, at the signal, all hands left off, and went into their huts, made their fires, made their corn-meal into hominy or cake, ate it, and went to work again at the signal of the horn, and worked until night, or until their tasks were done. Some cooked their breakfast in the field while at work. Each slave must grind his own corn in a hand-mill after he has done his work at night. There is generally one hand-mill on every plantation for the use of the slaves.

Some of the planters have no corn; others often get out. The substitute for it is the equivalent of one peck of corn, either in rice or sweet potatoes, neither of which is as good for the slaves as corn. They complain more of being faint when fed on rice or potatoes than when fed on corn. I was with one man a few weeks who gave me his hands to do a job of work, and, to save time, one cooked for all the rest. The following course was taken:—Two crotched sticks were driven down at one end of the yard, and a small pole being laid on the crotches, they swung a large iron kettle on the middle of the pole; then made up a fire under the kettle, and boiled the hominy; when ready, the hands were called around this kettle with their wooden plates and spoons. They dipped out and ate, standing around the kettle, or sitting upon the ground, as best suited their convenience. When they had potatoes, they took them out with their hands, and ate them.

— *Slavery As It Is,* p. 18. Thomas Clay, Esq., a slaveholder of Georgia, and a most benevolent man, and who interested himself very successfully in endeavouring to promote the improvement of the negroes, in his address before the Georgia Presbytery, 1833, says of their food, "The quantity allowed by custom is a *peck of corn a week*."

The *Maryland Journal and Baltimore Advertiser,* May 30, 1788, says, "A single peck of corn, or the same measure of rice, is the ordinary provision for a hard-working slave, to which a small quantity of meat is occasionally though rarely added."

Captain William Ladd, of Minot, Maine, formerly a slave-holder in Florida, says, "The usual allowance of food was a quart of corn a day to a full-task hand, with a modicum of salt. *Kind* masters allowed a peck of corn a week."

The law of North Carolina provides that the master shall give his slave a quart of corn a day, which is less than a peck a week by one quart.—*Haywood's Manual,* 525; *Slavery as It is,* p. 29. The master, therefore, who gave a peck a week would feel that he was going beyond the law, and giving a quart for generosity.

This condition of things will appear far more probable in the section of country where the scene of the story is laid. It is in the South-western States, where no provision is *raised* on the plantations, but the supply for the slaves is all purchased from the more Northern States.

Let the reader now imagine the various temptations which might occur to retrench the allowance of the slaves, under these circumstances; scarcity of money, financial embarrassment, high price of provisions, and various causes of the kind, bring a great influence upon the master or overseer.

At the time when it was discussed whether the State of Missouri should be admitted as a slave State, the measure, like all measures for the advancement of this horrible system, was advocated on the good old plea of humanity to the negroes. Thus Mr. Alexander Smyth, in his speech on the slavery question, January 21, 1820, says—

By confining the slaves to the Southern States, where crops are raised for exportation, and bread and meat are purchased, you *doom them to scarcity and hunger*. It is proposed to hem in the blacks where they are ILL FED.

— *Slavery as It is,* p. 28. This is a simple recognition of the state of things we have adverted to. To the same purport, Mr. Asa A. Stone, a theological student, who resided near Natchez, Mississippi, in 1834-5, says—

On almost every plantation, the hands suffer more or less from hunger at some seasons of almost every year. There is always a *good deal of suffering* from hunger. On many plantations, and particularly in Louisiana, the slaves are in a condition of *almost utter famishment* during a great portion of the year.

— *Ibid.* Mr. Tobias Baudinot, St. Albans, Ohio, a member of the Methodist Church, who for some years was a navigator on the Mississippi, says:—

The slaves down the Mississippi are *half-starved*. The boats, when they stop at night, are constantly boarded by slaves, begging for something to eat.

— *Ibid.* On the whole, while it is freely and cheerfully admitted that many individuals have made most commendable advances in regard to the provision for the physical comfort of the slave, still it is to be feared that the picture of the accommodations on Legree's plantation has yet too many counterparts. Lest, however, the author should be suspected of keeping back anything which might serve to throw light on the subject, she will insert in full the following incidents on the other side, from the pen of the accomplished Professor Ingraham. How far these may be regarded as exceptional cases, or as pictures of the general mode of providing for slaves, may safely be left to the good sense of the reader. The professor's anecdotes are as follows:—

CHAPTER X.

"What can you do with so much tobacco?" said a gentleman—who related the circumstance to me—on hearing a planter, whom he was visiting, give an order to his teamster to bring two hogsheads of tobacco out to the estate from the "Landing."

"I purchase it for my negroes; it is a harmless indulgence, which it gives me pleasure to afford them."

"Why are you at the trouble and expense of having high-post bedsteads for your negroes?" said a gentleman from the North, while walking through the handsome "quarters," or village, for the slaves, then in progress on a plantation near Natchez—addressing the proprietor.

"To suspend their 'bars' from, that they may not be troubled with mosquitoes."

"Master, me would like, if you please, a little bit gallery front my house."

"For what, Peter?"

"'Cause, master, the sun too hot (an odd reason for a negro to give) that side, and when he rain, we no able to keep de door open."

"Well, well, when a carpenter gets a little leisure, you shall have one."

A few weeks after, I was at the plantation, and riding past the quarters one Sabbath morning, beheld Peter, his wife and children, with his old father, all sunning themselves in the new gallery.

"Missus, you promise me a Chrismus gif'."

"Well, Jane, there is a new calico frock for you."

"It werry pretty, missus," said Jane, eyeing it at a distance without touching it, "but me prefer muslin, if you please: muslin de fashion dis Chrismus."

"Very well, Jane, call to-morrow, and you shall have a muslin."

The writer would not think of controverting the truth of these anecdotes. Any probable amount of high-post bedsteads and mosquito "bars," of tobacco distributed as gratuity, and verandahs constructed by leisurely carpenters for the sunning of fastidious negroes, may be conceded, and they do in no whit impair the truth of the other facts. When the reader remembers that the "gang" of some opulent owners amounts to from 500 to 700 working hands, besides children, he can judge how extensively these accommodations are likely to be provided. Let them be safely thrown into the account for what they are worth.

At all events, it is pleasing to end off so disagreeable a chapter with some more agreeable images. (See Appendix.)

CHAPTER XI.

SELECT INCIDENTS OF LAWFUL TRADE.

IN this chapter of *Uncle Tom's Cabin* were recorded some of the most highly-wrought and touching incidents of the slave-trade. It will be well to authenticate a few of them.

One of the first sketches presented to view is an account of the separation of a very old decrepit negro woman from her young son, by a sheriff's sale. The writer is sorry to say that not the slightest credit for invention is due to her in this incident. She found it, almost exactly as it stands, in the published journal of a young Southerner, related as a scene to which he was eye-witness. The only circumstance which she has omitted in the narrative was one of additional inhumanity and painfulness which he had delineated. He represents the boy as being bought by a planter, who fettered his hands, and tied a rope round his neck which he attached to the neck of his horse, thus compelling the child to trot by his side. This incident alone was suppressed by the author.

Another scene of fraud and cruelty, in the same chapter, is described as perpetrated by a Kentucky slave-master, who sells a woman to a trader, and induces her to go with him by the deceitful assertion that she is to be taken down the river a short distance, to work at the same hotel with her husband. This was an instance which occurred under the writer's own observation, some years since, when she was going down the Ohio river. The woman was very respectable, both in appearance and dress. The writer recalls her image now with distinctness, attired with great neatness in a white wrapper, her clothing and hair all arranged with evident care, and having with her a prettily-dressed boy about seven years of age. She had also a hair-trunk of clothing, which showed that she had been carefully and respectably brought up. It will be seen, in perusing the account, that the incident is somewhat altered to suit the purpose of the story, the woman being there represented as carrying with her a young infant.

The custom of unceremoniously separating the infant from its mother, when the latter is about to be taken from a Northern to a Southern market, is a matter of every-day notoriety in the trade. It is not done occasionally and sometimes, but always, whenever there is occasion for it; and the mother's agonies are no more regarded than those of a cow when her calf is separated from her.

The reason of this is, that the care and raising of children is no part of the intention or provision of a Southern plantation. They are a trouble; they detract from the value of the mother as a field-hand, and it is more expensive to raise them than to buy them ready raised; they are therefore left behind in making up of a coffle. Not longer ago than last summer, the writer was conversing with Thomas Strother, a slave minister of the gospel in St. Louis, for whose emancipation she was making some effort. He incidentally mentioned to her a scene which he had witnessed but a short time before, in which a young woman of his acquaintance came to him almost in a state of distraction, telling him that she had been sold to go South with a trader, and leave behind her a nursing infant.

In Lewis Clark's narrative he mentions that a master in his neighbourhood sold a woman and child to a trader, with the charge that he should not sell the child from its mother. The man, however, traded off the child in the very next town, in payment of his tavern-bill.

The following testimony is from a gentleman who writes from New Orleans to the *National Era*.

This writer says:—

While at Robinson, or Eyree Springs, twenty miles from Nashville, on the borders of Kentucky and Tennessee, my hostess said to me, one day, "Yonder comes a gang of slaves chained." I went to the road-side and viewed them. For the better answering my purpose of observation, I stopped the white man in front, who was at his ease in a one-horse waggon, and asked him if those slaves were for sale. I counted them and observed their position. They were divided by three one-horse waggons, each containing a man-merchant, so arranged as to command the whole gang. Some were unchained; sixty were chained in two companies, thirty in each, the right hand of the one to the left hand of the other opposite one, making fifteen each side of a large ox-chain, to which every hand was fastened, and necessarily compelled to hold up—men and women promiscuously, and about in equal proportions—all young people. No children here, except a few in a waggon behind, which were the only children in the four gangs. I said to a respectable mulatto woman in the house, "Is it true that the negro-traders take mothers from their babies?" "Massa, it is true; for here, last week, such a girl (naming her), who lives about a mile off, was taken after dinner— knew nothing of it in the morning— sold, put into the gang, and her baby given away to a neighbour. She was a stout young woman, and brought a good price."

Nor is the pitiful lie to be regarded which says that these unhappy mothers and fathers, husbands and wives, do not feel when the most sacred ties are thus severed. Every day and hour bears living witness of the falsehood of this slander, the more false because spoken of a race peculiarly affectionate, and strong, vivacious and vehement, in the expression of their feelings.

The case which the writer supposed of the woman's throwing herself overboard is not by any means a singular one. Witness the following recent fact, which appeared under the head of

ANOTHER INCIDENT FOR "UNCLE TOM'S CABIN."

The editorial correspondent of the *Oneida* (N. Y.) *Telegraph,* writing from a steamer on the Mississippi river, gives the following sad story:—

"At Louisville, a gentleman took passage, having with him a family of blacks —husband, wife, and children. The master was bound for Memphis, Tennessee, at which place he intended to take all except the man ashore. The latter was handcuffed, and although his master said nothing of his intention, the negro made up his mind, from appearances, as well as from the remarks of those around him, that he was destined for the *Southern market.* We reached Memphis during the night, and whilst within sight of the town, just before landing, the negro caused his wife to divide their things, as though resigned to the intended separation, and then, taking a moment when his master's back was turned, ran forward and jumped into the river. Of course he sank, and his master was several hundred dollars poorer than a moment before. That was all; at least, scarcely any one mentioned it the next morning. I was obliged to get my information from the deck hands, and did not hear a remark concerning it in the cabin. In justice to the master, I should say that, after the occurrence, he disclaimed any intention to separate them. Appearances, however, are quite against him, if I have been rightly informed. This sad affair needs no comment. It is an argument, however, that I might have used to-day, with some effect, whilst talking with a highly-intelligent Southerner of the evils of slavery. He had been reading *Uncle Tom's Cabin,* and spoke of it as a *novel,* which, like other romances, was well calculated to excite the sympathies, by the recital of heart-touching incidents which *never had an existence,* except in the imagination of the writer."

Instances have occurred where mothers, whose children were about to be sold from them, have, in their desperation, murdered their own offspring, to save them from this worst kind of orphanage. A case of this kind has been recently tried in the United States, and was alluded to, a week or two ago, by Mr. Giddings, in his speech on the floor of Congress.

An American gentleman from Italy, complaining of the effect of *Uncle Tom's Cabin* on the Italian mind, states that images of fathers dragged from their families to be sold into slavery, and of babes torn from the breasts of weeping mothers, are constantly presented before the minds of the people as scenes of every-day life in America. The author can only say, sorrowfully, that it is *only the truth* which is thus presented.

These things *are,* every day, part and parcel of one of *the most thriving trades that is carried on in America.* The only difference between us and foreign nations is, that we have got used to it, and they have not. The thing has been done, and done again, day after day, and year after year, reported and lamented over in every variety of way; but it is *going on this day* with more briskness than ever before, and no doubt; the other, and such scenes as we have described are enacted oftener, as the author will prove when she comes to the chapter on the internal slave-trade.

The incident in this same chapter which describes the scene where the wife of the unfortunate article, catalogued as "John, aged 30," rushed on board the boat and threw her arms around him, with moans and lamentations, was a real incident. The gentleman who related it was so stirred in his spirit at the sight, that he addressed the trader in the exact words which the writer represents the young minister as having used in her narrative.

My friend, how can you, how dare you, carry on a trade like this? Look at those poor creatures! Here I am, rejoicing in my heart that I am going home to my wife and child; and the same bell which is the signal to carry me onward towards them will part this poor man and his wife for ever. Depend upon it, God will bring you into judgment for this.

If that gentleman has read the work, as perhaps he has before now, he has probably recognised his own words. One affecting incident in the narrative, as it really occurred, ought to be mentioned. The wife was passionately bemoaning her husband's fate, as about to be for ever separated from all that he held dear, to be sold to the hard usage of a Southern plantation. The husband, in reply, used that very simple but sublime expression which the writer has placed in the mouth of Uncle Tom, in similar circumstances:—"*There'll be the same God there that there is here*."

One other incident mentioned in *Uncle Tom's Cabin* may, perhaps, be as well verified in this place as in any other.

The case of old Prue was related by a brother and sister of the writer as follows:—She was the woman who supplied *rusks* and other articles of the kind at the house where they boarded. Her manners, appearance, and character were just as described. One day another servant came in her place, bringing the rusks. The sister of the writer inquired what had become of *Prue*. She seemed reluctant to answer for some time, but at last said that they had taken her into the cellar and beaten her, and that the flies had got at her and she was dead!

It is well known that there are no *cellars,* properly so called, in New Orleans, the nature of the ground being such as to forbid digging. The slave who used the word had probably been imported from some State where cellars were in use, and applied the term to the place which was used for the ordinary purposes of a cellar. A cook who lived in the writer's family, having lived most of her life on a plantation, always applied the descriptive terms of the plantation to the very limited enclosures and retinue of a very plain house and yard.

This same lady, while living in the same place, used frequently to have her compassion excited by hearing the wailings of a sickly baby in a house adjoining their own, as also the objurgations and tyrannical abuse of a ferocious virago upon its mother. She once got an opportunity to speak to its mother, who appeared heart-broken and dejected, and inquired what was the matter with her child. Her answer was, that she had had a fever, and that her milk was all dried away; and that her mistress was set against her child, and would not buy milk for it. She had tried to feed it on her own coarse food, but it pined and cried continually; and in witness of this she brought the baby to her. It was emaciated to a skeleton. The lady took the little thing to a friend of hers in the house who had been recently confined, and who was suffering from a redundancy of milk, and begged her to nurse it. The miserable sight of the little, famished, wasted thing affected the mother so as to overcome all other considerations, and she placed it to her breast, when it revived, and took food with an eagerness which showed how much it had suffered. But the child was so reduced that this proved only a transient alleviation. It was after this almost impossible to get sight of the woman, and the violent temper of her mistress was such as to make it difficult to interfere in the case. The lady secretly afforded what aid she could, though, as she confessed, with a sort of misgiving that it was a cruelty to try to hold back the poor little sufferer from the refuge of the grave; and it was a relief to her when at last its wailings ceased, and it went where the weary are at rest. This is one of those cases which go to show that the *interest* of the owner will not always insure kind treatment of the slave.

There is one other incident, which the writer interwove into the history of the mulatto woman who was bought by Legree for his plantation. The reader will remember that, in telling her story to Emmeline, she says:—

"My mas'r was Mr. Ellis—lived in Levee-street. P'raps you've seen the house."

"Was he good to you?" said Emmeline.

"Mostly, till he tuk sick. He's lain sick, off and on, more than six months, and been orful oneasy. 'Pears like he warn't willin' to have nobody rest, day nor night; and got so cur'ous, there couldn't nobody suit him. 'Pears like he just grew crosser every day; kep me up nights till I got fairly beat out, and couldn't keep awake no longer; and 'cause I got to sleep one night, Lors! he talk so orful to me, and he tell me he'd sell me to just the hardest master he could find; and he'd promised me my freedom, too, when he died!"

An incident of this sort came under the author's observation in the following manner. A quadroon slave family, liberated by the will of the master, settled on Walnut Hills, near her residence, and their children were received into her family school, taught in her house. In this family was a little quadroon boy, four or five years of age, with a sad, dejected appearance, who excited their interest.

The history of this child, as narrated by his friends, was simply this: his mother had been the indefatigable nurse of her master, during a lingering and painful sickness which at last terminated his life. She had borne all the fatigue of the nursing both by night and by day, sustained in it by his promise that she should be rewarded for it by her liberty, at his death. Overcome by exhaustion and fatigue, she one night fell asleep, and he was unable to rouse her. The next day, after violently upbraiding her, he altered the directions of his will, and sold her to a man who was noted in all the region round as a cruel master, which sale, immediately on his death, which was shortly after, took effect. The only mitigation of her sentence was that her child was not to be taken with her into this dreaded lot, but was given to this quadroon family to be brought into a free State.

CHAPTER XI.

The writer very well remembers hearing this story narrated among a group of liberated negroes, and their comments on it. A peculiar form of grave and solemn irony often characterises the communications of this class of people. It is a habit engendered in slavery to comment upon proceedings of this kind in language apparently respectful to the perpetrators, and which is felt to be irony only by a certain peculiarity of manner, difficult to describe. After the relation of this story, when the writer expressed her indignation in no measured terms, one of the oldest of the sable circle remarked, gravely—

"The man was a mighty great Christian, anyhow."

The writer warmly expressed her dissent from this view, when another of the same circle added—

"Went to glory, anyhow."

And another continued—

"Had the greatest kind of a time when he was a-dyin'; said he was goin' straight into heaven."

And when the writer remarked that many people thought so who never got there, a singular smile of grim approval passed round the circle, but no further comments were made. This incident has often recurred to the writer's mind, as showing the danger to the welfare of the master's soul from the possession of absolute power. A man of justice and humanity when in health, is often tempted to become unjust, exacting, and exorbitant in sickness. If, in these circumstances, he is surrounded by inferiors, from whom law and public opinion have taken away the rights of common humanity, how is he tempted to the exercise of the most despotic passions, and, like this unfortunate man, to leave the world with the weight of these awful words upon his head: "If ye forgive not men their trespasses, neither will your Father forgive your trespasses."

CHAPTER XII.

TOPSY.

TOPSY stands as the representative of a large class of the children who are growing up under the institution of slavery—quick, active, subtle and ingenious, apparently utterly devoid of principle and conscience, keenly penetrating, by an instinct which exists in the childish mind, the degradation of their condition, and the utter hopelessness of rising above it; feeling the black skin on them, like the mark of Cain, to be a sign of reprobation and infamy, and urged on by a kind of secret desperation to make their "calling and election" in sin "sure."

Christian people have often been perfectly astonished and discouraged, as Miss Ophelia was, in the attempt to bring up such children decently and Christianly, under a state of things which takes away every stimulant which God meant should operate healthfully on the human mind.

We are not now speaking of the Southern States merely, but of the New England States; for, startling as it may appear, *slavery is not yet wholly abolished in the free States of the North.* The most unchristian part of it, that which gives to it all the bitterness and all the sting, is yet, in a great measure, unrepealed; it is the practical denial to the negro of the rights of human brotherhood. In consequence of this, Topsy is a character which may be found at the North as well as at the South.

In conducting the education of negro, mulatto, and quadroon children, the writer has often observed this fact—that, for a certain time, and up to a certain age, they kept equal pace with, and were often superior to, the white children with whom they were associated; but that there came a time when they became indifferent to learning, and made no further progress. This was invariably at the age when they were old enough to reflect upon life, and to perceive that society had no place to offer them for which anything more would be requisite than the rudest and most elementary knowledge.

Let us consider how it is with our own children; how few of them would ever acquire an education from the mere love of learning.

In the process necessary to acquire a handsome style of handwriting, to master the intricacies of any language, or to conquer the difficulties of mathematical study, how often does the perseverance of the child flag, and need to be stimulated by his parents and teachers by such considerations as these: "It will be necessary for you, in such or such a position in life, to possess this or that acquirement or accomplishment. How could you ever become a merchant without understanding accounts? How could you enter the learned professions without understanding languages? If you are ignorant and uninformed, you cannot take rank as a gentleman in society."

Does not everyone know that, without the stimulus which teachers and parents thus continually present, multitudes of children would never gain a tolerable education? And is it not the absence of all such stimulus which has prevented the negro child from an equal advance?

It is often objected to the negro race that they are frivolous and vain, passionately fond of show, and are interested only in trifles. And who is to blame for all this? Take away all high aims, all noble ambition, from any class, and what is left for them to be interested in *but* trifles?

The present Attorney-General of Liberia, Mr. Lewis, is a man who commands the highest respect for talent and ability in his position; yet, while he was in America, it is said that, like many other young coloured men, he was distinguished only for foppery and frivolity. What made the change in Lewis after he went to Liberia? Who does not see the answer? Does anyone wish to know what is inscribed on the seal which keeps the great stone over the sepulchre of African mind? It is this—which was so truly said by poor Topsy—"NOTHING BUT A NIGGER!"

It is this, burnt into the soul by the branding-iron of cruel and unchristian scorn, that is a sorer and deeper wound than all the physical evils of slavery together.

There never was a slave who did not feel it. Deep, deep down in the dark still waters of his soul is the conviction, heavier, bitterer than all others, that he is *not regarded as a man.* On this point may be introduced the testimony of one who has known the wormwood and the gall of slavery by bitter experience. The following letter has been received from Dr. Pennington, in relation to some inquiries of the author:—

New York, 50, *Laurens-street, November* 30, 1852.

ESTEEMED MADAM,—I have duly received your kind letter in answer to mine of the 15th instant, in which you state that you "have an intense curiosity to know how far you have rightly divined the heart of the slave." You give me your idea in these words: "There lies buried down in the heart of the most seemingly careless and stupid slave a *bleeding spot* that bleeds and aches, though he could scarcely tell why; and that this sore spot is the *degradation* of his position."

After escaping from the plantation of Dr. Tilghman, in Washington County, Md., where I was held as a slave, and worked as a blacksmith, I came to the State of Pennsylvania, and, after experiencing there some of the vicissitudes referred to in my little published narrative, I came into New York State, bringing in my mind a certain indescribable feeling of wretchedness. They used to say of me at Dr.

Tilghman's, “That blacksmith Jemmy is a 'cute fellow; still water runs deep.” But I confess that “blacksmith Jemmy” was not 'cute enough to understand the cause of his own wretchedness. The current of the still water may have run deep, but it did not reach down to that awful bed of lava.

At times I thought it occasioned by the lurking fear of betrayal. There was no Vigilance Committee at the time—there were but anti-slavery men. I came North with my counsels in my own cautious breast. I married a wife, and did not tell her I was a fugitive. None of my friends knew it. I knew not the means of safety, and hence I was constantly in fear of meeting with some one who would betray me.

It was fully two years before I could hold up my head; but still that feeling was in my mind. In 1846, after opening my bosom as a fugitive to John Hooker, Esq., I felt this much relief—“Thank God, there is one brother man in hard old Connecticut that knows my troubles.”

Soon after this, when I sailed to the island of Jamaica, and on landing there saw coloured men in all the stations of civil, social, commercial life, where I had seen white men in this country, that feeling of wretchedness experienced a sensible relief, as if some feverish sore had been just reached by just the right kind of balm. There was before my eye evidence that a coloured man is more than “a nigger.” I went into the House of Assembly at Spanishtown, where fifteen out of forty-five members were coloured men. I went into the courts, where I saw in the jury-box coloured and white men together, coloured and white lawyers at the bar. I went into the Common Council of Kingston; there I found men of different colours. So in all the counting-rooms,&c.&c.

But still there was this drawback. Somebody says, “This is nothing but a nigger island.” Now, then, my old trouble came back again, “a nigger among niggers is but a nigger still.”

In 1849, when I undertook my second visit to Great Britain, I resolved to prolong and extend my travel and intercourse with the best class of men, with a view to see if I could banish that troublesome old ghost entirely out of my mind. In England, Scotland, Wales, France, Germany, Belgium, and Prussia, my whole power has been concentrated on this object: “I'll be a man, and I'll kill off this enemy which has haunted me these twenty years and more.” I believe I have succeeded in some good degree; at least, I have now no more trouble on the score of equal manhood with the whites. My European tour was certainly useful, because there the trial was fair and honourable. I had nothing to complain of. I got what was due to man, and I was expected to do what was due from man to man. I sought not to be treated as a pet. I put myself into the harness, and wrought manfully in the first pulpits, and the platforms in peace congresses, conventions, anniversaries, commencements, &c.; and in these exercises that rusty old iron came out of my soul, and went “clean away.”

You say again you have never seen a slave, however careless and merryhearted, who had not this sore place, and that did not shrink or get angry if a finger was laid on it. I see that you have been a close observer of negro nature.

CHAPTER XII.

So far as I understand your idea, I think you are perfectly correct in the impression you have received, as explained in your note.

O Mrs. Stowe, slavery is an awful system! It takes man as God made him; it demolishes him, and then mis-creates him, or perhaps I should say mal-creates him!

Wishing you good health and good success in your arduous work,

I am yours, respectfully, J. W. C. PENNINGTON.

Mrs. H. B. Stowe.

People of intelligence, who have had the care of slaves, have often made this remark to the writer: "They are a singular, whimsical people; you can do a great deal more with them by humouring some of their prejudices than by bestowing on them the most substantial favours." On inquiring what these prejudices were, the reply would be, "They like to have their weddings elegantly celebrated, and to have a good deal of notice taken of their funerals, and to give and go to parties dressed and appearing like white people; and they will often put up with material inconveniences, and suffer themselves to be worked very hard, if they are humoured in these respects."

Can anyone think of this without compassion? Poor souls! willing to bear with so much for simply this slight acknowledgment of their common humanity. To honour their weddings and funerals is, in some sort, acknowledging that they are human, and therefore they prize it. Hence we see the reason of the passionate attachment which often exists in a faithful slave to a good master; it is, in fact, a transfer of his identity to his master. A stern law, and an unchristian public sentiment, has taken away his birthright of humanity, erased his name from the catalogue of men, and made him an anomalous creature—neither man nor brute. When a kind master recognises his humanity, and treats him as a humble companion and a friend, there is no end to the devotion and gratitude which he thus excites. He is to the slave a deliverer and a saviour from the curse which lies on his hapless race. Deprived of all legal rights and privileges, all opportunity or hope of personal advancement or honour, he transfers, as it were, his whole existence into his master's, and appropriates his rights, his position, his honour, as his own; and thus enjoys a kind of reflected sense of what it might be to be a man himself. Hence it is that the appeal to the more generous part of the negro character is seldom made in vain.

An acquaintance of the writer was married to a gentleman in Louisiana, who was the proprietor of some eight hundred slaves. He, of course, had a large train of servants in his domestic establishment. When about to enter upon her duties, she was warned that the servants were all so thievish that she would be under the necessity, in common with all other housekeepers, of keeping everything under lock and key. She, however, announced her intention of training her servants in such a manner as to make this unnecessary. Her ideas were ridiculed as chimerical, but she resolved to carry them into practice. The course she pursued was as follows:—She called all the family servants together; told them that it would be a great burden and restraint upon her to be obliged to keep everything locked from them; that she had heard that they were not at all to be trusted, but that she could not help hoping that they were much better than they had been represented. She told them that she should provide abundantly for all their wants, and then that she should leave her stores unlocked, and trust to their honour.

The idea that they were supposed capable of having any honour struck a new chord at once in every heart. The servants appeared most grateful for the trust, and there was much public spirit excited, the older and graver ones exerting themselves to watch over the children, that nothing might be done to destroy this new-found treasure of honour.

At last, however, the lady discovered that some depredations had been made on her cake by some of the juvenile part of the establishment; she, therefore, convened all the servants, and stated the fact to them. She remarked that it was not on account of the value of the cake that she felt annoyed, but that they must be sensible that it would not be pleasant for her to have it indiscriminately fingered and handled, and that, therefore, she should set some cake out upon a table, or some convenient place, and beg that all those who were disposed to take it would go there and help themselves, and allow the rest to remain undisturbed in the closet. She states that the cake stood upon the table and dried, without a morsel of it being touched, and that she never afterwards had any trouble in this respect.

A little time after, a new carriage was bought, and one night the leather boot of it was found to be missing. Before her husband had time to take any steps on the subject, the servants of the family had called a convention among themselves, and instituted an inquiry into the offence. The boot was found and promptly restored, though they would not reveal to their master and mistress the name of the offender.

One other anecdote which this lady related illustrates that peculiar devotion of a slave to a good master, to which allusion has been made. Her husband met with his death by a sudden and melancholy accident. He had a personal attendant and confidential servant who had grown up with him from childhood. This servant was so overwhelmed with grief as to be almost stupified. On the day of the funeral a brother of his deceased master inquired of him if he had performed a certain commission for his mistress. The servant said that he had forgotten it. Not perceiving his feelings at the moment, the gentleman replied, "I am surprised that you should neglect any command of your mistress, when she is in such affliction."

This remark was the last drop in the full cup. The poor fellow fell to the ground entirely insensible, and the family were obliged to spend nearly two hours employing various means to restore his vitality. The physician accounted for his situation by saying that there had been such a rush of all the blood in the body towards the heart, that there was actual danger of a rupture of that organ—a literal death by a broken heart.

Some thoughts may be suggested by Miss Ophelia's conscientious but unsuccessful efforts in the education of Topsy.

CHAPTER XII.

Society has yet need of a great deal of enlightening as to the means of restoring the vicious and degraded to virtue.

It has been erroneously supposed that with brutal and degraded natures only coarse and brutal measures could avail; and yet it has been found, by those who have most experience, that their success with this class of society has been just in proportion to the delicacy and kindliness with which they have treated them.

Lord Shaftesbury, who has won so honourable a fame by his benevolent interest in the efforts made for the degraded lower classes of his own land, says, in a recent letter to the author:—

You are right about Topsy; our ragged schools will afford you many instances of poor children, hardened by kicks, insults and neglect, moved to tears and docility by the first word of kindness. It opens new feelings, developes, as it were a new nature, and brings the wretched outcast into the family of man.

Recent efforts which have been made among unfortunate females in some of the worst districts of New York show the same thing. What is it that rankles deepest in the breast of fallen woman, that makes her so hopeless and irreclaimable? It is that burning consciousness of degradation which stings worse than cold or hunger, and makes her shrink from the face of the missionary and the philanthropist. They who have visited these haunts of despair and wretchedness have learned that they must touch gently the shattered harp of the human soul, if they would string it again to divine music; that they must encourage self-respect, and hope, and sense of character, or the bonds of death can never be broken.

Let us examine the gospel of Christ, and see on what principles its appeals are constructed. Of what nature are those motives which have melted *our* hearts and renewed *our* wills? Are they not appeals to the most generous and noble instincts of our nature? Are we not told of One fairer than the sons of men—One reigning in immortal glory, who loved us so that he could bear pain, and want, and shame, and death itself, for our sake?

When Christ speaks to the soul, does he crush one of its nobler faculties? Does he taunt us with our degradation, our selfishness, our narrowness of view, and feebleness of intellect, compared with his own? Is it not true that he not only saves us from our sins, but saves us in a way most considerate, most tender, most regardful of our feelings and sufferings? Does not the Bible tell us that, in order to fulfil his office of Redeemer the more perfectly, he took upon him the condition of humanity, and endured the pains, and wants, and temptations of a mortal existence, that he might be to us a sympathising, appreciating friend, "touched with the feelings of our infirmities," and cheering us gently on in the hard path of returning virtue?

Oh, when shall we, who have received so much of Jesus Christ, learn to repay it in acts of kindness to our poor brethren? When shall we be Christ-like, and not man-like, in our efforts to reclaim the fallen and wandering?

CHAPTER XIII.

THE QUAKERS.

THE writer's sketch of the character of this people has been drawn from personal observation. There are several settlements of these people in Ohio; and the manner of living, the tone of sentiment, and the habits of life, as represented in her book, are not at all exaggerated.

These settlements have always been refuges for the oppressed and outlawed slave. The character of Rachel Halliday was a real one, but she has passed away to her reward. Simeon Halliday, calmly risking fine and imprisonment for his love to God and man, has had in this country many counterparts among the sect.

The writer had in mind, at the time of writing, the scenes in the trial of John Garret, of Wilmington, Delaware, for the crime of hiring a hack to convey a mother and four children from Newcastle jail to Wilmington, a distance of *five miles*.

The writer has received the facts in this case, in a letter from John Garret himself, from which some extracts will be made.

Wilmington, Delaware,, 1st month 18th, 1853.

MY DEAR FRIEND, HARRIET BEECHER STOWE,—I have this day received a request from Charles K. Whipple, of Boston, to furnish thee with a statement, authentic and circumstantial, of the trouble and losses which have been brought upon myself and others of my friends from the aid we had rendered to fugitive slaves, in order, if thought of sufficient importance, to be published in a work thee is now preparing for the press.

I will now endeavour to give thee a statement of what John Hunn and myself suffered by aiding a family of slaves, a few years since. I will give the facts as they occurred, and thee may condense and publish so much as thee may think useful in thy work, and no more.

In the 12th month, year 1846, a family, consisting of Samuel Hawkins, a freeman, his wife Emeline, and six children, who were afterwards *proved slaves,* stopped at the house of a friend named John Hunn, near Middletown, in this State, in the evening about sunset, to procure food and lodging for the night. They were seen by some of Hunn's pro-slavery neighbours, who soon came with a constable, and had them taken before a magistrate. Hunn had left the slaves in his kitchen when he went to the village of Middletown, half a mile distant. When the officer came with a warrant for them, he met Hunn at the kitchen-door, and asked for the blacks. Hunn, with truth, said he did not know where they were. Hunn's wife, thinking they would be safer, had sent them up stairs during his absence, where they were found. Hunn made no resistance, and they were taken before the magistrate, and from his office direct to Newcastle jail, where they arrived about one o'clock on 7th day morning.

The sheriff and his daughter, being kind, humane people, inquired of Hawkins and wife the facts of their case; and his daughter wrote to a lady here, to request me to go to Newcastle and inquire into the case, as her father and self really believed they were most of them, if not all, entitled to their *freedom*. Next morning I went to Newcastle; had the family of coloured people brought into the parlour, and the sheriff and myself came to the conclusion that the parents and four youngest children were by law entitled to their freedom. I prevailed on the sheriff to show me the commitment of the magistrate, which I found was defective, and not in due form according to law. I procured a copy, and handed it to a lawyer. He pronounced the commitment irregular, and agreed to go next morning to Newcastle, and have the whole family taken before Judge Booth, Chief Justice of the State, by *habeas corpus,* when the following admission was made by Samuel Hawkins and wife: they admitted that the two eldest boys were held by one Charles Glaudin, of Queen Anne County, Maryland, as slaves; that after the birth of these two children, Elizabeth Turner, also of Queen Anne, the mistress of their mother, had set her free, and permitted her to go and live with her husband, near twenty miles from her residence, after which the four youngest children were born; that her mistress during all that time, eleven or twelve years, had never contributed one dollar to their support, or come to see them. After examining the commitment in their case, and consulting with my attorney, the judge set the whole family at liberty. The day was wet and cold; one of the children, three years old, was a cripple from white swelling, and could not walk a step; another, eleven months old, at the breast; and the parents being desirous of getting to Wilmington, five miles distant, I asked the judge if there would be any risk or impropriety in my hiring a conveyance for the mother and four young children to Wilmington. His reply, in the presence of the sheriff and my attorney, was, there would not be any. I then requested the sheriff to procure a hack to take them over to Wilmington.

The whole family escaped. John Hunn and John Garret were brought up to trial for having practically fulfilled those words of Christ, which read, “I was a stranger and ye took me in, I was sick and in prison and ye came unto me.” For John Hunn's part of this crime he was fined two thousand five hundred dollars, and John Garret was fined five thousand four hundred. Three thousand five hundred of this was the fine for hiring a hack for them, and one thousand nine hundred was assessed on him as the value of the slaves! Our European friends will infer from this that it costs something to obey Christ in America, as well as in Europe.

After John Garret's trial was over, and this heavy judgment had been given against him, he calmly rose in the court-room, and requested leave to address a few words to the court and audience.

Leave being granted, he spoke as follows:—

I have a few words which I wish to address to the court, jury, and prosecutors, in the several suits that have been brought against me during the sittings of this court, in order to determine the amount of penalty I must pay for doing what my feelings prompted me to do as a lawful and meritorious act; a simple act of humanity and justice, as I believed, to eight of that oppressed race, the people of colour, whom I found in the Newcastle jail, in the 12th month, 1845. I will now endeavour to state the facts of those cases, for your consideration and reflection after you return home to your families and friends. You will then have time to ponder on what has transpired here since the sitting of this court, and I believe that your verdict will then be unanimous, that the law of the United States, as explained by our venerable judge, when compared with the act committed by me, was cruel and oppressive, and needs remodelling.

Here follows a very brief and clear statement of the facts in the case, of which the reader is already apprised.

After showing conclusively that he had no reason to suppose the family to be slaves, and that they had all been discharged by the judge, he nobly adds the following words:—

Had I believed every one of them to be slaves, I should have done the same thing. I should have done violence to my convictions of duty, had I not made use of all the lawful means in my power to liberate those people, and assist them to become men and women, rather than leave them in the condition of chattels personal.

I am called an Abolitionist; once a name of reproach, but one I have ever been proud to be considered worthy of being called. For the last twenty-five years I have been engaged in the cause of this despised and much-injured race, and consider their cause worth suffering for; but, owing to a multiplicity of other engagements, I could not devote so much of my time and mind to their cause as I otherwise should have done.

The impositions and persecutions practised on those unoffending and innocent brethren are extreme beyond endurance. I am now placed in a situation in which I have not so much to claim my attention as formerly; and I now pledge myself, in the presence of this assembly, to use all lawful and honourable means to lessen the burdens of this oppressed people, and endeavour, according to ability furnished, to burst their chains asunder, and set them free; not relaxing my efforts on their behalf while blessed with health and a slave remains to tread the soil of the State of my adoption—Delaware.

After mature reflection, I can assure this assembly it is my opinion at this time that the verdicts you have given the prosecutors against John Hunn and myself, within the past few days, will have a tendency to raise a spirit of inquiry throughout the length and breadth of the land, respecting this monster evil (slavery), in many minds that have not heretofore investigated the subject. The reports of those trials will be published by editors from Maine to Texas, and the far West; and what must be the effect produced? It will, no doubt, add hundreds, perhaps thousands, to the present large and rapidly increasing army of Abolitionists. The injury is great to us who are the immediate sufferers by your verdict; but I believe the verdicts you have given against us within the last few days will have a powerful effect in bringing about the abolition of slavery in this country—this land of boasted freedom, where not only the slave is fettered at the South by his lordly master, but the white man at the North is bound as in chains to do the bidding of his Southern masters.

In his letter to the writer John Garret adds that, after this speech, a young man who had served as juryman came across the room, and taking him by the hand, said—

"Old gentleman, I believe every statement that you have made. I came from home prejudiced against you, and I now acknowledge that I have helped to do you injustice."

Thus calmly and simply did this Quaker confess Christ before men, according as it is written of them of old—"He esteemed the reproach of Christ greater riches than all the treasures of Egypt."

Christ has said, "Whosoever shall be ashamed of me and my words, of him shall the Son of Man be ashamed." In our days it is not customary to be ashamed of Christ personally, but of *his words* many are ashamed. But when they meet Him in judgment they will have cause to remember them; for heaven and earth shall pass away, but his words shall not pass away.

Another case of the same kind is of a more affecting character.

Richard Dillingham was the son of a respectable Quaker family in Morrow County, Ohio. His pious mother brought him up in the full belief of the doctrine of St. John, that the love of God and the love of man are inseparable. He was diligently taught in such theological notions as are implied in such passages as these: "Hereby perceive we the love of God, because he laid down his life for us; and we ought also to lay down our lives for the brethren.—But whoso hath this world's goods and seeth his brother have need, and shutteth up his bowels of compassion from him, how dwelleth the love of God in him?—My little children, let us not love in word and in tongue, but in deed and in truth."

In accordance with these precepts, Richard Dillingham, in early manhood, was found in Cincinnati teaching the coloured people, and visiting in the prisons, and doing what in him lay to "love in deed and in truth."

Some unfortunate families among the coloured people had dear friends who were slaves in Nashville, Tennessee. Richard was so interested in their story, that when he went into Tennessee he was actually taken up and caught in the very fact of helping certain poor people to escape to their friends.

He was seized and thrown into prison. In the language of this world he was imprisoned as a "negro-stealer." His own account is given in the following letter to his parents:—

Nashville Jail, 12*th mo:* 15*th,* 1849.

DEAR PARENTS,—I presume you have heard of my arrest and imprisonment in the Nashville jail, under a charge of aiding in an attempted escape of slaves from the city of Nashville, on the 5th inst. I was arrested by M. D. Maddox (district constable), aided by Frederick Marshal, watchman at the Nashville Inn, and the bridge-keeper, at the bridge across the Cumberland river. When they arrested me, I had rode up to the bridge on horseback and paid the toll for myself and for the hack to pass over, in which three coloured persons, who were said to be slaves, were found by the men who arrested me. The driver of the hack (who is a free coloured man of this city), and the persons in the hack, were also arrested; and after being taken to the Nashville Inn and searched, we were all taken to jail. My arrest took place about eleven o'clock at night.

In another letter he says:—

At the bridge, Maddox said to me, "You are just the man we wanted. We will make an example of you." As soon as we were safe in the bar-room of the Inn, Maddox took a candle and looked me in the face, to see if he could recognise my countenance; and looking intently at me a few moments, he said, "Well, you are too good-looking a young man to be engaged in such an affair as this." The bystanders asked me several questions, to which I replied that, under the present circumstances, I would rather be excused from answering any questions relating to my case; upon which they desisted from further inquiry. Some threats and malicious wishes were uttered against me by the ruffian part of the assembly, being about twenty-five persons. I was put in a cell which had six persons in it, and I can assure thee that they were very far from being agreeable companions to me, although they were kind. But thou knows that I do not relish cursing and swearing, and, worst of all, loathsome and obscene blasphemy and of such was most of the conversation of my prison mates when I was first put in here. The jailors are kind enough to me, but the jail is so constructed that it cannot be warmed, and we have either to warm ourselves by walking in our cell, which is twelve by fifteen feet, or by lying in bed. I went out on my trial on the 16th of last month, and put it off till the next term of the court, which will be commenced on the second of next 4th month. I put it off on the ground of excitement.

Dear brother, I have no hopes of getting clear of being convicted and sentenced to the Penitentiary; but do not think that I am without comfort in my afflictions, for I assure thee that I have many reflections that give me sweet consolation in the midst of my grief. I have a clear conscience before my God, which is my greatest comfort and support through all my troubles and afflictions. An approving conscience none can know but those who enjoy it. It nerves us in the hour of trial to bear our sufferings with fortitude and even with cheerfulness. The greatest affliction I have is the reflection of the sorrow and anxiety my friends will have to endure on my account. But I can assure thee, brother, that, with the exception of this reflection, I am far, very far, from being one of the most miserable of men. Nay, to the contrary, I am not terrified at the prospect before me, though I am grieved about it; but all have enough to grieve about in this unfriendly wilderness of sin and woe. My hopes are not fixed in this world, and therefore I have a source of consolation that will never fail me, so long as I slight not the offers of mercy, comfort, and peace, which my blessed Saviour constantly privileges me with.

One source of almost constant annoyance to my feelings is the profanity and vulgarity, and the bad, disagreeable temper, of two or three fellow-prisoners of my cell. They show me considerable kindness and respect; but they cannot do otherwise, when treated with the civility and kindness with which I treat them. If it be my fate to go to the Penitentiary for eight or ten years, I can, I believe, meet my doom without shedding a tear. I have not yet shed a tear, though there may be many in store. My bail-bonds were set at seven thousand dollars, If I should be bailed out, I should return to my trial, unless my security were rich, and did not wish me to return; for *I am Richard yet,* although I am in the prison of my enemy, and will not flinch from what I believe to be right and honourable. These are the principles which, in carrying out, have lodged me here; for there was a time, at my arrest, that I might have, in all probability, escaped the police, but it would have subjected those who were arrested with me to punishment, perhaps even to death, in order to find out who I was; and if they had not told more than they could have done in truth, they would probably have been punished without mercy; and I am determined no one shall suffer for me. I am now a prisoner, but those who were arrested with me are all at liberty, and I believe without whipping. I now stand alone before the Commonwealth of Tennessee to answer for the affair. Tell my friends I am in the midst of consolation here.

Richard was engaged to a young lady of amiable disposition and fine mental endowments.

To her he thus writes:—

Oh, dearest! Canst thou upbraid me? canst thou call it crime? wouldst thou call it crime, or couldst thou upbraid me, for rescuing, or attempting to rescue, *thy* father, mother, or brother and sister, or even friends, from a captivity among a cruel race of oppressors? Oh, couldst thou only see what I have seen, and hear what I have heard, of the sad, vexatious, degrading, and soul-trying situation of as noble minds as ever the Anglo-Saxon race were possessed of, mourning in vain for that universal heaven-born boon of freedom which an all-wise and beneficent Creator has designed for all, thou couldst not censure, but wouldst deeply sympathise with me! Take all these things into consideration, and the thousands of poor mortals who are dragging out far more miserable lives than mine will be, even at ten years in the Penitentiary, and thou wilt not look upon my fate with so much horror as thou would at first thought.

In another letter he adds:—

Have happy hours here, and I should not be miserable if I could only know you were not sorrowing for me at home. It would give me more satisfaction to hear that you were not grieving about me than anything else.

The nearer I live to the principle of the commandment, "Love thy neighbour as thyself," the more enjoyment I have of this life. None can know the enjoyments that flow from feelings of good-will towards our fellow-beings, both friends and enemies, but those who cultivate them. Even in my prison-cell I may be happy, if I will. For the Christian's consolation cannot be shut out from him by enemies or iron gates.

In another letter to the lady before alluded to he says:—

By what I am able to learn, I believe thy "Richard" has not fallen altogether unlamented; and the satisfaction it gives me is sufficient to make my prison life more pleasant and desirable than even a life of liberty without the esteem and respect of my friends. But it gives bitterness to the cup of my afflictions to think that my dear friends and relatives have to suffer such grief and sorrow for me.

* * * * *

Though persecution ever so severe be my lot, yet I will not allow my indignation ever to ripen into revenge even against my bitterest enemies; for there will be a time when all things must be revealed before Him who has said, "Vengeance is mine, I will repay." Yes, my heart shall ever glow with love for my poor fellow-mortals, who are hastening rapidly on to their final destination—the awful tomb and the solemn judgment.

Perhaps it will give thee some consolation for me to tell thee that I believe there is a considerable sympathy existing in the minds of some of the better portion of the citizens here, which may be of some benefit to me. But all that can be done in my behalf will still leave my case a sad one. Think not, however, that it is all loss to me, for by my calamity I have learned many good and useful lessons, which I hope may yet prove both temporal and spiritual blessings to me.

"Behind a frowning Providence
He hides a smiling face."

Therefore, I hope thou and my dear distressed parents will be somewhat comforted about me, for I know you regard my spiritual welfare far more than anything else.

In his next letter to the same friend, he says:—

Since I wrote my last, I have had a severe moral conflict, in which, I believe, the right conquered, and has completely gained the ascendancy. The matter was this:—A man with whom I have become acquainted since my imprisonment offered to bail me out and let me stay away from my trial, and pay the bail-bonds for me, and was very anxious to do it. [Here he mentions that the funds held by this individual had been placed in his hands by a person who obtained them by dishonest means.] But having learned the above facts, which he in confidence made known to me, I declined accepting his offer, giving him my reasons in full. The matter rests with him, my attorneys, and myself. My attorneys do not know who he is; but, with his permission, I in confidence informed them of the nature of the case, after I came to a conclusion upon the subject, and had determined not to accept the offer; which was approved by them. I also had an offer of iron saws, and files, and other tools, by which I could break jail; but I refused them also, as I do not wish to pursue any such underhanded course to extricate myself from my present difficulties; for when I leave Tennessee—if ever I do—I am determined to leave it a free man. Thou need not fear that I shall ever stoop to dishonourable means to avoid my severe impending fate. When I meet thee again, I want to meet thee with a clear conscience, and a character unspotted by disgrace.

In another place he says, in view of his nearly approaching trial:—

O dear parents! The principles of love for my fellow-beings which you have instilled into my mind are some of the greatest consolations I have in my imprisonment, and they give me resignation to bear whatever may be inflicted upon me without feeling any malice or bitterness toward my vigilant prosecutors. If they show me mercy, it will be accepted by me with gratitude; but if they do not, I will endeavour to bear whatever they may inflict with Christian fortitude and resignation, and try not to murmur at my lot; but it is hard to obey the commandment, "Love your enemies."

The day of his trial at length came.

His youth, his engaging manners, frank address, and invariable gentleness to all who approached him, had won many friends, and the trial excited much interest.

His mother and her brother, Asa Williams, went a distance of 750 miles to attend his trial. They carried with them a certificate of his character, drawn up by Dr. Brisbane, and numerously signed by his friends and acquaintances, and officially countersigned by civil officers. This was done at the suggestion of his counsel, and exhibited by them in court. When brought to the bar it is said "that his demeanour was calm, dignified, and manly." His mother sat by his side. The prosecuting attorney waived his plea, and left the ground clear for Richard's counsel. Their defence was eloquent and pathetic. After they closed, Richard rose, and in a calm and dignified manner spoke extemporaneously as follows:—

"By the kind permission of the court, for which I am sincerely thankful, I avail myself of the privilege of adding a few words to the remarks already made by my counsel. And although I stand, by my own confession, as a criminal in the eyes of your violated laws, yet I feel confident that I am addressing those who have hearts to feel; and in meting out the punishment that I am about to suffer, I hope you will be lenient; for it is a new situation in which I am placed. Never before, in the whole course of my life, have I been charged with a dishonest act. And from my childhood, kind parents, whose names I deeply reverence, have instilled into my mind a desire to be virtuous and honourable; and it has ever been my aim so to conduct myself as to merit the confidence and esteem of my fellow-men. But, gentlemen, I have violated your laws. This offence I did commit; and I now stand before you, to my sorrow and regret, as a criminal. But I was prompted to it by feelings of humanity. It has been suspected, as I was informed, that I am leagued with a fraternity who are combined for the purpose of committing such offences as the one with which I am charged. But gentlemen, the impression is false. I alone am guilty—I alone committed the offence—and I alone must suffer the penalty. My parents, my friends, my relatives, are as innocent of any participation in or knowledge of my offence as the babe unborn. My parents are still living, though advanced in years, and, in the course of nature, a few more years will terminate their earthly existence. In their old age and infirmity they will need a stay and protection; and, if you can, consistently with your ideas of justice, make my term of imprisonment a short one, you will receive the lasting gratitude of a son who reverences his parents, and the prayers and blessings of an aged father and mother who love their child."

A great deal of sensation now appeared in the court-room, and most of the jury are said to have wept. They retired for a few moments, and refurned a verdict for three years' imprisonment in the Penitentiary.

The *Nashville Daily Gazette* of April 13, 1849, contains the following notice:—

"THE KIDNAPPING CASE.

"Richard Dillingham, who was arrested on the 5th day of September last, having in his possession three slaves, whom he intended to convey with him to a free State, was arraigned yesterday and tried in the Criminal Court. The prisoner confessed his guilt, and made a short speech in palliation of his offence. He avowed that the act was undertaken by himself without instigation from any source, and he alone was responsible for the error into which his education had led him. He had, he said, no other motive than the good of the slaves, and did not expect to claim any advantage by freeing them. He was sentenced to three years' imprisonment in the Penitentiary, the least time the law allows for the offence committed. Mr. Dillingham is a Quaker from Ohio, and has been a teacher in that State. He belongs to a respectable family, and he is not without the sympathy of those who attended the trial. It was a fool-hardy enterprise in which he embarked, and dearly has he paid for his rashness."

His mother, before leaving Nashville, visited the governor, and had an interview with him in regard to pardoning her son. He gave her some encouragement, but thought she had better postpone her petition for the present. After the lapse of several months, she wrote to him about it; but he seemed to have changed his mind, as the following letter will show:—

Nashville, August 29, 1849

"DEAR MADAM,—Your letter of the 6th of the 7th mo. was received, and would have been noticed earlier but for my absence from home. Your solicitude for your son is natural, and it would be gratifying to be able to reward it by releasing him, if it were in my power. But the offence for which he is suffering was clearly made out, and its tendency here is very hurtful to our rights, and our peace as a people. He is doomed to the shortest period known to our statute. And, at all events, I could not interfere with his case for some time to come; and, to be frank with you, I do not see how his time can be lessened at all. But my term of office will expire soon, and the Governor elect, Gen. William Trousdale, will take my place. To him you will make any future appeal.

"Yours,&c., "N. L. BROWN."

The warden of the Penitentiary, John McIntosh, was much prejudiced against him. He thought the sentence was too light, and, being of a stern bearing, Richard had not much to expect from his kindness. But the same sterling inegrity and ingenuousness which had ever, under all circumstances, marked his conduct, soon wrought a change in the minds of his keepers, and of his enemies generally. He became a favourite with McIntosh and some of the guard. According to the rules of the prison, he was not allowed to write oftener than once in three months, and what he wrote had, of course, to be inspected by the warden.

He was at first put to sawing and scrubbing rock; but, as the delicacy of his frame unfitted him for such labours, and the spotless sanctity of his life won the reverence of his jailors, he was soon promoted to be steward of the prison hospital. In a letter to a friend he thus announces this change in his situation:

I suppose thou art, ere this time, informed of the change in my situation, having been placed in the hospital of the Penitentiary as steward..... I feel but poorly qualified to fill the situation they have assigned me, but will try to do the best I can..... I enjoy the comforts of a good fire and a warm room, and am allowed to sit up evenings and read, which I prize as a great privilege..... I have now been here nearly nine months, and have twenty-seven more to stay. It seems to me a long time in prospect. I try to be as patient as I can, but sometimes I get low-spirited. I throw off the thoughts of home and friends as much as possible; for, when indulged in, they only increase my melancholy feelings. And what wounds my feelings most is the reflection of what you all suffer of grief and anxiety for me. Cease to grieve for me, for I am unworthy of it; and it only causes pain for you, without availing aught for me..... As ever, thine in the bonds of affection,

R. D.

He had been in prison little more than a year when the cholera invaded Nashville, and broke out among the inmates; Richard was up day and night in attendance on the sick, his disinterested and sympathetic nature leading him to labours to which his delicate constitution, impaired by confinement, was altogether inadequate.

Beside the bed where parting life was laid,
And sorrow, grief, and pain, by turns dismayed,
The youthful champion stood: at his control
Despair and anguish fled the trembling soul,
Comfort came down the dying wretch to raise,
And his last faltering accents whispered praise.

Worn with these labours, the gentle, patient lover of God and of his brother sank at last overwearied, and passed peacefully away to a world where all are lovely and loving.

Though his correspondence with her he most loved was interrupted, from his unwillingness to subject his letters to the surveillance of the warden, yet a note reached her, conveyed through the hands of a prisoner whose time was out. In this letter, the last which any earthly friend ever received, he says:—

I oft-times, yea, *all* times, think of thee; if I did not, I should cease to exist.

What must that system be which makes it necessary to imprison with convicted felons a man like this, because he loves his brother man, "not wisely but too well?"

On his death Whittier wrote the following:—

"Si crucem libenter portes, te portabit."— *Imit. Christ.*

"The Cross, if freely borne, shall be
No burthen, but support, to thee."
So, moved of old time for our sake,
The holy man of Kempen spake.
Thou brave and true one, upon whom
Was laid the Cross of Martyrdom,
How didst thou, in thy faithful youth,
Bear witness to this blessed truth!
Thy cross of suffering and of shame
A staff within thy hands became,
In paths where Faith alone could see
The Master's steps upholding thee.
Thine was the seed-time: God alone
Beholds the end of what is sown;
Beyond our vision, weak and dim,
The harvest-time is hid with Him.
Yet, unforgotten where it lies,
That seed of generous sacrifice,
Though seeming on the desert cast,
Shall rise with bloom and fruit at last.
J. G. WHITTIER.

Amesbury, Second mo. 18*th,* 1852.

CHAPTER XIV. THE SPIRIT OF ST. CLARE.

THE general tone of the press and of the community in the slave States, so far as it has been made known at the North, has been loudly condemnatory of the representations of "Uncle Tom's Cabin." Still, it would be unjust to the character of the South to refuse to acknowledge that she has many sons with candour enough to perceive, and courage enough to avow, the evils of her "peculiar institutions." The manly independence exhibited by these men, in communities where popular sentiment rules despotically, either by law or in spite of law, should be duly honoured. The sympathy of such minds as these is a high encouragement to philanthropic effort.

The author inserts a few testimonials from Southern men, not without some pride in being thus kindly judged by those who might have been naturally expected to read her book with prejudice against it.

The *Jefferson Inquirer,* published at Jefferson City, Missouri, October 23, 1852, contains the following communication:—

UNCLE TOM'S CABIN.

I have lately read this celebrated book, which, perhaps, has gone through more editions, and been sold in greater numbers, than any work from the American press, in the same length of time. It is a work of high literary finish, and its several characters are drawn with great power and truthfulness, although, like the characters in most novels and works of fiction, in some instances too highly coloured. There is no attack on slave-holders as such, but, on the contrary, many of them are represented as highly noble, generous, humane, and benevolent. Nor is there any attack upon them as a class. It sets forth many of the evils of slavery, as *an institution established by law,* but without charging these evils on those who hold the slaves, and seems fully to appreciate the difficulties in finding a remedy. Its effect upon the slave-holder is to make him a kinder and better master; to which none can object. This is said without any intention to indorse everything contained in the book, or, indeed, in any novel or work of fiction. But, if I mistake not, there are few, excepting those who are greatly prejudiced, that will rise from a perusal of the book without being a truer and better Christian, and a more humane and benevolent man. As a slave-holder, I do not feel the least aggrieved. How Mrs. Stowe, the authoress, has obtained her extremely accurate knowledge of the negroes, their character, dialect, habits,&c., is beyond my comprehension, as she never resided—as appears from the preface—in a slave State, or among slaves or negroes. But they are certainly admirably delineated. The book is highly interesting and amusing, and will afford a rich treat to its reader.

THOMAS JEFFERSON. The opinion of the editor himself is given in these words:—

UNCLE TOM'S CABIN.

Well, like a good portion of "the world and the rest of mankind," we have read the book of Mrs. Stowe bearing the above title.

From numerous statements, newspaper paragraphs and rumours, we supposed the book was all that fanaticism and heresy could invent, and were, therefore, greatly prejudiced against it. But, on reading it, we cannot refrain from saying that it is a work of more than ordinary moral worth, and is entitled to consideration. We do not regard it as a "corruption of moral sentiment," and a gross "libel on a portion of our people." The authoress seems disposed to treat the subject fairly, though, in some particulars, the scenes are too highly coloured, and too strongly drawn from the imagination. The book, however, may lead its readers at a distance to misapprehend some of the general and better features of "Southern life as it is" (which, by the way, we, as an individual, prefer to Northern life); yet it is a perfect mirror of several classes of people we have in our mind's eye, who are not free from "all the ills that flesh is heir to." It has been feared that the book would result in injury to the slaveholding interests of the country; but we apprehend no such thing, and hesitate not to recommend it to the perusal of our friends and the public generally.

Mrs. Stowe has exhibited a knowledge of many peculiarities of Southern society which is really wonderful when we consider that she is a Northern lady by birth and residence.

We hope, then, before our friends form any harsh opinions of the merits of "Uncle Tom's Cabin," and make up any judgment against us for pronouncing in its favour (barring some objections to it), that they will give it a careful perusal; and, in so speaking, we may say that we yield to no man in his devotion to Southern rights and interests.

The editor of the *St. Louis* (Missouri) *Battery* pronounces the following judgment:—

We took up this work, a few evenings since, with just such prejudices against it as we presume many others have, and commenced reading it. We have been so much in contact with ultra abolitionists—have had so much evidence that their benevolence was much more hatred for the master than love for the slave, accompanied with a profound ignorance of the circumstances surrounding both, and a most consummate, supreme disgust for the whole negro race—that we had about concluded that anything but rant and nonsense was out of the question from a Northern writer on the subject of slavery.

Mrs. Stowe, in these delineations of life among the lowly, has convinced us to the contrary.

She brings to the discussion of her subject a perfectly cool, calculating judgment, a wide, all-comprehending intellectual vision, and a deep, warm, sea-like woman's soul, over all of which is flung a perfect iris-like imagination, which makes the light of her pictures stronger and more beautiful, as their shades are darker and terror-striking.

We do not wonder that the copy before us is of the seventieth thousand. And seventy thousand more will not supply the demand, or we mistake the appreciation of the American people of the real merits of literary productions. Mrs. Stowe has, in “Uncle Tom's Cabin,” set up for herself a monument more enduring than marble. It will stand amid the wastes of slavery as the Memnon stands amid the sands of the African desert, telling both the white man and the negro of the approach of morning. The book is not an abolitionist work, in the offensive sense of the word. It is, as we have intimated, free from everything like fanaticism, no matter what amount of enthusiasm vivifies every page, and runs like electricity along every thread of the story. It presents at one view the excellences and the evils of the system of slavery, and breathes the true spirit of Christian benevolence for the slave, and charity for the master.

The next witness gives his testimony in a letter to the *New York Evening Post:*—

LIGHT IN THE SOUTH.

The subjoined communication comes to us post-marked New Orleans, June 19, 1852.

“I have just been reading 'Uncle Tom's Cabin, or, Scenes in Lowly Life,' by Mrs. Harriet Beecher Stowe. It found its way to me through the channel of a young student, who purchased it at the North, to read on his homeward passage to New Orleans. He was entirely unacquainted with its character; he was attracted by its title, supposing it might amuse him while travelling. Through his family it was shown to me, as something that I would probably like. I looked at the author's name, and said, 'Oh, yes; anything from that lady I will read;' otherwise I should have disregarded a work of fiction without such a title.

“The remarks from persons present were, that it was a most amusing work, and the scenes most admirably drawn to life. I accepted the offer of a perusal of it, and brought it home with me. Although I have not read every sentence, I have looked over the whole of it, and I now wish to bear my testimony to its just delineation of the position that the slave occupies. Colourings in the work there are, but no colourings of the actual and real position of the slave worse than really exist. Whippings to death do occur; I know it to be so. Painful separations of master and slave, under circumstances creditable to the master's feelings of humanity, do also occur. I know that, too; many families, after having brought up their children in entire dependence on slaves to do everything for them, and after having been indulged in elegances and luxuries, have exhausted all their means; and the black people only being left, whom they must sell for further support. Running away, everybody knows, is the worst crime a slave can commit, in the eyes of his master, except it be a humane master; and from such few slaves care to run away.

"I am a slaveholder myself. I have long been dissatisfied with the system particularly since I have made the Bible my criterion for judging of it. I am convinced, from what I read there, slavery is not in accordance with what God delights to honour in his creatures. I am altogether opposed to the system; and I intend always to use whatever influence I may have against it. I feel very bold in speaking against it, though living in the midst of it, because I am backed by a powerful man, that can overturn and overrule the strongest efforts that the determined friends of slavery are now making for its continuance.

"I sincerely hope that more of Mrs. Stowes may be found, to show up the reality of slavery. It needs master minds to show it as it is, that it may rest upon its own merits.

"Like Mrs. Stowe, I feel that, since so many and good people, too, at the North have quietly consented to leave the slave to his fate, by acquiescing in and approving the late measures of government, those who do feel differently should bestir themselves. Christian effort must do the work; and soon it would be done if Christians would unite, not to destroy the Union States, but honestly to speak out, and speak freely, against that they know is wrong. They are not aware what countenance they give to slaveholders to hold on to their prey. Troubled consciences can be easily quieted by the sympathies of pious people, particularly when interest and inclination come in as aids.

"I am told there is to be a reply made to 'Uncle Tom's Cabin,' entitled 'Uncle Tom's Cabin as It is.' I am glad of it. Investigation is what is wanted.

"You will wonder why this communication is made to you by an unknown. It is simply made to encourage your heart, and strengthen your determination to persevere, and do all you can to put the emancipation of the slave in progress. Who I am you will never know; nor do I wish you to know, nor anyone else. I am a

"REPUBLICAN."

The following facts make the fiction of "Uncle Tom's Cabin" appear tame in the comparison. They are from the *New York Evangelist.*

UNCLE TOM'S CABIN.

MR. EDITOR,—I see in your paper that some persons deny the statements of Mrs. Stowe. I have read her book, *every word of it*. I was born in East Tennessee, near Knoxville, and, *we thought,* in an enlightened part of the Union, much favoured in our social, political, and religious privileges,&c.&c. Well, I think about the year 1829, or, perhaps '28, a good old German Methodist owned a black man named Robin, a Methodist preacher, and the manager of farm, distillery,&c., salesman and financier. This good old German Methodist had a son named Willey, a schoolmate of mine, and, as times were, a first-rate fellow. The old man also owned a keen, bright-eyed mulatto girl; and Willey—the naughty boy— became enamoured of the poor girl. The result was soon discovered; and our good German Methodist told his brother Robin to flog the girl for her wickedness. Brother Robin said he could not and would not perform such an act of cruelty as to flog the girl for what she could not help; and for that act of disobedience old

Robin was flogged by the good old German brother until he could not stand. He was carried to bed; and some three weeks thereafter, when my father left the State, he was still confined to his bed from the effects of that flogging.

Again: in the fall of 1836, I went South for my health, stopped at a village in Mississippi, and obtained employment in the largest house in the county, as a book-keeper, with a firm from Louisville, Kentucky. A man residing near the village—a bachelor, thirty years of age—became embarrassed, and executed a mortgage to my employer on a fine, likely boy, weighing about two hundred pounds—quick-witted, active, obedient, and remarkably faithful, trusty, and honest; so much so, that he was held up as an example. He had a wife that he loved; his owner cast his eyes upon her, and she became his paramour. His boy remonstrated with his master; told him that he tried faithfully to perform his every duty, that he was a good and faithful "nigger" to him; and it was hard, after he had toiled hard all day, and till ten o'clock at night, for him to have his domestic relations broken up and interfered with. The white man denied the charge, and the wife also denied it. One night, about the first of September, the boy came home earlier than usual, say about nine o'clock. It was a wet, dismal night; he made a fire in his cabin, went to get his supper, and found ocular demonstration of the guilt of his master. He became enraged, as I suppose any man would, seized a butcher-knife, and cut his master's throat, stabbed his wife in twenty-seven places, came to the village, and knocked at the office door. I told him to come in. He did so, and asked for my employer. I called him. The boy then told him that he had killed his master and his wife, and what for. My employer locked him up, and he, a doctor and myself, went out to the house of the old bachelor, and found him dead, and the boy's wife nearly so; she, however, lived. We (my employer and myself) returned to the village, watched the boy until about sunrise, left him locked up, and went to get our breakfasts, intending to take the boy to jail (as it was my employer' interest, if possible, to save the boy, having one thousand dollars at stake in him) but whilst we were eating, some persons who had heard of the murder broke open the door, took the poor fellow, put a log-chain round his neck, and started him for the woods at the point of the bayonet, marching by where we were eating, with a great deal of noise. My employer hearing it, ran out, and rescued the boy. The mob again broke in and took the boy, and marched him, as before stated, out of town.

My employer then begged them not to disgrace their town in such a manner, but to appoint a jury of twelve *sober* men to decide what should be done. And twelve as sober men as could be found (I was not sober) said he must be hanged. They then tied a rope round his neck, and set him on an old horse. He made a speech to the mob, which I at the time thought, if it had come from some senator, would have been received with rounds of applause; and, withal, he was more calm than I am now in writing this. And after he had told all about the deed and its causes, he then kicked the horse out from under him, and was launched into eternity. My employer has often remarked that he never saw anything more noble in his whole life than the conduct of that boy.

Now, Mr. Editor, I have given you facts, and can give you names and dates. You can do what you think is best for the cause of humanity. I hope I have seen the evil of my former practices, and will endeavour to reform.

Very respectfully, JAMES L. HILL.

Springfield, Illinois, Sept. 17*th,* 1852.

"The opinion of a Southerner," given below, appeared in the *National Era,* published at Washington. This is an anti-slavery journal, but by its generous tone and eminent ability it commands the respect and patronage of many readers in the slave States:

The following communication comes enclosed in an envelope from Louisiana.— *Ed. Era.*

THE OPINION OF A SOUTHERNER.

To the Editor of the National Era.

I have just been reading, in the *New York Observer* of the 12th of August, an article from the *Southern Free Press,* headed by an editorial one from the *Observer,* that has for its caption, "*Progress in the Right Quarter.*"

The editor of the *New York Observer* says that the *Southern Free Press* has been an able and earnest defender of Southern institutions, but that he now advocates the passage of a law to prohibit the separation of families, and recommends instruction to a portion of slaves that are most honest and faithful. The *Observer* further adds: "It was such language as this that was becoming common before Northern fanaticism ruined the prospects of emancipation." It is not so! Northern fanaticism, as he calls it, has done everything that has been done for bettering the condition of the slave. Every one who knows anything of slavery for the last thirty years will recollect that about that time since, the condition of the slave in Louisiana—for about Louisiana only do I speak, because about Louisiana only do I know—was as depressed and miserable as any of the accounts of the abolitionists that ever I have seen have made it. I say abolitionists; I mean friends and advocates of freedom in a fair and honourable way. If any doubt my assertion, let them seek for information; let them get the black laws of Louisiana, and read them; let them get facts from individuals of veracity, on whose statements they would rely.

This wretched condition of slaves roused the friends of humanity, who, like men and Christian men, came fearlessly forward and told truths, indignantly expressing their abhorrence of their oppressors. Such measures of course brought forth strife, which caused the cries of humanity to sound louder and louder throughout the land. The friends of freedom gained the ascendancy in the hearts of the people, and the slaveholders were brought to a stand. Some, through fear of consequences, lessened their cruelties, while others were made to think that, perhaps, were not unwilling to do so when it was urged upon them. Cruelties were not only refrained from, but the slave's comforts were increased. A retrograde treatment now was not practicable; fears of rebellion kept them to it. The slaves had found friends, and they were watchful. It was, however, soon discovered, that too many privileges, too much leniency, and giving knowledge, would destroy the power to keep down the slave, and tend to weaken, if not destroy the system. Accordingly, stringent laws had to be passed, and a penalty attached to them. No one must teach, or cause to be taught, a slave, without incurring the penalty. The law is now in force. These necessary laws, as they are called, are all put down to the account of the friends of freedom; to their interference. I do suppose that they do justly belong to their interference; for who that studies the history of the world's transactions does not know that in all contests with power the weak, until successful, will be dealt with more rigorously? Lose not sight, however, of their former condition. Law after law has since been passed to draw the cord tighter around the poor slave, and all attributed to the abolitionists. Well, anyhow, progress is being made. Here comes out the *Southern Press,* and make some honourable concessions. He says: "The assaults upon slavery, made for the last twenty years by the North, have increased the evils of it. The treatment of slaves has undoubtedly become a delicate and difficult question. The South has a great and moral conflict to wage; and it is for her to put on *the most invulnerable moral panoply*." He then thinks the availability of slave property would not be injured by passing a law to prohibit the separation of slave families; for he says, "Although cases sometimes occur which we observe are seized by these Northern fanatics as characteristic of the system,"&c. Nonsense! there are no "cases sometimes" occurring; no such thing! They are every day's occurrences, though there are families that form the exception, and many, I would hope, that would not do it. While I am writing, I can call before me three men that were brought here by negro traders from Virginia, each having left six or seven children, with their wives, from whom they have never heard. One other died here a short time since, who left the same number in Carolina, from whom he had never heard.

I spent the summer of 1845 in Nashville. During the month of September six hundred slaves passed through that place, in four different gangs, for New Orleans; final destination, probably, Texas. A goodly proportion were women; young women, of course; many mothers must have left not only their children, but their babies. One gang only had a few children. I made some excursions to the different watering-places around Nashville; and while at Robinson or Tyree Springs, twenty miles from Nashville, on the borders of Kentucky and Tennessee, my hostess said to me one day, "Yonder comes a gang of slaves chained." I went to the roadside, and viewed them. For the better answering my purpose of observation, I stopped the white man in front, who was at his ease in a one-horse waggon, and asked him if those slaves were for sale. I counted them and observed their position. They were divided by three one-horse waggons, each containing a man-merchant, so arranged as to command the whole gang. Some were unchained; sixty were chained in two companies, thirty in each, the right hand of one to the left hand of the other opposite one, making fifteen each side of a large ox-chain, to which every hand was fastened, and necessarily compelled to hold up—men and women promiscuously, and about in equal proportions—all young people. No children here, except a few in a waggon behind, which were the only children in the four gangs. I said to a respectable mulatto woman in the house, "Is it true that the negro traders take mothers from their babies?" "Missis, it is true; for here, last week, such a girl (naming her), who lives about a mile off, was taken after dinner—knew nothing of it in the morning—sold, put into the gang, and her baby was given away to a neighbour. She was a stout young woman and brought a good price."

The annexation of Texas induced the spirited traffic that summer. Coming down home in a small boat, water low, a negro trader on board had forty-five men and women crammed into a little spot, some handcuffed. One respectable-looking man had left a wife and seven children in Nashville. Near Memphis the boat stopped at a plantation by previous arrangement, to take in thirty more. An hour's delay was the stipulated time with the captain of the boat. Thirty young men and women came down the bank of the Mississippi, looking Wretcheduess personified, just from the field; in appearance dirty, disconsolate and oppressed some with an old shawl under their arm; a few had blankets; some had nothing at all—looked as though they cared for nothing. I calculated, while looking at them coming down the bank, that I could hold in a bundle all that the whole of them had. The short notice that was given them, when about to leave, was in consequence of the fears entertained that they would slip one side. They all looked distressed, leaving all that was dear to them behind, to be put under the hammer, for the property of the highest bidder. No children here! The whole seventy-five were crammed into a little space on the boat, men and women all together.

I am happy to see that morality is rearing its head with advocates for slavery, and that a "most invulnerable moral panoply" is thought to be necessary. I hope it may not prove to be like Mr. Clay's compromises. The *Southern Press* says: As, for caricatures of slavery in 'Uncle Tom's Cabin' and the 'White Slave,' all founded in imaginary circumstances, &c., we consider them highly incendiary. He who undertakes to stir up strife between two individual neighbours, by detraction, is justly regarded, by all men and all moral codes, as a criminal." Then he quotes the Ninth Commandment, and adds: "But to bear false witness against whole States, and millions of people,&c., would seem to be a crime as much deeper in turpitude as the mischief is greater and the provocation less." In the first place, I will put the *Southern Press* upon proof that Mrs. Harriet Beecher Stowe has told one falsehood. If she has told truth, she has, indeed, a powerful engine of "assault on slavery," such as these Northern fanatics have made for the "last twenty years." The number against whom she offends, in the editor's opinion, seems to increase the turpitude of her crime. This is good reasoning! I hope the editor will be brought to feel that wholesale wickedness is worse than single-handed, and is infinitely harder to reach, particularly if of long standing. It gathers boldness and strength when it is sanctioned by the authority of time, and aided by numbers that are interested in supporting it. Such is slavery; and Mrs. Harriet Beecher Stowe deserves the gratitude of "States and millions of people" for her talented work, in showing it up in its true light. She has advocated truth, justice, and humanity, and they will back her efforts. Her work will be read by "States and millions of people;" and when the *Southern Press* attempts to malign her, by bringing forward her own avowal, "that the subject of slavery had been so painful to her, that she had abstained from conversing on it for several years," and that, in his opinion, "it accounts for the intensity of the venom of her book," his *really* envenomed shafts will fall harmless at her feet; for readers will judge for themselves, and be very apt to conclude that more venom comes from the *Southern Press* than from her. She advocates what is right, and has a straight road, which "few get lost on;" he advocates what is wrong, and has, consequently, to tack, concede, deny, slander, and all sorts of things.

With all due deference to whatever of just principles the *Southern Press* may have advanced in favour of the slave, I am a poor judge of human nature, if I mistake in saying that Mrs. Stowe has done much to draw from him those concessions; and the putting forth of this "*most invulnerable moral panoply,*" that has just come into his head as a bulwark of safety for slavery, owes its impetus to her and other like efforts. I hope the *Southern Press* will not imitate the spoiled child, who refused to eat his pie for spite.

The "White Slave" I have not seen. I guess its character; for I made a passage to New York, some fourteen or fifteen years since, in a packet-ship, with a young woman whose face was enveloped in a profusion of light-brown curls, and who sat at the table with the passengers all the way as a white woman. When at the quarantine, Staten Island, the captain received a letter, sent by express mail, from a person in New Orleans, claiming her as his slave, and threatening the captain with the penalty of the existing law if she was not immediately returned. The streaming eyes of the poor unfortunate girl told the truth, when the captain reluctantly broke it to her. She unhesitatingly confessed that she had run away, and that a friend had paid her passage. Proper measures were taken, and she was conveyed to a packet-ship that was at Sandy Hook, bound for New Orleans.

"Uncle Tom's Cabin," I think, is a just delineation of slavery. The incidents are coloured, but the position that the slave is made to hold is just. I did not read every page of it, my object being to ascertain what position the slave occupied. I could state a case of whipping to death that would equal Uncle Tom's; still, such cases are not very frequent.

The stirring up of strife between neighbours, that the *Southern Press* complains of, deserves notice. Who are neighbours? The most explicit answer to this question will be found in the reply Christ made to the lawyer, when he asked it of him. Another question will arise, Whether, in Christ's judgment, Mrs. Stowe would be considered a neighbour or an incendiary? As the Almighty Ruler of the universe and the Maker of man has said that He has made all the nations of the earth of one blood, and man in His own image, the black man, irrespective of his colour, would seem to be a neighbour who has fallen among his enemies, that have deprived him of the fruits of his labour, his liberty, his right to his wife and children, his right to obtain the knowledge to read, or to anything that earth holds dear, except such portions of food and raiment as will fit him for his despoiler's purposes. Let not the apologists for slavery bring up the isolated cases of leniency, giving instruction, and affectionate attachment, that are found among some masters, as specimens of slavery! It is unfair! They form exceptions, and much do I respect them; but they are not the rules of slavery. The strife that is being stirred up is not to take away anything that belongs to another—neither their silver nor gold, their fine linen or purple, their houses or land, their horses or cattle, or anything that is their property; but to rescue a neighbour from their unmanly cupidity.

A REPUBLICAN. No introduction is necessary to explain the following correspondence, and no commendation will be required to secure for it a respectful attention from thinking readers:—

Washington City, D. C., Dec. 6, 1852.

DEAR SIR,—I understand that you are a North Carolinian, and have always resided in the South; you must, consequently, be acquainted with the workings of the institution of slavery. You have doubtless also read that world-renowned book, "Uncle Tom's Cabin," by Mrs. Stowe. The apologists for slavery deny that this book is a truthful picture of slavery. They say that its representations are exaggerated, its scenes and incidents unfounded, and, in a word, that the whole book is a *caricature*. They also deny that families are separated—that children are sold from parents, wives from their husbands,&c. Under these circumstances, I am induced to ask your opinion of Mrs. Stowe's book, and whether or not, in your opinion, her statements are entitled to credit.

I have the honour to be, yours truly, A. M. GANGEWER.

D. R. Goodloe, Esq.

Washington, Dec. 8, 1852.

DEAR SIR,—Your letter of the 6th inst., asking my opinion of "Uncle Tom's Cabin," has been received; and there being no reason why I should withhold unless it be the fear of public opinion (your object being, as I understand, the publication of my reply), I proceed to give it in some detail.

A book of fiction, to be worth reading, must necessarily be filled with rare and striking incidents, and the leading characters must be remarkable, some for great virtues—others, perhaps, for great vices or follies. A narrative of the ordinary events in the lives of common-place people would be insufferably dull and insipid, and a book made up of such materials would be, to the elegant and graphic pictures of life and manners which we have in the writings of Sir Walter Scott and Dickens, what a surveyor's plot of a ten-acre field is to a painted landscape, in which the eye is charmed by a thousand varieties of hill and dale, of green shrubbery and transparent water, of light and shade, at a glance. In order to determine whether a novel is a fair picture of society, it is not necessary to ask if its chief personages are to be met with every day; but whether they are characteristic of the times and country—whether they embody the prevalent sentiments, virtues, vices, follies, and peculiarities—and whether the events, tragic or otherwise, are such as may and do occasionally occur.

Judging "Uncle Tom's Cabin" by these principles, I have no hesitation in saying that it is a faithful portraiture of Southern life and institutions. There is nothing in the book inconsistent with the laws and usages of the slave-holding States; the virtues, vices, and peculiar hues of character and manners are all

Southern, and must be recognised at once by everyone who reads the book. I may never have seen such depravity in one man as that exhibited in the character of Legree, though I have ten thousand times witnessed the various shades of in different individuals. On the other hand, I have never seen so many perfections concentrated in one human being as Mrs. Stowe has conferred upon the daughter of a slave-holder. Evangeline is an image of beauty and goodness which can never be effaced from the mind, whatever may be its prejudices; yet her whole character is fragrant of the South: her generous sympathy, her beauty and delicacy, her sensibility, are all Southern. They are "to the manner born," and embodying as they do the Southern ideal of beauty and loveliness, cannot be ostracised from Southern hearts, even by the power of the Vigilance Committees.

The character of St. Clare cannot fail to inspire love and admiration. He is the *beau idéal* of a Southern gentleman—honourable, generous, and humane—of accomplished manners, liberal education, and easy fortune. In his treatment of his slaves, he errs on the side of lenity, rather than rigour; and is always their kind protector, from a natural impulse of goodness, without much reflection upon what may befall them when death or misfortune shall deprive them of his friendship.

Mr. Shelby, the original owner of Uncle Tom, and who sells him to a trader from the pressure of a sort of pecuniary necessity, is by no means a bad character his wife and son are whatever honour and humanity could wish; and, in a word, the only white persons who make any considerable figure in the book to a disadvantage are the villain Legree, who is a Vermonter by birth, and the oily-tongued slave-trader Haley, who has the accent of a Northerner. It is, therefore, evident that Mrs. Stowe's object in writing "Uncle Tom's Cabin" has not been to disparage Southern character. A careful analysis of the book would authorise the opposite inference—that she had studied to shield the Southern people from opprobrium, and even to convey an elevated idea of Southern society, at the moment of exposing the evils of the system of slavery. She directs her batteries against the institution, not against individuals; and generously makes a renegade Vermonter stand for her most hideous picture of a brutal tyrant.

Invidious as the duty may be, I cannot withhold my testimony to the fact that families of slaves are often separated. I know not how any man can have the hardihood to deny it. The thing is notorious, and is often the subject of painful remark in the Southern States. I have often heard the practice of separating husband and wife, parent and child, defended, apologised for, palliated in a thousand ways, but have never heard it denied. How could it be denied, in fact, when probably the very circumstance which elicited the conversation was a case of cruel separation then transpiring? No, sir! the denial of this fact by mercenary scribblers may deceive persons at a distance, but it can impose upon no one at the South.

In all the slaveholding States the relation of matrimony between slaves, or between a slave and free person, is merely voluntary. There is no law sanctioning it, or recognising it in any shape, directly or indirectly. In a word, it is illicit, and binds no one—neither the slaves themselves nor their masters. In separating husband and wife, or parent and child, the trader or owner violates no law of the

State—neither statute nor common law. He buys or sells at auction or privately, that which the majesty of the law has declared to be property. The victims may writhe in agony, and the tender-hearted spectator may look on with gloomy sorrow and indignation, but it is to no purpose. The promptings of mercy and justice in the heart are only in rebellion against the law of the land.

The law itself not unfrequently performs the most cruel separations of families, almost without the intervention of individual agency. This happens in the case of persons who die insolvent, or who become so during life-time. The estate, real and personal, must be disposed of at auction to the highest bidder; and the executor, administrator, sheriff, trustee, or other person whose duty it is to dispose of the property, although he may possess the most humane intentions in the world, cannot prevent the final severance of the most endearing ties of kindred. The illustration given by Mrs. Stowe, in the sale of Uncle Tom by Mr. Shelby, is a very common case. Pecuniary embarrassment is a most fruitful source of misfortune to the slave as well as the master; and instances of family ties broken from this cause are of daily occurrence.

It often happens that great abuses exist in violation of law, and in spite of the efforts of the authorities to suppress them; such is the case with drunkenness gambling, and other vices. But here is a law common to all the slaveholding States, which upholds and gives countenance to the wrongdoer, while its blackest terrors are reserved for those who would interpose to protect the innocent Statesmen of elevated and honourable characters, from a vague notion of state necessity, have defended this law in the abstract, while they would, without hesitation, condemn every instance of its application as unjust.

In one respect I am glad to see it publicly denied that the families of slaves are separated; for while it argues a disreputable want of candour, it at the same time evinces a commendable sense of shame, and induces the hope that the public opinion at the South will not much longer tolerate this most odious, though not essential part, of the system of slavery.

In this connection I will call to your recollection a remark of the editor of the *Southern Press,* in one of the last numbers of that paper, which acknowledges the existence of the abuse in question, and recommends its correction. He says:—

"The South has a great moral conflict to wage; and it is for her to put on the most invulnerable moral panoply. Hence it is her duty, as well as interest, to mitigate or remove whatever of evil that results incidentally from the institution. The separation of husband and wife, parent and child, is one of these evils, which we know is generally avoided and repudiated there—although cases sometimes occur which we observe are seized by these Northern fanatics as characteristic illustrations of the system. Now, we can see no great evil or inconvenience, but much good, in the prohibition by law of such occurrences. Let the husband and wife be sold together, and the parents and minor children. Such a law would affect but slightly the general value or availability of slave property, and would prevent in some cases the violence done to the feelings of such connections by sales either compulsory or voluntary. We are satisfied that it would be beneficial to the master and slave to promote marriage, and the observance of all its duties and relations."

Much as I have differed from the editor of the *Southern Press* in his general views of public policy, I am disposed to forgive him past errors in consideration of his public acknowledgment of this "incidental evil," and his frank recommendation of its removal. A Southern newspaper less devoted than the *Southern Press* to the maintenance of slavery would be seriously compromised by such a suggestion, and its advice would be far less likely to be heeded; I think, therefore, that Mr. Fisher deserves the thanks of every good man, North and South, for thus boldly pointing out the necessity of reform.

The picture which Mrs. Stowe has drawn of slavery as an institution is anything but favourable. She has illustrated the frightful cruelty and oppression that must result from a law which gives to one class of society almost absolute and irresponsible power over another. Yet the very machinery she has employed for this purpose shows that all who are parties to the system are not necessarily culpable. It is a high virtue in St. Clare to purchase Uncle Tom. He is actuated by no selfish or improper motive. Moved by a desire to gratify his daughter, and prompted by his own humane feelings, he purchases a slave, in order to rescue him from a hard fate on the plantations. If he had not been a slave-holder before, it was now his duty to become one; this, I think, is the moral to be drawn from the story of St. Clare, and the South have a right to claim the authority of Mrs. Stowe in defence of slave-holding to this extent.

It may be said that it was the duty of St. Clare to emancipate Uncle Tom, but the wealth of the Rothschilds would not enable a man to act out his benevolent instincts at such a price; and if such was his duty, it is not equally the duty of every monied man in the free States to attend the New Orleans slave-mart with the same benevolent purpose in view? It seems to me that to purchase a slave with the purpose of saving him for a hard and cruel fate, and without any view to emancipation, is itself a good action. If the slave should subsequently become able to redeem himself, it would doubtless be the duty of the owner to emancipate him, and it would be but even-handed justice to set down every dollar of the slave's earnings, above the expense of his maintenance, to his credit, until the price paid for him should be fully restored. This is all that justice could exact of the slaveholder.

Those who have railed against "Uncle Tom's Cabin" as an incendiary publication, have singularly (supposing that they have read the book) overlooked the moral of the hero's life. Uncle Tom is the most faithful of servants. He literally "obeyed in all things" his "masters according to the flesh; not with eye-service, as men-pleasers, but in singleness of heart, fearing God." If his conduct exhibits the slightest departure from a literal fulfillment of this injunction of Scripture, it is in a case which must command the approbation of the most rigid casuist, for the injunction of obedience extends, of course, only to lawful commands. It is only when the monster Legree commands him to inflict undeserved chastisement upon his fellow-servants that Uncle Tom refuses obedience. He would not listen to a proposition of escaping into Ohio with the young woman Eliza, on the night after they were sold by Mr. Shelby to the trader Haley. He thought it would be bad faith to his late master, whom he had nursed in his arms, and might be the means of bringing him into difficulty. He offered no resistance to Haley, and obeyed even Legree in every legitimate command; but when he was required to be the instrument of his master's cruelty, he chose rather to die, with the courage and resolution of a Christian martyr, than to save his life by a guilty compliance. Such was Uncle Tom—not a bad example for the imitation of man or master.

I am, sir, very respectfully, Your ob't serv't, DANIEL R. GOODLOE.

A. M. Gangewer, Esq., Washington, D. C.

The writer has received permission to publish the following extract from a letter received by a lady at the North from the editor of a Southern paper. The mind and character of the author will speak for themselves, in the reading of it:

Charleston, Sunday, 25th July, 1852.

The books, I infer, are Mrs. Beecher Stowe's "Uncle Tom's Cabin." The book was furnished me by— —, about a fortnight ago, and you may be assured I read it with an attentive interest. "Now, what is your opinion of it?" you will ask; and, knowing my preconceived opinions upon the question of slavery, and the embodiment of my principles, which I have so long supported, in regard to that *peculiar* institution, you may be prepared to meet an indirect answer. This my own consciousness of truth would not allow in the present instance. The book is a truthful picture of life, with the dark outlines beautifully portrayed. The life (the characteristics, incidents, and the dialogues) is life itself reduced to paper. In her Appendix she rather evades the question whether it was taken from actual scenes, but says there are many counterparts. In this she is correct beyond doubt. Had she changed the picture of Legree, on Red River, for — —, on—Island, South Carolina, she could not have drawn a more admirable portrait. I am led to question whether she had not some knowledge of this beast, as he is known to be, and made the transposition for effect.

My position in connexion with the extreme party, both in Georgia and South Carolina, would constitute a restraint to the full expression of my feelings upon several of the governing principles of the institution. I have studied slavery in all its different phases—have been thrown in contact with the negro in different parts of the world, and made it my aim to study his nature, so far as my limited abilities would give me light—and, whatever my opinions have been, they were based upon what I supposed to be honest convictions.

During the last three years you well know what my opportunities have been to examine all the sectional bearings of an institution which now holds the great and most momentous question of our federal well-being. These opportunities I have not let pass, but have given myself, body and soul, to a knowledge of its vast intricacies—to its constitutional compact and its individual hardships. Its wrongs are in the constituted rights of the master, and the *blank letter* of those laws which pretend to govern the bondman's rights. What legislative act, based upon the construction of self-protection for the very men who contemplate the laws—even though their intention was amelioration—could be enforced, when the legislated object is held as the *bond property* of the legislator? The very fact of constituting a law for the amelioration of property becomes an absurdity so far as carrying it out is concerned. A law which is intended to govern, and gives the governed no means of seeking its protection, is like the clustering together of so many useless words for vain show. But why talk of law? That which is considered the popular rights of a people, and every tenacious prejudice set forth to protect its property interest, creates its own power against every weaker vessel. Laws which interfere with this become unpopular, repugnant to a forcible will, and a dead letter in effect. So long as the voice of the governed cannot be heard, and his wrongs are felt beyond the jurisdiction or domain of the law, as nine-tenths are, where is the hope of redress? The master is the powerful vessel; the negro feels his dependence, and, fearing the consequences of an appeal for his rights, submits to the cruelty of his master in preference to the dread of something more cruel. It is in those dissected cases of cruelty we find the wrongs of slavery, and in those governing laws which give power to bad Northern men to become the most cruel task-masters. Do not judge from my observations that I am seeking consolation for the Abolitionists. Such is not my intention; but truth to a cause which calls loudly for reformation constrains me to say that humanity calls for some law to govern the force and absolute will of the master, and to reform no part is more requisite than that which regards the slave's food and raiment. A person must live years at the South before he can become fully acquainted with the many workings of slavery. A Northern man, not prominently interested in the political and social weal of the South, may live for years, in it, and pass from town to town in his every-day pursuits, and yet see but the polished side of slavery. With me it has been different. Its effect upon the negro himself, and its effect upon the social and commercial well-being of Southern society has been laid broadly open to me, and I have seen more of its workings within the past year than was disclosed to me all the time before. It is with these feelings that I am constrained to do credit to Mrs. Stowe's book, which I consider must have been written by one who derived the materials, from a thorough acquaintance with the subject. The character of the slave-dealer, the bankrupt owner in Kentucky, and the New Orleans merchant, are simple every-day occurrences in these parts. Editors may speak of the dramatic effect as they please; the tale is not told them, and the occurrences of common reality would form a picture more glaring. I could write a work, with date and incontrovertible facts, of abuses which stand recorded in the knowledge of the community in which they were transacted, that would need no dramatic effect, and would stand out ten-fold more horrible than anything Mrs. Stowe has described.

I have read two columns in the *Southern Press* of Mrs. Eastman's "Aunt Phillis's Cabin, or Southern Life as It is," with the remarks of the editor. I have no comments to make upon it, that being done by itself. The editor might have saved himself being writ down an ass by the public if he had withheld his nonsense. If the two columns are a specimen of Mrs. Eastman's book, I pity her attempt and her name as an author.

PART II

CHAPTER I.

THE New York *Courier and Inquirer,* of November 5th, contained an article which has been quite valuable to the author, as summing up, in a clear, concise, and intelligible form, the principal objections which may be urged to "Uncle Tom's Cabin." It is here quoted in full, as the foundation of the remarks in the following pages.

The author of "Uncle Tom's Cabin," that writer states, has committed false witness against thousands and millions of her fellow-men.

She has done it [he says] by attaching to them as slaveholders, in the eyes of the world, the guilt of the abuses of an institution of which they are absolutely guiltless. Her story is so devised as to present slavery in three dark aspects: first, the *cruel treatment* of the slaves; second, the *separation of families;* and, third, their *want of religious instruction.*

To show the first, she causes a reward to be offered for the recovery of a runaway slave, "dead or alive," when no reward with such an alternative was ever heard of, or dreamed of, south of Mason and Dixon's line, and it has been decided over the over again in Southern courts that "a slave who is merely flying away cannot be killed." She puts such language as this into the mouth of one of her speakers:—"The master who goes furthest and does the worst only uses within limits the power that the law gives him;" when, in fact, the civil code of the very State where it is represented the language was uttered—Louisiana—declares that—

"The slave is entirely subject to the will of his master, who may correct and chastise him, *though not with unusual rigour, nor so as to maim or mutilate him, on to expose him to the danger of loss of life, or to cause his death.*"

And provides for a compulsory sale—

"When the master shall be convicted of cruel treatment of his slaves, and the judge shall deem proper to pronounce, besides the penalty established for such cases, that the slave be sold at public auction, *in order to place him out of the reach of the power which the master has abused.*"

"If any person whatsoever shall wilfully kill his slave, or the slave of another person, the said person, being convicted thereof, shall be tried and condemned agreeably to the laws."

In the General Court of Virginia, last year, in the case of Souther *v.* Commonwealth, it was held that the killing of a slave by his master and owner, by wilful and excessive whipping, is murder in the first degree, *though it may not have been the purpose of the master and owner to kill the slave!* And it is not six months since Governor Johnson, of Virginia, pardoned a slave who killed his master, who was beating him with brutal severity.

And yet, in the face of such laws and decisions as these, Mrs. Stowe winds up a long series of cruelties upon her other black personages, by causing her faultless hero, Tom, to be literally whipped to death in Louisiana, by his master, Legree; and these acts, which the laws make criminal, and punish as such, she sets forth in the most repulsive colours, to illustrate the institution of slavery.

So, too, in reference to the separation of children from their parents. A considerable part of the plot is made to hinge upon the selling, in Louisiana, of the child Eliza, "eight or nine years old," away from her mother; when, had its inventor looked in the statute-book of Louisiana, she would have found the following language:—

"Every person is expressly prohibited from selling separately from their mothers *the children who shall not have attained the full age of ten years.*

"*Be it further enacted,* That if any person or persons shall sell the mother of any slave child or children *under the age of ten years, separate from said child or children, or shall, the mother living, sell any slave child or children of ten years of age, or under, separate from said mother,* said person or persons shall be fined not less than one thousand nor more than two thousand dollars, and be imprisoned in the public jail for a period of not less than six months nor more than one year."

The privation of religious instruction, as represented by Mrs. Stowe, is utterly unfounded in fact. The largest churches in the Union consist entirely of slaves. The first African church in Louisville, which numbers fifteen hundred persons, and the first African church in Augusta, which numbers thirteen hundred, are specimens. On multitudes of large plantations in the different parts of the South, the ordinances of the gospel are as regularly maintained, by competent ministers, as in any other communities, north or south. A larger proportion of the slave population are in communion with some Christian church than of the white population in any part of the country. A very considerable portion of every Southern congregation, either in city or country, is sure to consist of blacks; whereas, of our Northern churches, not a coloured person is to be seen in one out of fifty.

The peculiar falsity of this whole book consists in making exceptional or impossible cases the representatives of the system. By the same process which she has used, it would not be difficult to frame a fatal argument against the relation of husband and wife, or parent and child, or of guardian and ward; for thousands of wives and children, and wards, have been maltreated, and even murdered. It is wrong, unpardonably wrong, to impute to any relation of life those enormities which spring only out of the worst depravity of human nature. A ridiculously extravagant spirit of generalisation pervades this fiction from beginning to end. The Uncle Tom of the authoress is a perfect angel, and her blacks generally are half angels; her Simon Legree is a perfect demon, and her whites generally are half demons. She has quite a peculiar spite against the clergy; and, of the many she introduces at different times into the scenes, all, save an insignificant exception, are Pharisees or hypocrites. One who could know nothing of the United States and its people, except by what he might gather from this book, would judge that it was some region just on the confines of the infernal world. We do not say that Mrs. Stowe was actuated by wrong motives in the preparation of this work, but we do say that she has done a wrong which no ignorance can excuse, and no penance can expiate.

A much valued correspondent of the author, writing from Richmond, Virginia, also uses the following language:—

I will venture this morning to make a few suggestions which have occurred to me in regard to future editions of your work, "Uncle Tom's Cabin," which I desire should have all the influence of which your genius renders it capable, not only abroad, but in the local sphere of slavery, where it has been hitherto repudiated. Possessing already the great requisites of artistic beauty and of sympathetic affection, it may yet be improved in regard to accuracy of statement, without being at all enfeebled. For example, you do less than justice to the formalised laws of the Southern States, while you give more credit than is due to the virtue of public or private sentiment in restricting the evil which the laws permit.

I enclose the following extracts from a Southern paper:—

" 'I'll manage that ar; they's young in the business, and must 'spect to work cheap,' said Marks, as he continued to read. 'Thar's three on 'em easy cases, 'cause all you've got to do is to shoot 'em, or swear they is shot; they couldn't, of course, charge much for that.'

"The reader will observe that two charges against the South are involved in this precious discourse; one, that it is the habit of Southern masters to offer a reward, with the alternative of 'dead or alive,' for their fugitive slaves; and the other, that it is usual for pursuers to shoot them. Indeed, we are led to infer that, as the shooting is the easier mode of obtaining the reward, it is the more frequently employed in such cases. Now, when a Southern master offers a reward for his runaway slave, it is because he has lost a certain amount of property, represented by the negro which he wishes to recover. What man of Vermont, having an ox or an ass that had gone astray, would forthwith offer half the full value of the animal, not for the carcass, which might be turned to some useful purpose, but for the unavailing satisfaction of its head? Yet are the two cases exactly parallel. With regard to the assumption that men are permitted to go about, at the South, with double-barrelled guns, shooting down runaway negroes, in preference to apprehending them, we can only say that it is as wicked and wilful as it is ridiculous. Such Thugs there may have been as Marks and Loker, who have killed negroes in this unprovoked manner; but, if they have escaped the gallows, they are probably to be found within the walls of our State Penitentiaries, where they are comfortably provided for at public expense. The laws of the Southern States, which are designed, as in all good governments, for the protection of persons and property, have not been so loosely framed as to fail of their object where person and property are one.

"The law with regard to the killing of runaways is laid down with so much clearness and precision by a South Carolina judge, that we cannot forbear quoting his dictum as directly in point. In the case of Witsell *v.* Earnest and Parker Colcock, J., delivered the opinion of the court:

"By the statute of 1740, any white man may apprehend, and moderately correct, any slave who may be found out of the plantation at which he is employed; and if the slave assaults the white person, he may be killed; but a slave who is merely flying away cannot be killed. Nor can the defendants be justified by the common law if we consider the negro as a person; for they were not clothed with the authority of the law to apprehend him as a felon, and without such authority he could not be killed.'

[Jan. Term, 1818. 1 Nott. & M'Cord's S. C. Rep., 182.]

" 'It's commonly supposed that the *property* interest is a sufficient guard in these cases. If people choose to ruin their possessions, I don't know what's to be done. It seems the poor creature was a thief and a drunkard; and so there won't be much hope to get up sympathy for her.'

" 'It is perfectly outrageous—it is horrid, Augustine! It will certainly bring down vengeance upon you.'

" 'My dear cousin, I didn't do it, and I can't help it; I would, if I could. If low-minded, brutal people will act like themselves, what am I to do? *They have absolute control; they are irresponsible despots.* There would be no use in interfering; *there is no law that amounts to anything practically, for such a case.* The best we can do is to shut our eyes and ears, and let it alone. It's the only re source left us.'

"In a subsequent part of the same conversation St. Clare says—

" 'For pity's sake, for shame's sake, because we are men born of women, and not savage beasts, many of us do not, and dare not—we would *scorn* to use the full power which our savage laws put into our hands. *And he who goes furthest and does the worst only uses within limits the power that the law gives him.*'

"Mrs. Stowe tells us, through St. Clare, that 'there is no law that amounts to anything' in such cases, and that he who goes furthest in severity towards his slave—that is, to the deprivation of an eye or a limb, or even the destruction of life—'only uses within limits the power that the law gives him.' This is an awful and tremendous charge, which, lightly and unwarrantably made, must subject the maker to a fearful accountability. Let us see how the matter stands upon the statute-book of Louisiana. By referring to the civil code of that State, chapter 3rd, article 173, the reader will find this general declaration:—

" 'The slave is entirely subject to the will of his master, who may correct and chastise him, *though not with unusual rigour, nor so as to maim or mutilate him, or to expose him to the danger of loss of life, or to cause his death.*'

"On a subsequent page of the same volume and chapter, article 192, we find provision made for the slave's protection against his master's cruelty, in the statement that one of two cases, in which a master can be compelled to sell his slave, is—

" 'When the master shall be convicted of cruel treatment of his slave, and the judge shall deem proper to pronounce, *besides the penalty established for such cases,* that the slave shall be sold at public auction, *in order to place him out of the reach of the power which the master has abused.*'

"A code thus watchful of the negro's safety in life and limb confines not its guardianship to inhibitory clauses, but proscribes extreme penalties in case of their infraction. In the *Code Noir* (Black Code) of Louisiana, under head of Crimes and Offences, No. 55, sec. xvi., it is laid down that—

" 'If any person whatsoever shall wilfully kill his slave, or the slave of another person, the said person, being convicted thereof, shall be tried and condemned agreeably to the laws.'

"And because negro testimony is inadmissible in the court of the State, an therefore the evidence of such crimes might be with difficulty supplied, it is further provided that—

" 'If any slave be mutilated, beaten, or ill-treated, contrary to the true intent and meaning of this Act, when no one shall be present, in such case the owner, or other person having the management of said slave thus mutilated, shall be deemed responsible and guilty of the said offence, and shall be prosecuted without further evidence, unless the said owner, or other person so as aforesaid, can prove the contrary by means of good and sufficient evidence, or can clear himself by his own oath, which said oath every court, under the cognisance of which such offence shall have been examined and tried, is by this Act authorised to administer.'

[Code Noir. Crimes and Offences, 56, xvii.]

"Enough has been quoted to establish the utter falsity of the statement, made by our authoress through St. Clare, that brutal masters are 'irresponsible despots' —at least, in Louisiana. It would extend our review to a most unreasonable length, should we undertake to give the law, with regard to the murder of slaves, as it stands in each of the Southern States. The crime is a rare one, and therefore the reporters have had few cases to record. We may refer, however, to two. In Fields *v.* The State of Tennessee, the plaintiff in error was indicted in the Circuit Court of Maury county for the murder of a negro slave. He pleaded not guilty; and at the trial was found guilty of wilful and felonious slaying of the slave. From this sentence he prosecuted his writ of error, which was disallowed by the court affirming the original judgment. The opinion of the court, as given by Peck J. overflows with the spirit of enlightened humanity. He concludes thus:—

" 'It is well said by one of the judges of North Carolina, that the master has a right to exact the labour of his slave; thus far, the rights of the slave are suspended; but this gives the master no right over the life of his slave. I add to the saying of the judge, that law which says Thou shalt not kill, protects the slave; and he is within its very letter. Law, reason, Christianity, and common humanity, all point but one way.'

[1 Yerger's Tenn. Rep. 156.]

"In the General Court of Virginia, June Term, 1851, in Souther *v.* The Commonwealth, it was held that 'the killing of a slave by his master and owner, by wilful and excessive whipping, is murder in the first degree; *though it may not have been the purpose of the master and owner to kill the slave*. The writer shows, also, an ignorance of the law of contracts, as it affects slavery in the South, in making George's master take him from the factory against the proprietor's consent. George, by virtue of the contract of hiring, had become the property of the proprietor for the time being, and his master could no more have taken him away forcibly than the owner of a house in Massachusetts can dispossess his lessee, at any moment, from mere whim or caprice. There is no court in Kentucky, where the hirer's rights, in this regard, would not be enforced.

[7 Grattan's Rep. 673.]

" 'No. Father bought her once, in one of his trips to New Orleans, and brought her up as a present to mother. She was about eight or nine years old then. Father would never tell mother what he gave for her; but, the other day, in looking over his old papers, we came across the bill of sale. He paid an extravagant sum for her, to be sure. I suppose, on account of her extraordinary beauty.'

" 'George sat with his back to Cassy, and did not see the absorbed expression of her countenance, as he was giving these details.

" 'At this point in the story, she touched his arm, and, with a face perfectly white with interest, said, 'Do you know the names of the people he bought her of?'

" 'A man of the name of Simmons, I think, was the principal in the transaction. At least, I think that was the name in the bill of sale.'

" 'O my God!' said Cassy, and fell insensible on the floor of the cabin.'

"Of course Eliza turns out to be Cassy's child, and we are soon entertained with the family meeting in Montreal, where George Harris is living, five or six years after the opening of the story, in great comfort.

"Now, the reader will perhaps be surprised to know that such an incident as the sale of Cassy apart from Eliza, upon which the whole interest of the foregoing narrative hinges, never could have taken place in Louisiana, and that the bill of sale for Eliza would not have been worth the paper it was written on. Observe. George Shelby states that Eliza was *eight or nine years old* at the time his father purchased her in New Orleans. Let us again look at the statute-book of Louisiana.

"In the *Code Noir* we find it set down that—

" 'Every person is expressly prohibited from selling separately from their mothers *the children who shall not have attained the full age of ten years*.'

"And this humane provision is strengthened by a statute, one clause of which runs as follows:—

" 'Be it further enacted, That if any person or persons shall sell the mother of any slave child or children *under the age of ten years, separate from said child or children, or shall, the mother living, sell any slave child or children of ten years of age or under, separate from said mother,* such person or persons shall incur the penalty of the sixth section of this Act.'

CHAPTER I.

"This penalty is a fine of not less than one thousand nor more than two thousand dollars, and imprisonment in the public jail for a period of not less than six months, nor more than one year.—*Vide Act of Louisiana,* 1 *Session, 9th Legislature,* 1828, 1829, No. 24, Section 16."

The author makes here a remark. Scattered through all the Southern States are slaveholders who are such only in name. They have no pleasure in the system, they consider it one of wrong altogether, and they hold the legal relation still, only because not yet clear with regard to the best way of changing it, so as to better the condition of those held. Such are most earnest advocates for State emancipation, and are friends of anything, written in a right spirit, which tends in that direction. From such the author ever receives criticisms with pleasure.

She has endeavoured to lay before the world, in the fullest manner all that can be objected to her work, that both sides may have an opportunity of impartial hearing.

When writing "Uncle Tom's Cabin," though entirely unaware and unexpectant of the importance which would be attached to its statements and opinions, the author of that work was anxious, from love of consistency, to have some understanding of the laws of the slave system. She had on hand for reference, while writing, the *Code Noir* of Louisiana, and a sketch of the laws relating to slavery in the different States, by Judge Stroud of Philadelphia. This work, professing to have been compiled with great care from the latest editions of the statute-books of the several States, the author supposed to be a sufficient guide for the writing of a work of fiction. As the accuracy of those statements which relate to the slave-laws has been particularly contested, a more especial inquiry has been made in this direction. Under the guidance and with the assistance of legal gentlemen of high standing, the writer has proceeded to examine the statements of Judge Stroud with regard to statute-law, and to follow them up with some inquiry into the decisions of Courts. The result has been an increasing conviction on her part that the impressions first derived from Judge Stroud's work were correct; and the author now can only give the words of St. Clare, as the best possible expression of the sentiments and opinion which this course of reading has awakened in her mind.

This cursed business, accursed of God and man—what is it? Strip it of all its ornament, run it down to the root and nucleus of the whole, and what is it? Why, because my brother Quashy is ignorant and weak, and I am intelligent and strong —because I know how, and *can* do it—therefore I may steal all he has, keep it, and give him only such and so much as suits my fancy! Whatever is too hard, too dirty, too disagreeable for me, I may set Quashy to doing. Because I don't like work, Quashy shall work. Because the sun burns me, Quashy shall stay in the sun. Quashy shall earn the money, and I will spend it. Quashy shall lie down in every puddle, that I may walk over dry-shod. Quashy shall do my will, and not his, all the days of his mortal life, and have such a chance of getting to heaven at last as I find convenient. This I take to be about what slavery is. I defy anybody on earth to read our slave-code, as it stands in our law books, and make anything else of it.

Talk of the *abuses* of slavery! Humbug! The *thing itself* is the essence of all abuse. And the only reason why the land don't sink under it, like Sodom and Gomorrah, is because it is *used* in a way infinitely better than it is. For pity's sake, for shame's sake, because we are men born of women, and not savage beasts, many of us do not, and dare not—we would *scorn* to use the full power which our savage laws put into our hands. And he who goes the furthest, and does the worst, only uses within limits the power that the law gives him!

The author still holds to the opinion that slavery in itself, as legally defined in law-books and expressed in the records of Courts, *is* the SUM AND ESSENCE OF ALL ABUSE; and she still clings to the hope that there are *many* men at the South *infinitely* better than their laws; and after the reader has read all the extracts which she has to make, for the sake of a common humanity they will hope the same. The author must state, with regard to some pages which she must quote, that the language of certain enactments was so incredible that she would not take it on the authority of any compilation whatever, but copied it with her own hand from the latest edition of the statute-book where it stood and still stands.

CHAPTER II.

WHAT IS SLAVERY?

THE author will now enter into a consideration of slavery as it stands revealed in slave law.

What is it according to the definition of law-books and legal interpreters? "A slave," says the law of Louisiana, "is one who is in the power of a master to whom he belongs. The master may sell him, dispose of his person, his industry, and his labour; he can do nothing, possess nothing, nor acquire anything, but what must belong to his master. [Civil Code, Art. 35.] " South Carolina says: "Slaves shall be deemed, sold, taken, reputed, and adjudged in law, to be chattels personal in the hands of their owners and possessors, and their executors, administrators, and assigns, TO ALL INTENTS, constructions and purposes whatsoever. [2 Brev. Dig. 229 Prince's Digest, 446.] " The law of Georgia is similar.

Let the reader reflect on the extent of the meaning in this last clause. Judge Ruffin, pronouncing the opinion of the Supreme Court of North Carolina, says a slave is "one doomed in his own person, and his posterity, to live without knowledge, and without the capacity to make anything his own, and to toil that another may reap the fruits.' [Wheeler's Law of Slavery, 246, State *v.* Mann.]

This is what slavery *is,* this is what it is to be a slave! The slave-code, then, of the Southern States, is designed to keep millions of human beings in the condition of chattels personal; to keep them in a condition in which the master may sell them, dispose of their time, person, and labour; in which they can do nothing, possess nothing, and acquire nothing, except for the benefit of the master; in which they are doomed in themselves and in their posterity to live without knowledge, without the power to make anything their own, to toil that another may reap. The laws of the slave-code are designed to work out this problem, consistently with the peace of the community, and the safety of that superior race which is constantly to perpetrate this outrage.

From this simple statement of what the laws of slavery are designed to do—from a consideration that the class thus to be reduced, and oppressed, and made the subjects of a perpetual robbery, are *men* of like passions with our own, men originally made in the image of God as much as ourselves, men partakers of that same humanity of which Jesus Christ is the highest ideal and expression—when we consider that the material thus to be acted upon is that fearfully explosive element, the soul of man; that soul elastic, upspringing, immortal, whose free will even the Omnipotence of God refuses to coerce, we may form some idea of the tremendous force which is necessary to keep this mightiest of elements in the state of repression which is contemplated in the definition of slavery.

Of course, the system necessary to consummate and perpetuate such a work, from age to age, must be a fearfully stringent one; and our readers will find that it is so. Men who make the laws, and men who interpret them, may be fully sensible of their terrible severity and inhumanity; but if they are going to preserve the THING, they have no resource but to make the laws and to execute them faithfully after they are made. They may say with the Hon. Judge Ruffin, of North Carolina, when solemnly from the bench announcing this great foundation principle of slavery, that "THE POWER OF THE MASTER MUST BE ABSOLUTE, TO RENDER THE SUBMISSION OF THE SLAVE PERFECT—they may say with him, "I most freely confess my sense of the harshness of this proposition; I feel it as deeply as any man can; and, as a principle of moral right, every person in his retirement must repudiate it;" but they will also be obliged to add, with him, "But in the *actual condition* of things IT MUST BE SO. This discipline belongs to the state of slavery. It is INHERENT in the relation of master and slave."

And, like Judge Ruffin, men of honour, men of humanity, men of kindest and gentlest feelings, are *obliged* to interpret these severe laws with inflexible severity. In the perpetual reaction of that awful force of human passion and human will, which necessarily meets the compressive power of slavery—in that seething, boiling tide, never wholly repressed, which rolls its volcanic stream underneath the whole framework of society so constituted, ready to find vent at the least rent or fissure or unguarded aperture—there is a constant necessity which urges to severity of law, and inflexibility of execution. So Judge Ruffin says, "We cannot allow the *right* of the master to be brought into discussion in the courts of justice. The slave, to remain a slave, must be made sensible that there is NO APPEAL FROM HIS MASTER." Accordingly, we find in the more southern States, where the slave population is most accumulated, and slave property most necessary and valuable, and, of course, the determination to abide by the system the most decided, *there* the enactments are most severe, and the interpretation of Courts the most inflexible. And, when legal decisions of a contrary character begin to be made, it would appear that it is a symptom of leaning towards emancipation. So abhorrent is the slave-code to every feeling of humanity, that just as soon as there is any hesitancy in the community about perpetuating the institution of slavery, judges begin to listen to the voice of their more honourable nature, and by favourable interpretations to soften its necessary severities.

Such decisions do not commend themselves to the professional admiration of legal gentlemen. But in the workings of the slave system, when the irresponsible power which it guarantees comes to be used by men of the most brutal nature, cases sometimes arise for trial where the consistent exposition of the law involves results so loathsome and frightful that the judge prefers to be illogical, rather than inhuman. Like a spring out-gushing in the desert, some noble man, now and then, from the fulness of his own better nature, throws out a legal decision, generously inconsistent with every principle and precedent of slave jurisprudence, and we bless God for it. All we wish is that there were more of them, for then should we hope that the day of redemption was drawing nigh.

The reader is now prepared to enter with us on the proof of this proposition: That the slave-code is designed *only for the security of the master, and not with regard to the welfare of the slave.*

This is implied in the whole current of law-making and law-administration, and is often asserted in distinct form, with a precision and clearness of legal accuracy which, in a literary point of view, are quite admirable. Thus, Judge Ruffin, after stating that considerations restricting the power of the master had often been drawn from a comparison of slavery with the relation of parent and child, master and apprentice, tutor and pupil, says distinctly:

The Court does not recognise their application. There is no likeness between the cases. They are in opposition to each other, and there is an impassable gulf between them. In the one [case], the end in view is the *happiness of the youth,* born to equal rights with that governor on whom the duty devolves of training the young to usefulness, in a station which he is afterwards to assume among freemen. [Wheeler's Law of Slavery, p. 246.] With slavery it is far otherwise. The *end is the profit of the master* his security and the public safety.

Not only is this principle distinctly asserted in so many words, but it is more distinctly implied in multitudes of the arguings and reasonings which are given as grounds of legal decisions. Even such provisions as seem to be for the benefit of the slave we often find carefully interpreted so as to show that it is only on account of his property value to his master that he is thus protected, and not from any consideration of humanity towards himself. [Wheeler's Law of Slavery, p. 239.] Thus it has been decided that a master can bring no action for assault and battery on his slave, *unless the injury be such as to produce a loss of service.*

The spirit in which this question is discussed is worthy of remark. We give a brief statement of the case, as presented in Wheeler, p. 239.

It was an action for assault and battery committed by Dale on one Cornfute's slave. It was contended by Cornfute's counsel that it was not necessary to *prove loss of service,* in order that the action should be sustained [Cornfute *v.* Dale, April Term, 1800. 1 Har. and Johns. Rep. 4.]; that an action might be supported for beating plaintiff's *horse;* and that the lord might have an action for the battery of his villein, which is founded on this principle, that, as the villein could not support the action, *the injury would be without redress unless the lord could* [2 Lutw. 1481. 20 Viner's Abr. 454.]. On the other side, it was said that Lord Chief Justice Raymond had decided that an assault on a horse was no cause of action, unless accompanied with *a special damage of the animal,* which would impair his value.

Chief Justice Chase decided that no redress could be obtained in the case, because the value of the slave had not been impaired; *without injury or wrong to the master* no action could be sustained; and assigned this among other reasons for it, that there was no reciprocity in the case, as the master was not liable for assault and battery committed by his slave, neither could he gain redress for one committed upon his slave.

Let any reader now imagine what an amount of wanton cruelty and indignity may be heaped upon a slave man or woman or child without actually impairing their power to do service to the master, and he will have a full sense of the cruelty of this decision.

In the same spirit it has been held in North Carolina that patrols (night watchmen) are not liable to the master for inflicting punishment on the slave, unless their conduct clearly demonstrates *malice against the master*. [Tate *v*. O'Neal, 1 Hawks, 418, U.S. Dig. Sup. 2, p. 797, s. 121.]

The cool-bloodedness of some of these legal discussions is forcibly shown by two decisions in Wheeler's Law of Slavery, p. 243. On the question whether the criminal offence of assault and battery can be committed on a slave, there are two decisions of the two States of South and North Carolina [State *v*. Maner, 2 Hill's Rep. 453. Wheeler's Law of Slavery, p. 243.]; and it is difficult to say which of these decisions has the pre-eminence for cool legal inhumanity. That of South Carolina reads thus. Judge O'Neill says:

The criminal offence of assault and battery cannot, at common law, be committed upon the person of a slave. For notwithstanding (for some purposes) a slave is regarded by law as a *person,* yet generally he is a mere chattel personal, and his right or personal protection belongs to his master, who can maintain an action of trespass for the battery of his slave. There can be therefore no offence against the State for a *mere beating of a slave unaccompanied with any circumstances of cruelty*(!!), or an attempt to kill and murder. The peace of the State *is not thereby broken;* for a slave is not generally regarded as legally capable of being within the peace of the State. He is not a citizen, and is not in that character entitled to her protection.

What declaration of the utter indifference of the State to the sufferings of the slave could be more elegantly cool and clear? [See State *v*. Hale. Wheeler, p. 239. 2 Hawk. N.C. Rep. 582.] But in North Carolina it appears that the case is argued still more elaborately.

Chief Justice Taylor thus shows that, after all, there are reasons why an assault and battery upon the slave may, on the whole, have some such general connection with the comfort and security of the community, that it may be construed into a breach of the peace, and should be treated as an indictable offence.

The instinct of a slave may be, and generally is, tamed into subservience to his master's will, and from him he receives chastisement, whether it be merited or not, with perfect submission; for he knows the extent of the dominion assumed over him, and that the law ratifies the claim. But when the same authority is wantonly usurped by a stranger, Nature is disposed to assert her rights, and to prompt the slave to a resistance, often momentarily successful, sometimes fatally so. The public peace is thus broken, as much as if a free man had been beaten; for the party of the aggressor is always the strongest, and such contests usually terminate by overpowering the slave, and inflicting on him a severe chastisement, without regard to the original cause of the conflict. There is, consequently, as much reason for making such offences indictable as if a white man had been the victim. A wanton injury committed on a slave is a great provocation to the owner. awakens his resentment, and has a direct tendency to a breach of the peace, by inciting him to seek immediate vengeance. If resented in the heat of blood, it would probably extenuate a homicide to manslaughter, upon the same principle with the case stated by Lord Hale that if, A riding on the road, B had whipped his horse out of the track, and then A had alighted and killed B. These offences are usually committed by men of dissolute habits, hanging loose upon society, who, being repelled from association with well-disposed citizens, take refuge in the company of coloured persons and slaves, whom they deprave by their example, embolden by their familiarity, and then beat, under the expectation that a slave dare not resent a blow from a white man. If such offences may be committed with impunity, the public peace will not only be rendered extremely insecure, but the value of slave property must be much impaired, for the offenders can seldom make any reparation in damages. Nor is it necessary, in any case, that a person who has received an injury, real or imaginary, from a slave, should carve out his own justice; for the law has made ample and summary provision [1 Rev. Code, 448.] for the punishment of all trivial offences committed by slaves, by carrying them before a justice, who is authorised to pass sentence for their being publicly whipped. This provision, while it excludes the necessity of private vengeance, would seem to forbid its legality, since it effectually protects all persons from the insolence of slaves, even where their masters are unwilling to correct them upon complaint being made. The common law has often been called into efficient operation, for the punishment of public cruelty inflicted upon animals, for needless and wanton barbarity exercised even by masters upon their slaves, and for various violations of decency, morals, and comfort. Reason and analogy seem to require that a human being, although the subject of property, should be so far protected as the public might be injured through him.

For all purposes necessary to enforce the obedience of the slave, and to render him useful as property, the law secures to the master a complete authority over him, and it will not lightly interfere with the relation thus established. It is a more effectual guarantee of his right of property, when the slave is protected from wanton abuse from those who have no power over him; for it cannot be disputed that a slave is rendered less capable of performing his master's service, when he finds himself exposed by the law to the capricious violence of every turbulent man in the community.

If this is not a scrupulous disclaimer of all humane intention in the decision, as far as the slave is concerned, and an explicit declaration that he is protected only out of regard to the comfort of the community, and his property value to his master, it is difficult to see how such a declaration could be made. After all this cold-blooded course of remark, it is somewhat curious to come upon the following certainly most unexpected declaration, which occurs in the very next paragraph:—

Mitigated as slavery is by the *humanity of our laws,* the refinement of manners, and by *public opinion, which revolts at every instance of cruelty towards* them, it would be an anomaly in the system of police which affects them, if the offence stated in the verdict were not indictable.

The reader will please to notice that this remarkable declaration is made of the State of North Carolina. We shall have occasion again to refer to it by and by, when we extract from the statute-book of North Carolina some specimens of these humane laws.

In the same spirit it is decided, under the law of Louisiana, that if an individual injures another's slave so as to make him *entirely useless,*— and the owner recovers from him the full value of the slave, the slave by that act becomes thenceforth the property of the person who injured him.

[Jourdain *v.* Patton, July Term, 1818. 5 Martin's Louis. Rep. 615.] A decision to this effect is given in Wheeler's Law of Slavery, p. 249. A woman sued for an injury done to her slave by the slave of the defendant. The injury was such as to render him entirely useless, his *only* eye being put out. The parish court decreed that she should recover 1200 dollars, that the defendant should pay a further sum of 25 dollars a month from the time of the injury; also the physician's bill, and 200 dollars for the sustenance of the slave during his life, and that he should remain for ever in the possession of his mistress.

The case was appealed. The judge reversed the decision, and delivered the slave into the possession of the man whose slave had committed the outrage. In the course of the decision, the judge remarks, with that calm legal explicitness for which many decisions of this kind are remarkable, that

The principle of humanity, which would lead us to suppose that the mistress, whom he had long served, would treat her miserable blind slave with more kindness than the defendant, to whom the judgment ought to transfer him, cannot be taken into consideration in deciding this case.

[Jan. Term, 1828. 9 Martin La. Rep. 350.] Another case reported in Wheeler's Law, p. 198, the author thus summarily abridges. It is Dorothee *v.* Coquillon *et al.* A young girl, by will of her mistress, was to have her freedom at twenty-one; and it was required by the will that in the mean time she should be educated in such a manner as to enable her to earn her living when free, her services in the mean time being bequeathed to the daughter of the defendant. Her mother (a free woman) entered complaint that no care was taken of the child's education, and that she was cruelly treated. The prayer of the petition was that the child be declared free at twenty-one, and in the mean time hired out by the sheriff. The suit was decided against the mother, on this ground—that she could not sue *for* her daughter in a case where the daughter could not sue for herself were she of age—the object of the suit being *relief from ill treatment during the time of her slavery, which a slave cannot sue for.*

CHAPTER II.

Observe, now, the following case of Jennings *v.* Fundeberg [Jan. Term, 1827. 4 M'Cord's Rep. 161. Wheeler's Law of Slavery, p. 201.]. It seems Jennings brings an action of trespass against Fundeberg for killing his slave. The case was thus:—Fundeberg, with others, being out hunting runaway negroes, surprised them in their camp, and, as the report says, "*fired his gun towards them,* as they were running away, *to induce them to stop.*" One of them being shot through the head was thus *induced to stop*— and the master of the boy brought action for trespass against the firer for killing his slave.

The decision of the inferior Court was as follows:—

The Court "thought the killing accidental, and that the defendant ought not to be made answerable as a trespasser. When one is lawfully interfering with the property of another, and accidentally destroys it, he is no trespasser, and ought not to be answerable for the value of the property. In this case, the defendant was engaged in a lawful and *meritorious* service, and if he really fired his gun in the manner stated, it was an allowable act."

The superior judge reversed the decision, on the ground that in dealing with another person's property one is responsible for any injury which he could have avoided by any degree of circumspection. "The firing was *rash* and *incautious.*" Does not the whole spirit of this discussion speak for itself?

[Jan. Term, 1827. 4 M'Cord's Rep. 156.]

See also the very next case in Wheeler's Law. Richardson *v.* Dukes, p. 202.

Trespass for killing the plaintiff's slave. It appeared the slave was stealing potatoes from a bank near the defendant's house. The defendant fired upon him with a gun loaded with buckshot, and killed him. The jury found a verdict for plaintiff for one dollar. Motion for a new trial.

The Court, Nott J., held, there must be a new trial; that the jury ought to have given the plaintiff the value of the slave. That if the jury were of opinion the slave was of bad character, some deduction from the usual price ought to be made, but the plaintiff was certainly entitled to his actual damage for killing his slave. Where property is in question, the value of the article, as nearly as it can be ascertained, furnishes a rule from which they are not at liberty to depart.

It seems that the value of this unfortunate piece of property was somewhat reduced from the circumstance of his "stealing potatoes [Wheeler's Law of Slavery. p. 220.]." Doubtless he had his own best reasons for this; so, at least, we should infer from the following remark, which occurs in one of the reasonings of Judge Taylor of North Carolina.

The act of 1786 (Iredell's Revisal, p. 588) does, in the preamble, recognise the fact, that many persons, *by cruel treatment to their slaves, cause* them to commit crimes for which they are executed. The cruel treatment here alluded to must consist in *withholding from them the necessaries of life;* and the crimes thus resulting are such as are calculated to *furnish them with food and raiment.*

Perhaps "stealing potatoes" in this case was one of the class of crimes alluded to.

Again we have the following case:—

[Whitsell *v.* Earnest & Parker. Wheeler, p. 202.]

The defendants went to the plantation of Mrs. Whitsell for the purpose of hunting for runaway negroes; there being many in the neighbourhood, and the place in considerable alarm. As they approached the house with loaded guns, a negro ran from the house, or near the house, towards a swamp, when they fired and killed him.

The judge charged the jury, that such circumstances might exist, by the excitement and alarm of the neighbourhood, as to authorise the killing of a negro without the sanction of the magistrate.

This decision was reversed in the Superior Court, in the following language:

By the statute of 1740, any white man may apprehend and moderately correct any slave who may be found out of the plantation at which he is employed, and if the slave assaults the white person, *he may be killed;* but a slave who is merely flying away cannot be killed. Nor can the defendants be justified by common law, IF *we consider the negro as a person;* for they were not clothed with the authority of the law to apprehend him as a felon, and without such authority he could not be killed.

IF *we consider the negro a person,* says the judge; and, from his decision in the case, he evidently intimates that he has a strong leaning to his opinion, though it has been contested by so many eminent legal authorities that he puts forth his sentiments modestly, and in an hypothetical form. The reader, perhaps, will need to be informed that the question whether the slave is to be considered a person or a human being in any respect has been extensively and ably argued on both sides in legal courts, and it may be a comfort to know that the balance of legal opinion inclines in favour of the slave. Judge Clarke, of Mississippi, is quite clear on the point, and argues very ably and earnestly, [Wheeler, p. 252. June T. 1820. Walker's Rep. 83.] though, as he confesses, against very respectable legal authorities, that the slave *is* a person—that he *is* a reasonable creature. The reasoning occurs in the case State of Mississippi *v.* Jones, and is worthy of attention as a literary curiosity.

It seems that a case of murder of a slave had been clearly made out and proved in the lower Court, and that judgment was arrested, and the case appealed on the ground whether, in that State, murder could be committed on a slave. Judge Clarke thus ably and earnestly argues:—

The question in this case is, whether murder can be committed on a slave. Because individuals may have been deprived of many of their rights by society, it does not follow that they have been deprived of all their rights. In some respects, slaves may be considered as chattels; but in others they are regarded as men. The law views them as capable of committing crimes. This can only be upon the principle, that they are *men* and rational beings. The Roman law has been much relied on by the counsel of the defendant. That law was confined to the Roman empire, giving the power of life and death over captives in war, as slaves; but it no more extended here, than the similar power given to parents over the lives of their children. Much stress has also been laid, by the defendant's counsel, on the case cited from Taylor's Reports, decided in North Carolina; yet, in that case, two judges against one were of opinion, that killing a slave was murder. Judge Hall, who delivered the dissenting opinion in the above case, based his conclusions, as we conceive, upon erroneous principles, by considering the laws of Rome applicable here. His inference, also, that a person cannot be condemned capitally, because he may be liable in a civil action, is not sustained by reason or authority, but appears to us to be in direct opposition to both. At a very early period in Virginia, the power of life over slaves was given by statute; but Tucker observes, that as soon as these statutes were repealed, it was at once considered by their Courts that the killing of a slave might be murder. (Commonwealth *v.* Dolly Chapman: indictment for maliciously stabbing a slave, under a statute.) It has been determined in Virginia that slaves are persons. In the constitution of the United States, slaves are expressly designated as "persons." In this State the legislature have considered slaves as reasonable and accountable beings; and it would be a stigma upon the character of the State, and a reproach to the administration of justice, if the life of a slave could be taken with impunity, or if he could be murdered in cold blood, without subjecting the offender to the highest penalty known to the criminal jurisprudence of the country. Has the slave no rights, because he is deprived of his freedom? He is still a human being, and possesses all those rights of which he is not *deprived by the positive provisions of the law;* but in vain shall we look for any law passed by the enlightened and philanthropic legislature of this State, giving even to the master, much less to a stranger, power over the life of a slave. Such a statute would be worthy the age of Draco or Caligula, and would be condemned by the unanimous voice of the people of this State, where even cruelty to slaves, much [more] the taking away of life, meets with universal reprobation. By the provisions of our law, a slave may commit murder, and be punished with death; why, then, is it not murder to kill a slave? Can a mere chattel commit murder, and be subject to punishment?

* * * * * *

The right of the master exists not by force of the law of nature or nations, but by virtue only of the positive law of the State; and although that gives to the master the right to command the services of the slave, requiring the master to feed and clothe the slave from infancy till death, yet it gives the master no right to take the life of the slave; and, if the offence be not murder, it is not a crime, and subjects the offender to no punishment.

The taking away the life of a reasonable creature, under the king's peace, with malice aforethought, expressed or implied, is murder at common law. Is not a slave a reasonable creature—is he not a human being? And the meaning of this phrase, "reasonable creature," is a human being. For the killing a lunatic, an idiot, or even a child unborn, is murder, as much as the killing a philosopher; and has not the slave as much reason as a lunatic, an idiot, or an unborn child?

Thus triumphantly, in this nineteenth century of the Christian era, and in the State of Mississippi, has it been made to appear that the slave is a reasonable creature—a human being!

What sort of system, what sort of a public sentiment, was that which made this argument *necessary!*

And let us look at some of the admissions of this argument with regard to the *nature* of slavery. According to the judge, it is depriving human beings of *many of their rights*. Thus he says: "Because individuals may have been deprived of many of their rights by society, it does not follow that they have been deprived of *all* their rights." Again, he says of the slave: "He is still a human being, and possesses all those *rights* of which he is not deprived by *positive provisions of the law*." Here he admits that the provisions of law deprive the slave of natural *rights*. Again he says: "The right of the master exists not by force of the law of nature or of nations, but by virtue only of the positive law of the State." According to the decision of this judge, therefore, slavery exists by the same right that robbery or oppression of any kind does—the right of *ability*. A gang of robbers associated into a society have rights over all the neighbouring property that they can acquire, of precisely the same kind.

With the same unconscious serenity does the law apply that principle of force and robbery which is the essence of slavery, and show how far the master may proceed in appropriating another human being as his property.

The question arises, May a master give a woman to one person, and her *unborn children* to another one? [Wheeler, p. 28. Banks, Adm'r *v.* Marksbury. Spring T., 1823. 3 Little's Rep. 275] Let us hear the case argued. The unfortunate mother, selected as the test point of this interesting legal principle, comes to our view in the will of one Samuel Marksbury, under the style and denomination of "my negro wench, Pen." Said Samuel states in his will that, for the good-will and love he bears to his *own* children, he gives said negro wench, Pen, to son Samuel, and all her future increase to daughter Rachael. When daughter Rachael, therefore, marries, her husband sets up a claim for this increase, as it is stated, quite off-hand, that the "wench had several children." Here comes a beautifully interesting case, quite stimulating to legal acumen. Inferior Court decides that Samuel Marksbury could not have given away unborn children, on the strength of the legal maxim, *"Nemo dat quod non habet"—i. e.,* "Nobody can give what he has not got"—which certainly one should think sensible and satisfactory enough. The case, however, is appealed, and reversed in the superior Court; and now let us hear the reasoning.

The judge acknowledges the force of the maxim above quoted —says, as one would think any man might say, that it is quite a correct maxim—the only difficulty being that it does not at all apply to the present case. Let us hear him:

He who is the absolute owner of a *thing* owns all its faculties for profit or increase; and he may, no doubt, grant the profits or increase, as well as the *thing* itself. Thus, it is every day's practice to grant the future rents or profits of real estate; and it is held that a man may grant the wool of a flock of sheep for years.

See also p. 33, Fanny *v.* Bryant, 4 J. J. Marshall's Rep., 368. In this almost precisely the same language is used. If the reader will proceed, he will find also this principle applied with equal clearness to the hiring, selling, mortgaging of unborn children; and the perfect legal *nonchalance* of these discussions is only comparable to running a dissecting-knife through the course of all the heart-strings of a living subject, for the purpose of demonstrating the laws of nervous contraction.

Judge Stroud, in his sketch of the slave-laws, page 99, lays down for proof the following assertion:—That the penal codes of the slave States bear much more severely on slaves than on white persons. He introduces his consideration of this proposition by the following humane and sensible remarks:—

A being, ignorant of letters, unenlightened by religion, and deriving but little instruction from good example, cannot be supposed to have right conceptions as to the nature and extent of moral or political obligations. This remark, with but a slight qualification, is applicable to the condition of the slave. It has been just shown that the benefits of education are not conferred upon him, while his *chance* of acquiring a knowledge of the precepts of the gospel is so remote as scarcely to be appreciated. He may be regarded, therefore, as almost without the capacity to comprehend the force of laws; and, on this account, such as are designed for his government should be recommended by their simplicity and mildness.

His condition suggests another motive for tenderness on his behalf in these particulars. *He is unable to read;* and holding little or no communication with those who are better informed than himself, how is he to become acquainted with the fact that a law for his observance has been made? To exact obedience to a law which has not been promulgated, which is unknown to the subject of it, has ever been deemed most unjust and tyrannical. The reign of Caligula, were it obnoxious to no other reproach than this, would never cease to be remembered with abhorrence.

The lawgivers of the slave-holding States seem, in the formation of their penal codes, to have been uninfluenced by these claims of the slave upon their compassionate consideration. The *hardened convict* moves their sympathy, and is to be *taught* the laws *before* he is expected to obey them; yet the *guiltless slave* is subjected to an extensive system of cruel enactments, of no part of which probably has he ever heard.

Parts of this system apply to the slave exclusively, and for every infraction a large retribution is demanded; while with respect to offences for which whites as well as slaves are amenable, *punishments of much greater severity are inflicted upon the latter* than upon the former.

This heavy charge of Judge Stroud is sustained by twenty pages of proof, showing the very great disproportion between the number of offences made capital for slaves, and those that are so for whites. Concerning this, we find the following cool remark in Wheeler's Law of Slavery, page 222, note.

Much has been said of the disparity of punishment between the white inhabitants and the slaves and negroes of the same State; that slaves are punished with much more severity, for the commission of similar crimes, by white persons, than the latter. The charge is undoubtedly true to a considerable extent. It must be remembered that the primary object of the enactment of penal laws is the protection and security of those who make them. The slave has no agency in making them.

He is, indeed, one cause of the apprehended evils to the other class, which those laws are expected to remedy. That he should be held amenable for a violation of those rules established for the security of the other is the natural result of the state in which he is placed. And the severity of those rules will always bear a relation to that danger, real or ideal, of the other class.

It has been so among all nations, and will ever continue to be so, while the disparity between bond and free remains.

[The State *v.* Mann, Dec. Term, 1829. 2 Devereux's N. Carolina Rep. 263.]

A striking example of a legal decision to this purport is given in Wheeler's Law of Slavery, page 224. The case, apart from legal technicalities, may be thus briefly stated:—

The defendant, Mann, had hired a slave-woman for a year. During this time the slave committed some slight offence, for which the defendant undertook to chastise her. While in the act of doing so, the slave ran off, whereat he shot at and wounded her. The judge in the inferior Court charged the jury that if they believed the punishment was cruel and unwarrantable, and disproportioned to the offence, in law the defendant was guilty, *as he had only a special property in the slave.* The jury finding evidence that the punishment *had* been cruel, un-warrantable, and *disproportioned to the offence,* found verdict against the defendant. But on what ground? Because, according to the law of North Carolina, cruel, unwarrantable, disproportionate punishment of a slave from a master, is an indictable offence? No. They decided against the defendant, not because the punishment was cruel and unwarrantable, but because *he* was not the person who had the right to inflict it, "as he had only a SPECIAL *right of property in the slave.*"

The defendant appealed to a higher Court, and the decision was reversed, on the ground that the hirer has for the time being all the rights of the master. The remarks of Judge Ruffin are so characteristic, and so strongly express the conflict between the feelings of the humane judge and the logical necessity of a strict interpreter of slave-law, that we shall quote largely from it. One cannot but admire the unflinching calmness with which a man, evidently possessed of honourable and humane feelings, walks through the most extreme and terrible results and conclusions, in obedience to the laws of legal truth. Thus he says:—

A judge cannot but lament when such cases as the present are brought into judgment. It is impossible that the reasons on which they go can be appreciated, but where institutions similar to our own exist, and are *thoroughly understood.* The struggle, too, in the judge's own breast, between the feelings of the man and the duty of the magistrate, is a severe one, presenting strong temptations to put aside such questions, if it be possible. It is useless, however, to complain of things inherent in our political state; and it is criminal in a Court to avoid any responsibility which the laws impose. With whatever reluctance, therefore, it is done, the Court is compelled to express an opinion upon the extent of the dominion of the master over the slave in North Carolina. The indictment charges a battery on Lydia, a slave of Elizabeth Jones. The inquiry here is, whether a cruel and unreasonable battery on a slave by the hirer is indictable. The judge below instructed the jury that it is. He seems to have put it on the ground that the defendant had but a special property. Our laws uniformly treat the master, or other person having the possession and command of the slave, as entitled to the same extent of authority. The object is the same, the service of the slave; and the same powers must be confided. In a criminal proceeding, and, indeed, in reference to all other persons but the general owner, the hirer and possessor of the slave, in relation to both rights and duties, is, for the time being, the owner. But upon the general question whether the owner is answerable *criminaliter* for a battery upon his own slave, or other exercise of authority of force not forbidden by the statute, the Court entertains but little doubt. That he is so liable has never been decided; nor, as far as is known, been hitherto contended. There has been no prosecution of the sort. The established habits and uniform practice of the country in this respect is the best evidence of the portion of power deemed by the whole community requisite to the preservation of the master's dominion. If we thought differently, we could not set our notions in array against the judgment of everybody else, and say that this or that authority may be safely lopped off. This has indeed been assimilated at the bar to the other domestic relations; and arguments drawn from the well-established principles, which confer and restrain the authority of the parent over the child, the tutor over the pupil, the master over the apprentice, have been pressed on us.

The Court does not recognise their application; there is no likeness between the cases; they are in opposition to each other, and there is an impassable gulf between them. The difference is that which exists between freedom and slavery, and a greater cannot be imagined. In the one, the end in view is the happiness of the youth, born to equal rights with that governor on whom the duty devolves of training the young to usefulness in a station which he is afterwards to assume among freemen. To such an end, and with such a subject, moral and intellectual instruction seem the natural means, and, for the most part, they are found to suffice. Moderate force is superadded only to make the others effectual. If that fail, it is better to leave the party to his own headstrong passions, and the ultimate correction of the law, than to allow it to be immoderately inflicted by a private person. With slavery it is far otherwise. The end is the profit of the master, his security, and the public safety; the subject, one doomed, in his own person and his posterity, to live without knowledge, and without the capacity to make anything his own, and to toil that another may reap the fruits. What moral considerations shall be addressed to such a being to convince him, what it is impossible but that the most stupid must feel and know can never be true, that he is thus to labour upon a principle of natural duty, or for the sake of his own personal happiness? Such services can only be expected from one who has no will of his own; who surrenders his will in implicit obedience to that of another. Such obedience is the consequence only of uncontrolled authority over the body. There is nothing else which can operate to produce the effect. THE POWER OF THE MASTER MUST BE ABSOLUTE, TO RENDER THE SUBMISSION TO THE SLAVE PERFECT. I most freely confess my sense of the harshness of this proposition. I feel it as deeply as any man can; and as a principle of moral right, every person in his retirement must repudiate it; but, in the actual condition of things, it must be so; there is no remedy. This discipline belongs to the state of slavery. They cannot be disunited without abrogating at once the rights of the master, and absolving the slave from his subjection. It constitutes the curse of slavery to both the bond and the free portions of our population; but it is *inherent in the relation* of master and slave. That there may be particular instances of cruelty and deliberate barbarity, where in conscience the law might properly interfere, is most probable. The difficulty is to determine where *a Court* may properly begin. Merely in the abstract, it may well be asked which power of the master accords with right. The answer will probably sweep away all of them. But we cannot look at the matter in that light. The truth is, that we are forbidden to enter upon a train of general reasoning on the subject. We cannot allow the right of the master to be brought into discussion in the courts of justice. The slave, to remain a slave, must be made sensible that there is no appeal from his master; that his power is, in no instance, usurped on, is conferred by the laws of man at least, if not by the law of God. The danger would be great, indeed, if the tribunals of justice should be called on to graduate the punishment appropriate to every temper and every dereliction of menial duty.

No man can anticipate the many and aggravated provocations of the master which the slave would be constantly stimulated by his own passions, or the instigation of others, to give; or the consequent wrath of the master, prompting him to bloody vengeance upon the turbulent traitor; a vengeance *generally practised with impunity, by reason of its privacy.* The Court, therefore, disclaims the power of changing the relation in which these parts of our people stand to each other.

* * * * * * * * *

I repeat, that I would gladly have avoided this ungrateful question; but being brought to it, the Court is compelled to declare that while slavery exists amongst us in its present state, or until it shall seem fit to the legislature to interpose express enactments to the contrary, it will be the imperative *duty* of the judges *to recognise the full dominion of the owner over the slave,* except where the exercise of it is forbidden by statute.

And this we do upon the ground that *this dominion is essential to the value of slaves as property, to the security of the master and the public tranquillity, greatly dependant upon their subordination;* and, in fine, as most effectually securing the general protection and comfort of the slaves themselves. Judgment below reversed; and judgment entered for the defendant.

No one can read this decision, so fine and clear in expression, so dignified and solemn in its earnestness, and so dreadful in its results, without feeling at once deep respect for the man and horror for the system. The man, judging him from this short specimen, which is all the author knows, has one of that high order of minds which looks straight through all verbiage and sophistry to the heart of every subject which it encounters. He has, too, that noble scorn of dissimulation, that straightforward determination not to call a bad thing by a good name, even when most popular, and reputable, and legal, which it is to be wished could be more frequently seen, both in our Northern and Southern States. There is but one sole regret; and that is, that such a man, with such a mind, should have been merely an *expositor,* and not a *reformer* of law.

CHAPTER III.

SOUTHER V. THE COMMONWEALTH—THE NE PLUS ULTRA OF LEGAL HUMANITY.

"Yet in the face of *such* laws and decisions as *these,* Mrs. Stowe," &c.

—*Courier and Enquirer.*

THE case of Souther *v.* the Commonwealth has been cited by the *Courier and Enquirer* as a particularly favourable specimen of judicial proceedings under the slave code, with the following remark:—

And yet, in the face of such laws and decisions as these, Mrs. Stowe winds up a long series of cruelties upon her other black personages, by causing her faultless hero, Tom, to be literally whipped to death in Louisiana, by his master, Legree; and these acts, which the laws make criminal, and punish as such, she sets forth in the most repulsive colours, to illustrate the institution of slavery!

By the above language the author was led into the supposition that this case had been conducted in a manner so creditable to the feelings of our common humanity as to present a fairer side of criminal jurisprudence in this respect. She accordingly took the pains to procure a report of the case, designing to publish it as an offset to the many barbarities which research into this branch of the subject obliges one to unfold. A legal gentleman has copied the case from Grattan's Reports, and it is here given. If the reader is astounded at it, he cannot be more so than was the writer.

Souther v. The Commonwealth. 7 Grattan, 673, 1851.

The killing of a slave by his master and owner, by wilful and excessive whipping, is murder in the first degree; though it may not have been the purpose and intention of the master and owner to kill the slave.

Simeon Souther was indicted at the October Term, 1850, of the Circuit Court for the County of Hanover, for the murder of his own slave. The indictment contained fifteen counts, in which the various modes of punishment and torture by which the homicide was charged to have been committed were stated singly, and in various combinations. The fifteenth count unites them all: and, as the Court certifies that the *indictment was sustained by the evidence,* the giving the facts stated in that count will show what was the charge against the prisoner, and what was the proof to sustain it.

The count charged that on the 1st day of September, 1849, the prisoner tied his negro slave, Sam, with ropes about his wrists, neck, body, legs, and ankles, to a tree. That whilst so tied, the prisoner first whipped the slave with switches. That he next beat and cobbed the slave with a shingle, and compelled two of his slaves, a man and a woman, also to cob the deceased with the shingle. That whilst the deceased was so tied to the tree, the prisoner did strike, knock, kick, stamp, and beat him upon various parts of his head, face, and body; that he applied fire to his body; that he then washed his body with warm water, in which pods of red pepper had been put and steeped; and he compelled his two slaves aforesaid to wash him with this same preparation of warm water and red pepper. That after the tying, whipping, cobbing, striking, beating, knocking, kicking, stamping, wounding, bruising, lacerating, burning, washing, and torturing, as aforesaid, the prisoner untied the deceased from the tree, in such a way as to throw him with violence to the ground; and he then and there did knock, kick, stamp, and beat the deceased upon his head, temples, and various parts of his body. That the prisoner then had the deceased carried into a shed-room of his house, and there he compelled one of his slaves, in his presence, to confine the deceased's feet in stocks, by making his legs fast to a piece of timber, and to tie a rope about the neck of the deceased, and fasten it to a bed-post in the room, thereby strangling, choking, and suffocating the deceased. And that whilst the deceased was thus made fast in stocks as aforesaid, the prisoner did kick, knock, stamp, and beat him upon his head, face, breast, belly, sides, back, and body; and he again compelled his two slaves to apply fire to the body of the deceased, whilst he was so made fast as aforesaid. And the count charged, that from these various modes of punishment and torture the slave Sam then and there died. It appeared that the prisoner commenced the punishment of the deceased in the morning, and that it was continued throughout the day; and that the deceased died in the presence of the prisoner, and one of his slaves, and one of the witnesses, whilst the punishment was still progressing.

Field, J., delivered the opinion of the Court.

The prisoner was indicted and convicted of *murder in the second degree,* in the Circuit Court of Hanover, at its April term last past, and was sentenced to the *Penitentiary for five years,* the period of time ascertained by the jury. The murder consisted in the killing of a negro man-slave by the name of Sam, the property of the prisoner, by cruel and excessive whipping and torture, inflicted by Souther, aided by two of his other slaves, on the 1st day of September, 1849 The prisoner moved for a new trial, upon the ground that the offence, *if any,* amounted only to manslaughter. The motion for a new trial was overruled, and a bill of exceptions taken to the opinion of the Court, setting forth the facts proved, or as many of them as were deemed material for the consideration of the application for a new trial. The bill of exception states: That the slave Sam, in the indictment mentioned, was the slave and property of the prisoner. That for the purpose of chastising the slave for the offence of getting drunk, and dealing as the slave confessed and alleged with Henry and Stone, two of the witnesses for the Commonwealth, he caused him to be tied and punished in the presence of the said witnesses, with the exception of slight whipping with peach or apple-tree switches, before the said witnesses arrived at the scene after they were sent for by the prisoner (who were present by request from the defendant), and of several slaves of the prisoner, in the manner and by the means charged in the indictment; and the said slave died under and from the infliction of the said punishment, in the presence of the prisoner, one of his slaves, and one of the witnesses for the Commonwealth. But it did not appear that it was the design of the prisoner to kill the said slave, unless such design be properly inferable from the manner, means, and duration of the punishment. And, on the contrary, it did appear that the prisoner frequently declared, while the said slave was undergoing the punishment, that he believed the said slave was feigning, and pretending to be suffering and injured when he was not. The judge certifies that the slave was punished in the manner and by the means charged in the indictment. The indictment contains fifteen counts, and sets forth a case of the most cruel and excessive whipping and torture.

* * * * * * * *

It is believed that the records of criminal jurisprudence do not contain a case of more atrocious and wicked cruelty than was presented upon the trial of Souther; and yet it has been gravely and earnestly contended here by his counsel that his offence amounts to manslaughter only.

It has been contended by the counsel of the prisoner that a man cannot be indicted and prosecuted for the cruel and excessive whipping of his own slave. That it is lawful for the master to chastise his slave, and that if death ensues from such chastisement, unless it was intended to produce death, it is like the case of homicide which is committed by a man in the performance of a lawful act, which is manslaughter only. It has been decided by this Court in Turner's case, 5 Rand, that the owner of a slave, for the malicious, cruel, and excessive beating of his own slave, cannot be indicted; yet it by no means follows, when such malicious, cruel, and excessive beating results in death, though not intended and premeditated, that the beating is to be regarded as lawful for the purpose of reducing the crime to manslaughter, when the whipping is inflicted for the sole purpose of chastisement. It is the policy of the law, in respect to the relation of master and slave, and for the sake of securing proper subordination and obedience on the part of the slave, to protect the master from prosecution in all such cases, even if the whipping and punishment be malicious, cruel, and excessive. But in so inflicting punishment for the sake of punishment, the owner of the slave acts at his peril; and if death ensues in consequence of such punishment, the relation of master and slave affords no ground of excuse or palliation. The principles of the common law, in relation to homicide, apply to his case without qualification or exception; and according to those principles, the act of the prisoner, in the case under consideration, amounted to murder. The crime of the prisoner is not manslaughter, but murder in the first degree.

CHAPTER III.

On the case now presented there are some remarks to be made.

This scene of torture, it seems, occupied about twelve hours. It occurred in the State of Virginia, in the county of Hanover. Two white men were witnesses to nearly the whole proceeding, and, so far as we can see, made no effort to arouse the neighbourhood, and bring in help to stop the outrage. What sort of an education, what habits of thought, does this presuppose in these men?

The case was brought to trial. It requires no ordinary nerve to read over the counts of this indictment. Nobody, one would suppose, could willingly read them twice. One would think that it would have laid a cold hand of horror on every heart— that the community would have risen, by an universal sentiment, to shake out the man, as Paul shook the viper from his hand. It seems, however, that they were quite self-possessed; that lawyers calmly sat, and examined, and cross-examined, on particulars known before only in the records of the Inquisition; that it was "ably and earnestly argued" by educated intelligent American men, that this catalogue of horrors did not amount to a murder! and, in the cool language of legal precision, that "the offence, IF ANY, amounted to manslaughter;" and that an American jury found that the offence was murder *in the second degree*. Anyone who reads the indictment will certainly think that, if this be murder in the *second degree,* in Virginia, one might earnestly pray to be murdered in the first degree to begin with. Had Souther walked up to the man, and shot him through the head with a pistol, before white witnesses, *that* would have been murder in the *first* degree. As he preferred to spend *twelve hours* in killing him by torture, under the name of "*chastisement,*" that, says the verdict, is murder in the second degree; "*because,*" says the bill of exceptions, with admirable coolness, "*it did not appear that it was the design of the prisoner to kill the slave,* UNLESS SUCH DESIGN BE PROPERLY INFERABLE FROM THE MANNER, MEANS, AND DURATION OF THE PUNISHMENT."

The bill evidently seems to have a leaning to the idea that twelve hours spent in beating, stamping, scalding, burning, and mutilating a human being might possibly be considered as presumption of something beyond the limits of lawful chastisement. So startling an opinion, however, is expressed cautiously, and with a becoming diffidence, and is balanced by the very striking fact, which is also quoted in this remarkable paper, that the prisoner frequently declared, while the slave was undergoing the punishment, that he believed the slave was feigning and pretending to be suffering, when he was not. This view appears to have struck the Court as eminently probable—as going a long way to prove the propriety of Souther's intentions, making it at least extremely probable that only *correction* was intended.

It seems also that Souther, so far from being crushed by the united opinion of the community, found those to back him who considered five years in the Penitentiary an unjust severity for his crime, and hence the bill of exceptions from which we have quoted, and the appeal to the Superior Court; and hence the form in which the case stands in law-books, "*Souther* v. *the Commonwealth.*" Souther evidently considers himself an ill-used man, and it is in this character that he appears before the Superior Court.

As yet there has been no particular overflow of humanity in the treatment of the ease. The manner in which it has been discussed so far reminds one of nothing so much as of some discussions which the reader may have seen quoted from the records of the Inquisition, with regard to the propriety of roasting the feet of children who have not arrived at the age of thirteen years, with a view to eliciting evidence.

Let us now come to the decision of the Superior Court, which the editor of the *Courier and Enquirer* thinks so particularly enlightened and humane. Judge Field thinks that the case is a very atrocious one, and in this respect he seems to differ materially from judge, jury, and lawyers of the Court below. Furthermore, he doubts whether the annals of jurisprudence furnish a case of equal atrocity, wherein certainly he appears to be not far wrong; and he also states unequivocally the principle that killing a slave by torture under the name of correction is murder in the first degree; and here too, certainly, everybody will think that he is also right; the only wonder being that any man could ever have been called to express such an opinion, judicially. But he states, quite as unequivocally as Judge Ruffin, that awful principle of slave-laws, that the law cannot interfere with the master for any amount of torture inflicted on his slave which does not result in death. The decision, if it establishes anything, establishes this principle quite as strongly as it does the other. Let us hear the words of the decision:—

It has been decided by this Court, in Turner's case, that *the owner of a slave, for the malicious, cruel, and excessive beating of his own slave, cannot be indicted.*

* * * * * *

It is the policy of the law, in respect to the relation of master and slave, and for the sake of securing proper subordination and obedience on the part of the slave, to protect the master from prosecution in all such cases, even if the whipping and punishment be malicious, cruel, and excessive

What follows as a corollary from this remarkable declaration is this—that if the victim of this twelve hours' torture had only possessed a little stronger constitution, and had not actually died under it, there is no law in Virginia by which Souther could even have been indicted for misdemeanour.

If this is not filling out the measure of the language of St. Clare, that "he who goes the furthest, and does the worst, only uses within limits the power which the law gives him," how could this language be verified? Which is "*the worst,*" death outright, or torture indefinitely prolonged? This decision, in so many words, gives every master the power of indefinite torture, and takes from him only the power of terminating the agony by merciful death. And this is the judicial decision which the *Courier and Enquirer* cites as a perfectly convincing specimen of legal humanity. It must be hoped that the editor never read the decision, else he never would have cited it. Of all who knock at the charnel-house of legal precedents, with the hope of disinterring any evidence of humanity in the slave system, it may be said, in the awful words of the Hebrew poet:

> He knoweth not that the dead are there,
> And that her guests are in the depths of hell.

The upshot of this case was, that Souther, instead of getting off from his five years' imprisonment, got simply a judicial *opinion* from the Superior Court that he ought to be hung; but he could not be tried over again, and as we may infer from all the facts in the case that he was a man of tolerably resolute nerves and not very exquisite sensibility, it is not likely that the *opinion* gave him any very serious uneasiness. He has probably made up his mind to get over his five years with what grace he may. When he comes out, there is no law in Virginia to prevent his buying as many more negroes as he chooses, and going over the same scene with any one of them at a future time, if only he profit by the information which has been so explicitly conveyed to him in this decision, that he must take care and stop his tortures short of the point of death—a matter about which, as the history of the Inquisition shows, men, by careful practice, can be able to judge with considerable precision. Probably, also, the next time, he will not be so foolish as to send out and request the attendance of two white witnesses, even though they may be so complacently interested in the proceeding as to spend the whole day in witnessing them without effort at prevention.

Slavery, as defined in American law, is no more capable of being regulated in its administration by principles of humanity than the torture system of the Inquisition. Every act of humanity of every individual owner is an illogical result from the legal definition; and the reason why the slave-code of America is more atrocious than any ever before exhibited under the sun, is that the Anglo-Saxon race are a more coldly and strictly logical race, and have an unflinching courage to meet the consequences of every premise which they lay down, and to work out an accursed principle, with mathematical accuracy, to its most accursed results. The decisions in American law-books show nothing so much as this severe, unflinching accuracy of logic. It is often and evidently, not because judges are inhuman or partial, but because they are logical and truthful, that they announce from the bench, in the calmest manner, decisions which one would think might make the earth shudder, and the sun turn pale.

The French and the Spanish nations are, by constitution, more impulsive, passionate, and poetic, than logical; hence it will be found that while there may be more instances of individual barbarity, as might be expected among impulsive and passionate people, there is in their slave-code more exhibition of humanity. The code of the State of Louisiana contains more really humane provisions, were there any means of enforcing them, than that of any other state in the Union.

It is believed that there is no code of laws in the world which contains such a perfect cabinet crystallisation of every tear and every drop of blood which can be wrung from humanity, so accurately, elegantly, and scientifically arranged, as the slave-code of America. It is a case of elegant surgical instruments for the work of dissecting the living human heart; every instrument wrought with exactest temper and polish, and adapted with exquisite care, and labelled with the name of the nerve or artery or muscle which it is designed to sever. The instruments of the anatomist are instruments of earthly steel and wood, designed to operate at most on perishable and corruptible matter; but these are instruments of keener temper, and more ethereal workmanship, designed in the most precise and scientific manner to DESTROY THE IMMORTAL SOUL, and carefully and gradually to reduce man from the high position of a free agent, a social, religious, accountable being, down to the condition of the brute, or of inanimate matter.

CHAPTER IV.

PROTECTIVE STATUTES.

Apprentices protected. Outlawry. Melodrama of Prue in the Swamp. Harry the Carpenter, a Romance of Real Life.

BUT the question now occurs, Are there not protective statutes, the avowed object of which is the protection of the life and limb of the slave? We answer, there are; and these protective statutes are some of the most remarkable pieces of legislation extant.

That they were dictated by a spirit of humanity, charity, which hopeth *all* things, would lead us to hope; but no newspaper stories of bloody murders and shocking outrages convey to the mind so dreadful a picture of the numbness of public sentiment caused by slavery as these so-called protective statutes. The author copies the following from the statutes of North Carolina. Section 3rd of the Act passed in 1798 runs thus:—

Whereas by another Act of the Assembly, passed in 1774, the killing of a slave, however wanton, cruel, and deliberate, is only punishable in the first instance by imprisonment, and paying the value thereof to the owner, which distinction of criminality between the murder of a white person and one who is equally a human creature, but merely of a different complexion, is DISGRACEFUL TO HUMANITY, AND DEGRADING IN THE HIGHEST DEGREE TO THE LAWS AND PRINCIPLES OF A FREE, CHRISTIAN, AND ENLIGHTENED COUNTRY; Be it enacted,&c., That if any person shall hereafter be guilty of wilfully and maliciously killing a slave such offender shall, upon the first conviction thereof, be adjudged guilty of murder, and shall suffer the same punishment as if he had killed a free man: Provided always, this Act shall not extended to the person killing a slave OUTLAWED BY VIRTUE OF ANY ACT OF ASSEMBLY OF THIS STATE, or to any slave in the act of resistance to his lawful owner or master, or to any slave dying under moderate correction.

A law with a like proviso, except the outlawry clause, exists in Tennessee. See *Caruthers and Nicholson's Compilation,* 1836, p. 676.

The language of the constitution of Georgia, art. iv, sec. 12, is as follows:

Any person who shall maliciously dismember, or deprive a slave of life, shall suffer such punishment as would be inflicted in case the like offence had been committed on a free white person, and on the like proof, except in case of insurrection by such slave, and unless such death should happen by accident in giving such slave moderate correction. —*Cobb's Dig.,* 1851, p. 1125.

Let now any Englishman or New Englander imagine that such laws with regard to apprentices had ever been proposed in Parliament or State Legislature under the head of *protective acts;*—laws which in so many words permit the killing of the subject in three cases, and those comprising all the acts which would generally occur under the law; namely, if the slave resist, if he be outlawed, or if he die under *moderate* correction.

What rule in the world will ever prove correction immoderate, if the fact that the subject *dies* under it is not held as proof? How many such "accidents" would have to happen in Old England or New England, before Parliament or Legislature would hear from such a protective law?

"But," some one may ask, "what is the *outlawry* spoken of in this Act? The question is pertinent, and must be answered. The author has copied the following from the Revised Statutes of North Carolina, chap. cxi, sec. 22. It may be remarked in passing that the preamble to this law presents rather a new view of slavery to those who have formed their ideas from certain pictures of blissful contentment and Arcadian repose, which have been much in vogue of late.

Whereas, MANY TIMES slaves run away and lie out, hid and lurking in swamps, woods, and other obscure places, killing cattle and hogs, and committing other injuries to the inhabitants of this State; in all such cases, upon intelligence of any slave or slaves lying out as aforesaid, any two justices of the peace for the county wherein such slave or slaves is or are supposed to lurk or do mischief, shall, and they are hereby empowered and required to issue proclamation against such slave or slaves (reciting his or their names, and the name or names of the owner or owners, if known), thereby requiring him or them, and every of them, forthwith to surrender him or themselves; and also to empower and require the sheriff of the said county to take such power with him as he shall think fit and necessary for going in search and pursuit of, and effectually apprehending, such outlying slave or slaves; which proclamation shall be published at the door of the court-house, and at such other places as said justices shall direct. And if any slave or slaves, against whom proclamation hath been thus issued stay out, and do not immediately return home, it shall be lawful for any person or persons whatsoever to kill and destroy such slave or slaves by such ways and means as he shall think fit, without accusation or impeachment of any crime for the same.

What ways and means *have been* thought fit, in actual experience, for the destruction of the slave? What was done with the negro McIntosh, in the streets of St. Louis, in open daylight, and endorsed at the next sitting of the Supreme Court of the State, as transcending the sphere of law, because it was "an act of the majority of her most respectable citizens?" If these things are done in the green tree, what will be done in the dry? If these things have once been done in the open streets of St. Louis, by "a majority of her most respectable citizens," what will be done in the lonely swamps of North Carolina, by men of the stamp of Souther and Legree?

This passage of the Revised Statutes of North Carolina is more terribly suggestive to the imagination than any particulars into which the author of "Uncle Tom's Cabin" has thought fit to enter. Let us suppose a little melodrama quite possible to have occurred under this Act of the Legislature. Suppose some luckless Prue or Peg, as in the case we have just quoted, in State *v.* Mann, getting tired of the discipline of whipping, breaks from the overseer, clears the dogs, and gets into the swamp, and there "lies out," as the Act above graphically says. The Act which we are considering says that *many* slaves do this, and doubtless they have their own best reasons for it. We all know what fascinating places to "lie out" in these Southern swamps are. What with alligators and moccasin snakes, mud and water, and poisonous vines, one would be apt to think the situation not particularly eligible; but still Prue "lies out" there. Perhaps in the night some husband or brother goes to see her, taking a hog or some animal of the plantation stock, which he has ventured his life in killing, that she may not perish with hunger. Master overseer walks up to master proprietor, and reports the accident; master proprietor mounts his horse, and assembles to his aid two justices of the peace.

In the intervals between drinking brandy and smoking cigars a proclamation is duly drawn up, summoning the contumacious Prue to surrender, and requiring sheriff of said county to take such power as he shall think fit to go in search and pursuit of said slave; which proclamation, for Prue's further enlightenment, is solemnly published at the door of the court-house, and "at such other places as said justices shall direct." Let us suppose, now, that Prue, given over to hardness of heart and blindness of mind, pays no attention to all these means of grace, put forth to draw her to the protective shadow of the patriarchal roof. Suppose, further, as a final effort of long-suffering, and to leave her utterly without excuse, the worthy magistrate rides forth in full force—man, horse, dog, and gun—to the very verge of the swamp, and there proclaims aloud the merciful mandate. Suppose that, hearing the yelping of the dogs and the proclamation of the sheriffs mingled together, and the shouts of Loker, Marks, Sambo and Quimbo, and other such posse, black and white, as a sheriff can generally summon on such a hunt, this very ignorant and contumacious Prue only runs deeper into the swamp, and continues obstinately "lying out," as aforesaid; now she is by Act of the Assembly *outlawed,* and, in the astounding words of the Act, "it shall be lawful for any person or persons whatsoever to kill and destroy her, by such ways and means as he shall think fit, without accusation or impeachment of any crime for the same." What awful possibilities rise to the imagination under the fearfully suggestive clause, "*by such ways and means as he shall think fit!*" Such ways and means as ANY man shall think fit, of *any* character, of *any* degree of fiendish barbarity!! Such a permission to kill even a dog, by "any ways and means which anybody should think fit," never ought to stand on the law-books of a Christian nation; and yet this stands against one bearing that same humanity which Jesus Christ bore—

against one, perhaps, who, though blinded, darkened, and ignorant, he will not be ashamed to own, when he shall come in the glory of his Father, and all his holy angels with him!

That this law has not been a dead letter there is sufficient proof. In 1836 the following proclamation and advertisement appeared in the "Newbern (N. C.) Spectator."

STATE OF NORTH CAROLINA, LENOIR COUNTY.

Whereas complaint hath been this day made to us, two of the justices of the peace for the said county, by William D. Cobb, of Jones County, that two negro slaves belonging to him, named Ben (commonly known by the name of Ben Fox), and Rigdon, have absented themselves from their said master's service, and are lurking about in the Counties of Lenoir and Jones, committing acts of felony; these are, in the name of the State, to command the said slaves forthwith to surrender themselves and turn home to their said master. And we do hereby also require the sheriff of said County of Lenoir to make diligent search and pursuit after the above-mentioned slaves. And we do hereby, by virtue of an Act of Assembly of this State concerning servants and slaves, intimate and declare, if the said slaves do not surrender themselves and return home to their master immediately after the publication of these presents, that any person may kill or destroy said slaves by such means as he or they may think fit, without accusation or impeachment of any crime or offence for so doing, or without incurring any penalty or forfeiture thereby.

Given under our hands and seals, this 12th of November, 1836.

B. COLEMAN, J. P. [Seal.]
JAS. JONES, J. P. [Seal.]

200 DOLLARS REWARD.—Ran away from the subscriber, about three years ago, a certain negro man, named Ben, commonly known by the name of Ben Fox; also one other negro, by the name of Rigdon, who ran away on the 8th of this month.

I will give the reward of 100 dollars for each of the above negroes, to be delivered to me, or confined in the jail of Lenoir or Jones County, or for the killing of them, so that I can see them.

Nov. 12, 1836.

W. D. COBB.

That this Act was *not* a dead letter, also, was plainly implied in the protective Act first quoted. If slaves were not, as a matter of fact, ever outlawed, why does the Act formally recognise such a class?—"provided that this Act shall not extend to the killing of any slave *outlawed* by any Act of the Assembly." This language sufficiently indicates the existence of the custom.

Further than this, the statute-book of 1821 contained two Acts: the first of which provides that all masters in certain counties, who have had slaves killed in consequence of outlawry, shall have a claim on the treasury of the State for their value, unless cruel treatment of the slave be proved on the part of the master: the second Act extends the benefits of the latter provision to all the counties in the State.

Finally, there is evidence that this Act of outlawry was executed so recently as the year 1850, the year in which "Uncle Tom's Cabin" was written. See the following from the *Wilmington Journal* of December 13, 1850:—

STATE OF NORTH CAROLINA, NEW HANOVER COUNTY.

Whereas complaint upon oath has this day been made to us, two of the justices of the peace for the said State and county aforesaid, by Guilford Horn, of Edgecombe County, that a certain male slave belonging to him, named Harry, a carpenter by trade, about forty years old, five feet five inches high, or thereabouts; yellow complexion; stout built; with a scar on his left leg (from the cut of an axe); has very thick lips; eyes deep sunk in his head; forehead very square; tolerably loud voice; has lost one or two of his upper teeth; and has a very dark spot on his jaw, supposed to be a mark—hath absented himself from his master's service, and is supposed to be lurking about in this county, committing acts of felony or other misdeeds; these are, therefore, in the name of the State aforesaid, to command the said slave forthwith to surrender himself, and return home to his said master; and we do hereby, by virtue of the Act of Assembly in such cases made and provided, intimate and declare, that if the said slave Harry doth not surrender himself and return home immediately after the publication of these presents, that any person or persons may KILL and DESTROY the said slave by such means as he or they may think fit, without accusation or impeachment of any crime or offence for so doing, and without incurring any penalty or forfeiture thereby.

Given under our hands and seals, this 29th day of June, 1850.

JAMES T. MILLER, J. P. [Seal.]
W. C. BETTENCOURT, J. P. [Seal.]

ONE HUNDRED AND TWENTY-FIVE DOLLARS REWARD will be paid for the delivery of the said Harry to me at Tosnott Depot, Edgecombe County, or for his confinement in any jail in the State, so that I can get him; or One Hundred and Fifty Dollars will be given for his head.

He was lately heard from in Newbern, where he called himself Henry Barnes (or Burns), and will be likely to continue the same name, or assume that of Copage or Farmer. He has a free mulatto woman for a wife, by the name of Sally Bozeman, who has lately removed to Wilmington, and lives in that part of the town called Texas, where he will likely be lurking.

Masters of vessels are particularly cautioned against harbouring or concealing the said negro on board their vessels, as the full penalty of the law will be rigorously enforced.

June 29th, 1850. GUILFORD HORN.

There is an inkling of history and romance about the description of this same Harry, who is thus publicly set up to be killed in any way that any of the negro-hunters of the swamps may think the most piquant and enlivening. It seems he is a carpenter—a powerfully-made man, whose thews and sinews might be a profitable acquisition to himself. It appears also that he has a wife, and the advertiser intimates that possibly he may be caught prowling about somewhere in her vicinity. This indicates sagacity in the writer, certainly. Married men generally have a way of liking the society of their wives; and it strikes us, from what we know of the nature of carpenters here in New England, that Harry was not peculiar in this respect. Let us further notice the portrait of Harry:—"*Eyes deep sunk in his head; forehead very square*." This picture reminds us of what a persecuting old ecclesiastic once said in the days of the Port-Royalists, of a certain truculent abbess, who stood obstinately to a certain course, in the face of the whole power, temporal and spiritual, of the Romish Church, in spite of fining, imprisoning, starving, whipping, beating, and other enlightening argumentative processes, not wholly peculiar, it seems, to that age. "You will never subdue that woman," said the ecclesiastic, who was a phrenologist before his age; "she's got a *square head,* and I have always noticed that people with *square heads* never can be turned out of their course." We think it very probable that Harry, with his "square head," is just one of this sort. He is probably one of those articles which would be extremely valuable, if the owner could only get the use of him. His head is well enough, but he will use it for himself. It is of no use to anyone but the wearer; and the master seems to symbolise this state of things, by offering twenty-five dollars more for the head without the body, than he is willing to give for head, man, and all. Poor Harry! We wonder whether they have caught him yet; or whether the impenetrable thickets, the poisonous miasma, the deadly snakes, and the unwieldy alligators of the swamps, more humane than the slave-hunter, have interposed their uncouth and loathsome forms to guard the only fastness in Carolina where a slave can live in freedom.

It is not, then, in mere poetic fiction that the humane and graceful pen of Longfellow has drawn the following picture:—

In the dark fens of the Dismal Swamp
The hunted negro lay;
He saw the fire of the midnight camp,
And heard at times the horse's tramp,
And a bloodhound's distant bay.
Where will-o'-the-wisps and glow-worms shine,
In bulrush and in brake;
Where waving mosses shroud the pine,
And the cedar grows, and the poisonous vine
Is spotted like the snake;
Where hardly a human foot could pass,
Or a human heart would dare,—
On the quaking turf of the green morass
He crouched in the rank and tangled grass,
Like a wild beast in his lair.
A poor old slave! infirm and lame,
Great scars deformed his face;
On his forehead he bore the brand of shame,

And the rags that hid his mangled frame
Were the livery of disgrace.
All things above were bright and fair,
All things were glad and free;
Lithe squirrels darted here and there,
And wild birds filled the echoing air
With songs of liberty!
On him alone was the doom of pain,
From the morning of his birth;
On him alone the curse of Cain
Fell like the flail on the garnered grain,
And struck him to the earth.

The civilized world may and will ask, in what State this law has been drawn, and passed, and revised, and allowed to appear at the present day on the revised statute-book, and to be executed in the year of Our Lord 1850, as the above-cited extracts from its most respectable journals show. Is it some heathen, Kurdish tribe, some nest of pirates, some horde of barbarians, where destructive gods are worshipped, and libations to their honour poured from human skulls? The civilized world will not believe it, but it is actually a fact, that this law has been made, and is still kept in force, by men in every other respect than what relates to their slave code, as high-minded, as enlightened, as humane, as any men in Christendom; by citizens of a State which glories in the blood and hereditary Christian institutions of Scotland. Curiosity to know what sort of men the legislators of North Carolina might be, led the writer to examine with some attention the proceedings and debates of the convention of that State, called to amend its constitution, which assembled at Raleigh, June 4th, 1835. It is but justice to say that in these proceedings, in which all the different and perhaps conflicting interests of the various parts of the State were discussed, there was an exhibition of candour, fairness, and moderation, of gentlemanly honour and courtesy in the treatment of opposing claims, and of an overruling sense of the obligations of law and religion, which certainly have not always been equally conspicuous in the proceedings of deliberative bodies in such cases. It simply goes to show that one can judge nothing of the religion or of the humanity of individuals from what seems to us objectionable practice, where they have been educated under a system entirely incompatible with both. Such is the very equivocal character of what we call virtue.

It could not be for a moment supposed that such men as Judge Ruffin, or many of the gentlemen who figure in the debates alluded to, would ever think of availing themselves of the savage permissions of such a law. But what then? It follows that the law is a direct permission, letting loose upon the defenceless slave that class of men who exist in every community, who have no conscience, no honour, no shame; who are too far below public opinion to be restrained by that, and from whom accordingly this provision of the law takes away the only available restraint of their fiendish natures. Such men are not peculiar to the South. It is unhappily too notorious that they exist everywhere—in England, in New England, and the world over; but they can only arrive at full maturity in wickedness under a system where the law clothes them with absolute and irresponsible power.

CHAPTER V.

PROTECTIVE ACTS OF SOUTH CAROLINA AND LOUISIANA—THE IRON COLLAR OF LOUISIANA AND NORTH CAROLINA.

THUS far by way of considering the protective Acts of North Carolina, Georgia, and Tennessee.

Certain miscellaneous protective Acts of various other States will now be cited, merely as specimens of the spirit of legislation.

In South Carolina, the Act of 1740 punished the wilful, deliberate murder of a slave by disfranchisement, and by a fine of seven hundred pounds current money, or, in default of payment, imprisonment for seven years. [Stroud, p. 39. 2 Brevard's Digest, p.241.] But the wilful murder of a slave, in the sense contemplated in this law, is a crime which would not often occur. The kind of murder which was most frequent among masters or overseers was guarded against by another section of the same Act—*how adequately* the reader will judge for himself from the following quotation:—

[Stroud's Sketch, p. 40. 2 Brevard's Digest, 241. James' Digest, 392.] If any person shall, on a sudden heat or passion, or by undue correction, kill his own slave, or the slave of any other person, he shall forfeit the sum of three hundred and fifty pounds current money.

In 1821 the Act punishing the wilful murder of the slave only with fine or imprisonment was mainly repealed, and it was enacted that such crime should be punished by death; but the latter section, which relates to killing the slave in sudden heat or passion, or by undue correction, has been altered only by *diminishing* the pecuniary penalty to a fine of five hundred dollars, authorising also imprisonment for six months.

The next protective statute to be noticed is the following from the Act of 1740, South Carolina:—

In case any person shall wilfully cut out the tongue, put out the eye,

Stroud, p.240 2 Brevard's Digest, 241.

or cruelly scald, burn, or deprive any slave of any limb or member, or shall inflict any other cruel punishment, other than by whipping or beating with a horsewhip, cow-skin, switch, or small stick, or by putting irons on, or confining or imprisoning such slave, every such person shall, for every such offence, forfeit the sum of one hundred pounds, current money.

The language of this law, like many other of these protective enactments, is exceedingly suggestive. The first suggestion that occurs is, What sort of an institution, and what sort of a state of society is it, that called out a law worded like this? Laws are generally not made against practices that do not exist, and exist with some degree of frequency.

The advocates of slavery are very fond of comparing it to the apprentice system of England and America. Let us suppose that in the British Parliament, or in a New England Legislature, the following law is proposed, under the title of "An Act for the Protection of Apprentices," &c.:—

In case any person shall wilfully cut out the tongue, put out the eye, or cruelly scald, burn, or deprive any apprentice of any limb or member, or shall inflict any other cruel punishment, other than by whipping or beating with a horsewhip, cow-skin, switch, or small stick, or by putting irons on, or confining or imprisoning such apprentice, every such person shall, for every such offence, forfeit the sum of one hundred pounds, current money.

What a sensation such a proposed law would make in England may be best left for Englishmen to say; but in New England it would simply constitute the proposer a candidate for Bedlam. Yet that such a statute is necessary in South Carolina is evident enough, if we reflect that, because there is no such statute in Virginia, it has been decided that a wretch who perpetrates all these enormities on a slave cannot even be indicted for it, unless the slave dies.

But let us look further. What is to be the penalty when any of these fiendish things are done?

Why, the man forfeits a hundred pounds, current money. Surely he ought to pay as much as that for doing so very unnecessary an act, when the Legislature bountifully allows him to inflict any torture which revengeful ingenuity could devise, by means of horsewhip, cowskin, switch, or small stick, or putting irons on, or confining and imprisoning. One would surely think that here was sufficient scope and variety of legalised means of torture to satisfy any ordinary appetite for vengeance. It would appear decidedly that any more piquant varieties of agony ought to be an extra charge. The advocates of slavery are fond of comparing the situation of the slave with that of the English labourer. We are not aware that the English labourer has been so unfortunate as to be protected by any enactment like this since the days of villeinage.

Judge Stroud says that the same law, substantially, has been

Stroud's Sketch, p.41.

1 Mar. Digest, 654.

adopted in Louisiana. It is true that the civil code of Louisiana thus expresses its humane intentions:—

The slave is entirely subject to the will of his master, who may correct and chastise him, though not with unusual rigour, nor so as to maim or mutilate him, or to expose him to the danger of loss of life, or to cause his death. —*Civil Code of Louisiana, Article* 173.

The expression "unusual rigour" is suggestive again. It will afford large latitude for a jury, in States where slaves are in the habit of *dying* under *moderate* correction; where outlawed slaves may be killed by any means which any person thinks fit; and where laws have to be specifically made against scalding, burning, cutting out the tongue, putting out the eye,&c. What will be thought unusual rigour? This is a question, certainly, upon which persons in States not so constituted can have no means of forming an opinion.

In one of the newspaper extracts with which we prefaced our account, the following protective Act of Louisiana is alluded to as being particularly satisfactory and efficient. We give it as quoted by Judge Stroud in his Sketch, p. 58, giving his reference:—

No master shall be compelled to sell his slave, but in one of two cases, to wit: the first, when, being only co-proprietor of the slave, his co-proprietor demands the sale, in order to make partition of the property; second, when the master shall be CONVICTED of cruel treatment of his slave, AND THE JUDGE SHALL DEEM IT PROPER TO PRONOUNCE, besides the penalty established for such cases, that the slave shall be sold at public auction, in order to place him out of the reach of the power which his master has abused. —*Civil Code, Article* 192.

The question for a jury to determine in this case is, What is cruel treatment of a slave? Now, if all these barbarities which have been sanctioned by the legislative Acts which we have quoted are not held to be cruel treatment, the question is, What *is* cruel treatment of a slave?

Everything that fiendish barbarity could desire can be effected under the protection of the law of South Carolina, which, as we have just shown, exists also in Louisiana. It is true the law restrains from some particular forms of cruelty. If any person has a mind to scald or burn his slave—and it seems, by the statute, that there have been such people—these statutes merely provide that he shall do it in decent privacy; for, as the very keystone of Southern jurisprudence is the rejection of coloured, testimony, such an outrage, if perpetrated most deliberately in the presence of hundreds of slaves, could not be proved upon the master.

It is to be supposed that the fiendish people whom such statutes have in view will generally have enough of common sense not to perform it in the presence of white witnesses, since this simple act of prudence will render them entirely safe in doing whatever they have a mind to. We are told, it is true, as we have been reminded by our friend in the newspaper before quoted, that in Louisiana the deficiency caused by the rejection of negro testimony is supplied by the following most remarkable provision of the Code Noir:—

If any slave be mutilated, beaten, or ill-treated, contrary to the true intent and meaning of this section, when no one shall be present, in such case the owner or other person having the charge or management of said slave thus mutilated, shall be deemed responsible and guilty of the said offence, and shall be prosecuted without further evidence, unless the said owner, or other person so as aforesaid, can prove the contrary by means of good and sufficient evidence, or can clear himself by his own oath, which said oath every Court under the cognizance of which such offence shall have been examined and tried is by this Act authorised to administer. —*Code Noir. Crimes and Offences,* 56, xvii. *Rev. Stat.* 1852, p. 550, s. 141.

Would one have supposed that sensible people could ever publish as a law such a specimen of utter legislative nonsense—so ridiculous on the very face of it!

The object is to bring to justice those fiendish people who burn, scald, mutilate,&c. How is this done? Why, it is enacted that the fact of finding the slave in this condition shall be held presumption against the owner or overseer, unless—unless what? Why, unless he will prove to the contrary—or swear to the contrary, it is no matter which—either will answer the purpose. The question is, If a man is bad enough to do these things, will he not be bad enough to swear falsely? As if men who are the incarnation of cruelty, as supposed by the deeds in question, would not have sufficient intrepidity of conscience to compass a false oath!

What was this law ever made for? Can any one imagine?

Upon this whole subject we may quote the language of Judge Stroud, who thus sums up the whole amount of the protective laws for the slave in the United States of America:—

Upon a fair review of what has been written on the subject of this proposition, the result is found to be—that the master's power to inflict corporal punishment to any extent, short of life and limb, is fully sanctioned by law, in all the slave-holding States; that the master, in at least two States, is expressly protected in using the horse-whip and cowskin as instruments for beating his slave; that he may with entire impunity, in the same States, load his slave with irons, or subject him to perpetual imprisonment, whenever he may so choose; that, for cruelly scalding, wilfully cutting out the tongue, putting out an eye, and for any other dismemberment, if proved, a fine of one hundred pounds currency only is incurred in South Carolina; that, though in all the States the wilful, deliberate, and malicious murder of the slave is now directed to be punished with death, yet, as in the case of a white offender, none except whites can give evidence, a conviction can seldom, if ever, take place.—*Stroud's Sketch,* p. 43.

One very singular antithesis of two laws of Louisiana will still further show that deadness of public sentiment on cruelty to the slave which is an inseparable attendant on the system. It will be recollected that the remarkable *protective* law of South Carolina, with respect to scalding, burning, cutting out the tongue, and putting out the eye of the slave, has been substantially enacted in Louisiana; and that the penalty for a man's doing these things there, if he has not sense enough to do it privately, is not more than five hundred dollars.

Now, compare this other statute of Louisiana (Rev. Stat. 1852, p. 552, § 151):—

If any person or persons,&c., shall cut or break any iron chain or collar, which any master of slaves shall have used, in order to prevent the running away or escape of any such slave or slaves, such person or persons so offending shall, on conviction,&c., be fined not less than two hundred dollars, nor exceeding one thousand dollars [Stroud, p. 41.]; and suffer imprisonment for a term not exceeding two years, nor less than six months.—*Act of Assembly of March* 6, 1819. *Pamphlet,* p. 64.

Some Englishmen may naturally ask, "What is this iron collar which the Legislature have thought worthy of being protected by a special Act?" On this subject will be presented the testimony of an unimpeachable witness, Miss Sarah M. Grimké, a personal friend of the author. "Miss Grimké is a daughter of the late Judge Grimké, of the Supreme Court of South Carolina, and sister of the late Hon. Thomas S. Grimké." She is now a member of the Society of Friends, and resides in Bellville, New Jersey. The statement given is of a kind that its author did not mean to give, nor wish to give, and never would have given, had it not been made necessary to illustrate this passage in the slave-law. The account occurs in a statement which Miss Grimké furnished to her brother-in-law, Mr. Weld, and has been before the public ever since 1839, in his work entitled *Slavery as It is,* p. 22.

A handsome mulatto woman, about eighteen or twenty years of age, whose independent spirit could not brook the degradation of slavery, was in the habit of running away: for this offence she had been repeatedly sent by her master and mistress to be whipped by the keeper of the Charleston workhouse. This had been done with such inhuman severity as to lacerate her back in a most shocking manner; a finger could not be laid between the cuts. But the love of liberty was too strong to be annihilated by torture; and, as a last resort, she was whipped at several different times, and kept a close prisoner. A heavy iron collar, with three long prongs projecting from it, was placed round her neck, and a strong and sound front tooth was extracted, to serve as a mark to describe her, in case of escape. Her sufferings at this time were agonizing; she could lie in no position but on her back, which was sore from scourgings, as I can testify from personal inspection; and her only place of rest was the floor, on a blanket. These outrages were committed in a family where the mistress daily read the Scriptures, and assembled her children for family worship. She was accounted, and was really, so far as almsgiving was concerned, a charitable woman, and tender-hearted to the poor; and yet this suffering slave, who was the seamstress of the family, was continually in her presence, sitting in her chamber to sew, or engaged in her other household work, with her lacerated and bleeding back, her mutilated mouth, and heavy iron collar, without, so far as appeared, exciting any feelings of compassion.

This iron collar the author has often heard of from sources equally authentic. That one will meet with it every day in walking the streets, is not probable; but that it must have been used with some great degree of frequency, is evident from the fact of a law being thought necessary to protect it. But look at the penalty of the two *protective* laws! The fiendish cruelties described in the Act of South Carolina cost the perpetrator not more than five hundred dollars, if he does them before white people. The act of humanity costs from two hundred to one thousand dollars, and imprisonment from six months to two years, according to discretion of Court! What public sentiment was it which made these laws?

CHAPTER VI.

PROTECTIVE ACTS WITH REGARD TO FOOD AND RAIMENT, LABOUR, ETC.

Illustrative Drama of Tom *v.* Legree, under the Law of South Carolina.— Separation of Parent and Child.

HAVING finished the consideration of the laws which protect the life and limb of the slave, the reader may feel a curiosity to know something of the provisions by which he is protected in regard to food and clothing, and from the exactions of excessive labour. It is true, there are multitudes of men in the Northern States who would say, at once, that such enactments, on the very face of them, must be superfluous and absurd. "What!" they say, "are not the slaves property? and is it likely that any man will impair the market value of his own property by not giving them sufficient food or clothing, or by overworking them?" This process of reasoning appears to have been less convincing to the legislators of Southern States than to gentlemen generally at the North; since, as Judge Taylor says, [Wheeler, p. 220. State *v.* Sue, Cameron & Norwood's C. Rep. 54.] "the Act of 1786 (Iredell's Revisal, p. 588) does, in the preamble, recognise the fact, that *many* persons, by cruel treatment of their slaves, cause them to commit crimes for which they are executed; and the judge further explains this language, by saying, "The cruel treatment here alluded to must consist in withholding from them the necessaries of life; and the crimes thus resulting are such as are necessary to furnish them with food and raiment."

The State of South Carolina, in the Act of 1740 (see Stroud's Sketch, p. 28), had a section with the following language in its preamble: [Stroud, p. 29] —

Whereas many owners of slaves, and others who have the care, management, and overseeing of slaves, do confine them so closely to hard labour that they have not sufficient time for natural rest;—

and the law goes on to enact that the slave shall not work more than fifteen hours a day in summer, and fourteen in winter. Judge Stroud makes it appear that in three of the slave States the time allotted for work to convicts in prison, whose punishment is to consist in hard labour, cannot exceed *ten* hours, even in the summer months.

This was the protective Act of South Carolina, designed to reform the abusive practices of masters who confined their slaves so closely that they had not time for natural rest! What sort of habits of thought do these humane provisions show, in the makers of them? In order to protect the slave from what they consider undue exaction, they humanely provide that he shall be obliged to work only four or five hours longer than the convicts in the prison of the neighbouring State! In the Island of Jamaica, besides many holidays which were accorded by law to the slave, ten hours a day was the extent to which he was compelled by law ordinarily to work.—See *Stroud,* p. 29.

With regard to protective Acts concerning food and clothing, Judge Stroud gives the following example from the legislation of South Carolina. The author gives it as quoted by Stroud, p. 32.

In case any person,&c., who shall be the owner or who shall have the care, government, or charge of any slave or slaves, shall deny, neglect, or refuse to allow such slave or slaves,&c., sufficient clothing, covering, or food, it shall and may be lawful for any person or persons, on behalf of such slave or slaves, to make complaint to the next neighbouring justice in the parish where such slave or slaves live, or are usually employed, and the said justice shall summon the party against whom such complaint shall be made, and shall inquire of, hear, and determine the same; and if the said justice shall find the said complaint to be true, or that such person will not exculpate or clear himself from the charge, by his or her own oath, which such person shall be at liberty to do in all cases where positive proof is not given of the offence, such justice shall and may make such orders upon the same, for the relief of such slave or slaves, as he in his discretion shall think fit; and shall and may set and impose a fine or penalty on any person who shall offend in the premises, in any sum not exceeding twenty pounds current money, for each offence. —2 *Brevard's Dig.* 241. Also *Cobb's Dig.* 827.

A similar law obtains in Louisiana.—(Rev. Stat. 1852, p. 557, § 166.)

Now, would not anybody think, from the virtuous solemnity and gravity of this Act, that it was intended in some way to amount to something? Let us give a little sketch, to show how much it does amount to. Angelina Grimké Weld, sister to Sarah Grimké, before quoted, gives the following account of the situation of slaves on plantations:

And here let me say, that the treatment of plantation slaves cannot be fully known, except by the poor sufferers themselves, and their drivers and overseers. In a multitude of instances, even the master can know very little of the actual condition of his own field-slaves, and his wife and daughters far less. A few facts concerning my own family will show this. Our permanent residence was in Charleston; our country seat (Bellemont) was two hundred miles distant, in the north-western part of the State, where, for some years, our family spent a few months annually. Our plantation was three miles from this family mansion. There all the field-slaves lived and worked. Occasionally—once a month, perhaps — some of the family would ride over to the plantation; but I never visited the fields where the slaves were at work, and knew almost nothing of their condition; but this I do know, that the overseers who had charge of them were generally unprincipled and intemperate men. But I rejoice to know that the general treatment of slaves in that region of country was far milder than on the plantations in the lower country.

Throughout all the eastern and middle portions of the State, the planters very rarely reside permanently on their plantations. They have almost invariably *two* residences, and spend less than half the year on their estates. Even while spending a few months on them, politics, field-sports, races, speculations, journeys, visits, company, literary pursuits,&c., absorb so much of their time, that they must, to a considerable extent, take the condition of their slaves on *trust,* from the reports of their overseers. I make this statement, because these slaveholders (the wealthier class) are, I believe, almost the only ones who visit the North with their families; and Northern opinions of slavery are based chiefly on their testimony.

With regard to overseers, Miss Grimké's testimony is further borne out by the universal acknowledgment of Southern owners. A description of this class of beings is furnished by Mr. Wirt, in his life of Patrick Henry, page 34. "Last and lowest," he says [of different classes of society], "a *feculum* of beings called overseers—a most abject, degraded, unprincipled race." Now, suppose, while the master is in Charleston, enjoying literary leisure, the slaves on some Bellemont or other plantation, getting tired of being hungry and cold, form themselves into a committee of the whole, to see what is to be done. A broad-shouldered, courageous fellow, whom we will call Tom, declares it is too bad, and he won't stand it any longer; and having by some means become acquainted with this benevolent protective Act, resolves to make an appeal to the horns of this legislative altar. Tom talks stoutly, having just been bought on to the place, and been used to better quarters elsewhere. The women and children perhaps admire, but the venerable elders of the plantation— Sambo, Cudge, Pomp, and old Aunt Dinah—tell him, "he better mind himself, and keep clar o' dat ar." Tom, being young and progressive, does not regard these conservative maxims; he is determined that, if there be such a thing as justice to be got, he will have it. After considerable research, he finds some white man in the neighbourhood verdant enough to enter the complaint for him. Master Legree finds himself, one sun-shiny, pleasant morning, walked off to some Justice Dogberry's, to answer to the charge of not giving his niggers enough to eat and wear. We will call the infatuated white man who has undertaken this fool's errand Master Shallow. Let us imagine a scene: Legree standing carelessly with his hands in his pockets, rolling a quid of tobacco in his mouth; Justice Dogberry, seated, in all the majesty of law, reinforced by a decanter of whiskey and some tumblers, intended to assist in illuminating the intellect in such obscure cases.

Justice Dogberry. Come, gentlemen, take a little something, to begin with. Mr. Legree, sit down; sit down, Mr.—a what's-your-name?—Mr. Shallow.

Mr. Legree and Mr. Shallow each sit down, and take their tumbler of whiskey and water. After some little conversation, the justice introduces the business as follows:—

"Now, about this nigger business. Gentlemen, you know the Act of —um—um—where the deuce *is* that Act? [*Fumbling an old law-book.*] How plagued did you ever hear of that Act, Shallow? I'm sure I'm forgot all about it; Oh! here 'tis. Well, Mr. Shallow, the Act says you must make proof, you observe.

Mr. Shallow. [*Stuttering and hesitating.*] Good laud! why, don't everybody see that them ar niggers are most starved? Only see how ragged they are!

Justice. I can't say as I've observed it particular. Seem to be very well contented.

Shallow. [*Eagerly.*] But just ask Pomp, or Sambo, or Dinah, or Tom!

Justice Dogberry. [*With dignity.*] I'm astonished at you, Mr. Shallow! You think of producing negro testimony? I hope I know the law better than that! We must have direct proof, you know.

Shallow is posed; Legree significantly takes another tumbler of whiskey and water, and Justice Dogberry gives a long ahe-a-um. After a few moments the justice speaks:—

"Well, after all, I suppose, Mr. Legree, you wouldn't have any objections to swarin' off; that settles it all, you know."

As swearing is what Mr. Legree is rather more accustomed to do than anything else that could be named, a more appropriate termination of the affair could not be suggested; and he swears, accordingly, to any extent, and with any fulness and variety of oath that could be desired; and thus the little affair terminates. But it does not terminate thus for Tom or Sambo, Dinah, or any others who have been alluded to for authority. What will happen to them, when Mr. Legree comes home, had better be left to conjecture.

It is claimed, by the author of certain paragraphs quoted at the commencement of Part II., that there exist in Louisiana ample protective Acts to prevent the separation of young children from their mothers. This writer appears to be in the enjoyment of an amiable ignorance and unsophisticated innocence with regard to the workings of human society generally, which is, on the whole, rather refreshing. For, on a certain incident in "Uncle Tom's Cabin," which represented Cassy's little daughter as having been sold from her, he makes the following *naïve* remark:—

Now, the reader will perhaps be surprised to know that such an incident as the sale of Cassy apart from Eliza, upon which the whole interest of the foregoing narrative hinges, never could have taken place in Louisiana, and that the bill of sale for Eliza would not have been worth the paper it was written on. Observe, George Shelby states that Eliza was eight or nine years old at the time his father purchased her in New Orleans. Let us again look at the statute-book of Louisiana.

In the *Code Noir* we find it set down that—

"Every person is expressly prohibited from selling separately from their mothers the children who shall not have attained the full age of ten years."

And this humane provision is strengthened by a statute, one clause of which runs as follows:—

CHAPTER VI.

"Be it further enacted, that if any person or persons shall sell the mother of any slave child or children under the age of ten years, separate from said child or children, or shall, the mother living, sell any slave child or children of ten years of age or under, separate from said mother, such person or persons shall incur the penalty of the sixth section of this Act."

This penalty is a fine of not less than one thousand nor more than two thousand dollars, and imprisonment in the public jail for a period of not less than six months nor more than one year. —Vide Acts of Louisiana, 1 Session, 9th Legislature, 1828-9, No. 24, section 16. (Rev. Stat. 1850, p. 550, sec. 143.)

What a charming freshness of nature is suggested by this assertion! A thing could not have happened in a certain State, because there is a law against it!

Has there not been for two years a law forbidding to succour fugitives, or to hinder their arrest? and has not this thing been done thousands of times in all the Northern States, and is not it more and more likely to be done every year? What is a law against the whole public sentiment of society? and will anybody venture to say that the public sentiment of Louisiana *practically* goes against separation of families?

But let us examine a case more minutely, remembering the bearing on it of two great foundation principles of slave jurisprudence: namely, that a slave cannot bring a suit in any case, except in a suit for personal freedom, and this in some States must be brought by a guardian; and that a slave cannot bear testimony in any case in which whites are implicated.

Suppose Butler wants to sell Cassy's child of nine years. There is a statute forbidding to sell under ten years; what is Cassy to do? She cannot bring suit. Will the State prosecute? Suppose it does; what then? Butler says the child is ten years old; if he pleases, he will say she is ten and a half, or eleven. What is Cassy to do? She cannot testify; besides, she is utterly in Butler's power. He may tell her that if she offers to stir in the affair, he will whip the child within an inch of its life; and she knows he can do it, and that there is no help for it; he may lock her up in a dungeon, sell her on to a distant plantation, or do any other despotic thing he chooses, and there is nobody to say—Nay.

How much does the protective statute amount to for Cassy? It may be very well as a piece of advice to the public, or as a decorous expression of opinion; but one might as well try to stop the current of the Mississippi with a bulrush as the tide of trade in human beings with such a regulation.

We think that, by this time, the reader will agree with us that the less the defenders of slavery say about protective statutes the better.

CHAPTER VII.
THE EXECUTION OF JUSTICE.
State *v.* Eliza Rowand.—The "Ægis of Protection" to the Slave's Life.

> "We cannot but regard the fact of this trial as a salutary occurrence."
>
> — *Charleston Courier.*

HAVING given some account of what sort of statutes are to be found on the law-books of slavery, the reader will hardly be satisfied without knowing what sort of trials are held under them. We will quote one specimen of a trial, reported in the *Charleston Courier* of May 6th, 1847. The *Charleston Courier* is one of the leading papers of South Carolina, and the case is reported with the utmost apparent innocence that there was anything about the trial that could reflect in the least on the character of the State for the utmost legal impartiality. In fact, the *Charleston Courier* ushers it into public view with the following flourish of trumpets, as something which is for ever to confound those who say that South Carolina does not protect the life of the slave:—

THE TRIAL FOR MURDER.

Our community was deeply interested and excited yesterday, by a case of great importance and also of entire novelty in our jurisprudence. It was the trial of a lady of respectable family and the mother of a large family, charged with the murder of her own or her husband's slave. The court-house was thronged with spectators of the exciting drama, who remained, with unabated interest and undiminished numbers, until the verdict was rendered acquitting the prisoner. We cannot but regard the fact of this trial as a salutary, although in itself lamentable occurrence, as it will show to the world that, however panoplied in station and wealth, and although challenging those sympathies which are the right and inheritance of the female sex, no one will be suffered, in this community, to escape the most sifting scrutiny, at the risk of even an ignominious death, who stands charged with the suspicion of murdering a slave—to whose life our law now extends the ægis of protection, in the same manner as it does to that of the white man, save only in the character of the evidence necessary for conviction or defence. While evil-disposed persons at home are thus taught that they may expect rigorous trial and condign punishment, when, actuated by malignant passions, they invade the life of the humble slave, the enemies of our domestic institution abroad will find, their calumnies to the contrary notwithstanding, that we are resolved in this particular to do the full measure of our duty to the laws of humanity. We subjoin a report of the case.

The proceedings of the trial are thus given:—

TRIAL FOR THE MURDER OF A SLAVE.*State* v. *Eliza Rowand.—Spring Term, May* 5, 1847. Tried before his Honour Judge O'Neall.

The prisoner was brought to the bar and arraigned, attended by her husband and mother, and humanely supported, during the trying scene, by the sheriff, J. B. Irving, Esq. On her arraignment she pleaded "Not Guilty," and for her trial, placed herself upon "God and her country." After challenging John M. Deas, James Bancroft, H. F. Harbers, C. J. Beckman, E. R. Cowperthwaite, Parker J. Holland, Moses D. Hyams, Thomas Glaze, John Lawrence, B. Archer, J. S. Addison, B. P. Colburn, B. M. Jenkins, Carl Houseman, George Jackson, and Joseph Coppenberg, the prisoner accepted the subjoined panel, who were duly sworn, and charged with the case: 1. John L. Nowell, foreman; 2. Elias Whilden; 3. Jesse Coward; 4. Effington Wagner; 5. William Whaley; 6. James Culbert; 7. R. L.

Baker; 8. S. Wiley; 9. W. S. Chisholm; 10. T. M. Howard; 11. John Bickley; 12. John Y. Stock.

The following is the indictment on which the prisoner was arraigned for trial:—

The State v. *Eliza Rowand.—Indictment for Murder of a Slave.*

STATE OF SOUTH CAROLINA,
Charleston District,
to wit:

At a Court of General Sessions, begun and holden in and for the district of Charleston, in the State of South Carolina, at Charleston, in the district and State aforesaid, on Monday, the third day of May, in the year of our Lord one thousand eight hundred and forty-seven:

The jurors of and for the district of Charleston aforesaid, in the State of South Carolina aforesaid, upon their oath present, that Eliza Rowand, the wife of Robert Rowand Esq., not having the fear of God before her eyes, but being moved and seduced by the instigation of the devil, on the sixth day of January, in the year of our Lord one thousand eight hundred and forty-seven, with force and arms, at Charleston, in the district of Charleston, and State aforesaid, in and upon a certain female slave of the said Robert Rowand, named Maria, in the peace of God, and of the said State, then and there being feloniously, maliciously, wilfully, deliberately, and of her malice aforethought, did make an assault; and that a certain other slave of the said Robert Rowand, named Richard, then and there, being then and there in the presence and by the command of the said Eliza Rowand, with a certain piece of wood, which he the said Richard in both his hands then and there had and held, the said Maria did beat and strike in and upon the head of her the said Maria, then and there giving to her the said Maria, by such striking and beating as aforesaid, with the piece of wood aforesaid, divers mortal bruises on the top, back, and sides of the head of her the said Maria, of which several mortal bruises she, the said Maria, then and there instantly died; and that the said Eliza Rowand was then and there present, and then and there feloniously, maliciously, wilfully, deliberately, and of her malice aforethought, did order, command, and require the said slave named Richard the murder and felony aforesaid, in manner and form aforesaid, to do and commit. And as the jurors aforesaid, upon their oaths aforesaid, do say, that the said Eliza Rowand, her the said slave named Maria, in the manner and by the means aforesaid, feloniously, maliciously, wilfully, deliberately, and of her malice aforethought, did kill and murder, against the form of the Act of the General Assembly of the said State in such case made and provided, and against the peace and dignity of the same State aforesaid.

And the jurors aforesaid, upon their oaths aforesaid, do further present, that the said Eliza Rowand, not having the fear of God before her eyes, but being moved and seduced by the instigation of the devil, on the sixth day of January, in the year of our Lord one thousand eight hundred and forty-seven, with force and arms, at Charleston, in the district of Charleston, and State aforesaid, in and upon a certain other female slave of Robert Rowand, named Maria, in the peace of God, and of the said State, then and there being, feloniously, maliciously, wilfully, deliberately, and of her malice aforethought, did make an assault; and that the said Eliza Rowand, with a certain piece of wood, which she, the said Eliza Rowand, in both her hands then and there had and held, her the said last-mentioned slave named Maria did then and there strike, and beat, in and upon the head of her the said Maria, then and there giving to her the said Maria, by such striking and beating aforesaid, with the piece of wood aforesaid, divers mortal bruises, on the top, back, and side of the head, of her the said Maria, of which said several mortal bruises she the said Maria then and there instantly died. And so the jurors aforesaid, upon their oaths aforesaid, do say, that the said Eliza Rowand her the said last-mentioned slave named Maria, in the manner and by the means last mentioned, feloniously, maliciously, wilfully, deliberately, and of her malice aforethought, did kill and murder, against the form of the Act of the General Assembly of the said State in such case made and provided, and against the peace and dignity of the same State aforesaid.

H. BAILEY, Attorney-General.

As some of our readers may not have been in the habit of endeavouring to extract anything like common sense or information from documents so very concisely and luminously worded, the author will just state her own opinion that the above document is intended to charge Mrs. Eliza Rowand with having killed her slave Maria, in one of two ways: either with beating her on the head with her own hands, or having the same deed performed by proxy, by her slave-man Richard. The whole case is now presented. In order to make the reader clearly understand the arguments, it is necessary that he bear in mind that the law of 1740, as we have before shown, punished the murder of the slave only with fine and disfranchisement, while the law of 1821 punishes it with death.

On motion of Mr. Petigru, the prisoner was allowed to remove from the bar, and take her place by her counsel; the Judge saying he granted the motion only because the prisoner was a woman, but that no such privilege would have been extended by him to any man.

The Attorney-General, Henry Bailey, Esq., then rose and opened the case for the State, in substance as follows: he said that, after months of anxiety and expectation, the curtain had at length risen, and he and the jury were about to bear their part in the sad drama of real life, which had so long engrossed the public mind. He and they were called to the discharge of an important, painful, and solemn duty. They were to pass between the prisoner and the State—to take an inquisition of blood; on their decision hung the life or death, the honour or ignominy of the prisoner; yet he trusted he and they would have strength and ability to perform their duty faithfully; and, whatever might be the result, their consciences would be consoled and quieted by that reflection. He bade the jury pause and reflect on the great sanctions and solemn responsibilities under which they were acting. The constitution of the State invested them with power over all that affected the life, and was dear to the family of the unfortunate lady on trial before them. They were charged too, with the sacred care of the law of the land; and to their solution was submitted one of the most solemn questions ever intrusted to the arbitrament of man. They should pursue a direct and straightforward course, turning neither to the right hand nor to the left—influenced neither by prejudice against the prisoner, nor by a morbid sensibility in her behalf. Some of them might practically and personally be strangers to their present duty; but they were all familiar with the laws, and must be aware of the responsibilities of jurymen. It was scarcely necessary to tell them that, if evidence fixed guilt on this prisoner, they should not hesitate to record a verdict of guilty, although they should write that verdict in tears of blood. They should let no sickly sentimentality, or morbid feeling on the subject of capital punishments, deter them from the discharge of their plain and obvious duty. They were to administer, not to make, the law; they were called on to enforce the law, by sanctioning the highest duty to God and to their country. If any of them were disturbed with doubts or scruples on this point, he scarcely supposed they would have gone into the jury-box. The law had awarded capital punishment as the meet retribution for the crime under investigation, and they were sworn to administer that law. It had, too, the full sanction of Holy Writ; we were there told that "the land cannot be cleansed of the blood shed therein, except by the blood of him that shed it." He felt assured, then, that they would be swayed only by a firm resolve to act on this occasion in obedience to the dictates of sound judgments and enlightened consciences. The prisoner, however, had claims on them, as well as the community; she was entitled to a fair and impartial trial. By the wise and humane principles of our law, they were bound to hold the prisoner innocent, and she stood guiltless before them, until proved guilty, by legal, competent, and satisfactory evidence. Deaf alike to the voice of sickly humanity and heated prejudice, they should proceed to their task with minds perfectly equipoised and impartial; they should weigh the circumstances of the case with a nice and careful hand; and if, by legal evidence circumstantial and satisfactory, although not positive, guilt be established, they should unhesitatingly, fearlessly, and faithfully record the result of their convictions. He would next call their attention to certain legal distinctions, but would not say a word of the facts; he would leave *them* to the lips of the witnesses, unaffected by any previous comments of his own. The prisoner stood indicted for the murder of a slave. This was supposed not be murder at common law. At least, it was not murder by our former statute; but the Act of 1821 had placed the killing of the white man and the black man on the same footing. He read the Act of 1821, declaring that "any person who shall wilfully, deliberately, and maliciously murder a slave, shall, on conviction thereof, suffer death without benefit of clergy." The rules applicable to murder at common law were generally applicable, however, to the present case. The inquiries to be made may be reduced to two. 1. Is the party charged guilty of the fact of killing? This must be clearly made out by proof. If she be not guilty of killing, there is an end to the case. 2. The character of that killing, or of the offence. Was it done with malice aforethought? Malice is the essential ingredient of the crime. Where killing takes place, malice is presumed, unless the contrary appear; and this must be gathered from the attending circumstances. Malice is a technical term, importing a different meaning from that conveyed by the same word in common parlance. According to the learned Michael Foster, it consists not in "malevolence to particulars," it does not mean hatred to any particular individual, but is general in its import and application. But even killing, with intention to kill, is not always murder; there may be justifiable and excusable homicide, and killing in sudden heat and passion is so modified to manslaughter. Yet there may be murder when there is no ill-feeling—nay, perfect indifference to the slain—as in the case of the robber who slays to conceal his crime. Malice aforethought is that depraved feeling of the heart, which makes one regardless of social duty, and fatally bent on mischief. It is fulfilled by that recklessness of law and human life which is indicated by shooting into a crowd, and thus doing murder on even an unknown object. Such a feeling the law regards as hateful, and visits, in its practical exhibition, with condign punishment, because opposed to the very existence of law and society. One may do fatal mischief without this recklessness; but when the act is done, regardless of consequences, and death ensues, it is murder in the eye of the law. If the facts to be proved in this case should not come up to these requisitions, he implored the jury to acquit the accused, as at once due to law and justice. They should note every fact with scrutinising eye, and ascertain whether the fatal result proceeded from passing accident or from brooding revenge, which the law stamped with the odious name of malice. He would make no further preliminary remarks, but proceed at once to lay the facts before them, from the mouths of the witnesses.

Evidence.

J. Porteous Deveaux sworn.—He is the coroner of Charleston district; held the inquest on the 7th of January last, on the body of the deceased slave, *Maria,* the slave of Robert Rowand, at the residence of Mrs. T. C. Bee (the mother of the prisoner), in Logan-street. The body was found in an out-building—a kitchen; it was the body of an old and emaciated person, between fifty and sixty years of age; it was not examined in his presence by physicians; saw some few scratches about the face; adjourned to the City Hall. Mrs. Rowand was examined; her examination was in writing; it was here produced and read, as follows:—

"Mrs. Eliza Rowand sworn.—Says Maria is her nurse, and had misbehaved on yesterday morning; deponent sent Maria to Mr. Rowand's house, to be corrected by Simon; deponent sent Maria from the house about seven o'clock, A.M.; she returned to her about nine o'clock; came into her chamber; Simon did not come into the chamber at any time previous to the death of Maria; deponent says Maria fell down in the chamber; deponent had her seated up by Richard, who was then in the chamber, and deponent gave Maria some asafoetida; deponent then left the room; Richard came down and said Maria was dead; deponent says Richard did not strike Maria, nor did any one else strike her in deponent's chamber. Richard left the chamber immediately with deponent; Maria was about fifty-two years of age; deponent sent Maria by Richard to Simon, to Mr. Rowand's house, to be corrected; Mr. Rowand was absent from the city; Maria died about twelve o'clock;

Richard and Maria were on good terms; deponent was in the chamber all the while that Richard and Maria were there together.

"ELIZA ROWAND.

"Sworn to before me this seventh January, 1847. "J. P. DEVEAUX, Coroner, D.C."

Witness went to the chamber of prisoner, where the death occurred; saw nothing particular; some pieces of wood in a box set in the chimney; his attention was called to one piece in particular, eighteen inches long, three inches wide, and about one and a half inch thick; did not measure it; the jury of inquest did; it was not a light-wood knot; thinks it was of oak; there was some pine-wood and some split oak. Doctor Peter Porcher was called to examine the body professionally, who did so out of witness's presence.

Before this witness left the stand, B. F. Hunt, Esq., one of the counsel for the prisoner, rose and opened the defence before the Jury, in substance as follows:—

He said that the scene before them was a very novel one, and whether for, good or evil he would not pretend to prophesy. It was the first time in the history of this State that a lady of good character and respectable connexions stood arraigned at the bar, and had been put on trial for her life, on facts arising out of her domestic relations to her own slave. It was a spectacle consoling and cheering, perhaps, to those who owed no good-will to the institutions of our country, but calculated only to excite pain and regret among ourselves. He would not state a proposition so revolting to humanity as that crime should go unpunished; but judicial interference between the slave and the owner was a matter at once of delicacy and danger. It was the first time he had ever stood between a slave-owner and the public prosecutor, and his sensations were anything but pleasant. This is an entirely different case from homicide between equals in society. Subordination is indispensable where slavery exists, and in this there is no new principle involved. The same principle prevails in every country; on shipboard and in the army a large discretion is always left to the superior. Charges by inferiors against their superiors were always to be viewed with great circumspection at least, and especially when the latter are charged with cruelty or crime against subordinates. In the relation of owner and slave there is an absence of the usual motives for murder, and strong inducements against it on the part of the former. Life is usually taken from avarice or passion. The master gains nothing, but loses much, by the death of a slave; and when he takes the life of the latter deliberately, there must be more than ordinary malice to instigate the deed. The policy of altering the old law of 1740, which punished the killing of a slave with fine and political disfranchisement, was more than doubtful. It was the law of our colonial ancestors; it conformed to their policy, and was approved by their wisdom; and it continued undisturbed by their posterity until the year 1821. It was engrafted on our policy in counteraction of the schemes and machinations, or in deference to the clamours, of those who formed plans for our improvement, although not interested in nor understanding our institutions, and whose interference led to the tragedy of 1822. He here adverted to the views of Chancellor Harper on this subject, who, in his able and philosophical Memoir on Slavery, said —"It is a somewhat singular fact, that when there existed in our State no law for punishing the murder of a slave, other than a pecuniary fine, there were, I will venture to say, at least ten murders of freemen for one murder of a slave. Yet it is supposed that they are less protected than their masters. The change was made in subserviency to the opinions and clamour of others, who were utterly incompetent to form an opinion on the subject; and a wise act is seldom the result of legislation in this spirit. From the fact I have stated it is plain they need less protection. Juries are, therefore, less willing to convict, and it may sometimes happen that the guilty will escape all punishment. Security is one of the compensations of their humble position. We challenge the comparison, that with us there have been fewer murders of slaves than of parents, children, apprentices, and other murders, cruel and unnatural, in society where slavery does not exist."

Such was the opinion of Chancellor Harper on this subject, who had profoundly studied it, and whose views had been extensively read on this continent and in Europe. Fortunately, the jury, he said, were of the country, acquainted with our policy and practice; composed of men too independent and honourable to be led astray by the noise and clamour out of doors. All was now as it should be; at least a Court of justice had assembled to which his client had fled for refuge and safety. Its threshold was sacred; no profane clamours entered there; but legal investigation was had of facts derived from the testimony of sworn witnesses. And this should teach the community to shut their bosoms against sickly humanity, and their ears to imaginary tales of blood and horror, the food of a depraved appetite. He warned the jury that they were to listen to no testimony but that of free white persons, given on oath in open Court. They were to imagine none that came not from them. It was for this that they were selected, their intelligence putting them beyond the influence of unfounded accusations, unsustained by legal proof; of legends of aggravated cruelty, founded on the evidence of negroes, and arising from weak and wicked falsehoods. Were slaves permitted to testify against their owner, it would cut the cord that unites them in peace and harmony, and enable them to sacrifice their masters to their ill-will or revenge. Whole crews had been often leagued to charge captains of vessels with foulest murder, but judicial trial had exposed the falsehood. Truth has been distorted in this case, and murder manufactured out of what was nothing more than ordinary domestic discipline. Chastisement must be inflicted until subordination is produced; and the extent of the punishment is not to be judged by one's neighbours, but by himself. The event in this case has been unfortunate and sad, but there was no motive for the taking of life. There is no pecuniary interest in the owner to destroy his slave; the murder of his slave can only happen from ferocious passions of the master, filling his own bosom with anguish and contrition. This case has no other basis but unfounded rumour, commonly believed, on evidence that will not venture here, the offspring of that passion and depravity which makes up falsehood. The hope of freedom, of change of owners, revenge, are all motives with slave-witnesses to malign their owners; and to credit such testimony would be to dissolve human society. Where deliberate, wilful, and malicious murder is done, whether by male or female, the retribution of the law is a debt to God and man; but the jury should beware lest it fall upon the innocent. The offence charged was not strictly murder at common law. The Act of 1740 was founded on the practical good sense of our old planters, and its spirit still prevails. The Act of 1821 is, by its terms, an Act only to increase the punishment of persons convicted of murdering a slave; and this is a refinement in humanity of doubtful policy. But, by the Act of 1821, the murder must be wilful, deliberate, and malicious; and, when punishment is due to the slave, the master must not be held to strict account for going an inch beyond the mark; whether for doing so he shall be a felon is a question for the jury to solve. The master must conquer a refractory slave; and deliberation, so as to render clear the existence of malice, is necessary to bring the master within the provisions of the Act. He bade the jury remember the words of Him who spake as never man spake—"Let him that has never sinned throw the first stone." They, as masters, might regret excesses to which they have themselves carried punishment. He was not at all surprised at the course of the Attorney-General, it was his wont to treat every case with perfect fairness. He (Colonel H.) agreed that the inquiry should be—

1. Into the fact of the death.
2. The character or motive of the act.

The examination of the prisoner showed conclusively that the slave died a natural death, and not from personal violence. She was chastised with a lawful weapon; was in weak health, nervous, made angry by her punishment; excited. The story was then a plain one; the community had been misled by the creations of imagination, or the statements of interested slaves. The negro came into her mistress's chamber; fell on the floor; medicine was given her; it was supposed she was asleep, but she slept the sleep of death. To show the wisdom and policy of the old Act of 1740 (this indictment is under both Acts, the punishment only altered by that of 1821), he urged that a case like this was not murder at common law, nor is the same evidence applicable at common law. There, murder was presumed from killing; not so in the case of a slave. The Act of 1740 permits a master, when his slave is killed in his presence, there being no other white person present, to exculpate himself by his own oath; and this exculpation is complete, unless clearly contravened by the evidence of two white witnesses. This is exactly what the prisoner has done; she has, as the law permits, by calling on God, exculpated herself. And her oath is good, at least against the slander of her own slaves. Which, then, should prevail—the clamours of others, or the policy of the law established by our colonial ancestors? There would not be a tittle of positive evidence against the prisoner, nothing but circumstantial evidence; and ingenious combination might be made to lead to any conclusion. Justice was all that his client asked. She appealed to liberal and high-minded men, and she rejoiced in the privilege of doing so, to accord her that justice they would demand for themselves.

Mr. Deveaux was not cross-examined.

Evidence resumed.

Dr. E. W. North sworn.—(*Cautioned by Attorney-General to avoid hearsay evidence.*) Was the family physician of Mrs. Rowand. Went on the 6th January, at Mrs. Rowand's request, to see her at her mother's, in Logan-street; found her down stairs in sitting-room; she was in a nervous and excited state; had been so for a month before; he had attended her; she said nothing to witness of slave Maria; found Maria in a chamber, up stairs, about one o'clock P.M.; she was dead; she appeared to have been dead about an hour and a half; his attention was attracted to a piece of pine-wood on a trunk or table in the room; it had a large knot on one end; had it been used on Maria it must have caused considerable contusion; other pieces of wood were in a box, and much smaller ones; the corpse was lying one side in the chamber; it was not laid out; presumed she died there; the marks on the body were, to witness's view, very slight, some scratches about the face; he purposely avoided making an examination; observed no injuries about the head; had no conversation with Mrs. Rowand about Maria; left the house; it was on the 6th January last, the day before the inquest; knew the slave before, but had never attended her.

Cross-examined.—Mrs. Rowand was in feeble health, and nervous; the slave Maria was weak and emaciated in appearance; sudden death of such a person, in such a state, from apoplexy or action of nervous system, not unlikely; her sudden death would not imply violence; had prescribed asafoetida for Mrs. Rowand on a former visit; it is an appropriate remedy for nervous disorders; Mrs. Rowand was not of bodily strength to handle the pine knot so as to give a severe blow; Mrs. Rowand has five or six children, the elder of them large enough to have carried pieces of the wood about the room; there must have been a severe contusion, and much extravasation of blood, to infer death from violence in this case; apoplexy is frequently attended with extravasation of blood; there were two Marias in the family.

In reply.—Mrs. Rowand could have raised the pine knot, but could not have struck a blow with it; such a piece of wood could have produced death, but it would have left its mark; saw the fellow Richard; he was quite capable of giving such a blow.

Dr. Peter Porcher.—Was called in by the coroner's jury to examine Maria's body; found it in the wash-kitchen; it was the corpse of one feeble and emaciated; partly prepared for burial; had the clothes removed; the body was lacerated with stripes; abrasions about face and knuckles; skin knocked of; passed his hand over the head; no bone broken; on request opened her thorax, and examined the viscera; found them healthy; heart unusually so for one of her age; no particular odour; some undigested food; no inflammation; removed the scalp, and found considerable extravasation between scalp and skull; scalp bloodshot; just under the scalp, found the effects of a single blow, just over the right ear; after removing the scalp, lifted the bone; no rupture of any blood-vessel; some softening of the brain in the upper hemisphere; there was considerable extravasation under the scalp, the result of a succession of blows on the top of the head; this extravasation was general, but that over the ear was a single spot; the buttend of a cow-hide would have sufficed for this purpose; an ordinary stick, a heavy one, would have done it; a succession of blows on the head, in a feeble woman, would lead to death, when, in a stronger one, it would not; saw no other appearance about her person to account for her death, except those blows.

Cross-examined.—To a patient in this woman's condition the blows would probably cause death; they were not such as were calculated to kill an ordinary person; witness saw the body twenty-four hours after her death; it was winter, and bitter cold; no disorganisation, and the examination was therefore to be relied on; the blow behind the ear might have resulted from a fall, but not the blow on the top of the head, unless she fell head foremost; came to the conclusion of a succession of blows, from the extent of the extravasation; a single blow would have shown a distinct spot, with a gradual spreading or diffusion; one large blow could not account for it, as the head was spherical; no blood on the brain; the softening of the brain did not amount to much; in an ordinary dissection would have passed it over; anger sometimes produces apoplexy, which results in death; blood between the scalp and the bone of the skull; it was evidently a fresh extravasation; twenty-four hours would scarcely have made any change; knew nothing of this negro before; even after examination, the cause of death is sometimes inscrutable; not usual, however.

In reply.—Does not attribute the softening of the brain to the blows; it was slight, and might have been the result of age; it was some evidence of impairment of vital powers by advancing age.

Dr. A. P. Hayne.—At request of the coroner, acted with Dr. Porcher; was shown into an out-house; saw on the back of the corpse evidences of contusion; arms swollen and enlarged; laceration of body; contusions on head and neck; between scalp and skull extravasation of blood, on the top of head, and behind the right ear; a burn on the hand; the brain presented healthy appearance; opened the body, and no evidences of disease in the chest or viscera; attributed the extravasation of blood to external injury from blows—blows from a large and broad and blunt instrument; attributes the death to those blows; supposes they were adequate to cause death, as she was old, weak, and emaciated.

Cross-examined.—Would not have caused death in a young and robust person.

The evidence for the prosecution here closed, and no witnesses were called for the defence.

The jury were then successively addressed, ably and eloquently, by J. L. Petigru and James S. Rhett, Esqrs., on behalf of the prisoner, and H. Bailey, Esq., on behalf of the State; and by B.F. Hunt, Esq., in reply. Of those speeches, and also of the judge's charge, we have taken full notes, but have neither time nor space to insert them here.

His Honour, Judge O'Neall, then charged the jury eloquently and ably on the facts, vindicating the existing law, making death the penalty for the murder of a slave; but, on the law, intimated to the jury that he held the Act of 1740 so far still in force as to admit of the prisoner's exculpation by her own oath, unless clearly disproved by the oaths of two witnesses; and that they were, therefore, in his opinion, bound to acquit; although he left it to them, wholly, to say whether the prisoner was guilty of murder, killing in sudden heat and passion, or not guilty.

The jury then retired, and, in about twenty or thirty minutes, returned with a verdict of "Not Guilty."

There are some points which appear in this statement of the trial, especially in the plea for the defence. Particular attention is called to the following passage:—

Fortunately (said the lawyer), the jury were of the country; acquainted with our policy and practice; composed of men too honourable to be led astray by the noise and clamour out of doors. All was now as it should be; at least, a court of justice had assembled to which his client had fled for refuge and safety; its threshold was sacred; no profane clamours entered there; but legal investigation was had of facts.

From this it plainly appears that the case was a notorious one; so notorious and atrocious as to break through all the apathy which slave-holding institutions tend to produce, and to surround the court-house with noise and clamour.

From another intimation in the same speech, it would appear that there was abundant testimony of slaves to the direct fact— testimony which left no kind of doubt on the popular mind. Why else does he thus earnestly warn the jury?

He warned the jury that they were to listen to no evidence but that of free white persons, given on oath in open Court; they were to imagine none that came not from them. It was for this that they were selected; their intelligence putting them beyond the influence of unfounded accusations, unsustained by legal proof; of legends of aggravated cruelty, founded on the evidence of negroes, and arising from weak and wicked falsehoods.

See also this remarkable admission: "Truth had been distorted in this case, and murder manufactured out of what was nothing more than ORDINARY DOMESTIC DISCIPLINE." If the reader refers to the testimony, he will find it testified that the woman appeared to be about sixty years old; that she was much emaciated; that there had been a succession of blows on the top of her head, and one violent one over the ear; and that, in the opinion of a surgeon, these blows were sufficient to cause death. Yet the lawyer for the defence coolly remarks that "murder had been *manufactured* out of what was *ordinary domestic discipline*." Are we to understand that beating feeble old women on the head, in this manner, is a specimen of *ordinary domestic discipline* in Charleston? What would have been said if any anti-slavery newspaper at the North had made such an assertion as this? Yet the *Charleston Courier* reports this statement without comment or denial. But let us hear the lady's lawyer go still further in vindication of this ordinary domestic discipline: "Chastisement must be inflicted until subordination is produced; and the extent of the punishment is not to be judged by one's neighbours, but by himself. The event, IN THIS CASE, has been unfortunate and sad." The lawyer admits that the result of thumping a feeble old woman on the head has, *in this case,* been "unfortunate and sad." The old thing had not strength to bear it, and had no greater regard for the convenience of the family and the reputation of "the institution" than to die, and so get the family and the community generally into trouble. It will appear from this that in most cases where old women are thumped on the head, they have stronger constitutions—or more consideration.

Again he says, "When punishment is due to the slave, the master must not be held to strict account *for going an inch beyond the mark.*" And finally, and most astounding of all, comes this: "*He bade the jury remember the words of Him who spake as never man spake*—LET HIM THAT HATH NEVER SINNED THROW THE FIRST STONE. They, as masters, might regret excesses to which they themselves might have carried punishment."

What sort of an insinuation is this? Did he mean to say that almost all the jurymen had probably done things of the same sort, and therefore could have nothing to say in this case? and did no member of the jury get up and resent such a charge? From all that appears, the jury acquiesced in it as quite a matter of course; and the *Charleston Courier* quotes it without comment, in the record of a trial which it says "will show to the world HOW the law extends the ægis of her protection alike over the white man and the humblest slave."

Lastly, notice the decision of the judge, which has become law in South Carolina. What point does it establish? That the simple oath of the master, in face of all circumstantial evidence to the contrary, may clear him, when the murder of a slave is the question. And this trial is paraded as a triumphant specimen of legal impartiality and equity! "If the *light* that is in thee be darkness, how great is that darkness!"

CHAPTER VIII.

THE GOOD OLD TIMES.

"A refinement in humanity of doubtful policy."
— B. F. HUNT.

THE author takes no pleasure in presenting to her readers the shocking details of the following case. But it seems necessary to exhibit what were the actual workings of the ancient law of South Carolina, which has been characterised as one "conformed to the policy, and approved by the wisdom," of the fathers of that State, and the reform of which has been called "a refinement in humanity of doubtful policy."

It is well, also, to add the charge of Judge Wilds, partly for its intrinsic literary merit and the nobleness of its sentiments, but principally because it exhibits such a contrast as could scarcely be found elsewhere between the judge's high and indignant sense of justice and the shameful impotence and imbecility of the laws under which he acted.

The case was brought to the author's knowledge by a letter from a gentleman of Pennsylvania, from which the following is an extract:—

Some time between the years 1807 and 1810, there was lying in the harbour of Charleston a ship commanded by a man named Slater. His crew were slaves; one of them committed some offence, not specified in the narrative. The captain ordered him to be bound and laid upon the deck; and there, in the harbour of Charleston, in the broad daylight, compelled another slave-sailor to chop off his head. The affair was public—notorious. A prosecution was commenced against him; the offence was proved beyond all doubt—perhaps, indeed, it was not denied—and the judge, in a most eloquent charge or rebuke of the defendant, expressed his sincere regret that he could inflict no punishment, under the laws of the State.

I was studying law when the case was published in "Hall's American Law Journal," vol. i. I have not seen the book for twenty-five or thirty years. I may be in error as to names,&c., but while I have life and my senses the facts of the case cannot be forgotten.

CHAPTER VIII.

The following is the "charge" alluded to in the above letter. It was pronounced by the Honourable Judge Wilds, of South Carolina, and is copied from Hall's Law Journal, i. 67:—

John Slater! You have been convicted by a jury of your country of the wilful murder of your own slave; and I am sorry to say, the short, impressive, and uncontradicted testimony on which that conviction was founded, leaves but too little room to doubt its propriety.

The annals of human depravity might be safely challenged for a parallel to this unfeeling, bloody, and diabolical transaction.

You caused your unoffending, unresisting slave to be bound hand and foot, and, by a refinement in cruelty, compelled his companion, perhaps the friend of his heart, to chop his head with an axe, and to cast his body, yet convulsing with the agonies of death, into the water! And this deed you dared to perpetrate in the very harbour of Charleston, within a few yards of the shore, unblushingly, in the face of open day. Had your murderous arm been raised against your equals, whom the laws of self-defence and the more efficacious law of the land unite to protect, your crimes would not have been without precedent, and would have seemed less horrid. Your personal risk would at least have proved that, though a murderer, you were not a coward. But you too well knew that this unfortunate man, whom chance had subjected to your caprice, had not, like yourself, chartered to him by the laws of the land the sacred rights of nature; and that a stern but necessary policy had disarmed him of the rights of self-defence. Too well you knew that to you alone he could look for protection; and that your arm alone could shield him from oppression, or avenge his wrongs; yet that arm you cruelly stretched out for his destruction.

The counsel who generously volunteered his services in your behalf, shocked at the enormity of your offence, endeavoured to find a refuge, as well for his own feelings as for those of all who heard your trial, in a derangement of your intellect. Several witnesses were examined to establish this fact; but the result of their testimony, it is apprehended, was as little satisfactory to his mind as to those of the jury to whom it was addressed. I sincerely wish this defence had proved successful, not from any desire to save you from the punishment which awaits you, and which you so richly merit, but from the desire of saving my country from the foul reproach of having in its bosom such a monster.

From the peculiar situation of this country, our fathers felt themselves justified in subjecting to a very slight punishment he who murders a slave. Whether the present state of society require a continuation of this policy, so opposite to the apparent rights of humanity, it remains for a subsequent legislature to decide. Their attention would ere this have been directed to this subject, but, for the honour of human nature, such hardened sinners as yourself are rarely found to disturb the repose of society. The grand jury of this district, deeply impressed with your daring outrage against the laws both of God and man, have made a very strong expression of their feelings on the subject to the legislature; and, from the wisdom and justice of that body, the friends of humanity may confidently hope soon to see this blackest in the catalogue of human crimes pursued by appropriate punishment.

In proceeding to pass the sentence which the law provides for your offence, I confess I never felt more forcibly the want of power to make respected the laws of my country, whose minister I am. You have already violated the majesty of those laws. You have profanely pleaded the law under which you stand convicted, as a justification of your crime. You have held that law in one hand, and brandished your bloody axe in the other, impiously contending that the *one* gave a license to the unrestrained use of the *other*.

But, though you will go off unhurt in person, by the present sentence, expect not to escape with impunity. Your bloody deed has set a mark upon you, which I fear the good actions of your future life will not efface. You will be held in abhorrence by an impartial world, and shunned as a monster by every honest man. Your unoffending posterity will be visited, for your iniquity, by the stigma of deriving their origin from an unfeeling murderer. Your days, which will be but few, will be spent in wretchedness; and if your conscience be not steeled against every virtuous emotion, if you be not entirely abandoned to hardness of heart, the mangled, mutilated corpse of your murdered slave will ever be present in your imagination, obtrude itself into all your amusements, and haunt you in the hours of silence and repose.

But, should you disregard the reproaches of an offended world, should you hear with callous insensibility the gnawings of a guilty conscience, yet remember, I charge you, remember, that an awful period is fast approaching, and with you is close at hand, when you must appear before a tribunal whose want of power can afford you no prospect of impunity; when you must raise your bloody hands at the bar of an impartial omniscient Judge! Remember, I pray you, remember, whilst yet you have time, that God is just, and that his vengeance will not sleep for ever!

The penalty that followed this solemn denunciation was a fine of *seven hundred pounds,* current money, or, in default of payment, imprisonment for seven years.

And yet it seems that there have not been wanting those who consider the reform of this law "*a refinement in humanity of doubtful policy!*" To this sentiment, so high an authority as that of Chancellor Harper is quoted, as the reader will see by referring to the speech of Mr. Hunt in the last chapter. And, as is very common in such cases, the old law is vindicated as being, on the whole, a surer protection to the life of the slave than the new one. From the results of the last two trials, there would seem to be a fair show of plausibility in the argument; for under the old law it seems that Slater had at least to pay seven hundred pounds, while under the new Eliza Rowand comes off with only the penalty of "a most sifting scrutiny."

Thus it appears that the penalty of the law goes with the murderer of the slave.

How is it executed in the cases which concern the life of the master? Look at this short notice of a recent trial of this kind, which is given in the *Alexandria*

(Virginia) *Gazette* of October 23, 1852, as an extract from the *Charleston* (Virginia) *Free Press:*—

TRIAL OF NEGRO HENRY.

The trial of this slave for an attack, with intent to kill, on the person of Mr. Harrison Anderson, was commenced on Monday and concluded on Tuesday evening. His Honour, Braxton Davenport, Esq., chief justice of the county, with four associate gentlemen justices, composed the Court.

The commonwealth was represented by its attorney, Charles B. Harding, Esq., and the accused ably and eloquently defended by Wm. C. Worthington, and John A. Thompson, Esqrs. The evidence of the prisoner's guilt was conclusive. A majority of the Court thought that he ought to suffer the extreme penalty of the law; but, as this required a unanimous agreement, he was sentenced to receive 500 lashes, not more than thirty-nine at one time. The physician of the gaol was instructed to see that they should not be administered too frequently, and only when, in his opinion, he could bear them.

In another paper we are told that the *Free Press* says:—

A majority of the Court thought that he ought to suffer the extreme penalty of the law; but, as this required a unanimous agreement, he was sentenced to receive 500 lashes, not more than thirty-nine at any one time. The physician of the gaol was instructed to see that they should not to be administered too frequently, and *only* when, in his opinion, he could bear them. This *may seem* to be harsh and inhuman punishment; but when we take into consideration that it is in accordance with the *law of the land,* and the further fact that the insubordination among the slaves of that State has become truly alarming, we cannot question the righteousness of the judgment.

Will anybody say that the master's life is in more danger from the slave than the slave's from the master, that this disproportionate retribution is meted out? Those who countenance such legislation will do well to ponder the solemn words of an ancient book, inspired by One who is no respecter of persons:—

> "If I have refused justice to my man-servant or maid-servant,
> When they had a cause with me,
> What shall I do when God riseth up?
> And when He visiteth, what shall I answer him?
> Did not He that made me in the womb make him?
> Did not the same God fashion us in the womb?"
> JOB xxxi. 13—1

CHAPTER IX.

MODERATE CORRECTION AND ACCIDENTAL DEATH— STATE V. CASTLEMAN.

THE author remarks that the record of the following trial was read by her a little time before writing the account of the death of Uncle Tom. The shocking particulars haunted her mind and were in her thoughts when the following sentence was written:—

What man has nerve to do, man has not nerve to hear. What brother man and brother Christian must suffer, cannot be told us, even in our secret chamber, it so harrows up the soul. And yet, O my country, these things are done under the shadow of thy laws! O Christ, thy church sees them almost in silence!

It is given precisely as prepared by Dr. G. Bailey, the very liberal and fair-minded editor of the *National Era.*

From the "National Era," Washington, November 6, 1851. HOMICIDE CASE IN CLARKE COUNTY, VIRGINIA.

Some time since, the newspapers of Virginia contained an account of a horrible tragedy, enacted in Clarke County, of that State. A slave of Colonel James Castleman, it was stated, had been chained by the neck, and whipped to death by his master, on the charge of stealing. The whole neighbourhood in which the transaction occurred was incensed; the Virginia papers abounded in denunciations of the cruel act; and the people of the North were called upon to bear witness to the justice which would surely be meted in a slave State to the master of a slave. We did not publish the account. The case was horrible; it was, we were confident, exceptional; it should not be taken as evidence of the general treatment of slaves; we chose to delay any notice of it till the courts should pronounce their judgment, and we could announce at once the crime and its punishment, so that the State might stand acquitted of the foul deed.

Those who were so shocked at the transaction will be surprised and mortified to hear that the actors in it have been tried and acquitted; and when they read the following account of the trial and verdict published at the instance of the friends of the accused, their mortification will deepen into bitter indignation.

From the "Spirit of Jefferson."

CHAPTER IX.

"COLONEL JAMES CASTLEMAN.—The following statement, understood to have been drawn up by counsel, since the trial, has been placed by the friends of this gentleman in our hands for publication.

"At the Circuit Superior Court of Clarke County, commencing on the 13th of October, Judge Samuels presiding, James Castleman and his son Stephen D. Castleman were indicted jointly for the murder of negro Lewis, property of the latter. By advice of their counsel, the parties elected to be tried separately, and the attorney for the commonwealth directed that James Castleman should be tried first.

"It was proved on this trial, that for many months previous to the occurrence the money drawer of the tavern kept by Stephen D. Castleman, and the liquors kept in large quantities in his cellar, had been pillaged from time to time, until the thefts had attained to a considerable amount. Suspicion had, from various causes, been directed to Lewis, and another negro, named Reuben (a blacksmith), the property of James Castleman; but by the aid of two of the house-servants they had eluded the most vigilant watch.

"On the 20th of August last, in the afternoon, S. D. Castleman accidentally discovered a clue, by means of which, and through one of the house-servants implicated, he was enabled fully to detect the depredators, and to ascertain the manner in which the theft had been committed. He immediately sent for his father, living near him, and after communicating what he had discovered, it was determined that the offenders should be punished at once, and before they should know of the discovery that had been made.

"Lewis was punished first; and in a manner, as was fully shown, to preclude all risk of injury to his person, by stripes with a broad leathern strap. He was punished severely, but to an extent by no means disproportionate to his offence; nor was it pretended in any quarter that this punishment implicated either his life or health. He confessed the offence, and admitted that it had been effected by false keys furnished by the blacksmith Reuben.

"The latter servant was punished immediately afterwards. It was believed that he was the principal offender, and he was found to be more obdurate and contumacious than Lewis had been in reference to the offence. Thus it was proved, both by the prosecution and the defence, that he was punished with greater severity than his accomplice. It resulted in a like confession on his part, and he produced the false key, one fashioned by himself, by which the theft had been effected.

"It was further shown, on the trial, that Lewis was whipped in the upper room of a warehouse, connected with Stephen Castleman's store, and near the public road, where he was at work at the time; that after he had been flogged, to secure his person, whilst they went after Reuben, he was confined by a chain around his neck, which was attached to a joist above his head. The length of this chain, the breadth and thickness of the joist, its height from the floor, and the circlet of chain on the neck, were accurately measured; and it was thus shown that the chain unoccupied by the circlet and the joist was a foot and a half longer than the space between the shoulders of the man and the joist above, or to that extent the chain hung loose above him; that the circlet (which was fastened so as to prevent its contraction) rested on the shoulders and breast, the chain being sufficiently drawn only to prevent being slipped over his head, and that there was no other place in the room to which he could be fastened, except to one of the joists above. His hands were tied in front; a white man who had been at work with Lewis during the day was left with him by the Messrs. Castleman, the better to insure his detention, whilst they were absent after Reuben. It was proved by this man (who was a witness for the prosecution) that Lewis asked for a box to stand on, or for something that he could jump off from; that after the Castlemans had left him he expressed a fear that when they came back he would be whipped again; and said, if he had a knife, and could get one hand loose, he would cut his throat. The witness stated that the negro 'stood firm on his feet,' that he could turn freely in whatever direction he wished, and that he made no complaint of the mode of his confinement. This man stated that he remained with Lewis about half an hour, and then left there to go home.

"After punishing Reuben, the Castlemans returned to the warehouse, bringing him with them; their object being to confront the two men, in the hope that by further examination of them jointly, all their accomplices might be detected.

"They were not absent more than half an hour. When they entered the room above, Lewis was found hanging by the neck, his feet thrown behind him, his knees a few inches from the floor, and his head thrown forward—the body warm and supple (or relaxed), but life was extinct.

"It was proved by the surgeons who made a post-mortem examination before the coroner's inquest, that the death was caused by strangulation by hanging; and other eminent surgeons were examined to show, from the appearance of the brain and its blood-vessels after death (as exhibited at the post-mortem examination), that the subject could not have fainted before strangulation.

"After the evidence was finished on both sides, the jury from their box and of their own motion, without a word from counsel on either side, informed the Court that they had agreed upon their verdict. The counsel assented to its being thus received, and a verdict of "Not Guilty" was immediately rendered. The attorney for the commonwealth then informed the Court that all the evidence for the prosecution had been laid before the jury; and as no new evidence could be offered on the trial of Stephen D. Castleman, he submitted to the Court the propriety of entering a *nolle prosequi*. The judge replied that the case had been fully and fairly laid before the jury upon the evidence; that the Court was not only satisfied with the verdict, but, if any other had been rendered, it must have been set aside; and that if no further evidence was to be adduced on the trial of Stephen, the attorney for the commonwealth would exercise a proper discretion in entering a *nolle prosequi* as to him, and the Court would approve of its being done. A *nolle prosequi* was entered accordingly, and both gentlemen discharged.

"It may be added that two days were consumed in exhibiting the evidence, and that the trial was by a jury of Clarke County. Both the parties had been on bail from the time of their arrest, and were continued on bail whilst the trial was depending.'

Let us admit that the evidence does not prove the legal crime of homicide: what candid man can doubt, after reading this *ex parte* version of it, that the slave died in consequence of the punishment inflicted upon him?

In criminal prosecutions the federal constitution guarantees to the accused the right to a public trial by an impartial jury; the right to be informed of the nature and cause of the accusation; to be confronted with the witnesses against him; to have compulsory process for obtaining witness in his favour; and to have the assistance of counsel; guarantees necessary to secure innocence against hasty or vindictive judgment—absolutely necessary to prevent injustice. Grant that they were not intended for slaves; every master of a slave must feel that they are still morally binding upon him. He is the sole judge; he alone determines the offence, the proof requisite to establish it, and the amount of the punishment. The slave, then, has a peculiar claim upon him for justice. When charged with a crime, common humanity requires that he should be informed of it—that he should be confronted with the witnesses against him—that he should be permitted to show evidence in favour of his innocence.

But how was poor Lewis treated? The son of Castleman said he had discovered who stole the money; and it was forthwith "determined that the offenders should be punished at once, and before they should know of the discovery that had been made." Punished without a hearing! Punished on the testimony of a house-servant, the nature of which does not appear to have been inquired into by the Court! Not a word is said which authorises the belief that any careful examination was made as it respects their guilt. Lewis and Reuben were assumed, on loose evidence, without deliberate investigation, to be guilty; and then, without allowing them to attempt to show their evidence, they were whipped until a confession of guilt was extorted by bodily pain.

Is this Virginia justice?

Lewis was punished with a "broad leathern strap;" he was "punished severely:" this we do not need to be told. A "broad leathern strap" is well adapted to severity of punishment. "Nor was it pretended," the account says, "in any quarter that this punishment implicated either his life or his health." This is false; it was expressly stated in the newspaper accounts at the time, and such was the general impression in the neighbourhood, that the punishment did very severely implicate his life. But more of this anon.

Lewis was left. A chain was fastened around his neck, so as not to choke him, and secured to the joist above, leaving a slack of about a foot and a half. Remaining in an upright position, he was secure against strangulation, but he could neither sit nor kneel; and should he faint he would be choked to death. The account says that they fastened him thus for the purpose of securing him. If this had been the sole object, it could have been accomplished by safer and less cruel methods, as every reader must know. This mode of securing him was intended probably to intimidate him, and, at the same time, afforded some gratification to the vindictive feeling which controlled the actors in this foul transaction. The man whom they left to watch Lewis said that, after remaining there about half an hour, he went home; and Lewis was then alive. The Castlemans say that, after punishing Reuben, they returned, having been absent not more than half an hour, and they found him hanging by the neck, dead. We direct attention to this part of the testimony to show how loose the statements were which went to make up the evidence.

Why was Lewis chained at all, and a man left to watch him? "To secure him," say the Castlemans. Is it customary to chain slaves in this manner, and set a watch over them, after severe punishment, to prevent their running away? If the punishment of Lewis had not been unusual, and if he had not been threatened with another infliction on their return, there would have been no necessity for chaining him.

The testimony of the man left to watch represents him as desperate, apparently with pain and fright. "Lewis asked for a box to stand on." Why? Was he not suffering from pain and exhaustion, and did he not wish to rest himself without danger of slow strangulation? Again: he asked for "something he could jump off from." "After the Castlemans left, he expressed a fear when they came back that he would be whipped again; and said, if he had a knife, and could get one hand loose, he would cut his throat."

The punishment that could drive him to such desperation must have been horrible.

How long they were absent we know not, for the testimony on this point is contradictory. They found him hanging by the neck, dead, "his feet thrown behind him, his knees a few inches from the floor, and his head thrown forward;" just the position he would naturally fall into had he sunk from exhaustion. They wish it to appear that he hung himself. Could this be proved (we need hardly say that it is not) it would relieve but slightly the dark picture of their guilt. The probability is that he sank, exhausted by suffering, fatigue, and fear. As to the testimony of "surgeons," founded upon a post-mortem examination of the brain and blood-vessels, "that the subject could not have fainted before strangulation," it is not worthy of consideration. We know something of the fallacies and fooleries of such examinations.

From all we can learn; the only evidence relied on by the prosecution was that white man employed by the Castlemans. He was dependent upon them for work. Other evidence might have been obtained; why it was not is for the prosecuting attorney to explain. To prove what we say, and to show that justice has not been done in this horrible affair, we publish the following communication from an old and highly-respectable citizen of this place, and who is very far from being an Abolitionist. The slaveholders whom he mentions are well known here, and would have promptly appeared in the case had the prosecution, which was aware of their readiness, summoned them.

"*To the Editor of the Era.*

CHAPTER IX.

"I see that Castleman, who lately had a trial for whipping a slave to death, in Virginia, was 'triumphantly acquitted'—as many expected. There are three persons in this city, with whom I am acquainted, who stayed at Castleman's the same night in which this awful tragedy was enacted. They heard the dreadful lashing and the heart-rending screams and entreaties of the sufferer. They implored the only white man they could find on the premises, not engaged in the bloody work, to interpose; but for a long time he refused, on the ground that he was a dependant, and was afraid to give offence; and that, moreover, they had been drinking, and he was in fear for his own life, should he say a word that would be displeasing to them. He did, however, venture, and returned and reported the cruel manner in which the slaves were chained, and lashed, and secured in a blacksmith's vice. In the morning, when they ascertained that one of the slaves was dead, they were so shocked and indignant that they refused to eat in the house, and reproached Castleman with his cruelty. He expressed his regret that the slave had died, and especially as he had ascertained that he was innocent of the accusation for which he had suffered. The idea was that he had fainted from exhaustion; and, the chain being round his neck, he was strangled. The persons I refer to are themselves slaveholders—but their feelings were so harrowed and lacerated that they could not sleep (two of them are ladies); and for many nights afterwards their rest was disturbed, and their dreams made frightful, by the appalling recollection.

"These persons would have been material witnesses, and would have willingly attended on the part of the prosecution. The knowledge they had of the case was communicated to the proper authorities, yet their attendance was not required. The only witness was that dependant who considered his own life in danger.

"Yours,&c., J. F."

The account, as published by the friends of the accused parties, shows a case of extreme cruelty. The statements made by our correspondent prove that the truth has not been fully revealed, and that justice has been baffled. The result of the trial shows how irresponsible is the power of a master over his slave; and that, whatever security the latter has, is to be sought in the humanity of the former, not in the guarantees of law. Against the cruelty of an inhuman master he has really no safeguard.

Our conduct in relation to this case, deferring all notice of it in our columns till a legal investigation could be had, shows that we are not disposed to be captious towards our slaveholding countrymen. In no unkind spirit have we examined this lamentable case; but we must expose the utter repugnance of the slave system to the proper administration of justice. The newspapers of Virginia generally publish the account from the "Spirit of Jefferson," without comment. They are evidently not satisfied that justice was done; they, doubtless, will deny that the accused were guilty of homicide, legally; but they will not deny that they were guilty of an atrocity which should brand them for ever in a Christian country.

CHAPTER X.

PRINCIPLES ESTABLISHED—STATE V. LEGREE; A CASE NOT IN THE BOOKS.

FROM a review of all the legal cases which have hitherto been presented, and of the principles established in the judicial decisions upon them, the following facts must be apparent to the reader:—

First. That masters do, now and then, kill slaves by the torture.

Second. That the fact of so killing a slave is not of itself held presumption of murder in slave jurisprudence.

Third. That the slave in the act of resistance to his master may always be killed.

From these things it will be seen to follow that, if the facts of the death of Tom had been fully proved by two white witnesses in open court, Legree could not have been held by any *consistent* interpreter of slave-law to be a murderer, for Tom was in the act of resistance to the will of his master. His master had laid a command on him in the presence of other slaves. Tom had deliberately refused to obey the command. The master commenced chastisement, to reduce him to obedience. And it is evident, at the first glance, to every one, that if the law does not sustain him in enforcing obedience in such a case, there is an end of the whole slave power. No Southern Court would dare to decide that Legree did wrong to continue the punishment as long as Tom continued the insubordination. Legree stood by him every moment of the time, pressing him to yield, and offering to let him go as soon as he did yield. Tom's resistance was *insurrection.* It was an example which could not be allowed for a moment on any Southern plantation. By the express words of the constitution of Georgia, and by the understanding and usage of all slave-law, the power of life and death is always left in the hands of the master, in exigencies like this. This is not a case like that of Souther *v.* the Commonwealth. The victim of Souther was not in a state of resistance or insurrection. The punishment, in his case, was a simple vengeance for a past offence, and not an attempt to reduce him to subordination.

There is no principle of slave jurisprudence by which a man could be pronounced a murderer, for acting as Legree did, in his circumstances. Everybody must see that such an admission would strike at the foundations of the slave system. To be sure, Tom was in a state of insurrection for conscience's sake. But the law does not, and cannot, contemplate that the negro shall have a conscience independent of his master's. To allow that the negro may refuse to obey his master whenever he thinks that obedience would be wrong, would be to produce universal anarchy. If Tom had been allowed to disobey his master in this case, for conscience's sake, the next day Sambo would have had a case of conscience, and Quimbo the next. Several of them might very justly have thought that it was a sin to work as they did. The mulatto woman would have remembered that the command of God forbade her to take another husband. Mothers might have considered that it was more their duty to stay at home and take care of their children, when they were young and feeble, than to work for Mr. Legree in the cotton-field. There would be no end to the havoc made upon cotton-growing operations, were the negro allowed the right of maintaining his own conscience on moral subjects. If the slave system is a right system, and ought to be maintained, Mr. Legree ought not to be blamed for his conduct in this case; for he did only what was absolutely essential to maintain the system; and Tom died in fanatical and foolhardy resistance to “the powers that be, which are ordained of God.” He followed a sentimental impulse of his desperately depraved heart, and neglected those “solid teachings of the written word,” which, as recently elucidated, have proved so refreshing to eminent political men.

CHAPTER XI.

THE TRIUMPH OF JUSTICE OVER LAW.

HAVING been obliged to record so many trials in which justice has been turned away backward by the hand of law, and equity and common humanity have been kept out by the bolt and bar of logic, it is a relief to the mind to find one recent trial recorded in North Carolina, in which the nobler feelings of the human heart have burst over formalised limits, and where the prosecution appears to have been conducted by *men* who were not ashamed of possessing in their bosoms that very dangerous and most illogical agitator, a human heart. It is true that, in giving this trial, very sorrowful but inevitable inferences will force themselves upon the mind, as to that state of public feeling which allowed such outrages to be perpetrated in open daylight, in the capital of North Carolina, upon a hapless woman. It would seem that the public were too truly instructed in the awful doctrine pronounced by Judge Ruffin, that "THE POWER OF THE MASTER MUST BE ABSOLUTE," to think of interfering while the poor creature was dragged barefoot and bleeding at a horse's neck, at the rate of five miles an hour, through the streets of Raleigh. It seems, also, that the most horrible brutalities and enormities that could be conceived of were *witnessed,* without any efficient interference, by a number of the citizens, among whom we see the name of the Hon. W. H. Haywood, of Raleigh. It is a comfort to find the Attorney-General in this case speaking as a man ought to speak. Certainly there can be no occasion to wish to pervert or overstate the dread workings of the slave system, or to leave out the few comforting and encouraging features, however small the encouragement of them may be.

The case is now presented, as narrated from the published reports by Dr. Bailey, editor of the *National Era,* a man whose candour and fairness need no indorsing, as every line that he writes speaks for itself.

The reader may at first be surprised to find slave testimony in the Court, till he recollects that it is a slave that is on trial, the testimony of slaves being only null when it concerns whites,

AN INTERESTING TRIAL.

CHAPTER XI.

We find in one of the Raleigh (North Carolina) papers, of June 5, 1851, a report of an interesting trial, at the spring term of the Superior Court. Mima, a slave, was indicted for the murder of her master, William Smith, of Johnston County, on the night of the 29th of November, 1850. The evidence for the prosecution was Sydney, a slave-boy, twelve years old, who testified that, in the night, he and a slave-girl, named Jane, were roused from sleep by the call of their master, Smith, who had returned home. They went out, and found Mima tied to his horse's neck, with two ropes, one round her neck, the other round her hands. Deceased carried her into the house, jerking the rope fastened to her neck, and tied her to a post. He called for something to eat, threw her a piece of bread, and, after he had done, beat her on her naked back with a large piece of light-wood, giving her many hard blows. In a short time, deceased went out of the house, for a special purpose, witness accompanying him with a torch-light, and hearing him say that he intended "to use the prisoner up." The light was extinguished, and he re-entered the house for the purpose of lighting it. Jane was there; but the prisoner had been untied, and was not there. While lighting his torch, he heard blows outside, and heard the deceased cry out, two or three times, "O Leah! O Leah!" Witness and Jane went out, saw the deceased bloody and struggling, were frightened, ran back, and shut themselves up. Leah, it seems, was mother of the prisoner, and had run off two years, on account of cruel treatment by the deceased.

Smith was speechless and unconscious till he died, the following morning, of the wounds inflicted on him.

It was proved on the trial that Carroll, a white man, living about a mile from the house of the deceased, and whose wife was said to be the illegitimate daughter of Smith, had in his possession, the morning of the murder, the receipt given the deceased by Sheriff High the day before, for jail fees, and a note for thirty-five dollars, due deceased from one Wiley Price, which Carroll collected a short time thereafter; also the chest keys of the deceased; and no proof was offered to show how Carroll came into possession of these articles.

The following portion of the testimony discloses facts so horrible, and so disgraceful to the people who tolerated, in broad daylight, conduct which would have shamed the devil, that we copy it just as we find it in the Raleigh paper. The scene, remember, is the city of Raleigh.

"The defence was then opened. James Harris, C. W. D. Hutchings and Hon. W. H. Haywood, of Raleigh; John Cooper, of Wake; Joseph Hane and others, of Johnston, were examined for the prisoner. The substance of their testimony was as follows:—On the forenoon of Friday, 29th of November last, deceased took prisoner from Raleigh jail, tied her round the neck and wrist; ropes were then latched to the horse's neck; he cursed the prisoner several times, got on his horse, and started off. When he got opposite the Telegraph-office, on Fayetteville-street, he pulled her shoes and stockings off, cursed her again, went off in a swift trot, the prisoner running after him, doing apparently all she could to keep up; passed round by Peck's store; prisoner seemed very humble and submissive; took down the street east of the Capitol, going at the rate of five miles an hour; continued this gait until he passed O. Rork's corner, about half or three-quarters of a mile from the Capitol; that he reached Cooper's (one of the witnesses), thirteen miles from Raleigh, about four o'clock, P.M.; that it was raining very hard; deceased got off his horse, turned it loose with prisoner tied to its neck; witness went to take deceased's horse to stable; heard great lamentations at the house; hurried back; saw his little daughter running through the rain from the house, much frightened; got there; deceased was gouging prisoner in the eyes, and she making outcries; made him stop; became vexed, and insisted upon leaving; did leave in a short time, in the rain, sun about an hour high; when he left prisoner was tied as she was before; her arms and fingers were very much swollen; the rope around her wrist was small, and had sunk deep into the flesh, almost covered with it; that around the neck was large, and tied in a slip-knot; deceased would jerk it every now and then; when jerked it would choke prisoner; she was barefoot and bleeding; deceased was met some time after dark, in about six miles of home, being twenty-four or twenty-five from Raleigh."

Why did they not strike the monster to the earth, and punish him for his infernal brutality?

The Attorney-general conducted the prosecution with evident loathing. The defence argued, first, that the evidence was insufficient to fasten the crime upon the prisoner; secondly, that, should the jury be satisfied beyond a rational doubt that the prisoner committed the act charged, it would yet be only manslaughter.

"A single blow between equals would mitigate a killing instanter from murder to manslaughter. It could not, in law, be anything more, if done under the *furor brevis* of passion; but the rule was different as between master and slave. It was necessary that this should be, to preserve the subordination of the slave. The prisoner's counsel then examined the authorities at length, and contended that the prisoner's case came within the rule laid down in the State *v.* Will (1 Dev. and Bat. 121). The rule there given by Judge Gaston is this: 'If a slave, in defence of his life, and under circumstances strongly calculated to excite his passions of terror and resentment, kill his overseer or master, the homicide is, by such circumstances, mitigated to manslaughter.' The cruelties of the deceased to the prisoner were grievous and long-continued; they would have shocked a barbarian. The savage loves and thirsts for blood, but the arts of civilized life have not afforded him such refinement of torture as was here exhibited."

The Attorney-general, after discussing the law, appealed to the jury "not to suffer the prejudice which the counsel for the defence had attempted to create against the deceased (whose conduct he admitted was disgraceful to human nature) to influence their judgments in deciding whether the act of the prisoner was criminal or not, and what degree of criminality attached to it. He desired the prisoner to have a fair and impartial trial. He wished her to receive the benefit of every rational doubt. It was her right, however humble her condition; he hoped he had not that heart, as he certainly had not the right, by virtue of his office, to ask in her case for anything more than he would ask for the highest and proudest of the land on trial, that the jury should decide according to the evidence, and vindicate the violated law."

These were honourable sentiments.

After an able charge by Judge Ellis, the jury retired, and after having remained out several hours, returned with a verdict of NOT GUILTY. Of course, we see not how they could hesitate to come to this verdict at once.

The correspondent who furnishes the *Register* with a report of the case, says,

"It excited an intense interest in the community in which it occurred, and, although it developes a series of cruelties shocking to human nature, the result of the trial, nevertheless, vindicates the benignity and justice of our laws towards that class of our population whose condition Northern fanaticism has so carefully and grossly misrepresented, for their own purposes of selfishness, agitation, and crime."

We have no disposition to misrepresent the condition of the slaves, or to disparage the laws of North Carolina; but we ask, with a sincere desire to know the truth, Do the *laws* of North Carolina allow a master to practise such horrible cruelties upon his slaves as Smith was guilty of? and would the *public sentiment* of the city of Raleigh permit a repetition of such enormities as were perpetrated in its streets, in the light of day, by that miscreant?

In conclusion, as the accounts of these various trials contain so many shocking incidents and particulars, the author desires to enter a caution against certain mistaken uses which may be made of them, by well-intending persons. The crimes themselves, which form the foundation of the trials, are not to be considered and spoken of as specimens of the *common* working of the slave system. They are, it is true, the logical and legitimate fruits of a system which makes every individual owner an irresponsible despot. But the actual number of them, compared with the whole number of masters, we take pleasure in saying, is small. It is an injury to the cause of freedom to ground the argument against slavery upon the *frequency* with which such scenes as these occur. It misleads the popular mind as to the real issue of the subject. To hear many men talk, one would think that they supposed that unless negroes actually were whipped or burned alive, at the rate of two or three dozen a week, there was no harm in slavery. They seem to see nothing in the system, but its gross bodily abuses. If these are absent, they think there is no harm in it. They do not consider that the twelve hours' torture of some poor victim, bleeding away his life, drop by drop, under the hands of a SOUTHER, is only a symbol of that more atrocious process by which the divine, immortal soul is mangled, burned, lacerated, thrown down, stamped upon, and suffocated, by the fiend-like force of the tyrant Slavery. And as, when the torturing work was done, and the poor soul flew up to the judgment-seat, to stand there in awful witness, there was not a vestige of humanity left in that dishonoured body, nor anything by which it could be said, "See, this was a man!"—so, when Slavery has finished her legitimate work upon the soul, and trodden out every spark of manliness, and honour, and self-respect, and natural affection, and conscience, and religious sentiment, then there is nothing left *in the soul,* by which to say, "This was a man!"— and it becomes necessary for judges to construct grave legal arguments to prove that the slave is a human being.

Such *extreme* cases of bodily abuse from the despotic power of slavery are comparatively rare. Perhaps they may be paralleled by cases brought to light in the criminal jurisprudence of other countries. They might, perhaps, have happened anywhere; at any rate, we will concede that they might. But where under the sun did *such* TRIALS, of such cases, ever take place, in any nation professing to be free and Christian? The reader of English history will, perhaps, recur to the trials under Judge Jeffreys as a parallel. A moment's reflection will convince him that there is no parallel between the cases. The decisions of Jeffreys were the decisions of a monster, who violently wrested law from its legitimate course to gratify his own fiendish nature. The decisions of American slave-law have been, for the most part, the decisions of honourable and humane men, who have wrested from their natural course the most humane feelings, to fulfil the mandates of a cruel law.

In the case of Jeffreys, the sacred forms of the administration of justice were violated. In the case of the American decisions, every form has been maintained. Revolting to humanity as these decisions appear, they are strictly logical and legal.

Therefore, again, we say, Where, ever, in any nation professing to be civilised and Christian, did *such* TRIALS of *such cases* take place? When were ever *such* legal arguments made? When, ever, such legal principles judicially affirmed? Was ever such a trial held in England as that in Virginia, of SOUTHER *v.* THE COMMONWEALTH? Was it ever necessary in England for a judge to declare on the bench, contrary to the opinion of a lower Court, that the death of an apprentice, by twelve hours' torture from his master, *did* amount to murder in the first degree? Was such a decision, if given, accompanied by the affirmation of the principle, that any amount of torture inflicted by the master, *short of the point of death,* was not indictable? Not being read in English law, the writer cannot say; but there is strong impression from within that such a decision as this would have shaken the whole island of Great Britain; and that such a case as *Souther* v. *The Commonwealth* would never have been forgotten under the sun. Yet it is probable that very few persons in the United States ever heard of the case, or ever would have heard of it, had it not been quoted by the New York *Courier and Enquirer* as an overwhelming example of legal humanity.

The horror of the whole matter is, that more than one such case should ever need to happen in a country, in order to make the whole community feel, as one man, that such power ought not to be left in the hands of a master. How many such cases do people *wish* to have happen?—how many *must* happen, before they will learn that utter despotic power is not to be trusted in any hands? If one white man's son or brother had been treated in this way, under the law of *apprenticeship,* the whole country would have trembled, from Louisiana to Maine, till that law had been altered. They forget that the black man has also a Father. It is "He that sitteth upon the circle of the heavens, who bringeth the princes to nothing, and maketh the judges of the earth as vanity." He hath said that, "When he maketh inquisition for blood, he FORGETTETH NOT the cry of the humble." That blood which has fallen so despised to the earth—that blood which lawyers have quibbled over, in the quiet of legal nonchalance, discussing in great ease whether it fell by murder in the first or second degree—HE will one day reckon for as the blood of his own child. He "is not slack concerning his promises, as some men count slackness, but is long-suffering to usward;" but the day of vengeance is surely coming, and the year of his redeemed is in his heart.

Another Court will sit upon these trials, when the Son of Man shall come in his glory. It will be not alone Souther, and no doubt the other, and such as he, that will be arraigned there; but all those in this nation, North and South, who have abetted the system, and made the laws which MADE Souther what he was. In *that* Court negro testimony will be received, if never before; and the judges, and the counsellors, and the chief men, and the mighty men, marshalled to that awful bar, will say to the mountains and the rocks, "Fall on us and hide us from the face of Him that sitteth on the throne, and from the wrath of the Lamb."

The wrath of the Lamb! Think of it! Think that Jesus Christ has been present, a witness—a silent witness through every such scene of torture and anguish—a silent witness in every such Court, calmly hearing the evidence given in the lawyers pleading, the bills filed, and cases appealed! And think what a heart Jesus Christ has, and with what age-long patience he has suffered! What awful depths are there in that word LONG-SUFFERING! and what must be that wrath, when, after ages of endurance, this dread accumulation of wrong and anguish comes up at last to judgment!

CHAPTER XII.

A COMPARISON OF THE ROMAN LAW OF SLAVERY WITH THE AMERICAN.

THE writer has expressed the opinion that the American law of slavery, taken throughout, is a more severe one than that of any other civilised nation, ancient or modern, if we except, perhaps, that of the Spartans. She has not at hand the means of comparing French and Spanish slave-codes; but, as it is a common remark that Roman slavery was much more severe than any that has ever existed in America, it will be well to compare the Roman with the American law. We therefore present a description of the Roman slave-law, as quoted by William Jay, Esq., from Blair's "Inquiry into the State of Slavery among the Romans," giving such references to *American authorities* as will enable the reader to make his own comparison, and to draw his own inferences.

I. The slave had no protection against the avarice, rage, or lust of the master, whose authority was founded in absolute property; and the bondman was viewed less as a human being subject to arbitrary dominion, than as an inferior animal dependent wholly on the will of his owner.

See law of South Carolina, in Stroud's "Sketch of the Laws of Slavery," p. 23.

Slaves shall be deemed, sold, taken, reputed and adjudged in law to be chattels personal in the hands of their owners and possessors, and their executors, administrators, and assigns, to all intents, constructions, and purposes whatever. [2 Brev. Dig. 219. Prince's Dig. 446. Cobb's Dig. 971.]

A slave is one who is in the power of a master to whom he belongs. [Lou. Civil Code, art. 35. Stroud's Sketch, p. 22.]

Such obedience is the consequence only of uncontrolled authority over the body. There is nothing else which can operate to produce the effect. The power of the master must be absolute, to render the submission of the slave perfect. [Judge Ruffin's Decision in the Case of The State *v.* Mann. Wheeler's Law of Slavery, 246.]

II. At first, the master possessed the uncontrolled power of life and death. At a very early period in Virginia, the power of life over slaves was given by statute. [Judge Clarke, in case of State of Miss. *v.* Jones. Wheeler, 252.]

III. He might kill, mutilate, or torture his slaves, for any or no offence; he might force them to become gladiators or prostitutes.

The privilege of killing is now somewhat abridged; as to mutilation and torture, see the case of *Souther* v. *The Commonwealth, 7 Grattan,* 673, quoted in Chapter III. above. Also, *State* v. *Mann,* in the same chapter, from Wheeler, p. 244.

IV. The temporary unions of male with female slaves were formed and dissolved at his command; families and friends were separated when he pleased.

See the decision of Judge Mathews, in the case of *Girod* v. *Lewis,* Wheeler, 199:

It is clear that slaves have no legal capacity to assent to any contract. With the consent of their master, they may marry, and their moral power to agree to such a contract or connexion as that of marriage cannot be doubted; but whilst in a state of slavery it cannot produce any civil effect, because slaves are deprived of all civil rights.

See also the chapter below on "the Separation of Families," and the files of *any* Southern newspaper, *passim.*

V. The laws recognised no obligation upon the owners of slaves, to furnish them with food and clothing, or to take care of them in sickness.

The extent to which this deficiency in the Roman law has been supplied in the American, by *"protective Acts,"* has been exhibited above.

VI. Slaves could have no property but by the sufferance of their master, for whom they acquired everything, and with whom they could form no engagements which could be binding on him.

The following chapter will show how far American legislation is in advance of that of the Romans, in that it makes it a penal offence on the part of the master to permit his slave to hold property, and a crime on the part of the slave to be so permitted. For the present purpose, we give an extract from the Civil Code of Louisiana, as quoted by Judge Stroud:—

A slave is one who is in the power of a master to whom he belongs. The master may sell him, dispose of his person, his industry and his labour; he can do nothing, possess nothing, nor acquire anything but what must belong to his master. [Civil Code, Article 35. Stroud, p. 22.]

According to Judge Ruffin, a slave is "one doomed in his own person, and his posterity, to live without knowledge, and without the capacity to make anything his own, and to toil that another may reap the fruits." [Wheeler's Law of Slavery, p. 246. State *v.* Mann.]

With reference to the binding power of engagements between master and slave, the following decisions from the United States Digest are in point (7, p. 449):—

All the acquisitions of the slave in possession are the property of his master,

Gist v. Toohey, 2 Rich. 424.

notwithstanding the promise of his master that the slave shall have certain of them.

A slave paid money which he had earned over and above his wages, for
Ibid.
the purchase of his children, into the hands of B, and B purchased such children with the money. Held that the master of such slave was entitled to recover the money of B.

VII. The master might transfer his rights by either sale or gift, or might bequeath them by will.

Slaves shall be deemed, sold, taken, reputed, and adjudged in law, to be chattelspersonal in the hands of their owners and possessors, and their executors, administrators, and assigns, to all intents, constructions, and purposes whatsoever. [Law of S. Carolina. Cobb's Digest, 971.]

VIII. A master selling, giving, or bequeathing a slave, sometimes made it a provision that he should never be carried abroad, or that he should be manumitted on a fixed day; or that, on the other hand, he should never be emancipated, or that he should be kept in chains for life.

We hardly think that a provision that a slave should never be emancipated, or that he should be kept in chains for life, would be sustained. A provision that the slave should not be carried out of the State, or sold, and that on the happening of either event he should be free, has been sustained. [Williams *v.* Ash, 1 How, U. S. Rep. 1. 5 U. S. Dig. 792, s. 5.]

The remainder of Blair's account of Roman slavery is devoted rather to the practices of masters than the state of the law itself. Surely the writer is not called upon to exhibit in the society of enlightened, republican and Christian America, in the nineteenth century, a parallel to the atrocities committed in pagan Rome, under the sceptre of the persecuting Cæsars, when the amphitheatre was the favourite resort of the most refined of her citizens, as well as the great "school of morals" for the multitude. A few references only will show, as far as we desire to show, how much safer it is now to trust man with absolute power over his fellow, than it was then.

IX. While slaves turned the handmill they were generally chained, and had a broad wooden collar, to prevent them from eating the grain. The FURCA, which in later language means a gibbet, was, in older dialect, used to denote a wooden fork or collar, which was made to bear upon their shoulders, or around their necks, as a mark of disgrace, as much as an uneasy burden.

The reader has already seen in Chapter V., that this instrument of degradation has been in use in our own day, in certain of the slave States, under the express sanction and protection of statute laws; although the material is different, and the construction doubtless improved by modern ingenuity.

X. Fetters and chains were much used for punishment or restraint, and were, in some instances, worn by slaves during life, through the sole authority of the master. Porters at the gates of the rich were generally chained. Field-labourers worked for the most part in irons posterior to the first ages of the republic.

The legislature of South Carolina specially sanctions the same practices, by excepting them in the *"protective enactment,"* which inflicts the penalty of *one hundred pounds* "in case any person shall wilfully cut out the tongue," &c., of a slave, "or shall inflict *any other cruel* punishment *other than* by whipping or beating with a horse-whip, cowskin, switch, or small stick, *or by putting irons on, or confining or imprisoning such slave*."

XI. Some persons made it their business to catch runaway slaves.

That such a profession, constituted by the highest legislative authority in the nation, and rendered respectable by the commendation expressed or implied of statesmen and divines, and of newspapers political and religious, exists in our midst, *especially in the free States,* is a fact which is, day by day, making itself too apparent to need testimony. The matter seems, however, to be managed in a more perfectly open and business-like manner in the State of Alabama than elsewhere. Mr. Jay cites the following advertisement from the *Sumpter County* (Ala.) *Whig:*—

NEGRO DOGS.

The undersigned having bought the entire pack of Negro Dogs (of the Hay and Allen Stock), he now proposes to catch runaway negroes. His charges will be Three Dollars per day for hunting, and Fifteen Dollars for catching a runaway. He resides three and one-half miles north of Livingston, near the lower Jones Bluff-road.

WILLIAM GAMBEL. Nov. 6, 1845. 6m.

The following is copied, *verbatim et literatim,* from the *Dadeville* (Ala.) *Banner,* of November, 1852. The *Dadeville Banner* is "*devoted to politics, literature, education, agriculture, &c.*"

NOTICE.

The undersigned having an excellent pack of Hounds, for trailing and catching runaway slaves, informs the public that his prices in future will be as follows for such services:—

Dollars.
For each day employed in hunting or trailing 2.50
For catching each slave 10.00
For going over ten miles and catching slaves 20.00

If sent for, the above prices will be exacted in cash. The subscriber resides one mile and a half south of Dadeville, Ala.

B. BLACK. Dadeville, Sept. 1, 1852. 1tf.

XII. The runaway, when taken, was severely punished by authority of the master, or by the judge at his desire; sometimes with crucifixion, amputation of a foot, or by being sent to fight as a gladiator with wild beasts; but most frequently by being branded on the brow with letters indicative of his crime.

That severe punishment would be the lot of the recaptured runaway, every one would suppose, from the *"absolute power"* of the master to inflict it. That it *is* inflicted in many cases, it is equally easy and needless to prove. The peculiar forms of punishment mentioned above are now very much out of vogue, but the following advertisement by Mr. Micajah Ricks, in the *Raleigh* (N. C.) *Standard* of July 18th, 1838, shows that something of classic taste in torture still lingers in our degenerate days.

Run away, a negro woman and two children. A few days before she went off, I burnt her with a hot iron, on the left side of her face. I tried to make the letter M.

It is charming to notice the *naïf* betrayal of literary pride on the part of Mr. Ricks. He did not wish that letter M to be taken as a specimen of what he could do in the way of writing. The creature would not hold still, and he fears the M may be illegible.

The above is only one of a long list of advertisements of maimed, cropped, and branded negroes, in the book of Mr. Weld, entitled *American Slavery as It is,* p. 77.

XIII. Cruel masters sometimes hired torturers by profession, or had such persons in their establishments, to assist them in punishing their slaves. The noses and ears, and teeth of slaves, were often in danger from an enraged owner; and sometimes the eyes of a great offender were put out. Crucifixion was very frequently made the fate of a wretched slave for a trifling misconduct, or from mere caprice.

For justification of such practices as these, we refer again to that horrible list of maimed and mutilated men, advertised by slaveholders themselves, in Weld's *American Slavery as It is,* p. 77. We recall the reader's attention to the evidence of the monster Kephart, given in Part I. As to crucifixion, we presume that there are wretches whose religious scruples would deter them from this particular form of torture, who would not hesitate to inflict equal cruelties by other means; as the Greek pirate, during a massacre in the season of Lent, was conscience-striken at having tasted a drop of blood. We presume?—Let any one but read again, if he can, the sickening details of that twelve hours' torture of Souther's slave, and say how much more merciful is American slavery than Roman.

The last item in Blair's description of Roman slavery is the following:—

By a decree passed by the Senate, if a master was murdered when his slaves might possibly have aided him, all his household within reach were held as implicated, and deserving of death; and Tacitus relates an instance in which a family of four hundred were all executed.

To this alone, of all the atrocities of the slavery of old heathen Rome, do we fail to find a parallel in the slavery of the United States of America.

There are other respects, in which American legislation has reached a refinement in tyranny of which the despots of those early days never conceived. The following is the language of Gibbon:—

Hope, the best comfort of our imperfect condition, was not denied to the Roman slave; and if he had any opportunity of rendering himself either useful or agreeable, he might very naturally expect that the diligence and fidelity of a few years would be rewarded with the inestimable gift of freedom. Without destroying the distinction of ranks, a distant prospect of freedom and honours was presented even to those whom pride and prejudice almost disdained to number among the human species.

The youths of promising genius were instructed in the arts and sciences, and their price was ascertained by the degree of their skill and talents. Almost every profession, either liberal or mechanical, might be found in the household of an opulent senator.

The following chapter will show how "the best comfort" which Gibbon knew for human adversity is taken away from the American slave; how he is denied the commonest privileges of education and mental improvement, and how the whole tendency of the unhappy system, under which he is in bondage, is to take from him the consolations of religion itself, and to degrade him from our common humanity, and common brotherhood with the Son of God.

CHAPTER XIII.

THE MEN BETTER THAN THEIR LAWS.

Judgment is turned away backward,
And Justice standeth afar off;
For Truth is fallen in the street,
And Equity cannot enter.
Yea, Truth faileth;
And HE THAT DEPARTETH FROM EVIL MAKETH HIMSELF A PREY.
ISAIAH lix. 14, 15.

THERE is one very remarkable class of laws yet to be considered.

So full of cruelty and of unmerciful severity is the slave-code—such an atrocity is the institution of which it is the legal definition—that there are multitudes of individuals too generous and too just to be willing to go to the full extent of its restrictions and deprivations.

A generous man, instead of regarding the poor slave as a piece of property, dead, and void of rights, is tempted to regard him rather as a helpless younger brother, or as a defenceless child, and to extend to him, by his own good right arm, that protection and those rights which the law denies him. A religious man, who, by the theory of his belief, regards all men as brothers, and considers his Christian slave, with himself, as a member of Jesus Christ—as of one body, one spirit, and called in one hope of his calling—cannot willingly see him "doomed to live without knowledge," without the power of reading the written Word, and to raise up his children after him in the same darkness.

Hence, if left to itself, individual humanity would, in many cases, practically abrogate the slave-code. Individual humanity would teach the slave to read and write, would build school-houses for his children, and would, in very, very many cases, enfranchise him.

The result of all this has been foreseen. It has been foreseen that the result of education would be general intelligence; that the result of intelligence would be a knowledge of personal rights; and that an inquiry into the doctrine of personal rights would be fatal to the system. It has been foreseen, also, that the example of disinterestedness and generosity, in emancipation, might carry with it a generous contagion, until it should become universal; that the example of educated and emancipated slaves would prove a dangerous excitement to those still in bondage.

For this reason, the American slave-code, which, as we have already seen, embraces, substantially, all the barbarities of that of ancient Rome, has added to it a set of laws more cruel than any which ancient and heathen Rome ever knew—laws designed to shut against the slave his last refuge—the humanity of his master. The master, in ancient Rome, might give his slave whatever advantages of education he chose, or at any time emancipate him, and the State did not interfere to prevent.

But in America the laws, throughout all the slave States, most rigorously forbid, in the first place, the *education* of the slave. We do not profess to give all these laws, but a few striking specimens may be presented. Our authority is Judge Stroud's "Sketch of the Laws of Slavery."

The legislature of South Carolina, in 1740, enounced the following preamble: [Stroud's Sketch, p. 88.]

"Whereas, the having of slaves taught to write, or suffering them to be employed in writing, may be attended with *great inconveniences;*" and enacted that the crime of teaching a slave to write, or of employing a slave as a scribe, should be punished by a fine of *one hundred pounds,* current money. If the reader will turn now to the infamous "protective" statute, enacted by the same legislature, in the same year, he will find that the *same penalty* has been appointed for the cutting out of the tongue, putting out of the eye, cruel scalding,&c., of any slave, as for the offence of teaching him to write! That is to say, that to teach him to write, and to put out his eyes, are to be regarded as equally reprehensible.

That there might be no doubt of the "great and fundamental policy" of the State, and that there might be full security against the "*great inconveniences*" of "having of slaves taught to write," it was enacted, in 1800, "That assemblies of slaves, free negroes,&c., for the purpose of *mental instruction,* in a confined or secret place,&c.&c., is [are] declared to be an unlawful meeting;" and the officers are required to enter such confined places, and disperse the "unlawful assemblage," inflicting, at their discretion, "*such corporal punishment,* not exceeding twenty lashes, upon such slaves, free negroes,&c., as they may judge *necessary for deterring them from the like unlawful assemblage in future.*" [Stroud's Sketch, p. 89. 2 Brevard's Digest, pp. 254-5.]

The statute-book of Virginia is adorned with a law similar to the one last quoted. [Stroud, pp. 88, 89.]

The offence of teaching a slave to write was early punished, in Georgia as in South Carolina, by a pecuniary fine. But the city of Savannah seems to have found this penalty insufficient to protect it from "*great inconveniences,*" and we learn, by a quotation in the work of Judge Stroud, from a number of *The Portfolio,* that "the city has passed an ordinance, [Stroud's Sketch, pp. 89, 90.] by which any person that teaches any person of colour, *slave or free,* to *read or write,* or causes such person to be so taught, is subjected to a fine of thirty dollars for *each* offence; and every person of colour who shall keep a school, to teach reading or writing, is subject to a fine of thirty dollars, or to be imprisoned ten days, and whipped thirty-nine lashes."

Secondly. In regard to religious privileges:—

The State of Georgia has enacted a law, "to *protect* religious societies in the exercise of their religious duties." This law, after appointing rigorous penalties for the offence of interrupting or disturbing a congregation of *white persons,* concludes in the following words:—

No congregation or company of negroes, shall, under pretence of divine worship, assemble themselves, contrary to the Act regulating patrols. [Stroud, p. 92. Prince's Digest, p. 342.]

"The Act regulating patrols," as quoted by the editor of *Prince's Digest,* empowers *every justice of the peace to disperse* ANY *assembly or meeting of slaves* which *may* disturb the peace,&c., of His Majesty's subjects, and permits that every slave found at such a meeting shall "*immediately* be corrected, WITHOUT TRIAL, *by receiving on the bare back twenty-five stripes with a whip, switch, or cow-skin*." [Stroud, p. 93. Prince's Digest, p. 447.]

The history of legislation in South Carolina is significant. An Act was passed in 1800, containing the following section:—

[Stroud, p. 93. 2 Brevard's Digest, 254, 255.]

It shall not be lawful for any number of slaves, free negroes, mulattoes, or mestizoes, even in company with white persons, to meet together and assemble for the purpose of mental instruction or religious worship, either before the rising of the sun, or after the going down of the same. And all magistrates, sheriffs, militia officers&c.,&c., are hereby invested with power, &c., for dispersing such assemblies,&c.

The law just quoted seems somehow to have had a prejudicial effect upon the religious interests of the "slaves, free negroes," &c., specified in it; for, three years afterwards, on the petition of certain religious societies, a "*protective Act,*" was passed, which should secure them this *great religious privilege;* to wit, that it should be unlawful, before nine o'clock, "to break into a place of meeting, wherein shall be assembled the members of any religious society of this State, *provided a majority of them shall be white persons,* or otherwise to disturb their devotion, *unless* such person shall have first obtained a warrant,&c."

Thirdly. It appears that many masters, who are disposed to treat their slaves generously, have allowed them to accumulate property, to raise domestic animals for their own use, and, in the case of intelligent servants, to go at large, to hire their own time, and to trade upon their own account. Upon all these practices the law comes down with unmerciful severity. A penalty is inflicted on the owner, but, with a rigour quite accordant with the tenor of slave-law, the offence is considered, in law, as that of the slave, rather than that of the master; so that, if the master is generous enough not to regard the penalty which is imposed upon himself, he may be restrained by the fear of bringing a greater evil upon his dependant. These laws are, in some cases, so constructed as to make it for the interest of the lowest and most brutal part of society that they be enforced, by offering half the profits to the informer. We give the following, as specimens of slave legislation on this subject:—

The law of South Carolina.

It shall not be lawful for any slave to buy, sell, trade,&c., for any goods, &c., without a license from the owner,&c.; nor shall any slave be permitted to keep any boat, periauger, or canoe, or raise and breed, for the benefit of such slave, any horses, mares, cattle, sheep, or hogs, under pain of forfeiting all the goods, &c., and all the boats, periaugers, or canoes, horses, mares, cattle, sheep, or hogs. [Stroud, pp. 46, 47. James' Digest, 385, 386, Act of 1740.] And it shall be lawful for any person whatsoever to seize and take away from any slave all such goods, &c., boats, &c., &c., and to deliver the same into the hands of any justice of the peace, nearest to the place where the seizure shall be made; and no doubt the other, and such justice shall take the oath of the person making such seizure concerning the manner thereof; and if the said justice shall be satisfied that such seizure has been made according to law, he shall pronounce and declare the goods so seized to be forfeited, and order the same to be sold at public outcry, one half of the money arising from such sale to go to the State, and the other half to him or them that sue for the same.

The laws in many other States are similar to the above; but the State of Georgia has an additional provision [2 Cobbs, Sig. 284.], against permitting the slave to hire himself to another for his own benefit; a penalty of thirty dollars is imposed for every weekly offence on the part of the master, unless the labour be done on his own premises. Savannah, Augusta, and Sunbury, are places excepted.

In Virginia, "if the master shall permit his slave to hire himself out," the *slave* is to be apprehended,&c. [Stroud, p 47.], and the *master* to be fined.

In an early Act of the Legislature of the orthodox and Presbyterian State of North Carolina, it is gratifying to see how the judicious course of public policy is made to subserve the interests of Christian charity—how, in a single ingenious sentence, provision is made for punishing the offender against society, rewarding the patriotic informer, and feeding the poor and destitute:—

All horses, cattle, hogs, or sheep that, one month after the passing of this Act, shall belong to any slave, or be of any slave's mark, in this State, shall be seized and sold by the county wardens, and by them applied, the one half to the support of the poor of the county, and the other half to the informer. [Stroud's Sketch, 47.]

In Mississippi, a fine of fifty dollars is imposed upon the master who permits his slave to cultivate cotton for his own use; or who licences his slave to go at large and trade as a freeman; or who is *convicted* of permitting his slave to keep "*stock of any description*." [Stroud, p. 48.]

To show how the above law has been interpreted by the highest judicial tribunal of the sovereign State of Mississippi, we repeat here a portion of a decision of Chief Justice Sharkey, which we have elsewhere given more in full.

Independent of the principles laid down in adjudicated cases, our statute-law prohibits slaves from owning certain kinds of property; and it may be inferred that the legislature supposed they were extending the Act as far as it could be necessary to exclude them from owning any property, as the prohibition includes that kind of property which they would most likely be permitted to own without interruption, to wit: hogs, horses, cattle, &c. They cannot be prohibited from holding such property, in consequence of its being of a dangerous or offensive character, but because it was deemed impolitic for them to hold property of any description.

It was asserted, at the beginning of this head, that the permission of the master to a slave to hire his own time is, by law, considered the offence of the slave; the slave being subject to prosecution therefore, not the master. This is evident from the tenor of some of the laws quoted and alluded to above. It will be still further illustrated by the following decisions of the Courts of North Carolina. They are copied from the Supplement to the U.S. Digest, vol. ii. p. 798:—

139. An indictment charging that a certain negro did hire her own time [The State *v*. Clarissa, 5 Iredell,221.], contrary to the form of the statute,&c., is defective, and must be quashed, because it was omitted to be charged that she was permitted by her master to go at large, which is one essential part of the offence.

140. Under the first clause of the thirty-first section of the 111th chapter of the Revised Statutes, prohibiting masters from hiring to slaves their own time, the master is not indictable; he is only subject to a penalty of forty dollars. Nor is the master indictable under the second clause of that section; the process being against the slave, not against the master.—Ib.

142. To constitute the offence under section 32 (Rev. Stat. c. xi. § 32) it is not necessary that the slave should have hired his time; it is sufficient if the master permits him to go at large as a freeman.

This is maintaining the ground that "*the master can do no wrong*" with great consistency and thoroughness. But it is in perfect keeping, both in form and spirit, with the whole course of slave-law, which always upholds the supremacy of the master, and always depresses the slave.

Fourthly. Stringent laws against emancipation exist in nearly all the slave States.

[Stroud, 147. Prince's Dig. 456. James' Dig. 98. Toulmin's Dig. 632. Miss. Rev. Code, 386.]

In four of the States—South Carolina, Georgia, Alabama, and Mississippi—emancipation cannot be effected, except by a special act of the legislature of the State.

In Georgia, the *offence* of setting free "any slave, or slaves, in any other manner and form than the one prescribed," was punishable, according to the law of 1801, by the forfeiture of two hundred dollars, to be recovered by action *or indictment;* the slaves in question still remaining, "*to all intents and purposes, as much in a state of slavery as before they were manumitted.*"

Believers in human progress will be interested to know that since the law of 1801 there has been a reform introduced into this part of the legislation of the republic of Georgia. In 1818 a new law was passed, which, as will be seen, contains a grand remedy for the abuses of the old. In this it is provided, with endless variety of specifications and synonyms, as if to "let suspicion double-lock the door" against any possible evasion, that, "All and every will, testament, and deed, whether by way of trust or otherwise, contract, or agreement, or stipulation, or other instrument in writing or by parole, made and executed for the purpose of effecting, or endeavouring to effect, the manumission of any slave or slaves, either directly or indirectly, or virtually,&c.,&c., shall be, and the same are hereby declared to be, utterly null and void." And the guilty author of the outrage against the peace of the State, contemplated in such deed, &c., &c., "and all and every person or persons concerned in giving or attempting to give effect thereto in any way or manner whatsoever, shall be severally liable to a penalty not exceeding one thousand dollars."

It would be quite anomalous in slave-law, and contrary to the "great and fundamental policy" of slave States, if the negroes who, not having the fear of God before their eyes, but being instigated by the devil, should be guilty of being thus manumitted, were suffered to go unpunished; accordingly, the law very properly and judiciously provides [Stroud's Sketch, pp. 147-8. Prince's Dig. 466.] that "each and every slave or slaves in whose behalf such will or testament, &c., &c., shall have been made, shall be liable to be *arrested* by warrant, &c.; and, *being thereof convicted,*&c., shall be liable to be sold as a slave or slaves by public outcry; and the proceeds of such slaves shall be appropriated, &c., &c."

Judge Stroud gives the following account of the law of Mississippi:—

The emancipation must be by an instrument in writing, a last will or deed, &c., under seal attested by at least two credible witnesses, or acknowledged in the court of the county or corporation where the emancipator resides [Stroud's Sketch, p. 149. Miss. Rev. Code, p. 385-6 (Act June 18, 1822).]; proof satisfactory to the General Assembly must be adduced that the slave has done some meritorious act for the benefit of his master, or rendered some distinguished service to the State; all which circumstances are but prerequisites, and are of no efficacy until a special Act of Assembly sanctions the emancipation; to which may be added, as has been already stated, a saving of the rights of creditors, and the protection of the widow's thirds.

The same *pre-requisite* of "*meritorious services,* to be adjudged of and allowed by the county court," is exacted by an Act of the General Assembly of North Carolina; and all slaves emancipated contrary to the provisions of this Act are to be committed to the jail of the county, and at the next court held for that county are to be sold to the highest bidder.

But the law of North Carolina does not refuse opportunity for repentance, even after the crime has been proved: accordingly—

The sheriff is directed [Stroud's Sketch, 148. Haywood's Manual, 525, 526, 529, 537.], five days before the time for the sale of the *emancipated* negro, to give notice, in writing, to the person by whom the emancipation was made, to the end—

and with the hope that, smitten by remorse of conscience, and brought to a sense of his guilt before God and man—

such person may, if he thinks proper, renew his claim to the negro so emancipated by him; on failure to do which, the sale is to be made by the sheriff, and one-fifth part of the net proceeds is to become the property of the freeholder by whom the apprehension was made, and the remaining four-fifths are to be paid into the public treasury.

It is proper to add that we have given examples of the laws of States whose legislation on this subject has been most severe. [Stroud, pp. 148-154.] The laws of Virginia, Maryland, Missouri, Kentucky, and Louisiana, are much less stringent.

A Striking case, which shows how inexorably the law contends with the kind designs of the master, is on record in the reports of legal decisions in the State of Mississippi. The circumstances of the case have been thus briefly stated in the *New York Evening Post,* edited by Mr. William Cullen Bryant. They are a romance of themselves.

A man of the name of Elisha Brazealle, a planter in Jefferson County, Mississippi, was attacked with a loathsome disease. During his illness he was faithfully nursed by a mulatto slave, to whose assiduous attentions he felt that he owed his life. He was duly impressed by her devotion, and soon after his recovery took her to Ohio, and had her educated. She was very intelligent, and improved her advantages so rapidly that when he visited her again he determined to marry her. He executed a deed for her emancipation, and had it recorded both in the States of Ohio and Mississippi, and made her his wife.

Mr. Brazealle returned with her to Mississippi, and in process of time had a son. After a few years he sickened and died, leaving a will, in which, after reciting the deed of emancipation, he declared his intention to ratify it, and devised all his property to this lad, acknowledging him in the will to be such.

Some poor and distant relations in North Carolina, whom he did not know, and for whom he did not care, hearing of his death, came on to Mississippi, and claimed the property thus devised. They instituted a suit for its recovery, and the case (it is reported in Howard's Mississippi Reports, vol. ii.,.p. 837) came before Judge Sharkey, our new consul at Havana. He decided it, and in that decision declared the act of emancipation an offence against morality, and pernicious and detestable as an example. He set aside the will; gave the property of Brazealle to his distant relations, condemned Brazealle's son, and his wife, that son's mother, again to bondage, and made them the slaves of these North Carolina kinsmen, as part of the assets of the estate.

Chief Justice Sharkey, after narrating the circumstances of the case, declares the validity of the deed of emancipation to be the main question in the controversy. He then argues that, although according to principles of national comity "contracts are to be construed according to the laws of the country or State where they are made," yet these principles are not to be followed when they lead to conclusions in conflict with "the great and fundamental policy of the State." What this "great and fundamental policy" is, in Mississippi, may be gathered from the remainder of the decision, which we give in full.

CHAPTER XIII.

Let us apply these principles to the deed of emancipation. To give it validity would be, in the first place, a violation of the declared policy, and contrary to a positive law of the State.

The policy of a State is indicated by the general course of legislation on a given subject; and we find that free negroes are deemed offensive, because they are not permitted to emigrate to or remain in the State. They are allowed few privileges, and subject to heavy penalties for offences. They are required to leave the State within thirty days after notice, and in the meantime give security for good behaviour; and those of them who can lawfully remain must register and carry with them their certificates, or they may be committed to jail. It would also violate a positive law, passed by the legislature, expressly to maintain this settled policy, and to prevent emancipation. No owner can emancipate his slave, but by deed or will properly attested, or acknowledged in Court, and proof to the legislature that such slave has performed some meritorious act for the benefit of the master, or some distinguished service for the State; and the deed or will can have no validity until ratified by special act of legislature. It is believed that this law and policy are too essentially important to the interests of our citizens to permit them to be evaded.

The state of the case shows conclusively that the contract had its origin in an offence against morality, pernicious and detestable as an example. But, above all, it seems to have been planned and executed with a fixed design to evade the rigour of the laws of the State. The acts of the party in going to Ohio with the slaves, and there executing the deed, and his immediate return with them to this State, point with unerring certainty to his purpose and object. The laws of this State cannot be thus defrauded of their operation by one of our own citizens. If we could have any doubts about the principle, the case reported in 1 Randolph, 15, would remove them.

As we think the validity of the deed must depend upon the laws of this State, it becomes unnecessary to inquire whether it could have any force by the laws of Ohio. If it were even valid there, it can have no force here. The consequence is, that the negroes, John Monroe and his mother, are still slaves, and a part of the estate of Elisha Brazealle. They have not acquired a right to their freedom under the will; for, even if the clause in the will were sufficient for that purpose, their emancipation has not been consummated by an act of the legislature.

John Monroe, being a slave, cannot take the property as devisee; and I apprehend it is equally clear that it cannot be held in trust for him. 4 Desans. Rep. 266. Independent of the principles laid down in adjudicated cases, our statute law prohibits slaves from owning certain kinds of property; and it may be inferred that the legislature supposed they were extending the act as far as it could be necessary to exclude them from owning any property, as the prohibition includes that kind of property which they would most likely be permitted to own without interruption, to wit, hogs, horses, cattle,&c. They cannot be prohibited from holding such property in consequence of its being of a dangerous or offensive character, but because it was deemed impolitic for them to hold property of any description. It follows, therefore, that his heirs are entitled to the property.

As the deed was void, and the devisee could not take under the will, the heirs might, perhaps, have had a remedy at law; but, as an account must be taken for the rents and profits, and for the final settlement of the estate, I see no good reason why they should be sent back to law. The remedy is, doubtless, more full and complete than it could be at law. The decree of the Chancellor overruling the demurrer must be affirmed, and the cause remanded for further proceedings.

The Chief Justice Sharkey who pronounced this decision is stated by the *Evening Post* to have been a principal agent in the passage of the severe law under which this horrible inhumanity was perpetrated.

Nothing more forcibly shows the absolute despotism of the slave-law over all the kindest feelings and intentions of the master, and the determination of courts to carry these severities to their full length, than this cruel deed, which precipitated a young man who had been educated to consider himself free, and his mother, an educated woman, back into the bottomless abyss of slavery. Had this case been chosen for the theme of a novel, or a tragedy, the world would have cried out upon it as a plot of monstrous improbability. As it stands in the law-book, it is only a specimen of that awful kind of truth, stranger than fiction, which is all the time evolving, in one form or another, from the workings of this anomalous system.

This view of the subject is a very important one, and ought to be earnestly and gravely pondered by those in foreign countries, who are too apt to fasten their condemnation and opprobrium rather on the *person* of the slave-holder than on the horrors of the legal system. In some slave States it seems as if there was very little that the benevolent owner could do which should permanently benefit his slave, unless he should seek *to alter the laws*. Here it is that the highest obligation of the Southern Christian lies. Nor will the world or God hold *them* guiltless who, with the elective franchise in their hands, and the full power to speak, write, and discuss, suffer this monstrous system of legalised cruelty to go on from age to age.

CHAPTER XIV.

THE HEBREW SLAVE-LAW COMPARED WITH THE AMERICAN SLAVE-LAW.

HAVING compared the American law with the Roman, we will now compare it with one other code of slave-laws, to wit, the Hebrew.

This comparison is the more important, because American slavery has been defended on the ground of God's permitting Hebrew slavery.

The inquiry now arises, What kind of slavery was it that was permitted among the Hebrews? for in different nations very different systems have been called by the general name of slavery.

That the patriarchal state of servitude which existed in the time of Abraham was a very different thing from American slavery, a few graphic incidents in the Scripture narrative show; for we read that when the angels came to visit Abraham, although he had three hundred servants born in his house, it is said that *Abraham* hasted, and took a calf, and killed it, and gave it to a young man to dress; and that he told *Sarah* to take three measures of meal and knead it into cakes; and that when all was done, he himself set it before his guests.

From various other incidents which appear in the patriarchal narrative, it would seem that these servants bore more the relation of the members of a Scotch clan to their feudal lord than that of an American slave to his master; thus it seems that if Abraham had died without children his head servant would have been his heir.—Gen. xv. 3.

Of what species, then, was the slavery which God permitted among the Hebrews? By what laws was it regulated?

In the New Testament the whole Hebrew system of administration is spoken of as a relatively imperfect one, and as superseded by the Christian dispensation.—Heb. viii. 13.

We are taught thus to regard the Hebrew system as an educational system, by which a debased, half-civilised race, which had been degraded by slavery in its worst form among the Egyptians, was gradually elevated to refinement and humanity.

As they went from the land of Egypt, it would appear that the most disgusting personal habits, the most unheard-of and unnatural impurities, prevailed among them; so that it was necessary to make laws with relations to things of which Christianity has banished the very name from the earth.

Beside all this, polygamy, war, and slavery, were the universal custom of nations.

It is represented in the New Testament that God, in educating this people, proceeded in the same gradual manner in which a wise father would proceed with a family of children.

He selected a few of the most vital points of evil practice, and forbade them by positive statute, under rigorous penalties.

The worship of any other god was, by the Jewish law, constituted high treason, and rigorously punished with death.

As the knowledge of the true God and religious instruction could not then, as now, be afforded by printing and books, one day in the week had to be set apart for preserving in the minds of the people a sense of His being, and their obligations to Him. The devoting of this day to any other purpose was also punished with death; and the reason is obvious, that its sacredness was the principal means relied on for preserving the allegiance of the nation to their king and God, and its desecration, of course, led directly to high treason against the head of the State.

With regard to many other practices which prevailed among the Jews, as among other heathen nations, we find the Divine Being taking the same course which wise human legislators have taken.

When Lycurgus wished to banish money and its attendant luxuries from Sparta, he did not forbid it by direct statute-law, but he instituted a currency so clumsy and uncomfortable that, as we are informed by Rollin, it took a cart and pair of oxen to carry home the price of a very moderate estate.

In the same manner the Divine Being surrounded the customs of polygamy, war, blood-revenge, and slavery, with regulations which gradually and certainly tended to abolish them entirely.

No one would pretend that the laws which God established in relation to polygamy, cities of refuge, &c., have any application to Christian nations now.

The following summary of some of these laws of the Mosaic code is given by Dr. C. E. Stowe, Professor of Biblical Literature in Andover Theological Seminary:—

1. It commanded a Hebrew, even though a married man, with wife and children living, to take the childless widow of a deceased brother, and beget children with her.—Deut. xxv. 5-10.
2. The Hebrews, under certain restrictions, were allowed to make concubines, or wives for a limited time, of women taken in war.—Deut. xxi. 10-19.
3. A Hebrew who already had a wife was allowed to take another also, provided he still continued his intercourse with the first as her husband, and treated her kindly and affectionately.—Exodus xxi. 9-11.

4. By the Mosaic law, the nearest relative of a murdered Hebrew could pursue and slay the murderer, unless he could escape to the city of refuge; and the same permission was given in case of accidental homicide.—Num. xxxv. 9-39.
5. The Israelites were commanded to exterminate the Canaanites, men, women, and children.—Deut. ix. 12; xx. 16-18.

Any one, or all, of the above practices, can be justified by the Mosaic Law, as well as the practice of slaveholding.

Each of these laws, although in its time it was an ameliorating law, designed to take the place of some barbarous abuse, and to be a connecting link by which some higher state of society might be introduced, belongs confessedly to that system which St. Paul says made nothing perfect. They are a part of the commandment which he says was annulled for the weakness and unprofitableness thereof, and which, in the time which he wrote, was waxing old, and ready to vanish away. And Christ himself says, with regard to certain permissions of this system, that they were given on account of the "hardness of their hearts"—because the attempt to enforce a more stringent system at that time, owing to human depravity, would have only produced greater abuses.

The following view of the Hebrew laws of slavery is compiled from Barnes' work on slavery, and from Professor Stowe's manuscript lectures.

The legislation commenced by making the great and common source of slavery—kidnapping—a capital crime.

The enactment is as follows: "He that stealeth a man and selleth him, or if he be found in his hand, he shall surely be put to death."—Exodus xxi. 16.

The sources from which slaves were to be obtained were thus reduced to two: first, the voluntary sale of an individual by himself, which certainly does not come under the designation of involuntary servitude; second, the appropriation of captives taken in war, and the buying from the heathen.

With regard to the servitude of the Hebrew by a voluntary sale of himself, such servitude, by the statute-law of the land, came to an end once in seven years; so that the worst that could be made of it was that it was a voluntary contract to labour for a certain time.

With regard to the servants bought of the heathen, or of foreigners in the land, there was a statute by which their servitude was annulled once in fifty years.

It has been supposed, from a disconnected view of one particular passage in the Mosaic code, that God directly countenanced the treating of a slave, who was a stranger and foreigner, with more rigour and severity than a Hebrew slave. That this was not the case will appear from the following enactments, which have express reference to strangers:—

The stranger that dwelleth with you shall be unto you as one born among you and thou shalt love him as thyself.—Lev. xix. 34.

Thou shalt neither vex a stranger nor oppress him; for ye were strangers in the land of Egypt.—Exodus xxii. 21.

Thou shalt not oppress a stranger, for ye know the heart of a stranger.—Exodus xxiii. 9.

The Lord your God regardeth not persons. He doth execute the judgment of the fatherless and the widow, and loveth the stranger in giving him food and raiment; love ye therefore the stranger.—Deut. x. 17-19.

Judge righteously between every man and his brother, and the stranger that is with him. Deut. i. 16.

Cursed be he that perverteth the judgment of the stranger.—Deut. xxvii. 19.

Instead of making slavery an oppressive institution with regard to the stranger, it was made by God a system within which heathen were adopted into the Jewish state, educated and instructed in the worship of the true God, and in due time emancipated.

In the first place, they were protected by law from personal violence. The loss of an eye or a tooth, through the violence of his master, took the slave out of that master's power entirely, and gave him his liberty. Then, further than this, if a master's conduct towards a slave was such as to induce him to run away, it was enjoined that nobody should assist in retaking him, and that he should dwell wherever he chose in the land, without molestation. Third, the law secured to the slave a very considerable portion of time, which was to be at his own disposal. Every seventh year was to be at his own disposal.—Lev. xxv. 4-6. Every seventh day was, of course, secured to him.—Ex. xx. 10.

The servant had the privilege of attending the three great national festivals, when all the males of the nation were required to appear before God in Jerusalem.—Ex. xxxiv. 23.

Each of these festivals, it is computed, took up about three weeks. The slave also was to be a guest in the family festivals. In Deut. xii. 12, it is said, "Ye shall rejoice before the Lord your God, ye, and your sons, and your daughters, and your men-servants, and your maid-servants, and the Levite that is within your gates.

Dr. Barnes estimates that the whole amount of time which a servant could have to himself would amount to about twenty-three years out of fifty, or nearly one-half his time.

Again, the servant was placed on an exact equality with his master in all that concerned his religious relations.

Now, if we recollect that in the time of Moses, the God and the king of the nation were one and the same person, and that the civil and religious relation were one and the same, it will appear that the slave and his master stood on an equality in their civil relation with regard to the state.

Thus in Deuteronomy xxix. is described a solemn national convocation, which took place before the death of Moses, when the whole nation were called upon, after a solemn review of their national history, to renew their constitutional oath of allegiance to their supreme Magistrate and Lord.

On this occasion, Moses addressed them thus:—"Ye stand this day, all of you, before the Lord your God; your captains of your tribes, your elders, and your officers, with all the men of Israel, your little ones, your wives, and thy stranger that is in thy camp, *from the hewer of thy wood unto the drawer of thy water;* that *thou* shouldest enter into covenant with the Lord thy God, and into his oath, which the Lord thy God maketh with thee this day."

How different is this from the cool and explicit declaration of South Carolina with regard to the position of the American slave!—"A slave is not generally regarded as legally *capable of being within the peace of the State*. He is not a citizen, and is not in that character entitled to her protection." [Wheeler's Law of Slavery, p. 243.]

In all the religious services, which, as we have seen by the constitution of the nation, were civil services, the slave and the master mingled on terms of strict equality. There was none of the distinction which appertains to a distinct class or caste. "There was no special service appointed for them at unusual seasons. There were no particular seats assigned to them, to keep up the idea that they were a degraded class. There was no withholding from them the instruction which the Word of God gave about the equal rights of mankind."

Fifthly. It was always contemplated that the slave would, as a matter of course, choose the Jewish religion, and the service of God, and enter willingly into all the obligations and services of the Jewish polity.

Mr. Barnes cites the words of Maimonides, to show how this was commonly understood by the Hebrews.—*Inquiry into the Scriptural Views of Slavery,* by Albert Barnes, p. 132.

Whether a servant be born in the power of an Israelite, or whether he be purchased from the heathen, the master is to bring them both into the covenant.

But he that is in the house is entered on the eighth day; and he that is bought with money, on the day on which his master receives him, unless the slave be unwilling. For if the master receive a grown slave, and he be unwilling, his master is to bear with him, to seek to win him over by instruction, and by love and kindness, for one year. After which, should he refuse so long, it is forbidden to keep him longer than a year. And the master must send him back to the strangers from whence he came; for the God of Jacob will not accept any other than the worship of a willing heart. —*Maimon. Hilcoth Miloth,* chap. i. sec. 8.

A sixth fundamental arrangement with regard to the Hebrew slave was that he *could never be sold*. Concerning this Mr. Barnes remarks:—

A man, in certain circumstances, might be bought by a Hebrew; but when once bought, that was an end of the matter. There is not the slightest evidence that any Hebrew ever sold a slave; and any provision contemplating that was unknown to the constitution of the commonwealth. It is said of Abraham that he had "servants bought with money;" but there is no record of his having ever sold one, nor is there any account of its ever having been done by Isaac or Jacob. The only instance of a sale of this kind among the patriarchs is that act of the brothers of Joseph, which is held up to so strong reprobation, by which they sold him to the Ishmaelites. Permission is given in the law of Moses to buy a servant, but none is given to sell him again; and the fact that no such permission is given is full proof that it was not contemplated. When he entered into that relation it became certain that there could be no change, unless it was voluntary on his part (comp. Ex. xxi.

5, 6), or unless his master gave him his freedom, until the not distant period fixed by law when he could be free. There is no arrangement in the law of Moses by which servants were to be taken in payment of their master's debts, by which they were to be given as pledges, by which they were to be consigned to the keeping of others, or by which they were to be given away as presents. There are no instances occurring in the Jewish history in which any of these things were done. This law is positive in regard to the Hebrew servant, and the principle of the law would apply to all others. Lev. xxv. 42 "They shall not be sold as bondmen." In all these respects there was a marked difference, and there was doubtless intended to be, between the estimate affixed to servants and to property. —*Inquiry,* &c., pp. 133, 134.

As to the practical workings of this system, as they are developed in the incidents of sacred history, they are precisely what we should expect from such a system of laws. For instance, we find it mentioned incidentally in the ninth chapter of the first book of Samuel, that when Saul and his servant came to see Samuel, that Samuel, in anticipation of his being crowned king, made a great feast for him; and in verse twenty-second the history says, "And Samuel took Saul *and his servant,* and brought them into the parlour, and made *them* sit in the chiefest place."

We read, also, in 2 Samuel ix. 10, of a servant of Saul who had large estates, and twenty servants of his own.

We find in 1 Chron. ii. 34, the following incident related: —"Now, Sheshan had no sons, but daughters. And Sheshan had a servant, an Egyptian, whose name was Jarha. And Sheshan gave his daughter to Jarha, his servant, to wife."

Does this resemble American slavery?

We find, moreover, that this connexion was not considered at all disgraceful, for the son of this very daughter was enrolled among the valiant men of David's army.—1 Chron. ii. 41.

In fine, we are not surprised to discover that the institutions of Moses in effect so obliterated all the characteristics of slavery, that it had ceased to exist among the Jews long before the time of Christ. Mr. Barnes asks:—

On what evidence would a man rely to prove that slavery existed at all in the land in the time of the later prophets of the Maccabees, or when the Saviour appeared? There are abundant proofs, as we shall see, that it existed in Greece and Rome; but what is the evidence that it existed in Judea? So far as I have been able to ascertain, there are no declarations that it did to be found in the canonical books of the Old Testament or in Josephus. There are no allusion to laws and customs which imply that it was prevalent; there are no coins or medals which suppose it; there are no facts which do not admit of an easy explanation on the supposition that slavery had ceased. —*Inquiry,*&c., p. 226.

Two objections have been urged to the interpretations which have been given of two of the enactments before quoted.

CHAPTER XIV.

1. It is said that the enactment, "Thou shalt not return to his master the servant that has escaped," &c., relates only to servants escaping from heathen masters to the Jewish nation.

The following remarks on this passage are from Professor Stowe's lectures:

Deuteronomy xxiii. 15, 16.—These words make a statute which, like every other statute, is to be strictly construed. There is nothing in the language to limit its meaning; there is nothing in the connexion in which it stands to limit its meaning; nor is there anything in the history of the Mosaic legislation to limit the application of this statute to the case of servants escaping from foreign masters. The assumption that it is thus limited is wholly gratuitous, and, so far as the Bible is concerned, unsustained by any evidence whatever. It is said that it would be absurd for Moses to enact such a law while servitude existed among the Hebrews. It would indeed be absurd, were it the object of the Mosaic legislation to sustain and perpetuate slavery; but if it were the object of Moses to limit and to restrain, and finally to extinguish slavery, this statute was admirably adapted to his purpose. That it was the object of Moses to extinguish and not to perpetuate slavery is perfectly clear from the whole course of his legislation on the subject. Every slave was to have all the religious privileges and instruction to which his master's children were entitled. Every seventh year released the Hebrew slave, and every fiftieth year produced universal emancipation. If a master, by an accidental or an angry blow, deprived the slave of a tooth, the slave, by that act, was for ever free. And so by the statute, in question, if the slave felt himself oppressed, he could make his escape, and, though the master was not forbidden to retake him if he could, every one was forbidden to aid his master in doing it. This statute, in fact, made the servitude voluntary, and that was what Moses intended.

Moses dealt with slavery precisely as he dealt with polygamy and with war—without directly prohibiting, he so restricted as to destroy it; instead of cutting down the poison-tree, he girdled it, and left it to die of itself. There is a statute in regard to military expeditions precisely analogous to this celebrated fugitive slave-law. Had Moses designed to perpetuate a warlike spirit among the Hebrews, the statute would have been pre-eminently absurd; but, if it was his design to crush it, and to render foreign wars almost impossible, the statute was exactly adapted to his purpose. It rendered foreign military service, in effect, entirely voluntary, just as the fugitive-law rendered domestic servitude, in effect, voluntary.

The law may be found at length in Deuteronomy xx. 5-10; and let it be carefully read and compared with the fugitive slave-law already adverted to. Just when the men are drawn up ready for the expedition—just at the moment when even the hearts of brave men are apt to fail them—the officers are commanded to address the soldiers thus:—

What man of you is there that hath built a new house, and hath not dedicated it? Let him go and return to his house, lest he die in the battle, and another man dedicate it.

And what man is he that hath planted a vineyard and hath not yet eaten of it? Let him also go and return to his house, lest he die in the battle, and another man eat of it.

And what man is there that hath betrothed a wife, and hath not taken her? Let him go and return unto his house, lest he die in the battle, and another man take her.

And the officers shall speak further unto the people, and they shall say, What man is there that is fearful and faint-hearted? Let him go and return unto his house, lest his brethren's heart faint, as well as his heart.

Now, consider that the Hebrews were exclusively an agricultural people, that warlike parties necessarily consist mainly of young men, and that by this statute every man who had built a house which he had not yet lived in, and every man who had planted a vineyard from which he had not yet gathered fruit, and every man who had engaged a wife whom he had not yet married, and everyone who felt timid and faint-hearted, was permitted and commanded to go home—how many would there probably be left? Especially when the officers, instead of exciting their military ardour by visions of glory and of splendour, were commanded to repeat it over and over again, that they would probably die in the battle and never get home, and hold this idea up before them as if it were the only idea suitable for their purpose, how excessively absurd is the whole statute considered as a military law—just as absurd as the Mosaic fugitive-law, understood in its widest application, is, considered as a slave-law!

It is clearly the object of this military law to put an end to military expeditions; for, with this law in force, such expeditions must always be entirely volunteer expeditions. Just as clearly was it the object of the fugitive slave-law to put an end to compulsory servitude; for, with that law in force, the servitude must in effect be, to a great extent, voluntary—and that is just what the legislator intended. There is no possibility of limiting the law, on account of its absurdity, when understood in its widest sense, except by proving that the Mosaic legislation was designed to perpetuate and not to limit slavery; and this certainly cannot be proved, for it is directly contrary to the plain matter of fact.

I repeat it, then, again—there is nothing in the language of this statute, there is nothing in the connexion in which it stands, there is nothing in the history of the Mosaic legislation on this subject, to limit the application of the law to the case of servants escaping from foreign masters; but every consideration from every legitimate source leads us to a conclusion directly the opposite. Such a limitation is the arbitrary, unsupported *stet voluntas pro ratione* assumption of the commentator, and nothing else. The only shadow of a philological argument that I can see, for limiting the statute, is found in the use of the words *to thee,* in the fifteenth verse. It may be said that the pronoun *thee* is used in a *national* and not *individual* sense, implying an escape from some other nation to the Hebrews. But examine the statute immediately preceding this, and observe the use of the pronoun *thee* in the thirteenth verse. Most obviously, the pronouns in these statutes are used with reference to the *individuals* addressed, and not in a collective or national sense exclusively; very rarely, if ever, can this sense be given to them in the way claimed by the argument referred to.

2. It is said that the proclamation, "Thou shalt proclaim liberty through the land to all the inhabitants thereof," related only to Hebrew slaves. This assumption is based entirely on the supposition that the slave was not considered in Hebrew law as a person, as an inhabitant of the land, and a member of the State; but we have just proved that in the most solemn transaction of the State the hewer of wood and drawer of water is expressly designated as being just as much an actor and participator as his master; and it would be absurd to suppose that, in a statute addressed to all the inhabitants of the land, he is not included as an inhabitant.

Barnes enforces this idea by some pages of quotations from Jewish writers, which will fully satisfy anyone who reads his work.

From a review, then, of all that relates to the Hebrew slave-law, it will appear that it was a very well-considered and wisely adapted system of education and gradual emancipation. No rational man can doubt that if the same laws were enacted and the same practices prevailed with regard to slavery in the United States, that the system of American slavery might be considered, to all intents and purposes, practically at an end. If there is any doubt of this fact, and it is still thought that the permission of slavery among the Hebrews justifies American slavery, in all fairness the experiment of making the two systems alike ought to be tried, and we should then see what would be the result.

CHAPTER XV.

SLAVERY IS DESPOTISM.

IT is always important, in discussing a thing, to keep before our minds exactly what it is.

The only means of understanding precisely what a civil institution is, are an examination of the laws which regulate it. In different ages and nations, very different things have been called by the name of slavery. Patriarchal servitude was one thing, Hebrew servitude was another, Greek and Roman servitude still a third; and these institutions differed very much from each other. What, then, is American slavery, as we have seen it exhibited by law, and by the decision of Courts?

Let us begin by stating what it is not:—

1. It is not apprenticeship.
2. It is not guardianship.
3. It is in no sense a system for the education of a weaker race by a stronger.
4. The happiness of the governed is in no sense its object.
5. The temporal improvement or the eternal well-being of the governed is in no sense its object.

The object of it has been distinctly stated in one sentence by Judge Ruffin—"The end is the profit of the master, his security, and the public safety."

Slavery, then, is absolute despotism, of the most unmitigated form.

It would, however, be doing injustice to the absolutism of any *civilised* country to liken American slavery to it. The absolute governments of Europe none of them pretend to be founded on a *property* right of the governor to the persons and entire capabilities of the governed.

This is a form of despotism which exists only in some of the most savage countries of the world; as, for example, in Dahomey.

The European absolutism or despotism, now, does, to some extent, recognise the happiness and welfare of the *governed* as the foundation of government; and the ruler is considered as invested with power *for the benefit of the people;* and his right to rule is supposed to be in somewhat predicated upon the idea that he better understands how to promote the good of the people than they themselves do. No government in the *civilised* world now presents the pure despotic idea, as it existed in the old days of the Persian and Assyrian rule.

The arguments which defend slavery must be substantially the same as those which defend despotism of any other kind; and the objections which are to be urged against it are precisely those which can be urged against despotism of any other kind. The customs and practices to which it gives rise are precisely those to which despotisms in all ages have given rise.

Is the slave suspected of a crime? His master has the power to examine him by torture (see State *v*. Castleman). His master has, in fact, in most cases, the power of life and death, owing to the exclusion of the slave's evidence. He has the power of banishing the slave, at any time, and without giving an account to anybody, to an exile as dreadful as that of Siberia, and to labours as severe as those of the galleys. He has also unlimited power over the character of his slave. He can accuse him of any crime, yet withhold from him all right of trial or investigation, and sell him into captivity, with his name blackened by an unexamined imputation.

These are all abuses for which despotic governments are blamed. They are powers which good men who are despotic rulers are beginning to disuse; but, under the flag of every slaveholding State, and under the flag of the whole United States in the District of Columbia, they are committed indiscriminately to men of any character.

But the worst kind of despotism has been said to be that which extends alike over the body and over the soul; which can bind the liberty of the conscience, and deprive a man of all right of choice in respect to the manner in which he shall learn the will of God, and worship him. In other days, kings on their thrones, and cottagers by their fire-sides, alike trembled before a despotism which declared itself able to bind and to loose, to open and to shut the kingdom of heaven.

Yet this power to control the conscience, to control the religious privileges, and all the opportunities which man has of acquaintanceship with his Maker, and of learning to do his will, is, under the flag of every slave State, and under the flag of the United States, placed in the hands of any men of any character who can afford to pay for it.

It is a most awful and most solemn truth that the greatest republic in the world does sustain under her national flag the worst system of despotism which can possibly exist.

With regard to one point to which we have adverted—the power of the master to deprive the slave of a legal trial while accusing him of crime—a very striking instance has occurred in the District of Columbia, within a year or two. The particulars of the case, as stated at the time, in several papers, were briefly these: A gentleman in Washington, our national capital—an elder in the Presbyterian church—held a female slave, who had, for some years, supported a good character in a Baptist church of that city. He accused her of an attempt to poison his family, and immediately placed her in the hands of a slave-dealer, who took her over and imprisoned her in the slave-pen at Alexandria, to await the departure of a coffle. The poor girl had a mother, who felt as any mother would naturally feel.

When apprised of the situation of her daughter she flew to the pen, and, with tears, besought an interview with her only child; but she was cruelly repulsed, and told to be gone! She then tried to see the elder, but failed. She had the promise of money sufficient to purchase her daughter, but the owner would listen to no terms of compromise.

In her distress, the mother repaired to a lawyer in the city, and begged him to give form to her petition in writing. She stated to him what she wished to have said, and he arranged it for her in such a form as she herself might have presented it in, had not the benefits of education been denied her. The following is the letter:—

Washington, July 25, 1851.

SIR,—I address you as a rich Christian freeman and father, while I am myself but a poor slave-mother. I come to plead with you for an only child whom I love, who is a professor of the Christian religion with yourself, and a member of a Christian church; and who, by your act of ownership, now pines in her imprisonment in a loathsome man-warehouse, where she is held for sale. I come to plead with you for the exercise of that blessed law, "Whatsoever ye would that men should do unto you, do ye even so to them."

With great labour, I have found friends who are willing to aid me in the purchase of my child, to save us from a cruel separation. You, as a father, can judge of my feelings when I was told that you had decreed her banishment to distant as well as to hopeless bondage!

For nearly six years my child has done for you the hard labour of a slave; from the age of sixteen to twenty-two she has done the hard work of your chamber, kitchen, cellar, and stables. By night and by day, your will and your commands have been her highest law; and all this has been unrequited toil. If in all this time her scanty allowance of tea and coffee has been sweetened, it has been at the cost of her slave-mother, and not at yours.

You are an office-bearer in the church, and a man of prayer. As such, and as the absolute owner of my child, I ask candidly whether she has enjoyed such mild and gentle treatment, and amiable example, as she ought to have had, to encourage her in her monotonous bondage? Has she received at your hands, in faithful religious instruction in the Word of God, a full and fair compensation for all her toil? It is not to me alone that you must answer these questions. You acknowledge the high authority of His laws who preached a deliverance to the captive, and who commands you to give to your servant "that which is just and equal." Oh, I entreat you, withhold not, at this trying hour, from my child that which will cut off her last hope, and which may endanger your own soul!

It has been said that you charge my daughter with crime. Can this be really so? Can it be that you would set aside the obligations of honour and good citizenship—that you would dare to sell the guilty one away for money, rather than bring her to trial, which you know she is ready to meet? What would you say, if you were accused of guilt and refused a trial? Is not her fair name as precious to her, in the church to which she belongs, as yours can be to you?

CHAPTER XV.

Suppose, now, for a moment, that your daughter, whom you love, instead of mine, was in these hot days incarcerated in a negro-pen, subject to my control, fed on the coarsest food, committed to the entire will of a brute, denied the privilege commonly allowed even to the murderer—that of seeing the face of his friends? Oh, then you would FEEL!—feel soon, then, for a poor slave-mother and her child, and do for us as you shall wish you had done when we shall meet before the Great Judge, and when it shall be your greatest joy to say, "I *did* let the oppressed free!"

ELLEN BROWN. Mr.—

The girl, however, was sent off to the Southern market.

The writer has received these incidents from the gentleman who wrote the letter. Whether the course pursued by the master was strictly legal is a point upon which we are not entirely certain; that it was a course in which the law did not in fact interfere, is quite plain, and it is also very apparent that it was a course against which public sentiment did not remonstrate. The man who exercised this power was a professedly religious man, enjoying a position of importance in a Christian church; and it does not appear, from any movements in the Christian community about him, that they did not consider his course a justifiable one.

Yet is not this kind of power the very one at which we are so shocked when we see it exercised by foreign despots?

Do we not read with shuddering that in Russia, or in Austria, a man accused of crime is seized upon, separated from his friends, allowed no opportunities of trial or of self-defence, but hurried off to Siberia, or some other dreaded exile?

Why is despotism any worse in the governor of a State than in a private individual?

There is a great controversy now going on in the world between the despotic and the republican principle. All the common arguments used in support of slavery are arguments that apply with equal strength to despotic government, and there are some arguments in favour of despotic governments that do not apply to individual slavery.

There are arguments, and quite plausible ones, in favour of despotic government. Nobody can deny that it possesses a certain kind of efficiency, compactness, and promptness of movement, which cannot, from the nature of things, belong to a republic. Despotism has established and sustained much more efficient systems of police than ever a republic did. The late King of Prussia, by the possession of absolute despotic power, was enabled to carry out a much more efficient system of popular education than we ever have succeeded in carrying out in America. He districted his kingdom in the most thorough manner, and obliged every parent, whether he would or not, to have his children thoroughly educated.

If we reply to all this, as we do, that the possession of absolute power in a man qualified to use it right is undoubtedly calculated for the good of the state, but that there are so few men that know how to use it, that this form of government is not, on the whole, a safe one, then we have stated an argument that goes to over-throw slavery as much as it does a despotic government; for certainly the chances are much greater of finding one man, in the course of fifty years, who is capable of wisely using this power, than of finding thousands of men every day in our streets, who can be trusted with such power. It is a painful and most serious fact, that America trusts to the hands of the most brutal men of her country, equally with the best, that despotic power which she thinks an unsafe thing even in the hands of the enlightened, educated, and cultivated Emperor of the Russias.

With all our republican prejudices, we cannot deny that Nicholas is a man of talent, with a mind liberalised by education; we have been informed, also, that he is a man of serious and religious character; he certainly, acting as he does in the eye of all the world, must have great restraint upon him from public opinion, and a high sense of character. But who is the man to whom American laws intrust powers more absolute than those of Nicholas of Russia, or Ferdinand of Naples? He may have been a pirate on the high seas; he may be a drunkard; he may, like Souther, have been convicted of a brutality at which humanity turns pale; but, for all that, American slave-law will none the less trust him with this irresponsible power,—power over the body, and power over the soul.

On which side, then, stands the American nation, in the great controversy which is now going on between self-government and despotism? On which side does America stand, in the great controversy for liberty of conscience?

Do foreign governments exclude their population from the reading of the Bible? The slave of America is excluded by the most effectual means possible. Do we say, "Ah! but we read the Bible to our slaves, and present the gospel orally?" This is precisely what religious despotism in Italy says. Do we say that we have no objection to our slaves reading the Bible, if they will stop there; but that with this there will come in a flood of general intelligence, which will upset the existing state of things? This is precisely what is said in Italy.

Do we say we should be willing that the slave should read his Bible, but that he, in his ignorance, will draw false and erroneous conclusions from it, and for that reason we prefer to impart its truths to him orally? This, also, is precisely what the religious despotism of Europe says.

Do we say in our vainglory that despotic government dreads the coming in of anything calculated to elevate and educate the people? And is there not the same dread through all the despotic slave governments of America?

On which side, then, does the American nation stand, in the great, last QUESTION of the age?

THE MINISTER'S WOOING.

INTRODUCTION.

THE author has endeavoured in this story to paint a style of life and manners which existed in New England in the earlier days of her national existence.

Some of the principal characters are historic: the leading events of the story are founded on actual facts, although the author has taken the liberty to arrange and vary them for the purposes of the story.

The author has executed the work with a reverential tenderness for those great and religious minds who laid in New England the foundations of many generations, and for those institutions and habits of life from which, as from a fruitful germ, sprang all the present prosperity of America.

Such as it is, it is commended to the kindly thoughts of that British fireside from which the fathers and mothers of America first went out to give to English ideas and institutions a new growth in a new world.

H. B. STOWE.

18 Montague Street, Russell Square,
August 25, 1859.

CHAPTER I.

MRS. KATY SCUDDER had invited Mrs. Brown, and Mrs. Jones, and Deacon Twitchel's wife to take tea with her on the afternoon of June second, A. D. 17—.

When one has a story to tell, one is always puzzled which end of it to begin at. You have a whole corps of people to introduce that *you* know and your reader doesn't; and one thing so presupposes another, that, whichever way you turn your patchwork, the figures still seem ill-arranged. The small item that I have given will do as well as any other to begin with, as it certainly will lead you to ask, 'Pray, who was Mrs. Katy Scudder?'—and this will start me systematically on my story.

You must understand that in the then small seaport-town of Newport, at that time unconscious of its present fashion and fame, there lived nobody in those days who did not know 'the Widow Scudder.'

In New England settlements a custom has obtained, which is wholesome and touching, of ennobling the woman whom God has made desolate, by a sort of brevet rank which continually speaks for her as a claim on the respect and consideration of the community. The Widow Jones, or Brown, or Smith, is one of the fixed institutions of every New England village,—and doubtless the designation acts as a continual plea for one whom bereavement, like the lightning of heaven, has made sacred.

The Widow Scudder, however, was one of the sort of women who reign queens in whatever society they move in; nobody was more quoted, more deferred to, or enjoyed more unquestioned position than she. She was not rich,—a small farm, with a modest, 'gambrel-roofed,' one-story cottage, was her sole domain; but she was one of the much-admired class who, in the speech of New England, are said to have 'faculty,'—a gift which, among that shrewd people, commands more esteem than beauty, riches, learning, or any other worldly endowment. *Faculty* is Yankee for *savoir faire*, and the opposite virtue to shiftlessness. Faculty is the greatest virtue, and shiftlessness the greatest vice, of Yankee man and woman. To her who has faculty nothing shall be impossible. She shall scrub floors, wash, wring, bake, brew, and yet her hands shall be small and white; she shall have no perceptible income, yet always be handsomely dressed; she shall not have a servant in her house,—with a dairy to manage, hired men to feed, a boarder or two to care for, unheard-of pickling and preserving to do,—and yet you commonly see her every afternoon sitting at her shady parlour-window behind the lilacs, cool and easy, hemming muslin cap-strings, or reading the last new book. She who hath faculty is never in a hurry, never behindhand. She can always step over to distressed Mrs. Smith, whose jelly won't come,—and stop to show Mrs. Jones how she makes her pickles so green,—and be ready to watch with poor old Mrs. Simpkins, who is down with the rheumatism.

Of this genus was the Widow Scudder,—or, as the neighbours would have said of her, she that *was* Katy Stephens. Katy was the only daughter of a shipmaster, sailing from Newport harbour, who was wrecked off the coast one cold December night, and left small fortune to his widow and only child. Katy grew up, however, a tall, straight, black-eyed girl, with eyebrows drawn true as a bow, a foot arched like a Spanish woman's, and a little hand which never saw the thing it could not do,—quick of speech, ready of wit, and, as such girls have a right to be, somewhat positive withal. Katy could harness a chaise, or row a boat; she could saddle and ride any horse in the neighbourhood; she could cut any garment that ever was seen or thought of; make cake, jelly, and wine, from her earliest years, in most precocious style; all without seeming to derange a sort of trim, well-kept air of ladyhood that sat jauntily on her.

Of course, being young and lively, she had her admirers, and some well-to-do in worldly affairs laid their lands and houses at Katy's feet; but, to the wonder of all, she would not even pick them up to look at them. People shook their heads, and wondered whom Katy Stephens expected to get, and talked about going through the wood to pick up a crooked stick,—till one day she astonished her world by marrying a man that nobody ever thought of her taking.

George Scudder was a grave, thoughtful young man,—not given to talking, and silent in the society of women, with that kind of reverential bashfulness which sometimes shows a pure, unworldly nature. How Katy came to fancy him everybody wondered,—for he never talked to her, never so much as picked up her glove when it fell, never asked her to ride or sail; in short, everybody said she must have wanted him from sheer wilfulness, because he of all the young men of the neighbourhood never courted her. But Katy, having very sharp eyes, saw some things that nobody else saw. For example, you must know she discovered by mere accident that George Scudder always was looking at her, wherever she moved, though he looked away in a moment if discovered,—and that an accidental touch of her hand or brush of her dress would send the blood into his cheek like the spirit in the tube of a thermometer; and so, as women are curious, you know, Katy amused herself with investigating the causes of these little phenomena, and, before she knew it, got her foot caught in a cobweb that held her fast, and constrained her, whether she would or no, to marry a poor man that nobody cared much for but herself.

George was, in truth, one of the sort who evidently have made some mistake in coming into this world at all, as their internal furniture is in no way suited to its general courses and currents. He was of the order of dumb poets,—most wretched when put to the grind of the hard and actual; for if he who would utter poetry stretches out his hand to a gainsaying world, he is worse off still who is possessed with the desire of living it. Especially is this the case if he be born poor, and with a dire necessity upon him of making immediate efforts in the hard and actual. George had a helpless invalid mother to support; so, though he loved reading and silent thought above all things, he put to instant use the only convertible worldly talent he possessed, which was a mechanical genius, and shipped at sixteen as a ship-carpenter. He studied navigation in the forecastle, and found in its calm diagrams and tranquil eternal signs food for his thoughtful nature, and a refuge from the brutality and coarseness of sea life. He had a healthful, kindly animal nature, and so his inwardness did not ferment and turn to Byronic sourness and bitterness; nor did he needlessly parade to everybody in his vicinity the great gulf which lay between him and them. He was called a good fellow,—only a little lumpish,—and as he was brave and faithful, he rose in time to be a shipmaster. But when came the business of making money, the aptitude for accumulating, George found himself distanced by many a one with not half his general powers.

What shall a man do with a sublime tier of moral faculties, when the most profitable business out of his port is the slave-trade? So it was in Newport in those days. George's first voyage was on a slaver, and he wished himself dead many a time before it was over,—and ever after would talk like a man beside himself if the subject was named. He declared that the gold made in it was distilled from human blood, from mothers' tears, from the agonies and dying groans of gasping, suffocating men and women, and that it would sear and blister the soul of him that touched it: in short, he talked as whole-souled, unpractical fellows are apt to talk about what respectable people sometimes do. Nobody had ever instructed him that a slave-ship, with a procession of expectant sharks in its wake, is a missionary institution, by which closely-packed heathens are brought over to enjoy the light of the gospel.

So, though George was acknowledged to be a good fellow, and honest as the noon-mark on the kitchen floor, he let slip so many chances of making money as seriously to compromise his reputation among thriving folks. He was wastefully generous,—insisted on treating every poor dog that came in his way, in any foreign port, as a brother,—absolutely refused to be party in cheating or deceiving the heathen on any shore, or in skin of any colour,—and also took pains, as far as in him lay, to spoil any bargains which any of his subordinates founded on the ignorance or weakness of his fellow-men. So he made voyage after voyage, and gained only his wages and the reputation among his employers of an incorruptibly honest fellow.

To be sure, it was said that he carried out books in his ship, and read and studied, and wrote observations on all the countries he saw, which Parson Smith told Miss Dolly Persimmon would really do credit to a printed book; but then they never *were* printed, or, as Miss Dolly remarked of them, they never seemed to come to anything—and coming to anything, as she understood it, meant standing in definite relations to bread and butter.

George never cared, however, for money. He made enough to keep his mother comfortable, and that was enough for him, till he fell in love with Katy Stephens. He looked at her through those glasses which such men carry in their souls, and she was a mortal woman no longer, but a transfigured, glorified creature,—an object of awe and wonder. He was actually afraid of her; her glove, her shoe, her needle, thread, and thimble, her bonnet-string, everything, in short, she wore or touched became invested with a mysterious charm. He wondered at the impudence of men that could walk up and talk to her,—that could ask her to dance with such an assured air. *Now* he wished he were rich; he dreamed impossible chances of his coming home a millionnaire to lay unknown wealth at Katy's feet; and when Miss Persimmon, the ambulatory dressmaker of the neighbourhood, in making up a new black gown for his mother, recounted how Captain Blatherem had sent Katy Stephens ''most the splendidest India shawl that ever she did see,' he was ready to tear his hair at the thought of his poverty. But even in that hour of temptation he did not repent that he had refused all part and lot in the ship by which Captain Blatherem's money was made, for he knew every timber of it to be seasoned by the groans and saturated with the sweat of human agony. True love is a natural sacrament; and if ever a young man thanks God for having saved what is noble and manly in his soul, it is when he thinks of offering it to the woman he loves. Nevertheless, the India-shawl story cost him a night's rest; nor was it till Miss Persimmon had ascertained, by a private confabulation with Katy's mother, that she had indignantly rejected it, and that she treated the captain 'real ridiculous,' that he began to take heart. 'He ought not,' he said, 'to stand in her way now, when he had nothing to offer. No, he would leave Katy free to do better, if she could; he would try his luck, and if, when he came home from the next voyage, Katy was disengaged, why, then he would lay all at her feet.'

And so George was going to sea with a secret shrine in his soul, at which he was to burn unsuspected incense.

But, after all, the mortal maiden whom he adored suspected this private arrangement, and contrived—as women will—to get her own key into the lock of his secret temple; because, as girls say, 'she was *determined* to know what was there.' So, one night, she met him quite accidentally on the sea-sands, struck up a little conversation, and begged him in such a pretty way to bring her a spotted shell from the South Sea, like the one on his mother's mantelpiece, and looked so simple and childlike in saying it, that our young man very imprudently committed himself by remarking, that, 'When people had rich friends to bring them all the world from foreign parts, he never dreamed of her wanting so trivial a thing.'

Of course Katy 'didn't know what he meant,—she hadn't heard of any rich friends.' And then came something about Captain Blatherem; and Katy tossed her head, and said, 'If anybody wanted to insult her, they might talk to her about Captain Blatherem,'—and then followed this, that, and the other, till finally, as you might expect, out came all that never was to have been said; and Katy was almost frightened at the terrible earnestness of the spirit she had evoked. She tried to laugh, and ended by crying, and saying she hardly knew what; but when she came to herself in her own room at home, she found on her finger a ring of African gold that George had put there, which she did not send back like Captain Blatherem's presents.

Katy was like many intensely matter-of-fact and practical women, who have not in themselves a bit of poetry or a particle of ideality, but who yet worship these qualities in others with the homage which the Indians paid to the unknown tongue of the first whites. They are secretly weary of a certain conscious dryness of nature in themselves, and this weariness predisposes them to idolize the man who brings them this unknown gift. Naturalists say that every defect of organization has its compensation, and men of ideal natures find in the favour of women the equivalent for their disabilities among men.

Do you remember, at Niagara, a little cataract on the American side, which throws its silver sheeny veil over a cave called the Grot of Rainbows? Whoever stands on a rock in that grotto sees himself in the centre of a rainbow-circle, above, below, around. In like manner, merry, chatty, positive, busy, housewifely Katy saw herself standing in a rainbow-shrine in her lover's inner soul, and liked to see herself so. A woman, by-the-by, must be very insensible who is not moved to come upon a higher plane of being, herself, by seeing how undoubtingly she is insphered in the heart of a good and noble man. A good man's faith in you, fair lady, if you ever have it, will make you better and nobler even before you know it.

Katy made an excellent wife: she took home her husband's old mother, and nursed her with a dutifulness and energy worthy of all praise, and made her own keen outward faculties and deft handiness a compensation for the defects in worldly estate. Nothing would make Katy's bright eyes flash quicker than any reflections on her husband's want of luck in the material line. 'She didn't know whose business it was, if *she* was satisfied. She hated these sharp, gimlet, gouging sort of men that would put a screw between body and soul for money. George had that in him that nobody understood. She would rather be his wife on bread and water than to take Captain Blatherem's house, carriages, and horses, and all,—and she *might* have had 'em fast enough, dear knows. She was sick of making money when she saw what sort of men could make it,'—and so on. All which talk did her infinite credit, because *at bottom* she *did* care, and was naturally as proud and ambitious a little minx as ever breathed, and was thoroughly grieved at heart at George's want of worldly success; but, like a nice little Robin Redbreast, she covered up the grave of her worldliness with the leaves of true love, and sang a 'Who cares for that?' above it.

Her thrifty management of the money her husband brought her soon bought a snug little farm, and put up the little brown gambrel-roofed cottage to which we directed your attention in the first of our story. Children were born to them, and George found, in short intervals between voyages, his home an earthly paradise. He was still sailing, with the fond illusion, in every voyage, of making enough to remain at home,—when the yellow fever smote him under the line, and the ship returned to Newport without its captain.

George was a Christian man;—he had been one of the first to attach himself to the unpopular and unworldly ministry of the celebrated Dr. H., and to appreciate the sublime ideality and unselfishness of those teachings which then were awakening new sensations in the theological mind of New England. Katy, too, had become a professor with her husband in the same church, and his death, in the midst of life, deepened the power of her religious impressions. She became absorbed in religion, after the fashion of New England, where devotion is doctrinal, not ritual. As she grew older, her energy of character, her vigour and good judgment, caused her to be regarded as a mother in Israel; the minister boarded at her house, and it was she who was first to be consulted in all matters relating to the well-being of the church. No woman could more manfully breast a long sermon, or bring a more determined faith to the reception of a difficult doctrine. To say the truth, there lay at the bottom of her doctrinal system this stable corner-stone,—'Mr. Scudder used to believe it,—I will.' And after all that is said about independent thought, isn't the fact that a just and good soul has thus or thus believed, a more respectable argument than many that often are adduced? If it be not, more's the pity,—since two-thirds of the faith in the world is built on no better foundation.

In time, George's old mother was gathered to her son, and two sons and a daughter followed their father to the invisible—one only remaining of the flock, and she a person with whom you and I, good reader, have joint concern in the further unfolding of our story.

CHAPTER II.

AS I before remarked, Mrs. Katy Scudder had invited company to tea. Strictly speaking, it is necessary to begin with the creation of the world, in order to give a full account of anything. But for popular use, something less may serve one's turn, and therefore I shall let the past chapter suffice to introduce my story, and shall proceed to arrange my scenery and act my little play on the supposition that you know enough to understand things and persons.

Being asked to tea in our New England in the year 17— meant something very different from the same invitation in our more sophisticated days. In those times, people held to the singular opinion, that the night was made to sleep in; they inferred it from a general confidence they had in the wisdom of Mother Nature, supposing that she did not put out her lights and draw her bed-curtains, and hush all noise in her great world-house without strongly intending that her children should go to sleep; and the consequence was, that very soon after sunset, the whole community very generally set their faces bedward, and the tolling of the nine-o'clock evening-bell had an awful solemnity in it, sounding to the full. Good society in New England in those days very generally took its breakfast at six, its dinner at twelve, and its tea at six. 'Company tea,' however, among thrifty, industrious folk, was often taken an hour earlier, because each of the inviteés had children to put to bed, or other domestic cares at home, and as in those simple times people were invited because you wanted to see them, a tea-party assembled themselves at three and held session till sundown, when each matron rolled up her knitting-work and wended soberly home.

Though Newport, even in those early times, was not without its families which affected state and splendour, rolled about in carriages with armorial emblazonments, and had servants in abundance to every turn within-doors, yet there, as elsewhere in New England, the majority of the people lived with the wholesome, thrifty simplicity of the olden time, when labour and intelligence went hand in hand in perhaps a greater harmony than the world has ever seen.

Our scene opens in the great old-fashioned kitchen, which, on ordinary occasions, is the family dining and sitting room of the Scudder family. I know fastidious moderns think that the working-room, wherein are carried on the culinary operations of a large family, must necessarily be an untidy and comfortless sitting-place; but it is only because they are ignorant of the marvellous workings which pertain to the organ of 'faculty,' on which we have before insisted. The kitchen of a New England matron was her throne-room, her pride; it was the habit of her life to produce the greatest possible results there with the slightest possible discomposure; and what any woman could do, Mrs. Katy Scudder could do *par excellence*. Everything there seemed to be always done, and never doing. Washing and baking, those formidable disturbers of the composure of families, were all over within those two or three morning-hours when we are composing ourselves for a last nap,—and only the fluttering of linen over the green-yard, on Monday mornings, proclaimed that the dreaded solemnity of a wash had transpired. A breakfast arose there as by magic; and in an incredibly short space after, every knife, fork, spoon, and trencher, clean and shining, was looking as innocent and unconscious in its place as if it never had been used and never expected to be.

The floor,—perhaps, sir, you remember your grandmother's floor, of snowy boards sanded with whitest sand; you remember the ancient fireplace stretching quite across one end,—a vast cavern, in each corner of which a cozy seat might be found, distant enough to enjoy the crackle of the great jolly wood-fire; across the room ran a dresser, on which was displayed great store of shining pewter dishes and plates, which always shone with the same mysterious brightness; and by the side of the fire a commodious wooden 'settee,' or settle, offered repose to people too little accustomed to luxury to ask for a cushion. Oh, that kitchen of the olden times, the old, clean, roomy New England kitchen! Who that has breakfasted, dined, and supped in one has not cheery visions of its thrift, its warmth, its coolness? The noon-mark on its floor was a dial that told of some of the happiest days; thereby did we right up the shortcomings of the solemn old clock that tick-tacked in the corner, and whose ticks seemed mysterious prophecies of unknown good yet to arise out of the hours of life. How dreamy the winter twilight came in there!—as yet the candles were not lighted,—when the crickets chirped around the dark stone hearth, and shifting tongues of flame flickered and cast dancing shadows and elfish lights on the walls, while grandmother nodded over her knitting-work, and puss purred, and old Rover lay dreamily opening now one eye and then the other on the family group! With all our ceiled houses, let us not forget our grandmothers' kitchens!

But we must pull up, however, and back to our subject-matter, which is in the kitchen of Mrs. Katy Scudder, who has just put into the oven, by the fireplace, some wondrous tea-rusks, for whose composition she is renowned. She has examined and pronounced perfect a loaf of cake which has been prepared for the occasion, and which, as usual, is done exactly right. The best room, too, has been opened and aired,—the white window-curtains saluted with a friendly little shake, as when one says, 'How d'ye do?' to a friend; for you must know, clean as our kitchen is, we are genteel, and have something better for company. Our best room in here has a polished little mahogany tea-table, and six mahogany chairs, with claw talons grasping balls; the white sanded floor is crinkled in curious little waves, like those on the sea-beach; and right across the corner stands the 'buffet,' as it is called, with its transparent glass doors, wherein are displayed the solemn appurtenances of company tea-table. There you may see a set of real China teacups, which George bought in Canton, and had marked with his and his wife's joint initials,—a small silver cream-pitcher, which has come down as an heirloom from unknown generations,—silver spoons and delicate China cake-plates, which have been all carefully reviewed and wiped on napkins of Mrs. Scudder's own weaving.

Her cares now over, she stands drying her hands on a roller-towel in the kitchen, while her only daughter, the gentle Mary, stands in the doorway with the afternoon sun streaming in spots of flickering golden light on her smooth pale-brown hair,—a *petite* figure, in a full stuff petticoat and white short-gown, she stands reaching up one hand and cooing to something among the apple-blossoms,—and now a Java dove comes whirring down and settles on her finger,—and we, that have seen pictures, think, as we look on her girlish face, with its lines of statuesque beauty,—on the tremulous, half-infantine expression of her lovely mouth, and the general air of simplicity and purity,—of some old pictures of the girlhood of the Virgin. But Mrs. Scudder was thinking of no such Popish matter, I can assure you,—not she! I don't think you could have done her a greater indignity than to mention her daughter in any such connection. She had never seen a painting in her life, and therefore was not to be reminded of them; and furthermore, the dove was evidently, for some reason, no favourite,—for she said, in a quick, imperative tone, 'Come, come, child! don't fool with that bird, it's high time we were dressed and ready,'—and Mary, blushing, as it would seem, even to her hair, gave a little toss, and sent the bird, like a silver fluttering cloud, up among the rosy apple-blossoms. And now she and her mother have gone to their respective little bedrooms for the adjustment of their toilets, and while the door is shut and nobody hears us, we shall talk to you about Mary.

Newport at the present day blooms like a flower-garden with young ladies of the best *ton*,—lovely girls, hopes of their families, possessed of amiable tempers and immensely large trunks, and capable of sporting ninety changes in thirty days, and otherwise rapidly emptying the purses of distressed fathers, and whom yet travellers and the world in general look upon as genuine specimens of the kind of girls formed by American institutions.

We fancy such a one lying in a rustling silk *négligé*, and, amid a gentle generality of rings, ribbons, puffs, laces, beaux, and dinner-discussion, reading our humble sketch;—and what favour shall our poor heroine find in her eyes? For though her mother was a world of energy and 'faculty,' in herself considered, and had bestowed on this one little lone chick all the vigour and all the care and all the training which would have sufficed for a family of sixteen, there were no results produced which could be made appreciable in the eyes of such company. She could not waltz, or polk, or speak bad French, or sing Italian songs; but, nevertheless, we must proceed to say what was her education and what her accomplishments.

Well, then, she could both read and write fluently in the mother-tongue. She could spin both on the little and the great wheel, and there were numberless towels, napkins, sheets, and pillow-cases in the household store that could attest the skill of her pretty fingers. She had worked several samplers of such rare merit, that they hung framed in different rooms of the house, exhibiting every variety and style of possible letter in the best marking-stitch. She was skilful in all sewing and embroidery, in all shaping and cutting, with a quiet and deft handiness that constantly surprised her energetic mother, who could not conceive that so much could be done with so little noise. In fact, in all household lore she was a veritable good fairy; her knowledge seemed unerring and intuitive: and whether she washed or ironed, or moulded biscuit or conserved plums, her gentle beauty seemed to turn to poetry all the prose of life.

There was something in Mary, however, which divided her as by an appreciable line from ordinary girls of her age. From her father she had inherited a deep and thoughtful nature, predisposed to moral and religious exaltation. Had she been born in Italy, under the dissolving influences of that sunny, dreamy clime, beneath the shadow of cathedrals, and where pictured saints and angels smiled in clouds of painting from every arch and altar, she might, like fair St. Catherine of Siena, have seen beatific visions in the sunset skies, and a silver dove descending upon her as she prayed; but, unfolding in the clear, keen, cold New England clime, and nurtured in its abstract and positive theologies, her religious faculties took other forms. Instead of lying entranced in mysterious raptures at the foot of altars, she read and pondered treatises on the Will, and listened in rapt attention while her spiritual guide, the venerated Dr. H., unfolded to her the theories of the great Edwards on the nature of true virtue. Womanlike, she felt the subtle poetry of these sublime abstractions which dealt with such infinite and unknown quantities,—which spoke of the universe, of its great Architect, of men, of angels, as matters of intimate and daily contemplation; and her teacher, a grand-minded and simple-hearted man as ever lived, was often amazed at the tread with which this fair young child walked through these high regions of abstract thought,—often comprehending through an ethereal clearness of nature what he had laboriously and heavily reasoned out; and sometimes, when she turned her grave, childlike face upon him with some question or reply, the good man started as if an angel had looked suddenly out upon him from a cloud. Unconsciously to himself, he often seemed to follow her, as Dante followed the flight of Beatrice, through the ascending circles of the celestial spheres.

When her mother questioned him, anxiously, of her daughter's spiritual estate, he answered, that she was a child of a strange graciousness of nature, and of a singular genius; to which Katy responded, with a woman's pride, that she was all her father over again. It is only now and then that a matter-of-fact woman is sublimated by a real love; but if she is, it is affecting to see how impossible it is for death to quench it; for in the child the mother feels that she has a mysterious and undying repossession of the father.

But, in truth, Mary was only a recast in feminine form of her father's nature. The elixir of the spirit that sparkled within her was of that quality of which the souls of poets and artists are made; but the keen New England air crystallizes emotions into ideas, and restricts many a poetic soul to the necessity of expressing itself only in practical living.

The rigid theological discipline of New England is fitted to produce rather strength and purity than enjoyment. It was not fitted to make a sensitive and thoughtful nature happy, however it might ennoble and exalt.

The system of Dr. H. was one that could only have had its origin in a soul at once reverential and logical,—a soul, moreover, trained from its earliest years in the habits of thought engendered by monarchical institutions. For although he, like other ministers, took an active part as a patriot in the Revolution, still he was brought up under the shadow of a throne; and a man cannot ravel out the stitches in which early days have knit him. His theology, was, in fact, the turning to an invisible Sovereign of that spirit of loyalty and unquestioning subjugation which is one of the noblest capabilities of our nature. And as a gallant soldier renounces life and personal aims in the cause of his king and country, and holds himself ready to be drafted for a forlorn hope, to be shot down, or help make a bridge of his mangled body, over which the more fortunate shall pass to victory and glory, so he regarded himself as devoted to the King Eternal, ready in His hands to be used to illustrate and build up an Eternal Commonwealth, either by being sacrificed as a lost spirit or glorified as a redeemed one, ready to throw not merely his mortal life, but his immortality even, into the forlorn hope, to bridge with a never-dying soul the chasm over which white-robed victors should pass to a commonwealth of glory and splendour, whose vastness should dwarf the misery of all the lost to an infinitesimal.

It is not in our line to imply the truth or the falsehood of those systems of philosophic theology which seem for many years to have been the principal outlet for the proclivities of the New England mind, but as psychological developments they have an intense interest. He who does not see a grand side to these strivings of the soul cannot understand one of the noblest capabilities of humanity.

No real artist or philosopher ever lived who has not at some hours risen to the height of utter self-abnegation for the glory of the invisible. There have been painters who would have been crucified to demonstrate the action of a muscle,—chemists who would gladly have melted themselves and all humanity in their crucible, if so a new discovery might arise out of its fumes. Even persons of mere artistic sensibility are at times raised by music, painting, or poetry to a momentary trance of self-oblivion, in which they would offer their whole being before the shrine of an invisible loveliness. These hard old New England divines were the poets of metaphysical philosophy, who built systems in an artistic fervour, and felt self exhale from beneath them as they rose into the higher regions of thought. But where theorists and philosophers tread with sublime assurance, woman often follows with bleeding footsteps;—women are always turning from the abstract to the individual, and feeling where the philosopher only thinks.

It was easy enough for Mary to believe in *self*-renunciation, for she was one with a born vocation for martyrdom; and so, when the idea was put to her of suffering eternal pains for the glory of God and the good of being in general, she responded to it with a sort of sublime thrill, such as it is given to some natures to feel in view of uttermost sacrifice. But when she looked around on the warm, living faces of friends, acquaintances, and neighbours, viewing them as possible candidates for dooms so fearfully different, she sometimes felt the walls of her faith closing round her as an iron shroud,—she wondered that the sun could shine so brightly, that flowers could flaunt such dazzling colours, that sweet airs could breathe, and little children play, and youth love and hope, and a thousand intoxicating influences combine to cheat the victims from the thought that their next step might be into an abyss of horrors without end. The blood of youth and hope was saddened by this great sorrow, which lay ever on her heart,—and her life, unknown to herself, was a sweet tune in the minor key; it was only in prayer, or deeds of love and charity, or in rapt contemplation of that beautiful millennial day which her spiritual guide most delighted to speak of, that the tone of her feelings ever rose to the height of joy.

Among Mary's young associates was one who had been as a brother to her childhood. He was her mother's cousin's son,—and so, by a sort of family immunity, had always a free access to her mother's house. He took to the sea, as the most bold and resolute young men will, and brought home from foreign parts those new modes of speech, those other eyes for received opinions and established things, which so often shock established prejudices,—so that he was held as little better than an infidel and a castaway by the stricter religious circles in his native place. Mary's mother, now that Mary was grown up to woman's estate, looked with a severe eye on her cousin. She warned her daughter against too free an association with him,—and so—— We all know what comes to pass when girls are constantly warned not to think of a man. The most conscientious and obedient little person in the world, Mary resolved to be very careful. She never would think of James, except, of course, in her prayers; but as these were constant, it may easily be seen it was not easy to forget him.

All that was so often told her of his carelessness, his trifling, his contempt of orthodox opinions, and his startling and bold expressions, only wrote his name deeper in her heart,—for was not his soul in peril? Could she look in his frank, joyous face, and listen to his thoughtless laugh, and then think that a fall from a mast-head, or one night's storm, might——Ah, with what images her faith filled the blank! Could she believe all this and forget him?

You see, instead of getting our tea ready, as we promised at the beginning of this chapter, we have filled it with descriptions and meditations,—and now we foresee that the next chapter will be equally far from the point. But have patience with us; for we can write only as we are driven, and never know exactly where we are going to land.

CHAPTER III.

A QUIET, maiden-like place was Mary's little room. The window looked out under the overarching boughs of a thick apple orchard, now all in a blush with blossoms and pink-tipped buds, and the light came golden-green, strained through flickering leaves,—and an ever-gentle rustle and whirr of branches and blossoms, a chitter of birds, and an indefinite whispering motion, as the long heads of orchard-grass nodded and bowed to each other under the trees, seemed to give the room the quiet hush of some little side chapel in a cathedral, where green and golden glass softens the sunlight, and only the sigh and rustle of kneeling worshippers break the stillness of the aisles. It was small enough for a nun's apartment, and dainty in its neatness as the waxen cell of a bee. The bed and low window were draped in spotless white, with fringes of Mary's own knotting. A small table under the looking-glass bore the library of a well-taught young woman of those times. The 'Spectator,' 'Paradise Lost,' Shakspeare, and 'Robinson Crusoe,' stood for the admitted secular literature, and beside them the Bible and the works then published of Mr. Jonathan Edwards. Laid a little to one side, as if of doubtful reputation, was the only novel which the stricter people in those days allowed for the reading of their daughters: that seven-volumed, trailing, tedious, delightful old bore, 'Sir Charles Grandison,'—a book whose influence in those times was so universal, that it may be traced in the epistolary style even of the gravest divines. Our little heroine was mortal, with all her divinity, and had an imagination which sometimes wandered to the things of earth; and this glorious hero in lace and embroidery, who blended rank, gallantry, spirit, knowledge of the world, disinterestedness, constancy, and piety, sometimes walked before her, while she sat spinning at her wheel, till she sighed, she hardly knew why, that no such men walked the earth now. Yet it is to be confessed, this occasional raid of the romantic into Mary's balanced and well-ordered mind was soon energetically put to rout, and the book, as we have said, remained on her table under protest,—protected by being her father's gift to her mother during their days of courtship. The small looking-glass was curiously wreathed with corals and foreign shells, so disposed as to indicate an artistic eye and skilful hand; and some curious Chinese paintings of birds and flowers gave rather a piquant and foreign air to the otherwise homely neatness of the apartment.

Here in this little retreat, Mary spent those few hours which her exacting conscience would allow her to spare from her busy-fingered household-life; here she read and wrote and thought and prayed;—and here she stands now, arraying herself for the tea company that afternoon. Dress, which in our day is becoming in some cases the whole of woman, was in those times a remarkably simple affair. True, every person of a certain degree of respectability had state and festival robes; and a certain camphor-wood brass-bound trunk, which was always kept solemnly locked in Mrs. Katy Scudder's apartment, if it could have spoken, might have given off quite a catalogue of brocade satin and laces. The wedding-suit there slumbered in all the unsullied whiteness of its stiff ground broidered with heavy knots of flowers; and there were scarfs of wrought India muslin and embroidered crape, each of which had its history,—for each had been brought into the door with beating heart on some return voyage of one who, alas! should return no more. The old trunk stood with its histories, its imprisoned remembrances,—and a thousand tender thoughts seemed to be shaping out of every rustling fold of silk and embroidery, on the few yearly occasions when all were brought out to be aired, their history related, and then solemnly locked up again. Nevertheless, the possession of these things gave to the women of an establishment a certain innate dignity, like a good conscience, so that in that larger portion of existence commonly denominated among them 'every day,' they were content with plain stuff and homespun. Mary's toilet, therefore, was sooner made than those of Newport belles of the present day; it simply consisted in changing her ordinary 'short-gown and petticoat' for another of somewhat nicer materials, a skirt of India chintz and a striped jaconet short-gown. Her hair was of the kind which always lies like satin; but, nevertheless, girls never think their toilet complete unless the smoothest hair has been shaken down and rearranged. A few moments, however, served to braid its shining folds and dispose them in their simple knot on the back of the head; and having given a final stroke to each side with her little dimpled hands, she sat down a moment at the window, thoughtfully watching where the afternoon sun was creeping through the slates of the fence in long lines of gold among the tall, tremulous orchard-grass, and unconsciously she began warbling, in a low, gurgling voice, the words of a familiar hymn, whose grave earnestness accorded well with the general tone of her life and education:—

> 'Life is the time to serve the Lord,
> The time t' insure the great reward.'

There was a swish and rustle in the orchard-grass, and a tramp of elastic steps; then the branches were brushed aside, and a young man suddenly emerged from the trees a little behind Mary. He was apparently about twenty-five, dressed in the holiday rig of a sailor on shore, which well set off his fine athletic figure, and accorded with a sort of easy, dashing, and confident air which sat not unhandsomely on him. For the rest, a high forehead shaded by rings of the blackest hair, a keen, dark eye, a firm and determined mouth, gave the impression of one who had engaged to do battle with life, not only with a will, but with shrewdness and ability.

CHAPTER III.

He introduced the colloquy by stepping deliberately behind Mary, putting his arms round her neck, and kissing her.

'Why, James!' said Mary, starting up and blushing, 'Come, now!'

'I have come, haven't I?' said the young man, leaning his elbow on the window-seat and looking at her with an air of comic determined frankness, which yet had in it such wholesome honesty that it was scarcely possible to be angry. 'The fact is, Mary,' he added, with a sudden earnest darkening of the face, 'I won't stand this nonsense any longer. Aunt Katy has been holding me at arm's length ever since I got home; and what have I done? Haven't I been to every prayer-meeting and lecture and sermon, since I got into port, just as regular as a psalm-book? and not a bit of a word could I get with you, and no chance even so much as to give you my arm. Aunt Katy always comes between us and says, "Here, Mary, you take my arm." What does she think I go to meeting for, and almost break my jaws keeping down the gapes? I never even go to sleep, and yet I am treated in this way! It's too bad! What's the row? What's anybody been saying about me? I always have waited on you ever since you were that high. Didn't I always draw you to school on my sled? didn't we always use to do our sums together? didn't I always wait on you to singing school? and I've been made free to run in and out as if I were your brother;—and now she is as glum and stiff, and always stays in the room every minute of the time that I am there, as if she was afraid I should be in some mischief. It's too bad!'

'Oh, James, I am sorry that you only go to meeting for the sake of seeing me; you feel no real interest in religious things; and besides, mother thinks now I am grown so old that—Why, you know, things are different now,—at least, we mustn't, you know, always do as we did when we were children. But I wish you did feel more interested in good things.'

'I *am* interested in one or two good things, Mary,—principally in you, who are the best I know of. Besides,' he said quickly, and scanning her face attentively to see the effect of his words, 'don't you think there is more merit in my sitting out all these meetings, when they bore me so confoundedly, than there is in your and Aunt Katy's doing it, who really seem to find something to like in them? I believe you have a sixth sense, quite unknown to me, for it's all a maze,—I can't find top, nor bottom, nor side, nor up, nor down to it,—it's you can and you can't, you shall and you shan't, you will and you won't,—'

'James!'

'You needn't look at me so. I'm not going to say the rest of it. But, seriously, it's all anywhere and nowhere to me; it don't touch me, it don't help me, and I think it rather makes me worse; and then they tell me it's because I'm a natural man, and the natural man understandeth not the things of the Spirit. Well, I *am* a natural man,—how's a fellow to help it?'

'Well, James, why need you talk everywhere as you do? You joke, and jest, and trifle, till it seems to everybody that you don't believe in anything. I'm afraid mother thinks you are an infidel, but I *know* it can't be; yet we hear all sorts of things that you say.'

'I suppose you mean my telling Deacon Twitchel that I had seen as good Christians among the Mahometans as any in Newport. *Didn't* I make him open his eyes? It's true, too!'

'In every nation, he that feareth God and worketh righteousness is accepted of Him,' said Mary; 'and if there are better Christians than us among the Mahometans, I am sure I am glad of it. But, after all, the great question is, "Are we Christians ourselves?" Oh, James, if you only were a real, true, noble Christian!'

'Well, Mary, you have got into that harbour, through all the sandbars and rocks and crooked channels; and now do you think it right to leave a fellow beating about outside, and not go out to help him in? This way of drawing up, among your good people, and leaving us sinners to ourselves, isn't generous. You might care a little for the soul of an old friend, anyhow!'

'And don't I care, James? How many days and nights have been one prayer for you! If I could take my hopes of heaven out of my own heart and give them to you, I would. Dr. H. preached last Sunday on the text, "I could wish myself accursed from Christ for my brethren, my kinsmen;" and he went on to show how we must be willing to give up even our own salvation, if necessary, for the good of others. People said it was hard doctrine, but I could feel my way through it very well. Yes, I would give my soul for yours; I wish I could.'

There was a solemnity and pathos in Mary's manner which checked the conversation. James was the more touched because he felt it all so real, from one whose words were always yea and nay, so true, so inflexibly simple. Her eyes filled with tears, her face kindled with a sad earnestness, and James thought, as he looked, of a picture he had once seen in a European cathedral, where the youthful Mother of Sorrows is represented,

'Radiant and grave, as pitying man's decline;
All youth, but with an aspect beyond time; Mournful, but mournful of another's crime;

She looked as if she sat by Eden's door,

And grieved for those who should return no more.'

James had thought he loved Mary; he had admired her remarkable beauty; he had been proud of a certain right in her before that of other young men, her associates; he had thought of her as the keeper of his home; he had wished to appropriate her wholly to himself;—but in all this there had been, after all, only the thought of what she was to be to him; and this, for this poor measure of what he called love, she was ready to offer an infinite sacrifice.

As a subtle flash of lightning will show in a moment a whole landscape—tower, town, winding stream, and distant sea—so that one subtle ray of feeling seemed in a moment to reveal to James the whole of his past life; and it seemed to him so poor, so meagre, so shallow, by the side of that childlike woman, to whom the noblest of feelings were unconscious matters of course, that a sort of awe awoke in him: like the Apostles of old, he 'feared as he entered into the cloud:' it seemed as if the deepest string of some eternal sorrow had vibrated between them.

CHAPTER III.

After a moment's pause, he spoke in a low and altered voice:—

'Mary, I am a sinner. No psalm or sermon ever taught it to me, but I see it now. Your mother is quite right, Mary; you are too good for me; I am no mate for you. Oh, what would you think of me, if you knew me wholly? I have lived a mean, miserable, shallow, unworthy life. You are worthy, you are a saint, and walk in white! Oh, what upon earth, could ever make you care so much for me?'

'Well, then, James, you will be good? Won't you talk with Dr. H.?'

'Hang Dr. H.!' said James. 'Now Mary, I beg your pardon, but I can't make head or tail of a word Dr. H. says. I don't get hold of it, or know what he would be at. You girls and women don't know your power. Why, Mary, you are a living gospel. You have always had a strange power over us boys. You never talked religion much; but I have seen high fellows come away from being with you as still and quiet as one feels when one goes into a church. I can't understand all the hang of predestination, and moral ability, and natural ability, and God's efficiency, and man's agency, which Dr. H. is so engaged about; but I can understand *you*—*you* can do me good!'

'Oh, James, can I?'

'Mary I am going to confess my sins. I saw that, somehow or other, the wind was against me in Aunt Katy's quarter, and you know we fellows who take up the world in both fists don't like to be beat. If there's opposition, it sets us on. Now I confess I never did care much about religion, but I thought, without being really a hypocrite, I'd just let you try to save my soul for the sake of getting you; for there's nothing surer to hook a woman than trying to save a fellow's soul. It's a dead-shot, generally, that. Now our ship sails to-night, and I thought I'd just come across this path in the orchard to speak to you. You know I used always to bring you peaches and juneatings across this way, and once I brought you a ribbon.'

'Yes, I've got it yet, James.'

'Well, now, Mary, all this seems mean to me,—mean to try and trick and snare you, who are so much too good for me. I felt very proud this morning that I was to go out first mate this time, and that I should command a ship next voyage. I meant to have asked you for a promise, but I don't. Only, Mary, just give me your little Bible, and I'll promise to read it all through soberly, and see what it all comes to. And pray for me; and if, while I'm gone, a good man comes who loves you, and is worthy of you, why take him, Mary,—that's my advice.'

'James, I'm not thinking of any such things; I don't ever mean to be married. And I'm glad you don't ask me for any promise, because it would be wrong to give it; mother don't even like me to be much with you. But I'm sure all I have said to you to-day is right; I shall tell her exactly all I have said.'

'If Aunt Katy knew what things we fellows are pitched into, who take the world head-foremost, she wouldn't be so selfish. Mary, you girls and women don't know the world you live in; you ought to be pure and good; you are not as we are. You don't know what men, what women,—no, they're not women!—what creatures, beset us in every foreign port, and boarding-houses that are gates of hell; and then, if a fellow comes back from all this and don't walk exactly straight, you just draw up the hems of your garments and stand close to the wall, for fear he should touch you when he passes. I don't mean you, Mary, for you are different from most; but if you would do what you could, you might save us.—But it's no use talking, Mary. Give me the Bible; and please be kind to my dove,—for I had a hard time getting him across the water, and I don't want him to die.'

If Mary had spoken all that welled up in her little heart at that moment, she might have said too much; but duty had its habitual seal upon her lips. She took the little Bible from her table and gave it with a trembling hand, and James turned to go. In a moment he turned back and stood irresolute.

'Mary,' he said, 'we are cousins; I may never come back: you might kiss me this once.'

The kiss was given and received in silence, and James disappeared among the thick trees.

'Come, child,' said Aunt Katy, looking in, 'there is Deacon Twitchel's chaise in sight,—are you ready?'

'Yes, mother.'

CHAPTER IV.

THEOLOGICAL TEA.

AT the call of her mother, Mary hurried into the 'best room, with a strange discomposure of spirit she had never felt before. From childhood, her love for James had been so deep, equable, and intense, that it had never disturbed her with thrills and yearnings; it had grown up in sisterly calmness, and, quietly expanding, had taken possession of her whole nature without her once dreaming of its power. But this last interview seemed to have struck some great nerve of her being,—and calm as she usually was, from habit, principle, and good health, she shivered and trembled as she heard his retreating footsteps, and saw the orchard-grass fly back from under his feet. It was as if each step trod on a nerve,—as if the very sound of the rustling grass was stirring something living and sensitive in her soul. And, strangest of all, a vague impression of guilt hovered over her. *Had* she done anything wrong? She did not ask him there; she had not spoken love to him; no, she had only talked to him of his soul, and how she would give hers for his,—oh, so willingly!—and that was not love; it was only what Dr. H. said Christians must always feel.

'Child, what *have* you been doing?' said Aunt Katy, who sat in full flowing chintz petticoat and spotless dimity short-gown, with her company knitting-work in her hands; 'your cheeks are as red as peonies. Have you been crying? What's the matter?'

'There is the Deacon's wife, mother,' said Mary, turning confusedly, and darting to the entry-door.

Enter Mrs. Twitchel,—a soft, pillowy, little elderly lady, whose whole air and dress reminded one of a sack of feathers tied in the middle with a string. A large, comfortable pocket, hung upon the side, disclosed her knitting-work ready for operation; and she zealously cleansed herself with a checked handkerchief from the dust which had accumulated during her ride in the old 'one-hoss shay,' answering the hospitable salutation of Katy Scudder in that plaintive, motherly voice which belongs to certain nice old ladies, who appear to live in a state of mild chronic compassion for the sins and sorrows of this mortal life generally.

'Why, yes, Miss Scudder, I'm pretty tol'able. I keep goin', and goin'. That's my way. I's a-tellin' the Deacon, this mornin', I didn't see how I *was* to come here this afternoon; but then I *did* want to see Miss Scudder, and talk a little about that precious sermon, Sunday. How is the Doctor? blessed man! Well, his reward must be great in heaven, if not on earth, as I was a-tellin' the Deacon; and he says to me, says he, "Polly, we mustn't be man-worshippers." There, dear,' (*to Mary,*) 'don't trouble yourself about my bonnet; it a'n't my Sunday one, but I thought 'twould do. Says I to Cerinthy Ann, "Miss Scudder won't mind, 'cause her heart's set on better things." I always like to drop a word in season to Cerinthy Ann, 'cause she's clean took up with vanity and dress. Oh, dear! oh, dear me! so different from your blessed daughter, Miss Scudder! Well, it's a great blessin' to be called in one's youth, like Samuel and Timothy; but then we doesn't know the Lord's ways. Sometimes I gets clean discouraged with my children,—but then ag'in I don't know; none on us does. Cerinthy Ann is one of the most master hands to turn off work; she takes hold and goes along like a woman, and nobody never knows when that gal finds the time to do all she does do; and I don't know nothin' what I *should* do without her. Deacon was saying, if ever she was called, she'd be a Martha, and not a Mary: but then she's dreadful opposed to the doctrines. Oh, dear me! oh, dear me! Somehow they seem to rile her all up; and she was a-tellin' me yesterday, when she was a-hangin' out clothes, that she never should get reconciled to Decrees and 'Lection, 'cause she can't see, if things is certain, how folks is to help 'emselves. Says I, "Cerinthy Ann, folks a'n't to help themselves; they's to submit unconditional." And she jest slammed down the clothes-basket and went into the house.'

When Mrs. Twitchel began to talk, it flowed a steady stream, as when one turns a faucet, that never ceases running till some hand turns it back again; and the occasion that cut the flood short at present was the entrance of Mrs. Brown.

Mr. Simeon Brown was a thriving ship-owner of Newport, who lived in a large house, owned several negro-servants and a span of horses, and affected some state and style in his worldly appearance. A passion for metaphysical Orthodoxy had drawn Simeon to the congregation of Dr. H., and his wife of course stood by right in a high place there. She was a tall, angular, somewhat hard-favoured body, dressed in a style rather above the simple habits of her neighbours, and her whole air spoke the great woman, who in right of her thousands expected to have her say in all that was going on in the world, whether she understood it or not.

On her entrance, mild little Mrs. Twitchel fled from the cushioned rocking-chair, and stood with the quivering air of one who feels she has no business to be anywhere in the world, until Mrs. Brown's bonnet was taken and she was seated, when Mrs. Twitchel subsided into a corner and rattled her knitting-needles to conceal her emotion.

New England has been called the land of equality; but what land upon earth is wholly so? Even the mites in a bit of cheese, naturalists say, have great tumblings and strivings about position and rank: he who has ten pounds will always be a nobleman to him who has but one, let him strive as manfully as he may; and therefore let us forgive meek little Mrs. Twitchel from melting into nothing in her own eyes when Mrs. Brown came in, and let us forgive Mrs. Brown that she sat down in the rocking-chair with an easy grandeur, as one who thought it her duty to be affable and meant to be. It was, however, rather difficult for Mrs. Brown, with her money, house, negroes, and all, to patronise Mrs. Katy Scudder, who was one of those women whose natures seems to sit on thrones, and who dispense patronage and favour by an inborn right and aptitude, whatever be their social advantages. It was one of Mrs. Brown's trials of life, this secret, strange quality in her neighbour, who stood apparently so far below her in worldly goods. Even the quiet positive style of Mrs. Katy's knitting made her nervous; it was an implication of independence of her sway; and though on the present occasion every customary courtesy was bestowed, she still felt, as she always did when Mrs. Katy's guest, a secret uneasiness. She mentally contrasted the neat little parlour, with its white sanded floor and muslin curtains, with her own grand front-room, which boasted the then uncommon luxuries of Turkey carpet and Persian rug, and wondered if Mrs. Katy did really feel as cool and easy in receiving her as she appeared.

You must not understand that this was what Mrs. Brown *supposed* herself to be thinking about; oh, no! by no means! All the little, mean work of our nature is generally done in a small dark closet just a little back of the subject we are talking about, on which subject we suppose ourselves of course to be thinking;—of course we *are* thinking of it; how else could we talk about it?

The subject in discussion, and what Mrs. Brown supposed to be in her own thoughts, was the last Sunday's sermon, on the doctrine of entire Disinterested Benevolence, in which good Doctor H. had proclaimed to the citizens of Newport their duty of being so wholly absorbed in the general good of the universe as even to acquiesce in their own final and eternal destruction, if the greater good of the whole might thereby be accomplished.

'Well, now, dear me!' said Mrs. Twitchel, while her knitting-needles trotted contentedly to the mournful tone of her voice,—'I was tellin' the Deacon, if we only could get there! Sometimes I think I get a little way,—but then ag'in I don't know; but the Deacon he's quite down,—he don't see no evidences in himself. Sometimes he says he don't feel as if he ought to keep his place in the church,—but then ag'in he don't know. He keeps a-turnin' and turnin' on't over in his mind, and a-tryin' himself this way and that way; and he says he don't see nothin' but what's selfish, no way.

''Member one night last winter, after the Deacon got warm in bed, there come a rap at the door; and who should it be but old Beulah Ward wantin' to see the Deacon—'twas her boy she sent, and he said Beulah was sick and hadn't no more wood nor candles. Now I know'd the Deacon had carried that critter half a cord of wood, if he had one stick, since Thanksgivin', and I'd sent her two o' my best moulds of candles,—nice ones that Cerinthy Ann run when we killed a crittur; but nothin' would do but the Deacon must get right out his warm bed and dress himself, and hitch up his team to carry over some wood to Beulah. Says I, "Father, you know you'll be down with the rheumatis for this; besides, Beulah is real aggravatin'. I know she trades off what we send her to the store for rum, and you never get no thanks. She 'xpects, 'cause we has done for her, we always must; and more we do, more we may do." And says he to me, says he, "That's jest the way we sarves the Lord, Polly; and what if He shouldn't hear us when we call on Him in our troubles?" So I shet up; and the next day he was down with the rheumatis. And Cerinthy Ann, says she, "Well, father, *now* I hope you'll own you have got *some* disinterested benevolence," says she; and the Deacon he thought it over a spell, and then he says, "I'm 'fraid it's all selfish. I'm jest a-makin' a righteousness of it." And Cerinthy Ann she come out, declarin' that the best folks never had no comfort in religion; and for her part she didn't mean to trouble her head about it, but have jest as good a time as she could while she's young, 'cause if she was 'lected to be saved she should be, and if she wa'n't she couldn't help it, any how.'

'Mr. Brown says he came on to Dr. H.'s ground years ago' said Mrs. Brown, giving a nervous twitch to her yarn, and speaking in a sharp, hard, didactic voice, which made little Mrs. Twitchel give a gentle quiver, and look humble and apologetic. 'Mr. Brown's a master thinker; there's nothing pleases that man better than a hard doctrine; he says you can't get 'em too hard for him. He don't find any difficulty in bringing his mind up; he just reasons it out all plain; and he says, people have no need to be in the dark; and that's *my* opinion. "If folks know they ought to come up to anything, why *don't* they?" he says; and I say so too.'

'Mr. Scudder used to say that it took great afflictions to bring his mind to that place,' said Mrs. Katy. 'He used to say that an old paper-maker told him once, that paper that was shaken only one way in the making would tear across the other, and the best paper had to be shaken every way; and so he said we couldn't tell, till we had been turned and shaken and tried every way, where we should tear.'

Mrs. Twitchel responded to this sentiment with a gentle series of groans, such as were her general expression of approbation, swaying herself backward and forward; while Mrs. Brown gave a sort of toss and snort, and said that for her part she always thought people knew what they did know,—but she guessed she was mistaken.

The conversation was here interrupted by the civilities attendant on the reception of Mrs. Jones,—a broad, buxom, hearty soul, who had come on horseback from a farm about three miles distant.

Smiling with rosy content, she presented Mrs. Katy a small pot of golden butter,—the result of her forenoon's churning.

There are some people so evidently broadly and heartily of this world, that their coming into a room always materializes the conversation. We wish to be understood that we mean no disparaging reflection on such persons;—they are as necessary to make up a world as cabbages to make up a garden; the great healthy principles of cheerfulness and animal life seem to exist in them in the gross; they are wedges and ingots of solid, contented vitality. Certain kinds of virtues and Christian graces thrive in such people as the first crop of corn does in the bottomlands of the Ohio. Mrs. Jones was a church-member, a regular church-goer, and planted her comely person plump in front of Dr. H. every Sunday, and listened to his searching and discriminating sermons with broad, honest smiles of satisfaction. Those keen distinctions as to motives, those awful warnings and urgent expostulations, which made poor Deacon Twitchel weep, she listened to with great, round, satisfied eyes, making to all, and after all, the same remark,—that it was good, and she liked it, and the Doctor was a good man; and on the present occasion, she announced her pot of butter as one fruit of her reflections after the last discourse.

'You see,' she said, 'as I was a-settin' in the spring-house, this mornin', a-workin' my butter, I says to Dinah,—"I'm goin' to carry a pot of this down to Miss Scudder for the Doctor,—I got so much good out of his Sunday's sermon." And Dinah she says to me, says she,—"Laws, Miss Jones, I thought you was asleep, for sartin!" But I wasn't; only I forgot to take any carraway-seed in the mornin', and so I kinder missed it; you know it 'livens one up. But I never lost myself so but what I kinder heerd him goin' on, on, sort o' like,—and it sounded *all* sort o' *good;* and so I thought of the Doctor to-day.'

'Well, I'm sure,' said Aunt Katy, 'this will be a treat; we all know about your butter, Mrs. Jones. I sha'n't think of putting any of mine on table to-night, I'm sure.'

'Law, now don't!' said Mrs. Jones. 'Why you re'lly make me ashamed, Miss Scudder. To be sure, folks does like our butter, and it always fetches a pretty good price,—*he's* very proud on't. I tell him he oughtn't to be,—we oughtn't to be proud of anything.'

And now Mrs. Katy, giving a look at the old clock, told Mary it was time to set the tea-table; and forthwith there was a gentle movement of expectancy. The little mahogany tea-table opened its brown wings, and from a drawer came forth the snowy damask covering. It was etiquette, on such occasions, to compliment every article of the establishment successively as it appeared; so the Deacon's wife began at the table-cloth.

'Well, I do declare, Miss Scudder beats us all in her table-cloths,' she said, taking up a corner of the damask, admiringly; and Mrs. Jones forthwith jumped up and seized the other corner.

'Why, this 'ere must have come from the Old Country. It's most the beautiflest thing I ever did see.'

'It's my own spinning,' replied Mrs. Katy, with conscious dignity. 'There was an Irish weaver came to Newport the year before I was married, who wove beautifully,—just the Old-Country patterns,—and I'd been spinning some uncommonly fine flax then. I remember Mr. Scudder used to read to me while I was spinning,'—and Aunt Katy looked afar, as one whose thoughts are in the past, and dropped out the last words with a little sigh, unconsciously, as to herself.

'Wall, now, I must say,' said Mrs. Jones, 'this goes quite beyond me. I thought I could spin some; but I shan't never dare to show mine.'

'I'm sure, Mrs. Jones, your towels that you had out bleaching, this spring, were wonderful,' said Aunt Katy. 'But I don't pretend to do much now,' she continued, straightening her trim figure. 'I'm getting old, you know; we must let the young folks take up these things. Mary spins better now than I ever did; Mary, hand out those napkins.'

And so Mary's napkins passed from hand to hand.

'Well, well,' said Mrs. Twitchel to Mary, 'it's easy to see that *your* linen-chest will be pretty full by the time *he* comes along; won't it, Miss Jones?'—and Mrs Twitchel looked pleasantly facetious, as elderly ladies generally do, when suggesting such possibilities to younger ones.

Mary was vexed to feel the blood boil up in her cheeks in a most unexpected and provoking way at the suggestion; whereat Mrs. Twitchel nodded knowingly at Mrs. Jones, and whispered something in a mysterious aside, to which plump Mrs. Jones answered,—'Why, do tell! now I never!'

'It's strange,' said Mrs. Twitchel, taking up her parable again, in such a plaintive tone that all knew something pathetic was coming, 'what mistakes some folks will make, a-fetchin' up girls. Now there's your Mary, Miss Scudder,—why, there a'n't nothin' she can't do: but law, I was down to Miss Skinner's, last week, a-watchin' with her, and re'lly it 'most broke my heart to see her. Her mother was a most amazin' smart woman; but she brought Suky up, for all the world, as if she'd been a wax doll, to be kept in the drawer,—and sure enough, she was a pretty cretur,—and now she's married, what is she? She ha'n't no more idee how to take hold than nothin'. The poor child means well enough, and she works so hard she 'most kills herself; but then she is in the suds from mornin' till night,—she's one the sort whose work's never done,—and poor George Skinner's clean discouraged.'

'There's everything in *knowing how*,' said Mrs. Katy. 'Nobody ought to be always working; it's a bad sign. I tell Mary,—"Always do up your work in the forenoon." Girls must learn that. I never work afternoons, after my dinner dishes are got away; I never did and never would.'

'Nor I, neither,' chimed in Mrs. Jones and Mrs. Twitchel,—both anxious to show themselves clear on this leading point of New-England housekeeping.

'There's another thing I always tell Mary,' said Mrs. Katy, impressively. '"Never say there isn't time for a thing that ought to be done. If a thing is *necessary*, why, life is long enough to find a place for it. That's my doctrine. When anybody tells me they can't *find time* for this or that, I don't think much of 'em. I think they don't know how to work,—that's all."'

Here Mrs. Twitchel looked up from her knitting, with apologetic giggle at Mrs. Brown.

'Law, now, there's Miss Brown, she don't know nothin' about it, 'cause she's got her servants to every turn. I s'pose she thinks it queer to hear us talkin' about our work. Miss Brown must have her time all to herself. I was tellin' the Deacon the other day that she was a privileged woman.'

CHAPTER IV.

'I'm sure, those that have servants find work enough following 'em 'round,' said Mrs. Brown,—who, like all other human beings, resented the implication of not having as many trials in life as her neighbours. 'As to getting the work done up in the forenoon, that's a thing I never can teach 'em; they'd rather not. Chloe likes to keep her work 'round, and do it by snacks, any time, day or night, when the notion takes her.'

'And it was just for that reason I never would have one of those creatures 'round,' said Mrs. Katy. 'Mr. Scudder was principled against buying negroes,—but if he had *not* been, I should not have wanted any of *their* work. I know what's to be done, and most help is no help to me. I want people to stand out of my way and let me get done. I've tried keeping a girl once or twice, and I never worked so hard in my life. When Mary and I do all ourselves, we can calculate everything to a minute; and we get our time to sew and read and spin and visit, and live just as we want to.'

Here, again, Mrs. Brown looked uneasy. To what use was it that she was rich and owned servants, when this Mordecai in her gate utterly despised her prosperity? In her secret heart she thought Mrs. Katy must be envious, and rather comforted herself on this view of the subject,—sweetly unconscious of any inconsistency in the feeling with her views of utter self-abnegation just announced.

Meanwhile the tea-table had been silently gathering on its snowy plateau the delicate china, the golden butter, the loaf of faultless cake, a plate of crullers or wonders, as a sort of sweet fried cake was commonly called,—tea-rusks, light as a puff, and shining on top with a varnish of eggs,—jellies of apple and quince quivering in amber clearness,—whitest and purest honey in the comb,—in short, everything that could go to the getting-up of a most faultless tea.

'I don't see,' said Mrs. Jones, resuming the gentle pæans of the occasion, 'how Miss Scudder's loaf-cake always comes out just so. It don't rise neither to one side nor t'other, but just even all 'round; and it a'n't white one side and burnt the other, but just a good brown all over; and it don't have any heavy streak in it.'

'Jest what Cerinthy Ann was sayin', the other day,' said Mrs. Twichel. 'She says she can't never be sure how hers is a-comin' out. Do what she can, it will be either too much or too little; but Miss Scudder's is always jest so. "Law," says I, "Cerinthy Ann, it's *faculty*,—that's it;—them that has it has it, and them that hasn't—why, they've got to work hard, and not do half so well, neither."'

Mrs. Katy took all these praises as matter of course. Since she was thirteen years old, she had never put her hand to anything that she had not been held to do better than other folks, and therefore she accepted her praises with the quiet repose and serenity of assured reputation: though, of course, she used the usual polite disclaimers of 'Oh, it's nothing, nothing at all; I'm sure I don't know how I do it, and was not aware it was so good,' and so on. All which things are proper for gentlewomen to observe, in like cases, in every walk of life.

'Do you think the Deacon will be along soon?' said Mrs. Katy, when Mary, returning from the kitchen, announced the important fact, that the tea-kettle was boiling.

'Why, yes,' said Mrs. Twitchel. 'I'm a-lookin' for him every minute. He told me, that he and the men should be plantin' up to the eight-acre lot, but he'd keep the colt up there to come down on; and so I laid him out a clean shirt, and says, "Now, father, you be sure and be there by five, so that Miss Scudder may know when to put her tea a-drawin'."—There he is, I believe,' she added, as a horse's tramp was heard without, and, after a few moments, the desired Deacon entered.

He was a gentle, soft-spoken man, low, sinewy, thin, with black hair showing lines and patches of silver. His keen, thoughtful dark eye marked the nervous and melancholic temperament. A mild and pensive humility of manner seemed to brood over him, like the shadow of a cloud. Everything in his dress, air, and motions indicated punctilious exactness and accuracy, at times rising to the point of nervous anxiety.

Immediately after the bustle of his entrance had subsided, Mr. Simeon Brown followed. He was a tall, lank individual, with high-cheek bones, thin, sharp features, small, keen, hard eyes, and large hands and feet.

Simeon was, as we have before remarked, a keen theologian, and had the scent of a hound for a metaphysical distinction. True, he was a man of business, being a thriving trader to the coast of Africa, whence he imported negroes for the American market; and no man was held to understand that branch of traffic better,—he having, in his earlier days, commanded ships in the business, and thus learned it from the root. In his private life, Simeon was severe and dictatorial. He was one of that class of people who, of a freezing day, will plant themselves directly between you and the fire, and there stand and argue to prove that selfishness is the root of moral evil. Simeon said he always had thought so; and his neighbours sometimes supposed that nobody could enjoy better experimental advantages for understanding the subject. He was one of those men who suppose themselves submissive to the Divine will, to the uttermost extent demanded by the extreme theology of that day, simply because they have no nerves to feel, no imagination to conceive, what endless happiness or suffering is, and who deal therefore with the great question of the salvation or damnation of myriads as a problem of theological algebra, to be worked out by their inevitable *x*, *y*, *z*.

But we must not spend too much time with our analysis of character, for matters at the tea-table are drawing to a crisis. Mrs. Jones has announced that she does not think '*he*' can come this afternoon; by which significant mode of expression she conveyed the dutiful idea that there was for her but one male person in the world. And now Mrs. Katy says, 'Mary, dear, knock at the Doctor's door and tell him that tea is ready.'

The Doctor was sitting in his shady study, in the room on the other side of the little entry. The windows were dark and fragrant with the shade and perfume of blossoming lilacs, whose tremulous shadow, mingled with spots of afternoon sunlight, danced on the scattered papers of a great writing-table covered with pamphlets and heavily-bound volumes of theology, where the Doctor was sitting.

CHAPTER IV.

A man of gigantic proportions, over six feet in height, and built every way with an amplitude corresponding to his height, sitting bent over his writing, so absorbed that he did not hear the gentle sound of Mary's entrance.

'Doctor,' said the maiden, gently, 'tea is ready.'

No motion, no sound, except the quick tracing of the pen over the paper.

'Doctor! Doctor!' a little louder, and with another step into the apartment,—'tea is ready.'

The Doctor stretched his head forward to a paper which lay before him, and responded in a low, murmuring voice, as reading something.

'Firstly,—if underived virtue be peculiar to the Deity, can it be the duty of a creature to have it?'

Here a little waxen hand came with a very gentle tap on his huge shoulder, and 'Doctor, tea is ready,' penetrated drowsily to the nerve of his ear, as a sound heard in sleep. He rose suddenly with a start, opened a pair of great blue eyes, which shone abstractedly under the dome of a capacious and lofty forehead, and fixed them on the maiden, who by this time was looking up rather archly, and yet with an attitude of the most profound respect, while her venerated friend was assembling together his earthly faculties.

'Tea is ready, if you please. Mother wished me to call you.'

'Oh!—ah!—yes!—indeed!' he said, looking confusedly about, and starting for the door in his study gown.

'If you please, sir,' said Mary, standing in his way, 'would you not like to put on your coat and wig?'

The Doctor gave a hurried glance at his study gown, put his hand to his head, which, in place of the ample curls of his full-bottomed wig, was decked only with a very ordinary cap, and seemed to come at once to full comprehension. He smiled a kind of conscious, benignant smile, which adorned his high cheek-bones and hard features as sunshine adorns the side of a rock, and said, kindly, 'Ah, well, child, I understand now; I'll be out in a moment.'

And Mary, sure that he was now on the right track, went back to the tea-room with the announcement that the Doctor was coming.

In a few moments he entered, majestic and proper, in all the dignity of full-buttomed, powdered wig, full, flowing coat, with ample cuffs, silver knee and shoe buckles, as became the gravity and majesty of the minister of those days.

He saluted all the company with a benignity which had a touch of the majestic, and also of the rustic in it; for at heart the Doctor was a bashful man, that is, he had somewhere in his mental camp that treacherous fellow whom John Bunyan anathematizes under the name of Shame. The company rose on his entrance; the men bowed and the women curtsied, and all remained standing while he addressed to each, with punctilious decorum, those inquiries in regard to health and well-being which preface a social interview. Then, at a dignified sigh from Mrs. Katy, he advanced to the table, and all following his example, stood, while, with one hand uplifted, he went through a devotional exercise which, for length, more resembled a prayer than a grace,—after which the company were seated.

'Well, Doctor,' said Mr. Brown, who, as a householder of substance, felt a conscious right to be first in open conversation with the minister, 'people are beginning to make a noise about your views. I was talking with Deacon Timmins the other day down on the wharf, and he said Dr. Stiles said that it was entirely new doctrine—entirely so,—and for his part he wanted the good old ways.'

'They say so, do they?' said the Doctor, kindling up from an abstraction into which he seemed to be gradually subsiding. 'Well, let them. I had rather publish *new* divinity than any other, and the more of it the better,—*if it be but true*. I should think it hardly worth while to write, if I had nothing *new* to say.'

'Well,' said Deacon Twitchel,—his meek face flushing with awe of his minister—'Doctor, there's all sorts of things said about you. Now the other day I was at the mill with a load of corn, and while I was a-waitin', Amariah Wadsworth come along with his'n; and so while we were waitin', he says to me, "Why, they say your minister is gettin' to be an Arminian;" and he went on a-tellin' how old Ma'am Badger told him that you interpreted some parts of Paul's Epistles clear on the Arminian side. You know Ma'am Badger's a master-hand at doctrines, and she's 'most an uncommon Calvinist.'

'That does not frighten me at all,' said the sturdy Doctor. 'Supposing I do interpret some texts like the Arminians. Can't Arminians have anything right about them? Who wouldn't rather go with the Arminians when they are *right*, than with the Calvinists when they are wrong?'

'That's it,—you've hit it, Doctor,' said Simeon Brown. 'That's what I always say. I say, 'Don't he *prove* it? and how are you going to answer him?' That gravels 'em.'

'Well,' said Deacon Twitchel, 'Brother Seth—you know Brother Seth,—he says you deny depravity. He's all for imputation of Adam's sin, you know; and I have long talks with Seth about it, every time he comes to see me; and he says, that if we did not sin in Adam, it's givin' up the whole ground altogether; and then he insists you're clean wrong about the unregenerate doings.'

'Not at all,—not in the least,' said the Doctor, promptly.

'I wish Seth could talk with you some time, Doctor. Along in the spring, he was down helpin' me to lay stone fence,—it was when we was fencin' off the south-pastur' lot,—and we talked pretty nigh all day; and it really did seem to me that the longer we talked, the sotter Seth grew. He's a master-hand at readin'; and when he heard that your remarks on Dr. Mayhew had come out, Seth tackled up o' purpose and come up to Newport to get them, and spent all his time, last winter, studyin' on it and makin' his remarks: and I tell you, sir, he's a tight fellow to argue with. Why, that day, what with layin' stone wall and what with arguin' with Seth, I come home quite beat out,—Miss Twitchel will remember.'

'That he was!' said his helpmeet. 'I 'member, when he came home, says I, "Father, you seem clean used up;" and I stirred 'round lively like, to get him his tea. But he jest went into the bedroom and laid down afore supper; and I says to Cerinthy Ann, "That's a thing I ha'n't seen your father do since he was took with the typhus." And Cerinthy Ann, she said she knew 'twa'n't anything but them old doctrines,—that it was always so when Uncle Seth come down. And after tea father was kinder chirked up a little, and he and Seth set by the fire, and was a-beginnin' it ag'in, and I jest spoke out and said,—"Now, Seth, these 'ere things doesn't hurt you; but the Deacon is weakly, and if he gets his mind riled after supper, he don't sleep none all night. So," says I, "you'd better jest let matters stop where they be; 'cause," says I, "'twon't make no difference, for to-night, which on ye's got the right on't;—reckon the Lord'll go on his own way without you; and we shall find out, by'm-by, what that is."'

'Mr. Scudder used to think a great deal on these points,' said Mrs. Katy, 'and the last time he was home he wrote out his views. I haven't ever shown them to you, Doctor; but I should be pleased to know what you think of them.'

'Mr. Scudder was a good man, with a clear head,' said the Doctor; 'and I should be much pleased to see anything that he wrote.'

A flush of gratified feeling passed over Mrs. Katy's face;—for one flower laid on the shrine which we keep in our hearts for the dead is worth more than any gift to our living selves.

We will not now pursue our party further, lest you, Reader, get more theological tea than you can drink. We will not recount the numerous nice points raised by Mr. Simeon Brown and adjusted by the Doctor,—and how Simeon invariably declared, that that was the way in which he disposed of them himself, and how he had thought it out ten years ago.

We will not relate, either, too minutely, how Mary changed colour and grew pale and red in quick succession, when Mr. Simeon Brown incidentally remarked that the 'Monsoon' was going to set sail that very afternoon for her three-years' voyage. Nobody noticed—in the busy amenities—the sudden welling and ebbing of that one poor little heart-fountain.

So we go,—so little knowing what we touch and what touches us as we talk! We drop out a common piece of news,—'Mr. So-and-so is dead,—Miss Such-a-one is married,—such a ship has sailed,'—and lo, on our right hand or our left, some heart has sunk under the news silently,—gone down in the great ocean of Fate, without even a bubble rising to tell its drowning pang. And this—God help us!—is what we call living!

CHAPTER V.

THE LETTER.

MARY returned to the quietude of her room. The red of twilight had faded, and the silver moon, round and fair, was rising behind the thick boughs of the apple-trees. She sat down in the window, thoughtful and sad, and listened to the crickets, whose ignorant jollity often sounds as mournfully to us mortals as ours may to superior beings. There the little hoarse, black wretches were scraping and creaking, as if life and death were invented solely for their pleasure, and the world were created only to give them a good time in it. Now and then a little wind shivered among the boughs, and brought down a shower of white petals which shimmered in the slant beams of the moonlight; and now a ray touched some tall head of grass, and forthwith it blossomed into silver, and stirred itself with a quiet joy, like a new-born saint just awaking in Paradise. And ever and anon came on the still air the soft, eternal pulsations of the distant sea,—sound mournfullest, most mysterious, of all the harpings of Nature. It was the sea,—the deep, eternal sea,—the treacherous, soft, dreadful, inexplicable sea; and he was perhaps at this moment being borne away on it,—away, away,—to what sorrows, to what temptations, to what dangers, she knew not. She looked along the old, familiar, beaten path by which he came, by which he went, and thought, 'What if he *never* should come back?' There was a little path through the orchard out to a small elevation in the pasture-lot behind, whence the sea was distinctly visible, and Mary had often used her low-silled window as a door when she wanted to pass out thither; so now she stepped out, and, gathering her skirts back from the dewy grass, walked thoughtfully along the path and gained the hill. Newport harbour lay stretched out in the distance, with the rising moon casting a long, wavering track of silver upon it; and vessels, like silver-winged moths, were turning and shifting slowly to and fro upon it, and one stately ship in full sail passing fairly out under her white canvas, graceful as some grand, snowy bird. Mary's beating heart told her that *there* was passing away from her one who carried a portion of her existence with him. She sat down under a lonely tree that stood there, and, resting her elbow on her knee, followed the ship with silent prayers, as it passed, like a graceful, cloudy dream, out of her sight.

CHAPTER V.

Then she thoughtfully retraced her way to her chamber; and as she was entering, observed in the now clearer moonlight what she had not seen before,—something white, like a letter, lying on the floor. Immediately she struck a light, and there, sure enough, it was,—a letter in James's handsome, dashing hand; and the little puss, before she knew what she was about, actually kissed it, with a fervour which would much have astonished the writer, could he at that moment have been clairvoyant. But Mary felt as one who finds, in the emptiness after a friend's death, an unexpected message or memento; and all alone in the white, calm stillness of her little room her heart took sudden possession of her. She opened the letter with trembling hands, and read what of course we shall let you read. We got it out of a bundle of old, smoky, yellow letters, years after all the parties concerned were gone on the eternal journey beyond earth.

> 'My dear Mary,—
>
> 'I cannot leave you so. I have about two hundred things to say to you, and it's a shame I could not have had longer to see you; but blessed be ink and paper! I am writing and seeing to fifty things besides; so you musn't wonder if my letter has rather a confused appearance.
>
> 'I have been thinking that perhaps I gave you a wrong impression of myself, this afternoon. I am going to speak to you from my heart, as if I were confessing on my death-bed. Well, then, I do not confess to being what is commonly called a bad young man. I should be willing that men of the world generally, even strict ones, should look my life through and know all about it. It is only in your presence, Mary, that I feel that I am bad and low and shallow and mean, because you represent to me a sphere higher and holier than any in which I have ever moved, and stir up a sort of sighing and longing in my heart to come towards it. In all countries, in all temptations, Mary, your image has stood between me and low, gross vice. When I have been with fellows roaring drunken, beastly songs,—suddenly I have seemed to see you as you used to sit beside me in the singing-school, and your voice has been like an angel's in my ear, and I have got up and gone out sick and disgusted. Your face has risen up calm and white and still, between the faces of poor lost creatures who know no better way of life than to tempt us to sin. And sometimes, Mary, when I have seen girls that, had they been cared for by good, pious mothers, might have been like you, I have felt as if I could cry for them. Poor women are abused all the world over; and it's no wonder they turn round and revenge themselves on us.
>
> 'No, I have not been bad, Mary, as the world calls badness. I have been kept by you. But do you remember you told me once, that, when the snow first fell and lay so dazzling and pure and soft, all about, you always felt as if the spreads and window-curtains that seemed white before were dirty? Well, it's just like that with me.

Your presence makes me feel that I am not pure,—that I am low and unworthy,—not worthy to touch the hem of your garment. Your good Dr. H. spent a whole half-day, the other Sunday, trying to tell us about the beauty of holiness; and he cut, and pared, and peeled, and sliced, and told us what it wasn't, and what was *like* it, and wasn't; and then he built up an exact definition, and fortified and bricked it up all round; and I thought to myself that he'd better tell 'em to look at Mary Scudder, and they'd understand all about it. That was what I was thinking when you talked to me for looking at you in church instead of looking towards the pulpit. It really made me laugh in myself to see what a good little ignorant, unconscious way you had of looking up at the Doctor, as if he knew more about that than you did.

'And now as to your Doctor that you think so much of, I like him for certain things, in certain ways. He is a great, grand, large pattern of a man,—a man who isn't afraid to think, and to speak anything he does think; but then I do believe, if he would take a voyage round the world in the forecastle of a whaler, he would know more about what to say to people than he does now; it would certainly give him several new points to be considered. Much of his preaching about men is as like live men as Chinese pictures of trees and rocks and gardens,—no nearer the reality than that. All I can say is, "It isn't so; and you'd know it, Sir, if you knew men." He has got what they call a *system*,—just so many bricks put together just so; but it is too narrow to take in all I see in my wanderings round this world of ours. Nobody that has a soul, and goes round the world as I do, can help feeling it at times, and thinking, as he sees all the races of men and their ways, who made them, and what they were made for. To doubt the existence of a God seems to me like a want of common sense. There is a Maker and a Ruler, doubtless; but then, Mary, all this invisible world of religion is unreal to me. I can see we must be good, somehow,—that if we are not, we shall not be happy here or hereafter. As to all the metaphysics of your good Doctor, you can't tell how they tire me. I'm not the sort of person that they can touch. I must have real things,—real people; abstractions are nothing to me. Then I think that he systematically contradicts on one Sunday what he preaches on another. One Sunday he tells us that God is the immediate efficient Author of every act of will; the next he tells us that we are entire free agents. I see no sense in it, and can't take the trouble to put it together. But then he and you have something in you that I call religion,—something that makes you *good*. When I see a man working away on an entirely honest, unworldly, disinterested pattern, as he does, and when I see you, Mary, as I said before, I should like at least to *be* as you are, whether I could believe as you do or not.

CHAPTER V.

'How could you so care for me, and waste on one so unworthy of you such love? Oh, Mary, some better man must win you; I never shall and never can;—but then you must not quite forget me; you must be my friend, my saint. If, through your prayers, your Bible, your friendship, you can bring me to your state, I am willing to be brought there,—nay, desirous. God has put the key of my soul into your hands.

'So, dear Mary, good-bye! Pray still for your naughty, loving

'COUSIN JAMES.'

Mary read this letter, and re-read it, with more pain than pleasure. To feel the immortality of a beloved soul hanging upon us, to feel that its only communications with Heaven must be through us, is the most solemn and touching thought that can pervade a mind. It was without one particle of gratified vanity, with even a throb of pain, that she read such exalted praises of herself from one blind to the glories of a far higher loveliness.

Yet was she at that moment, unknown to herself, one of the great company scattered through earth who are priests unto God,—ministering between the Divine One, who has unveiled himself unto them, and those who as yet stand in the outer courts of the great sanctuary of truth and holiness. Many a heart, wrung, pierced, bleeding with the sins and sorrows of earth, longing to depart, stands in this mournful and beautiful ministry, but stands unconscious of the glory of the work in which it waits and suffers. God's kings and priests are crowned with thorns, walking the earth with bleeding feet and comprehending not the work they are performing.

Mary took from a drawer a small pocket-book, from which dropped a lock of black hair,—a glossy curl, which seemed to have a sort of wicked, wilful life in every shining ring, just as she had often seen it shake naughtily on the owner's head. She felt a strange tenderness towards the little wilful thing, and, as she leaned over it, made in her heart a thousand fond apologies for every fault and error.

She was standing thus when Mrs. Scudder entered the room to see if her daughter had yet retired.

'What are you doing there, Mary?' she said, as her eye fell on the letter. 'What is it you are reading?'

Mary felt herself grow pale: it was the first time in her whole life that her mother had asked her a question that she was not from the heart ready to answer. Her loyalty to her only parent had gone on even-handed with that she gave to her God; she felt, somehow, that the revelations of that afternoon had opened a gulf between them, and the consciousness overpowered her.

Mrs. Scudder was astonished at her evident embarrassment, her trembling, and paleness. She was a woman of prompt, imperative temperament, and the slightest hesitation in rendering to her a full, outspoken confidence had never before occurred in their intercourse. Her child was the core of her heart, the apple of her eye, and intense love is always near neighbour to anger; there was therefore an involuntary flash from her eye and a heightening of her colour, as she said,—'Mary, are you concealing anything from your mother?'

In that moment Mary had grown calm again. The wonted serene, balanced nature had found its habitual poise, and she looked up innocently, though with tears in her large blue eyes, and said,—'No, mother,—I have nothing that I do not mean to tell you fully. This letter came from James Marvyn; he came here to see me this afternoon.'

'Here?—when? I did not see him.'

'After dinner. I was sitting here in the window, and suddenly he came up behind me through the orchard-path.'

Mrs. Katy sat down with a flushed cheek and a discomposed air; but Mary seemed actually to bear her down by the candid clearness of the large blue eye which she turned on her as she stood perfectly collected, with her deadly-pale face and a brilliant spot burning on each cheek.

'James came to say good-bye. He complained that he had not had a chance to see me alone since he came home.'

'And what should he want to see you alone for?' said Mrs. Scudder, in a dry, disturbed tone.

'Mother,—everybody has things at times which they would like to say to some one person alone,' said Mary.

'Well, tell me what he said.'

'I will try. In the first place he said that he always had been free, all his life, to run in and out of our house, and to wait on me like a brother.'

'Hum!' said Mrs. Scudder; 'but he isn't your brother for all that.'

'Well, then he wanted to know why you were so cold to him, and why you never let him walk with me from meetings, or see me alone as we often used to. And I told him why,—that we were not children now, and that you thought it was not best; and then I talked with him about religion, and tried to persuade him to attend to the concerns of his soul; and I never felt so much hope for him as I do now.'

Aunt Katy looked sceptical, and remarked,—'If he really felt a disposition for religious instruction, Dr. H. could guide him much better than you could.'

'Yes,—so I told him, and I tried to persuade him to talk with Dr. H.; but he was very unwilling. He said, I could have more influence over him than anybody else,—that nobody could do him any good but me.'

'Yes, yes,—I understand all that,' said Aunt Katy,—'I have heard young men say *that* before, and I know just what it amounts to.'

'But, mother, I do think James was moved very much, this afternoon. I never heard him speak so seriously; he seemed really in earnest, and he asked me to give him my Bible.'

'Couldn't he read any Bible but yours?'

'Why, naturally, you know, mother, he would like my Bible better, because it would put him in mind of me. He promised faithfully to read it all through.'

'And then, it seems, he wrote you a letter.' 'Yes, mother.'

CHAPTER V.

Mary shrank from showing this letter, from the natural sense of honour which makes us feel it indelicate to expose to an unsympathising eye the confidential outpourings of another heart; and then, she felt quite sure that there was no such intercessor for James in her mother's heart as in her own. But over all this reluctance rose the determined force of duty; and she handed the letter in silence to her mother.

Mrs. Scudder took it, laid it deliberately in her lap, and then began searching in the pocket of her chintz petticoat for her spectacles. These being found, she wiped them, accurately adjusted them, opened the letter and spread it on her lap, brushing out its folds and straightening it, that she might read with the greater ease. After this she read it carefully and deliberately; and all this while there was such a stillness, that the sound of the tall varnished clock in the best room could be heard through the half-opened door.

After reading it with the most tiresome, torturing slowness, she rose, and laying it on the table under Mary's eye, and, pressing down her finger on two lines in the letter, said, 'Mary, have you told James that you loved him?'

'Yes, mother, always. I always loved him, and he always knew it.'

'But, Mary, this that he speaks of is something different. What has passed between——'

'Why, mother, he was saying that we who were Christians drew to ourselves and did not care for the salvation of our friends; and then I told him how I had always prayed for him, and how I should be willing even to give up my hopes in heaven, if he might be saved.'

'Child,—what do you mean?'

'I mean, if only one of us two could go to heaven, I had rather it should be him than me,' said Mary.

'Oh, child! child!' said Mrs. Scudder, with a sort of groan,—'has it gone with you so far as this? Poor child!—after all my care, you *are* in love with this boy,—your heart is set on him.'

'Mother, I am not. I never expect to see him much,—never expect to marry him or anybody else;—only he seems to me to have so much more life and soul and spirit than most people,—I think him so noble and grand,—that is, that he *could* be, if he were all he ought to be,—that, somehow, I never think of myself in thinking of him, and his salvation seems worth more than mine;—men can do so much more!—they can live such splendid lives!—oh, a real noble man is so glorious!'

'And you would like to see him well married, would you not?' said Mrs. Scudder, sending, with a true woman's aim, this keen arrow into the midst of the cloud of enthusiasm which enveloped her daughter. 'I think,' she added, 'that Jane Spencer would make him an excellent wife.'

Mary was astonished at a strange, new pain that shot through her at these words. She drew in her breath and turned herself uneasily, as one who had literally felt a keen dividing blade piercing between soul and spirit. Till this moment, she had never been conscious of herself; but the shaft had torn the veil. She covered her face with her hands; the hot blood flushed scarlet over neck and brow; at last, with a beseeching look, she threw herself into her mother's arms.

'Oh, mother, mother, I am selfish, after all!'

Mrs. Scudder folded her silently to her heart, and said, 'My daughter, that is not at all what I wished it to be; I see how it is;—but then you have been a good child; I don't blame you. We can't always help ourselves. We don't always really know how we do feel. I didn't know, for a long while, that I loved your father. I thought I was only curious about him, because he had a strange way of treating me, different from other men; but, one day, I remember, Julian Simons told me that it was reported that his mother was making a match for him with Susan Emery, and I was astonished to find how I felt. I saw him that evening, and the moment he looked at me I saw it wasn't true; all at once I knew something I never knew before,—and that was, that I should be very unhappy, if he loved any one else better than me. But then, my child, your father was a different man from James;—he was as much better than I was as you are than James. I was a foolish, thoughtless young thing then. I never should have been anything at all, but for him. Somehow, when I loved him, I grew more serious, and then he always guided and led me. Mary, your father was a wonderful man; he was one of the sort that the world knows not of; sometime I must show you his letters. I always hoped, my daughter, that you would marry such a man.'

'Don't speak of marrying, mother. I never shall marry.'

'You certainly should not, unless you can marry in the Lord. Remember the words, "Be ye not unequally yoked together with unbelievers. For what fellowship hath righteousness with unrighteousness? and what communion hath light with darkness? and what concord hath Christ with Belial? or what part hath he that believeth with an infidel?"'

'Mother, James is not an infidel.'

'He certainly is an *unbeliever*, Mary, by his own confession; but then God is a Sovereign and hath mercy on whom He will. You do right to pray for him; but if he does not come out on the Lord's side, you must not let your heart mislead you. He is going to be gone three years, and you must try to think as little of him as possible;—put your mind upon your duties, like a good girl, and God will bless you. Don't believe too much in your power over him:—young men, when they are in love, will promise anything, and really think they mean it; but nothing is a saving change, except what is wrought in them by sovereign grace.'

'But, mother, does not God use the love we have to each other as a means of doing us good? Did you not say that it was by your love to father that you first were led to think seriously?'

'That is true, my child,' said Mrs. Scudder, who, like many of the rest of the world, was surprised to meet her own words walking out on a track where she had not expected them, but was yet too true of soul to cut their acquaintance because they were not going the way of her wishes. 'Yes, all that is true; but yet, Mary, when one has but one little ewe lamb in the world, one is jealous of it. I would give all the world, if you had never seen James. It is dreadful enough for a woman to love anybody as you can, but it is more to love a man of unsettled character and no religion. But then the Lord appoints all our goings: it is not in man that walketh to direct his steps;—I leave you, my child, in His hands.' And, with one solemn and long embrace, the mother and daughter parted for the night.

It is impossible to write a story of New England life and manners for a thoughtless, shallow-minded person. If we represent things as they are, their intensity, their depth, their unworldly gravity and earnestness, must inevitably repel lighter spirits, as the reverse pole of the magnet drives off sticks and straws.

In no other country were the soul and the spiritual life ever such intense realities, and everything contemplated so much (to use a current New-England phrase) 'in reference to eternity.' Mrs. Scudder was a strong clear-headed, practical woman. No one had a clearer estimate of the material and outward life, or could more minutely manage its smallest item; but then a tremendous, eternal future had so weighed down and compacted the fibres of her very soul, that all earthly things were but as dust in comparison to it. That her child should be one elected to walk in white, to reign with Christ when earth was a forgotten dream, was her one absorbing wish; and she looked on all the events of life only with reference to this. The way of life was narrow, the chances in favour of any child of Adam infinitely small; the best, the most seemingly pure and fair, was by nature a child of wrath, and could be saved only by a sovereign decree, by which it should be plucked as a brand from the burning. Therefore it was, that, weighing all things in one balance, there was the sincerity of her whole being in the dread which she felt at the thought of her daughter's marriage with an unbeliever.

Mrs. Scudder, after retiring to her room, took her Bible, in preparation for her habitual nightly exercise of devotion, before going to rest. She read and re-read a chapter, scarce thinking what she was reading,—aroused herself,—and then sat with the book in her hand in deep thought. James Marvyn was her cousin's son, and she had a strong feeling of respect and family attachment for his father. She had, too, a real kindness for the young man, whom she regarded as a well-meaning, wilful youngster; but that *he* should touch her saint, her Mary, that *he* should take from her the daughter who was her all, really embittered her heart towards him.

'After all,' she said to herself, 'there are three years,—three years in which there will be no letters, or perhaps only one or two,—and a great deal may be done in three years, if one is wise;'—and she felt within herself an arousing of all the shrewd womanly and motherly tact of her nature to meet this new emergency.

CHAPTER VI.

THE DOCTOR.

IT is seldom that man and woman come together in intimate association, unless influences are at work more subtle and mysterious than the subjects of them dream. Even in cases where the strongest ruling force of the two sexes seems out of the question, there is still something peculiar and insidious in their relationship. A fatherly old gentleman, who undertakes the care of a sprightly young girl, finds, to his astonishment, that little Miss spins all sorts of cobwebs round him. Grave professors and teachers cannot give lessons to their female pupils just as they give them to the coarser sex; and more than once has the fable of 'Cadenus and Vanessa' been acted over by the most unlikely performers.

The Doctor was a philosopher, a metaphysician, a philanthropist, and in the highest and most earnest sense a minister of good on earth. The New England clergy had no sentimental affectation of sanctity that segregated them from wholesome human relations; and, consequently, our good Doctor had always resolved, in a grave and thoughtful spirit, at a suitable time in his worldly affairs, to choose unto himself a helpmeet. Love, as treated of in romances, he held to be a foolish and profane matter, unworthy the attention of a serious and reasonable creature. All the language of poetry on this subject was to him an unknown tongue. He contemplated the entrance on married life somewhat in this wise:—That at a time and place suiting, he should look out unto himself a woman of a pleasant countenance and of good repute, a zealous, earnest Christian, and well skilled in the items of household management, whom, accosting as a stranger and pilgrim to a better life, he should loyally and lovingly entreat, as Isaac did Rebekah, to come under the shadow of his tent and be a helpmeet unto him in what yet remained of this mortal journey. But straitened circumstances, and the unsettled times of the Revolution, in which he had taken an earnest and zealous part, had delayed to a late bachelorhood the fulfilment of this resolution.

When once received under the shadow of Mrs. Scudder's roof, and within the provident sphere of her unfailing housekeeping, all material necessity for an immediate choice was taken away; for he was in exactly that situation dearest to every scholarly and thoughtful man, in which all that pertained to the outward life appeared to rise under his hand at the moment he wished for it, without his knowing how or why.

He was not at the head of a prosperous church and society, rich and well-to-do in the world,—but, as the pioneer leader of a new theology, in a country where theology was the all-absorbing interest, he had to breast the reaction that ever attends the advent of new ideas. His pulpit talents, too, were unattractive. His early training had been all logical, not in the least æsthetic; for, like the ministry of his country generally, he had been trained always to think more of what he should say than of how he should say it. Consequently, his style, though not without a certain massive greatness, which always comes from largeness of nature, had none of those attractions by which the common masses are beguiled into thinking. He gave only the results of thought, not its incipient processes; and the consequence was, that few could follow him. In like manner, his religious teachings were characterized by an ideality so high as quite to discourage ordinary virtue.

There is a ladder to heaven, whose base God has placed in human affections, tender instincts, symbolic feelings, sacraments of love, through which the soul rises higher and higher, refining as she goes, till she outgrows the human, and changes, as she rises, into the image of the divine. At the very top of this ladder, at the threshold of Paradise, blazes dazzling and crystalline that celestial grade where the soul knows self no more, having learned, through a long experience of devotion, how blest it is to lose herself in that eternal Love and Beauty of which all earthly fairness and grandeur are but the dim type, the distant shadow. This highest step, this saintly elevation, which but few selectest spirits ever on earth attain, to raise the soul to which the Eternal Father organized every relation of human existence and strung every chord of human love, for which this world is one long discipline, for which the soul's human education is constantly varied, for which it is now torn by sorrow, now flooded by joy, to which all its multiplied powers tend with upward hands of dumb and ignorant aspiration,—this Ultima Thule of virtue had been seized upon by our sage as the *all* of religion. He knocked out every round of the ladder but the highest, and then, pointing to its hopeless splendour, said to the world, 'Go up thither and be saved!'

Short of that absolute self-abnegation, that unconditional surrender to the Infinite, there was nothing meritorious,—because, if *that* were commanded, every moment of refusal was rebellion. Every prayer, not based on such consecration, he held to be an insult to the Divine Majesty;—the reading of the Word, the conscientious conduct of life, the performance of the duties of man to man, being, without this, the deeds of a creature in conscious rebellion to its Eternal Sovereign, were all vitiated and made void. Nothing was to be preached to the sinner, but his ability and obligation to rise immediately to this height.

It is not wonderful that teaching of this sort should seem to many unendurable, and that the multitude should desert the preacher with the cry, 'This is an hard saying; who can hear it?' The young and gay were wearied by the dryness of metaphysical discussions which to them were as unintelligible as a statement of the last results of the mathematician to the child commencing the multiplication-table.

There remained around him only a select circle,—shrewd, hard thinkers, who delighted in metaphysical subtleties,—deep-hearted, devoted natures, who sympathized with the unworldly purity of his life, his active philanthropy and untiring benevolence,—courageous men, who admired his independence of thought and freedom in breasting received opinions,—and those unperceiving, dull, good people who are content to go to church anywhere as convenience and circumstances may drift them,—people who serve, among the keen-feeling and thinking portion of the world, much the same purpose as adipose matter in the human system, as a soft cushion between the nerves of feeling and the muscles of activity.

There was something affecting in the pertinacity with which the good Doctor persevered in saying his say to his discouraging minority of hearers. His salary was small; his meeting-house, damaged during the Revolutionary struggle, was dilapidated and forlorn,—fireless in winter, and in summer admitting a flood of sun and dust through those great windows which formed so principal a feature in those first efforts of Puritan architecture.

Still, grand in his humility, he preached on,—and as a soldier never asks why, but stands at apparently the most useless post, so he went on from Sunday to Sunday, comforting himself with the reflection that no one could think more meanly of his ministrations than he did himself. 'I am like Moses only in not being eloquent,' he said in his simplicity. 'My preaching is barren and dull, my voice is hard and harsh; but then the Lord is a Sovereign, and may work through me. He fed Elijah once through a raven, and he may feed some poor wandering soul through me.'

The only mistake made by the good man was that of supposing that the elaboration of theology was preaching the gospel. The gospel he was preaching constantly, by his pure, unworldly living, by his visitations to homes of poverty and sorrow, by his searching out of the lowly African slaves, his teaching of those whom no one else in those days had thought of teaching, and by the grand humanity, outrunning his age, in which he protested against the then admitted system of slavery and the slave-trade. But when, rising in the pulpit, he followed trains of thought suited only to the desk of the theological lecture-room, he did it blindly, following that law of self-development by which minds of a certain amount of fervour *must* utter what is in them, whether men will hear or whether they will forbear.

But the place where our Doctor was happiest was his study. There he explored, and wandered, and read, and thought, and lived a life as wholly ideal and intellectual as heart could conceive.

And could *Love* enter a reverend doctor's study, and find his way into a heart empty and swept of all those shreds of poetry and romance in which he usually finds the material of his incantations? Even so;—but he came so thoughtfully, so reverently, with so wise and cautious a footfall, that the good Doctor never even raised his spectacles to see who was there. The first that he knew, poor man, he was breathing an air of strange and subtile sweetness,—from what Paradise he never stopped his studies to inquire. He was like a great, rugged elm, with all its lacings and archings of boughs and twigs, which has stood cold and frozen against the metallic blue of winter sky, forgetful of leaves, and patient in its bareness, calmly content in its naked strength and crystalline definiteness of outline. But in April there is a rising and stirring within the grand old monster,—a whispering of knotted buds, a mounting of sap coursing ethereally from bough to bough with a warm and gentle life; and though the old elm knows it not, a new creation is at hand. Just so, ever since the good man had lived at Mrs. Scudder's, and had the gentle Mary for his catechumen, a richer life seemed to have coloured his thoughts,—his mind seemed to work with a pleasure never felt before.

Whoever looked on the forehead of the good Doctor must have seen the squareness of ideality giving marked effect to its outline. As yet ideality had dealt only with the intellectual and invisible, leading to subtile refinements of argument and exalted ideas of morals. But there was lying in him, crude and unworked, a whole mine of those artistic feelings and perceptions which are awakened and developed only by the touch of beauty. Had he been born beneath the shadow of the great Duomo of Florence, where Giotto's Campanile rises like the slender stalk of a celestial lily, where varied marbles and rainbow glass and gorgeous paintings and lofty statuary call forth, even from childhood, the soul's reminiscences of the bygone glories of its pristine state, his would have been a soul as rounded and full in its sphere of faculties as that of Da Vinci or Michael Angelo. But of all that he was as ignorant as a child; and the first revelation of his dormant nature was to come to him through the face of woman,—that work of the Mighty Master which is to be found in all lands and ages.

What makes the love of a great mind something fearful in its inception is, that it is often the unsealing of a hitherto undeveloped portion of a large and powerful being: the woman may or may not seem to other eyes adequate to the effect produced, but the man cannot forget her, because with her came a change which makes him for ever a different being. So it was with our friend. A woman it was that was destined to awaken in him all that consciousness which music, painting, poetry awaken in more evenly-developed minds; and it is the silent breathing of her creative presence that is even now creating him anew, while as yet he knows it not.

He never thought, this good old soul, whether Mary were beautiful or not; he never even knew that he looked at her; nor did he know why it was that the truths of his theology, when uttered by her tongue, had such a wondrous beauty as he never felt before. He did not know why it was, that, when she silently sat by him, copying tangled manuscript for the press, as she sometimes did, his whole study seemed so full of some divine influence, as if, like St. Dorothea, she had worn in her bosom, invisibly, the celestial roses of Paradise. He recorded honestly in his diary what marvellous freshness of spirit the Lord had given him, and how he seemed to be uplifted in his communings with heaven, without once thinking from the robes of what angel this sweetness had exhaled.

On Sundays, when he saw good Mrs. Jones asleep, and Simon Brown's hard, sharp eyes, and Deacon Twitchel mournfully rocking to and fro, and his wife handing fennel to keep the children awake, his eye glanced across to the front gallery, where one earnest young face, ever kindling with feeling and bright with intellect, followed on his way, and he felt uplifted and comforted. On Sunday mornings, when Mary came out of her little room, in clean white dress, with her singing-book and psalm-book in her hands, her deep eyes solemn from recent prayer, he thought of that fair and mystical bride, the Lamb's wife, whose union with her Divine Redeemer in a future millenial age was a frequent and favourite subject of his musings; yet he knew not that this celestial bride, clothed in fine linen, clean and white, veiled in humility and meekness, bore in his mind those earthly features. No, he never had dreamed of that! But only after she had passed by, that mystical vision seemed to him more radiant, more easy to be conceived.

It is said that, if a grape-vine be planted in the neighbourhood of a well, its roots, running silently under ground, wreathe themselves in a network around the cold clear waters, and the vine's putting on outward greenness and unwonted clusters and fruit is all that tells where every root and fibre of its being has been silently stealing. So those loves are most fatal, most absorbing, in which, with unheeded quietness, every thought and fibre of our life twines gradually around some human soul, to us the unsuspected well-spring of our being. Fearful it is, because so often the vine must be uprooted, and all its fibres wrenched away; but till the hour of discovery comes, how is it transfigured by a new and beautiful life!

There is nothing in life more beautiful than that trancelike quiet dawn which precedes the rising of love in the soul. When the whole being is pervaded imperceptibly and tranquilly by another being, and we are happy, we know not and ask not why, the soul is then receiving all and asking nothing. At a later day she becomes self-conscious, and then come craving exactions, endless questions,—the whole world of the material comes in with its hard counsels and consultations, and the beautiful trance fades for ever.

Of course all this is not so to *you*, my good friends, who read it without the most distant idea what it can mean; but there are people in the world to whom it has meant and will mean much, and who will see in the present happiness of our respectable friend something even ominous and sorrowful.

It had not escaped the keen eye of the mother how quickly and innocently the good Doctor was absorbed by her daughter, and thereupon had come long trains of practical reflections.

The Doctor, though not popular indeed as a preacher, was a noted man in his age. Her deceased husband had regarded him with something of the same veneration which might have been accorded to a divine messenger, and Mrs. Scudder had received and kept this veneration as a precious legacy. Then, although not handsome, the Doctor had decidedly a grand and imposing appearance. There was nothing common or insignificant about him. Indeed, it had been said, that, when, just after the declaration of peace, he walked through the town in the commemorative procession side by side with General Washington, the minister, in the majesty of his gown, bands, cocked hat, and full flowing wig, was thought by many to be the more majestic and personable figure of the two.

In those days, the minister united in himself all those ideas of superior position and cultivation with which the theocratic system of the New England community had invested him. Mrs. Scudder's notions of social rank could reach no higher than to place her daughter on the throne of such pre-eminence.

Her Mary, she pondered, was no common girl. In those days it was a rare thing for young persons to devote themselves to religion or make any professions of devout life. The church, or that body of people who professed to have passed through a divine regeneration, was almost entirely confined to middle-aged and elderly people, and it was looked upon as a singular and unwonted call of divine grace when young persons came forward to attach themselves to it. When Mary, therefore, at quite an early age, in all the bloom of her youthful beauty, arose, according to the simple and impressive New England rite, to consecrate herself publicly to a religious life, and to join the company of professing Christians, she was regarded with a species of deference amounting even to awe. Had it not been for the childlike, unconscious simplicity of her manners, the young people of her age would have shrunk away from her, as from one entirely out of their line of thought and feeling; but a certain natural and innocent playfulness and amiable self-forgetfulness made her a general favourite.

Nevertheless, Mrs. Scudder knew no young man whom she deemed worthy to have and hold a heart which she prized so highly. As to James, he stood at double disadvantage, because, as her cousin's son, he had grown up from childhood under her eye, and all those sins and iniquities into which gay and adventurous youngsters will be falling had come to her knowledge. She felt kindly to the youth; she wished him well; but as to giving him her Mary!—the very suggestion made her dislike him. She was quite sure he must have tried to beguile her—he must have tampered with her feelings to arouse in her pure and well-ordered mind so much emotion and devotedness as she had witnessed.

How encouraging a Providence, then, was it that he was gone to sea for three years!—how fortunate that Mary had been prevented in any way from committing herself with him!—how encouraging that the only man in those parts, in the least fitted to appreciate her, seemed so greatly pleased and absorbed in her society!—how easily might Mary's dutiful reverence be changed to a warmer sentiment, when she should find that so great a man could descend from his lofty thoughts to think of her!

In fact, before Mrs. Scudder had gone to sleep the first night after James's departure, she had settled upon the house where the minister and his young wife were to live, had reviewed the window-curtains and bed-quilts for each room, and glanced complacently at an improved receipt for wedding-cake, which might be brought out to glorify a certain occasion!

CHAPTER VII.

THE FRIENDS AND RELATIONS OF JAMES.

MR. ZEBEDEE MARVYN, the father of James, was the sample of an individuality so purely the result of New England society and education that he must be embodied in our story as a representative man of the times.

He owned a large farm in the immediate vicinity of Newport, which he worked with his own hands and kept under the most careful cultivation. He was a man past the middle of life, with a white head, a keen blue eye, and a face graven deeply with the lines of energy and thought. His was one of those clearly-cut minds which New England forms among her farmers, as she forms quartz crystals in her mountains, by a sort of gradual influence flowing through every pore of her soil and system.

His education, properly so called, had been merely that of those common schools and academies with which the States are thickly sown, and which are the springs of so much intellectual activity. Here he had learned to think and to inquire,—a process which had not ceased with his schooldays. Though toiling daily with his sons and hired man in all the minutiæ of a farmer's life, he kept an observant eye on the field of literature, and there was not a new publication heard of that he did not immediately find means to add it to his yearly increasing stock of books. In particular was he a well-read and careful theologian, and all the controversial tracts, sermons, and books, with which then, as ever since, New England has abounded, not only lay on his shelves, but had his pencilled annotations, queries, and comments thickly scattered along their margins. There was scarce an office of public trust which had not at one time or another been filled by him. He was deacon of the church, chairman of the school committee, justice of the peace, had been twice representative in the State legislature, and was in permanence a sort of adviser-general in all cases between neighbour and neighbour. Among other acquisitions, he had gained some knowledge of the general forms of law, and his advice was often asked in preference to that of the regular practitioners.

His dwelling was one of those large, square, white, green-blinded mansions—cool, clean, and roomy—wherein the respectability of New England in those days rejoiced. The windows were shaded by clumps of lilacs; the deep yard with its white fence enclosed a sweep of clean, short grass and a few fruit-trees. Opposite the house was a small blacksmith's shed, which, of a wet day, was sparkling and lively with bellows and ringing forge, while Mr. Zebedee and his sons were hammering and pounding and putting in order anything that was out of the way in farming-tools or establishments. Not unfrequently the latest scientific work or the last tractate of theology lay open by his side, the contents of which would be discussed with a neighbour or two as they entered; for, to say the truth, many a neighbour, less forehanded and thrifty, felt the benefit of this arrangement of Mr. Zebedee, and would drop in to see if he 'wouldn't just tighten that rivet,' or 'kind o'ease out that 'ere brace,' or 'let a feller have a turn with his bellows or a stroke or two on his anvil,'—to all which the good man consented with a grave obligingness. The fact was, that as nothing in the establishment of Mr. Marvyn was often broken or lost or out of place, he had frequent applications to lend to those less fortunate persons, always to be found, who supply their own lack of considerateness from the abundance of their neighbours.

He who is known always to be in hand, and always obliging, in a neighbourhood, stands the chance sometimes of having nothing for himself. Mr. Zebedee reflected quietly on this subject, taking it, as he did all others, into grave and orderly consideration, and finally provided a complete set of tools, which he kept for the purpose of lending; and when any of these were lent, he told the next applicant quietly that the axe or the hoe was already out, and thus he reconciled the Scripture which commanded him to 'do good and lend' with that law of order which was written in his nature.

Early in life Mr. Marvyn had married one of the handsomest girls of his acquaintance, who had brought him a thriving and healthy family of children, of whom James was the youngest. Mrs. Marvyn was, at this time, a tall, sad-eyed, gentle-mannered woman, thoughtful, earnest, deep-natured, though sparing in the matter of words. In all her household arrangements, she had the same thrift and order which characterized her husband; but hers was a mind of a finer and higher stamp than his.

In her bedroom, near by her work-basket, stood a table covered with books,—and so systematic were her household arrangements, that she never any day missed her regular hours for reading. One who should have looked over this table would have seen there how eager and hungry a mind was hid behind the silent eyes of this quiet woman. History, biography, mathematics, volumes of the encyclopædia, poetry, novels, all alike found their time and place there,—and while she pursued her household labours, the busy, active soul within travelled cycles and cycles of thought, few of which ever found expression in words. What might be that marvellous music of the *Miserere*, of which she read, that it convulsed crowds and drew groans and tears from the most obdurate? What might be those wondrous pictures of Raphael and Leonardo da Vinci? What would it be to see the Apollo, the Venus? What was the charm that enchanted the old marbles—charm untold and inconceivable to one who had never seen even the slightest approach to a work of art? Then those glaciers of Switzerland, that grand, unapproachable mixture of beauty and sublimity in her mountains!—what would it be to one who could see it? Then what were all those harmonies of which she read,—masses, fugues, symphonies? Oh, could she once hear the Miserere of Mozart, just to know what music was like! And the cathedrals, what were they? How wonderful they must be, with their forests of arches, many-coloured as autumn-woods with painted glass, and the chants and anthems rolling down their long aisles! On all these things she pondered quietly, as she sat often on Sundays in the old staring, rattle-windowed meeting-house, and looked at the uncouth old pulpit, and heard the choir fa-sol-la-ing or singing fuguing tunes; but of all this she said nothing.

Sometimes, for days, her thoughts would turn from these subjects and be absorbed in mathematical or metaphysical studies. 'I have been following that treatise on Optics for a week, and never understood it till to-day,' she once said to her husband. 'I have found now that there has been a mistake in drawing the diagrams. I have corrected it, and now the demonstration is complete.—Dinah, take care, that wood is hickory, and it takes only seven sticks of that size to heat the oven.'

It is not to be supposed that a woman of this sort was an inattentive listener to preaching so stimulating to the intellect as that of Dr. H. No pair of eyes followed the web of his reasonings with a keener and more anxious watchfulness than those sad, deep-set, hazel ones; and as she was drawn along the train of its inevitable logic, a close observer might have seen how the shadows deepened over them. For, while others listened for the clearness of the thought, for the acuteness of the argument, she listened as a soul wide, fine-strung, acute, repressed, whose every fibre is a nerve, listens to the problem of its own destiny,—listened as the mother of a family listens, to know what were the possibilities, the probabilities of this mysterious existence of ours to herself and those dearer to her than herself.

The consequence of all her listening was a history of deep inward sadness. That exultant joy, or that entire submission, with which others seemed to view the scheme of the universe, as thus unfolded, did not visit her mind. Everything to her seemed shrouded in gloom and mystery; and that darkness she received as a token of unregeneracy, as a sign that she was one of those who are destined, by a mysterious decree, never to receive the light of the glorious gospel of Christ. Hence, while her husband was a deacon of the church, she for years had sat in her pew while the sacramental elements were distributed, a mournful spectator. Punctilious in every duty, exact, reverential, she still regarded herself as a child of wrath, an enemy to God, and an heir of perdition; nor could she see any hope of remedy, except in the sovereign, mysterious decree of an Infinite and Unknown Power, a mercy for which she waited with the sickness of hope deferred.

Her children had grown up successively around her, intelligent and exemplary. Her eldest son was mathematical professor in one of the leading colleges of New England. Her second son, who jointly with his father superintended the farm, was a man of wide literary culture and of fine mathematical genius; and not unfrequently, on winter evenings, the son, father, and mother worked together, by their kitchen fireside, over the calculations for the almanac for the ensuing year, which the son had been appointed to edit.

Everything in the family arrangements was marked by a sober precision, a grave and quiet self-possession. There was little demonstrativeness of affection between parents and children, brothers and sisters, though great mutual affection and confidence. It was not pride, nor sternness, but a sort of habitual shamefacedness, that kept far back in each soul those feelings which are the most beautiful in their outcome; but after a while, the habit became so fixed a nature, that a caressing or affectionate expression could not have passed the lips of one to another without a painful awkwardness. Love was understood, once for all, to be the basis on which their life was built. Once for all, they loved each other, and after that, the less said the better. It had cost the woman's heart of Mrs. Marvyn some pangs, in the earlier part of her wedlock, to accept of this *once for all*, in place of those daily out-gushings which every woman desires should be like God's loving kindness, 'new every morning;' but hers, too, was a nature strongly inclining inward, and, after a few tremulous movements, the needle of her soul settled, and her life-lot was accepted,—not as what she would like or could conceive, but as a reasonable and good one. Life was a picture painted in low, cool tones, but in perfect keeping; and though another and brighter style might have pleased better, she did not quarrel with this.

Into this steady, decorous, highly-respectable circle, the youngest child, James, made a formidable irruption. One sometimes sees launched into a family circle a child of so different a nature from all the rest, that it might seem as if, like an aërolite, he had fallen out of another sphere. All the other babies of the Marvyn family had been of that orderly, contented sort who sleep till it is convenient to take them up, and while awake suck their thumbs contentedly and look up with large, round eyes at the ceiling when it is not convenient for their elders and betters that they should do anything else. In farther advanced childhood, they had been quiet and decorous children, who could be all dressed and set up in chairs, like so many dolls, of a Sunday morning, patiently awaiting the stroke of the church-bell to be carried out and put into the waggon which took them over the two miles' road to church. Possessed of such tranquil, orderly, and exemplary young offshoots, Mrs. Marvyn had been considered eminent for her 'faculty' in bringing up children.

But James was destined to put 'faculty,' and every other talent which his mother possessed, to rout. He was an infant of moods and tenses, and those not of any regular verb. He would cry of nights, and he would be taken up of mornings, and he would not suck his thumb, nor a bundle of caraway-seed tied in a rag and dipped in sweet milk, with which the good gossips in vain endeavoured to pacify him. He fought manfully with his two great fat fists the battle of babyhood, utterly reversed all nursery maxims, and reigned as baby over the whole prostrate household. When old enough to run alone, his splendid black eyes and glossy rings of hair were seen flashing and bobbing in every forbidden place and occupation. Now trailing on his mother's gown, he assisted her in salting her butter by throwing in small contributions of snuff or sugar, as the case might be; and again, after one of those mysterious periods of silence which are of most ominous significance in nursery experience, he would rise from the demolition of her indigo-bag, showing a face ghastly with blue streaks, and looking more like a gnome than the son of a respectable mother. There was not a pitcher of any description of contents left within reach of his little tiptoes and busy fingers that was not pulled over upon his giddy head without in the least seeming to improve its steadiness. In short, his mother remarked that she was thankful every night when she had fairly gotten him into bed and asleep: James had really got through one more day and killed neither himself nor any one else.

As a boy, the case was little better. He did not take to study, yawned over books, and cut out moulds for running anchors when he should have been thinking of his columns of words in four syllables. No mortal knew how he learned to read, for he never seemed to stop running long enough to learn anything; and yet he did learn, and used the talent in conning over travels, sea-voyages, and lives of heroes and naval commanders. Spite of father, mother, and brother, he seemed to possess the most extraordinary faculty of running up unsavoury acquaintances. He was a hail-fellow well-met with every Tom and Jack and Jim and Ben and Dick that strolled on the wharves, and astonished his father with minutest particulars of every ship, schooner, and brig in the harbour, together with biographical notes of the different Toms, Dicks, and Harrys, by whom they were worked.

There was but one member of the family that seemed to know at all what to make of James, and that was their negro servant, Candace.

In those days, when domestic slavery prevailed in New England, it was quite a different thing in its aspects from the same institution in more southern latitudes. The hard soil, unyielding to any but the most considerate culture, the thrifty, close, shrewd habits of the people, and their untiring activity and industry, prevented, among the mass of the people, any great reliance on slave labour. It was something foreign, grotesque, and picturesque in a life of the most matter-of-fact sameness: it was even as if one should see clusters of palm-trees scattered here and there among Yankee wooden meeting-houses, or open one's eyes on clumps of yellow-striped aloes growing among hardhack and huckleberry bushes in the pastures.

Added to this, there were from the very first, in New England, serious doubts in the minds of thoughtful and conscientious people in reference to the lawfulness of slavery; and this scruple prevented many from availing themselves of it, and proved a restraint on all, so that nothing like plantation-life existed, and what servants were owned were scattered among different families, of which they came to be regarded and to regard themselves as a legitimate part and portion,—Mr. Marvyn, as a man of substance, numbering two or three in his establishment, among whom Candace reigned chief. The presence of these tropical specimens of humanity, with their wide, joyous, rich physical abundance of nature and their hearty *abandon* of outward expression, was a relief to the still clear-cut lines in which the picture of New England life was drawn, which an artist must appreciate.

No race has ever shown such infinite and rich capabilities of adaptation to varying soil and circumstances as the negro. Alike to them the snows of Canada, the hard, rocky land of New England, with its set lines and orderly ways, or the gorgeous profusion and loose abundance of the Southern States. Sambo and Cuffy expand under them all. New England yet preserves among her hills and valleys the lingering echoes of the jokes and jollities of various sable worthies, who saw alike in orthodoxy and heterodoxy, in Dr. This-side and Dr. That-side, only food for more abundant merriment;—in fact, the minister of those days not unfrequently had his black shadow, a sort of African Boswell, who powdered his wig, brushed his boots, defended and patronized his sermons, and strutted complacently about, as if through virtue of his blackness he had absorbed every ray of his master's dignity and wisdom. In families, the presence of these exotics was a godsend to the children, supplying from the abundant outwardness and demonstrativeness of their nature that aliment of sympathy so dear to childhood, which the repressed and quiet habits of New England education denied. Many and many a New Englander counts among his pleasantest early recollections the memory of some of these genial creatures, who by their warmth of nature were the first and most potent mesmerizers of his childish mind.

Candace was a powerfully built, majestic black woman, corpulent, heavy, with a swinging majesty of motion like that of a ship in a ground swell. Her shining black skin and glistening white teeth were indications of perfect physical vigour which had never known a day's sickness; her turban, of broad red and yellow bandanna stripes, had even a warm tropical glow; and her ample skirts were always ready to be spread over every childish transgression of her youngest pet and favourite, James.

She used to hold him entranced long winter evenings, while she sat knitting in the chimney-corner, and crooned to him strange, wild African legends of the things that she had seen in her childhood and early days,—for she had been stolen when about fifteen years of age; and these weird, dreamy talks increased the fervour of his roving imagination, and his desire to explore the wonders of the wide and unknown world. When rebuked or chastised, it was she who had secret bowels of mercy for him, and hid doughnuts in her ample bosom to be secretly administered to him in mitigation of the sentence that sent him supperless to bed; and many a triangle of pie, many a wedge of cake, had conveyed to him surreptitious consolations which his more conscientious mother longed, but dared not, to impart. In fact, these ministrations, if suspected, were winked at by Mrs. Marvyn, for two reasons: first, that mothers are generally glad of any loving-kindness to an erring boy, which they are not responsible for; and second, that Candace was so set in her ways and opinions that one might as well come in front of a ship under full sail as endeavour to stop her in a matter where her heart was engaged.

To be sure, she had her own private and special quarrels with 'Massa James,' when he disputed any of her sovereign orders in the kitchen, and would sometimes pursue him with uplifted rolling-pin and floury hands when he had snatched a gingernut or cooky without suitable deference or supplication, and would declare, roundly, that there 'never was sich an aggravatin' young-un.' But if, on the strength of this, any one else ventured a reproof, Candace was immediately round on the other side: 'Dat ar chile gwin' to be spiled, 'cause dey's allers a'pickin' on him; he's well enough on'y let him alone.'

Well, under this miscellaneous assortment of influences,—through the order and gravity and solemn monotone of life at home, with the unceasing tick-tack of the clock for ever resounding through clean, empty-seeming rooms,—through the sea, ever shining, ever smiling, dimpling, soliciting, like a magical charger who comes saddled and bridled and offers to take you to fairyland,—through acquaintance with all sorts of foreign, outlandish ragamuffins among the ships in the harbour,—from disgust of slow-moving oxen, and long-drawn, endless furrows round the fifteen-acre lot,—from misunderstandings with grave elder brothers, and feeling somehow as if, he knew not why, he grieved his mother all the time just by being what he was and couldn't help being,—and, finally, by a bitter break with his father, in which came that last wrench for an individual existence which some time or other the young growing mind will give to old authority,—by all these united, was the lot at length cast; for one evening James was missing at supper, missing by the fireside, gone all night, not at home to breakfast,—till, finally, a strange, weird, most heathenish-looking cabin-boy, who had often been forbidden the premises by Mr. Marvyn, brought in a letter, half-defiant, half-penitent, which announced that James had sailed in the 'Ariel' the evening before.

Mr. Zebedee Marvyn set his face as a flint, and said, 'He went out from us because he was not of us,'—whereat old Candace lifted her great floury fist from the kneading-trough, and, shaking it like a large snowball, said, 'Oh, you go 'long, Massa Marvyn; ye'll live to count dat ar boy for de staff o' your old age yet, now I tell ye; got de makin' o' ten or'nary men in him; kittles dat's full allers will bile over; good yeast will blow out de cork,—lucky ef it don't bust de bottle. Tell ye, der's angels has der hooks in sich, and when de Lord wants him dey'll haul him in safe and sound.' And Candace concluded her speech by giving a lift to her whole batch of dough, and flinging it down in the trough with an emphasis that made the pewter on the dresser rattle.

This apparently irreverent way of expressing her mind, so contrary to the deferential habits studiously inculcated in family discipline, had grown to be so much a matter of course to all the family that nobody ever thought of rebuking it. There was a sort of savage freedom about her, which they excused in right of her having been born and bred a heathen, and of course not to be expected to come at once under the yoke of civilization. In fact, you must all have noticed, my dear readers, that there are some sorts of people for whom everybody turns out as they would for a railroad-car, without stopping to ask why—and Candace was one of them.

Moreover, Mr. Marvyn was not displeased with this defence of James, as might be inferred from his mentioning it four or five times in the course of the morning, to say how foolish it was,—wondering why it was that Candace and everybody else got so infatuated with that boy,—and ending, at last, after a long period of thought, with the remark that these poor African creatures often seemed to have a great deal of shrewdness in them, and that he was often astonished at the penetration that Candace showed.

At the end of the year James came home, more quiet and manly than he had ever been known before,—so handsome with his sunburnt face, and his keen, dark eyes and glossy curls, that half the girls in the front gallery lost their hearts the first Sunday he appeared in church. He was tender as a woman to his mother, and followed her with his eyes, like a lover, wherever she went: he made due and manly acknowledgments to his father, but declared his fixed and settled intention to abide by the profession he had chosen; and he brought home all sorts of strange foreign gifts for every member of the household. Candace was glorified with a flaming red and yellow turban of Moorish stuff from Mogadore, together with a pair of gorgeous yellow morocco slippers with peaked toes, which, though there appeared no call to wear them in her common course of life, she would put on her fat feet, and contemplate with daily satisfaction. She became increasingly strengthened thereby in the conviction that the angels who had their hooks in Massa James's jacket were already beginning to shorten the line.

CHAPTER VIII.

WHICH TREATS OF ROMANCE.

THERE is no word in the English language more unceremoniously and indefinitely kicked and cuffed about, by what are called sensible people, than the word *romance*. When Mr. Smith or Mr. Stubbs has brought every wheel of life into such range and order that it is one steady, daily grind,—when they themselves have come into the habits and attitudes of the patient donkey, who steps round and round the endlessly turning wheel of some machinery—then they fancy that they have gotten 'the victory that overcometh the world.'

All but this dead grind, and the dollars that come through the mill, is by them thrown into one waste 'catch-all' and labelled *romance*. Perhaps there was a time in Mr. Smith's youth,—he remembers it now,—when he read poetry, when his cheek was wet with strange tears, when a little song, ground out by an organ-grinder in the street, had power to set his heart beating and bring a mist before his eyes. Ah, in those days he had a vision!—a pair of soft eyes stirred him strangely; a little weak hand was laid on his manhood, and it shook and trembled; and then came all the humility, the aspiration, the fear, the hope, the high desire, the troubling of the waters by the descending angel of love,—and a little more and Mr. Smith might have become a man, instead of a banker! He thinks of it now, sometimes, as he looks across the fireplace after dinner and sees Mrs. Smith asleep, innocently shaking the bouquet of pink bows and Brussels lace that waves over her placid red countenance.

Mrs. Smith wasn't his first love, nor, indeed, any love at all; but they agreed reasonably well. And as for poor Nellie,—well, she is dead and buried,—all that was stuff and romance. Mrs. Smith's money set him up in business, and Mrs. Smith is a capital manager, and he thanks God that he isn't romantic, and tells Smith Junior not to read poetry or novels, and to stick to realities.

'This is the victory that overcometh the world,'—to learn to be fat and tranquil, to have warm fires and good dinners, to hang your hat on the same peg at the same hour every day, to sleep soundly all night, and never to trouble your head with a thought or imagining beyond.

CHAPTER VIII.

But there are many people besides Mr. Smith who have gained this victory,—who have strangled their higher nature and buried it, and built over its grave the structure of their life, the better to keep it down.

The fascinating Mrs. T., whose life is a whirl between ball and opera, point-lace, diamonds, and schemings of admiration for herself, and of establishments for her daughters,—there was a time, if you will believe me, when that proud, worldly woman was so humbled, under the touch of some mighty power, that she actually thought herself capable of being a poor man's wife. She thought she could live in a little, mean house, on no-matter-what-street, with one servant, and make her own bonnets, and mend her own clothes, and sweep the house Mondays, while Betty washed,—all for what? All because she thought that there was a man so noble, so true, so good, so high-minded, that to live with him in poverty, to be guided by him in adversity, to lean on him in every rough place of life, was a something nobler, better, purer, more satisfying, than French laces, opera-boxes, and even Madame Roget's best gowns.

Unfortunately, this was all romance,—there was no such man. There was, indeed, a person of very common, self-interested aims and worldly nature, whom she had credited at sight with an unlimited draft on all her better nature; and when the hour of discovery came, she awoke from her dream with a start and a laugh, and ever since has despised aspiration, and been busy with the *realities* of life, and feeds poor little Mary Jane, who sits by her in the opera-box there, with all the fruit which she has picked from the bitter tree of knowledge. There is no end of the epigrams and witticisms which she can throw out, this elegant Mrs. T., on people who marry for love, lead prosy, worky lives, and put on their best cap with pink ribbons for Sunday. 'Mary Jane shall never make a fool of herself;' but, even as she speaks, poor Mary Jane's heart is dying within her at the vanishing of a pair of whiskers from an opposite box, which whiskers the poor little fool has credited with a *résumé* drawn from her own imaginings of all that is grandest and most heroic, most worshipful in man. By-and-by, when Mrs. T. finds the glamour has fallen on her daughter, she wonders; she has 'tried to keep novels out of the girl's way,—where did she get these notions?'

All prosaic, and all bitter, disenchanted people talk as if poets and novelists *made* romance. They do—just as much as craters make volcanoes,—no more. What is romance? whence comes it? Plato spoke to the subject wisely, in his quaint way, some two thousand years ago, when he said, 'Man's soul, in a former state, was winged and soared among the gods; and so it comes to pass, that, in this life, when the soul, by the power of music or poetry, or the sight of beauty, hath her remembrance quickened, forthwith there is a struggling and a pricking pain as of wings trying to come forth,—even as children in teething.' And if an old heathen, two thousand years ago, discoursed thus gravely of the romantic part of our nature, whence comes it that in Christian lands we think in so pagan a way of it, and turn the whole care of it to ballad-makers, romancers, and opera-singers?

Let us look up in fear and reverence, and say, 'GOD is the great maker of romance. HE, from whose hand came man and woman,—HE, who strung the great harp of Existence with all its wild and wonderful and manifold chords, and attuned them to one another,—HE is the great Poet of life.' Every impulse of beauty, of heroism, and every craving for purer love, fairer perfection, nobler type and style of being than that which closes like a prison-house around us, in the dim, daily walk of life, is God's breath, God's impulse, God's reminder to the soul that there is something higher, sweeter, purer, yet to be attained.

Therefore, man or woman, when thy ideal is shattered—as shattered a thousand times it must be; when the vision fades, the rapture burns out, turn not away in scepticism and bitterness, saying, 'There is nothing better for a man than that he should eat and drink,' but rather cherish the revelations of those hours as prophecies and fore-shadowings of something real and possible, yet to be attained in the manhood of immortality. The scoffing spirit that laughs at romance, is an apple of the Devil's own handing from the bitter tree of knowledge;—it opens the eyes only to see eternal nakedness.

If ever you have had a romantic, uncalculating friendship—a boundless worship and belief in some hero of your soul; if ever you have so loved, that all cold prudence, all selfish worldly considerations, have gone down like drift-wood before a river flooded with new rain from heaven, so that you even forgot yourself, and were ready to cast your whole being into the chasm of existence, as an offering before the feet of another, and all for nothing,—if you awoke bitterly betrayed and deceived, still give thanks to God that you have had one glimpse of heaven. The door now shut will open again. Rejoice that the noblest capability of your eternal inheritance has been made known to you; treasure it, as the highest honour of your being, that ever you could so feel,—that so divine a guest ever possessed your soul.

By such experiences are we taught the pathos, the sacredness of life; and if we use them wisely, our eyes will ever after be anointed to see what poems, what romances, what sublime tragedies lie around us in the daily walk of life, 'written not with ink, but in fleshly tables of the heart.' The dullest street of the most prosaic town has matter in it for more smiles, more tears, more intense excitement, than ever were written in story or sung in poem; the reality is there, of which the romancer is the second-hand recorder.

So much of a plea we put in boldly, because we foresee grave heads beginning to shake over our history, and doubts rising in reverend and discreet minds whether this history is going to prove anything but a love-story, after all.

We do assure you, right reverend Sir, and you, most discreet Madam, that it is not going to prove anything else; and you will find, if you will follow us, that there is as much romance burning under the snow-banks of cold Puritan preciseness as if Dr. H. had been brought up to attend operas instead of metaphysical preaching; and Mary had been nourished on Byron's poetry instead of 'Edwards on the Affections.'

The innocent credulities, the subtle deceptions, that were quietly at work under the grave, white curls of the Doctor's wig, were exactly of the kind which have beguiled man in all ages, when near the sovereign presence of her who is born for his destiny;—and as for Mary, what did it avail her that she could say the Assembly's Catechism from end to end without tripping, and that every habit of her life beat time to practical realities, steadily as the parlour clock? The wildest Italian singer or dancer, nursed on nothing but excitement from her cradle, never was more thoroughly possessed by the awful and solemn mystery of woman's life, than this Puritan girl.

It is quite true, that, the next morning after James's departure, she rose as usual in the dim gray, and was to be seen opening the kitchen-door just at the moment when the birds were giving the first little drowsy stir and chirp,—and that she went on setting the breakfast-table for the two hired men, who were bound to the fields with the oxen,—and that then she went on skimming cream for the butter, and getting ready to churn, and making up biscuit for the Doctor's breakfast, when he and they should sit down together at a somewhat later hour; and as she moved about, doing all these things, she sung various scraps of old psalm-tunes; and the good Doctor, who was then busy with his early exercises of devotion, listened, as he heard the voice, now here, now there, and thought about angels and the Millennium. Solemnly and tenderly there floated in at his open study-window, through the breezy lilacs, mixed with low of kine, and bleat of sheep, and hum of early wakening life, the little silvery ripples of that singing, somewhat mournful in its cadence, as if a gentle soul were striving to hush itself to rest. The words were those of the rough old version of the psalms then in use:—

'Truly my waiting soul relies
In silence God upon: Because from him there doth arise

All my salvation.'

And then came the busy patter of the little footsteps without, the moving of chairs, the clink of plates, as busy hands were arranging the table; and then again there was a pause, and he thought she seemed to come near to the open window of the adjoining room, for the voice floated in clearer and sadder:—

'O God, to me be merciful,
Be merciful to me! Because my soul for shelter safe,

Betakes itself to thee.

'Yea, in the shadow of thy wings

My refuge have I placed,
Until these sore calamities
Shall quite be overpast.'

The tone of life in New England, so habitually earnest and solemn, breathed itself in the grave and plaintive melodies of the tunes then sung in the churches; and so these words, though in the saddest minor key, did not suggest to the listening ear of the auditor anything more than that pensive religious calm in which he delighted to repose. A contrast indeed they were, in their melancholy earnestness, to the exuberant carollings of a robin, who, apparently attracted by them, perched himself hard by in the lilacs, and struck up such a merry *roulade* as quite diverted the attention of the fair singer; in fact, the intoxication breathed in the strain of this little messenger, whom God had feathered and winged and filled to the throat with ignorant joy, came in singular contrast with the sadder notes breathed by that creature of so much higher mould and fairer clay,—that creature born for an immortal life.

But the good Doctor was inly pleased when she sung; and when she stopped, looked up from his Bible wistfully, as missing something, he knew not what; for he scarce thought how pleasant the little voice was, or knew he had been listening to it,—and yet he was in a manner enchanted by it, so thankful and happy that he exclaimed with fervour, 'The lines are fallen unto me in pleasant places; yea, I have a goodly heritage.'

So went the world with him, full of joy and praise, because the voice and the presence wherein lay his unsuspected life, were securely near,—so certainly and constantly a part of his daily walk, that he had not even the trouble to wish for them. But in that other heart how was it?—how with the sweet saint that was talking to herself in psalms and hymns and spiritual songs?

The good child had remembered her mother's parting words the night before,—'Put your mind upon your duties,'—and had begun her first conscious exercise of thought with a prayer that grace might be given her to do it. But even as she spoke, mingling and interweaving with that golden thread of prayer was another consciousness, a life in another soul, as she prayed that the grace of God might overshadow him, shield him from temptation, and lead him up to heaven; and this prayer so got the start of the other, that, ere she was aware, she had quite forgotten self, and was feeling, living, thinking in that other life.

The first discovery she made, when she looked out into the fragrant orchard, whose perfumes steamed in at her window, and listened to the first chirping of birds among the old apple-trees, was one that has astonished many a person before her;—it was this: she found that all that had made life interesting to her was suddenly gone. She herself had not known that, for the month past, since James came from sea, she had been living in an enchanted land; that Newport harbour, and every rock and stone, and every mat of yellow seaweed on the shore, that the two-mile road between the cottage and the white house of Zebedee Marvyn, every mullein-stalk, every juniper-tree, had all had a light and a charm which were suddenly gone. There had not been an hour in the day for the last four weeks that had not had its unsuspected interest,—because he was at the White House; because, possibly, he might be going by, or coming in: nay, even in church, when she stood up to sing, and thought she was thinking only of God, had she not been conscious of that tenor voice that poured itself out by her side? and though afraid to turn her head that way, had she not felt that he was there every moment?—heard every word of the sermon and prayer for him? The very vigilant care which her mother had taken to prevent private interviews had only served to increase the interest by throwing over it the veil of constraint and mystery. Silent looks, involuntary starts, things indicated, not expressed—these are the most dangerous, the most seductive aliment of thought to a delicate and sensitive nature. If things were said out, they might not be said wisely,—they might repel by their freedom, or disturb by their unfitness; but what is only looked is sent into the soul through the imagination, which makes of it all that the ideal faculties desire.

In a refined and exalted nature it is very seldom that the feeling of love, when once thoroughly aroused, bears any sort of relation to the reality of the object. It is commonly an enkindling of the whole power of the soul's love for whatever she considers highest and fairest; it is, in fact, the love of something divine and unearthly, which, by a sort of illusion, connects itself with a personality. Properly speaking, there is but One true, eternal Object of all that the mind conceives in this trance of its exaltation. Disenchantment must come, of course; and in a love which terminates in happy marriage there is a tender and gracious process, by which, without shock or violence, the ideal is gradually sunk in the real, which, though found faulty and earthly, is still ever tenderly remembered as it seemed under the morning light of that enchantment.

What Mary loved so passionately, that which came between her and God in every prayer, was not the gay, young, dashing sailor,—sudden in anger, imprudent of speech, and, though generous in heart, yet worldly in plans and schemings,—but her own ideal of a grand and noble man, such a man as she thought he might become. He stood glorified before her—an image of the strength that overcomes things physical; of the power of command which controls men and circumstances; of the courage which disdains fear; of the honour which cannot lie; of constancy which knows no shadow of turning; of tenderness which protects the weak; and, lastly, of religious loyalty, which should lay the golden crown of its perfected manhood at the feet of a Sovereign Lord and Redeemer. This was the man she loved; and with this regal mantle of glories she invested the person called James Marvyn: and all that she saw and felt to be wanting, she prayed for with the faith of a believing woman.

Nor was she wrong; for, as to every leaf and every flower there is an ideal to which the growth of the plant is constantly urging, so is there an ideal to every human being,—a perfect form in which it might appear, were every defect removed and every characteristic excellence stimulated to the highest point. Once, in an age, God sends to some of us a friend who loves in us, *not* a false imagining, an unreal character, but, looking through all the rubbish of our imperfections, loves in us the divine ideal of our nature,—loves, not the man that we are, but the angel that we may be. Such friends seem inspired by a divine gift of prophecy,—like the mother of St. Augustine, who, in the midst of the wayward, reckless youth of her son, beheld him in a vision, standing, clothed in white, a ministering priest at the right hand of God—as he has stood for long ages since. Could a mysterious foresight unveil to us this resurrection form of the friends with whom we daily walk, compassed about with mortal infirmity, we should follow them with faith and reverence through all the disguises of human faults and weaknesses, 'waiting for the manifestation of the sons of God.'

But these wonderful soul-friends, to whom God grants such perception, are the exceptions in life; yet, sometimes are we blessed with one who sees through us, as Michel Angelo saw through a block of marble when he attacked it in a divine fervour, declaring that an angel was imprisoned within it: and it is often the resolute and delicate hand of such a friend that sets the angel free.

There be soul-artists, who go through this world, looking among their fellows with reverence, as one looks amid the dust and rubbish of old shops for hidden works of Titian and Leonardo; and, finding them, however cracked or torn, or painted over with tawdry daubs of pretenders, immediately recognise the divine original, and set themselves to cleanse and restore. Such be God's real priests, whose ordination and anointing are from the Holy Spirit; and he who hath not this enthusiasm is not ordained of God, though whole synods of bishops laid hands on him.

Many such priests there be among women; for to this silent ministry their nature calls them, endowed, as it is, with fineness of fibre and a subtile keenness of perception outrunning slow-footed reason,—and she of whom we write was one of these.

At this very moment, while the crimson wings of morning were casting delicate reflections on tree, and bush, and rock, they were also reddening innumerable waves round a ship that sailed alone, with a wide horizon stretching like an eternity around it; and in the advancing morning stood a young man, thoughtfully looking off into the ocean, with a book in his hand—James Marvyn,—as truly and heartily a creature of this material world as Mary was of the invisible and heavenly.

There are some who seem made to *live*,—life is such a joy to them; their senses are so fully *en rapport* with all outward things; the world is so keenly appreciable, so much a part of themselves; they are so conscious of power and victory in the government and control of material things, that the moral and invisible life often seems to hang tremulous and unreal in their minds, like the pale, faded moon in the light of a gorgeous sunrise. When brought face to face with the great truths of the invisible world, they stand related to the higher wisdom much like the gorgeous, gay Alcibiades to the divine Socrates, or like the young man in Holy Writ to Him for whose appearing Socrates longed;—they gaze, imperfectly comprehending, and at the call of ambition or riches turn away sorrowing.

So it was with James: in full tide of worldly energy and ambition there had been forming over his mind that hard crust—that scepticism of the spiritual and exalted which men of the world delight to call practical sense. He had been suddenly arrested and humbled by the revelation of a nature so much nobler than his own that he seemed worthless in his own eyes: he had asked for love; but when *such* love unveiled itself, he felt like the disciple of old in the view of a diviner tenderness,—'Depart from me, for I am a sinful man.'

But it is not often that all the current of a life is reversed in one hour: and now, as James stood on the ship's deck, with life passing around him, and everything drawing upon the strings of old habits, Mary and her religion recurred to his mind, as some fair, sweet, inexplicable vision. Where she stood he saw; but how *he* was ever to get there seemed as incomprehensible as how a mortal man should pillow his form on sunset clouds.

He held the little Bible in his hand as if it were some amulet charmed by the touch of a superior being; but when he strove to read it, his thoughts wandered, and he shut it, troubled and unsatisfied. Yet there were within him yearnings and cravings, wants never felt before, the beginning of that trouble which must ever precede the soul's rise to a higher plan of being.

There we leave him. We have shown you now our three different characters, each one in its separate sphere, feeling the force of that strongest and holiest power with which it has pleased our great Author to glorify this mortal life.

CHAPTER IX.

WHICH TREATS OF THINGS SEEN.

AS, for example, the breakfast. It is six o'clock,—the hired men and oxen are gone,—the breakfast-table stands before the open kitchen-door, snowy with its fresh cloth, the old silver coffee-pot steaming up a refreshing perfume,—and the Doctor sits on one side, sipping his coffee and looking across the table at Mary, who is innocently pleased at the kindly beaming in his placid blue eyes,—and Aunt Katy Scudder discourses of housekeeping, and fancies something must have disturbed the rising of the cream, as it is not so thick and yellow as wont.

Now the Doctor, it is to be confessed, was apt to fall into a way of looking at people such as pertains to philosophers and scholars generally, that is, as if he were looking through them into the infinite,—in which case, his gaze became so earnest and intent that it would quite embarrass an uninitiated person; but Mary, being used to this style of contemplation, was only quietly amused, and waited till some great thought should loom up before his mental vision,—in which case, she hoped to hear from him.

The good man swallowed his first cup of coffee and spoke:—

'In the Millennium, I suppose, there will be such a fulness and plenty of all the necessaries and conveniences of life, that it will not be necessary for men and women to spend the greater part of their lives in labour in order to procure a living. It will not be necessary for each one to labour more than two or three hours a day,—not more than will conduce to health of body and vigour of mind; and the rest of their time they will spend in reading and conversation, and such exercises as are necessary and proper to improve their minds and make progress in knowledge.'

New England presents probably the only example of a successful commonwealth founded on a theory, as a distinct experiment in the problem of society. It was for this reason that the minds of its great thinkers dwelt so much on the final solution of that problem in this world. The fact of a future Millennium was a favourite doctrine of the great leading theologians of New England, and Dr. H. dwelt upon it with a peculiar partiality. Indeed, it was the solace and refuge of his soul, when oppressed with the discouragements which always attend things actual, to dwell upon and draw out in detail the splendours of this perfect future which was destined to glorify the world.

Nobody, therefore, at the cottage was in the least surprised when there dropped into the flow of their daily life these sparkling bits of ore, which their friend had dug in his explorations of a future Canaan,—in fact, they served to raise the hackneyed present out of the level of mere commonplace.

'But how will it be possible,' inquired Mrs. Scudder, 'that so much less work will suffice in those days to do all that is to be done?'

'Because of the great advance of arts and sciences which will take place before those days,' said the Doctor, 'whereby everything shall be performed with so much greater ease,—also the great increase of disinterested love, whereby the skill and talents of those who have much shall make up for the weakness of those who have less.

'Yes,'—he continued, after a pause,—'all the careful Marthas in those days will have no excuse for not sitting at the feet of Jesus; there will be no cumbering with much serving; the church will have only Maries in those days.'

This remark, made without the slightest personal intention, called a curious smile into Mrs. Scudder's face, which was reflected in a slight blush from Mary's, when the crack of a whip and the rattling of waggon-wheels disturbed the conversation and drew all eyes to the door.

There appeared the vision of Mr. Zebedee Marvyn's farm-waggon, stored with barrels, boxes, and baskets, over which Candace sat throned triumphant, her black face and yellow-striped turban glowing in the fresh morning with a hearty, joyous light, as she pulled up the reins, and shouted to the horse to stop with a voice that might have done credit to any man living.

'Dear me, if there isn't Candace!' said Mary.

'Queen of Ethiopia,' said the Doctor, who sometimes adventured a very placid joke.

The Doctor was universally known in all the neighbourhood as a sort of friend and patron-saint of the negro race; he had devoted himself to their interests with a zeal unusual in those days. His church numbered more of them than any in Newport; and his hours of leisure from study were often spent in lowliest visitations among them, hearing their stories, consoling their sorrows, advising and directing their plans, teaching them reading and writing, and he often drew hard on his slender salary to assist them in their emergencies and distresses.

This unusual condescension on his part was repaid on theirs with all the warmth of their race; and Candace, in particular, devoted herself to the Doctor with all the force of her being.

There was a legend current in the neighbourhood, that the first efforts to catechize Candace were not eminently successful, her modes of contemplating theological tenets being so peculiarly from her own individual point of view that it was hard to get her subscription to a received opinion. On the venerable clause in the Catechism, in particular, which declares that all men sinned in Adam and fell with him, Candace made a dead halt:—

'I didn't do dat ar', for one, I knows. I's got good mem'ry,—allers knows what I does,—nebber did eat dat ar' apple,—nebber eat a bit ob him. Don't tell me!'

It was of no use, of course, to tell Candace of all the explanations of this redoubtable passage,—of potential presence, and representative presence, and representative identity, and federal headship. She met all with the dogged,—

'Nebber did it, I knows; should 'ave 'membered, if I had. Don't tell me!'

And even in the catechizing class of the Doctor himself, if this answer came to her, she sat black and frowning in stony silence even in his reverend presence.

Candace was often reminded that the Doctor believed the Catechism, and that she was differing from a great and good man; but the argument made no manner of impression on her, till, one day, a far-off cousin of hers, whose condition under a hard master had often moved her compassion, came in overjoyed to recount to her how, owing to Dr. H.'s exertions, he had gained his freedom. The Doctor himself had in person gone from house to house, raising the sum for his redemption; and when more yet was wanting, supplied it by paying half his last quarter's limited salary.

'He do dat ar'?' said Candace, dropping the fork wherewith she was spearing doughnuts. 'Den I'm gwine to b'liebe ebery word *he* does!'

And accordingly, at the next catechizing, the Doctor's astonishment was great when Candace pressed up to him, exclaiming,—

'De Lord bress you, Doctor, for opening de prison for dem dat is bound! I b'liebes in you now, Doctor. I's gwine to b'liebe ebery word you say. I'll say de Catechize now,—fix it any way you like. I *did* eat dat ar' apple,—I eat de whole tree, an' swallowed ebery bit ob it, if you say so.'

And this very thorough profession of faith was followed, on the part of Candace, by years of the most strenuous orthodoxy. Her general mode of expressing her mind on the subject was short and definitive.

'Law me! what's de use? I's set out to b'liebe de Catechize, an' I'm gwine to b'liebe it,—so!'

While we have been telling you all this about her, she has fastened her horse, and is swinging leisurely up to the house with a basket on either arm.

'Good morning, Candace,' said Mrs. Scudder. 'What brings you so early?'

'Come down 'fore light to sell my chickens an' eggs,—got a lot o' money for 'em, too. Missy Marvyn she sent Miss Scudder some turkey-eggs, an' I brought down some o' my doughnuts for de Doctor. Good folks must lib, you know, as well as wicked ones,'—and Candace gave a hearty, unctuous laugh. 'No reason why Doctors shouldn't hab good tings as well as sinners, is dere?'—and she shook in great billows, and showed her white teeth in the *abandon* of her laugh. 'Lor' bress ye, honey, chile!' she said, turning to Mary, 'why, ye looks like a new rose, ebery bit! Don't wonder *somebody* was allers pryin' an' spyin' about here!'

'How is your mistress, Candace?' said Mrs. Scudder, by way of changing the subject.

'Well, porly,—rader porly. When Massa Jim goes, 'pears like takin' de light right out her eyes. Dat ar' boy trains roun' arter his mudder like a cosset, he does.

Lor', de house seems so still widout him!—can't a fly scratch his ear but it starts a body. Missy Marvyn she sent down, an' says, would you and de Doctor an' Miss Mary please come to tea dis arternoon?'

'Thank your mistress, Candace,' said Mrs. Scudder; 'Mary and I will come,—and the Doctor, perhaps,' looking at the good man, who had relapsed into meditation, and was eating his breakfast without taking note of anything going on. 'It will be time enough to tell him of it,' she said to Mary, 'when we have to wake him up to dress; so we won't disturb him now.'

To Mary the prospect of the visit was a pleasant one, for reasons which she scarce gave a definite form to. Of course, like a good girl, she had come to a fixed and settled resolution to think of James as little as possible; but when the path of duty lay directly along scenes and among people fitted to recall him, it was more agreeable than if it had lain in another direction. Added to this, a very tender and silent friendship subsisted between Mrs. Marvyn and Mary; in which, besides similarity of mind and intellectual pursuits, there was a deep, unspoken element of sympathy.

Candace watched the light in Mary's eyes with the instinctive shrewdness by which her race seem to divine the thoughts and feelings of their superiors, and chuckled to herself internally. Without ever having been made a *confidante* by any party, or having a word said to or before her, still the whole position of affairs was as clear to her as if she had seen it on a map. She had appreciated at once Mrs. Scudder's coolness, James's devotion, and Mary's perplexity,—and inly resolved, that, if the little maiden did not think of James in his absence, it should not be her fault.

'Laws, Miss Scudder,' she said, 'I's right glad you's comin', 'cause you hasn't seen how we's kind o' splendified since Massa Jim come home. You wouldn't know it. Why, he's got mats from Mogadore on all de entries, and a great big 'un on de parlour; and ye ought to see de shawl he brought Missus, an' all de cur'us kind o' tings to de Squire. 'Tell ye, dat ar' boy honours his fader and mudder, ef he don't do nuffin else,—an' dat's de fus' commandment wid promise, ma'am; and to see him a-settin' up ebery day in prayer-time, so handsome, holdin' Missus's han', an' lookin' right into her eyes all de time! Why, dat ar' boy is one o' de 'lect,—it's jest as clare to me; and de 'lect has got to come in,—dat's what I say. My faith's strong,—real clare, 'tell ye,' she added, with the triumphant laugh which usually chorused her conversation, and turning to the Doctor, who, aroused by her loud and vigorous strain, was attending with interest to her.

'Well, Candace,' he said, 'we all hope you are right.'

'*Hope*, Doctor!—I don't hope,—I *knows*. 'Tell ye, when I pray for him, don't I feel enlarged? 'Tell ye, it goes wid a rush. I can feel it gwine up like a rushin', mighty wind. I feels strong, I do.'

'That's right, Candace,' said the Doctor, 'keep on; your prayers stand as much chance with God as if you were a crowned queen. The Lord is no respecter of persons.'

'Dat's what he a'n't, Doctor,—an' dere's where I 'gree wid him,' said Candace, as she gathered her baskets vigorously together, and, after a sweeping curtsy, went sailing down to her waggon, full laden with content, shouting a hearty 'Good mornin', Missus,' with the full power of her cheerful lungs, as she rode off.

As the Doctor looked after her, the simple, pleased expression with which he had watched her, gradually faded, and there passed over his broad, good face, a shadow, as of a cloud on a mountain-side.

'What a shame it is,' he said; 'what a scandal and disgrace to the Protestant religion, that Christians of America should openly practise and countenance this enslaving of the Africans! I have for a long time holden my peace—may the Lord forgive me!—but I believe the time is coming when I must utter my voice. I cannot go down to the wharves, or among the shipping, without these poor dumb creatures look at me so that I am ashamed; as if they asked me what I, a Christian minister, was doing, that I did not come to their help. I must testify.'

Mrs. Scudder looked grave at this earnest announcement; she had heard many like it before, and they always filled her with alarm, because——Shall we tell you why?

Well, then, it was not because she was not a thoroughly indoctrinated anti-slavery woman. Her husband, who did all her thinking for her, had been a man of ideas beyond his day, and never for a moment countenanced the right of slavery so far as to buy or own a servant or attendant of any kind: and Mrs. Scudder had always followed decidedly along the path of his opinions and practice, and never hesitated to declare the reasons for the faith that was in her. But if any of us could imagine an angel dropped down out of heaven, with wings, ideas, notions, manners, and customs all fresh from that very different country, we might easily suppose that the most pious and orthodox family might find the task of presenting him in general society, and piloting him along the courses of this world, a very delicate and embarrassing one. However much they might reverence him on their own private account, their hearts would probably sink within them at the idea of allowing him to expand himself according to his previous nature and habits in the great world without. In like manner, men of high, unworldly natures are often reverenced by those who are somewhat puzzled what to do with them practically.

Mrs. Scudder considered the Doctor as a superior being, possessed by a holy helplessness in all things material and temporal, which imposed on her the necessity of thinking and caring for him, and prevising the earthly and material aspects of his affairs.

There was not in Newport a more thriving and reputable business at that time than the slave-trade. Large fortunes were constantly being turned out in it, and what better Providential witness of its justice could most people require?

Beside this, in their own little church, she reflected with alarm, that Simeon Brown, the richest and most liberal supporter of the society, had been, and was then, drawing all his wealth from this source; and rapidly there flashed before her mind a picture of one and another, influential persons, who were holders of slaves. Therefore, when the Doctor announced, 'I must testify,' she rattled her tea-spoon uneasily, and answered,—

'In what way, Doctor, do you think of bearing testimony? The subject, I think, is a very difficult one.'

'Difficult? I think no subject can be clearer. If we were right in our war for liberty, we are wrong in making slaves or keeping them.'

'Oh, I did not mean,' said Mrs. Scudder, 'that it was difficult to understand the subject; the *right* of the matter is clear, but what to *do* is the thing.'

'I shall preach about it,' said the Doctor; 'my mind has run upon it some time. I shall show to the house of Judah their sin in this matter.'

'I fear there will be great offence given,' said Mrs. Scudder. 'There's Simeon Brown, one of our largest supporters,—he is in the trade.'

'Ah, yes,—but he will come out of it,—of course he will,—he is all right, all clear. I was delighted with the clearness of his views the other night, and thought then of bringing them to bear on this point,—only, as others were present, I deferred it. But I can show him that it follows logically from his principles; I am confident of that.'

'I think you'll be disappointed in him, Doctor;—I think he'll be angry, and get up a commotion, and leave the church.'

'Madam,' said the Doctor, 'do you suppose that a man who would be willing even to give up his eternal salvation for the greatest good of the universe could hesitate about a few paltry thousands that perish in the using?'

'He may feel willing to give up his soul,' said Mrs. Scudder, naïvely, 'but I don't think he'll give up his ships,—that's quite another matter,—he won't see it to be his duty.'

'Then, ma'am, he'll be a hypocrite, a gross hypocrite, if he won't,' said the Doctor. 'It is not Christian charity to think it of him. I shall call upon him this morning and tell him my intentions.'

'But, Doctor,' exclaimed Mrs. Scudder, with a start, 'pray, think a little more of it. You know a great many things depend on him. Why! he has subscribed for twenty copies of your "System of Theology." I hope you'll remember that.'

'And why should I remember that?' said the Doctor,—hastily turning round, suddenly enkindled, his blue eyes flashing out of their usual misty calm,—'what has my "System of Theology" to do with the matter?'

'Why,' said Mrs. Scudder, 'it's of more importance to get right views of the gospel before the world than anything else, is it not?—and if, by any imprudence in treating influential people, this should be prevented, more harm than good would be done.'

'Madam,' said the Doctor, 'I'd sooner my system should be sunk in the sea than it should be a millstone round my neck to keep me from my duty. Let God take care of my theology; I must do my duty.'

And as the Doctor spoke, he straightened himself to the full dignity of his height, his face kindling with an unconscious majesty, and, as he turned, his eye fell on Mary, who was standing with her slender figure dilated, her large blue eye wide and bright, in a sort of trance of solemn feeling, half-smiles, half-tears,—and the strong, heroic man started, to see this answer to his higher soul in the sweet, tremulous mirror of womanhood. One of those lightning glances passed between his eyes and hers which are the freemasonry of noble spirits,—and, by a sudden impulse, they approached each other. He took both her outstretched hands, looked down into her face with a look full of admiration, and a sort of naïve wonder,—then, as if her inspired silence had been a voice to him, he laid his hand on her head, and said,—

'God bless you, child! "Out of the mouth of babes and sucklings hast thou ordained strength because of thine enemies, that thou mightest still the enemy and the avenger."'

In a moment he was gone.

'Mary,' said Mrs. Scudder, laying her hand on her daughter's arm, 'the Doctor loves you!'

'I know he does, mother,' said Mary, innocently; 'and I love him,—dearly!—he is a noble, grand man!'

Mrs. Scudder looked keenly at her daughter. Mary's eye was as calm as a June sky, and she began, composedly, gathering up the teacups.

'She did not understand me,' thought the mother.

CHAPTER X.

THE TEST OF THEOLOGY.

THE Doctor went immediately to his study and put on his best coat and his wig, and, surmounting them by his cocked hat, walked manfully out of the house, with his gold-headed cane in his hand.

'There he goes!' said Mrs. Scudder, looking regretfully after him. 'He is *such* a good man!—but he has not the least idea how to get along in the world. He never thinks of anything but what is true; he hasn't a particle of management about him.'

'Seems to me,' said Mary, 'that is like an Apostle. You know, mother, St. Paul says, "In simplicity and godly sincerity, not with fleshly wisdom, but by the grace of God, we have had our conversation in the world."'

'To be sure,—that is just the Doctor,' said Mrs. Scudder; 'that's as like him as if it had been written for him. But that kind of way, somehow, don't seem to do in our times; it won't answer with Simeon Brown,—I know the man. I know just as well, now, how it will all seem to him, and what will be the upshot of this talk, if the Doctor goes there! It won't do any good; if it would I would be willing. I feel as much desire to have this horrid trade in slaves stopped as anybody; your father, I'm sure, said enough about it in his time; but then I know it's no use trying. Just as if Simeon Brown, when he is making his hundreds of thousands in it, is going to be persuaded to give it up! He won't—he'll only turn against the Doctor, and won't pay his part of the salary, and will use his influence to get up a party against him, and our church will be broken up and the Doctor driven away,—that's all that will come of it; and all the good that he is now doing to these poor negroes will be overthrown,—and they never did have so good a friend. If he would stay here and work gradually, and get his System of Theology printed,—and Simeon Brown would help at that,—and only drop words in season here and there, till people are brought along with him, why, by-and-by something might be done; but now, it's just the most imprudent thing a man could undertake.'

'But, mother, if it really is a sin to trade in slaves and hold them, I don't see how he can help himself. I quite agree with him. I don't see how he came to let it go so long as he has.'

'Well,' said Mrs. Scudder, 'if worst comes to worst, and he will do it, I, for one, shall stand by him to the last.'

'And I, for another,' said Mary.

'I would like him to talk with Cousin Zebedee about it,' said Mrs. Scudder. 'When we are up there this afternoon, we will introduce the conversation. He is a good sound man, and the Doctor thinks much of him, and perhaps he may shed some light upon this matter.'

Meanwhile the Doctor was making the best of his way in the strength of his purpose to test the orthodoxy of Simeon Brown.

Honest old granite boulder that he was, no sooner did he perceive a truth than he rolled after it with all the massive gravitation of his being, inconsiderate as to what might lie in his way:—from which it is to be inferred, that, with all his intellect and goodness, he would have been a very clumsy and troublesome inmate of the modern American Church. How many societies, boards, colleges, and other good institutions, have reason to congratulate themselves that he has long been among the saints!

With him logic was everything; and to perceive a truth and not act in logical sequence from it a thing so incredible, that he had not yet enlarged his capacity to take it in as a possibility. That a man should refuse to hear truth, he could understand. In fact, he had good reason to think the majority of his townsmen had no leisure to give to that purpose. That men hearing truth should dispute it and argue stoutly against it, he could also understand; but that a man could admit a truth and not admit the plain practice resulting from it was to him a thing incomprehensible. Therefore, spite of Mrs. Katy Scudder's discouraging observations, our good Doctor walked stoutly, and with a trusting heart.

At the moment when the Doctor, with a silent uplifting of his soul to his invisible Sovereign, passed out of his study, on this errand, where was the disciple whom he went to seek?

In a small, dirty room, down by the wharf, the windows veiled by cobwebs and dingy with the accumulated dust of ages, he sat in a greasy, leathern chair by a rickety office-table, on which were a great pewter inkstand, an account-book, and divers papers tied with red tape.

Opposite to him was seated a square-built individual,—a man of about forty, whose round head, shaggy eyebrows, small, keen eyes, broad chest, and heavy muscles, showed a preponderance of the animal and brutal over the intellectual and spiritual. This was Mr. Scroggs, the agent of a rice plantation, who had come on, bringing an order for a new relay of negroes to supply the deficit occasioned by fever, dysentery, and other causes, in their last year's stock.

'The fact is,' said Simeon, 'this last ship-load wasn't as good a one as usual; we lost more than a third of it, so we can't afford to put them a penny lower.'

'Ay,' said the other—'but then there are so many women!'

'Well,' said Simeon, 'women a'n't so strong perhaps to start with; but then they stan' it out, perhaps, in the long run, better. They're more patient;—some of these men, the Mandingoes particularly, are pretty troublesome to manage. We lost a splendid fellow, coming over, on this very voyage. Let 'em on deck for air, and this fellow managed to get himself loose and fought like a dragon. He settled one of our men with his fist, and another with a marlinespike that he caught,—and, in fact, they had to shoot him down. You'll have his wife; there's his son, too,—fine fellow, fifteen year old by his teeth.'

'What! that lame one?'

'Oh, he a'n't lame!—it's nothing but the cramps from stowing. You know, of course, they are more or less stiff. He's as sound as a nut.'

'Don't much like to buy relations, on account of their hatching up mischief together,' said Mr. Scroggs.

'Oh, that's all humbug! You must keep 'em from coming together, anyway. It's about as broad as 'tis long. There'll be wives and husbands and children among 'em before long, start 'em as you will. And then this woman will work better for having the boy; she's kinder set on him; she jabbers lots of lingo to him, day and night.'

'Too much, I doubt,' said the overseer, with a shrug.

'Well, well,—I'll tell you,' said Simeon, rising. 'I've got a few errands up town, and you just step over with Matlock and look over the stock;—just set aside any that you want, and when I see 'em all together, I'll tell you just what you shall have 'em for. I'll be back in an hour or two.'

And so saying, Simeon Brown called an underling from an adjoining room, and, committing his customer to his care, took his way up-town, in a serene frame of mind, like a man who comes from the calm performance of duty.

Just as he came upon the street where was situated his own large and somewhat pretentious mansion, the tall figure of the Doctor loomed in sight, sailing majestically down upon him, making a signal to attract his attention.

'Good morning, Doctor,' said Simeon.

'Good morning, Mr. Brown,' said the Doctor. 'I was looking for you. I did not quite finish the subject we were talking about at Mrs. Scudder's table last night. I thought I should like to go on with it a little.'

'With all my heart, Doctor,' said Simeon, not a little flattered. 'Turn right in. Mrs. Brown will be about her house business, and we will have the keeping-room all to ourselves. Come right in.'

The 'keeping-room' of Mr. Simeon Brown's house was an intermediate apartment between the ineffable glories of the front parlour and that court of the Gentiles, the kitchen; for the presence of a large train of negro servants made the latter apartment an altogether different institution from the throne-room of Mrs. Katy Scudder.

This keeping-room was a low-studded apartment, finished with the heavy oaken beams of the wall left full in sight, boarded over and painted. Two windows looked out on the street, and another into a sort of court-yard, where three black wenches, each with a broom, pretended to be sweeping, but were, in fact, chattering and laughing, like so many crows.

On one side of the room stood a heavy mahogany sideboard, covered with decanters, labelled Gin, Brandy, Rum, &c.; for Simeon was held to be a provider of none but the best, in his housekeeping. Heavy mahogany chairs, with crewel coverings, stood sentry about the room; and the fireplace was flanked by two broad arm-chairs, covered with stamped leather.

On ushering the Doctor into this apartment, Simeon courteously led him to the sideboard.

'We mus'n't make our discussions too *dry*, Doctor,' he said; 'what will you take?'

'Thank you, sir,' said the Doctor, with a wave of his hand,—'nothing this morning.'

And, depositing his cocked hat in a chair, he settled himself into one of the leathern easy chairs, and, dropping his hands upon his knees, looked fixedly before him, like a man who is studying how to enter upon an inwardly absorbing subject.

'Well, Doctor,' said Simeon, seating himself opposite, sipping comfortably at a glass of rum-and-water, 'our views appear to be making a noise in the world. Everything is preparing for your volumes; and when they appear, the battle of New Divinity, I think, may fairly be considered as won.'

Let us consider, that, though a woman may forget her firstborn, yet a man cannot forget his own system of theology,—because, therein, if he be a true man, is the very elixir and essence of all that is valuable and hopeful to the universe; and considering this, let us appreciate the settled purpose of our friend, whom even this tempting bait did not swerve from the end which he had in view.

'Mr. Brown,' he said, 'all our theology is as a drop in the ocean of God's majesty, to whose glory we must be ready to make any and every sacrifice.'

'Certainly,' said Mr. Brown, not exactly comprehending the turn the Doctor's thoughts were taking.

'And the glory of God consisteth in the happiness of all his rational universe, each in his proportion, according to his separate amount of being; so that, when we devote ourselves to God's glory, it is the same as saying that we devote ourselves to the highest happiness of his created universe.'

'That's clear, sir,' said Simeon, rubbing his hands, and taking out his watch to see the time.

The Doctor hitherto had spoken in a laborious manner, like a man who is slowly lifting a heavy bucket of thought out of an internal well.

'I am glad to find your mind so clear on this all-important point, Mr. Brown, the more so as I feel that we must immediately proceed to apply our principles, at whatever sacrifice of worldly goods; and I trust, sir, that you are one who, at the call of your Master, would not hesitate even to lay down all your worldly possessions for the greater good of the universe.'

'I trust so, sir,' said Simeon, rather uneasily, and without the most distant idea what could be coming next in the mind of his reverend friend.

CHAPTER X.

'Did it never occur to you, my friend,' said the Doctor, 'that the enslaving of the African race is a clear violation of the great law which commands us to love our neighbour as ourselves,—and a dishonour upon the Christian religion, more particularly in us Americans, whom the Lord hath so marvellously protected, in our recent struggle for our own liberty?'

Simeon started at the first words of this address, much as if some one had dashed a bucket of water on his head, and after that rose uneasily, walking the room and playing with the seals of his watch.

'I—I never regarded it in this light,' he said.

'Possibly not, my friend' said the Doctor,—'so much doth established custom blind the minds of the best of men. But since I have given more particular attention to the case of the poor negroes here in Newport, the thought has more and more laboured in my mind,—more especially as our own struggles for liberty have turned my attention to the rights which every human creature hath before God,—so that I find much in my former blindness and the comparative dumbness I have heretofore maintained on this subject wherewith to reproach myself; for, though I have borne somewhat of a testimony, I have not given it that force which so important a subject required. I am humbled before God for my neglect, and resolved now, by his grace, to leave no stone unturned till this iniquity be purged away from our Zion.'

'Well, Doctor,' said Simeon, 'you are certainly touching on a very dark and difficult subject, and one in which it is hard to find out the path of duty. Perhaps it will be well to bear it in mind, and by looking at it prayerfully some light may arise. There are such great obstacles in the way, that I do not see at present what can be done; do you, Doctor?'

'I intend to preach on the subject next Sunday, and hereafter devote my best energies in the most public way to this great work,' said the Doctor.

'You, Doctor?—and now, immediately? Why, it appears to me you cannot do it. You are the most unfit man possible. Whosoever's duty it may be, it does not seem to me to be yours. You already have more on your shoulders than you can carry; you are hardly able to keep your ground now, with all the odium of this new theology upon you. Such an effort would break up your church,—destroy the chance you have to do good here,—prevent the publication of your system.'

'If it's nobody's system but mine, the world won't lose much, if it never be published; but if it be God's system, nothing can hinder its appearing. Besides, Mr. Brown, I ought not to be one man alone. I count on your help. I hold it as a special providence, Mr. Brown, that in our own church an opportunity will be given to testify to the reality of disinterested benevolence. How glorious the opportunity for a man to come out and testify by sacrificing his worldly living and business! If you, Mr. Brown, will at once, at whatever sacrifice, quit all connection with this detestable and diabolical slave-trade, you will exhibit a spectacle over which angels will rejoice, and which will strengthen and encourage me to preach and write and testify.'

Mr. Simeon Brown's usual demeanour was that of the most leathery imperturbability. In calm theological reasoning, he could demonstrate, in the dryest tone, that, if the eternal torment of six bodies and souls were absolutely the necessary means for preserving the eternal blessedness of thirty-six, benevolence would require us to rejoice in it, not in itself considered, but in view of greater good. And when he spoke, not a nerve quivered; the great mysterious sorrow with which the creation groaneth and travaileth, the sorrow from which angels veil their faces, never had touched one vibrating chord either of body or soul; and he laid down the obligations of man to unconditional submission in a style which would have affected a person of delicate sensibility much like being mentally sawn in sunder. Benevolence, when Simeon Brown spoke of it, seemed the grimmest and unloveliest of Gorgons; for his mind seemed to resemble those fountains which petrify everything that falls into them. But the hardest-shelled animals have a vital and sensitive part, though only so large as the point of a needle; and the Doctor's innocent proposition to Simeon, to abandon his whole worldly estate for his principles, touched this spot.

When benevolence required but the acquiescence in certain possible things which might be supposed to happen to his soul, which, after all, he was comfortably certain never would happen, or the acquiescence in certain suppositious sacrifices for the good of that most intangible of all abstractions, Being in general, it was a dry, calm subject. But when it concerned the immediate giving up of his slave-ships and a transfer of business, attended with all that confusion and loss which he foresaw at a glance, then he *felt*, and felt too much to see clearly. His swarthy face flushed, his little blue eye kindled, he walked up to the Doctor, and began speaking in the short, energetic sentences of a man thoroughly awake to what he is talking about.

'Doctor, you're too fast. You are not a practical man, Doctor. You are good in your pulpit;—nobody better. Your theology is clear;—nobody can argue better. But come to practical matters, why, business has its laws, Doctor. Ministers are the most unfit men in the world to talk on such subjects; it's departing from their sphere; they talk about what they don't understand. Besides, you take too much for granted. I'm not sure that this trade is an evil. I want to be convinced of it. I'm sure it's a favour to these poor creatures to bring them to a Christian land. They are a thousand times better off. Here they can hear the gospel and have some chance of salvation.'

'If we want to get the gospel to the Africans,' said the Doctor, 'why not send whole ship-loads of missionaries to them, and carry civilization and the arts and Christianity to Africa, instead of stirring up wars, tempting them to ravage each other's territories, that we may get the booty? Think of the numbers killed in the wars,—of all that die on the passage! Is there any need of killing ninety-nine men to give the hundredth one the gospel, when we could give the gospel to them all? Ah, Mr. Brown, what if all the money spent in fitting out ships to bring the poor negroes here, so prejudiced against Christianity that they regard it with fear and aversion, had been spent in sending it to them, Africa would have been covered with towns and villages, rejoicing in civilization and Christianity!'

'Doctor, you are a dreamer,' replied Simeon, 'an unpractical man. Your situation prevents your knowing anything of real life.'

'Amen! the Lord be praised there for!' said the Doctor, with a slowly-increasing flush mounting to his cheek, showing the burning brand of a smouldering fire of indignation.

'Now let me just talk common-sense, Doctor,—which has its time and place, just as much as theology; and if you have the most theology, I flatter myself I have the most common-sense: a business-man must have it. Now just look at your situation,—how you stand. You've got a most important work to do. In order to do it, you must keep your pulpit, you must keep our church together. We are few and weak. We are a minority. Now there's not an influential man in your society that don't either hold slaves or engage in the trade; and, if you open upon this subject as you are going to do, you'll just divide and destroy the church. All men are not like you; men are men, and will be, till they are thoroughly sanctified, which never happens in this life,—and there will be an instant and most unfavourable agitation. Minds will be turned off from the discussion of the great saving doctrines of the gospel to a side issue. You will be turned out; and you know, Doctor, you are not appreciated as you ought to be, and it won't be easy for you to get a new settlement; and then subscriptions will all drop off from your book, and you won't be able to get that out; and all this good will be lost to the world, just for want of common-sense.'

'There is a kind of wisdom in what you say, Mr. Brown,' replied the Doctor, naïvely; 'but I fear much that it is the wisdom spoken in James iii. 15, which "descendeth not from above, but is earthly, sensual, devilish." You avoid the very point of the argument, which is, Is this a sin against God? That it is, I am solemnly convinced; and shall I "use lightness? or the things that I purpose do I purpose according to the flesh, that with me there should be yea, yea, and nay, nay?" No, Mr. Brown, immediate repentance, unconditional submission, these are what I must preach as long as God gives me a pulpit to stand in, whether men will hear or whether they will forbear.'

'Well, Doctor,' said Simeon, shortly, 'you can do as you like; but I give you fair warning, that I, for one, shall stop my subscription, and go to Dr. Stiles's church.'

'Mr. Brown,' said the Doctor, solemnly, rising, and drawing his tall figure to its full height, while a vivid light gleamed from his blue eye, 'as to that, you can do as you like; but I think it my duty, as your pastor, to warn you that I have perceived, in my conversation with you this morning, such a want of true spiritual illumination and discernment as leads me to believe that you are yet in the flesh, blinded by that "carnal mind" which "is not subject to the law of God, neither indeed can be." I much fear you have no part nor lot in this matter, and that you have need, seriously, to set yourself to search into the foundations of your hope; for you may be like him of whom it is written, (Isaiah xliv. 20,) "He feedeth on ashes: a deceived heart hath turned him aside, that he cannot deliver his soul, nor say, is there not a lie in my right hand?'"

The Doctor delivered this address to his man of influence with the calmness of an ambassador charged with a message from a sovereign, for which he is no otherwise responsible than to speak it in the most intelligible manner; and then, taking up his hat and cane, he bade him good morning, leaving Simeon Brown in a tumult of excitement which no previous theological discussion had ever raised in him.

CHAPTER XI.

THE PRACTICAL TEST.

THE hens cackled drowsily in the barn-yard of the white Marvyn-house; in the blue June-afternoon sky sported great sailing islands of cloud, whose white, glistening heads looked in and out through the green apertures of maple and blossoming apple-boughs; the shadows of the trees had already turned eastward, when the one-horse waggon of Mrs. Katy Scudder appeared at the door, where Mrs. Marvyn stood, with a pleased, quiet welcome in her soft brown eyes. Mrs. Scudder herself drove, sitting on a seat in front,—while the Doctor, apparelled in the most faultless style, with white wrist-ruffles, plaited shirt-bosom, immaculate wig, and well-brushed coat, sat by Mary's side, serenely unconscious how many feminine cares had gone to his getting-up. He did not know of the privy consultations, the sewings, stitchings, and starchings, the ironings, the brushings, the foldings and unfoldings and timely arrangements, that gave such dignity and respectability to his outer man, any more than the serene moon rising tranquilly behind a purple mountain-top troubles her calm head with treatises on astronomy; it is enough for her to shine,—she thinks not how or why.

There is a vast amount of latent gratitude to women lying undeveloped in the hearts of men, which would come out plentifully, if they only knew what they did for them. The Doctor was so used to being well dressed, that he never asked why. That his wig always sat straight, and even around his ample forehead, not facetiously poked to one side, nor assuming rakish airs, unsuited to clerical dignity, was entirely owing to Mrs. Katy Scudder. That his best broadcloth coat was not illustrated with shreds and patches, fluff and dust, and hanging in ungainly folds, was owing to the same. That his long silk stockings never had a treacherous stitch allowed to break out into a long running ladder was due to her watchfulness; and that he wore spotless ruffles on his wrists or at his bosom was her doing also. The Doctor little thought, while he, in common with good ministers generally, gently traduced the Scriptural Martha and insisted on the duty of heavenly abstractedness, how much of his own leisure for spiritual contemplation was due to the Martha-like talents of his hostess. But then, the good soul had it in him to be grateful, and would have been unboundedly so, if he had known his indebtedness,—as, we trust, most of our magnanimous masters would be.

Mr. Zebedee Marvyn was quietly sitting in the front summer parlour, listening to the story of two of his brother church-members, between whom some difficulty had arisen in the settling of accounts: Jim Bigelow, a small, dry, dapper little individual, known as general jobber and factotum, and Abram Griswold, a stolid, wealthy, well-to-do farmer. And the fragments of conversation we catch are not uninteresting, as showing Mr. Zebedee's habits of thought and mode of treating those who came to him for advice.

'I could 'ave got along better, if he'd 'a' paid me regular every night,' said the squeaky voice of little Jim;—'but he was allers puttin' me off till it come even change, he said.'

'Well, 't'aint always handy,' replied the other; 'one doesn't like to break into a five-pound note for nothing; and I like to let it run till it comes even change.'

'But, brother,' said Mr. Zebedee, turning over the great Bible that lay on the mahogany stand in the corner, 'we must go to the law and to the testimony,'—and, turning over the leaves, he read from Deuteronomy xxiv.:—

'Thou shalt not oppress an hired servant that is poor and needy, whether he be of thy brethren or of thy strangers that are in thy land within thy gates. At his day thou shalt give him his hire, neither shall the sun go down upon it; for he is poor, and setteth his heart upon it: lest he cry against thee unto the Lord, and it be sin unto thee.'

'You see what the Bible has to say on the matter,' he said.

'Well, now, Deacon, I rather think you've got me in a tight place,' said Mr. Griswold, rising; and turning confusedly round, he saw the placid figure of the Doctor, who had entered the room unobserved in the midst of the conversation, and was staring with that look of calm, dreamy abstraction which often led people to suppose that he heard and saw nothing of what was going forward.

All rose reverently; and while Mr. Zebedee was shaking hands with the Doctor, and welcoming him to his house, the other two silently withdrew, making respectful obeisance.

Mrs. Marvyn had drawn Mary's hand gently under her arm and taken her to her own sleeping-room, as it was her general habit to do, that she might show her the last book she had been reading, and pour into her ear the thoughts that had been kindled up by it.

Mrs. Scudder, after carefully brushing every speck of dust from the Doctor's coat and seeing him seated in an arm-chair by the open window, took out a long stocking of blue-mixed yarn which she was knitting for his winter-wear, and, pinning her knitting-sheath on her side, was soon trotting her needles contentedly in front of him.

The ill-success of the Doctor's morning attempt at enforcing his theology in practice rather depressed his spirits. There was a noble innocence of nature in him which looked at hypocrisy with a puzzled and incredulous astonishment. How a man *could* do so and be so was to him a problem at which his thoughts vainly laboured. Not that he was in the least discouraged or hesitating in regard to his own course. When he had made up his mind to perform a duty, the question of success no more entered his thoughts than those of the granite boulder to which we have before compared him. When the time came for him to roll, he did roll with the whole force of his being;—where he was to land was not his concern.

Mildly and placidly he sat with his hands resting on his knees, while Mr. Zebedee and Mrs. Scudder compared notes respecting the relative prospects of corn, flax, and buckwheat, and thence passed to the doings of Congress and the last proclamation of General Washington, pausing once in a while, if, peradventure, the Doctor might take up the conversation. Still he sat dreamily eyeing the flies as they fizzed down the panes of the half-open window.

'I think,' said Mr. Zebedee, 'the prospects of the Federal party were never brighter.'

The Doctor was a stanch Federalist, and generally warmed to this allurement; but it did not serve this time.

Suddenly drawing himself up, a light came into his blue eyes, and he said to Mr. Marvyn,—

'I'm thinking, Deacon, if it is wrong to keep back the wages of a servant till after the going down of the sun, what those are to do who keep them back all their lives.'

There was a way the Doctor had of hearing and seeing when he looked as if his soul were afar off, and bringing suddenly into present conversation some fragment of the past on which he had been leisurely hammering in the quiet chambers of his brain, which was sometimes quite startling.

This allusion to a passage of Scripture which Mr. Marvyn was reading when he came in, and which nobody supposed he had attended to, startled Mrs. Scudder, who thought, mentally, 'Now for it!' and laid down her knitting-work, and eyed her cousin anxiously. Mrs. Marvyn and Mary, who had glided in and joined the circle, looking interested; and a slight flush rose and overspread the thin cheeks of Mr. Marvyn, and his blue eyes deepened in a moment with a thoughtful shadow, as he looked inquiringly at the Doctor, who proceeded:—

'My mind labours with this subject of the enslaving of the Africans, Mr. Marvyn. We have just been declaring to the world that all men are born with an inalienable right to liberty. We have fought for it, and the Lord of Hosts has been with us; and can we stand before Him, with our foot upon our brother's neck?'

A generous, upright nature is always more sensitive to blame than another,—sensitive in proportion to the amount of its reverence for good,—and Mr. Marvyn's face flushed, his eye kindled, and his compressed respiration showed how deeply the subject moved him. Mrs. Marvyn's eyes turned on him an anxious look of inquiry. He answered, however, calmly:—

'Doctor, I have thought of the subject myself. Mrs. Marvyn has lately been reading a pamphlet of Mr. Thomas Clarkson's on the slave-trade, and she was saying to me only last night, that she did not see but the argument extended equally to holding slaves. One thing, I confess, stumbles me:—Was there not an express permission given to Israel to buy and hold slaves of old?'

'Doubtless,' said the Doctor; 'but many permissions were given to them which were local and temporary; for if we hold them to apply to the human race, the Turks might quote the Bible for making slaves of us, if they could,—and the Algerines have the Scripture all on their side,—and our own blacks, at some future time, if they can get the power, might justify themselves in making slaves of us.'

'I assure you, sir,' said Mr. Marvyn, 'if I speak, it is not to excuse myself. But I am quite sure my servants do not desire liberty, and would not take it, if it were offered.'

'Call them in and try it,' said the Doctor. 'If they refuse, it is their own matter.'

There was a gentle movement in the group at the directness of this personal application; but Mr. Marvyn replied, calmly,—

'Cato is up at the eight-acre lot, but you may call in Candace. My dear, call Candace, and let the Doctor put the question to her.'

Candace was at this moment sitting before the ample fireplace in the kitchen, with two iron kettles before her, nestled each in its bed of hickory coals, which gleamed out from their white ashes like sleepy, red eyes, opening and shutting. In one was coffee, which she was burning, stirring vigorously with a pudding-stick,—and in the other, puffy dough-nuts, in shapes of rings, hearts, and marvellous twists, which Candace had such a special proclivity for making, that Mrs. Marvyn's table and closets never knew an intermission of their presence.

'Candace, the Doctor wishes to see you,' said Mrs. Marvyn.

'Bress his heart!' said Candace, looking up, perplexed. 'Wants to see me, does he? Can't nobody hab me till dis yer coffee's done; a minnit's a minnit in coffee;—but I'll be in dereckly,' she added, in a patronising tone. 'Missis, you jes' go 'long in, an' I'll be dar dereckly.'

A few moments after Candace joined the group in the sitting-room, having hastily tied a clean white apron over her blue linsey working-dress, and donned the brilliant Madras which James had lately given her, and which she had a barbaric fashion of arranging so as to give to her head the air of a gigantic butterfly. She sunk a dutiful curtsy, and stood twirling her thumbs, while the Doctor surveyed her gravely.

'Candace,' said he, 'do you think it right that the black race should be slaves to the white?'

The face and air of Candace presented a curious picture at this moment; a sort of rude sense of delicacy embarrassed her, and she turned a deprecating look, first on Mrs. Marvyn and then on her master.

'Don't mind us, Candace,' said Mrs. Marvyn; 'tell the Doctor the exact truth.'

Candace stood still a moment, and the spectators saw a deeper shadow roll over her sable face, like a cloud over a dark pool of water, and her immense person heaved with her laboured breathing.

'Ef I must speak I must,' she said. 'No,—I neber did tink 'twas right. When General Washington was here, I hearn 'em read de Declaration ob Independence and Bill o' Rights; an' I tole Cato den, says I, "Ef dat ar' true, you an' I are as free as anybody." It stands to reason. Why, look at me,—I a'n't a critter. I's neider huffs nor horns. I's a reasonable bein',—a woman,—as much a woman as any-body,' she said, holding up her head with an air as majestic as a palm-tree;—'an' Cato,—he's a man born free an' equal, ef dar's any truth in what you read,—dat's all.'

'But, Candace, you've always been contented and happy with us, have you not?' said Mr. Marvyn.

'Yes, Mass'r,—I ha'n't got nuffin to complain of in dat matter. I couldn't hab no better friends 'n you an' Missis.'

'Would you like your liberty, if you could get it, though?' said Mr. Marvyn. 'Answer me honestly.'

'Why, to be sure I should! Who wouldn't? Mind ye,' she said, earnestly raising her black, heavy hand, ''ta'n't dat I want to go off, or want to shirk work; but I want to *feel free*. Dem dat isn't free has nuffin to give to nobody;—dey can't show what dey would do.'

'Well, Candace, from this day you are free,' said Mr. Marvyn, solemnly.

Candace covered her face with both her fat hands, and shook and trembled, and, finally, throwing her apron over her head, made a desperate rush for the door, and threw herself down in the kitchen in a perfect tropical torrent of tears and sobs.

'You see,' said the Doctor, 'what freedom is to every human creature. The blessing of the Lord will be on this deed, Mr. Marvyn. "The steps of a just man are ordered by the Lord, and he delighteth in his way."'

At this moment, Candace reappeared at the door, her butterfly turban somewhat deranged with the violence of her prostration, giving a whimsical air to her portly person.

'I want ye all to know,' she said, with a clearing-up snuff, 'dat it's my will 'an pleasure to go right on doin' my work jes' de same; an', Missis, please, I'll allers put three eggs in de crullers, now; an' I won't turn de wash-basin down in de sink, but hang it jam-up on de nail; an' I won't pick up chips in a milkpan, ef I'm in ever so big a hurry;—I'll do eberyting jes' as ye tells me. Now you try me and see ef I won't!'

Candace here alluded to some of the little private wilfulnesses which she had always obstinately cherished as reserved rights, in pursuing domestic matters with her mistress.

'I intend,' said Mr. Marvyn, 'to make the same offer to your husband, when he returns from work to night.'

'Laus, Mass'r,—why, Cato he'll do jes' as I do,—dere a'n't no kind o' need o' askin' him. 'Course he will.'

A smile passed round the circle, because between Candace and her husband there existed one of those whimsical contrasts which one sometimes sees in married life. Cato was a small-built, thin, softly-spoken negro, addicted to a gentle chronic cough; and, though a faithful and skilful servant, seemed, in relation to his better half, much like a hill of potatoes under a spreading apple-tree. Candace held to him with a vehement and patronizing fondness, so devoid of conjugal reverence as to excite the comments of her friends.

'You must remember, Candace,' said a good deacon to her one day, when she was ordering him about at a catechizing, 'you ought to give honour to your husband; the wife is the weaker vessel.'

'*I* de weaker vessel?' said Candace, looking down from the tower of her ample corpulence on the small, quiet man whom she had been fledging with the ample folds of a worsted comforter, out of which his little head and shining bead-eyes looked much like a blackbird in a nest,—'*I* de weaker vessel? Umph!'

A whole-woman's-rights' convention could not have expressed more in a day than was given in that single look and word. Candace considered a husband as a thing to be taken care of,—a rather inconsequent and somewhat troublesome species of pet, to be humoured, nursed, fed, clothed, and guided in the way that he was to go,—an animal that was always losing of buttons, catching colds, wearing his best coat every day, and getting on his Sunday hat in a surreptitious manner for week-day occasions; but she often condescended to express it as her opinion that he was a blessing, and that she didn't know what she should do if it wasn't for Cato. In fact, he seemed to supply her that which we are told is the great want in woman's situation,—an object in life. She sometimes was heard expressing herself very energetically in disapprobation of the conduct of one of her sable friends, named Jinny Stiles, who, after being presented with her own freedom, worked several years to buy that of her husband, but became afterwards so disgusted with her acquisition that she declared she would, 'neber buy anoder nigger.'

'Now Jinny don't know what she's talkin' about,' she would say. 'S'pose he does cough and keep her awake nights, and take a little too much sometimes, a'n't he better'n no husband at all? A body wouldn't seem to hab nuffin to lib for, ef dey hadn't an ole man to look arter. Men is nate'lly foolish about some tings,—but dey's good deal better'n nuffin.'

And Candace, after this condescending remark, would lift off with one hand a brass kettle in which poor Cato might have been drowned, and fly across the kitchen with it as if it were a feather.

CHAPTER XII.

MISS PRISSY.

WILL our little Mary really fall in love with the Doctor?—The question reaches us in anxious tones from all the circle of our readers; and what especially shocks us is, that grave doctors of divinity, and serious, stocking-knitting matrons, seem to be the class who are particularly set against the success of our excellent orthodox hero, and bent on reminding us of the claims of that unregenerate James, whom we have sent to sea on purpose that our heroine may recover herself of that foolish partiality for him which all the Christian world seems bent on perpetuating.

'Now, really,' says the Rev. Mrs. Q., looking up from her bundle of Sewing-Society work, 'you are *not* going to let Mary marry the Doctor?'

My dear Madam, is not that just what you did, yourself, after having turned off three or four fascinating young sinners as good as James any day? Don't make us believe that you are sorry for it now!

'Is it possible,' says Dr. Theophrastus, who is himself a stanch Hopkinsian divine, and who is at present recovering from his last grand effort on Natural and Moral Ability,—'is it possible that you are going to let Mary forget that poor young man and marry Dr. H.? That will never do in the world!'

Dear Doctor, consider what would have become of you, if some lady at a certain time had not had the sense and discernment to fall in love with the *man* who came to her disguised as a theologian.

'But he's so old!' says Aunt Maria.

Not at all. Old? What do you mean? Forty is the very season of ripeness,—the very meridian of manly lustre and splendour.

'But he wears a wig.'

My dear Madam, so did Sir Charles Grandison, and Lovelace, and all the other fine fellows of those days: the wig was the distinguishing mark of a gentleman.

No,—spite of all you may say and declare, we do insist that our Doctor is a very proper and probable subject for a young lady to fall in love with.

If women have one weakness more marked than another, it is towards veneration. They are born worshippers,—makers of silver shrines for some divinity or other, which, of course, they always think fell straight down from heaven.

The first step towards their falling in love with an ordinary mortal is generally to dress him out with all manner of real or fancied superiority; and having made him up, they worship him.

Now a truly great man, a man really grand and noble in heart and intellect, has this advantage with women, that he is an idol ready-made to hand; and so that very painstaking and ingenious sex have less labour in getting him up, and can be ready to worship him on shorter notice.

In particular is this the case where a sacred profession and a moral supremacy are added to the intellectual. Just think of the career of celebrated preachers and divines in all ages. Have they not stood like the image that 'Nebuchadnezzar the king set up,' and all womankind, coquettes and flirts not excepted, been ready to fall down and worship, even before the sound of cornet, flute, harp, sackbut, and so forth? Is not the faithful Paula, with her beautiful face, prostrate in reverence before poor, old, lean, haggard, dying St. Jerome, in the most splendid painting of the world, an emblem and sign of woman's eternal power of self-sacrifice to what she deems noblest in man? Does not old Richard Baxter tell us, with delightful single-heartedness, how his wife fell in love with him first, spite of his long, pale face,—and how she confessed, dear soul, after many years of married life, that she had found him *less* sour and bitter than she had expected?

The fact is, women are burdened with fealty, faith, reverence, more than they know what to do with; they stand like a hedge of sweet-peas, throwing out fluttering tendrils everywhere for something high and strong to climb by,—and when they find it, be it ever so rough in the bark, they catch upon it. And instances are not wanting of those who have turned away from the flattery of admirers to prostrate themselves at the feet of a genuine hero who never wooed them except by heroic deeds and the rhetoric of a noble life.

Never was there a distinguished man whose greatness could sustain the test of minute domestic inspection better than our Doctor. Strong in a single-hearted humility, a perfect unconsciousness of self, an honest and sincere absorption in high and holy themes and objects, there was in him what we so seldom see,—a perfect logic of life; his minutest deeds were the true results of his sublimest principles. His whole nature, moral, physical, and intellectual, was simple, pure, and cleanly. He was temperate as an anchorite in all matters of living,—avoiding, from a healthy instinct, all those intoxicating stimuli then common among the clergy. In his early youth, indeed, he had formed an attachment to the almost universal clerical pipe,—but, observing a delicate woman once nauseated by coming into the atmosphere which he and his brethren had polluted, he set himself gravely to reflect that that which could so offend a woman must needs be uncomely and unworthy a Christian man; wherefore he laid his pipe on the mantelpiece, and never afterwards resumed the indulgence.

CHAPTER XII.

In all his relations with womanhood he was delicate and reverential, forming his manners by that old precept, 'The elder women entreat as mothers, the younger as sisters,'—which rule, short and simple as it is, is nevertheless the most perfect *résumé* of all true gentlemanliness. Then, as for person, the Doctor was not handsome, to be sure; but he was what sometimes serves with woman better,—majestic and manly, and, when animated by thought and feeling, having even a commanding grandeur of mien. Add to all this, that our valiant hero is now on the straight road to bring him into that situation most likely to engage the warm partisanship of a true woman,—namely, that of a man unjustly abused for right-doing,—and one may see that it is ten to one our Mary may fall in love with him yet, before she knows it.

If it were not for this mysterious selfness-and-sameness which makes this wild, wandering, uncanonical sailor, James Marvyn, so intimate and internal,—if his thread were not knit up with the thread of her life,—were it not for the old habit of feeling for him, thinking for him, praying for him, hoping for him, fearing for him, which—woe is us!—is the unfortunate habit of womankind,—if it were not for that fatal something which neither judgment, nor wishes, nor reason, nor common sense shows any great skill in unravelling,—we are quite sure that Mary would be in love with the Doctor within the next six months; as it is, we leave you all to infer from your own heart and consciousness what his chances are.

A new sort of scene is about to open on our heroine, and we shall show her to you, for an evening at least, in new associations, and with a different background from that homely and rural one in which she has fluttered as a white dove amid leafy and congenial surroundings.

As we have before intimated, Newport presented a *résumé* of many different phases of society, all brought upon a social level by the then universally admitted principle of equality.

There were scattered about in the settlement lordly mansions, whose owners rolled in emblazoned carriages, and whose wide halls were the scenes of a showy and almost princely hospitality. By her husband's side, Mrs. Katy Scudder was allied to one of these families of wealthy planters, and often recognized the connection with a quiet undertone of satisfaction, as a dignified and self-respecting woman should. She liked, once in a while, quietly to let people know, that, although they lived in the plain little cottage and made no pretensions, yet they had good blood in their veins,—that Mr. Scudder's mother was a Wilcox, and that the Wilcoxes were, she supposed, as high as anybody,—generally ending the remark with the observation, that 'all these things, to be sure, were matters of small consequence, since at last it would be of far more importance to have been a true Christian than to have been connected with the highest families of the land.'

Nevertheless, Mrs. Scudder was not a little pleased to have in her possession a card of invitation to a splendid wedding-party that was going to be given on Friday at the Wilcox Manor. She thought it a very becoming mark of respect to the deceased Mr. Scudder that his widow and daughter should be brought to mind,—

so becoming and praiseworthy, in fact, that, 'though an old woman,' as she said, with a complacent straightening of her tall, lithe figure, she really thought she must make an effort to go.

Accordingly, early one morning, after all domestic duties had been fulfilled, and the clock, loudly ticking through the empty rooms, told that all needful bustle had died down to silence, Mrs. Katy, Mary, and Miss Prissy Diamond, the dress-maker, might have been observed sitting in solemn senate around the camphor-wood trunk, before spoken of, and which exhaled vague foreign and Indian perfumes of silk and sandalwood.

You may have heard of dignitaries, my good reader,—but, I assure you, you know very little of a situation of trust or importance compared to that of *the* dressmaker in a small New England town.

What important interests does she hold in her hands! How is she besieged, courted, deferred to! Three months beforehand, all her days and nights are spoken for; and the simple statement, that *only* on that day you can have Miss Clippers, is of itself an apology for any omission of attention elsewhere,—it strikes home at once to the deepest consciousness of every woman, married or single. How thoughtfully is everything arranged, weeks beforehand, for the golden, important season when Miss Clippers can come! On that day, there is to be no extra sweeping, dusting, cleaning, cooking, no visiting, no receiving, no reading or writing, but all with one heart and soul are to wait upon her, intent to forward the great work which she graciously affords a day's leisure to direct. Seated in her chair of state, with her well-worn cushion bristling with pins and needles at her side, her ready roll of patterns and her scissors, she hears, judges, and decides *ex cathedrâ* on the possible or not possible, in that important art on which depends the right presentation of the floral part of Nature's great horticultural show. She alone is competent to say whether there is any available remedy for the stained breadth in Jane's dress—whether the fatal spot by any magical hocus-pocus can be cut out from the fulness, or turned up and smothered from view in the gathers, or concealed by some new fashion of trimming falling with generous appropriateness exactly across the fatal weak point. She can tell you whether that remnant of velvet will make you a basque,—whether mamma's old silk can reappear in juvenile grace for Miss Lucy. What marvels follow her, wherever she goes! What wonderful results does she contrive from the most unlikely materials, as everybody after her departure wonders to see old things become so much better than new!

Among the most influential and happy of her class was Miss Prissy Diamond,—a little, dapper, doll-like body, quick in her motions and nimble in her tongue, whose delicate complexion, flaxen curls, merry flow of spirits, and ready abundance of gaiety, song, and story, apart from her professional accomplishments, made her a welcome guest in every family in the neighbourhood. Miss Prissy laughingly boasted being past forty, sure that the avowal would always draw down on her quite a storm of compliments, on the freshness of her sweet-pea complexion and the brightness of her merry blue eyes. She was well pleased to hear dawning girls wondering why with so many advantages she had never married. At such remarks, Miss Prissy always laughed loudly, and declared that she had always had such a string of engagements with the women that she never found half an hour to listen to what any *man* living would say to her, supposing she could stop to hear him. 'Besides, if I were to get married, nobody else could,' she would say. 'What would become of all the wedding-clothes for everybody else?' But sometimes, when Miss Prissy felt extremely gracious, she would draw out of her little chest, just the faintest tip-end of a sigh, and tell some young lady, in a confidential undertone, that one of these days she would tell her something,—and then there would come a wink of her blue eyes, and a fluttering of the pink ribbons in her cap, quite stimulating to youthful inquisitiveness, though we have never been able to learn by any of our antiquarian researches that the expectations thus excited were ever gratified.

In her professional prowess she felt a pardonable pride. What feats could she relate of wonderful dresses got out of impossibly small patterns of silk! what marvels of silks turned that could not be told from new! what reclaimings of waists that other dressmakers had hopelessly spoiled! Had not Mrs. General Wilcox once been obliged to call in her aid on a dress sent to her from Paris? and did not Miss Prissy work three days and nights on that dress, and make every stitch of that trimming over with her own hands, before it was fit to be seen? And when Mrs. Governor Dexter's best silver-gray brocade was spoiled by Miss Pimlico, and there wasn't another scrap to pattern it with, didn't she make a new waist out of the cape, and piece one of the sleeves twenty-nine times, and yet nobody would ever have known that there was a joining in it?

In fact, though Miss Prissy enjoyed the fair average plain-sailing of her work, she might be said to *revel* in difficulties. A full pattern with trimming, all ample and ready, awoke a moderate enjoyment; but the resurrection of anything half-worn or imperfectly made, the brilliant success, when, after turning, twisting, piecing, contriving, and, by unheard-of inventions of trimming, a dress faded and defaced was restored to more than pristine splendour,—*that* was a triumph worth enjoying.

It was true, Miss Prissy, like most of her nomadic compeers, was a little given to gossip; but, after all, it was innocent gossip,—not a bit of malice in it; it was only all the particulars about Mrs. Thus-and-So's wardrobe,—all the statistics of Mrs. That-and-T'other's china-closet,—all the minute items of Miss Simpkins's wedding-clothes,—and how her mother cried the morning of the wedding, and said that she didn't know anything how she could spare Louisa Jane, only that Edward was such a good boy that she felt she could love him like an own son,—and what a providence it seemed that the very ring that was put into the bride-loaf was one that he gave her when he first went to sea, when she wouldn't be engaged to him because she thought she loved Thomas Strickland better, but that was only because she hadn't found him out, you know,—and so forth, and so forth. Sometimes, too, her narrations assumed a solemn cast, and brought to mind the hush of funerals, and told of words spoken in faint whispers, when hands were clasped for the last time,—and of utterances crushed out from hearts, when the hammer of a great sorrow strikes out sparks of the Divine, even from common stone; and there would be real tears in the little blue eyes, and the pink bows would flutter tremulously, like the last three leaves on a bare scarlet maple in autumn. In fact, dear reader, *gossip*, like romance, has its noble side to it. How can you love your neighbour as yourself, and not feel a little curiosity as to how he fares, what he wears, where he goes, and how he takes the great life tragi-comedy, at which you and he are both more than spectators? Show me a person who lives in a country-village absolutely without curiosity or interest on these subjects, and I will show you a cold, fat oyster, to whom the tide-mud of propriety is the whole of existence.

As one of our esteemed collaborators remarks,—'A dull town, where there is neither theatre nor circus nor opera, must have some excitement, and the real tragedy and comedy of life *must* come in place of the second-hand. Hence the noted gossiping propensities of country-places, which, so long as they are not poisoned by envy or ill-will, have a respectable and picturesque side to them,—an undoubted leave to be, as probably has almost everything, which obstinately and always insists on being, except sin!'

As it is, it must be confessed that the arrival of Miss Prissy in a family was much like the setting up of a domestic showcase, through which you could look into all the families in the neighbourhood, and see the never-ending drama of life,—births, marriages, deaths,—joy of new-made mothers, whose babes weighed just eight pounds and three quarters, and had hair that would part with a comb,—and tears of Rachels who wept for their children, and would not be comforted because they were not. Was there a tragedy, a mystery, in all Newport, whose secret closet had not been unlocked by Miss Prissy? She thought not; and you always wondered, with an uncertain curiosity, what those things might be over which she gravely shook her head, declaring, with such a look,—'Oh, if you only *could* know!'—and ending with a general sigh and lamentation, like the confidential chorus of a Greek tragedy.

We have been thus minute in sketching Miss Prissy's portrait, because we rather like her. She has great power, we admit; and were she a sour-faced, angular, energetic body, with a heart whose secretions had all become acrid by disappointment and dyspepsia, she might be a fearful gnome, against whose family visitations one ought to watch and pray. As it was, she came into the house rather like one of those breezy days of spring, which burst all the blossoms, set all the doors and windows open, make the hens cackle and the turtles peep,—filling a solemn Puritan dwelling with as much bustle and chatter as if a box of martins were setting up housekeeping in it.

Let us now introduce you to the sanctuary of Mrs. Scudder's own private bedroom, where the committee of exigencies, with Miss Prissy at their head, are seated in solemn session around the camphor-wood trunk.

'Dress, you know, is of *some* importance after all,' said Mrs. Scudder, in that apologetic way in which sensible people generally acknowledge a secret leaning towards anything so very mundane. While the good lady spoke, she was reverentially unpinning and shaking out of their fragrant folds creamy crape shawls of rich Chinese embroidery,—India muslin, scarfs, and aprons; and already her hands were undoing the pins of a silvery damask linen in which was wrapped her own wedding-dress. 'I have always told Mary,' she continued, 'that, though our hearts ought not to be set on these things, yet they had their importance.'

'Certainly, certainly, ma'am,' chimed in Miss Prissy. 'I was saying to Miss General Wilcox, the other day, *I* didn't see how we could "consider the lilies of the field," without seeing the importance of looking pretty. I've got a flower-de-luce in my garden now, from one of the new roots that old Major Seaforth brought over from France, which is just the most beautiful thing you ever did see; and I was thinking, as I looked at it to-day, that if women's dresses only grew on 'em as handsome and well-fitting as that, why, there wouldn't be any need of me; but as it is, why, we *must think*, if we want to look well. Now peach-trees, I s'pose, might bear just as good peaches without the pink blows; but then who would want 'em to? Miss Deacon Twitchel, when I was up there the other day, kept kind o' sighin', 'cause Cerintha Ann is getting a new pink silk made up, 'cause she said it was such a dying world it didn't seem right to call off our attention: but I told her it wasn't any pinker than the apple-blossoms; and what with robins and blue-birds, and one thing or another, the Lord is always calling off our attention; and I think we ought to observe the Lord's works and take a lesson from 'em.'

'Yes, you are quite right,' said Mrs. Scudder, rising and shaking out a splendid white brocade, on which bunches of moss-roses were looped to bunches of violets by graceful fillets of blue ribbons. 'This was my wedding-dress,' she said.

Little Miss Prissy sprang up and clapped her hands in an ecstasy.

'Well, now, Miss Scudder, really!—did I ever see anything more beautiful? It really goes beyond anything *I* ever saw. I don't think, in all the brocades I ever made up, I ever saw so pretty a pattern as this.'

'Mr. Scudder chose it for me himself, at the silk-factory in Lyons,' said Mrs. Scudder, with pardonable pride, 'and I want it tried on to Mary.'

'Really, Miss Scudder, this ought to be kept for *her* wedding-dress,' said Miss Prissy, as she delightedly bustled about the congenial task. 'I was up to Miss Marvyn's, a-working, last week,' she said, as she threw the dress over Mary's head, 'and she said that James expected to make his fortune in that voyage, and come home and settle down.'

Mary's fair head emerged from the rustling folds of the brocade, her cheeks crimson as one of the moss-roses,—while her mother's face assumed a severe gravity, as she remarked that she believed James had been much pleased with Jane Spencer, and that, for her part, she should be very glad when he came home, if he could marry such a steady, sensible girl, and settle down to a useful, Christian life.

'Ah, yes,—just so,—a very excellent idea, certainly,' said Miss Prissy. 'It wants a little taken in here on the shoulders, and a little under the arms. The biases are all right; the sleeves will want altering, Miss Scudder. I hope you will have a hot iron ready for pressing.'

Mrs. Scudder rose immediately, to see the command obeyed; and as her back was turned, Miss Prissy went on in a low tone,—

'Now *I*, for my part, don't think there's a word of truth in that story about James Marvyn and Jane Spencer, for I was down there at work one day when he called, and I *know* there couldn't have been anything between them,—besides, Miss Spencer, her mother, told me there wasn't. There, Miss Scudder, you see that is a good fit. It's astonishing how near it comes to fitting, just as it was. I didn't think Mary was so near what you were, when you were a girl, Miss Scudder. The other day, when I was up to General Wilcox's, the General he was in the room when I was a-trying on Miss Wilcox's cherry velvet, and she was asking couldn't I come this week for her, and I mentioned I was coming to Miss Scudder; and the General, says he,—"I used to know her when she was a girl. I tell you, she was one of the handsomest girls in Newport, by George!" says he. And says I,—"General, you ought to see her daughter." And the General,—you know his jolly way,—he laughed, and says he,—"If she is as handsome as her mother was, I don't want to see her," says he. "I tell you, wife," says he, "I but just missed falling in love with Katy Stephens."'

'I could have told her more than that,' said Mrs. Scudder, with a flash of her old coquette girlhood for a moment lighting her eyes and straightening her lithe form. 'I guess, if I should show a letter he wrote me once——. But what am I talking about?' she said, suddenly stiffening back into a sensible woman. 'Miss Prissy, do you think it will be necessary to cut it off at the bottom? It seems a pity to cut such rich silk.'

'So it does, I declare. Well, I believe it will do to turn it up.'

'I depend on you to put it a little into modern fashion, you know,' said Mrs. Scudder. 'It is many a year, you know, since it was made.'

'Oh, never you fear! You leave all that to me,' said Miss Prissy. 'Now, there never was anything so lucky as that, just before all these wedding-dresses had to be fixed, I got a letter from my sister Martha, that works for all the first families of Boston. And Martha, she is really unusually privileged, because she works for Miss Cranch, and Miss Cranch gets letters from Miss Adams,—you know Mr. Adams is Ambassador now at the Court of St. James, and Miss Adams writes home all the particulars about the court-dresses; and Martha, she heard one of the letters read, and she told Miss Cranch that she would give the best five-pound note she had, if she could just copy that description to send to Prissy. Well, Miss Cranch let her do it, and I've got a copy of the letter here in my work-pocket. I read it up to Miss General Wilcox's, and to Major Seaforth's, and I'll read it to you.'

Mrs. Katy Scudder was a born subject of a crown, and, though now a republican matron, had not outlived the reverence, from childhood implanted, for the high and stately doings of courts, lords, ladies, queens, and princesses, and therefore it was not without some awe that she saw Miss Prissy produce from her little black work-bag, the well-worn epistle.

'Here it is,' said Miss Prissy, at last. 'I only copied out the parts about being presented at Court. She says:—

'"One is obliged here to attend the circles of the Queen, which are held once a fortnight; and what renders it very expensive is, that you cannot go twice in the same dress, and a court-dress you cannot make use of elsewhere. I directed my mantua-maker to let my dress be elegant, but plain as I could possibly appear with decency. Accordingly, it is white lutestring, covered and full-trimmed with white crape, festooned with lilac ribbon and mock point-lace, over a hoop of enormous size. There is only a narrow train, about three yards in length to the gown-waist, which is put into a ribbon on the left side,—the Queen only having her train borne. Ruffled cuffs for married ladies,—treble lace ruffles, a very dress cap with long lace lappets, two white plumes, and a blonde lace handkerchief. This is my rigging."'

Miss Prissy here stopped to adjust her spectacles. Her audience expressed a breathless interest.

'You see,' she said, 'I used to know her when she was Nabby Smith. She was Parson Smith's daughter, at Weymouth, and as handsome a girl as ever I wanted to see,—just as graceful as a sweet-brier bush. I don't believe any of those English ladies looked one bit better than she did. She was always a master-hand at writing. Everything she writes about, she puts it right before you. You feel as if you'd been there. Now, here she goes on to tell about her daughter's dress. She says:—

'"My head is dressed for St. James's, and in my opinion looks very tasty. Whilst my daughter is undergoing the same operation, I set myself down composedly to write you a few lines. Well, methinks I hear Betsy and Lucy say, 'What is cousin's dress?' *White*, my dear girls, like your aunt's, only differently trimmed and ornamented,—her train being wholly of white crape, and trimmed with white ribbon; the petticoat, which is the most showy part of the dress, covered and drawn up in what are called festoons, with light wreaths of beautiful flowers; the sleeves, white crape drawn over the silk, with a row of lace round the sleeve near the shoulder, another half-way down the arm, and a third upon the top of the ruffle,—a little stuck between,—a kind of hat-cap with three large feathers and a bunch of flowers,—a wreath of flowers on the hair."'

Miss Prissy concluded this relishing description with a little smack of the lips, such as people sometimes give when reading things that are particularly to their taste.

'Now, I was a-thinking,' she added, 'that it would be an excellent way to trim Mary's sleeves,—three rows of lace, with a sprig to each row.'

All this while, our Mary, with her white short-gown and blue stuff-petticoat, her shining pale brown hair and serious large blue eyes, sat innocently looking first at her mother, then at Miss Prissy, and then at the finery.

We do not claim for her any superhuman exemption from girlish feelings. She was innocently dazzled with the vision of courtly halls and princely splendours, and thought Mrs. Adams's descriptions almost a perfect realization of things she had read in 'Sir Charles Grandison.' If her mother thought it right and proper she should be dressed and made fine, she was glad of it; only there came a heavy, leaden feeling in her little heart, which she did not understand, but we who know womankind will translate for you: it was, that a certain pair of dark eyes would not see her after she was dressed; and so, after all, what was the use of looking pretty?

'I wonder what James *would* think,' passed through her head; for Mary had never changed a ribbon, or altered the braid of her hair, or pinned a flower in her bosom, that she had not quickly seen the effect of the change mirrored in those dark eyes. It was a pity, of course, now she had found out that she ought not to think about him, that so many thought-strings were twisted round him.

So while Miss Prissy turned over her papers, and read out of others extracts about Lord Caermarthen and Sir Clement Cotterel Dormer, and the Princess Royal, and Princess Augusta, in black and silver, with a silver netting upon the coat, and a head stuck full of diamond pins,—and Lady Salisbury and Lady Talbot, and the Duchess of Devonshire, and scarlet satin sacks and diamonds and ostrich-plumes, and the King's kissing Mrs. Adams,—little Mary's blue eyes grew larger and larger, seeing far off on the salt green sea, and her ears heard only the ripple and murmur of those waters that carried her heart away,—till, by-and-by, Miss Prissy gave her a smart little tap, which awakened her to the fact that she was wanted again to try on the dress which Miss Prissy's nimble fingers had basted.

So passed the day,—Miss Prissy busily chattering, clipping, basting,—Mary patiently trying on to an unheard-of extent,—and Mrs. Scudder's neat room whipped into a perfect froth and foam of gauze, lace, artificial flowers, linings, and other aids, accessories, and abetments.

At dinner, the Doctor, who had been all the morning studying out his Treatise on the Millennium, discoursed tranquilly as usual, innocently ignorant of the unusual cares which were distracting the minds of his listeners. What should he know of dressmakers, good soul? Encouraged by the respectful silence of his auditors, he calmly expanded and soliloquized on his favourite topic, the last golden age of Time, the Marriage Supper of the Lamb, when the purified Earth, like a repentant Psyche, shall be restored to the long-lost favour of a celestial Bridegroom, and glorified saints and angels shall walk familiarly as wedding-guests among men.

'Sakes alive!' said little Miss Prissy, after dinner, 'did I ever hear any one go on like that blessed man?—such a spiritual mind! Oh, Miss Scudder, how you are privileged in having him here! I do really think it is a shame such a blessed man a'n't thought more of. Why, I could just sit and hear him talk all day. Miss Scudder, I wish sometimes you'd just let me make a ruffled shirt for him, and do it all up myself, and put a stitch in the hem that I learned from my sister Martha, who learned it from a French young lady who was educated in a convent;—nuns, you know, poor things, can do *some* things right; and I think *I* never saw such hemstitching as they do there;—and I should like to hemstitch the Doctor's ruffles; he is *so* spiritually-minded, it really makes me love him. Why, hearing him talk put me in mind of a real beautiful song of Mr. Watts,—I don't know as I could remember the tune.'

And Miss Prissy, whose musical talent was one of her special *fortes*, tuned her voice, a little cracked and quavering, and sang, with a vigorous accent on each accented syllable,—

'From *the* third heaven, where God resides,
That holy, happy place, The New Jerusalem comes down,

Adorned with shining grace.

'Attending angels shout for joy,

And the bright armies sing,—
"Mortals! behold the sacred seat
Of your descending King!"'

'Take care, Miss Scudder!—that silk must be cut exactly on the bias;' and Miss Prissy, hastily finishing her last quaver, caught the silk and the scissors out of Mrs. Scudder's hand, and fell down at once from the Millennium into a discourse on her own particular way of covering piping-cord.

So we go, dear reader,—so long as we have a body and a soul. Two worlds must mingle,—the great and the little, the solemn and the trivial, wreathing in and out, like the grotesque carvings on a Gothic shrine;—only, did we know it rightly, nothing is trivial; since the human soul, with its awful shadow, makes all things sacred. Have not ribbons, cast-off flowers, soiled bits of gauze, trivial, trashy fragments of millinery, sometimes had an awful meaning, a deadly power, when they belonged to one who should wear them no more, and whose beautiful form, frail and crushed as they, is a hidden and a vanished thing for all time? For so sacred and individual is a human being, that, of all the million-peopled earth, no one form ever restores another. The mould of each mortal type is broken at the grave; and never, never, though you look through all the faces on earth, shall the exact form you mourn ever meet your eyes again! You are living your daily life among trifles that one death-stroke may make relics. One false step, one luckless accident, an obstacle on the track of a train, the tangling of the cord in shifting a sail, and the penknife, the pen, the papers, the trivial articles of dress and clothing, which to-day you toss idly and jestingly from hand to hand, may become dread memorials of that awful tragedy whose deep abyss ever underlies our common life.

CHAPTER XIII.

THE PARTY.

WELL, let us proceed to tell how the eventful evening drew on,—how Mary, by Miss Prissy's care, stood at last in a long-waisted gown flowered with rosebuds and violets, opening in front to display a white satin skirt trimmed with lace and flowers,—how her little feet were put into high-heeled shoes, and a little jaunty cap with a wreath of moss rosebuds was fastened over her shining hair,—and how Miss Prissy, delighted, turned her round and round, and then declared that she must go and get the Doctor to look at her. She knew he must be a man of taste, he talked so beautifully about the Millennium; and so, bursting into his study, she actually chattered him back into the visible world, and, leading the blushing Mary to the door, asked him, point blank, if he ever saw anything prettier.

The Doctor, being now wide awake, gravely gave his mind to the subject, and, after some consideration, said, gravely, 'No,—he didn't think he ever did.' For the Doctor was not a man of compliment, and had a habit of always thinking, before he spoke, whether what he was going to say was exactly true; and having lived some time in the family of President Edwards, renowned for beautiful daughters, he naturally thought them over.

The Doctor looked innocent and helpless, while Miss Prissy, having got him now quite into her power, went on volubly to expatiate on the difficulties overcome in adapting the ancient wedding-dress to its present modern fit. He told her that it was very nice,—said, 'Yes, ma'am,' at proper places,—and, being a very obliging man, looked at whatever he was directed to, with round, blank eyes; but ended all with a long gaze on the laughing, blushing face, that, half in shame and half in perplexed mirth, appeared and disappeared as Miss Prissy in her warmth turned her round and showed her.

'Now, don't she look beautiful?' Miss Prissy reiterated for the twentieth time, as Mary left the room.

The Doctor, looking after her musingly, said to himself,—'"The king's daughter is all glorious within; her clothing is of wrought gold; she shall be brought into the king in raiment of needlework."'

CHAPTER XIII.

'Now, did I ever?' said Miss Prissy, rushing out. 'How that good man does turn everything! I believe you couldn't get anything, that he wouldn't find a text right out of the Bible about it. I mean to get the linen for that shirt this very week, with the Miss Wilcox's money; they always pay well, those Wilcoxes,—and I've worked for them, off and on, sixteen days and a quarter. To be sure, Miss Scudder, there's no real need of my doing it, for I must say you keep him looking like a pink; but only I feel as if I must do something for such a good man.'

The good Doctor was brushed up for the evening with zealous care and energy; and if he did *not* look like a pink, it was certainly no fault of his hostess.

Well, we cannot reproduce in detail the faded glories of that entertainment, nor relate how the Wilcox Manor and gardens were illuminated,—how the bride wore a veil of real point-lace,—how carriages rolled and grated on the gravel walks, and negro servants, in white kid gloves, handed out ladies in velvet and satin.

To Mary's inexperienced eye it seemed like an enchanted dream,—a realization of all she had dreamed of grand and high society. She had her little triumph of an evening; for everybody asked who that beautiful girl was, and more than one gallant of the old Newport first families felt himself adorned and distinguished to walk with her on his arm. Busy, officious dowagers repeated to Mrs. Scudder the applauding whispers that followed her wherever she went.

'Really, Mrs. Scudder,' said gallant old General Wilcox, 'where have you kept such a beauty all this time? It's a sin and a shame to hide such a light under a bushel.'

And Mrs. Scudder, though, of course, like you and me, sensible reader, properly apprised of the perishable nature of such fleeting honours, was, like us, too, but a mortal, and smiled condescendingly on the follies of the scene.

The house was divided by a wide hall opening by doors, the front one upon the street, the back into a large garden, the broad central walk of which, edged on each side with high clipped hedges of box, now resplendent with coloured lamps, seemed to continue the prospect in a brilliant vista.

The old-fashioned garden was lighted in every part, and the company dispersed themselves about it in picturesque groups.

We have the image in our mind of Mary as she stood with her little hat and wreath of rosebuds, her fluttering ribbons and rich brocade, as it were a picture framed in the doorway, with her back to the illuminated garden, and her calm, innocent face regarding with a pleased wonder the unaccustomed gaieties within.

Her dress, which, under Miss Prissy's forming hand, had been made to assume that appearance of style and fashion which more particularly characterised the mode of those times, formed a singular, but not unpleasing, contrast to the sort of dewy freshness of air and mien which was characteristic of her style of beauty. It seemed so to represent a being who was in the world, yet not of it,—who, though living habitually in a higher region of thought and feeling, was artlessly curious, and innocently pleased with a fresh experience in an altogether untried sphere. The feeling of being in a circle to which she did not belong, where her presence was in a manner an accident, and where she felt none of the responsibilities which come from being a component part of a society, gave to her a quiet, disengaged air, which produced all the effect of the perfect ease of high breeding.

While she stands there, there comes out of the door of the bridal reception-room a gentleman with a stylishly-dressed lady on either arm, with whom he seems wholly absorbed. He is of middle height, peculiarly graceful in form and moulding, with that indescribable air of high breeding which marks the polished man of the world. His beautifully-formed head, delicate profile, fascinating sweetness of smile, and, above all, an eye which seemed to have an almost mesmeric power of attraction, were traits which distinguished one of the most celebrated men of the time, and one whose peculiar history yet lives not only in our national records, but in the private annals of many an American family.

'Good Heavens!' he said, suddenly pausing in conversation, as his eye accidentally fell upon Mary. 'Who is that lovely creature?'

'Oh, that,' said Mrs. Wilcox,—'why, that is Mary Scudder. Her father was a family connection of the General's. The family are in rather modest circumstances, but highly respectable.'

After a few moments more of ordinary chit-chat, in which from time to time he darted upon her glances of rapid and piercing observation, the gentleman might have been observed to disembarrass himself of one of the ladies on his arm, by passing her with a compliment and a bow to another gallant, and after a few moments more, he spoke something to Mrs. Wilcox, in a low voice, and with that gentle air of deferential sweetness which always made everybody well satisfied to do his will. The consequence was, that in a few moments Mary was startled from her calm speculations by the voice of Mrs. Wilcox, saying at her elbow, in a formal tone:—

'Miss Scudder, I have the honour to present to your acquaintance Colonel Burr, of the United States Senate.'

CHAPTER XIV.

AT the period of which we are speaking, no name in the new republic was associated with ideas of more brilliant promise, or invested with a greater prestige of popularity and success, than that of Colonel Aaron Burr.

Sprung of a line distinguished for intellectual ability, the grandson of a man whose genius has swayed New England from that day to this—the son of parents eminent in their day for influential and popular talent, he united in himself the quickest perceptions and keenest delicacy of fibre with the most diamond hardness and unflinching steadiness of purpose. Apt, subtle, dazzling, adroit, no man in his time ever began life with fairer chances for success and fame. His name, as it fell on the ear of our heroine, carried with it the suggestion of all this; and when, with his peculiarly engaging smile, he offered his arm, she felt a little of the flutter natural to a modest young person unexpectedly honoured with the notice of the distinguished of the earth, whom it is seldom the lot of humble individuals to know except by distant report.

But although Mary was a blushing and sensitive person, she was not what is commonly called a diffident girl: her nerves had that steady poise which gave her presence of mind in the most unwonted circumstances.

The first few sentences addressed to her by her new companion were in a tone and style altogether different from any in which she had ever been approached—different from the dashing frankness of her sailor lover, and from the rustic gallantry of her other admirers. That indescribable mixture of ease and deference, guided by a fine tact, which shows the practised, high-bred man of the world, made its impression on her immediately, as the breeze on the chords of a wind harp. She felt herself pleasantly swayed and breathed upon: it was as if an atmosphere were around her in which she felt a perfect ease and freedom—an assurance that her lightest word might launch forth safely, as a tiny boat on the smooth glassy mirror of her listener's pleased attention.

'I came to Newport only on a visit of business,' he said, after a few moments of introductory conversation; 'I was not prepared for its many attractions.'

'Newport has a great deal of beautiful scenery,' said Mary.

'I have heard that it was celebrated for the beauty of its scenery and of its ladies,' he answered; 'but,' he added, with a quick flash of his dark eye, 'I never realised the fact before.'

The glance of the eye pointed and limited the compliment; at the same time there was a wary shrewdness in it: he was measuring how deeply his shaft had sunk, as he always instinctively measured the person he talked with.

Mary had been told of her beauty since her childhood, notwithstanding her mother had assayed all that transparent, respectable hoaxing by which discreet mothers endeavour to blind their daughters to the real facts in such cases; but in her own calm, balanced mind she had accepted what she was so often told as a quiet verity, and therefore she neither fluttered nor blushed on this occasion; but regarded her auditor with a pleased attention, as one who was saying obliging things.

'Cool,' he thought to himself. 'Hum—a little rustic belle, I suppose, well aware of her own value; rather piquante, upon my word.'

'Shall we walk in the garden?' he said; 'the evening is so beautiful.'

They passed out the door, and began promenading the long walk. At the bottom of the alley he stopped, and, turning, looked up the vista of box, ending in the brilliantly-lighted rooms, where gentlemen with powdered heads, lace ruffles, and glittering knee-buckles were handing ladies in stiff brocades, whose towering heads were shaded by ostrich feathers and sparkling with gems.

'Quite court-like, on my word,' he said: 'tell me, do you often have such brilliant entertainments as these?'

'I suppose they do,' said Mary; 'I never was at one before, but I sometimes hear of them.'

'And *you* do not attend?' said the gentleman, with an accent which made the inquiry a marked compliment.

'No, I do not,' said Mary; 'these people generally do not visit us.'

'What a pity,' he said, 'that their parties should want such an ornament! but,' he added, 'this night must make them aware of their oversight: if you are not always in society after this, it will surely not be from want of solicitation.'

'You are very kind to think so,' replied Mary; 'but even if it were to be so, I should not see my way clear to be often in such scenes as this.'

Her companion looked at her with a glance a little doubtful and amused, and said—

'And pray, why not, if the inquiry be not presumptuous?'

'Because,' said Mary, 'I should be afraid they would take too much time and thought, and lead me to forget the great object of life.'

The simple gravity with which this was said, as if quite assured of the sympathy of her auditor, appeared to give him a secret amusement. His bright dark eyes danced as if he suppressed some quick repartee; but, drooping his long lashes deferentially, he said, in gentle tones—

'I should like to know what so beautiful a young lady considers the great object of life?'

Mary answered reverentially, in those words familiar from infancy to every Puritan child, 'To glorify God, and enjoy Him for ever.'

CHAPTER XIV.

'*Really?*' he said, looking straight into her eyes with that penetrating glance with which he was accustomed to take the gauge of every one with whom he conversed.

'Is it not?' said Mary, looking back, calm and firm, into the sparkling, restless depths of his eye.

In that moment, two souls, going with the whole force of their being in two opposite directions, looked out of their windows at each other with a fixed and earnest recognition.

Burr was practised in every act of gallantry; he had made womankind a study: he never saw a beautiful face and form without a sort of restless desire to experiment upon it, and try his power over the interior inhabitant. But just at this moment something streamed into his soul from those blue, earnest eyes, which brought back to his mind what pious people had so often told him of his mother—the beautiful and early-sainted Esther Burr.

He was one of those persons who systematically managed and played upon himself and others, as a skilful musician on an instrument. Yet one secret of his fascination was the naïveté with which at some moments he would abandon himself to some little impulse of a nature originally sensitive and tender. Had the strain of feeling which now awoke in him come over him elsewhere, he would have shut down some spring in his mind, and excluded it in a moment; but talking with a beautiful creature whom he wished to please, he gave way at once to the emotion: real tears stood in his fine eyes; he raised Mary's hand to his lips and kissed it, saying—

'Thank you, my beautiful child, for so good a thought! it is truly a noble sentiment, though practicable only to those gifted with angelic natures.'

'Oh, I trust not!' said Mary, earnestly, touched and wrought upon more than she herself knew by the beautiful eyes, the modulated voice, the charm of manner, which seemed to enfold her like an Italian summer.

Burr sighed—a real sigh of his better nature, but passed out with all the more freedom that he felt it would interest his fair companion, who, for the time being, was the one woman in the world to him.

'Pure, artless souls like yours,' he said, 'cannot measure the temptations of those who are called to the real battle of life. In a world like this, how many nobler aspirations fall withered in the fierce heat and struggle of the conflict!'

He was saying then what he really felt—often bitterly felt; but using this real feeling advisedly, and with skilful tact, for the purpose of the hour.

What was this purpose? to win the regard, the esteem, the tenderness of a religious exalted nature, shrined in a beautiful form—to gain and hold ascendency: it was a life-long habit; one of those forms of refined self-indulgence which he pursued, reckless of consequences. He had found now the key-note of the character: it was a beautiful instrument, and he was well-pleased to play on it.

'I think, sir,' said Mary, modestly, 'that you forget the great provision made for our weakness.'

'How?' said he.

'They that wait on the Lord shall renew their strength,' she replied, gently.

He looked at her as she spoke these words with a pleased, artistic perception of the contrast between her worldly attire and the simple religious earnestness of her words.

'She is entrancing,' he thought to himself; 'so altogether fresh and naïve.'

'My sweet saint,' he said, 'such as you are the appointed guardians of us coarser beings: the prayers of a soul given up to worldliness and ambition effect little; you must intercede for us. I am very orthodox, you see,' he added, with that subtle smile which sometimes irradiated his features. 'I am fully aware of all that your reverend Doctor tells you of the worthlessness of unregenerate doings; and so, when I see angels walking below, I try to secure a "friend at court."'

He saw that Mary looked embarrassed and pained at this banter, and therefore added, with a delicate shading of earnestness—

'In truth, my fair young friend, I hope you will sometimes pray for me. I am sure if I have any chance of good, it must come to me in such ways.'

'Indeed I will,' said Mary, fervently, her little heart full, tears in her eyes, her breath coming quick; and she added, with a deepening colour, 'I am sure, Mr. Burr, there should be a covenant blessing for you, if for any one, for you are the son of a holy ancestry.'

'Eh bien, mon ami, qu'est-ce que tu fais ici?' said a gay voice behind a clump of box, and immediately there started out, like a French picture from its frame, a dark-eyed figure, dressed like a marquise of Louis Fourteenth's time, with powdered hair, sparkling with diamonds.

'Rien que m'amuser,' he replied, with ready presence of mind, in the same tone, and then added—

'Permit me, madame, to present to you a charming specimen of our genuine New England flowers. Miss Scudder, I have the honour to present you to the acquaintance of Madame de Frontignac.'

'I am very happy,' said the lady, with a sweet lisping accentuation of English, which well became her lovely mouth. 'Miss Scudder, I hope, is very well?'

Mary replied affirmatively, her eyes resting the while, with pleased admiration, on the brilliant speaking face and diamond-bright eyes which seemed looking her through.

'Monsieur la trouve bien séduisante apparemment,' said the stranger in a low, rapid voice to the gentleman, in a manner which showed a mingling of pique and admiration.

'Petite jalouse, t'assure toi,' he replied, with a look and manner into which, with that mobile force which was peculiar to himself, he threw the most tender and passionate devotion. 'Ne suis-je pas à toi tout-à-fait?' and as he spoke he offered her his other arm.

'Allow me to be an unworthy link between the beauty of France and America.'

The lady swept a proud curtsy backward, bridled her beautiful neck, and signed for them to pass.

'I am waiting here for a friend,' she said.

CHAPTER XIV.

'Your will is always mine,' replied Burr, bowing with proud humility, and passing on with Mary to the supper-room.

Here the company were fast assembling in that high tide of good-humour which generally sets in at this crisis of the evening. The scene, in truth, was a specimen of a range of society which in those times could have been assembled nowhere else but in Newport. There stood Dr. H., in the tranquil majesty of his lordly form, and by his side the alert, compact figure of his cotemporary and theological opponent, Dr. Styles, who, animated by the social spirit of the hour, was dispensing courtesies to the right and left with the debonair grace of the trained gentleman of the old school. Near by, and engaging from time to time in conversation with them, stood a Jewish Rabbi with one or two wealthy bankers of the same race, whose olive complexion, keen eyes, and aquiline profile spoke their descent, and gave a picturesque and foreign grace to the scene.

Colonel Burr, one of the most brilliant and distinguished of the rising men of the new republic, and Colonel de Frontignac, who had won for himself laurels in the corps of Lafayette during the recent revolutionary struggle, with his brilliant and accomplished wife, were all unexpected and distinguished additions to the circle.

Burr gently cleared the way for his fair companion, and purposely placing her where the full light of the wax chandeliers set off her beauty to the best advantage, devoted himself to her with a subserviency as deferential as if she had been a goddess.

For all that, he was not unobservant when, a few moments after, Madame de Frontignac was led in on the arm of a distinguished senator, with whom she was presently in full flirtation.

He observed, with a quiet, furtive smile, that, while she rattled and fanned herself, and listened with apparent attention to the flatteries addressed to her, she darted every now and then a glance keen as a steel blade towards him and his companion. He was perfectly adroit in playing off one woman against another, and it struck him with a pleasant sense of oddity, how perfectly unconscious his sweet and saintly neighbour was of the position in which she was supposed to stand by her rival.

And poor Mary all this while, in her simplicity, really thought she had seen traces of what she would have called 'the strivings of the Spirit in his soul.'

Alas! that a phrase weighed down with such a mysterious truth and meaning should ever come to fall on the ear as mere empty cant: with Mary it was a living form, as were all her words, for in nothing was the Puritan education more marked than in the earnest reality and truthfulness which it gave to language. And even now, as she stands by his side, her large blue eye is occasionally fixed in dreamy reverie, as she thinks what a triumph of divine grace it would be if these inward movings of her companion's mind should lead him, as all the pious of New England hoped, to follow in the footsteps of President Edwards.

She wishes that she could some time see him alone, where she could talk with him undisturbed. She was too humble, too modest, fully to accept the delicious flattery which he had breathed, in implying that her hand had power to unseal the fountains of good in his soul; but still it thrilled through all the sensitive strings of her nature, a tremulous flutter of suggestion.

She had read instances of striking and wonderful conversions from words dropped by children and women; and suppose some such thing should happen to her, that this so charming, distinguished, and powerful being should be called into the fold of Christ's church by her means! No, it was too much to be hoped; but the very possibility was thrilling.

When, after supper, Mrs. Scudder and the Doctor made their adieus, Burr's devotion was still unabated: with an enchanting mixture of reverence and fatherly protection, he waited on her to the last, shawled her with delicate care, and handed her into the small one-horse waggon as if it had been the coach of a duchess.

'I have pleasant recollections connected with this kind of an establishment,' he said, as, after looking carefully at the harness, he passed the reins into Mrs. Scudder's hands; 'it reminds me of school-days and old times. I hope your horse is quite safe, madam?'

'Oh, yes,' said Mrs. Scudder; 'I perfectly understand him.'

'Pardon the suggestion,' he replied, 'what is there that a New England matron does not understand? Doctor, I must call by-and-by and have a little talk with you; my theologies, you know, need a little straightening.'

'We should all be happy to see you, Colonel Burr,' said Mrs. Scudder; 'we live in a very plain way it is true.'

'But can always find a place for a friend; that, I trust, is what you meant to say,' he replied, bowing with his own peculiar grace as the carriage drove off.

'Really, a most charming person is this Colonel Burr,' said Mrs. Scudder.

'He seems a very frank, ingenuous young person,' said the Doctor; 'one cannot but mourn that the son of such gracious parents should be left to wander into infidelity.'

'Oh, he is not an infidel,' said Mary: 'he is far from it; though I think that his mind is a little darkened on some points.'

'Ah!' said the Doctor, 'have you had any special religious conversation with him?'

'A little,' said Mary; 'and it seems to me, that his mind is perplexed somewhat in regard to the doings of the unregenerate. I fear that it has rather proved a stumbling-block in his way; but he showed so much feeling! I could really see the tears in his eyes.'

'His mother was a most godly woman, Mary,' said the Doctor; 'she was called from her youth, and her beautiful person became a temple for the indwelling of the Holy Spirit. Aaron Burr is a child of many prayers, and therefore there is hope that he may yet be effectually called. He studied awhile with Bellamy,' he added, musingly; 'I have often doubted whether Bellamy took just the right course with him.'

'I hope he will call and talk with you,' said Mary, earnestly. 'What a blessing to the world if such talents as his could become wholly consecrated!'

CHAPTER XIV.

'Not many rich, not many mighty, not many noble are called,' said the Doctor. 'Yet, if it would please the Lord to employ my instrumentality and prayers, how much should I rejoice! I was struck,' he added, 'to-night, when I saw those Jews present, with the thought that it was, as it were, a type of that last ingathering, when both Jew and Gentile should sit down lovingly together at the gospel feast. It is only by passing over and forgetting these present years, when so few are called, and the gospel makes such slow progress, and looking forward to that glorious time that I find comfort. If the Lord but use me as a dumb stepping-stone to that heavenly Jerusalem, I shall be content.'

Thus they talked while the waggon jogged slowly homeward, while the frogs and turtles and the distant ripple of the sea made a drowsy mingling concert in the summer-evening air.

Meanwhile Colonel Burr had returned to the lighted rooms; and it was not long before his quick eye sought out Madame de Frontignac, standing pensively in a window-recess, half hid by the curtain. He stole up softly behind her, and whispered something in her ear.

In a moment she turned on him a face glowing with anger, and drew back haughtily; but Burr remarked the glitter of tears, not quite dried even by the angry flash of her eyes.

'In what have I had the misfortune to offend?' he said, crossing his arms upon his breast. 'I stand at the bar and plead not guilty.'

He spoke in French, and she replied in the same smooth accents—

'It was not for her to dispute monsieur's right to amuse himself.'

Burr drew nearer, and spoke in those persuasive, pleading tones which he had ever at command, and in that language whose very structure, in its delicate tu toi, gives such opportunity for gliding on through shade after shade of intimacy and tenderness, till gradually the haughty fire of the eyes was quenched in tears; and in the sudden revulsion of a strong impulsive nature, she poured out to him what she called words of friendship, but which carried with them all the warmth of that sacred fire which is given to woman to light and warm the temple of home, and which sears and scars when kindled for any other shrine; and yet this woman was the wife of his friend and associate.

Monsieur de Frontignac was a grave and dignified man of forty-five. Virginie de Frontignac had been given him to wife when but eighteen; a beautiful, generous, impulsive, wilful girl.

She had accepted him gladly for very substantial reasons. First, that she might come out of the convent where she was kept for the very purpose of educating her in ignorance of the world she was to live in. Second, that she might wear velvet, lace, cashmere, and jewels. Third, that she might be a madame, free to go and come, ride, walk, and talk, without surveillance. Fourth, and consequent upon this, that she might go into company, and have admirers and adorers.

She supposed, of course, she loved her husband—whom else should she love? he was the only man except her father and brothers that she had ever seen; and in the fortnight that preceded their marriage, did he not send her the most splendid bons-bons every day, with bouquets of every pattern that ever taxed the brain of a Parisian artiste? Was not the corbeille de mariage a wonder and an envy to all her acquaintance? and after marriage had she not found him always a steady, indulgent friend, easy to be coaxed as any grave papa?

On his part, Monsieur de Frontignac cherished his young wife as a beautiful, though somewhat absurd little pet; and amused himself with her frolics and gambols, as the gravest person often will with those of a kitten.

It was not until she knew Aaron Burr that poor Virginie de Frontignac came to that great awakening of her being which teaches woman what she is, and transforms her from a careless child to a deep-hearted, thinking, suffering, human being.

For the first time, in his society, she became aware of the charm of a polished and cultivated mind; able, with exquisite tact, to adapt itself to hers; to draw forth her inquiries; to excite her tastes; to stimulate her observation. A new world awoke around her—the world of literature, of taste, of art, of sentiment. She felt somehow as if she had gained the growth of years in a few months. She felt within herself the stirring of dim aspiration—the uprising of a new power of self-devotion and self sacrifice; a trance of hero worship; a cloud of high ideal images; the lighting up, in short, of all that God has laid ready to be enkindled in woman's nature when the time comes to sanctify her as the pure priestess of a domestic temple.

But, alas! it was kindled by one who did it only for an experiment; because he felt an artistic pleasure in the beautiful light and heat which had burned a soul away.

Burr was one of those men, willing to play with any charming woman the game of those navigators who give to simple natives glass beads and feathers in return for gold and diamonds; to accept from a woman her heart's blood in return for such odds, ends, and clippings as he could afford her from the serious ambitions of life.

Look in with us one moment, now that the party is over, and the busy hum of voices and blaze of lights have died down to midnight silence and darkness. We make you clairvoyant; and you may look through the walls of this stately old mansion, still known as that where Rochambeau held his headquarters, into this room, where two wax candles are burning on a toilette-table before an old-fashioned mirror.

The slumbrous folds of the curtains are drawn with stately gloom around a high bed, where Colonel de Frontignac has been for many hours quietly asleep. But opposite, resting with one elbow on the toilette-table, her long black hair hanging down over her night-dress, and the brush hanging listlessly in her hand, sits Virginie, looking fixedly into the dreamy depths of the mirror.

Scarcely twenty yet; all unwarned of the world of power and passion that lay slumbering in her girl's heart; led, in the meshes of custom and society, to utter vows and take responsibilities of whose nature she was no more apprised than is a slumbering babe, and now at last fully awake, feeling the whole power of that mysterious and awful force which we call love, yet shuddering to call it by its name; yet by its light beginning to understand all she is capable of, and all that marriage should have been to her!

She struggles feebly and confusedly with her fate, still clinging to the name of duty, and baptizing as friendship the strange new feeling which makes her tremble through all her being. How can she dream of danger in such a feeling, when it seems to her the awakening of all that is highest and noblest within her? She remembers when she thought of nothing beyond an opera ticket or a new dress; and now she feels that there might be to her a friend for whose sake she would try to be noble and great and good; for whom all self-denial, all high endeavour, all difficult virtue, would become possible; who would be to her life, inspiration, order, beauty.

She sees him, as woman always sees the one she loves—noble, great, and good; for when did a loving woman ever believe a man otherwise? too noble, too great, too high, too good, she thinks for her, poor, trivial, ignorant coquette—poor, trifling, childish Virginie! Has he not commanded armies? she thinks; is he not eloquent in the senate? and yet, what interest he has taken in her, a poor, unformed, ignorant creature! She never tried to improve herself till since she knew him: and he is so considerate too; so respectful; so thoughtful and kind; so manly and honourable; and has such a tender friendship for her; such a brotherly, fatherly solicitude. And yet, if she is haughty, or imperious, or severe, how humbled and grieved he looks! How strange that she could have power over such a man!

It is one of the saddest truths of this sad mystery of life, that woman is often never so much an angel as just the moment before she falls into the bottomless depths of perdition; and what shall we say of the man who leads her up to this spot as an experiment? who amuses himself with taking woman after woman up these dazzling, delusive heights, knowing, as he certainly must, where they lead?

We have been told, in extenuation of the course of Aaron Burr, that he was not a man of gross passions or of coarse indulgence, but in the most consummate and refined sense a man of gallantry: this, then, is the descriptive name which polite society has invented for the man who does this thing.

Of old it was thought that one who administered poison in the sacramental bread and wine had touched the very height of impious sacrilege; but this crime is white by the side of his who poisons God's eternal sacrament of *love*, and destroys woman's soul through her noblest and purest affections.

We have given you the after view of most of the actors of our little scene to-night, and therefore it is but fair that you should have a peep over the Colonel's shoulder as he sums up the evening in a letter to a friend.

> 'MY DEAR ——,
>
> 'As to the business, it gets on rather slowly: L—— and T—— are away, and the coalition cannot be formed without them; they set out a week ago from Philadelphia, and are yet on the road.
>
> 'Meanwhile, we have some providential alleviations; as, for example, a wedding-party to-night at the Wilcox's, which was really

quite an affair. I saw the prettiest little Puritan there that I have set eyes on for many a day. I really couldn't help getting up a flirtation with her, though it was much like flirting with a small copy of the Assembly's catechism, of which I had enough years ago, heaven knows. But really, such a naïve, earnest little saint, who has such a real, deadly belief, and opens such blue pitying eyes on one, is quite a stimulating novelty. I got myself well scolded by the fair madame (as angels scold), and had to plead like a lawyer to make my peace.

'After all, *that* woman really enchains me. Don't shake your head wisely. "What is going to be the end of it?" I am sure I don't know; we'll see when the time comes.

'Meanwhile, push the business ahead with all your might. I shall not be idle.

'D—— must canvass the Senate thoroughly. I wish I could be in two places at once, and I would do it myself. Au revoir.

'Ever yours,

'BURR.'

CHAPTER XV.

'AND now, Mary,' said Mrs. Scudder, at five o'clock the next morning, 'today, you know, is the doctor's fast, and so we won't get any dinner, and it will be a good time to do up all our little odd jobs. Miss Prissy promised to come in for two or three hours this morning, to alter the waist of that black silk, and I shouldn't be surprised if we could get it all done and ready to wear by Sunday.'

We will remark, by way of explanation to a part of this conversation, that our doctor, who was a specimen of life in earnest, made a practice through the greater part of his pulpit course of spending every Saturday as a day of fasting and retirement in preparation for the duties of the Sabbath.

Accordingly, the early breakfast things were no sooner disposed of than Miss Prissy's quick footsteps might have been heard pattering in the kitchen.

'Well, Miss Scudder, how *do* you do this morning? and how *do* you do, Mary? Well, if you aint the beaters! up just as early as ever, and everything cleared away! I was telling Miss Wilcox that there didn't ever seem to be anything done in Miss Scudder's kitchen, and I did verily believe you made your beds before you got up in the morning. Well, well; wasn't that a party last night!' she said, as she sat down with the black silk and prepared her ripping-knife. 'I must rip this myself, Miss Scudder; for there's a great deal in ripping silk, so as not to let anybody know where it has been sewed.

'You didn't know that I was at the party, did you? Well, I was. You see, I thought I'd just step round there to see about that money to get the doctor's shirt with, and there I found Miss Wilcox with so many things on her mind, and says she, "Miss Prissy, you don't know how much it would help me if I had somebody like you just to look after things a little here;" and says I, "Miss Wilcox, you just go right to your room and dress, and don't you give yourself one minute's thought about anything, and you see if I don't have everything just right." And so there I was in for it, and I just stayed through; and it was well I did, for Dinah, she wouldn't have put ne'er enough egg in the coffee if it hadn't been for me. Why, I just went and beat up four eggs with my own hand, and stirred 'em into the grounds.

'Well, but really; wasn't I behind the door, and didn't I peep into the supper-room! I saw who was a-waitin' on Miss Mary. Well, they do say he's the handsomest, most fascinating man; why, all the ladies in Philadelphia are in a perfect quarrel about him; and I heard he said that he hadn't seen such a beauty, he didn't remember when.'

'We all know that beauty is of small consequence,' said Mrs. Scudder. 'I hope Mary has been brought up to feel that.'

'Oh, of course,' said Miss Prissy; 'it's just like a fading flower; all is to be good and useful, and that's what she is; and I told 'em that her beauty was the least part of her, though I must say that dress did fit like a biscuit, if it was my own fitting. But, Miss Scudder, what do you think I heard 'em saying about the good old doctor?'

'I am sure I don't know,' said Mrs. Scudder; 'I only know they couldn't say anything bad.'

'Well, no, not bad exactly,' said Miss Prissy; 'but they say he's getting such strange notions in his head; why, I heard some of 'em say he was going to come out and preach against the slave trade; and I'm sure I don't know what Newport folks will do if that's wicked; there aint hardly any money here that's made any other way: it'll certainly make a great noise and talk, and make everybody angry; and I hope the Doctor aint a-going to do anything of that sort.'

'I believe he is, Miss Prissy,' said Mrs. Scudder; 'he thinks it's a great sin that ought to be rebuked, and I think so too,' she said, bracing herself resolutely; 'that was Mr. Scudder's opinion when I first married him, and it's mine.'

'Oh, ah, yes. Well, if it's a sin, of course,' said Miss Prissy; 'but then, dear me! Why, just think how many great houses are living on it. Why, there's General Wilcox himself, and he's a very nice man; and then there's Major Seaforth; and why, I could count you off now a dozen—all our very first people. Why, Doctor Styles doesn't think so, and I'm sure he's a good Christian. Doctor Styles thinks it's a dispensation for giving the light of the gospel to the Africans; why, now I'm sure, when I was a-working at Deacon Stebbins', I stopped over Sunday once, 'cause Miss Stebbins she was weakly; 'twas when she was getting up after Samuel was born. No, on the whole, I believe 'twas Nehemiah, 'cause I remember he had curly hair; but any way, I remember I stayed there, and I remember as plain as if 'twas yesterday, just after breakfast, how a man went driving by in a chaise, and the Deacon, he went out and stopped him for travelling on the Lord's day ('cause, you know, he was a justice of the peace), and who should it be but Tom Seaforth, and he told the Deacon his father had got a shipload of negroes just come in, and the Deacon he just let him go, 'cause I remember he said *that* was a plain work of necessity and mercy[1]. Well now, who would have thought it? I believe the Doctor is better than most folks; but then the best people may be mistaken, you know.'

'The Doctor has made up his mind that it's his duty,' said Mrs. Scudder. 'I'm afraid it'll make him very unpopular; but I, for one, shall stand by him.'

'Oh, certainly, Miss Scudder, you're doing just right, exactly. Well, there's one comfort, he'll have a great crowd to hear him preach, 'cause as I was going

---

[1] A fact.

round through the entries last night, I heard 'em talking about it; and Colonel Burr said he should be there, and so did the General, and so did Mr. What's-his-name there, that senator from Philadelphia. I tell you you'll have a full house.'

It was to be confessed that Mrs. Scudder's heart rather sank than otherwise at this announcement, and those who have felt what it is to be almost alone in the right, in the face of all the 'first families' of their acquaintance, may perhaps find some compassion for her; since after all, truth is invisible, but 'first families' are very evident. First families are often very agreeable, undeniably respectable—fearfully virtuous; and it takes great faith to resist an evil principle which incarnates itself in the suavities of their breeding and amiability; and therefore it was that Mrs. Scudder felt her heart heavy within her, and could with a very good grace have joined the Doctor's Saturday fast.

As for the Doctor, he sat the while tranquil in his study, with his great Bible and his Concordance open before him, culling, with that patient assiduity for which he was remarkable, all the terrible texts which that very unceremonious and old-fashioned book rains down so unsparingly on the sin of oppressing the weak. First families, whether in Newport or elsewhere, were as invisible to him as they were to Moses during the forty days that he spent with God on the Mount. He was merely thinking of his message, thinking only how he should shape it so as not to leave one word of it unsaid, not even imagining in the least what the result of it was to be: he was but a voice, but an instrument,—a passive instrument through which an Almighty will was to reveal itself: and the sublime fatalism of his faith made him as dead to all human considerations as if he had been a portion of the immutable laws of nature herself.

So the next morning, although all his friends trembled for him when he rose in the pulpit, he never thought of trembling for himself: he had come in the covered way of silence from the secret place of the Most High, and felt himself still abiding under the shadow of the Almighty. It was alike to him whether the house was full or empty. Whoever were decreed to hear the message would be there; whether they would hear or forbear was already settled in the counsels of a mightier will than his: he had the simple duty of utterance.

The ruinous old meeting-house was never so radiant with station and gentility as on that morning: a June sun shone brightly, the sea sparkled with a thousand little eyes, the birds sang all along the way, and all the notables turned out to hear the Doctor.

Mrs. Scudder received into her pew, with dignified politeness, Colonel Burr, and Colonel and Madame de Frontignac.

General Wilcox and his portly dame, Major Seaforth, and we know not, what not of Vernons and De Wolfs, and other grand old names were present there. Stiff silks rustled, Chinese fans fluttered, and the last court fashion stood revealed in bonnets; everybody was looking fresh and amiable: a charming and respectable set of sinners come to hear what the Doctor would find to tell them about their transgressions.

Mrs. Scudder was calculating consequences, and, shutting her eyes on the too evident world about her, prayed that the Lord would overrule all for good: the Doctor prayed that he might have grace to speak the truth, and the whole truth.

We have yet on record, in his published works, the great argument of that day, through which he moved with that calm appeal to the reason, which made his results always so weighty.

'If these things be true,' he said, after a condensed statement of the facts of the case, 'then the following terrible consequences, which may well make all shudder and tremble who realize them, force themselves upon us, that all who have had any hand in this iniquitous business, whether directly or indirectly, or have used their influence to promote it, or have consented to it, or even connived at it, or have not opposed it by all proper exertions of which they are capable—all these are in a greater or less degree chargeable with the injuries and miseries which millions have suffered and are suffering, and are guilty of the blood of millions who lost their lives by this traffic in the human species. Not only the merchants who have been engaged in this trade, and the captains who have been tempted by the love of money to engage in this cruel work, and the slaveholders of every description, are guilty of shedding rivers of blood, but all the legislatures who have authorized, encouraged, or even neglected to suppress it to the utmost of their power, and all the individuals in private stations who have in any way aided in this business, consented to it, or have not opposed it to the utmost of their ability, have a share in this guilt. This trade in the human species has been the first wheel of commerce in Newport, on which every other movement in business has chiefly depended. This town has been built up and flourished in times past at the expense of the blood, the liberty, and the happiness of the poor Africans; and the inhabitants have lived on this, and by it have gotten most of their wealth and riches. If a bitter woe is pronounced on him who buildeth his house by unrighteousness and his chambers by wrong (Jer. xxii. 13), to him who buildeth a town by blood, and establisheth a city by iniquity (Hab. ii. 12), to the bloody city (Ezek. xxiv. 6), what a heavy, dreadful woe hangs over the heads of all those whose hands are defiled by the blood of the Africans—especially the inhabitants of this state and this town, who have had a distinguished share in this unrighteous and bloody commerce!' He went over the recent history of the country; expatiated on the national declaration so lately made, that all men are born equally free and independent, and have a natural and inalienable right to liberty, and asked with what face a nation declaring such things could continue to hold thousands of their fellow-men in abject slavery.

He pointed out signs of national disaster which foreboded the wrath of heaven: the increase of public and private debts; the spirit of murmuring and jealousy of rulers among the people; divisions and contentions and bitter party alienations; the jealous irritation of England constantly endeavouring to hamper our trade; the Indians making war on the frontiers; the Algerines taking captive our ships, and making slaves of our citizens; all evident tokens of the displeasure and impending judgment of an offended justice.

CHAPTER XV.

The sermon rolled over the heads of the gay audience deep and dark as a thunder-cloud which in a few moments changes a summer sky into heaviest gloom. Gradually an expression of intense interest and deep concern spread over the listeners; it was the magnetism of a strong mind, which held them for a time under the shadow of his own awful sense of God's almighty justice.

It is said that a little child once described his appearance in the pulpit by saying, 'I saw God there, and I was afraid.'

Something of the same effect was produced on the audience now, and it was not till after sermon, prayer, and benediction were all over, that the respectables of Newport began gradually to unstiffen themselves from the spell, and to look into each other's eyes for comfort, and to reassure themselves that after all they were the first families, eminently respectable, and going on in the good old way the world had always gone, and that the Doctor, of course, was a Radical and a fanatic.

When the audience streamed out, crowding the broad aisle, Mary descended from the singers' seat, and stood with her psalm book in hand, waiting at the door to be joined by her mother and the Doctor. She overheard many hard words from people who an evening or two before had smiled so graciously upon them. It was, therefore, with no little determination of manner that she advanced and took the Doctor's arm, as if anxious to associate herself with his well-earned unpopularity; and just at this moment she caught the eye and smile of Colonel Burr, as he bowed gracefully, yet not without a suggestion of something sarcastic in his eye.

CHAPTER XVI.

WE suppose the heroine of a novel, among other privileges and immunities, has a prescriptive right to her own private boudoir, where, as a French writer has it, 'she appears like a lovely picture in its frame.'

Well, our little Mary is not without this luxury, and to its sacred precincts we will give you this morning a ticket of admission. Know, then, that the garret of this gambrel-roofed cottage had a projecting window on the seaward side, which opened into an immensely large old apple-tree, and was a look-out as leafy and secluded as a robin's nest.

Garrets are delicious places, in any case, for people of thoughtful, imaginative temperament. Who has not loved a garret in the twilight days of childhood, with its endless stores of quaint, cast-off, suggestive antiquity,—old worm-eaten chests,—rickety chairs,—boxes and casks full of old comminglings, out of which, with tiny, childish hands, we fished wonderful hoards of fairy treasure? What peep-holes, and hiding-places, and undiscoverable retreats we made to ourselves,—where we sat rejoicing in our security, and bidding defiance to the vague, distant cry which summoned us to school, or to some unsavoury every-day task! How deliciously the rain came pattering on the roof over head, or the red twilight streamed in at the window, while we sat snugly ensconced over the delicious pages of some romance, which careful aunts had packed away at the bottom of all things, to be sure we should never read it! If you have anything, beloved friends, which you wish your Charlie or your Susie to be sure and read, pack it mysteriously away at the bottom of a trunk of stimulating rubbish, in the darkest corner of your garret;—in that case, if the book be at all readable, one that by any possible chance can make its way into a young mind, you may be sure that it will not only be read, but remembered to the longest day they have to live.

Mrs. Katy Scudder's garret was not an exception to the general rule. Those quaint little people who touch with so airy a grace all the lights and shadows of great beams, bare rafters, and unplastered walls, had not failed in their work there. Was there not there a grand easy-chair of stamped-leather, minus two of its hinder legs, which had genealogical associations through the Wilcoxes with the Vernons, and through the Vernons quite across the water with Old England? and was there not a dusky picture, in an old tarnished frame, of a woman of whose tragic end strange stories were whispered,—one of the sufferers in the time when witches were unceremoniously helped out of the world, instead of being, as now-a-days, helped to make their fortune in it by table-turning?

Yes, there were all these things, and many more which we will not stay to recount, but bring you to the boudoir which Mary has constructed for herself around the dormer-window which looks into the whispering old apple-tree.

The enclosure was formed by blankets and bed-spreads, which, by reason of their antiquity, had been pensioned off to an undisturbed old age in the garret,—not *common* blankets or bed-spreads, either,—bought, as you buy yours, out of a shop,—spun or woven by machinery,—without individuality or history. Every one of these curtains had its story. The one on the right, nearest the window, and already falling into holes, is a Chinese linen, and even now displays unfaded, quaint patterns of sleepy-looking Chinamen, in conical hats, standing on the leaves of most singular herbage, and with hands for ever raised in act to strike bells, which never are struck and never will be till the end of time. These, Mrs. Katy Scudder had often instructed Mary, were brought from the Indies by her great-great-grandfather, and were her grandmother's wedding-curtains,—the grandmother who had blue eyes like hers, and was just about her height.

The next spread was spun and woven by Mrs. Katy's beloved Aunt Eunice,—a mythical personage, of whom Mary gathered vague accounts that she was disappointed in love, and that this very article was part of a bridal outfit, prepared in vain, against the return of one from sea, who never came back,—and she heard of how she sat wearily and patiently at her work, this poor Aunt Eunice, month after month, starting every time she heard the gate shut, every time she heard the tramp of a horse's hoof, every time she heard the news of a sail in sight,—her colour, meanwhile, fading and fading as life and hope bled away at an inward wound,—till at last she found comfort and reunion beyond the veil.

Next to this was a bed-quilt pieced in tiny blocks, none of them bigger than a sixpence, containing, as Mrs. Katy said, pieces of the gowns of all her grandmothers, aunts, cousins, and female relatives for years back,—and mated to it was one of the blankets which had served Mrs. Scudder's uncle in his bivouac at Valley Forge, when the American soldiers went on the snows with bleeding feet, and had scarce anything for daily bread except a morning message of patriotism and hope from George Washington.

Such were the memories woven into the tapestry of our little boudoir. Within, fronting the window, stands the large spinning-wheel, one end adorned with a snowy pile of fleecy rolls,—and beside it, a reel and a basket of skeins of yarn,—and open, with its face down on the beam of the wheel, lay always a book, with which the intervals of work were beguiled.

The dusky picture of which we have spoken hung against the rough wall in one place, and in another appeared an old engraved head of one of the Madonnas of Leonardo da Vinci, a picture which to Mary had a mysterious interest, from the fact of its having been cast on shore after a furious storm, and found like a waif lying in the sea-weed; and Mrs. Marvyn, who had deciphered the signature, had not ceased exploring till she found for her, in an Encyclopædia, a life of that wonderful man, whose greatness enlarges our ideas of what is possible to humanity,—and Mary, pondering thereon, felt the sea-worn picture as a constant vague inspiration.

Here our heroine spun for hours, and hours with intervals, when, crouched on a low seat in the window, she pored over her book, and then, returning again to her work, thought of what she had read to the lulling burr of the sounding wheel.

By chance a robin had built its nest so that from her retreat she could see the five little blue eggs whenever the patient brooding mother left them for a moment uncovered. And sometimes, as she sat in dreamy reverie, resting her small, round arms on the window-sill, she fancied that the little feathered watcher gave her familiar nods and winks of a confidential nature,—cocking the small head first to one side and then to the other, to get a better view of her gentle human neighbour.

I dare say it seems to you, reader, that we have travelled, in our story, over a long space of time, because we have talked so much, and introduced so many personages and reflections; but, in fact, it is only Wednesday week since James sailed, and the eggs which were brooded when he went are still unhatched in the nest, and the apple-tree has changed only in having now a majority of white blossoms over the pink buds.

This one week has been a critical one to our Mary: in it she has made the great discovery that she loves; and she has made her first step into the gay world; and now she comes back to her retirement to think the whole over by herself. It seems a dream to her, that she who sits there now reeling yarn in her stuff petticoat and white short-gown is the same who took the arm of Colonel Burr amid the blaze of wax-lights, and the sweep of silks and rustle of plumes. She wonders dreamily as she remembers the dark, lovely face of the foreign madame, so brilliant under its powdered hair and flashing gems,—the sweet, foreign accents of the voice,—the tiny, jewelled fan, with its glancing pictures and sparkling tassels, whence exhaled vague and floating perfumes; then she hears again that manly voice, softened to tones so seductive, and sees those fine eyes with the tears in them, and wonders within herself that *he* could have kissed her hand with such veneration, as if she had been a throned queen.

But here the sound of busy, pattering footsteps is heard on the old, creaking staircase, and soon the bows of Miss Prissy's bonnet part the folds of the boudoir drapery, and her merry, May-day face looks in.

'Well, really, Mary, how do you do, to be sure? You wonder to see me, don't you? but I thought I must just run in a minute on my way up to Miss Marvyn's. I promised her at least a half a day, though I didn't see how I was to spare it,—for I tell Miss Wilcox I just run and run till it does seem as if my feet would drop off; but I thought I must just step in to say, that I, for my part, *do admire* the Doctor more than ever, and I was telling your mother we mus'n't mind too much what people say. I 'most made Miss Wilcox angry, standing up for him; but I put it right to her, and says I, "Miss Wilcox, you know folks *must* speak what's on their mind,—in particular ministers must; and you know, Miss Wilcox," I says, "that the Doctor *is* a good man, and lives up to his teaching, if anybody in this world does, and gives away every dollar he can lay hands on to those poor negroes, and works over 'em and teaches 'em as if they were his brothers;" and says I, "Miss Wilcox, you know I don't spare myself, night nor day, trying to please you and do your work to give satisfaction; but when it comes to my conscience," says I, "Miss Wilcox, you know I always must speak out, and if it was the last word I had to say on my dying bed, I'd say that I think the Doctor is right." Why! what things he told about the slave-ships, and packing those poor creatures so that they couldn't move nor breathe!—why, I declare, every time I turned over and stretched in bed, I thought of it; and says I, "Miss Wilcox, I do believe that the judgments of God will come down on us, if something a'n't done, and I shall always stand by the Doctor," says I;—and if you'll believe me, just then I turned round and saw the General; and the General, he just haw-hawed right out, and says he, "Good for you, Miss Prissy! that's real grit," says he, "and I like you better for it."'—'Laws,' added Miss Prissy, reflectively, 'I sha'n't lose by it, for Miss Wilcox knows she never can get anybody to do the work for her that I will.'

'Do you think,' said Mary, 'that there are a great many made angry?'

'Why, bless your heart, child, haven't you heard? Why, there never was such a talk in all Newport. Why, you know Mr. Simeon Brown is gone clear off to Doctor Stiles; and Miss Brown, I was making up her plum-coloured satin a' Monday, and you ought to 'a' heard her talk. But, I tell you, I fought her. She used to talk to me,' said Miss Prissy, sinking her voice to a mysterious whisper, ''cause I never could come to it to say that I was willin' to be lost, if it was for the glory of God; and she always told me folks could just bring their minds right up to anything they knew they must; and I just got the tables turned on her, for they talked and abused the Doctor till they fairly wore me out, and says I, "Well, Miss Brown, I'll give in, that you and Mr. Brown *do* act up to your principles; you certainly *act* as if you were willing to be damned;"—and so do all those folks who will live on the blood and groans of the poor Africans, as the Doctor said; and I should think, by the way Newport people are making their money, that they were all pretty willing to go that way, though, whether it's for the glory of God, or not, I'm doubting. But you see, Mary,' said Miss Prissy, sinking her voice again to a solemn whisper, 'I never was *clear* on that point; it always did seem to me a dreadful high place to come to, and it didn't seem to be given to me; but I thought, perhaps, if it *was* necessary, it would be given, you know,—for the Lord always has been so good to me that I've faith to believe that, and so I just say, "The Lord is my shepherd, I shall not want;"'—and Miss Prissy hastily whisked a little drop out of her blue eye with her handkerchief.

At this moment Mrs. Scudder came into the boudoir with a face expressive of some anxiety.

'I suppose Miss Prissy has told you,' she said, 'the news about the Browns. That'll make a great falling off in the Doctor's salary; and I feel for him, because I know it will come hard to him not to be able to help and do, especially for these poor negroes, just when he will. But then we must put everything on the most economical scale we can, and just try, all of us, to make it up to him. I was speaking to Cousin Zebedee about it, when he was down here, on Monday, and he is all clear;—he has made out three papers for Candace and Cato and Dinah, and they couldn't, one of 'em, be hired to leave him; and he says, from what he's seen already, he has no doubt but they'll do enough more to pay for their wages.'

'Well,' said Miss Prissy, 'I haven't got anybody to care for but myself. I was telling sister Elizabeth, one time (she's married and got four children), that I could take a storm a good deal easier than she could, 'cause I hadn't near so many sails to pull down; and now, you just look to me for the Doctor's shirts, 'cause, after this, they shall all come in ready to put on, if I have to sit up till morning. And I hope, Miss Scudder, you can trust me to make them; for if I do say it myself, I a'n't afraid to do fine stitching 'longside of anybody,—and hemstitching ruffles, too; and I haven't shown you yet that French stitch I learned of the nuns;—but you just set your heart at rest about the Doctor's shirts. I always thought,' continued Miss Prissy, laughing, 'that I should have made a famous hand about getting up that tabernacle in the wilderness, with the blue and the purple and fine-twined linen; it's one of my favourite passages, that is;—different things, you know, are useful to different people.'

'Well,' said Mrs. Scudder, 'I see that it's our call to be a remnant small and despised, but I hope we sha'n't shrink from it. I thought, when I saw all those fashionable people go out Sunday, tossing their heads and looking so scornful, that I hoped grace would be given me to be faithful.'

'And what does the Doctor say?' said Miss Prissy.

'He hasn't said a word; his mind seems to be very much lifted above all these things.'

'La, yes,' said Miss Prissy, 'that's one comfort; he'll never know where his shirts come from; and besides that, Miss Scudder,' she said, sinking her voice to a whisper, 'as you know, I haven't any children to provide for,—though I was telling Elizabeth t'other day, when I was making up frocks for her children, that I believed old maids, first and last, did more providing for children than married women: but still I do contrive to slip away a pound-note, now and then, in my little old silver teapot that was given to me when they settled old Mrs. Simpson's property (I nursed her all through her last sickness, and laid her out with my own hands), and, as I was saying, if ever the Doctor should want money, you just let me know.'

'Thank you, Miss Prissy,' said Mrs. Scudder; 'we all know where your heart is.'

'And now,' added Miss Prissy, 'what do you suppose they say? Why, they say Colonel Burr is struck dead in love with our Mary; and you know his wife's dead, and he's a widower; and they do say that he'll get to be the next President. Sakes alive! Well, Mary must be careful, if she don't want to be carried off; for they do say that there can't any woman resist him, that sees enough of him. Why, there's that poor Frenchwoman, Madame —— what do you call her, that's staying with the Vernons?—they say she's over head and ears in love with him.'

'But she's a married woman,' said Mary; 'it can't be possible!'

CHAPTER XVI.

Mrs. Scudder looked reprovingly at Miss Prissy, and for a few moments there was great shaking of heads and a whispered conference between the two ladies, ending in Miss Prissy's going off, saying, as she went down stairs,—

'Well, if women will do so, I, for my part, can't blame the men.'

In a few moments Miss Prissy rushed back as much discomposed as a clucking hen who has seen a hawk.

'Well, Miss Scudder, what do you think? Here's Colonel Burr come to call on the ladies!'

Mrs. Scudder's first movement, in common with all middle-aged gentlewomen, was to put her hand to her head and reflect that she had not on her best cap; and Mary looked down at her dimpled hands, which were blue from the contact with mixed yarn she had just been spinning.

'Now, I'll tell you what,' said Miss Prissy,—'wasn't it lucky you had me here? for I first saw him coming in at the gate, and I whipped in quick as a wink and opened the best room window-shutters, and then I was back at the door, and he bowed to me as if I'd been a queen, and says he, "Miss Prissy, how fresh you're looking this morning!" You see, I was in working at the Vernons', but I never thought as he'd noticed me. And then he inquired in the handsomest way for the ladies and the Doctor, and so I took him into the parlour and settled him down, and then I ran into the study, and you may depend upon it I flew round lively for a few minutes. I got the Doctor's study-gown off, and got his best coat on, and put on his wig for him, and started him up kinder lively,—you know it takes me to get him down into this world,—and so there he's in talking with him; and so you can just slip down and dress yourselves,—easy as not.'

Meanwhile Colonel Burr was entertaining the simple-minded Doctor with all the grace of a young neophyte come to sit at the feet of superior truth. There are some people who receive from Nature as a gift a sort of graceful facility of sympathy by which they incline to take on, for the time being, the sentiments and opinions of those with whom they converse, as the chameleon was fabled to change its hue with every surrounding. Such are often supposed to be wilfully acting a part, as exerting themselves to flatter and deceive, when in fact they are only framed so sensitive to the sphere of mental emanation which surrounds others that it would require an exertion *not* in some measure to harmonize with it. In approaching others in conversation, they are like a musician who joins a performer on an instrument,—it is impossible for them to strike a discord; their very nature urges them to bring into play faculties according in vibration with those which another is exerting. It was as natural as possible for Burr to commence talking with the Doctor on scenes and incidents in the family of President Edwards, and his old tutor, Dr. Bellamy,—and thence to glide on to the points of difference and agreement in theology, with a suavity and deference which acted on the good man like a June sun on a budding elm-tree. The Doctor was soon wide awake, talking with fervent animation on the topic of disinterested benevolence,—Burr the meanwhile studying him with the quiet interest of an observer of natural history, who sees a new species developing before him. At all the best possible points he interposed suggestive questions, and set up objections in the quietest manner for the Doctor to knock down, smiling ever the while as a man may who truly and genuinely does not care a *sou* for truth on any subject not practically connected with his own schemes in life. He therefore gently guided the Doctor to sail down the stream of his own thoughts till his bark glided out into the smooth waters of the Millennium, on which, with great simplicity, he gave his views at length.

It was just in the midst of this that Mary and her mother entered. Burr interrupted the conversation to pay them the compliments of the morning,—to inquire for their health, and hope they suffered no inconvenience from their night ride from the party; then, seeing the Doctor still looking eager to go on, he contrived with gentle dexterity to tie again the broken thread of conversation.

'Our excellent friend,' he said, 'was explaining to me his views of a future Millennium. I assure you, ladies, that we sometimes find ourselves in company which enables us to believe in the perfectibility of the human species. We see family retreats, so unaffected, so charming in their simplicity, where industry and piety so go hand in hand! One has only to suppose all families such, to imagine a Millennium!'

There was no disclaiming this compliment, because so delicately worded, that, while perfectly clear to the internal sense, it was, in a manner, veiled and unspoken.

Meanwhile, the Doctor, who sat ready to begin where he left off, turned to his complaisant listener and resumed an exposition of the Apocalypse.

'To my mind, it is certain,' he said, 'as it is now three hundred years since the fifth vial was poured out, there is good reason to suppose that the sixth vial began to be poured out at the beginning of the last century, and has been running for a hundred years or more, so that it is run nearly out; the seventh and last vial will begin to run early in the next century.'

'You anticipate, then, no rest for the world for some time to come?' said Burr.

'Certainly not,' said the Doctor, definitively; 'there will be no rest from overturnings till He whose right it is shall come.'

'The passage,' he added, 'concerning the drying up of the river Euphrates, under the sixth vial, has a distinct reference, I think, to the account in ancient writers of the taking of Babylon, and prefigures, in like manner, that the resources of that modern Babylon, the Popish power, shall continue to be drained off, as they have now been drying up for a century or more, till, at last, there will come a sudden and final downfall of that power. And after that will come the first triumphs of truth and righteousness,—the marriage-supper of the Lamb.'

'These investigations must undoubtedly possess a deep interest for you, sir,' said Burr; 'the hope of a future as well as the tradition of a past age of gold seems to have been one of the most cherished conceptions of the human breast.'

'In those times,' continued the Doctor, 'the whole earth will be of one language.'

'Which language, sir, do you suppose will be considered worthy of such preeminence?' inquired his listener.

CHAPTER XVI.

'That will probably be decided by an amicable conference of all nations,' said the Doctor; 'and the one universally considered most valuable will be adopted; and the literature of all other nations being translated into it, they will gradually drop all other tongues. Brother Stiles thinks it will be the Hebrew. I am not clear on that point. The Hebrew seems to me too inflexible, and not sufficiently copious. I do not think,' he added, after some consideration, 'that it will be the Hebrew tongue.'

'I am most happy to hear it, sir,' said Burr, gravely; 'I never felt much attracted to that language. But, ladies,' he added, starting up with animation, 'I must improve this fine weather to ask you to show me the view of the sea from this little hill beyond your house, it is evidently so fine;—I trust I am not intruding too far on your morning?'

'By no means, sir,' said Mrs. Scudder, rising; 'we will go with you in a moment.'

And soon Colonel Burr, with one on either arm, was to be seen on the top of the hill beyond the house,—the very one from which Mary, the week before, had seen the retreating sail we all wot of. Hence, though her companion contrived, with the adroitness of a practised man of gallantry, to direct his words and looks as constantly to her as if they had been in a *tête-à-tête*, and although nothing could be more graceful, more delicately flattering, more engaging, still the little heart kept equal poise; for where a true love has once bolted the door, a false one serenades in vain under the window.

Some fine, instinctive perceptions of the real character of the man beside her seemed to have dawned on Mary's mind in the conversation of the morning;—she had felt the covert and subtile irony that lurked beneath his polished smile, felt the utter want of faith or sympathy in what she and her revered friend deemed holiest, and therefore there was a calm dignity in her manner of receiving his attentions which rather piqued and stimulated his curiosity. He had been wont to boast that he could subdue any woman, if he could only see enough of her: in the first interview in the garden, he had made her colour come and go, and brought tears to her eyes in a manner that interested his fancy, and he could not resist the impulse to experiment again. It was a new sensation to him, to find himself quietly studied and calmly measured by those thoughtful blue eyes; he felt, with his fine instinctive tact, that the soul within was enfolded in some crystalline sphere of protection, transparent, but adamantine, so that he could not touch it. What was that secret poise, that calm, immutable centre on which she rested, that made her, in her rustic simplicity, so unapproachable and so strong?

Burr remembered once finding in his grandfather's study, among a mass of old letters, one in which that great man, in early youth, described his future wife, then known to him only by distant report. With his keen natural sense of everything fine and poetic, he had been struck with this passage, as so beautifully expressing an ideal womanhood, that he had in his earlier days copied it in his private *recueil*.

'They say,' it ran, 'that there is a young lady who is beloved of that Great Being who made and rules the world, and that there are certain seasons in which this Great Being, in some way or other invisible, comes to her and fills her mind with such exceeding sweet delight, that she hardly cares for anything except to meditate on Him; that she expects, after a while, to be received up where He is, to be raised up out of the world and caught up into heaven, being assured that He loves her too well to let her remain at a distance from Him always. Therefore, if you present all the world before her, with the richest of its treasures, she disregards it. She has a strange sweetness in her mind, and singular purity in her affections; and you could not persuade her to do anything wrong or sinful, if you should give her all the world. She is of a wonderful sweetness, calmness, and universal benevolence of mind, especially after this great God has manifested Himself to her mind. She will sometimes go from place to place singing sweetly, and seems to be always full of joy and pleasure; and no one knows for what. She loves to be alone, walking in fields and groves, and seems to have some invisible one always conversing with her.'

A shadowy recollection of this description crossed his mind more than once, as he looked into those calm and candid eyes. Was there, then, a truth in that inner union of chosen souls with God, of which his mother and her mother before her had borne meek witness,—their souls shining out as sacred lamps through the alabaster walls of a temple?

But then, again, had he not logically met and demonstrated, to his own satisfaction, the nullity of the religious dogmas on which New England faith was based? There could be no such inner life, he said to himself,—he had demonstrated it as an absurdity. What was it, then,—this charm, so subtile and so strong, by which this fair child, his inferior in age, cultivation, and knowledge of the world, held him in a certain awe, and made him feel her spirit so unapproachable? His curiosity was piqued. He felt stimulated to employ all his powers of pleasing. He was determined that, sooner or later, she should feel his power.

With Mrs. Scudder his success was immediate: she was completely won over by the deferential manner with which he constantly referred himself to her matronly judgments; and, on returning to the house, she warmly pressed him to stay to dinner.

Burr accepted the invitation with a frank and almost boyish *abandon*, declaring that he had not seen anything for years that so reminded him of old times. He praised everything at table,—the smoking brown bread, the baked beans steaming from the oven, where they had been quietly simmering during the morning walk, and the Indian pudding, with its gelatinous softness, matured by long and patient brooding in the motherly old oven. He declared that there was no style of living to be compared with the simple, dignified order of a true New England home, where servants were excluded, and everything came direct from the polished and cultured hand of a lady. It realized the dreams of Arcadian romance. A man, he declared, must be unworthy the name, who did not rise to lofty sentiments and heroic deeds, when even his animal wants were provided for by the ministrations of the most delicate and exalted portion of the creation.

After dinner he would be taken into all the family interests. Gentle and pliable as oil, he seemed to penetrate every joint of the *ménage* by a subtile and seductive sympathy. He was interested in the spinning, in the weaving,—and, in fact, nobody knows how it was done, but before the afternoon shadows had turned, he was sitting in the cracked arm-chair of Mary's garret-boudoir, gravely giving judgment on several specimens of her spinning, which Mrs. Scudder had presented to his notice.

With that ease with which he could at will glide into the character of the superior and elder brother, he had, without seeming to ask questions, drawn from Mary an account of her reading, her studies, her acquaintances.

'You read French, I presume?' he said to her, with easy negligence.

Mary coloured deeply, and then, as one who recollects one's self, answered, gravely,—

'No, Mr. Burr, I know no language but my own.'

'But you should learn French, my child,' said Burr, with that gentle dictatorship which he could at times so gracefully assume.

'I should be delighted to learn,' said Mary, 'but have no opportunity.'

'Yes,' said Mrs. Scudder, 'Mary has always had a taste for study, and would be glad to improve in any way.'

'Pardon me, madam, if I take the liberty of making a suggestion. There is a most excellent man, the Abbé Léfon, now in Newport, driven here by the political disturbances in France; he is anxious to obtain a few scholars, and I am interested that he should succeed, for he is a most worthy man.'

'Is he a Roman Catholic?'

'He is, madam; but there could be no manner of danger with a person so admirably instructed as your daughter. If you please to see him, madam, I will call with him some time.'

'Mrs. Marvyn will, perhaps, join me,' said Mary. 'She has been studying French by herself for some time, in order to read a treatise on astronomy, which she found in that language. I will go over to-morrow and see her about it.'

Before Colonel Burr departed, the doctor requested him to step a moment with him into his study. Burr, who had had frequent occasions during his life to experience the sort of paternal freedom which the clergy of his country took with him in right of his clerical descent, began to summon together his faculties of address for the avoidance of a kind of conversation which he was not disposed to meet. He was agreeably disappointed, however, when, taking a paper from the table, and presenting it to him, the Doctor said,—

'I feel myself, my dear sir, under a burden of obligation for benefits received from your family, so that I never see a member of it without casting about in my own mind how I may in some measure express my good-will towards him. You are aware that the papers of your distinguished grandfather have fallen into my hands, and from them I have taken the liberty to make a copy of those maxims by which he guided a life which was a blessing to his country and to the world. May I ask the favour that you will read them with attention? and if you find anything contrary to right reason or sober sense, I shall be happy to hear of it on a future occasion.'

'Thank you, Doctor,' said Burr, bowing, 'I shall always be sensible of the kindness of the motive which has led you to take this trouble on my account. Believe me, sir, I am truly obliged to you for it.'

And thus the interview terminated.

That night, the Doctor, before retiring, offered fervent prayers for the grandson of his revered master and friend, praying that his father's and mother's God might bless him and make him a living stone in the Eternal Temple.

Meanwhile, the object of these prayers was sitting by a table in dressing-gown and slippers, thinking over the events of the day. The paper which Dr. H. had handed him contained the celebrated 'Resolutions' by which his ancestor led a life nobler than any mere dogmas can possibly be. By its side lay a perfumed note from Madame de Frontignac,—one of those womanly notes, so beautiful, so sacred in themselves, but so mournful to a right-minded person who sees whither they are tending. Burr opened and perused it,—laid it by,—opened the document which the Doctor had given, and thoughtfully read the first of the 'Resolutions':—

'Resolved, That I will do whatsoever I think to be most to God's glory, and my own good profit and pleasure *in the whole of my duration*, without any consideration of time, whether now or never so many myriad ages hence.

'Resolved, To do whatever I think to be my duty and most for the good and advantage of mankind in general.

'Resolved, To do this, whatsoever difficulties I meet with, and how many and how great soever.'

Burr read the whole paper through attentively once or twice, and paused thoughtfully over many parts of it. He sat for some time after, lost in reflection; the paper dropped from his hand, and then followed one of those long, deep seasons of fixed reverie, when the soul thinks by pictures and goes over endless distances in moments. In him, originally, every moral faculty and sensibility was as keenly strung as in any member of that remarkable family from which he was descended, and which has, whether in good or ill, borne no common stamp. Two possible lives flashed before his mind at that moment, rapidly as when a train sweeps by with flashing lamps in the night. The life of worldly expediency, the life of eternal rectitude,—the life of seventy years, and that life eternal in which the event of death is no disturbance. Suddenly he roused himself up, picked up the paper, filed and dated it carefully, and laid it by; and in that moment was renewed again that governing purpose which sealed him, with all his beautiful capabilities, as the slave of the fleeting and the temporary, which sent him, at last, a shipwrecked man, to a nameless, dishonoured grave.

He took his pen and gave to a friend his own views of the events of the day.

'MY DEAR ——,

CHAPTER XVI.

'We are still in Newport, conjugating the verb *s'ennuyer*, which I, for one, have put through all the moods and tenses. *Pour passer le temps*, however, I have *la belle Française* and my sweet little Puritan. I visited there this morning. She lives with her mother, a little walk out toward the sea-side in a cottage quite prettily sequestered among blossoming apple-trees, and the great hierarch of modern theology, Dr. H., keeps guard over them. No chance here for any indiscretions, you see.

'By-the-by, the good Doctor astonished our *monde* here on Sunday last, by treating us to a solemn onslaught on slavery and the slave-trade. He had all the chief captains and counsellors to hear him, and smote them hip and thigh, and pursued them even unto Shur.

'He is one of those great, honest fellows, without the smallest notion of the world we live in, who think, in dealing with men, that you must go to work and prove the right and wrong of a matter; just as if anybody cared for that! Supposing he is right,—which appears very probable to me,—what is he going to do about it? No moral argument, since the world began, ever prevailed over twenty-five per cent. profit.

'However, he is the spiritual director of *la belle Puritaine*, and was a resident in my grandfather's family, so I did the agreeable with him as well as such an uncircumcised Ishmaelite could. I discoursed theology,—sat with the most docile air possible while he explained to me all the ins and outs in his system of the universe, past, present, and future,—heard him dilate calmly on the Millennium, and expound prophetic symbols, marching out before me his whole apocalyptic menagerie of beasts and dragons with heads and horns innumerable, to all which I gave edifying attention, taking occasion now and then to turn a compliment in favour of the ladies,—never lost, you know.

'Really, he is a worthy old soul, and actually believes all these things with his whole heart, attaching unheard-of importance to the most abstract ideas, and embarking his whole being in his ideal view of a grand Millennial *finale* to the human race. I look at him and at myself, and ask, Can human beings be made so unlike?

'My little Mary to-day was in a mood of "sweet austere composure" quite becoming to her style of beauty; her *naïve nonchalance* at times is rather stimulating. What a contrast between her and *la belle Française!*—all the difference that there is between a diamond and a flower. I find the little thing has a cultivated mind, enriched by reading, and more by a still, quaint habit of thinking, which is new and charming. But a truce to this.

'I have seen our friends at last. We have had three or four meetings, and are waiting to hear from Philadelphia,—matters are getting in train. If Messrs. T. and S. dare to repeat what they said again, let me know; they will find in me a man not to be trifled with. I shall be with you in a week or ten days at farthest. Meanwhile, stand to your guns.

'Ever yours,

'BURR.'

CHAPTER XVII.

THE next morning, before the early dews had yet dried off the grass, Mary started to go and see her friend Mrs. Marvyn. It was one of those charming, invigorating days, familiar to those of Newport experience, when the sea lies shimmering and glittering in deep blue and gold, and the sky above is firm and cloudless, and every breeze that comes landward seems to bear health and energy upon its wings.

As Mary approached the house, she heard loud sounds of discussion from the open kitchen-door, and, looking in, saw a rather original scene acting.

Candace, armed with a long oven-shovel, stood before the open door of the oven, whence she had just been removing an army of good things which appeared ranged around on the dresser. Cato, in the undress of a red flannel shirt and tow-cloth trousers, was cuddled, in a consoled and protected attitude, in the corner of the wooden settle, with a mug of flip in his hand, which Candace had prepared, and, calling him in from his work, authoritatively ordered him to drink, on the showing that he had kept her awake the night before with his cough, and she was sure he was going to be sick. Of course, worse things may happen to a man than to be vigorously taken care of by his wife, and Cato had a salutary conviction of this fact, so that he resigned himself to his comfortable corner and his flip with edifying serenity.

Opposite to Candace stood a well-built, corpulent negro man, dressed with considerable care, and with the air of a person on excellent terms with himself. This was no other than Digo, the house-servant and factotum of Dr. Stiles, who considered himself as the guardian of his master's estate, his title, his honour, his literary character, his professional position, and his religious creed.

Digo was ready to assert before all the world, that one and all of these were under his special protection, and that whoever had anything to say to the contrary of any of these must expect to take issue with him. Digo not only swallowed all his master's opinions whole, but seemed to have the stomach of an ostrich in their digestion. He believed everything, no matter what, the moment he understood that the Doctor held it. He believed that Hebrew was the language of heaven,—that the ten tribes of the Jews had reappeared in the North American Indians,—that there was no such thing as disinterested benevolence, and that the doings of the unregenerate had some value,—that slavery was a divine ordinance, and that Dr.

H. was a Radical, who did more harm than good,—and, finally, that there never was so great a man as Dr. Stiles: and as Dr. Stiles belonged to him in the capacity of master, why, he, Digo, owned the greatest man in America. Of course, as Candace held precisely similar opinions in regard to Dr. H., the two never could meet without a discharge of the opposite electricities. Digo had, it is true, come ostensibly on a mere worldly errand from his mistress to Mrs. Marvyn, who had promised to send her some turkeys' eggs, but he had inly resolved with himself that he would give Candace his opinion,—that is, what Dr. Stiles had said at dinner the day before about Dr. H.'s Sunday's discourse. Dr. Stiles had not heard it, but Digo had. He had felt it due to the responsibilities of his position to be present on so very important an occasion.

Therefore, after receiving his eggs, he opened hostilities by remarking, in a general way, that he had attended the Doctor's preaching on Sunday, and that there was quite a crowded house. Candace immediately began mentally to bristle her feathers like a hen who sees a hawk in the distance, and responded with decision:—

'Den you *heard* sometin', for once in your life!'

'I must say,' said Digo, with suavity, 'dat I can't give my 'proval to such sentiments.'

'More shame for you,' said Candace, grimly. '*You* a man, and not stan' by your colour, and flunk under to mean white ways! Ef you was *half* a man, your heart would 'a' bounded like a cannon-ball at dat 'ar sermon.'

'Dr. Stiles and me we talked it over after church,' said Digo,—'and de Doctor was of my 'pinion, dat Providence didn't intend—'

'Oh, you go 'long wid your Providence! Guess, ef white folks had let us alone, Providence wouldn't trouble us.'

'Well,' said Digo, 'Dr. Stiles is clear dat dis yer's a-fulfillin' de prophecies and bringin' in de fulness of de Gentiles.'

'Fulness of de fiddlesticks!' said Candace, irreverently. 'Now what a way dat ar' is of talkin'! Go look at one o' dem ships we come over in,—sweatin' and groanin'—in de dark and dirt,—cryin' and dyin',—howlin' for breath till de sweat run off us,—livin' and dead chained together,—prayin' like de rich man in hell for a drop o' water to cool our tongues! Call dat ar' a-bringin' de fulness of de Gentiles, do ye?—Ugh!'

And Candace ended with a guttural howl, and stood frowning and gloomy over the top of her long kitchen-shovel, like a black Bellona leaning on her spear of battle.

Digo recoiled a little, but stood too well in his own esteem to give up; so he shifted his attack.

'Well, for my part, I must say I never was 'clined to your Doctor's 'pinions. Why, now, Dr. Stiles says, notin' couldn't be more absurd dan what he says 'bout disinterested benevolence. *My* Doctor says, dere a'n't no such ting!'

CHAPTER XVII.

'I should tink it's likely!' said Candace, drawing herself up with superb disdain. '*Our* Doctor knows dere *is*,—and why? 'cause he's got it IN HERE,' said she, giving her ample chest a knock which resounded like the boom from a barrel.

'Candace,' said Cato, gently, 'you's gettin' too hot.'

'Cato, you shut up!' said Candace, turning sharp round. 'What did I make you dat ar' flip for, 'cept you was so hoarse you oughtn' for to say a word? Pootty business, you go to agitatin' *your*-self wid dese yer! Ef you wear out your poor old throat talkin', you may get de 'sumption; and den what'd become o' me?'

Cato, thus lovingly pitched *hors de combat*, sipped the sweetened cup in quietness of soul, while Candace returned to the charge.

'Now, I tell ye what,' she said to Digo,—'jest 'cause you wear your master's old coats and hats, you tink you must go in for all dese yer old, mean, white 'pinions. A'n't ye 'shamed—you, a black man—to have no more pluck and make cause wid de Egyptians? Now, 'ta'n't what my Doctor gives me,—he never giv' me the snip of a finger-nail,—but it's what he does for *mine;* and when de poor critturs lands dar, tumbled out like bales on de wharves, ha'n't dey seen his great cocked hat, like a lighthouse, and his big eyes lookin' sort o' pitiful at 'em, as ef he felt o' one blood wid 'em? Why, de very looks of de man is worth everyting; and who ever thought o' doin' anyting for deir souls, or cared ef dey had souls, till he begun it?'

'Well, at any rate,' said Digo, brightening up, 'I don't believe his doctrine about de doings of de unregenerate,—it's quite clear he's wrong dar.'

'Who cares?' said Candace,—'generate or unregenerate, it's all one to me. I believe a man dat *acts* as he does. Him as stands up for de poor,—him as pleads for de weak,—he's my man. I'll believe straight through anyting he's a mind to put at me.'

At this juncture, Mary's fair face appearing at the door put a stop to the discussion.

'Bress *you*, Miss Mary! comin' here like a fresh June rose! it makes a body's eyes dance in deir head! Come right in! I got Cato up from de lot, 'cause he's rader poorly dis mornin'; his cough makes me a sight o' concern; he's allers a-pullin' off his jacket de wrong time, or doin' sometin' I tell him not to,—and it just keeps him hack, hack, hackin', all de time.'

During this speech, Cato stood meekly bowing, feeling that he was being apologized for in the best possible manner; for long years of instruction had fixed the idea in his mind, that he was an ignorant sinner, who had not the smallest notion how to conduct himself in this world, and that, if it were not for his wife's distinguishing grace, he would long since have been in the shades of oblivion.

'Missis is spinnin' up in de north chamber,' said Candace; 'but I'll run up and fetch her down.'

Candace, who was about the size of a puncheon, was fond of this familiar manner of representing her mode of ascending the stairs; but Mary, suppressing a smile, said, 'Oh, no, Candace; don't for the world disturb her. I know just where she is.' And before Candace could stop her, Mary's light foot was on the top step of the staircase that led up from the kitchen.

The north room was a large chamber, overlooking a splendid reach of sea-prospect. A moving panorama of blue water and gliding sails was unrolled before its three windows, so that stepping into the room gave one an instant and breezy sense of expansion. Mrs. Marvyn was standing at the large wheel, spinning wool,—a reel and basket of spools on her side. Her large brown eyes had an eager joy in them when Mary entered; but they seemed to calm down again, and she received her only with that placid, sincere air which was her habit. Everything about this woman showed an ardent soul, repressed by timidity and by a certain dumbness in the faculties of outward expression; but her eyes had, at times, that earnest, appealing language which is so pathetic in the silence of inferior animals. One sometimes sees such eyes, and wonders whether the story they intimate will ever be spoken in mortal language.

Mary began eagerly detailing to her all that had interested her since they last met: the party,—her acquaintance with Burr,—his visit to the cottage,—his inquiries into her education and reading,—and, finally, the proposal that they should study French together.

'My dear,' said Mrs. Marvyn, 'let us begin at once;—such an opportunity is not to be lost. I studied a little with James, when he was last at home.'

'With James?' said Mary, with an air of timid surprise.

'Yes,—the dear boy has become, what I never expected, quite a student. He employs all his spare time now in reading and studying;—the second mate is a Frenchman, and James has got so that he can both speak and read. He is studying Spanish, too.'

Ever since the last conversation, with her mother on the subject of James, Mary had felt a sort of guilty constraint when any one spoke of him; instead of answering frankly, as she once did when anything brought his name up, she fell at once into a grave, embarrassed silence.

Mrs. Marvyn was so constantly thinking of him, that it was difficult to begin on any topic that did not in some manner or other knit itself into the one ever present in her thoughts. None of the peculiar developments of the female nature have a more exquisite vitality than the sentiment of a frail, delicate, repressed, timid woman, for a strong, manly, generous son. There is her ideal expressed; there is the out-speaking and out-acting of all she trembles to think, yet burns to say or do; here is the hero that shall speak for her, the heart into which she has poured hers, and that shall give to her tremulous and hidden aspirations a strong and victorious expression. 'I have gotten a *man* from the Lord,' she says to herself; and each outburst of his manliness, his vigour, his self-confidence, his superb vitality, fills her with a strange, wondering pleasure, and she has a secret tenderness and pride even in his wilfulness and waywardness. 'What a creature he is!' she says, when he flouts at sober argument and pitches all received opinions hither and thither in the wild capriciousness of youthful paradox. She looks grave and reproving; but he reads the concealed triumph in her eyes,—he knows that in her heart she is full of admiration all the time. First love of womanhood is something wonderful and mysterious,—but in this second love it rises again, idealized and refined: she loves the father and herself united and made one in this young heir of life and hope.

Such was Mrs. Marvyn's still intense, passionate love for her son. Not a tone of his manly voice, not a flash of his dark eyes, not one of the deep, shadowy dimples that came and went as he laughed, not a ring of his glossy black hair, that was not studied, got by heart, and dwelt on in the inner shrine of her thoughts: he was the romance of her life. His strong, daring nature carried her with it beyond those narrow, daily bounds where her soul was weary of treading; and just as his voyages had given to the trite prose of her *ménage* a poetry of strange, foreign perfumes, of quaint objects of interest, speaking of many a far-off shore, so his mind and life were a constant channel of outreach through which her soul held converse with the active and stirring world. Mrs. Marvyn had known all the story of her son's love; and to no other woman would she have been willing to resign him: but her love to Mary was so deep, that she thought of his union with her more as gaining a daughter than as losing a son. She would not speak of the subject: she knew the feelings of Mary's mother; and the name of James fell so often from her lips, simply because it was so ever-present in her heart that it could not be helped.

Before Mary left, it was arranged that they should study together, and that the lessons should be given alternately at each other's houses; and with this understanding they parted.

CHAPTER XVIII.

THE Doctor sat at his study-table. It was evening, and the slant beams of the setting sun shot their golden arrows through the healthy purple clusters of lilacs that veiled the windows. There had been a shower that filled them with drops of rain, which every now and then tattooed with a slender rat-tat on the window-sill, as a breeze would shake the leaves and bear in perfume on its wings. Sweet, fragrance-laden airs tripped stirringly to and fro about the study-table, making gentle confusions, fluttering papers on moral ability, agitating treatises on the great end of creation, mixing up subtile distinctions between amiable instincts and true holiness, and, in short, conducting themselves like very unappreciative and unphilosophical little breezes.

The Doctor patiently smoothed back and rearranged, while opposite to him sat Mary, bending over some copying she was doing for him. One stray sunbeam fell on her light-brown hair, tinging it to gold; her long, drooping lashes lay over the wax-like pink of her cheeks, as she wrote on.

'Mary,' said the Doctor, pushing the papers from him.

'Sir,' she answered, looking up, the blood just perceptibly rising in her cheeks.

'Do you ever have any periods in which your evidences seem not altogether clear?'

Nothing could show more forcibly the grave, earnest character of thought in New England at this time than the fact that this use of the term 'evidences' had become universally significant and understood as relating to one's right of citizenship in a celestial, invisible commonwealth.

So Mary understood it, and it was with a deepened flush she answered gently, 'No, sir.'

'What! never any doubts?' said the Doctor.

'I am sorry,' said Mary, apologetically; 'but I do not see how I *can* have; I never could.'

'Ah!' said the Doctor, musingly, 'would I could say so! There are times, indeed, when I hope I have an interest in the precious Redeemer, and behold an infinite loveliness and beauty in Him, apart from anything I expect or hope. But even then how deceitful is the human heart! how insensibly might a mere selfish love take the place of that disinterested complacency which regards Him for what

He is in Himself, apart from what He is to us! Say, my dear friend, does not this thought sometimes make you tremble?'

Poor Mary was truth itself, and this question distressed her; she must answer the truth. The fact was, that it had never come into her blessed little heart to tremble, for she was one of those children of the bride-chamber who cannot mourn, because the bridegroom is ever with them; but then, when she saw the man for whom her reverence was almost like that for her God thus distrustful, thus lowly, she could not but feel that her too calm repose might, after all, be the shallow, treacherous calm of an ignorant, ill-grounded spirit, and therefore, with a deep blush and a faltering voice, she said,—

'Indeed, I am afraid something must be wrong with me. I *cannot* have any fears,—I never could; I try sometimes, but the thought of God's goodness comes all around me, and I am so happy before I think of it!'

'Such exercises, my dear friend, I have also had,' said the Doctor; 'but before I rest on them as evidences, I feel constrained to make the following inquiries:—Is this gratitude that swells my bosom the result of a mere natural sensibility? Does it arise in a particular manner because God has done me good? or do I love God for what He *is*, as well as for what He has done? and for what He has done for others, as well as for what He has done for me? Love to God, which is built on nothing but good received, is not incompatible with a disposition so horrid as even to curse God to His face. If God is not to be loved except when He does good, then in affliction we are free. If doing *us* good is all that renders God lovely to us, then not doing us good divests Him of His glory, and dispenses us from obligation to love Him. But there must be, undoubtedly, some permanent reason why God is to be loved by all: and if not doing us good divests Him of His glory so as to free *us* from our obligation to love, it equally frees the universe; so that, in fact, the universe of happiness if ours be not included, reflects no glory on its Author.'

The Doctor had practised his subtile mental analysis till his instruments were so fine-pointed and keen-edged that he scarce ever allowed a flower of sacred emotion to spring in his soul without picking it to pieces to see if its genera and species were correct. Love, gratitude, reverence, benevolence,—which all moved in mighty tides in his soul—were all compelled to pause midway while he rubbed up his optical instruments to see whether they were rising in right order. Mary, on the contrary, had the blessed gift of womanhood,—that vivid life in the soul and sentiment which resists the chills of analysis, as a healthful human heart resists cold; yet still, all humbly, she thought this perhaps was a defect in herself, and therefore, having confessed, in a depreciating tone, her habits of unanalysed faith and love, she added,—

'But, my dear sir, you are my best friend. I trust you will be faithful to me. If I am deceiving myself, undeceive me; you cannot be too severe with me.'

'Alas!' said the Doctor, 'I fear that I may be only a blind leader of the blind. What, after all, if I be only a miserable self-deceiver? What if some thought of self has come in to poison all my prayers and strivings? It is true, I think,—yes, I *think,*' said the Doctor, speaking very slowly and with intense earnestness,—'I think, that, if I knew at this moment that my name never would be written among those of the elect, I could still see God to be infinitely amiable and glorious, and could feel sure that He *could* not do me wrong, and that it was infinitely becoming and right that He should dispose of me according to His sovereign pleasure. I *think* so;—but still my deceitful heart!—after all, I might find it rising in rebellion. Say, my dear friend, are you sure, that, should you discover yourself to be for ever condemned by His justice, you would not find your heart rising up against Him?'

'Against *Him?*' said Mary, with a tremulous, sorrowful expression on her face,—'against my Heavenly Father?'

Her face flushed and faded; her eyes kindled eagerly, as if she had something to say, and then grew misty with tears. At last she said,—

'Thank you, my dear, faithful friend! I will think about this; *perhaps* I may have been deceived. How very difficult it must be to know one's self perfectly!'

Mary went into her own little room, and sat leaning for a long time with her elbow on the window-seat, watching the pale shells of the apple-blossoms as they sailed and fluttered downward into the grass, and listened to a chippering conversation in which the birds in the nest above were settling up their small housekeeping accounts for the day.

After a while, she took her pen and wrote the following, which the Doctor found the next morning lying on his study-table:—

> 'MY DEAR, HONOURED FRIEND,—How can I sufficiently thank you for your faithfulness with me? All you say to me seems true and excellent; and yet, my dear sir, permit me to try to express to you some of the many thoughts to which our conversation this evening has given rise. To love God because He is good to me you seem to think is not a right kind of love; and yet every moment of my life I have experienced His goodness. When recollection brings back the past, where can I look that I see not His goodness? What moment of my life presents not instances of merciful kindness to me, as well as to every creature, more and greater than I can express, than my mind is able to take in? How, then, can I help loving God because He is good to me? Were I not an object of God's mercy and goodness, I cannot have any conception what would be my feeling. Imagination never yet placed me in a situation not to experience the goodness of God in some way or other; and if I do love Him, how can it be but because He is good, and to me good? Do not God's children love Him because He first loved them?
>
> 'If I called nothing goodness which did not happen to suit my inclination, and could not believe the Deity to be gracious and merciful except when the course of events was so ordered as to agree with my humour, so far from imagining that I had any love to God, I must conclude myself wholly destitute of anything good. A love founded

on nothing but good received is not, you say, incompatible with a disposition so horrid as even to curse God. I am not sensible that I ever in my life imagined anything *but* good could come from the hand of God. From a Being infinite in goodness everything *must* be good, though we do not always comprehend how it is so. Are not afflictions good? Does He not even in judgment remember mercy? Sensible that "afflictions are but blessings in disguise," I would bless the hand that, with infinite kindness, wounds only to heal, and love and adore the goodness of God equally in suffering as in rejoicing.

'The disinterested love to God, which you think is alone the genuine love, I see not how we can be certain we possess, when our love of happiness and our love of God are so inseparably connected. The joys arising from a consciousness that God is a benefactor to me and my friends (and when I think of God every creature is my friend), if arising from a selfish motive, it does not seem to me possible could be changed into hate, even supposing God my enemy, whilst I regarded Him as a Being infinitely just as well as good. If God is my enemy, it must be because I deserve He should be such; and it does not seem to me *possible* that I should hate Him, even if I knew He would always be so.

'In what you say of willingness to suffer eternal punishment, I don't know that I understand what the feeling is. Is it wickedness in me that I do not feel a willingness to be left to eternal sin? Can any one joyfully acquiesce in being thus left? When I pray for a new heart and a right spirit, must I be willing to be denied, and rejoice that my prayer is not heard? Could any real Christian rejoice in this? But he fears it not,—he knows it will never be,—he therefore can cheerfully leave it with God; and so can I.

'Such, my dear friend, are my thoughts, poor and unworthy; yet they seem to me as certain as my life, or as anything I see. Am I unduly confident? I ask your prayers that I may be guided aright.

'Your affectionate friend,

'MARY.'

There are in this world two kinds of natures,—those that have wings, and those that have feet,—the winged and the walking spirits. The walking are the logicians; the winged are the instinctive and poetic. Natures that must always walk find many a bog, many a thicket, many a tangled brake, which God's happy little winged birds flit over by one noiseless flight. Nay, when a man has toiled till his feet weigh too heavily with the mud of earth to enable him to walk another step, these little birds will often cleave the air in a right line towards the bosom of God, and show the way where he could never have found it.

The Doctor paused in his ponderous and heavy reasonings to read this real woman's letter; and being a loving man, he felt as if he could have kissed the hem of her garment who wrote it. He recorded it in his journal, and after it this significant passage from the Canticles:—

'I charge you, O ye daughters of Jerusalem, by the roes, and by the hinds of the field, that ye stir not up nor awake this lovely one till she please.'

Mrs. Scudder's motherly eye noticed, with satisfaction, these quiet communings. 'Let it alone,' she said to herself; 'before she knows it, she will find herself wholly under his influence.' Mrs. Scudder was a wise woman.

CHAPTER XIX.

IN the course of a day or two, a handsome carriage drew up in front of Mrs. Scudder's cottage, and a brilliant party alighted. They were Colonel and Madame de Frontignac, the Abbé Léfon, and Colonel Burr. Mrs. Scudder and her daughter, being prepared for the call, sat in afternoon dignity and tranquillity, in the best room, with their knitting-work.

Madame de Frontignac had divined, with the lightning-like tact which belongs to women in the positive, and to French women in the superlative degree, that there was something in the cottage-girl, whom she had passingly seen at the party, which powerfully affected the man whom she loved with all the jealous intensity of a strong nature, and hence she embraced eagerly the opportunity to see her,—yes, to see her, to study her, to dart her keen French wit through her, and detect the secret of her charm, that she, too, might practise it.

Madame de Frontignac was one of those women whose beauty is so striking and imposing, that they seem to kindle up, even in the most prosaic apartment, an atmosphere of enchantment. All the pomp and splendour of high life, the wit, the refinements, the nameless graces and luxuries of courts, seemed to breathe in invisible airs around her, and she made a Faubourg St. Germain of the darkest room into which she entered. Mary thought, when she came in, that she had never seen anything so splendid. She was dressed in a black velvet riding-habit, buttoned to the throat with coral; her riding-hat drooped with its long plumes so as to cast a shadow over her animated face, out of which her dark eyes shone like jewels, and her pomegranate cheeks glowed with the rich shaded radiance of one of Rembrandt's pictures. Something quaint and foreign, something poetic and strange, marked each turn of her figure, each article of her dress, down to the sculptured hand on which glittered singular and costly rings,—and the riding-glove, embroidered with seed-pearls, that fell carelessly beside her on the floor.

In Antwerp one sees a picture in which Rubens, who felt more than any other artist the glory of the physical life, has embodied his conception of the Madonna, in opposition to the faded, cold ideals of the Middle Ages, from which he revolted with such a bound. *His* Mary is a superb Oriental sultana, with lustrous dark eyes, redundant form, jewelled turban, standing leaning on the balustrade of a princely terrace, and bearing on her hand, *not* the silver dove, but a gorgeous paroquet. The two styles, in this instance, were both in the same room; and as Burr sat looking from one to the other, he felt, for a moment, as one would who should put a sketch of Overbeck's beside a splendid painting of Titian's.

For a few moments, everything in the room seemed faded and cold, in contrast with the tropical atmosphere of this regal beauty. Burr watched Mary with a keen eye, to see if she were dazzled and overawed. He saw nothing but the most innocent surprise and delight. All the slumbering poetry within her seemed to awaken at the presence of her beautiful neighbour,—as when one, for the first time, stands before the great revelations of Art. Mary's cheek glowed, her eyes seemed to grow deep with the enthusiasm of admiration, and, after a few moments, it seemed as if her delicate face and figure reflected the glowing loveliness of her visitor, just as the virgin snows of the Alps become incarnadine as they stand opposite the glorious radiance of a sunset sky.

Madame de Frontignac was accustomed to the effect of her charms; but there was so much love in the admiration now directed towards her, that her own warm nature was touched, and she threw out the glow of her feelings with a magnetic power. Mary never felt the cold, habitual reserve of her education so suddenly melt, never felt herself so naturally falling into language of confidence and endearment with a stranger; and as her face, so delicate and spiritual, grew bright with love, Madame de Frontignac thought she had never seen anything so beautiful, and stretching out her hands towards her, she exclaimed, in her own language,—

'*Mais, mon Dieu! mon enfant, que tu es belle!*'

Mary's deep blush, at her ignorance of the language in which her visitor spoke, recalled her to herself;—she laughed a clear, silvery laugh, and laid her jewelled little hand on Mary's with a caressing movement.

'*He* shall not teach you French, *ma toute belle*,' she said, indicating the Abbé, by a pretty, wilful gesture; '*I* will teach you;—and you shall teach me English. Oh I shall try *so* hard to learn!' she said.

There was something inexpressibly pretty and quaint in the childish lisp with which she pronounced English. Mary was completely won over. She could have fallen into the arms of this wondrously beautiful fairy princess, expecting to be carried away by her to Dreamland.

Meanwhile, Mrs. Scudder was gravely discoursing with Colonel Burr and M. de Frontignac; and the Abbé, a small and gentlemanly personage, with clear black eye, delicately-cut features, and powdered hair, appeared to be absorbed in his efforts to follow the current of a conversation imperfectly understood. Burr, the while, though seeming to be entirely and politely absorbed in the conversation he was conducting, lost not a glimpse of the picturesque aside which was being enacted between the two fair ones whom he had thus brought together. He smiled quietly when he saw the effect Madame de Frontignac produced on Mary.

'After all, the child has flesh and blood!' he thought, 'and may feel that there are more things in heaven and earth than she has dreamed of yet. A few French ideas won't hurt her.'

CHAPTER XIX.

The arrangements about lessons being completed, the party returned to the carriage. Madame de Frontignac was enthusiastic in Mary's praise.

'*Cependant*,' she said, leaning back, thoughtfully, after having exhausted herself in superlatives,—'*cependant elle est dévote,—et à dix-neuf comment cela se peut-il?*'

'It is the effect of her austere education,' said Burr. 'It is not possible for you to conceive how young people are trained in the religious families of this country.'

'But yet,' said Madame, 'it gives her a grace altogether peculiar; something in her looks went to my heart. I could find it very easy to love her, because she is really good.'

'The Queen of Hearts should know all that is possible in loving,' said Burr.

Somehow, of late, the compliments which fell so readily from those graceful lips had brought with them an unsatisfying pain. Until a woman really *loves*, flattery and compliment are often like her native air; but when that deeper feeling has once awakened in her, her instincts become marvellously acute to detect the false from the true. Madame de Frontignac longed for one strong, unguarded, real, earnest word from the man who had stolen from her her whole being. She was beginning to feel in some dim wise what an untold treasure she was daily giving for tinsel and dross. She leaned back in the carriage, with a restless, burning cheek, and wondered why she was born to be so miserable. The thought of Mary's saintly face and tender eyes rose before her as the moon rises on the eyes of some hot and fevered invalid, inspiring vague yearnings after an unknown, unattainable peace.

Could some friendly power once have made her at that time clairvoyant and shown her the *reality* of the man whom she was seeing through the prismatic glass of her own enkindled ideality! Could she have seen the calculating quietness in which, during the intervals of a restless and sleepless ambition, he played upon her heart-strings, as one uses a musical instrument to beguile a passing hour,—how his only embarrassment was the fear that the feelings he was pleased to excite might become too warm and too strong, while as yet his relations to her husband were such as to make it dangerous to arouse his jealousy! And if he could have seen that pure ideal conception of himself which alone gave him power in the heart of this woman,—that spotless, glorified image of a hero without fear, without reproach,—would he have felt a moment's shame and abasement at its utter falsehood?

The poet says that the Evil Spirit stood abashed when he saw virtue in an angel form! How would a man, then, stand, who meets face to face his own glorified, spotless ideal, made living by the boundless faith of some believing heart? The best must needs lay his hand on his mouth at this apparition; but woe to him who feels no redeeming power in the sacredness of this believing dream,—who with calculating shrewdness *uses* this most touching miracle of love only to corrupt and destroy the loving! For him there is no sacrifice for sin, no place for repentance. His very mother might shrink in her grave to have him laid beside her.

Madame de Frontignac had the high, honourable nature of the old blood of France, and a touch of its romance. She was strung heroically, and educated according to the notions of her caste and church, purely and religiously. True it is, that one can scarcely call *that* education which teaches woman everything except herself,—*except* the things that relate to her own peculiar womanly destiny, and, on plea of the holiness of ignorance, sends her without one word of just counsel into the temptations of life. Incredible as it may seem, Virginie de Frontignac had never read a romance or work of fiction of which love was the staple; the *régime* of the convent in this regard was inexorable; at eighteen she was more thoroughly a child than most American girls at thirteen. On entrance into life, she was at first so dazzled and bewildered by the mere contrast of fashionable excitement with the quietness of the scenes in which she had hitherto grown up, that she had no time for reading or thought,—all was one intoxicating frolic of existence, one dazzling, bewildering dream.

He whose eye had measured her for his victim verified, if ever man did, the proverbial expression of the iron hand under the velvet glove. Under all his gentle suavities there was a fixed, inflexible will, a calm self-restraint, and a composed philosophical measurement of others, that fitted him to bear despotic rule over an impulsive, unguarded nature. The position, at once accorded to him, of her instructor in the English language and literature, gave him a thousand daily opportunities to touch and stimulate all that class of finer faculties, so restless and so perilous, and which a good man approaches always with a certain awe. It is said that he once asserted that he never beguiled a woman who did not come halfway to meet him,—an observation much the same as a serpent might make in regard to his birds.

The visit of the morning was followed by several others. Madame de Frontignac seemed to conceive for Mary one of those passionate attachments which women often conceive for anything fair and sympathizing, at those periods when their whole inner being is made vital by the approaches of a grand passion. It took only a few visits to make her as familiar as a child at the cottage; and the whole air of the Faubourg St. Germain seemed to melt away from her, as, with the pliability peculiar to her nation, she blended herself with the quiet pursuits of the family. Sometimes, in simple straw hat and white wrapper, she would lie down in the grass under the apple-trees, or join Mary in an expedition to the barn for hen's eggs, or a run along the sea-beach for shells; and her childish eagerness and delight on these occasions used to arouse the unqualified astonishment of Mrs. Katy Scudder.

The Doctor she regarded with a *naïve* astonishment, slightly tinctured with apprehension. She knew he was very religious, and stretched her comprehension to imagine what he might be like. She thought of Bossuet's sermons walking about under a Protestant coat, and felt vaguely alarmed and sinful in his presence, as she used to when entering under the shadows of a cathedral. In her the religious sentiment, though vague, was strong. Nothing in the character of Burr had ever awakened so much disapprobation as his occasional sneers at religion. On such occasions she always reproved him with warmth, but excused him in her heart, because he was brought up a heretic. She held a special theological conversation with the Abbé, whether salvation were possible to one outside of the True Church,—and had added to her daily prayer a particular invocation to the Virgin for him.

The French lessons with her assistance proceeded prosperously. She became an inmate in Mrs. Marvyn's family also. The brown-eyed, sensitive woman loved her as a new poem; she felt enchanted by her; and the prosaic details of her household seemed touched to poetic life by her innocent interest and admiration. The young Madame insisted on being taught to spin at the great wheel; and a very pretty picture she made of it, too, with her earnest gravity of endeavour, her deepening cheek, her graceful form, with some strange foreign scarf or jewelry waving and flashing in odd contrast with her work.

'Do you know,' she said, one day, while thus employed in the north room at Mrs. Marvyn's,—'do you know Burr told me that princesses used to spin? He read me a beautiful story from the "Odyssey," about how Penelope cheated her lovers with her spinning, while she was waiting for her husband to come home;—*he* was gone to sea, Mary,—her *true* love,—you understand.'

She turned on Mary a wicked glance, so full of intelligence that the snowdrop grew red as the inside of a sea-shell.

'*Mon enfant!* thou hast a thought *deep in here!*' she said to Mary, one day, as they sat together in the grass under the apple-trees.

'Why, what?' said Mary, with a startled and guilty look.

'Why, what? *petite!*' said the fairy princess, whimsically mimicking her accent. '*Ah! ah! ma belle!* you think I have no eyes;—Virginie sees deep in here!' she said, laying her hand playfully on Mary's heart. '*Ah, petite!*' she said, gravely, and almost sorrowfully, 'if you love him, wait for him,—*don't marry another!* It is dreadful not to have one's heart go with one's duty.'

'I shall never marry anybody,' said Mary.

'Nevare marrie anybodie!' said the lady, imitating her accents in tones much like those of a bobolink. 'Ah! ah! my little saint, you cannot always live on nothing but the prayers, though prayers are verie good. But, *ma chère*,' she added, in a low tone, 'don't you ever marry that good man in there; priests should not marry.'

'Ours are not priests,—they are ministers,' said Mary. 'But why do you speak of him?—he is like my father.'

'Virginie sees something!' said the lady, shaking her head gravely; 'she sees he loves little Mary.'

'Of course he does!'

'Of-course-he-does?—ah, yes; and by-and-by comes the mamma, and she takes this little hand, and she says, "Come, Mary!" and then she gives it to him; and then the poor *jeune homme*, when he comes back, finds not a bird in his poor little nest. *Oh, c'est ennuyeux cela!*' she said, throwing herself back in the grass till the clover heads and buttercups closed over her.

'I do assure you, dear Madame!'—

'I do assure you, dear Mary, *Virginie knows*. So lock up her words in your little heart; you will want them some day.'

There was a pause of some moments, while the lady was watching the course of a cricket through the clover. At last, lifting her head, she spoke very gravely,—

'My little cat! it is *dreadful* to be married to a good man, and want to be good, and want to love him, and yet never like to have him take your hand, and be more glad when he is away than when he is at home; and then to think how different it would all be, if it was only somebody else. That will be the way with you, if you let them lead you into this; so don't you do it, *mon enfant*.'

A thought seemed to cross Mary's mind, as she turned to Madame de Frontignac, and said, earnestly,—

'If a good man were my husband, I would never think of another,—I wouldn't let myself.'

'How could you help it, *mignonne?* Can you stop your thinking?'

Mary said, after a moment's blush,—

'I can *try!*'

'Ah, yes! But to try all one's life,—oh, Mary, that is too hard! Never do it, darling!'

And then Madame de Frontignac broke out into a carolling little French song, which started all the birds around into a general orchestral accompaniment.

This conversation occurred just before Madame de Frontignac started for Philadelphia, whither her husband had been summoned as an agent in some of the ambitious intrigues of Burr.

It was with a sigh of regret that she parted from her friends at the cottage. She made them a hasty good-bye call,—alighting from a splendid barouche with two white horses, and filling their simple best room with the light of her presence for a last half-hour. When she bade good-bye to Mary, she folded her warmly to her heart, and her long lashes drooped heavily with tears.

After her absence, the lessons were still pursued with the gentle, quiet little Abbé, who seemed the most patient and assiduous of teachers; but, in both houses, there was that vague *ennui*, that sense of want, which follows the fading of one of life's beautiful dreams! We bid her adieu for a season;—we may see her again.

CHAPTER XX.

THE summer passed over the cottage, noiselessly, as our summers pass. There were white clouds walking in saintly troops over blue mirrors of sea,—there were purple mornings, choral with bird-singing,—there were golden evenings, with long, eastward shadows. Apple-blossoms died quietly in the deep orchard-grass, and tiny apples waxed and rounded and ripened and gained stripes of gold and carmine; and the blue eggs broke into young robins, that grew from gaping, yellow-mouthed youth to fledged and outflying maturity. Came autumn, with its long Indian summer, and winter, with its flinty, sparkling snows, under which all Nature lay a sealed and beautiful corpse. Came once more the spring winds, the lengthening days, the opening flowers, and the ever-renewing miracle of buds and blossoms on the apple-trees around the cottage. A year had passed since the June afternoon when first we showed you Mary standing under the spotty shadows of the tree, with the white dove on her hand,—a year in which not many outward changes have been made in the relations of the actors of our story.

Mary calmly spun and read and thought; now and then composing with care very English-French letters, to be sent to Philadelphia to Madame de Frontignac, and receiving short missives of very French-English in return.

The cautions of Madame, in regard to the Doctor, had not rippled the current of their calm, confiding intercourse; and the Doctor, so very satisfied and happy in her constant society and affection, scarcely as yet meditated distinctly that he needed to draw her more closely to himself. If he had a passage to read, a page to be copied, a thought to express, was she not ever there, gentle, patient, unselfish? and scarce by the absence of a day did she let him perceive that his need of her was becoming so absolute that his hold on her must needs be made permanent.

As to his salary and temporal concerns, they had suffered somewhat for his unpopular warfare with reigning sins,—a fact which had rather reconciled Mrs. Scudder to the dilatory movement of her cherished hopes. Since James was gone, what need to press imprudently to new arrangements? Better give the little heart time to grow over before starting a subject which a certain womanly instinct told her might be met with a struggle. Somehow she never thought without a certain heart-sinking of Mary's look and tone the night she spoke with her about James; she had an awful presentiment that that tone of voice belonged to the things that cannot be shaken. But yet, Mary seemed so even, so quiet, her delicate form filled out and rounded so beautifully, and she sang so cheerfully at her work, and, above all, she was so entirely silent about James, that Mrs. Scudder had hope.

Ah, that silence! Do not listen to hear whom a woman praises, to know where her heart is! do not ask for whom she expresses the most earnest enthusiasm! but if there be one she once knew well, whose name she never speaks,—if she seem to have an instinct to avoid every occasion of its mention,—if, when you speak, she drops into silence and changes the subject,—why, look there for something! just as, when going through deep meadow-grass, a bird flies ostentatiously up before you, you may know her nest is not there, but far off, under distant tufts of fern and buttercup, through which she has crept with a silent flutter in her spotted breast, to act her pretty little falsehood before you.

Poor Mary's little nest was along the sedgy margin of the sea-shore, where grow the tufts of golden-rod, where wave the reeds, where crimson, green, and purple sea-weeds float up, like torn fringes of Nereid vestures, and gold and silver shells lie on the wet wrinkles of the sands.

The sea had become to her like a friend, with its ever-varying monotony. Somehow she loved this old, fresh, blue, babbling, restless giant, who had carried away her heart's love to hide him in some far off palmy island, such as she had often heard him tell of in his sea romances. Sometimes she would wander out for an afternoon's stroll on the rocks, and pause by the great spouting cave, now famous to Newport *dilettanti*, but then a sacred and impressive solitude. There the rising tide bursts with deafening strokes through a narrow opening into some inner cavern, which, with a deep thunder-boom, like the voice of an angry lion, casts it back in a high jet of foam into the sea.

Mary often sat and listened to this hollow noise, and watched the ever-rising columns of spray as they reddened with the transpiercing beams of the afternoon sun; and thence her eye travelled far, far off over the shimmering starry blue, where sails looked no bigger than miller's wings; and it seemed sometimes as if a door were opening by which her soul might go out into some eternity,—some abyss, so wide and deep, that fathomless lines of thought could not sound it. She was no longer a girl in a mortal body, but an infinite spirit, the adoring companion of Infinite Beauty and Infinite Love.

As there was an hour when the fishermen of Galilee saw their Master transfigured, his raiment white and glistening, and his face like the light, so are there hours when our whole mortal life stands forth in a celestial radiance. From our daily lot falls off every weed of care,—from our heart-friends every speck and stain of earthly infirmity. Our horizon widens, and blue, and amethyst, and gold touch every object. Absent friends and friends gone on the last long journey stand once more together, bright with an immortal glow, and, like the disciples who saw their Master floating in the clouds above them, we say, 'Lord, it is good to be here!' How fair the wife, the husband, the absent mother, the gray-haired father, the manly son, the bright-eyed daughter! Seen in the actual present, all have some fault, some flaw; but absent, we see them in their permanent and better selves. Of our distant home we remember not one dark day, not one servile care, nothing but the echo of its holy hymns and the radiance of its brightest days,—of our father, not one hasty word, but only the fulness of his manly vigour and noble tenderness,—of our mother, nothing of mortal weakness, but a glorified form of love,—of our brother, not one teasing, provoking word of brotherly freedom, but the proud beauty of his noblest hours,—of our sister, our child, only what is fairest and sweetest.

This is to life the true ideal, the calm glass, wherein looking, we shall see, that, whatever defects cling to us, they are not, after all, permanent, and that we are tending to something nobler than we yet are;—it is 'the earnest of our inheritance until the redemption of the purchased possession.' In the resurrection we shall see our friends for ever as we see them in these clairvoyant hours.

We are writing thus on and on, linking image and thought and feeling, and lingering over every flower, and listening to every bird, because just before us there lies a dark valley, and we shrink and tremble to enter it.

But it *must* come, and why do we delay?

Towards evening, one afternoon in the latter part of June, Mary returned from one of these lonely walks by the sea, and entered the kitchen. It was still in its calm and sober cleanness;—the tall clock ticked with a startling distinctness. From the half-closed door of her mother's bedroom, which stood ajar, she heard the chipper of Miss Prissy's voice. She stayed her light footsteps, and the words that fell on her ear were these:—

'Miss Marvyn fainted dead away;—she stood it till he came to *that;* but then she just clapped both hands together, as if she'd been shot, and fell right forward on the floor in a faint!'

What could this be? There was a quick, intense whirl of thoughts in Mary's mind, and then came one of those awful moments when the powers of life seem to make a dead pause and all things stand still; and then all seemed to fail under her, and the life to sink down, down, down, till nothing was but one dim, vague, miserable consciousness.

Mrs. Scudder and Miss Prissy were sitting, talking earnestly, on the foot of the bed, when the door opened noiselessly, and Mary glided to them like a spirit,—no colour in cheek or lip,—her blue eyes wide with calm horror; and laying her little hand, with a nervous grasp, on Miss Prissy's arm, she said,—

'Tell me,—what is it?—is it?—is he—dead?'

The two women looked at each other, and then Mrs. Scudder opened her arms.

'My daughter!'

'Oh! mother! mother!'

Then fell that long, hopeless silence, broken only by hysteric sobs from Miss Prissy, and answering ones from the mother; but *she* lay still and quiet, her blue eyes wide and clear, making an inarticulate moan.

'Oh! are they *sure?—can* it be?—*is* he dead?' at last she gasped.

'My child, it is too true; all we can say is, "Be still, and know that I am God!"'

'I shall *try* to be still, mother,' said Mary, with a piteous, hopeless voice, like the bleat of a dying lamb; 'but I did not think he *could* die!—I never thought of that!—I never *thought* of it!—Oh! mother! mother! mother! oh! what shall I do?'

They laid her on her mother's bed,—the first and last resting-place of broken hearts,—and the mother sat down by her in silence. Miss Prissy stole away into the Doctor's study, and told him all that had happened.

'It's the same to her,' said Miss Prissy, with womanly reserve, 'as if he'd been an own brother.'

'What was his spiritual state?' said the Doctor, musingly.

Miss Prissy looked blank, and answered mournfully,—

'I don't know.'

The Doctor entered the room where Mary was lying with closed eyes. Those few moments seemed to have done the work of years,—so pale, and faded, and sunken she looked; nothing but the painful flutter of the eyelids and lips showed that she yet breathed. At a sign from Mrs. Scudder, he kneeled by the bed, and began to pray,—'Lord, thou hast been our dwelling-place in all generations,'—prayer deep, mournful, upheaving like the swell of the ocean, surging upward, under the pressure of mighty sorrows, towards an Almighty heart.

The truly good are of one language in prayer. Whatever lines or angles of thought may separate them in other hours, *when they pray in extremity*, all good men pray alike. The Emperor Charles V. and Martin Luther, two great generals of opposite faiths, breathed out their dying struggle in the self-same words.

There be many tongues and many languages of men,—but the language of prayer is one by itself, *in* all and *above* all. It is the inspiration of that Spirit that is ever working with our spirit, and constantly lifting us higher than we know, and, by our wants, by our woes, by our tears, by our yearnings, by our poverty, urging us, with mightier and mightier force, against those chains of sin which keep us from our God. We speak not of *things* conventionally called prayers,—vain mutterings of unawakened spirits talking drowsily in sleep,—but of such prayers as come when flesh and heart fail, in mighty straits;—*then* he who prays is a prophet, and a Mightier than he speaks in him; for the '*Spirit* helpeth our infirmities; for we know not what we should pray for as we ought; but the Spirit itself maketh intercession for us, with groanings which cannot be uttered.'

So the voice of supplication, upheaving from that great heart, so childlike in its humility, rose with a wisdom and a pathos beyond what he dreamed in his intellectual hours; it uprose even as a strong angel, whose brow is solemnly calm, and whose wings shed healing dews of paradise.

CHAPTER XXI.

THE next day broke calm and fair. The robins sang remorselessly in the apple-tree, and were answered by bobolink, oriole, and a whole tribe of ignorant little bits of feathered, happiness that danced among the leaves. Golden and glorious unclosed those purple eyelids of the East, and regally came up the sun; and the treacherous sea broke into ten thousand smiles, laughing and dancing with every ripple, as unconsciously as if no form dear to human hearts had gone down beneath it. Oh! treacherous, deceiving beauty of outward things! beauty, wherein throbs not one answering nerve to human pain!

Mary rose early and was about her morning work. Her education was that of the soldier, who must know himself no more, whom no personal pain must swerve from the slightest minutiæ of duty. So she was there, at her usual hour, dressed with the same cool neatness, her brown hair parted in satin bands, and only the colourless cheek and lip differing from the Mary of yesterday.

How strange this external habit of living! One thinks how to stick in a pin, and how to tie a string,—one busies one's self with folding robes, and putting away napkins, the day after some stroke that has cut the inner life in two, with the heart's blood dropping quietly at every step.

Yet it is better so! Happy those whom stern principle or long habit or hard necessity calls from the darkened room, the languid trance of pain, in which the wearied heart longs to indulge, and gives this trite prose of common life, at which our weak and wearied appetites so revolt!

Mary never thought of such a thing as self-indulgence;—this daughter of the Puritans had her seed within her. Aërial in her delicacy, as the blue-eyed flax-flower with which they sowed their fields, she had yet its strong fibre, which no stroke of the flail could break; bruising and hackling only made it fitter for uses of homely utility. Mary, therefore, opened the kitchen-door at dawn, and, after standing one moment to breathe the freshness, began spreading the cloth for an early breakfast. Mrs. Scudder, the meanwhile, was kneading the bread that had been set to rise over-night; and the oven was crackling and roaring with a large-throated, honest garrulousness.

But, ever and anon, as the mother worked, she followed the motions of her child anxiously.

'Mary, my dear,' she said, 'the eggs are giving out; hadn't you better run to the barn and get a few?'

Most mothers are instinctive philosophers. No treatise on the laws of nervous fluids could have taught Mrs. Scudder a better *rôle* for this morning, than her tender gravity, and her constant expedients to break and ripple, by changing employments, that deep, deadly under-current of thoughts which she feared might undermine her child's life.

Mary went into the barn, stopped a moment, and took out a handful of corn to throw to her hens, who had a habit of running towards her and cocking an expectant eye to her little hand whenever she appeared. All came at once flying towards her,—speckled, white, and gleamy with hues between of tawny orange-gold,—the cocks, magnificent with the blade-like waving of their tails,—and, as they chattered and cackled and pressed and crowded about her, pecking the corn even where it lodged in the edge of her little shoes, she said, 'Poor things, I am glad they enjoy it!'—and even this one little act of love to the ignorant fellowship below her carried away some of the choking pain which seemed all the while suffocating her heart. Then, climbing into the hay, she sought the nest and filled her little basket with eggs, warm, translucent, pinky-white in their freshness. She felt, for a moment, the customary animation in surveying her new treasures; but suddenly, like a vision rising before her, came a remembrance of once when she and James were children together and had been seeking eggs just there. He flashed before her eyes, the bright boy with the long black lashes, the dimpled cheeks, the merry eyes, just as he stood and threw the hay over her when they tumbled and laughed together,—and she sat down with a sick faintness, and then turned and walked wearily in.

CHAPTER XXII.

MARY returned to the house with her basket of warm, fresh eggs, which she set down mournfully upon the table. In her heart there was one conscious want and yearning, and that was to go to the friends of him she had lost—to go to his mother. The first impulse of bereavement is to stretch out the hands towards what was nearest and dearest to the departed.

Her dove came fluttering down out of the tree and settled on her hand, and began asking in his dumb way to be noticed. Mary stroked his white feathers, and bent her head down over them till they were wet with tears. 'Oh, birdie, you live, but he is gone!' she said. Then suddenly putting it gently from her, and going near and throwing her arms around her mother's neck,—'Mother,' she said, 'I want to go up to Cousin Ellen's.' (This was the familiar name by which she always called Mrs. Marvyn.) 'Can't you go with me, mother?'

'My daughter, I have thought of it. I hurried about my baking this morning, and sent word to Mr. Jenkyns that he needn't come to see about the chimney, because I expected to go as soon as breakfast should be out of the way. So hurry, now, boil some eggs, and get on the cold beef and potatoes, for I see Solomon and Amaziah coming in with the milk. They'll want their breakfast immediately.'

The breakfast for the hired men was soon arranged on the table, and Mary sat down to preside while her mother was going on with her baking, introducing various loaves of white and brown bread into the capacious oven by means of a long iron shovel, and discoursing at intervals with Solomon with regard to the different farming operations which he had in hand for the day.

Solomon was a tall, large-boned man, brawny and angular, with a face tanned by the sun, and graven with those considerate lines which New England so early writes on the faces of her sons. He was reputed an oracle in matters of agriculture and cattle, and, like oracles generally, was prudently sparing of his responses. Amaziah was one of those uncouth over-grown boys of eighteen, whose physical bulk appears to have so suddenly developed that the soul has more matter than she has learned to recognize, so that the hapless individual is always awkwardly conscious of too much limb; and in Amaziah's case this consciousness grew particularly distressing when Mary was in the room. He liked to have her there, he said, 'but somehow she was so white and pretty, she made him feel sort o' awful-like.'

Of course, as such poor mortals always do, he must, on this particular morning, blunder into precisely the wrong subject.

'S'pose you've heerd the news that Jeduthan Pettibone brought home in the "Flying Scud," 'bout the wreck o' the "Monsoon;" it's an awful providence, that 'ar' is—a'n't it? Why Jeduthan says she jest crushed like an egg-shell'—and with that Amaziah illustrated the fact by crushing an egg-shell in his great brown hand.

Mary did not answer. She could not grow any paler than she was before; a dreadful curiosity came over her, but her lips could frame no question. Amaziah went on:

'Ye see, the cap'en he got killed with a spar when the blow fust come on, and Jim Marvyn he commanded; and Jeduthan says that he seemed to have the spirit of ten men in him. He worked, and he watched, and he was everywhere at once, and he kep' 'em all up for three days, till finally they lost their rudder, and went drivin' right onto the rocks. When they come in sight, he come up on deck, and says he, "Well, my boys, we're headin' right into eternity," says he, "and our chances for this world a'n't worth mentionin', any on us; but we'll all have one try for our lives. Boys, I've tried to do my duty by you and the ship—but God's will be done! All I have to ask now is, that if any of you git to shore, you'll find my mother and tell her I died thinkin' of her and father and my dear friends." That was the last Jeduthan saw of him, for in a few minutes more the ship struck, and then it was every man for himself. Laws! Jeduthan says there couldn't nobody have stood beatin' agin them rocks unless they was all leather and inger-rubber like him. Why, he says the waves would take strong men and jest crush 'em against the rocks like smashin' a pie-plate!'

Here Mary's paleness became livid; she made a hasty motion to rise from the table, and Solomon trod on the foot of the narrator.

'You seem to forget that friends and relations has feelin's,' he said, as Mary hastily went into her own room.

Amaziah, suddenly awakened to the fact that he had been trespassing, sat with mouth half open and a stupefied look of perplexity on his face for a moment, and then, rising hastily, said: 'Well, Sol, I guess I'll go an' yoke up the steers.'

At eight o'clock all the morning toils were over, the wide kitchen cool and still, and the one-horse waggon standing at the door, into which climbed Mary, her mother, and the Doctor, for, though invested with no spiritual authority, and charged with no ritual or form for hours of affliction, the religion of New England always expects her minister as a first visitor in every house of mourning.

The ride was a sorrowful and silent one. The Doctor, propped upon his cane, seemed to reflect deeply.

'Have you been at all conversant with the exercises of our young friend's mind on the subject of religion?' he asked.

Mrs. Scudder did not at first reply. The remembrance of James's last letter flashed over her mind, and she felt the vibration of the frail child beside her, in whom every nerve was quivering. After a moment she said: 'It does not become us to judge the spiritual state of any one. James's mind was in an unsettled way when he left; but who can say what wonders may have been effected by Divine grace since then?'

This conversation fell on the soul of Mary like the sound of clods falling on a coffin to the ear of one buried alive; she heard it with a dull, smothering sense of suffocation. *That* question to be raised!—and about one, too, for whom she could have given her own soul! At this moment she felt how idle is the mere hope or promise of personal salvation made to one who has passed beyond the life of self, and struck deep the roots of his existence in others. She did not utter a word—how could she? A doubt—the faintest shadow of a doubt—in such a case, falls on the soul with the weight of mountain certainty, and in that short ride she felt what an infinite pain may be locked in one small, silent breast.

The waggon drew up to the house of mourning. Cato stood at the gate, and came forward, officiously, to help them out. 'Mass'r and Missis will be glad to see you,' he said. 'It's a dreffful stroke has come upon 'em.'

Candace appeared at the door. There was a majesty of sorrow in her bearing as she received them. She said not a word, but pointed with her finger towards the inner room; but as Mary lifted up her faded, weary face to hers, her whole soul seemed to heave towards her like a billow, and she took her up in her arms and broke forth into sobbing, and, carrying her in, as if she had been a child, set her down in the inner room and sat down beside her.

Mrs. Marvyn and her husband sat together, holding each other's hands, the open Bible between them. For a few moments nothing was to be heard but sobs and unrestrained weeping, and then all kneeled down while the Doctor prayed.

After they rose up, Mr. Zebedee Marvyn stood for a moment thoughtfully, and then said: 'If it had pleased the Lord to give me a sure evidence of my son's salvation, I could have given him up with all my heart; but now, whatever there may be, I have seen none.' He stood in an attitude of hopeless, heart-smitten dejection, which contrasted painfully with his usual upright carriage and the firm lines of his face.

Mrs. Marvyn started as if a sword had pierced her, passed her arm round Mary's waist, with a strong, nervous clasp, unlike her usual calm self, and said, 'Stay with me, daughter, to-day!—stay with me!'

'Mary can stay as long as you wish, cousin,' said Mrs. Scudder; 'we have nothing to call her home.'

'*Come* with me!' said Mrs. Marvyn to Mary, opening an adjoining door into her bedroom, and drawing her in with a sort of suppressed vehemence, 'I want you!—I must have you!'

'Mrs. Marvyn's state alarms me,' said her husband, looking apprehensively after her when the door was closed; 'she has not shed any tears nor slept any since she heard this news. You know that her mind has been in a peculiar and unhappy state with regard to religious things for many years. I was in hopes she might feel free to open her exercises of mind to the Doctor.'

'Perhaps she will feel more freedom with Mary,' said the Doctor. 'There is no healing for such troubles except in unconditional submission to Infinite Wisdom and Goodness. The Lord reigneth, and will at last bring infinite good out of evil, whether *our* small portion of existence be included or not.'

After a few moments more of conference, Mrs. Scudder and the Doctor departed, leaving Mary alone in the house of mourning.

CHAPTER XXIII.

WE have said before, what we now repeat, that it is impossible to write a story of New England life and manners for superficial thought or shallow feeling. They who would fully understand the springs which moved the characters with whom we now associate must go down with us to the very depths.

Never was there a community where the roots of common life shot down so deeply, and were so intensely grappled around things sublime and eternal. The founders of it were a body of confessors and martyrs, who turned their backs on the whole glory of the visible to found in the wilderness a republic of which the God of heaven and earth should be the sovereign power. For the first hundred years grew this community, shut out by a fathomless ocean from the existing world, and divided by an antagonism not less deep from all the reigning ideas of nominal Christendom.

In a community thus unworldly must have arisen a mode of thought, energetic, original, and sublime. The leaders of thought and feeling were the ministry, and we boldly assert that the spectacle of the early ministry of New England was one to which the world gives no parallel. Living an intense, earnest, practical life, mostly tilling the earth with their own hands, they yet carried on the most startling and original religious investigations with a simplicity that might have been deemed audacious, were it not so reverential. All old issues relating to government, religion, ritual, and forms of church organization having for them passed away, they went straight to the heart of things, and boldly confronted the problem of universal being. They had come out from the world as witnesses to the most solemn and sacred of human rights. They had accustomed themselves boldly to challenge and dispute all sham pretensions and idolatries of past ages—to question the right of kings in the State and of prelates in the Church; and now they turned the same bold inquiries towards the Eternal Throne, and threw down their glove in the lists as authorized defenders of every mystery in the Eternal Government. The task they proposed to themselves was that of reconciling the most tremendous facts of sin and evil, present and eternal, with those conceptions of Infinite Power and Benevolence which their own strong and generous natures enabled them so vividly to realize. In the intervals of planting and harvesting they were busy with the toils of adjusting the laws of a universe. Solemnly simple, they made long journeys in their old one-horse chaises to settle with each other some nice point of celestial jurisprudence, and to compare their maps of the Infinite. Their letters to each other form a literature altogether unique. Hopkins sends to Edwards the younger his scheme of the universe, in which he starts with the proposition that God is infinitely above all obligations of any kind to his creatures. Edwards replies with the brusque comment:—'This is wrong; God has no more right to injure a creature than a creature has to injure God;' and each probably about that time preached a sermon on his own views, which was discussed by every farmer, in intervals of plough and hoe, by every woman and girl, at loom, spinning-wheel, or wash-tub. New England was one vast sea, surging from depths to heights with thought and discussion on the most insoluble of mysteries. And it is to be added that no man or woman accepted any theory or speculation simply *as* theory or speculation; all was profoundly real and vital—a foundation on which actual life was based with intensest earnestness.

The views of human existence which resulted from this course of training were gloomy enough to oppress any heart which did not rise above them by triumphant faith, or sink below them by brutish insensibility; for they included every moral problem of natural or revealed religion, divested of all those softening poetries and tender draperies which, forms, ceremonies, and rituals had thrown around them in other parts and ages of Christendom. The human race, without exception, coming into existence 'under God's wrath and curse,' with a nature so fatally disordered, that, although perfect free agents, men were infallibly certain to do nothing to Divine acceptance until regenerated by the supernatural aid of God's Spirit, this aid being given to a certain decreed number of the human race only; the rest, with enough free agency to make them responsible, but without this indispensable assistance exposed to the malignant assaults of evil spirits versed in every art of temptation, were sure to fall hopelessly into perdition. The standard of what constituted a true regeneration, as presented in such treatises as Edwards on the Affections, and others of the times, made this change to be something so high, disinterested, and superhuman, so removed from all natural and common habits and feelings, that the most earnest and devoted, whose whole life had been a constant travail of endeavour, a tissue of almost unearthly disinterestedness, often lived and died with only a glimmering hope of its attainment.

According to any views then entertained of the evidences of a true regeneration, the number of the whole human race who could be supposed as yet to have received this grace was so small, that, as to any numerical valuation, it must have been expressed by an infinitesimal. Dr. Hopkins, in many places, distinctly recognizes the fact, that the greater part of the human race, up to his time, had been eternally lost; and boldly assumes the ground, that this amount of sin and suffering, being the best and most necessary means of the greatest final amount of happiness, was not merely permitted, but distinctly chosen, decreed, and provided for, as essential in the schemes of Infinite Benevolence. He held that this decree not only *permitted* each individual act of sin, but also took measures to make it certain, though, by an exercise of infinite skill, it accomplished this result without violating human free agency.

CHAPTER XXIII.

The preaching of those times was animated by an unflinching consistency which never shrank from carrying an idea to its remotest logical verge. The sufferings of the lost were not kept from view, but proclaimed with a terrible power. Dr. Hopkins boldly asserts, that 'all the use which God will have for them is to suffer; this is all the end they can answer; therefore all their faculties, and their whole capacities, will be employed and used for this end.... The body can by omnipotence be made capable of suffering the greatest imaginable pain without producing dissolution, or abating the least degree of life or sensibility.... One way in which God will show his power in the punishment of the wicked, will be in strengthening and upholding their bodies and souls in torments which otherwise would be intolerable.'

The sermons preached by President Edwards on this subject are so terrific in their refined poetry of torture, that very few persons of quick sensibility could read them through without agony; and it is related that when in those calm and tender tones, which never rose to passionate enunciation, he read these discourses, the house was often filled with shrieks and wailings, and that a brother minister once laid hold of his skirts, exclaiming, in an involuntary agony, 'Oh! Mr. Edwards! Mr. Edwards! is God not a God of mercy?'

Not that these men were indifferent or insensible to the dread words they spoke; their whole lives and deportment bore thrilling witness to their sincerity. Edwards set apart special days of fasting, in view of the dreadful doom of the lost, in which he was wont to walk the floor, weeping and wringing his hands. Hopkins fasted every Saturday. David Brainerd gave up every refinement of civilized life to weep and pray at the feet of hardened savages, if by any means he might save *one*. All, by lives of eminent purity and earnestness, gave awful weight and sanction to their words.

If we add to this statement the fact, that it was always proposed to every inquiring soul, as an evidence of regeneration, that it should truly and heartily accept all the ways of God thus declared right and lovely, and from the heart submit to Him as the only just and good, it will be seen what materials of tremendous internal conflict and agitation were all the while working in every bosom. Almost all the histories of religious experience of those times relate paroxysms of opposition to God and fierce rebellion, expressed in language which appals the very soul, followed at length by mysterious elevations of faith and reactions of confiding love, the result of Divine interposition, which carried the soul far above the region of the intellect, into that of direct spiritual intuition.

President Edwards records that he was once in this state of enmity, that the facts of the Divine administration seemed horrible to him, and that this opposition was overcome by no course of reasoning, but by an '*inward and sweet sense*' which came to him once when walking alone in the fields, and, looking up into the blue sky, he saw the blending of the Divine majesty with a calm, sweet, and almost infinite meekness.

The piety which grew up under such a system was, of necessity, energetic; it was the uprousing of the whole energy of the human soul, pierced and wrenched and probed from her lowest depths to her topmost heights, with every awful life-force possible to existence. He whose faith in God came clear through these terrible tests, would be sure never to know greater ones. He might certainly challenge earth or heaven, things present or things to come, to swerve him from this grand allegiance.

But it is to be conceded that these systems, so admirable in relation to the energy, earnestness, and acuteness of their authors, when received as absolute truth, and as a basis of actual life, had, on minds of a certain class, the effect of a slow poison, producing life-habits of morbid action very different from any which ever followed the simple reading of the Bible. They differ from the New Testament as the living embrace of a friend does from his lifeless body, mapped out under the knife of the anatomical demonstrator; every nerve and muscle is there, but to a sensitive spirit there is the very chill of death in the analysis.

All systems that deal with the infinite are, besides, exposed to danger from small, unsuspected admixtures of human error, which become deadly when carried to such vast results. The smallest speck of earth's dust, in the focus of an infinite lens, appears magnified among the heavenly orbs as a frightful monster.

Thus it happened that while strong spirits walked, palm-crowned, with victorious hymns, along these sublime paths, feebler and more sensitive ones lay along the track, bleeding away in life-long despair. Fearful to them were the shadows that lay over the cradle and the grave. The mother clasped her babe to her bosom, and looked with shuddering to the awful coming trial of free agency, with its terrible responsibilities and risks, and, as she thought of the infinite chances against her beloved, almost wished it might die in infancy. But when the stroke of death came, and some young, thoughtless head was laid suddenly low, who can say what silent anguish of loving hearts sounded the dread depths of eternity with the awful question, *Where?*

In no other time or place of Christendom have so fearful issues been presented to the mind. Some church interposed its protecting shield; the Christian born and baptized child was supposed in some wise rescued from the curse of the fall, and related to the great redemption, to be a member of Christ's family, and, if ever so sinful, still infolded in some vague sphere of hope and protection. Augustine solaced the dread anxieties of trembling love by prayers offered for the dead, in times when the Church above and on earth presented itself to the eye of the mourner as a great assembly with one accord lifting interceding hands for the parted soul.

But the clear logic and intense individualism of New England deepened the problems of the Augustinian faith, while they swept away all those softening provisions so earnestly clasped to the throbbing heart of that great poet of theology. No rite, no form, no paternal relation, no faith or prayer of church, earthly or heavenly, interposed the slightest shield between the trembling spirit and Eternal Justice. The individual entered eternity alone, as if he had no interceding relation the universe.

CHAPTER XXIII.

This, then, was the awful dread which was constantly underlying life. This it was which caused the tolling bell in green hollows and lonely dells to be a sound which shook the soul and searched the heart with fearful questions. And this it was that was lying with mountain weight on the soul of the mother, too keenly agonized to feel that doubt in such a case was any less a torture than the most dreadful certainty.

Hers was a nature more reasoning than creative and poetic; and whatever she believed bound her mind in strictest chains to its logical results. She delighted in the regions of mathematical knowledge, and walked them as a native home; but the commerce with abstract certainties fitted her mind still more to be stiffened and enchained by glacial reasonings, in regions where spiritual intuitions are as necessary as wings to birds.

Mary was by nature of the class who never reason abstractly, whose intellections all begin in the heart, which sends them coloured with its warm life-tint to the brain. Her perceptions of the same subjects were as different from Mrs. Marvyn's as his who revels only in colour from his who is busy with the dry details of mere outline. The one mind was arranged like a map, and the other like a picture. In all the system which had been explained to her, her mind selected points on which it seized with intense sympathy, which it dwelt upon and expanded till all else fell away. The sublimity of disinterested benevolence, the harmony and order of a system tending in its final results to infinite happiness, the goodness of God, the love of a self-sacrificing Redeemer, were all so many glorious pictures, which she revolved in her mind with small care for their logical relations.

Mrs. Marvyn had never, in all the course of their intimacy, opened her mouth to Mary on the subject of religion. It was not an uncommon incident of those times for persons of great elevation and purity of character to be familiarly known and spoken of as living under a cloud of religious gloom; and it was simply regarded as one more mysterious instance of the workings of that infinite decree which denied to them the special illumination of the Spirit.

When Mrs. Marvyn had drawn Mary with her into her room, she seemed like a person almost in frenzy. She shut and bolted the door, drew her to the foot of the bed, and, throwing her arms round her, rested her hot and throbbing forehead on her shoulder. She pressed her thin hand over her eyes, and then, suddenly drawing back, looked her in the face as one resolved to speak something long suppressed. Her soft brown eyes had a flash of despairing wildness in them, like that of a hunted animal turning in its death-struggle on its pursuer.

'Mary,' she said, 'I can't help it,—don't mind what I say, but I must speak or die! Mary, I cannot, will not, be resigned!—it is all hard, unjust, cruel!—to all eternity I will say so! To me there is no goodness, no justice, no mercy in anything! Life seems to me the most tremendous doom that can be inflicted on a helpless being! *What had we done* that it should be sent upon us? Why were we made to love so, to hope so,—our hearts so full of feeling, and all the laws of Nature marching over us,—never stopping for our agony? Why, we can suffer so in this life that we had better never have been born!

'But, Mary, think what a moment life is! think of those awful ages of eternity! and then think of all God's power and knowledge used on the lost to make them suffer! think that all but the merest fragment of mankind have gone into this, are in it now! The number of the elect is so small we can scarce count them for anything! Think what noble minds, what warm, generous hearts, what splendid natures are wrecked and thrown away by thousands and tens of thousands! How we love each other! how our hearts weave into each other! how more than glad we should be to die for each other! And all this ends—O God, how must it end? Mary! it isn't *my* sorrow only! What right have I to mourn? Is *my* son any better than any other mother's son? Thousands of thousands, whose mothers loved them as I loved mine, are gone there! Oh, my wedding-day! Why did they rejoice? Brides should wear mourning, the bells should toll for every wedding; every new family is built over this awful pit of despair, and only one in a thousand escapes!'

Pale, aghast, horror-stricken, Mary stood dumb, as one who in the dark and storm sees by the sudden glare of lightning a chasm yawning under foot. It was amazement and dimness of anguish; the dreadful words struck on the very centre where her soul rested. She felt as if the point of a wedge were being driven between her life and her life's life, between her and her God. She clasped her hands instinctively on her bosom, as if to hold there some cherished image, and said in a piercing voice of supplication, '*My* God! *my* God! oh, where art Thou?'

Mrs. Marvyn walked up and down the room with a vivid spot of red in each cheek and a baleful fire in her eyes, talking in rapid soliloquy, scarcely regarding her listener, absorbed in her own enkindled thoughts.

'Dr. Hopkins says that this is all best, better than it would have been in any other possible way; that God *chose* it because it was for a greater final good; that He not only chose it, but took means to make it certain, that He ordains every sin, and does all that is necessary to make it certain; that He creates the vessels of wrath and fits them for destruction; and that He has an infinite knowledge by which He can do it without violating their free agency. So much the worse! What a use of infinite knowledge! What if men should do so? What if a father should take means to make it certain that his poor little child should be an abandoned wretch, without violating his free agency? So much the worse, I say! They say He does this so that He may show to all eternity, by their example, the evil nature of sin and its consequences! This is all that the greater part of the human race have been used for yet; and it is all right, because an overplus of infinite happiness is yet to be wrought out by it! It is *not* right! No possible amount of good to ever so many can make it right to deprave ever so few; happiness and misery cannot be measured so! I never can think it right, never! Yet they say our salvation depends on our loving God, loving Him better than ourselves, loving Him better than our dearest friends. It is impossible! it is contrary to the laws of my nature! I can never love God! I can never praise Him! I am lost! lost! lost! And what is worse, I cannot redeem my friends! Oh, I *could* suffer for ever, how willingly! if I could save *him!* But oh, eternity, eternity! Frightful, unspeakable woe! No end! no bottom! no shore! no hope! O God! O God!'

Mrs. Marvyn's eyes grew wilder,—she walked the floor, wringing her hands,—and her words, mingled with shrieks and moans, became whirling and confused, as when in autumn a storm drives the leaves in dizzy mazes.

Mary was alarmed,—the ecstasy of despair was just verging on insanity. She rushed out and called Mr. Marvyn.

'Oh! come in! do! quick!—I'm afraid her mind is going!' she said.

'It is what I feared,' he said, rising from where he sat reading his great Bible, with an air of heartbroken dejection. 'Since she heard this news, she has not slept nor shed a tear. The Lord hath covered us with a cloud in the day of His fierce anger.'

He came into the room, and tried to take his wife to his arms. She pushed him violently back, her eyes glistening with a fierce light. 'Leave me alone!' she said,—'I am a lost spirit!'

These words were uttered in a shriek that went through Mary's heart like an arrow.

At this moment, Candace, who had been anxiously listening at the door for an hour past, suddenly burst into the room.

'Lor' bress ye, Squire Marvyn, we won't hab her goin' on dis yer way,' she said. 'Do talk *gospel* to her, can't ye—ef you can't, I will.'

'Come, ye poor little lamb,' she said, walking straight up to Mrs. Marvyn, 'come to ole Candace!'—and with that she gathered the pale form to her bosom, and sat down and began rocking her, as if she had been a babe. 'Honey, darlin', ye a'n't right, dar's a drefful mistake somewhar,' she said. 'Why, de Lord a'n't like what ye tink,—He *loves* ye, honey! Why, jes' feel how *I* loves ye,—poor ole black Candace,—an' I a'n't better'n Him as made me! Who was it wore de crown o' thorns, lamb?—who was it sweat great drops o' blood?—who was it said, "Father, forgive dem"? Say, honey!—wasn't it de Lord dat made ye?—Dar, dar, now ye'r' cryin'!—cry away, and ease yer poor little heart! He died for Mass'r Jim,—loved him and *died* for him,—jes' give up His sweet, precious body and soul for him on de cross! Laws, jes' *leave* him in Jesus' hands! Why, honey, dar's de very print o' de nails in his hands now!'

The flood-gates were rent; and healing sobs and tears shook the frail form, as a faded lily shakes under the soft rains of summer. All in the room wept together.

'Now, honey,' said Candace, after a pause of some minutes, 'I knows our Doctor's a mighty good man, an' larned,—an' in fair weather I ha'n't no 'bjection to yer hearin' all about dese yer great an' mighty tings he's got to say. But, honey, dey won't do for you now; sick folks mus'n't hab strong meat; an' times like dese, dar jest a'n't but one ting to come to, an' dat ar's *Jesus*. Jes' come right down to whar poor ole black Candace has to stay allers,—it's a good place, darlin'! *Look right at Jesus.* Tell ye, honey, ye can't live no other way now. Don't ye 'member how He looked on His mother, when she stood faintin' an' tremblin' under de cross, jes' like you? He knows all about mothers' hearts; He won't break yours. It was jes' 'cause He know'd we'd come into straits like dis yer, dat He went through all dese tings,—Him, de Lord o' Glory! Is dis Him you was a-talkin' about?—Him you can't love? Look at Him, an' see ef you can't. Look an' see what He is!—don't ask no questions, and don't go to no reasonin's,—jes' look at *Him*, hangin' dar, so sweet and patient, on de cross! All dey could do couldn't stop his lovin' 'em; He prayed for 'em wid all de breath He had. Dar's a God you can love, a'n't dar? Candace loves Him,—poor, ole, foolish, black, wicked Candace,—and she knows He loves her,'—and here Candace broke down into torrents of weeping.

They laid the mother, faint and weary, on her bed, and beneath the shadow of that suffering cross came down a healing sleep on those weary eyelids.

'Honey,' said Candace, mysteriously, after she had drawn Mary out of the room, 'don't ye go for to troublin' yer mind wid dis yer. I'm clar Mass'r James is one o' de 'lect; and I'm clar dar's consid'able more o' de 'lect dan people tink. Why, Jesus didn't die for nothin',—all dat love a'n't gwine to be wasted. De 'lect is more'n you or I knows, honey! Dar's de *Spirit,*—He'll give it to 'em; and ef Mass'r James *is* called an' took, depend upon it de Lord has got him ready,—course He has,—so don't ye go to layin' on yer poor heart what no mortal creetur can live under; 'cause, as we's got to live in dis yer world, it's quite clar de Lord must ha' fixed it so we *can;* and ef tings was as some folks suppose, why, we *couldn't* live, and dar wouldn't be no sense in anyting dat goes on.'

The sudden shock of these scenes was followed, in Mrs. Marvyn's case, by a low, lingering fever. Her room was darkened, and she lay on her bed, a pale, suffering form, with scarcely the ability to raise her hand. The shimmering twilight of the sick-room fell on white napkins, spread over stands, where constantly appeared new vials, big and little, as the physician made his daily visit, and prescribed now this drug and now that, for a wound that had struck through the soul.

Mary remained many days at the white house, because, to the invalid, no step, no voice, no hand was like hers. We see her there now, as she sits in the glimmering by the bed-curtains,—her head a little drooped, as droops a snowdrop over a grave;—one ray of light from a round hole in the closed shutters falls on her smooth-parted hair, her small hands clasped on her knees, her mouth has lines of sad compression, and in her eyes are infinite questionings.

CHAPTER XXIV.

WHEN Mrs. Marvyn began to amend, Mary returned to the home cottage, and resumed the details of her industrious and quiet life.

Between her and her two best friends had fallen a curtain of silence. The subject that filled all her thoughts could not be named between them. The Doctor often looked at her pale cheeks and drooping form with a face of honest sorrow, and heaved deep sighs as she passed; but he did not find any power within himself by which he could approach her. When he would speak, and she turned her sad, patient eyes so gently on him, the words went back again to his heart, and there, taking a second thought, spread upward wing in prayer.

Mrs. Scudder sometimes came to her room after she was gone to bed, and found her weeping; and when gently she urged her to sleep, she would wipe her eyes so patiently and turn her head with such obedient sweetness, that her mother's heart utterly failed her. For hours Mary sat in her room with James's last letter spread out before her. How anxiously had she studied every word and phrase in it, weighing them to see if the hope of eternal life were in them! How she dwelt on those last promises! Had he kept them? Ah! to die without one word more! Would no angel tell her?—would not the loving God, who knew all, just whisper one word? He must have read the little Bible! What had he thought? What did he feel in that awful hour when he felt himself drifting on to that fearful eternity? Perhaps he had been regenerated,—perhaps there had been a sudden change;—who knows?—she had read of such things;—*perhaps*——Ah, in that perhaps lies a world of anguish! Love will not hear of it. Love *dies* for certainty. Against an uncertainty who can brace the soul? We put all our forces of faith and prayer against it, and it goes down just as a buoy sinks in the water, and the next moment it is up again. The soul fatigues itself with efforts which come and go in waves; and when with laborious care she has adjusted all things in the light of hope, back flows the tide, and sweeps all away. In such struggles life spends itself fast; an inward wound does not carry one deathward more surely than this worst wound of the soul. God has made us so mercifully that there is no *certainty*, however dreadful, to which life-forces do not in time adjust themselves,—but to uncertainty there is no possible adjustment. Where is he? Oh, question of questions!—question which we suppress, but which a power of infinite force still urges on the soul, who feels a part of herself torn away.

Mary sat at her window in evening hours, and watched the slanting sunbeams through the green blades of grass, and thought one year ago he stood there, with his well-knit, manly form, his bright eye, his buoyant hope, his victorious mastery of life! And where was he now? Was his heart as sick, longing for her, as hers for him? Was he looking back to earth and its joys with pangs of unutterable regret? or had a divine power interpenetrated his soul, and lighted there the flame of a celestial love which bore him far above earth? If he were among the lost, in what age of eternity could she ever be blessed? Could Christ be happy, if those who were one with Him were sinful and accursed? and could Christ's own loved ones be happy, when those with whom they have exchanged being, in whom they live and feel, are as wandering stars, for whom is reserved the mist of darkness for ever? She had been taught that the agonies of the lost would be for ever in sight of the saints, without abating in the least their eternal joys; nay, that they would find in it increasing motives to praise and adoration. Could it be so? Would the last act of the great Bridegroom of the Church be to strike from the heart of his purified Bride those yearnings of self-devoting love which His whole example had taught her, and in which she reflected, as in a glass, His own nature? If not, is there not some provision by which those roots of deathless love which Christ's betrothed ones strike into other hearts shall have a divine, redeeming power? Question vital as life-blood to ten thousand hearts,—fathers, mothers, wives, husbands,—to all who feel the infinite sacredness of love!

After the first interview with Mrs. Marvyn, the subject which had so agitated them was not renewed. She had risen at last from her sick-bed, as thin and shadowy as a faded moon after sunrise. Candace often shook her head mournfully, as her eyes followed her about her daily tasks. Once only, with Mary, she alluded to the conversation which had passed between them;—it was one day when they were together, spinning, in the north upper room that looked out upon the sea. It was a glorious day. A ship was coming in under full sail, with white gleaming wings. Mrs. Marvyn watched it a few moments,—the gay creature, so full of exultant life,—and then smothered down an inward groan, and Mary thought she heard her saying, 'Thy will be done!'

'Mary,' she said, gently, 'I hope you will forget all I said to you that dreadful day. It had to be said, or I should have died. Mary, I begin to think that it is not best to stretch our minds with reasonings where we are so limited, where we can know so little. I am quite sure there must be dreadful mistakes somewhere.

'It seems to me irreverent and shocking that a child should oppose a father, or a creature its Creator. I never should have done it, only that, where direct questions are presented to the judgment, one cannot help judging. If one is required to praise a being as just and good, one must judge of his actions by some standard of right,—and we have no standard but such as our Creator has placed in us. I have been told it was my duty to attend to these subjects, and I have tried to,—and the result has been that the facts presented seem wholly irreconcilable with any notions of justice or mercy that I am able to form. If these be the facts, I can only say that my nature is made entirely opposed to them. If I followed the standard of right they present, and acted according to my small mortal powers on the same principles, I should be a very bad person. Any father, who should make such use of power over his children as they say the Deity does with regard to us, would be looked upon as a monster by our very imperfect moral sense. Yet I cannot say that the facts are not so. When I heard the Doctor's sermons on "Sin a Necessary Means of the Greatest Good," I could not extricate myself from the reasoning.

'I have thought, in desperate moments, of giving up the Bible itself. But what do I gain? Do I not see the same difficulty in Nature? I see everywhere a Being whose main ends seem to be beneficent, but whose good purposes are worked out at terrible expense of suffering, and apparently by the total sacrifice of myriads of sensitive creatures. I see unflinching order, general good-will, but no sympathy, no mercy. Storms, earthquakes, volcanoes, sickness, death, go on without regarding us. Everywhere I see the most hopeless, unrelieved suffering,—and for aught I see, it may be eternal. Immortality is a dreadful chance, and I would rather never have been.—The Doctor's dreadful system is, I confess, much like the laws of Nature, about what one may reason out from them.

'There is but just one thing remaining, and that is, as Candace said, the cross of Christ. If God so loved us,—if He died for us,—greater love hath no man than this. It seems to me that love is shown here in the two highest forms possible to our comprehension. We see a Being who gives himself for us,—and more than that, harder than that, a Being who consents to the suffering of a dearer than self. Mary, I feel that I must love more, to give up one of my children to suffer, than to consent to suffer myself. There is a world of comfort to me in the words, "He that spared not his own Son, but delivered him up for us all, how shall he not with him also freely give us all things?" These words speak to my heart. I can interpret them by my own nature, and I rest on them. If there is a fathomless mystery of sin and sorrow, there is a deeper mystery of God's love. So, Mary, I try Candace's way,—I look at Christ,—I pray to Him. If he that hath seen Him hath seen the Father, it is enough. I rest there,—I wait. What I know not now I shall know hereafter.'

Mary kept all things and pondered them in her heart. She could speak to no one,—not to her mother, nor to her spiritual guide, for had she not passed to a region beyond theirs? As well might those on the hither side of mortality instruct the souls gone beyond the veil as souls outside a great affliction guide those who are struggling in it. That is a mighty baptism, and only Christ can go down with us into those waters.

Mrs. Scudder and the Doctor only marked that she was more than ever conscientious in every duty, and that she brought to life's daily realities something of the calmness and disengagedness of one whose soul has been wrenched by a mighty shock from all moorings here below. Hopes did not excite, fears did not alarm her; life had no force strong enough to awaken a thrill within; and the only subjects on which she ever spoke with any degree of ardour were religious subjects.

One who should have seen moving about the daily ministrations of the cottage a pale girl, whose steps were firm, whose eye was calm, whose hands were ever busy, would scarce imagine that through that silent heart were passing tides of thought that measured a universe; but it was even so. Through that one gap of sorrow flowed in the whole awful mystery of existence, and silently, as she spun and sewed, she thought over and over again all that she had ever been taught, and compared and revolved it by the light of a dawning inward revelation.

Sorrow is the great birth-agony of immortal powers; sorrow is the great searcher and revealer of hearts, the great test of truth; for Plato has wisely said, sorrow will not endure sophisms; all shams and unrealities melt in the fire of that awful furnace. Sorrow reveals forces in ourselves we never dreamed of. The soul, a bound and sleeping prisoner, hears her knock on her cell-door, and wakens. Oh, how narrow the walls! oh, how close and dark the grated window! how the long useless wings beat against the impassable barriers! Where are we? What *is* this prison? What *is* beyond? Oh for more air, more light! When will the door be opened? The soul seems to itself to widen and to deepen; it trembles at its own dreadful forces; it gathers up in waves that break with wailing, only to flow back into the everlasting void. The calmest and most centred natures are sometimes thrown by the shock of a great sorrow into a tumultuous amazement. All things are changed. The earth no longer seems solid, the skies no longer secure; a deep abyss seems underlying every joyous scene of life. The soul, struck with this awful inspiration, is a mournful Cassandra; she sees blood on every threshold, and shudders in the midst of mirth and festival with the weight of a terrible wisdom.

Who shall dare be glad any more, that has once seen the frail foundations on which love and joy are built? Our brighter hours, have they only been weaving a network of agonizing remembrances for this day of bereavement? The heart is pierced with every past joy, with every hope of its ignorant prosperity. Behind every scale in music, the gayest and cheeriest, the grandest, the most triumphant, lies its dark relative minor; the notes are the same, but the change of a semitone changes all to gloom; all our gayest hours are tunes that have a modulation into these dreary keys ever possible; at any moment the key-note may be struck.

The firmest, best-prepared natures are often beside themselves with astonishment and dismay, when they are called to this dread initiation. They thought it a very happy world before,—a glorious universe. Now it is darkened with the shadow of insoluble mysteries. Why this everlasting tramp of inevitable laws on quivering life? If the wheels must roll, why must the crushed be so living and sensitive?

And yet sorrow is god-like, sorrow is grand and great, sorrow is wise and far-seeing. Our own instinctive valuations, the intense sympathy which we give to the tragedy which God has inwoven into the laws of Nature, show us that it is with no slavish dread, no cowardly shrinking, that we should approach her divine mysteries. What are the natures that cannot suffer? Who values them? From the fat oyster, over which the silver tide rises and falls without one pulse upon its fleshy ear, to the hero who stands with quivering nerve parting with wife and child and home for country and God, all the way up is an ascending scale, marked by increasing power to suffer; and when we look to the Head of all being, up through principalities and powers and princedoms, with dazzling orders and celestial blazonry, to behold by what emblem the Infinite Sovereign chooses to reveal himself, we behold, in the midst of the throne, 'a lamb as it had been slain.'

Sorrow is divine. Sorrow is reigning on the throne of the universe, and the crown of all crowns has been one of thorns. There have been many books that treat of the mystery of sorrow, but only one that bids us glory in tribulation, and count it all joy when we fall into divers afflictions, that so we may be associated with that great fellowship of suffering of which the Incarnate God is the head, and through which He is carrying a redemptive conflict to a glorious victory over evil. If we suffer with Him, we shall also reign with Him.

Even in the very making up of our physical nature, God puts suggestions of such a result. 'Weeping may endure for a night, but joy cometh in the morning.' There are victorious powers in our nature which are all the while working for us in our deepest pain. It is said, that after the sufferings of the rack, there ensues a period in which the simple repose from torture produces a beatific trance; it is the reaction of Nature, asserting the benignant intentions of her Creator. So, after great mental conflicts and agonies must come a reaction, and the Divine Spirit, co-working with our spirit, seizes the favourable moment, and, interpenetrating natural laws with a celestial vitality, carries up the soul to joys beyond the ordinary possibilities of mortality.

It is said that gardeners, sometimes, when they would bring a rose to richer flowering, deprive it for a season of light and moisture. Silent and dark it stands, dropping one fading leaf after another, and seeming to go down patiently to death. But when every leaf is dropped, and the plant stands stripped to the uttermost, a new life is even then working in the buds, from which shall spring a tender foliage and a brighter wealth of flowers. So, often in celestial gardening, every leaf of earthly joy must drop, before a new and divine bloom visits the soul.

Gradually, as months passed away, the floods grew still; the mighty rushes of the inner tide ceased to dash. There came first a delicious calmness, and then a celestial inner clearness, in which the soul seemed to lie quiet as an untroubled ocean, reflecting heaven. Then came the fulness of mysterious communion given to the pure in heart, that advent of the Comforter in the soul, teaching all things and bringing all things to remembrance; and Mary moved in a world transfigured by a celestial radiance. Her face, so long mournfully calm, like some chiselled statue of Patience, now wore a radiance, as when one places a light behind some alabaster screen sculptured with mysterious and holy emblems, and words of strange sweetness broke from her, as if one should hear snatches of music from a door suddenly opened in heaven. Something wise and strong and sacred gave an involuntary impression of awe in her looks and words; it was not the child-like loveliness of early days, looking with dove-like, ignorant eyes on sin and sorrow; but the victorious sweetness of that great multitude who have come out of great tribulation, having washed their robes and made them white in the blood of the

Lamb. In her eyes there was that nameless depth that one sees with awe in the Sistine Madonna; eyes that have measured infinite sorrow and looked through it to an infinite peace.

'My dear madam,' said the Doctor to Mrs. Scudder, 'I cannot but think there must be some uncommonly gracious exercises passing in the mind of your daughter; for I observe, that, though she is not inclined to conversation, she seems to be much in prayer; and I have of late felt the sense of a Divine Presence with her in a most unusual degree. Has she opened her mind to you?'

'Mary was always a silent girl,' said Mrs. Scudder, 'and not given to speaking of her own feelings; indeed, until she gave you an account of her spiritual state, on joining the church, I never knew what her exercises were. Hers is a most singular case. I never knew the time when she did not seem to love God more than anything else. It has disturbed me sometimes, because I did not know but it might be mere natural sensibility, instead of gracious affection.'

'Do not disturb yourself, madam,' said the Doctor. 'The Spirit worketh when, where, and how He will; and, undoubtedly, there have been cases where His operations commence exceedingly early. Mr. Edwards relates a case of a young person who experienced a marked conversion when three years of age, and Jeremiah was called from the womb. (Jeremiah i. 5.) In all cases we must test the quality of the evidence without relation to the time of its commencement. I do not generally lay much stress on our impressions, which are often uncertain and delusive; yet I have had an impression that the Lord would be pleased to make some singular manifestations of His grace through this young person. In the economy of grace there is neither male nor female; and Peter says (Acts ii. 17) that the Spirit of the Lord shall be poured out, and your sons and your daughters shall prophesy. Yet, if we consider that the Son of God, as to His human nature, was made of a woman, it leads us to see that in matters of grace God sets a special value on woman's nature and designs to put special honour upon it. Accordingly there have been in the Church, in all ages, holy women who have received the Spirit, and been called to a ministration in the things of God—such as Deborah, Huldah, and Anna the prophetess. In our own days most uncommon manifestations of divine grace have been given to holy women. It was my privilege to be in the family of President Edwards at a time when Northampton was specially visited, and his wife seemed and spoke more like a glorified spirit than a mortal woman, and multitudes flocked to the house to hear her wonderful words. She seemed to have such a sense of the Divine love as was almost beyond the powers of nature to endure. Just to speak the words, "Our Father who art in heaven," would overcome her with such a manifestation that she would become cold and almost faint; and though she uttered much, yet she told us that the divinest things she saw could not be spoken. These things could not be fanaticism, for she was a person of a singular evenness of nature, and of great skill and discretion in temporal matters, and of an exceeding humility, sweetness, and quietness of disposition.'

'I have observed of late,' said Mrs. Scudder, 'that in our praying circles Mary seemed much carried out of herself, and often as if she would speak, and with difficulty holding herself back. I have not urged her, because I thought it best to wait till she should feel full liberty.'

'Therein you do rightly, madam,' said the Doctor, 'but I am persuaded you will hear from her yet.'

It came at length, the hour of utterance. And one day, in a praying circle of the women of the church, all were startled by the clear silver tones of one who sat among them and spoke with the unconscious simplicity of an angel child, calling God her Father, and speaking of an ineffable union in Christ, binding all things together in one, and making all complete in Him. She spoke of a love passing knowledge—passing all love of lovers or of mothers—a love for ever spending, yet never spent—a love ever pierced and bleeding, yet ever constant and triumphant, rejoicing with infinite joy to bear in its own body the sins and sorrows of a universe—conquering, victorious love, rejoicing to endure, panting to give, and offering its whole self with an infinite joyfulness for our salvation. And when, kneeling, she poured out her soul in prayer, her words seemed so many winged angels, musical with unearthly harpings of an untold blessedness. They who heard her had the sensation of rising in the air, of feeling a celestial light and warmth descending into their souls; and when, rising, she stood silent and with downcast drooping eyelids, there were tears in all eyes, and a hush in all movements as she passed, as if something celestial were passing out.

Miss Prissy came rushing homeward, to hold a private congratulatory talk with the Doctor and Mrs. Scudder, while Mary was tranquilly setting the tea-table and cutting bread for supper.

'To see her now, certainly,' said Miss Prissy, 'moving round so thoughtful, not forgetting anything, and doing everything so calm, you wouldn't 'a' thought it could be her that spoke those blessed words and made that prayer! Well, certainly, that prayer seemed to take us all right up and put us down in heaven; and when I opened my eyes, and saw the roses and asparagus-bushes on the manteltree-piece, I had to ask myself, "Where have I been?" Oh! Miss Scudder, her afflictions have been sanctified to her! And really, when I see her going on so, I feel she can't be long for us. They say dying grace is for dying hours; and I'm sure this seems more like dying grace than anything that I ever yet saw.'

'She is a precious gift,' said the Doctor; 'let us thank the Lord for His grace through her. She has evidently had a manifestation of the Beloved, and feedeth among the lilies (Canticles vi. 3); and we will not question the Lord's further dispensations concerning her.'

'Certainly,' said Miss Prissy, briskly, 'it's never best to borrow trouble; "sufficient unto the day" is enough, to be sure. And now, Miss Scudder, I thought I'd just take a look at that dove-coloured silk of yours to-night, to see what would have to be done with it, because I must make every minute tell, and you know I lose half a day every week for the prayer-meeting. Though I ought not to say I lose it, either, for I was telling Miss General Wilcox I wouldn't give up that meeting for bags and bags of gold. She wanted me to come and sew for her one Wednesday, and says I, "Miss Wilcox, I'm poor and have to live by my work, but

I a'n't so poor but what I have some comforts, and I can't give up my prayer-meeting for any money—for you see, if one gets a little lift there, it makes all the work go lighter, but then I have to be particular to save up every scrap and end of time."'

Mrs. Scudder and Miss Prissy crossed the kitchen and entered the bedroom, and soon had the dove-coloured silk under consideration.

'Well, Miss Scudder,' said Miss Prissy, after mature investigation, 'here's a broad hem, not cut at all on the edge, as I see, and that might be turned down, and so cut off the worn spot up by the waist, and then, if it is turned, it will look every bit and grain as well as a new silk. I'll sit right down now and go to ripping. I put my ripping-knife into my pocket when I put on this dress to go to prayer-meeting, because, says I to myself, there'll be something to do at Miss Scudder's to-night. You just get an iron to the fire, and we'll have it all ripped and pressed out before dark.'

Miss Prissy seated herself at the open window, as cheery as a fresh apple-blossom, and began busily plying her knife, looking at the garment she was ripping with an astute air, as if she were about to circumvent it into being a new dress by some surprising act of legerdemain. Mrs. Scudder walked to the looking-glass and began changing her bonnet-cap for a tea-table one.

Miss Prissy, after a while, commenced in a mysterious tone:

'Miss Scudder, I know folks like me shouldn't have their eyes open too wide, but then I can't help noticing some things. Did you see the Doctor's face when we was talking to him about Mary? Why, he coloured all up and the tears came into his eyes. It's my belief that that blessed man worships the ground she treads on. I don't mean *worships*, either, 'cause that would be wicked, and he's too good a man to make a graven image of anything; but it's clear to see that there a'n't anybody in the world like Mary to him. I always did think so, but I used to think Mary was such a little poppet—that she'd do better for——Well, you know, I thought about some younger man—but, laws, now I see how she rises up to be ahead of everybody, and is so kind of solemn-like. I can't but see the leadings of Providence. What a minister's wife she'd be, Miss Scudder! Why, all the ladies coming out of prayer-meeting were speaking of it. You see, they want the Doctor to get married: it seems more comfortable-like to have ministers married; one feels more free to open their exercises of mind; and, as Miss Deacon Twitchel said to me—"If the Lord had made a woman o' purpose, as he did for Adam, he wouldn't have made her a bit different from Mary Scudder." Why, the oldest of us would follow her lead, 'cause she goes before us without knowing it.'

'I feel that the Lord has greatly blessed me in such a child,' said Mrs. Scudder, 'and I feel disposed to wait the leadings of Providence.'

'Just exactly,' said Miss Prissy, giving a shake to her silk; 'and as Miss Twitchel said, in this case every providence seems to p'int. I felt dreadfully for her along six months back; but now I see how she's been brought out, I begin to see that things are for the best, perhaps, after all. I can't help feeling that Jim Marvyn is gone to heaven, poor fellow! His father is a deacon,—and such a good man!—and Jim, though he did make a great laugh wherever he went, and sometimes laughed where he hadn't ought to, was a noble-hearted fellow. Now, to be sure, as the Doctor says, "amiable instincts a'n't true holiness;" but then they are better than unamiable ones, like Simeon Brown's. I do think, if that man is a Christian, he is a dreadful ugly one; he snapped me short up about my change, when he settled with me last Tuesday; and if I hadn't felt that it was a sinful rising, I should have told him I'd never put foot in his house again; I'm glad, for my part, he's gone out of our church. Now Jim Marvyn was like a prince to poor people; and I remember once his mother told him to settle with me, and he gave me 'most double, and wouldn't let me make change. "Confound it all, Miss Prissy," says he, "I wouldn't stitch as you do from morning to night for double that money." Now I know we can't do anything to recommend ourselves to the Lord, but then I can't help feeling some sorts of folks must be by nature more pleasing to Him than others. David was a man after God's own heart, and he was a generous, whole-souled fellow, like Jim Marvyn, though he did get carried away by his spirits sometimes and do wrong things; and so I hope the Lord saw fit to make Jim one of the elect. We don't ever know what God's grace has done for folks. I think a great many are converted when we know nothing about it, as Miss Twitchel told poor old Miss Tyrrel, who was mourning about her son, a dreadful wild boy, who was killed falling from mast-head; she says, that from the mast-head to the deck was time enough for divine grace to do the work.'

'I have always had a trembling hope for poor James,' said Mrs. Scudder,—'not on account of any of his good deeds or amiable traits, because election is without foresight of any good works,—but I felt he was a child of the covenant, at least by the father's side, and I hope the Lord has heard his prayer. These are dark providences; the world is full of them; and all we can do is to have faith that the Lord will bring infinite good out of finite evil, and make everything better than if the evil had not happened. That's what our good Doctor is always repeating; and we must try to rejoice, in view of the happiness of the universe, without considering whether we or our friends are to be included in it or not.'

'Well, dear me!' said Miss Prissy, 'I hope, if that is necessary, it will please the Lord to give it to me; for I don't seem to find any power in me to get up to it. But all's for the best, at any rate,—and that's a comfort.'

Just at this moment Mary's clear voice at the door announced that tea was on the table.

'Coming, this very minute,' said Miss Prissy, bustling up and pulling off her spectacles. Then, running across the room, she shut the door mysteriously, and turned to Mrs. Scudder with the air of an impending secret. Miss Prissy was subject to sudden impulses of confidence, in which she was so very cautious that not the thickest oak-plank door seemed secure enough, and her voice dropped to its lowest key. The most important and critical words were entirely omitted, or supplied by a knowing wink and a slight stamp of the foot.

In this mood she now approached Mrs. Scudder, and, holding up her hand on the door side, to prevent consequences, if, after all, she should be betrayed into a loud word, she said, 'I thought I'd just say, Miss Scudder, that, in case Mary should —— the Doctor,—in case, you know, there should be a —— in the house, you *must* just contrive it so as to give me a month's notice, so that I could give you a whole fortnight to fix her up as such a good man's —— ought to be. Now I know how spiritually-minded our blessed Doctor is; but, bless you, Ma'am, he's got eyes. I tell you, Miss Scudder, these men, the best of 'em, *feel* what's what, though they don't *know* much. I saw the Doctor look at Mary that night I dressed her for the wedding-party. I tell you he'd like to have his wife look pretty well, and he'll get up some blessed text or other about it, just as he did that night about being brought unto the king in raiment of needle-work. That is an encouraging thought to us sewing-women.

'But this thing was spoken of after the meeting. Miss Twitchel and Miss Jones were talking about it; and they all say that there would be the best setting-out got for her that was ever seen in Newport, if it should happen. Why, there's reason in it. She ought to have at least two real good India silks that will stand alone,—and you'll see she'll have 'em too; you let me alone for that; and I was thinking, as I lay awake last night, of a new way of making up, that you will say is just the sweetest that ever you did see. And Miss Jones was saying that she hoped there wouldn't anything happen without her knowing it, because her husband's sister in Philadelphia has sent her a new receipt for cake, and she has tried it and it came out beautifully, and she says she'll send some in.'

All the time that this stream was flowing, Mrs. Scudder stood with the properly reserved air of a discreet matron, who leaves all such matters to Providence, and is not supposed unduly to anticipate the future; and, in reply, she warmly pressed Miss Prissy's hand, and remarked, that no one could tell what a day might bring forth,—and other general observations on the uncertainty of mortal prospects, which form a becoming shield when people do not wish to say more exactly what they are thinking of.

CHAPTER XXV.

NOTHING is more striking in the light and shadow of the human drama than to compare the inner life and thoughts of an elevated and silent nature, with the thoughts and plans which those by whom they are surrounded have of and for them. Little thought Mary of any of the speculations that busied the friendly head of Miss Prissy, or that lay in the provident forecastings of her prudent mother. When a life into which all our life nerves have run is cut suddenly away, there follows, after the first long bleeding is healed, an internal paralysis of certain portions of our nature. It was so with Mary: the thousand fibres that bind youth and womanhood to earthly love and life were all in her still as the grave, and only the spiritual and divine part of her being was active. Her hopes, desires, and aspirations were all such as she could have had in greater perfection, as a disembodied spirit than as a mortal woman. The small stake for self which she had invested in life was gone,—and henceforward all personal matters were to her so indifferent that she scarce was conscious of a wish in relation to her own individual happiness. She was through the sudden crush of a great affliction in that state of self-abnegation to which the mystics brought themselves by fastings and self-imposed penances,—a state not purely healthy, nor realizing the divine ideal of a perfect human being, made to exist in the relations of human life,—but one of those exceptional conditions, which, like the hours that often precede dissolution, seem to impart to the subject of them a peculiar aptitude for delicate and refined spiritual impressions. We could not afford to have it always night—and we must think that broad, gay morning light, when meadow-lark and robin and bobolink are singing in chorus with a thousand insects and the waving of a thousand breezes, is on the whole the most in accordance with the average wants of those who have a material life to live and material work to do. But then we reverence that clear-obscure of midnight, when everything is still and dewy—then sing the nightingales which cannot be heard by day—then shine the mysterious stars. So when all earthly voices are hushed in the soul, all earthly lights darkened, music and colour float in from a higher sphere.

No veiled nun, with her shrouded forehead and downcast eyes, ever moved about a convent with a spirit more utterly divided from the world, than Mary moved about her daily employments. Her care about the details of life seemed more than ever minute; she was always anticipating her mother in every direction, and striving by a thousand gentle preveniences, to spare her from fatigue and care; there was even a tenderness about her ministrations, as if the daughter had changed feelings and places with the mother.

The Doctor, too, felt a change in her manner towards him, which, always considerate and kind, was now invested with a tender thoughtfulness, and anxious solicitude to serve, which often brought tears to his eyes. All the neighbours who had been in the habit of visiting at the house, received from her almost daily, in one little form or another, some proof of her thoughtful remembrance.

She seemed in particular to attach herself to Mrs. Marvyn; throwing her cares around that fragile and wounded nature, as a generous vine will sometimes embrace with tender leaves and flowers a dying tree.

But her heart seemed to have yearnings beyond even the circle of home and friends. She longed for the sorrowful and the afflicted; she would go down to the forgotten and the oppressed, and made herself the companion of the Doctor's secret walks and explorings among the poor victims of the slave-ships, and entered with zeal as teacher among his African catechumens.

Nothing but the limits of bodily strength could check her zeal to do and suffer for others,—a river of love had suddenly been checked in her heart, and it needed all these channels to drain off the waters that otherwise must have drowned her in the suffocating agonies of repression.

Sometimes, indeed, there would be a returning thrill of the old wound, one of those overpowering moments when some turn in life brings back anew a great anguish. She would find unexpectedly in a book a mark that he had placed there, or a turn in conversation would bring back a tone of his voice, or she would see on some thoughtless young head, curls just like those which were swaying to and fro down among the wavering seaweeds, and then her heart gave one great throb of pain, and turned for relief to some immediate act of love to some living being. They who saw her in one of these moments, felt a surging of her heart towards them, a moisture of the eye, a sense of some inexpressible yearning, and knew not from what pain that love was wrung, and what poor heart was seeking to still its own throbbings in blessing them.

By what name shall we call this beautiful twilight, this night of the soul, so starry with heavenly mysteries, *not* happiness, but blessedness? They who have it, walk among men as sorrowful, yet always rejoicing; as poor, yet making many rich; as having nothing, and yet possessing all things.

The Doctor, as we have seen, had always that reverential spirit towards women which accompanies a healthy and great nature; but in the constant converse which he now held with a beautiful being, from whom every particle of selfish feeling or mortal weakness seemed sublimed, he appeared to yield his soul up to her leading, with a wondering humility, as to some fair miraculous messenger of heaven. All questions of internal experience, all delicate shadings of the spiritual history, with which his pastoral communings in his flock made him conversant, he brought to her to be resolved with the purest simplicity of trust.

CHAPTER XXV.

'She is one of the Lord's rarities,' he said one day to Mrs. Scudder, 'and I find it difficult to maintain the bonds of Christian faithfulness in talking with her. It is a charm of the Lord's hidden ones that they know not their own beauty; and God forbid that I should tempt a creature made so perfect by divine grace, to self-exultation, or lay my hand, unadvisedly, as Uzzah did, upon the ark of God, by my inconsiderate praises.'

'Well, Doctor,' said Miss Prissy, who sat in the corner sewing on the dove-coloured silk, 'I do wish you could come into one of our meetings and hear those blessed prayers. I don't think you nor anybody else ever heard anything like 'em.'

'I would, indeed, that I might with propriety enjoy the privilege,' said the Doctor.

'Well, I'll tell you what' said Miss Prissy, 'next week they're going to meet here, and I'll leave the door just ajar, and you can hear every word, just by standing in the entry.'

'Thank you, madam,' said the Doctor, 'it would certainly be a blessed privilege, but I cannot persuade myself that such an act would be consistent with Christian propriety.'

'Ah, now do hear that good man,' said Miss Prissy, after he had left the room; 'if he ha'n't got the making of a real gentleman in him as well as a real Christian, though I always did say, for my part, that a real Christian will be a gentleman. But I don't believe all the temptations in the world could stir that blessed man one jot or grain to do the least thing that he thinks is wrong or out of the way. Well, I must say, I never saw such a good man; he is the only man I ever saw good enough for our Mary.'

Another spring came round, and brought its roses, and the apple-trees blossomed for the third time since the commencement of our story; and the robins had repaired the old nest, and began to lay their blue eggs in it; and Mary still walked her calm course, as a sanctified priestess of the great worship of sorrow. Many were the hearts now dependent on her, the spiritual histories, the thread of which were held in her loving hand,—many the souls burdened with sins, or oppressed with sorrow, who found in her bosom at once confessional and sanctuary.

So many sought her prayers, that her hours of intercession were full, and needed to be lengthened often to embrace all for whom she would plead. United to the good Doctor by a constant friendship and fellowship, she had gradually grown accustomed to the more and more intimate manner in which he regarded her, which had risen from a 'simple dear child and dear Mary,' to 'dear friend,' and at last 'dearest of all friends,' which he frequently called her, and encouraged by the calm, confiding sweetness of those still, blue eyes and that gentle smile which came without one varying flutter of the pulse or the rising of the slightest flush on the marble cheek.

One day a letter was brought in, post-marked 'Philadelphia.' It was from Madame de Frontignac; it was in French, and ran as follows:—

'MY DEAR LITTLE WHITE ROSE:—

'I am longing to see you once more, and before long I shall be in Newport. Dear little Mary, I am sad, very sad; the days seem all of them too long; and every morning I look out of my window and wonder why I was born. I am not so happy as I used to be, when I cared for nothing but to sing and smooth my feathers like the birds. That is the best kind of life for us women; if we love anything better than our clothes, it is sure to bring us great sorrow. For all that, I can't help thinking it is very noble and beautiful to love,—love is very beautiful, but very, very sad. My poor dear little white cat, I should like to hold you a little while to my heart,—it is so cold all the time, and aches so, I wish I were dead; but then I am not good enough to die. The Abbé says, we must offer up our sorrow to God, as a satisfaction for our sins. I have a good deal to offer, because my nature is strong and I can feel a great deal. But I am very selfish, dear little Mary, to think only of myself, when I know how you must suffer. Ah, but you knew he loved you truly, the poor dear boy, that is something. I pray daily for his soul; don't think it wrong of me, you know it is our religion, we should all do our best for each other.

'Remember me tenderly to Mrs. Marvyn. Poor mother! the bleeding heart of the Mother of God alone can understand such sorrows.

'I am coming in a week or two, and then I have many things to say to *ma belle rose blanche;* till then I kiss her little hands.

'VERGINIE DE FRONTIGNAC.'

One beautiful afternoon, not long after, a carriage stopped at the cottage, and Madame de Frontignac alighted. Mary was spinning in her garret boudoir, and Mrs. Scudder was at that moment at a little distance from the house, sprinkling some linen, which was laid out to bleach on the green turf of the clothes yard.

Madame de Frontignac sent away the carriage, and ran up the stairway, pursuing the sound of Mary's spinning wheel, mingled with her song; and in a moment, throwing aside the curtain, she seized Mary in her arms, and kissed her on either cheek, laughing and crying both at once.

'I knew where I should find you, *ma blanche;* I heard the wheel of my poor little princess, it's a good while since we spun together, *mimi*. Ah, Mary darling, little do we know what we spin; life is hard and bitter, isn't it? Ah, how white your cheeks are, poor child!'

Madame de Frontignac spoke with tears in her own eyes, passing her hand caressingly over the fair cheeks.

'And you have grown pale, too, dear Madame,' said Mary, looking up, and struck with the change in the once brilliant face.

'Have I, *petite?* I don't know why not. We women have secret places where our life runs out. At home I wear *rouge;* that makes all right; but I don't put it on for you, Mary; you see me just as I am.'

Mary could not but notice the want of that brilliant colour and roundness in the cheek, that made so glowing a picture; the eyes seemed larger and tremulous with a pathetic depth, and around them those bluish circles that speak of languor and pain; yet still, changed as she was, Madame de Frontignac seemed only more strikingly interesting and fascinating than ever. Still she had those thousand pretty movements, those nameless graces of manner, those wavering shades of expression, that irresistibly enchained the eye and the imagination; true Frenchwoman as she was, always in one rainbow shimmer of fancy, and feeling like one of those cloud-spotted April days, which give you flowers and rain, sun and shadow, and snatches of bird-singing all at once.

'I have sent away my carriage, Mary, and come to stay with you. You want me, *n'est-ce pas?*' she said, coaxingly, with her arms round Mary's neck; 'if you don't, *tant pis;* for I am the bad penny you English speak of, you cannot get me off.'

'I am sure, dear friend,' said Mary, earnestly, 'we don't want to put you off.'

'I know it; you are true, you *mean* what you say; you are all good real gold, down to your hearts; that is why I love you; but you, my poor Mary, your cheeks are very white; poor little heart, you suffer.'

'No,' said Mary; 'I do not suffer now. Christ has given me the victory over sorrow.'

There was something sadly sublime in the manner in which this was said, and something so sacred in the expression of Mary's face, that Madame de Frontignac crossed herself, as she had been wont before a shrine; and then said, 'Sweet Mary, pray for me; I am not at peace; I cannot get the victory over sorrow.'

'What sorrow can you have?' said Mary; 'you, so beautiful, so rich, so admired; whom everybody must love.'

'That is what I came to tell you; I came to confess to you. But you must sit down *there*,' she said, placing Mary on a low seat in the garret window, 'and Verginie will sit here,' she said, drawing a bundle of uncarded wool towards her, and sitting down at Mary's feet.

'Dear Madame,' said Mary, 'let me get you a better seat.'

'No, no, *mignonne*, this is best. I want to lay my head in your lap;' and she took off her riding-hat with its streaming plume, and tossed it carelessly from her, and laid her head down on Mary's lap. 'Now don't call me Madame any more. Do you know,' she said, raising her head with a sudden brightening of cheek and eye, 'do you know that there are two *me's* to this person?—one is Verginie, and the other is Madame de Frontignac. Everybody in Philadelphia knows Madame de Frontignac; she is very gay, very careless, very happy; she never has any serious hours, or any sad thoughts; she wears powder and diamonds, and dances all night, and never prays—that is Madame. But Verginie is quite another thing. She is tired of all this; tired of the balls and the dancing, and the diamonds, and the beaux; and she likes true people, and would like to live very quiet with somebody that she loved. She is very unhappy, and she prays too, sometimes, in a poor little way, like the birds in your nest out there, who don't know much, but chipper and cry because they are hungry—this is your Verginie—Madame never comes here; never call me Madame.'

'Dear Verginie,' said Mary, 'how I love you!'

'Do you, Mary—*bien sur?* you are my good angel. I felt a good impulse from you when I first saw you, and have always been stronger to do right when I got one of your pretty little letters. Oh, Mary, darling! I have been very foolish and very miserable, and sometimes tempted to be very, very bad. Oh, sometimes I thought I would not care for God or anything else—it was very bad of me—but I was like a foolish little fly, caught in a spider's net before he knows it.'

Mary's eyes questioned her companion with an expression of eager sympathy, somewhat blended with curiosity.

'I can't make you understand me quite,' said Madame de Frontignac, 'unless I go back a good many years. You see, dear Mary, my dear angel mamma died when I was very little, and I was sent to be educated at the Sacré Cœur, in Paris. I was very happy and very good in those days—the sisters loved me, and I loved them, and I used to be so pious, and loved God dearly. When I took my first communion, Sister Agatha prepared me. She was a true saint, and is in heaven now; and I remember when I came to her, all dressed like a bride, with my white crown and white veil, that she looked at me so sadly, and said she hoped I would never love anybody better than God, and then I should be happy. I didn't think much of those words then, but oh, I have since, many times. They used to tell me always that I had a husband who was away in the army, and who would come to marry me when I was seventeen, and that he would give me all sorts of beautiful things, and show me everything I wanted to see in the world, and that I must love and honour him.

'Well, I was married at last, and Monsieur de Frontignac is a good, brave man, although he seemed to me very old and sober; but he was always kind to me, and gave me nobody knows how many sets of jewelry, and let me do everything I wanted to, and so I liked him very much; but I thought there was no danger I should love him, or anybody else better than God. I didn't *love* anybody in those days, I only liked people, and some people more than others. All the men I saw professed to be lovers, and I liked to lead them about and see what foolish things I could make them do, because it pleased my vanity; but I laughed at the very idea of love.

'Well, Mary, when we came to Philadelphia I heard everybody speaking of Colonel Burr—and what a fascinating man he was, and I thought it would be a pretty thing to have him in my train—and so I did all I could to charm him. I tried all my little arts—and if it is a sin for us women to do such things, I am sure I have been punished for it. Mary, he was stronger than I was. These men, they are not satisfied with having the whole earth under their feet, and having all the strength and all the glory, but they must even take away our poor little reign—it's too bad.

'I can't tell you how it was. I didn't know myself, but it seemed to me that he took my very life away from me; and it was all done before I knew it. He called himself my friend—my brother—he offered to teach me English—he read with me, and by-and-by he controlled my whole life. I that used to be so haughty, so proud—I that used to laugh to think how independent I was of everybody. I was entirely under his control, though I tried not to show it. I didn't well know where I was, for he talked friendship, and I talked friendship; he talked about sympathetic natures that are made for each other, and I thought how beautiful it all was; it was living in a new world. Monsieur de Frontignac was as much charmed with him as I was; he often told me that he was his best friend; that he was his hero—his model man; and I thought, oh Mary, you would wonder to hear me say what I thought! I thought he was a Bayard, a Sully, a Montmorenci; everything grand and noble and good. I loved him with a religion. I would have died for him; I sometimes thought how I might lay down my life to save his, like women I read of in history. I did not know myself. I was astonished I could feel so; and I did not dream that this could be wrong. How could I, when it made me feel more religious than anything in my whole life? Everything in the world seemed to grow sacred. I thought if men could be so good and admirable, life was a holy thing, and not to be trifled with. But our good Abbé is a faithful shepherd, and when I told him these things in confession, he told me I was in great danger—danger of falling into mortal sin. Oh, Mary! it was as if the earth opened under me. He told me, too, that this noble man, this man so dear, was a heretic, and that if he died he would go to dreadful pains. Oh, Mary! I dare not tell you half what he told me; dreadful things that make me shiver when I think of them; and then he said that I must offer myself a sacrifice for him; that if I would put down all this love, and overcome it, that God would perhaps accept it as a satisfaction, and bring him into the true church at last.

'Then I began to try. Oh, Mary! we never know how we love till we try to unlove; it seemed like taking my heart out of my breast, and separating life from life. How can one do it? I wish any one would tell me. The Abbé said I must do it by prayer; but it seemed to me prayer only made me think the more of him.

'But at last I had a great shock; everything broke up like a great, grand, noble dream; and I waked out of it just as weak and wretched as one feels when one has overslept. Oh, Mary! I found I was mistaken in him—all, all, wholly!'

Madame de Frontignac laid her forehead on Mary's knee, and her long chestnut hair drooped down over her face.

'He was going somewhere with my husband, to explore out in the regions of the Ohio, where he had some splendid schemes of founding a state; and I was all interest; and one day, as they were preparing, Monsieur de Frontignac gave me a quantity of papers to read and arrange, and among them was a part of a letter; I never could imagine how it got there; it was to one of his confidential friends; I read it at first, wondering what it meant, till I came to two or three sentences about me.' Madame de Frontignac paused a moment; and then said, rising with sudden energy, 'Mary, that man never loved me; he cannot love; he does not know what love is; what I felt he cannot know; he cannot even dream of it, because he never felt anything like it; such men never know us women; we are as high as heaven above them; it is true enough that my heart was wholly in his power, but why? Because I adored him as something divine, incapable of dishonour, incapable of selfishness, incapable of even a thought that was not perfectly noble and heroic. If he had been all that, I would have been proud to have been even a poor little flower that should exhale away, to give him an hour's pleasure; I would have offered my whole life to God as a sacrifice for such a glorious soul; and all this time, what was he thinking of me?

'He was *using* my feelings to carry his plans; he was admiring me like a picture; he was considering what he should do with me; and were it not for his interests with my husband, *he* would have tried his power to make me sacrifice this world and the next to his pleasure. But he does not know me. My mother was a Montmorenci, and I have the blood of her house in my veins; we are princesses; we can give all; but he must be a god that we give it for.'

Mary's enchanted eye followed the beautiful narrator, as she enacted before her this poetry and tragedy of real life, so much beyond what dramatic art can ever furnish. Her eyes grew splendid in their depths and brilliancy; sometimes they were full of tears, and sometimes they flashed out like lightnings; her whole form seemed to be a plastic vehicle which translated every emotion of her soul; and Mary sat and looked at her with the intense absorption that one gives to the highest and deepest in art or nature.

'*Enfin—que faire?*' she said at last, suddenly stopping, and drooping in every limb. 'Mary, I have lived on this dream so long—never thought of anything else—now all is gone, and what shall I do? I think,' she added, pointing to the nest in the tree, 'Mary, I see my life in many things. My heart was once still and quiet, like the round little eggs that were in your nest,—now it has broken out of its shell, and cries with cold and hunger: I want my dream again,—I wish it all back,—or that my heart could go back into its shell. If I only could drop this year out of my life, and care for nothing, as I used to,—I have tried to do that—I can't—I cannot get back where I was before.'

'*Would* you do it, dear Verginie,' said Mary; 'would you if you could?'

'It was very noble and sweet, all that,' said Verginie; 'it gave me higher thoughts than ever I had before. I think my feelings were beautiful,—but now they are like little birds that have no mother—they kill me with their crying.'

'Dear Verginie, there is a real friend in heaven, who is all you can ask or think,—nobler, better, purer, who cannot change, and cannot die, and who loved you and gave himself for you.'

'You mean Jesus,' said Verginie. 'Ah, I know it; and I say the offices to him daily, but my heart is very wild and starts away from my words. I say, "My God, I give myself to you,"—and after all, I don't give myself, and I don't feel comforted. Dear Mary, you must have suffered too—for you loved really—I saw it,—when we feel a thing ourselves we can see very quick the same in others,—and it was a dreadful blow to come so all at once.'

'Yes it was,' said Mary; 'I thought I must die; but Christ has given me peace.'

These words were spoken with that long-breathed sigh with which we always speak of peace,—a sigh that told of storms and sorrows past,—the sighing of the wave that falls spent and broken on the shores of eternal rest. There was a little pause in the conversation, and then Verginie raised her head and spoke in a sprightlier tone.

'Well, my little fairy cat,—my white doe,—I have come to you. Poor Verginie wants something to hold to her heart; let me have you,' she said, throwing her arms round Mary.

'Dear, dear Verginie, indeed you shall,' said Mary; 'I will love you dearly, and pray for you. I always have prayed for you ever since the first day I knew you.'

'I knew it,—I felt your prayers in my heart. Mary, I have many thoughts that I dare not tell to any one, lately,—but I cannot help feeling that some are real Christians who are not in the true Church. You are as true a saint as Saint Catharine; indeed, I always think of you when I think of our dear lady; and yet they say there is no salvation out of the Church.'

This was a new view of the subject to Mary, who had grown up with the familiar idea that the Romish Church was Babylon and anti-Christ, and who had during the conversation been revolving the same surmises with regard to her friend. She turned her grave, blue eyes on Madame de Frontignac, with a somewhat surprised look, which melted into a half-smile. But the latter still went on with a puzzled air, as if trying to talk herself out of some mental perplexity. 'Now, Burr is a heretic,—and more than that, he is an infidel,—he has no religion in his heart, I saw that often,—it made me tremble for him. It ought to have put me on my guard,—but you, dear Mary, you love Jesus as your life. I think you love Him just as much as sister Agatha, who was a saint. The Abbé says that there is nothing so dangerous as to begin to use our reason in religion,—that if we once begin we never know where it may carry us; but I can't help using mine a very little. I must think there are some saints that are not in the true Church.'

'All are one who love Christ,' said Mary; 'we are one in Him.'

'I should not dare to tell the Abbé,' said Madame de Frontignac; and Mary queried in her heart whether Dr. Hopkins would feel satisfied that she could bring this wanderer to the fold of Christ, without undertaking to batter down the walls of her creed; and yet, there they were, the Catholic and the Puritan, each strong in her respective faith, yet melting together in that embrace of love and sorrow, joined in the great communion of suffering. Mary took up her Testament, and read the fourteenth of John:—

'Let not your heart be troubled; ye believe in God, believe also in me; in my Father's house are many mansions; if it were not so, I would have told you; I go to prepare a place for you; and if I go to prepare a place for you, I will come again and receive you unto myself, that where I am there you may be also.'

Mary read on through the chapter, through the next wonderful prayer; her face grew solemnly transparent, as of an angel; for her soul was lifted from earth by the words, and walked with Christ far above all things, over that starry pavement where each footstep is on a world.

The greatest moral effects are like those of music, not wrought out by sharp-sided intellectual propositions, but melted in by a divine fusion, by words that have mysterious indefinite fulness of meaning, made living by sweet voices, which seem to be the out-throbbings of angelic hearts; so one verse in the Bible read by a mother in some hour of tender prayer has a significance deeper and higher than the most elaborate of sermons, the most acute of arguments.

Verginie Frontignac sat as one divinely enchanted, while that sweet voice read on; and when the silence fell between them she gave a long sigh as we do when sweet music stops. They heard between them the soft stir of summer leaves, the distant songs of birds, the breezy hum when some afternoon wind shivered through many branches, and the silver sea chimed in; Verginie rose at last, and kissed Mary on the forehead. 'That is a beautiful book,' she said, 'and to read it all by one's self must be lovely; I cannot understand why it should be dangerous; it has not injured you.

'Sweet saint,' she added, 'let me stay with you; you shall read to me every day; do you know I came here to get you to take me; I want you to show me how to find peace where you do; will you let me be your sister?'

'Yes, indeed,' said Mary, with a cheek brighter than it had been for many a day; her heart feeling a throb of more real human pleasure than for long months.

'Will you get your mamma to let me stay?' said Verginie, with the bashfulness of a child; 'haven't you a little place like yours, with white curtains, and sanded floor, to give to poor little Verginie to learn to be good in?'

'Why, do you really want to stay here with us,' said Mary, 'in this little house?'

'Do I really?' said Virginie, mimicking her voice with a start of her old playfulness; '*don't* I really? Come now, *mimi*, coax the good mamma for me, tell her I shall try to be very good. I shall help you with the spinning; you know I spin beautifully,—and I shall make butter, and milk the cow, and set the tables. Oh, I will be so useful, you can't spare me!'

'I should love to have you dearly,' said Mary, warmly; 'but you would soon be dull for want of society here.'

'*Quelle idée! ma petite drole*,' said the lady, who with the mobility of her nation had already recovered some of the saucy mocking grace that was habitual to her, as she began teasing Mary with a thousand little childish motions. 'Indeed, *mimi*, you must keep me hid up here, or may be the wolf will find me and eat me up; who knows?' Mary looked at her with inquiring eyes.

'What do you mean?'

'I mean, Mary,—I mean that when *he* comes back to Philadelphia he thinks he will find me there; he thought I should stay while my husband was gone; and when he finds I am gone he may come to Newport; and I never want to see him again without you; you must let me stay with you.'

'Have you told him,' said Mary, 'what you think?'

'I wrote to him, Mary, but oh, I can't trust my heart! I want so much to believe him; it kills me so to think evil of him that it will never do for me to see him. If he looks at me with those eyes of his I am all gone; I shall believe anything he tells me; he will draw me to him as a great magnet draws a poor little grain of steel.'

CHAPTER XXV.

'But now you know his unworthiness, his baseness,' said Mary, 'I should think it would break all his power.'

'*Should* you think so? Ah, Mary, we cannot unlove in a minute; love is a great while dying. I do not worship him now as I did. I know what he is. I know he is bad, and I am sorry for it. I would like to cover it from all the world, even from you, Mary, since I see it makes you dislike him; it hurts me to hear any one else blame him; but sometimes I do so long to think I am mistaken, that I know if I should see him I should catch at anything he might tell me, as a drowning man at straws; I should shut my eyes and think after all that it was all my fault, and ask a thousand pardons for all the evil he has done. No. Mary, you must keep your blue eyes upon me, or I shall be gone.'

At this moment Mrs. Scudder's voice was heard, calling Mary below.

'Go down now, darling, and tell mamma; make a good little talk to her, *ma reine;* ah, you are queen here; all do as you say, even the good priest there; you have a little hand, but it leads all; so go, *petite.*'

Mrs. Scudder was somewhat flurried and discomposed at the proposition; there were the *pros* and the *cons* in her nature, such as we all have.

In the first place, Madame de Frontignac belonged to high society, and that was *pro;* for Mrs. Scudder prayed daily against worldly vanities, because she felt a little traitor in her heart that was ready to open its door to them if not constantly talked down. In the second place, Madame de Frontignac was French, there was a *con;* for Mrs. Scudder had enough of her father John Bull in her heart to have a very wary look-out on anything French. But then, in the third place, she was out of health and unhappy, and there was a *pro* again; for Mrs. Scudder was as kind and motherly a soul as ever breathed. But then she was a Catholic, *con.* But the Doctor and Mary might convert her, *pro.* And then Mary wanted her, *pro.* And she was a pretty, bewitching, loveable creature, *pro.* The *pros* had it; and it was agreed that Madame de Frontignac should be installed as proprietress of the spare chamber, and she sat down to the tea-table that evening in the great kitchen.

CHAPTER XXVI.

THE domesticating of Madame de Frontignac as an inmate of the cottage, added a new element of vivacity to that still and unvaried life. One of the most beautiful traits of French nature is that fine gift of appreciation, which seizes at once the picturesque side of every condition of life, and finds in its own varied storehouse something to assort with it. As compared with the Anglo-Saxon, the French appear to be gifted with a *naïve* childhood of nature, and to have the power that children have of gilding every scene of life with some of their own poetic fancies.

Madame de Frontignac was in raptures with the sanded floor of her little room, which commanded, through the apple-boughs, a little morsel of a sea-view. She could fancy it was a nymph's cave, she said.

'Yes, *ma* Marie, I will play Calypso, and you shall play Telemachus, and Dr. Hopkins shall be Mentor. Mentor was so very, very good, only a little bit—*dull*,' she said, pronouncing the last word with a wicked accent, and lifting her hands with a whimsical gesture like a naughty child who expects a correction.

Mary could not but laugh; and as she laughed more colour rose in her waxen cheeks than for many days before.

Madame de Frontignac looked triumphant as a child who has made its mother laugh, and went on laying things out of her trunk into her drawers with a zeal that was quite amusing to see.

'You see, *ma blanche*, I have left all *Madame's* clothes at Philadelphia, and brought only those that belong to Verginie,—no *tromperie*, no feathers, no gauzes, no diamonds, only white dresses and my straw hat *en bergère*. I brought one string of pearls that was my mother's; but pearls, you know, belong to the sea-nymphs. I will trim my hat with sea-weed and buttercups together, and we will go out on the beach to-night and get some gold and silver shells to dress *ma miroir*.'

'Oh, I have ever so many now,' said Mary, running into her room, and coming back with a little bag. They both sat on the bed together, and began pouring them out, Madame de Frontignac showering childish exclamations of delight.

Suddenly Mary put her hand to her heart as if she had been struck with something; and Madame de Frontignac heard her say, in a low voice of sudden pain, 'Oh, dear!'

'What is it, mimi?' she said, looking up quickly.

CHAPTER XXVI.

'Nothing,' said Mary, turning her head. Madame de Frontignac looked down, and saw among the sea-treasures a necklace of Venetian shells that she knew never grew on the shores of Newport. She held it up.

'Ah, I see,' she said. 'He gave you this. Ah, *ma pauvrette*,' she said, clasping Mary in her arms, 'thy sorrow meets thee everywhere. May I be a comfort to thee, just a little one.'

'Dear, dear friend,' said Mary, weeping. 'I know not how it is. Sometimes I think this sorrow is all gone; but then, for a moment, it comes back again. But I am at peace; it is all right, all right; I would not have it otherwise. But oh, if he could have spoken one word to me before! He gave me this,' she added, 'when he came home from his first voyage to the Mediterranean. I did not know it was in this bag. I had looked for it everywhere.'

'Sister Agatha would have told you to make a rosary of it,' said Madame de Frontignac; 'but you pray without a rosary. It is all one,' she added; 'there will be a prayer for every shell, though you do not count them. But come, *ma chère*, get your bonnet, and let us go out on the beach.'

That evening, before retiring, Mrs. Scudder came into Mary's room. Her manner was grave and tender, her eyes had tears in them; and although her usual habits were not caressing, she came to Mary and put her arms around and kissed her. It was an unusual manner, and Mary's gentle eyes seemed to ask the reason of it.

'My daughter,' said her mother, 'I have just had a long and very interesting talk with our dear good friend, the Doctor; ah, Mary, very few people know how good he is.'

'True, mother,' said Mary, warmly; 'he is the best, the noblest, and yet the humblest man in the world.'

'You love him very much, do you not?' said her mother.

'Very dearly,' said Mary.

'Mary, he has asked me this evening if you would be willing to be his wife.'

'His *wife*, mother?' said Mary in the tone of one confused with a new and strange thought.

'Yes, daughter; I have long seen that he was preparing to make you this proposal.'

'You have, mother?'

'Yes, daughter; have you never thought of it?'

'Never, mother.'

There was a long pause, Mary standing just as she had been interrupted in her night toilette, with her long, light hair streaming down over her white dress, and the comb held mechanically in her hand. She sat down after a moment, and clasping both hands over her knees, fixed her eyes intently on the floor; and there fell between the two a silence so intense, that the tickings of the clock in the next room seemed to knock upon the door. Mrs. Scudder sat with anxious eyes watching that silent face, pale as sculptured marble.

'Well, Mary,' she said at last.

A deep sigh was the only answer. The violent throbbings of her heart could be seen undulating the long hair as the moaning sea tosses the rockweed.

'My daughter!' again said Mrs. Scudder.

Mary gave a great sigh, like that of a sleeper awakening from a dream, and looking on her mother, said: 'Do you suppose he really *loves* me, mother?'

'Indeed he does, Mary, as much as man ever loved woman.'

'Does he indeed?' said Mary, relapsing into thoughtfulness.

'And you love him, do you not?' said her mother.

'Oh yes, I love him!'

'You love him better than any man in the world, don't you?'

'Oh, mother, mother! yes!' said Mary, throwing herself passionately forward, and bursting into sobs; 'yes, there is no one else now that I love better,—no one,—no one!'

'My darling, my daughter!' said Mrs. Scudder, coming and taking her in her arms.

'Oh, mother, mother!' she said, sobbing distressfully, 'let me cry, just for a little,—oh, mother, mother, mother!'

What was there hidden under that despairing wail?—it was the parting of the last strand of the cord of youthful hope.

Mrs. Scudder soothed and caressed her daughter, but maintained still in her breast a tender pertinacity of purpose, such as mothers will, who think they are conducting a child through some natural sorrow into a happier state.

Mary was not one either to yield long to emotion of any kind. Her rigid education had taught her to look upon all such outbursts as a species of weakness, and she struggled for composure, and soon seemed entirely calm.

'If he really loves me, mother, it would give him great pain if I refuse,' said Mary, thoughtfully.

'Certainly it would; and, Mary, you have allowed him to act as a very near friend for a long time; and it is quite natural that he should have hopes that you loved him.'

'I do love him, mother,—better than anybody in the world except you. Do you think that will do?'

'Will do?' said her mother; 'I don't understand you.'

'Why, is that loving enough to marry? I shall love him more perhaps after, shall I, mother?'

'Certainly you will; every one does.'

'I wish he did not want to marry me, mother,' said Mary, after a pause. 'I liked it a great deal better as we were before.'

'All girls feel so, Mary, at first; it is very natural.'

'Is that the way you felt about father, mother?'

Mrs. Scudder's heart smote her when she thought of her own early love,—that great love that asked no questions; that had no doubts, no fears, no hesitations; nothing but one great, outsweeping impulse, which swallowed her life in that of another. She was silent; and after a moment, she said, 'I was of a different disposition from you, Mary. I was of a strong, wilful, positive nature. I either liked or disliked with all my might; and besides, Mary, there never was a man like your father.'

The matron uttered this first article in the great confession of woman's faith with the most unconscious simplicity.

'Well, mother, I will do whatever is my duty. I want to be guided. If I can make that good man happy, and help him to do some good in the world,—After all, life is short, and the great thing is to do for others.'

'I am sure, Mary, if you could have heard how he spoke, you would be sure you could make him happy. He had not spoken before, because he felt so unworthy of such a blessing: he said I was to tell you that he should love and honour you all the same, whether you could feel to be his wife or not; but that nothing this side of heaven would be so blessed a gift; that it would make up for every trial that could possibly come upon him,—and you know, Mary, he has a great many discouragements and trials;—people don't appreciate him; his efforts to do good are misunderstood, and misconstrued; they look down on him, and despise him, and tell all sorts of evil things about him; and sometimes he gets quite discouraged.'

'Yes, mother, I will marry him,' said Mary. 'Yes, I will.'

'My darling daughter,' said Mrs. Scudder, 'this has been the hope of my life.'

'Has it, mother?' said Mary, with a faint smile; 'I shall make you happier then?'

'Yes, dear, you will; and think what a prospect of usefulness opens before you; you can take a position as his wife which will enable you to do even more good than you do now; and you will have the happiness of seeing every day how much you comfort the hearts and encourage the hands of God's dear people.'

'Mother, I ought to be very glad I can do it,' said Mary; 'and I trust I am. God orders all things for the best.'

'Well, my child, sleep to-night, and to-morrow we will talk more about it.'

CHAPTER XXVII.

MRS. SCUDDER kissed her daughter, and left her. After a moment's thought, Mary gathered the long silky folds of hair around her head, and knotted them for the night. Then leaning forward on her toilet-table, she folded her hands together, and stood regarding the reflection of herself in the mirror.

Nothing is capable of more ghostly effect than such a silent, lonely contemplation of that mysterious image of ourselves which seems to look out of an infinite depth in the mirror, as if it were our own soul beckoning to us visibly from unknown regions. Those eyes look into our own with an expression sometimes vaguely sad and inquiring. The face wears weird and tremulous lights and shadows; it asks us mysterious questions, and troubles us with the suggestions of our relations to some dim unknown. The sad, blue eyes that gazed into Mary's had that look of calm initiation, of melancholy comprehension, peculiar to eyes made clairvoyant by 'great and critical' sorrow. They seemed to say to her, 'Fulfil thy mission; life is made for sacrifice; the flower must fall before fruit can perfect itself.' A vague shuddering of mystery gave intensity to her reverie. It seemed as if those mirror depths were another world; she heard the far-off dashing of sea-green waves; she felt a yearning impulse towards that dear soul gone out into the infinite unknown.

Her word just passed had in her eyes all the sacred force of the most solemnly-attested vow; and she felt as if that vow had shut some before open door between her and him; and she had a kind of shadowy sense of a throbbing and yearning nature that seemed to call on her,—that seemed surging towards her with an imperative, protesting force that shook her heart to its depths.

Perhaps it is so, that souls once intimately related have ever after this strange power of affecting each other,—a power that neither absence nor death can annul. How else can we interpret these mysterious hours, in which the power of departed love seems to overshadow us, making our souls vital with such longings, with such wild throbbings, with such unutterable sighings, that a little more might burst the mortal band? Is it not deep calling unto deep? the free soul singing outside the cage to her mate, beating against the bars within?

Mary even for a moment fancied that a voice called her name, and started, shivering. Then the habits of her positive and sensible education returned at once, and she came out of her reverie as one breaks from a dream, and lifted all these sad thoughts with one heavy sigh from her breast; and opening her Bible, she read: 'They that trust in the Lord shall be as Mount Zion that cannot be moved. As the mountains are round about Jerusalem, so the Lord is about His people from this time henceforth and for evermore.'

Then she kneeled by her bedside, and offered her whole life a sacrifice to the loving God who had offered His life a sacrifice for her. She prayed for grace to be true to her promise—to be faithful to the new relation she had accepted. She prayed that all vain regrets for the past might be taken away, and that her soul might vibrate without discord in unison with the will of Eternal Love. So praying, she rose calm, and with that clearness of spirit which follows an act of uttermost self-sacrifice; and so calmly she lay down and slept, with her two hands crossed upon her breast, her head slightly turned on the pillow, her cheek pale as marble, and her long dark lashes lying drooping, with a sweet expression, as if under that mystic veil of sleep the soul were seeing things forbidden to the waking eye. Only the gentlest heaving of the quiet breast told that the heavenly spirit within had not gone where it was hourly aspiring to go.

Meanwhile Mrs. Scudder had left Mary's room, and entered the Doctor's study, holding a candle in her hand. The good man was sitting alone in the dark, with his head bowed upon his Bible. When Mrs. Scudder entered, he rose and regarded her wistfully, but did not speak. He had something just then in his heart for which he had no words; so he only looked as a man does who hopes and fears for the answer of a decided question.

Mrs. Scudder felt some of the natural reserve which becomes a matron coming charged with a gift in which lies the whole sacredness of her own existence, and which she puts from her hands with a jealous reverence.

She therefore measured the man with her woman's and mother's eye, and said, with a little stateliness,—

'My dear sir, I come to tell you the result of my conversation with Mary.'

She made a little pause, and the Doctor stood before her as humbly as if he had not weighed and measured the universe; because he knew that though he might weigh the mountains in scales, and the hills in a balance, yet it was a far subtler power which must possess him of one small woman's heart. In fact, he felt to himself like a great awkward, clumsy, mountainous earthite asking of a white-robed angel to help him up a ladder of cloud. He was perfectly sure for the moment that he was going to be refused, and he looked humbly firm—he would take it like a man. His large blue eyes, generally so misty in their calm, had a resolute clearness, rather mournful than otherwise. Of course no such celestial experience was going to happen to him.

He cleared his throat and said,—

'Well, Madam?'

Mrs. Scudder's womanly dignity was appeased; she reached out her hand cheerfully, and said,—

'*She has accepted.*'

The Doctor drew his hand suddenly away, turned quickly round, and walked to the window, although, as it was ten o'clock at night and quite dark, there was evidently nothing to be seen there. He stood there quietly, swallowing very hard, and raising his handkerchief several times to his eyes. There was enough went on under the black coat just then to make quite a little figure in a romance if it had been uttered; but he belonged to a class who *lived* romance, but never spoke it. In a few moments he returned to Mrs. Scudder and said,—

'I trust, dear madam, that this very dear friend may never have reason to think me ungrateful for her wonderful goodness; and whatever sins my evil heart may lead me into, I *hope* I may never fall so low as to forget the undeserved mercy of this hour. If ever I shrink from duty or murmur at trials, while so sweet a friend is mine, I shall be vile indeed.'

The Doctor, in general, viewed himself on the discouraging side, and had berated and snubbed himself all his life as a most flagitious and evil-disposed individual—a person to be narrowly watched, and capable of breaking at any moment into the most flagrant iniquity; and therefore it was that he received his good fortune in so different a spirit from many of the Lords of Creation in similar circumstances.

'I am sensible,' he added, 'that a poor minister, without much power of eloquence, and commissioned of the Lord to speak unpopular truths, and whose worldly condition, in consequence, is never likely to be very prosperous, that such a one could scarcely be deemed a suitable partner for so very beautiful a young woman, who might expect proposals, in a temporal point of view, of a much more advantageous nature; and I am therefore the more struck and overpowered with this blessed result.'

These last words caught in the Doctor's throat, as if he were overpowered in very deed.

'In regard to *her* happiness,' said the Doctor, with a touch of awe in his voice, 'I would not have presumed to become the guardian of it, were it not that I am persuaded it is assured by a Higher Power; for when He giveth peace, who then can make trouble? (Job xxxv. 29.) But I trust I may say no effort on my part shall be wanting to secure it.'

Mrs. Scudder was a mother, and come to that spot in life where mothers always feel tears rising behind their smiles. She pressed the Doctor's hand, silently, and they parted for the night.

We know not how we can acquit ourselves to our friends of the great world for the details of such an unfashionable courtship, so well as by giving them, before they retire for the night, a dip into a more modish view of things.

The Doctor was evidently green; green in his faith, green in his simplicity, green in his general belief of the divine in woman, green in his particular, humble faith in one small Puritan maiden, whom a knowing fellow might at least have manœuvred so skilfully as to break up her saintly superiority, discompose her, rout her ideas, and lead her up and down a swamp of hopes and fears and conjectures, till she was wholly bewildered and ready to take him at last—if he made up his mind to have her at all—as a great bargain for which she was to be sensibly grateful.

Yes, the Doctor was green, *immortally* green, as a cedar of Lebanon which, waving its broad archangel wings over some fast-rooted eternal old solitude, and seeing from its sublime height the vastness of the universe, veils its kingly head with humility before God's infinite majesty.

He has gone to bed now, simple old soul, first apologizing to Mrs. Scudder for having kept her up to so dissipated and unparalleled an hour as ten o'clock on his personal matters.

Meanwhile our Asmodeus will transport us to an easily furnished apartment in one of the most fashionable hotels of Philadelphia, where Col. Aaron Burr, just returned from his trip to the then aboriginal wilds of Ohio, is seated before a table covered with maps, letters, books, and papers. His keen eye runs over the addresses of the letters, and he eagerly seizes one from Madame de Frontignac, and reads it; and as no one but ourselves is looking at him now his face has no need to wear its habitual mask. First comes an expression of profound astonishment; then of chagrin and mortification; then of deepening concern; there were stops where the dark eyelashes flashed together as if to brush a tear out of the view of the keen-sighted eyes; and then a red flush rose even to his forehead, and his delicate lips wore a sarcastic smile. He laid down the letter and made one or two turns through the room.

The man had felt the dashing against his own of a strong, generous, indignant woman's heart fully awakened, and speaking with that impassioned vigour with which a French regiment charges in battle. There were those picturesque, winged words, those condensed expressions, those subtle piercings of meaning, and above all, that simple pathos for which the French tongue has no superior; and for the moment the woman had the victory; she shook his heart. But Burr resembled the marvel with which chemists amuse themselves. His heart was a vase filled with boiling passions, while his *will*, a still, cold, unmelted lump of ice, lay at the bottom.

Self-denial is not peculiar to Christians. They who go downward often put forth as much force to kill a noble nature as another does to annihilate a sinful one. There was something in this letter so keen, so searching, so self-revealing, that it brought on one of those interior crises in which a man is convulsed with the struggle of two natures—the godlike and the demoniac, and from which he must pass out more wholly to the dominion of the one or the other.

Nobody knew the true better than Burr. He *knew* the god-like and the pure, he had *felt* its beauty and its force to the very depths of his being, as the demoniac knew at once the fair man of Nazareth; and even now he felt the voice within that said, 'What have I to do with thee?' and the rending of a struggle of heavenly life with fast-coming eternal death.

That letter had told him what he might be, and what he was. It was as if his dead mother's hand had held up before him a glass in which he saw himself, white robed and crowned, and so dazzling in purity that he loathed his present self.

As he walked up and down the room perturbed, he sometimes wiped tears from his eyes, and then set his teeth, and compressed his lips. At last his face grew calm and settled in its expression, his mouth wore a sardonic smile; he came and took the letter, and folding it leisurely, laid it on the table, and put a heavy paper weight over it, as if to hold it down and bury it. Then drawing to himself some maps of new territories, he set himself vigorously to some columns of arithmetical calculations on the margin; and thus he worked for an hour or two till his mind was as dry, and his pulse as calm as a machine; then he drew the ink-stand towards him, and scribbled hastily the following letter to his most confidential associate—a letter which told no more of the conflict that preceded it, than do the dry sands and civil gossip of the sea-waves to-day of the storm and wreck of last week.

> 'Dear——. *Nous voilà* once more in Philadelphia. Our schemes in Ohio prosper. Frontignac remains there to superintend. He answers our purpose *passablement*. On the whole I don't see as we could do better than retain him; he is, beside, a gentlemanly, agreeable person, and wholly devoted to me—a point certainly not to be overlooked.
>
> 'As to your railleries about the fair Madame, I must say, in justice both to her and myself, that any grace with which she has been pleased to honour me is not to be misconstrued. You are not to imagine any but the most Platonic of "*liaisons*." She is as high strung as an Arabian steed; proud,—heroic, romantic, and *French!* and such must be permitted to take their own time and way, which we in our *gaucherie* can only humbly wonder at. I have ever professed myself her abject slave, ready to follow any whim, and obeying the slightest signal of the jewelled hand. As that is her sacred pleasure, I have been inhabiting the most abstract realms of heroic sentiment, living on the most diluted moonshine, and spinning out elaborately all those charming and seraphic distinctions between tweedle-dum and tweedle-dee with which these ecstatic creatures delight themselves in certain stages of "*affaires du cœur*."
>
> 'The last development on the part of my goddess is a fit of celestial anger, of the cause of which I am in the most innocent ignorance. She writes me three pages of French sublimities, writing as only a French woman can, bids me an eternal adieu, and informs me she is going to Newport.
>
> 'Of course the affair becomes stimulating. I am not to presume to dispute her sentence, or doubt a lady's perfect sincerity in wishing never to see me again; but yet I think I shall try to pacify the
>
> "tantas in animis celestibus iras."
>
> If a woman hates you it is only her love turned wrong side out, and you may turn it back with due care. The pretty creatures know

how becoming a *grande* passion is, and take care to keep themselves in mind; a quarrel serves their turn when all else fails.

'To another point. I wish you to advertise S——, that his insinuations in regard to me, in the Aurora, have been observed, and that I require that they be promptly retracted. He knows me well enough to attend to this hint. I am in earnest when I speak; if the word does nothing, the blow will come, and if I strike once no second blow will be needed; yet I do not wish to get him on my hands needlessly; a duel and a love affair and hot weather, coming on together, might prove too much even for me. N.B. Thermometer stands at 85. I am resolved on Newport next week.

'Yours ever,

'BURR.

'P.S. I forgot to say that, oddly enough, my goddess has gone and placed herself under the wing of the pretty Puritan I saw in Newport. Fancy the *melange;* could anything be more piquant?—that cart-load of goodness, the old Doctor,—that sweet little saint and Madame Faubourg St. Germain shaken up together!—fancy her listening with well-bred astonishment to a critique on the doings of the unregenerate, or flirting that little jewelled fan of hers in Mrs. Scudder's square pew of a Sunday. Probably they will carry her to the weekly prayer-meeting, which of course she will find some fine French subtlety for admiring, and "*trouve ravissante*." I fancy I see it.'

When Burr had finished this letter, he had actually written himself into a sort of persuasion of its truth. When a finely-constituted nature wishes to go into baseness, it has first to bribe itself. Evil is never embraced undisguised as evil, but under some fiction which the mind accepts, and with which it has the singular power of blinding itself in the face of daylight. The power of imposing on one's self is an essential preliminary to imposing on others. The man first argues himself down, and then he is ready to put the whole weight of his nature to deceiving others. This letter ran so smoothly, so plausibly, that it produced on the writer of it the effect of a work of fiction, which we *know* to be unreal, but *feel* to be true. Long habits of this kind of self-delusion in time produce a paralysis in the vital nerves of truth, so that one becomes habitually unable to see things in their verity, and realizes the awful words of scripture, 'He feedeth on ashes; a deceived heart hath turned him aside, so that he cannot deliver his soul, nor say, is there not a lie in my right hand?'

CHAPTER XXVIII.

BETWEEN three and four the next morning, the robin in the nest above Mary's room stretched out his left wing, opened one eye, and gave a short and rather drowsy chirp, which broke up his night's rest and restored him to the full consciousness that he was a bird with wings and feathers—a large apple-tree to live in, and all heaven for an estate—and so, on these fortunate premises, he broke into a gush of singing, clear and loud, which Mary without waking heard in her slumbers.

Scarcely conscious, she lay in that dim clairvoyant state, when the half-sleep of the outward senses permits a delicious dewy clearness of the soul; that perfect ethereal rest and freshness of faculties, comparable only to what we imagine of the spiritual state. Season of celestial enchantment, in which the heavy weight 'of all this unintelligible world' drops off, and the soul, divinely charmed, nestles like a wind-tossed bird in the protecting bosom of the One all Perfect, all Beautiful. What visions then come to the inner eye have often no words corresponding in mortal vocabularies. The poet, the artist, and the prophet in such hours become possessed of divine *certainties*, which all their lives they struggle, with pencil or song, or burning words, to make evident to their fellows. The world around wonders, but *they* are unsatisfied, because they have *seen the glory* and know how inadequate the copy. But not merely to selectest spirits come these hours, but to those (humble poets) ungifted with utterance, who are among men as fountains sealed; whose song can be wrought out only by the harmony of deeds; the patient, pathetic melodies of tender endurance, or the heroic chant of undiscouraged labour. The poor slave woman last night parted from her only boy, and weary with the cotton-picking; the captive pining in his cell; the patient wife of the drunkard, saddened by a consciousness of the growing vileness of one once so dear; the delicate spirit doomed to harsh and uncongenial surroundings;—all in such hours feel the soothings of a celestial harmony, the tenderness of more than a mother's love. It is by such hours as these often, more than by reasonings or disputings, that doubts are resolved in the region of religious faith. The All-Father treats us as the mother does her 'infant crying in the dark;' He does not reason with our fears, or demonstrate their fallacy, but draws us silently to His bosom, and we are at peace. Nay, there have been those undoubtedly who have known God falsely with the intellect, yet felt Him truly with the heart; and there may be many, principally among the unlettered little ones of Christ's flock, who positively *know* that much that is dogmatically propounded to them of their Redeemer is cold, barren, unsatisfying, and even utterly false, who yet can give no account of their certainties better than that of the inspired fisherman, 'We know Him, and have seen Him.'

It was in such hours as these that Mary's deadly fears for the soul of her beloved had passed away, passed out of her, as if some warm healing nature of tenderest vitality had drawn out of her heart all pain and coldness, and warmed it with the breath of an eternal summer. So, while the purple shadows spread their gauzy veils inwove with fire along the sky, and the gloom of the sea broke out here and there into lines of light, and thousands of birds were answering to each other from apple-tree, and meadow-grass, and top of jagged rock, or trooping in bands hither and thither like angels on loving messages, Mary lay there with the flickering light through the leaves fluttering over her face, and the glow of dawn warming the snow-white draperies of the bed, and giving a tender rose hue to the calm cheek. She lay half conscious, smiling the while, as one who sleeps while the heart waketh, and who hears in dreams the voice of the One Eternally Beautiful and Beloved.

Mrs. Scudder entered her room, and thinking that she still slept, stood and looked down upon her. She felt as one does who has parted with some precious possession, a sudden sense of its value coming over her; and she queried in herself whether any living mortal were worthy of so perfect a gift; and nothing but a remembrance of the Doctor's prostrate humility at all reconciled her to the sacrifice she was making.

'Mary, dear,' she said, bending over her with an unusual infusion of emotion in her voice; 'darling child.'

The arms moved instinctively, even before the eyes unclosed, and drew her mother down to her with a warm clinging embrace.

Love in Puritan families was often like latent caloric,—an all-pervading force that affected no visible thermometer, shown chiefly by a noble, silent confidence, a ready helpfulness, but seldom out-breathed in caresses,—yet natures like Mary's always craved these outward demonstrations, and sprang towards them as a trailing vine sways to the nearest support. It was delightful for once fully to *feel* how much her mother loved her, as well as to *know* it.

'Dear, precious mother, do you love me so very much?'

'I live and breathe in you, Mary,' said Mrs. Scudder, giving vent to herself in one of those trenchant short-hand expressions, wherein positive natures incline to résumé *all* when they must speak at all.

Mary held her mother silently to her breast, her heart shining through her face with a quiet radiance of love.

'Do you feel happy this morning?' said Mrs. Scudder.

'Very, very, *very* happy, mother.'

'I am so glad to hear you say so,' said Mrs. Scudder, who, to say the truth, had entertained many doubts at her pillow the night before.

Mary began dressing herself in a state of calm exaltation. Every trembling leaf on the tree, every sunbeam was like a loving smile of God, every fluttering breeze like His voice, full of encouragement and hope.

'Mother, did you tell the Doctor what I said last night?'

'I did, my darling.'

'Then, mother, I would like to see him a few moments alone.'

'Well, Mary, he is in his study at his morning devotions.'

'That is just the time. I will go to him.'

The Doctor was sitting by the window, and the honest-hearted motherly lilacs, a-bloom for the third time since our story began, were filling the air with their sweetness. Suddenly the door opened, and Mary entered in her simple white short-gown and skirt, her eyes calmly radiant, and her whole manner having something serious and celestial. She came directly towards him, and put out both her little hands with a smile half child-like, half angelic, and the Doctor bowed his head, and covered his face with his hands.

'Dear friend,' said Mary, kneeling, and taking his hands, 'if you want me, I am come. Life is but a moment. There is an eternal blessedness just beyond us, and for the little time between, I will be all I can to you if you will only show me how.'

And the Doctor—— No, young man, the study door closed just then, and no one heard those words from a quaint old oriental book which told that all the poetry of that grand old soul had burst into flower, as the aloe blossoms once in a hundred years. The ripples of that great heart might have fallen unconsciously into phrases from that one love poem of the Bible which these men read so purely and devoutly, and which warmed the icy clearness of their intellects with the myrrh and spices of ardent lands, where earthly and heavenly love meet and blend in one indistinguishable horizon line, like sea and sky.

'Who is she that looketh forth as the morning, fair as the moon? clear as the sun? My dove, my undefiled, is but one. She is the only one of her mother—thou art all fair, my beloved, there is no spot in thee.'

The Doctor might have said all this, we will not say he did, nor will we say he did not; all we know is, that when the breakfast-table was ready they came out cheerfully together. Madame de Frontignac stood in a fresh white wrapper, with a few buttercups in her hair, waiting for the breakfast. She was startled to see the Doctor entering all radiant, leading in Mary by the hand, and looking as if he thought she were some dream-miracle which might dissolve under his eyes unless he kept fast hold of her. The keen eyes shot their arrowy glance, which went at once to the heart of the matter. Madame de Frontignac knew they were engaged, and regarded Mary with attention.

The calm, sweet, elevated expression of her face struck her; it struck her also that *that* was not the light of any earthly love, that it had no thrill, no blush, no tremor, but only the calmness of a soul that knows itself no more, and she sighed involuntarily.

CHAPTER XXVIII.

She looked at the Doctor, and seemed to study attentively a face which happiness had made this morning as genial and attractive as it was generally strong and fine.

There was little said at the breakfast-table this morning; and yet the loud singing of the birds, the brightness of the sunshine, the life and vigour of all things, seemed to make up for the silence of those who were too well pleased to speak.

'*Eh bien, ma chère*,' said Madame, after breakfast, drawing Mary into her little room. '*C'est fini?*'

'Yes,' said Mary, cheerfully.

'Thou art content,' said Madame, passing her arm around her; 'well then, I should be: but, Mary, it is like a marriage with the altar, like taking the veil, is it not?'

'No,' said Mary, 'it is not taking the veil, it is beginning a cheerful, reasonable life with a kind, noble friend who will always love me truly, and whom I hope to make as happy as he deserves.'

'I think well of him, my little cat,' said Madame, reflectively; 'but—,' she stopped something she was going to say, and kissed Mary's forehead; after a moment's pause, she added,

'One must have love or refuge, Mary; this is thy refuge, child; thou wilt have peace in it;' she sighed again.

'*Enfin*,' she said, resuming her gay tone, 'what shall be *la toilette de noce?* Thou shalt have Verginie's pearls, my fair one, and look like a sea-born Venus; *tiens!* let me try them in thy hair.'

And in a few moments she had Mary's long hair down, and was chattering like a blackbird, wreathing the pearls in and out, and saying a thousand pretty nothings, weaving grace and poetry into the strait thread of Puritan life.

CHAPTER XXIX.

THE QUILTING.

THE announcement of the definite engagement of two such bright particular stars in the hemisphere of the Doctor's small parish excited the interest that such events usually create among the faithful of the flock.

There was a general rustle and flutter, as when a covey of wild pigeons has been started, and all the little elves who rejoice in the name of 'says he,' and 'says I,' and 'do tell,' and 'have you heard,' were speedily flying through the consecrated air of the parish.

The fact was discussed by matrons and maidens at the spinning-wheel and in the green clothes-yard, or at the foaming wash-tub, out of which arose a new birth of weekly freshness and beauty. Many a rustic Venus of the foam, as she splashed her dimpled elbows in the rainbow-tinted froth, talked what should be done for the forthcoming solemnities, and wondered what Mary would have on when she was married, and whether she (the Venus) should get an invitation to the wedding, and whether 'Ethan' would go—not that she cared in the least whether he did or not.

Grave elderly matrons talked about the 'prosperity of Zion,' which they imagined intimately connected with the event of their minister's marriage; and descending from 'Zion,' speculated on bed-quilts and table-cloths, and rummaged their own clean, sweet-smelling stores, fragrant with balm and rose-leaves, to lay out a bureau cover, or a pair of sheets, or a dozen napkins for the wedding outfit.

The solemnest of solemn quiltings was resolved upon.

Miss Prissy declared that she fairly couldn't sleep nights with the responsibility of the wedding-dresses in her mind; but yet she 'must give one day to getting on that quilt.' The *grande monde* also was in motion. Mrs. General Wilcox called in her own particular carriage, bearing the present of a cashmere shawl for the bride, with the General's best compliments, and also an oak-leaf pattern for quilting, which had been sent her from England, and which was authentically established to be that used on a petticoat belonging to the Princess Royal; and Mrs. Major Seaforth came also, bearing a scarf of worked Indian muslin; and Mrs. Vernon sent a splendid Indian china punch-bowl. Indeed, to say the truth, the notables high and mighty of Newport, whom the Doctor had so unceremoniously accused of building their houses with blood, and establishing their city with iniquity, considering that nobody seemed to take his words to heart, and that they were making money as fast as old Tyre, rather assumed the magnanimous, and patted themselves on the shoulder for this opportunity to show the Doctor that, after all, they were good fellows, and bore him no malice, though they did make money at the expense of thirty per cent. human life.

Simeon Brown was the only exception: he stood aloof, grim and sarcastic, and informed some good, middle-aged ladies who came to see if he would, as they phrased it, 'esteem it a privilege' to add his mite to the Doctor's outfit, that he would give him a likely negro boy if he wanted, and if he was too conscientious to keep him, he might sell him at a fair profit; a happy stroke of humour, which he was fond of relating many years after.

The quilting was in these days considered as the most solemn and important recognition of a betrothal; and for the benefit of those not to the manner born, a little preliminary instruction may be necessary.

The good wives of New England, impressed with that thrifty orthodoxy of economy which forbids to waste the merest trifle, had a habit of saving every scrap and fragment clipped out in the fashioning of household garments; and these they cut into fanciful patterns, and constructed of them rainbow shapes and quaint traceries, the arrangement of which became one of their few fine arts. Many a maiden, as she sorted and arranged fluttering bits of green, yellow, red, and blue, felt rising in her breast a passion for somewhat vague and unknown, which came out at length in a new pattern of patchwork; and collections of these tiny fragments were always ready to fill an hour when there was nothing else to do; and as the maiden chatted with her beaux, her busy, flying needle stitched together the pretty morsels, which, little in themselves, were destined by gradual unions and accretions to bring about at last substantial beauty, warmth, and comfort; emblems thus of that household life which is to be brought to stability and beauty by reverent economy in husbanding, and tact in arranging the little, useful, and agreeable morsels of daily existence.

When a wedding was forthcoming, then there was a solemn review of the stores of beauty and utility thus provided, and the patchwork-spread best worthy of such distinction was chosen for the quilting.

Thereto, duly summoned, trooped all intimate female friends of the bride, and the quilt being spread on a frame, and wadded with cotton, each vied with the other in the delicacy of the quilting they could put upon it; for quilting also was a fine art, and had its delicacies and nice points, concerning which, grave, elderly matrons discussed with judicious care. The quilting generally began at an early hour in the afternoon, and ended at dusk with a great supper and general jubilee, in which that ignorant and incapable sex who could not quilt were allowed to appear, and put in claims for consideration of another nature. It may perhaps be surmised that this expected reinforcement was often alluded to by the younger maidens, whose wickedly coquettish toilettes exhibited suspicious marks of that willingness to get a chance to say 'No,' which has been slanderously attributed to mischievous maidens.

In consequence of the tremendous responsibilities involved in this quilting, the reader will not be surprised to learn that the evening before Miss Prissy made her appearance at the brown cottage, armed with thimble, scissors, and pincushion, in order to relieve her mind by a little preliminary confabulation.

'You see me, Miss Scudder, run almost to death,' she said; 'but I thought I would just run up to Mrs. Major Seaforth's and see her best bedroom quilt, 'cause I wanted to have all the ideas we possibly could before I decided on the pattern. Hers is in shells—just common shells; nothing to be compared with Miss Wilcox's oak-leaves; and I suppose there isn't the least doubt that Miss Wilcox's sister in London did get that from a lady who had a cousin who was governess in the royal family, and I just quilted a little bit to-day on an old piece of silk, and it comes out beautiful, and so I thought I would just come and ask you if you did not think it was best for us to have the oak-leaves.'

'Well, certainly, Miss Prissy, if you think so,' said Mrs. Scudder, who was as pliant to the opinions of this wise woman of the parish as New England matrons generally are to a reigning dressmaker and factotum.

Miss Prissy had the happy consciousness always that her early advent under any roof was considered a matter of special grace, and therefore it was with rather a patronizing tone that she announced that she would stay and spend the night with them.

'I knew,' she added, 'that your spare chamber was full with that Madame de What-you-call-her (if I was to die I could not remember the woman's name). Well, I thought I could just crawl in with you, Mary, most anywhere.'

'That's right, Miss Prissy,' said Mary, 'you shall be welcome to half my bed any time.'

'Well, I knew you would say so, Mary; I never saw the thing you would not give away half of since you was that high,' said Miss Prissy, illustrating her words by placing her hand about two feet from the floor.

Just at this moment Madame de Frontignac entered and asked Mary to come into her room, and give her advice as to a piece of embroidery. When she was gone out, Miss Prissy looked after her, and sank her voice once more to the confidential whisper which we before described.

'I have heard strange stories about that French woman,' she said; 'but as she was here with you and Mary, I suppose there cannot be any truth in them. Dear me! the world is so censorious about women! But then, you know, we don't expect much from French women. I suppose she is a Roman Catholic, and worships pictures and stone images; but then, after all, she has got an immortal soul, and I can't help hoping Mary's influence may be blest to her. They say when she speaks French she swears every few minutes; but if that is the way she was brought up, maybe she isn't accountable. I think we can't be too charitable for people that a'n't privileged as we are. Miss Vernon's Polly told me she has seen her sew Sabbath day. She came into her room of a sudden, and she was working on her embroidery there, and she never winked, nor blushed, nor offered to put it away, but sat there just as easy! Polly said she never was so beat in all her life; she felt kind o' scared every time she thought of it. But now she has come here, who knows but she may be converted?'

'Mary has not said much about her state of mind,' said Mrs. Scudder; 'but something of deep interest has passed between them. Mary is such an uncommon child that I trust everything to her.'

We will not dwell further on the particulars of this evening, nor describe how Madame de Frontignac reconnoitred Miss Prissy with keen, amused eyes; nor how Miss Prissy apprised Mary, in the confidential solitude of her chamber, that her fingers just itched to get hold of that trimming on that Madame de Frogsneck's dress, because she was pretty nigh sure she could make some just like it; for she never saw any trimming she could not make.

The robin that lived in the apple-tree was fairly out-generalled the next morning, for Miss Prissy was up before him, tripping about the chamber on the points of her toes, and knocking down all the moveable things in the room in her efforts to be still, so as not to waken Mary; and it was not until she had finally upset the stand by the bed, with the candlestick, snuffers, and Bible on it, that Mary opened her eyes.

'Miss Prissy! dear me! What is it you are doing?'

'Why I am trying to be still, Mary, so as not to wake you up, and it seems to me as if everything was possessed to tumble down so. But it is only half-past three, so you turn over and go to sleep.'

'But, Miss Prissy,' said Mary, sitting up in bed, 'you are all dressed; where are you going?'

'Well, to tell the truth, Mary, I am just one of those people that can't sleep when they have got responsibility on their minds; and I've been lying awake more than an hour here, thinking about that quilt. There is a new way of getting it on to the frame that I want to try, 'cause you know when we quilted Cerinthy Stebbins' it would trouble us in the rolling; and I have got a new way that I want to try, and I mean just to get it into the frame before breakfast. I was in hopes I should get out without waking any of you; and now I don't know as I shall get by your mother's door without waking her ('cause I know she works hard, and needs her rest); but that bedroom door squawks like a cat—enough to raise the dead!

'Mary,' she added, with sudden energy, 'if I had the least drop of oil in a teacup, and a bit of quill, I'd stop that door making such a noise.' And Miss Prissy's eyes glowed with resolution.

'I don't know where you could find any at this time,' said Mary.

'Well, never mind, I'll just go and open the door as slow and careful as I can,' said Miss Prissy, as she trotted out of the apartment.

The result of her carefulness was very soon announced to Mary by a protracted sound resembling the mewing of a hoarse cat, accompanied with sundry audible grunts from Miss Prissy, terminating in a grand finale of clatter, occasioned by her knocking down all the pieces of the quilt-frame that stood in a corner of the room, with a concussion that roused everybody in the house.

'What is that?' called out Mrs. Scudder from her bedroom.

She was answered by two streams of laughter; one from Mary, sitting up in bed, and the other from Miss Prissy, holding her sides, as she sat dissolved in merriment on the sanded floor.

CHAPTER XXX.

BY six o'clock in the morning, Miss Prissy came out of the best room to the breakfast-table, with the air of a general who has arranged a campaign, her face glowing with satisfaction. All sat down together to their morning meal. The outside door was open into the green, turfy yard, and the apple-tree, now nursing stores of fine yellow jennetings, looked in at the window. Every once in a while, as a breeze shook the leaves, a fully ripe apple might be heard falling to the ground, at which Miss Prissy would bustle up from the table and rush to secure the treasure.

As the meal waxed to its close, the rattling of wheels was heard at the gate, and Candace was discerned, seated aloft in the one-horse waggon, with her usual complements of baskets and bags.

'Well, now, dear me! if there is not Candace,' said Miss Prissy; 'I do believe Mrs. Marvyn has sent her with something for the quilting;' and out she flew as nimble as a humming-bird, while those in the house heard various exclamations of admiration, as Candace, with stately dignity, disinterred from the waggon one basket after another, and exhibited to Miss Prissy's enraptured eyes sly peeps under the white napkins by which they were covered. And then, lodging a large basket on either arm, she rolled majestically towards the house, like a heavy-laden Indiaman coming in after a fat voyage.

'Good morning, Mrs. Scudder. Good morning, Doctor,' she said, dropping her curtsy on the door-step; 'good morning, Miss Mary. You see our folks were stirring pretty early this morning, and Mrs. Marvyn sent me down with two or three little things.' Setting down her baskets on the floor, and seating herself between them, she proceeded to develop their contents with ill-concealed triumph. One basket was devoted to cakes of every species, from the great Mont Blanc loaf-cake, with its snowy glaciers of frosting, to the twisted cruller and puffy dough-nut. In the other basket lay pots of golden butter curiously stamped, reposing on a bed of fresh green leaves, while currants, red and white, and delicious cherries and raspberries, gave a final finish to the picture. From a basket which Miss Prissy brought in from the rear, appeared cold fowl and tongue, delicately prepared, and shaded with feathers of parsley. Candace, whose rollicking delight in the good things of this life was conspicuous in every emotion, might have famished to a painter, as she sat in a brilliant turban, an idea for an African genius of plenty.

'Why, really, Candace,' said Mrs. Scudder, 'you are overwhelming us!'

'Ho! ho! ho!' said Candace, 'I'se tellin' Miss Marvyn folks don't get married but once in their lives (gen'rally speaking, that is), and then they ought to have plenty to do it with.'

'Well, I must say,' said Miss Prissy, taking out the loaf-cake with busy assiduity, 'I must say, Candace, this does beat all!'

'I should rather think it ought,' said Candace, bridling herself with proud consciousness; 'if it don't it a'n't 'cause old Candace ha'n't put enough into it. I tell ye, I didn't do nothing all day yesterday but just make dat ar cake. Cato, when he got up, he begun to talk something about his shirt buttons, and I just shet him right up. Says I, "Cato, when I'se really got cake to make for a great 'casion, I want my mind *just* as quiet and *just* as serene as if I was agoin' to the meetin'. I don't want no earthly cares on it. Now," says I, "Cato, the old Doctor is going to be married, and dis yer is his quiltin' cake, and Miss Mary, she's going to be married, and dis yer is *her* quiltin' cake. And dare'll be everybody to dat ar quiltin', and if de cake a'n't right, why, 'twould be puttin' a candle under a bushel. And so, says I, Cato, your buttons must wait." And Cato, he sees the 'priety of it, 'cause though he can't make cake like me, he's a mazin' good judge of it, and is dre'ful tickled when I slip out a little loaf for his supper.'

'How is Mrs. Marvyn?' said Mrs. Scudder.

'Kinder thin and shimmery, but she is about, havin' her eyes everywhere and looking into everything. She just touches things with the tips of her fingers and they seem to go like. She'll be down to the quiltin' this afternoon. But she told me to take the things and come down and spend the day here; for Mrs. Marvyn and I both knows how many steps must be taken such times, and we agreed you ought to favour yourselves all you could.'

'Well, now,' said Miss Prissy, lifting up her hands, 'if that a'n't what 'tis to have friends! Why, that was one of the things I was thinking of as I lay awake last night: because you know at times like these people run their feet off before the time begins, and then they are all limpsey and lop-sided when the time comes. Now, I say, Candace, all Mrs. Scudder and Mary have to do is to give everything up to us, and we'll put it through straight.'

'That's what we will,' said Candace. 'Just show me what's to be done, and I'll do it.'

Candace and Miss Prissy soon disappeared together into the pantry with the baskets, whose contents they began busily to arrange. Candace shut the door that no sound might escape, and began a confidential outpouring to Miss Prissy.

'You see,' she said, 'I has *feelin's* all the while for Miss Marvyn; 'cause, yer see, she was expectin', if ever Mary was married—well—that it would be to somebody else, you know.'

Miss Prissy responded with a sympathetic groan.

'Well,' said Candace, 'if it had been anybody but the Doctor, *I* would not have been resigned. But after all he has done for my colour, there a'n't nothing I could find it in my heart to grudge him. But then I was tellin' Cato the other day, says I,

"Cato, I don't know about the rest of the world, but I ha'n't never felt it in my bones that Master James is really dead, for sartin. Now I feels things *gen'rally*, but *some* things I feels *in my bones*, and them always comes true. And that ar is a feelin' I ha'n't had about Master Jim yet, and that ar is what I'm waitin' for 'fore I clear make up my mind. Tho' I know, 'cordin' to all white folks' way o' thinkin', there a'n't no hope, 'cause 'Squire Marvyn he had that Jeduth Pettibone up to his house, a questioning on him off and on, nigh about three hours. And reely I didn't see no hope no way, except just this, as I was tellin' Cato, *I can't feel it in my bones*."'

Candace was not versed enough in the wisdom of the world to know that she belonged to a large and respectable school of philosophers in this particular mode of testing evidence, which, after all, the reader will perceive has its conveniences.

'Another thing,' said Candace, 'as much as a dozen times, dis yer last year, when I have been a-scourin' knives, a fork has fell and stuck straight up in the floor: and the last time I pinted it out to Miss Marvyn, and she only just said, "Why, what of that, Candace?"'

'Well,' said Miss Prissy, 'I don't believe in *signs*, but then strange things do happen. Now about dogs howling under windows; why, I don't believe in it a bit, but I never knew it fail that there was a death in the house after.'

'Ah, I tell ye what,' said Candace, looking mysterious, 'dogs knows a heap more than they likes to tell!'

'Just so,' said Miss Prissy; 'now I remember one night, when I was watching with Miss Colonel Andrews, after Martha Ann was born, that we heard the *mournfullest* howling that ever you did hear. It seemed to come from right under the front stoop; and Miss Andrews, she just dropped the spoon in her gruel, and says she, "Miss Prissy, do for pity's sake just go down and see what that noise is." And I went down, and lifted up one of the loose boards of the stoop, and what should I see there but their Newfoundland pup; there that creature had dug a grave, and was a-sitting by it crying.'

Candace drew near to Miss Prissy, dark with expressive interest, as her voice, in this awful narration, sank to a whisper.

'Well,' said Candace, after Miss Prissy had made something of a pause.

'Well, I told Miss Andrews I didn't think there was anything in it,' said Miss Prissy; 'but,' she added, impressively, 'she lost a very dear brother six months after, and I laid him out with my own hands—yes, laid him out in white flannel.'

'Some folks say,' said Candace, 'that dreaming about white horses is a certain sign. Jinny Styles is very strong about that. Now she came down one morning crying, 'cause she had been dreaming about white horses, and she was sure she should hear some friend was dead. And sure enough, a man came in that day and told her that her son was drown'd out in the harbour. And Jinny said, "There, she was sure that sign never would fail." But then, ye see, that night he came home. Jinny wan't reely disappointed, but she always insisted he was *as good as drowned*, any way, "'cause he sank three times."'

'Well, I tell you,' said Miss Prissy, 'there are a great many more things in this world than folks know about.'

'So they are,' said Candace. 'Now, I ha'n't never opened my mind to nobody; but there's a dream I've had, three mornings running, lately. I dreamed I see Jim Marvyn a-sinking in the water, and stretching up his hands. And then I dreamed that I see the Lord Jesus come a-walking on the water, and take hold of his hand, and says He, "O thou of little faith, wherefore didst thou doubt?" And then He lifted him right out. And I ha'n't said nothing to nobody, 'cause you know the Doctor,—he says people must not mind nothing about their dreams, 'cause dreams belong to the old 'spensation.'

'Well! well! well!' said Miss Prissy, 'I am sure I don't know what to think. What time in the morning was it that you dreamed it?'

'Why,' said Candace, 'it was just after bird-peep. I kinder always wakes myself then, and turns over, and what comes after that is apt to run clear.'

'Well! well! well!' said Miss Prissy, 'I don't know what to think. You see, it may have reference to the state of his soul.'

'I know that,' said Candace; 'but as nigh as I could judge in my dream,' she added, sinking her voice and looking mysterious, 'as nigh as I can judge, *that boy's soul was in his body!*'

'Why, how do you know?' said Miss Prissy, looking astonished at the confidence with which Candace expressed her opinion.

'Well, ye see,' said Candace, rather mysteriously, 'the Doctor he don't like to have us talk much about these things, 'cause he thinks it's kind o' heathenish. But then, folks as is used to seein' such things, knows the look of a sperit *out* of the body, from the look of a sperit in the body, just as easy as you can tell Mary from the Doctor.'

At this moment Mrs. Scudder opened the pantry-door and put an end to this mysterious conversation, which had already so affected Miss Prissy that, in the eagerness of her interest, she had rubbed up her cap border and ribbon into rather an elfin and goblin style, as if they had been ruffled up by a breeze from the land of spirits; and she flew around for a few moments in a state of great nervous agitation, upsetting dishes, knocking down plates, and huddling up contrary suggestions as to what ought to be done first, in such impossible relations, that Mrs. Katy Scudder stood in dignified surprise at this strange freak of conduct in the wise woman of the parish.

A dim consciousness of something not quite canny in herself appeared to strike her, for she made a vigorous effort to appear composed; and facing Mrs. Scudder, with an air of dignified suavity, inquired if it would not be best to put Jim Marvyn in the oven now, while Candace was getting the pies ready, meaning of course a large turkey which was to be the first in an indefinite series to be baked that morning; and discovering, by Mrs. Scudder's dazed expression and a vigorous pinch from Candace, that somehow she had not improved matters, she rubbed her spectacles in a diagonal manner across her eyes and stood glaring through them, with a helpless expression, which in a less judicious person might have suggested the idea of a state of slight intoxication.

But the exigencies of an immediate temporal dispensation put an end to Miss Prissy's unwonted vagaries, and she was soon to be seen flying round like a meteor, dusting, shaking curtains, counting napkins, wiping and sorting china, all with such rapidity as to give rise to the idea that she actually existed in forty places at once.

Candace, whom the limits of her corporeal frame restricted to an altogether different style of locomotion, often rolled the whites of her eyes after her, and gave vent to her views of her proceedings in sententious expressions.

'Do you know why *dat ar* never was married?' she said to Mary, as she stood looking after her. Miss Prissy had made one of those rapid transits through the apartment.

'No,' answered Mary, innocently; 'why was not she?'

'Because never was a man could run fast enough to catch her,' said Candace; and then her portly person shook with the impulse of her own wit.

By two o'clock a goodly company began to assemble. Mrs. Deacon Twitchel arrived, soft, pillowy, and plaintive as ever, accompanied by Cerinthy Ann, a comely damsel, tall and trim, with a bright black eye and a most vigorous and determined style of movement.

Good Mrs. Jones, broad, expansive, and solid, having vegetated tranquilly on in the cabbage garden of the virtues since three years ago when she graced our tea-party, was now as well preserved as ever, and brought some fresh butter, a tin pail of cream, and a loaf of cake made on a new Philadelphia receipt. The tall, spare, angular figure of Mrs. Simeon Brown only was wanting; but she patronized Mrs. Scudder no more, and tossed her head with a becoming pride when her name was mentioned.

The quilt-pattern was gloriously drawn in oak-leaves, done in indigo; and soon all the company, young and old, were passing busy fingers over it; and conversation went on briskly.

Madame de Frontignac, we must not forget to say, had entered with hearty *abandon* into the spirit of the day. She had dressed the tall china vases on the mantelpieces; and, departing from the usual rule of an equal mixture of roses and asparagus bushes, had constructed two quaint and graceful bouquets, where garden flowers were mingled with drooping grasses and trailing wild vines, forming a graceful combination, which excited the surprise of all who saw it.

'It's the very first time in my life that I ever saw grass put into a flower-pot,' said Miss Prissy; 'but I must say it looks as handsome as a pictur'. Mary, I must say,' she added in an aside, 'I think that Madame de Frongenac is the sweetest dressing and appearing creature I ever saw: she don't dress up nor put on airs, but she seems to see in a minute how things ought to go; and if it's only a bit of grass, or leaf, or wild vine, that she puts in her hair, why it seems to come just right. I should like to make her a dress, for I know she would understand my fit; do speak to her, Mary, in case she should want a dress fitted here, to let me try it.'

At the quilting, Madame de Frontignac would have her seat, and soon won the respect of the party by the dexterity with which she used her needle; though, when it was whispered that she learned to quilt among the nuns, some of the elderly ladies exhibited a slight uneasiness, as being rather doubtful whether they might not be encouraging papistical opinions by allowing her an equal share in the work of getting up their minister's bed-quilt; but the younger part of the company were quite captivated by her foreign air, and the pretty manner in which she lisped her English; and Cerinthy Ann even went so far as to horrify her mother, by saying that she wished she'd been educated in a convent herself,—a declaration which arose less from native depravity, than from a certain vigorous disposition, which often shows itself in young people, to shock the current opinions of their elders and betters. Of course the conversation took a general turn, somewhat in unison with the spirit of the occasion; and whenever it flagged, some allusion to a forthcoming wedding, or some sly hint to the future young Madam of the parish, was sufficient to awake the dormant animation of the company.

Cerinthy Ann contrived to produce an agreeable electric shock, by declaring that for her part she never could see into it, how any girl could marry a minister—that she should as soon think of setting up housekeeping in a meeting-house.

'O, Cerinthy Ann!' exclaimed her mother, 'how can you go on so?'

'It's a fact,' said the adventurous damsel; 'now other men let you have some peace, but a minister's always round under your feet.'

'So you think the less you see of a husband the better?' said one of the ladies.

'Just my views,' said Cerinthy, giving a decided snip to her thread with her scissors; 'I like the Nantucketers that go off on four years' voyages, and leave their wives a clear field. If ever I get married I'm going up to have one of those fellows.'

It is to be remarked, in passing, that Miss Cerinthy Ann was at this very time receiving surreptitious visits from a consumptive-looking, conscientious, young theological candidate who came occasionally to preach in the vicinity, and put up at the house of the Deacon, her father. This good young man, being violently attacked on the doctrine of election by Miss Cerinthy, had been drawn on to illustrate it in a most practical manner, to her comprehension; and it was the consciousness of the weak and tottering state of the internal garrison, that added vigour to the young lady's tones. As Mary had been the chosen confidant of the progress of this affair, she was quietly amused at the demonstration.

'You'd better take care, Cerinthy Ann,' said her mother; 'they say that "those who sing before breakfast, will cry before night." Girls talk about getting married,' she said, relapsing into a gentle didactic melancholy, 'without realizing its awful responsibilities.'

'Oh! as to that,' said Cerinthy, 'I've been practising on my pudding now these six years, and I shouldn't be afraid to throw one up chimney with any girl.' This speech was founded on a tradition, current in those times, 'that no young lady was fit to be married till she could construct a boiled Indian-pudding, of such durability, that it could be thrown up chimney and come down on the ground, outside, without breaking;' and the consequence of Cerinthy Ann's sally was a general laugh.

'Girls a'n't what they used to be in my day,' sententiously remarked an elderly lady. 'I remember my mother told me when she was thirteen she could knit a long cotton stocking in a day.'

'I haven't much faith in these stories of old times; have you, girls?' said Cerinthy, appealing to the younger members at the frame.

'At any rate,' said Mrs. Twitchel, 'our minister's wife will be a pattern; I don't know anybody as goes beyond her either in spinning or fine stitching.'

Mary sat as placid and disengaged as the new moon, and listened to the chatter of old and young, with the easy quietness of a young heart that has early outlived life, and looks on everything in the world from some gentle, restful eminence far on towards a better home. She smiled at everybody's word, had a quick eye for everybody's wants, and was ready with thimble, scissors, or thread, whenever any one needed them; but once when there was a pause in the conversation, she and Mrs. Marvyn were both discovered to be stolen away. They were seated on the bed in Mary's little room, with their arms around each other, communing in low and gentle tones. 'Mary, my dear child,' said her friend, 'this event is very pleasant to me, because it places you permanently near me. I did not know but eventually this sweet face might lead to my losing you, who are in some respects the dearest friend I have.'

'You might be sure,' said Mary, 'I never would have married, except that my mother's happiness and the happiness of so good a friend seem to depend on it. When we renounce self in anything, we have reason to hope God's blessing; and so I feel assured of a peaceful life in the course I have taken. You will always be as a mother to me,' she added, laying her head on her friend's shoulder.

'Yes,' said Mrs. Marvyn; 'and I must not let myself think a moment how dear it might have been to have you *more* my own. If you feel really, truly happy, if you can enter on this life without any misgivings—'

'I can,' said Mary, firmly.

At this instant, very strangely, the string which confined a wreath of sea-shells around her glass, having been long undermined by moths, suddenly broke and fell down, scattering the shells upon the floor.

Both women started, for the string of shells had been placed there by James; and though neither were superstitious, this was one of those odd coincidences that make hearts throb.

'Dear boy,' said Mary, gathering the shells up tenderly; 'wherever he is, I shall never cease to love him; it makes me feel sad to see this come down; but it is only an accident; nothing of him will ever fail out of my heart.'

Mrs. Marvyn clasped Mary closer to her, with tears in her eyes.

'I'll tell you what, Mary; it must have been the moths did that,' said Miss Prissy, who had been standing, unobserved, at the door for a moment back; 'moths will eat away strings just so. Last week Mrs. Vernon's great family picture fell down because the moths eat through the cord; people ought to use twine or cotton string always. But I came to tell you that the supper is all set, and the Doctor out of his study, and all the people are wondering where you are.'

Mary and Mrs. Marvyn gave a hasty glance at themselves in the glass, to be assured of their good keeping, and went into the great kitchen, where a long table stood exhibiting all that plenitude of provision which the immortal description of Washington Irving has saved us the trouble of representing in detail.

The husbands, brothers, and lovers had come in, and the scene was redolent of gaiety. When Mary made her appearance, there was a moment's pause, till she was conducted to the side of the Doctor; when, raising his hand, he invoked a grace upon the loaded board.

Unrestrained gaieties followed. Groups of young men and maidens chatted together, and all the gallantries of the times were enacted. Serious matrons commented on the cake, and told each other high and particular secrets in the culinary art, which they drew from remote family archives. One might have learned in that instructive assembly how best to keep moths out of blankets, how to make fritters of Indian corn undistinguishable from oysters: how to bring up babies by hand, and how to mend a cracked teapot, and how to take out grease from a brocade, and how to reconcile absolute decrees with free will, and how to make five yards of cloth answer the purpose of six, and how to put down the democratic party. All were busy, earnest, and certain, just as a swarm of men and women, old and young, are in 1859.

Miss Prissy was in her glory; every bow of her best cap was alive with excitement, and she presented to the eyes of astonished Newport gentry an animated receipt-book. Some of the information she communicated, indeed, was so valuable and important, that she could not trust the air with it, but whispered the most important portions in a confidential tone. Among the crowd Cerinthy Ann's theological admirer was observed in deeply reflective attitude; and that high-spirited young lady added further to his convictions of the total depravity of the species, by vexing and discomposing him in those thousand ways in which a lively, ill-conditioned young woman will put to rout a serious, well-disposed young man, comforting herself with the reflection that by-and-by she would repent of all her sins in a lump together.

Vain, transitory splendours! Even this evening, so glorious, so heart-cheering, so fruitful in instruction and amusement, could not last for ever. Gradually the company broke up; the matrons mounted soberly on horseback behind their spouses; and Cerinthy consoled her clerical friend by giving him an opportunity to read her a lecture on the way home, if he found the courage to do so.

Mr. and Mrs. Marvyn and Candace wound their way soberly homeward; the Doctor returned to his study for nightly devotions; and before long, sleep settled down on the brown cottage.

'I'll tell you what, Cato,' said Candace, before composing herself to sleep, 'I can't feel it in my bones dat dis yer wedding is going to come off yet.'

CHAPTER XXXI.

A DAY or two after, Madame de Frontignac and Mary went out to gather shells and seaweed on the beach. It was four o'clock; and the afternoon sun was hanging in the sultry sky of July with a hot and vaporous stillness. The whole air was full of blue haze, that softened the outlines of objects without hiding them. The sea lay like so much glass; every ship and boat was double; every line, and rope, and spar had its counterpart; and it seemed hard to say which was the most real, the under or the upper world. Madame de Frontignac and Mary had brought along a little basket, which they were filling with shells and sea-mosses. The former was in high spirits. She ran, and shouted, and exclaimed, and wondered at each new marvel thrown out upon the shore, with the *abandon* of a little child. Mary could not but wonder whether this indeed were she whose strong words had pierced and wrung her sympathies the other night, and whether a deep life-wound could lie bleeding under those brilliant eyes and that infantine exuberance of gaiety; yet surely all that which seemed so strong, so true, so real, could not be gone so soon,—and it could not be so soon consoled. Mary wondered at her, as the Anglo-Saxon constitution, with its strong, firm intensity, its singleness of nature, wonders at the mobile, many-sided existence of warmer races, whose versatility of emotion on the surface is not incompatible with the most intense sameness lower down.

Mary's was one of those indulgent and tolerant natures which seem to form the most favourable base for the play of other minds, rather than to be itself salient,—and something about her tender calmness always seemed to provoke the spirit of frolic in her friend. She would laugh at her, kiss her, gambol round her, dress her hair with fantastic *coiffures*, and call her all sorts of fanciful and poetic names in French or English, while Mary surveyed her with a pleased and innocent surprise, as a revelation of character altogether new and different from anything to which she had been hitherto accustomed. She was to her a living pantomime, and brought into her unembellished life the charms of opera, and theatre, and romance.

After wearying themselves with their researches, they climbed round a point of rock that stretched some way out into the sea, and attained to a little kind of grotto, where the high cliffs shut out the rays of the sun. They sat down to rest upon the rocks. A fresh breeze of declining day was springing up, and bringing the rising tide landward,—each several line of waves with their white crest coming up and breaking gracefully on the hard, sparkling sand-beach at their feet.

Mary's eyes fixed themselves, as they were apt to do, in a mournful reverie, on the infinite expanse of waters, which was now broken and chopped into thousand incoming waves by the fresh afternoon breeze. Madame de Frontignac noticed the expression, and began to play with her as if she had been a child. She pulled the comb from her hair, and let down its long silky waves upon her shoulders.

'Now,' said she, 'let us make a Miranda of thee. This is our cave. I will be Prince Ferdinand. Burr told me all about that,—he reads beautifully, and explained it all to me. What a lovely story that is;—you must be so happy who know how to read Shakspeare without learning. *Tenez!* I will put this shell on your forehead,—it has a hole here, and I will pass this gold chain through—now! What a pity this seaweed will not be pretty out of water; it has no effect; but there is some green that will do,—let me fasten it so. Now, fair Miranda, look at thyself.'

Where is the girl so angelic as not to feel a slight curiosity to know how she shall look in a new and strange costume? Mary bent over the rock where a little pool of water lay in a brown hollow above the fluctuations of the tide, dark and still, like a mirror,—and saw a fair face, with a white shell above the forehead, and drooping wreaths of green seaweed in the silken hair; and a faint blush and smile rose on the cheek, giving the last finish to the picture.

'How do you find yourself?' said Madame; 'confess now that I have a true talent in coiffure. Now I will be Ferdinand.' She turned quickly, and her eye was caught by something that Mary did not see; she only saw the smile fade suddenly from Madame de Frontignac's cheek, and her lips grow deadly white, while her heart beat so that Mary could notice its flutterings under her black silk bodice.

'Will the sea-nymphs punish the rash presumption of a mortal who intrudes?' said Colonel Burr, stepping before them with a grace as invincible and assured as if he had never had any past history with either.

Mary started with a guilty blush, like a child detected in an unseemly frolic, and put her hand to her head to take off the unwonted adornments.

'Let me protest, in the name of the graces,' said Burr, who by that time stood with easy calmness at her side; and as he spoke he stayed her hand with that gentle air of authority which made it the natural impulse of most people to obey him. 'It would be treason against the picturesque,' he added, 'to spoil that toilet so charmingly uniting the wearer to the scene.'

Mary was taken by surprise, and discomposed, as every one is who finds one's self masquerading in attire foreign to their usual habits and character; and therefore, when she would persist in taking it to pieces, Burr found sufficient to alleviate the embarrassment of Madame de Frontignac's utter silence in a playful run of protestations and compliments.

'I think, Mary,' said Madame de Frontignac, 'that we had better be returning to the house.'

CHAPTER XXXI.

This was said in the haughtiest and coolest tone imaginable, looking at the place where Burr stood, as if there were nothing there but empty air. Mary rose to go; Madame de Frontignac offered her arm.

'Permit me to remark, ladies,' said Burr, with the quiet suavity which never forsook him, 'that your very agreeable occupations have caused time to pass more rapidly than you are aware. I think you will find that the tide has risen so as to intercept the path by which you came here. You will hardly be able to get around the point of rocks without some assistance.'

Mary looked a few paces ahead, and saw, a little before them, a fresh afternoon breeze driving the rising tide high on to the side of the rocks, at whose foot their course had lain. The nook in which they had been sporting formed a part of a shelving ledge which inclined over their heads, and which it was just barely possible could be climbed by a strong and agile person, but which would be wholly inaccessible to a frail, unaided woman.

'There is no time to be lost,' said Burr, coolly, measuring the possibilities with that keen eye that was never discomposed by any exigency. 'I am at your service, ladies; I can either carry you in my arms around this point, or assist you up these rocks.' He paused and waited for their answer.

Madame de Frontignac stood pale, cold, and silent, hearing only the wild beating of her heart.

'I think,' said Mary, 'that we should try the rocks.'

'Very well,' said Burr; and placing his gloved hand on a fragment of rock, somewhat above their heads, he swung himself on to it with an easy agility; from this he stretched himself down as far as possible towards them, and extending his hand, directed Mary, who stood foremost, to set her foot on a slight projection, and give him both her hands; she did so, and he seemed to draw her up as easily as if she had been a feather. He placed her by him on a shelf of rock, and turned again to Madame de Frontignac: she folded her arms and turned resolutely away towards the sea.

Just at that moment a coming wave broke at her feet.

'There is no time to be lost,' said Burr; 'there's a tremendous wave coming in, and the next wave may carry you out.'

'*Tant mieux*,' she responded, without turning her head.

'Oh, Verginie! Verginie!' exclaimed Mary,—kneeling and stretching her arms over the rock; but another voice called Verginie, in a tone which went to her heart. She turned and saw those dark eyes full of tears.

'Oh, come,' he said, with that voice which she could never resist.

She put her cold, trembling hands into his, and he drew her up and placed her safely beside Mary. A few moments of difficult climbing followed, in which his arm was thrown now around one and then around the other, and they felt themselves carried with a force, as if the slight and graceful form were strung with steel.

Placed in safety on the top of the bank, there was a natural gush of grateful feeling towards their deliverer. The severest resentment, the coolest moral disapprobation, are necessarily somewhat softened when the object of them has just laid one under a personal obligation.

Burr did not seem disposed to press his advantage, and treated the incident as the most matter-of-course affair in the world. He offered an arm to each lady, with the air of a well-bred gentleman, who offers a necessary support; and each took it, because neither wished, under the circumstances, to refuse.

He walked along leisurely homeward, talking in that easy, quiet, natural way in which he excelled, addressing no very particular remark to either one, and at the door of the cottage took his leave, saying, as he bowed, that he hoped neither of them would feel any inconvenience from their exertions, and that he should do himself the pleasure to call soon, and inquire after their health.

Madame de Frontignac made no reply; but curtsied with a stately grace, turned and went into her little room, whither Mary, after a few minutes, followed her.

She found her thrown upon the bed, her face buried in the pillow, her breast heaving as if she were sobbing; but when at Mary's entrance she raised her head, her eyes were bright and dry.

'It is just as I told you, Mary,—that man holds me. I love him yet, in spite of myself. It is in vain to be angry. What is the use of striking your right hand with your left? When we *love* one more than ourselves, we only hurt ourselves with our anger.'

'But,' said Mary, 'love is founded on respect and esteem; and when that is gone——'

'Why, then,' said Madame, 'we are very sorry; but we love yet; do we stop loving ourselves when we have lost our own self-respect? No! it is so disagreeable to see, we shut our eyes and ask to have the bandage put on,—you know *that*, poor little heart; you can think how it would have been with you, if you had found that he was not what you thought.'

The word struck home to Mary's consciousness, but she sat down and took her friend in her arms with an air, self-controlled, serious, rational.

'I see and feel it all, dear Verginie, but I must stand firm for you. You are in the waves, and I on the shore. If you are so weak at heart, you must not see this man any more.'

'But he will call.'

'I will see him for you.'

'What will you tell him, my heart,—tell him that I am ill, perhaps?'

'No; I will tell him the truth,—that you do not wish to see him.'

'That is hard,—he will wonder.'

'I think not,' said Mary, resolutely; 'and furthermore I shall say to him that, while Madame de Frontignac is at the cottage, it will not be agreeable for us to receive calls from him.'

'Mary, *ma chère*, you astonish me!'

'My dear friend,' said Mary, 'it is the only way. This man,—this cruel, wicked, deceitful man,—must not be allowed to trifle with you in this way. I will protect you.' And she rose up with flashing eye and glowing cheek, looking as her father looked when he protested against the slave-trade.

'Thou art my Saint Catherine,' said Verginie, rising up, excited by Mary's enthusiasm, 'and hast the sword as well as the palm; but, dear saint, don't think so very, very badly of him,—he has a noble nature; he has the angel in him.'

'The greater his sin,' said Mary; 'he sins against light and love.'

'But I think his heart is touched,—I think he is sorry. Oh, Mary, if you had only seen how he looked at me, when he put out his hands on the rocks,—there were tears in his eyes.'

'Well there might be,' said Mary; 'I do not think he is quite a fiend; no one could look at those cheeks, dear Verginie, and not feel sad, that saw you a few months ago.'

'Am I so changed?' she said, rising and looking at herself in the mirror. 'Sure enough, my neck used to be quite round,—now you can see those two little bones, like rocks at low tide. Poor Verginie! her summer is gone, and the leaves are falling; poor little cat;'—and Verginie stroked her own chestnut head, as if she had been pitying another, and began humming a little Norman air, with a refrain that sounded like the murmur of a brook over the stones.

The more Mary was touched by these little poetic ways, which ran just on an even line between the gay and the pathetic, the more indignant she grew with the man that had brought all this sorrow. She felt a saintly vindictiveness, and a determination to place herself as an adamantine shield between him and her friend. There is no courage and no anger like that of a gentle woman when once fully roused; if ever you have occasion to meet it, you will certainly remember the hour.

CHAPTER XXXII.

MARY revolved the affairs of her friend in her mind during the night. The intensity of the mental crisis through which she herself had just passed, had developed her in many inward respects, so that she looked upon life no longer as a timid girl, but as a strong, experienced woman. She had thought, and suffered, and held converse with eternal realities, until thousands of mere earthly hesitations and timidities, that often restrain a young and untried nature, had entirely lost their hold upon her. Besides, Mary had at heart the Puritan seed of heroism,—never absent from the souls of true New England women. Her essentially Hebrew education, trained in daily converse with the words of prophets and seers, and with the modes of thought of a grave and heroic people, predisposed her to a kind of exaltation which, in times of great trial, might rise to the heights of the religious sublime, in which the impulse of self-devotion and protection took a form essentially commanding. The very intensity of the repression under which her faculties developed seemed as it were to produce a surplus of hidden strength, which came out in exigencies. Her reading, though restricted to few volumes, had been of the kind that vitalized and stimulated a poetic nature, and laid up in its chambers vigorous words and trenchant phrases, for the use of an excited feeling—so that eloquence came to her as a native gift. She realized, in short, in her higher hours, the last touch with which Milton finishes his portrait of an ideal woman:—

> 'Greatness of mind and nobleness, their seat
> Build in her loftiest, and create an awe About her as a guard angelic placed.'

The next morning, Colonel Burr called at the cottage. Mary was spinning in the garret, and Madame de Frontignac was reeling yarn, when Mrs. Scudder brought this announcement.

'Mother,' said Mary, 'I wish to see Mr. Burr alone; Madame de Frontignac will not go down.'

Mrs. Scudder looked surprised, but asked no questions. When she was gone down, Mary stood a moment reflecting; Madame de Frontignac looked eager and agitated. 'Remember and notice all he says, and just how he looks, Mary, so as to tell me; and be sure and say that “I thank him for his kindness yesterday;” we must own he appeared very well there; did he not?’

‘Certainly,’ said Mary; ‘but no man could have done less.’

‘Ah! but Mary, not every man could have done it as he did; now don’t be too hard on him, Mary; I have said dreadful things to him; I am afraid I have been too severe. After all, these distinguished men are so tempted; we don’t know how much they are tempted; and who can wonder that they are a little spoiled; so, my angel, you must be merciful.’

‘Merciful!’ said Mary, kissing the pale cheek and feeling the cold little hands that trembled in hers.

‘So you will go down in your little spinning toilette, ma *mie;* I fancy you look as Joan of Arc did when she was keeping her sheep at Doremi. Go, and God bless thee!’ and Madame de Frontignac pushed her playfully forward.

Mary entered the room where Burr was seated, and wished him good morning, in a serious and placid manner, in which there was not the slightest trace of embarrassment or discomposure.

‘Shall I have the pleasure of seeing your fair companion this morning?’ said Burr, after some moments of indifferent conversation.

‘No, sir; Madame de Frontignac desires me to excuse her to you.’

‘Is she ill?’ said Burr, with a look of concern.

‘No, Mr. Burr, she prefers not to see you.’ Burr gave a start of well-bred surprise; and Mary added:—

‘Madame de Frontignac has made me familiar with the history of your acquaintance with her; and you will therefore understand what I mean, Mr. Burr, when I say that, during the time of her stay with us, we would prefer not to receive calls from you.’

‘Your language, Miss Scudder, has certainly the merit of explicitness.’

‘I intend it shall have, sir,’ said Mary, tranquilly; ‘half the misery of the world comes of want of courage to speak and to hear the truth plainly, and in a spirit of love.’

‘I am gratified that you insert the last clause, Miss Scudder; I might not otherwise recognize the gentle being whom I have always regarded as the impersonation of all that is softest in woman. I have not the honour of understanding in the least the reason of this apparently capricious sentence, but I bow to it in submission.’

‘Mr. Burr,’ said Mary, walking up to him, and looking him full in the eyes with an energy that for the moment bore down his practised air of easy superiority, ‘I wish to speak to you for a moment, as one immortal soul should to another, without any of those false glosses and deceits which men call ceremony and good manners. You have done a very great injury to a lovely lady, whose weakness ought to have been sacred in your eyes. Precisely, because you are what you are,—strong, keen, penetrating, able to control and govern all who come near you; because you have the power to make yourself agreeable, interesting, fascinating, and to win esteem and love,—just for that reason you ought to hold yourself the guardian of every woman, and treat her as you would wish any man to treat your own daughter. I leave it to your own conscience whether this is the manner in which you have treated Madame de Frontignac.'

'Upon my word, Miss Scudder,' began Burr, 'I cannot imagine what representations our mutual friend may have been making. I assure you, our intercourse has been as irreproachable as the most scrupulous could desire.'

'Irreproachable! innocent! Mr. Burr, you know that you have taken the very life out of her; you men can have everything, ambition, wealth, power; a thousand ways are open to you; and women have nothing but their hearts, and when that is gone, all is gone. Mr. Burr, you remember the rich man that had flocks and herds, but nothing would do for him but he must have the one little ewe lamb which was all his poor neighbour had. Thou art the man! You have stolen all the love she has to give, all that she had to make a happy home; and you can never give her anything in return without endangering her purity and her soul, and you knew you could not. I know you men *think* this is a light matter; but it is death to us; what will this woman's life be? one long struggle to forget; and when you have forgotten her, and are going on gay and happy, when you have thrown her very name away as a faded flower, she will be praying, hoping, fearing for you; though all men deny you, yet will not she. Yes, Mr. Burr, if ever your popularity and prosperity should leave you, and those who now flatter should despise and curse you, she will always be interceding with her own heart and with God for you, and making a thousand excuses when she cannot deny; and if you die, as I fear you have lived, unreconciled to the God of your fathers, it will be in her heart to offer up her very soul for you, and to pray that God will impute all your sins to her, and give you heaven. Oh, I know this because I have felt it in my own heart!' and Mary threw herself passionately down into a chair, and broke into an agony of uncontrolled sobbing.

Burr turned away, and stood looking through the window; tears were dropping silently, unchecked by the cold, hard pride which was the evil demon of his life.

It is due to our human nature to believe that no man could ever have been so passionately and enduringly loved and revered by both men and women as he was, without a beautiful and lovable nature; no man ever demonstrated more forcibly the truth, that it is not a man's natural constitution, but the *use* he makes of it which stamps him as good or evil.

The diviner part of him was weeping, and the cold, proud, demon was struggling to regain his lost ascendency. Every sob of the fair, inspired child who had been speaking to him seemed to shake his heart; he felt as if he could have fallen on his knees to her; and yet that stoical habit, which was the boast of his life, which was the highest wisdom he taught to his only and beautiful daughter, was slowly stealing back round his heart, and he pressed his lips together, resolved that no word should escape till he had fully mastered himself.

In a few moments Mary rose with renewed calmness and dignity, and approaching him, said, 'Before I wish you a good morning, Mr. Burr, I must ask pardon for the liberty I have taken in speaking so very plainly.'

CHAPTER XXXII.

'There is no pardon needed, my dear child,' said Burr, turning and speaking very gently, and with a face expressive of a softened concern; 'if you have told me harsh truths, it was with gentle intentions; I only hope that I may prove, at least by the future, that I am not altogether so bad as you imagine. As to the friend whose name has been passed between us, no man can go beyond me in a sense of her real nobleness; I am sensible how little I can ever deserve the sentiment with which she honours me. I am ready, in my future course, to obey any commands that you and she may think proper to lay upon me.'

'The only kindness you can now do her,' said Mary, 'is to leave her. It is impossible that you can be merely friends,—it is impossible, without violating the holiest bonds, that you can be more. The injury done is irreparable, but you can avoid adding another and greater one to it.'

Burr looked thoughtful.

'May I say one thing more?' said Mary, the colour rising in her cheeks.

Burr looked at her with that smile that always drew out the confidence of every heart.

'Mr. Burr,' she said, 'you will pardon me, but I cannot help saying this: You have, I am told, wholly renounced the Christian faith of your fathers, and build your whole life on quite another foundation. I cannot help feeling that this is a great and terrible mistake. I cannot help wishing that you would examine and reconsider.'

'My dear child, I am extremely grateful to you for your remark, and appreciate fully the purity of the source from which it springs. Unfortunately, our intellectual beliefs are not subject to the control of our will. I have examined, and the examination has, I regret to say, not had the effect you would desire.'

Mary looked at him wistfully; he smiled and bowed, all himself again; and stopping at the door, he said, with a proud humility, 'Do me the favour to present my devoted regard to your friend; believe me, that hereafter you shall have less reason to complain of me.' He bowed and was gone.

An eye-witness of the scene has related that when Burr resigned his seat as president of his country's senate, he was an object of peculiar political bitterness and obloquy. Almost all who listened to him had made up their minds that he was an utterly faithless, unprincipled man; and yet, such was his singular and peculiar personal power, that his short farewell address melted the whole assembly into tears; and his most embittered adversaries were charmed into a momentary enthusiasm of admiration.

It must not be wondered at, therefore, if our simple-hearted, loving Mary strangely found all her indignation against him gone, and herself little disposed to criticise the impassioned tenderness with which Madame de Frontignac still regarded him.

We have one thing more that we cannot avoid saying of two men so singularly in juxtaposition, as Aaron Burr and Dr. Hopkins.

Both had a perfect *logic* of life, and guided themselves with an inflexible rigidity by it. Burr assumed individual pleasure to be the great object of human existence; and Dr. Hopkins placed it in a life altogether beyond self. Burr rejected all sacrifice, Hopkins considered sacrifice as the foundation of all existence. To live as far as possible without a disagreeable sensation was an object which Burr proposed to himself as the *summum bonum*, for which he drilled down and subjugated a nature of singular richness. Hopkins, on the other hand, smoothed the asperities of a temperament naturally violent and fiery by a rigid discipline, which guided it entirely above the plane of self-indulgence; and, in the pursuance of their great end, the one watched against his better nature as the other did against his worse. It is but fair, then, to take their lives as the practical workings of their respective ethical creeds.

CHAPTER XXXIII.

'*Enfin, chère Sibylle,*' said Madame de Frontignac when Mary came out of the room with her cheeks glowing and her eyes flashing with a still unsubdued light. '*Te voilà encore!* What did he say, *mimi?* did he ask for me?'

'Yes,' said Mary, 'he asked for you.'

'What did you tell him?'

'I told him that you wished me to excuse you.'

'How did he look then? Did he look surprised?'

'A good deal so, I thought,' said Mary.

'*Allons, mimi,* tell me all you said and all he said.'

'Oh,' said Mary, 'I am the worst person in the world; in fact, I cannot remember anything that I have said; but I told him that he must leave you and never see you any more.'

'Oh, *mimi!* never!'

Madame de Frontignac sat down on the side of the bed with such a look of utter despair as went to Mary's heart.

'You know that that is best, Verginie, do you not?'

'Oh! yes, I know it; but it is like death to me! Ah, well, what shall Verginie do now?'

'You have your husband,' said Mary.

'I do not love him,' said Madame de Frontignac.

'Yes; but he is a good and honourable man, and you should love him.'

'Love is not in our power,' said Madame de Frontignac.

'Not *every kind* of love,' said Mary, 'but *some* kinds. If you have an indulgent friend who protects you, and cares for you, you can be grateful to him; you can try to make him happy, and in time you may come to love him very much. He is a thousand times nobler man, if what you say is true, than the one who has injured you so.'

'Oh, Mary,' said Madame de Frontignac, 'there are some cases where we find it too easy to love our enemies.'

'More than that,' said Mary; 'I believe that if you were to go on patiently in the way of duty, and pray daily to God, that at last He will take out of your heart this painful love, and give you a true and healthy one. As you say, such feelings are very sweet and noble; but they are not the only ones we have to live by. We can find happiness in duty, in self-sacrifice, in calm, sincere, honest friendship. That is what you can feel for your husband.'

'Your words cool me,' said Madame de Frontignac. 'Thou art a sweet snow-maiden, and my heart is hot and tired. I like to feel thee in my arms,' she said, putting her arms around Mary, and resting her head upon her shoulder. 'Talk to me so every day, and read me good, cool verses out of that beautiful book, and perhaps by-and-by I shall grow still and quiet like you.'

Thus Mary soothed her friend; but every few days this soothing had to be done over, as long as Burr remained in Newport. When he was finally gone, she grew more calm. The simple, homely ways of the cottage, the healthful routine of daily domestic toils, into which she delighted to enter, brought refreshment to her spirits. That fine tact and exquisite social sympathy which distinguishes the French above other nations, caused her at once to enter into the spirit of the life in which she moved; so that she no longer shocked any one's religious feelings by acts forbidden to the Puritan idea of the sabbath, or failed in any of the exterior proprieties of religious life.

She also read and studied with avidity the English Bible, which came to her with the novelty of a wholly new book, and in a new language; nor was she without a certain artistic valuation of the austere precision and gravity of the religious life by which she was surrounded.

'It is sublime, but a little "glaciale," like the Alps,' she sometimes said to Mary and Mrs. Marvyn, when speaking of it; 'but then,' she added, playfully, 'there are the flowers—*les roses des Alpes;* and the air is very strengthening, and it is near to heaven—*il faut avouer*.'

We have shown how she appeared to the eye of New England life; it may not be uninteresting to give a letter to one of her friends, which showed how the same appeared to her.

It was not a friend with whom she felt on such terms that her intimacy with Burr would furnish any allusions to her correspondence.

'You behold me, my charming Gabrielle, quite pastoral; recruiting from the dissipations of my Philadelphia life in a lovely, quiet cottage, with most worthy, excellent people, whom I have learnt to love very much. They are good and true, as pious as the saints themselves, although they do not belong to the true Church, a thing which I am sorry for; but then let us hope that if the world is wide, heaven is wider, and that all worthy and religious people will find room at last. This is Verginie's own little pet private heresy, and when I tell it to the Abbé, he only smiles; and so I think, somehow, that it is not so very bad as it might be.

'We have had a very gay life in Philadelphia, and now I am growing tired of the world, and think I shall retire to my cheese, like La Fontaine's rat. These people in the country here in America have a character quite their own; very different from the life of cities, where one sees, for the most part, only a continuation of the forms of good society which exist in the old world.

'In the country these people seem simple, grave, severe; always industrious; cold and reserved in their manners towards each other, but with great warmth of heart. They are all obedient to the word of their priest, whom they call a minister, and who lives among them just like any other man, and marries and has children. Everything in their worship is plain and austere. Their churches are perfectly desolate; they have no chants, no pictures, no carvings; only a most disconsolate, bare building, where they meet together and sing one or two hymns, and the minister makes one or two prayers all out of his own thoughts; and then gives them a long, long discourse about things which I cannot understand English enough to comprehend.

'There is a very beautiful, charming young girl here, the daughter of my hostess, who is as lovely and as saintly as St. Catharine, and has such a genius for religion that if she had been in our Church she would certainly have made a saint. Her mother is a respectable and worthy matron, and the good priest lives in the family. I think he is a man of very sublime religion, as much above this world as a great mountain; but he has the true sense of liberty and fraternity, for he has dared to oppose with all his might this detestable and cruel trade in poor negroes; which makes us, who are so proud of the example of America in asserting the rights of man, so ashamed for her inconsistencies.

'Well, now, there is a little romance getting up in the cottage; for the good priest has fixed his eyes on the pretty saint, and has discovered, what he must be blind not to see, that she is very lovely. And so, as he can marry, he wants to make her his wife; and her mamma, who adores him as if he were God, is quite set upon it. The sweet Marie, however, has had a lover of her own in her little heart, a beautiful young man who went to sea, as heroes always do, to seek his fortune. And the cruel sea has drowned him, and the poor little saint has wept and prayed her very life out on his grave; till she is so thin, and sweet, and mournful, that it makes one's heart ache to see her smile. In our Church, Gabrielle, she would have gone into a convent; but she makes a vocation of her daily life, and goes round the house so sweetly, doing all the little work that is to be done, as sacredly as the nuns pray at the altar. For you must know, here in New England the people for the most part keep no servants, but perform all the household work themselves, with no end of spinning and sewing besides. It is the true Arcadia, where you find refined and cultivated natures busying themselves with the simplest toils. For these people are well-read and well-bred, and truly ladies in all things. And so, my little Marie and I, we feed the hens and chickens together, and we search for eggs in the hay in the barn; and they have taught me to spin at their great wheel, and a little one, too, which makes a noise like the humming of a bee. But where am I? Oh, I was telling about the romance. Well, so the good priest has proposed for my Marie, and the dear soul has accepted him, as the nun accepts the veil; for she only loves him filially and religiously. And now they are going on, in their way, with preparations for the wedding. They had what they call "a quilting" here the other night, to prepare the bride's quilt, and all the friends in the neighbourhood came—it was very amusing to see. The morals of this people are so austere that young men and girls are allowed the greatest freedom. They associate and talk freely together, and the young men walk home alone with the girls after evening parties. And most generally the young people, I am told, arrange their marriages among themselves before the consent of the parents is asked. This is very strange to us. I must not weary you, however, with the details. I watch my little romance daily, and will let you hear further as it progresses.

'With a thousand kisses, I am ever your loving

'VERGINIE.'

CHAPTER XXXIV.

MEANWHILE wedding proceedings were going on at the cottage with that consistent vigour with which Yankee people always drive operations when they know precisely what they are about. The wedding-day was definitively fixed for the 1st of August, and every one of the two weeks between had its particular significance and value precisely marked out and arranged in Mrs. Katy Scudder's comprehensive and systematic schemes. It was settled that the newly-wedded pair were, for a while at least, to reside at the cottage. It might have been imagined, therefore, that no great external changes were in contemplation; but it is astonishing to see the amount of grave discussion, the amount of consulting, advising, and running abstractedly to and fro, which can be made to result out of an apparently slight change in the relative position of two people in the same house.

Dr. Hopkins really opened his eyes with calm amazement—good modest soul! he had never imagined himself the hero of so much preparation. He heard his name constantly from morning to night occurring in busy consultations that seemed to be going on between Miss Prissy, and Mrs. Deacon Twitchel, and Mrs. Scudder, and Mrs. Jones, and quietly wondered what they could have so much more than usual to say about him. For a while it seemed to him that the whole house was about to be torn to pieces. He was even requested to step out of his study one day, into which immediately entered, in his absence, two of the most vigorous women of the parish, who proceeded to uttermost measures, first pitching everything into pie, so that the Doctor, who returned disconsolately to look for a book, at once gave up himself and his system of divinity as entirely lost, until assured by one of the ladies in a condescending manner that he knew nothing about the matter, and that if he would return after half a day he would find everything right again: a declaration in which he tried to have unlimited faith, and where he found the advantage of a mind accustomed to believe in mysteries. And it is to be remarked, that on his return he actually found his table in most perfect order, with not a single one of his papers missing; in fact, to his ignorant eye, the room looked exactly as it did before; and when Miss Prissy eloquently demonstrated to him that every inch of that paint had been scrubbed, and the windows taken out and washed inside and out, and rinsed through three waters, and that the curtains had been taken down and washed and put through a blue water, and starched and ironed, and put up again, he only innocently wondered in his ignorance what there was in a man's being married that made all these ceremonies necessary; but the Doctor was a wise man, and in cases of difficulty kept his mind much to himself, and therefore he only informed those energetic practitioners that 'he was extremely obliged to them,' accepting the matter by simple faith, an example which we recommend to all good men in similar circumstances.

The house throughout was subjected to similar renovations. Everything in every chest, or trunk, or box, was vigorously pulled out and hung out on lines in the clothes-yard to air, for when once the spirit of enterprise has fairly possessed a group of women, it assumes the form of a 'prophetic fury,' and carries them beyond themselves. Let not any ignorant mortal of the masculine gender, at such hours, rashly dare to question the promptings of the genius that inspires them! Spite of all the treatises that have lately appeared to demonstrate that there is no particular inherent diversity between men and women, we hold to the opinion that one thorough season of house-cleansing is sufficient to demonstrate the existence of awful and mysterious differences between the sexes, and of subtle and reserved forces in the female line, before which the lords of creation can only veil their faces with a discreet reverence as our Doctor has done.

In fact, his whole deportment on the occasion was characterized by humility so edifying as really to touch the hearts of the whole synod of matrons; and Miss Prissy rewarded him by declaring impressively her opinion that he was worthy to have a voice in the choosing the wedding-dress, and she actually swooped him up, just in a very critical part of a distinction between natural and moral ability, and conveyed him bodily (as fairy sprites know how to convey the most ponderous of mortals) into the best room, where three specimens of brocade lay spread out upon a table for inspection.

Mary stood by the side of the table, her pretty head bent reflectively downward, her cheek just resting upon the tip of one of her fingers, as she stood looking thoughtfully *through* the brocades at something deeper that seemed to lie under them; and when the Doctor was required to give judgment on the articles, it was observed by the matrons that his large blue eyes were resting upon Mary with an expression that almost glorified his face; and it was not until his elbow was repeatedly shaken by Miss Prissy that he gave a sudden start and fixed his attention as was requested upon the silks. It had been one of Miss Prissy's favourite theories, that 'that dear blessed man *had taste enough if he would only give his mind to things;*' and in fact the Doctor rather verified the remark on the present occasion, for he looked very conscientiously and soberly at the silks, and even handled them cautiously and respectfully with his fingers, and listened with grave attention to all that Miss Prissy told him of their price and properties, and then laid his finger down on one whose snow-white ground was embellished with a pattern representing lilies of the valley on a background of green leaves. 'This is the one,' he said, with an air of decision, and then he looked at Mary and smiled, and a murmur of universal approbation broke out. A chorus of loud acclamations, in which Miss Prissy's voice took the lead, conveyed to the innocent-minded Doctor the idea that in some mysterious way he had distinguished himself in the eyes of his feminine friends, whereat he retired to his study, slightly marvelling, but on the whole well pleased, as men generally are when they do better than they expect; and Miss Prissy, turning out all profaner persons from the apartment, held a solemn consultation, to which only Mary, Mrs. Scudder, and Madame de Frontignac were admitted; for it is to be observed that the latter had risen daily and hourly in Miss Prissy's esteem since her entrance into the cottage, and she declared that if she only would give her a few hints, she didn't believe but that she could make that dress look just like a Paris one, and rather intimated that in such a case she might almost be ready to resign all mortal ambitions.

The afternoon of this day, just at that cool hour when the clock ticks so quietly in a New England kitchen, and everything is so clean and put away that there seems to be nothing to do in the house, Mary sat quietly down in her room to hem a ruffle. Everybody had gone out of the house on various errands. The Doctor, with implicit faith, had surrendered himself to Mrs. Scudder and Miss Prissy, to be conveyed up to Newport, and attend to various appointments in relation to his outer man, which he was informed would be indispensable in the forthcoming solemnities.

Madame de Frontignac had also gone to spend the day with some of her Newport friends; and Mary, quite well pleased with the placid and orderly stillness which reigned through the house, sat pleasantly murmuring a little tune to her sewing, when suddenly the trip of a merry, brisk foot was heard in the kitchen, and Miss Cerinthy Ann Twitchel made her appearance at the door, her healthy, glowing cheek wearing a still brighter colour, from the exercise of a three-mile walk in a July day.

'Why, Cerinthy,' said Mary, 'how glad I am to see you!'

'Well!' said Cerinthy; 'I have been meaning to come down all this week, but there is so much to do in haying-time; but to-day I told mother I *must* come. I brought these down,' she said, unfolding a dozen of snowy damask napkins, 'that I spun myself, and was thinking of you almost all the while I spun them; so I suppose they ain't quite so wicked as they might be.'

We will remark here that Cerinthy Ann, in virtue of having a high stock of animal spirits, and great fulness of physical vigour, had very small proclivities towards the unseen and spiritual; but still always indulged a secret resentment at being classed as a sinner above many others, who as church-members made such professions, and were, as she remarked, 'not a bit better than she was.'

She always, however, had cherished an unbounded veneration for Mary, and had made her the confidante of most of her important secrets; and it soon became very evident that she had come with one on her mind now.

'Don't you want to come and sit out in the lot?' she said to her, after sitting awhile, twirling her bonnet-strings with the air of one who has something to say and does not know exactly how to begin upon it.

Mary cheerfully gathered up her thread, scissors, and ruffling, and the two stepped over the window-sill, and soon found themselves seated cozily under the boughs of a large apple-tree, whose descending branches, meeting the tops of the high grass all around, formed a perfect seclusion, as private as heart could desire.

They sat down, pushing away a place in the grass; and Cerinthy Ann took off her bonnet, and threw it among the clover, exhibiting to view her glossy black hair, always trimly arranged in shining braids, except where some curls fell over the rich, high colour of her cheeks. Something appeared to discompose her this afternoon; there were those evident signs of a consultation impending, which to an experienced eye are as unmistakeable as the coming up of a shower in summer.

Cerinthy began by passionately demolishing several heads of clover, remarking as she did so that 'she didn't see, for her part, how Mary could keep so calm when things were coming so near;' and as Mary answered to this only with a quiet smile, she broke out again:—

'I don't see, for my part, how a young girl *could* marry a minister anyhow; but then I think *you* are just cut out for it. But what would anybody say if *I* should do such a thing?'

'I don't know,' said Mary, innocently.

'Well, I suppose everybody would hold up their hands; and yet if I *do* say it myself,' she added, colouring, 'there are not many girls who could make a better minister's wife than I could if I had a mind to try.'

'That I am sure of,' said Mary, warmly.

'I guess you are the only one that ever thought so,' said Cerinthy, giving an impatient toss; 'there's father all the while mourning over me, and mother too, and yet I don't see but that I do pretty much all that is done in the house. And they say I am a great comfort in a temporal point of view; but oh! the groanings and the sighings that there are over me!

'I don't think it is pleasant to think that your best friends are thinking such awful things about you when you are working your fingers off to help them; it is kind o' discouraging, but I don't know what to do about it;' and for a few moments Cerinthy sat demolishing buttercups and throwing them up in the air, till her shiny black head was covered with golden flakes, while her cheek grew redder with something that she was going to say next.

'Now, Mary, there is *that creature;* well—you know—he won't take "no" for an answer. What shall I do?'

'Suppose then you try "yes,"' said Mary, rather archly.

'Oh, pshaw, Mary Scudder! You know better than that now. I look like it, don't I?'

'Why, yes,' said Mary, looking at Cerinthy deliberately, 'on the whole I think you do.'

'Well, one thing I must say,' said Cerinthy, 'I can't see what *he* finds in me. I think he is a thousand times too good for me. Why, you have no idea, Mary, how I *have* plagued him. I believe that man *really is a Christian*,' she added, while something like a penitent tear actually glistened in those sharp, saucy, black eyes; 'besides,' she added, 'I have told him everything I could think of to discourage him. I told him that I had a bad temper, and didn't believe the doctrines, and couldn't promise that I ever should. And after all, that creature keeps right on, and I don't know what to tell him.'

'Well,' said Mary, mildly; 'do you think you really love him?'

'Love him,' said Cerinthy, giving a great flounce, 'to be sure I don't—catch me loving *any* man. I told him last night I didn't, but it didn't do a bit of good. I used to think that man was bashful, but I declare I have altered my mind. He will talk and talk, 'till I don't know what to do. I tell you, Mary, he talks beautifully too, sometimes.' Here Cerinthy turned quickly away, and began reaching passionately after clover heads. After a few moments she resumed. 'The fact is, Mary, that man *needs* somebody to take care of him, for he never thinks of himself. They say he has got the consumption, but he hasn't any more than I have. It is just the way he neglects himself!—preaching, talking, and visiting—nobody to take care of him, and see to his clothes, and nurse him up when he gets a little hoarse and run down. Well, I suppose if I *am* unregenerate, I do know how to keep things in order; and if I should keep *such* a man's soul in his body, I suppose I should be doing some good in the world; because if a minister don't *live*, of course he can't convert anybody. Just think of his saying that I could be a comfort to *him!* I told him that it was perfectly ridiculous, "and besides," says I, "what will everybody think?" I thought that I had really talked him out of the notion of it last night; but there he was in again this morning; and told me he had derived great encouragement from what I said. Well, the poor man really is lonesome, his mother's dead, and he hasn't any sisters. I asked him why he didn't go and take Miss Olladine Hocum. Everybody says she would make a first-rate minister's wife.'

'Well; and what did he say to that?' said Mary.

'Well, something really silly about my looks,' said Cerinthy, looking down.

Mary looked up and remarked the shining black hair, the long dark lashes, lying down over the glowing cheek, where two arch dimples were nestling, and said quietly, 'Probably he is a man of taste, Cerinthy. I advise you to leave the matter entirely to his judgment.'

'You don't really, Mary,' said the damsel, looking up; 'don't you think it would injure *him* if I should?'

'I think not materially,' said Mary.

'Well,' said Cerinthy, rising, 'the men will be coming home from mowing before I get home, and want their supper. Mother has one of her headaches on this afternoon, so I can't stop any longer: there isn't a soul in the house knows where anything is when I am gone. If I should ever take it into my head to go off, I don't know what would become of father and mother. I was telling mother the other day that I thought unregenerate folks were of some use in *this* world any way.'

'Does your mother know anything about it?' said Mary.

'Oh, as to mother, I believe she has been hoping and praying about it these three months. She thinks that I am such a desperate case, it is the only way I am to be brought in, as she calls it. That's what set me against him at first; but the fact is, if girls will let a man argue with them, he always contrives to get the best of it.

I am provoked about it too; but dear me! he is so meek there is no use of getting provoked at him. Well, I guess I will go home and think about it.'

As she turned to go she looked really pretty. Her long lashes were wet with a twinkling moisture, like meadow-grass after a shower; and there was a softened, child-like expression stealing over the careless gaiety of her face. Mary put her arms round her with a gentle caressing movement, which the other returned with a hearty embrace. They stood locked in each other's arms; the bright, vigorous, strong-hearted girl, with that pale, spiritual face resting on her breast, as when the morning, songful and radiant, clasps the pale silver moon to her glowing bosom.

'Look here now, Mary,' said Cerinthy; 'your folks are all gone, you may as well walk with me. It's pleasant now.'

'Yes, I will,' said Mary; 'wait a moment till I get my bonnet.'

In a few moments the two girls were walking together in one of those little pasture foot-tracks which run cosily among huckleberry and juniper bushes, while Cerinthy eagerly pursued the subject she could not leave thinking of.

Their path now wound over high ground that overlooked the distant sea, now lost itself in little copses of cedar and pitch-pine; and now there came on the air the pleasant breath of new hay, which mowers were harvesting in adjoining meadows.

They walked on and on as girls will; because when a young lady has once fairly launched on the enterprise of telling another all that *he* said, and just how *he* looked for the last three months, walks are apt to be indefinitely extended.

Mary was besides one of the most seductive little confidantes in the world. She was so pure from all *selfism*, so heartily and innocently interested in what another was telling her, that people in talking with her found the subject constantly increasing in interest; although if they had really been called upon afterwards to state the exact portion in *words* which she added to the conversation, they would have been surprised to find it so small.

In fact, before Cerinthy Ann had quite finished her confessions, they were more than a mile from the cottage, and Mary began to think of returning, saying that her mother would wonder where she was when she came home.

CHAPTER XXXV.

THE sun was just setting, and the whole air and sea seemed flooded with rosy rays. Even the crags and rocks of the sea-shore took purple and lilac tints, and savins and junipers, had a painter been required to represent them, would have been found not without a suffusion of the same tints. Through the tremulous rosy sea of the upper air, the silver full moon looked out like some calm superior presence which waits only for the flush of a temporary excitement to die away, to make its tranquillizing influence felt.

Mary, as she walked homeward with this dreamy light about her, moved with a slower step than when borne along by the vigorous arm and determined motion of her young friend.

It is said that a musical sound, uttered with decision by one instrument, always makes vibrate the corresponding chord of another, and Mary felt, as she left her positive but warm-hearted friend, a plaintive vibration of something in her own self of which she was conscious her calm friendship for her future husband had no part. She fell into one of those reveries which she thought she had for ever forbidden to herself, and there arose before her mind, like a picture, the idea of a marriage ceremony; but the eyes of the bridegroom were dark, and his curls were clustering in raven ringlets, and her hand throbbed in his as it had never throbbed in any other.

It was just as she was coming out of a little grove of cedars, where the high land overlooks the sea, and the dream which came to her overcame her with a vague and yearning sense of pain. Suddenly she heard footsteps behind her, and some one said 'Mary!' It was spoken in a choked voice, as one speaks in the crisis of a great emotion, and she turned and saw those very eyes!—that very hair!—yes, and the cold little hand throbbed with that very throb in that strong, living, manly hand, and 'whether in the body or out of the body' she knew not; she felt herself borne in those arms, and words that spoke themselves in her inner heart—words profaned by being repeated, were on her ear.

'Oh, is this a dream!—is it a dream! James, are we in heaven? Oh, I have lived through such an agony—I have been so worn out! Oh, I thought you never would come!' And then the eyes closed, and heaven and earth faded away together in a trance of blissful rest.

But it was no dream, for an hour later you might have seen a manly form sitting in that self-same place, bearing in his arms a pale girl, whom he cherished as tenderly as a mother her babe. And they were talking together—talking in low tones; and in all this wide universe neither of them knew or felt anything but the great joy of being thus side by side. They spoke of love, mightier than death, which many waters cannot quench. They spoke of yearnings, each for the other—of longing prayers—of hopes deferred—and then of this great joy: for *she* had hardly yet returned to the visible world. Scarce wakened from deadly faintness, she had not come back fully to the realm of life, *only* to that of love. And therefore it was, that without knowing that she spoke, she had said all, and compressed the history of those three years into one hour.

But at last, thoughtful for her health and provident of her weakness, he rose up and passed his arm around her to convey her home. And as he did so, he spoke *one* word that broke the whole charm.

'You will allow me, Mary, the right of a future husband, to watch over your life and health?'

Then came back the visible world—recollection, consciousness, and the great battle of duty; and Mary drew away a little and said—

'Oh, James! you are too late! *that* can never be!'

He drew back from her.

'Mary, are you married?'

'Before God I am!' she said. 'My word is pledged. I cannot retract it. I have suffered a good man to place his whole faith upon it—a man who loves me with his whole soul!'

'But, Mary! you do not love *him! That* is impossible!' said James, holding her off from him, and looking at her with an agonized eagerness. 'After what you have just said, it is not possible.'

'Oh! James, I'm sure I don't know what I have said. It was all so sudden, and I didn't know what I was saying—but things that I must never say again. The day is fixed for next week. It is all the same as if you had found me his wife!'

'NOT QUITE,' said James, his voice cutting the air with a decided, manly ring. '*I* have some words to say to that yet.'

'Oh, James, will you be selfish? Will *you* tempt me to do a mean, dishonourable thing—to be false to my word deliberately given?'

'But,' said James, eagerly, 'you know, Mary, you *never* would have given it if you had known that I was living.'

'That is true, James; but I *did* give it. I have suffered him to build all his hopes of life upon it. I *beg* you not to tempt me. Help me to do right.'

'But, Mary, did you not get my letter?'

'Your letter!'

'Yes! that long letter that I wrote you.'

'I never got any letter, James.'

'Strange,' he said; 'no wonder it seems sudden to you.'

CHAPTER XXXV.

'Have you seen your mother?' said Mary, who was conscious this moment only of a dizzy instinct to turn the conversation from the spot where she felt too weak to bear it.

'No! Do you suppose I should see anybody before you?'

'Oh, then you must go to her!' said Mary. 'Oh, James, you don't know how she has suffered!'

They were drawing near to the cottage gate.

'Do, pray,' said Mary. 'Go—hurry to your mother—don't be too sudden either, for she's very weak; she is almost worn out with sorrow. Go, my dear brother. *Dear* you always will be to me!'

James helped her into the house, and they parted. All the house was yet still. The open kitchen door let in a sober square of moonlight on the floor; the very stir of the leaves in the trees could be heard. Mary went into her little room, and threw herself upon the bed, weak, weary, yet happy; for deeper and higher above all other feelings was the great relief that *he* was living still. After a little while she heard the rattling of the waggon, and then the quick patter of Miss Prissy's feet, and her mother's considerate tones, and the Doctor's grave voice, and quite unexpectedly to herself she was shocked to find herself turning with an inward shudder from the idea of meeting him.

How very wicked! she thought; how ungrateful! and she prayed that God would give her strength to check the first rising of such feelings.

Then there was her mother, so ignorant and innocent, busy putting away baskets of things that she had bought in provision for the wedding-day. Mary almost felt as if she had a guilty secret. But when she looked back upon the last two hours, she felt no wish to take them back. Two little hours of joy and rest they had been, so pure, so perfect, she thought God must have given them to her as a keepsake, to remind her of His love, and to strengthen her in the way of duty.

Some will perhaps think it an unnatural thing that Mary should have regarded her pledge to the Doctor as of so absolute and binding a force, but they must remember the rigidity of her education. Self-denial and self-sacrifice had been the daily bread of her life. Every prayer, hymn, and sermon from her childhood had warned her to distrust her inclinations and regard her feelings as traitors. In particular had she been brought up within a superstitious tenacity in regard to the sacredness of a promise, and in this case the promise involved so deeply the happiness of a friend whom she had loved and revered all her life, that she never thought of any way of escape from it. She had been taught that there was no feeling so strong but that it might be immediately repressed at the call of duty, and if the idea arose to her of this great love to another as standing in her way, she immediately answered it by saying—'How would it have been if I had been married? As I could have overcome then, so I can now.'

Mrs. Scudder came into her room with a candle in her hand, and Mary, accustomed to read the expressions of her mother's face, saw at a glance a visible discomposure there. She held the light so that it shone upon Mary's face.

'Are you asleep?' she said.

'No, mother.'

'Are you unwell?'

'No, mother; only a little tired.'

Mrs. Scudder set down the candle and shut the door, and after a moment's hesitation, said,

'My daughter, I have some news to tell you, which I want you to prepare your mind for. Keep yourself quite quiet.

'Oh, mother,' said Mary, stretching out her hands towards her, 'I know it, James has come home.'

'How did you hear?' said her mother with astonishment.

'I have seen him, mother.'

Mrs. Scudder's countenance fell.

'Where?'

'I went to walk home with Cerinthy Twitchel, and as I was coming back he came up behind me just at Savin Rock.'

Mrs. Scudder sat down on the bed, and took her daughter's hand.

'I trust, my dear child,' she said—and stopped.

'I think I know what you are going to say, mother. It is a great joy and a great relief, but of course I shall be true to my engagement with the Doctor.'

Mrs. Scudder's face brightened.

'That is my own daughter! I might have known that you would do so. You would not, certainly, so cruelly disappoint a noble man that has set his whole faith on you.'

'No, mother, I shall *not* disappoint him. I told James that I should be true to my word.'

'He will probably see the justice of it,' said Mrs. Scudder, in that easy tone with which elderly people are apt to dispose of the feelings of young persons.

'Perhaps it may be something of a trial at first.'

Mary looked at her mother with incredulous blue eyes. The idea that feelings which made her hold her breath when she thought of them could be so summarily disposed of, struck her as almost an absurdity. She turned her face weariedly to the wall with a deep sigh, and said,

'After all, mother, it is mercy enough and comfort enough to think that he is living. Poor cousin Ellen, too, what a relief to her! it is like life from the dead. Oh! I shall be happy enough, no fear of that.'

'And you know,' said Mrs. Scudder, 'that there has *never* existed *any engagement of any kind* between you and James. He had no right to found any expectations on anything you ever told him.'

'That is true also, mother,' said Mary; 'I had never thought of such a thing as marriage in relation to James.'

'Of course,' pursued Mrs. Scudder, 'he will always be to you as a near friend.'

Mary assented wearily.

'There is but a week now before your wedding,' continued Mrs. Scudder, 'and I think cousin James, if he is reasonable, will see the propriety of your mind being kept as quiet as possible. I heard the news this afternoon in town,' pursued Mrs. Scudder, 'from Captain Staunton, and, by a curious coincidence, I received this letter from him from James, which came from New York by post. The brig that brought it must have been delayed out of the harbour.'

'Oh, *please* mother, give it to me!' said Mary, rising up with animation; 'he mentioned having sent me one.'

'Perhaps you had better wait till morning,' said Mrs. Scudder; 'you are tired and excited.'

'Oh, mother, I think I shall be more composed when I know all that is in it,' said Mary, still stretching out her hand.

'Well, my daughter, you are the best judge,' said Mrs. Scudder; and she set down the candle on the table, and left Mary alone. It was a very thick letter, of many pages, dated in Canton, and ran as follows:

CHAPTER XXXVI.

'MY DEAREST MARY,—I have lived through many wonderful scenes since I saw you last; my life has been so adventurous that I scarcely know myself when I think of it. But it is not of *that* I am going now to write; I have written all that to mother, and she will show it to you: but since I parted from you there has been another history going on within me, and *that* is what I wish to make you understand if I can.

'It seems to me that I have been a changed man from that afternoon when I came to your window where we parted. I have never forgotten how you looked then, nor what you said; nothing in my life ever had such an effect on me. I thought that I loved you before; but I went away feeling that *love* was something so deep, and high, and sacred, that *I* was not worthy to name it to you; I cannot think of the man in the world that *is* worthy of what you said you felt for me. From *that* hour there was a new purpose in my soul—a purpose which has led me upward ever since.

'I thought to myself in this way, "There is some secret source from whence this inner life springs;" and I knew that it was connected with the Bible which you gave me, and so I thought I would read it carefully and deliberately, to see what I could make of it. I began with the beginning; it impressed me with a sense of something quaint and strange—something rather fragmentary; and yet there were spots all along that went right to the heart of a man who has to deal with life and things as I did.

'Now I must say that the Doctor's preaching, as I told you, never impressed me much in any way. I could not make any connection between it and the men I had to manage, and the things I had to do in my daily life. But there were things in the Bible that struck me otherwise; there was *one* passage in particular, and that was where Jacob started off from all his friends, to go off and seek his fortune in a strange country, and lay down to sleep all alone in the field, with only a stone for his pillow. It seemed to me exactly the image of what every young man is like when he leaves his home, and goes out to shift for himself in this hard world. I tell you, Mary, that *one man alone* on the great ocean of life feels himself a very weak thing: we are held up by each other more than we know, till we go off by ourselves into this great experiment. Well, there he was, as lonesome as *I* upon the deck of my ship; and so lying with this stone under his head, he saw a ladder in his sleep between him and heaven, and angels going up and down. That was a sight which came to the very point of his necessities; he saw that there was a way between him and God, and that there were those above who did care for him, and who could come to him to help him.

'Well, so the next morning he got up, and set up the stone to mark the place; and it says "Jacob vowed a vow, saying, If God will be with me, and will keep me in this way that I go, and will give me bread to eat and raiment to put on, so that I come again to my father's house in peace, *then* shall the Lord be my God." Now there was something that looked to me like a tangible foundation to begin on.

'If I understand Dr. Hopkins, I believe he would have called that all selfishness. At first sight it does look a little so, but then I thought of it in this way. Here he was, all alone; God was entirely invisible to him, and how could he feel certain that He really existed unless he could come into some kind of connection with Him? The point that he wanted to be sure of was more than merely to know that there was a God who made the world; he wanted to know whether He cared anything about men, and would do anything to help them. And so, in fact, it was saying "If there is a God who interests himself at all in me, and will be my friend and protector, I will obey Him so far as I can find out His will."

'I thought to myself, "This is the great experiment, and I will try it." I made in my heart exactly the same resolution, and just quietly resolved to assume for a while, as a fact, that there *was* such a God, and whenever I came to a place where I could not help myself, just to ask His help honestly in so many words, and see what would come of it.

'Well, as I went on reading through the Old Testament, I was more and more convinced that all the men of those times had tried this experiment, and found that it would bear them; and, in fact, I did begin to find in my own experience a great many things happening so remarkably that I could not but think that somebody did attend even to my prayers: I began to feel a trembling faith that *somebody* was guiding me, and that the events of my life were not happening by accident, but working themselves out by His will.

'Well, as I went on in this way there were other and higher thoughts kept rising in my mind. I wanted to be better than I was; I had a sense of a life much nobler and purer than anything I had ever lived, that I wanted to come up to. But in the world of men, as I found it, such feelings are always laughed down as romantic and impracticable and impossible. But about this time I began to read the New Testament, and then the idea came to me that the same Power that helped me in the lower sphere of life would help me carry out these higher aspirations. Perhaps the Gospels would not have interested me so much if I had begun with them first; but my Old Testament life seemed to have schooled me, and brought me to a place where I wanted, something higher, and I began to notice that my prayers now were more that I might be noble, and patient, and self-denying, and constant in my duty, than for any other kind of help. And then I understood what met me in the very first of Matthew, "He shall be called Jesus, for He shall save His people from their sins."

'I began now to live a new life, a life in which I felt myself coming into sympathy with you; for, Mary, when I began to read the gospels I took knowledge of you, that you had been with Jesus.

'The crisis of my life was that dreadful night of the shipwreck. It was as dreadful as the day of judgment. No words of mine can describe to you what I felt when I knew that our rudder was gone, and saw those hopeless rocks before us—what I felt for our poor men!—but in the midst of it all the words came into my mind, "And Jesus was in the hinder part of the vessel asleep on a pillow," and at once I felt He *was* there; and when the ship struck, I was only conscious of an intense going out of my soul to Him, like Peter's when he threw himself from the ship to meet Him in the waters.

'I will not recapitulate what I have already written—the wonderful manner in which I was saved, and in which friends, and help, and prosperity, and worldly success came to me again after life had seemed all lost, but now I am ready to return to my country, and I feel as Jacob did when he said, "With my staff I passed over this Jordan, but now am I become two bands." I do not need any arguments now to convince me that the Bible is from above. There is a great deal in it that I cannot understand—a great deal that seems to me inexplicable; but all I can say is, that I have tried its directions, and find that in my case they do work; that it is a book that I can *live* by, and that is enough for me.

'And now, Mary, I am coming home again quite another man from what I went out; with a whole new world of thought and feeling in my heart, and a new purpose, by which, please God, I mean to shape my life. All this, under God, I owe to you; and if you will let me devote my whole life to you, it will be a small return for what you have done for me.

'You know I left you wholly free: others must have seen your loveliness and felt your worth, and you may have learnt to love some better man than I; but I know not what hope tells me that this will not be, and I shall find true what the Bible says of love, that "many waters cannot quench it, nor floods drown." In any case I shall be always from my very heart yours, and yours only, till death.

'JAMES MARVYN.'

Mary rose after reading this letter wrapped into a divine state of exaltation,—the pure joy in contemplating an infinite good to another, in which the question of self was utterly forgotten. He was then what she had always hoped and prayed he would be, and she pressed the thought triumphantly to her heart. He was that true and victorious man; that Christian able to subdue life, and to show in a perfect and healthy manly nature a reflection of the image of the superhuman excellence. Her prayers that night were aspirations and praises; and she felt how possible it might be so to appropriate the good, and the joy, and the nobleness of others, so as to have in them an eternal and satisfying pleasure. And with this came the dearer thought that she in her weakness and solitude had been permitted to put her hand to the beginning of a work so noble. The consciousness of good done to an immortal spirit is wealth that neither life nor death can take away.

CHAPTER XXXVI.

And so, having prayed, she lay down with that sleep which God giveth to His beloved.

CHAPTER XXXVII.

IT is a hard condition of our existence here, that every exaltation must have its depression. God will not let us have heaven here below, but only such glimpses and faint showings as parents sometimes give to children when they show them beforehand the jewelry and pictures, and stores of rare and curious treasures, which they hold in store for the possession of their riper years. So it very often happens that the man who, entranced by some rapturous excitement, has gone to bed an angel, feeling as if all sin were for ever vanquished, and he himself immutably grounded in love, may wake the next morning with a sick headache; and if he be not careful may scold about his breakfast like a miserable sinner.

We will not say that our dear little Mary rose in this condition next morning; for although she had the headache, she had one of those natures in which somehow or other the combative element seems to be left out, so that no one ever knew her to speak a fretful word. But still, as we have observed, she had the headache and the depression, and then came the slow, creeping sense of a wakening-up through all her heart and soul, of a thousand thousand things that could be said only to *one* person, and that person one that it would be temptation and danger to say them to.

She came out of her room to her morning work with a face resolved and calm, but expressive of languor, with slight signs of some inward struggle.

Madame de Frontignac, who had already heard the intelligence, threw two or three of her bright glances upon her at breakfast, and at once divined how the matter stood. She was of a nature so delicately sensitive to the most refined shades of honour, that she apprehended at once that there must be a conflict; though, judging by her own impulsive nature, she made no doubt that all would at once go down before the mighty force of reawakened love.

After breakfast she would insist upon following Mary about through all her avocations. She possessed herself of a towel, and would wipe the teacups and saucers while Mary washed. She clinked the glasses and rattled the cups and spoons, and stepped about as briskly as if she had two or three breezes to carry her train; and chattered half-English and half-French, for the sake of bringing into Mary's cheek the shy, slow dimples that she liked to watch. But still Mrs. Scudder was around, with an air as provident and forbidding as that of a setting hen who watches her nest; nor was it till after all things had been cleared away in the house, and Mary had gone up into her little attic to spin, that the opportunity long sought came, of diving to the bottom of this mystery.

'*Enfin, Marie, nous voilà!* are you not going to tell me anything, when I have turned my heart out to you like a bag? *Chère enfant!* how happy you must be!' she said, embracing her.

'Yes, I am very happy,' said Mary, with calm gravity.

'*Very happy!*' said Madame de Frontignac, mimicking her manner. 'Is that the way you American girls show it when you are very happy? Come, come, *ma belle*, tell little Verginie something. Thou hast seen this hero, this wandering Ulysses. He has come back at last—the tapestry will not be quite as long as Penelope's. Speak to me of him. Has he beautiful black eyes, and hair that curls like a grape-vine? Tell me, *ma belle*.'

'I only saw him a little while,' said Mary; 'and I *felt* a great deal more than I saw. He could not have been any clearer to me than he always has been in my mind.'

'But I think,' said Madame de Frontignac, seating Mary as was her wont, and sitting down at her feet, 'I think you are a little "*triste*" about this! Very likely you pity the poor priest! It is sad for him, but a good priest has the church for his bride, you know.'

'You do not think,' said Mary, speaking seriously, 'that I shall break my promise, given before God, to this good man?'

'*Mon Dieu, mon enfant!* You do not mean to marry the priest after all! *Quelle idée!*'

'But I *promised* him,' said Mary.

Madame de Frontignac threw up her hands with an expression of vexation.

'What a pity, my little one, you are not in the true Church! Any good priest could dispense you from that.'

'I do not believe,' said Mary, 'in any earthly power that can dispense us from solemn obligations which we have assumed before God, and on which we have suffered others to build the most precious hopes. If James had won the affections of some girl, thinking as I do, I should not feel it right for him to leave her and come to me. The Bible says that the just man is he that sweareth to his own hurt and changeth not.'

'This is the sublime of duty!' said Madame de Frontignac, who, with the airy facility of her race, never lost her appreciation of the fine points of anything that went on under her eyes. But nevertheless she was inwardly resolved, that picturesque as this 'sublime of duty' was, it must not be allowed to pass beyond the limits of a fine art, and so she recommenced.

'*Mais c'est absurde!* This beautiful young man, with his black eyes and his curls—a real hero—a *Theseus*, Mary; just come home from killing a Minotaur—and loves you with his whole heart—and this dreadful promise! Why haven't you any sort of people in your Church that can unbind you from promises? I should think the good priest himself would do it!'

'Perhaps he would,' said Mary, 'if I would ask him; but that would be equivalent to a breach of it. Of course no man would marry a woman that asked to be dispensed.'

'You are an angel of delicacy, my child; *c'est admirable!* but after all, Mary, this is not well! Listen now to me: you are a very sweet saint, and very strong in goodness. I think you must have a very strong angel that takes care of you; but think, *chère enfant*, *think* what it is to marry one man while you love another.'

'But I love the Doctor,' said Mary, evasively.

'*Love!*' said Madame de Frontignac. 'Oh, Marie! you may love him well, but you and I both know that there is something deeper than that! What will you *do* with this young man? Must he move away from this place, and not be with his poor mother any more? Or can you see him, and hear him, and be with him after your marriage, and not feel that you love him more than your husband?'

'I should hope that God would help me to feel right,' said Mary.

'I am very much afraid He will not, *ma chère*' said Madame. 'I asked Him a great many times to help *me* when I found how wrong it all was, and He did not. You remember what you told *me* the other day, "that if I would do right I must not *see* that man any more." You will have to ask him to go away from this place. You can never see him, for this love will never die till *you* die! That you may be sure of. Is it wise? Is it right, dear little one? *Must* he leave his home for ever for you? Or must you struggle always, and grow whiter and whiter and whiter, and fade away into heaven like the moon this morning, and nobody know what is the matter? People will say you have the liver-complaint, or the consumption, or something. Nobody ever knows what we women die of.'

Poor Mary's conscience was fairly posed. This appeal struck upon her sense of right, as having its grounds. She felt inexpressibly confused and distressed.

'Oh, I wish somebody would tell me exactly what *is* right!' she said.

'Well, *I* will!' said Madame de Frontignac. 'Go down to the dear priest and tell him the whole truth. My dear child, do you think if he should ever find it out after your marriage, he would think you used him right?'

'And yet *mother* does not think so! Mother does not wish me to tell him!'

'*Pauvrette!* Always the mother! Yes, it is always the mothers that stand in the way of the lovers. Why cannot she marry the priest herself?' she said, between her teeth, and then looked up, startled and guilty, to see if Mary had heard her.

'I *cannot!*' said Mary. 'I cannot go against my conscience, and my mother, and my best friend—'

At this moment the conference was cut short by Mrs. Scudder's provident footstep on the garret stairs. A vague suspicion of something *French* had haunted her during her dairy-work, and she resolved to come and put a stop to the interview by telling Mary that Miss Prissy wanted her to come and be measured for the skirt of her dress.

Mrs. Scudder, by the use of that sixth sense peculiar to mothers, had divined that there had been some agitating conference, and had she been questioned about it, her guesses as to what it might be, would probably have given no bad *résumé* of the real state of the case. She was inwardly resolved that there should be no more such for the present, and kept Mary employed about various matters relating to the dresses so scrupulously, that there was no opportunity for anything more of the sort that day.

In the evening James Marvyn came down, and was welcomed with the greatest demonstrations of joy by all but Mary, who sat distant and embarrassed after the first salutations had passed.

The Doctor was innocently parental; but we fear there was small reciprocation of the sentiments he expressed on the part of the young man.

Miss Prissy, indeed, had had her heart somewhat touched, as good little women's hearts are apt to be by a true love story, and had hinted something of her feelings to Mrs. Scudder in a manner which brought such a severe rejoinder as quite humbled and abashed her, so that she coweringly took refuge under her former declaration, that 'to be sure there couldn't be any man in the world better *worthy* of Mary than the Doctor.' While still at her heart she was possessed with that troublesome preference for unworthy people which stands in the way of so many excellent things. But she went on vigorously sewing on the wedding-dress, and pursing up her small mouth into the most perfect and guarded expression of non-committal, though, she said afterwards 'it went to her heart to see how that poor young man did look sitting there, just as noble and as handsome as a pictur'. She didn't see for *her* part how anybody's heart *could* stand it. Then, to be sure, as Mrs. Scudder said, the poor Doctor ought to be thought about. Dear, blessed man! What a pity it was things *would* turn out so! Not that it was a pity that Jim came home! *That* was a great providence! But a pity they hadn't known about it sooner. Well, for her part, she didn't pretend to say; the path of duty did have a great many hard places in it,' &c.

As for James, during his interview at the cottage, he waited and tried in vain for one moment's solitary conversation. Mrs. Scudder was immovable in her motherly kindness, sitting there smiling and chatting with him, but never stirring from her place by Mary.

Madame de Frontignac was out of all patience, and determined in her small way to do something to discompose the fixed state of things. So, retreating to her room, she contrived, in very desperation, to upset and break a wash-pitcher, shrieking violently in French and English at the deluge which came upon the sanded floor and the little piece of carpet by the bedside.

What housekeeper's instincts are proof against the crash of breaking china? Mrs. Scudder fled from her seat, followed by Miss Prissy—

'Ah, then and there was hurrying to and fro'

—while Mary sat, quiet as a statue, bending over her sewing, and James, knowing that it must be now or never, was, like a flash, in the empty chair by her side, with his black moustache very near the bent, brown head.

'Mary,' he said, 'you *must* let me see you once more. All is not said! is it? Just hear me—hear me once alone!'

'Oh, James! I am too weak! I dare not! I am afraid of myself.'

'You think,' he said, 'that you *must* take this course, because it is right; but *is* it right? *Is* it right to marry *one* man when you love another better? I don't put this to your inclination, Mary; I know it would be of no use. I put it to your conscience.'

'Oh, I never was so perplexed before!' said Mary. 'I don't know what I *do* think. I must have time to reflect. And you, oh, James! you *must* let me do right. There will never be any happiness for me if I do wrong—nor for you either.'

All this while the sounds of running and hurrying in Madame de Frontignac's room had been unintermitted, and Miss Prissy, not without some glimmerings of perception into the state of things, was holding tight on to Mrs. Scudder's gown, detailing to her a most capital receipt for mending broken china, the history of which she traced regularly through all the families in which she had ever worked, varying the details with small items of family history, and little incidents as to the births, marriages, and deaths of different people for whom it had been employed, with all the particulars of how, where, and when, so that the time of James for conversation was by this means indefinitely extended.

'Now,' he said to Mary, 'let me propose one thing. Let *me* go to the Doctor and tell him the truth.'

'James, it does not seem to me that I can. A friend who has been so considerate, so kind, so self-sacrificing and disinterested, and whom I have allowed to go on with this implicit faith in me so long. Should *you*, James, think of *yourself* only?'

'I do not, I trust, think of myself only,' said James. 'I hope that I am calm enough and have a heart to think for others. But I ask you, is it doing right to *him* to let him marry you in ignorance of the state of your feelings? Is it a kindness to a good and noble man to give yourself to him only seemingly, when the best and noblest part of your affection is gone wholly beyond your control. I am quite sure of *that*, Mary. I know you do love him very well, that you would make a most true, affectionate, constant wife to him, but what I *know* you feel for me is something wholly out of your power to give to him, is it not now?'

'I think it is,' said Mary, looking gravely and deeply thoughtful. 'But then, James, I ask myself, what if all this had happened a week hence? My feelings would have been just the same, because they are feelings over which I have no more control than over my existence. I can only control the expression of them. But in *that* case you would not have asked me to break my marriage vow, and why now shall I break a solemn vow deliberately made before God? If what I can give him will content him, and he never knows that which would give him pain, what wrong is done him?'

'I should think the deepest possible wrong done me,' said James, 'if, when I thought I had married a wife with a whole heart, I found that the greater part of it had been before that given to another. If you tell him, or if I tell him, or your mother, who is the more proper person, and he chooses to hold you to your promise, then, Mary, I have no more to say. I shall sail in a few weeks again, and carry your image for ever in my heart; nobody can take that away, and *that* dear shadow will be the only wife I shall ever know.'

At this moment Miss Prissy came rattling along towards the door, talking, we suspect designedly, in quite a high key. Mary hastily said,

'Wait, James, let me think. To-morrow is the Sabbath-day. Monday I will send you word or see you.'

And when Miss Prissy returned into the best room, James was sitting at one window and Mary at another, he making remarks in a style of most admirable commonplace on a copy of Milton's Paradise Lost, which he had picked up in the confusion of the moment, and which at the time Mrs. Katy Scudder entered, he was declaring to be a most excellent book, and a really truly valuable work.

Mrs. Scudder looked keenly from one to the other, and saw that Mary's cheek was glowing like the deepest heart of a pink shell, while in all other respects she was as cold and calm. On the whole she felt satisfied that no mischief had been done.

We hope our readers will do Mrs. Scudder justice. It is true that she yet wore on her third finger the marriage ring of a sailor lover, and his memory was yet fresh in her heart; but even mothers who have married for love themselves somehow so blend their daughter's existence with their own as to conceive that she must marry *their* love and not her own.

Beside this, Mrs. Scudder was an Old Testament woman, brought up with that scrupulous exactitude of fidelity in relation to promises which would naturally come from familiarity with a book where covenant-keeping is represented as one of the highest attributes of Deity, and covenant-breaking as one of the vilest sins of humanity. To break the word that had gone forth out of one's mouth was to lose self-respect and all claim to the respect of others, and to sin against eternal rectitude.

As we have said before, it is almost impossible to make our light-minded modern times comprehend the earnestness with which these people lived. It was in the beginning no vulgar nor mercenary ambition that made Mrs. Scudder desire the Doctor as a husband for her daughter. He was poor, and she had had offers from richer men. He was often unpopular, but he was the man in the world she most revered, the man she believed in with the most implicit faith, the man who embodied her highest idea of the good; and therefore it was that she was willing to resign her child to him.

As to James, she had felt truly sympathetic with his mother and with Mary in the dreadful hour when they supposed him lost, and had it not been for the great perplexity occasioned by his return she would have received him as a relative with open arms. But now she felt it her duty to be on the defensive, an attitude not the most favourable for cherishing pleasing associations in regard to another. She had read the letter giving an account of his spiritual experience with very sincere pleasure as a good woman should, but not without an internal perception how very much it endangered her favourite plans. But when Mary had calmly reiterated her determination, she felt sure of her. For had she ever known her to say a thing she did not do?

The uneasiness she felt at present was not the doubt of her daughter’s steadiness, but the fear that she might have been unsuitably harassed or annoyed.

CHAPTER XXXVIII.

THE next morning rose calm and fair. It was the Sabbath-day; the *last* Sabbath in Mary's maiden life if her promises and plans were fulfilled.

Mary dressed herself in white—her hands trembling with unusual agitation, her sensitive nature divided between two opposing consciences and two opposing affections. Her devoted filial love towards the Doctor made her feel the keenest sensitiveness at the thought of giving him pain. At the same time, the questions which James had proposed to her had raised serious doubts in her mind whether it was altogether right to suffer him blindly to enter into this union. So after she was all prepared, she bolted the door of her chamber, and opening her Bible, read, 'If any man lack wisdom, let him ask of God, who giveth to all liberally and upbraideth not, and it shall be given;' and then kneeling down by the bed, she asked that God would give her some immediate light in her present perplexity. So praying, her mind grew calm and steady, and she rose up at the sound of the bell which marked that it was time to set forward for church.

Everybody noticed, as she came into the church that morning, how beautiful Mary Scudder looked. It was no longer the beauty of the carved statue, the pale alabaster shrine, the sainted virgin, but a warm, bright, living light, that spoke of some summer breath breathing within her soul.

When she took her place in the singers' seat she knew, without turning her head, that *he* was in his old place not far from her side, and those whose eyes followed her to the gallery marvelled at her face, where—

'The pure and eloquent blood
Spoke in her cheeks, and so divinely wrought That you might almost say her body thought;'

for a thousand delicate nerves were becoming vital once more, as the holy mystery of womanhood wrought within her.

When they rose to sing, the tune must needs be one which Mary and James had often sung together out of the same book at the singing school—one of those wild, pleading tunes dear to the heart of New England, born, if we may credit the report, in the rocky hollow of its mountains, and whose notes have a kind of grand and mournful triumph in their warbling wail. The different parts of the harmony, set contrary to all the canons of musical pharisaism, had still a singular and romantic effect, which a true musical genius would not have failed to recognize. The four parts, tenor, treble, bass, and counter, as they were then called, rose and swelled and wildly mingled with the fitful strangeness of an Æolian harp, or of winds in mountain hollows, or the vague moanings of the sea on lone, forsaken shores. And Mary, while her voice rose over the waves of the treble, and trembled with a pathetic richness, felt to her inmost heart the deep accord of that other voice which came to meet hers so wildly melancholy, as if the soul in that manly breast had come forth to meet her soul in the disembodied shadowy verity of eternity. That grand old tune, called by our fathers 'China,' never, with its dirge-like melody, drew two souls more out of themselves and entwined them more nearly with each other.

The last verse of the hymn spoke of the resurrection of the saints with Christ—

'Then let the last dread trumpet sound,
And bid the dead arise; Awake, ye nations underground,

Ye saints, ascend the skies.'

And as Mary sang she felt sublimely upborn with the idea that life is but a moment and love is immortal, and seemed in a shadowy trance to feel herself and him past this mortal pain far over on the shores of that other life, ascending with Christ all glorified, all tears wiped away, and with full permission to love and to be loved for ever. And as she sang, the Doctor looked upward and marvelled at the light in her eyes and the rich bloom on her cheek, for where she stood a sunbeam, streaming aslant through the dusty panes of the window, touched her head with a kind of glory, and the thought he then received outbreathed itself in the yet more fervent adoration of his prayer.

CHAPTER XXXIX.

OUR fathers believed in special answers to prayer. They were not stumbled by the objection about the inflexibility of the laws of nature, because they had the idea that when the Creator of the world promised to answer human prayers, He probably understood the laws of nature as well as they did; at any rate, the laws of nature were His affairs and not theirs. They were men very apt, as the Duke of Wellington said, to 'look to their marching-orders;' which, being found to read, 'be careful for nothing, but in everything by prayer and supplication let your requests be made known unto God,' they did it. 'They looked unto Him, and were likened, and their faces were not ashamed.' One reads in the memoirs of Dr. Hopkins how Newport Gardner, one of his African catechumens, a negro of singular genius and ability, being desirous of his freedom, that he might be a missionary to Africa, and having long worked without being able to raise the amount required, was counselled by Dr. Hopkins that it might be a shorter way to seek his freedom from the Lord by a day of solemn fasting and prayer. The historical fact is, that on the evening of a day so consecrated his master returned from church, called Newport to him, and presented him with his freedom. Is it not possible that He who made the world may have established laws for prayer, as invariable as those for the sowing of seed and raising of grain? Is it not as legitimate a subject of inquiry when petitions are not answered, *which* of these laws has been neglected?

But be that as it may, certain it is, that a train of events were set in operation this day which went directly towards answering Mary's morning supplication for guidance. Candace, who on this particular morning had contrived to place herself where she could see Mary and James in the singers' seat, had certain thoughts 'borne in' on her mind, which bore fruit afterwards in a solemn and select conversation held with Miss Prissy at the end of the horse-shed by the meeting-house, during the intermission between the morning and afternoon sermons.

Candace sat on a fragment of a granite boulder which lay there, her black face relieved against a clump of yellow mulleins, then in majestic altitude. On her lap was spread a check pocket-handkerchief, containing rich slices of cheese and a store of her favourite brown dough-nuts.

'Now, Miss Prissy,' she said, 'der's *reason* in all things; and a good deal *more* in some things dan der is in others. Dere's a good deal more reason in two young, handsome folks coming together dan der is in——'

Candace finished the sentence by an emphatic flourish of her dough-nut.

'Now as long as everybody thought Massa Jim was dead, dere wa'n't nothin' in de world else *to be* done *but* for Miss Mary to marry the Doctor. But, good Lord! I heard him a-talkin' to Mrs. Marvyn last night; it kinder most broke my heart. Why dem two poor creeturs—dey's just as onhappy's dey can be; and she's got too much feelin' for the Doctor to say a word, and *I* say *he orter be told on't;* dat's what I say,' said Candace, giving a decisive bite to her dough-nut.

'I say so too,' said Miss Prissy: 'why I never had such feelings in my life as I did yesterday when that young man came down to our house; he was just as pale as a cloth. I tried to say a word to Mrs. Scudder, but she snapped me up so; she's an awful decided woman when her mind's made up. I was telling Cerinthy Ann Twitchel, she come round me this noon, that it didn't exactly seem to me right that things should go on as they're gone to; and says I, "Cerinthy Ann, I don't know anything what to do." And says she, "If I was you, Miss Prissy, I know what I'd do; I'd tell the Doctor." Says she, "Nobody ever takes offence at anything *you* do, Miss Prissy." To be sure,' added Miss Prissy, 'I *have* talked to people about a good many things that it's rather strange I should, 'cause I ain't one somehow that can let things go that seem to want doing. I always told folks that I should spoil a novel before it got half-way through the first volume, by blirting out some of those things that they let go trailing on till everybody gets so mixed up they don't know what they're doing.'

'Well, now, honey,' said Candace, authoritatively, 'ef you've got any notion o' that kind, I think it must a come from de good Lord; and I 'vise ye to be 'tendin' to it right away. You just go 'long and tell de Doctor yo'self all you knows, and den let's see what'll come on't. I tell you I b'lieves it'll be one o' the best day's works *you* ever did in your life.'

'Well,' said Miss Prissy, 'I guess to-night before I go to bed I'll make a dive at him. When a thing's once out it's out, and can't be got in again, even if people don't like it, and that's a mercy anyhow. It really makes me feel most wicked to think of it, for the Doctor is the blessedest man.'

'That's what he *is*,' said Candace. 'But den de blessedest men in the world ought fur to know de truth, that's what *I* think.'

'Yes, true enough,' said Miss Prissy, 'I'll tell him anyway.'

Miss Prissy was as good as her word, for that evening when the Doctor had retired to his study, she took her light in her hand, and walking softly as a cat, tapped rather timidly at the study door, which the Doctor opening, said benignantly—

'Ah! Miss Prissy!'

'If you please, sir,' said Miss Prissy, 'I'd like a little conversation.'

The Doctor was well enough used to such requests from the female members of his church, which generally were the prelude to some disclosures of internal difficulties or spiritual experiences. He therefore graciously motioned her to a chair.

CHAPTER XXXIX.

'I thought I must come in,' she began, busily twirling a bit of her Sunday gown. 'I thought—that is I felt it my duty—I thought—perhaps—I ought to tell you—that perhaps you ought to know—'

The Doctor looked civilly concerned. He did not know but Miss Prissy's wits were taking leave of her. He replied, however, with his usual honest stateliness,

'I trust, dear madam, that you will feel at perfect freedom to open to me any exercises of mind that you may have.'

'It isn't about myself,' said Prissy. 'If you please, it's about *you*, sir, and Mary.'

The Doctor *now* looked awake in right earnest, and very much astonished besides; and he looked eagerly at Miss Prissy to have her go on.

'I don't know how you would view such a matter,' said Miss Prissy; 'but the fact is, that James Marvyn and Mary always did love each other ever since they were children.'

Still the Doctor was unawakened to the real meaning of the words, and he answered, simply,—

'I should be far from wishing to interfere with so very natural and innocent a sentiment, which I make no doubt is all quite as it should be.'

'No! but,' said Miss Prissy, 'you don't understand what I mean. I mean that James Marvyn wanted to marry Mary, and that she was—well! she wasn't engaged to him—but—'

'MADAM!!' said the Doctor, in a voice that frightened Miss Prissy out of her chair, while a blaze like sheet-lightning shot from his eyes and his face flushed crimson.

'Mercy on us! Doctor, I hope you'll excuse me, but there, the fact is out! I've said it out; the fact is they wa'n't engaged, but that Mary loved him ever since he was a boy, as she never will and never can love any man again in this world, is what I'm just as sure of as that I'm standing here; and I've felt you ought to know it, 'cause I'm quite sure that if he'd been alive, she'd never given the promise she has—the promise that she means to keep if her heart breaks and his too; there wouldn't anybody tell you, and I thought I must tell you, 'cause I thought you'd know what was right to do about it.'

During all this latter speech the Doctor was standing with his back to Miss Prissy and his face to the window, just as he did some time before when Mrs. Scudder came to tell him of Mary's consent. He made a gesture backward, without speaking, that she should leave the apartment; and Miss Prissy left with a guilty kind of feeling, as if she had been plunging a knife in her pastor; and rushing distractedly across the entry into Mary's little bedroom, she bolted the door, threw herself on the bed, and began to cry.

'Well! I've done it,' she said to herself. 'He's a very strong, hearty man,' she soliloquized, 'so I hope it won't put him in a consumption. Men do go in a consumption about such things sometimes. I remember Abner Seaforth did—but then he was always narrow-chested, and had the liver complaint, or something. I don't know what Mrs. Scudder *will* say, but I've done it. Poor man! such a good man too! I declare I feel just like Herod taking off John the Baptist's head. Well! well! it's done, and can't be helped.'

Just at this moment Miss Prissy heard a gentle tap at the door, and started as if it had been a ghost—not being able to rid herself of the impression that somehow she had committed a great crime, for which retribution was knocking at the door.

It was Mary, who said, in her sweetest and most natural tones, 'Miss Prissy, the Doctor would like to see you.' Mary was much astonished at the frightened, discomposed manner with which Miss Prissy received this announcement, and said, 'I'm afraid I've waked you up out of sleep. I don't think there's the least hurry.'

Miss Prissy didn't either; but she reflected afterwards that she might as well get through with it at once, and therefore, smoothing her tumbled cap-border, she went to the Doctor's study. This time he was quite composed, and received her with a mournful gravity, and requested her to be seated.

'I beg, madam,' he said, 'you will excuse the abruptness of my manner in our late interview. I was so little prepared for the communication you had to make that I was perhaps unsuitably discomposed. Will you allow me to ask whether you were requested by any of the parties to communicate to me what you did?'

'No, sir,' said Miss Prissy.

'Have any of the parties ever communicated with you on the subject at all?' said the Doctor.

'No, sir,' said Miss Prissy.

'That is all,' said the Doctor. 'I will not detain you. I am very much obliged to you, madam.'

He rose and opened the door for her to pass out, and Miss Prissy, overawed by the stately gravity of his manner, went out in silence.

CHAPTER XL.

WHEN Miss Prissy left the room the Doctor sat down by the table, and covered his face with his hands. He had a large, passionate, determined nature; and he had just come to one of those cruel crises in life, in the which it is apt to seem to us that the whole force of our being—all that we can hope, or wish, or feel—has been suffered to gather itself into one great wave, only to break upon some cold rock of inevitable fate, and go back moaning into emptiness.

In such hours men and women have cursed God and life, and thrown violently down and trampled under their feet what yet was left of life's blessings in the fierce bitterness of despair. This or nothing! the soul shrieks in her frenzy.

At just such points as these men have plunged into intemperance and wild excess; they have gone to be shot down in battle; they have broken life, and thrown it away like an empty goblet; and gone like wailing ghosts out into the dread unknown.

The possibility of all this lay in that heart which had just received that stunning blow. Exercised and disciplined as he had been by years of sacrifice, by constant, unsleeping self-vigilance, there was rising there in that great heart an ocean-tempest of passion; and for a while his cries unto God seemed as empty and as vague as the screams of birds tossed and buffeted in the clouds of mighty tempests.

The will that he thought wholly subdued seemed to rise under him as a rebellious giant. A few hours before he thought himself established in an invincible submission to God that nothing could shake. Now, he looked into himself as into a seething vortex of rebellion; and against all the passionate cries of his lower nature, he could only (in the language of an old saint) 'cling to God by the naked force of his will.' That will was as determined and firm as that of Aaron Burr. It rested unmelted amid the boiling sea of passion, waiting its hour of renewed sway. He walked the room for hours; and then sat down to his Bible, and wakened once or twice to find his head leaning on its pages, and his mind far gone in thoughts from which he woke with a bitter throb. Then he determined to set himself to some definite work; and taking his Concordance, began busily tracing out and numbering all the proof-texts for one of the chapters of his theological system; till at last he worked himself down to such calmness that he could pray; and then he schooled and reasoned with himself in a style not unlike, in its spirit, to what a great modern author has addressed to suffering humanity,—'What is it that thou art fretting and self-tormenting about? Is it because *thou* art not happy? Who told thee that thou wast to be happy? Is there any ordinance of the universe that *thou* shouldst be happy? Art thou nothing but a vulture screaming for prey? Canst thou not do without happiness? Yea, thou canst do without happiness, and instead thereof find blessedness.'

The Doctor came lastly to the conclusion that '*blessedness*,' which was all the portion his Master had on earth, might do for him also. And therefore he kissed and blessed that silver dove of happiness, which he saw was weary of sailing in his clumsy old ark, and let it go out of his hand without a tear.

He slept little that night, but when he came to breakfast all noticed an unusual gentleness and benignity of manner; and Mary, she knew not why, saw tears rising in his eyes when he looked at her.

After breakfast he requested Mrs. Scudder to step with him into his study; and Miss Prissy shook in her little shoes as she saw the matron entering. The door was shut for a long time, and two voices could be heard in earnest conversation.

Meanwhile James Marvyn entered the cottage, prompt to remind Mary of her promise, that she would talk with him again this morning.

They had talked with each other but a few moments, by the sweetbriar-shaded window in the best room, when Mrs. Scudder appeared at the door of the apartment, with traces of tears upon her cheeks. 'Good morning, James,' she said. 'The Doctor wishes to see you and Mary a moment together.' Both looked sufficiently astounded, knowing from Mrs. Scudder's looks that something was impending. They followed Mrs. Scudder, scarcely feeling the ground they trod on.

The Doctor was sitting at his table with his favourite large-print Bible open before him. He rose to receive them with a manner at once gentle and grave. There was a pause of some minutes, during which he sat with his head leaning upon his hand. 'You all know,' he said, turning towards Mary who sat very near him, 'the near and dear relation in which I have been expected to stand towards this friend; I should not have been worthy of that relation if I had not felt in my heart the true love of a husband as set forth in the New Testament; who should "love his wife even as Christ loved the church and gave Himself for it;" and if in case any peril or danger threatened this dear soul, and I could not give myself for her, I had never been worthy the honour she has done me. For I take it, wherever there is a cross or burden to be borne by one or the other, that the man who is made in the image of God, as to strength and endurance, should take it upon himself, and not lay it upon her that is weaker; for he is therefore strong, not that he may tyrannize over the weak, but bear their burdens for them, even as Christ for His church. I have just discovered,' he added, looking kindly upon Mary, 'that there is a great cross and burden which must come, either on this dear child or on myself, through no fault of either of us, but through God's good providence; and, therefore, let *me* bear it.

'Mary, my dear child,' he said, 'I will be to thee as a father; but I will not force thy heart.'

CHAPTER XL.

At this moment, Mary, by a sudden, impulsive movement, threw her arms around his neck and kissed him, and lay sobbing on his shoulder. 'No, no,' she said, 'I will marry you as I said.'

'Not if I will not, dear,' he said, with a benign smile. 'Come here, young man,' he said, with some authority, to James, 'I give thee this maiden to wife,' and he lifted her from his shoulder and placed her gently in the arms of the young man, who, overawed and overcome, pressed her silently to his heart. 'There, children, it is over,' he said. 'God bless you!'

'Take her away,' he added, 'she will be more composed soon.'

Before James left, he grasped the Doctor's hand in his and said, 'Sir, this tells on my heart more than any sermon you ever preached, I shall never forget it. God bless you, sir!'

The Doctor saw them slowly quit the apartment, and following them, closed the door, and thus ended

THE MINISTER'S WOOING.

CHAPTER XLI.

OF the events which followed this scene, we are happy to give our readers more minute and graphic details than we ourselves could furnish, by transcribing for their edification an autograph letter of Miss Prissy's, still preserved in a black oaken cabinet of our great-grandmother's, and with which we take no further liberties than the correction of a somewhat peculiar orthography.

It is written to that sister 'Martha' in Boston, of whom she made such frequent mention, and who, it appears, it was her custom to keep posted up in all the gossip of her immediate sphere.

> 'MY DEAR SISTER,
>
> 'You wonder, I s'pose, why I haven't written you; but the fact is, I've been run just off my feet and worked till the flesh aches so, it seems as if it would drop off my bones with this wedding of Mary Scudder's. And, after all, you'll be astonished to hear that she ha'n't married the Doctor, but that Jim Marvyn that I told you about, who had such a wonderful escape from shipwreck. You see, he came home a week before the wedding was to be, and Mary, she was so conscientious, she thought 'twa'n't right to break off with the Doctor, and so she was for going right on with it; and Mrs. Scudder, she was for going on more yet; and the poor young man, he couldn't get a word in edgeways; and there wouldn't anybody tell the Doctor a word about it, and there 'twas drifting along, and both on 'em feeling dreadfully; and so I thought to myself I'll just take my life in my hand like Queen Esther, and go in and tell the Doctor all about it. And so I did. I'm scared to death always when I think of it. But that dear, blessed man! he took it like a saint. He just gave her up as serene and calm as a psalm-book, and called James in and told him to take her. Jim was fairly over-crowed—it really made him feel small, and he says he'll agree that there is more in the Doctor's religion than most men's, which shows how important it is for professing Christians to bear testimony in their works—as I was telling Cerinthy Ann Twitchel, and she said there wa'n't anything made her want to be a Christian so much, if that was what religion would do for peo-

ple. Well, you see, when this came out, it wanted just three days of the wedding, which was to be Thursday; and that wedding-dress I told you about, that had lilies of the valley on a white ground, was pretty much made, except puffing the gauze round the neck, which I do with white satin piping cord, and it looks beautiful too. And so Mrs. Scudder and I, we were thinking 'twould do just as well, when in came Jim Marvyn bringing the sweetest thing you ever saw, that he had got in China, and I think I never did see anything lovelier. It was a white silk, as thick as a board, and so stiff that it would stand alone, and overshot with little fine dots of silver, so that it shone when you moved it just like frost-work. And when I saw it I just clapped my hands and jumped up from the floor; and says I, "If I have to sit up all night that dress shall be made, and made well too." For, you know, I thought I could get Miss Ollodine Hocum to run the breadth and do such parts, so that I could devote myself to the fine work; and that French woman I told you about, she said she'd help, and she's a master-hand for touching things up. There seems to be work provided for all kinds of people, and French people seem to have a gift in all sorts of dressy things, and 'tisn't a bad gift either. Well, as I was saying, we agreed that this was to be cut open with a train, and a petticoat of just the palest, sweetest, loveliest, blue that ever you saw, and gauze puffings down the edgings each side, fastened in, every once in a while, with lilies of the valley; and 'twas cut square in the neck, with puffing and flowers to match; and then, tight sleeves with full ruffles of that old Mechlin lace that you remember Mrs. Katy Scudder showed you once in that great camphor-wood trunk. Well, you see, come to get all things together that were to be done, we concluded to put off the wedding till Tuesday; and Madame de Frontignac she would dress the best room for it herself, and she spent nobody knows what time in going round and getting evergreens, and making wreaths, and putting up green boughs over the pictures, so that the room looked just like the Episcopal Church at Christmas. In fact, Mrs. Scudder said if it had been Christmas she wouldn't have felt it right, because it would be like encouraging prelacy; but as it was, she didn't think anybody would think it any harm. Well, Tuesday night I and Madame de Frontignac we dressed Mary ourselves, and I tell you the dress fitted as if 'twas grown on her; and Madame de Frontignac she dressed her hair, and she had on a wreath of lilies of the valley, and a gauze veil that came a'most down to her feet and came all around her like a cloud, and you could see her white shining dress through it every time she moved. And she looked just as white as a snowberry; but there were two little pink spots that came coming and going in her cheeks, that kind o' lightened up when she smiled, and then faded down again. And the

French lady put a string of real pearls round her neck, with a cross of pearls, which went down and lay hid in her bosom. She was mighty calm-like while she was being dressed; but just as I was putting in the last pin, she started, for she heard the rumbling of a coach down stairs, for Jim Marvyn had got a real elegant carriage to carry her over to his father's in, and so she knew he was come; and pretty soon Mrs. Marvyn came in the room, and when she saw Mary, her brown eyes kind o' danced, and she lifted up both hands to see how beautiful she looked; and Jim Marvyn he was standing at the door, and they told him it wasn't proper that he should see till the time come.

'But he begged so hard that he might just have one peep, that I let him come in, and he looked at her as if she was something he wouldn't dare to touch, and he said to me softly, says he, "I'm 'most afraid she has got wings somewhere that will fly away from me, or that I shall wake up and find it is a dream."

'Well, Cerinthy Ann Twitchel was the bridesmaid, and she came next with that young man she is engaged to. It is all out now that she is engaged, and she don't deny it.

'And Cerinthy, she looked handsomer than I ever saw her, in a white brocade with rosebuds on it, which I guess she got in reference to the future, for they say she is going to be married next month.

'Well, we all filled up the room pretty well, till Mrs. Scudder came in to tell us that the company were all together, and then they took hold of arms, and they had a little time practising how they must stand; and Cerinthy Ann's beau would always get her on the wrong side, 'cause he's rather bashful, and don't know very well what he's about; and Cerinthy Ann declared she was afraid that she should laugh out in prayer-time, 'cause she always did laugh when she knew she mus'n't.

'But, finally, Mrs. Scudder told us we must go in, and looked so reprovingly at Cerinthy that she had to hold her mouth with her pocket-handkerchief.

'Well, the old Doctor was standing there in the very silk gown that the ladies gave him to be married in himself, poor, dear man! and he smiled kind o' peaceful on 'em when they came in and walked up to a kind o' bower of evergreens and flowers that Madame de Frontignac had fixed for them to stand in. Mary grew rather white as if she was going to faint; but Jim Marvyn stood up just as firm and looked as proud and handsome as a prince, and he kind o' looked down at her, 'cause you know he is a great deal taller, kind o' wondering as if he wanted to know if it was really so. Well, when they got all placed, they let the doors stand open, and Cato and Candace came and stood in the door. And Candace had on her great splendid

Mogadore turban, and a crimson and yellow shawl that she seemed to take comfort in wearing, although it was pretty hot.

'Well, so when they were all fixed, the Doctor he began his prayer; and as most all of us knew what a great sacrifice he had made, I don't believe there was a dry eye in the room; and when he had done there was a great time—people blowing their noses and wiping their eyes as if it had been a funeral.

'Then Cerinthy Ann she pulled off Mary's glove pretty quick; but that poor beau of hers, he made such work of James's that he had to pull it off himself after all, and Cerinthy Ann she like to have laughed out loud.

'And so, when the Doctor told them to join hands, Jim took hold of Mary's hand as if he didn't mean to let go very soon; and so they were married, and I was the first one that kissed the bride after Mrs. Scudder. I got that promise out of Mary when I was making the dress. And Jim Marvyn he insisted upon kissing me, 'cause, says he, Miss Prissy, you are as young and handsome as any of them. And I told him he was a saucy fellow, and I'd box his ears if I could reach them.

'That French lady looked lovely, dressed in pale pink silk, with long pink wreaths of flowers in her hair; and she came up and kissed Mary, and said something to her in French.

'And, after a while, old Candace came up, and Mary kissed her; and then Candace put her arms round Jim's neck and gave him a real hearty smack, so that everybody laughed.

'And then the cake and the wine was passed round, and everybody had good times till we heard the nine-o'clock bell ring. And then the coach came up to the door, and Mrs. Scudder she wrapped Mary up, kissing her and crying over her; while Mrs. Marvyn stood stretching her arms out of the coach after her.

'And then Cato and Candace went after in the waggon behind, and so they all went off together, and that was the end of the wedding. And ever since then we ha'n't any of us done much but rest, for we were pretty much tired out. So no more at present from your affectionate sister

'PRISSY.

'P.S. (to Miss Prissy's letter).—I forgot to tell you that Jim Marvyn has come home quite rich. He fell in with a man in China who was at the head of one of their great merchant-houses, whom he nursed through a long fever, and took care of his business, and so when he got well nothing would do but he must have him for a partner, and now he is going to live in this country and attend to the business of the house here. They say he is going to build a house as grand as the Vernons'; and we hope he has experienced religion, and he means to join our church, which is a providence, for he is twice as rich and generous as that old Simon Brown that snapped me up so about my wages. I never believed in him for all his talk. I was down to Miss Scudder's when the Doctor examined Jim about his evidences. At first the Doctor seemed a little anxious 'cause he didn't talk in the regular way, for you know Jim always did have his own way of talking, and never could say things in other people's words; and sometimes he makes folks laugh when he himself don't know what they laugh at, because he hits the nail on the head in some strange way they ar'n't expecting. If I was to have died I couldn't help laughing at some things he said, and yet I don't think I ever felt more solemnized. He sat up there in a sort o' grand, straightforward, noble way, and told us all the way the Lord had been leading of him, and all the exercises of his mind; and all about the dreadful shipwreck, and how he was saved, and the loving-kindness of the Lord, till the Doctor's spectacles got all blinded with tears, and he couldn't see the notes he made to examine him by; and we all cried, Miss Scudder, and Mary, and I; and as to Miss Marvyn, she just sat with her hands clasped, looking into her son's eyes, like a picture of the Virgin Mary; and when Jim got through there wa'n't nothing to be heard for some minutes, and the Doctor he wiped his eyes and wiped his glasses, and he looked over his papers, but he couldn't bring out a word, and at last, says he, "Let us pray," for that was all there was to be said, for I think sometimes things so kind o' fills folks up that there a'n't nothin' to be done but pray, which the Lord be praised we are privileged to do always. Between you and I, Martha, I never could understand all the distinctions our dear, blessed Doctor sets up; and when he publishes his system, if I work my fingers to the bone, I mean to buy one and study it out, because he is such a blessed man; though after all's said I have to come back to my old place, and trust in the loving-kindness of the Lord, who takes care of the sparrow on the house-top and all small, lone creatures like me; though I can't say I'm lone either, because nobody need say that so long as there's folks to be done for; so if I *don't* understand the Doctor's theology, or don't get eyes to read it on account of the fine stitching on his shirt ruffles I've been trying to do, still I hope I may be accepted on account of the Lord's great goodness; for if we can't trust that, it's all over with us all.'

CHAPTER XLII.

LAST WORDS.

WE know it is fashionable to drop the curtain over a new-married pair as they recede from the altar, but we cannot but hope our readers may have by this time enough of interest in our little history to wish for a few words on the lot of the personages whose acquaintance they have thereby made.

The conjectures of Miss Prissy in regard to the house which was to be built for the new-married pair were as speedily as possible realized. On a beautiful elevation, a little out of the town of Newport, rose a fair and stately mansion, whose windows overlooked the harbour, and whose wide cool rooms were adorned by the constant presence of the sweet face and form which has been the guiding-star of our story. The fair poetic maiden, the seeress, the saint, has passed into that appointed shrine for woman, more holy than cloister, more saintly and pure than church or altar—*a Christian home*. Priestess, wife, and mother, there she ministers daily in holy works of household peace, and by faith and prayer and love redeems from grossness and earthliness the common toils and wants of life.

The gentle guiding force that led James Marvyn from the maxims and habits and ways of this world to the higher conception of an heroic and Christ-like manhood was still ever present with him, gently touching the springs of life, brooding peacefully with dove-like wings over his soul, and he grew up under it noble in purpose and strong in spirit. He was one of the most energetic and fearless supporters of the Doctor in his life-long warfare against an inhumanity which was entrenched in all the mercantile interest of the day, and which at last fell before the force of conscience and moral appeal.

Candace, in time, transferred her allegiance to the growing family of her young master and mistress; and predominated proudly, in gorgeous raiment and butterfly turban, over a rising race of young Marvyns. All the cares not needed by them were bestowed on the somewhat garrulous old age of Cato, whose never-failing cough furnished occupation for all her spare hours and thought.

As for our friend the Doctor, we trust our readers will appreciate the magnanimity with which he proved a real and disinterested love, in a point where so many men experience only the graspings of a selfish one. A mind so severely trained as his had been brings to a great crisis, involving severe self-denial, an amount of reserved moral force quite inexplicable to those less habituated to self-control. He was like a warrior whose sleep even was in armour, always ready to be roused to the conflict.

In regard to his feelings for Mary, he made the sacrifice of himself to her happiness so wholly and thoroughly that there was not a moment of weak hesitation—no going back over the past—no vain regret. Generous and brave souls find a support in such actions, because the very exertion raises them to a higher and purer plane of existence.

His diary records the event only in these very calm and temperate words:—'It was a trial to me—a *very great* trial; but as she did not deceive me, I shall never lose my friendship for her.'

The Doctor was always a welcome inmate in the house of Mary and James, as a friend revered and dear. Nor did he want in time a hearthstone of his own, where a bright and loving face made him daily welcome; for we find that he married at last a woman of a fair countenance, and that sons and daughters grew up around him.

In time, also, his theological system was published. In that day it was customary to dedicate new or important works to the patronage of some distinguished or powerful individual. The Doctor had no earthly patron. Four or five simple lines are found in the commencement of his work, in which, in a spirit reverential and affectionate, he dedicates it to our Lord Jesus Christ, praying Him to accept the good, and to overrule the errors to His glory.

Quite unexpectedly to himself the work proved a success, not only in public acceptance and esteem, but even in a temporal view, bringing to him at last a modest competence, which he accepted with surprise and gratitude. To the last of a very long life he was the same steady undiscouraged worker, the same calm witness against popular sins and proclaimer of unpopular truths, ever saying and doing what he saw to be eternally true and right, without the slightest consultation with worldly expediency or earthly gain, nor did his words cease to work in New England till the evils he opposed were finally done away.

Colonel Burr leaves the scene of our story to pursue those brilliant and unscrupulous political intrigues so well known to the historian of those times, and whose results were so disastrous to himself. His duel with the ill-fated Hamilton, and the awful retribution of public opinion that followed—the slow downward course of a doomed life, are all on record. Chased from society, pointed at everywhere by the finger of hatred, so accursed in common esteem that even the publican who lodged him for a night refused to accept his money when he knew his name, heart-stricken in his domestic relation, his only daughter taken by pirates, and dying in untold horrors,—one seems to see in a doom so much above that of other men the power of an avenging Nemesis for sins beyond those of ordinary humanity.

But we who have learned of Christ may humbly hope that these crushing miseries in this life came not because he was a sinner above others, not in wrath alone, but that the prayers of the sweet saint who gave him to God even before his birth brought to him those friendly adversities that thus might be slain in his soul the evil demon of pride, which had been the opposing force to all that was noble within him. Nothing is more affecting than the account of the last hours of this man, whom a woman took in and cherished in his poverty and weakness with that same heroic enthusiasm with which it was his lot to inspire so many women. This humble keeper of lodgings was told that if she retained Aaron Burr all her other lodgers would leave—'Let them do it then,' she said, 'but he shall remain.' In the same uncomplaining and inscrutable silence in which he had borne the reverses and miseries of his life did this singular being pass through the shades of the dark valley. The New Testament was always under his pillow, and when alone he was often found reading it attentively, but of the result of that communion with higher powers he said nothing. Patient, gentle, and grateful he was, as to all his inner history, entirely silent and impenetrable. He died with the request, which has a touching significance, that he might be buried at the feet of those parents whose sainted lives had finished so differently from his own.

> 'No farther seek his errors to disclose,
> Or draw his frailties from their dread abode.'

Shortly after Mary's marriage Madame de Frontignac sailed with her husband to France, where they lived in a very retired way on a large estate in the south of France. A close correspondence was kept up between her and Mary for many years, from which we shall give our readers a few extracts. The first is dated shortly after their return to France.

'At last, my sweet Marie, you behold us in peace after our wanderings. I wish you could see our lovely nest in the hills, which overlooks the Mediterranean, whose blue waters remind me of Newport harbour and our old days there. Ah, my sweet saint, blessed was the day I first learned to know you! for it was you more than anything else that kept me back from sin and misery. I call you my Sibyl, dearest, because the Sibyl was a prophetess of divine things out of the church; and so are you. The Abbé says that all true, devout persons in all persuasions belong to the true Catholic Apostolic Church, and will in the end be enlightened to know it; what do you think of that, *ma belle?* I fancy I see you look at me with your grave, innocent eyes, just as you used to; but you say nothing.

'I am far happier, *ma* Marie, than I ever thought I could be. I took your advice, and told my husband all I had felt and suffered. It was a very hard thing to do; but I felt how true it was, as you said, there could be no real friendship without perfect truth at bottom; so I told him all, and he was very good, and noble, and helpful to me; and since then he has been so gentle, and patient, and thoughtful, that no mother could be kinder, and I should be a very bad woman if I did not love him truly and dearly—I do.

'I must confess that there is still a weak, bleeding place in my heart that aches yet, but I try to bear it bravely; and when I am tempted to think myself very miserable, I remember how patiently you used to go about your housework and spinning in those sad days when you thought your heart was drowned in the sea;

and I try to do like you. I have many duties to my servants and tenants, and mean to be a good châtelaine; and I find when I nurse the sick and comfort the poor that my sorrows seem lighter. For after all, Mary, I have lost nothing that ever was mine—only my foolish heart has grown to something that it should not, and bleeds at being torn away. Nobody but Christ and His dear mother can tell what this sorrow is; but they know, and that is enough.'

The next letter is dated some three years after.

'You see me now, my Marie, a proud and happy woman. I was truly envious when you wrote me of the birth of your little son; but now the dear good God has sent a sweet little angel to me, to comfort my sorrows and lie close to my heart; and since he came all pain is gone. Ah, if you could see him! he has black eyes and lashes like silk, and such little hands!—even his finger-nails are all perfect, like little gems; and when he puts his little hand on my bosom I tremble with joy. Since he came I pray always, and the good God seems very near to me. Now I realize as I never did before the sublime thought that God revealed himself in the infant Jesus; and I bow before the manger of Bethlehem where the Holy Babe was laid. What comfort, what adorable condescension for us mothers in that scene! My husband is so moved he can scarce stay an hour from the cradle! He seems to look at me with a sort of awe, because I know how to care for this precious treasure that he adores without daring to touch. We are going to call him Henri, which is my husband's name and that of his ancestors for many generations back. I vow for him an eternal friendship with the son of my little Marie; and I shall try and train him up to be a brave man and a true Christian. Ah, Marie, this gives me something to live for. My heart is full—a whole new life opens before me!'

Somewhat later, another letter announces the birth of a daughter, and later still, that of another son; but we shall only add one more, written some years after, on hearing of the great reverse of popular feeling towards Burr, subsequently to his duel with the ill-fated Hamilton.

'*Ma chère Marie*—Your letter has filled me with grief. My noble Henri, who already begins to talk of himself as my protector (these boys feel their manhood so soon, *ma Marie*), saw by my face when I read your letter that something pained me, and he would not rest till I told him something about it. Ah, Marie, how thankful I then felt that I had nothing to blush for before my son! how thankful for those dear children whose little hands had healed all the morbid places of my heart, so that I could think of all the past without a pang! I told Henri that the letter brought bad news of an old friend, but that it pained me to speak of it; and you would have thought by the grave and tender way he talked to his mamma that the boy was an experienced man of forty, to say the least.

'But Marie, how unjust is the world; how unjust both in praise and blame! Poor Burr was the petted child of society: yesterday she doted on him, flattered him, smiled on his faults, and let him do what he would without reproof; to-day she flouts, and scorns, and scoffs him, and refuses to see the least good in him. I know that man, Mary, and I know that sinful as he may be before Infinite Purity, he is not so much worse than all the other men of his time. Have I not been in

America? I know Jefferson; I knew poor Hamilton—peace be with the dead! Neither of them had lives that could bear the sort of trial to which Burr's is subjected. When every secret fault, failing, and sin is dragged out and held up without mercy, what man can stand?

'But I know what irritates the world is that proud, disdainful calm which will neither give sigh nor tear. It was not that he killed poor Hamilton, but that he never seemed to care! Ah, there is that evil demon of his life!—that cold, stoical pride, which haunts him like a fate. But I know he *does* feel; I know he is *not* as hard at heart as he tries to be; I have seen too many real acts of pity to the unfortunate, of tenderness to the weak, of real love to his friends to believe that. Great have been his sins against our sex, and God forbid that the mother of children should speak lightly of them; but is not so susceptible a temperament, and so singular a power to charm as he possessed, to be taken into account in estimating his temptations? Because he is a sinning man, it does not follow that he is a demon. If any should have cause to think bitterly of him, I should. He trifled inexcusably with my deepest feelings; he caused me years of conflict and anguish, such as he little knows. I was almost shipwrecked; yet I will still say to the last that what I loved in him was a better self—something really noble and good, however concealed and perverted by pride, ambition, and self-will. Though all the world reject him, I still have faith in this better nature, and prayers that he may be led right at last. There is at least one heart that will always intercede with God for him.'

It is well known that for many years after Burr's death the odium that covered his name was so great that no monument was erected, lest it should become a mark for popular violence. Subsequently, however, in a mysterious manner a plain granite slab marked his grave; by whom erected has been never known. It was placed in the night by some friendly, unknown hand. A labourer in the vicinity, who first discovered it, found lying near the spot a small porte-monnaie, which had perhaps been used in paying for the workmanship. It contained no papers that could throw any light on the subject, except the fragment of the address of a letter, on which was written 'Henri de Frontignac.'

THE PEARL OF ORR'S ISLAND

A Story of the Coast of Maine

INTRODUCTORY NOTE

The publication of *Uncle Tom's Cabin*, though much more than an incident in an author's career, seems to have determined Mrs. Stowe more surely in her purpose to devote herself to literature. During the summer following its appearance, she was in Andover, making over the house which she and her husband were to occupy upon leaving Brunswick; and yet, busy as she was, she was writing articles for *The Independent* and *The National Era*. The following extract from a letter written at that time, July 29, 1852, intimates that she already was sketching the outline of the story which later grew into *The Pearl of Orr's Island*:—

"I seem to have so much to fill my time, and yet there is my Maine story waiting. However, I am composing it every day, only I greatly need living studies for the filling in of my sketches. There is old Jonas, my "fish father," a sturdy, independent fisherman farmer, who in his youth sailed all over the world and made up his mind about everything. In his old age he attends prayer-meetings and reads the *Missionary Herald*. He also has plenty of money in an old brown sea-chest. He is a great heart with an inflexible will and iron muscles. I must go to Orr's Island and see him again." The story seems to have remained in her mind, for we are told by her son that she worked upon it by turns with *The Minister's Wooing*.

It was not, however, until eight years later, after *The Minister's Wooing* had been published and *Agnes of Sorrento* was well begun, that she took up her old story in earnest and set about making it into a short serial. It would seem that her first intention was to confine herself to a sketch of the childhood of her chief characters, with a view to delineating the influences at work upon them; but, as she herself expressed it, "Out of the simple history of the little Pearl of Orr's Island as it had shaped itself in her mind, rose up a Captain Kittridge with his garrulous yarns, and Misses Roxy and Ruey, given to talk, and a whole pigeon roost of yet undreamed of fancies and dreams which would insist on being written." So it came about that the story as originally planned came to a stopping place at the end of Chapter XVII., as the reader may see when he reaches that place. The childish life of her characters ended there, and a lapse of ten years was assumed before their story was taken up again in the next chapter. The book when published had no chapter headings. These have been supplied in the present edition.

CHAPTER I

NAOMI

On the road to the Kennebec, below the town of Bath, in the State of Maine, might have been seen, on a certain autumnal afternoon, a one-horse wagon, in which two persons were sitting. One was an old man, with the peculiarly hard but expressive physiognomy which characterizes the seafaring population of the New England shores. A clear blue eye, evidently practiced in habits of keen observation, white hair, bronzed, weather-beaten cheeks, and a face deeply lined with the furrows of shrewd thought and anxious care, were points of the portrait that made themselves felt at a glance.

By his side sat a young woman of two-and-twenty, of a marked and peculiar personal appearance. Her hair was black, and smoothly parted on a broad forehead, to which a pair of penciled dark eyebrows gave a striking and definite outline. Beneath, lay a pair of large black eyes, remarkable for tremulous expression of melancholy and timidity. The cheek was white and bloodless as a snowberry, though with the clear and perfect oval of good health; the mouth was delicately formed, with a certain sad quiet in its lines, which indicated a habitually repressed and sensitive nature.

The dress of this young person, as often happens in New England, was, in refinement and even elegance, a marked contrast to that of her male companion and to the humble vehicle in which she rode. There was not only the most fastidious neatness, but a delicacy in the choice of colors, an indication of elegant tastes in the whole arrangement, and the quietest suggestion in the world of an acquaintance with the usages of fashion, which struck one oddly in those wild and dreary surroundings. On the whole, she impressed one like those fragile wild-flowers which in April cast their fluttering shadows from the mossy crevices of the old New England granite,—an existence in which colorless delicacy is united to a sort of elastic hardihood of life, fit for the rocky soil and harsh winds it is born to encounter.

The scenery of the road along which the two were riding was wild and bare. Only savins and mulleins, with their dark pyramids or white spires of velvet leaves, diversified the sandy wayside; but out at sea was a wide sweep of blue, reaching far to the open ocean, which lay rolling, tossing, and breaking into white caps of foam in the bright sunshine. For two or three days a northeast storm had been raging, and the sea was in all the commotion which such a general upturning creates.

The two travelers reached a point of elevated land, where they paused a moment, and the man drew up the jogging, stiff-jointed old farm-horse, and raised himself upon his feet to look out at the prospect.

There might be seen in the distance the blue Kennebec sweeping out toward the ocean through its picturesque rocky shores, docked with cedars and other dusky evergreens, which were illuminated by the orange and flame-colored trees of Indian summer. Here and there scarlet creepers swung long trailing garlands over the faces of the dark rock, and fringes of goldenrod above swayed with the brisk blowing wind that was driving the blue waters seaward, in face of the upcoming ocean tide,—a conflict which caused them to rise in great foam-crested waves. There are two channels into this river from the open sea, navigable for ships which are coming in to the city of Bath; one is broad and shallow, the other narrow and deep, and these are divided by a steep ledge of rocks.

Where the spectators of this scene were sitting, they could see in the distance a ship borne with tremendous force by the rising tide into the mouth of the river, and encountering a northwest wind which had succeeded the gale, as northwest winds often do on this coast. The ship, from what might be observed in the distance, seemed struggling to make the wider channel, but was constantly driven off by the baffling force of the wind.

"There she is, Naomi," said the old fisherman, eagerly, to his companion, "coming right in." The young woman was one of the sort that never start, and never exclaim, but with all deeper emotions grow still. The color slowly mounted into her cheek, her lips parted, and her eyes dilated with a wide, bright expression; her breathing came in thick gasps, but she said nothing.

The old fisherman stood up in the wagon, his coarse, butternut-colored coat-flaps fluttering and snapping in the breeze, while his interest seemed to be so intense in the efforts of the ship that he made involuntary and eager movements as if to direct her course. A moment passed, and his keen, practiced eye discovered a change in her movements, for he cried out involuntarily,—

"*Don't* take the narrow channel to-day!" and a moment after, "O Lord! O Lord! have mercy,—there they go! Look! look! look!"

And, in fact, the ship rose on a great wave clear out of the water, and the next second seemed to leap with a desperate plunge into the narrow passage; for a moment there was a shivering of the masts and the rigging, and she went down and was gone.

"They're split to pieces!" cried the fisherman. "Oh, my poor girl—my poor girl—they're gone! O Lord, have mercy!"

The woman lifted up no voice, but, as one who has been shot through the heart falls with no cry, she fell back,—a mist rose up over her great mournful eyes,—she had fainted.

CHAPTER I

The story of this wreck of a home-bound ship just entering the harbor is yet told in many a family on this coast. A few hours after, the unfortunate crew were washed ashore in all the joyous holiday rig in which they had attired themselves that morning to go to their sisters, wives, and mothers.

This is the first scene in our story.

CHAPTER II

MARA

Down near the end of Orr's Island, facing the open ocean, stands a brown house of the kind that the natives call "lean-to," or "linter,"—one of those large, comfortable structures, barren in the ideal, but rich in the practical, which the workingman of New England can always command. The waters of the ocean came up within a rod of this house, and the sound of its moaning waves was even now filling the clear autumn starlight. Evidently something was going on within, for candles fluttered and winked from window to window, like fireflies in a dark meadow, and sounds as of quick footsteps, and the flutter of brushing garments, might be heard.

Something unusual is certainly going on within the dwelling of Zephaniah Pennel to-night.

Let us enter the dark front-door. We feel our way to the right, where a solitary ray of light comes from the chink of a half-opened door. Here is the front room of the house, set apart as its place of especial social hilarity and sanctity,—the "best room," with its low studded walls, white dimity window-curtains, rag carpet, and polished wood chairs. It is now lit by the dim gleam of a solitary tallow candle, which seems in the gloom to make only a feeble circle of light around itself, leaving all the rest of the apartment in shadow.

In the centre of the room, stretched upon a table, and covered partially by a sea-cloak, lies the body of a man of twenty-five,—lies, too, evidently as one of whom it is written, "He shall return to his house no more, neither shall his place know him any more." A splendid manhood has suddenly been called to forsake that lifeless form, leaving it, like a deserted palace, beautiful in its desolation. The hair, dripping with the salt wave, curled in glossy abundance on the finely-formed head; the flat, broad brow; the closed eye, with its long black lashes; the firm, manly mouth; the strongly-moulded chin,—all, all were sealed with that seal which is never to be broken till the great resurrection day.

He was lying in a full suit of broadcloth, with a white vest and smart blue neck-tie, fastened with a pin, in which was some braided hair under a crystal. All his clothing, as well as his hair, was saturated with sea-water, which trickled from time to time, and struck with a leaden and dropping sound into a sullen pool which lay under the table.

This was the body of James Lincoln, ship-master of the brig Flying Scud, who that morning had dressed himself gayly in his state-room to go on shore and meet his wife,—singing and jesting as he did so.

This is all that you have to learn in the room below; but as we stand there, we hear a trampling of feet in the apartment above,—the quick yet careful opening and shutting of doors,—and voices come and go about the house, and whisper consultations on the stairs. Now comes the roll of wheels, and the Doctor's gig drives up to the door; and, as he goes creaking up with his heavy boots, we will follow and gain admission to the dimly-lighted chamber.

Two gossips are sitting in earnest, whispering conversation over a small bundle done up in an old flannel petticoat. To them the doctor is about to address himself cheerily, but is repelled by sundry signs and sounds which warn him not to speak. Moderating his heavy boots as well as he is able to a pace of quiet, he advances for a moment, and the petticoat is unfolded for him to glance at its contents; while a low, eager, whispered conversation, attended with much head-shaking, warns him that his first duty is with somebody behind the checked curtains of a bed in the farther corner of the room. He steps on tiptoe, and draws the curtain; and there, with closed eye, and cheek as white as wintry snow, lies the same face over which passed the shadow of death when that ill-fated ship went down.

This woman was wife to him who lies below, and within the hour has been made mother to a frail little human existence, which the storm of a great anguish has driven untimely on the shores of life,—a precious pearl cast up from the past eternity upon the wet, wave-ribbed sand of the present. Now, weary with her moanings, and beaten out with the wrench of a double anguish, she lies with closed eyes in that passive apathy which precedes deeper shadows and longer rest.

Over against her, on the other side of the bed, sits an aged woman in an attitude of deep dejection, and the old man we saw with her in the morning is standing with an anxious, awestruck face at the foot of the bed.

The doctor feels the pulse of the woman, or rather lays an inquiring finger where the slightest thread of vital current is scarcely throbbing, and shakes his head mournfully. The touch of his hand rouses her,—her large wild, melancholy eyes fix themselves on him with an inquiring glance, then she shivers and moans,—

"Oh, Doctor, Doctor!—Jamie, Jamie!"

"Come, come!" said the doctor, "cheer up, my girl, you've got a fine little daughter,—the Lord mingles mercies with his afflictions."

Her eyes closed, her head moved with a mournful but decided dissent.

A moment after she spoke in the sad old words of the Hebrew Scripture,—

"Call her not Naomi; call her Mara, for the Almighty hath dealt very bitterly with me."

And as she spoke, there passed over her face the sharp frost of the last winter; but even as it passed there broke out a smile, as if a flower had been thrown down from Paradise, and she said,—

"Not my will, but thy will," and so was gone.

Aunt Roxy and Aunt Ruey were soon left alone in the chamber of death.

"She'll make a beautiful corpse," said Aunt Roxy, surveying the still, white form contemplatively, with her head in an artistic attitude.

"She was a pretty girl," said Aunt Ruey; "dear me, what a Providence! I 'member the wedd'n down in that lower room, and what a handsome couple they were."

"They were lovely and pleasant in their lives, and in their deaths they were not divided," said Aunt Roxy, sententiously.

"What was it she said, did ye hear?" said Aunt Ruey.

"She called the baby 'Mary.'"

"Ah! sure enough, her mother's name afore her. What a still, softly-spoken thing she always was!"

"A pity the poor baby didn't go with her," said Aunt Roxy; "seven-months' children are so hard to raise."

"'Tis a pity," said the other.

But babies will live, and all the more when everybody says that it is a pity they should. Life goes on as inexorably in this world as death. It was ordered by THE WILL above that out of these two graves should spring one frail, trembling autumn flower,—the "Mara" whose poor little roots first struck deep in the salt, bitter waters of our mortal life.

CHAPTER III

THE BAPTISM AND THE BURIAL

Now, I cannot think of anything more unlikely and uninteresting to make a story of than that old brown "linter" house of Captain Zephaniah Pennel, down on the south end of Orr's Island.

Zephaniah and Mary Pennel, like Zacharias and Elizabeth, are a pair of worthy, God-fearing people, walking in all the commandments and ordinances of the Lord blameless; but that is no great recommendation to a world gaping for sensation and calling for something stimulating. This worthy couple never read anything but the Bible, the "Missionary Herald," and the "Christian Mirror,"—never went anywhere except in the round of daily business. He owned a fishing-smack, in which he labored after the apostolic fashion; and she washed, and ironed, and scrubbed, and brewed, and baked, in her contented round, week in and out. The only recreation they ever enjoyed was the going once a week, in good weather, to a prayer-meeting in a little old brown school-house, about a mile from their dwelling; and making a weekly excursion every Sunday, in their fishing craft, to the church opposite, on Harpswell Neck.

To be sure, Zephaniah had read many wide leaves of God's great book of Nature, for, like most Maine sea-captains, he had been wherever ship can go,—to all usual and unusual ports. His hard, shrewd, weather-beaten visage had been seen looking over the railings of his brig in the port of Genoa, swept round by its splendid crescent of palaces and its snow-crested Apennines. It had looked out in the Lagoons of Venice at that wavy floor which in evening seems a sea of glass mingled with fire, and out of which rise temples, and palaces, and churches, and distant silvery Alps, like so many fabrics of dreamland. He had been through the Skagerrack and Cattegat,—into the Baltic, and away round to Archangel, and there chewed a bit of chip, and considered and calculated what bargains it was best to make. He had walked the streets of Calcutta in his shirt-sleeves, with his best Sunday vest, backed with black glazed cambric, which six months before came from the hands of Miss Roxy, and was pronounced by her to be as good as any tailor could make; and in all these places he was just Zephaniah Pennel,—a chip of old Maine,—thrifty, careful, shrewd, honest, God-fearing, and carrying an instinctive knowledge of men and things under a face of rustic simplicity.

It was once, returning from one of his voyages, that he found his wife with a black-eyed, curly-headed little creature, who called him papa, and climbed on his knee, nestled under his coat, rifled his pockets, and woke him every morning by pulling open his eyes with little fingers, and jabbering unintelligible dialects in his ears.

"We will call this child Naomi, wife," he said, after consulting his old Bible; "for that means pleasant, and I'm sure I never see anything beat her for pleasantness. I never knew as children was so engagin'!"

It was to be remarked that Zephaniah after this made shorter and shorter voyages, being somehow conscious of a string around his heart which pulled him harder and harder, till one Sunday, when the little Naomi was five years old, he said to his wife,—

"I hope I ain't a-pervertin' Scriptur' nor nuthin', but I can't help thinkin' of one passage, 'The kingdom of heaven is like a merchantman seeking goodly pearls, and when he hath found one pearl of great price, for joy thereof he goeth and selleth all that he hath, and buyeth that pearl.' Well, Mary, I've been and sold my brig last week," he said, folding his daughter's little quiet head under his coat, "'cause it seems to me the Lord's given us this pearl of great price, and it's enough for us. I don't want to be rambling round the world after riches. We'll have a little farm down on Orr's Island, and I'll have a little fishing-smack, and we'll live and be happy together."

And so Mary, who in those days was a pretty young married woman, felt herself rich and happy,—no duchess richer or happier. The two contentedly delved and toiled, and the little Naomi was their princess. The wise men of the East at the feet of an infant, offering gifts, gold, frankincense, and myrrh, is just a parable of what goes on in every house where there is a young child. All the hard and the harsh, and the common and the disagreeable, is for the parents,—all the bright and beautiful for their child.

When the fishing-smack went to Portland to sell mackerel, there came home in Zephaniah's fishy coat pocket strings of coral beads, tiny gaiter boots, brilliant silks and ribbons for the little fairy princess,—his Pearl of the Island; and sometimes, when a stray party from the neighboring town of Brunswick came down to explore the romantic scenery of the solitary island, they would be startled by the apparition of this still, graceful, dark-eyed child exquisitely dressed in the best and brightest that the shops of a neighboring city could afford,—sitting like some tropical bird on a lonely rock, where the sea came dashing up into the edges of arbor vitæ, or tripping along the wet sands for shells and seaweed.

Many children would have been spoiled by such unlimited indulgence; but there are natures sent down into this harsh world so timorous, and sensitive, and helpless in themselves, that the utmost stretch of indulgence and kindness is needed for their development,—like plants which the warmest shelf of the green-house and the most careful watch of the gardener alone can bring into flower. The pale child, with her large, lustrous, dark eyes, and sensitive organization, was nursed and brooded into a beautiful womanhood, and then found a protector in a high-spirited, manly young ship-master, and she became his wife.

And now we see in the best room—the walls lined with serious faces—men, women, and children, that have come to pay the last tribute of sympathy to the living and the dead. The house looked so utterly alone and solitary in that wild, sea-girt island, that one would have as soon expected the sea-waves to rise and walk in, as so many neighbors; but they had come from neighboring points, crossing the glassy sea in their little crafts, whose white sails looked like millers' wings, or walking miles from distant parts of the island.

Some writer calls a funeral one of the amusements of a New England population. Must we call it an amusement to go and see the acted despair of Medea? or the dying agonies of poor Adrienne Lecouvreur? It is something of the same awful interest in life's tragedy, which makes an untaught and primitive people gather to a funeral,—a tragedy where there is no acting,—and one which each one feels must come at some time to his own dwelling.

Be that as it may, here was a roomful. Not only Aunt Roxy and Aunt Ruey, who by a prescriptive right presided over all the births, deaths, and marriages of the neighborhood, but there was Captain Kittridge, a long, dry, weather-beaten old sea-captain, who sat as if tied in a double bow-knot, with his little fussy old wife, with a great Leghorn bonnet, and eyes like black glass beads shining through in the bows of her horn spectacles, and her hymn-book in her hand ready to lead the psalm. There were aunts, uncles, cousins, and brethren of the deceased; and in the midst stood two coffins, where the two united in death lay sleeping tenderly, as those to whom rest is good. All was still as death, except a chance whisper from some busy neighbor, or a creak of an old lady's great black fan, or the fizz of a fly down the window-pane, and then a stifled sound of deep-drawn breath and weeping from under a cloud of heavy black crape veils, that were together in the group which country-people call the mourners.

A gleam of autumn sunlight streamed through the white curtains, and fell on a silver baptismal vase that stood on the mother's coffin, as the minister rose and said, "The ordinance of baptism will now be administered." A few moments more, and on a baby brow had fallen a few drops of water, and the little pilgrim of a new life had been called Mara in the name of the Father, Son, and Holy Ghost,—the minister slowly repeating thereafter those beautiful words of Holy Writ, "A father of the fatherless is God in his holy habitation,"—as if the baptism of that bereaved one had been a solemn adoption into the infinite heart of the Lord.

With something of the quaint pathos which distinguishes the primitive and Biblical people of that lonely shore, the minister read the passage in Ruth from which the name of the little stranger was drawn, and which describes the return of the bereaved Naomi to her native land. His voice trembled, and there were tears in many eyes as he read, "And it came to pass as she came to Bethlehem, all the city was moved about them; and they said, Is this Naomi? And she said unto them,

Call me not Naomi; call me Mara; for the Almighty hath dealt very bitterly with me. I went out full, and the Lord hath brought me home again empty: why then call ye me Naomi, seeing the Lord hath testified against me, and the Almighty hath afflicted me?"

Deep, heavy sobs from the mourners were for a few moments the only answer to these sad words, till the minister raised the old funeral psalm of New England,—

"Why do we mourn departing friends,
Or shake at Death's alarms?
'Tis but the voice that Jesus sends
To call them to his arms.
"Are we not tending upward too,
As fast as time can move?
And should we wish the hours more slow
That bear us to our love?"

The words rose in old "China,"—that strange, wild warble, whose quaintly blended harmonies might have been learned of moaning seas or wailing winds, so strange and grand they rose, full of that intense pathos which rises over every defect of execution; and as they sung, Zephaniah Pennel straightened his tall form, before bowed on his hands, and looked heavenward, his cheeks wet with tears, but something sublime and immortal shining upward through his blue eyes; and at the last verse he came forward involuntarily, and stood by his dead, and his voice rose over all the others as he sung,—

"Then let the last loud trumpet sound,
And bid the dead arise!
Awake, ye nations under ground!
Ye saints, ascend the skies!"

The sunbeam through the window-curtain fell on his silver hair, and they that looked beheld his face as it were the face of an angel; he had gotten a sight of the city whose foundation is jasper, and whose every gate is a separate pearl.

CHAPTER IV

AUNT ROXY AND AUNT RUEY

The sea lay like an unbroken mirror all around the pine-girt, lonely shores of Orr's Island. Tall, kingly spruces wore their regal crowns of cones high in air, sparkling with diamonds of clear exuded gum; vast old hemlocks of primeval growth stood darkling in their forest shadows, their branches hung with long hoary moss; while feathery larches, turned to brilliant gold by autumn frosts, lighted up the darker shadows of the evergreens. It was one of those hazy, calm, dissolving days of Indian summer, when everything is so quiet that the faintest kiss of the wave on the beach can be heard, and white clouds seem to faint into the blue of the sky, and soft swathing bands of violet vapor make all earth look dreamy, and give to the sharp, clear-cut outlines of the northern landscape all those mysteries of light and shade which impart such tenderness to Italian scenery.

The funeral was over; the tread of many feet, bearing the heavy burden of two broken lives, had been to the lonely graveyard, and had come back again,—each footstep lighter and more unconstrained as each one went his way from the great old tragedy of Death to the common cheerful walks of Life.

The solemn black clock stood swaying with its eternal "tick-tock, tick-tock," in the kitchen of the brown house on Orr's Island. There was there that sense of a stillness that can be felt,—such as settles down on a dwelling when any of its inmates have passed through its doors for the last time, to go whence they shall not return. The best room was shut up and darkened, with only so much light as could fall through a little heart-shaped hole in the window-shutter,—for except on solemn visits, or prayer meetings, or weddings, or funerals, that room formed no part of the daily family scenery.

The kitchen was clean and ample, with a great open fireplace and wide stone hearth, and oven on one side, and rows of old-fashioned splint-bottomed chairs against the wall. A table scoured to snowy whiteness, and a little work-stand whereon lay the Bible, the "Missionary Herald" and the "Weekly Christian Mirror," before named, formed the principal furniture. One feature, however, must not be forgotten,—a great sea-chest, which had been the companion of Zephaniah through all the countries of the earth. Old, and battered, and unsightly it looked, yet report said that there was good store within of that which men for the most part respect more than anything else; and, indeed, it proved often when a deed of grace was to be done,—when a woman was suddenly made a widow in a coast gale, or a fishing-smack was run down in the fogs off the banks, leaving in some neighboring cottage a family of orphans,—in all such cases, the opening of this sea-chest was an event of good omen to the bereaved; for Zephaniah had a large heart and a large hand, and was apt to take it out full of silver dollars when once it went in. So the ark of the covenant could not have been looked on with more reverence than the neighbors usually showed to Captain Pennel's sea-chest.

The afternoon sun is shining in a square of light through the open kitchen-door, whence one dreamily disposed might look far out to sea, and behold ships coming and going in every variety of shape and size.

But Aunt Roxy and Aunt Ruey, who for the present were sole occupants of the premises, were not people of the dreamy kind, and consequently were not gazing off to sea, but attending to very terrestrial matters that in all cases somebody must attend to. The afternoon was warm and balmy, but a few smouldering sticks were kept in the great chimney, and thrust deep into the embers was a mongrel species of snub-nosed tea-pot, which fumed strongly of catnip-tea, a little of which gracious beverage Miss Roxy was preparing in an old-fashioned cracked India china tea-cup, tasting it as she did so with the air of a connoisseur.

Apparently this was for the benefit of a small something in long white clothes, that lay face downward under a little blanket of very blue new flannel, and which something Aunt Roxy, when not otherwise engaged, constantly patted with a gentle tattoo, in tune to the steady trot of her knee. All babies knew Miss Roxy's tattoo on their backs, and never thought of taking it in ill part. On the contrary, it had a vital and mesmeric effect of sovereign force against colic, and all other disturbers of the nursery; and never was infant known so pressed with those internal troubles which infants cry about, as not speedily to give over and sink to slumber at this soothing appliance.

At a little distance sat Aunt Ruey, with a quantity of black crape strewed on two chairs about her, very busily employed in getting up a mourning-bonnet, at which she snipped, and clipped, and worked, zealously singing, in a high cracked voice, from time to time, certain verses of a funeral psalm.

Miss Roxy and Miss Ruey Toothacre were two brisk old bodies of the feminine gender and singular number, well known in all the region of Harpswell Neck and Middle Bay, and such was their fame that it had even reached the town of Brunswick, eighteen miles away.

They were of that class of females who might be denominated, in the Old Testament language, "cunning women,"—that is, gifted with an infinite diversity of practical "faculty," which made them an essential requisite in every family for miles and miles around. It was impossible to say what they could not do: they could make dresses, and make shirts and vests and pantaloons, and cut out boys' jackets, and braid straw, and bleach and trim bonnets, and cook and wash, and iron and mend, could upholster and quilt, could nurse all kinds of sicknesses, and in default of a doctor, who was often miles away, were supposed to be infallible medical oracles. Many a human being had been ushered into life under their auspices,—trotted, chirruped in babyhood on their knees, clothed by their handiwork in garments gradually enlarging from year to year, watched by them in the last sickness, and finally arrayed for the long repose by their hands.

These universally useful persons receive among us the title of "aunt" by a sort of general consent, showing the strong ties of relationship which bind them to the whole human family. They are nobody's aunts in particular, but aunts to human nature generally. The idea of restricting their usefulness to any one family, would strike dismay through a whole community. Nobody would be so unprincipled as to think of such a thing as having their services more than a week or two at most. Your country factotum knows better than anybody else how absurd it would be

"To give to a part what was meant for mankind."

Nobody knew very well the ages of these useful sisters. In that cold, clear, severe climate of the North, the roots of human existence are hard to strike; but, if once people do take to living, they come in time to a place where they seem never to grow any older, but can always be found, like last year's mullein stalks, upright, dry, and seedy, warranted to last for any length of time.

Miss Roxy Toothacre, who sits trotting the baby, is a tall, thin, angular woman, with sharp black eyes, and hair once black, but now well streaked with gray. These ravages of time, however, were concealed by an ample mohair frisette of glossy blackness woven on each side into a heap of stiff little curls, which pushed up her cap border in rather a bristling and decisive way. In all her movements and personal habits, even to her tone of voice and manner of speaking, Miss Roxy was vigorous, spicy, and decided. Her mind on all subjects was made up, and she spoke generally as one having authority; and who should, if she should not? Was she not a sort of priestess and sibyl in all the most awful straits and mysteries of life? How many births, and weddings, and deaths had come and gone under her jurisdiction! And amid weeping or rejoicing, was not Miss Roxy still the master-spirit,—consulted, referred to by all?—was not her word law and precedent? Her younger sister, Miss Ruey, a pliant, cozy, easy-to-be-entreated personage, plump and cushiony, revolved around her as a humble satellite. Miss Roxy looked on Miss Ruey as quite a frisky young thing, though under her ample frisette of carroty hair her head might be seen white with the same snow that had powdered that of her sister. Aunt Ruey had a face much resembling the kind of one you may see, reader, by looking at yourself in the convex side of a silver milk-pitcher. If you try the experiment, this description will need no further amplification.

The two almost always went together, for the variety of talent comprised in their stock could always find employment in the varying wants of a family. While one nursed the sick, the other made clothes for the well; and thus they were always chippering and chatting to each other, like a pair of antiquated house-sparrows, retailing over harmless gossips, and moralizing in that gentle jogtrot which befits serious old women. In fact, they had talked over everything in Nature, and said everything they could think of to each other so often, that the opinions of one were as like those of the other as two sides of a pea-pod. But as often happens in cases of the sort, this was not because the two were in all respects exactly alike, but because the stronger one had mesmerized the weaker into consent.

Miss Roxy was the master-spirit of the two, and, like the great coining machine of a mint, came down with her own sharp, heavy stamp on every opinion her sister put out. She was matter-of-fact, positive, and declarative to the highest degree, while her sister was naturally inclined to the elegiac and the pathetic, indulging herself in sentimental poetry, and keeping a store thereof in her thread-case, which she had cut from the "Christian Mirror." Miss Roxy sometimes, in her brusque way, popped out observations on life and things, with a droll, hard quaintness that took one's breath a little, yet never failed to have a sharp crystallization of truth,—frosty though it were. She was one of those sensible, practical creatures who tear every veil, and lay their fingers on every spot in pure business-like good-will; and if we shiver at them at times, as at the first plunge of a cold bath, we confess to an invigorating power in them after all.

"Well, now," said Miss Roxy, giving a decisive push to the tea-pot, which buried it yet deeper in the embers, "ain't it all a strange kind o' providence that this 'ere little thing is left behind so; and then their callin' on her by such a strange, mournful kind of name,—Mara. I thought sure as could be 'twas Mary, till the minister read the passage from Scriptur'. Seems to me it's kind o' odd. I'd call it Maria, or I'd put an Ann on to it. Mara-ann, now, wouldn't sound so strange."

"It's a Scriptur' name, sister," said Aunt Ruey, "and that ought to be enough for us."

"Well, I don't know," said Aunt Roxy. "Now there was Miss Jones down on Mure P'int called her twins Tiglath-Pileser and Shalmaneser,—Scriptur' names both, but I never liked 'em. The boys used to call 'em, Tiggy and Shally, so no mortal could guess they was Scriptur'."

"Well," said Aunt Ruey, drawing a sigh which caused her plump proportions to be agitated in gentle waves, "'tain't much matter, after all, *what* they call the little thing, for 'tain't 'tall likely it's goin' to live,—cried and worried all night, and kep' a-suckin' my cheek and my night-gown, poor little thing! This 'ere's a baby that won't get along without its mother. What Mis' Pennel's a-goin' to do with it when we is gone, I'm sure I don't know. It comes kind o' hard on old people to be broke o' their rest. If it's goin' to be called home, it's a pity, as I said, it didn't go with its mother"—

"And save the expense of another funeral," said Aunt Roxy. "Now when Mis' Pennel's sister asked her what she was going to do with Naomi's clothes, I couldn't help wonderin' when she said she should keep 'em for the child."

"She had a sight of things, Naomi did," said Aunt Ruey. "Nothin' was never too much for her. I don't believe that Cap'n Pennel ever went to Bath or Portland without havin' it in his mind to bring Naomi somethin'."

CHAPTER IV

"Yes, and she had a faculty of puttin' of 'em on," said Miss Roxy, with a decisive shake of the head. "Naomi was a still girl, but her faculty was uncommon; and I tell you, Ruey, 'tain't everybody hes faculty as hes things."

"The poor Cap'n," said Miss Ruey, "he seemed greatly supported at the funeral, but he's dreadful broke down since. I went into Naomi's room this morning, and there the old man was a-sittin' by her bed, and he had a pair of her shoes in his hand,—you know what a leetle bit of a foot she had. I never saw nothin' look so kind o' solitary as that poor old man did!"

"Well," said Miss Roxy, "she was a master-hand for keepin' things, Naomi was; her drawers is just a sight; she's got all the little presents and things they ever give her since she was a baby, in one drawer. There's a little pair of red shoes there that she had when she wa'n't more'n five year old. You 'member, Ruey, the Cap'n brought 'em over from Portland when we was to the house a-makin' Mis' Pennel's figured black silk that he brought from Calcutty. You 'member they cost just five and sixpence; but, law! the Cap'n he never grudged the money when 'twas for Naomi. And so she's got all her husband's keepsakes and things just as nice as when he give 'em to her."

"It's real affectin'," said Miss Ruey, "I can't all the while help a-thinkin' of the Psalm,—

"'So fades the lovely blooming flower,—
Frail, smiling solace of an hour;
So quick our transient comforts fly,
And pleasure only blooms to die.'"

"Yes," said Miss Roxy; "and, Ruey, I was a-thinkin' whether or no it wa'n't best to pack away them things, 'cause Naomi hadn't fixed no baby drawers, and we seem to want some."

"I was kind o' hintin' that to Mis' Pennel this morning," said Ruey, "but she can't seem to want to have 'em touched."

"Well, we may just as well come to such things first as last," said Aunt Roxy; "'cause if the Lord takes our friends, he does take 'em; and we can't lose 'em and have 'em too, and we may as well give right up at first, and done with it, that they are gone, and we've got to do without 'em, and not to be hangin' on to keep things just as they was."

"So I was a-tellin' Mis' Pennel," said Miss Ruey, "but she'll come to it by and by. I wish the baby might live, and kind o' grow up into her mother's place."

"Well," said Miss Roxy, "I wish it might, but there'd be a sight o' trouble fetchin' on it up. Folks can do pretty well with children when they're young and spry, if they do get 'em up nights; but come to grandchildren, it's pretty tough."

"I'm a-thinkin', sister," said Miss Ruey, taking off her spectacles and rubbing her nose thoughtfully, "whether or no cow's milk ain't goin' to be too hearty for it, it's such a pindlin' little thing. Now, Mis' Badger she brought up a seven-months' child, and she told me she gave it nothin' but these 'ere little seed cookies, wet in water, and it throve nicely,—and the seed is good for wind."

"Oh, don't tell me none of Mis' Badger's stories," said Miss Roxy, "I don't believe in 'em. Cows is the Lord's ordinances for bringing up babies that's lost their mothers; it stands to reason they should be,—and babies that can't eat milk, why they can't be fetched up; but babies can eat milk, and this un will if it lives, and if it can't it won't live." So saying, Miss Roxy drummed away on the little back of the party in question, authoritatively, as if to pound in a wholesome conviction at the outset.

"I hope," said Miss Ruey, holding up a strip of black crape, and looking through it from end to end so as to test its capabilities, "I hope the Cap'n and Mis' Pennel'll get some support at the prayer-meetin' this afternoon."

"It's the right place to go to," said Miss Roxy, with decision.

"Mis' Pennel said this mornin' that she was just beat out tryin' to submit; and the more she said, 'Thy will be done,' the more she didn't seem to feel it."

"Them's common feelin's among mourners, Ruey. These 'ere forty years that I've been round nussin', and layin'-out, and tendin' funerals, I've watched people's exercises. People's sometimes supported wonderfully just at the time, and maybe at the funeral; but the three or four weeks after, most everybody, if they's to say what they feel, is unreconciled."

"The Cap'n, he don't say nothin'," said Miss Ruey.

"No, he don't, but he looks it in his eyes," said Miss Roxy; "he's one of the kind o' mourners as takes it deep; that kind don't cry; it's a kind o' dry, deep pain; them's the worst to get over it,—sometimes they just says nothin', and in about six months they send for you to nuss 'em in consumption or somethin'. Now, Mis' Pennel, she can cry and she can talk,—well, she'll get over it; but *he* won't get no support unless the Lord reaches right down and lifts him up over the world. I've seen that happen sometimes, and I tell you, Ruey, that sort makes powerful Christians."

At that moment the old pair entered the door. Zephaniah Pennel came and stood quietly by the pillow where the little form was laid, and lifted a corner of the blanket. The tiny head was turned to one side, showing the soft, warm cheek, and the little hand was holding tightly a morsel of the flannel blanket. He stood swallowing hard for a few moments. At last he said, with deep humility, to the wise and mighty woman who held her, "I'll tell you what it is, Miss Roxy, I'll give all there is in my old chest yonder if you'll only make her—live."

CHAPTER V

THE KITTRIDGES

It did live. The little life, so frail, so unprofitable in every mere material view, so precious in the eyes of love, expanded and flowered at last into fair childhood. Not without much watching and weariness. Many a night the old fisherman walked the floor with the little thing in his arms, talking to it that jargon of tender nonsense which fairies bring as love-gifts to all who tend a cradle. Many a day the good little old grandmother called the aid of gossips about her, trying various experiments of catnip, and sweet fern, and bayberry, and other teas of rustic reputation for baby frailties.

At the end of three years, the two graves in the lonely graveyard were sodded and cemented down by smooth velvet turf, and playing round the door of the brown houses was a slender child, with ways and manners so still and singular as often to remind the neighbors that she was not like other children,—a bud of hope and joy,—but the outcome of a great sorrow,—a pearl washed ashore by a mighty, uprooting tempest. They that looked at her remembered that her father's eye had never beheld her, and her baptismal cup had rested on her mother's coffin.

She was small of stature, beyond the wont of children of her age, and moulded with a fine waxen delicacy that won admiration from all eyes. Her hair was curly and golden, but her eyes were dark like her mother's, and the lids drooped over them in that manner which gives a peculiar expression of dreamy wistfulness. Every one of us must remember eyes that have a strange, peculiar expression of pathos and desire, as if the spirit that looked out of them were pressed with vague remembrances of a past, or but dimly comprehended the mystery of its present life. Even when the baby lay in its cradle, and its dark, inquiring eyes would follow now one object and now another, the gossips would say the child was longing for something, and Miss Roxy would still further venture to predict that that child always would long and never would know exactly what she was after.

That dignitary sits at this minute enthroned in the kitchen corner, looking majestically over the press-board on her knee, where she is pressing the next year's Sunday vest of Zephaniah Pennel. As she makes her heavy tailor's goose squeak on the work, her eyes follow the little delicate fairy form which trips about the kitchen, busily and silently arranging a little grotto of gold and silver shells and seaweed. The child sings to herself as she works in a low chant, like the prattle of a brook, but ever and anon she rests her little arms on a chair and looks through the open kitchen-door far, far off where the horizon line of the blue sea dissolves in the blue sky.

"See that child now, Roxy," said Miss Ruey, who sat stitching beside her; "do look at her eyes. She's as handsome as a pictur', but 't ain't an ordinary look she has neither; she seems a contented little thing; but what makes her eyes always look so kind o' wishful?"

"Wa'n't her mother always a-longin' and a-lookin' to sea, and watchin' the ships, afore she was born?" said Miss Roxy; "and didn't her heart break afore she was born? Babies like that is marked always. They don't know what ails 'em, nor nobody."

"It's her mother she's after," said Miss Ruey.

"The Lord only knows," said Miss Roxy; "but them kind o' children always seem homesick to go back where they come from. They're mostly grave and old-fashioned like this 'un. If they gets past seven years, why they live; but it's always in 'em to long; they don't seem to be really unhappy neither, but if anything's ever the matter with 'em, it seems a great deal easier for 'em to die than to live. Some say it's the mothers longin' after 'em makes 'em feel so, and some say it's them longin' after their mothers; but dear knows, Ruey, what anything is or what makes anything. Children's mysterious, that's my mind."

"Mara, dear," said Miss Ruey, interrupting the child's steady lookout, "what you thinking of?"

"Me want somefin'," said the little one.

"That's what she's always sayin'," said Miss Roxy.

"Me want somebody to pay wis'," continued the little one.

"Want somebody to play with," said old Dame Pennel, as she came in from the back-room with her hands yet floury with kneading bread; "sure enough, she does. Our house stands in such a lonesome place, and there ain't any children. But I never saw such a quiet little thing—always still and always busy."

"I'll take her down with me to Cap'n Kittridge's," said Miss Roxy, "and let her play with their little girl; she'll chirk her up, I'll warrant. She's a regular little witch, Sally is, but she'll chirk her up. It ain't good for children to be so still and old-fashioned; children ought to be children. Sally takes to Mara just 'cause she's so different."

"Well, now, you may," said Dame Pennel; "to be sure *he* can't bear her out of his sight a minute after he comes in; but after all, old folks can't be company for children."

Accordingly, that afternoon, the little Mara was arrayed in a little blue flounced dress, which stood out like a balloon, made by Miss Roxy in first-rate style, from a French fashion-plate; her golden hair was twined in manifold curls by Dame Pennel, who, restricted in her ideas of ornamentation, spared, nevertheless, neither time nor money to enhance the charms of this single ornament to her dwelling. Mara was her picture-gallery, who gave her in the twenty-four hours as many Murillos or Greuzes as a lover of art could desire; and as she tied over the child's golden curls a little flat hat, and saw her go dancing off along the sea-sands, holding to Miss Roxy's bony finger, she felt she had in her what galleries of pictures could not buy.

It was a good mile to the one story, gambrel-roofed cottage where lived Captain Kittridge,—the long, lean, brown man, with his good wife of the great Leghorn bonnet, round, black bead eyes, and psalm-book, whom we told you of at the funeral. The Captain, too, had followed the sea in his early life, but being not, as he expressed it, "very rugged," in time changed his ship for a tight little cottage on the seashore, and devoted himself to boat-building, which he found sufficiently lucrative to furnish his brown cottage with all that his wife's heart desired, besides extra money for knick-knacks when she chose to go up to Brunswick or over to Portland to shop.

The Captain himself was a welcome guest at all the firesides round, being a chatty body, and disposed to make the most of his foreign experiences, in which he took the usual advantages of a traveler. In fact, it was said, whether slanderously or not, that the Captain's yarns were spun to order; and as, when pressed to relate his foreign adventures, he always responded with, "What would you like to hear?" it was thought that he fabricated his article to suit his market. In short, there was no species of experience, finny, fishy, or aquatic,—no legend of strange and unaccountable incident of fire or flood,—no romance of foreign scenery and productions, to which his tongue was not competent, when he had once seated himself in a double bow-knot at a neighbor's evening fireside.

His good wife, a sharp-eyed, literal body, and a vigorous church-member, felt some concern of conscience on the score of these narrations; for, being their constant auditor, she, better than any one else, could perceive the variations and discrepancies of text which showed their mythical character, and oftentimes her black eyes would snap and her knitting-needles rattle with an admonitory vigor as he went on, and sometimes she would unmercifully come in at the end of a narrative with,—

"Well, now, the Cap'n's told them ar stories till he begins to b'lieve 'em himself, I think."

But works of fiction, as we all know, if only well gotten up, have always their advantages in the hearts of listeners over plain, homely truth; and so Captain Kittridge's yarns were marketable fireside commodities still, despite the skepticisms which attended them.

The afternoon sunbeams at this moment are painting the gambrel-roof with a golden brown. It is September again, as it was three years ago when our story commenced, and the sea and sky are purple and amethystine with its Italian haziness of atmosphere.

The brown house stands on a little knoll, about a hundred yards from the open ocean. Behind it rises a ledge of rocks, where cedars and hemlocks make deep shadows into which the sun shoots golden shafts of light, illuminating the scarlet feathers of the sumach, which throw themselves jauntily forth from the crevices; while down below, in deep, damp, mossy recesses, rise ferns which autumn has just begun to tinge with yellow and brown. The little knoll where the cottage stood had on its right hand a tiny bay, where the ocean water made up amid picturesque rocks—shaggy and solemn. Here trees of the primeval forest, grand and lordly, looked down silently into the waters which ebbed and flowed daily into this little pool. Every variety of those beautiful evergreens which feather the coast of Maine, and dip their wings in the very spray of its ocean foam, found here a representative. There were aspiring black spruces, crowned on the very top with heavy coronets of cones; there were balsamic firs, whose young buds breathe the scent of strawberries; there were cedars, black as midnight clouds, and white pines with their swaying plumage of needle-like leaves, strewing the ground beneath with a golden, fragrant matting; and there were the gigantic, wide-winged hemlocks, hundreds of years old, and with long, swaying, gray beards of moss, looking white and ghostly under the deep shadows of their boughs. And beneath, creeping round trunk and matting over stones, were many and many of those wild, beautiful things which embellish the shadows of these northern forests. Long, feathery wreaths of what are called ground-pines ran here and there in little ruffles of green, and the prince's pine raised its oriental feather, with a mimic cone on the top, as if it conceived itself to be a grown-up tree. Whole patches of partridge-berry wove their evergreen matting, dotted plentifully with brilliant scarlet berries. Here and there, the rocks were covered with a curiously inwoven tapestry of moss, overshot with the exquisite vine of the Linnea borealis, which in early spring rings its two fairy bells on the end of every spray; while elsewhere the wrinkled leaves of the mayflower wove themselves through and through deep beds of moss, meditating silently thoughts of the thousand little cups of pink shell which they had it in hand to make when the time of miracles should come round next spring.

Nothing, in short, could be more quaintly fresh, wild, and beautiful than the surroundings of this little cove which Captain Kittridge had thought fit to dedicate to his boat-building operations,—where he had set up his tar-kettle between two great rocks above the highest tide-mark, and where, at the present moment, he had a boat upon the stocks.

Mrs. Kittridge, at this hour, was sitting in her clean kitchen, very busily engaged in ripping up a silk dress, which Miss Roxy had engaged to come and make into a new one; and, as she ripped, she cast now and then an eye at the face of a tall, black clock, whose solemn tick-tock was the only sound that could be heard in the kitchen.

By her side, on a low stool, sat a vigorous, healthy girl of six years, whose employment evidently did not please her, for her well-marked black eyebrows were bent in a frown, and her large black eyes looked surly and wrathful, and one versed in children's grievances could easily see what the matter was,—she was turning a sheet! Perhaps, happy young female reader, you don't know what that is,—most likely not; for in these degenerate days the strait and narrow ways of self-denial, formerly thought so wholesome for little feet, are quite grass-grown with neglect. Childhood nowadays is unceasingly fêted and caressed, the principal difficulty of the grown people seeming to be to discover what the little dears want,—a thing not always clear to the little dears themselves. But in old times, turning sheets was thought a most especial and wholesome discipline for young girls; in the first place, because it took off the hands of their betters a very uninteresting and monotonous labor; and in the second place, because it was such a long, straight, unending turnpike, that the youthful travelers, once started thereupon, could go on indefinitely, without requiring guidance and direction of their elders. For these reasons, also, the task was held in special detestation by children in direct proportion to their amount of life, and their ingenuity and love of variety. A dull child took it tolerably well; but to a lively, energetic one, it was a perfect torture.

"I don't see the use of sewing up sheets one side, and ripping up the other," at last said Sally, breaking the monotonous tick-tock of the clock by an observation which has probably occurred to every child in similar circumstances.

"Sally Kittridge, if you say another word about that ar sheet, I'll whip you," was the very explicit rejoinder; and there was a snap of Mrs. Kittridge's black eyes, that seemed to make it likely that she would keep her word. It was answered by another snap from the six-year-old eyes, as Sally comforted herself with thinking that when she was a woman she'd speak her mind out in pay for all this.

At this moment a burst of silvery child-laughter rang out, and there appeared in the doorway, illuminated by the afternoon sunbeams, the vision of Miss Roxy's tall, lank figure, with the little golden-haired, blue-robed fairy, hanging like a gay butterfly upon the tip of a thorn-bush. Sally dropped the sheet and clapped her hands, unnoticed by her mother, who rose to pay her respects to the "cunning woman" of the neighborhood.

"Well, now, Miss Roxy, I was 'mazin' afraid you wer'n't a-comin'. I'd just been an' got my silk ripped up, and didn't know how to get a step farther without you."

"Well, I was finishin' up Cap'n Pennel's best pantaloons," said Miss Roxy; "and I've got 'em along so, Ruey can go on with 'em; and I told Mis' Pennel I must come to you, if 'twas only for a day; and I fetched the little girl down, 'cause the little thing's so kind o' lonesome like. I thought Sally could play with her, and chirk her up a little."

"Well, Sally," said Mrs. Kittridge, "stick in your needle, fold up your sheet, put your thimble in your work-pocket, and then you may take the little Mara down to the cove to play; but be sure you don't let her go near the tar, nor wet her shoes. D'ye hear?"

"Yes, ma'am," said Sally, who had sprung up in light and radiance, like a translated creature, at this unexpected turn of fortune, and performed the welcome orders with a celerity which showed how agreeable they were; and then, stooping and catching the little one in her arms, disappeared through the door, with the golden curls fluttering over her own crow-black hair.

The fact was, that Sally, at that moment, was as happy as human creature could be, with a keenness of happiness that children who have never been made to turn sheets of a bright afternoon can never realize. The sun was yet an hour high, as she saw, by the flash of her shrewd, time-keeping eye, and she could bear her little prize down to the cove, and collect unknown quantities of gold and silver shells, and starfish, and salad-dish shells, and white pebbles for her, besides quantities of well turned shavings, brown and white, from the pile which constantly was falling under her father's joiner's bench, and with which she would make long extemporaneous tresses, so that they might play at being mermaids, like those that she had heard her father tell about in some of his sea-stories.

"Now, railly, Sally, what you got there?" said Captain Kittridge, as he stood in his shirt-sleeves peering over his joiner's bench, to watch the little one whom Sally had dumped down into a nest of clean white shavings. "Wal', wal', I should think you'd a-stolen the big doll I see in a shop-window the last time I was to Portland. So this is Pennel's little girl?—poor child!"

"Yes, father, and we want some nice shavings."

"Stay a bit, I'll make ye a few a-purpose," said the old man, reaching his long, bony arm, with the greatest ease, to the farther part of his bench, and bringing up a board, from which he proceeded to roll off shavings in fine satin rings, which perfectly delighted the hearts of the children, and made them dance with glee; and, truth to say, reader, there are coarser and homelier things in the world than a well turned shaving.

"There, go now," he said, when both of them stood with both hands full; "go now and play; and mind you don't let the baby wet her feet, Sally; them shoes o' hern must have cost five-and-sixpence at the very least."

That sunny hour before sundown seemed as long to Sally as the whole seam of the sheet; for childhood's joys are all pure gold; and as she ran up and down the white sands, shouting at every shell she found, or darted up into the overhanging forest for checkerberries and ground-pine, all the sorrows of the morning came no more into her remembrance.

The little Mara had one of those sensitive, excitable natures, on which every external influence acts with immediate power. Stimulated by the society of her energetic, buoyant little neighbor, she no longer seemed wishful or pensive, but kindled into a perfect flame of wild delight, and gamboled about the shore like a blue and gold-winged fly; while her bursts of laughter made the squirrels and blue jays look out inquisitively from their fastnesses in the old evergreens. Gradually the sunbeams faded from the pines, and the waves of the tide in the little cove came in, solemnly tinted with purple, flaked with orange and crimson, borne in from a great rippling sea of fire, into which the sun had just sunk.

"Mercy on us—them children!" said Miss Roxy.

"*He's* bringin' 'em along," said Mrs. Kittridge, as she looked out of the window and saw the tall, lank form of the Captain, with one child seated on either shoulder, and holding on by his head.

CHAPTER V

The two children were both in the highest state of excitement, but never was there a more marked contrast of nature. The one seemed a perfect type of well-developed childish health and vigor, good solid flesh and bones, with glowing skin, brilliant eyes, shining teeth, well-knit, supple limbs,—vigorously and healthily beautiful; while the other appeared one of those aerial mixtures of cloud and fire, whose radiance seems scarcely earthly. A physiologist, looking at the child, would shake his head, seeing one of those perilous organizations, all nerve and brain, which come to life under the clear, stimulating skies of America, and, burning with the intensity of lighted phosphorus, waste themselves too early.

The little Mara seemed like a fairy sprite, possessed with a wild spirit of glee. She laughed and clapped her hands incessantly, and when set down on the kitchen-floor spun round like a little elf; and that night it was late and long before her wide, wakeful eyes could be veiled in sleep.

"Company jist sets this 'ere child crazy," said Miss Roxy; "it's jist her lonely way of livin'; a pity Mis' Pennel hadn't another child to keep company along with her."

"Mis' Pennel oughter be trainin' of her up to work," said Mrs. Kittridge. "Sally could oversew and hem when she wa'n't more'n three years old; nothin' straightens out children like work. Mis' Pennel she just keeps that ar child to look at."

"All children ain't alike, Mis' Kittridge," said Miss Roxy, sententiously. "This 'un ain't like your Sally. 'A hen and a bumble-bee can't be fetched up alike, fix it how you will!'"

CHAPTER VI

GRANDPARENTS

Zephaniah Pennel came back to his house in the evening, after Miss Roxy had taken the little Mara away. He looked for the flowery face and golden hair as he came towards the door, and put his hand in his vest-pocket, where he had deposited a small store of very choice shells and sea curiosities, thinking of the widening of those dark, soft eyes when he should present them.

"Where's Mara?" was the first inquiry after he had crossed the threshold.

"Why, Roxy's been an' taken her down to Cap'n Kittridge's to spend the night," said Miss Ruey. "Roxy's gone to help Mis' Kittridge to turn her spotted gray and black silk. We was talking this mornin' whether 'no 't would turn, 'cause *I* thought the spot was overshot, and wouldn't make up on the wrong side; but Roxy she says it's one of them ar Calcutty silks that has two sides to 'em, like the one you bought Miss Pennel, that we made up for her, you know;" and Miss Ruey arose and gave a finishing snap to the Sunday pantaloons, which she had been left to "finish off,"—which snap said, as plainly as words could say that there was a good job disposed of.

Zephaniah stood looking as helpless as animals of the male kind generally do when appealed to with such prolixity on feminine details; in reply to it all, only he asked meekly,—

"Where's Mary?"

"Mis' Pennel? Why, she's up chamber. She'll be down in a minute, she said; she thought she'd have time afore supper to get to the bottom of the big chist, and see if that 'ere vest pattern ain't there, and them sticks o' twist for the button-holes, 'cause Roxy she says she never see nothin' so rotten as that 'ere twist we've been a-workin' with, that Mis' Pennel got over to Portland; it's a clear cheat, and Mis' Pennel she give more'n half a cent a stick more for 't than what Roxy got for her up to Brunswick; so you see these 'ere Portland stores charge up, and their things want lookin' after."

Here Mrs. Pennel entered the room, "the Captain" addressing her eagerly,—

"How came you to let Aunt Roxy take Mara off so far, and be gone so long?"

CHAPTER VI

"Why, law me, Captain Pennel! the little thing seems kind o' lonesome. Chil'en want chil'en; Miss Roxy says she's altogether too sort o' still and old-fashioned, and must have child's company to chirk her up, and so she took her down to play with Sally Kittridge; there's no manner of danger or harm in it, and she'll be back to-morrow afternoon, and Mara will have a real good time."

"Wal', now, really," said the good man, "but it's 'mazin' lonesome."

"Cap'n Pennel, you're gettin' to make an idol of that 'ere child," said Miss Ruey. "We have to watch our hearts. It minds me of the hymn,—

"'The fondness of a creature's love,
How strong it strikes the sense,—
Thither the warm affections move,
Nor can we call them hence.'"

Miss Ruey's mode of getting off poetry, in a sort of high-pitched canter, with a strong thump on every accented syllable, might have provoked a smile in more sophisticated society, but Zephaniah listened to her with deep gravity, and answered,—

"I'm 'fraid there's truth in what you say, Aunt Ruey. When her mother was called away, I thought that was a warning I never should forget; but now I seem to be like Jonah,—I'm restin' in the shadow of my gourd, and my heart is glad because of it. I kind o' trembled at the prayer meetin' when we was a-singin',—

"'The dearest idol I have known,
Whate'er that idol be,
Help me to tear it from Thy throne,
And worship only Thee.'"

"Yes," said Miss Ruey, "Roxy says if the Lord should take us up short on our prayers, it would make sad work with us sometimes."

"Somehow," said Mrs. Pennel, "it seems to me just her mother over again. She don't look like her. I think her hair and complexion comes from the Badger blood; my mother had that sort o' hair and skin,—but then she has ways like Naomi,—and it seems as if the Lord had kind o' given Naomi back to us; so I hope she's goin' to be spared to us."

Mrs. Pennel had one of those natures—gentle, trustful, and hopeful, because not very deep; she was one of the little children of the world whose faith rests on child-like ignorance, and who know not the deeper needs of deeper natures; such see only the sunshine and forget the storm.

This conversation had been going on to the accompaniment of a clatter of plates and spoons and dishes, and the fizzling of sausages, prefacing the evening meal, to which all now sat down after a lengthened grace from Zephaniah.

"There's a tremendous gale a-brewin'," he said, as they sat at table. "I noticed the clouds to-night as I was comin' home, and somehow I felt kind o' as if I wanted all our folks snug in-doors."

"Why, law, husband, Cap'n Kittridge's house is as good as ours, if it does blow. You never can seem to remember that houses don't run aground or strike on rocks in storms."

"The Cap'n puts me in mind of old Cap'n Jeduth Scranton," said Miss Ruey, "that built that queer house down by Middle Bay. The Cap'n he would insist on havin' on't jist like a ship, and the closet-shelves had holes for the tumblers and dishes, and he had all his tables and chairs battened down, and so when it came a gale, they say the old Cap'n used to sit in his chair and hold on to hear the wind blow."

"Well, I tell you," said Captain, "those that has followed the seas hears the wind with different ears from lands-people. When you lie with only a plank between you and eternity, and hear the voice of the Lord on the waters, it don't sound as it does on shore."

And in truth, as they were speaking, a fitful gust swept by the house, wailing and screaming and rattling the windows, and after it came the heavy, hollow moan of the surf on the beach, like the wild, angry howl of some savage animal just beginning to be lashed into fury.

"Sure enough, the wind is rising," said Miss Ruey, getting up from the table, and flattening her snub nose against the window-pane. "Dear me, how dark it is! Mercy on us, how the waves come in!—all of a sheet of foam. I pity the ships that's comin' on coast such a night."

The storm seemed to have burst out with a sudden fury, as if myriads of howling demons had all at once been loosened in the air. Now they piped and whistled with eldritch screech round the corners of the house—now they thundered down the chimney—and now they shook the door and rattled the casement—and anon mustering their forces with wild ado, seemed to career over the house, and sail high up into the murky air. The dash of the rising tide came with successive crash upon crash like the discharge of heavy artillery, seeming to shake the very house, and the spray borne by the wind dashed whizzing against the window-panes.

Zephaniah, rising from supper, drew up the little stand that had the family Bible on it, and the three old time-worn people sat themselves as seriously down to evening worship as if they had been an extensive congregation. They raised the old psalm-tune which our fathers called "Complaint," and the cracked, wavering voices of the women, with the deep, rough bass of the old sea-captain, rose in the uproar of the storm with a ghostly, strange wildness, like the scream of the curlew or the wailing of the wind:—

"Spare us, O Lord, aloud we pray,
Nor let our sun go down at noon:
Thy years are an eternal day,
And must thy children die so soon!"

Miss Ruey valued herself on singing a certain weird and exalted part which in ancient days used to be called counter, and which wailed and gyrated in unimaginable heights of the scale, much as you may hear a shrill, fine-voiced wind over a chimney-top; but altogether, the deep and earnest gravity with which the three filled up the pauses in the storm with their quaint minor key, had something singularly impressive. When the singing was over, Zephaniah read to the accompaniment of wind and sea, the words of poetry made on old Hebrew shores, in the dim, gray dawn of the world:—

"The voice of the Lord is upon the waters; the God of glory thundereth; the Lord is upon many waters. The voice of the Lord shaketh the wilderness; the Lord shaketh the wilderness of Kadesh. The Lord sitteth upon the floods, yea, the Lord sitteth King forever. The Lord will give strength to his people; yea, the Lord will bless his people with peace."

How natural and home-born sounded this old piece of Oriental poetry in the ears of the three! The wilderness of Kadesh, with its great cedars, was doubtless Orr's Island, where even now the goodly fellowship of black-winged trees were groaning and swaying, and creaking as the breath of the Lord passed over them.

And the three old people kneeling by their smouldering fireside, amid the general uproar, Zephaniah began in the words of a prayer which Moses the man of God made long ago under the shadows of Egyptian pyramids: "Lord, thou hast been our dwelling-place in all generations. Before the mountains were brought forth, or ever thou hadst formed the earth and the world, even from everlasting to everlasting, thou art God."

We hear sometimes in these days that the Bible is no more inspired of God than many other books of historic and poetic merit. It is a fact, however, that the Bible answers a strange and wholly exceptional purpose by thousands of firesides on all shores of the earth; and, till some other book can be found to do the same thing, it will not be surprising if a belief of its Divine origin be one of the ineffaceable ideas of the popular mind. It will be a long while before a translation from Homer or a chapter in the Koran, or any of the beauties of Shakespeare, will be read in a stormy night on Orr's Island with the same sense of a Divine presence as the Psalms of David, or the prayer of Moses, the man of God.

Boom! boom! "What's that?" said Zephaniah, starting, as they rose up from prayer. "Hark! again, that's a gun,—there's a ship in distress."

"Poor souls," said Miss Ruey; "it's an awful night!"

The captain began to put on his sea-coat.

"You ain't a-goin' out?" said his wife.

"I must go out along the beach a spell, and see if I can hear any more of that ship."

"Mercy on us; the wind'll blow you over!" said Aunt Ruey.

"I rayther think I've stood wind before in my day," said Zephaniah, a grim smile stealing over his weather-beaten cheeks. In fact, the man felt a sort of secret relationship to the storm, as if it were in some manner a family connection—a wild, roystering cousin, who drew him out by a rough attraction of comradeship.

"Well, at any rate," said Mrs. Pennel, producing a large tin lantern perforated with many holes, in which she placed a tallow candle, "take this with you, and don't stay out long."

The kitchen door opened, and the first gust of wind took off the old man's hat and nearly blew him prostrate. He came back and shut the door. "I ought to have known better," he said, knotting his pocket-handkerchief over his head, after which he waited for a momentary lull, and went out into the storm.

Miss Ruey looked through the window-pane, and saw the light go twinkling far down into the gloom, and ever and anon came the mournful boom of distant guns.

"Certainly there is a ship in trouble somewhere," she said.

"He never can be easy when he hears these guns," said Mrs. Pennel; "but what can he do, or anybody, in such a storm, the wind blowing right on to shore?"

"I shouldn't wonder if Cap'n Kittridge should be out on the beach, too," said Miss Ruey; "but laws, he ain't much more than one of these 'ere old grasshoppers you see after frost comes. Well, any way, there *ain't* much help in man if a ship comes ashore in such a gale as this, such a dark night too."

"It's kind o' lonesome to have poor little Mara away such a night as this is," said Mrs. Pennel; "but who would a-thought it this afternoon, when Aunt Roxy took her?"

"I 'member my grandmother had a silver cream-pitcher that come ashore in a storm on Mare P'int," said Miss Ruey, as she sat trotting her knitting-needles. "Grand'ther found it, half full of sand, under a knot of seaweed way up on the beach. It had a coat of arms on it,—might have belonged to some grand family, that pitcher; in the Toothacre family yet."

"I remember when I was a girl," said Mrs. Pennel, "seeing the hull of a ship that went on Eagle Island; it run way up in a sort of gully between two rocks, and lay there years. They split pieces off it sometimes to make fires, when they wanted to make a chowder down on the beach."

"My aunt, Lois Toothacre, that lives down by Middle Bay," said Miss Ruey, "used to tell about a dreadful blow they had once in time of the equinoctial storm; and what was remarkable, she insisted that she heard a baby cryin' out in the storm,—she heard it just as plain as could be."

"Laws a-mercy," said Mrs. Pennel, nervously, "it was nothing but the wind,—it always screeches like a child crying; or maybe it was the seals; seals will cry just like babes."

"So they told her; but no,—she insisted she knew the difference,—it *was* a baby. Well, what do you think, when the storm cleared off, they found a baby's cradle washed ashore sure enough!"

"But they didn't find any baby," said Mrs. Pennel, nervously.

"No; they searched the beach far and near, and that cradle was all they found. Aunt Lois took it in—it was a very good cradle, and she took it to use, but every time there came up a gale, that ar cradle would rock, rock, jist as if somebody was a-sittin' by it; and you could stand across the room and see there wa'n't nobody there."

"You make me all of a shiver," said Mrs. Pennel.

This, of course, was just what Miss Ruey intended, and she went on:—

"Wal', you see they kind o' got used to it; they found there wa'n't no harm come of its rockin', and so they didn't mind; but Aunt Lois had a sister Cerinthy that was a weakly girl, and had the janders. Cerinthy was one of the sort that's born with veils over their faces, and can see sperits; and one time Cerinthy was a-visitin' Lois after her second baby was born, and there came up a blow, and Cerinthy comes out of the keepin'-room, where the cradle was a-standin', and says, 'Sister,' says she, 'who's that woman sittin' rockin' the cradle?' and Aunt Lois says she, 'Why, there ain't nobody. That ar cradle always will rock in a gale, but I've got used to it, and don't mind it.' 'Well,' says Cerinthy, 'jist as true as you live, I just saw a woman with a silk gown on, and long black hair a-hangin' down, and her face was pale as a sheet, sittin' rockin' that ar cradle, and she looked round at me with her great black eyes kind o' mournful and wishful, and then she stooped down over the cradle.' 'Well,' says Lois, 'I ain't goin' to have no such doin's in my house,' and she went right in and took up the baby, and the very next day she jist had the cradle split up for kindlin'; and that night, if you'll believe, when they was a-burnin' of it, they heard, jist as plain as could be, a baby scream, scream, screamin' round the house; but after that they never heard it no more."

"I don't like such stories," said Dame Pennel, "'specially to-night, when Mara's away. I shall get to hearing all sorts of noises in the wind. I wonder when Cap'n Pennel will be back."

And the good woman put more wood on the fire, and as the tongues of flame streamed up high and clear, she approached her face to the window-pane and started back with half a scream, as a pale, anxious visage with sad dark eyes seemed to approach her. It took a moment or two for her to discover that she had seen only the reflection of her own anxious, excited face, the pitchy blackness without having converted the window into a sort of dark mirror.

Miss Ruey meanwhile began solacing herself by singing, in her chimney-corner, a very favorite sacred melody, which contrasted oddly enough with the driving storm and howling sea:—

"Haste, my beloved, haste away,
Cut short the hours of thy delay;
Fly like the bounding hart or roe,
Over the hills where spices grow."

The tune was called "Invitation,"—one of those profusely florid in runs, and trills, and quavers, which delighted the ears of a former generation; and Miss Ruey, innocently unconscious of the effect of old age on her voice, ran them up and down, and out and in, in a way that would have made a laugh, had there been anybody there to notice or to laugh.

"I remember singin' that ar to Mary Jane Wilson the very night she died," said Aunt Ruey, stopping. "She wanted me to sing to her, and it was jist between two and three in the mornin'; there was jist the least red streak of daylight, and I opened the window and sat there and sung, and when I come to 'over the hills where spices grow,' I looked round and there was a change in Mary Jane, and I went to the bed, and says she very bright, 'Aunt Ruey, the Beloved has come,' and she was gone afore I could raise her up on her pillow. I always think of Mary Jane at them words; if ever there was a broken-hearted crittur took home, it was her."

At this moment Mrs. Pennel caught sight through the window of the gleam of the returning lantern, and in a moment Captain Pennel entered, dripping with rain and spray.

"Why, Cap'n! you're e'en a'most drowned," said Aunt Ruey.

"How long have you been gone? You must have been a great ways," said Mrs. Pennel.

"Yes, I have been down to Cap'n Kittridge's. I met Kittridge out on the beach. We heard the guns plain enough, but couldn't see anything. I went on down to Kittridge's to get a look at little Mara."

"Well, she's all well enough?" said Mrs. Pennel, anxiously.

"Oh, yes, well enough. Miss Roxy showed her to me in the trundle-bed, 'long with Sally. The little thing was lying smiling in her sleep, with her cheek right up against Sally's. I took comfort looking at her. I couldn't help thinking: 'So he giveth his beloved sleep!'"

CHAPTER VII

FROM THE SEA

During the night and storm, the little Mara had lain sleeping as quietly as if the cruel sea, that had made her an orphan from her birth, were her kind-tempered old grandfather singing her to sleep, as he often did,—with a somewhat hoarse voice truly, but with ever an undertone of protecting love. But toward daybreak, there came very clear and bright into her childish mind a dream, having that vivid distinctness which often characterizes the dreams of early childhood.

She thought she saw before her the little cove where she and Sally had been playing the day before, with its broad sparkling white beach of sand curving round its blue sea-mirror, and studded thickly with gold and silver shells. She saw the boat of Captain Kittridge upon the stocks, and his tar-kettle with the smouldering fires flickering under it; but, as often happens in dreams, a certain rainbow vividness and clearness invested everything, and she and Sally were jumping for joy at the beautiful things they found on the beach.

Suddenly, there stood before them a woman, dressed in a long white garment. She was very pale, with sweet, serious dark eyes, and she led by the hand a black-eyed boy, who seemed to be crying and looking about as for something lost. She dreamed that she stood still, and the woman came toward her, looking at her with sweet, sad eyes, till the child seemed to feel them in every fibre of her frame. The woman laid her hand on her head as if in blessing, and then put the boy's hand in hers, and said, "Take him, Mara, he is a playmate for you;" and with that the little boy's face flashed out into a merry laugh. The woman faded away, and the three children remained playing together, gathering shells and pebbles of a wonderful brightness. So vivid was this vision, that the little one awoke laughing with pleasure, and searched under her pillows for the strange and beautiful things that she had been gathering in dreamland.

"What's Mara looking after?" said Sally, sitting up in her trundle-bed, and speaking in the patronizing motherly tone she commonly used to her little playmate.

"All gone, pitty boy—all gone!" said the child, looking round regretfully, and shaking her golden head; "pitty lady all gone!"

"How queer she talks!" said Sally, who had awakened with the project of building a sheet-house with her fairy neighbor, and was beginning to loosen the upper sheet and dispose the pillows with a view to this species of architecture. "Come, Mara, let's make a pretty house!" she said.

"Pitty boy out dere—out dere!" said the little one, pointing to the window, with a deeper expression than ever of wishfulness in her eyes.

"Come, Sally Kittridge, get up this minute!" said the voice of her mother, entering the door at this moment; "and here, put these clothes on to Mara, the child mustn't run round in her best; it's strange, now, Mary Pennel never thinks of such things."

Sally, who was of an efficient temperament, was preparing energetically to second these commands of her mother, and endue her little neighbor with a coarse brown stuff dress, somewhat faded and patched, which she herself had outgrown when of Mara's age; with shoes, which had been coarsely made to begin with, and very much battered by time; but, quite to her surprise, the child, generally so passive and tractable, opposed a most unexpected and desperate resistance to this operation. She began to cry and to sob and shake her curly head, throwing her tiny hands out in a wild species of freakish opposition, which had, notwithstanding, a quaint and singular grace about it, while she stated her objections in all the little English at her command.

"Mara don't want—Mara want pitty boo des—and *pitty* shoes."

"Why, was ever anything like it?" said Mrs. Kittridge to Miss Roxy, as they both were drawn to the door by the outcry; "here's this child won't have decent every-day clothes put on her,—she must be kept dressed up like a princess. Now, that ar's French calico!" said Mrs. Kittridge, holding up the controverted blue dress, "and that ar never cost a cent under five-and-sixpence a yard; it takes a yard and a half to make it, and it must have been a good day's work to make it up; call that three-and-sixpence more, and with them pearl buttons and thread and all, that ar dress never cost less than a dollar and seventy-five, and here she's goin' to run out every day in it!"

"Well, well!" said Miss Roxy, who had taken the sobbing fair one in her lap, "you know, Mis' Kittridge, this 'ere's a kind o' pet lamb, an old-folks' darling, and things be with her as they be, and we can't make her over, and she's such a nervous little thing we mustn't cross her." Saying which, she proceeded to dress the child in her own clothes.

"If you had a good large checked apron, I wouldn't mind putting that on her!" added Miss Roxy, after she had arrayed the child.

"Here's one," said Mrs. Kittridge; "that may save her clothes some."

Miss Roxy began to put on the wholesome garment; but, rather to her mortification, the little fairy began to weep again in a most heart-broken manner.

"Don't want che't apon."

"Why don't Mara want nice checked apron?" said Miss Roxy, in that extra cheerful tone by which children are to be made to believe they have mistaken their own mind.

CHAPTER VII

"Don't want it!" with a decided wave of the little hand; "I's too pitty to wear che't apon."

"Well! well!" said Mrs. Kittridge, rolling up her eyes, "did I ever! no, I never did. If there ain't depraved natur' a-comin' out early. Well, if she says she's pretty now, what'll it be when she's fifteen?"

"She'll learn to tell a lie about it by that time," said Miss Roxy, "and say she thinks she's horrid. The child *is* pretty, and the truth comes uppermost with her now."

"Haw! haw! haw!" burst with a great crash from Captain Kittridge, who had come in behind, and stood silently listening during this conversation; "that's musical now; come here, my little maid, you *are* too pretty for checked aprons, and no mistake;" and seizing the child in his long arms, he tossed her up like a butterfly, while her sunny curls shone in the morning light.

"There's one comfort about the child, Miss Kittridge," said Aunt Roxy: "she's one of them that dirt won't stick to. I never knew her to stain or tear her clothes,—she always come in jist so nice."

"She ain't much like Sally, then!" said Mrs. Kittridge. "That girl'll run through more clothes! Only last week she walked the crown out of my old black straw bonnet, and left it hanging on the top of a blackberry-bush."

"Wal', wal'," said Captain Kittridge, "as to dressin' this 'ere child,—why, ef Pennel's a mind to dress her in cloth of gold, it's none of our business! He's rich enough for all he wants to do, and so let's eat our breakfast and mind our own business."

After breakfast Captain Kittridge took the two children down to the cove, to investigate the state of his boat and tar-kettle, set high above the highest tide-mark. The sun had risen gloriously, the sky was of an intense, vivid blue, and only great snowy islands of clouds, lying in silver banks on the horizon, showed vestiges of last night's storm. The whole wide sea was one glorious scene of forming and dissolving mountains of blue and purple, breaking at the crest into brilliant silver. All round the island the waves were constantly leaping and springing into jets and columns of brilliant foam, throwing themselves high up, in silvery cataracts, into the very arms of the solemn evergreen forests which overhung the shore.

The sands of the little cove seemed harder and whiter than ever, and were thickly bestrewn with the shells and seaweed which the upturnings of the night had brought in. There lay what might have been fringes and fragments of sea-gods' vestures,—blue, crimson, purple, and orange seaweeds, wreathed in tangled ropes of kelp and sea-grass, or lying separately scattered on the sands. The children ran wildly, shouting as they began gathering sea-treasures; and Sally, with the air of an experienced hand in the business, untwisted the coils of rosy seaweed, from which every moment she disengaged some new treasure, in some rarer shell or smoother pebble.

Suddenly, the child shook out something from a knotted mass of sea-grass, which she held up with a perfect shriek of delight. It was a bracelet of hair, fastened by a brilliant clasp of green, sparkling stones, such as she had never seen before. She redoubled her cries of delight, as she saw it sparkle between her and the sun, calling upon her father.

"Father! father! do come here, and see what I've found!"

He came quickly, and took the bracelet from the child's hand; but, at the same moment, looking over her head, he caught sight of an object partially concealed behind a projecting rock. He took a step forward, and uttered an exclamation,—

"Well, well! sure enough! poor things!"

There lay, bedded in sand and seaweed, a woman with a little boy clasped in her arms! Both had been carefully lashed to a spar, but the child was held to the bosom of the woman, with a pressure closer than any knot that mortal hands could tie. Both were deep sunk in the sand, into which had streamed the woman's long, dark hair, which sparkled with glittering morsels of sand and pebbles, and with those tiny, brilliant, yellow shells which are so numerous on that shore.

The woman was both young and beautiful. The forehead, damp with ocean-spray, was like sculptured marble,—the eyebrows dark and decided in their outline; but the long, heavy, black fringes had shut down, as a solemn curtain, over all the history of mortal joy or sorrow that those eyes had looked upon. A wedding-ring gleamed on the marble hand; but the sea had divorced all human ties, and taken her as a bride to itself. And, in truth, it seemed to have made to her a worthy bed, for she was all folded and inwreathed in sand and shells and seaweeds, and a great, weird-looking leaf of kelp, some yards in length, lay twined around her like a shroud. The child that lay in her bosom had hair, and face, and eyelashes like her own, and his little hands were holding tightly a portion of the black dress which she wore.

"Cold,—cold,—stone dead!" was the muttered exclamation of the old seaman, as he bent over the woman.

"She must have struck her head there," he mused, as he laid his finger on a dark, bruised spot on her temple. He laid his hand on the child's heart, and put one finger under the arm to see if there was any lingering vital heat, and then hastily cut the lashings that bound the pair to the spar, and with difficulty disengaged the child from the cold clasp in which dying love had bound him to a heart which should beat no more with mortal joy or sorrow.

Sally, after the first moment, had run screaming toward the house, with all a child's forward eagerness, to be the bearer of news; but the little Mara stood, looking anxiously, with a wishful earnestness of face.

"Pitty boy,—pitty boy,—come!" she said often; but the old man was so busy, he scarcely regarded her.

"Now, Cap'n Kittridge, do tell!" said Miss Roxy, meeting him in all haste, with a cap-border stiff in air, while Dame Kittridge exclaimed,—

"Now, you don't! Well, well! didn't I say that was a ship last night? And what a solemnizing thought it was that souls might be goin' into eternity!"

"We must have blankets and hot bottles, right away," said Miss Roxy, who always took the earthly view of matters, and who was, in her own person, a personified humane society. "Miss Kittridge, you jist dip out your dishwater into the smallest tub, and we'll put him in. Stand away, Mara! Sally, you take her out of the way! We'll fetch this child to, perhaps. I've fetched 'em to, when they's seemed to be dead as door-nails!"

"Cap'n Kittridge, you're sure the woman's dead?"

"Laws, yes; she had a blow right on her temple here. There's no bringing her to till the resurrection."

"Well, then, you jist go and get Cap'n Pennel to come down and help you, and get the body into the house, and we'll attend to layin' it out by and by. Tell Ruey to come down."

Aunt Roxy issued her orders with all the military vigor and precision of a general in case of a sudden attack. It was her habit. Sickness and death were her opportunities; where they were, she felt herself at home, and she addressed herself to the task before her with undoubting faith.

Before many hours a pair of large, dark eyes slowly emerged from under the black-fringed lids of the little drowned boy,—they rolled dreamily round for a moment, and dropped again in heavy languor.

The little Mara had, with the quiet persistence which formed a trait in her baby character, dragged stools and chairs to the back of the bed, which she at last succeeded in scaling, and sat opposite to where the child lay, grave and still, watching with intense earnestness the process that was going on. At the moment when the eyes had opened, she stretched forth her little arms, and said, eagerly, "Pitty boy, come,"—and then, as they closed again, she dropped her hands with a sigh of disappointment. Yet, before night, the little stranger sat up in bed, and laughed with pleasure at the treasures of shells and pebbles which the children spread out on the bed before him.

He was a vigorous, well-made, handsome child, with brilliant eyes and teeth, but the few words that he spoke were in a language unknown to most present. Captain Kittridge declared it to be Spanish, and that a call which he most passionately and often repeated was for his mother. But he was of that happy age when sorrow can be easily effaced, and the efforts of the children called forth joyous smiles. When his playthings did not go to his liking, he showed sparkles of a fiery, irascible spirit.

The little Mara seemed to appropriate him in feminine fashion, as a chosen idol and graven image. She gave him at once all her slender stock of infantine treasures, and seemed to watch with an ecstatic devotion his every movement,—often repeating, as she looked delightedly around, "Pitty boy, come."

She had no words to explain the strange dream of the morning; it lay in her, struggling for expression, and giving her an interest in the new-comer as in something belonging to herself. Whence it came,—whence come multitudes like it, which spring up as strange, enchanted flowers, every now and then in the dull, material pathway of life,—who knows? It may be that our present faculties have among them a rudimentary one, like the germs of wings in the chrysalis, by which the spiritual world becomes sometimes an object of perception; there may be natures in which the walls of the material are so fine and translucent that the spiritual is seen through them as through a glass darkly. It may be, too, that the love which is stronger than death has a power sometimes to make itself heard and felt through the walls of our mortality, when it would plead for the defenseless ones it has left behind. All these things *may* be,—who knows?

"There," said Miss Roxy, coming out of the keeping-room at sunset; "I wouldn't ask to see a better-lookin' corpse. That ar woman was a sight to behold this morning. I guess I shook a double handful of stones and them little shells out of her hair,—now she reely looks beautiful. Captain Kittridge has made a coffin out o' some cedar-boards he happened to have, and I lined it with bleached cotton, and stuffed the pillow nice and full, and when we come to get her in, she reely will look lovely."

"I s'pose, Mis' Kittridge, you'll have the funeral to-morrow,—it's Sunday."

"Why, yes, Aunt Roxy,—I think everybody must want to improve such a dispensation. Have you took little Mara in to look at the corpse?"

"Well, no," said Miss Roxy; "Mis' Pennel's gettin' ready to take her home."

"I think it's an opportunity we ought to improve," said Mrs. Kittridge, "to learn children what death is. I think we can't begin to solemnize their minds too young."

At this moment Sally and the little Mara entered the room.

"Come here, children," said Mrs. Kittridge, taking a hand of either one, and leading them to the closed door of the keeping-room; "I've got somethin' to show you."

The room looked ghostly and dim,—the rays of light fell through the closed shutter on an object mysteriously muffled in a white sheet.

Sally's bright face expressed only the vague curiosity of a child to see something new; but the little Mara resisted and hung back with all her force, so that Mrs. Kittridge was obliged to take her up and hold her.

She folded back the sheet from the chill and wintry form which lay so icily, lonely, and cold. Sally walked around it, and gratified her curiosity by seeing it from every point of view, and laying her warm, busy hand on the lifeless and cold one; but Mara clung to Mrs. Kittridge, with eyes that expressed a distressed astonishment. The good woman stooped over and placed the child's little hand for a moment on the icy forehead. The little one gave a piercing scream, and struggled to get away; and as soon as she was put down, she ran and hid her face in Aunt Roxy's dress, sobbing bitterly.

"That child'll grow up to follow vanity," said Mrs. Kittridge; "her little head is full of dress now, and she hates anything serious,—it's easy to see that."

The little Mara had no words to tell what a strange, distressful chill had passed up her arm and through her brain, as she felt that icy cold of death,—that cold so different from all others. It was an impression of fear and pain that lasted weeks and months, so that she would start out of sleep and cry with a terror which she had not yet a sufficiency of language to describe.

CHAPTER VII

"You seem to forget, Mis' Kittridge, that this 'ere child ain't rugged like our Sally," said Aunt Roxy, as she raised the little Mara in her arms. "She was a seven-months' baby, and hard to raise at all, and a shivery, scary little creature."

"Well, then, she ought to be hardened," said Dame Kittridge. "But Mary Pennel never had no sort of idea of bringin' up children; 'twas jist so with Naomi,—the girl never had no sort o' resolution, and she just died for want o' resolution,—that's what came of it. I tell ye, children's got to learn to take the world as it is; and 'tain't no use bringin' on 'em up too tender. Teach 'em to begin as they've got to go out,—that's my maxim."

"Mis' Kittridge," said Aunt Roxy, "there's reason in all things, and there's difference in children. 'What's one's meat's another's pison.' You couldn't fetch up Mis' Pennel's children, and she couldn't fetch up your'n,—so let's say no more 'bout it."

"I'm always a-tellin' my wife that ar," said Captain Kittridge; "she's always wantin' to make everybody over after her pattern."

"Cap'n Kittridge, I don't think *you* need to speak," resumed his wife. "When such a loud providence is a-knockin' at *your* door, I think you'd better be a-searchin' your own heart,—here it is the eleventh hour, and you hain't come into the Lord's vineyard yet."

"Oh! come, come, Mis' Kittridge, don't twit a feller afore folks," said the Captain. "I'm goin' over to Harpswell Neck this blessed minute after the minister to 'tend the funeral,—so we'll let *him* preach."

CHAPTER VIII

THE SEEN AND THE UNSEEN

Life on any shore is a dull affair,—ever degenerating into commonplace; and this may account for the eagerness with which even a great calamity is sometimes accepted in a neighborhood, as affording wherewithal to stir the deeper feelings of our nature. Thus, though Mrs. Kittridge was by no means a hard-hearted woman, and would not for the world have had a ship wrecked on her particular account, yet since a ship had been wrecked and a body floated ashore at her very door, as it were, it afforded her no inconsiderable satisfaction to dwell on the details and to arrange for the funeral.

It was something to talk about and to think of, and likely to furnish subject-matter for talk for years to come when she should go out to tea with any of her acquaintances who lived at Middle Bay, or Maquoit, or Harpswell Neck. For although in those days,—the number of light-houses being much smaller than it is now,—it was no uncommon thing for ships to be driven on shore in storms, yet this incident had undeniably more that was stirring and romantic in it than any within the memory of any tea-table gossip in the vicinity. Mrs. Kittridge, therefore, looked forward to the funeral services on Sunday afternoon as to a species of solemn fête, which imparted a sort of consequence to her dwelling and herself. Notice of it was to be given out in "meeting" after service, and she might expect both keeping-room and kitchen to be full. Mrs. Pennel had offered to do her share of Christian and neighborly kindness, in taking home to her own dwelling the little boy. In fact, it became necessary to do so in order to appease the feelings of the little Mara, who clung to the new acquisition with most devoted fondness, and wept bitterly when he was separated from her even for a few moments. Therefore, in the afternoon of the day when the body was found, Mrs. Pennel, who had come down to assist, went back in company with Aunt Ruey and the two children.

The September evening set in brisk and chill, and the cheerful fire that snapped and roared up the ample chimney of Captain Kittridge's kitchen was a pleasing feature. The days of our story were before the advent of those sullen gnomes, the "air-tights," or even those more sociable and cheery domestic genii, the cooking-stoves. They were the days of the genial open kitchen-fire, with the crane, the pot-hooks, and trammels,—where hissed and boiled the social tea-kettle, where steamed the huge dinner-pot, in whose ample depths beets, carrots, potatoes, and turnips boiled in jolly sociability with the pork or corned beef which they were destined to flank at the coming meal.

On the present evening, Miss Roxy sat bolt upright, as was her wont, in one corner of the fireplace, with her spectacles on her nose, and an unwonted show of candles on the little stand beside her, having resumed the task of the silk dress which had been for a season interrupted. Mrs. Kittridge, with her spectacles also mounted, was carefully and warily "running-up breadths," stopping every few minutes to examine her work, and to inquire submissively of Miss Roxy if "it will do?"

Captain Kittridge sat in the other corner busily whittling on a little boat which he was shaping to please Sally, who sat on a low stool by his side with her knitting, evidently more intent on what her father was producing than on the evening task of "ten bouts," which her mother exacted before she could freely give her mind to anything on her own account. As Sally was rigorously sent to bed exactly at eight o'clock, it became her to be diligent if she wished to do anything for her own amusement before that hour.

And in the next room, cold and still, was lying that faded image of youth and beauty which the sea had so strangely given up. Without a name, without a history, without a single accompaniment from which her past could even be surmised,—there she lay, sealed in eternal silence.

"It's strange," said Captain Kittridge, as he whittled away,—"it's very strange we don't find anything more of that ar ship. I've been all up and down the beach a-lookin'. There was a spar and some broken bits of boards and timbers come ashore down on the beach, but nothin' to speak of."

"It won't be known till the sea gives up its dead," said Miss Roxy, shaking her head solemnly, "and there'll be a great givin' up then, I'm a-thinkin'."

"Yes, indeed," said Mrs. Kittridge, with an emphatic nod.

"Father," said Sally, "how many, many things there must be at the bottom of the sea,—so many ships are sunk with all their fine things on board. Why don't people contrive some way to go down and get them?"

"They do, child," said Captain Kittridge; "they have diving-bells, and men go down in 'em with caps over their faces, and long tubes to get the air through, and they walk about on the bottom of the ocean."

"Did you ever go down in one, father?"

"Why, yes, child, to be sure; and strange enough it was, to be sure. There you could see great big sea critters, with ever so many eyes and long arms, swimming right up to catch you, and all you could do would be to muddy the water on the bottom, so they couldn't see you."

"I never heard of that, Cap'n Kittridge," said his wife, drawing herself up with a reproving coolness.

"Wal', Mis' Kittridge, you hain't heard of everything that ever happened," said the Captain, imperturbably, "though you *do* know a sight."

"And how does the bottom of the ocean look, father?" said Sally.

"Laws, child, why trees and bushes grow there, just as they do on land; and great plants,—blue and purple and green and yellow, and lots of great pearls lie round. I've seen 'em big as chippin'-birds' eggs."

"Cap'n Kittridge!" said his wife.

"I have, and big as robins' eggs, too, but them was off the coast of Ceylon and Malabar, and way round the Equator," said the Captain, prudently resolved to throw his romance to a sufficient distance.

"It's a pity you didn't get a few of them pearls," said his wife, with an indignant appearance of scorn.

"I did get lots on 'em, and traded 'em off to the Nabobs in the interior for Cashmere shawls and India silks and sich," said the Captain, composedly; "and brought 'em home and sold 'em at a good figure, too."

"Oh, father!" said Sally, earnestly, "I wish you had saved just one or two for us."

"Laws, child, I wish now I had," said the Captain, good-naturedly. "Why, when I was in India, I went up to Lucknow, and Benares, and round, and saw all the Nabobs and Biggums,—why, they don't make no more of gold and silver and precious stones than we do of the shells we find on the beach. Why, I've seen one of them fellers with a diamond in his turban as big as my fist."

"Cap'n Kittridge, what are you telling?" said his wife once more.

"Fact,—as big as my fist," said the Captain, obdurately; "and all the clothes he wore was jist a stiff crust of pearls and precious stones. I tell you, he looked like something in the Revelations,—a real New Jerusalem look he had."

"I call that ar talk wicked, Cap'n Kittridge, usin' Scriptur' that ar way," said his wife.

"Why, don't it tell about all sorts of gold and precious stones in the Revelations?" said the Captain; "that's all I meant. Them ar countries off in Asia ain't like our'n,—stands to reason they shouldn't be; them's Scripture countries, and everything is different there."

"Father, didn't you ever get any of those splendid things?" said Sally.

"Laws, yes, child. Why, I had a great green ring, an emerald, that one of the princes giv' me, and ever so many pearls and diamonds. I used to go with 'em rattlin' loose in my vest pocket. I was young and gay in them days, and thought of bringin' of 'em home for the gals, but somehow I always got opportunities for swappin' of 'em off for goods and sich. That ar shawl your mother keeps in her camfire chist was what I got for one on 'em."

"Well, well," said Mrs. Kittridge, "there's never any catchin' you, 'cause you've been where we haven't."

"You've caught me once, and that ought'r do," said the Captain, with unruffled good-nature. "I tell you, Sally, your mother was the handsomest gal in Harpswell in them days."

"I should think you was too old for such nonsense, Cap'n," said Mrs. Kittridge, with a toss of her head, and a voice that sounded far less inexorable than her former admonition. In fact, though the old Captain was as unmanageable under his wife's fireside *régime* as any brisk old cricket that skipped and sang around the hearth, and though he hopped over all moral boundaries with a cheerful alertness of conscience that was quite discouraging, still there was no resisting the spell of his inexhaustible good-nature.

By this time he had finished the little boat, and to Sally's great delight, began sailing it for her in a pail of water.

"I wonder," said Mrs. Kittridge, "what's to be done with that ar child. I suppose the selectmen will take care on't; it'll be brought up by the town."

"I shouldn't wonder," said Miss Roxy, "if Cap'n Pennel should adopt it."

"You don't think so," said Mrs. Kittridge. "'Twould be taking a great care and expense on their hands at their time of life."

"I wouldn't want no better fun than to bring up that little shaver," said Captain Kittridge; "he's a bright un, I promise you."

"You, Cap'n Kittridge! I wonder you can talk so," said his wife. "It's an awful responsibility, and I wonder you don't think whether or no you're fit for it."

"Why, down here on the shore, I'd as lives undertake a boy as a Newfoundland pup," said the Captain. "Plenty in the sea to eat, drink, and wear. That ar young un may be the staff of their old age yet."

"You see," said Miss Roxy, "I think they'll adopt it to be company for little Mara; they're bound up in her, and the little thing pines bein' alone."

"Well, they make a real graven image of that ar child," said Mrs. Kittridge, "and fairly bow down to her and worship her."

"Well, it's natural," said Miss Roxy. "Besides, the little thing is cunnin'; she's about the cunnin'est little crittur that I ever saw, and has such enticin' ways."

The fact was, as the reader may perceive, that Miss Roxy had been thawed into an unusual attachment for the little Mara, and this affection was beginning to spread a warming element though her whole being. It was as if a rough granite rock had suddenly awakened to a passionate consciousness of the beauty of some fluttering white anemone that nestled in its cleft, and felt warm thrills running through all its veins at every tender motion and shadow. A word spoken against the little one seemed to rouse her combativeness. Nor did Dame Kittridge bear the child the slightest ill-will, but she was one of those naturally care-taking people whom Providence seems to design to perform the picket duties for the rest of society, and who, therefore, challenge everybody and everything to stand and give an account of themselves. Miss Roxy herself belonged to this class, but sometimes found herself so stoutly overhauled by the guns of Mrs. Kittridge's battery, that she could only stand modestly on the defensive.

One of Mrs. Kittridge's favorite hobbies was education, or, as she phrased it, the "fetchin' up" of children, which she held should be performed to the letter of the old stiff rule. In this manner she had already trained up six sons, who were all following their fortunes upon the seas, and, on this account, she had no small conceit of her abilities; and when she thought she discerned a lamb being left to frisk heedlessly out of bounds, her zeal was stirred to bring it under proper sheepfold regulations.

"Come, Sally, it's eight o'clock," said the good woman.

Sally's dark brows lowered over her large, black eyes, and she gave an appealing look to her father.

"Law, mother, let the child sit up a quarter of an hour later, jist for once."

"Cap'n Kittridge, if I was to hear to you, there'd never be no rule in this house. Sally, you go 'long this minute, and be sure you put your knittin' away in its place."

The Captain gave a humorous nod of submissive good-nature to his daughter as she went out. In fact, putting Sally to bed was taking away his plaything, and leaving him nothing to do but study faces in the coals, or watch the fleeting sparks which chased each other in flocks up the sooty back of the chimney.

It was Saturday night, and the morrow was Sunday,—never a very pleasant prospect to the poor Captain, who, having, unfortunately, no spiritual tastes, found it very difficult to get through the day in compliance with his wife's views of propriety, for he, alas! soared no higher in his aims.

"I b'lieve, on the hull, Polly, I'll go to bed, too," said he, suddenly starting up.

"Well, father, your clean shirt is in the right-hand corner of the upper drawer, and your Sunday clothes on the back of the chair by the bed."

The fact was that the Captain promised himself the pleasure of a long conversation with Sally, who nestled in the trundle-bed under the paternal couch, to whom he could relate long, many-colored yarns, without the danger of interruption from her mother's sharp, truth-seeking voice.

A moralist might, perhaps, be puzzled exactly what account to make of the Captain's disposition to romancing and embroidery. In all real, matter-of-fact transactions, as between man and man, his word was as good as another's, and he was held to be honest and just in his dealings. It was only when he mounted the stilts of foreign travel that his paces became so enormous. Perhaps, after all, a rude poetic and artistic faculty possessed the man. He might have been a humbler phase of the "mute, inglorious Milton." Perhaps his narrations required the privileges and allowances due to the inventive arts generally. Certain it was that, in common with other artists, he required an atmosphere of sympathy and confidence in which to develop himself fully; and, when left alone with children, his mind ran such riot, that the bounds between the real and unreal became foggier than the banks of Newfoundland.

The two women sat up, and the night wore on apace, while they kept together that customary vigil which it was thought necessary to hold over the lifeless casket from which an immortal jewel had recently been withdrawn.

"I re'lly did hope," said Mrs. Kittridge, mournfully, "that this 'ere solemn Providence would have been sent home to the Cap'n's mind; but he seems jist as light and triflin' as ever."

"There don't nobody see these 'ere things unless they's effectually called," said Miss Roxy, "and the Cap'n's time ain't come."

CHAPTER VIII

"It's gettin' to be t'ward the eleventh hour," said Mrs. Kittridge, "as I was a-tellin' him this afternoon."

"Well," said Miss Roxy, "you know

"'While the lamp holds out to burn,
The vilest sinner may return.'"

"Yes, I know that," said Mrs. Kittridge, rising and taking up the candle. "Don't you think, Aunt Roxy, we may as well give a look in there at the corpse?"

It was past midnight as they went together into the keeping-room. All was so still that the clash of the rising tide and the ticking of the clock assumed that solemn and mournful distinctness which even tones less impressive take on in the night-watches. Miss Roxy went mechanically through with certain arrangements of the white drapery around the cold sleeper, and uncovering the face and bust for a moment, looked critically at the still, unconscious countenance.

"Not one thing to let us know who or what she is," she said; "that boy, if he lives, would give a good deal to know, some day."

"What is it one's duty to do about this bracelet?" said Mrs. Kittridge, taking from a drawer the article in question, which had been found on the beach in the morning.

"Well, I s'pose it belongs to the child, whatever it's worth," said Miss Roxy.

"Then if the Pennels conclude to take him, I may as well give it to them," said Mrs. Kittridge, laying it back in the drawer.

Miss Roxy folded the cloth back over the face, and the two went out into the kitchen. The fire had sunk low—the crickets were chirruping gleefully. Mrs. Kittridge added more wood, and put on the tea-kettle that their watching might be refreshed by the aid of its talkative and inspiring beverage. The two solemn, hard-visaged women drew up to each other by the fire, and insensibly their very voices assumed a tone of drowsy and confidential mystery.

"If this 'ere poor woman was hopefully pious, and could see what was goin' on here," said Mrs. Kittridge, "it would seem to be a comfort to her that her child has fallen into such good hands. It seems a'most a pity she couldn't know it."

"How do you know she don't?" said Miss Roxy, brusquely.

"Why, you know the hymn," said Mrs. Kittridge, quoting those somewhat sadducaical lines from the popular psalm-book:—

"'The living know that they must die,
But all the dead forgotten lie—
Their memory and their senses gone,
Alike unknowing and unknown.'"

"Well, I don't know 'bout that," said Miss Roxy, flavoring her cup of tea; "hymn-book ain't Scriptur', and I'm pretty sure that ar ain't true always;" and she nodded her head as if she could say more if she chose.

Now Miss Roxy's reputation of vast experience in all the facts relating to those last fateful hours, which are the only certain event in every human existence, caused her to be regarded as a sort of Delphic oracle in such matters, and therefore Mrs. Kittridge, not without a share of the latent superstition to which each human heart must confess at some hours, drew confidentially near to Miss Roxy, and asked if she had anything particular on her mind.

"Well, Mis' Kittridge," said Miss Roxy, "I ain't one of the sort as likes to make a talk of what I've seen, but mebbe if I was, I've seen some things *as* remarkable as anybody. I tell you, Mis' Kittridge, folks don't tend the sick and dyin' bed year in and out, at all hours, day and night, and not see some remarkable things; that's my opinion."

"Well, Miss Roxy, did you ever see a sperit?"

"I won't say as I have, and I won't say as I haven't," said Miss Roxy; "only as I have seen some remarkable things."

There was a pause, in which Mrs. Kittridge stirred her tea, looking intensely curious, while the old kitchen-clock seemed to tick with one of those fits of loud insistence which seem to take clocks at times when all is still, as if they had something that they were getting ready to say pretty soon, if nobody else spoke.

But Miss Roxy evidently had something to say, and so she began:—

"Mis' Kittridge, this 'ere's a very particular subject to be talkin' of. I've had opportunities to observe that most haven't, and I don't care if I jist say to you, that I'm pretty sure spirits that has left the body do come to their friends sometimes."

The clock ticked with still more *empressement*, and Mrs. Kittridge glared through the horn bows of her glasses with eyes of eager curiosity.

"Now, you remember Cap'n Titcomb's wife, that died fifteen years ago when her husband had gone to Archangel; and you remember that he took her son John out with him—and of all her boys, John was the one she was particular sot on."

"Yes, and John died at Archangel; I remember that."

"Jes' so," said Miss Roxy, laying her hand on Mrs. Kittridge's; "he died at Archangel the very day his mother died, and jist the hour, for the Cap'n had it down in his log-book."

"You don't say so!"

"Yes, I do. Well, now," said Miss Roxy, sinking her voice, "this 'ere was remarkable. Mis' Titcomb was one of the fearful sort, tho' one of the best women that ever lived. Our minister used to call her 'Mis' Muchafraid'—you know, in the 'Pilgrim's Progress'—but he was satisfied with her evidences, and told her so; she used to say she was 'afraid of the dark valley,' and she told our minister so when he went out, that ar last day he called; and his last words, as he stood with his hand on the knob of the door, was 'Mis' Titcomb, the Lord will find ways to bring you thro' the dark valley.' Well, she sunk away about three o'clock in the morning. I remember the time, 'cause the Cap'n's chronometer watch that he left with her lay on the stand for her to take her drops by. I heard her kind o' restless, and I went up, and I saw she was struck with death, and she looked sort o' anxious and distressed.

"'Oh, Aunt Roxy,' says she, 'it's so dark, who will go with me?' and in a minute her whole face brightened up, and says she, 'John is going with me,' and she jist gave the least little sigh and never breathed no more—she jist died as easy as a bird. I told our minister of it next morning, and he asked if I'd made a note of the hour, and I told him I had, and says he, 'You did right, Aunt Roxy.'"

"What did he seem to think of it?"

"Well, he didn't seem inclined to speak freely. 'Miss Roxy,' says he, 'all natur's in the Lord's hands, and there's no saying why he uses this or that; them that's strong enough to go by faith, he lets 'em, but there's no saying what he won't do for the weak ones.'"

"Wa'n't the Cap'n overcome when you told him?" said Mrs. Kittridge.

"Indeed he was; he was jist as white as a sheet."

Miss Roxy now proceeded to pour out another cup of tea, and having mixed and flavored it, she looked in a weird and sibylline manner across it, and inquired,—

"Mis' Kittridge, do you remember that ar Mr. Wadkins that come to Brunswick twenty years ago, in President Averill's days?"

"Yes, I remember the pale, thin, long-nosed gentleman that used to sit in President Averill's pew at church. Nobody knew who he was, or where he came from. The college students used to call him Thaddeus of Warsaw. Nobody knew who he was but the President, 'cause he could speak all the foreign tongues—one about as well as another; but the President he knew his story, and said he was a good man, and he used to stay to the sacrament regular, I remember."

"Yes," said Miss Roxy, "he used to live in a room all alone, and keep himself. Folks said he was quite a gentleman, too, and fond of reading."

"I heard Cap'n Atkins tell," said Mrs. Kittridge, "how they came to take him up on the shores of Holland. You see, when he was somewhere in a port in Denmark, some men come to him and offered him a pretty good sum of money if he'd be at such a place on the coast of Holland on such a day, and take whoever should come. So the Cap'n he went, and sure enough on that day there come a troop of men on horseback down to the beach with this man, and they all bid him good-by, and seemed to make much of him, but he never told 'em nothin' on board ship, only he seemed kind o' sad and pinin'."

"Well," said Miss Roxy; "Ruey and I we took care o' that man in his last sickness, and we watched with him the night he died, and there was something quite remarkable."

"Do tell now," said Mrs. Kittridge.

"Well, you see," said Miss Roxy, "he'd been low and poorly all day, kind o' tossin' and restless, and a little light-headed, and the Doctor said he thought he wouldn't last till morning, and so Ruey and I we set up with him, and between twelve and one Ruey said she thought she'd jist lop down a few minutes on the old sofa at the foot of the bed, and I made me a cup of tea like as I'm a-doin' now, and set with my back to him."

"Well?" said Mrs. Kittridge, eagerly.

"Well, you see he kept a-tossin' and throwin' off the clothes, and I kept a-gettin' up to straighten 'em; and once he threw out his arms, and something bright fell out on to the pillow, and I went and looked, and it was a likeness that he wore by a ribbon round his neck. It was a woman—a real handsome one—and she had on a low-necked black dress, of the cut they used to call Marie Louise, and she had a string of pearls round her neck, and her hair curled with pearls in it, and very wide blue eyes. Well, you see, I didn't look but a minute before he seemed to wake up, and he caught at it and hid it in his clothes. Well, I went and sat down, and I grew kind o' sleepy over the fire; but pretty soon I heard him speak out very clear, and kind o' surprised, in a tongue I didn't understand, and I looked round."

Miss Roxy here made a pause, and put another lump of sugar into her tea.

"Well?" said Mrs. Kittridge, ready to burst with curiosity.

"Well, now, I don't like to tell about these 'ere things, and you mustn't never speak about it; but as sure as you live, Polly Kittridge, I see that ar very woman standin' at the back of the bed, right in the partin' of the curtains, jist as she looked in the pictur'—blue eyes and curly hair and pearls on her neck, and black dress."

"What did you do?" said Mrs. Kittridge.

"Do? Why, I jist held my breath and looked, and in a minute it kind o' faded away, and I got up and went to the bed, but the man was gone. He lay there with the pleasantest smile on his face that ever you see; and I woke up Ruey, and told her about it."

Mrs. Kittridge drew a long breath. "What do you think it was?"

"Well," said Miss Roxy, "I know what I think, but I don't think best to tell. I told Doctor Meritts, and he said there were more things in heaven and earth than folks knew about—and so I think."

Meanwhile, on this same evening, the little Mara frisked like a household fairy round the hearth of Zephaniah Pennel.

The boy was a strong-limbed, merry-hearted little urchin, and did full justice to the abundant hospitalities of Mrs. Pennel's tea-table; and after supper little Mara employed herself in bringing apronful after apronful of her choicest treasures, and laying them down at his feet. His great black eyes flashed with pleasure, and he gamboled about the hearth with his new playmate in perfect forgetfulness, apparently, of all the past night of fear and anguish.

When the great family Bible was brought out for prayers, and little Mara composed herself on a low stool by her grandmother's side, he, however, did not conduct himself as a babe of grace. He resisted all Miss Ruey's efforts to make him sit down beside her, and stood staring with his great, black, irreverent eyes during the Bible-reading, and laughed out in the most inappropriate manner when the psalm-singing began, and seemed disposed to mingle incoherent remarks of his own even in the prayers.

"This is a pretty self-willed youngster," said Miss Ruey, as they rose from the exercises, "and I shouldn't think he'd been used to religious privileges."

"Perhaps not," said Zephaniah Pennel; "but who can say but what this providence is a message of the Lord to us—such as Pharaoh's daughter sent about Moses, 'Take this child, and bring him up for me'?"

CHAPTER VIII

"I'd like to take him, if I thought I was capable," said Mrs. Pennel, timidly. "It seems a real providence to give Mara some company; the poor child pines so for want of it."

"Well, then, Mary, if you say so, we will bring him up with our little Mara," said Zephaniah, drawing the child toward him. "May the Lord bless him!" he added, laying his great brown hands on the shining black curls of the child.

CHAPTER IX

MOSES

Sunday morning rose clear and bright on Harpswell Bay. The whole sea was a waveless, blue looking-glass, streaked with bands of white, and flecked with sailing cloud-shadows from the skies above. Orr's Island, with its blue-black spruces, its silver firs, its golden larches, its scarlet sumachs, lay on the bosom of the deep like a great many-colored gem on an enchanted mirror. A vague, dreamlike sense of rest and Sabbath stillness seemed to brood in the air. The very spruce-trees seemed to know that it was Sunday, and to point solemnly upward with their dusky fingers; and the small tide-waves that chased each other up on the shelly beach, or broke against projecting rocks, seemed to do it with a chastened decorum, as if each blue-haired wave whispered to his brother, "Be still—be still."

Yes, Sunday it was along all the beautiful shores of Maine—netted in green and azure by its thousand islands, all glorious with their majestic pines, all musical and silvery with the caresses of the sea-waves, that loved to wander and lose themselves in their numberless shelly coves and tiny beaches among their cedar shadows.

Not merely as a burdensome restraint, or a weary endurance, came the shadow of that Puritan Sabbath. It brought with it all the sweetness that belongs to rest, all the sacredness that hallows home, all the memories of patient thrift, of sober order, of chastened yet intense family feeling, of calmness, purity, and self-respecting dignity which distinguish the Puritan household. It seemed a solemn pause in all the sights and sounds of earth. And he whose moral nature was not yet enough developed to fill the blank with visions of heaven was yet wholesomely instructed by his weariness into the secret of his own spiritual poverty.

Zephaniah Pennel, in his best Sunday clothes, with his hard visage glowing with a sort of interior tenderness, ministered this morning at his family-altar—one of those thousand priests of God's ordaining that tend the sacred fire in as many families of New England. He had risen with the morning star and been forth to meditate, and came in with his mind softened and glowing. The trance-like calm of earth and sea found a solemn answer with him, as he read what a poet wrote by the sea-shores of the Mediterranean, ages ago: "Bless the Lord, O my soul. O

Lord my God, thou art very great; thou art clothed with honor and majesty. Who coverest thyself with light as with a garment: who stretchest out the heavens like a curtain: who layeth the beams of his chambers in the waters: who maketh the clouds his chariot: who walketh upon the wings of the wind. The trees of the Lord are full of sap; the cedars of Lebanon, which he hath planted; where the birds make their nests; as for the stork, the fir-trees are her house. O Lord, how manifold are thy works! in wisdom hast thou made them all."

Ages ago the cedars that the poet saw have rotted into dust, and from their cones have risen generations of others, wide-winged and grand. But the words of that poet have been wafted like seed to our days, and sprung up in flowers of trust and faith in a thousand households.

"Well, now," said Miss Ruey, when the morning rite was over, "Mis' Pennel, I s'pose you and the Cap'n will be wantin' to go to the meetin', so don't you gin yourse'ves a mite of trouble about the children, for I'll stay at home with 'em. The little feller was starty and fretful in his sleep last night, and didn't seem to be quite well."

"No wonder, poor dear," said Mrs. Pennel; "it's a wonder children can forget as they do."

"Yes," said Miss Ruey; "you know them lines in the 'English Reader,'—

'Gay hope is theirs by fancy led,
Least pleasing when possessed;
The tear forgot as soon as shed,
The sunshine of the breast.'

Them lines all'ys seemed to me affectin'."

Miss Ruey's sentiment was here interrupted by a loud cry from the bedroom, and something between a sneeze and a howl.

"Massy! what is that ar young un up to!" she exclaimed, rushing into the adjoining bedroom.

There stood the young Master Hopeful of our story, with streaming eyes and much-bedaubed face, having just, after much labor, succeeded in making Miss Ruey's snuff-box fly open, which he did with such force as to send the contents in a perfect cloud into eyes, nose, and mouth. The scene of struggling and confusion that ensued cannot be described. The washings, and wipings, and sobbings, and exhortings, and the sympathetic sobs of the little Mara, formed a small tempest for the time being that was rather appalling.

"Well, this 'ere's a youngster that's a-goin' to make work," said Miss Ruey, when all things were tolerably restored. "Seems to make himself at home first thing."

"Poor little dear," said Mrs. Pennel, in the excess of loving-kindness, "I hope he will; he's welcome, I'm sure."

"Not to my snuff-box," said Miss Ruey, who had felt herself attacked in a very tender point.

"He's got the notion of lookin' into things pretty early," said Captain Pennel, with an indulgent smile.

"Well, Aunt Ruey," said Mrs. Pennel, when this disturbance was somewhat abated, "I feel kind o' sorry to deprive you of your privileges to-day."

"Oh! never mind me," said Miss Ruey, briskly. "I've got the big Bible, and I can sing a hymn or two by myself. My voice ain't quite what it used to be, but then I get a good deal of pleasure out of it." Aunt Ruey, it must be known, had in her youth been one of the foremost leaders in the "singers' seats," and now was in the habit of speaking of herself much as a retired *prima donna* might, whose past successes were yet in the minds of her generation.

After giving a look out of the window, to see that the children were within sight, she opened the big Bible at the story of the ten plagues of Egypt, and adjusting her horn spectacles with a sort of sideway twist on her little pug nose, she seemed intent on her Sunday duties. A moment after she looked up and said, "I don't know but I must send a message by you over to Mis' Deacon Badger, about a worldly matter, if 'tis Sunday; but I've been thinkin', Mis' Pennel, that there'll have to be clothes made up for this 'ere child next week, and so perhaps Roxy and I had better stop here a day or two longer, and you tell Mis' Badger that we'll come to her a Wednesday, and so she'll have time to have that new press-board done,—the old one used to pester me so."

"Well, I'll remember," said Mrs. Pennel.

"It seems a'most impossible to prevent one's thoughts wanderin' Sundays," said Aunt Ruey; "but I couldn't help a-thinkin' I could get such a nice pair o' trousers out of them old Sunday ones of the Cap'n's in the garret. I was a-lookin' at 'em last Thursday, and thinkin' what a pity 'twas you hadn't nobody to cut down for; but this 'ere young un's going to be such a tearer, he'll want somethin' real stout; but I'll try and put it out of my mind till Monday. Mis' Pennel, you'll be sure to ask Mis' Titcomb how Harriet's toothache is, and whether them drops cured her that I gin her last Sunday; and ef you'll jist look in a minute at Major Broad's, and tell 'em to use bayberry wax for his blister, it's so healin'; and do jist ask if Sally's baby's eye-tooth has come through yet."

"Well, Aunt Ruey, I'll try to remember all," said Mrs. Pennel, as she stood at the glass in her bedroom, carefully adjusting the respectable black silk shawl over her shoulders, and tying her neat bonnet-strings.

"I s'pose," said Aunt Ruey, "that the notice of the funeral'll be gin out after sermon."

"Yes, I think so," said Mrs. Pennel.

"It's another loud call," said Miss Ruey, "and I hope it will turn the young people from their thoughts of dress and vanity,—there's Mary Jane Sanborn was all took up with gettin' feathers and velvet for her fall bonnet. I don't think I shall get no bonnet this year till snow comes. My bonnet's respectable enough,—don't you think so?"

"Certainly, Aunt Ruey, it looks very well."

"Well, I'll have the pork and beans and brown-bread all hot on table agin you come back," said Miss Ruey, "and then after dinner we'll all go down to the funeral together. Mis' Pennel, there's one thing on my mind,—what you goin' to call this 'ere boy?"

"Father and I've been thinkin' that over," said Mrs. Pennel.

"Wouldn't think of giv'n him the Cap'n's name?" said Aunt Ruey.

"He must have a name of his own," said Captain Pennel. "Come here, sonny," he called to the child, who was playing just beside the door.

The child lowered his head, shook down his long black curls, and looked through them as elfishly as a Skye terrier, but showed no inclination to come.

"One thing he hasn't learned, evidently," said Captain Pennel, "and that is to mind."

"Here!" he said, turning to the boy with a little of the tone he had used of old on the quarter-deck, and taking his small hand firmly.

The child surrendered, and let the good man lift him on his knee and stroke aside the clustering curls; the boy then looked fixedly at him with his great gloomy black eyes, his little firm-set mouth and bridled chin,—a perfect little miniature of proud manliness.

"What's your name, little boy?"

The great eyes continued looking in the same solemn quiet.

"Law, he don't understand a word," said Zephaniah, putting his hand kindly on the child's head; "our tongue is all strange to him. Kittridge says he's a Spanish child; may be from the West Indies; but nobody knows,—we never shall know his name."

"Well, I dare say it was some Popish nonsense or other," said Aunt Ruey; "and now he's come to a land of Christian privileges, we ought to give him a good Scripture name, and start him well in the world."

"Let's call him Moses," said Zephaniah, "because we drew him out of the water."

"Now, did I ever!" said Miss Ruey; "there's something in the Bible to fit everything, ain't there?"

"I like Moses, because I had a brother of that name," said Mrs. Pennel.

The child had slid down from his protector's knee, and stood looking from one to the other gravely while this discussion was going on. What change of destiny was then going on for him in this simple formula of adoption, none could tell; but, surely, never orphan stranded on a foreign shore found home with hearts more true and loving.

"Well, wife, I suppose we must be goin'," said Zephaniah.

About a stone's throw from the open door, the little fishing-craft lay courtesying daintily on the small tide-waves that came licking up the white pebbly shore. Mrs. Pennel seated herself in the end of the boat, and a pretty placid picture she was, with her smooth, parted hair, her modest, cool, drab bonnet, and her bright hazel eyes, in which was the Sabbath calm of a loving and tender heart. Zephaniah loosed the sail, and the two children stood on the beach and saw them go off. A pleasant little wind carried them away, and back on the breeze came the sound of Zephaniah's Sunday-morning psalm:—

"Lord, in the morning thou shalt hear
My voice ascending high;
To thee will I direct my prayer,
To thee lift up mine eye.
"Unto thy house will I resort.
To taste thy mercies there;
I will frequent thy holy court,
And worship in thy fear."

The surface of the glassy bay was dotted here and there with the white sails of other little craft bound for the same point and for the same purpose. It was as pleasant a sight as one might wish to see.

Left in charge of the house, Miss Ruey drew a long breath, took a consoling pinch of snuff, sang "Bridgewater" in an uncommonly high key, and then began reading in the prophecies. With her good head full of the "daughter of Zion" and the house of Israel and Judah, she was recalled to terrestrial things by loud screams from the barn, accompanied by a general flutter and cackling among the hens.

Away plodded the good soul, and opening the barn-door saw the little boy perched on the top of the hay-mow, screaming and shrieking,—his face the picture of dismay,—while poor little Mara's cries came in a more muffled manner from some unexplored lower region. In fact, she was found to have slipped through a hole in the hay-mow into the nest of a very domestic sitting-hen, whose clamors at the invasion of her family privacy added no little to the general confusion.

The little princess, whose nicety as to her dress and sensitiveness as to anything unpleasant about her pretty person we have seen, was lifted up streaming with tears and broken eggs, but otherwise not seriously injured, having fallen on the very substantial substratum of hay which Dame Poulet had selected as the foundation of her domestic hopes.

"Well, now, did I ever!" said Miss Ruey, when she had ascertained that no bones were broken; "if that ar young un isn't a limb! I declare for't I pity Mis' Pennel,—she don't know what she's undertook. How upon 'arth the critter managed to get Mara on to the hay, I'm sure I can't tell,—that ar little thing never got into no such scrapes before."

Far from seeming impressed with any wholesome remorse of conscience, the little culprit frowned fierce defiance at Miss Ruey, when, after having repaired the damages of little Mara's toilet, she essayed the good old plan of shutting him into the closet. He fought and struggled so fiercely that Aunt Ruey's carroty frisette came off in the skirmish, and her head-gear, always rather original, assumed an aspect verging on the supernatural. Miss Ruey thought of Philistines and Moabites, and all the other terrible people she had been reading about that morning, and came as near getting into a passion with the little elf as so good-humored and Christian an old body could possibly do. Human virtue is frail, and every one has some vulnerable point. The old Roman senator could not control himself when his beard was invaded, and the like sensitiveness resides in an old woman's cap; and when young master irreverently clawed off her Sunday best, Aunt Ruey, in her confusion of mind, administered a sound cuff on either ear.

Little Mara, who had screamed loudly through the whole scene, now conceiving that her precious new-found treasure was endangered, flew at poor Miss Ruey with both little hands; and throwing her arms round her "boy," as she constantly called him, she drew him backward, and looked defiance at the common enemy. Miss Ruey was dumb-struck.

"I declare for't, I b'lieve he's bewitched her," she said, stupefied, having never seen anything like the martial expression which now gleamed from those soft brown eyes. "Why, Mara dear,—putty little Mara."

But Mara was busy wiping away the angry tears that stood on the hot, glowing cheeks of the boy, and offering her little rosebud of a mouth to kiss him, as she stood on tiptoe.

"Poor boy,—no kie,—Mara's boy," she said; "Mara love boy;" and then giving an angry glance at Aunt Ruey, who sat much disheartened and confused, she struck out her little pearly hand, and cried, "Go way,—go way, naughty!"

The child jabbered unintelligibly and earnestly to Mara, and she seemed to have the air of being perfectly satisfied with his view of the case, and both regarded Miss Ruey with frowning looks. Under these peculiar circumstances, the good soul began to bethink her of some mode of compromise, and going to the closet took out a couple of slices of cake, which she offered to the little rebels with pacificatory words.

Mara was appeased at once, and ran to Aunt Ruey; but the boy struck the cake out of her hand, and looked at her with steady defiance. The little one picked it up, and with much chippering and many little feminine manœuvres, at last succeeded in making him taste it, after which appetite got the better of his valorous resolutions,—he ate and was comforted; and after a little time, the three were on the best possible footing. And Miss Ruey having smoothed her hair, and arranged her frisette and cap, began to reflect upon herself as the cause of the whole disturbance. If she had not let them run while she indulged in reading and singing, this would not have happened. So the toilful good soul kept them at her knee for the next hour or two, while they looked through all the pictures in the old family Bible.

The evening of that day witnessed a crowded funeral in the small rooms of Captain Kittridge. Mrs. Kittridge was in her glory. Solemn and lugubrious to the last degree, she supplied in her own proper person the want of the whole corps of mourners, who generally attract sympathy on such occasions. But what drew artless pity from all was the unconscious orphan, who came in, led by Mrs. Pennel by the one hand, and with the little Mara by the other.

The simple rite of baptism administered to the wondering little creature so strongly recalled that other scene three years before, that Mrs. Pennel hid her face in her handkerchief, and Zephaniah's firm hand shook a little as he took the boy to offer him to the rite. The child received the ceremony with a look of grave surprise, put up his hand quickly and wiped the holy drops from his brow, as if they annoyed him; and shrinking back, seized hold of the gown of Mrs. Pennel. His great beauty, and, still more, the air of haughty, defiant firmness with which he regarded the company, drew all eyes, and many were the whispered comments.

"Pennel'll have his hands full with that ar chap," said Captain Kittridge to Miss Roxy.

Mrs. Kittridge darted an admonitory glance at her husband, to remind him that she was looking at him, and immediately he collapsed into solemnity.

The evening sunbeams slanted over the blackberry bushes and mullein stalks of the graveyard, when the lonely voyager was lowered to the rest from which she should not rise till the heavens be no more. As the purple sea at that hour retained no trace of the ships that had furrowed its waves, so of this mortal traveler no trace remained, not even in that infant soul that was to her so passionately dear.

CHAPTER X

THE MINISTER

Mrs. Kittridge's advantages and immunities resulting from the shipwreck were not yet at an end. Not only had one of the most "solemn providences" known within the memory of the neighborhood fallen out at her door,—not only had the most interesting funeral that had occurred for three or four years taken place in her parlor, but she was still further to be distinguished in having the minister to tea after the performances were all over. To this end she had risen early, and taken down her best china tea-cups, which had been marked with her and her husband's joint initials in Canton, and which only came forth on high and solemn occasions. In view of this probable distinction, on Saturday, immediately after the discovery of the calamity, Mrs. Kittridge had found time to rush to her kitchen, and make up a loaf of pound-cake and some doughnuts, that the great occasion which she foresaw might not find her below her reputation as a forehanded housewife.

It was a fine golden hour when the minister and funeral train turned away from the grave. Unlike other funerals, there was no draught on the sympathies in favor of mourners—no wife, or husband, or parent, left a heart in that grave; and so when the rites were all over, they turned with the more cheerfulness back into life, from the contrast of its freshness with those shadows into which, for the hour, they had been gazing.

The Rev. Theophilus Sewell was one of the few ministers who preserved the costume of a former generation, with something of that imposing dignity with which, in earlier times, the habits of the clergy were invested. He was tall and majestic in stature, and carried to advantage the powdered wig and three-cornered hat, the broad-skirted coat, knee-breeches, high shoes, and plated buckles of the ancient costume. There was just a sufficient degree of the formality of olden times to give a certain quaintness to all he said and did. He was a man of a considerable degree of talent, force, and originality, and in fact had been held in his day to be one of the most promising graduates of Harvard University. But, being a good man, he had proposed to himself no higher ambition than to succeed to the pulpit of his father in Harpswell.

His parish included not only a somewhat scattered seafaring population on the mainland, but also the care of several islands. Like many other of the New England clergy of those times, he united in himself numerous different offices for the benefit of the people whom he served. As there was neither lawyer nor physician in the town, he had acquired by his reading, and still more by his experience, enough knowledge in both these departments to enable him to administer to the ordinary wants of a very healthy and peaceable people.

It was said that most of the deeds and legal conveyances in his parish were in his handwriting, and in the medical line his authority was only rivaled by that of Miss Roxy, who claimed a very obvious advantage over him in a certain class of cases, from the fact of her being a woman, which was still further increased by the circumstance that the good man had retained steadfastly his bachelor estate. "So, of course," Miss Roxy used to say, "poor man! what could he know about a woman, you know?"

This state of bachelorhood gave occasion to much surmising; but when spoken to about it, he was accustomed to remark with gallantry, that he should have too much regard for any lady whom he could think of as a wife, to ask her to share his straitened circumstances. His income, indeed, consisted of only about two hundred dollars a year; but upon this he and a very brisk, cheerful maiden sister contrived to keep up a thrifty and comfortable establishment, in which everything appeared to be pervaded by a spirit of quaint cheerfulness.

In fact, the man might be seen to be an original in his way, and all the springs of his life were kept oiled by a quiet humor, which sometimes broke out in playful sparkles, despite the gravity of the pulpit and the awfulness of the cocked hat. He had a placid way of amusing himself with the quaint and picturesque side of life, as it appeared in all his visitings among a very primitive, yet very shrewd-minded people.

There are those people who possess a peculiar faculty of mingling in the affairs of this life as spectators as well as actors. It does not, of course, suppose any coldness of nature or want of human interest or sympathy—nay, it often exists most completely with people of the tenderest human feeling. It rather seems to be a kind of distinct faculty working harmoniously with all the others; but he who possesses it needs never to be at a loss for interest or amusement; he is always a spectator at a tragedy or comedy, and sees in real life a humor and a pathos beyond anything he can find shadowed in books.

Mr. Sewell sometimes, in his pastoral visitations, took a quiet pleasure in playing upon these simple minds, and amusing himself with the odd harmonies and singular resolutions of chords which started out under his fingers. Surely he had a right to something in addition to his limited salary, and this innocent, unsuspected entertainment helped to make up the balance for his many labors.

His sister was one of the best-hearted and most unsuspicious of the class of female idolaters, and worshiped her brother with the most undoubting faith and devotion—wholly ignorant of the constant amusement she gave him by a thousand little feminine peculiarities, which struck him with a continual sense of oddity. It was infinitely diverting to him to see the solemnity of her interest in his shirts and stockings, and Sunday clothes, and to listen to the subtle distinctions which she would draw between best and second-best, and every-day; to receive her somewhat prolix admonition how he was to demean himself in respect of the wearing of each one; for Miss Emily Sewell was a gentlewoman, and held rigidly to various traditions of gentility which had been handed down in the Sewell family, and which afforded her brother too much quiet amusement to be disturbed. He would not have overthrown one of her quiddities for the world; it would be taking away a part of his capital in existence.

Miss Emily was a trim, genteel little person, with dancing black eyes, and cheeks which had the roses of youth well dried into them. It was easy to see that she had been quite pretty in her days; and her neat figure, her brisk little vivacious ways, her unceasing good-nature and kindness of heart, still made her an object both of admiration and interest in the parish. She was great in drying herbs and preparing recipes; in knitting and sewing, and cutting and contriving; in saving every possible snip and chip either of food or clothing; and no less liberal was she in bestowing advice and aid in the parish, where she moved about with all the sense of consequence which her brother's position warranted.

The fact of his bachelorhood caused his relations to the female part of his flock to be even more shrouded in sacredness and mystery than is commonly the case with the great man of the parish; but Miss Emily delighted to act as interpreter. She was charmed to serve out to the willing ears of his parish from time to time such scraps of information as regarded his life, habits, and opinions as might gratify their ever new curiosity. Instructed by her, all the good wives knew the difference between his very best long silk stocking and his second best, and how carefully the first had to be kept under lock and key, where he could not get at them; for he was understood, good as he was, to have concealed in him all the thriftless and pernicious inconsiderateness of the male nature, ready at any moment to break out into unheard-of improprieties. But the good man submitted himself to Miss Emily's rule, and suffered himself to be led about by her with an air of half whimsical consciousness.

Mrs. Kittridge that day had felt the full delicacy of the compliment when she ascertained by a hasty glance, before the first prayer, that the good man had been brought out to her funeral in all his very best things, not excepting the long silk stockings, for she knew the second-best pair by means of a certain skillful darn which Miss Emily had once shown her, which commemorated the spot where a hole had been. The absence of this darn struck to Mrs. Kittridge's heart at once as a delicate attention.

"Mis' Simpkins," said Mrs. Kittridge to her pastor, as they were seated at the tea-table, "told me that she wished when you were going home that you would call in to see Mary Jane; she couldn't come out to the funeral on account of a dreffle sore throat. I was tellin' on her to gargle it with blackberry-root tea—don't you think that is a good gargle, Mr. Sewell?"

"Yes, I think it a very good gargle," replied the minister, gravely.

"Ma'sh rosemary is the gargle that I always use," said Miss Roxy; "it cleans out your throat so."

"Marsh rosemary is a very excellent gargle," said Mr. Sewell.

"Why, brother, don't you think that rose leaves and vitriol is a good gargle?" said little Miss Emily; "I always thought that you liked rose leaves and vitriol for a gargle."

"So I do," said the imperturbable Mr. Sewell, drinking his tea with the air of a sphinx.

"Well, now, you'll have to tell which on 'em will be most likely to cure Mary Jane," said Captain Kittridge, "or there'll be a pullin' of caps, I'm thinkin'; or else the poor girl will have to drink them all, which is generally the way."

"There won't any of them cure Mary Jane's throat," said the minister, quietly.

"Why, brother!" "Why, Mr. Sewell!" "Why, you don't!" burst in different tones from each of the women.

"I thought you said that blackberry-root tea was good," said Mrs. Kittridge.

"I understood that you 'proved of ma'sh rosemary," said Miss Roxy, touched in her professional pride.

"And I am sure, brother, that I have heard you say, often and often, that there wasn't a better gargle than rose leaves and vitriol," said Miss Emily.

"You are quite right, ladies, all of you. I think these are all good gargles—excellent ones."

"But I thought you said that they didn't do any good?" said all the ladies in a breath.

"No, they don't—not the least in the world," said Mr. Sewell; "but they are all excellent gargles, and as long as people must have gargles, I think one is about as good as another."

"Now you have got it," said Captain Kittridge.

"Brother, you do say the strangest things," said Miss Emily.

"Well, I must say," said Miss Roxy, "it is a new idea to me, long as I've been nussin', and I nussed through one season of scarlet fever when sometimes there was five died in one house; and if ma'sh rosemary didn't do good then, I should like to know what did."

"So would a good many others," said the minister.

"Law, now, Miss Roxy, you mus'n't mind him. Do you know that I believe he says these sort of things just to hear us talk? Of course he wouldn't think of puttin' his experience against yours."

"But, Mis' Kittridge," said Miss Emily, with a view of summoning a less controverted subject, "what a beautiful little boy that was, and what a striking providence that brought him into such a good family!"

"Yes," said Mrs. Kittridge; "but I'm sure I don't see what Mary Pennel is goin' to do with that boy, for she ain't got no more government than a twisted tow-string."

"Oh, the Cap'n, he'll lend a hand," said Miss Roxy, "it won't be easy gettin' roun' him; Cap'n bears a pretty steady hand when he sets out to drive."

CHAPTER X

"Well," said Miss Emily, "I do think that bringin' up children is the most awful responsibility, and I always wonder when I hear that any one dares to undertake it."

"It requires a great deal of resolution, certainly," said Mrs. Kittridge; "I'm sure I used to get a'most discouraged when my boys was young: they was a reg'lar set of wild ass's colts," she added, not perceiving the reflection on their paternity.

But the countenance of Mr. Sewell was all aglow with merriment, which did not break into a smile.

"Wal', Mis' Kittridge," said the Captain, "strikes me that you're gettin' pussonal."

"No, I ain't neither," said the literal Mrs. Kittridge, ignorant of the cause of the amusement which she saw around her; "but you wa'n't no help to me, you know; you was always off to sea, and the whole wear and tear on't came on me."

"Well, well, Polly, all's well that ends well; don't you think so, Mr. Sewell?"

"I haven't much experience in these matters," said Mr. Sewell, politely.

"No, indeed, that's what he hasn't, for he never will have a child round the house that he don't turn everything topsy-turvy for them," said Miss Emily.

"But I was going to remark," said Mr. Sewell, "that a friend of mine said once, that the woman that had brought up six boys deserved a seat among the martyrs; and that is rather my opinion."

"Wal', Polly, if you git up there, I hope you'll keep a seat for me."

"Cap'n Kittridge, what levity!" said his wife.

"I didn't begin it, anyhow," said the Captain.

Miss Emily interposed, and led the conversation back to the subject. "What a pity it is," she said, "that this poor child's family can never know anything about him. There may be those who would give all the world to know what has become of him; and when he comes to grow up, how sad he will feel to have no father and mother!"

"Sister," said Mr. Sewell, "you cannot think that a child brought up by Captain Pennel and his wife would ever feel as without father and mother."

"Why, no, brother, to be sure not. There's no doubt he will have everything done for him that a child could. But then it's a loss to lose one's real home."

"It may be a gracious deliverance," said Mr. Sewell—"who knows? We may as well take a cheerful view, and think that some kind wave has drifted the child away from an unfortunate destiny to a family where we are quite sure he will be brought up industriously and soberly, and in the fear of God."

"Well, I never thought of that," said Miss Roxy.

Miss Emily, looking at her brother, saw that he was speaking with a suppressed vehemence, as if some inner fountain of recollection at the moment were disturbed. But Miss Emily knew no more of the deeper parts of her brother's nature than a little bird that dips its beak into the sunny waters of some spring knows of its depths of coldness and shadow.

"Mis' Pennel was a-sayin' to me," said Mrs. Kittridge, "that I should ask you what was to be done about the bracelet they found. We don't know whether 'tis real gold and precious stones, or only glass and pinchbeck. Cap'n Kittridge he thinks it's real; and if 'tis, why then the question is, whether or no to try to sell it, or keep it for the boy agin he grows up. It may help find out who and what he is."

"And why should he want to find out?" said Mr. Sewell. "Why should he not grow up and think himself the son of Captain and Mrs. Pennel? What better lot could a boy be born to?"

"That may be, brother, but it can't be kept from him. Everybody knows how he was found, and you may be sure every bird of the air will tell him, and he'll grow up restless and wanting to know. Mis' Kittridge, have you got the bracelet handy?"

The fact was, little Miss Emily was just dying with curiosity to set her dancing black eyes upon it.

"Here it is," said Mrs. Kittridge, taking it from a drawer.

It was a bracelet of hair, of some curious foreign workmanship. A green enameled serpent, studded thickly with emeralds and with eyes of ruby, was curled around the clasp. A crystal plate covered a wide flat braid of hair, on which the letters "D.M." were curiously embroidered in a cipher of seed pearls. The whole was in style and workmanship quite different from any jewelry which ordinarily meets one's eye.

But what was remarkable was the expression in Mr. Sewell's face when this bracelet was put into his hand. Miss Emily had risen from table and brought it to him, leaning over him as she did so, and he turned his head a little to hold it in the light from the window, so that only she remarked the sudden expression of blank surprise and startled recognition which fell upon it. He seemed like a man who chokes down an exclamation; and rising hastily, he took the bracelet to the window, and standing with his back to the company, seemed to examine it with the minutest interest. After a few moments he turned and said, in a very composed tone, as if the subject were of no particular interest,—

"It is a singular article, so far as workmanship is concerned. The value of the gems in themselves is not great enough to make it worth while to sell it. It will be worth more as a curiosity than anything else. It will doubtless be an interesting relic to keep for the boy when he grows up."

"Well, Mr. Sewell, you keep it," said Mrs. Kittridge; "the Pennels told me to give it into your care."

"I shall commit it to Emily here; women have a native sympathy with anything in the jewelry line. She'll be sure to lay it up so securely that she won't even know where it is herself."

"Brother!"

"Come, Emily," said Mr. Sewell, "your hens will all go to roost on the wrong perch if you are not at home to see to them; so, if the Captain will set us across to Harpswell, I think we may as well be going."

"Why, what's your hurry?" said Mrs. Kittridge.

CHAPTER X

"Well," said Mr. Sewell, "firstly, there's the hens; secondly, the pigs; and lastly, the cow. Besides I shouldn't wonder if some of Emily's admirers should call on her this evening,—never any saying when Captain Broad may come in."

"Now, brother, you are too bad," said Miss Emily, as she bustled about her bonnet and shawl. "Now, that's all made up out of whole cloth. Captain Broad called last week a Monday, to talk to you about the pews, and hardly spoke a word to me. You oughtn't to say such things, 'cause it raises reports."

"Ah, well, then, I won't again," said her brother. "I believe, after all, it was Captain Badger that called twice."

"Brother!"

"And left you a basket of apples the second time."

"Brother, you know he only called to get some of my hoarhound for Mehitable's cough."

"Oh, yes, I remember."

"If you don't take care," said Miss Emily, "I'll tell where you call."

"Come, Miss Emily, you must not mind him," said Miss Roxy; "we all know his ways."

And now took place the grand leave-taking, which consisted first of the three women's standing in a knot and all talking at once, as if their very lives depended upon saying everything they could possibly think of before they separated, while Mr. Sewell and Captain Kittridge stood patiently waiting with the resigned air which the male sex commonly assume on such occasions; and when, after two or three "Come, Emily's," the group broke up only to form again on the door-step, where they were at it harder than ever, and a third occasion of the same sort took place at the bottom of the steps, Mr. Sewell was at last obliged by main force to drag his sister away in the middle of a sentence.

Miss Emily watched her brother shrewdly all the way home, but all traces of any uncommon feeling had passed away; and yet, with the restlessness of female curiosity, she felt quite sure that she had laid hold of the end of some skein of mystery, could she only find skill enough to unwind it.

She took up the bracelet, and held it in the fading evening light, and broke into various observations with regard to the singularity of the workmanship. Her brother seemed entirely absorbed in talking with Captain Kittridge about the brig Anna Maria, which was going to be launched from Pennel's wharf next Wednesday. But she, therefore, internally resolved to lie in wait for the secret in that confidential hour which usually preceded going to bed. Therefore, as soon as she had arrived at their quiet dwelling, she put in operation the most seducing little fire that ever crackled and snapped in a chimney, well knowing that nothing was more calculated to throw light into any hidden or concealed chamber of the soul than that enlivening blaze, which danced so merrily on her well-polished andirons, and made the old chintz sofa and the time-worn furniture so rich in remembrances of family comfort.

She then proceeded to divest her brother of his wig and his dress-coat, and to induct him into the flowing ease of a study-gown, crowning his well-shaven head with a black cap, and placing his slippers before the corner of a sofa nearest the fire. She observed him with satisfaction sliding into his seat, and then she trotted to a closet with a glass door in the corner of the room, and took down an old, quaintly-shaped silver cup, which had been an heirloom in their family, and was the only piece of plate which their modern domestic establishment could boast; and with this, down cellar she tripped, her little heels tapping lightly on each stair, and the hum of a song coming back after her as she sought the cider-barrel. Up again she came, and set the silver cup, with its clear amber contents, down by the fire, and then busied herself in making just the crispest, nicest square of toast to be eaten with it; for Miss Emily had conceived the idea that some little ceremony of this sort was absolutely necessary to do away all possible ill effects from a day's labor, and secure an uninterrupted night's repose. Having done all this, she took her knitting-work, and stationed herself just opposite to her brother.

It was fortunate for Miss Emily that the era of daily journals had not yet arisen upon the earth, because if it had, after all her care and pains, her brother would probably have taken up the evening paper, and holding it between his face and her, have read an hour or so in silence; but Mr. Sewell had not this resort. He knew perfectly well that he had excited his sister's curiosity on a subject where he could not gratify it, and therefore he took refuge in a kind of mild, abstracted air of quietude which bid defiance to all her little suggestions.

After in vain trying every indirect form, Miss Emily approached the subject more pointedly. "I thought that you looked very much interested in that poor woman to-day."

"She had an interesting face," said her brother, dryly.

"Was it like anybody that you ever saw?" said Miss Emily.

Her brother did not seem to hear her, but, taking the tongs, picked up the two ends of a stick that had just fallen apart, and arranged them so as to make a new blaze.

Miss Emily was obliged to repeat her question, whereat he started as one awakened out of a dream, and said,—

"Why, yes, he didn't know but she did; there were a good many women with black eyes and black hair,—Mrs. Kittridge, for instance."

"Why, I don't think that she looked like Mrs. Kittridge in the least," said Miss Emily, warmly.

"Oh, well! I didn't say she did," said her brother, looking drowsily at his watch; "why, Emily, it's getting rather late."

"What made you look so when I showed you that bracelet?" said Miss Emily, determined now to push the war to the heart of the enemy's country.

"Look how?" said her brother, leisurely moistening a bit of toast in his cider.

"Why, I never saw anybody look more wild and astonished than you did for a minute or two."

"I did, did I?" said her brother, in the same indifferent tone. "My dear child, what an active imagination you have. Did you ever look through a prism, Emily?"

"Why, no, Theophilus; what do you mean?"

"Well, if you should, you would see everybody and everything with a nice little bordering of rainbow around them; now the rainbow isn't on the things, but in the prism."

"Well, what's that to the purpose?" said Miss Emily, rather bewildered.

"Why, just this: you women are so nervous and excitable, that you are very apt to see your friends and the world in general with some coloring just as unreal. I am sorry for you, childie, but really I can't help you to get up a romance out of this bracelet. Well, good-night, Emily; take good care of yourself and go to bed;" and Mr. Sewell went to his room, leaving poor Miss Emily almost persuaded out of the sight of her own eyes.

CHAPTER XI

LITTLE ADVENTURERS

The little boy who had been added to the family of Zephaniah Pennel and his wife soon became a source of grave solicitude to that mild and long-suffering woman. For, as the reader may have seen, he was a resolute, self-willed little elf, and whatever his former life may have been, it was quite evident that these traits had been developed without any restraint.

Mrs. Pennel, whose whole domestic experience had consisted in rearing one very sensitive and timid daughter, who needed for her development only an extreme of tenderness, and whose conscientiousness was a law unto herself, stood utterly confounded before the turbulent little spirit to which her loving-kindness had opened so ready an asylum, and she soon discovered that it is one thing to take a human being to bring up, and another to know what to do with it after it is taken.

The child had the instinctive awe of Zephaniah which his manly nature and habits of command were fitted to inspire, so that morning and evening, when he was at home, he was demure enough; but while the good man was away all day, and sometimes on fishing excursions which often lasted a week, there was a chronic state of domestic warfare—a succession of skirmishes, pitched battles, long treaties, with divers articles of capitulation, ending, as treaties are apt to do, in open rupture on the first convenient opportunity.

Mrs. Pennel sometimes reflected with herself mournfully, and with many self-disparaging sighs, what was the reason that young master somehow contrived to keep her far more in awe of him than he was of her. Was she not evidently, as yet at least, bigger and stronger than he, able to hold his rebellious little hands, to lift and carry him, and to shut him up, if so she willed, in a dark closet, and even to administer to him that discipline of the birch which Mrs. Kittridge often and forcibly recommended as the great secret of her family prosperity? Was it not her duty, as everybody told her, to break his will while he was young?—a duty which hung like a millstone round the peaceable creature's neck, and weighed her down with a distressing sense of responsibility.

CHAPTER XI

Now, Mrs. Pennel was one of the people to whom self-sacrifice is constitutionally so much a nature, that self-denial for her must have consisted in standing up for her own rights, or having her own way when it crossed the will and pleasure of any one around her. All she wanted of a child, or in fact of any human creature, was something to love and serve. We leave it entirely to theologians to reconcile such facts with the theory of total depravity; but it is a fact that there are a considerable number of women of this class. Their life would flow on very naturally if it might consist only in giving, never in withholding—only in praise, never in blame—only in acquiescence, never in conflict; and the chief comfort of such women in religion is that it gives them at last an object for love without criticism, and for whom the utmost degree of self-abandonment is not idolatry, but worship.

Mrs. Pennel would gladly have placed herself and all she possessed at the disposition of the children; they might have broken her china, dug in the garden with her silver spoons, made turf alleys in her best room, drummed on her mahogany tea-table, filled her muslin drawer with their choicest shells and seaweed; only Mrs. Pennel knew that such kindness was no kindness, and that in the dreadful word responsibility, familiar to every New England mother's ear, there lay an awful summons to deny and to conflict where she could so much easier have conceded.

She saw that the tyrant little will would reign without mercy, if it reigned at all; and ever present with her was the uneasy sense that it was her duty to bring this erratic little comet within the laws of a well-ordered solar system,—a task to which she felt about as competent as to make a new ring for Saturn. Then, too, there was a secret feeling, if the truth must be told, of what Mrs. Kittridge would think about it; for duty is never more formidable than when she gets on the cap and gown of a neighbor; and Mrs. Kittridge, with her resolute voice and declamatory family government, had always been a secret source of uneasiness to poor Mrs. Pennel, who was one of those sensitive souls who can feel for a mile or more the sphere of a stronger neighbor. During all the years that they had lived side by side, there had been this shadowy, unconfessed feeling on the part of poor Mrs. Pennel, that Mrs. Kittridge thought her deficient in her favorite virtue of "resolution," as, in fact, in her inmost soul she knew she was;—but who wants to have one's weak places looked into by the sharp eyes of a neighbor who is strong precisely where we are weak? The trouble that one neighbor may give to another, simply by living within a mile of one, is incredible; but until this new accession to her family, Mrs. Pennel had always been able to comfort herself with the idea that the child under her particular training was as well-behaved as any of those of her more demonstrative friend. But now, all this consolation had been put to flight; she could not meet Mrs. Kittridge without most humiliating recollections.

On Sundays, when those sharp black eyes gleamed upon her through the rails of the neighboring pew, her very soul shrank within her, as she recollected all the compromises and defeats of the week before. It seemed to her that Mrs. Kittridge saw it all,—how she had ingloriously bought peace with gingerbread, instead of maintaining it by rightful authority,—how young master had sat up till nine o'clock on divers occasions, and even kept little Mara up for his lordly pleasure.

How she trembled at every movement of the child in the pew, dreading some patent and open impropriety which should bring scandal on her government! This was the more to be feared, as the first effort to initiate the youthful neophyte in the decorums of the sanctuary had proved anything but a success,—insomuch that Zephaniah Pennel had been obliged to carry him out from the church; therefore, poor Mrs. Pennel was thankful every Sunday when she got her little charge home without any distinct scandal and breach of the peace.

But, after all, he was such a handsome and engaging little wretch, attracting all eyes wherever he went, and so full of saucy drolleries, that it seemed to Mrs. Pennel that everything and everybody conspired to help her spoil him. There are two classes of human beings in this world: one class seem made to give love, and the other to take it. Now Mrs. Pennel and Mara belonged to the first class, and little Master Moses to the latter.

It was, perhaps, of service to the little girl to give to her delicate, shrinking, highly nervous organization the constant support of a companion so courageous, so richly blooded, and highly vitalized as the boy seemed to be. There was a fervid, tropical richness in his air that gave one a sense of warmth in looking at him, and made his Oriental name seem in good-keeping. He seemed an exotic that might have waked up under fervid Egyptian suns, and been found cradled among the lotus blossoms of old Nile; and the fair golden-haired girl seemed to be gladdened by his companionship, as if he supplied an element of vital warmth to her being. She seemed to incline toward him as naturally as a needle to a magnet.

The child's quickness of ear and the facility with which he picked up English were marvelous to observe. Evidently, he had been somewhat accustomed to the sound of it before, for there dropped out of his vocabulary, after he began to speak, phrases which would seem to betoken a longer familiarity with its idioms than could be equally accounted for by his present experience. Though the English evidently was not his native language, there had yet apparently been some effort to teach it to him, although the terror and confusion of the shipwreck seemed at first to have washed every former impression from his mind.

But whenever any attempt was made to draw him to speak of the past, of his mother, or of where he came from, his brow lowered gloomily, and he assumed that kind of moody, impenetrable gravity, which children at times will so strangely put on, and which baffle all attempts to look within them. Zephaniah Pennel used to call it putting up his dead-lights. Perhaps it was the dreadful association of agony and terror connected with the shipwreck, that thus confused and darkened the mirror of his mind the moment it was turned backward; but it was thought wisest by his new friends to avoid that class of subjects altogether—indeed, it was their wish that he might forget the past entirely, and remember them as his only parents.

Miss Roxy and Miss Ruey came duly, as appointed, to initiate the young pilgrim into the habiliments of a Yankee boy, endeavoring, at the same time, to drop into his mind such seeds of moral wisdom as might make the internal economy in time correspond to the exterior. But Miss Roxy declared that "of all the children that ever she see, he beat all for finding out new mischief,—the moment you'd make him understand he mustn't do one thing, he was right at another."

One of his exploits, however, had very nearly been the means of cutting short the materials of our story in the outset.

It was a warm, sunny afternoon, and the three women, being busy together with their stitching, had tied a sun-bonnet on little Mara, and turned the two loose upon the beach to pick up shells. All was serene, and quiet, and retired, and no possible danger could be apprehended. So up and down they trotted, till the spirit of adventure which ever burned in the breast of little Moses caught sight of a small canoe which had been moored just under the shadow of a cedar-covered rock. Forthwith he persuaded his little neighbor to go into it, and for a while they made themselves very gay, rocking it from side to side.

The tide was going out, and each retreating wave washed the boat up and down, till it came into the boy's curly head how beautiful it would be to sail out as he had seen men do,—and so, with much puffing and earnest tugging of his little brown hands, the boat at last was loosed from her moorings and pushed out on the tide, when both children laughed gayly to find themselves swinging and balancing on the amber surface, and watching the rings and sparkles of sunshine and the white pebbles below. Little Moses was glorious,—his adventures had begun,—and with a fairy-princess in his boat, he was going to stretch away to some of the islands of dreamland. He persuaded Mara to give him her pink sun-bonnet, which he placed for a pennon on a stick at the end of the boat, while he made a vehement dashing with another, first on one side of the boat and then on the other,—spattering the water in diamond showers, to the infinite amusement of the little maiden.

Meanwhile the tide waves danced them out and still outward, and as they went farther and farther from shore, the more glorious felt the boy. He had got Mara all to himself, and was going away with her from all grown people, who wouldn't let children do as they pleased,—who made them sit still in prayer-time, and took them to meeting, and kept so many things which they must not touch, or open, or play with. Two white sea-gulls came flying toward the children, and they stretched their little arms in welcome, nothing doubting but these fair creatures were coming at once to take passage with them for fairy-land. But the birds only dived and shifted and veered, turning their silvery sides toward the sun, and careering in circles round the children. A brisk little breeze, that came hurrying down from the land, seemed disposed to favor their unsubstantial enterprise,—for your winds, being a fanciful, uncertain tribe of people, are always for falling in with anything that is contrary to common sense. So the wind trolled them merrily along, nothing doubting that there might be time, if they hurried, to land their boat on the shore of some of the low-banked red clouds that lay in the sunset, where they could pick up shells,—blue and pink and purple,—enough to make them rich for life. The children were all excitement at the rapidity with which their little bark danced and rocked, as it floated outward to the broad, open ocean; at the blue, freshening waves, at the silver-glancing gulls, at the floating, white-winged ships, and at vague expectations of going rapidly somewhere, to something more beautiful still. And what is the happiness of the brightest hours of grown people more than this?

"Roxy," said Aunt Ruey innocently, "seems to me I haven't heard nothin' o' them children lately. They're so still, I'm 'fraid there's some mischief."

"Well, Ruey, you jist go and give a look at 'em," said Miss Roxy. "I declare, that boy! I never know what he will do next; but there didn't seem to be nothin' to get into out there but the sea, and the beach is so shelving, a body can't well fall into that."

Alas! good Miss Roxy, the children are at this moment tilting up and down on the waves, half a mile out to sea, as airily happy as the sea-gulls; and little Moses now thinks, with glorious scorn, of you and your press-board, as of grim shadows of restraint and bondage that shall never darken his free life more.

Both Miss Roxy and Mrs. Pennel were, however, startled into a paroxysm of alarm when poor Miss Ruey came screaming, as she entered the door,—

"As sure as you're alive, them chil'en are off in the boat,—they're out to sea, sure as I'm alive! What shall we do? The boat'll upset, and the sharks'll get 'em."

Miss Roxy ran to the window, and saw dancing and courtesying on the blue waves the little pinnace, with its fanciful pink pennon fluttered gayly by the indiscreet and flattering wind.

Poor Mrs. Pennel ran to the shore, and stretched her arms wildly, as if she would have followed them across the treacherous blue floor that heaved and sparkled between them.

"Oh, Mara, Mara! Oh, my poor little girl! Oh, poor children!"

"Well, if ever I see such a young un as that," soliloquized Miss Roxy from the chamber-window; "there they be, dancin' and giggitin' about; they'll have the boat upset in a minit, and the sharks are waitin' for 'em, no doubt. *I* b'lieve that ar young un's helped by the Evil One,—not a boat round, else I'd push off after 'em. Well, I don't see but we must trust in the Lord,—there don't seem to be much else to trust to," said the spinster, as she drew her head in grimly.

To say the truth, there was some reason for the terror of these most fearful suggestions; for not far from the place where the children embarked was Zephaniah's fish-drying ground, and multitudes of sharks came up with every rising tide, allured by the offal that was here constantly thrown into the sea. Two of these prowlers, outward-bound from their quest, were even now assiduously attending the little boat, and the children derived no small amusement from watching their motions in the pellucid water,—the boy occasionally almost upsetting the boat by valorous plunges at them with his stick. It was the most exhilarating and piquant entertainment he had found for many a day; and little Mara laughed in chorus at every lunge that he made.

What would have been the end of it all, it is difficult to say, had not some mortal power interfered before they had sailed finally away into the sunset. But it so happened, on this very afternoon, Rev. Mr. Sewell was out in a boat, busy in the very apostolic employment of catching fish, and looking up from one of the contemplative pauses which his occupation induced, he rubbed his eyes at the apparition which presented itself. A tiny little shell of a boat came drifting toward him, in which was a black-eyed boy, with cheeks like a pomegranate and lustrous tendrils of silky dark hair, and a little golden-haired girl, white as a water-lily, and looking ethereal enough to have risen out of the sea-foam. Both were in the very sparkle and effervescence of that fanciful glee which bubbles up from the golden, untried fountains of early childhood. Mr. Sewell, at a glance, comprehended the whole, and at once overhauling the tiny craft, he broke the spell of fairy-land, and constrained the little people to return to the confines, dull and dreary, of real and actual life.

Neither of them had known a doubt or a fear in that joyous trance of forbidden pleasure which shadowed with so many fears the wiser and more far-seeing heads and hearts of the grown people; nor was there enough language yet in common between the two classes to make the little ones comprehend the risk they had run. Perhaps so do our elder brothers, in our Father's house, look anxiously out when we are sailing gayly over life's sea,—over unknown depths,—amid threatening monsters,—but want words to tell us why what seems so bright is so dangerous.

Duty herself could not have worn a more rigid aspect than Miss Roxy, as she stood on the beach, press-board in hand; for she had forgotten to lay it down in the eagerness of her anxiety. She essayed to lay hold of the little hand of Moses to pull him from the boat, but he drew back, and, looking at her with a world of defiance in his great eyes, jumped magnanimously upon the beach. The spirit of Sir Francis Drake and of Christopher Columbus was swelling in his little body, and was he to be brought under by a dry-visaged woman with a press-board? In fact, nothing is more ludicrous about the escapades of children than the utter insensibility they feel to the dangers they have run, and the light esteem in which they hold the deep tragedy they create.

That night, when Zephaniah, in his evening exercise, poured forth most fervent thanksgivings for the deliverance, while Mrs. Pennel was sobbing in her handkerchief, Miss Roxy was much scandalized by seeing the young cause of all the disturbance sitting upon his heels, regarding the emotion of the kneeling party with his wide bright eyes, without a wink of compunction.

"Well, for her part," she said, "she hoped Cap'n Pennel would be blessed in takin' that ar boy; but she was sure she didn't see much that looked like it now."

The Rev. Mr. Sewell fished no more that day, for the draught from fairy-land with which he had filled his boat brought up many thoughts into his mind, which he pondered anxiously.

"Strange ways of God," he thought, "that should send to my door this child, and should wash upon the beach the only sign by which he could be identified. To what end or purpose? Hath the Lord a will in this matter, and what is it?"

So he thought as he slowly rowed homeward, and so did his thoughts work upon him that half way across the bay to Harpswell he slackened his oar without knowing it, and the boat lay drifting on the purple and gold-tinted mirror, like a speck between two eternities. Under such circumstances, even heads that have worn the clerical wig for years at times get a little dizzy and dreamy. Perhaps it was because of the impression made upon him by the sudden apparition of those great dark eyes and sable curls, that he now thought of the boy that he had found floating that afternoon, looking as if some tropical flower had been washed landward by a monsoon; and as the boat rocked and tilted, and the minister gazed dreamily downward into the wavering rings of purple, orange, and gold which spread out and out from it, gradually it seemed to him that a face much like the child's formed itself in the waters; but it was the face of a girl, young and radiantly beautiful, yet with those same eyes and curls,—he saw her distinctly, with her thousand rings of silky hair, bound with strings of pearls and clasped with strange gems, and she raised one arm imploringly to him, and on the wrist he saw the bracelet embroidered with seed pearls, and the letters D.M. "Ah, Dolores," he said, "well wert thou called so. Poor Dolores! I cannot help thee."

"What am I dreaming of?" said the Rev. Mr. Sewell. "It is my Thursday evening lecture on Justification, and Emily has got tea ready, and here I am catching cold out on the bay."

CHAPTER XII

SEA TALES

Mr. Sewell, as the reader may perhaps have inferred, was of a nature profoundly secretive. It was in most things quite as pleasant for him to keep matters to himself, as it was to Miss Emily to tell them to somebody else. She resembled more than anything one of those trotting, chattering little brooks that enliven the "back lot" of many a New England home, while he was like one of those wells you shall sometimes see by a deserted homestead, so long unused that ferns and lichens feather every stone down to the dark, cool water.

Dear to him was the stillness and coolness of inner thoughts with which no stranger intermeddles; dear to him every pendent fern-leaf of memory, every dripping moss of old recollection; and though the waters of his soul came up healthy and refreshing enough when one really must have them, yet one had to go armed with bucket and line and draw them up,—they never flowed. One of his favorite maxims was, that the only way to keep a secret was never to let any one suspect that you have one. And as he had one now, he had, as you have seen, done his best to baffle and put to sleep the feminine curiosity of his sister.

He rather wanted to tell her, too, for he was a good-natured brother, and would have liked to have given her the amount of pleasure the confidence would have produced; but then he reflected with dismay on the number of women in his parish with whom Miss Emily was on tea-drinking terms,—he thought of the wondrous solvent powers of that beverage in whose amber depths so many resolutions yea, and solemn vows, of utter silence have been dissolved like Cleopatra's pearls. He knew that an infusion of his secret would steam up from every cup of tea Emily should drink for six months to come, till gradually every particle would be dissolved and float in the air of common fame. No; it would not do.

You would have thought, however, that something was the matter with Mr. Sewell, had you seen him after he retired for the night, after he had so very indifferently dismissed the subject of Miss Emily's inquiries. For instead of retiring quietly to bed, as had been his habit for years at that hour, he locked his door, and then unlocked a desk of private papers, and emptied certain pigeon-holes of their contents, and for an hour or two sat unfolding and looking over old letters and papers; and when all this was done, he pushed them from him, and sat for a long time buried in thoughts which went down very, very deep into that dark and mossy well of which we have spoken.

Then he took a pen and wrote a letter, and addressed it to a direction for which he had searched through many piles of paper, and having done so, seemed to ponder, uncertainly, whether to send it or not. The Harpswell post-office was kept in Mr. Silas Perrit's store, and the letters were every one of them carefully and curiously investigated by all the gossips of the village, and as this was addressed to St. Augustine in Florida, he foresaw that before Sunday the news would be in every mouth in the parish that the minister had written to so and so in Florida, "and what do you s'pose it's about?"

"No, no," he said to himself, "that will never do; but at all events there is no hurry," and he put back the papers in order, put the letter with them, and locking his desk, looked at his watch and found it to be two o'clock, and so he went to bed to think the matter over.

Now, there may be some reader so simple as to feel a portion of Miss Emily's curiosity. But, my friend, restrain it, for Mr. Sewell will certainly, as we foresee, become less rather than more communicative on this subject, as he thinks upon it. Nevertheless, whatever it be that he knows or suspects, it is something which leads him to contemplate with more than usual interest this little mortal waif that has so strangely come ashore in his parish. He mentally resolves to study the child as minutely as possible, without betraying that he has any particular reason for being interested in him.

Therefore, in the latter part of this mild November afternoon, which he has devoted to pastoral visiting, about two months after the funeral, he steps into his little sail-boat, and stretches away for the shores of Orr's Island. He knows the sun will be down before he reaches there; but he sees, in the opposite horizon, the spectral, shadowy moon, only waiting for daylight to be gone to come out, calm and radiant, like a saintly friend neglected in the flush of prosperity, who waits patiently to enliven our hours of darkness.

As his boat-keel grazed the sands on the other side, a shout of laughter came upon his oar from behind a cedar-covered rock, and soon emerged Captain Kittridge, as long and lean and brown as the Ancient Mariner, carrying little Mara on one shoulder, while Sally and little Moses Pennel trotted on before.

It was difficult to say who in this whole group was in the highest spirits. The fact was that Mrs. Kittridge had gone to a tea-drinking over at Maquoit, and left the Captain as housekeeper and general overseer; and little Mara and Moses and Sally had been gloriously keeping holiday with him down by the boat-cove, where, to say the truth, few shavings were made, except those necessary to adorn the children's heads with flowing suits of curls of a most extraordinary effect. The aprons of all of them were full of these most unsubstantial specimens of woody treasure, which hung out in long festoons, looking of a yellow transparency in the evening light. But the delight of the children in their acquisitions was only equaled by that of grown-up people in possessions equally fanciful in value.

The mirth of the little party, however, came to a sudden pause as they met the minister. Mara clung tight to the Captain's neck, and looked out slyly under her curls. But the little Moses made a step forward, and fixed his bold, dark, inquisitive eyes upon him. The fact was, that the minister had been impressed upon the boy, in his few visits to the "meeting," as such a grand and mysterious reason for good behavior, that he seemed resolved to embrace the first opportunity to study him close at hand.

"Well, my little man," said Mr. Sewell, with an affability which he could readily assume with children, "you seem to like to look at me."

"I do like to look at you," said the boy gravely, continuing to fix his great black eyes upon him.

"I see you do, my little fellow."

"Are you the Lord?" said the child, solemnly.

"Am I what?"

"The Lord," said the boy.

"No, indeed, my lad," said Mr. Sewell, smiling. "Why, what put that into your little head?"

"I thought you were," said the boy, still continuing to study the pastor with attention. "Miss Roxy said so."

"It's curious what notions chil'en will get in their heads," said Captain Kittridge. "They put this and that together and think it over, and come out with such queer things."

"But," said the minister, "I have brought something for you all;" saying which he drew from his pocket three little bright-cheeked apples, and gave one to each child; and then taking the hand of the little Moses in his own, he walked with him toward the house-door.

Mrs. Pennel was sitting in her clean kitchen, busily spinning at the little wheel, and rose flushed with pleasure at the honor that was done her.

"Pray, walk in, Mr. Sewell," she said, rising, and leading the way toward the penetralia of the best room.

"Now, Mrs. Pennel, I am come here for a good sit-down by your kitchen-fire, this evening," said Mr. Sewell. "Emily has gone out to sit with old Mrs. Broad, who is laid up with the rheumatism, and so I am turned loose to pick up my living on the parish, and you must give me a seat for a while in your kitchen corner. Best rooms are always cold."

"The minister's right," said Captain Kittridge. "When rooms ain't much set in, folks never feel so kind o' natural in 'em. So you jist let me put on a good back-log and forestick, and build up a fire to tell stories by this evening. My wife's gone out to tea, too," he said, with an elastic skip.

And in a few moments the Captain had produced in the great cavernous chimney a foundation for a fire that promised breadth, solidity, and continuance. A great back-log, embroidered here and there with tufts of green or grayish moss, was first flung into the capacious arms of the fireplace, and a smaller log placed above it. "Now, all you young uns go out and bring in chips," said the Captain. "There's capital ones out to the wood-pile."

Mr. Sewell was pleased to see the flash that came from the eyes of little Moses at this order, how energetically he ran before the others, and came with glowing cheeks and distended arms, throwing down great white chips with their green mossy bark, scattering tufts on the floor. "Good," said he softly to himself, as he leaned on the top of his gold-headed cane; "there's energy, ambition, muscle;" and he nodded his head once or twice to some internal decision.

"There!" said the Captain, rising out of a perfect whirlwind of chips and pine kindlings with which in his zeal he had bestrown the wide, black stone hearth, and pointing to the tongues of flame that were leaping and blazing up through the crevices of the dry pine wood which he had intermingled plentifully with the more substantial fuel,—"there, Mis' Pennel, ain't I a master-hand at a fire? But I'm really sorry I've dirtied your floor," he said, as he brushed down his pantaloons, which were covered with bits of grizzly moss, and looked on the surrounding desolations; "give me a broom, I can sweep up now as well as any woman."

"Oh, never mind," said Mrs. Pennel, laughing, "I'll sweep up."

"Well, now, Mis' Pennel, you're one of the women that don't get put out easy; ain't ye?" said the Captain, still contemplating his fire with a proud and watchful eye.

"Law me!" he exclaimed, glancing through the window, "there's the Cap'n a-comin'. I'm jist goin' to give a look at what he's brought in. Come, chil'en," and the Captain disappeared with all three of the children at his heels, to go down to examine the treasures of the fishing-smack.

Mr. Sewell seated himself cozily in the chimney corner and sank into a state of half-dreamy reverie; his eyes fixed on the fairest sight one can see of a frosty autumn twilight—a crackling wood-fire.

Mrs. Pennel moved soft-footed to and fro, arraying her tea-table in her own finest and pure damask, and bringing from hidden stores her best china and newest silver, her choicest sweetmeats and cake—whatever was fairest and nicest in her house—to honor her unexpected guest.

Mr. Sewell's eyes followed her occasionally about the room, with an expression of pleased and curious satisfaction. He was taking it all in as an artistic picture—that simple, kindly hearth, with its mossy logs, yet steaming with the moisture of the wild woods; the table so neat, so cheery with its many little delicacies, and refinements of appointment, and its ample varieties to tempt the appetite; and then the Captain coming in, yet fresh and hungry from his afternoon's toil, with the children trotting before him.

"And this is the inheritance he comes into," he murmured; "healthy—wholesome—cheerful—secure: how much better than hot, stifling luxury!"

Here the minister's meditations were interrupted by the entrance of all the children, joyful and loquacious. Little Moses held up a string of mackerel, with their graceful bodies and elegantly cut fins.

CHAPTER XII

"Just a specimen of the best, Mary," said Captain Pennel. "I thought I'd bring 'em for Miss Emily."

"Miss Emily will be a thousand times obliged to you," said Mr. Sewell, rising up.

As to Mara and Sally, they were reveling in apronfuls of shells and seaweed, which they bustled into the other room to bestow in their spacious baby-house.

And now, after due time for Zephaniah to assume a land toilet, all sat down to the evening meal.

After supper was over, the Captain was besieged by the children. Little Mara mounted first into his lap, and nestled herself quietly under his coat—Moses and Sally stood at each knee.

"Come, now," said Moses, "you said you would tell us about the mermen to-night."

"Yes, and the mermaids," said Sally. "Tell them all you told me the other night in the trundle-bed."

Sally valued herself no little on the score of the Captain's talent as a romancer.

"You see, Moses," she said, volubly, "father saw mermen and mermaids a plenty of them in the West Indies."

"Oh, never mind about 'em now," said Captain Kittridge, looking at Mr. Sewell's corner.

"Why not, father? mother isn't here," said Sally, innocently.

A smile passed round the faces of the company, and Mr. Sewell said, "Come, Captain, no modesty; we all know you have as good a faculty for telling a story as for making a fire."

"Do tell me what mermen are," said Moses.

"Wal'," said the Captain, sinking his voice confidentially, and hitching his chair a little around, "mermen and maids is a kind o' people that have their world jist like our'n, only it's down in the bottom of the sea, 'cause the bottom of the sea has its mountains and its valleys, and its trees and its bushes, and it stands to reason there should be people there too."

Moses opened his broad black eyes wider than usual, and looked absorbed attention.

"Tell 'em about how you saw 'em," said Sally.

"Wal', yes," said Captain Kittridge; "once when I was to the Bahamas,—it was one Sunday morning in June, the first Sunday in the month,—we cast anchor pretty nigh a reef of coral, and I was jist a-sittin' down to read my Bible, when up comes a merman over the side of the ship, all dressed as fine as any old beau that ever ye see, with cocked hat and silk stockings, and shoe-buckles, and his clothes were sea-green, and his shoe-buckles shone like diamonds."

"Do you suppose they were diamonds, really?" said Sally.

"Wal', child, I didn't ask him, but I shouldn't be surprised, from all I know of their ways, if they was," said the Captain, who had now got so wholly into the spirit of his fiction that he no longer felt embarrassed by the minister's presence, nor saw the look of amusement with which he was listening to him in his chimney-corner. "But, as I was sayin', he came up to me, and made the politest bow that ever ye see, and says he, 'Cap'n Kittridge, I presume,' and says I, 'Yes, sir.' 'I'm sorry to interrupt your reading,' says he; and says I, 'Oh, no matter, sir.' 'But,' says he, 'if you would only be so good as to move your anchor. You've cast anchor right before my front-door, and my wife and family can't get out to go to meetin'.'"

"Why, do they go to meeting in the bottom of the sea?" said Moses.

"Law, bless you sonny, yes. Why, Sunday morning, when the sea was all still, I used to hear the bass-viol a-soundin' down under the waters, jist as plain as could be,—and psalms and preachin'. I've reason to think there's as many hopefully pious mermaids as there be folks," said the Captain.

"But," said Moses, "you said the anchor was before the front-door, so the family couldn't get out,—how did the merman get out?"

"Oh! he got out of the scuttle on the roof," said the Captain, promptly.

"And did you move your anchor?" said Moses.

"Why, child, yes, to be sure I did; he was such a gentleman I wanted to oblige him,—it shows you how important it is always to be polite," said the Captain, by way of giving a moral turn to his narrative.

Mr. Sewell, during the progress of this story, examined the Captain with eyes of amused curiosity. His countenance was as fixed and steady, and his whole manner of reciting as matter-of-fact and collected, as if he were relating some of the every-day affairs of his boat-building.

"Wal', Sally," said the Captain, rising, after his yarn had proceeded for an indefinite length in this manner, "you and I must be goin'. I promised your ma you shouldn't be up late, and we have a long walk home,—besides it's time these little folks was in bed."

The children all clung round the Captain, and could hardly be persuaded to let him go.

When he was gone, Mrs. Pennel took the little ones to their nest in an adjoining room.

Mr. Sewell approached his chair to that of Captain Pennel, and began talking to him in a tone of voice so low, that we have never been able to make out exactly what he was saying. Whatever it might be, however, it seemed to give rise to an anxious consultation. "I did not think it advisable to tell *any* one this but yourself, Captain Pennel. It is for you to decide, in view of the probabilities I have told you, what you will do."

"Well," said Zephaniah, "since you leave it to me, I say, let us keep him. It certainly seems a marked providence that he has been thrown upon us as he has, and the Lord seemed to prepare a way for him in our hearts. I am well able to afford it, and Mis' Pennel, she agrees to it, and on the whole I don't think we'd best go back on our steps; besides, our little Mara has thrived since he came under our roof. He is, to be sure, kind o' masterful, and I shall have to take him off Mis' Pennel's hands before long, and put him into the sloop. But, after all, there seems to be the makin' of a man in him, and when we are called away, why he'll be as a brother to poor little Mara. Yes, I think it's best as 'tis."

The minister, as he flitted across the bay by moonlight, felt relieved of a burden. His secret was locked up as safe in the breast of Zephaniah Pennel as it could be in his own.

CHAPTER XIII

BOY AND GIRL

Zephaniah Pennel was what might be called a Hebrew of the Hebrews.

New England, in her earlier days, founding her institutions on the Hebrew Scriptures, bred better Jews than Moses could, because she read Moses with the amendments of Christ.

The state of society in some of the districts of Maine, in these days, much resembled in its spirit that which Moses labored to produce in ruder ages. It was entirely democratic, simple, grave, hearty, and sincere,—solemn and religious in its daily tone, and yet, as to all material good, full of wholesome thrift and prosperity. Perhaps, taking the average mass of the people, a more healthful and desirable state of society never existed. Its better specimens had a simple Doric grandeur unsurpassed in any age. The bringing up a child in this state of society was a far more simple enterprise than in our modern times, when the factious wants and aspirations are so much more developed.

Zephaniah Pennel was as high as anybody in the land. He owned not only the neat little schooner, "Brilliant," with divers small fishing-boats, but also a snug farm, adjoining the brown house, together with some fresh, juicy pasture-lots on neighboring islands, where he raised mutton, unsurpassed even by the English South-down, and wool, which furnished homespun to clothe his family on all every-day occasions.

Mrs. Pennel, to be sure, had silks and satins, and flowered India chintz, and even a Cashmere shawl, the fruits of some of her husband's earlier voyages, which were, however, carefully stowed away for occasions so high and mighty, that they seldom saw the light. *Not to wear best things every day* was a maxim of New England thrift as little disputed as any verse of the catechism; and so Mrs. Pennel found the stuff gown of her own dyeing and spinning so respectable for most purposes, that it figured even in the meeting-house itself, except on the very finest of Sundays, when heaven and earth seemed alike propitious. A person can well afford to wear homespun stuff to meeting, who is buoyed up by a secret consciousness of an abundance of fine things that could be worn, if one were so disposed, and everybody respected Mrs. Pennel's homespun the more, because they thought of the things she didn't wear.

As to advantages of education, the island, like all other New England districts, had its common school, where one got the key of knowledge,—for having learned to read, write, and cipher, the young fellow of those regions commonly regarded himself as in possession of all that a man needs, to help himself to any further acquisitions he might desire. The boys then made fishing voyages to the Banks, and those who were so disposed took their books with them. If a boy did not wish to be bored with study, there was nobody to force him; but if a bright one saw visions of future success in life lying through the avenues of knowledge, he found many a leisure hour to pore over his books, and work out the problems of navigation directly over the element they were meant to control.

Four years having glided by since the commencement of our story, we find in the brown house of Zephaniah Pennel a tall, well-knit, handsome boy of ten years, who knows no fear of wind or sea; who can set you over from Orr's Island to Harpswell, either in sail or row-boat, he thinks, as well as any man living; who knows every rope of the schooner Brilliant, and fancies he could command it as well as "father" himself; and is supporting himself this spring, during the tamer drudgeries of driving plough, and dropping potatoes, with the glorious vision of being taken this year on the annual trip to "the Banks," which comes on after planting. He reads fluently,—witness the "Robinson Crusoe," which never departs from under his pillow, and Goldsmith's "History of Greece and Rome," which good Mr. Sewell has lent him,—and he often brings shrewd criticisms on the character and course of Romulus or Alexander into the common current of every-day life, in a way that brings a smile over the grave face of Zephaniah, and makes Mrs. Pennel think the boy certainly ought to be sent to college.

As for Mara, she is now a child of seven, still adorned with long golden curls, still looking dreamily out of soft hazel eyes into some unknown future not her own. She has no dreams for herself—they are all for Moses. For his sake she has learned all the womanly little accomplishments which Mrs. Kittridge has dragooned into Sally. She knits his mittens and his stockings, and hems his pocket-handkerchiefs, and aspires to make his shirts all herself. Whatever book Moses reads, forthwith she aspires to read too, and though three years younger, reads with a far more precocious insight.

Her little form is slight and frail, and her cheek has a clear transparent brilliancy quite different from the rounded one of the boy; she looks not exactly in ill health, but has that sort of transparent appearance which one fancies might be an attribute of fairies and sylphs. All her outward senses are finer and more acute than his, and finer and more delicate all the attributes of her mind. Those who contend against giving woman the same education as man do it on the ground that it would make the woman unfeminine, as if Nature had done her work so slightly that it could be so easily raveled and knit over. In fact, there is a masculine and a feminine element in all knowledge, and a man and a woman put to the same study extract only what their nature fits them to see, so that knowledge can be fully orbed only when the two unite in the search and share the spoils.

When Moses was full of Romulus and Numa, Mara pondered the story of the nymph Egeria—sweet parable, in which lies all we have been saying. Her trust in him was boundless. He was a constant hero in her eyes, and in her he found a steadfast believer as to all possible feats and exploits to which he felt himself competent, for the boy often had privately assured her that he could command the Brilliant as well as father himself.

Spring had already come, loosing the chains of ice in all the bays and coves round Harpswell, Orr's Island, Maquoit, and Middle Bay. The magnificent spruces stood forth in their gala-dresses, tipped on every point with vivid emerald; the silver firs exuded from their tender shoots the fragrance of ripe pineapple; the white pines shot forth long weird fingers at the end of their fringy boughs; and even every little mimic evergreen in the shadows at their feet was made beautiful by the addition of a vivid border of green on the sombre coloring of its last year's leaves. Arbutus, fragrant with its clean, wholesome odors, gave forth its thousand dewy pink blossoms, and the trailing Linnea borealis hung its pendent twin bells round every mossy stump and old rock damp with green forest mould. The green and vermilion matting of the partridge-berry was impearled with white velvet blossoms, the checkerberry hung forth a translucent bell under its varnished green leaf, and a thousand more fairy bells, white or red, hung on blueberry and huckleberry bushes. The little Pearl of Orr's Island had wandered many an hour gathering bouquets of all these, to fill the brown house with sweetness when her grandfather and Moses should come in from work.

The love of flowers seemed to be one of her earliest characteristics, and the young spring flowers of New England, in their airy delicacy and fragility, were much like herself; and so strong seemed the affinity between them, that not only Mrs. Pennel's best India china vases on the keeping-room mantel were filled, but here stood a tumbler of scarlet rock columbine, and there a bowl of blue and white violets, and in another place a saucer of shell-tinted crowfoot, blue liverwort, and white anemone, so that Zephaniah Pennel was wont to say there wasn't a drink of water to be got, for Mara's flowers; but he always said it with a smile that made his weather-beaten, hard features look like a rock lit up by a sunbeam. Little Mara was the pearl of the old seaman's life, every finer particle of his nature came out in her concentrated and polished, and he often wondered at a creature so ethereal belonging to him—as if down on some shaggy sea-green rock an old pearl oyster should muse and marvel on the strange silvery mystery of beauty that was growing in the silence of his heart.

But May has passed; the arbutus and the Linnea are gone from the woods, and the pine tips have grown into young shoots, which wilt at noon under a direct reflection from sun and sea, and the blue sky has that metallic clearness and brilliancy which distinguishes those regions, and the planting is at last over, and this very morning Moses is to set off in the Brilliant for his first voyage to the Banks. Glorious knight he! the world all before him, and the blood of ten years racing and throbbing in his veins as he talks knowingly of hooks, and sinkers, and bait, and lines, and wears proudly the red flannel shirt which Mara had just finished for him.

"How I do wish I were going with you!" she says. "I could do something, couldn't I—take care of your hooks, or something?"

"Pooh!" said Moses, sublimely regarding her while he settled the collar of his shirt, "you're a girl; and what can girls do at sea? you never like to catch fish—it always makes you cry to see 'em flop."

"Oh, yes, poor fish!" said Mara, perplexed between her sympathy for the fish and her desire for the glory of her hero, which must be founded on their pain; "I can't help feeling sorry when they gasp so."

"Well, and what do you suppose you would do when the men are pulling up twenty and forty pounder?" said Moses, striding sublimely. "Why, they flop so, they'd knock you over in a minute."

"Do they? Oh, Moses, do be careful. What if they should hurt you?"

"Hurt me!" said Moses, laughing; "that's a good one. I'd like to see a fish that could hurt me."

"Do hear that boy talk!" said Mrs. Pennel to her husband, as they stood within their chamber-door.

"Yes, yes," said Captain Pennel, smiling; "he's full of the matter. I believe he'd take the command of the schooner this morning, if I'd let him."

The Brilliant lay all this while courtesying on the waves, which kissed and whispered to the little coquettish craft. A fairer June morning had not risen on the shores that week; the blue mirror of the ocean was all dotted over with the tiny white sails of fishing-craft bound on the same errand, and the breeze that was just crisping the waters had the very spirit of energy and adventure in it.

Everything and everybody was now on board, and she began to spread her fair wings, and slowly and gracefully to retreat from the shore. Little Moses stood on the deck, his black curls blowing in the wind, and his large eyes dancing with excitement,—his clear olive complexion and glowing cheeks well set off by his red shirt.

Mrs. Pennel stood with Mara on the shore to see them go. The fair little golden-haired Ariadne shaded her eyes with one arm, and stretched the other after her Theseus, till the vessel grew smaller, and finally seemed to melt away into the eternal blue. Many be the wives and lovers that have watched those little fishing-craft as they went gayly out like this, but have waited long—too long—and seen them again no more. In night and fog they have gone down under the keel of some ocean packet or Indiaman, and sunk with brave hearts and hands, like a bubble in the mighty waters. Yet Mrs. Pennel did not turn back to her house in apprehension of this. Her husband had made so many voyages, and always returned safely, that she confidently expected before long to see them home again.

The next Sunday the seat of Zephaniah Pennel was vacant in church. According to custom, a note was put up asking prayers for his safe return, and then everybody knew that he was gone to the Banks; and as the roguish, handsome face of Moses was also missing, Miss Roxy whispered to Miss Ruey, "There! Captain Pennel's took Moses on his first voyage. We must contrive to call round on Mis' Pennel afore long. She'll be lonesome."

Sunday evening Mrs. Pennel was sitting pensively with little Mara by the kitchen hearth, where they had been boiling the tea-kettle for their solitary meal. They heard a brisk step without, and soon Captain and Mrs. Kittridge made their appearance.

"Good evening, Mis' Pennel," said the Captain; "I's a-tellin' my good woman we must come down and see how you's a-getting along. It's raly a work of necessity and mercy proper for the Lord's day. Rather lonesome, now the Captain's gone, ain't ye? Took little Moses, too, I see. Wasn't at meetin' to-day, so I says, Mis' Kittridge, we'll just step down and chirk 'em up a little."

"I didn't really know how to come," said Mrs. Kittridge, as she allowed Mrs. Pennel to take her bonnet; "but Aunt Roxy's to our house now, and she said she'd see to Sally. So you've let the boy go to the Banks? He's young, ain't he, for that?"

"Not a bit of it," said Captain Kittridge. "Why, I was off to the Banks long afore I was his age, and a capital time we had of it, too. Golly! how them fish did bite! We stood up to our knees in fish before we'd fished half an hour."

Mara, who had always a shy affinity for the Captain, now drew towards him and climbed on his knee. "Did the wind blow very hard?" she said.

"What, my little maid?"

"Does the wind blow at the Banks?"

"Why, yes, my little girl, that it does, sometimes; but then there ain't the least danger. Our craft ride out storms like live creatures. I've stood it out in gales that was tight enough, I'm sure. 'Member once I turned in 'tween twelve and one, and hadn't more'n got asleep, afore I came *clump* out of my berth, and found everything upside down. And 'stead of goin' upstairs to get on deck, I had to go right down. Fact was, that 'ere vessel jist turned clean over in the water, and come right side up like a duck."

"Well, now, Cap'n, I wouldn't be tellin' such a story as that," said his helpmeet.

"Why, Polly, what do you know about it? you never was to sea. We did turn clear over, for I 'member I saw a bunch of seaweed big as a peck measure stickin' top of the mast next day. Jist shows how safe them ar little fishing craft is,—for all they look like an egg-shell on the mighty deep, as Parson Sewell calls it."

"I was very much pleased with Mr. Sewell's exercise in prayer this morning," said Mrs. Kittridge; "it must have been a comfort to you, Mis' Pennel."

"It was, to be sure," said Mrs. Pennel.

"Puts me in mind of poor Mary Jane Simpson. Her husband went out, you know, last June, and hain't been heard of since. Mary Jane don't really know whether to put on mourning or not."

"Law! I don't think Mary Jane need give up yet," said the Captain. "'Member one year I was out, we got blowed clear up to Baffin's Bay, and got shut up in the ice, and had to go ashore and live jist as we could among them Esquimaux. Didn't get home for a year. Old folks had clean giv' us up. Don't need never despair of folks gone to sea, for they's sure to turn up, first or last."

"But I hope," said Mara, apprehensively, "that grandpapa won't get blown up to Baffin's Bay. I've seen that on his chart,—it's a good ways."

"And then there's them 'ere icebergs," said Mrs. Kittridge; "I'm always 'fraid of running into them in the fog."

"Law!" said Captain Kittridge, "I've met 'em bigger than all the colleges up to Brunswick,—great white bears on 'em,—hungry as Time in the Primer. Once we came kersmash on to one of 'em, and if the Flying Betsey hadn't been made of whalebone and injer-rubber, she'd a-been stove all to pieces. Them white bears, they was so hungry, that they stood there with the water jist runnin' out of their chops in a perfect stream."

"Oh, dear, dear," said Mara, with wide round eyes, "what will Moses do if they get on the icebergs?"

"Yes," said Mrs. Kittridge, looking solemnly at the child through the black bows of her spectacles, "we can truly say:—

"'Dangers stand thick through all the ground,
To push us to the tomb,'

as the hymn-book says."

The kind-hearted Captain, feeling the fluttering heart of little Mara, and seeing the tears start in her eyes, addressed himself forthwith to consolation. "Oh, never you mind, Mara," he said, "there won't nothing hurt 'em. Look at me. Why, I've been everywhere on the face of the earth. I've been on icebergs, and among white bears and Indians, and seen storms that would blow the very hair off your head, and here I am, dry and tight as ever. You'll see 'em back before long."

The cheerful laugh with which the Captain was wont to chorus his sentences sounded like the crackling of dry pine wood on the social hearth. One would hardly hear it without being lightened in heart; and little Mara gazed at his long, dry, ropy figure, and wrinkled thin face, as a sort of monument of hope; and his uproarious laugh, which Mrs. Kittridge sometimes ungraciously compared to "the crackling of thorns under a pot," seemed to her the most delightful thing in the world.

"Mary Jane was a-tellin' me," resumed Mrs. Kittridge, "that when her husband had been out a month, she dreamed she see him, and three other men, a-floatin' on an iceberg."

"Laws," said Captain Kittridge, "that's jist what my old mother dreamed about me, and 'twas true enough, too, till we got off the ice on to the shore up in the Esquimaux territory, as I was a-tellin'. So you tell Mary Jane she needn't look out for a second husband *yet*, for that ar dream's a sartin sign he'll be back."

"Cap'n Kittridge!" said his helpmeet, drawing herself up, and giving him an austere glance over her spectacles; "how often must I tell you that there *is* subjects which shouldn't be treated with levity?"

"Who's been a-treatin' of 'em with levity?" said the Captain. "I'm sure I ain't. Mary Jane's good-lookin', and there's plenty of young fellows as sees it as well as me. I declare, she looked as pretty as any young gal when she ris up in the singers' seats to-day. Put me in mind of you, Polly, when I first come home from the Injies."

"Oh, come now, Cap'n Kittridge! we're gettin' too old for that sort o' talk."

"We ain't too old, be we, Mara?" said the Captain, trotting the little girl gayly on his knee; "and we ain't afraid of icebergs and no sich, be we? I tell you they's a fine sight of a bright day; they has millions of steeples, all white and glistering, like the New Jerusalem, and the white bears have capital times trampin' round on 'em. Wouldn't little Mara like a great, nice white bear to ride on, with his white fur, so soft and warm, and a saddle made of pearls, and a gold bridle?"

"You haven't seen any little girls ride so," said Mara, doubtfully.

"I shouldn't wonder if I had; but you see, Mis' Kittridge there, she won't let me tell all I know," said the Captain, sinking his voice to a confidential tone; "you jist wait till we get alone."

"But, you are sure," said Mara, confidingly, in return, "that white bears will be kind to Moses?"

"Lord bless you, yes, child, the kindest critturs in the world they be, if you only get the right side of 'em," said the Captain.

"Oh, yes! because," said Mara, "I know how good a wolf was to Romulus and Remus once, and nursed them when they were cast out to die. I read that in the Roman history."

"Jist so," said the Captain, enchanted at this historic confirmation of his apocrypha.

"And so," said Mara, "if Moses should happen to get on an iceberg, a bear might take care of him, you know."

"Jist so, jist so," said the Captain; "so don't you worry your little curly head one bit. Some time when you come down to see Sally, we'll go down to the cove, and I'll tell you lots of stories about chil'en that have been fetched up by white bears, jist like Romulus and what's his name there."

"Come, Mis' Kittridge," added the cheery Captain; "you and I mustn't be keepin' the folks up till nine o'clock."

"Well now," said Mrs. Kittridge, in a doleful tone, as she began to put on her bonnet, "Mis' Pennel, you must keep up your spirits—it's one's duty to take cheerful views of things. I'm sure many's the night, when the Captain's been gone to sea, I've laid and shook in my bed, hearin' the wind blow, and thinking what if I should be left a lone widow."

"There'd a-been a dozen fellows a-wanting to get you in six months, Polly," interposed the Captain. "Well, good-night, Mis' Pennel; there'll be a splendid haul of fish at the Banks this year, or there's no truth in signs. Come, my little Mara, got a kiss for the dry old daddy? That's my good girl. Well, good night, and the Lord bless you."

And so the cheery Captain took up his line of march homeward, leaving little Mara's head full of dazzling visions of the land of romance to which Moses had gone. She was yet on that shadowy boundary between the dreamland of childhood and the real land of life; so all things looked to her quite possible; and gentle white bears, with warm, soft fur and pearl and gold saddles, walked through her dreams, and the victorious curls of Moses appeared, with his bright eyes and cheeks, over glittering pinnacles of frost in the ice-land.

CHAPTER XIV

THE ENCHANTED ISLAND

June and July passed, and the lonely two lived a quiet life in the brown house. Everything was so still and fair—no sound but the coming and going tide, and the swaying wind among the pine-trees, and the tick of the clock, and the whirr of the little wheel as Mrs. Pennel sat spinning in her door in the mild weather. Mara read the Roman history through again, and began it a third time, and read over and over again the stories and prophecies that pleased her in the Bible, and pondered the wood-cuts and texts in a very old edition of Æsop's Fables; and as she wandered in the woods, picking fragrant bayberries and gathering hemlock, checkerberry, and sassafras to put in the beer which her grandmother brewed, she mused on the things that she read till her little mind became a tabernacle of solemn, quaint, dreamy forms, where old Judean kings and prophets, and Roman senators and warriors, marched in and out in shadowy rounds. She invented long dramas and conversations in which they performed imaginary parts, and it would not have appeared to the child in the least degree surprising either to have met an angel in the woods, or to have formed an intimacy with some talking wolf or bear, such as she read of in Æsop's Fables.

One day, as she was exploring the garret, she found in an old barrel of cast-off rubbish a bit of reading which she begged of her grandmother for her own. It was the play of the "Tempest," torn from an old edition of Shakespeare, and was in that delightfully fragmentary condition which most particularly pleases children, because they conceive a mutilated treasure thus found to be more especially their own property—something like a rare wild-flower or sea-shell. The pleasure which thoughtful and imaginative children sometimes take in reading that which they do not and cannot fully comprehend is one of the most common and curious phenomena of childhood.

And so little Mara would lie for hours stretched out on the pebbly beach, with the broad open ocean before her and the whispering pines and hemlocks behind her, and pore over this poem, from which she collected dim, delightful images of a lonely island, an old enchanter, a beautiful girl, and a spirit not quite like those in the Bible, but a very probable one to her mode of thinking. As for old Caliban, she fancied him with a face much like that of a huge skate-fish she had once seen drawn ashore in one of her grandfather's nets; and then there was the beautiful young Prince Ferdinand, much like what Moses would be when he was grown up—and how glad she would be to pile up his wood for him, if any old enchanter should set him to work!

One attribute of the child was a peculiar shamefacedness and shyness about her inner thoughts, and therefore the wonder that this new treasure excited, the host of surmises and dreams to which it gave rise, were never mentioned to anybody. That it was all of it as much authentic fact as the Roman history, she did not doubt, but whether it had happened on Orr's Island or some of the neighboring ones, she had not exactly made up her mind. She resolved at her earliest leisure to consult Captain Kittridge on the subject, wisely considering that it much resembled some of his fishy and aquatic experiences.

Some of the little songs fixed themselves in her memory, and she would hum them as she wandered up and down the beach.

"Come unto these yellow sands,
And then take hands;
Courtsied when you have and kissed
The wild waves whist,
Foot it featly here and there;
And, sweet sprites, the burthen bear."

And another which pleased her still more:—

"Full fathom five thy father lies;
Of his bones are coral made,
Those are pearls that were his eyes:
Nothing of him that can fade
But doth suffer a sea-change
Into something rich and strange;
Sea-nymphs hourly ring his knell:
Hark, now I hear them—ding-dong, bell."

These words she pondered very long, gravely revolving in her little head whether they described the usual course of things in the mysterious under-world that lay beneath that blue spangled floor of the sea; whether everybody's eyes changed to pearl, and their bones to coral, if they sunk down there; and whether the sea-nymphs spoken of were the same as the mermaids that Captain Kittridge had told of. Had he not said that the bell rung for church of a Sunday morning down under the waters?

Mara vividly remembered the scene on the sea-beach, the finding of little Moses and his mother, the dream of the pale lady that seemed to bring him to her; and not one of the conversations that had transpired before her among different gossips had been lost on her quiet, listening little ears. These pale, still children that play without making any noise are deep wells into which drop many things which lie long and quietly on the bottom, and come up in after years whole and new, when everybody else has forgotten them.

So she had heard surmises as to the remaining crew of that unfortunate ship, where, perhaps, Moses had a father. And sometimes she wondered if *he* were lying fathoms deep with sea-nymphs ringing his knell, and whether Moses ever thought about him; and yet she could no more have asked him a question about it than if she had been born dumb. She decided that she should never show him this poetry—it might make him feel unhappy.

One bright afternoon, when the sea lay all dead asleep, and the long, steady respiration of its tides scarcely disturbed the glassy tranquillity of its bosom, Mrs. Pennel sat at her kitchen-door spinning, when Captain Kittridge appeared.

"Good afternoon, Mis' Pennel; how ye gettin' along?"

"Oh, pretty well, Captain; won't you walk in and have a glass of beer?"

"Well, thank you," said the Captain, raising his hat and wiping his forehead, "I be pretty dry, it's a fact."

Mrs. Pennel hastened to a cask which was kept standing in a corner of the kitchen, and drew from thence a mug of her own home-brewed, fragrant with the smell of juniper, hemlock, and wintergreen, which she presented to the Captain, who sat down in the doorway and discussed it in leisurely sips.

"Wal', s'pose it's most time to be lookin' for 'em home, ain't it?" he said.

"I *am* lookin' every day," said Mrs. Pennel, involuntarily glancing upward at the sea.

At the word appeared the vision of little Mara, who rose up like a spirit from a dusky corner, where she had been stooping over her reading.

"Why, little Mara," said the Captain, "you ris up like a ghost all of a sudden. I thought you's out to play. I come down a-purpose arter you. Mis' Kittridge has gone shoppin' up to Brunswick, and left Sally a 'stent' to do; and I promised her if she'd clap to and do it quick, I'd go up and fetch you down, and we'd have a play in the cove."

Mara's eyes brightened, as they always did at this prospect, and Mrs. Pennel said, "Well, I'm glad to have the child go; she seems so kind o' still and lonesome since Moses went away; really one feels as if that boy took all the noise there was with him. I get tired myself sometimes hearing the clock tick. Mara, when she's alone, takes to her book more than's good for a child."

"She does, does she? Well, we'll see about that. Come, little Mara, get on your sun-bonnet. Sally's sewin' fast as ever she can, and we're goin' to dig some clams, and make a fire, and have a chowder; that'll be nice, won't it? Don't you want to come, too, Mis' Pennel?"

"Oh, thank you, Captain, but I've got so many things on hand to do afore they come home, I don't really think I can. I'll trust Mara to you any day."

Mara had run into her own little room and secured her precious fragment of treasure, which she wrapped up carefully in her handkerchief, resolving to enlighten Sally with the story, and to consult the Captain on any nice points of criticism. Arrived at the cove, they found Sally already there in advance of them, clapping her hands and dancing in a manner which made her black elf-locks fly like those of a distracted creature.

CHAPTER XIV

"Now, Sally," said the Captain, imitating, in a humble way, his wife's manner, "are you sure you've finished your work well?"

"Yes, father, every stitch on't."

"And stuck in your needle, and folded it up, and put it in the drawer, and put away your thimble, and shet the drawer, and all the rest on't?" said the Captain.

"Yes, father," said Sally, gleefully, "I've done everything I could think of."

"'Cause you know your ma'll be arter ye, if you don't leave everything straight."

"Oh, never you fear, father, I've done it all half an hour ago, and I've found the most capital bed of clams just round the point here; and you take care of Mara there, and make up a fire while I dig 'em. If she comes, she'll be sure to wet her shoes, or spoil her frock, or something."

"Wal', she likes no better fun now," said the Captain, watching Sally, as she disappeared round the rock with a bright tin pan.

He then proceeded to construct an extemporary fireplace of loose stones, and to put together chips and shavings for the fire,—in which work little Mara eagerly assisted; but the fire was crackling and burning cheerily long before Sally appeared with her clams, and so the Captain, with a pile of hemlock boughs by his side, sat on a stone feeding the fire leisurely from time to time with crackling boughs. Now was the time for Mara to make her inquiries; her heart beat, she knew not why, for she was full of those little timidities and shames that so often embarrass children in their attempts to get at the meanings of things in this great world, where they are such ignorant spectators.

"Captain Kittridge," she said at last, "do the mermaids toll any bells for people when they are drowned?"

Now the Captain had never been known to indicate the least ignorance on any subject in heaven or earth, which any one wished his opinion on; he therefore leisurely poked another great crackling bough of green hemlock into the fire, and, Yankee-like, answered one question by asking another.

"What put that into your curly pate?" he said.

"A book I've been reading says they do,—that is, sea-nymphs do. Ain't sea-nymphs and mermaids the same thing?"

"Wal', I guess they be, pretty much," said the Captain, rubbing down his pantaloons; "yes, they be," he added, after reflection.

"And when people are drowned, how long does it take for their bones to turn into coral, and their eyes into pearl?" said little Mara.

"Well, that depends upon circumstances," said the Captain, who wasn't going to be posed; "but let me jist see your book you've been reading these things out of."

"I found it in a barrel up garret, and grandma gave it to me," said Mara, unrolling her handkerchief; "it's a beautiful book,—it tells about an island, and there was an old enchanter lived on it, and he had one daughter, and there was a spirit they called Ariel, whom a wicked old witch fastened in a split of a pine-tree, till the enchanter got him out. He was a beautiful spirit, and rode in the curled clouds and hung in flowers,—because he could make himself big or little, you see."

"Ah, yes, I see, to be sure," said the Captain, nodding his head.

"Well, that about sea-nymphs ringing his knell is here," Mara added, beginning to read the passage with wide, dilated eyes and great emphasis. "You see," she went on speaking very fast, "this enchanter had been a prince, and a wicked brother had contrived to send him to sea with his poor little daughter, in a ship so leaky that the very rats had left it."

"Bad business that!" said the Captain, attentively.

"Well," said Mara, "they got cast ashore on this desolate island, where they lived together. But once, when a ship was going by on the sea that had his wicked brother and his son—a real good, handsome young prince—in it, why then he made a storm by magic arts."

"Jist so," said the Captain; "that's been often done, to my sartin knowledge."

"And he made the ship be wrecked, and all the people thrown ashore, but there wasn't any of 'em drowned, and this handsome prince heard Ariel singing this song about his father, and it made him think he was dead."

"Well, what became of 'em?" interposed Sally, who had come up with her pan of clams in time to hear this story, to which she had listened with breathless interest.

"Oh, the beautiful young prince married the beautiful young lady," said Mara.

"Wal'," said the Captain, who by this time had found his soundings; "that you've been a-tellin' is what they call a play, and I've seen 'em act it at a theatre, when I was to Liverpool once. I know all about it. Shakespeare wrote it, and he's a great English poet."

"But did it ever happen?" said Mara, trembling between hope and fear. "Is it like the Bible and Roman history?"

"Why, no," said Captain Kittridge, "not exactly; but things jist like it, you know. Mermaids and sich is common in foreign parts, and they has funerals for drowned sailors. 'Member once when we was sailing near the Bermudas by a reef where the Lively Fanny went down, and I heard a kind o' ding-dongin',—and the waters there is clear as the sky,—and I looked down and see the coral all a-growin', and the sea-plants a-wavin' as handsome as a pictur', and the mermaids they was a-singin'. It was beautiful; they sung kind o' mournful; and Jack Hubbard, he would have it they was a-singin' for the poor fellows that was a-lyin' there round under the seaweed."

"But," said Mara, "did you ever see an enchanter that could make storms?"

"Wal', there be witches and conjurers that make storms. 'Member once when we was crossin' the line, about twelve o'clock at night, there was an old man with a long white beard that shone like silver, came and stood at the masthead, and he had a pitchfork in one hand, and a lantern in the other, and there was great balls of fire as big as my fist came out all round in the rigging. And I'll tell you if we didn't get a blow that ar night! I thought to my soul we should all go to the bottom."

CHAPTER XIV

"Why," said Mara, her eyes staring with excitement, "that was just like this shipwreck; and 'twas Ariel made those balls of fire; he says so; he said he 'flamed amazement' all over the ship."

"I've heard Miss Roxy tell about witches that made storms," said Sally.

The Captain leisurely proceeded to open the clams, separating from the shells the contents, which he threw into a pan, meanwhile placing a black pot over the fire in which he had previously arranged certain slices of salt pork, which soon began frizzling in the heat.

"Now, Sally, you peel them potatoes, and mind you slice 'em thin," he said, and Sally soon was busy with her work.

"Yes," said the Captain, going on with his part of the arrangement, "there was old Polly Twitchell, that lived in that ar old tumble-down house on Mure P'int; people used to say she brewed storms, and went to sea in a sieve."

"Went in a sieve!" said both children; "why a sieve wouldn't swim!"

"No more it wouldn't, in any Christian way," said the Captain; "but that was to show what a great witch she was."

"But this was a good enchanter," said Mara, "and he did it all by a book and a rod."

"Yes, yes," said the Captain; "that ar's the gen'l way magicians do, ever since Moses's time in Egypt. 'Member once I was to Alexandria, in Egypt, and I saw a magician there that could jist see everything you ever did in your life in a drop of ink that he held in his hand."

"He could, father!"

"To be sure he could! told me all about the old folks at home; and described our house as natural as if he'd a-been there. He used to carry snakes round with him,—a kind so p'ison that it was certain death to have 'em bite you; but he played with 'em as if they was kittens."

"Well," said Mara, "my enchanter was a king; and when he got through all he wanted, and got his daughter married to the beautiful young prince, he said he would break his staff, and deeper than plummet sounded he would bury his book."

"It was pretty much the best thing he could do," said the Captain, "because the Bible is agin such things."

"Is it?" said Mara; "why, he was a real good man."

"Oh, well, you know, we all on us does what ain't quite right sometimes, when we gets pushed up," said the Captain, who now began arranging the clams and sliced potatoes in alternate layers with sea-biscuit, strewing in salt and pepper as he went on; and, in a few moments, a smell, fragrant to hungry senses, began to steam upward, and Sally began washing and preparing some mammoth clam-shells, to serve as ladles and plates for the future chowder.

Mara, who sat with her morsel of a book in her lap, seemed deeply pondering the past conversation. At last she said, "What did you mean by saying you'd seen 'em act that at a theatre?"

"Why, they make it all seem real; and they have a shipwreck, and you see it all jist right afore your eyes."

"And the Enchanter, and Ariel, and Caliban, and all?" said Mara.

"Yes, all on't,—plain as printing."

"Why, that is by magic, ain't it?" said Mara.

"No; they hes ways to jist make it up; but,"—added the Captain, "Sally, you needn't say nothin' to your ma 'bout the theatre, 'cause she wouldn't think I's fit to go to meetin' for six months arter, if she heard on't."

"Why, ain't theatres good?" said Sally.

"Wal', there's a middlin' sight o' bad things in 'em," said the Captain, "that I must say; but as long as folks *is* folks, why, they will be *folksy*;—but there's never any makin' women folk understand about them ar things."

"I am sorry they are bad," said Mara; "I want to see them."

"Wal', wal'," said the Captain, "on the hull I've seen real things a good deal more wonderful than all their shows, and they hain't no make-b'lieve to 'em; but theatres is takin' arter all. But, Sally, mind you don't say nothin' to Mis' Kittridge."

A few moments more and all discussion was lost in preparations for the meal, and each one, receiving a portion of the savory stew in a large shell, made a spoon of a small cockle, and with some slices of bread and butter, the evening meal went off merrily. The sun was sloping toward the ocean; the wide blue floor was bedropped here and there with rosy shadows of sailing clouds. Suddenly the Captain sprang up, calling out,—

"Sure as I'm alive, there they be!"

"Who?" exclaimed the children.

"Why, Captain Pennel and Moses; don't you see?"

And, in fact, on the outer circle of the horizon came drifting a line of small white-breasted vessels, looking like so many doves.

"Them's 'em," said the Captain, while Mara danced for joy.

"How soon will they be here?"

"Afore long," said the Captain; "so, Mara, I guess you'll want to be getting hum."

CHAPTER XV

THE HOME COMING

Mrs. Pennel, too, had seen the white, dove-like cloud on the horizon, and had hurried to make biscuits, and conduct other culinary preparations which should welcome the wanderers home.

The sun was just dipping into the great blue sea—a round ball of fire—and sending long, slanting tracks of light across the top of each wave, when a boat was moored at the beach, and the minister sprang out,—not in his suit of ceremony, but attired in fisherman's garb.

"Good afternoon, Mrs. Pennel," he said. "I was out fishing, and I thought I saw your husband's schooner in the distance. I thought I'd come and tell you."

"Thank you, Mr. Sewell. I thought I saw it, but I was not certain. Do come in; the Captain would be delighted to see you here."

"We miss your husband in our meetings," said Mr. Sewell; "it will be good news for us all when he comes home; he is one of those I depend on to help me preach."

"I'm sure you don't preach to anybody who enjoys it more," said Mrs. Pennel. "He often tells me that the greatest trouble about his voyages to the Banks is that he loses so many sanctuary privileges; though he always keeps Sunday on his ship, and reads and sings his psalms; but, he says, after all, there's nothing like going to Mount Zion."

"And little Moses has gone on his first voyage?" said the minister.

"Yes, indeed; the child has been teasing to go for more than a year. Finally the Cap'n told him if he'd be faithful in the ploughing and planting, he should go. You see, he's rather unsteady, and apt to be off after other things,—very different from Mara. Whatever you give her to do, she always keeps at it till it's done."

"And pray, where is the little lady?" said the minister; "is she gone?"

"Well, Cap'n Kittridge came in this afternoon to take her down to see Sally. The Cap'n's always so fond of Mara, and she has always taken to him ever since she was a baby."

"The Captain is a curious creature," said the minister, smiling.

Mrs. Pennel smiled also; and it is to be remarked that nobody ever mentioned the poor Captain's name without the same curious smile.

"The Cap'n is a good-hearted, obliging creature," said Mrs. Pennel, "and a master-hand for telling stories to the children."

"Yes, a perfect 'Arabian Nights' Entertainment,'" said Mr. Sewell.

"Well, I really believe the Cap'n believes his own stories," said Mrs. Pennel; "he always seems to, and certainly a more obliging man and a kinder neighbor couldn't be. He has been in and out almost every day since I've been alone, to see if I wanted anything. He would insist on chopping wood and splitting kindlings for me, though I told him the Cap'n and Moses had left a plenty to last till they came home."

At this moment the subject of their conversation appeared striding along the beach, with a large, red lobster in one hand, while with the other he held little Mara upon his shoulder, she the while clapping her hands and singing merrily, as she saw the Brilliant out on the open blue sea, its white sails looking of a rosy purple in the evening light, careering gayly homeward.

"There is Captain Kittridge this very minute," said Mrs. Pennel, setting down a tea-cup she had been wiping, and going to the door.

"Good evening, Mis' Pennel," said the Captain. "I s'pose you see your folks are comin'. I brought down one of these 'ere ready b'iled, 'cause I thought it might make out your supper."

"Thank you, Captain; you must stay and take some with us."

"Wal', me and the children have pooty much done our supper," said the Captain. "We made a real fust-rate chowder down there to the cove; but I'll jist stay and see what the Cap'n's luck is. Massy!" he added, as he looked in at the door, "if you hain't got the minister there! Wal', now, I come jist as I be," he added, with a glance down at his clothes.

"Never mind, Captain," said Mr. Sewell; "I'm in my fishing-clothes, so we're even."

As to little Mara, she had run down to the beach, and stood so near the sea, that every dash of the tide-wave forced her little feet to tread an inch backward, stretching out her hands eagerly toward the schooner, which was standing straight toward the small wharf, not far from their door. Already she could see on deck figures moving about, and her sharp little eyes made out a small personage in a red shirt that was among the most active. Soon all the figures grew distinct, and she could see her grandfather's gray head, and alert, active form, and could see, by the signs he made, that he had perceived the little blowy figure that stood, with hair streaming in the wind, like some flower bent seaward.

And now they are come nearer, and Moses shouts and dances on the deck, and the Captain and Mrs. Pennel come running from the house down to the shore, and a few minutes more, and all are landed safe and sound, and little Mara is carried up to the house in her grandfather's arms, while Captain Kittridge stops to have a few moments' gossip with Ben Halliday and Tom Scranton before they go to their own resting-places.

CHAPTER XV

Meanwhile Moses loses not a moment in boasting of his heroic exploits to Mara.

"Oh, Mara! you've no idea what times we've had! I can fish equal to any of 'em, and I can take in sail and tend the helm like anything, and I know all the names of everything; and you ought to have seen us catch fish! Why, they bit just as fast as we could throw; and it was just throw and bite,—throw and bite,—throw and bite; and my hands got blistered pulling in, but I didn't mind it,—I was determined no one should beat me."

"Oh! did you blister your hands?" said Mara, pitifully.

"Oh, to be sure! Now, you girls think that's a dreadful thing, but we men don't mind it. My hands are getting so hard, you've no idea. And, Mara, we caught a great shark."

"A shark!—oh, how dreadful! Isn't he dangerous?"

"Dangerous! I guess not. We served him out, I tell you. He'll never eat any more people, I tell you, the old wretch!"

"But, poor shark, it isn't his fault that he eats people. He was made so," said Mara, unconsciously touching a deep theological mystery.

"Well, I don't know but he was," said Moses; "but sharks that we catch never eat any more, I'll bet you."

"Oh, Moses, did you see any icebergs?"

"Icebergs! yes; we passed right by one,—a real grand one."

"Were there any bears on it?"

"Bears! No; we didn't see any."

"Captain Kittridge says there are white bears live on 'em."

"Oh, Captain Kittridge," said Moses, with a toss of superb contempt; "if you're going to believe all *he* says, you've got your hands full."

"Why, Moses, you don't think he tells lies?" said Mara, the tears actually starting in her eyes. "I think he is *real* good, and tells nothing but the truth."

"Well, well, you are young yet," said Moses, turning away with an air of easy grandeur, "and only a girl besides," he added.

Mara was nettled at this speech. First, it pained her to have her child's faith shaken in anything, and particularly in her good old friend, the Captain; and next, she felt, with more force than ever she did before, the continual disparaging tone in which Moses spoke of her girlhood.

"I'm sure," she said to herself, "he oughtn't to feel so about girls and women. There was Deborah was a prophetess, and judged Israel; and there was Egeria,—she taught Numa Pompilius all his wisdom."

But it was not the little maiden's way to speak when anything thwarted or hurt her, but rather to fold all her feelings and thoughts inward, as some insects, with fine gauzy wings, draw them under a coat of horny concealment. Somehow, there was a shivering sense of disappointment in all this meeting with Moses. She had dwelt upon it, and fancied so much, and had so many things to say to him; and he had come home so self-absorbed and glorious, and seemed to have had so little need of or thought for her, that she felt a cold, sad sinking at her heart; and walking away very still and white, sat down demurely by her grandfather's knee.

"Well, so my little girl is glad grandfather's come," he said, lifting her fondly in his arms, and putting her golden head under his coat, as he had been wont to do from infancy; "grandpa thought a great deal about his little Mara."

The small heart swelled against his. Kind, faithful old grandpa! how much more he thought about her than Moses; and yet she had thought so much of Moses. And there he sat, this same ungrateful Moses, bright-eyed and rosy-cheeked, full of talk and gayety, full of energy and vigor, as ignorant as possible of the wound he had given to the little loving heart that was silently brooding under her grandfather's butternut-colored sea-coat. Not only was he ignorant, but he had not even those conditions within himself which made knowledge possible. All that there was developed of him, at present, was a fund of energy, self-esteem, hope, courage, and daring, the love of action, life, and adventure; his life was in the outward and present, not in the inward and reflective; he was a true ten-year old boy, in its healthiest and most animal perfection. What she was, the small pearl with the golden hair, with her frail and high-strung organization, her sensitive nerves, her half-spiritual fibres, her ponderings, and marvels, and dreams, her power of love, and yearning for self-devotion, our readers may, perhaps, have seen. But if ever two children, or two grown people, thus organized, are thrown into intimate relations, it follows, from the very laws of their being, that one must hurt the other, simply by being itself; one must always hunger for what the other has not to give.

It was a merry meal, however, when they all sat down to the tea-table once more, and Mara by her grandfather's side, who often stopped what he was saying to stroke her head fondly. Moses bore a more prominent part in the conversation than he had been wont to do before this voyage, and all seemed to listen to him with a kind of indulgence elders often accord to a handsome, manly boy, in the first flush of some successful enterprise. That ignorant confidence in one's self and one's future, which comes in life's first dawn, has a sort of mournful charm in experienced eyes, who know how much it all amounts to.

Gradually, little Mara quieted herself with listening to and admiring him. It is not comfortable to have any heart-quarrel with one's cherished idol, and everything of the feminine nature, therefore, can speedily find fifty good reasons for seeing one's self in the wrong and one's graven image in the right; and little Mara soon had said to herself, without words, that, of course, Moses couldn't be expected to think as much of her as she of him. He was handsomer, cleverer, and had a thousand other things to do and to think of—he was a boy, in short, and going to be a glorious man and sail all over the world, while she could only hem handkerchiefs and knit stockings, and sit at home and wait for him to come back. This was about the *résumé* of life as it appeared to the little one, who went on from the moment worshiping her image with more undivided idolatry than ever, hoping that by and by he would think more of her.

CHAPTER XV

Mr. Sewell appeared to study Moses carefully and thoughtfully, and encouraged the wild, gleeful frankness which he had brought home from his first voyage, as a knowing jockey tries the paces of a high-mettled colt.

"Did you get any time to read?" he interposed once, when the boy stopped in his account of their adventures.

"No, sir," said Moses; "at least," he added, blushing very deeply, "I didn't feel like reading. I had so much to do, and there was so much to see."

"It's all new to him now," said Captain Pennel; "but when he comes to being, as I've been, day after day, with nothing but sea and sky, he'll be glad of a book, just to break the sameness."

"Laws, yes," said Captain Kittridge; "sailor's life ain't all apple-pie, as it seems when a boy first goes on a summer trip with his daddy—not by no manner o' means."

"But," said Mara, blushing and looking very eagerly at Mr. Sewell, "Moses has read a great deal. He read the Roman and the Grecian history through before he went away, and knows all about them."

"Indeed!" said Mr. Sewell, turning with an amused look towards the tiny little champion; "do you read them, too, my little maid?"

"Yes, indeed," said Mara, her eyes kindling; "I have read them a great deal since Moses went away—them and the Bible."

Mara did not dare to name her new-found treasure—there was something so mysterious about that, that she could not venture to produce it, except on the score of extreme intimacy.

"Come, sit by me, little Mara," said the minister, putting out his hand; "you and I must be friends, I see."

Mr. Sewell had a certain something of mesmeric power in his eyes which children seldom resisted; and with a shrinking movement, as if both attracted and repelled, the little girl got upon his knee.

"So you like the Bible and Roman history?" he said to her, making a little aside for her, while a brisk conversation was going on between Captain Kittridge and Captain Pennel on the fishing bounty for the year.

"Yes, sir," said Mara, blushing in a very guilty way.

"And which do you like the best?"

"I don't know, sir; I sometimes think it is the one, and sometimes the other."

"Well, what pleases you in the Roman history?"

"Oh, I like that about Quintus Curtius."

"Quintus Curtius?" said Mr. Sewell, pretending not to remember.

"Oh, don't you remember him? why, there was a great gulf opened in the Forum, and the Augurs said that the country would not be saved unless some one would offer himself up for it, and so he jumped right in, all on horseback. I think that was grand. I should like to have done that," said little Mara, her eyes blazing out with a kind of starry light which they had when she was excited.

"And how would you have liked it, if you had been a Roman girl, and Moses were Quintus Curtius? would you like to have him give himself up for the good of the country?"

"Oh, no, no!" said Mara, instinctively shuddering.

"Don't you think it would be very grand of him?"

"Oh, yes, sir."

"And shouldn't we wish our friends to do what is brave and grand?"

"Yes, sir; but then," she added, "it would be so dreadful *never* to see him any more," and a large tear rolled from the great soft eyes and fell on the minister's hand.

"Come, come," thought Mr. Sewell, "this sort of experimenting is too bad—too much nerve here, too much solitude, too much pine-whispering and sea-dashing are going to the making up of this little piece of workmanship."

"Tell me," he said, motioning Moses to sit by him, "how *you* like the Roman history."

"I like it first-rate," said Moses. "The Romans were such smashers, and beat everybody; nobody could stand against them; and I like Alexander, too—I think he was splendid."

"True boy," said Mr. Sewell to himself, "unreflecting brother of the wind and the sea, and all that is vigorous and active—no precocious development of the moral here."

"Now you have come," said Mr. Sewell, "I will lend you another book."

"Thank you, sir; I love to read them when I'm at home—it's so still here. I should be dull if I didn't."

Mara's eyes looked eagerly attentive. Mr. Sewell noticed their hungry look when a book was spoken of.

"And you must read it, too, my little girl," he said.

"Thank you, sir," said Mara; "I always want to read everything Moses does."

"What book is it?" said Moses.

"It is called Plutarch's 'Lives,'" said the minister; "it has more particular accounts of the men you read about in history."

"Are there any lives of women?" said Mara.

"No, my dear," said Mr. Sewell; "in the old times, women did not get their lives written, though I don't doubt many of them were much better worth writing than the men's."

"I should like to be a great general," said Moses, with a toss of his head.

"The way to be great lies through books, now, and not through battles," said the minister; "there is more done with pens than swords; so, if you want to do anything, you must read and study."

"Do you think of giving this boy a liberal education?" said Mr. Sewell some time later in the evening, after Moses and Mara were gone to bed.

"Depends on the boy," said Zephaniah. "I've been up to Brunswick, and seen the fellows there in the college. With a good many of 'em, going to college seems to be just nothing but a sort of ceremony; they go because they're sent, and don't learn anything more'n they can help. That's what I call waste of time and money."

"But don't you think Moses shows some taste for reading and study?"

"Pretty well, pretty well!" said Zephaniah; "jist keep him a little hungry; not let him get all he wants, you see, and he'll bite the sharper. If I want to catch cod, I don't begin with flingin' over a barrel o' bait. So with the boys, jist bait 'em with a book here and a book there, and kind o' let 'em feel their own way, and then, if nothin' will do but a fellow must go to college, give in to him—that'd be *my* way."

"And a very good one, too!" said Mr. Sewell. "I'll see if I can't bait my hook, so as to make Moses take after Latin this winter. I shall have plenty of time to teach him."

"Now, there's Mara!" said the Captain, his face becoming phosphorescent with a sort of mild radiance of pleasure as it usually was when he spoke of her; "she's real sharp set after books; she's ready to fly out of her little skin at the sight of one."

"That child thinks too much, and feels too much, and knows too much for her years!" said Mr. Sewell. "If she were a boy, and you would take her away cod-fishing, as you have Moses, the sea-winds would blow away some of the thinking, and her little body would grow stout, and her mind less delicate and sensitive. But she's a woman," he said, with a sigh, "and they are all alike. We can't do much for them, but let them come up as they will and make the best of it."

CHAPTER XVI

THE NATURAL AND THE SPIRITUAL

"Emily," said Mr. Sewell, "did you ever take much notice of that little Mara Lincoln?"

"No, brother; why?"

"Because I think her a very uncommon child."

"She is a pretty little creature," said Miss Emily, "but that is all I know; modest—blushing to her eyes when a stranger speaks to her."

"She has wonderful eyes," said Mr. Sewell; "when she gets excited, they grow so large and so bright, it seems almost unnatural."

"Dear me! has she?" said Miss Emily, in a tone of one who had been called upon to do something about it. "Well?" she added, inquiringly.

"That little thing is only seven years old," said Mr. Sewell; "and she is thinking and feeling herself all into mere spirit—brain and nerves all active, and her little body so frail. She reads incessantly, and thinks over and over what she reads."

"Well?" said Miss Emily, winding very swiftly on a skein of black silk, and giving a little twitch, every now and then, to a knot to make it subservient.

It was commonly the way when Mr. Sewell began to talk with Miss Emily, that she constantly answered him with the manner of one who expects some immediate, practical proposition to flow from every train of thought. Now Mr. Sewell was one of the reflecting kind of men, whose thoughts have a thousand meandering paths, that lead nowhere in particular. His sister's brisk little "Well's?" and "Ah's!" and "Indeed's!" were sometimes the least bit in the world annoying.

"What is to be done?" said Miss Emily; "shall we speak to Mrs. Pennel?"

"Mrs. Pennel would know nothing about her."

"How strangely you talk!—who should, if she doesn't?"

"I mean, she wouldn't understand the dangers of her case."

"Dangers! Do you think she has any disease? She seems to be a healthy child enough, I'm sure. She has a lovely color in her cheeks."

Mr. Sewell seemed suddenly to become immersed in a book he was reading.

CHAPTER XVI

"There now," said Miss Emily, with a little tone of pique, "that's the way you always do. You begin to talk with me, and just as I get interested in the conversation, you take up a book. It's too bad."

"Emily," said Mr. Sewell, laying down his book, "I think I shall begin to give Moses Pennel Latin lessons this winter."

"Why, what do you undertake that for?" said Miss Emily. "You have enough to do without that, I'm sure."

"He is an uncommonly bright boy, and he interests me."

"Now, brother, you needn't tell me; there is some mystery about the interest you take in that child, *you know* there is."

"I am fond of children," said Mr. Sewell, dryly.

"Well, but you don't take as much interest in other boys. I never heard of your teaching any of them Latin before."

"Well, Emily, he is an uncommonly interesting child, and the providential circumstances under which he came into our neighborhood"—

"Providential fiddlesticks!" said Miss Emily, with heightened color, "*I* believe you knew that boy's mother."

This sudden thrust brought a vivid color into Mr. Sewell's cheeks. To be interrupted so unceremoniously, in the midst of so very proper and ministerial a remark, was rather provoking, and he answered, with some asperity,—

"And suppose I had, Emily, and supposing there were any painful subject connected with this past event, you might have sufficient forbearance not to try to make me speak on what I do not wish to talk of."

Mr. Sewell was one of your gentle, dignified men, from whom Heaven deliver an inquisitive female friend! If such people would only get angry, and blow some unbecoming blast, one might make something of them; but speaking, as they always do, from the serene heights of immaculate propriety, one gets in the wrong before one knows it, and has nothing for it but to beg pardon. Miss Emily had, however, a feminine resource: she began to cry—wisely confining herself to the simple eloquence of tears and sobs. Mr. Sewell sat as awkwardly as if he had trodden on a kitten's toe, or brushed down a china cup, feeling as if he were a great, horrid, clumsy boor, and his poor little sister a martyr.

"Come, Emily," he said, in a softer tone, when the sobs subsided a little.

But Emily didn't "come," but went at it with a fresh burst. Mr. Sewell had a vision like that which drowning men are said to have, in which all Miss Emily's sisterly devotions, stocking-darnings, account-keepings, nursings and tendings, and infinite self-sacrifices, rose up before him: and there she was—crying!

"I'm sorry I spoke harshly, Emily. Come, come; that's a good girl."

"I'm a silly fool," said Miss Emily, lifting her head, and wiping the tears from her merry little eyes, as she went on winding her silk.

"Perhaps he will tell me now," she thought, as she wound.

But he didn't.

"What I was going to say, Emily," said her brother, "was, that I thought it would be a good plan for little Mara to come sometimes with Moses; and then, by observing her more particularly, you might be of use to her; her little, active mind needs good practical guidance like yours."

Mr. Sewell spoke in a gentle, flattering tone, and Miss Emily was flattered; but she soon saw that she had gained nothing by the whole breeze, except a little kind of dread, which made her inwardly resolve never to touch the knocker of his fortress again. But she entered into her brother's scheme with the facile alacrity with which she usually seconded any schemes of his proposing.

"I might teach her painting and embroidery," said Miss Emily, glancing, with a satisfied air, at a framed piece of her own work which hung over the mantelpiece, revealing the state of the fine arts in this country, as exhibited in the performances of well-instructed young ladies of that period. Miss Emily had performed it under the tuition of a celebrated teacher of female accomplishments. It represented a white marble obelisk, which an inscription, in legible India ink letters, stated to be "Sacred to the memory of Theophilus Sewell," etc. This obelisk stood in the midst of a ground made very green by an embroidery of different shades of chenille and silk, and was overshadowed by an embroidered weeping-willow. Leaning on it, with her face concealed in a plentiful flow of white handkerchief, was a female figure in deep mourning, designed to represent the desolate widow. A young girl, in a very black dress, knelt in front of it, and a very lugubrious-looking young man, standing bolt upright on the other side, seemed to hold in his hand one end of a wreath of roses, which the girl was presenting, as an appropriate decoration for the tomb. The girl and gentleman were, of course, the young Theophilus and Miss Emily, and the appalling grief conveyed by the expression of their faces was a triumph of the pictorial art.

Miss Emily had in her bedroom a similar funeral trophy, sacred to the memory of her deceased mother,—besides which there were, framed and glazed, in the little sitting-room, two embroidered shepherdesses standing with rueful faces, in charge of certain animals of an uncertain breed between sheep and pigs. The poor little soul had mentally resolved to make Mara the heiress of all the skill and knowledge of the arts by which she had been enabled to consummate these marvels.

"She is naturally a lady-like little thing," she said to herself, "and if I know anything of accomplishments, she shall have them."

Just about the time that Miss Emily came to this resolution, had she been clairvoyant, she might have seen Mara sitting very quietly, busy in the solitude of her own room with a little sprig of partridge-berry before her, whose round green leaves and brilliant scarlet berries she had been for hours trying to imitate, as appeared from the scattered sketches and fragments around her. In fact, before Zephaniah started on his spring fishing, he had caught her one day very busy at work of the same kind, with bits of charcoal, and some colors compounded out of wild berries; and so out of his capacious pocket, after his return, he drew a little box of water-colors and a lead-pencil and square of India-rubber, which he had bought for her in Portland on his way home.

CHAPTER XVI

Hour after hour the child works, so still, so fervent, so earnest,—going over and over, time after time, her simple, ignorant methods to make it "look like," and stopping, at times, to give the true artist's sigh, as the little green and scarlet fragment lies there hopelessly, unapproachably perfect. Ignorantly to herself, the hands of the little pilgrim are knocking at the very door where Giotto and Cimabue knocked in the innocent child-life of Italian art.

"Why won't it look round?" she said to Moses, who had come in behind her.

"Why, Mara, did you do these?" said Moses, astonished; "why, how well they are done! I should know in a minute what they were meant for."

Mara flushed up at being praised by Moses, but heaved a deep sigh as she looked back.

"It's so pretty, that sprig," she said; "if I only could make it just like"—

"Why, nobody expects *that*," said Moses, "it's like enough, if people only know what you mean it for. But come, now, get your bonnet, and come with me in the boat. Captain Kittridge has just brought down our new one, and I'm going to take you over to Eagle Island, and we'll take our dinner and stay all day; mother says so."

"Oh, how nice!" said the little girl, running cheerfully for her sun-bonnet.

At the house-door they met Mrs. Pennel, with a little closely covered tin pail.

"Here's your dinner, children; and, Moses, mind and take good care of her."

"Never fear *me* mother, I've been to the Banks; there wasn't a man there could manage a boat better than I could."

"Yes, grandmother," said Mara, "you ought to see how strong his arms are; I believe he will be like Samson one of these days if he keeps on."

So away they went. It was a glorious August forenoon, and the sombre spruces and shaggy hemlocks that dipped and rippled in the waters were penetrated to their deepest recesses with the clear brilliancy of the sky,—a true northern sky, without a cloud, without even a softening haze, defining every outline, revealing every minute point, cutting with sharp decision the form of every promontory and rock, and distant island.

The blue of the sea and the blue of the sky were so much the same, that when the children had rowed far out, the little boat seemed to float midway, poised in the centre of an azure sphere, with a firmament above and a firmament below. Mara leaned dreamily over the side of the boat, and drew her little hands through the waters as they rippled along to the swift oars' strokes, and she saw as the waves broke, and divided and shivered around the boat, a hundred little faces, with brown eyes and golden hair, gleaming up through the water, and dancing away over rippling waves, and thought that so the sea-nymphs might look who came up from the coral caves when they ring the knell of drowned people. Moses sat opposite to her, with his coat off, and his heavy black curls more wavy and glossy than ever, as the exercise made them damp with perspiration.

Eagle Island lay on the blue sea, a tangled thicket of evergreens,—white pine, spruce, arbor vitæ, and fragrant silver firs. A little strip of white beach bound it, like a silver setting to a gem. And there Moses at length moored his boat, and the children landed. The island was wholly solitary, and there is something to children quite delightful in feeling that they have a little lonely world all to themselves. Childhood is itself such an enchanted island, separated by mysterious depths from the mainland of nature, life, and reality.

Moses had subsided a little from the glorious heights on which he seemed to be in the first flush of his return, and he and Mara, in consequence, were the friends of old time. It is true he thought himself quite a man, but the manhood of a boy is only a tiny masquerade,—a fantastic, dreamy prevision of real manhood. It was curious that Mara, who was by all odds the most precociously developed of the two, never thought of asserting herself a woman; in fact, she seldom thought of herself at all, but dreamed and pondered of almost everything else.

"I declare," said Moses, looking up into a thick-branched, rugged old hemlock, which stood all shaggy, with heavy beards of gray moss drooping from its branches, "there's an eagle's nest up there; I mean to go and see." And up he went into the gloomy embrace of the old tree, crackling the dead branches, wrenching off handfuls of gray moss, rising higher and higher, every once in a while turning and showing to Mara his glowing face and curly hair through a dusky green frame of boughs, and then mounting again. "I'm coming to it," he kept exclaiming.

Meanwhile his proceedings seemed to create a sensation among the feathered house-keepers, one of whom rose and sailed screaming away into the air. In a moment after there was a swoop of wings, and two eagles returned and began flapping and screaming about the head of the boy.

Mara, who stood at the foot of the tree, could not see clearly what was going on, for the thickness of the boughs; she only heard a great commotion and rattling of the branches, the scream of the birds, and the swooping of their wings, and Moses's valorous exclamations, as he seemed to be laying about him with a branch which he had broken off.

At last he descended victorious, with the eggs in his pocket. Mara stood at the foot of the tree, with her sun-bonnet blown back, her hair streaming, and her little arms upstretched, as if to catch him if he fell.

"Oh, I was so afraid!" she said, as he set foot on the ground.

"Afraid? Pooh! Who's afraid? Why, you might know the old eagles couldn't beat me."

"Ah, well, I know how strong you are; but, you know, I couldn't help it. But the poor birds,—do hear 'em scream. Moses, don't you suppose they feel bad?"

"No, they're only mad, to think they couldn't beat me. I beat them just as the Romans used to beat folks,—I played their nest was a city, and I spoiled it."

"I shouldn't want to spoil cities!" said Mara.

"That's 'cause you are a girl,—I'm a man, and men always like war; I've taken one city this afternoon, and mean to take a great many more."

"But, Moses, do you think war is right?"

"Right? why, yes, to be sure; if it ain't, it's a pity; for it's all that has ever been done in this world. In the Bible, or out, certainly it's right. I wish I had a gun now, I'd stop those old eagles' screeching."

CHAPTER XVI

"But, Moses, we shouldn't want any one to come and steal all our things, and then shoot us."

"How long you do think about things!" said Moses, impatient at her pertinacity. "I am older than you, and when I tell you a thing's right, you ought to believe it. Besides, don't you take hens' eggs every day, in the barn? How do you suppose the hens like that?"

This was a home-thrust, and for the moment threw the little casuist off the track. She carefully folded up the idea, and laid it away on the inner shelves of her mind till she could think more about it. Pliable as she was to all outward appearances, the child had her own still, interior world, where all her little notions and opinions stood up crisp and fresh, like flowers that grow in cool, shady places. If anybody too rudely assailed a thought or suggestion she put forth, she drew it back again into this quiet inner chamber, and went on. Reader, there are some women of this habit; and there is no independence and pertinacity of opinion like that of these seemingly soft, quiet creatures, whom it is so easy to silence, and so difficult to convince. Mara, little and unformed as she yet was, belonged to the race of those spirits to whom is deputed the office of the angel in the Apocalypse, to whom was given the golden rod which measured the New Jerusalem. Infant though she was, she had ever in her hands that invisible measuring-rod, which she was laying to the foundations of all actions and thoughts. There may, perhaps, come a time when the saucy boy, who now steps so superbly, and predominates so proudly in virtue of his physical strength and daring, will learn to tremble at the golden measuring-rod, held in the hand of a woman.

"Howbeit, that is not first which is spiritual, but that which is natural." Moses is the type of the first unreflecting stage of development, in which are only the out-reachings of active faculties, the aspirations that tend toward manly accomplishments. Seldom do we meet sensitiveness of conscience or discriminating reflection as the indigenous growth of a very vigorous physical development. Your true healthy boy has the breezy, hearty virtues of a Newfoundland dog, the wild fullness of life of the young race-colt. Sentiment, sensibility, delicate perceptions, spiritual aspirations, are plants of later growth.

But there are, both of men and women, beings born into this world in whom from childhood the spiritual and the reflective predominate over the physical. In relation to other human beings, they seem to be organized much as birds are in relation to other animals. They are the artists, the poets, the unconscious seers, to whom the purer truths of spiritual instruction are open. Surveying man merely as an animal, these sensitively organized beings, with their feebler physical powers, are imperfect specimens of life. Looking from the spiritual side, they seem to have a noble strength, a divine force. The types of this latter class are more commonly among women than among men. Multitudes of them pass away in earlier years, and leave behind in many hearts the anxious wonder, why they came so fair only to mock the love they kindled. They who live to maturity are the priests and priestesses of the spiritual life, ordained of God to keep the balance between the rude but absolute necessities of physical life and the higher sphere to which that must at length give place.

CHAPTER XVII

LESSONS

Moses felt elevated some inches in the world by the gift of a new Latin grammar, which had been bought for him in Brunswick. It was a step upward in life; no graduate from a college ever felt more ennobled.

"Wal', now, I tell ye, Moses Pennel," said Miss Roxy, who, with her press-board and big flat-iron, was making her autumn sojourn in the brown house, "I tell ye Latin ain't just what you think 'tis, steppin' round so crank; you must remember what the king of Israel said to Benhadad, king of Syria."

"I don't remember; what did he say?"

"I remember," said the soft voice of Mara; "he said, 'Let not him that putteth on the harness boast as him that putteth it off.'"

"Good for you, Mara," said Miss Roxy; "if some other folks read their Bibles as much as you do, they'd know more."

Between Moses and Miss Roxy there had always been a state of sub-acute warfare since the days of his first arrival, she regarding him as an unhopeful interloper, and he regarding her as a grim-visaged, interfering gnome, whom he disliked with all the intense, unreasoning antipathy of childhood.

"I hate that old woman," he said to Mara, as he flung out of the door.

"Why, Moses, what for?" said Mara, who never could comprehend hating anybody.

"I do hate her, and Aunt Ruey, too. They are two old scratching cats; they hate me, and I hate them; they're always trying to bring me down, and I won't be brought down."

Mara had sufficient instinctive insight into the feminine rôle in the domestic concert not to adventure a direct argument just now in favor of her friends, and therefore she proposed that they should sit down together under a cedar hard by, and look over the first lesson.

"Miss Emily invited me to go over with you," she said, "and I should like so much to hear you recite."

Moses thought this very proper, as would any other male person, young or old, who has been habitually admired by any other female one. He did not doubt that, as in fishing and rowing, and all other things he had undertaken as yet, he should win himself distinguished honors.

"See here," he said; "Mr. Sewell told me I might go as far as I liked, and I mean to take all the declensions to begin with; there's five of 'em, and I shall learn them for the first lesson; then I shall take the adjectives next, and next the verbs, and so in a fortnight get into reading."

Mara heaved a sort of sigh. She wished she had been invited to share this glorious race; but she looked on admiring when Moses read, in a loud voice, "Penna, pennæ, pennæ, pennam," etc.

"There now, I believe I've got it," he said, handing Mara the book; and he was perfectly astonished to find that, with the book withdrawn, he boggled, and blundered, and stumbled ingloriously. In vain Mara softly prompted, and looked at him with pitiful eyes as he grew red in the face with his efforts to remember.

"Confound it all!" he said, with an angry flush, snatching back the book; "it's more trouble than it's worth."

Again he began the repetition, saying it very loud and plain; he said it over and over till his mind wandered far out to sea, and while his tongue repeated "penna, pennæ," he was counting the white sails of the fishing-smacks, and thinking of pulling up codfish at the Banks.

"There now, Mara, try me," he said, and handed her the book again; "I'm sure I *must* know it now."

But, alas! with the book the sounds glided away; and "penna" and "pennam" and "pennis" and "pennæ" were confusedly and indiscriminately mingled. He thought it must be Mara's fault; she didn't read right, or she told him just as he was going to say it, or she didn't tell him right; or was he a fool? or had he lost his senses?

That first declension has been a valley of humiliation to many a sturdy boy—to many a bright one, too; and often it is, that the more full of thought and vigor the mind is, the more difficult it is to narrow it down to the single dry issue of learning those sounds. Heinrich Heine said the Romans would never have found time to conquer the world, if they had had to learn their own language; but that, luckily for them, they were born into the knowledge of what nouns form their accusatives in "um."

Long before Moses had learned the first declension, Mara knew it by heart; for her intense anxiety for him, and the eagerness and zeal with which she listened for each termination, fixed them in her mind. Besides, she was naturally of a more quiet and scholar-like turn than he,—more intellectually developed. Moses began to think, before that memorable day was through, that there was some sense in Aunt Roxy's quotation of the saying of the King of Israel, and materially to retrench his expectations as to the time it might take to master the grammar; but still, his pride and will were both committed, and he worked away in this new sort of labor with energy.

It was a fine, frosty November morning, when he rowed Mara across the bay in a little boat to recite his first lesson to Mr. Sewell.

CHAPTER XVII

Miss Emily had provided a plate of seed-cake, otherwise called cookies, for the children, as was a kindly custom of old times, when the little people were expected. Miss Emily had a dim idea that she was to do something for Mara in her own department, while Moses was reciting his lesson; and therefore producing a large sampler, displaying every form and variety of marking-stitch, she began questioning the little girl, in a low tone, as to her proficiency in that useful accomplishment.

Presently, however, she discovered that the child was restless and uneasy, and that she answered without knowing what she was saying. The fact was that she was listening, with her whole soul in her eyes, and feeling through all her nerves, every word Moses was saying. She knew all the critical places, where he was likely to go wrong; and when at last, in one place, he gave the wrong termination, she involuntarily called out the right one, starting up and turning towards them. In a moment she blushed deeply, seeing Mr. Sewell and Miss Emily both looking at her with surprise.

"Come here, pussy," said Mr. Sewell, stretching out his hand to her. "Can you say this?"

"I believe I could, sir."

"Well, try it."

She went through without missing a word. Mr. Sewell then, for curiosity, heard her repeat all the other forms of the lesson. She had them perfectly.

"Very well, my little girl," he said, "have you been studying, too?"

"I heard Moses say them so often," said Mara, in an apologetic manner, "I couldn't help learning them."

"Would you like to recite with Moses every day?"

"Oh, yes, sir, so much."

"Well, you shall. It is better for him to have company."

Mara's face brightened, and Miss Emily looked with a puzzled air at her brother.

"So," she said, when the children had gone home, "I thought you wanted me to take Mara under my care. I was going to begin and teach her some marking stitches, and you put her up to studying Latin. I don't understand you."

"Well, Emily, the fact is, the child has a natural turn for study, that no child of her age ought to have; and I have done just as people always will with such children; there's no sense in it, but I wanted to do it. You can teach her marking and embroidery all the same; it would break her little heart, now, if I were to turn her back."

"I do not see of what use Latin can be to a woman."

"Of what use is embroidery?"

"Why, that is an accomplishment."

"Ah, indeed!" said Mr. Sewell, contemplating the weeping willow and tombstone trophy with a singular expression, which it was lucky for Miss Emily's peace she did not understand. The fact was, that Mr. Sewell had, at one period of his life, had an opportunity of studying and observing minutely some really fine works of art, and the remembrance of them sometimes rose up to his mind, in the presence of the *chefs-d'œuvre* on which his sister rested with so much complacency. It was a part of his quiet interior store of amusement to look at these bits of Byzantine embroidery round the room, which affected him always with a subtle sense of drollery.

"You see, brother," said Miss Emily, "it is far better for women to be accomplished than learned."

"You are quite right in the main," said Mr. Sewell, "only you must let me have my own way just for once. One can't be consistent always."

So another Latin grammar was bought, and Moses began to feel a secret respect for his little companion, that he had never done before, when he saw how easily she walked through the labyrinths which at first so confused him. Before this, the comparison had been wholly in points where superiority arose from physical daring and vigor; now he became aware of the existence of another kind of strength with which he had not measured himself. Mara's opinion in their mutual studies began to assume a value in his eyes that her opinions on other subjects had never done, and she saw and felt, with a secret gratification, that she was becoming more to him through their mutual pursuit. To say the truth, it required this fellowship to inspire Moses with the patience and perseverance necessary for this species of acquisition. His active, daring temperament little inclined him to patient, quiet study. For anything that could be done by two hands, he was always ready; but to hold hands still and work silently in the inner forces was to him a species of undertaking that seemed against his very nature; but then he would do it—he would not disgrace himself before Mr. Sewell, and let a girl younger than himself outdo him.

But the thing, after all, that absorbed more of Moses's thoughts than all his lessons was the building and rigging of a small schooner, at which he worked assiduously in all his leisure moments. He had dozens of blocks of wood, into which he had cut anchor moulds; and the melting of lead, the running and shaping of anchors, the whittling of masts and spars took up many an hour. Mara entered into all those things readily, and was too happy to make herself useful in hemming the sails.

When the schooner was finished, they built some ways down by the sea, and invited Sally Kittridge over to see it launched.

"There!" he said, when the little thing skimmed down prosperously into the sea and floated gayly on the waters, "when I'm a man, I'll have a big ship; I'll build her, and launch her, and command her, all myself; and I'll give you and Sally both a passage in it, and we'll go off to the East Indies—we'll sail round the world!"

None of the three doubted the feasibility of this scheme; the little vessel they had just launched seemed the visible prophecy of such a future; and how pleasant it would be to sail off, with the world all before them, and winds ready to blow them to any port they might wish!

The three children arranged some bread and cheese and doughnuts on a rock on the shore, to represent the collation that was usually spread in those parts at a ship launch, and felt quite like grown people—acting life beforehand in that sort of shadowy pantomime which so delights little people. Happy, happy days—when ships can be made with a jack-knife and anchors run in pine blocks, and three children together can launch a schooner, and the voyage of the world can all be made in one sunny Saturday afternoon!

"Mother says you are going to college," said Sally to Moses.

"Not I, indeed," said Moses; "as soon as I get old enough, I'm going up to Umbagog among the lumberers, and I'm going to cut real, splendid timber for my ship, and I'm going to get it on the stocks, and have it built to suit myself."

"What will you call her?" said Sally.

"I haven't thought of that," said Moses.

"Call her the Ariel," said Mara.

"What! after the spirit you were telling us about?" said Sally.

"Ariel is a pretty name," said Moses. "But what is that about a spirit?"

"Why," said Sally, "Mara read us a story about a ship that was wrecked, and a spirit called Ariel, that sang a song about the drowned mariners."

Mara gave a shy, apprehensive glance at Moses, to see if this allusion called up any painful recollections.

No; instead of this, he was following the motions of his little schooner on the waters with the briskest and most unconcerned air in the world.

"Why didn't you ever show me that story, Mara?" said Moses.

Mara colored and hesitated; the real reason she dared not say.

"Why, she read it to father and me down by the cove," said Sally, "the afternoon that you came home from the Banks; I remember how we saw you coming in; don't you, Mara?"

"What have you done with it?" said Moses.

"I've got it at home," said Mara, in a faint voice; "I'll show it to you, if you want to see it; there are such beautiful things in it."

That evening, as Moses sat busy, making some alterations in his darling schooner, Mara produced her treasure, and read and explained to him the story. He listened with interest, though without any of the extreme feeling which Mara had thought possible, and even interrupted her once in the middle of the celebrated—

"Full fathom five thy father lies,"

by asking her to hold up the mast a minute, while he drove in a peg to make it rake a little more. He was, evidently, thinking of no drowned father, and dreaming of no possible sea-caves, but acutely busy in fashioning a present reality; and yet he liked to hear Mara read, and, when she had done, told her that he thought it was a pretty—quite a pretty story, with such a total absence of recognition that the story had any affinities with his own history, that Mara was quite astonished.

She lay and thought about him hours, that night, after she had gone to bed; and he lay and thought about a new way of disposing a pulley for raising a sail, which he determined to try the effect of early in the morning.

What was the absolute truth in regard to the boy? Had he forgotten the scenes of his early life, the strange catastrophe that cast him into his present circumstances? To this we answer that all the efforts of Nature, during the early years of a healthy childhood, are bent on effacing and obliterating painful impressions, wiping out from each day the sorrows of the last, as the daily tide effaces the furrows on the seashore. The child that broods, day after day, over some fixed idea, is so far forth not a healthy one. It is Nature's way to make first a healthy animal, and then develop in it gradually higher faculties. We have seen our two children unequally matched hitherto, because unequally developed. There will come a time, by and by in the history of the boy, when the haze of dreamy curiosity will steam up likewise from his mind, and vague yearnings, and questionings, and longings possess and trouble him, but it must be some years hence.

Here for a season we leave both our child friends, and when ten years have passed over their heads,—when Moses shall be twenty, and Mara seventeen,—we will return again to tell their story, for then there will be one to tell. Let us suppose in the interval, how Moses and Mara read Virgil with the minister, and how Mara works a shepherdess with Miss Emily, which astonishes the neighborhood,—but how by herself she learns, after divers trials, to paint partridge, and checkerberry, and trailing arbutus,—how Moses makes better and better ships, and Sally grows up a handsome girl, and goes up to Brunswick to the high school,—how Captain Kittridge tells stories, and Miss Roxy and Miss Ruey nurse and cut and make and mend for the still rising generation,—how there are quiltings and tea-drinkings and prayer meetings and Sunday sermons,—how Zephaniah and Mary Pennel grow old gradually and graciously, as the sun rises and sets, and the eternal silver tide rises and falls around our little gem, Orr's Island.

CHAPTER XVIII

SALLY

"Now, where's Sally Kittridge! There's the clock striking five, and nobody to set the table. Sally, I say! Sally!"

"Why, Mis' Kittridge," said the Captain, "Sally's gone out more'n an hour ago, and I expect she's gone down to Pennel's to see Mara; 'cause, you know, she come home from Portland to-day."

"Well, if she's come home, I s'pose I may as well give up havin' any good of Sally, for that girl fairly bows down to Mara Lincoln and worships her."

"Well, good reason," said the Captain. "There ain't a puttier creature breathin'. I'm a'most a mind to worship her myself."

"Captain Kittridge, you ought to be ashamed of yourself, at your age, talking as you do."

"Why, laws, mother, I don't feel my age," said the frisky Captain, giving a sort of skip. "It don't seem more'n yesterday since you and I was a-courtin', Polly. What a life you did lead me in them days! I think you kep' me on the anxious seat a pretty middlin' spell."

"I do wish you wouldn't talk so. You ought to be ashamed to be triflin' round as you do. Come, now, can't you jest tramp over to Pennel's and tell Sally I want her?"

"Not I, mother. There ain't but two gals in two miles square here, and I ain't a-goin' to be the feller to shoo 'em apart. What's the use of bein' gals, and young, and putty, if they can't get together and talk about their new gownds and the fellers? That ar's what gals is for."

"I do wish you wouldn't talk in that way before Sally, father, for her head is full of all sorts of vanity now; and as to Mara, I never did see a more slack-twisted, flimsy thing than she's grown up to be. Now Sally's learnt to do something, thanks to me. She can brew, and she can make bread and cake and pickles, and spin, and cut, and make. But as to Mara, what does she do? Why, she paints pictur's. Mis' Pennel was a-showin' on me a blue-jay she painted, and I was a-thinkin' whether she could brile a bird fit to be eat if she tried; and she don't know the price of nothin'," continued Mrs. Kittridge, with wasteful profusion of negatives.

"Well," said the Captain, "the Lord makes some things jist to be looked at. Their work is to be putty, and that ar's Mara's sphere. It never seemed to me she was cut out for hard work; but she's got sweet ways and kind words for everybody, and it's as good as a psalm to look at her."

"And what sort of a wife'll she make, Captain Kittridge?"

"A real sweet, putty one," said the Captain, persistently.

"Well, as to beauty, I'd rather have our Sally any day," said Mrs. Kittridge; "and she looks strong and hearty, and seems to be good for use."

"So she is, so she is," said the Captain, with fatherly pride. "Sally's the very image of her ma at her age—black eyes, black hair, tall and trim as a spruce-tree, and steps off as if she had springs in her heels. I tell you, the feller'll have to be spry that catches her. There's two or three of 'em at it, I see; but Sally won't have nothin' to say to 'em. I hope she won't, yet awhile."

"Sally is a girl that has as good an eddication as money can give," said Mrs. Kittridge. "If I'd a-had her advantages at her age, I should a-been a great deal more'n I am. But we ha'n't spared nothin' for Sally; and when nothin' would do but Mara must be sent to Miss Plucher's school over in Portland, why, I sent Sally too—for all she's our seventh child, and Pennel hasn't but the one."

"You forget Moses," said the Captain.

"Well, he's settin' up on his own account, I guess. They did talk o' giving him college eddication; but he was so unstiddy, there weren't no use in trying. A real wild ass's colt he was."

"Wal', wal', Moses was in the right on't. He took the cross-lot track into life," said the Captain. "Colleges is well enough for your smooth, straight-grained lumber, for gen'ral buildin'; but come to fellers that's got knots, and streaks, and cross-grains, like Moses Pennel, and the best way is to let 'em eddicate 'emselves, as he's a-doin'. He's cut out for the sea, plain enough, and he'd better be up to Umbagog, cuttin' timber for his ship, than havin' rows with tutors, and blowin' the roof off the colleges, as one o' them 'ere kind o' fellers is apt to when he don't have work to use up his steam. Why, mother, there's more gas got up in them Brunswick buildin's, from young men that are spilin' for hard work, than you could shake a stick at! But Mis' Pennel told me yesterday she was 'spectin' Moses home to-day."

"Oho! that's at the bottom of Sally's bein' up there," said Mrs. Kittridge.

"Mis' Kittridge," said the Captain, "I take it you ain't the woman as would expect a daughter of your bringin' up to be a-runnin' after any young chap, be he who he may," said the Captain.

Mrs. Kittridge for once was fairly silenced by this home-thrust; nevertheless, she did not the less think it quite possible, from all that she knew of Sally; for although that young lady professed great hardness of heart and contempt for all the young male generation of her acquaintance, yet she had evidently a turn for observing their ways—probably purely in the way of philosophical inquiry.

CHAPTER XIX

EIGHTEEN

In fact, at this very moment our scene-shifter changes the picture. Away rolls the image of Mrs. Kittridge's kitchen, with its sanded floor, its scoured rows of bright pewter platters, its great, deep fireplace, with wide stone hearth, its little looking-glass with a bit of asparagus bush, like a green mist, over it. *Exeunt* the image of Mrs. Kittridge, with her hands floury from the bread she has been moulding, and the dry, ropy, lean Captain, who has been sitting tilting back in a splint-bottomed chair,—and the next scene comes rolling in. It is a chamber in the house of Zephaniah Pennel, whose windows present a blue panorama of sea and sky. Through two windows you look forth into the blue belt of Harpswell Bay, bordered on the farther edge by Harpswell Neck, dotted here and there with houses, among which rises the little white meeting-house, like a mother-bird among a flock of chickens. The third window, on the other side of the room, looks far out to sea, where only a group of low, rocky islands interrupts the clear sweep of the horizon line, with its blue infinitude of distance.

The furniture of this room, though of the barest and most frigid simplicity, is yet relieved by many of those touches of taste and fancy which the indwelling of a person of sensibility and imagination will shed off upon the physical surroundings. The bed was draped with a white spread, embroidered with a kind of knotted tracery, the working of which was considered among the female accomplishments of those days, and over the head of it was a painting of a bunch of crimson and white trillium, executed with a fidelity to Nature that showed the most delicate gifts of observation. Over the mantelpiece hung a painting of the Bay of Genoa, which had accidentally found a voyage home in Zephaniah Pennel's sea-chest, and which skillful fingers had surrounded with a frame curiously wrought of moss and sea-shells. Two vases of India china stood on the mantel, filled with spring flowers, crowfoot, anemones, and liverwort, with drooping bells of the twin-flower. The looking-glass that hung over the table in one corner of the room was fancifully webbed with long, drooping festoons of that gray moss which hangs in such graceful wreaths from the boughs of the pines in the deep forest shadows of Orr's Island. On the table below was a collection of books: a whole set of Shakespeare which Zephaniah Pennel had bought of a Portland bookseller; a selection, in prose and verse, from the best classic writers, presented to Mara Lincoln, the fly-leaf said, by her sincere friend, Theophilus Sewell; a Virgil, much thumbed, with an old, worn cover, which, however, some adroit fingers had concealed under a coating of delicately marbled paper;—there was a Latin dictionary, a set of Plutarch's Lives, the Mysteries of Udolpho, and Sir Charles Grandison, together with Edwards on the Affections, and Boston's Fourfold State;—there was an inkstand, curiously contrived from a sea-shell, with pens and paper in that phase of arrangement which betokened frequency of use; and, lastly, a little work-basket, containing a long strip of curious and delicate embroidery, in which the needle yet hanging showed that the work was in progress.

By a table at the sea-looking window sits our little Mara, now grown to the maturity of eighteen summers, but retaining still unmistakable signs of identity with the little golden-haired, dreamy, excitable, fanciful "Pearl" of Orr's *Island*.

She is not quite of a middle height, with something beautiful and child-like about the moulding of her delicate form. We still see those sad, wistful, hazel eyes, over which the lids droop with a dreamy languor, and whose dark lustre contrasts singularly with the golden hue of the abundant hair which waves in a thousand rippling undulations around her face. The impression she produces is not that of paleness, though there is no color in her cheek; but her complexion has everywhere that delicate pink tinting which one sees in healthy infants, and with the least emotion brightens into a fluttering bloom. Such a bloom is on her cheek at this moment, as she is working away, copying a bunch of scarlet rock-columbine which is in a wine-glass of water before her; every few moments stopping and holding her work at a distance, to contemplate its effect. At this moment there steps behind her chair a tall, lithe figure, a face with a rich Spanish complexion, large black eyes, glowing cheeks, marked eyebrows, and lustrous black hair arranged in shining braids around her head. It is our old friend, Sally Kittridge, whom common fame calls the handsomest girl of all the region round Harpswell, Maquoit, and Orr's Island. In truth, a wholesome, ruddy, blooming creature she was, the sight of whom cheered and warmed one like a good fire in December; and she seemed to have enough and to spare of the warmest gifts of vitality and joyous animal life. She had a well-formed mouth, but rather large, and a frank laugh which showed all her teeth sound—and a fortunate sight it was, considering that they were white and even as pearls; and the hand that she laid upon Mara's at this moment, though twice as large as that of the little artist, was yet in harmony with her vigorous, finely developed figure.

"Mara Lincoln," she said, "you are a witch, a perfect little witch, at painting. How you can make things look so like, I don't see. Now, I could paint the things we painted at Miss Plucher's; but then, dear me! they didn't look at all like flowers. One needed to write under them what they were made for."

"Does this look like to you, Sally?" said Mara. "I wish it would to me. Just see what a beautiful clear color that flower is. All I can do, I can't make one like it. My scarlet and yellows sink dead into the paper."

CHAPTER XIX

"Why, I think your flowers are wonderful! You are a real genius, that's what you are! I am only a common girl; I can't do things as you can."

"You can do things a thousand times more useful, Sally. I don't pretend to compare with you in the useful arts, and I am only a bungler in ornamental ones. Sally, I feel like a useless little creature. If I could go round as you can, and do business, and make bargains, and push ahead in the world, I should feel that I was good for something; but somehow I can't."

"To be sure you can't," said Sally, laughing. "I should like to see you try it."

"Now," pursued Mara, in a tone of lamentation, "I could no more get into a carriage and drive to Brunswick as you can, than I could fly. I can't drive, Sally—something is the matter with me; and the horses always know it the minute I take the reins; they always twitch their ears and stare round into the chaise at me, as much as to say, 'What! you there?' and I feel sure they never will mind me. And then how you can make those wonderful bargains you do, I can't see!—you talk up to the clerks and the men, and somehow you talk everybody round; but as for me, if I only open my mouth in the humblest way to dispute the price, everybody puts me down. I always tremble when I go into a store, and people talk to me just as if I was a little girl, and once or twice they have made me buy things that I knew I didn't want, just because they will talk me down."

"Oh, Mara, Mara," said Sally, laughing till the tears rolled down her cheeks, "what do *you* ever go a-shopping for?—of course you ought always to send me. Why, look at this dress—real India chintz; do you know I made old Pennywhistle's clerk up in Brunswick give it to me just for the price of common cotton? You see there was a yard of it had got faded by lying in the shop-window, and there were one or two holes and imperfections in it, and you ought to have heard the talk I made! I abused it to right and left, and actually at last I brought the poor wretch to believe that he ought to be grateful to me for taking it off his hands. Well, you see the dress I've made of it. The imperfections didn't hurt it the least in the world as I managed it,—and the faded breadth makes a good apron, so you see. And just so I got that red spotted flannel dress I wore last winter. It was moth-eaten in one or two places, and I made them let me have it at half-price;—made exactly as good a dress. But after all, Mara, I can't trim a bonnet as you can, and I can't come up to your embroidery, nor your lace-work, nor I can't draw and paint as you can, and I can't sing like you; and then as to all those things you talk with Mr. Sewell about, why they're beyond my depth,—that's all I've got to say. Now, you are made to have poetry written to you, and all that kind of thing one reads of in novels. Nobody would ever think of writing poetry to me, now, or sending me flowers and rings, and such things. If a fellow likes me, he gives me a quince, or a big apple; but, then, Mara, there ain't any fellows round here that are fit to speak to."

"I'm sure, Sally, there always is a train following you everywhere, at singing-school and Thursday lecture."

"Yes—but what do I care for 'em?" said Sally, with a toss of her head. "Why they follow me, I don't see. I don't do anything to make 'em, and I tell 'em all that they tire me to death; and still they will hang round. What is the reason, do you suppose?"

"What can it be?" said Mara, with a quiet kind of arch drollery which suffused her face, as she bent over her painting.

"Well, you know I can't bear fellows—I think they are hateful."

"What! even Tom Hiers?" said Mara, continuing her painting.

"Tom Hiers! Do you suppose I care for him? He would insist on waiting on me round all last winter, taking me over in his boat to Portland, and up in his sleigh to Brunswick; but I didn't care for him."

"Well, there's Jimmy Wilson, up at Brunswick."

"What! that little snip of a clerk! You don't suppose I care for him, do you?—only he almost runs his head off following me round when I go up there shopping; he's nothing but a little dressed-up yard-stick! I never saw a fellow yet that I'd cross the street to have another look at. By the by, Mara, Miss Roxy told me Sunday that Moses was coming down from Umbagog this week."

"Yes, he is," said Mara; "we are looking for him every day."

"You must want to see him. How long is it since you saw him?"

"It is three years," said Mara. "I scarcely know what he is like now. I was visiting in Boston when he came home from his three-years' voyage, and he was gone into the lumbering country when I came back. He seems almost a stranger to me."

"He's pretty good-looking," said Sally. "I saw him on Sunday when he was here, but he was off on Monday, and never called on old friends. Does he write to you often?"

"Not very," said Mara; "in fact, almost never; and when he does, there is so little in his letters."

"Well, I tell you, Mara, you must not expect fellows to write as girls can. They don't do it. Now, our boys, when they write home, they tell the latitude and longitude, and soil and productions, and such things. But if you or I were only there, don't you think we should find something more to say? Of course we should,—fifty thousand little things that they never think of."

Mara made no reply to this, but went on very intently with her painting. A close observer might have noticed a suppressed sigh that seemed to retreat far down into her heart. Sally did not notice it.

What was in that sigh? It was the sigh of a long, deep, inner history, unwritten and untold—such as are transpiring daily by thousands, and of which we take no heed.

CHAPTER XX

REBELLION

We have introduced Mara to our readers as she appears in her seventeenth year, at the time when she is expecting the return of Moses as a young man of twenty; but we cannot do justice to the feelings which are roused in her heart by this expectation, without giving a chapter or two to tracing the history of Moses since we left him as a boy commencing the study of the Latin grammar with Mr. Sewell. The reader must see the forces that acted upon his early development, and what they have made of him.

It is common for people who write treatises on education to give forth their rules and theories with a self-satisfied air, as if a human being were a thing to be made up, like a batch of bread, out of a given number of materials combined by an infallible recipe. Take your child, and do thus and so for a given number of years, and he comes out a thoroughly educated individual.

But in fact, education is in many cases nothing more than a blind struggle of parents and guardians with the evolutions of some strong, predetermined character, individual, obstinate, unreceptive, and seeking by an inevitable law of its being to develop itself and gain free expression in its own way. Captain Kittridge's confidence that he would as soon undertake a boy as a Newfoundland pup, is good for those whose idea of what is to be done for a human being are only what would be done for a dog, namely, give food, shelter, and world-room, and leave each to act out his own nature without let or hindrance.

But everybody takes an embryo human being with some plan of one's own what it shall do or be. The child's future shall shape out some darling purpose or plan, and fulfill some long unfulfilled expectation of the parent. And thus, though the wind of every generation sweeps its hopes and plans like forest-leaves, none are whirled and tossed with more piteous moans than those which come out green and fresh to shade the happy spring-time of the cradle. For the temperaments of children are often as oddly unsuited to parents as if capricious fairies had been filling cradles with changelings.

A meek member of the Peace Society, a tender, devout, poetical clergyman, receives an heir from heaven, and straightway devotes him to the Christian ministry. But lo! the boy proves a young war-horse, neighing for battle, burning for gunpowder and guns, for bowie-knives and revolvers, and for every form and expression of physical force;—he might make a splendid trapper, an energetic sea-captain, a bold, daring military man, but his whole boyhood is full of rebukes and disciplines for sins which are only the blind effort of the creature to express a nature which his parent does not and cannot understand. So again, the son that was to have upheld the old, proud merchant's time-honored firm, that should have been mighty in ledgers and great upon 'Change, breaks his father's heart by an unintelligible fancy for weaving poems and romances. A father of literary aspirations, balked of privileges of early education, bends over the cradle of his son with but one idea. This child shall have the full advantages of regular college-training; and so for years he battles with a boy abhorring study, and fitted only for a life of out-door energy and bold adventure,—on whom Latin forms and Greek quantities fall and melt aimless and useless, as snow-flakes on the hide of a buffalo. Then the secret agonies,—the long years of sorrowful watchings of those gentler nurses of humanity who receive the infant into their bosom out of the void unknown, and strive to read its horoscope through the mists of their prayers and tears!—what perplexities,—what confusion! Especially is this so in a community where the moral and religious sense is so cultivated as in New England, and frail, trembling, self-distrustful mothers are told that the shaping and ordering not only of this present life, but of an immortal destiny, is in their hands.

On the whole, those who succeed best in the rearing of children are the tolerant and easy persons who instinctively follow nature and accept without much inquiry whatever she sends; or that far smaller class, wise to discern spirits and apt to adopt means to their culture and development, who can prudently and carefully train every nature according to its true and characteristic ideal.

Zephaniah Pennel was a shrewd old Yankee, whose instincts taught him from the first, that the waif that had been so mysteriously washed out of the gloom of the sea into his family, was of some different class and lineage from that which might have filled a cradle of his own, and of a nature which he could not perfectly understand. So he prudently watched and waited, only using restraint enough to keep the boy anchored in society, and letting him otherwise grow up in the solitary freedom of his lonely seafaring life.

The boy was from childhood, although singularly attractive, of a moody, fitful, unrestful nature,—eager, earnest, but unsteady,—with varying phases of imprudent frankness and of the most stubborn and unfathomable secretiveness. He was a creature of unreasoning antipathies and attractions. As Zephaniah Pennel said of him, he was as full of hitches as an old bureau drawer. His peculiar beauty, and a certain electrical power of attraction, seemed to form a constant circle of protection and forgiveness around him in the home of his foster-parents; and great as was the anxiety and pain which he often gave them, they somehow never felt the charge of him as a weariness.

We left him a boy beginning Latin with Mr. Sewell in company with the little Mara. This arrangement progressed prosperously for a time, and the good clergyman, all whose ideas of education ran through the halls of a college, began to have hopes of turning out a choice scholar. But when the boy's ship of life came into the breakers of that narrow and intricate channel which divides boyhood from manhood, the difficulties that had always attended his guidance and management wore an intensified form. How much family happiness is wrecked just then and there! How many mothers' and sisters' hearts are broken in the wild and confused tossings and tearings of that stormy transition! A whole new nature is blindly upheaving itself, with cravings and clamorings, which neither the boy himself nor often surrounding friends understand.

A shrewd observer has significantly characterized the period as the time when the boy wishes he were dead, and everybody else wishes so too. The wretched, half-fledged, half-conscious, anomalous creature has all the desires of the man, and none of the rights; has a double and triple share of nervous edge and intensity in every part of his nature, and no definitely perceived objects on which to bestow it,—and, of course, all sorts of unreasonable moods and phases are the result.

One of the most common signs of this period, in some natures, is the love of contradiction and opposition,—a blind desire to go contrary to everything that is commonly received among the older people. The boy disparages the minister, quizzes the deacon, thinks the school-master an ass, and doesn't believe in the Bible, and seems to be rather pleased than otherwise with the shock and flutter that all these announcements create among peaceably disposed grown people. No respectable hen that ever hatched out a brood of ducks was more puzzled what to do with them than was poor Mrs. Pennel when her adopted nursling came into this state. Was he a boy? an immortal soul? a reasonable human being? or only a handsome goblin sent to torment her?

"What shall we do with him, father?" said she, one Sunday, to Zephaniah, as he stood shaving before the little looking-glass in their bedroom. "He can't be governed like a child, and he won't govern himself like a man."

Zephaniah stopped and strapped his razor reflectively.

"We must cast out anchor and wait for day," he answered. "Prayer is a long rope with a strong hold."

It was just at this critical period of life that Moses Pennel was drawn into associations which awoke the alarm of all his friends, and from which the characteristic willfulness of his nature made it difficult to attempt to extricate him.

In order that our readers may fully understand this part of our history, we must give some few particulars as to the peculiar scenery of Orr's Island and the state of the country at this time.

The coast of Maine, as we have elsewhere said, is remarkable for a singular interpenetration of the sea with the land, forming amid its dense primeval forests secluded bays, narrow and deep, into which vessels might float with the tide, and where they might nestle unseen and unsuspected amid the dense shadows of the overhanging forest.

At this time there was a very brisk business done all along the coast of Maine in the way of smuggling. Small vessels, lightly built and swift of sail, would run up into these sylvan fastnesses, and there make their deposits and transact their business so as entirely to elude the vigilance of government officers.

It may seem strange that practices of this kind should ever have obtained a strong foothold in a community peculiar for its rigid morality and its orderly submission to law; but in this case, as in many others, contempt of law grew out of weak and unworthy legislation. The celebrated embargo of Jefferson stopped at once the whole trade of New England, and condemned her thousand ships to rot at the wharves, and caused the ruin of thousands of families.

The merchants of the country regarded this as a flagrant, high-handed piece of injustice, expressly designed to cripple New England commerce, and evasions of this unjust law found everywhere a degree of sympathy, even in the breasts of well-disposed and conscientious people. In resistance to the law, vessels were constantly fitted out which ran upon trading voyages to the West Indies and other places; and although the practice was punishable as smuggling, yet it found extensive connivance. From this beginning smuggling of all kinds gradually grew up in the community, and gained such a foothold that even after the repeal of the embargo it still continued to be extensively practiced. Secret depositories of contraband goods still existed in many of the lonely haunts of islands off the coast of Maine. Hid in deep forest shadows, visited only in the darkness of the night, were these illegal stores of merchandise. And from these secluded resorts they found their way, no one knew or cared to say how, into houses for miles around.

There was no doubt that the practice, like all other illegal ones, was demoralizing to the community, and particularly fatal to the character of that class of bold, enterprising young men who would be most likely to be drawn into it.

Zephaniah Pennel, who was made of a kind of straight-grained, uncompromising oaken timber such as built the Mayflower of old, had always borne his testimony at home and abroad against any violations of the laws of the land, however veiled under the pretext of righting a wrong or resisting an injustice, and had done what he could in his neighborhood to enable government officers to detect and break up these unlawful depositories. This exposed him particularly to the hatred and ill-will of the operators concerned in such affairs, and a plot was laid by a few of the most daring and determined of them to establish one of their depositories on Orr's Island, and to implicate the family of Pennel himself in the trade. This would accomplish two purposes, as they hoped,—it would be a mortification and defeat to him,—a revenge which they coveted; and it would, they thought, insure his silence and complicity for the strongest reasons.

The situation and characteristics of Orr's Island peculiarly fitted it for the carrying out of a scheme of this kind, and for this purpose we must try to give our readers a more definite idea of it.

The traveler who wants a ride through scenery of more varied and singular beauty than can ordinarily be found on the shores of any land whatever, should start some fine clear day along the clean sandy road, ribboned with strips of green grass, that leads through the flat pitch-pine forests of Brunswick toward the sea. As he approaches the salt water, a succession of the most beautiful and picturesque lakes seems to be lying softly cradled in the arms of wild, rocky forest shores, whose outlines are ever changing with the windings of the road.

At a distance of about six or eight miles from Brunswick he crosses an arm of the sea, and comes upon the first of the interlacing group of islands which beautifies the shore. A ride across this island is a constant succession of pictures, whose wild and solitary beauty entirely distances all power of description. The magnificence of the evergreen forests,—their peculiar air of sombre stillness,—the rich intermingling ever and anon of groves of birch, beech, and oak, in picturesque knots and tufts, as if set for effect by some skillful landscape-gardener,—produce a sort of strange dreamy wonder; while the sea, breaking forth both on the right hand and the left of the road into the most romantic glimpses, seems to flash and glitter like some strange gem which every moment shows itself through the framework of a new setting. Here and there little secluded coves push in from the sea, around which lie soft tracts of green meadow-land, hemmed in and guarded by rocky pine-crowned ridges. In such sheltered spots may be seen neat white houses, nestling like sheltered doves in the beautiful solitude.

When one has ridden nearly to the end of Great Island, which is about four miles across, he sees rising before him, from the sea, a bold romantic point of land, uplifting a crown of rich evergreen and forest trees over shores of perpendicular rock. This is Orr's Island.

It was not an easy matter in the days of our past experience to guide a horse and carriage down the steep, wild shores of Great Island to the long bridge that connects it with Orr's. The sense of wild seclusion reaches here the highest degree; and one crosses the bridge with a feeling as if genii might have built it, and one might be going over it to fairy-land. From the bridge the path rises on to a high granite ridge, which runs from one end of the island to the other, and has been called the Devil's Back, with that superstitious generosity which seems to have abandoned all romantic places to so undeserving an owner.

By the side of this ridge of granite is a deep, narrow chasm, running a mile and a half or two miles parallel with the road, and veiled by the darkest and most solemn shadows of the primeval forest. Here scream the jays and the eagles, and fish-hawks make their nests undisturbed; and the tide rises and falls under black branches of evergreen, from which depend long, light festoons of delicate gray moss. The darkness of the forest is relieved by the delicate foliage and the silvery trunks of the great white birches, which the solitude of centuries has allowed to grow in this spot to a height and size seldom attained elsewhere.

It was this narrow, rocky cove that had been chosen by the smuggler Atkinson and his accomplices as a safe and secluded resort for their operations. He was a seafaring man of Bath, one of that class who always prefer uncertain and doubtful courses to those which are safe and reputable. He was possessed of many of those traits calculated to make him a hero in the eyes of young men; was dashing, free, and frank in his manners, with a fund of humor and an abundance of ready anecdote which made his society fascinating; but he concealed beneath all these attractions a character of hard, grasping, unscrupulous selfishness, and an utter destitution of moral principle.

Moses, now in his sixteenth year, and supposed to be in a general way doing well, under the care of the minister, was left free to come and go at his own pleasure, unwatched by Zephaniah, whose fishing operations often took him for weeks from home. Atkinson hung about the boy's path, engaging him first in fishing or hunting enterprises; plied him with choice preparations of liquor, with which he would enhance the hilarity of their expeditions; and finally worked on his love of adventure and that impatient restlessness incident to his period of life to draw him fully into his schemes. Moses lost all interest in his lessons, often neglecting them for days at a time—accounting for his negligence by excuses which were far from satisfactory. When Mara would expostulate with him about this, he would break out upon her with a fierce irritation. Was he always going to be tied to a girl's apron-string? He was tired of study, and tired of old Sewell, whom he declared an old granny in a white wig, who knew nothing of the world. He wasn't going to college—it was altogether too slow for him—he was going to see life and push ahead for himself.

Mara's life during this time was intensely wearing. A frail, slender, delicate girl of thirteen, she carried a heart prematurely old with the most distressing responsibility of mature life. Her love for Moses had always had in it a large admixture of that maternal and care-taking element which, in some shape or other, qualities the affection of woman to man. Ever since that dream of babyhood, when the vision of a pale mother had led the beautiful boy to her arms, Mara had accepted him as something exclusively her own, with an intensity of ownership that seemed almost to merge her personal identity with his. She felt, and saw, and enjoyed, and suffered in him, and yet was conscious of a higher nature in herself, by which unwillingly he was often judged and condemned. His faults affected her with a kind of guilty pain, as if they were her own; his sins were borne bleeding in her heart in silence, and with a jealous watchfulness to hide them from every eye but hers. She busied herself day and night interceding and making excuses for him, first to her own sensitive moral nature, and then with everybody around, for with one or another he was coming into constant collision. She felt at this time a fearful load of suspicion, which she dared not express to a human being.

Up to this period she had always been the only confidant of Moses, who poured into her ear without reserve all the good and the evil of his nature, and who loved her with all the intensity with which he was capable of loving anything. Nothing so much shows what a human being is in moral advancement as the quality of his love. Moses Pennel's love was egotistic, exacting, tyrannical, and capricious—sometimes venting itself in expressions of a passionate fondness, which had a savor of protecting generosity in them, and then receding to the icy pole of surly petulance. For all that, there was no resisting the magnetic attraction with which in his amiable moods he drew those whom he liked to himself.

Such people are not very wholesome companions for those who are sensitively organized and predisposed to self-sacrificing love. They keep the heart in a perpetual freeze and thaw, which, like the American northern climate, is so particularly fatal to plants of a delicate habit. They could live through the hot summer and the cold winter, but they cannot endure the three or four months when it freezes one day and melts the next,—when all the buds are started out by a week of genial sunshine, and then frozen for a fortnight. These fitful persons are of all others most engrossing, because you are always sure in their good moods that they are just going to be angels,—an expectation which no number of disappointments seems finally to do away. Mara believed in Moses's future as she did in her own existence. He was going to do something great and good,—that she was certain of. He would be a splendid man! Nobody, she thought, knew him as she did; nobody could know how good and generous he was *sometimes*, and how frankly he would confess his faults, and what noble aspirations he had!

But there was no concealing from her watchful sense that Moses was beginning to have secrets from her. He was cloudy and murky; and at some of the most harmless inquiries in the world, would flash out with a sudden temper, as if she had touched some sore spot. Her bedroom was opposite to his; and she became quite sure that night after night, while she lay thinking of him, she heard him steal down out of the house between two and three o'clock, and not return till a little before day-dawn. Where he went, and with whom, and what he was doing, was to her an awful mystery,—and it was one she dared not share with a human being. If she told her kind old grandfather, she feared that any inquiry from him would only light as a spark on that inflammable spirit of pride and insubordination that was rising within him, and bring on an instantaneous explosion. Mr. Sewell's influence she could hope little more from; and as to poor Mrs. Pennel, such communications would only weary and distress her, without doing any manner of good. There was, therefore, only that one unfailing Confidant—the Invisible Friend to whom the solitary child could pour out her heart, and whose inspirations of comfort and guidance never fail to come again in return to true souls.

One moonlight night, as she lay thus praying, her senses, sharpened by watching, discerned a sound of steps treading under her window, and then a low whistle. Her heart beat violently, and she soon heard the door of Moses's room open, and then the old chamber-stairs gave forth those inconsiderate creaks and snaps that garrulous old stairs always will when anybody is desirous of making them accomplices in a night-secret. Mara rose, and undrawing her curtain, saw three men standing before the house, and saw Moses come out and join them. Quick as thought she threw on her clothes and wrapping her little form in a dark cloak, with a hood, followed them out. She kept at a safe distance behind them,—so far back as just to keep them in sight. They never looked back, and seemed to say but little till they approached the edge of that deep belt of forest which shrouds so large a portion of the island. She hurried along, now nearer to them lest they should be lost to view in the deep shadows, while they went on crackling and plunging through the dense underbrush.

CHAPTER XXI

THE TEMPTER

It was well for Mara that so much of her life had been passed in wild forest rambles. She looked frail as the rays of moonbeam which slid down the old white-bearded hemlocks, but her limbs were agile and supple as steel; and while the party went crashing on before, she followed with such lightness that the slight sound of her movements was entirely lost in the heavy crackling plunges of the party. Her little heart was beating fast and hard; but could any one have seen her face, as it now and then came into a spot of moonshine, they might have seen it fixed in a deadly expression of resolve and determination. She was going after *him*—no matter where; she was resolved to know who and what it was that was leading him away, as her heart told her, to no good. Deeper and deeper into the shadows of the forest they went, and the child easily kept up with them.

Mara had often rambled for whole solitary days in this lonely wood, and knew all its rocks and dells the whole three miles to the long bridge at the other end of the island. But she had never before seen it under the solemn stillness of midnight moonlight, which gives to the most familiar objects such a strange, ghostly charm. After they had gone a mile into the forest, she could see through the black spruces silver gleams of the sea, and hear, amid the whirr and sway of the pine-tops, the dash of the ever restless tide which pushed up the long cove. It was at the full, as she could discern with a rapid glance of her practiced eye, expertly versed in the knowledge of every change of the solitary nature around.

And now the party began to plunge straight down the rocky ledge of the Devil's Back, on which they had been walking hitherto, into the deep ravine where lay the cove. It was a scrambling, precipitous way, over perpendicular walls of rock, whose crevices furnished anchoring-places for grand old hemlocks or silver-birches, and whose rough sides, leathery with black flaps of lichen, were all tangled and interlaced with thick netted bushes. The men plunged down laughing, shouting, and swearing at their occasional missteps, and silently as moonbeam or thistledown the light-footed shadow went down after them.

She suddenly paused behind a pile of rock, as, through an opening between two great spruces, the sea gleamed out like a sheet of looking-glass set in a black frame. And here the child saw a small vessel swinging at anchor, with the moonlight full on its slack sails, and she could hear the gentle gurgle and lick of the green-tongued waves as they dashed under it toward the rocky shore.

Mara stopped with a beating heart as she saw the company making for the schooner. The tide is high; will they go on board and sail away with him where she cannot follow? What could she do? In an ecstasy of fear she kneeled down and asked God not to let him go,—to give her at least one more chance to save him.

For the pure and pious child had heard enough of the words of these men, as she walked behind them, to fill her with horror. She had never before heard an oath, but there came back from these men coarse, brutal tones and words of blasphemy that froze her blood with horror. And Moses was going with them! She felt somehow as if they must be a company of fiends bearing him to his ruin.

For some time she kneeled there watching behind the rock, while Moses and his companions went on board the little schooner. She had no feeling of horror at the loneliness of her own situation, for her solitary life had made every woodland thing dear and familiar to her. She was cowering down, on a loose, spongy bed of moss, which was all threaded through and through with the green vines and pale pink blossoms of the mayflower, and she felt its fragrant breath streaming up in the moist moonlight. As she leaned forward to look through a rocky crevice, her arms rested on a bed of that brittle white moss she had often gathered with so much admiration, and a scarlet rock-columbine, such as she loved to paint, brushed her cheek,—and all these mute fair things seemed to strive to keep her company in her chill suspense of watchfulness. Two whippoorwills, from a clump of silvery birches, kept calling to each other in melancholy iteration, while she stayed there still listening, and knowing by an occasional sound of laughing, or the explosion of some oath, that the men were not yet gone. At last they all appeared again, and came to a cleared place among the dry leaves, quite near to the rock where she was concealed, and kindled a fire which they kept snapping and crackling by a constant supply of green resinous hemlock branches.

The red flame danced and leaped through the green fuel, and leaping upward in tongues of flame, cast ruddy bronze reflections on the old pine-trees with their long branches waving with boards of white moss,—and by the firelight Mara could see two men in sailor's dress with pistols in their belts, and the man Atkinson, whom she had recollected as having seen once or twice at her grandfather's. She remembered how she had always shrunk from him with a strange instinctive dislike, half fear, half disgust, when he had addressed her with that kind of free admiration which men of his class often feel themselves at liberty to express to a pretty girl of her early age. He was a man that might have been handsome, had it not been for a certain strange expression of covert wickedness. It was as if some vile evil spirit, walking, as the Scriptures say, through dry places, had lighted on a comely man's body, in which he had set up housekeeping, making it look like a fair house abused by an unclean owner.

As Mara watched his demeanor with Moses, she could think only of a loathsome black snake that she had once seen in those solitary rocks;—she felt as if his handsome but evil eye were charming him with an evil charm to his destruction.

"Well, Mo, my boy," she heard him say,—slapping Moses on the shoulder,—"this is something like. We'll have a 'tempus,' as the college fellows say,—put down the clams to roast, and I'll mix the punch," he said, setting over the fire a tea-kettle which they brought from the ship.

After their preparations were finished, all sat down to eat and drink. Mara listened with anxiety and horror to a conversation such as she never heard or conceived before. It is not often that women hear men talk in the undisguised manner which they use among themselves; but the conversation of men of unprincipled lives, and low, brutal habits, unchecked by the presence of respectable female society, might well convey to the horror-struck child a feeling as if she were listening at the mouth of hell. Almost every word was preceded or emphasized by an oath; and what struck with a death chill to her heart was, that Moses swore too, and seemed to show that desperate anxiety to seem *au fait* in the language of wickedness, which boys often do at that age, when they fancy that to be ignorant of vice is a mark of disgraceful greenness. Moses evidently was bent on showing that he was not green,—ignorant of the pure ear to which every such word came like the blast of death.

He drank a great deal, too, and the mirth among them grew furious and terrific. Mara, horrified and shocked as she was, did not, however, lose that intense and alert presence of mind, natural to persons in whom there is moral strength, however delicate be their physical frame. She felt at once that these men were playing upon Moses; that they had an object in view; that they were flattering and cajoling him, and leading him to drink, that they might work out some fiendish purpose of their own. The man called Atkinson related story after story of wild adventure, in which sudden fortunes had been made by men who, he said, were not afraid to take "the short cut across lots." He told of piratical adventures in the West Indies,—of the fun of chasing and overhauling ships,—and gave dazzling accounts of the treasures found on board. It was observable that all these stories were told on the line between joke and earnest,—as frolics, as specimens of good fun, and seeing life, etc.

At last came a suggestion,—What if they should start off together some fine day, "just for a spree," and try a cruise in the West Indies, to see what they could pick up? They had arms, and a gang of fine, whole-souled fellows. Moses had been tied to Ma'am Pennel's apron-string long enough. And "hark ye," said one of them, "Moses, they say old Pennel has lots of dollars in that old sea-chest of his'n. It would be a kindness to him to invest them for him in an adventure."

Moses answered with a streak of the boy innocence which often remains under the tramping of evil men, like ribbons of green turf in the middle of roads:—

"You don't know Father Pennel,—why, he'd no more come into it than"—

A perfect roar of laughter cut short this declaration, and Atkinson, slapping Moses on the back, said,—

CHAPTER XXI

"By ——, Mo! you are the jolliest green dog! I shall die a-laughing of your innocence some day. Why, my boy, can't you see? Pennel's money can be invested without asking him."

"Why, he keeps it locked," said Moses.

"And supposing you pick the lock?"

"Not I, indeed," said Moses, making a sudden movement to rise.

Mara almost screamed in her ecstasy, but she had sense enough to hold her breath.

"Ho! see him now," said Atkinson, lying back, and holding his sides while he laughed, and rolled over; "you can get off anything on that muff,—any hoax in the world,—he's so soft! Come, come, my dear boy, sit down. I was only seeing how wide I could make you open those great black eyes of your'n,—that's all."

"You'd better take care how you joke with me," said Moses, with that look of gloomy determination which Mara was quite familiar with of old. It was the rallying effort of a boy who had abandoned the first outworks of virtue to make a stand for the citadel. And Atkinson, like a prudent besieger after a repulse, returned to lie on his arms.

He began talking volubly on other subjects, telling stories, and singing songs, and pressing Moses to drink.

Mara was comforted to see that he declined drinking,—that he looked gloomy and thoughtful, in spite of the jokes of his companions; but she trembled to see, by the following conversation, how Atkinson was skillfully and prudently making apparent to Moses the extent to which he had him in his power. He seemed to Mara like an ugly spider skillfully weaving his web around a fly. She felt cold and faint; but within her there was a heroic strength.

She was not going to faint; she would make herself bear up. She was going to do something to get Moses out of this snare,—but what? At last they rose.

"It is past three o'clock," she heard one of them say.

"I say, Mo," said Atkinson, "you must make tracks for home, or you won't be in bed when Mother Pennel calls you."

The men all laughed at this joke, as they turned to go on board the schooner.

When they were gone, Moses threw himself down and hid his face in his hands. He knew not what pitying little face was looking down upon him from the hemlock shadows, what brave little heart was determined to save him. He was in one of those great crises of agony that boys pass through when they first awake from the fun and frolic of unlawful enterprises to find themselves sold under sin, and feel the terrible logic of evil which constrains them to pass from the less to greater crime. He felt that he was in the power of bad, unprincipled, heartless men, who, if he refused to do their bidding, had the power to expose him. All he had been doing would come out. His kind old foster-parents would know it. Mara would know it. Mr. Sewell and Miss Emily would know the secrets of his life that past month. He felt as if they were all looking at him now. He had disgraced himself,—had sunk below his education,—had been false to all his better knowledge and the past expectations of his friends, living a mean, miserable, dishonorable life,—and now the ground was fast sliding from under him, and the next plunge might be down a precipice from which there would be no return. What he had done up to this hour had been done in the roystering, inconsiderate gamesomeness of boyhood. It had been represented to himself only as "sowing wild oats," "having steep times," "seeing a little of life," and so on; but this night he had had propositions of piracy and robbery made to him, and he had not dared to knock down the man that made them,—had not dared at once to break away from his company. He must meet him again,—must go on with him, or—he groaned in agony at the thought.

It was a strong indication of that repressed, considerate habit of mind which love had wrought in the child, that when Mara heard the boy's sobs rising in the stillness, she did not, as she wished to, rush out and throw her arms around his neck and try to comfort him.

But she felt instinctively that she must not do this. She must not let him know that she had discovered his secret by stealing after him thus in the night shadows. She knew how nervously he had resented even the compassionate glances she had cast upon him in his restless, turbid intervals during the past few weeks, and the fierceness with which he had replied to a few timid inquiries. No,—though her heart was breaking for him, it was a shrewd, wise little heart, and resolved not to spoil all by yielding to its first untaught impulses. She repressed herself as the mother does who refrains from crying out when she sees her unconscious little one on the verge of a precipice.

When Moses rose and moodily began walking homeward, she followed at a distance. She could now keep farther off, for she knew the way through every part of the forest, and she only wanted to keep within sound of his footsteps to make sure that he was going home. When he emerged from the forest into the open moonlight, she sat down in its shadows and watched him as he walked over the open distance between her and the house. He went in; and then she waited a little longer for him to be quite retired. She thought he would throw himself on the bed, and then she could steal in after him. So she sat there quite in the shadows.

The grand full moon was riding high and calm in the purple sky, and Harpswell Bay on the one hand, and the wide, open ocean on the other, lay all in a silver shimmer of light. There was not a sound save the plash of the tide, now beginning to go out, and rolling and rattling the pebbles up and down as it came and went, and once in a while the distant, mournful intoning of the whippoorwill. There were silent lonely ships, sailing slowly to and fro far out to sea, turning their fair wings now into bright light and now into shadow, as they moved over the glassy stillness. Mara could see all the houses on Harpswell Neck and the white church as clear as in the daylight. It seemed to her some strange, unearthly dream.

As she sat there, she thought over her whole little life, all full of one thought, one purpose, one love, one prayer, for this being so strangely given to her out of that silent sea, which lay so like a still eternity around her,—and she revolved again what meant the vision of her childhood. Did it not mean that she was to watch over him and save him from some dreadful danger? That poor mother was lying now silent and peaceful under the turf in the little graveyard not far off, and *she* must care for her boy.

A strong motherly feeling swelled out the girl's heart,—she felt that she *must*, she would, somehow save that treasure which had so mysteriously been committed to her. So, when she thought she had given time enough for Moses to be quietly asleep in his room, she arose and ran with quick footsteps across the moonlit plain to the house.

The front-door was standing wide open, as was always the innocent fashion in these regions, with a half-angle of moonlight and shadow lying within its dusky depths. Mara listened a moment,—no sound: he had gone to bed then. "Poor boy," she said, "I hope he is asleep; how he must feel, poor fellow! It's all the fault of those dreadful men!" said the little dark shadow to herself, as she stole up the stairs past his room as guiltily as if she were the sinner. Once the stairs creaked, and her heart was in her mouth, but she gained her room and shut and bolted the door. She kneeled down by her little white bed, and thanked God that she had come in safe, and then prayed him to teach her what to do next. She felt chilly and shivering, and crept into bed, and lay with her great soft brown eyes wide open, intently thinking what she should do.

Should she tell her grandfather? Something instinctively said No; that the first word from him which showed Moses he was detected would at once send him off with those wicked men. "He would never, never bear to have this known," she said. Mr. Sewell?—ah, that was worse. She herself shrank from letting him know what Moses had been doing; she could not bear to lower him so much in his eyes. He could not make allowances, she thought. He is good, to be sure, but he is so old and grave, and doesn't know how much Moses has been tempted by these dreadful men; and then perhaps he would tell Miss Emily, and they never would want Moses to come there any more.

"What shall I do?" she said to herself. "I must get somebody to help me or tell me what to do. I can't tell grandmamma; it would only make her ill, and she wouldn't know what to do any more than I. Ah, I know what I will do,—I'll tell Captain Kittridge; he was always so kind to me; and he has been to sea and seen all sorts of men, and Moses won't care so much perhaps to have him know, because the Captain is such a funny man, and don't take everything so seriously. Yes, that's it. I'll go right down to the cove in the morning. God will bring me through, I know He will;" and the little weary head fell back on the pillow asleep. And as she slept, a smile settled over her face, perhaps a reflection from the face of her good angel, who always beholdeth the face of our Father in Heaven.

CHAPTER XXII

A FRIEND IN NEED

Mara was so wearied with her night walk and the agitation she had been through, that once asleep she slept long after the early breakfast hour of the family. She was surprised on awaking to hear the slow old clock downstairs striking eight. She hastily jumped up and looked around with a confused wonder, and then slowly the events of the past night came back upon her like a remembered dream. She dressed herself quickly, and went down to find the breakfast things all washed and put away, and Mrs. Pennel spinning.

"Why, dear heart," said the old lady, "how came you to sleep so?—I spoke to you twice, but I could not make you hear."

"Has Moses been down, grandma?" said Mara, intent on the sole thought in her heart.

"Why, yes, dear, long ago,—and cross enough he was; that boy does get to be a trial,—but come, dear, I've saved some hot cakes for you,—sit down now and eat your breakfast."

Mara made a feint of eating what her grandmother with fond officiousness would put before her, and then rising up she put on her sun-bonnet and started down toward the cove to find her old friend.

The queer, dry, lean old Captain had been to her all her life like a faithful kobold or brownie, an unquestioning servant of all her gentle biddings. She dared tell him anything without diffidence or shamefacedness; and she felt that in this trial of her life he might have in his sea-receptacle some odd old amulet or spell that should be of power to help her. Instinctively she avoided the house, lest Sally should see and fly out and seize her. She took a narrow path through the cedars down to the little boat cove where the old Captain worked so merrily ten years ago, in the beginning of our story, and where she found him now, with his coat off, busily planing a board.

"Wal', now,—if this 'ere don't beat all!" he said, looking up and seeing her; "why, you're looking after Sally, I s'pose? She's up to the house."

"No, Captain Kittridge, I'm come to see *you*."

CHAPTER XXII

"You *be*?" said the Captain, "I swow! if I ain't a lucky feller. But what's the matter?" he said, suddenly observing her pale face and the tears in her eyes. "Hain't nothin' bad happened,—hes there?"

"Oh! Captain Kittridge, something dreadful; and nobody but you can help me."

"Want to know, now!" said the Captain, with a grave face. "Well, come here, now, and sit down, and tell me all about it. Don't you cry, there's a good girl! Don't, now."

Mara began her story, and went through with it in a rapid and agitated manner; and the good Captain listened in a fidgety state of interest, occasionally relieving his mind by interjecting "Do tell, now!" "I swan,—if that ar ain't too bad."

"That ar's rediculous conduct in Atkinson. He ought to be talked to," said the Captain, when she had finished, and then he whistled and put a shaving in his mouth, which he chewed reflectively.

"Don't you be a mite worried, Mara," he said. "You did a great deal better to come to me than to go to Mr. Sewell or your grand'ther either; 'cause you see these 'ere wild chaps they'll take things from me they wouldn't from a church-member or a minister. Folks mustn't pull 'em up with *too* short a rein,—they must kind o' flatter 'em off. But that ar Atkinson's too rediculous for anything; and if he don't mind, I'll serve him out. I know a thing or two about him that I shall shake over his head if he don't behave. Now I don't think so much of smugglin' as some folks," said the Captain, lowering his voice to a confidential tone. "I reely don't, now; but come to goin' off piratin',—and tryin' to put a young boy up to robbin' his best friends,—why, there ain't no kind o' sense in that. It's p'ison mean of Atkinson. I shall tell him so, and I shall talk to Moses."

"Oh! I'm afraid to have you," said Mara, apprehensively.

"Why, chickabiddy," said the old Captain, "you don't understand me. I ain't goin' at him with no sermons,—I shall jest talk to him this way: Look here now, Moses, I shall say, there's Badger's ship goin' to sail in a fortnight for China, and they want likely fellers aboard, and I've got a hundred dollars that I'd like to send on a venture; if you'll take it and go, why, we'll share the profits. I shall talk like that, you know. Mebbe I sha'n't let him know what I know, and mebbe I shall; jest tip him a wink, you know; it depends on circumstances. But bless you, child, these 'ere fellers ain't none of 'em 'fraid o' me, you see, 'cause they know I know the ropes."

"And can you make that horrid man let him alone?" said Mara, fearfully.

"Calculate I can. 'Spect if I's to tell Atkinson a few things I know, he'd be for bein' scase in our parts. Now, you see, I hain't minded doin' a small bit o' trade now and then with them ar fellers myself; but this 'ere," said the Captain, stopping and looking extremely disgusted, "why, it's contemptible, it's rediculous!"

"Do you think I'd better tell grandpapa?" said Mara.

"Don't worry your little head. I'll step up and have a talk with Pennel, this evening. He knows as well as I that there is times when chaps must be seen to, and no remarks made. Pennel knows that ar. Why, now, Mis' Kittridge thinks our boys turned out so well all along of her bringin' up, and I let her think so; keeps her sort o' in spirits, you see. But Lord bless ye, child, there's been times with Job, and Sam, and Pass, and Dass, and Dile, and all on 'em finally, when, if I hadn't jest pulled a rope here and turned a screw there, and said nothin' to nobody, they'd a-been all gone to smash. I never told Mis' Kittridge none o' their didos; bless you, 'twouldn't been o' no use. I never told *them*, neither; but I jest kind o' worked 'em off, you know; and they's all putty 'spectable men now, as men go, you know; not like Parson Sewell, but good, honest mates and ship-masters,—kind o' middlin' people, you know. It takes a good many o' sich to make up a world, d'ye see."

"But oh, Captain Kittridge, did any of them use to swear?" said Mara, in a faltering voice.

"Wal', they did, consid'able," said the Captain;—then seeing the trembling of Mara's lip, he added,—

"Ef you could a-found this 'ere out any other way, it's most a pity you'd a-heard him; 'cause he wouldn't never have let out afore you. It don't do for gals to hear the fellers talk when they's alone, 'cause fellers,—wal', you see, fellers will be fellers, partic'larly when they're young. Some on 'em, they never gits over it all their lives finally."

"But oh! Captain Kittridge, that talk last night was so dreadfully wicked! and Moses!—oh, it was dreadful to hear him!"

"Wal', yes, it was," said the Captain, consolingly; "but don't you cry, and don't you break your little heart. I expect he'll come all right, and jine the church one of these days; 'cause there's old Pennel, he prays,—fact now, I think there's consid'able in some people's prayers, and he's one of the sort. And you pray, too; and I'm quite sure the good Lord *must* hear you. I declare sometimes I wish you'd jest say a good word to Him for me; I should like to get the hang o' things a little better than I do, somehow, I reely should. I've gi'n up swearing years ago. Mis' Kittridge, she broke me o' that, and now I don't never go further than 'I vum' or 'I swow,' or somethin' o' that sort; but you see I'm old;—Moses is young; but then he's got eddication and friends, and he'll come all right. Now you jest see ef he don't!"

This miscellaneous budget of personal experiences and friendly consolation which the good Captain conveyed to Mara may possibly make you laugh, my reader, but the good, ropy brown man was doing his best to console his little friend; and as Mara looked at him he was almost glorified in her eyes—he had power to save Moses, and he would do it. She went home to dinner that day with her heart considerably lightened. She refrained, in a guilty way, from even looking at Moses, who was gloomy and moody.

Mara had from nature a good endowment of that kind of innocent hypocrisy which is needed as a staple in the lives of women who bridge a thousand awful chasms with smiling, unconscious looks, and walk, singing and scattering flowers, over abysses of fear, while their hearts are dying within them.

She talked more volubly than was her wont with Mrs. Pennel, and with her old grandfather; she laughed and seemed in more than usual spirits, and only once did she look up and catch the gloomy eye of Moses. It had that murky, troubled look that one may see in the eye of a boy when those evil waters which cast up mire and dirt have once been stirred in his soul. They fell under her clear glance, and he made a rapid, impatient movement, as if it hurt him to be looked at. The evil spirit in boy or man cannot bear the "touch of celestial temper;" and the sensitiveness to eyebeams is one of the earliest signs of conscious, inward guilt.

Mara was relieved, as he flung out of the house after dinner, to see the long, dry figure of Captain Kittridge coming up and seizing Moses by the button. From the window she saw the Captain assuming a confidential air with him; and when they had talked together a few moments, she saw Moses going with great readiness after him down the road to his house.

In less than a fortnight, it was settled Moses was to sail for China, and Mara was deep in the preparations for his outfit. Once she would have felt this departure as the most dreadful trial of her life. Now it seemed to her a deliverance for him, and she worked with a cheerful alacrity, which seemed to Moses more than was proper, considering *he* was going away.

For Moses, like many others of his sex, boy or man, had quietly settled in his own mind that the whole love of Mara's heart was to be his, to have and to hold, to use and to draw on, when and as he liked. He reckoned on it as a sort of inexhaustible, uncounted treasure that was his own peculiar right and property, and therefore he felt abused at what he supposed was a disclosure of some deficiency on her part.

"You seem to be very glad to be rid of me," he said to her in a bitter tone one day, as she was earnestly busy in her preparations.

Now the fact was, that Moses had been assiduously making himself disagreeable to Mara for the fortnight past, by all sorts of unkind sayings and doings; and he knew it too; yet he felt a right to feel very much abused at the thought that she could possibly want him to be going. If she had been utterly desolate about it, and torn her hair and sobbed and wailed, he would have asked what she could be crying about, and begged not to be bored with scenes; but as it was, this cheerful composure was quite unfeeling.

Now pray don't suppose Moses to be a monster of an uncommon species. We take him to be an average specimen of a boy of a certain kind of temperament in the transition period of life. Everything is chaos within; the flesh lusteth against the spirit, and the spirit against the flesh, and "light and darkness, and mind and dust, and passion and pure thoughts, mingle and contend," without end or order. He wondered at himself sometimes that he could say such cruel things as he did to his faithful little friend—to one whom, after all, he did love and trust before all other human beings.

There is no saying why it is that a man or a boy, not radically destitute of generous comprehensions, will often cruelly torture and tyrannize over a woman whom he both loves and reveres, who stands in his soul in his best hours as the very impersonation of all that is good and beautiful. It is as if some evil spirit at times possessed him, and compelled him to utter words which were felt at the moment to be mean and hateful. Moses often wondered at himself, as he lay awake nights, how he could have said and done the things he had, and felt miserably resolved to make it up somehow before he went away; but he did not.

He could not say, "Mara, I have done wrong," though he every day meant to do it, and sometimes sat an hour in her presence, feeling murky and stony, as if possessed by a dumb spirit; then he would get up and fling stormily out of the house.

Poor Mara wondered if he really would go without one kind word. She thought of all the years they had been together, and how he had been her only thought and love. What had become of her brother?—the Moses that once she used to know—frank, careless, not ill-tempered, and who sometimes seemed to love her and think she was the best little girl in the world? Where was he gone to—this friend and brother of her childhood, and would he never come back?

At last came the evening before his parting; the sea-chest was all made up and packed; and Mara's fingers had been busy with everything, from more substantial garments down to all those little comforts and nameless conveniences that only a woman knows how to improvise. Mara thought certainly she should get a few kind words, as Moses looked it over. But he only said, "All right;" and then added that "there was a button off one of the shirts." Mara's busy fingers quickly replaced it, and Moses was annoyed at the tear that fell on the button. What was she crying for now? He knew very well, but he felt stubborn and cruel. Afterwards he lay awake many a night in his berth, and acted this last scene over differently. He took Mara in his arms and kissed her; he told her she was his best friend, his good angel, and that he was not worthy to kiss the hem of her garment; but the next day, when he thought of writing a letter to her, he didn't, and the good mood passed away. Boys do not acquire an ease of expression in letter-writing as early as girls, and a voyage to China furnished opportunities few and far between of sending letters.

Now and then, through some sailing ship, came missives which seemed to Mara altogether colder and more unsatisfactory than they would have done could she have appreciated the difference between a boy and a girl in power of epistolary expression; for the power of really representing one's heart on paper, which is one of the first spring flowers of early womanhood, is the latest blossom on the slow-growing tree of manhood. To do Moses justice, these seeming cold letters were often written with a choking lump in his throat, caused by thinking over his many sins against his little good angel; but then that past account was so long, and had so much that it pained him to think of, that he dashed it all off in the shortest fashion, and said to himself, "One of these days when I see her I'll make it all up."

No man—especially one that is living a rough, busy, out-of-doors life—can form the slightest conception of that veiled and secluded life which exists in the heart of a sensitive woman, whose sphere is narrow, whose external diversions are few, and whose mind, therefore, acts by a continual introversion upon itself. They know nothing how their careless words and actions are pondered and turned again in weary, quiet hours of fruitless questioning. What did he mean by this?

and what did he intend by that?—while he, the careless buffalo, meant nothing, or has forgotten what it was, if he did. Man's utter ignorance of woman's nature is a cause of a great deal of unsuspected cruelty which he practices toward her.

Mara found one or two opportunities of writing to Moses; but her letters were timid and constrained by a sort of frosty, discouraged sense of loneliness; and Moses, though he knew he had no earthly right to expect this to be otherwise, took upon him to feel as an abused individual, whom nobody loved—whose way in the world was destined to be lonely and desolate. So when, at the end of three years, he arrived suddenly at Brunswick in the beginning of winter, and came, all burning with impatience, to the home at Orr's Island, and found that Mara had gone to Boston on a visit, he resented it as a personal slight.

He might have inquired why she should expect him, and whether her whole life was to be spent in looking out of the window to watch for him. He might have remembered that he had warned her of his approach by no letter. But no. "Mara didn't care for him—she had forgotten all about him—she was having a good time in Boston, just as likely as not with some train of admirers, and he had been tossing on the stormy ocean, and she had thought nothing of it." How many things he had meant to say! He had never felt so good and so affectionate. He would have confessed all the sins of his life to her, and asked her pardon—and she wasn't there!

Mrs. Pennel suggested that he might go to Boston after her.

No, he was not going to do that. He would not intrude on her pleasures with the memory of a rough, hard-working sailor. He was alone in the world, and had his own way to make, and so best go at once up among lumbermen, and cut the timber for the ship that was to carry Cæsar and his fortunes.

When Mara was informed by a letter from Mrs. Pennel, expressed in the few brief words in which that good woman generally embodied her epistolary communications, that Moses had been at home, and gone to Umbagog without seeing her, she felt at her heart only a little closer stricture of cold, quiet pain, which had become a habit of her inner life.

"He did not love her—he was cold and selfish," said the inner voice. And faintly she pleaded, in answer, "He is a man—he has seen the world—and has so much to do and think of, no wonder."

In fact, during the last three years that had parted them, the great change of life had been consummated in both. They had parted boy and girl; they would meet man and woman. The time of this meeting had been announced.

And all this is the history of that sigh, so very quiet that Sally Kittridge never checked the rattling flow of her conversation to observe it.

CHAPTER XXIII

THE BEGINNING OF THE STORY

We have in the last three chapters brought up the history of our characters to the time when our story opens, when Mara and Sally Kittridge were discussing the expected return of Moses. Sally was persuaded by Mara to stay and spend the night with her, and did so without much fear of what her mother would say when she returned; for though Mrs. Kittridge still made bustling demonstrations of authority, it was quite evident to every one that the handsome grown-up girl had got the sceptre into her own hands, and was reigning in the full confidence of being, in one way or another, able to bring her mother into all her views.

So Sally stayed—to have one of those long night-talks in which girls delight, in the course of which all sorts of intimacies and confidences, that shun the daylight, open like the night-blooming cereus in strange successions. One often wonders by daylight at the things one says very naturally in the dark.

So the two girls talked about Moses, and Sally dilated upon his handsome, manly air the one Sunday that he had appeared in Harpswell meeting-house.

"He didn't know me at all, if you'll believe it," said Sally. "I was standing with father when he came out, and he shook hands with him, and looked at me as if I'd been an entire stranger."

"I'm not in the least surprised," said Mara; "you're grown so and altered."

"Well, now, you'd hardly know him, Mara," said Sally. "He is a man—a real man; everything about him is different; he holds up his head in such a proud way. Well, he always did that when he was a boy; but when he speaks, he has such a deep voice! How boys do alter in a year or two!"

"Do you think I have altered much, Sally?" said Mara; "at least, do you think *he* would think so?"

"Why, Mara, you and I have been together so much, I can't tell. We don't notice what goes on before us every day. I really should like to see what Moses Pennel will think when he sees you. At any rate, he can't order you about with such a grand air as he used to when you were younger."

"I think sometimes he has quite forgotten about me," said Mara.

CHAPTER XXIII

"Well, if I were you, I should put him in mind of myself by one or two little ways," said Sally. "I'd plague him and tease him. I'd lead him such a life that he couldn't forget me,—that's what I would."

"I don't doubt you would, Sally; and he might like you all the better for it. But you know that sort of thing isn't my way. People must act in character."

"Do you know, Mara," said Sally, "I always thought Moses was hateful in his treatment of you? Now I'd no more marry that fellow than I'd walk into the fire; but it would be a just punishment for his sins to have to marry me! Wouldn't I serve him out, though!"

With which threat of vengeance on her mind Sally Kittridge fell asleep, while Mara lay awake pondering,—wondering if Moses would come to-morrow, and what he would be like if he did come.

The next morning as the two girls were wiping breakfast dishes in a room adjoining the kitchen, a step was heard on the kitchen-floor, and the first that Mara knew she found herself lifted from the floor in the arms of a tall dark-eyed young man, who was kissing her just as if he had a right to. She knew it must be Moses, but it seemed strange as a dream, for all she had tried to imagine it beforehand.

He kissed her over and over, and then holding her off at arm's length, said, "Why, Mara, you have grown to be a beauty!"

"And what was she, I'd like to know, when you went away, Mr. Moses?" said Sally, who could not long keep out of a conversation. "She was handsome when you were only a great ugly boy."

"Thank you, Miss Sally!" said Moses, making a profound bow.

"Thank me for what?" said Sally, with a toss.

"For your intimation that I am a handsome young man now," said Moses, sitting with his arm around Mara, and her hand in his.

And in truth he was as handsome now for a man as he was in the promise of his early childhood. All the oafishness and surly awkwardness of the half-boy period was gone. His great black eyes were clear and confident: his dark hair clustering in short curls round his well-shaped head; his black lashes, and fine form, and a certain confident ease of manner, set him off to the greatest advantage.

Mara felt a peculiar dreamy sense of strangeness at this brother who was not a brother,—this Moses so different from the one she had known. The very tone of his voice, which when he left had the uncertain cracked notes which indicate the unformed man, were now mellowed and settled. Mara regarded him shyly as he talked, blushed uneasily, and drew away from his arm around her, as if this handsome, self-confident young man were being too familiar. In fact, she made apology to go out into the other room to call Mrs. Pennel.

Moses looked after her as she went with admiration. "What a little woman she has grown!" he said, naïvely.

"And what did you expect she would grow?" said Sally. "You didn't expect to find her a girl in short clothes, did you?"

"Not exactly, Miss Sally," said Moses, turning his attention to her; "and some other people are changed too."

"Like enough," said Sally, carelessly. "I should think so, since somebody never spoke a word to one the Sunday he was at meeting."

"Oh, you remember that, do you? On my word, Sally"—

"Miss Kittridge, if you please, sir," said Sally, turning round with the air of an empress.

"Well, then, Miss Kittridge," said Moses, making a bow; "now let me finish my sentence. I never dreamed who you were."

"Complimentary," said Sally, pouting.

"Well, hear me through," said Moses; "you had grown so handsome, Miss Kittridge."

"Oh! that indeed! I suppose you mean to say I was a fright when you left?"

"Not at all—not at all," said Moses; "but handsome things may grow handsomer, you know."

"I don't like flattery," said Sally.

"I never flatter, Miss Kittridge," said Moses.

Our young gentleman and young lady of Orr's Island went through with this customary little lie of civilized society with as much gravity as if they were practicing in the court of Versailles,—she looking out from the corner of her eye to watch the effect of her words, and he laying his hand on his heart in the most edifying gravity. They perfectly understood one another.

But, says the reader, seems to me Sally Kittridge does all the talking! So she does,—so she always will,—for it is her nature to be bright, noisy, and restless; and one of these girls always overcrows a timid and thoughtful one, and makes her, for the time, seem dim and faded, as does rose color when put beside scarlet.

Sally was a born coquette. It was as natural for her to want to flirt with every man she saw, as for a kitten to scamper after a pin-ball. Does the kitten care a fig for the pin-ball, or the dry leaves, which she whisks, and frisks, and boxes, and pats, and races round and round after? No; it's nothing but kittenhood; every hair of her fur is alive with it. Her sleepy green eyes, when she pretends to be dozing, are full of it; and though she looks wise a moment, and seems resolved to be a discreet young cat, let but a leaf sway—off she goes again, with a frisk and a rap. So, though Sally had scolded and flounced about Moses's inattention to Mara in advance, she contrived even in this first interview to keep him talking with nobody but herself;—not because she wanted to draw him from Mara, or meant to; not because she cared a pin for him; but because it was her nature, as a frisky young cat. And Moses let himself be drawn, between bantering and contradicting, and jest and earnest, at some moments almost to forget that Mara was in the room.

She took her sewing and sat with a pleased smile, sometimes breaking into the lively flow of conversation, or eagerly appealed to by both parties to settle some rising quarrel.

Once, as they were talking, Moses looked up and saw Mara's head, as a stray sunbeam falling upon the golden hair seemed to make a halo around her face. Her large eyes were fixed upon him with an expression so intense and penetrative, that he felt a sort of wincing uneasiness. "What makes you look at me so, Mara?" he said, suddenly.

A bright flush came in her cheek as she answered, "I didn't know I was looking. It all seems so strange to me. I am trying to make out who and what you are."

"It's not best to look too deep," Moses said, laughing, but with a slight shade of uneasiness.

When Sally, late in the afternoon, declared that she must go home, she couldn't stay another minute, Moses rose to go with her.

"What are you getting up for?" she said to Moses, as he took his hat.

"To go home with you, to be sure."

"Nobody asked you to," said Sally.

"I'm accustomed to asking myself," said Moses.

"Well, I suppose I must have you along," said Sally. "Father will be glad to see you, of course."

"You'll be back to tea, Moses," said Mara, "will you not? Grandfather will be home, and want to see you."

"Oh, I shall be right back," said Moses, "I have a little business to settle with Captain Kittridge."

But Moses, however, did stay at tea with Mrs. Kittridge, who looked graciously at him through the bows of her black horn spectacles, having heard her liege lord observe that Moses was a smart chap, and had done pretty well in a money way.

How came he to stay? Sally told him every other minute to go; and then when he had got fairly out of the door, called him back to tell him that there was something she had heard about him. And Moses of course came back; wanted to know what it was; and couldn't be told, it was a secret; and then he would be ordered off, and reminded that he promised to go straight home; and then when he got a little farther off she called after him a second time, to tell him that he would be very much surprised if he knew how she found it out, etc., etc.,—till at last tea being ready, there was no reason why he shouldn't have a cup. And so it was sober moonrise before Moses found himself going home.

"Hang that girl!" he said to himself; "don't she know what she's about, though?"

There our hero was mistaken. Sally never did know what she was about,—had no plan or purpose more than a blackbird; and when Moses was gone laughed to think how many times she had made him come back.

"Now, confound it all," said Moses, "I care more for our little Mara than a dozen of her; and what have I been fooling all this time for?—now Mara will think I don't love her."

And, in fact, our young gentleman rather set his heart on the sensation he was going to make when he got home. It is flattering, after all, to feel one's power over a susceptible nature; and Moses, remembering how entirely and devotedly Mara had loved him all through childhood, never doubted but he was the sole possessor of uncounted treasure in her heart, which he could develop at his leisure and use as he pleased. He did not calculate for one force which had grown up in the meanwhile between them,—and that was the power of womanhood. He did not know the intensity of that kind of pride, which is the very life of the female nature, and which is most vivid and vigorous in the most timid and retiring.

Our little Mara was tender, self-devoting, humble, and religious, but she was woman after all to the tips of her fingers,—quick to feel slights, and determined with the intensest determination, that no man should wrest from her one of those few humble rights and privileges, which Nature allows to woman. Something swelled and trembled in her when she felt the confident pressure of that bold arm around her waist,—like the instinct of a wild bird to fly. Something in the deep, manly voice, the determined, self-confident air, aroused a vague feeling of defiance and resistance in her which she could scarcely explain to herself. Was he to assume a right to her in this way without even asking? When he did not come to tea nor long after, and Mrs. Pennel and her grandfather wondered, she laughed, and said gayly,—

"Oh, he knows he'll have time enough to see me. Sally seems more like a stranger."

But when Moses came home after moonrise, determined to go and console Mara for his absence, he was surprised to hear the sound of a rapid and pleasant conversation, in which a masculine and feminine voice were intermingled in a lively duet. Coming a little nearer, he saw Mara sitting knitting in the doorway, and a very good-looking young man seated on a stone at her feet, with his straw hat flung on the ground, while he was looking up into her face, as young men often do into pretty faces seen by moonlight. Mara rose and introduced Mr. Adams of Boston to Mr. Moses Pennel.

Moses measured the young man with his eye as if he could have shot him with a good will. And his temper was not at all bettered as he observed that he had the easy air of a man of fashion and culture, and learned by a few moments of the succeeding conversation, that the acquaintance had commenced during Mara's winter visit to Boston.

"I was staying a day or two at Mr. Sewell's," he said, carelessly, "and the night was so fine I couldn't resist the temptation to row over."

It was now Moses's turn to listen to a conversation in which he could bear little part, it being about persons and places and things unfamiliar to him; and though he could give no earthly reason why the conversation was not the most proper in the world,—yet he found that it made him angry.

In the pauses, Mara inquired, prettily, how he found the Kittridges, and reproved him playfully for staying, in despite of his promise to come home. Moses answered with an effort to appear easy and playful, that there was no reason, it appeared, to hurry on her account, since she had been so pleasantly engaged.

"That is true," said Mara, quietly; "but then grandpapa and grandmamma expected you, and they have gone to bed, as you know they always do after tea."

"They'll keep till morning, I suppose," said Moses, rather gruffly.

"Oh yes; but then as you had been gone two or three months, naturally they wanted to see a little of you at first."

The stranger now joined in the conversation, and began talking with Moses about his experiences in foreign parts, in a manner which showed a man of sense and breeding. Moses had a jealous fear of people of breeding,—an apprehension lest they should look down on one whose life had been laid out of the course of their conventional ideas; and therefore, though he had sufficient ability and vigor of mind to acquit himself to advantage in this conversation, it gave him all the while a secret uneasiness. After a few moments, he rose up moodily, and saying that he was very much fatigued, he went into the house to retire.

Mr. Adams rose to go also, and Moses might have felt in a more Christian frame of mind, had he listened to the last words of the conversation between him and Mara.

"Do you remain long in Harpswell?" she asked.

"That depends on circumstances," he replied. "If I do, may I be permitted to visit you?"

"As a friend—yes," said Mara; "I shall always be happy to see you."

"No more?"

"No more," replied Mara.

"I had hoped," he said, "that you would reconsider."

"It is impossible," said she; and soft voices can pronounce that word, *impossible*, in a very fateful and decisive manner.

"Well, God bless you, then, Miss Lincoln," he said, and was gone.

Mara stood in the doorway and saw him loosen his boat from its moorings and float off in the moonlight, with a long train of silver sparkles behind.

A moment after Moses was looking gloomily over her shoulder.

"Who is that puppy?" he said.

"He is not a puppy, but a very fine young man," said Mara.

"Well, that very fine young man, then?"

"I thought I told you. He is a Mr. Adams of Boston, and a distant connection of the Sewells. I met him when I was visiting at Judge Sewell's in Boston."

"You seemed to be having a very pleasant time together?"

"We were," said Mara, quietly.

"It's a pity I came home as I did. I'm sorry I interrupted you," said Moses, with a sarcastic laugh.

"You didn't interrupt us; he had been here almost two hours."

Now Mara saw plainly enough that Moses was displeased and hurt, and had it been in the days of her fourteenth summer, she would have thrown her arms around his neck, and said, "Moses, I don't care a fig for that man, and I love you better than all the world." But this the young lady of eighteen would not do; so she wished him good-night very prettily, and pretended not to see anything about it.

Mara was as near being a saint as human dust ever is; but—she was a woman saint; and therefore may be excused for a little gentle vindictiveness. She was, in a merciful way, rather glad that Moses had gone to bed dissatisfied, and rather glad that he did not know what she might have told him—quite resolved that he should not know at present. Was he to know that she liked nobody so much as him? Not he, unless he loved her more than all the world, and said so first. Mara was resolved upon that. He might go where he liked—flirt with whom he liked—come back as late as he pleased; never would she, by word or look, give him reason to think she cared.

CHAPTER XXIV

DESIRES AND DREAMS

Moses passed rather a restless and uneasy night on his return to the home-roof which had sheltered his childhood. All his life past, and all his life expected, seemed to boil and seethe and ferment in his thoughts, and to go round and round in never-ceasing circles before him.

Moses was *par excellence* proud, ambitious, and willful. These words, generally supposed to describe positive vices of the mind, in fact are only the overaction of certain very valuable portions of our nature, since one can conceive all three to raise a man immensely in the scale of moral being, simply by being applied to right objects. He who is too proud even to admit a mean thought—who is ambitious only of ideal excellence—who has an inflexible will only in the pursuit of truth and righteousness—may be a saint and a hero.

But Moses was neither a saint nor a hero, but an undeveloped chaotic young man, whose pride made him sensitive and restless; whose ambition was fixed on wealth and worldly success; whose willfulness was for the most part a blind determination to compass his own points, with the leave of Providence or without. There was no God in his estimate of life—and a sort of secret unsuspected determination at the bottom of his heart that there should be none. He feared religion, from a suspicion which he entertained that it might hamper some of his future schemes. He did not wish to put himself under its rules, lest he might find them in some future time inconveniently strict.

With such determinations and feelings, the Bible—necessarily an excessively uninteresting book to him—he never read, and satisfied himself with determining in a general way that it was not worth reading, and, as was the custom with many young men in America at that period, announced himself as a skeptic, and seemed to value himself not a little on the distinction. Pride in skepticism is a peculiar distinction of young men. It takes years and maturity to make the discovery that the power of faith is nobler than the power of doubt; and that there is a celestial wisdom in the ingenuous propensity to trust, which belongs to honest and noble natures. Elderly skeptics generally regard their unbelief as a misfortune.

Not that Moses was, after all, without "the angel in him." He had a good deal of the susceptibility to poetic feeling, the power of vague and dreamy aspiration, the longing after the good and beautiful, which is God's witness in the soul. A noble sentiment in poetry, a fine scene in nature, had power to bring tears in his great dark eyes, and he had, under the influence of such things, brief inspired moments in which he vaguely longed to do, or be, something grand or noble. But this, however, was something apart from the real purpose of his life,—a sort of voice crying in the wilderness,—to which he gave little heed. Practically, he was determined with all his might, to have a good time in this life, whatever another might be,—if there were one; and that he would do it by the strength of his right arm. Wealth he saw to be the lamp of Aladdin, which commanded all other things. And the pursuit of wealth was therefore the first step in his programme.

As for plans of the heart and domestic life, Moses was one of that very common class who had more desire to be loved than power of loving. His cravings and dreams were not for somebody to be devoted to, but for somebody who should be devoted to him. And, like most people who possess this characteristic, he mistook it for an affectionate disposition.

Now the chief treasure of his heart had always been his little sister Mara, chiefly from his conviction that he was the one absorbing thought and love of her heart. He had never figured life to himself otherwise than with Mara at his side, his unquestioning, devoted friend. Of course he and his plans, his ways and wants, would always be in the future, as they always had been, her sole thought. These sleeping partnerships in the interchange of affection, which support one's heart with a basis of uncounted wealth, and leave one free to come and go, and buy and sell, without exaction or interference, are a convenience certainly, and the loss of them in any way is like the sudden breaking of a bank in which all one's deposits are laid.

It had never occurred to Moses how or in what capacity he should always stand banker to the whole wealth of love that there was in Mara's heart, and what provision he should make on his part for returning this incalculable debt. But the interview of this evening had raised a new thought in his mind. Mara, as he saw that day, was no longer a little girl in a pink sun-bonnet. She was a woman,—a little one, it is true, but every inch a woman,—and a woman invested with a singular poetic charm of appearance, which, more than beauty, has the power of awakening feeling in the other sex.

He felt in himself, in the experience of that one day, that there was something subtle and veiled about her, which set the imagination at work; that the wistful, plaintive expression of her dark eyes, and a thousand little shy and tremulous movements of her face, affected him more than the most brilliant of Sally Kittridge's sprightly sallies. Yes, there would be people falling in love with her fast enough, he thought even here, where she is as secluded as a pearl in an oyster-shell,—it seems means were found to come after her,—and then all the love of her heart, that priceless love, would go to another.

CHAPTER XXIV

Mara would be absorbed in some one else, would love some one else, as he knew she could, with heart and soul and mind and strength. When he thought of this, it affected him much as it would if one were turned out of a warm, smiling apartment into a bleak December storm. What should he do, if that treasure which he had taken most for granted in all his valuations of life should suddenly be found to belong to another? Who was this fellow that seemed so free to visit her, and what had passed between them? Was Mara in love with him, or going to be? There is no saying how the consideration of this question enhanced in our hero's opinion both her beauty and all her other good qualities.

Such a brave little heart! such a good, clear little head! and such a pretty hand and foot! She was always so cheerful, so unselfish, so devoted! When had he ever seen her angry, except when she had taken up some childish quarrel of his, and fought for him like a little Spartan? Then she was pious, too. She was born religious, thought our hero, who, in common with many men professing skepticism for their own particular part, set a great value on religion in that unknown future person whom they are fond of designating in advance as "my wife." Yes, Moses meant his wife should be pious, and pray for him, while he did as he pleased.

"Now there's that witch of a Sally Kittridge," he said to himself; "I wouldn't have such a girl for a wife. Nothing to her but foam and frisk,—no heart more than a bobolink! But isn't she amusing? By George! isn't she, though?"

"But," thought Moses, "it's time I settled this matter who is to be my wife. I won't marry till I'm rich,—that's flat. My wife isn't to rub and grub. So at it I must go to raise the wind. I wonder if old Sewell really does know anything about my parents. Miss Emily would have it that there was some mystery that he had the key of; but I never could get any thing from him. He always put me off in such a smooth way that I couldn't tell whether he did or he didn't. But, now, supposing I have relatives, family connections, then who knows but what there may be property coming to me? That's an idea worth looking after, surely."

There's no saying with what vividness ideas and images go through one's wakeful brain when the midnight moon is making an exact shadow of your window-sash, with panes of light, on your chamber-floor. How vividly we all have loved and hated and planned and hoped and feared and desired and dreamed, as we tossed and turned to and fro upon such watchful, still nights. In the stillness, the tide upon one side of the Island replied to the dash on the other side in unbroken symphony, and Moses began to remember all the stories gossips had told him of how he had floated ashore there, like a fragment of tropical seaweed borne landward by a great gale. He positively wondered at himself that he had never thought of it more, and the more he meditated, the more mysterious and inexplicable he felt. Then he had heard Miss Roxy once speaking something about a bracelet, he was sure he had; but afterwards it was hushed up, and no one seemed to know anything about it when he inquired. But in those days he was a boy,—he was nobody,—now he was a young man. He could go to Mr. Sewell, and demand as his right a fair answer to any questions he might ask. If he found, as was quite likely, that there was nothing to be known, his mind would be thus far settled,—he should trust only to his own resources.

So far as the state of the young man's finances were concerned, it would be considered in those simple times and regions an auspicious beginning of life. The sum intrusted to him by Captain Kittridge had been more than doubled by the liberality of Zephaniah Pennel, and Moses had traded upon it in foreign parts with a skill and energy that brought a very fair return, and gave him, in the eyes of the shrewd, thrifty neighbors, the prestige of a young man who was marked for success in the world.

He had already formed an advantageous arrangement with his grandfather and Captain Kittridge, by which a ship was to be built, which he should command, and thus the old Saturday afternoon dream of their childhood be fulfilled. As he thought of it, there arose in his mind a picture of Mara, with her golden hair and plaintive eyes and little white hands, reigning as a fairy queen in the captain's cabin, with a sort of wish to carry her off and make sure that no one else ever should get her from him.

But these midnight dreams were all sobered down by the plain matter-of-fact beams of the morning sun, and nothing remained of immediate definite purpose except the resolve, which came strongly upon Moses as he looked across the blue band of Harpswell Bay, that he would go that morning and have a talk with Mr. Sewell.

CHAPTER XXV

MISS EMILY

Miss Roxy Toothache was seated by the window of the little keeping-room where Miss Emily Sewell sat on every-day occasions. Around her were the insignia of her power and sway. Her big tailor's goose was heating between Miss Emily's bright brass fire-irons; her great pin-cushion was by her side, bristling with pins of all sizes, and with broken needles thriftily made into pins by heads of red sealing-wax, and with needles threaded with all varieties of cotton, silk, and linen; her scissors hung martially by her side; her black bombazette work-apron was on; and the expression of her iron features was that of deep responsibility, for she was making the minister a new Sunday vest!

The good soul looks not a day older than when we left her, ten years ago. Like the gray, weather-beaten rocks of her native shore, her strong features had an unchangeable identity beyond that of anything fair and blooming. There was of course no chance for a gray streak in her stiff, uncompromising mohair frisette, which still pushed up her cap-border bristlingly as of old, and the clear, high winds and bracing atmosphere of that rough coast kept her in an admirable state of preservation.

Miss Emily had now and then a white hair among her soft, pretty brown ones, and looked a little thinner; but the round, bright spot of bloom on each cheek was there just as of yore,—and just as of yore she was thinking of her brother, and filling her little head with endless calculations to keep him looking fresh and respectable, and his housekeeping comfortable and easy, on very limited means. She was now officiously and anxiously attending on Miss Roxy, who was in the midst of the responsible operation which should conduce greatly to this end.

"Does that twist work well?" she said, nervously; "because I believe I've got some other upstairs in my India box."

Miss Roxy surveyed the article; bit a fragment off, as if she meant to taste it; threaded a needle and made a few cabalistical stitches; and then pronounced, *ex cathedrâ*, that it would do. Miss Emily gave a sigh of relief. After buttons and tapes and linings, and various other items had been also discussed, the conversation began to flow into general channels.

"Did you know Moses Pennel had got home from Umbagog?" said Miss Roxy.

"Yes. Captain Kittridge told brother so this morning. I wonder he doesn't call over to see us."

"Your brother took a sight of interest in that boy," said Miss Roxy. "I was saying to Ruey, this morning, that if Moses Pennel ever did turn out well, he ought to have a large share of the credit."

"Brother always did feel a peculiar interest in him; it was such a strange providence that seemed to cast in his lot among us," said Miss Emily.

"As sure as you live, there he is a-coming to the front door," said Miss Roxy.

"Dear me," said Miss Emily, "and here I have on this old faded chintz. Just so sure as one puts on any old rag, and thinks nobody will come, company is sure to call."

"Law, I'm sure I shouldn't think of calling him company," said Miss Roxy.

A rap at the door put an end to this conversation, and very soon Miss Emily introduced our hero into the little sitting-room, in the midst of a perfect stream of apologies relating to her old dress and the littered condition of the sitting-room, for Miss Emily held to the doctrine of those who consider any sign of human occupation and existence in a room as being disorder—however reputable and respectable be the cause of it.

"Well, really," she said, after she had seated Moses by the fire, "how time does pass, to be sure; it don't seem more than yesterday since you used to come with your Latin books, and now here you are a grown man! I must run and tell Mr. Sewell. He will be so glad to see you."

Mr. Sewell soon appeared from his study in morning-gown and slippers, and seemed heartily responsive to the proposition which Moses soon made to him to have some private conversation with him in his study.

"I declare," said Miss Emily, as soon as the study-door had closed upon her brother and Moses, "what a handsome young man he is! and what a beautiful way he has with him!—so deferential! A great many young men nowadays seem to think nothing of their minister; but he comes to seek advice. Very proper. It isn't every young man that appreciates the privilege of having elderly friends. I declare, what a beautiful couple he and Mara Lincoln would make! Don't Providence seem in a peculiar way to have designed them for each other?"

"I hope not," said Miss Roxy, with her grimmest expression.

"You don't! Why not?"

"I never liked him," said Miss Roxy, who had possessed herself of her great heavy goose, and was now thumping and squeaking it emphatically on the press-board. "She's a thousand times too good for Moses Pennel,"—thump. "I ne'er had no faith in him,"—thump. "He's dreffle unstiddy,"—thump. "He's handsome, but he knows it,"—thump. "He won't never love nobody so much as he does himself,"—thump, *fortissimo con spirito.*

"Well, really now, Miss Roxy, you mustn't always remember the sins of his youth. Boys must sow their wild oats. He was unsteady for a while, but now everybody says he's doing well; and as to his knowing he's handsome, and all that, I don't see as he does. See how polite and deferential he was to us all, this morning; and he spoke so handsomely to you."

"I don't want none of his politeness," said Miss Roxy, inexorably; "and as to Mara Lincoln, she might have better than him any day. Miss Badger was a-tellin' Captain Brown, Sunday noon, that she was very much admired in Boston."

"So she was," said Miss Emily, bridling. "I never reveal secrets, or I might tell something,—but there has been a young man,—but I promised not to speak of it, and I sha'n't."

"If you mean Mr. Adams," said Miss Roxy, "you need n't worry about keepin' that secret, 'cause that ar was all talked over atween meetin's a-Sunday noon; for Mis' Kittridge she used to know his aunt Jerushy, her that married Solomon Peters, and Mis' Captain Badger she says that he has a very good property, and is a professor in the Old South church in Boston."

"Dear me," said Miss Emily, "how things do get about!"

"People will talk, there ain't no use trying to help it," said Miss Roxy; "but it's strongly borne in on my mind that it ain't Adams, nor 't ain't Moses Pennel that's to marry her. I've had peculiar exercises of mind about that ar child,—well I have;" and Miss Roxy pulled a large spotted bandanna handkerchief out of her pocket, and blew her nose like a trumpet, and then wiped the withered corners of her eyes, which were humid as some old Orr's Island rock wet with sea-spray.

Miss Emily had a secret love of romancing. It was one of the recreations of her quiet, monotonous life to build air-castles, which she furnished regardless of expense, and in which she set up at housekeeping her various friends and acquaintances, and she had always been bent on weaving a romance on the history of Mara and Moses Pennel. The good little body had done her best to second Mr. Sewell's attempts toward the education of the children. It was little busy Miss Emily who persuaded honest Zephaniah and Mary Pennel that talents such as Mara's ought to be cultivated, and that ended in sending her to Miss Plucher's school in Portland. There her artistic faculties were trained into creating funereal monuments out of chenille embroidery, fully equal to Miss Emily's own; also to painting landscapes, in which the ground and all the trees were one unvarying tint of blue-green; and also to creating flowers of a new and particular construction, which, as Sally Kittridge remarked, were pretty, but did not look like anything in heaven or earth. Mara had obediently and patiently done all these things; and solaced herself with copying flowers and birds and landscapes as near as possible like nature, as a recreation from these more dignified toils.

Miss Emily also had been the means of getting Mara invited to Boston, where she saw some really polished society, and gained as much knowledge of the forms of artificial life as a nature so wholly and strongly individual could obtain. So little Miss Emily regarded Mara as her godchild, and was intent on finishing her up into a romance in real life, of which a handsome young man, who had been washed ashore in a shipwreck, should be the hero.

What would she have said could she have heard the conversation that was passing in her brother's study? Little could she dream that the mystery, about which she had timidly nibbled for years, was now about to be unrolled;—but it was even so. But, upon what she does not see, good reader, you and I, following invisibly on tiptoe, will make our observations.

When Moses was first ushered into Mr. Sewell's study, and found himself quite alone, with the door shut, his heart beat so that he fancied the good man must hear it. He knew well what he wanted and meant to say, but he found in himself all that shrinking and nervous repugnance which always attends the proposing of any decisive question.

"I thought it proper," he began, "that I should call and express my sense of obligation to you, sir, for all the kindness you showed me when a boy. I'm afraid in those thoughtless days I did not seem to appreciate it so much as I do now."

As Moses said this, the color rose in his cheeks, and his fine eyes grew moist with a sort of subdued feeling that made his face for the moment more than usually beautiful.

Mr. Sewell looked at him with an expression of peculiar interest, which seemed to have something almost of pain in it, and answered with a degree of feeling more than he commonly showed,—

"It has been a pleasure to me to do anything I could for you, my young friend. I only wish it could have been more. I congratulate you on your present prospects in life. You have perfect health; you have energy and enterprise; you are courageous and self-reliant, and, I trust, your habits are pure and virtuous. It only remains that you add to all this that fear of the Lord which is the beginning of wisdom."

Moses bowed his head respectfully, and then sat silent a moment, as if he were looking through some cloud where he vainly tried to discover objects.

Mr. Sewell continued, gravely,—

"You have the greatest reason to bless the kind Providence which has cast your lot in such a family, in such a community. I have had some means in my youth of comparing other parts of the country with our New England, and it is my opinion that a young man could not ask a better introduction into life than the wholesome nurture of a Christian family in our favored land."

"Mr. Sewell," said Moses, raising his head, and suddenly looking him straight in the eyes, "do you know anything of my family?"

The question was so point-blank and sudden, that for a moment Mr. Sewell made a sort of motion as if he dodged a pistol-shot, and then his face assumed an expression of grave thoughtfulness, while Moses drew a long breath. It was out,—the question had been asked.

"My son," replied Mr. Sewell, "it has always been my intention, when you had arrived at years of discretion, to make you acquainted with all that I know or suspect in regard to your life. I trust that when I tell you all I do know, you will see that I have acted for the best in the matter. It has been my study and my prayer to do so."

Mr. Sewell then rose, and unlocking the cabinet, of which we have before made mention, in his apartment, drew forth a very yellow and time-worn package of papers, which he untied. From these he selected one which enveloped an old-fashioned miniature case.

"I am going to show you," he said, "what only you and my God know that I possess. I have not looked at it now for ten years, but I have no doubt that it is the likeness of your mother."

Moses took it in his hand, and for a few moments there came a mist over his eyes,—he could not see clearly. He walked to the window as if needing a clearer light.

What he saw was a painting of a beautiful young girl, with large melancholy eyes, and a clustering abundance of black, curly hair. The face was of a beautiful, clear oval, with that warm brunette tint in which the Italian painters delight. The black eyebrows were strongly and clearly defined, and there was in the face an indescribable expression of childish innocence and shyness, mingled with a kind of confiding frankness, that gave the picture the charm which sometimes fixes itself in faces for which we involuntarily make a history. She was represented as simply attired in a white muslin, made low in the neck, and the hands and arms were singularly beautiful. The picture, as Moses looked at it, seemed to stand smiling at him with a childish grace,—a tender, ignorant innocence which affected him deeply.

"My young friend," said Mr. Sewell, "I have written all that I know of the original of this picture, and the reasons I have for thinking her your mother.

"You will find it all in this paper, which, if I had been providentially removed, was to have been given you in your twenty-first year. You will see in the delicate nature of the narrative that it could not properly have been imparted to you till you had arrived at years of understanding. I trust when you know all that you will be satisfied with the course I have pursued. You will read it at your leisure, and after reading I shall be happy to see you again."

Moses took the package, and after exchanging salutations with Mr. Sewell, hastily left the house and sought his boat.

When one has suddenly come into possession of a letter or paper in which is known to be hidden the solution of some long-pondered secret, of the decision of fate with regard to some long-cherished desire, who has not been conscious of a sort of pain,—an unwillingness at once to know what is therein? We turn the letter again and again, we lay it by and return to it, and defer from moment to moment the opening of it. So Moses did not sit down in the first retired spot to ponder the paper. He put it in the breast pocket of his coat, and then, taking up his oars, rowed across the bay. He did not land at the house, but passed around the south point of the Island, and rowed up the other side to seek a solitary retreat in the rocks, which had always been a favorite with him in his early days.

The shores of the Island, as we have said, are a precipitous wall of rock, whose long, ribbed ledges extend far out into the sea. At high tide these ledges are covered with the smooth blue sea quite up to the precipitous shore. There was a place, however, where the rocky shore shelved over, forming between two ledges a sort of grotto, whose smooth floor of shells and many-colored pebbles was never wet by the rising tide. It had been the delight of Moses when a boy, to come here and watch the gradual rise of the tide till the grotto was entirely cut off from all approach, and then to look out in a sort of hermit-like security over the open ocean that stretched before him. Many an hour he had sat there and dreamed of all the possible fortunes that might be found for him when he should launch away into that blue smiling futurity.

It was now about half-tide, and Moses left his boat and made his way over the ledge of rocks toward his retreat. They were all shaggy and slippery with yellow seaweeds, with here and there among them wide crystal pools, where purple and lilac and green mosses unfolded their delicate threads, and thousands of curious little shell-fish were tranquilly pursuing their quiet life. The rocks where the pellucid water lay were in some places crusted with barnacles, which were opening and shutting the little white scaly doors of their tiny houses, and drawing in and out those delicate pink plumes which seem to be their nerves of enjoyment. Moses and Mara had rambled and played here many hours of their childhood, amusing themselves with catching crabs and young lobsters and various little fish for these rocky aquariums, and then studying at their leisure their various ways. Now he had come hither a man, to learn the secret of his life.

Moses stretched himself down on the clean pebbly shore of the grotto, and drew forth Mr. Sewell's letter.

CHAPTER XXVI

DOLORES

Mr. Sewell's letter ran as follows:—

My Dear Young Friend,—It has always been my intention when you arrived at years of maturity to acquaint you with some circumstances which have given me reason to conjecture your true parentage, and to let you know what steps I have taken to satisfy my own mind in relation to these conjectures. In order to do this, it will be necessary for me to go back to the earlier years of my life, and give you the history of some incidents which are known to none of my most intimate friends. I trust I may rely on your honor that they will ever remain as secrets with you.

I graduated from Harvard University in ——. At the time I was suffering somewhat from an affection of the lungs, which occasioned great alarm to my mother, many of whose family had died of consumption. In order to allay her uneasiness, and also for the purpose of raising funds for the pursuit of my professional studies, I accepted a position as tutor in the family of a wealthy gentleman at St. Augustine, in Florida.

I cannot do justice to myself,—to the motives which actuated me in the events which took place in this family, without speaking with the most undisguised freedom of the character of all the parties with whom I was connected.

Don José Mendoza was a Spanish gentleman of large property, who had emigrated from the Spanish West Indies to Florida, bringing with him an only daughter, who had been left an orphan by the death of her mother at a very early age. He brought to this country a large number of slaves;—and shortly after his arrival, married an American lady: a widow with three children. By her he had four other children. And thus it will appear that the family was made up of such a variety of elements as only the most judicious care could harmonize. But the character of the father and mother was such that judicious care was a thing not to be expected of either.

Don José was extremely ignorant and proud, and had lived a life of the grossest dissipation. Habits of absolute authority in the midst of a community of a very low moral standard had produced in him all the worst vices of despots. He was cruel, overbearing, and dreadfully passionate. His wife was a woman who had pretensions to beauty, and at times could make herself agreeable, and even fascinating, but she was possessed of a temper quite as violent and ungoverned as his own.

Imagine now two classes of slaves, the one belonging to the mistress, and the other brought into the country by the master, and each animated by a party spirit and jealousy;—imagine children of different marriages, inheriting from their parents violent tempers and stubborn wills, flattered and fawned on by slaves, and alternately petted or stormed at, now by this parent and now by that, and you will have some idea of the task which I undertook in being tutor in this family.

I was young and fearless in those days, as you are now, and the difficulties of the position, instead of exciting apprehension, only awakened the spirit of enterprise and adventure.

The whole arrangements of the household, to me fresh from the simplicity and order of New England, had a singular and wild sort of novelty which was attractive rather than otherwise. I was well recommended in the family by an influential and wealthy gentleman of Boston, who represented my family, as indeed it was, as among the oldest and most respectable of Boston, and spoke in such terms of me, personally, as I should not have ventured to use in relation to myself. When I arrived, I found that two or three tutors, who had endeavored to bear rule in this tempestuous family, had thrown up the command after a short trial, and that the parents felt some little apprehension of not being able to secure the services of another,—a circumstance which I did not fail to improve in making my preliminary arrangements. I assumed an air of grave hauteur, was very exacting in all my requisitions and stipulations, and would give no promise of doing more than to give the situation a temporary trial. I put on an air of supreme indifference as to my continuance, and acted in fact rather on the assumption that I should confer a favor by remaining.

In this way I succeeded in obtaining at the outset a position of more respect and deference than had been enjoyed by any of my predecessors. I had a fine apartment, a servant exclusively devoted to me, a horse for riding, and saw myself treated among the servants as a person of consideration and distinction.

Don José and his wife both had in fact a very strong desire to retain my services, when after the trial of a week or two, it was found that I really could make their discordant and turbulent children to some extent obedient and studious during certain portions of the day; and in fact I soon acquired in the whole family that ascendancy which a well-bred person who respects himself, and can keep his temper, must have over passionate and undisciplined natures.

I became the receptacle of the complaints of all, and a sort of confidential adviser. Don José imparted to me with more frankness than good taste his chagrins with regard to his wife's indolence, ill-temper, and bad management, and his wife in turn omitted no opportunity to vent complaints against her husband for similar reasons. I endeavored, to the best of my ability, to act a friendly part by both. It never was in my nature to see anything that needed to be done without trying to do it, and it was impossible to work at all without becoming so interested in my work as to do far more than I had agreed to do. I assisted Don José about many of his affairs; brought his neglected accounts into order; and suggested from time to time arrangements which relieved the difficulties which had been brought on by disorder and neglect. In fact, I became, as he said, quite a necessary of life to him.

In regard to the children, I had a more difficult task. The children of Don José by his present wife had been systematically stimulated by the negroes into a chronic habit of dislike and jealousy toward her children by a former husband. On the slightest pretext, they were constantly running to their father with complaints; and as the mother warmly espoused the cause of her first children, criminations and recriminations often convulsed the whole family.

In ill-regulated families in that region, the care of the children is from the first in the hands of half-barbarized negroes, whose power of moulding and assimilating childish minds is peculiar, so that the teacher has to contend constantly with a savage element in the children which seems to have been drawn in with the mother's milk. It is, in a modified way, something the same result as if the child had formed its manners in Dahomey or on the coast of Guinea. In the fierce quarrels which were carried on between the children of this family, I had frequent occasion to observe this strange, savage element, which sometimes led to expressions and actions which would seem incredible in civilized society.

The three children by Madame Mendoza's former husband were two girls of sixteen and eighteen and a boy of fourteen. The four children of the second marriage consisted of three boys and a daughter,—the eldest being not more than thirteen.

The natural capacity of all the children was good, although, from self-will and indolence, they had grown up in a degree of ignorance which could not have been tolerated except in a family living an isolated plantation life in the midst of barbarized dependents. Savage and untaught and passionate as they were, the work of teaching them was not without its interest to me. A power of control was with me a natural gift; and then that command of temper which is the common attribute of well-trained persons in the Northern states, was something so singular in this family as to invest its possessor with a certain awe; and my calm, energetic voice, and determined manner, often acted as a charm on their stormy natures.

But there was one member of the family of whom I have not yet spoken,—and yet all this letter is about her,—the daughter of Don José by his first marriage. Poor Dolores! poor child! God grant she may have entered into his rest!

I need not describe her. You have seen her picture. And in the wild, rude, discordant family, she always reminded me of the words, "a lily among thorns." She was in her nature unlike all the rest, and, I may say, unlike any one I ever saw. She seemed to live a lonely kind of life in this disorderly household, often marked out as the object of the spites and petty tyrannies of both parties. She was regarded with bitter hatred and jealousy by Madame Mendoza, who was sure to visit her with unsparing bitterness and cruelty after the occasional demonstrations of fondness she received from her father. Her exquisite beauty and the gentle softness of her manners made her such a contrast to her sisters as constantly excited their ill-will. Unlike them all, she was fastidiously neat in her personal habits, and orderly in all the little arrangements of life.

She seemed to me in this family to be like some shy, beautiful pet creature in the hands of rude, unappreciated owners, hunted from quarter to quarter, and finding rest only by stealth. Yet she seemed to have no perception of the harshness and cruelty with which she was treated. She had grown up with it; it was the habit of her life to study peaceable methods of averting or avoiding the various inconveniences and annoyances of her lot, and secure to herself a little quiet.

It not unfrequently happened, amid the cabals and storms which shook the family, that one party or the other took up and patronized Dolores for a while, more, as it would appear, out of hatred for the other than any real love to her. At such times it was really affecting to see with what warmth the poor child would receive these equivocal demonstrations of good-will—the nearest approaches to affection which she had ever known—and the bitterness with which she would mourn when they were capriciously withdrawn again. With a heart full of affection, she reminded me of some delicate, climbing plant trying vainly to ascend the slippery side of an inhospitable wall, and throwing its neglected tendrils around every weed for support.

Her only fast, unfailing friend was her old negro nurse, or Mammy, as the children called her. This old creature, with the cunning and subtlety which had grown up from years of servitude, watched and waited upon the interests of her little mistress, and contrived to carry many points for her in the confused household. Her young mistress was her one thought and purpose in living. She would have gone through fire and water to serve her; and this faithful, devoted heart, blind and ignorant though it were, was the only unfailing refuge and solace of the poor hunted child.

Dolores, of course, became my pupil among the rest. Like the others, she had suffered by the neglect and interruptions in the education of the family, but she was intelligent and docile, and learned with a surprising rapidity. It was not astonishing that she should soon have formed an enthusiastic attachment to me, as I was the only intelligent, cultivated person she had ever seen, and treated her with unvarying consideration and delicacy. The poor thing had been so accustomed to barbarous words and manners that simple politeness and the usages of good society seemed to her cause for the most boundless gratitude.

It is due to myself, in view of what follows, to say that I was from the first aware of the very obvious danger which lay in my path in finding myself brought into close and daily relations with a young creature so confiding, so attractive, and so singularly circumstanced. I knew that it would be in the highest degree dishonorable to make the slightest advances toward gaining from her that kind of affection which might interfere with her happiness in such future relations as her father might arrange for her. According to the European fashion, I know that Dolores was in her father's hands, to be disposed of for life according to his pleasure, as absolutely as if she had been one of his slaves. I had every reason to think that his plans on this subject were matured, and only waited for a little more teaching and training on my part, and her fuller development in womanhood, to be announced to her.

In looking back over the past, therefore, I have not to reproach myself with any dishonest and dishonorable breach of trust; for I was from the first upon my guard, and so much so that even the jealousy my other scholars never accused me of partiality. I was not in the habit of giving very warm praise, and was in my general management anxious rather to be just than conciliatory, knowing that with the kind of spirits I had to deal with, firmness and justice went farther than anything else. If I approved Dolores oftener than the rest, it was seen to be because she never failed in a duty; if I spent more time with her lessons, it was because her enthusiasm for study led her to learn longer ones and study more things; but I am sure there was never a look or a word toward her that went beyond the proprieties of my position.

But yet I could not so well guard my heart. I was young and full of feeling. She was beautiful; and more than that, there was something in her Spanish nature at once so warm and simple, so artless and yet so unconsciously poetic, that her presence was a continual charm. How well I remember her now,—all her little ways,—the movements of her pretty little hands,—the expression of her changeful face as she recited to me,—the grave, rapt earnestness with which she listened to all my instructions!

I had not been with her many weeks before I felt conscious that it was her presence that charmed the whole house, and made the otherwise perplexing and distasteful details of my situation agreeable. I had a dim perception that this growing passion was a dangerous thing for myself; but was it a reason, I asked, why I should relinquish a position in which I felt that I was useful, and when I could do for this lovely child what no one else could do? I call her a child,—she always impressed me as such,—though she was in her sixteenth year and had the early womanly development of Southern climates. She seemed to me like something frail and precious, needing to be guarded and cared for; and when reason told me that I risked my own happiness in holding my position, love argued on the other hand that I was her only friend, and that I should be willing to risk something myself for the sake of protecting and shielding her. For there was no doubt that my presence in the family was a restraint upon the passions which formerly vented themselves so recklessly on her, and established a sort of order in which she found more peace than she had ever known before.

For a long time in our intercourse I was in the habit of looking on myself as the only party in danger. It did not occur to me that this heart, so beautiful and so lonely, might, in the want of all natural and appropriate objects of attachment, fasten itself on me unsolicited, from the mere necessity of loving. She seemed to me so much too beautiful, too perfect, to belong to a lot in life like mine, that I could not suppose it possible this could occur without the most blameworthy solicitation on my part; and it is the saddest and most affecting proof to me how this poor child had been starved for sympathy and love, that she should have repaid such cold services as mine with such an entire devotion. At first her feelings were expressed openly toward me, with the dutiful air of a good child. She placed flowers on my desk in the morning, and made quaint little nosegays in the Spanish fashion, which she gave me, and busied her leisure with various ingenious little knick-knacks of fancy work, which she brought me. I treated them all as the offerings of a child while with her, but I kept them sacredly in my own room. To tell the truth, I have some of the poor little things now.

But after a while I could not help seeing how she loved me; and then I felt as if I ought to go; but how could I? The pain to myself I could have borne; but how could I leave her to all the misery of her bleak, ungenial position? She, poor thing, was so unconscious of what I knew,—for I was made clear-sighted by love. I tried the more strictly to keep to the path I had marked out for myself, but I fear I did not always do it; in fact, many things seemed to conspire to throw us together. The sisters, who were sometimes invited out to visit on neighboring estates, were glad enough to dispense with the presence and attractions of Dolores, and so she was frequently left at home to study with me in their absence. As to Don José, although he always treated me with civility, yet he had such an ingrained and deep-rooted idea of his own superiority of position, that I suppose he would as soon have imagined the possibility of his daughter's falling in love with one of his horses. I was a great convenience to him. I had a knack of governing and carrying points in his family that it had always troubled and fatigued him to endeavor to arrange,—and that was all. So that my intercourse with Dolores was as free and unwatched, and gave me as many opportunities of enjoying her undisturbed society, as heart could desire.

At last came the crisis, however. After breakfast one morning, Don José called Dolores into his library and announced to her that he had concluded for her a treaty of marriage, and expected her husband to arrive in a few days. He expected that this news would be received by her with the glee with which a young girl hears of a new dress or of a ball-ticket, and was quite confounded at the grave and mournful silence in which she received it. She said no word, made no opposition, but went out from the room and shut herself up in her own apartment, and spent the day in tears and sobs.

Don José, who had rather a greater regard for Dolores than for any creature living, and who had confidently expected to give great delight by the news he had imparted, was quite confounded by this turn of things. If there had been one word of either expostulation or argument, he would have blazed and stormed in a fury of passion; but as it was, this broken-hearted submission, though vexatious, was perplexing. He sent for me, and opened his mind, and begged me to talk with Dolores and show her the advantages of the alliance, which the poor foolish child, he said, did not seem to comprehend. The man was immensely rich, and had a splendid estate in Cuba. It was a most desirable thing.

I ventured to inquire whether his person and manners were such as would be pleasing to a young girl, and could gather only that he was a man of about fifty, who had been most of his life in the military service, and was now desirous of making an establishment for the repose of his latter days, at the head of which he would place a handsome and tractable woman, and do well by her.

I represented that it would perhaps be safer to say no more on the subject until Dolores had seen him, and to this he agreed. Madame Mendoza was very zealous in the affair, for the sake of getting clear of the presence of Dolores in the family, and her sisters laughed at her for her dejected appearance. They only wished, they said, that so much luck might happen to them. For myself, I endeavored to take as little notice as possible of the affair, though what I felt may be conjectured. I knew,—I was perfectly certain,—that Dolores loved me as I loved her. I knew that she had one of those simple and unworldly natures which wealth and splendor could not satisfy, and whose life would lie entirely in her affections. Sometimes I violently debated with myself whether honor required me to sacrifice her happiness as well as my own, and I felt the strongest temptation to ask her to be my wife and fly with me to the Northern states, where I did not doubt my ability to make for her a humble and happy home.

But the sense of honor is often stronger than all reasoning, and I felt that such a course would be the betrayal of a trust; and I determined at least to command myself till I should see the character of the man who was destined to be her husband.

Meanwhile the whole manner of Dolores was changed. She maintained a stony, gloomy silence, performed all her duties in a listless way, and occasionally, when I commented on anything in her lessons or exercises, would break into little flashes of petulance, most strange and unnatural in her. Sometimes I could feel that she was looking at me earnestly, but if I turned my eyes toward her, hers were instantly averted; but there was in her eyes a peculiar expression at times, such as I have seen in the eye of a hunted animal when it turned at bay,—a sort of desperate resistance,—which, taken in connection with her fragile form and lovely face, produced a mournful impression.

One morning I found Dolores sitting alone in the schoolroom, leaning her head on her arms. She had on her wrist a bracelet of peculiar workmanship, which she always wore,—the bracelet which was afterwards the means of confirming her identity. She sat thus some moments in silence, and then she raised her head and began turning this bracelet round and round upon her arm, while she looked fixedly before her. At last she spoke abruptly, and said,—

"Did I ever tell you that this was *my mother's* hair? It is my mother's hair,—and she was the only one that ever loved me; except poor old Mammy, nobody else loves me,—nobody ever will."

"My dear Miss Dolores," I began.

"Don't call me dear," she said; "you don't care for me,—nobody does,—papa doesn't, and I always loved him; everybody in the house wants to get rid of me, whether I like to go or not. I have always tried to be good and do all you wanted, and I should think *you* might care for me a little, but you don't."

"Dolores," I said, "I do care for you more than I do for any one in the world; I love you more than my own soul."

These were the very words I never meant to say, but somehow they seemed to utter themselves against my will. She looked at me for a moment as if she could not believe her hearing, and then the blood flushed her face, and she laid her head down on her arms.

At this moment Madame Mendoza and the other girls came into the room in a clamor of admiration about a diamond bracelet which had just arrived as a present from her future husband. It was a splendid thing, and had for its clasp his miniature, surrounded by the largest brilliants.

The enthusiasm of the party even at this moment could not say anything in favor of the beauty of this miniature, which, though painted on ivory, gave the impression of a coarse-featured man, with a scar across one eye.

"No matter for the beauty," said one of the girls, "so long as it is set with such diamonds."

"Come, Dolores," said another, giving her the present, "pull off that old hair bracelet, and try this on."

Dolores threw the diamond bracelet from her with a vehemence so unlike her gentle self as to startle every one.

"I shall not take off my mother's bracelet for a gift from a man I never knew," she said. "I hate diamonds. I wish those who like such things might have them."

"Was ever anything so odd?" said Madame Mendoza.

"Dolores always was odd," said another of the girls; "nobody ever could tell what she would like."

CHAPTER XXVII

HIDDEN THINGS

The next day Señor Don Guzman de Cardona arrived, and the whole house was in a commotion of excitement. There was to be no school, and everything was bustle and confusion. I passed my time in my own room in reflecting severely upon myself for the imprudent words by which I had thrown one more difficulty in the way of this poor harassed child.

Dolores this day seemed perfectly passive in the hands of her mother and sisters, who appeared disposed to show her great attention. She allowed them to array her in her most becoming dress, and made no objection to anything except removing the bracelet from her arm. "Nobody's gifts should take the place of her mother's," she said, and they were obliged to be content with her wearing of the diamond bracelet on the other arm.

Don Guzman was a large, plethoric man, with coarse features and heavy gait. Besides the scar I have spoken of, his face was adorned here and there with pimples, which were not set down in the miniature. In the course of the first hour's study, I saw him to be a man of much the same stamp as Dolores's father—sensual, tyrannical, passionate. He seemed in his own way to be much struck with the beauty of his intended wife, and was not wanting in efforts to please her. All that I could see in her was the settled, passive paleness of despair. She played, sang, exhibited her embroidery and painting, at the command of Madame Mendoza, with the air of an automaton; and Don Guzman remarked to her father on the passive obedience as a proper and hopeful trait. Once only when he, in presenting her a flower, took the liberty of kissing her cheek, did I observe the flashing of her eye and a movement of disgust and impatience, that she seemed scarcely able to restrain.

The marriage was announced to take place the next week, and a holiday was declared through the house. Nothing was talked of or discussed but the *corbeille de mariage* which the bridegroom had brought—the dresses, laces, sets of jewels, and cashmere shawls. Dolores never had been treated with such attention by the family in her life. She rose immeasurably in the eyes of all as the future possessor of such wealth and such an establishment as awaited her. Madame Mendoza had visions of future visits in Cuba rising before her mind, and overwhelmed her daughter-in-law with flatteries and caresses, which she received in the same passive silence as she did everything else.

For my own part, I tried to keep entirely by myself. I remained in my room reading, and took my daily rides, accompanied by my servant—seeing Dolores only at mealtimes, when I scarcely ventured to look at her. One night, however, as I was walking through a lonely part of the garden, Dolores suddenly stepped out from the shrubbery and stood before me. It was bright moonlight, by which her face and person were distinctly shown. How well I remember her as she looked then! She was dressed in white muslin, as she was fond of being, but it had been torn and disordered by the haste with which she had come through the shrubbery. Her face was fearfully pale, and her great, dark eyes had an unnatural brightness. She laid hold on my arm.

"Look here," she said, "I saw you and came down to speak with you."

She panted and trembled, so that for some moments she could not speak another word. "I want to ask you," she gasped, after a pause, "whether I heard you right? Did you say"—

"Yes, Dolores, you did. I did say what I had no right to say, like a dishonorable man."

"But is it true? Are you sure it is true?" she said, scarcely seeming to hear my words.

"God knows it is," said I despairingly.

"Then why don't you save me? Why do you let them sell me to this dreadful man? He don't love me—he never will. Can't you take me away?"

"Dolores, I am a poor man. I cannot give you any of these splendors your father desires for you."

"Do you think I care for them? I love you more than all the world together. And if you do really love me, why should we not be happy with each other?"

"Dolores," I said, with a last effort to keep calm, "I am much older than you, and know the world, and ought not to take advantage of your simplicity. You have been so accustomed to abundant wealth and all it can give, that you cannot form an idea of what the hardships and discomforts of marrying a poor man would be. You are unused to having the least care, or making the least exertion for yourself. All the world would say that I acted a very dishonorable part to take you from a position which offers you wealth, splendor, and ease, to one of comparative hardship. Perhaps some day you would think so yourself."

While I was speaking, Dolores turned me toward the moonlight, and fixed her great dark eyes piercingly upon me, as if she wanted to read my soul. "Is that all?" she said; "is that the only reason?"

"I do not understand you," said I.

She gave me such a desolate look, and answered in a tone of utter dejection, "Oh, I didn't know, but perhaps *you* might not want me. All the rest are so glad to sell me to anybody that will take me. But you really do love me, don't you?" she added, laying her hand on mine.

CHAPTER XXVII

What answer I made I cannot say. I only know that every vestige of what is called reason and common sense left me at that moment, and that there followed an hour of delirium in which I—we both were *very* happy—we forgot everything but each other, and we arranged all our plans for flight. There was fortunately a ship lying in the harbor of St. Augustine, the captain of which was known to me. In course of a day or two passage was taken, and my effects transported on board. Nobody seemed to suspect us. Everything went on quietly up to the day before that appointed for sailing. I took my usual rides, and did everything as much as possible in my ordinary way, to disarm suspicion, and none seemed to exist. The needed preparations went gayly forward. On the day I mentioned, when I had ridden some distance from the house, a messenger came post-haste after me. It was a boy who belonged specially to Dolores. He gave me a little hurried note. I copy it:—

> "Papa has found all out, and it is dreadful. No one else knows, and he means to kill you when you come back. Do, if you love me, hurry and get on board the ship. I shall never get over it, if evil comes on you for my sake. I shall let them do what they please with me, if God will only save *you*. I will try to be good. Perhaps if I bear my trials well, he will let me die soon. That is all I ask. I love you, and always shall, to death and after.
> DOLORES."

There was the end of it all. I escaped on the ship. I read the marriage in the paper. Incidentally I afterwards heard of her as living in Cuba, but I never saw her again till I saw her in her coffin. Sorrow and death had changed her so much that at first the sight of her awakened only a vague, painful remembrance. The sight of the hair bracelet which I had seen on her arm brought all back, and I felt sure that my poor Dolores had strangely come to sleep her last sleep near me.

Immediately after I became satisfied who you were, I felt a painful degree of responsibility for the knowledge. I wrote at once to a friend of mine in the neighborhood of St. Augustine, to find out any particulars of the Mendoza family. I learned that its history had been like that of many others in that region. Don José had died in a bilious fever, brought on by excessive dissipation, and at his death the estate was found to be so incumbered that the whole was sold at auction. The slaves were scattered hither and thither to different owners, and Madame Mendoza, with her children and remains of fortune, had gone to live in New Orleans.

Of Dolores he had heard but once since her marriage. A friend had visited Don Guzman's estates in Cuba. He was living in great splendor, but bore the character of a hard, cruel, tyrannical master, and an overbearing man. His wife was spoken of as being in very delicate health,—avoiding society and devoting herself to religion.

I would here take occasion to say that it was understood when I went into the family of Don José, that I should not in any way interfere with the religious faith of the children, the family being understood to belong to the Roman Catholic Church. There was so little like religion of any kind in the family, that the idea of their belonging to any faith savored something of the ludicrous. In the case of poor Dolores, however, it was different. The earnestness of her nature would always have made any religious form a reality to her. In her case I was glad to remember that the Romish Church, amid many corruptions, preserves all the essential beliefs necessary for our salvation, and that many holy souls have gone to heaven through its doors. I therefore was only careful to direct her principal attention to the more spiritual parts of her own faith, and to dwell on the great themes which all Christian people hold in common.

Many of my persuasion would not have felt free to do this, but my liberty of conscience in this respect was perfect. I have seen that if you break the cup out of which a soul has been used to take the wine of the gospel, you often spill the very wine itself. And after all, these forms are but shadows of which the substance is Christ.

I am free to say, therefore, that the thought that your poor mother was devoting herself earnestly to religion, although after the forms of a church with which I differ, was to me a source of great consolation, because I knew that in that way alone could a soul like hers find peace.

I have never rested from my efforts to obtain more information. A short time before the incident which cast you upon our shore, I conversed with a sea-captain who had returned from Cuba. He stated that there had been an attempt at insurrection among the slaves of Don Guzman, in which a large part of the buildings and out-houses of the estate had been consumed by fire. On subsequent inquiry I learned that Don Guzman had sold his estates and embarked for Boston with his wife and family, and that nothing had subsequently been heard of him.

Thus, my young friend, I have told you all that I know of those singular circumstances which have cast your lot on our shores. I do not expect at your time of life you will take the same view of this event that I do. You may possibly—very probably will—consider it a loss not to have been brought up as you might have been in the splendid establishment of Don Guzman, and found yourself heir to wealth and pleasure without labor or exertion. Yet I am quite sure in that case that your value as a human being would have been immeasurably less. I think I have seen in you the elements of passions, which luxury and idleness and the too early possession of irresponsible power, might have developed with fatal results. You have simply to reflect whether you would rather be an energetic, intelligent, self-controlled man, capable of guiding the affairs of life and of acquiring its prizes,—or to be the reverse of all this, with its prizes bought for you by the wealth of parents. I hope mature reflection will teach you to regard with gratitude that disposition of the All-Wise, which cast your lot as it has been cast.

Let me ask one thing in closing. I have written for you here many things most painful for me to remember, because I wanted you to love and honor the memory of your mother. I wanted that her memory should have something such a charm for you as it has for me. With me, her image has always stood between me and all other women; but I have never even intimated to a living being that such a passage in my history ever occurred,—no, not even to my sister, who is nearer to me than any other earthly creature.

In some respects I am a singular person in my habits, and having once written this, you will pardon me if I observe that it will never be agreeable to me to have the subject named between us. Look upon me always as a friend, who would regard nothing as a hardship by which he might serve the son of one so dear.

I have hesitated whether I ought to add one circumstance more. I think I will do so, trusting to your good sense not to give it any undue weight.

I have never ceased making inquiries in Cuba, as I found opportunity, in regard to your father's property, and late investigations have led me to the conclusion that he left a considerable sum of money in the hands of a notary, whose address I have, which, if your identity could be proved, would come in course of law to you. I have written an account of all the circumstances which, in my view, identify you as the son of Don Guzman de Cardona, and had them properly attested in legal form.

This, together with your mother's picture and the bracelet, I recommend you to take on your next voyage, and to see what may result from the attempt. How considerable the sum may be which will result from this, I cannot say, but as Don Guzman's fortune was very large, I am in hopes it may prove something worth attention.

At any time you may wish to call, I will have all these things ready for you.

I am, with warm regard,

Your sincere friend,

THEOPHILUS SEWELL.

When Moses had finished reading this letter, he laid it down on the pebbles beside him, and, leaning back against a rock, looked moodily out to sea. The tide had washed quite up to within a short distance of his feet, completely isolating the little grotto where he sat from all the surrounding scenery, and before him, passing and repassing on the blue bright solitude of the sea, were silent ships, going on their wondrous pathless ways to unknown lands. The letter had stirred all within him that was dreamy and poetic: he felt somehow like a leaf torn from a romance, and blown strangely into the hollow of those rocks. Something too of ambition and pride stirred within him. He had been born an heir of wealth and power, little as they had done for the happiness of his poor mother; and when he thought he might have had these two wild horses which have run away with so many young men, he felt, as young men all do, an impetuous desire for their possession, and he thought as so many do, "Give them to me, and I'll risk my character,—I'll risk my happiness."

The letter opened a future before him which was something to speculate upon, even though his reason told him it was uncertain, and he lay there dreamily piling one air-castle on another,—unsubstantial as the great islands of white cloud that sailed through the sky and dropped their shadows in the blue sea.

It was late in the afternoon when he bethought him he must return home, and so climbing from rock to rock he swung himself upward on to the island, and sought the brown cottage. As he passed by the open window he caught a glimpse of Mara sewing. He walked softly up to look in without her seeing him. She was sitting with the various articles of his wardrobe around her, quietly and deftly mending his linen, singing soft snatches of an old psalm-tune.

She seemed to have resumed quite naturally that quiet care of him and his, which she had in all the earlier years of their life. He noticed again her little hands,—they seemed a sort of wonder to him. Why had he never seen, when a boy, how pretty they were? And she had such dainty little ways of taking up and putting down things as she measured and clipped; it seemed so pleasant to have her handling his things; it was as if a good fairy were touching them, whose touch brought back peace. But then, he thought, by and by she will do all this for some one else. The thought made him angry. He really felt abused in anticipation. She was doing all this for him just in sisterly kindness, and likely as not thinking of somebody else whom she loved better all the time. It is astonishing how cool and dignified this consideration made our hero as he faced up to the window. He was, after all, in hopes she might blush, and look agitated at seeing him suddenly; but she did not. The foolish boy did not know the quick wits of a girl, and that all the while that he had supposed himself so sly, and been holding his breath to observe, Mara had been perfectly cognizant of his presence, and had been schooling herself to look as unconscious and natural as possible. So she did,—only saying,—

"Oh, Moses, is that you? Where have you been all day?"

"Oh, I went over to see Parson Sewell, and get my pastoral lecture, you know."

"And did you stay to dinner?"

"No; I came home and went rambling round the rocks, and got into our old cave, and never knew how the time passed."

"Why, then you've had no dinner, poor boy," said Mara, rising suddenly. "Come in quick, you must be fed, or you'll get dangerous and eat somebody."

"No, no, don't get anything," said Moses, "it's almost supper-time, and I'm not hungry."

And Moses threw himself into a chair, and began abstractedly snipping a piece of tape with Mara's very best scissors.

"If you please, sir, don't demolish that; I was going to stay one of your collars with it," said Mara.

"Oh, hang it, I'm always in mischief among girls' things," said Moses, putting down the scissors and picking up a bit of white wax, which with equal unconsciousness, he began kneading in his hands, while he was dreaming over the strange contents of the morning's letter.

"I hope Mr. Sewell didn't say anything to make you look so very gloomy," said Mara.

"Mr. Sewell?" said Moses, starting; "no, he didn't; in fact, I had a pleasant call there; and there was that confounded old sphinx of a Miss Roxy there. Why don't she die? She must be somewhere near a hundred years old by this time."

"Never thought to ask her why she didn't die," said Mara; "but I presume she has the best of reasons for living."

"Yes, that's so," said Moses; "every old toadstool, and burdock, and mullein lives and thrives and lasts; no danger of their dying."

"You seem to be in a charitable frame of mind," said Mara.

"Confound it all! I hate this world. If I could have my own way now,—if I could have just what I wanted, and do just as I please exactly, I might make a pretty good thing of it."

"And pray what would you have?" said Mara.

"Well, in the first place, riches."

"In the first place?"

"Yes, in the first place, I say; for money buys everything else."

"Well, supposing so," said Mara, "for argument's sake, what would you buy with it?"

"Position in society, respect, consideration,—and I'd have a splendid place, with everything elegant. I have ideas enough, only give me the means. And then I'd have a wife, of course."

"And how much would you pay for her?" said Mara, looking quite cool.

"I'd buy her with all the rest,—a girl that wouldn't look at *me* as I am,—would take me for all the rest, you know,—that's the way of the world."

"It is, is it?" said Mara. "I don't understand such matters much."

"Yes; it's the way with all you girls," said Moses; "it's the way you'll marry when you do."

"Don't be so fierce about it. I haven't done it yet," said Mara; "but now, really, I must go and set the supper-table when I have put these things away,"—and Mara gathered an armful of things together, and tripped singing upstairs, and arranged them in the drawer of Moses's room. "Will his wife like to do all these little things for him as I do?" she thought. "It's natural I should. I grew up with him, and love him, just as if he were my own brother,—he is all the brother I ever had. I love him more than anything else in the world, and this wife he talks about could do no more."

"She don't care a pin about me," thought Moses; "it's only a habit she has got, and her strict notions of duty, that's all. She is housewifely in her instincts, and seizes all neglected linen and garments as her lawful prey,—she would do it just the same for her grandfather;" and Moses drummed moodily on the window-pane.

CHAPTER XXVIII

A COQUETTE

The timbers of the ship which was to carry the fortunes of our hero were laid by the side of Middle Bay, and all these romantic shores could hardly present a lovelier scene. This beautiful sheet of water separates Harpswell from a portion of Brunswick. Its shores are rocky and pine-crowned, and display the most picturesque variety of outline. Eagle Island, Shelter Island, and one or two smaller ones, lie on the glassy surface like soft clouds of green foliage pierced through by the steel-blue tops of arrowy pine-trees.

There were a goodly number of shareholders in the projected vessel; some among the most substantial men in the vicinity. Zephaniah Pennel had invested there quite a solid sum, as had also our friend Captain Kittridge. Moses had placed therein the proceeds of his recent voyage, which enabled him to buy a certain number of shares, and he secretly revolved in his mind whether the sum of money left by his father might not enable him to buy the whole ship. Then a few prosperous voyages, and his fortune was made!

He went into the business of building the new vessel with all the enthusiasm with which he used, when a boy, to plan ships and mould anchors. Every day he was off at early dawn in his working-clothes, and labored steadily among the men till evening. No matter how early he rose, however, he always found that a good fairy had been before him and prepared his dinner, daintily sometimes adding thereto a fragrant little bunch of flowers. But when his boat returned home at evening, he no longer saw her as in the days of girlhood waiting far out on the farthest point of rock for his return. Not that she did not watch for it and run out many times toward sunset; but the moment she had made out that it was surely he, she would run back into the house, and very likely find an errand in her own room, where she would be so deeply engaged that it would be necessary for him to call her down before she could make her appearance. Then she came smiling, chatty, always gracious, and ready to go or to come as he requested,—the very cheerfulest of household fairies,—but yet for all that there was a cobweb invisible barrier around her that for some reason or other he could not break over. It vexed and perplexed him, and day after day he determined to whistle it down,—ride over it rough-shod,—and be as free as he chose with this apparently soft, unresistant, airy being, who seemed so accessible. Why shouldn't he kiss her when he chose, and sit with his arm around her waist, and draw her familiarly upon his knee,—this little child-woman, who was as a sister to him? Why, to be sure? Had she ever frowned or scolded as Sally Kittridge did when he attempted to pass the air-line that divides man from womanhood? Not at all. She had neither blushed nor laughed, nor ran away. If he kissed her, she took it with the most matter-of-fact composure; if he passed his arm around her, she let it remain with unmoved calmness; and so somehow he did these things less and less, and wondered why.

The fact is, our hero had begun an experiment with his little friend that we would never advise a young man to try on one of these intense, quiet, soft-seeming women, whose whole life is inward. He had determined to find out whether she loved him before he committed himself to her; and the strength of a whole book of martyrs is in women to endure and to bear without flinching before they will surrender the gate of this citadel of silence. Moreover, our hero had begun his siege with precisely the worst weapons.

For on the night that he returned and found Mara conversing with a stranger, the suspicion arose in his mind that somehow Mara might be particularly interested in him, and instead of asking her, which anybody might consider the most feasible step in the case, he asked Sally Kittridge.

Sally's inborn, inherent love of teasing was up in a moment. Did she know anything of that Mr. Adams? Of course she did,—a young lawyer of one of the best Boston families,—a splendid fellow; she wished any such luck might happen to her! Was Mara engaged to him? What would he give to know? Why didn't he ask Mara? Did he expect her to reveal her friend's secrets? Well, she shouldn't,—report said Mr. Adams was well-to-do in the world, and had expectations from an uncle,—and didn't Moses think he was interesting in conversation? Everybody said what a conquest it was for an Orr's Island girl, etc., etc. And Sally said the rest with many a malicious toss and wink and sly twinkle of the dimples of her cheek, which might mean more or less, as a young man of imaginative temperament was disposed to view it. Now this was all done in pure simple love of teasing. We incline to think phrenologists have as yet been very incomplete in their classification of faculties, or they would have appointed a separate organ for this propensity of human nature. Certain persons, often the most kind-hearted in the world, and who would not give pain in any serious matter, seem to have an insatiable appetite for those small annoyances we commonly denominate teasing,—and Sally was one of this number.

She diverted herself infinitely in playing upon the excitability of Moses,—in awaking his curiosity, and baffling it, and tormenting him with a whole phantasmagoria of suggestions and assertions, which played along so near the line of probability, that one could never tell which might be fancy and which might be fact.

Moses therefore pursued the line of tactics for such cases made and provided, and strove to awaken jealousy in Mara by paying marked and violent attentions to

Sally. He went there evening after evening, leaving Mara to sit alone at home. He made secrets with her, and alluded to them before Mara. He proposed calling his new vessel the Sally Kittridge; but whether all these things made Mara jealous or not, he could never determine. Mara had no peculiar gift for acting, except in this one point; but here all the vitality of nature rallied to her support, and enabled her to preserve an air of the most unperceiving serenity. If she shed any tears when she spent a long, lonesome evening, she was quite particular to be looking in a very placid frame when Moses returned, and to give such an account of the books, or the work, or paintings which had interested her, that Moses was sure to be vexed. Never were her inquiries for Sally more cordial,—never did she seem inspired by a more ardent affection for her.

Whatever may have been the result of this state of things in regard to Mara, it is certain that Moses succeeded in convincing the common fame of that district that he and Sally were destined for each other, and the thing was regularly discussed at quilting frolics and tea-drinkings around, much to Miss Emily's disgust and Aunt Roxy's grave satisfaction, who declared that "Mara was altogether too good for Moses Pennel, but Sally Kittridge would make him stand round,"—by which expression she was understood to intimate that Sally had in her the rudiments of the same kind of domestic discipline which had operated so favorably in the case of Captain Kittridge.

These things, of course, had come to Mara's ears. She had overheard the discussions on Sunday noons as the people between meetings sat over their doughnuts and cheese, and analyzed their neighbors' affairs, and she seemed to smile at them all. Sally only laughed, and declared that it was no such thing; that she would no more marry Moses Pennel, or any other fellow, than she would put her head into the fire. What did she want of any of them? She knew too much to get married,—that she did. She was going to have her liberty for one while yet to come, etc., etc.; but all these assertions were of course supposed to mean nothing but the usual declarations in such cases. Mara among the rest thought it quite likely that this thing was yet to be.

So she struggled and tried to reason down a pain which constantly ached in her heart when she thought of this. She ought to have foreseen that it must some time end in this way. Of course she must have known that Moses would some time choose a wife; and how fortunate that, instead of a stranger, he had chosen her most intimate friend. Sally was careless and thoughtless, to be sure, but she had a good generous heart at the bottom, and she hoped she would love Moses at least as well as *she* did, and then she would always live with them, and think of any little things that Sally might forget.

After all, Sally was so much more capable and efficient a person than herself,—so much more bustling and energetic, she would make altogether a better housekeeper, and doubtless a better wife for Moses. But then it was so hard that he did not tell her about it. Was she not his sister?—his confidant for all his childhood?—and why should he shut up his heart from her now? But then she must guard herself from being jealous,—that would be mean and wicked. So Mara, in her zeal of self-discipline, pushed on matters; invited Sally to tea to meet Moses; and when she came, left them alone together while she busied herself in hospitable cares. She sent Moses with errands and commissions to Sally, which he was sure to improve into protracted visits; and in short, no young match-maker ever showed more good-will to forward the union of two chosen friends than Mara showed to unite Moses and Sally.

So the flirtation went on all summer, like a ship under full sail, with prosperous breezes; and Mara, in the many hours that her two best friends were together, tried heroically to persuade herself that she was not unhappy. She said to herself constantly that she never had loved Moses other than as a brother, and repeated and dwelt upon the fact to her own mind with a pertinacity which might have led her to suspect the reality of the fact, had she had experience enough to look closer. True, it was rather lonely, she said, but that she was used to,—she always had been and always should be. Nobody would ever love her in return as she loved; which sentence she did not analyze very closely, or she might have remembered Mr. Adams and one or two others, who had professed more for her than she had found herself able to return. That general proposition about nobody is commonly found, if sifted to the bottom, to have specific relation to somebody whose name never appears in the record.

Nobody could have conjectured from Mara's calm, gentle cheerfulness of demeanor, that any sorrow lay at the bottom of her heart; she would not have owned it to herself.

There are griefs which grow with years, which have no marked beginnings,—no especial dates; they are not events, but slow perceptions of disappointment, which bear down on the heart with a constant and equable pressure like the weight of the atmosphere, and these things are never named or counted in words among life's sorrows; yet through them, as through an unsuspected inward wound, life, energy, and vigor slowly bleed away, and the persons, never owning even to themselves the weight of the pressure,—standing, to all appearance, fair and cheerful, are still undermined with a secret wear of this inner current, and ready to fall with the first external pressure.

There are persons often brought into near contact by the relations of life, and bound to each other by a love so close, that they are perfectly indispensable to each other, who yet act upon each other as a file upon a diamond, by a slow and gradual friction, the pain of which is so equable, so constantly diffused through life, as scarcely ever at any time to force itself upon the mind as a reality.

Such had been the history of the affection of Mara for Moses. It had been a deep, inward, concentrated passion that had almost absorbed self-consciousness, and made her keenly alive to all the moody, restless, passionate changes of his nature; it had brought with it that craving for sympathy and return which such love ever will, and yet it was fixed upon a nature so different and so uncomprehending that the action had for years been one of pain more than pleasure. Even now, when she had him at home with her and busied herself with constant cares for him, there was a sort of disturbing, unquiet element in the history of every day. The longing for him to come home at night,—the wish that he would stay with her,—the uncertainty whether he would or would not go and spend the evening with Sally,—the musing during the day over all that he had done and said the day before, were a constant interior excitement. For Moses, besides being in his moods quite variable and changeable, had also a good deal of the dramatic element in him, and put on sundry appearances in the way of experiment.

He would feign to have quarreled with Sally, that he might detect whether Mara would betray some gladness; but she only evinced concern and a desire to make up the difficulty. He would discuss her character and her fitness to make a man happy in matrimony in the style that young gentlemen use who think their happiness a point of great consequence in the creation; and Mara, always cool, and firm, and sensible, would talk with him in the most maternal style possible, and caution him against trifling with her affections. Then again he would be lavish in his praise of Sally's beauty, vivacity, and energy, and Mara would join with the most apparently unaffected delight. Sometimes he ventured, on the other side, to rally her on some future husband, and predict the days when all the attentions which she was daily bestowing on him would be for another; and here, as everywhere else, he found his little Sphinx perfectly inscrutable. Instinct teaches the grass-bird, who hides her eggs under long meadow grass, to creep timidly yards from the nest, and then fly up boldly in the wrong place; and a like instinct teaches shy girls all kinds of unconscious stratagems when the one secret of their life is approached. They may be as truthful in all other things as the strictest Puritan, but here they deceive by an infallible necessity. And meanwhile, where was Sally Kittridge in all this matter? Was her heart in the least touched by the black eyes and long lashes? Who can say? Had she a heart? Well, Sally was a good girl. When one got sufficiently far down through the foam and froth of the surface to find what was in the depths of her nature, there was abundance there of good womanly feeling, generous and strong, if one could but get at it.

She was the best and brightest of daughters to the old Captain, whose accounts she kept, whose clothes she mended, whose dinner she often dressed and carried to him, from loving choice; and Mrs. Kittridge regarded her housewifely accomplishments with pride, though she never spoke to her otherwise than in words of criticism and rebuke, as in her view an honest mother should who means to keep a flourishing sprig of a daughter within limits of a proper humility.

But as for any sentiment or love toward any person of the other sex, Sally, as yet, had it not. Her numerous admirers were only so many subjects for the exercise of her dear delight of teasing, and Moses Pennel, the last and most considerable, differed from the rest only in the fact that he was a match for her in this redoubtable art and science, and this made the game she was playing with him altogether more stimulating than that she had carried on with any other of her admirers. For Moses could sulk and storm for effect, and clear off as bright as Harpswell Bay after a thunder-storm—for effect also. Moses could play jealous, and make believe all those thousand-and-one shadowy nothings that coquettes, male and female, get up to carry their points with; and so their quarrels and their makings-up were as manifold as the sea-breezes that ruffled the ocean before the Captain's door.

There is but one danger in play of this kind, and that is, that deep down in the breast of every slippery, frothy, elfish Undine sleeps the germ of an unawakened soul, which suddenly, in the course of some such trafficking with the outward shows and seemings of affection, may wake up and make of the teasing, tricksy elf a sad and earnest woman—a creature of loves and self-denials and faithfulness unto death—in short, something altogether too good, too sacred to be trifled with; and when a man enters the game protected by a previous attachment which absorbs all his nature, and the woman awakes in all her depth and strength to feel the real meaning of love and life, she finds that she has played with one stronger than she, at a terrible disadvantage.

Is this mine lying dark and evil under the saucy little feet of our Sally? Well, we should not of course be surprised some day to find it so.

CHAPTER XXIX

NIGHT TALKS

October is come, and among the black glooms of the pine forests flare out the scarlet branches of the rock-maple, and the beech-groves are all arrayed in gold, through which the sunlight streams in subdued richness. October is come with long, bright, hazy days, swathing in purple mists the rainbow brightness of the forests, and blending the otherwise gaudy and flaunting colors into wondrous harmonies of splendor. And Moses Pennel's ship is all built and ready, waiting only a favorable day for her launching.

And just at this moment Moses is sauntering home from Captain Kittridge's in company with Sally, for Mara has sent him to bring her to tea with them. Moses is in high spirits; everything has succeeded to his wishes; and as the two walk along the high, bold, rocky shore, his eye glances out to the open ocean, where the sun is setting, and the fresh wind blowing, and the white sails flying, and already fancies himself a sea-king, commanding his own place, and going from land to land.

"There hasn't been a more beautiful ship built here these twenty years," he says, in triumph.

"Oho, Mr. Conceit," said Sally, "that's only because it's yours now—your geese are all swans. I wish you could have seen the Typhoon, that Ben Drummond sailed in—a real handsome fellow he was. What a pity there aren't more like him!"

"I don't enter on the merits of Ben Drummond's beauty," said Moses; "but I don't believe the Typhoon was one whit superior to our ship. Besides, Miss Sally, I thought you were going to take it under your especial patronage, and let me honor it with your name."

"How absurd you always will be talking about that—why don't you call it after Mara?"

"After Mara?" said Moses. "I don't want to—it wouldn't be appropriate—one wants a different kind of girl to name a ship after—something bold and bright and dashing!"

"Thank you, sir, but I prefer not to have my bold and dashing qualities immortalized in this way," said Sally; "besides, sir, how do I know that you wouldn't run me on a rock the very first thing? When I give my name to a ship, it must have an experienced commander," she added, maliciously, for she knew that Moses was specially vulnerable on this point.

"As you please," said Moses, with heightened color. "Allow me to remark that he who shall ever undertake to command the 'Sally Kittridge' will have need of all his experience—and then, perhaps, not be able to know the ways of the craft."

"See him now," said Sally, with a malicious laugh; "we are getting wrathy, are we?"

"Not I," said Moses; "it would cost altogether too much exertion to get angry at every teasing thing you choose to say, Miss Sally. By and by I shall be gone, and then won't your conscience trouble you?"

"My conscience is all easy, so far as you are concerned, sir; your self-esteem is too deep-rooted to suffer much from my poor little nips—they produce no more impression than a cat-bird pecking at the cones of that spruce-tree yonder. Now don't you put your hand where your heart is supposed to be—there's nobody at home there, you know. There's Mara coming to meet us;" and Sally bounded forward to meet Mara with all those demonstrations of extreme delight which young girls are fond of showering on each other.

"It's such a beautiful evening," said Mara, "and we are all in such good spirits about Moses's ship, and I told him you must come down and hold counsel with us as to what was to be done about the launching; and the name, you know, that is to be decided on—are you going to let it be called after you?"

"Not I, indeed. I should always be reading in the papers of horrible accidents that had happened to the 'Sally Kittridge.'"

"Sally has so set her heart on my being unlucky," said Moses, "that I believe if I make a prosperous voyage, the disappointment would injure her health."

"She doesn't mean what she says," said Mara; "but I think there are some objections in a young lady's name being given to a ship."

"Then I suppose, Mara," said Moses, "that you would not have yours either?"

"I would be glad to accommodate you in anything *but* that," said Mara, quietly; but she added, "Why need the ship be named for anybody? A ship is such a beautiful, graceful thing, it should have a fancy name."

"Well, suggest one," said Moses.

"Don't you remember," said Mara, "one Saturday afternoon, when you and Sally and I launched your little ship down in the cove after you had come from your first voyage at the Banks?"

"I do," said Sally. "We called that the Ariel, Mara, after that old torn play you were so fond of. That's a pretty name for a ship."

"Why not take that?" said Mara.

"I bow to the decree," said Moses. "The Ariel it shall be."

"Yes; and you remember," said Sally, "Mr. Moses here promised at that time that he would build a ship, and take us two round the world with him."

Moses's eyes fell upon Mara as Sally said these words with a sort of sudden earnestness of expression which struck her. He was really feeling very much about something, under all the bantering disguise of his demeanor, she said to herself. Could it be that he felt unhappy about his prospects with Sally? That careless liveliness of hers might wound him perhaps now, when he felt that he was soon to leave her.

Mara was conscious herself of a deep undercurrent of sadness as the time approached for the ship to sail that should carry Moses from her, and she could not but think some such feeling must possess her mind. In vain she looked into Sally's great Spanish eyes for any signs of a lurking softness or tenderness concealed under her sparkling vivacity. Sally's eyes were admirable windows of exactly the right size and color for an earnest, tender spirit to look out of, but just now there was nobody at the casement but a slippery elf peering out in tricksy defiance.

When the three arrived at the house, tea was waiting on the table for them. Mara fancied that Moses looked sad and preoccupied as they sat down to the tea-table, which Mrs. Pennel had set forth festively, with the best china and the finest tablecloth and the choicest sweetmeats. In fact, Moses did feel that sort of tumult and upheaving of the soul which a young man experiences when the great crisis comes which is to plunge him into the struggles of manhood. It is a time when he wants sympathy and is grated upon by uncomprehending merriment, and therefore his answers to Sally grew brief and even harsh at times, and Mara sometimes perceived him looking at herself with a singular fixedness of expression, though he withdrew his eyes whenever she turned hers to look on him. Like many another little woman, she had fixed a theory about her friends, into which she was steadily interweaving all the facts she saw. Sally *must* love Moses, because she had known her from childhood as a good and affectionate girl, and it was impossible that she could have been going on with Moses as she had for the last six months without loving him. She must evidently have seen that he cared for her; and in how many ways had she shown that she liked his society and him! But then evidently she did not understand him, and Mara felt a little womanly self-pluming on the thought that *she* knew him so much better. She was resolved that she would talk with Sally about it, and show her that she was disappointing Moses and hurting his feelings. Yes, she said to herself, Sally has a kind heart, and her coquettish desire to conceal from him the extent of her affection ought now to give way to the outspoken tenderness of real love.

So Mara pressed Sally with the old-times request to stay and sleep with her; for these two, the only young girls in so lonely a neighborhood, had no means of excitement or dissipation beyond this occasional sleeping together—by which is meant, of course, lying awake all night talking.

When they were alone together in their chamber, Sally let down her long black hair, and stood with her back to Mara brushing it. Mara sat looking out of the window, where the moon was making a wide sheet of silver-sparkling water. Everything was so quiet that the restless dash of the tide could be plainly heard. Sally was rattling away with her usual gayety.

"And so the launching is to come off next Thursday. What shall you wear?"

"I'm sure I haven't thought," said Mara.

"Well, I shall try and finish my blue merino for the occasion. What fun it will be! I never was on a ship when it was launched, and I think it will be something perfectly splendid!"

"But doesn't it sometimes seem sad to think that after all this Moses will leave us to be gone so long?"

"What do I care?" said Sally, tossing back her long hair as she brushed it, and then stopping to examine one of her eyelashes.

"Sally dear, you often speak in that way," said Mara, "but really and seriously, you do yourself great injustice. You could not certainly have been going on as you have these six months past with a man you did not care for."

"Well, I do care for him, 'sort o','" said Sally; "but is that any reason I should break my heart for his going?—that's too much for any man."

"But, Sally, you *must* know that Moses loves you."

"I'm not so sure," said Sally, freakishly tossing her head and laughing.

"If he did not," said Mara, "why has he sought you so much, and taken every opportunity to be with you? I'm sure I've been left here alone hour after hour, when my only comfort was that it was because my two best friends loved each other, as I know they must some time love some one better than they do me."

The most practiced self-control must fail some time, and Mara's voice faltered on these last words, and she put her hands over her eyes. Sally turned quickly and looked at her, then giving her hair a sudden fold round her shoulders, and running to her friend, she kneeled down on the floor by her, and put her arms round her waist, and looked up into her face with an air of more gravity than she commonly used.

"Now, Mara, what a wicked, inconsistent fool I have been! Did you feel lonesome?—did you care? I ought to have seen that; but I'm selfish, I love admiration, and I love to have some one to flatter me, and run after me; and so I've been going on and on in this silly way. But I didn't know you cared—indeed, I didn't—you are such a deep little thing. Nobody can ever tell what you feel. I never shall forgive myself, if you have been lonesome, for you are worth five hundred times as much as I am. You really do love Moses. I don't."

"I do love him as a dear brother," said Mara.

"Dear fiddlestick," said Sally. "Love is love; and when a person loves all she can, it isn't much use to talk so. I've been a wicked sinner, that I have. Love? Do you suppose I would bear with Moses Pennel all his ins and outs and ups and downs, and be always putting him before myself in everything, as you do? No, I couldn't; I haven't it in me; but you have. He's a sinner, too, and deserves to get me for a wife. But, Mara, I have tormented him well—there's some comfort in that."

"It's no comfort to me," said Mara. "I see his heart is set on you—the happiness of his life depends on you—and that he is pained and hurt when you give him only cold, trifling words when he needs real true love. It is a serious thing, dear, to have a strong man set his whole heart on you. It will do him a great good or a great evil, and you ought not to make light of it."

"Oh, pshaw, Mara, you don't know these fellows; they are only playing games with us. If they once catch us, they have no mercy; and for one here's a child that isn't going to be caught. I can see plain enough that Moses Pennel has been trying to get me in love with him, but he doesn't love me. No, he doesn't," said Sally, reflectively. "He only wants to make a conquest of me, and I'm just the same. I want to make a conquest of him,—at least I have been wanting to,—but now I see it's a false, wicked kind of way to do as we've been doing."

"And is it really possible, Sally, that you don't love him?" said Mara, her large, serious eyes looking into Sally's. "What! be with him so much,—seem to like him so much,—look at him as I have seen you do,—and not love him!"

"I can't help my eyes; they will look so," said Sally, hiding her face in Mara's lap with a sort of coquettish consciousness. "I tell you I've been silly and wicked; but he's just the same exactly."

"And you have worn his ring all summer?"

"Yes, and he has worn mine; and I have a lock of his hair, and he has a lock of mine; yet I don't believe he cares for them a bit. Oh, his heart is safe enough. If he has any, it isn't with me: that I know."

"But if you found it were, Sally? Suppose you found that, after all, you were the one love and hope of his life; that all he was doing and thinking was for you; that he was laboring, and toiling, and leaving home, so that he might some day offer you a heart and home, and be your best friend for life? Perhaps he dares not tell you how he really does feel."

"It's no such thing! it's no such thing!" said Sally, lifting up her head, with her eyes full of tears, which she dashed angrily away. "What am I crying for? I hate him. I'm glad he's going away. Lately it has been such a trouble to me to have things go on so. I'm really getting to dislike him. You are the one he ought to love. Perhaps all this time you are the one he does love," said Sally, with a sudden energy, as if a new thought had dawned in her mind.

"Oh, no; he does not even love me as he once did, when we were children," said Mara. "He is so shut up in himself, so reserved, I know nothing about what passes in his heart."

"No more does anybody," said Sally. "Moses Pennel isn't one that says and does things straightforward because he feels so; but he says and does them to see what *you* will do. That's his way. Nobody knows why he has been going on with me as he has. He has had his own reasons, doubtless, as I have had mine."

"He has admired you very much, Sally," said Mara, "and praised you to me very warmly. He thinks you are so handsome. I could tell you ever so many things he has said about you. He knows as I do that you are a more enterprising, practical sort of body than I am, too. Everybody thinks you are engaged. I have heard it spoken of everywhere."

"Everybody is mistaken, then, as usual," said Sally. "Perhaps Aunt Roxy was in the right of it when she said that Moses would never be in love with anybody but himself."

CHAPTER XXIX

"Aunt Roxy has always been prejudiced and unjust to Moses," said Mara, her cheeks flushing. "She never liked him from a child, and she never can be made to see anything good in him. I know that he has a deep heart,—a nature that craves affection and sympathy; and it is only because he is so sensitive that he is so reserved and conceals his feelings so much. He has a noble, kind heart, and I believe he truly loves you, Sally; it must be so."

Sally rose from the floor and went on arranging her hair without speaking. Something seemed to disturb her mind. She bit her lip, and threw down the brush and comb violently. In the clear depths of the little square of looking-glass a face looked into hers, whose eyes were perturbed as if with the shadows of some coming inward storm; the black brows were knit, and the lips quivered. She drew a long breath and burst out into a loud laugh.

"What *are* you laughing at now?" said Mara, who stood in her white night-dress by the window, with her hair falling in golden waves about her face.

"Oh, because these fellows are so funny," said Sally; "it's such fun to see their actions. Come now," she added, turning to Mara, "don't look so grave and sanctified. It's better to laugh than cry about things, any time. It's a great deal better to be made hard-hearted like me, and not care for anybody, than to be like you, for instance. The idea of any one's being in love is the drollest thing to me. I haven't the least idea how it feels. I wonder if I ever shall be in love!"

"It will come to you in its time, Sally."

"Oh, yes,—I suppose like the chicken-pox or the whooping cough," said Sally; "one of the things to be gone through with, and rather disagreeable while it lasts,—so I hope to put it off as long as possible."

"Well, come," said Mara, "we must not sit up all night."

After the two girls were nestled into bed and the light out, instead of the brisk chatter there fell a great silence between them. The full round moon cast the reflection of the window on the white bed, and the ever restless moan of the sea became more audible in the fixed stillness. The two faces, both young and fair, yet so different in their expression, lay each still on its pillow,—their wide-open eyes gleaming out in the shadow like mystical gems. Each was breathing softly, as if afraid of disturbing the other. At last Sally gave an impatient movement.

"How lonesome the sea sounds in the night," she said. "I wish it would ever be still."

"I like to hear it," said Mara. "When I was in Boston, for a while I thought I could not sleep, I used to miss it so much."

There was another silence, which lasted so long that each girl thought the other asleep, and moved softly, but at a restless movement from Sally, Mara spoke again.

"Sally,—you asleep?"

"No,—I thought you were."

"I wanted to ask you," said Mara, "did Moses ever say anything to you about me?—you know I told you how much he said about you."

"Yes; he asked me once if you were engaged to Mr. Adams."

"And what did you tell him?" said Mara, with increasing interest.

"Well, I only plagued him. I sometimes made him think you were, and sometimes that you were not; and then again, that there was a deep mystery in hand. But I praised and glorified Mr. Adams, and told him what a splendid match it would be, and put on any little bits of embroidery here and there that I could lay hands on. I used to make him sulky and gloomy for a whole evening sometimes. In that way it was one of the best weapons I had."

"Sally, what does make you love to tease people so?" said Mara.

"Why, you know the hymn says,—

'Let dogs delight to bark and bite,
For God hath made them so;
Let bears and lions growl and fight,
For 'tis their nature too.'

That's all the account I can give of it."

"But," said Mara, "I never can rest easy a moment when I see I am making a person uncomfortable."

"Well, I don't tease anybody but the men. I don't tease father or mother or you,—but men are fair game; they are such thumby, blundering creatures, and we can confuse them so."

"Take care, Sally, it's playing with edge tools; you may lose your heart some day in this kind of game."

"Never you fear," said Sally; "but aren't you sleepy?—let's go to sleep."

Both girls turned their faces resolutely in opposite directions, and remained for an hour with their large eyes looking out into the moonlit chamber, like the fixed stars over Harpswell Bay. At last sleep drew softly down the fringy curtains.

CHAPTER XXX

THE LAUNCH OF THE ARIEL

In the plain, simple regions we are describing,—where the sea is the great avenue of active life, and the pine forests are the great source of wealth,—shipbuilding is an engrossing interest, and there is no fête that calls forth the community like the launching of a vessel. And no wonder; for what is there belonging to this workaday world of ours that has such a never-failing fund of poetry and grace as a ship? A ship is a beauty and a mystery wherever we see it: its white wings touch the regions of the unknown and the imaginative; they seem to us full of the odors of quaint, strange, foreign shores, where life, we fondly dream, moves in brighter currents than the muddy, tranquil tides of every day.

Who that sees one bound outward, with her white breasts swelling and heaving, as if with a reaching expectancy, does not feel his own heart swell with a longing impulse to go with her to the far-off shores? Even at dingy, crowded wharves, amid the stir and tumult of great cities, the coming in of a ship is an event that never can lose its interest. But on these romantic shores of Maine, where all is so wild and still, and the blue sea lies embraced in the arms of dark, solitary forests, the sudden incoming of a ship from a distant voyage is a sort of romance. Who that has stood by the blue waters of Middle Bay, engirdled as it is by soft slopes of green farming land, interchanged here and there with heavy billows of forest-trees, or rocky, pine-crowned promontories, has not felt that sense of seclusion and solitude which is so delightful? And then what a wonder! There comes a ship from China, drifting in like a white cloud,—the gallant creature! how the waters hiss and foam before her! with what a great free, generous plash she throws out her anchors, as if she said a cheerful "Well done!" to some glorious work accomplished! The very life and spirit of strange romantic lands come with her; suggestions of sandal-wood and spice breathe through the pine-woods; she is an oriental queen, with hands full of mystical gifts; "all her garments smell of myrrh and cassia, out of the ivory palaces, whereby they have made her glad." No wonder men have loved ships like birds, and that there have been found brave, rough hearts that in fatal wrecks chose rather to go down with their ocean love than to leave her in the last throes of her death-agony.

A ship-building, a ship-sailing community has an unconscious poetry ever underlying its existence. Exotic ideas from foreign lands relieve the trite monotony of life; the ship-owner lives in communion with the whole world, and is less likely to fall into the petty commonplaces that infest the routine of inland life.

Never arose a clearer or lovelier October morning than that which was to start the Ariel on her watery pilgrimage. Moses had risen while the stars were yet twinkling over their own images in Middle Bay, to go down and see that everything was right; and in all the houses that we know in the vicinity, everybody woke with the one thought of being ready to go to the launching.

Mrs. Pennel and Mara were also up by starlight, busy over the provisions for the ample cold collation that was to be spread in a barn adjoining the scene,—the materials for which they were packing into baskets covered with nice clean linen cloths, ready for the little sail-boat which lay within a stone's throw of the door in the brightening dawn, her white sails looking rosy in the advancing light.

It had been agreed that the Pennels and the Kittridges should cross together in this boat with their contributions of good cheer.

The Kittridges, too, had been astir with the dawn, intent on their quota of the festive preparations, in which Dame Kittridge's housewifely reputation was involved,—for it had been a disputed point in the neighborhood whether she or Mrs. Pennel made the best doughnuts; and of course, with this fact before her mind, her efforts in this line had been all but superhuman.

The Captain skipped in and out in high feather,—occasionally pinching Sally's cheek, and asking if she were going as captain or mate upon the vessel after it was launched, for which he got in return a fillip of his sleeve or a sly twitch of his coat-tails, for Sally and her old father were on romping terms with each other from early childhood, a thing which drew frequent lectures from the always exhorting Mrs. Kittridge.

"Such levity!" she said, as she saw Sally in full chase after his retreating figure, in order to be revenged for some sly allusions he had whispered in her ear.

"Sally Kittridge! Sally Kittridge!" she called, "come back this minute. What are you about? I should think your father was old enough to know better."

"Lawful sakes, Polly, it kind o' renews one's youth to get a new ship done," said the Captain, skipping in at another door. "Sort o' puts me in mind o' that *I* went out cap'en in when I was jist beginning to court you, as somebody else is courtin' our Sally here."

"Now, father," said Sally, threateningly, "what did I tell you?"

"It's really *lemancholy*," said the Captain, "to think how it does distress gals to talk to 'em 'bout the fellers, when they ain't thinkin' o' nothin' else all the time. They can't even laugh without sayin' he-he-he!"

"Now, father, you know I've told you five hundred times that I don't care a cent for Moses Pennel,—that he's a hateful creature," said Sally, looking very red and determined.

"Yes, yes," said the Captain, "I take that ar's the reason you've ben a-wearin' the ring he gin you and them ribbins you've got on your neck this blessed minute, and why you've giggled off to singin'-school, and Lord knows where with him all summer,—that ar's clear now."

"But, father," said Sally, getting redder and more earnest, "I don't care for him really, and I've told him so. I keep telling him so, and he will run after me."

"Haw! haw!" laughed the Captain; "he will, will he? Jist so, Sally; that ar's jist the way your ma there talked to me, and it kind o' 'couraged me along. I knew that gals always has to be read back'ard jist like the writin' in the Barbary States."

"Captain Kittridge, will you stop such ridiculous talk?" said his helpmeet; "and jist carry this 'ere basket of cold chicken down to the landin' agin the Pennels come round in the boat; and you must step spry, for there's two more baskets a-comin'."

The Captain shouldered the basket and walked toward the sea with it, and Sally retired to her own little room to hold a farewell consultation with her mirror before she went.

You will perhaps think from the conversation that you heard the other night, that Sally now will cease all thought of coquettish allurement in her acquaintance with Moses, and cause him to see by an immediate and marked change her entire indifference. Probably, as she stands thoughtfully before her mirror, she is meditating on the propriety of laying aside the ribbons he gave her—perhaps she will alter that arrangement of her hair which is one that he himself particularly dictated as most becoming to the character of her face. She opens a little drawer, which looks like a flower garden, all full of little knots of pink and blue and red, and various fancies of the toilet, and looks into it reflectively. She looses the ribbon from her hair and chooses another,—but Moses gave her that too, and said, she remembers, that when she wore that "he should know she had been thinking of him." Sally is Sally yet—as full of sly dashes of coquetry as a tulip is of streaks.

"There's no reason I should make myself look like a fright because I don't care for him," she says; "besides, after all that he has said, he ought to say more,—he ought at least to give me a chance to say no,—he *shall*, too," said the gypsy, winking at the bright, elfish face in the glass.

"Sally Kittridge, Sally Kittridge," called her mother, "how long will you stay prinkin'?—come down this minute."

"Law now, mother," said the Captain, "gals must prink afore such times; it's as natural as for hens to dress their feathers afore a thunder-storm."

Sally at last appeared, all in a flutter of ribbons and scarfs, whose bright, high colors assorted well with the ultramarine blue of her dress, and the vivid pomegranate hue of her cheeks. The boat with its white sails flapping was balancing and courtesying up and down on the waters, and in the stern sat Mara; her shining white straw hat trimmed with blue ribbons set off her golden hair and pink shell complexion. The dark, even penciling of her eyebrows, and the beauty of the brow above, the brown translucent clearness of her thoughtful eyes, made her face striking even with its extreme delicacy of tone. She was unusually animated and excited, and her cheeks had a rich bloom of that pure deep rose-color which flushes up in fair complexions under excitement, and her eyes had a kind of intense expression, for which they had always been remarkable. All the deep secluded yearning of repressed nature was looking out of them, giving that pathos which every one has felt at times in the silence of eyes.

"Now bless that ar gal," said the Captain, when he saw her. "Our Sally here's handsome, but she's got the real New-Jerusalem look, she has—like them in the Revelations that wears the fine linen, clean and white."

"Bless you, Captain Kittridge! don't be a-makin' a fool of yourself about no girl at your time o' life," said Mrs. Kittridge, speaking under her breath in a nipping, energetic tone, for they were coming too near the boat to speak very loud.

"Good mornin', Mis' Pennel; we've got a good day, and a mercy it is so. 'Member when we launched the North Star, that it rained guns all the mornin', and the water got into the baskets when we was a-fetchin' the things over, and made a sight o' pester."

"Yes," said Mrs. Pennel, with an air of placid satisfaction, "everything seems to be going right about this vessel."

Mrs. Kittridge and Sally were soon accommodated with seats, and Zephaniah Pennel and the Captain began trimming sail. The day was one of those perfect gems of days which are to be found only in the jewel-casket of October, a day neither hot nor cold, with an air so clear that every distant pine-tree top stood out in vivid separateness, and every woody point and rocky island seemed cut out in crystalline clearness against the sky. There was so brisk a breeze that the boat slanted quite to the water's edge on one side, and Mara leaned over and pensively drew her little pearly hand through the water, and thought of the days when she and Moses took this sail together—she in her pink sun-bonnet, and he in his round straw hat, with a tin dinner-pail between them; and now, to-day the ship of her childish dreams was to be launched. That launching was something she regarded almost with superstitious awe. The ship, built on one element, but designed to have its life in another, seemed an image of the soul, framed and fashioned with many a weary hammer-stroke in this life, but finding its true element only when it sails out into the ocean of eternity. Such was her thought as she looked down the clear, translucent depths; but would it have been of any use to try to utter it to anybody?—to Sally Kittridge, for example, who sat all in a cheerful rustle of bright ribbons beside her, and who would have shown her white teeth all round at such a suggestion, and said, "Now, Mara, who but you would have thought of that?"

But there are souls sent into this world who seem to have always mysterious affinities for the invisible and the unknown—who see the face of everything beautiful through a thin veil of mystery and sadness. The Germans call this yearning of spirit home-sickness—the dim remembrances of a spirit once affiliated to some higher sphere, of whose lost brightness all things fair are the vague reminders. As Mara looked pensively into the water, it seemed to her that every incident of life came up out of its depths to meet her. Her own face reflected in a wavering image, sometimes shaped itself to her gaze in the likeness of the pale lady of her childhood, who seemed to look up at her from the waters with dark, mysterious eyes of tender longing. Once or twice this dreamy effect grew so vivid that she shivered, and drawing herself up from the water, tried to take an interest in a very minute account which Mrs. Kittridge was giving of the way to make corn-fritters which should taste exactly like oysters. The closing direction about the quantity of mace Mrs. Kittridge felt was too sacred for common ears, and therefore whispered it into Mrs. Pennel's bonnet with a knowing nod and a look from her black spectacles which would not have been bad for a priestess of Dodona in giving out an oracle. In this secret direction about the *mace* lay the whole mystery of corn-oysters; and who can say what consequences might ensue from casting it in an unguarded manner before the world?

And now the boat which has rounded Harpswell Point is skimming across to the head of Middle Bay, where the new ship can distinctly be discerned standing upon her ways, while moving clusters of people were walking up and down her decks or lining the shore in the vicinity. All sorts of gossiping and neighborly chit-chat is being interchanged in the little world assembling there.

"I hain't seen the Pennels nor the Kittridges yet," said Aunt Ruey, whose little roly-poly figure was made illustrious in her best cinnamon-colored dyed silk. "There's Moses Pennel a-goin' up that ar ladder. Dear me, what a beautiful feller he is! it's a pity he ain't a-goin' to marry Mara Lincoln, after all."

"Ruey, do hush up," said Miss Roxy, frowning sternly down from under the shadow of a preternatural black straw bonnet, trimmed with huge bows of black ribbon, which head-piece sat above her curls like a helmet. "Don't be a-gettin' sentimental, Ruey, whatever else you get—and talkin' like Miss Emily Sewell about match-makin'; I can't stand it; it rises on my stomach, such talk does. As to that ar Moses Pennel, folks ain't so certain as they thinks what he'll do. Sally Kittridge may think he's a-goin' to have her, because he's been a-foolin' round with her all summer, and Sally Kittridge may jist find she's mistaken, that's all."

"Yes," said Miss Ruey, "I 'member when I was a girl my old aunt, Jerushy Hopkins, used to be always a-dwellin' on this Scripture, and I've been havin' it brought up to me this mornin': 'There are three things which are too wonderful for me, yea, four, which I know not: the way of an eagle in the air, the way of a serpent upon a rock, the way of a ship in the sea, and the way of a man with a maid.' She used to say it as a kind o' caution to me when she used to think Abram Peters was bein' attentive to me. I've often reflected what a massy it was that ar never come to nothin', for he's a poor drunken critter now."

"Well, for my part," said Miss Roxy, fixing her eyes critically on the boat that was just at the landing, "I should say the ways of a maid with a man was full as particular as any of the rest of 'em. Do look at Sally Kittridge now. There's Tom Hiers a-helpin' her out of the boat; and did you see the look she gin Moses Pennel as she went by him? Wal', Moses has got Mara on his arm anyhow; there's a gal worth six-and-twenty of the other. Do see them ribbins and scarfs, and the furbelows, and the way that ar Sally Kittridge handles her eyes. She's one that one feller ain't never enough for."

Mara's heart beat fast when the boat touched the shore, and Moses and one or two other young men came to assist in their landing. Never had he looked more beautiful than at this moment, when flushed with excitement and satisfaction he stood on the shore, his straw hat off, and his black curls blowing in the sea-breeze. He looked at Sally with a look of frank admiration as she stood there dropping her long black lashes over her bright cheeks, and coquettishly looking out from under them, but she stepped forward with a little energy of movement, and took the offered hand of Tom Hiers, who was gazing at her too with undisguised rapture, and Moses, stepping into the boat, helped Mrs. Pennel on shore, and then took Mara on his arm, looking her over as he did so with a glance far less assured and direct than he had given to Sally.

"You won't be afraid to climb the ladders, Mara?" said he.

"Not if you help me," she said.

Sally and Tom Hiers had already walked on toward the vessel, she ostentatiously chatting and laughing with him. Moses's brow clouded a little, and Mara noticed it. Moses thought he did not care for Sally; he knew that the little hand that was now lying on his arm was the one he wanted, and yet he felt vexed when he saw Sally walk off triumphantly with another. It was the dog-in-the-manger feeling which possesses coquettes of both sexes. Sally, on all former occasions, had shown a marked preference for him, and professed supreme indifference to Tom Hiers.

"It's all well enough," he said to himself, and he helped Mara up the ladders with the greatest deference and tenderness. "This little woman is worth ten such girls as Sally, if one only could get her heart. Here we are on our ship, Mara," he said, as he lifted her over the last barrier and set her down on the deck. "Look over there, do you see Eagle Island? Did you dream when we used to go over there and spend the day that you ever would be on *my* ship, as you are to-day? You won't be afraid, will you, when the ship starts?"

"I am too much of a sea-girl to fear on anything that sails in water," said Mara with enthusiasm. "What a splendid ship! how nicely it all looks!"

"Come, let me take you over it," said Moses, "and show you my cabin."

Meanwhile the graceful little vessel was the subject of various comments by the crowd of spectators below, and the clatter of workmen's hammers busy in some of the last preparations could yet be heard like a shower of hail-stones under her.

"I hope the ways are well greased," said old Captain Eldritch. "'Member how the John Peters stuck in her ways for want of their being greased?"

"Don't you remember the Grand Turk, that keeled over five minutes after she was launched?" said the quavering voice of Miss Ruey; "there was jist such a company of thoughtless young creatures aboard as there is now."

"Well, there wasn't nobody hurt," said Captain Kittridge. "If Mis' Kittridge would let me, I'd be glad to go aboard this 'ere, and be launched with 'em."

"I tell the Cap'n he's too old to be climbin' round and mixin' with young folks' frolics," said Mrs. Kittridge.

"I suppose, Cap'n Pennel, you've seen that the ways is all right," said Captain Broad, returning to the old subject.

CHAPTER XXX

"Oh yes, it's all done as well as hands can do it," said Zephaniah. "Moses has been here since starlight this morning, and Moses has pretty good faculty about such matters."

"Where's Mr. Sewell and Miss Emily?" said Miss Ruey. "Oh, there they are over on that pile of rocks; they get a pretty fair view there."

Mr. Sewell and Miss Emily were sitting under a cedar-tree, with two or three others, on a projecting point whence they could have a clear view of the launching. They were so near that they could distinguish clearly the figures on deck, and see Moses standing with his hat off, the wind blowing his curls back, talking earnestly to the golden-haired little woman on his arm.

"It is a launch into life for him," said Mr. Sewell, with suppressed feeling.

"Yes, and he has Mara on his arm," said Miss Emily; "that's as it should be. Who is that that Sally Kittridge is flirting with now? Oh, Tom Hiers. Well! he's good enough for her. Why don't she take him?" said Miss Emily, in her zeal jogging her brother's elbow.

"I'm sure, Emily, I don't know," said Mr. Sewell dryly; "perhaps he won't be taken."

"Don't you think Moses looks handsome?" said Miss Emily. "I declare there is something quite romantic and Spanish about him; don't you think so, Theophilus?"

"Yes, I think so," said her brother, quietly looking, externally, the meekest and most matter-of-fact of persons, but deep within him a voice sighed, "Poor Dolores, be comforted, your boy is beautiful and prosperous!"

"There, there!" said Miss Emily, "I believe she is starting."

All eyes of the crowd were now fixed on the ship; the sound of hammers stopped; the workmen were seen flying in every direction to gain good positions to see her go,—that sight so often seen on those shores, yet to which use cannot dull the most insensible.

First came a slight, almost imperceptible, movement, then a swift exultant rush, a dash into the hissing water, and the air was rent with hurrahs as the beautiful ship went floating far out on the blue seas, where her fairer life was henceforth to be.

Mara was leaning on Moses's arm at the instant the ship began to move, but in the moment of the last dizzy rush she felt his arm go tightly round her, holding her so close that she could hear the beating of his heart.

"Hurrah!" he said, letting go his hold the moment the ship floated free, and swinging his hat in answer to the hats, scarfs, and handkerchiefs, which fluttered from the crowd on the shore. His eyes sparkled with a proud light as he stretched himself upward, raising his head and throwing back his shoulders with a triumphant movement. He looked like a young sea-king just crowned; and the fact is the less wonderful, therefore, that Mara felt her heart throb as she looked at him, and that a treacherous throb of the same nature shook the breezy ribbons fluttering over the careless heart of Sally. A handsome young sea-captain, treading the deck of his own vessel, is, in his time and place, a prince.

Moses looked haughtily across at Sally, and then passed a half-laughing defiant flash of eyes between them. He looked at Mara, who could certainly not have known what was in her eyes at the moment,—an expression that made his heart give a great throb, and wonder if he saw aright: but it was gone a moment after, as all gathered around in a knot exchanging congratulations on the fortunate way in which the affair had gone off. Then came the launching in boats to go back to the collation on shore, where were high merry-makings for the space of one or two hours: and thus was fulfilled the first part of Moses Pennel's Saturday afternoon prediction.

CHAPTER XXXI

GREEK MEETS GREEK

Moses was now within a day or two of the time of his sailing, and yet the distance between him and Mara seemed greater than ever. It is astonishing, when two people are once started on a wrong understanding with each other, how near they may live, how intimate they may be, how many things they may have in common, how many words they may speak, how closely they may seem to simulate intimacy, confidence, friendship, while yet there lies a gulf between them that neither crosses,—a reserve that neither explores.

Like most shy girls, Mara became more shy the more really she understood the nature of her own feelings. The conversation with Sally had opened her eyes to the secret of her own heart, and she had a guilty feeling as if what she had discovered must be discovered by every one else. Yes, it was clear she loved Moses in a way that made him, she thought, more necessary to her happiness than she could ever be to his,—in a way that made it impossible to think of him as wholly and for life devoted to another, without a constant inner conflict. In vain had been all her little stratagems practiced upon herself the whole summer long, to prove to herself that she was glad that the choice had fallen upon Sally. She saw clearly enough now that she was not glad,—that there was no woman or girl living, however dear, who could come for life between him and her, without casting on her heart the shuddering sorrow of a dim eclipse.

But now the truth was plain to herself, her whole force was directed toward the keeping of her secret. "I may suffer," she thought, "but I will have strength not to be silly and weak. Nobody shall know,—nobody shall dream it,—and in the long, long time that he is away, I shall have strength given me to overcome."

So Mara put on her most cheerful and matter-of-fact kind of face, and plunged into the making of shirts and knitting of stockings, and talked of the coming voyage with such a total absence of any concern, that Moses began to think, after all, there could be no depth to her feelings, or that the deeper ones were all absorbed by some one else.

"You really seem to enjoy the prospect of my going away," said he to her, one morning, as she was energetically busying herself with her preparations.

"Well, of course; you know your career must begin. You must make your fortune; and it is pleasant to think how favorably everything is shaping for you."

"One likes, however, to be a little regretted," said Moses, in a tone of pique.

"A little regretted!" Mara's heart beat at these words, but her hypocrisy was well practiced. She put down the rebellious throb, and assuming a look of open, sisterly friendliness, said, quite naturally, "Why, we shall all miss you, of course."

"Of course," said Moses,—"one would be glad to be missed some other way than *of course*."

"Oh, as to that, make yourself easy," said Mara. "We shall all be dull enough when you are gone to content the most exacting." Still she spoke, not stopping her stitching, and raising her soft brown eyes with a frank, open look into Moses's—no tremor, not even of an eyelid.

"You men must have everything," she continued, gayly, "the enterprise, the adventure, the novelty, the pleasure of feeling that you are something, and can do something in the world; and besides all this, you want the satisfaction of knowing that we women are following in chains behind your triumphal car!"

There was a dash of bitterness in this, which was a rare ingredient in Mara's conversation.

Moses took the word. "And you women sit easy at home, sewing and singing, and forming romantic pictures of our life as like its homely reality as romances generally are to reality; and while we are off in the hard struggle for position and the means of life, you hold your hearts ready for the first rich man that offers a fortune ready made."

"The first!" said Mara. "Oh, you naughty! sometimes we try two or three."

"Well, then, I suppose this is from one of them," said Moses, flapping down a letter from Boston, directed in a masculine hand, which he had got at the post-office that morning.

Now Mara knew that this letter was nothing in particular, but she was taken by surprise, and her skin was delicate as peach-blossom, and so she could not help a sudden blush, which rose even to her golden hair, vexed as she was to feel it coming. She put the letter quietly in her pocket, and for a moment seemed too discomposed to answer.

"You do well to keep your own counsel," said Moses. "No friend so near as one's self, is a good maxim. One does not expect young girls to learn it so early, but it seems they do."

"And why shouldn't they as well as young men?" said Mara. "Confidence begets confidence, they say."

"I have no ambition to play confidant," said Moses; "although as one who stands to you in the relation of older brother and guardian, and just on the verge of a long voyage, I might be supposed anxious to know."

"And I have no ambition to be confidant," said Mara, all her spirit sparkling in her eyes; "although when one stands to you in the relation of an only sister, I might be supposed perhaps to feel some interest to be in your confidence."

CHAPTER XXXI

The words "older brother" and "only sister" grated on the ears of both the combatants as a decisive sentence. Mara never looked so pretty in her life, for the whole force of her being was awake, glowing and watchful, to guard passage, door, and window of her soul, that no treacherous hint might escape. Had he not just reminded her that he was only an older brother? and what would he think if he knew the truth?—and Moses thought the words *only sister* unequivocal declaration of how the matter stood in her view, and so he rose, and saying, "I won't detain you longer from your letter," took his hat and went out.

"Are you going down to Sally's?" said Mara, coming to the door and looking out after him.

"Yes."

"Well, ask her to come home with you and spend the evening. I have ever so many things to tell her."

"I will," said Moses, as he lounged away.

"The thing is clear enough," said Moses to himself. "Why should I make a fool of myself any further? What possesses us men always to set our hearts precisely on what isn't to be had? There's Sally Kittridge likes me; I can see that plainly enough, for all her mincing; and why couldn't I have had the sense to fall in love with her? She will make a splendid, showy woman. She has talent and tact enough to rise to any position I may rise to, let me rise as high as I will. She will always have skill and energy in the conduct of life; and when all the froth and foam of youth has subsided, she will make a noble woman. Why, then, do I cling to this fancy? I feel that this little flossy cloud, this delicate, quiet little puff of thistledown, on which I have set my heart, is the only thing for me, and that without her my life will always be incomplete. I remember all our early life. It was she who sought me, and ran after me, and where has all that love gone to? Gone to this fellow; that's plain enough. When a girl like her is so comfortably cool and easy, it's because her heart is off somewhere else."

This conversation took place about four o'clock in as fine an October afternoon as you could wish to see. The sun, sloping westward, turned to gold the thousand blue scales of the ever-heaving sea, and soft, pine-scented winds were breathing everywhere through the forests, waving the long, swaying films of heavy moss, and twinkling the leaves of the silver birches that fluttered through the leafy gloom. The moon, already in the sky, gave promise of a fine moonlight night; and the wild and lonely stillness of the island, and the thoughts of leaving in a few days, all conspired to foster the restless excitement in our hero's mind into a kind of romantic unrest.

Now, in some such states, a man disappointed in one woman will turn to another, because, in a certain way and measure, her presence stills the craving and fills the void. It is a sort of supposititious courtship,—a saying to one woman, who is sympathetic and receptive, the words of longing and love that another will not receive. To be sure it is a game unworthy of any true man,—a piece of sheer, reckless, inconsiderate selfishness. But men do it, as they do many other unworthy things, from the mere promptings of present impulse, and let consequences take care of themselves. Moses met Sally that afternoon in just the frame to play the lover in this hypothetical, supposititious way, with words and looks and tones that came from feelings given to another. And as to Sally? Well, for once, Greek met Greek; for although Sally, as we showed her, was a girl of generous impulses, she was yet in no danger of immediate translation on account of superhuman goodness. In short, Sally had made up her mind that Moses should give her a chance to say that precious and golden *No*, which should enable her to count him as one of her captives,—and then he might go where he liked for all her.

So said the wicked elf, as she looked into her own great eyes in the little square of mirror shaded by a misty asparagus bush; and to this end there were various braidings and adornings of the lustrous black hair, and coquettish earrings were mounted that hung glancing and twinkling just by the smooth outline of her glowing cheek,—and then Sally looked at herself in a friendly way of approbation, and nodded at the bright dimpled shadow with a look of secret understanding. The real Sally and the Sally of the looking-glass were on admirable terms with each other, and both of one mind about the plan of campaign against the common enemy. Sally thought of him as he stood kingly and triumphant on the deck of his vessel, his great black eyes flashing confident glances into hers, and she felt a rebellious rustle of all her plumage. "No, sir," she said to herself, "you don't do it. You shall never find me among your slaves,"—"that you know of," added a doubtful voice within her. "Never to your knowledge," she said, as she turned away. "I wonder if he will come here this evening," she said, as she began to work upon a pillow-case,—one of a set which Mrs. Kittridge had confided to her nimble fingers. The seam was long, straight, and monotonous, and Sally was restless and fidgety; her thread would catch in knots, and when she tried to loosen it, would break, and the needle had to be threaded over. Somehow the work was terribly irksome to her, and the house looked so still and dim and lonesome, and the tick-tock of the kitchen-clock was insufferable, and Sally let her work fall in her lap and looked out of the open window, far to the open ocean, where a fresh breeze was blowing toward her, and her eyes grew deep and dreamy following the gliding ship sails. Sally was getting romantic. Had she been reading novels? Novels! What can a pretty woman find in a novel equal to the romance that is all the while weaving and unweaving about her, and of which no human foresight can tell her the catastrophe? It is *novels* that give false views of life. Is there not an eternal novel, with all these false, cheating views, written in the breast of every beautiful and attractive girl whose witcheries make every man that comes near her talk like a fool? Like a sovereign princess, she never hears the truth, unless it be from the one manly man in a thousand, who understands both himself and her. From all the rest she hears only flatteries more or less ingenious, according to the ability of the framer. Compare, for instance, what Tom Brown says to little Seraphina at the party to-night, with what Tom Brown sober says to sober sister Maria *about* her to-morrow. Tom remembers that he was a fool last night, and knows what he thinks and always has thought to-day; but pretty Seraphina thinks he adores her, so that no matter what she does he will never see a flaw, she is sure of that,—poor little puss! She does not know that philosophic Tom looks at her as he does at a glass of champagne, or a dose of exhilarating gas, and calculates how much it will do for him to take of the stimulus without interfering with his serious and settled plans of life, which, of course, he doesn't mean to give up for her. The one-thousand-and-first man in creation is he that can feel the fascination but will not flatter, and that tries to tell to the little tyrant the rare word of truth that may save her; he is, as we say, the one-thousand-and-first. Well, as Sally sat with her great dark eyes dreamily following the ship, she mentally thought over all the compliments Moses had paid her, expressed or understood, and those of all her other admirers, who had built up a sort of cloud-world around her, so that her little feet never rested on the soil of reality. Sally was shrewd and keen, and had a native mother-wit in the discernment of spirits, that made her feel that somehow this was all false coin; but still she counted it over, and it looked so pretty and bright that she sighed to think it was not real.

"If it only had been," she thought; "if there were only any truth to the creature; he is so handsome,—it's a pity. But I do believe in his secret heart he is in love with Mara; he is in love with some one, I know. I have seen looks that must come from something real; but they were not for me. I have a kind of power over him, though," she said, resuming her old wicked look, "and I'll puzzle him a little, and torment him. He shall find his match in me," and Sally nodded to a cat-bird that sat perched on a pine-tree, as if she had a secret understanding with him, and the cat-bird went off into a perfect roulade of imitations of all that was going on in the late bird-operas of the season.

Sally was roused from her revery by a spray of goldenrod that was thrown into her lap by an invisible hand, and Moses soon appeared at the window.

"There's a plume that would be becoming to your hair," he said; "stay, let me arrange it."

"No, no; you'll tumble my hair,—what can you know of such things?"

Moses held the spray aloft, and leaned toward her with a sort of quiet, determined insistence.

"By your leave, fair lady," he said, wreathing it in her hair, and then drawing back a little, he looked at her with so much admiration that Sally felt herself blush.

"Come, now, I dare say you've made a fright of me," she said, rising and instinctively turning to the looking-glass; but she had too much coquetry not to see how admirably the golden plume suited her black hair, and the brilliant eyes and cheeks; she turned to Moses again, and courtesied, saying "Thank you, sir," dropping her eyelashes with a mock humility.

"Come, now," said Moses; "I am sent after you to come and spend the evening; let's walk along the seashore, and get there by degrees."

And so they set out; but the path was circuitous, for Moses was always stopping, now at this point and now at that, and enacting some of those thousand little by-plays which a man can get up with a pretty woman. They searched for smooth pebbles where the waves had left them,—many-colored, pink and crimson and yellow and brown, all smooth and rounded by the eternal tossings of the old sea that had made playthings of them for centuries, and with every pebble given and taken were things said which should have meant more and more, had the play been earnest. Had Moses any idea of offering himself to Sally? No; but he was in one of those fluctuating, unresisting moods of mind in which he was willing to lie like a chip on the tide of present emotion, and let it rise and fall and dash him when it liked; and Sally never had seemed more beautiful and attractive to him than that afternoon, because there was a shade of reality and depth about her that he had never seen before.

"Come on, and let me show you my hermitage," said Moses, guiding her along the slippery projecting rocks, all covered with yellow tresses of seaweed. Sally often slipped on this treacherous footing, and Moses was obliged to hold her up, and instinctively he threw a meaning into his manner so much more than ever he had before, that by the time they had gained the little cove both were really agitated and excited. He felt that temporary delirium which is often the mesmeric effect of a strong womanly presence, and she felt that agitation which every woman must when a determined hand is striking on the great vital chord of her being. When they had stepped round the last point of rock they found themselves driven by the advancing tide up into the little lonely grotto,—and there they were with no lookout but the wide blue sea, all spread out in rose and gold under the twilight skies, with a silver moon looking down upon them.

"Sally," said Moses, in a low, earnest whisper, "you love me,—do you not?" and he tried to pass his arm around her.

She turned and flashed at him a look of mingled terror and defiance, and struck out her hands at him; then impetuously turning away and retreating to the other end of the grotto, she sat down on a rock and began to cry.

Moses came toward her, and kneeling, tried to take her hand. She raised her head angrily, and again repulsed him.

"Go!" she said. "What right had you to say that? What right had you even to think it?"

"Sally, you do love me. It cannot but be. You are a woman; you could not have been with me as we have and not feel more than friendship."

"Oh, you men!—your conceit passes understanding," said Sally. "You think we are born to be your bond slaves,—but for once you are mistaken, sir. I *don't* love you; and what's more, you don't love me,—you know you don't; you know that you love somebody else. You love Mara,—you know you do; there's no truth in you," she said, rising indignantly.

Moses felt himself color. There was an embarrassed pause, and then he answered,—

"Sally, why should I love Mara? Her heart is all given to another,—you yourself know it."

"I don't know it either," said Sally; "I know it isn't so."

"But you gave me to understand so."

"Well, sir, you put prying questions about what you ought to have asked her, and so what was I to do? Besides, I did want to show you how much better Mara could do than to take you; besides, I didn't know till lately. I never thought she could care much for any man more than I could."

"And you think she loves me?" said Moses, eagerly, a flash of joy illuminating his face; "do you, really?"

"There you are," said Sally; "it's a shame I have let you know! Yes, Moses Pennel, she loves you like an angel, as none of you men deserve to be loved,—as you in particular don't."

Moses sat down on a point of rock, and looked on the ground discountenanced. Sally stood up glowing and triumphant, as if she had her foot on the neck of her oppressor and meant to make the most of it.

"Now what do you think of yourself for all this summer's work?—for what you have just said, asking me if I didn't love you? Supposing, now, I had done as other girls would, played the fool and blushed, and said yes? Why, to-morrow you would have been thinking how to be rid of me! I shall save you all that trouble, sir."

"Sally, I own I have been acting like a fool," said Moses, humbly.

"You have done more than that,—you have acted wickedly," said Sally.

"And am I the only one to blame?" said Moses, lifting his head with a show of resistance.

"Listen, sir!" said Sally, energetically; "I have played the fool and acted wrong too, but there is just this difference between you and me: you had nothing to lose, and I a great deal; your heart, such as it was, was safely disposed of. But supposing you had won mine, what would you have done with it? That was the last thing you considered."

"Go on, Sally, don't spare; I'm a vile dog, unworthy of either of you," said Moses.

Sally looked down on her handsome penitent with some relenting, as he sat quite dejected, his strong arms drooping, and his long eyelashes cast down.

"I'll be friends with you," she said, "because, after all, I'm not so very much better than you. We have both done wrong, and made dear Mara very unhappy. But after all, I was not so much to blame as you; because, if there had been any reality in your love, I could have paid it honestly. I had a heart to give,—I have it now, and hope long to keep it," said Sally.

"Sally, you are a right noble girl. I never knew what you were till now," said Moses, looking at her with admiration.

"It's the first time for all these six months that we have either of us spoken a word of truth or sense to each other. I never did anything but trifle with you, and you the same. Now we've come to some plain dry land, we may walk on and be friends. So now help me up these rocks, and I will go home."

"And you'll not come home with me?"

"Of course not. I think you may now go home and have one talk with Mara without witnesses."

CHAPTER XXXII

THE BETROTHAL

Moses walked slowly home from his interview with Sally, in a sort of maze of confused thought. In general, men understand women only from the outside, and judge them with about as much real comprehension as an eagle might judge a canary-bird. The difficulty of real understanding intensifies in proportion as the man is distinctively manly, and the woman womanly. There are men with a large infusion of the feminine element in their composition who read the female nature with more understanding than commonly falls to the lot of men; but in general, when a man passes beyond the mere outside artifices and unrealities which lie between the two sexes, and really touches his finger to any vital chord in the heart of a fair neighbor, he is astonished at the quality of the vibration.

"I could not have dreamed there was so much in her," thought Moses, as he turned away from Sally Kittridge. He felt humbled as well as astonished by the moral lecture which this frisky elf with whom he had all summer been amusing himself, preached to him from the depths of a real woman's heart. What she said of Mara's loving him filled his eyes with remorseful tears,—and for the moment he asked himself whether this restless, jealous, exacting desire which he felt to appropriate her whole life and heart to himself were as really worthy of the name of love as the generous self-devotion with which she had, all her life, made all his interests her own.

Was he to go to her now and tell her that he loved her, and therefore he had teased and vexed her,—therefore he had seemed to prefer another before her,—therefore he had practiced and experimented upon her nature? A suspicion rather stole upon him that love which expresses itself principally in making exactions and giving pain is not exactly worthy of the name. And yet he had been secretly angry with her all summer for being the very reverse of this; for her apparent cheerful willingness to see him happy with another; for the absence of all signs of jealousy,—all desire of exclusive appropriation. It showed, he said to himself, that there was no love; and now when it dawned on him that this might be the very heroism of self-devotion, he asked himself which was best worthy to be called love.

CHAPTER XXXII

"She did love him, then!" The thought blazed up through the smouldering embers of thought in his heart like a tongue of flame. She loved him! He felt a sort of triumph in it, for he was sure Sally must know, they were so intimate. Well, he would go to her, and tell her all, confess all his sins, and be forgiven.

When he came back to the house, all was still evening. The moon, which was playing brightly on the distant sea, left one side of the brown house in shadow. Moses saw a light gleaming behind the curtain in the little room on the lower floor, which had been his peculiar sanctum during the summer past. He had made a sort of library of it, keeping there his books and papers. Upon the white curtain flitted, from time to time, a delicate, busy shadow; now it rose and now it stooped, and then it rose again—grew dim and vanished, and then came out again. His heart beat quick.

Mara was in his room, busy, as she always had been before his departures, in cares for him. How many things had she made for him, and done and arranged for him, all his life long! things which he had taken as much as a matter of course as the shining of that moon. His thought went back to the times of his first going to sea,—he a rough, chaotic boy, sensitive and surly, and she the ever thoughtful good angel of a little girl, whose loving-kindness he had felt free to use and to abuse. He remembered that he made her cry there when he should have spoken lovingly and gratefully to her, and that the words of acknowledgment that ought to have been spoken, never had been said,—remained unsaid to that hour. He stooped low, and came quite close to the muslin curtain. All was bright in the room, and shadowy without; he could see her movements as through a thin white haze. She was packing his sea-chest; his things were lying about her, folded or rolled nicely. Now he saw her on her knees writing something with a pencil in a book, and then she enveloped it very carefully in silk paper, and tied it trimly, and hid it away at the bottom of the chest. Then she remained a moment kneeling at the chest, her head resting in her hands. A sort of strange, sacred feeling came over him as he heard a low murmur, and knew that she felt a Presence that he never felt or acknowledged. He felt somehow that he was doing her a wrong thus to be prying upon moments when she thought herself alone with God; a sort of vague remorse filled him; he felt as if she were too good for him. He turned away, and entering the front door of the house, stepped noiselessly along and lifted the latch of the door. He heard a rustle as of one rising hastily as he opened it and stood before Mara. He had made up his mind what to say; but when she stood there before him, with her surprised, inquiring eyes, he felt confused.

"What, home so soon?" she said.

"You did not expect me, then?"

"Of course not,—not for these two hours; so," she said, looking about, "I found some mischief to do among your things. If you had waited as long as I expected, they would all have been quite right again, and you would never have known."

Moses sat down and drew her toward him, as if he were going to say something, and then stopped and began confusedly playing with her work-box.

"Now, please don't," said she, archly. "You know what a little old maid I am about my things!"

"Mara," said Moses, "people have asked you to marry them, have they not?"

"People asked me to marry them!" said Mara. "I hope not. What an odd question!"

"You know what I mean," said Moses; "you have had offers of marriage—from Mr. Adams, for example."

"And what if I have?"

"You did not accept him, Mara?" said Moses.

"No, I did not."

"And yet he was a fine man, I am told, and well fitted to make you happy."

"I believe he was," said Mara, quietly.

"And why were you so foolish?"

Mara was fretted at this question. She supposed Moses had come to tell her of his engagement to Sally, and that this was a kind of preface, and she answered,—

"I don't know why you call it foolish. I was a true friend to Mr. Adams. I saw intellectually that he might have the power of making any reasonable woman happy. I think now that the woman will be fortunate who becomes his wife; but I did not wish to marry him."

"Is there anybody you prefer to him, Mara?" said Moses.

She started up with glowing cheeks and sparkling eyes.

"You have no right to ask me that, though you are my brother."

"I am not your brother, Mara," said Moses, rising and going toward her, "and that is why I ask you. I feel I have a right to ask you."

"I do not understand you," she said, faintly.

"I can speak plainer, then. I wish to put in my poor venture. I love you, Mara—not as a brother. I wish you to be my wife, if you will."

While Moses was saying these words, Mara felt a sort of whirling in her head, and it grew dark before her eyes; but she had a strong, firm will, and she mastered herself and answered, after a moment, in a quiet, sorrowful tone, "How can I believe this, Moses? If it is true, why have you done as you have this summer?"

"Because I was a fool, Mara,—because I was jealous of Mr. Adams,—because I somehow hoped, after all, that you either loved me or that I might make you think more of me through jealousy of another. They say that love always is shown by jealousy."

"Not true love, I should think," said Mara. "How *could* you do so?—it was cruel to her,—cruel to me."

"I admit it,—anything, everything you can say. I have acted like a fool and a knave, if you will; but after all, Mara, I do love you. I know I am not worthy of you—never was—never can be; you are in all things a true, noble woman, and I have been unmanly."

It is not to be supposed that all this was spoken without accompaniments of looks, movements, and expressions of face such as we cannot give, but such as doubled their power to the parties concerned; and the "I love you" had its usual conclusive force as argument, apology, promise,—covering, like charity, a multitude of sins.

Half an hour after, you might have seen a youth and a maiden coming together out of the door of the brown house, and walking arm in arm toward the sea-beach.

It was one of those wonderfully clear moonlight evenings, when the ocean, like a great reflecting mirror, seems to double the brightness of the sky,—and its vast expanse lay all around them in its stillness, like an eternity of waveless peace. Mara remembered that time in her girlhood when she had followed Moses into the woods on just such a night,—how she had sat there under the shadows of the trees, and looked over to Harpswell and noticed the white houses and the meeting-house, all so bright and clear in the moonlight, and then off again on the other side of the island where silent ships were coming and going in the mysterious stillness. They were talking together now with that outflowing fullness which comes when the seal of some great reserve has just been broken,—going back over their lives from day to day, bringing up incidents of childhood, and turning them gleefully like two children.

And then Moses had all the story of his life to relate, and to tell Mara all he had learned of his mother,—going over with all the narrative contained in Mr. Sewell's letter.

"You see, Mara, that it was intended that you should be my fate," he ended; "so the winds and waves took me up and carried me to the lonely island where the magic princess dwelt."

"You are Prince Ferdinand," said Mara.

"And you are Miranda," said he.

"Ah!" she said with fervor, "how plainly we can see that our heavenly Father has been guiding our way! How good He is,—and how we must try to live for Him,—both of us."

A sort of cloud passed over Moses's brow. He looked embarrassed, and there was a pause between them, and then he turned the conversation.

Mara felt pained; it was like a sudden discord; such thoughts and feelings were the very breath of her life; she could not speak in perfect confidence and unreserve, as she then spoke, without uttering them; and her finely organized nature felt a sort of electric consciousness of repulsion and dissent. She grew abstracted, and they walked on in silence.

"I see now, Mara, I have pained you," said Moses, "but there are a class of feelings that you have that I have not and cannot have. No, I cannot feign anything. I can understand what religion is in you, I can admire its results. I can be happy, if it gives you any comfort; but people are differently constituted. I never can feel as you do."

"Oh, don't say never," said Mara, with an intensity that nearly startled him; "it has been the one prayer, the one hope, of my life, that you might have these comforts,—this peace."

"I need no comfort or peace except what I shall find in you," said Moses, drawing her to himself, and looking admiringly at her; "but pray for me still. I always thought that my wife must be one of the sort of women who pray."

"And why?" said Mara, in surprise.

"Because I need to be loved a great deal, and it is only that kind who pray who know how to love really. If you had not prayed for me all this time, you never would have loved me in spite of all my faults, as you did, and do, and will, as I know you will," he said, folding her in his arms, and in his secret heart he said, "Some of this intensity, this devotion, which went upward to heaven, will be mine one day. She will worship me."

"The fact is, Mara," he said, "I am a child of this world. I have no sympathy with things not seen. You are a half-spiritual creature,—a child of air; and but for the great woman's heart in you, I should feel that you were something uncanny and unnatural. I am selfish, I know; I frankly admit, I never disguised it; but I love your religion because it makes you love me. It is an incident to that loving, trusting nature which makes you all and wholly mine, as I want you to be. I want you all and wholly; every thought, every feeling,—the whole strength of your being. I don't care if I say it: I would not wish to be second in your heart even to God himself!"

"Oh, Moses!" said Mara, almost starting away from him, "such words are dreadful; they will surely bring evil upon us."

"I only breathed out my nature, as you did yours. Why should you love an unseen and distant Being more than you do one whom you can feel and see, who holds you in his arms, whose heart beats like your own?"

"Moses," said Mara, stopping and looking at him in the clear moonlight, "God has always been to me not so much like a father as like a dear and tender mother. Perhaps it was because I was a poor orphan, and my father and mother died at my birth, that He has been so loving to me. I never remember the time when I did not feel His presence in my joys and my sorrows. I never had a thought of joy and sorrow that I could not say to Him. I never woke in the night that I did not feel that He was loving and watching me, and that I loved Him in return. Oh, how many, many things I have said to Him about you! My heart would have broken years ago, had it not been for Him; because, though you did not know it, you often seemed unkind; you hurt me very often when you did not mean to. His love is so much a part of my life that I cannot conceive of life without it. It is the very air I breathe."

Moses stood still a moment, for Mara spoke with a fervor that affected him; then he drew her to his heart, and said,—

"Oh, what could ever make you love me?"

"He sent you and gave you to me," she answered, "to be mine in time and eternity."

The words were spoken in a kind of enthusiasm so different from the usual reserve of Mara, that they seemed like a prophecy. That night, for the first time in her life, had she broken the reserve which was her very nature, and spoken of that which was the intimate and hidden history of her soul.

CHAPTER XXXIII

AT A QUILTING

"And so," said Mrs. Captain Badger to Miss Roxy Toothacre, "it seems that Moses Pennel ain't going to have Sally Kittridge after all,—he's engaged to Mara Lincoln."

"More shame for him," said Miss Roxy, with a frown that made her mohair curls look really tremendous.

Miss Roxy and Mrs. Badger were the advance party at a quilting, to be holden at the house of Mr. Sewell, and had come at one o'clock to do the marking upon the quilt, which was to be filled up by the busy fingers of all the women in the parish. Said quilt was to have a bordering of a pattern commonly denominated in those parts clam-shell, and this Miss Roxy was diligently marking with indigo.

"What makes you say so, now?" said Mrs. Badger, a fat, comfortable, motherly matron, who always patronized the last matrimonial venture that put forth among the young people.

"What business had he to flirt and gallivant all summer with Sally Kittridge, and make everybody think he was going to have her, and then turn round to Mara Lincoln at the last minute? I wish I'd been in Mara's place."

In Miss Roxy's martial enthusiasm, she gave a sudden poke to her frisette, giving to it a diagonal bristle which extremely increased its usually severe expression; and any one contemplating her at the moment would have thought that for Moses Pennel, or any other young man, to come with tender propositions in that direction would have been indeed a venturesome enterprise.

"I tell you what 'tis, Mis' Badger," she said, "I've known Mara since she was born,—I may say I fetched her up myself, for if I hadn't trotted and tended her them first four weeks of her life, Mis' Pennel'd never have got her through; and I've watched her every year since; and havin' Moses Pennel is the only silly thing I ever knew her to do; but you never can tell what a girl will do when it comes to marryin',—never!"

"But he's a real stirrin', likely young man, and captain of a fine ship," said Mrs. Badger.

CHAPTER XXXIII

"Don't care if he's captain of twenty ships," said Miss Roxy, obdurately; "he ain't a professor of religion, and I believe he's an infidel, and she's one of the Lord's people."

"Well," said Mrs. Badger, "you know the unbelievin' husband shall be sanctified by the believin' wife."

"Much sanctifyin' he'll get," said Miss Roxy, contemptuously. "I don't believe he loves her any more than fancy; she's the last plaything, and when he's got her, he'll be tired of her, as he always was with anything he got ever since. I tell you, Moses Pennel is all for pride and ambition and the world; and his wife, when he gets used to her, 'll be only a circumstance,—that's all."

"Come, now, Miss Roxy," said Miss Emily, who in her best silk and smoothly-brushed hair had just come in, "we must *not* let you talk so. Moses Pennel has had long talks with brother, and he thinks him in a very hopeful way, and we are all delighted; and as to Mara, she is as fresh and happy as a little rose."

"So I tell Roxy," said Miss Ruey, who had been absent from the room to hold private consultations with Miss Emily concerning the biscuits and sponge-cake for tea, and who now sat down to the quilt and began to unroll a capacious and very limp calico thread-case; and placing her spectacles awry on her little pug nose, she began a series of ingenious dodges with her thread, designed to hit the eye of her needle.

"The old folks," she continued, "are e'en a'most tickled to pieces,—'cause they think it'll jist be the salvation of him to get Mara."

"I ain't one of the sort that wants to be a-usin' up girls for the salvation of fellers," said Miss Roxy, severely. "Ever since he nearly like to have got her eat up by sharks, by giggiting her off in the boat out to sea when she wa'n't more'n three years old, I always have thought he was a misfortin' in that family, and I think so now."

Here broke in Mrs. Eaton, a thrifty energetic widow of a deceased sea-captain, who had been left with a tidy little fortune which commanded the respect of the neighborhood. Mrs. Eaton had entered silently during the discussion, but of course had come, as every other woman had that afternoon, with views to be expressed upon the subject.

"For my part," she said, as she stuck a decisive needle into the first clam-shell pattern, "I ain't so sure that all the advantage in this match is on Moses Pennel's part. Mara Lincoln is a good little thing, but she ain't fitted to help a man along,—she'll always be wantin' somebody to help her. Why, I 'member goin' a voyage with Cap'n Eaton, when I saved the ship, if anybody did,—it was allowed on all hands. Cap'n Eaton wasn't hearty at that time, he was jist gettin' up from a fever,—it was when Marthy Ann was a baby, and I jist took her and went to sea and took care of him. I used to work the longitude for him and help him lay the ship's course when his head was bad,—and when we came on the coast, we were kept out of harbor beatin' about nearly three weeks, and all the ship's tacklin' was stiff with ice, and I tell you the men never would have stood it through and got the ship in, if it hadn't been for me. I kept their mittens and stockings all the while adryin' at my stove in the cabin, and hot coffee all the while a-boilin' for 'em, or I believe they'd a-frozen their hands and feet, and never been able to work the ship in. That's the way *I* did. Now Sally Kittridge is a great deal more like that than Mara."

"There's no doubt that Sally is smart," said Mrs. Badger, "but then it ain't every one can do like you, Mrs. Eaton."

"Oh no, oh no," was murmured from mouth to mouth; "Mrs. Eaton mustn't think she's any rule for others,—everybody knows she can do more than most people;" whereat the pacified Mrs. Eaton said "she didn't know as it was anything remarkable,—it showed what anybody might do, if they'd only *try* and have resolution; but that Mara never had been brought up to have resolution, and her mother never had resolution before her, it wasn't in any of Mary Pennel's family; she knew their grandmother and all their aunts, and they were all a weakly set, and not fitted to get along in life,—they were a kind of people that somehow didn't seem to know how to take hold of things."

At this moment the consultation was hushed up by the entrance of Sally Kittridge and Mara, evidently on the closest terms of intimacy, and more than usually demonstrative and affectionate; they would sit together and use each other's needles, scissors, thread, and thimbles interchangeably, as if anxious to express every minute the most overflowing confidence. Sly winks and didactic nods were covertly exchanged among the elderly people, and when Mrs. Kittridge entered with more than usual airs of impressive solemnity, several of these were covertly directed toward her, as a matron whose views in life must have been considerably darkened by the recent event.

Mrs. Kittridge, however, found an opportunity to whisper under her breath to Miss Ruey what a relief to her it was that the affair had taken such a turn. She had felt uneasy all summer for fear of what might come. Sally was so thoughtless and worldly, she felt afraid that he would lead her astray. She didn't see, for her part, how a professor of religion like Mara could make up her mind to such an unsettled kind of fellow, even if he did seem to be rich and well-to-do. But then she had done looking for consistency; and she sighed and vigorously applied herself to quilting like one who has done with the world.

In return, Miss Ruey sighed and took snuff, and related for the hundredth time to Mrs. Kittridge the great escape she once had from the addresses of Abraham Peters, who had turned out a "poor drunken creetur." But then it was only natural that Mara should be interested in Moses; and the good soul went off into her favorite verse:—

"The fondness of a creature's love,
How strong it strikes the sense!
Thither the warm affections move,
Nor can we drive them thence."

In fact, Miss Ruey's sentimental vein was in quite a gushing state, for she more than once extracted from the dark corners of the limp calico thread-case we have spoken of certain long-treasured *morceaux* of newspaper poetry, of a tender and sentimental cast, which she had laid up with true Yankee economy, in case any one should ever be in a situation to need them. They related principally to the union of kindred hearts, and the joys of reciprocated feeling and the pains of absence. Good Miss Ruey occasionally passed these to Mara, with glances full of meaning, which caused the poor old thing to resemble a sentimental goblin, keeping Sally Kittridge in a perfect hysterical tempest of suppressed laughter, and making it difficult for Mara to preserve the decencies of life toward her well-intending old friend. The trouble with poor Miss Ruey was that, while her body had grown old and crazy, her soul was just as juvenile as ever,—and a simple, juvenile soul disporting itself in a crazy, battered old body, is at great disadvantage. It was lucky for her, however, that she lived in the most sacred unconsciousness of the ludicrous effect of her little indulgences, and the pleasure she took in them was certainly of the most harmless kind. The world would be a far better and more enjoyable place than it is, if all people who are old and uncomely could find amusement as innocent and Christian-like as Miss Ruey's inoffensive thread-case collection of sentimental truisms.

This quilting of which we speak was a solemn, festive occasion of the parish, held a week after Moses had sailed away; and so *piquant* a morsel as a recent engagement could not, of course, fail to be served up for the company in every variety of garnishing which individual tastes might suggest.

It became an ascertained fact, however, in the course of the evening festivities, that the minister was serenely approbative of the event; that Captain Kittridge was at length brought to a sense of the errors of his way in supposing that Sally had ever cared a pin for Moses more than as a mutual friend and confidant; and the great affair was settled without more ripples of discomposure than usually attend similar announcements in more refined society.

CHAPTER XXXIV

FRIENDS

The quilting broke up at the primitive hour of nine o'clock, at which, in early New England days, all social gatherings always dispersed. Captain Kittridge rowed his helpmeet, with Mara and Sally, across the Bay to the island.

"Come and stay with me to-night, Sally," said Mara.

"I think Sally had best be at home," said Mrs. Kittridge. "There's no sense in girls talking all night."

"There ain't sense in nothin' else, mother," said the Captain. "Next to sparkin', which is the Christianist thing I knows on, comes gals' talks 'bout their sparks; they's as natural as crowsfoot and red columbines in the spring, and spring don't come but once a year neither,—and so let 'em take the comfort on't. I warrant now, Polly, you've laid awake nights and talked about me."

"We've all been foolish once," said Mrs. Kittridge.

"Well, mother, we want to be foolish too," said Sally.

"Well, you and your father are too much for me," said Mrs. Kittridge, plaintively; "you always get your own way."

"How lucky that my way is always a good one!" said Sally.

"Well, you know, Sally, you are going to make the beer to-morrow," still objected her mother.

"Oh, yes; that's another reason," said Sally. "Mara and I shall come home through the woods in the morning, and we can get whole apronfuls of young wintergreen, and besides, I know where there's a lot of sassafras root. We'll dig it, won't we, Mara?"

"Yes; and I'll come down and help you brew," said Mara. "Don't you remember the beer I made when Moses came home?"

"Yes, yes, I remember," said the Captain, "you sent us a couple of bottles."

"We can make better yet now," said Mara. "The wintergreen is young, and the green tips on the spruce boughs are so full of strength. Everything is lively and sunny now."

"Yes, yes," said the Captain, "and I 'spect I know why things do look pretty lively to some folks, don't they?"

CHAPTER XXXIV

"I don't know what sort of work you'll make of the beer among you," said Mrs. Kittridge; "but you must have it your own way."

Mrs. Kittridge, who never did anything else among her tea-drinking acquaintances but laud and magnify Sally's good traits and domestic acquirements, felt constantly bound to keep up a faint show of controversy and authority in her dealings with her,—the fading remains of the strict government of her childhood; but it was, nevertheless, very perfectly understood, in a general way, that Sally was to do as she pleased; and so, when the boat came to shore, she took the arm of Mara and started up toward the brown house.

The air was soft and balmy, and though the moon by which the troth of Mara and Moses had been plighted had waned into the latest hours of the night, still a thousand stars were lying in twinkling brightness, reflected from the undulating waves all around them, and the tide, as it rose and fell, made a sound as gentle and soft as the respiration of a peaceful sleeper.

"Well, Mara," said Sally, after an interval of silence, "all has come out right. You see that it was you whom he loved. What a lucky thing for me that I am made so heartless, or I might not be as glad as I am."

"You are not heartless, Sally," said Mara; "it's the enchanted princess asleep; the right one hasn't come to waken her."

"Maybe so," said Sally, with her old light laugh. "If I only were sure he would make you happy now,—half as happy as you deserve,—I'd forgive him his share of this summer's mischief. The fault was just half mine, you see, for I witched with him. I confess it. I have my own little spider-webs for these great lordly flies, and I like to hear them buzz."

"Take care, Sally; never do it again, or the spider-web may get round you," said Mara.

"Never fear me," said Sally. "But, Mara, I wish I felt sure that Moses could make you happy. Do you really, now, when you think seriously, feel as if he would?"

"I never thought seriously about it," said Mara; "but I know he needs me; that I can do for him what no one else can. I have always felt all my life that he was to be mine; that he was sent to me, ordained for me to care for and to love."

"You are well mated," said Sally. "He wants to be loved very much, and you want to love. There's the active and passive voice, as they used to say at Miss Plucher's. But yet in your natures you are opposite as any two could well be."

Mara felt that there was in these chance words of Sally more than she perceived. No one could feel as intensely as she could that the mind and heart so dear to her were yet, as to all that was most vital and real in her inner life, unsympathizing. To her the spiritual world was a reality; God an ever-present consciousness; and the line of this present life seemed so to melt and lose itself in the anticipation of a future and brighter one, that it was impossible for her to speak intimately and not unconsciously to betray the fact. To him there was only the life of this world: there was no present God; and from all thought of a future life he shrank with a shuddering aversion, as from something ghastly and unnatural. She had realized this difference more in the few days that followed her betrothal than all her life before, for now first the barrier of mutual constraint and misunderstanding having melted away, each spoke with an *abandon* and unreserve which made the acquaintance more vitally intimate than ever it had been before. It was then that Mara felt that while her sympathies could follow him through all his plans and interests, there was a whole world of thought and feeling in her heart where his could not follow her; and she asked herself, Would it be so always? Must she walk at his side forever repressing the utterance of that which was most sacred and intimate, living in a nominal and external communion only? How could it be that what was so lovely and clear in its reality to her, that which was to her as life-blood, that which was the vital air in which she lived and moved and had her being, could be absolutely nothing to him? Was it really possible, as he said, that God had no existence for him except in a nominal cold belief; that the spiritual world was to him only a land of pale shades and doubtful glooms, from which he shrank with dread, and the least allusion to which was distasteful? and would this always be so? and if so, could she be happy?

But Mara said the truth in saying that the question of personal happiness never entered her thoughts. She loved Moses in a way that made it necessary to her happiness to devote herself to him, to watch over and care for him; and though she knew not how, she felt a sort of presentiment that it was through her that he must be brought into sympathy with a spiritual and immortal life.

All this passed through Mara's mind in the reverie into which Sally's last words threw her, as she sat on the door-sill and looked off into the starry distance and heard the weird murmur of the sea.

"How lonesome the sea at night always is," said Sally. "I declare, Mara, I don't wonder you miss that creature, for, to tell the truth, I do a little bit. It was something, you know, to have somebody to come in, and to joke with, and to say how he liked one's hair and one's ribbons, and all that. I quite got up a friendship for Moses, so that I can feel how dull you must be;" and Sally gave a half sigh, and then whistled a tune as adroitly as a blackbird.

"Yes," said Mara, "we two girls down on this lonely island need some one to connect us with the great world; and he was so full of life, and so certain and confident, he seemed to open a way before one out into life."

"Well, of course, while he is gone there will be plenty to do getting ready to be married," said Sally. "By the by, when I was over to Portland the other day, Maria Potter showed me a new pattern for a bed-quilt, the sweetest thing you can imagine,—it is called the morning star. There is a great star in the centre, and little stars all around,—white on a blue ground. I mean to begin one for you."

"I am going to begin spinning some very fine flax next week," said Mara; "and have I shown you the new pattern I drew for a counterpane? it is to be morning-glories, leaves and flowers, you know,—a pretty idea, isn't it?"

And so, the conversation falling from the region of the sentimental to the practical, the two girls went in and spent an hour in discussions so purely feminine that we will not enlighten the reader further therewith. Sally seemed to be investing all her energies in the preparation of the wedding outfit of her friend, about which she talked with a constant and restless activity, and for which she formed a thousand plans, and projected shopping tours to Portland, Brunswick, and even to Boston,—this last being about as far off a venture at that time as Paris now seems to a Boston belle.

"When you are married," said Sally, "you'll have to take me to live with you; that creature sha'n't have you *all* to himself. I hate men, they are so exorbitant,—they spoil all our playmates; and what shall I do when *you* are gone?"

"You will go with Mr.—what's his name?" said Mara.

"Pshaw, I don't know him. I shall be an old maid," said Sally; "and really there isn't much harm in that, if one could have company,—if somebody or other wouldn't marry all one's friends,—that's lonesome," she said, winking a tear out of her black eyes and laughing. "If I were only a young fellow now, Mara, I'd have you myself, and that would be just the thing; and I'd shoot Moses, if he said a word; and I'd have money, and I'd have honors, and I'd carry you off to Europe, and take you to Paris and Rome, and nobody knows where; and we'd live in peace, as the story-books say."

"Come, Sally, how wild you are talking," said Mara, "and the clock has just struck one; let's try to go to sleep."

Sally put her face to Mara's and kissed her, and Mara felt a moist spot on her cheek,—could it be a tear?

CHAPTER XXXV

THE TOOTHACRE COTTAGE

Aunt Roxy and Aunt Ruey Toothacre lived in a little one-story gambrel-roofed cottage, on the side of Harpswell Bay, just at the head of the long cove which we have already described. The windows on two sides commanded the beautiful bay and the opposite shores, and on the other they looked out into the dense forest, through whose deep shadows of white birch and pine the silver rise and fall of the sea daily revealed itself.

The house itself was a miracle of neatness within, for the two thrifty sisters were worshipers of soap and sand, and these two tutelary deities had kept every board of the house-floor white and smooth, and also every table and bench and tub of household use. There was a sacred care over each article, however small and insignificant, which composed their slender household stock. The loss or breakage of one of them would have made a visible crack in the hearts of the worthy sisters,—for every plate, knife, fork, spoon, cup, or glass was as intimate with them, as instinct with home feeling, as if it had a soul; each defect or spot had its history, and a cracked dish or article of furniture received as tender and considerate medical treatment as if it were capable of understanding and feeling the attention.

It was now a warm, spicy day in June,—one of those which bring out the pine-apple fragrance from the fir-shoots, and cause the spruce and hemlocks to exude a warm, resinous perfume. The two sisters, for a wonder, were having a day to themselves, free from the numerous calls of the vicinity for twelve miles round. The room in which they were sitting was bestrewn with fragments of dresses and bonnets, which were being torn to pieces in a most wholesale way, with a view to a general rejuvenescence. A person of unsympathetic temperament, and disposed to take sarcastic views of life, might perhaps wonder what possible object these two battered and weather-beaten old bodies proposed to themselves in this process,—whether Miss Roxy's gaunt black-straw helmet, which she had worn defiantly all winter, was likely to receive much lustre from being pressed over and trimmed with an old green ribbon which that energetic female had colored black by a domestic recipe; and whether Miss Roxy's rusty bombazette would really seem to the world any fresher for being ripped, and washed, and turned, for the second or third time, and made over with every breadth in a different situation. Probably after a week of efficient labor, busily expended in bleaching, dyeing, pressing, sewing, and ripping, an unenlightened spectator, seeing them come into the meeting-house, would simply think, "There are those two old frights with the same old things on they have worn these fifty years." Happily the weird sisters were contentedly ignorant of any such remarks, for no duchesses could have enjoyed a more quiet belief in their own social position, and their semi-annual spring and fall rehabilitation was therefore entered into with the most simple-hearted satisfaction.

"I'm a-thinkin', Roxy," said Aunt Ruey, considerately turning and turning on her hand an old straw bonnet, on which were streaked all the marks of the former trimming in lighter lines, which revealed too clearly the effects of wind and weather,—"I'm a-thinkin' whether or no this 'ere mightn't as well be dyed and done with it as try to bleach it out. I've had it ten years last May, and it's kind o' losin' its freshness, you know. I don't believe these 'ere streaks will bleach out."

"Never mind, Ruey," said Miss Roxy, authoritatively, "I'm goin' to do Mis' Badger's leg'orn, and it won't cost nothin'; so hang your'n in the barrel along with it,—the same smoke'll do 'em both. Mis' Badger she finds the brimstone, and next fall you can put it in the dye when we do the yarn."

"That ar straw is a beautiful straw!" said Miss Ruey, in a plaintive tone, tenderly examining the battered old head-piece,—"I braided every stroke on it myself, and I don't know as I could do it ag'in. My fingers ain't quite so limber as they was! I don't think I shall put green ribbon on it ag'in; 'cause green is such a color to ruin, if a body gets caught out in a shower! There's these green streaks come that day I left my amberil at Captain Broad's, and went to meetin'. Mis' Broad she says to me, 'Aunt Ruey, it won't rain.' And says I to her, 'Well, Mis' Broad, I'll try it; though I never did leave my amberil at home but what it rained.' And so I went, and sure enough it rained cats and dogs, and streaked my bonnet all up; and them ar streaks won't bleach out, I'm feared."

"How long is it Mis' Badger has had that ar leg'orn?"

"Why, you know, the Cap'n he brought it home when he came from his voyage from Marseilles. That ar was when Phebe Ann was born, and she's fifteen year old. It was a most elegant thing when he brought it; but I think it kind o' led Mis' Badger on to extravagant ways,—for gettin' new trimmin' spring and fall so uses up money as fast as new bonnets; but Mis' Badger's got the money, and she's got a right to use it if she pleases; but if I'd a-had new trimmin's spring and fall, I shouldn't a-put away what I have in the bank."

"Have you seen the straw Sally Kittridge is braidin' for Mara Lincoln's weddin' bonnet?" said Miss Ruey. "It's jist the finest thing ever you did see,—and the whitest. I was a-tellin' Sally that I could do as well once myself, but my mantle was a-fallin' on her. Sally don't seem to act a bit like a disap'inted gal. She is as chipper as she can be about Mara's weddin', and seems like she couldn't do too much. But laws, everybody seems to want to be a-doin' for her. Miss Emily was a-showin' me a fine double damask tablecloth that she was goin' to give her; and Mis' Pennel, she's been a-spinnin' and layin' up sheets and towels and tablecloths all her life,—and then she has all Naomi's things. Mis' Pennel was talkin' to me the other day about bleachin' 'em out 'cause they'd got yellow a-lyin'. I kind o' felt as if 'twas unlucky to be a-fittin' out a bride with her dead mother's things, but I didn't like to say nothin'."

"Ruey," said Miss Roxy impressively, "I hain't never had but jist one mind about Mara Lincoln's weddin',—it's to be,—but it won't be the way people think. I hain't nussed and watched and sot up nights sixty years for nothin'. I can see beyond what most folks can,—her weddin' garments is bought and paid for, and she'll wear 'em, but she won't be Moses Pennel's wife,—now you see."

"Why, whose wife will she be then?" said Miss Ruey; "'cause that ar Mr. Adams is married. I saw it in the paper last week when I was up to Mis' Badger's."

Miss Roxy shut her lips with oracular sternness and went on with her sewing.

"Who's that comin' in the back door?" said Miss Ruey, as the sound of a footstep fell upon her ear. "Bless me," she added, as she started up to look, "if folks ain't always nearest when you're talkin' about 'em. Why, Mara; you come down here and catched us in all our dirt! Well now, we're glad to see you, if we be," said Miss Ruey.

CHAPTER XXXVI

THE SHADOW OF DEATH

It was in truth Mara herself who came and stood in the doorway. She appeared overwearied with her walk, for her cheeks had a vivid brightness unlike their usual tender pink. Her eyes had, too, a brilliancy almost painful to look upon. They seemed like ardent fires, in which the life was slowly burning away.

"Sit down, sit down, little Mara," said Aunt Ruey. "Why, how like a picture you look this mornin',—one needn't ask you how you do,—it's plain enough that you are pretty well."

"Yes, I am, Aunt Ruey," she answered, sinking into a chair; "only it is warm to-day, and the sun is so hot, that's all, I believe; but I am very tired."

"So you are now, poor thing," said Miss Ruey. "Roxy, where's my turkey-feather fan? Oh, here 'tis; there, take it, and fan you, child; and maybe you'll have a glass of our spruce beer?"

"Thank you, Aunt Roxy. I brought you some young wintergreen," said Mara, unrolling from her handkerchief a small knot of those fragrant leaves, which were wilted by the heat.

"Thank you, I'm sure," said Miss Ruey, in delight; "you always fetch something, Mara,—always would, ever since you could toddle. Roxy and I was jist talkin' about your weddin'. I s'pose you're gettin' things well along down to your house. Well, here's the beer. I don't hardly know whether you'll think it worked enough, though. I set it Saturday afternoon, for all Mis' Twitchell said it was wicked for beer to work Sundays," said Miss Ruey, with a feeble cackle at her own joke.

"Thank you, Aunt Ruey; it is excellent, as your things always are. I was very thirsty."

"I s'pose you hear from Moses pretty often now," said Aunt Ruey. "How kind o' providential it happened about his getting that property; he'll be a rich man now; and Mara, you'll come to grandeur, won't you? Well, I don't know anybody deserves it more,—I r'ally don't. Mis' Badger was a-sayin' so a-Sunday, and Cap'n Kittridge and all on 'em. I s'pose though we've got to lose you,—you'll be goin' off to Boston, or New York, or somewhere."

"We can't tell what may happen, Aunt Ruey," said Mara, and there was a slight tremor in her voice as she spoke.

Miss Roxy, who beyond the first salutations had taken no part in this conversation, had from time to time regarded Mara over the tops of her spectacles with looks of grave apprehension; and Mara, looking up, now encountered one of these glances.

"Have you taken the dock and dandelion tea I told you about?" said the wise woman, rather abruptly.

"Yes, Aunt Roxy, I have taken them faithfully for two weeks past."

"And do they seem to set you up any?" said Miss Roxy.

"No, I don't think they do. Grandma thinks I'm better, and grandpa, and I let them think so; but Miss Roxy, *can't* you think of something else?"

Miss Roxy laid aside the straw bonnet which she was ripping, and motioned Mara into the outer room,—the sink-room, as the sisters called it. It was the scullery of their little establishment,—the place where all dish-washing and clothes-washing was generally performed,—but the boards of the floor were white as snow, and the place had the odor of neatness. The open door looked out pleasantly into the deep forest, where the waters of the cove, now at high tide, could be seen glittering through the trees. Soft moving spots of sunlight fell, checkering the feathery ferns and small piney tribes of evergreen which ran in ruffling wreaths of green through the dry, brown matting of fallen pine needles. Birds were singing and calling to each other merrily from the green shadows of the forest,—everything had a sylvan fullness and freshness of life. There are moods of mind when the sight of the bloom and freshness of nature affects us painfully, like the want of sympathy in a dear friend. Mara had been all her days a child of the woods; her delicate life had grown up in them like one of their own cool shaded flowers; and there was not a moss, not a fern, not an upspringing thing that waved a leaf or threw forth a flower-bell, that was not a well-known friend to her; she had watched for years its haunts, known the time of its coming and its going, studied its shy and veiled habits, and interwoven with its life each year a portion of her own; and now she looked out into the old mossy woods, with their wavering spots of sun and shadow, with a yearning pain, as if she wanted help or sympathy to come from their silent recesses.

She sat down on the clean, scoured door-sill, and took off her straw hat. Her golden-brown hair was moist with the damps of fatigue, which made it curl and wave in darker little rings about her forehead; her eyes,—those longing, wistful eyes,—had a deeper pathos of sadness than ever they had worn before; and her delicate lips trembled with some strong suppressed emotion.

"Aunt Roxy," she said suddenly, "I *must* speak to somebody. I can't go on and keep up without telling some one, and it had better be you, because you have skill and experience, and can help me if anybody can. I've been going on for six months now, taking this and taking that, and trying to get better, but it's of no use. Aunt Roxy, I feel my life going,—going just as steadily and as quietly every day as the sand goes out of your hour-glass. I want to live,—oh, I never wanted to live so much, and I can't,—oh, I know I can't. Can I now,—do you think I can?"

Mara looked imploringly at Miss Roxy. The hard-visaged woman sat down on the wash-bench, and, covering her worn, stony visage with her checked apron, sobbed aloud.

Mara was confounded. This implacably withered, sensible, dry woman, beneficently impassive in sickness and sorrow, weeping!—it was awful, as if one of the Fates had laid down her fatal distaff to weep.

Mara sprung up impulsively and threw her arms round her neck.

"Now don't, Aunt Roxy, don't. I didn't think you would feel bad, or I wouldn't have told you; but oh, you don't know how hard it is to keep such a secret all to one's self. I have to make believe all the time that I am feeling well and getting better. I really say what isn't true every day, because, poor grandmamma, how could I bear to see her distress? and grandpapa,—oh, I wish people didn't love me so! Why cannot they let me go? And oh, Aunt Roxy, I had a letter only yesterday, and he is so sure we shall be married this fall,—and I know it cannot be." Mara's voice gave way in sobs, and the two wept together,—the old grim, gray woman holding the soft golden head against her breast with a convulsive grasp. "Oh, Aunt Roxy, do you love me, too?" said Mara. "I didn't know you did."

"Love ye, child?" said Miss Roxy; "yes, I love ye like my life. I ain't one that makes talk about things, but I do; you come into my arms fust of anybody's in this world,—and except poor little Hitty, I never loved nobody as I have you."

"Ah! that was your sister, whose grave I have seen," said Mara, speaking in a soothing, caressing tone, and putting her little thin hand against the grim, wasted cheek, which was now moist with tears.

"Jes' so, child, she died when she was a year younger than you be; she was not lost, for God took her. Poor Hitty! her life jest dried up like a brook in August,—jest so. Well, she was hopefully pious, and it was better for her."

"Did she go like me, Aunt Roxy?" said Mara.

"Well, yes, dear; she did begin jest so, and I gave her everything I could think of; and we had doctors for her far and near; but *'twasn't to be*,—that's all we could say; she was called, and her time was come."

"Well, now, Aunt Roxy," said Mara, "at any rate, it's a relief to speak out to some one. It's more than two months that I have felt every day more and more that there was no hope,—life has hung on me like a weight. I have had to *make* myself keep up, and make myself do everything, and no one knows how it has tried me. I am so tired all the time, I could cry; and yet when I go to bed nights I can't sleep, I lie in such a hot, restless way; and then before morning I am drenched with cold sweat, and feel so weak and wretched. I force myself to eat, and I force myself to talk and laugh, and it's all pretense; and it wears me out,—it would be better if I stopped trying,—it would be better to give up and act as weak as I feel; but how can I let them know?"

"My dear child," said Aunt Roxy, "the truth is the kindest thing we can give folks in the end. When folks know jest where they are, why they can walk; you'll all be supported; you must trust in the Lord. I have been more'n forty years with sick rooms and dyin' beds, and I never knew it fail that those that trusted in the Lord was brought through."

"Oh, Aunt Roxy, it is so hard for me to give up,—to give up hoping to live. There were a good many years when I thought I should love to depart,—not that I was really unhappy, but I longed to go to heaven, though I knew it was selfish, when I knew how lonesome I should leave my friends. But now, oh, life has looked so bright; I have clung to it so; I do now. I lie awake nights and pray, and try to give it up and be resigned, and I can't. Is it wicked?"

"Well, it's natur' to want to live," said Miss Roxy. "Life is sweet, and in a gen'l way we was made to live. Don't worry; the Lord'll bring you right when His time comes. Folks isn't always supported jest when they want to be, nor *as* they want to be; but yet they're supported fust and last. Ef I was to tell you how as I has hope in your case, I shouldn't be a-tellin' you the truth. I hasn't much of any; only all things is possible with God. If you could kind o' give it all up and rest easy in His hands, and keep a-doin' what you can,—why, while there's life there's hope, you know; and if you are to be made well, you will be all the sooner."

"Aunt Roxy, it's all right; I know it's all right. God knows best; He will do what is best; I know that; but my heart bleeds, and is sore. And when I get his letters,—I got one yesterday,—it brings it all back again. Everything is going on so well; he says he has done more than all he ever hoped; his letters are full of jokes, full of spirit. Ah, he little knows,—and how can I tell him?"

"Child, you needn't yet. You can jest kind o' prepare his mind a little."

"Aunt Roxy, have you spoken of my case to any one,—have you told what you know of me?"

"No, child, I hain't said nothin' more than that you was a little weakly now and then."

"I have such a color every afternoon," said Mara. "Grandpapa talks about my roses, and Captain Kittridge jokes me about growing so handsome; nobody seems to realize how I feel. I have kept up with all the strength I had. I have tried to shake it off, and to feel that nothing was the matter,—really there is nothing much, only this weakness. This morning I thought it would do me good to walk down here. I remember times when I could ramble whole days in the woods, but I was so tired before I got half way here that I had to stop a long while and rest. Aunt Roxy, if you would only tell grandpapa and grandmamma just how things are, and what the danger is, and let them stop talking to me about wedding things,—for really and truly I am too unwell to keep up any longer."

"Well, child, I will," said Miss Roxy. "Your grandfather will be supported, and hold you up, for he's one of the sort as has the secret of the Lord,—I remember him of old. Why, the day your father and mother was buried he stood up and sung old China, and his face was wonderful to see. He seemed to be standin' with the world under his feet and heaven opening. He's a master Christian, your grandfather is; and now you jest go and lie down in the little bedroom, and rest you a bit, and by and by, in the cool of the afternoon, I'll walk along home with you."

CHAPTER XXXVI

Miss Roxy opened the door of a little room, whose white fringy window-curtains were blown inward by breezes from the blue sea, and laid the child down to rest on a clean sweet-smelling bed with as deft and tender care as if she were not a bony, hard-visaged, angular female, in a black mohair frisette.

She stopped a moment wistfully before a little profile head, of a kind which resembles a black shadow on a white ground. "That was Hitty!" she said.

Mara had often seen in the graveyard a mound inscribed to this young person, and heard traditionally of a young and pretty sister of Miss Roxy who had died very many years before. But the grave was overgrown with blackberry-vines, and gray moss had grown into the crevices of the slab which served for a tombstone, and never before that day had she heard Miss Roxy speak of her. Miss Roxy took down the little black object and handed it to Mara. "You can't tell much by that, but she was a most beautiful creatur'. Well, it's all best as it is." Mara saw nothing but a little black shadow cast on white paper, yet she was affected by the perception how bright, how beautiful, was the image in the memory of that seemingly stern, commonplace woman, and how of all that in her mind's eye she saw and remembered, she could find no outward witness but this black block. "So some day my friends will speak of me as a distant shadow," she said, as with a sigh she turned her head on the pillow.

Miss Roxy shut the door gently as she went out, and betrayed the unwonted rush of softer feelings which had come over her only by being more dictatorial and commanding than usual in her treatment of her sister, who was sitting in fidgety curiosity to know what could have been the subject of the private conference.

"I s'pose Mara wanted to get some advice about makin' up her weddin' things," said Miss Ruey, with a sort of humble quiver, as Miss Roxy began ripping and tearing fiercely at her old straw bonnet, as if she really purposed its utter and immediate demolition.

"No she didn't, neither," said Miss Roxy, fiercely. "I declare, Ruey, you are silly; your head is always full of weddin's, weddin's, weddin's—nothin' else—from mornin' till night, and night till mornin'. I tell you there's other things have got to be thought of in this world besides weddin' clothes, and it would be well, if people would think more o' gettin' their weddin' garments ready for the kingdom of heaven. That's what Mara's got to think of; for, mark my words, Ruey, there is no marryin' and givin' in marriage for her in this world."

"Why, bless me, Roxy, now you don't say so!" said Miss Ruey; "why I knew she was kind o' weakly and ailin', but"—

"Kind o' weakly and ailin'!" said Miss Roxy, taking up Miss Ruey's words in a tone of high disgust, "I should rather think she was; and more'n that, too: she's marked for death, and that before long, too. It may be that Moses Pennel'll never see her again—he never half knew what she was worth—maybe he'll know when he's lost her, that's one comfort!"

"But," said Miss Ruey, "everybody has been a-sayin' what a beautiful color she was a-gettin' in her cheeks."

"Color in her cheeks!" snorted Miss Roxy; "so does a rock-maple get color in September and turn all scarlet, and what for? why, the frost has been at it, and its time is out. That's what your bright colors stand for. Hain't you noticed that little gravestone cough, jest the faintest in the world, and it don't come from a cold, and it hangs on. I tell you you can't cheat me, she's goin' jest as Mehitabel went, jest as Sally Ann Smith went, jest as Louisa Pearson went. I could count now on my fingers twenty girls that have gone that way. Nobody saw 'em goin' till they was gone."

"Well, now, I don't think the old folks have the least idea on't," said Miss Ruey. "Only last Saturday Mis' Pennel was a-talkin' to me about the sheets and tablecloths she's got out a-bleachin'; and she said that the weddin' dress was to be made over to Mis' Mosely's in Portland, 'cause Moses he's so particular about havin' things genteel."

"Well, Master Moses'll jest have to give up his particular notions," said Miss Roxy, "and come down in the dust, like all the rest on us, when the Lord sends an east wind and withers our gourds. Moses Pennel's one of the sort that expects to drive all before him with the strong arm, and sech has to learn that things ain't to go as they please in the Lord's world. Sech always has to come to spots that they can't get over nor under nor round, to have their own way, but jest has to give right up square."

"Well, Roxy," said Miss Ruey, "how does the poor little thing take it? Has she got reconciled?"

"Reconciled! Ruey, how you do ask questions!" said Miss Roxy, fiercely pulling a bandanna silk handkerchief out of her pocket, with which she wiped her eyes in a defiant manner. "Reconciled! It's easy enough to talk, Ruey, but how would you like it, when everything was goin' smooth and playin' into your hands, and all the world smooth and shiny, to be took short up? I guess you wouldn't be reconciled. That's what I guess."

"Dear me, Roxy, who said I should?" said Miss Ruey. "I wa'n't blamin' the poor child, not a grain."

"Well, who said you was, Ruey?" answered Miss Roxy, in the same high key.

"You needn't take my head off," said Aunt Ruey, roused as much as her adipose, comfortable nature could be. "You've been a-talkin' at me ever since you came in from the sink-room, as if I was to blame; and snappin' at me as if I hadn't a right to ask civil questions; and I won't stan' it," said Miss Ruey. "And while I'm about it, I'll say that you always have snubbed me and contradicted and ordered me round. I won't bear it no longer."

"Come, Ruey, don't make a fool of yourself at your time of life," said Miss Roxy. "Things is bad enough in this world without two lone sisters and church-members turnin' agin each other. You must take me as I am, Ruey; my bark's worse than my bite, as you know."

Miss Ruey sank back pacified into her usual state of pillowy dependence; it was so much easier to be good-natured than to contend. As for Miss Roxy, if you have ever carefully examined a chestnut-burr, you will remember that, hard as it is to handle, no plush of downiest texture can exceed the satin smoothness of the fibres which line its heart. There are a class of people in New England who betray the uprising of the softer feelings of our nature only by an increase of outward asperity—a sort of bashfulness and shyness leaves them no power of expression for these unwonted guests of the heart—they hurry them into inner chambers and slam the doors upon them, as if they were vexed at their appearance.

Now if poor Miss Roxy had been like you, my dear young lady—if her soul had been encased in a round, rosy, and comely body, and looked out of tender blue eyes shaded by golden hair, probably the grief and love she felt would have shown themselves only in bursts of feeling most graceful to see, and engaging the sympathy of all; but this same soul, imprisoned in a dry, angular body, stiff and old, and looking out under beetling eyebrows, over withered high cheek-bones, could only utter itself by a passionate tempest—unlovely utterance of a lovely impulse—dear only to Him who sees with a Father's heart the real beauty of spirits. It is our firm faith that bright solemn angels in celestial watchings were frequent guests in the homely room of the two sisters, and that passing by all accidents of age and poverty, withered skins, bony features, and grotesque movements and shabby clothing, they saw more real beauty there than in many a scented boudoir where seeming angels smile in lace and satin.

"Ruey," said Miss Roxy, in a more composed voice, while her hard, bony hands still trembled with excitement, "this 'ere's been on my mind a good while. I hain't said nothin' to nobody, but I've seen it a-comin'. I always thought that child wa'n't for a long life. Lives is run in different lengths, and nobody can say what's the matter with some folks, only that their thread's run out; there's more on one spool and less on another. I thought, when we laid Hitty in the grave, that I shouldn't never set my heart on nothin' else—but we can't jest say we will or we won't. Ef we are to be sorely afflicted at any time, the Lord lets us set our hearts before we know it. This 'ere's a great affliction to me, Ruey, but I must jest shoulder my cross and go through with it. I'm goin' down to-night to tell the old folks, and to make arrangements so that the poor little lamb may have the care she needs. She's been a-keepin' up so long, 'cause she dreaded to let 'em know, but this 'ere has got to be looked right in the face, and I hope there'll be grace given to do it."

CHAPTER XXXVII

THE VICTORY

Meanwhile Mara had been lying in the passive calm of fatigue and exhaustion, her eyes fixed on the window, where, as the white curtain drew inward, she could catch glimpses of the bay. Gradually her eyelids fell, and she dropped into that kind of half-waking doze, when the outer senses are at rest, and the mind is all the more calm and clear for their repose. In such hours a spiritual clairvoyance often seems to lift for a while the whole stifling cloud that lies like a confusing mist over the problem of life, and the soul has sudden glimpses of things unutterable which lie beyond. Then the narrow straits, that look so full of rocks and quick-sands, widen into a broad, clear passage, and one after another, rosy with a celestial dawn, and ringing silver bells of gladness, the isles of the blessed lift themselves up on the horizon, and the soul is flooded with an atmosphere of light and joy. As the burden of Christian fell off at the cross and was lost in the sepulchre, so in these hours of celestial vision the whole weight of life's anguish is lifted, and passes away like a dream; and the soul, seeing the boundless ocean of Divine love, wherein all human hopes and joys and sorrows lie so tenderly up-holden, comes and casts the one little drop of its personal will and personal existence with gladness into that Fatherly depth. Henceforth, with it, God and Saviour is no more word of mine and thine, for in that hour the child of earth feels himself heir of all things: "All things are yours, and ye are Christ's, and Christ is God's."

"The child is asleep," said Miss Roxy, as she stole on tiptoe into the room when their noon meal was prepared. A plate and knife had been laid for her, and they had placed for her a tumbler of quaint old engraved glass, reputed to have been brought over from foreign parts, and which had been given to Miss Roxy as her share in the effects of the mysterious Mr. Swadkins. Tea also was served in some egg-like India china cups, which saw the light only on the most high and festive occasions.

"Hadn't you better wake her?" said Miss Ruey; "a cup of hot tea would do her so much good."

CHAPTER XXXVII

Miss Ruey could conceive of few sorrows or ailments which would not be materially better for a cup of hot tea. If not the very elixir of life, it was indeed the next thing to it.

"Well," said Miss Roxy, after laying her hand for a moment with great gentleness on that of the sleeping girl, "she don't wake easy, and she's tired; and she seems to be enjoying it so. The Bible says, 'He giveth his beloved sleep,' and I won't interfere. I've seen more good come of sleep than most things in my nursin' experience," said Miss Roxy, and she shut the door gently, and the two sisters sat down to their noontide meal.

"How long the child does sleep!" said Miss Ruey as the old clock struck four.

"It was too much for her, this walk down here," said Aunt Roxy. "She's been doin' too much for a long time. I'm a-goin' to put an end to that. Well, nobody needn't say Mara hain't got resolution. I never see a little thing have more. She always did have, when she was the leastest little thing. She was always quiet and white and still, but she did whatever she sot out to."

At this moment, to their surprise, the door opened, and Mara came in, and both sisters were struck with a change that had passed over her. It was more than the result of mere physical repose. Not only had every sign of weariness and bodily languor vanished, but there was about her an air of solemn serenity and high repose that made her seem, as Miss Ruey afterwards said, "like an angel jest walked out of the big Bible."

"Why, dear child, how you have slept, and how bright and rested you look," said Miss Ruey.

"I am rested," said Mara; "oh how much! And happy," she added, laying her little hand on Miss Roxy's shoulder. "I thank you, dear friend, for all your kindness to me. I am sorry I made you feel so sadly; but now you mustn't feel so any more, for all is well—yes, all is well. I see now that it is so. I have passed beyond sorrow—yes, forever."

Soft-hearted Miss Ruey here broke into audible sobbing, hiding her face in her hands, and looking like a tumbled heap of old faded calico in a state of convulsion.

"Dear Aunt Ruey, you mustn't," said Mara, with a voice of gentle authority. "We mustn't any of us feel so any more. There is no harm done, no real evil is coming, only a good which we do not understand. I am perfectly satisfied—perfectly at rest now. I was foolish and weak to feel as I did this morning, but I shall not feel so any more. I shall comfort you all. Is it anything so dreadful for me to go to heaven? How little while it will be before you all come to me! Oh, how little—little while!"

"I told you, Mara, that you'd be supported in the Lord's time," said Miss Roxy, who watched her with an air of grave and solemn attention. "First and last, folks allers is supported; but sometimes there is a long wrestlin'. The Lord's give you the victory early."

"Victory!" said the girl, speaking as in a deep muse, and with a mysterious brightness in her eyes; "yes, that is the word—it *is* a victory—no other word expresses it. Come, Aunt Roxy, we will go home. I am not afraid now to tell grandpapa and grandmamma. God will care for them; He will wipe away all tears."

"Well, though, you mus'n't think of goin' till you've had a cup of tea," said Aunt Ruey, wiping her eyes. "I've kep' the tea-pot hot by the fire, and you must eat a little somethin', for it's long past dinner-time."

"Is it?" said Mara. "I had no idea I had slept so long—how thoughtful and kind you are!"

"I do wish I could only do more for you," said Miss Ruey. "I don't seem to get reconciled no ways; it seems dreffle hard—dreffle; but I'm glad you *can* feel so;" and the good old soul proceeded to press upon the child not only the tea, which she drank with feverish relish, but every hoarded dainty which their limited housekeeping commanded.

It was toward sunset before Miss Roxy and Mara started on their walk homeward. Their way lay over the high stony ridge which forms the central part of the island. On one side, through the pines, they looked out into the boundless blue of the ocean, and on the other caught glimpses of Harpswell Bay as it lay glorified in the evening light. The fresh cool breeze blowing landward brought with it an invigorating influence, which Mara felt through all her feverish frame. She walked with an energy to which she had long been a stranger. She said little, but there was a sweetness, a repose, in her manner contrasting singularly with the passionate melancholy which she had that morning expressed.

Miss Roxy did not interrupt her meditations. The nature of her profession had rendered her familiar with all the changing mental and physical phenomena that attend the development of disease and the gradual loosening of the silver cords of a present life. Certain well-understood phrases everywhere current among the mass of the people in New England, strikingly tell of the deep foundations of religious earnestness on which its daily life is built. "A triumphant death" was a matter often casually spoken of among the records of the neighborhood; and Miss Roxy felt that there was a vague and solemn charm about its approach. Yet the soul of the gray, dry woman was hot within her, for the conversation of the morning had probed depths in her own nature of whose existence she had never before been so conscious. The roughest and most matter-of-fact minds have a craving for the ideal somewhere; and often this craving, forbidden by uncomeliness and ungenial surroundings from having any personal history of its own, attaches itself to the fortune of some other one in a kind of strange disinterestedness. Some one young and beautiful is to live the life denied to them—to be the poem and the romance; it is the young mistress of the poor black slave—the pretty sister of the homely old spinster—or the clever son of the consciously ill-educated father. Something of this unconscious personal investment had there been on the part of Miss Roxy in the nursling whose singular loveliness she had watched for so many years, and on whose fair virgin orb she had marked the growing shadow of a fatal eclipse, and as she saw her glowing and serene, with that peculiar brightness that she felt came from no earthly presence or influence, she could scarcely keep the tears from her honest gray eyes.

CHAPTER XXXVII

When they arrived at the door of the house, Zephaniah Pennel was sitting in it, looking toward the sunset.

"Why, reely," he said, "Miss Roxy, we thought you must a-run away with Mara; she's been gone a'most all day."

"I expect she's had enough to talk with Aunt Roxy about," said Mrs. Pennel. "Girls goin' to get married have a deal to talk about, what with patterns and contrivin' and makin' up. But come in, Miss Roxy; we're glad to see you."

Mara turned to Miss Roxy, and gave her a look of peculiar meaning. "Aunt Roxy," she said, "you must tell them what we have been talking about to-day;" and then she went up to her room and shut the door.

Miss Roxy accomplished her task with a matter-of-fact distinctness to which her business-like habits of dealing with sickness and death had accustomed her, yet with a sympathetic tremor in her voice which softened the hard directness of her words. "You can take her over to Portland, if you say so, and get Dr. Wilson's opinion," she said, in conclusion. "It's best to have all done that can be, though in my mind the case is decided."

The silence that fell between the three was broken at last by the sound of a light footstep descending the stairs, and Mara entered among them.

She came forward and threw her arms round Mrs. Pennel's neck, and kissed her; and then turning, she nestled down in the arms of her old grandfather, as she had often done in the old days of childhood, and laid her hand upon his shoulder. There was no sound for a few moments but one of suppressed weeping; but *she* did not weep—she lay with bright calm eyes, as if looking upon some celestial vision.

"It is not so very sad," she said at last, in a gentle voice, "that I should go there; you are going, too, and grandmamma; we are all going; and we shall be forever with the Lord. Think of it! think of it!"

Many were the words spoken in that strange communing; and before Miss Roxy went away, a calmness of solemn rest had settled down on all. The old family Bible was brought forth, and Zephaniah Pennel read from it those strange words of strong consolation, which take the sting from death and the victory from the grave:—

"And I heard a great voice out of heaven. Behold the tabernacle of God is with men, and he will dwell with them, and they shall be his people; and God himself shall be with them and be their God. And God shall wipe away all tears from their eyes; and there shall be no more death, neither sorrow nor crying, for the former things are passed away."

CHAPTER XXXVIII

OPEN VISION

As Miss Roxy was leaving the dwelling of the Pennels, she met Sally Kittridge coming toward the house, laughing and singing, as was her wont. She raised her long, lean forefinger with a gesture of warning.

"What's the matter now, Aunt Roxy? You look as solemn as a hearse."

"None o' your jokin' now, Miss Sally; there *is* such a thing as serious things in this 'ere world of our'n, for all you girls never seems to know it."

"What is the matter, Aunt Roxy?—has anything happened?—is anything the matter with Mara?"

"Matter enough. I've known it a long time," said Miss Roxy. "She's been goin' down for three months now; and she's got that on her that will carry her off before the year's out."

"Pshaw, Aunt Roxy! how lugubriously you old nurses always talk! I hope now you haven't been filling Mara's head with any such notions—people can be frightened into anything."

"Sally Kittridge, don't be a-talkin' of what you don't know nothin' about! It stands to reason that a body that was bearin' the heat and burden of the day long before you was born or thought on in this world *should* know a thing or two more'n you. Why, I've laid you on your stomach and trotted you to trot up the wind many a day, and I was pretty experienced then, and it ain't likely that I'm a-goin' to take sa'ce from you. Mara Pennel is a gal as has every bit and grain as much resolution and ambition as you have, for all you flap your wings and crow so much louder, and she's one of the close-mouthed sort, that don't make no talk, and she's been a-bearin' up and bearin' up, and comin' to me on the sly for strengthenin' things. She's took camomile and orange-peel, and snake-root and boneset, and dash-root and dandelion—and there hain't nothin' done her no good. She told me to-day she couldn't keep up no longer, and I've been a-tellin' Mis' Pennel and her grand'ther. I tell you it has been a solemn time; and if you're goin' in, don't go in with none o' your light triflin' ways, 'cause 'as vinegar upon nitre is he that singeth songs on a heavy heart,' the Scriptur' says."

CHAPTER XXXVIII

"Oh, Miss Roxy, do tell me truly," said Sally, much moved. "What do you think is the matter with Mara? I've noticed myself that she got tired easy, and that she was short-breathed—but she seemed so cheerful. Can anything really be the matter?"

"It's consumption, Sally Kittridge," said Miss Roxy, "neither more nor less; that ar is the long and the short. They're going to take her over to Portland to see Dr. Wilson—it won't do no harm, and it won't do no good."

"You seem to be determined she shall die," said Sally in a tone of pique.

"Determined, am I? Is it I that determines that the maple leaves shall fall next October? Yet I know they will—folks can't help knowin' what they know, and shuttin' one's eyes won't alter one's road. I s'pose you think 'cause you're young and middlin' good-lookin' that you have feelin's and I hasn't; well, you're mistaken, that's all. I don't believe there's one person in the world that would go farther or do more to save Mara Pennel than I would,—and yet I've been in the world long enough to see that livin' ain't no great shakes neither. Ef one is hopefully prepared in the days of their youth, why they escape a good deal, ef they get took cross-lots into heaven."

Sally turned away thoughtfully into the house; there was no one in the kitchen, and the tick of the old clock sounded lonely and sepulchral. She went upstairs to Mara's room; the door was ajar. Mara was sitting at the open window that looked forth toward the ocean, busily engaged in writing. The glow of evening shone on the golden waves of her hair, and tinged the pearly outline of her cheek. Sally noticed the translucent clearness of her complexion, and the deep burning color and the transparency of the little hands, which seemed as if they might transmit the light like Sèvres porcelain. She was writing with an expression of tender calm, and sometimes stopping to consult an open letter that Sally knew came from Moses.

So fair and sweet and serene she looked that a painter might have chosen her for an embodiment of twilight, and one might not be surprised to see a clear star shining out over her forehead. Yet in the tender serenity of the face there dwelt a pathos of expression that spoke of struggles and sufferings past, like the traces of tears on the face of a restful infant that has grieved itself to sleep.

Sally came softly in on tiptoe, threw her arms around her, and kissed her, with a half laugh, then bursting into tears, sobbed upon her shoulder.

"Dear Sally, what is the matter?" said Mara, looking up.

"Oh, Mara, I just met Miss Roxy, and she told me"—

Sally only sobbed passionately.

"It is very sad to make all one's friends so unhappy," said Mara, in a soothing voice, stroking Sally's hair. "You don't know how much I have suffered dreading it. Sally, it is a long time since I began to expect and dread and fear. My time of anguish was then—then when I first felt that it could be possible that I should not live after all. There was a long time I dared not even think of it; I could not even tell such a fear to myself; and I did far more than I felt able to do to convince myself that I was not weak and failing. I have been often to Miss Roxy, and once, when nobody knew it, I went to a doctor in Brunswick, but then I was afraid to tell him half, lest he should say something about me, and it should get out; and so I went on getting worse and worse, and feeling every day as if I could not keep up, and yet afraid to lie down for fear grandmamma would suspect me. But this morning it was pleasant and bright, and something came over me that said I *must* tell somebody, and so, as it was cool and pleasant, I walked up to Aunt Roxy's and told her. I thought, you know, that she knew the most, and would feel it the least; but oh, Sally, she has such a feeling heart, and loves me so; it is strange she should."

"Is it?" said Sally, tightening her clasp around Mara's neck; and then with a hysterical shadow of gayety she said, "I suppose you think that you are such a hobgoblin that nobody could be expected to do that. After all, though, I should have as soon expected roses to bloom in a juniper clump as love from Aunt Roxy."

"Well, she does love me," said Mara. "No mother could be kinder. Poor thing, she really sobbed and cried when I told her. I was very tired, and she told me she would take care of me, and tell grandpapa and grandmamma,—*that* had been lying on my heart as such a dreadful thing to do,—and she laid me down to rest on her bed, and spoke so lovingly to me! I wish you could have seen her. And while I lay there, I fell into a strange, sweet sort of rest. I can't describe it; but since then everything has been changed. I wish I could tell any one how I saw things then."

"Do try to tell me, Mara," said Sally, "for I need comfort too, if there is any to be had."

"Well, then, I lay on the bed, and the wind drew in from the sea and just lifted the window-curtain, and I could see the sea shining and hear the waves making a pleasant little dash, and then my head seemed to swim. I thought I was walking out by the pleasant shore, and everything seemed so strangely beautiful, and grandpapa and grandmamma were there, and Moses had come home, and you were there, and we were all so happy. And then I felt a sort of strange sense that something was coming—some great trial or affliction—and I groaned and clung to Moses, and asked him to put his arm around me and hold me.

"Then it seemed to be not by our seashore that this was happening, but by the Sea of Galilee, just as it tells about it in the Bible, and there were fishermen mending their nets, and men sitting counting their money, and I saw Jesus come walking along, and heard him say to this one and that one, 'Leave all and follow me,' and it seemed that the moment he spoke they did it, and then he came to me, and I felt his eyes in my very soul, and he said, 'Wilt *thou* leave *all* and follow me?' I cannot tell now what a pain I felt—what an anguish. I wanted to leave all, but my heart felt as if it were tied and woven with a thousand threads, and while I waited he seemed to fade away, and I found myself then alone and unhappy, wishing that I could, and mourning that I had not; and then something shone out warm like the sun, and I looked up, and he stood there looking pitifully, and he said again just as he did before, 'Wilt thou leave all and follow me?' Every word was so gentle and full of pity, and I looked into his eyes and could not look away;

they drew me, they warmed me, and I felt a strange, wonderful sense of his greatness and sweetness. It seemed as if I felt within me cord after cord breaking, I felt so free, so happy; and I said, 'I will, I will, with all my heart;' and I woke then, so happy, so sure of God's love.

"I saw so clearly how his love is in everything, and these words came into my mind as if an angel had spoken them, 'God shall wipe away all tears from their eyes.' Since then I cannot be unhappy. I was so myself only this morning, and now I wonder that any one can have a grief when God is so loving and good, and cares so sweetly for us all. Why, Sally, if I could see Christ and hear him speak, I could not be more certain that he will make this sorrow such a blessing to us all that we shall never be able to thank him enough for it."

"Oh Mara," said Sally, sighing deeply, while her cheek was wet with tears, "it is beautiful to hear you talk; but there is one that I am sure will not and cannot feel so."

"God will care for him," said Mara; "oh, I am sure of it; He is love itself, and He values his love in us, and He never, never would have brought such a trial, if it had not been the true and only way to our best good. We shall not shed one needless tear. Yes, if God loved us so that he spared not his own Son, he will surely give us all the good here that we possibly can have without risking our eternal happiness."

"You are writing to Moses, now?" said Sally.

"Yes, I am answering his letter; it is so full of spirit and life and hope—but all hope in this world—all, all earthly, as much as if there was no God and no world to come. Sally, perhaps our Father saw that I could not have strength to live with him and keep my faith. I should be drawn by him earthward instead of drawing him heavenward; and so this is in mercy to us both."

"And are you telling him the whole truth, Mara?"

"Not all, no," said Mara; "he could not bear it at once. I only tell him that my health is failing, and that my friends are seriously alarmed, and then I speak as if it were doubtful, in my mind, what the result might be."

"I don't think you can make him feel as you do. Moses Pennel has a tremendous will, and he never yielded to any one. You bend, Mara, like the little blue harebells, and so the storm goes over you; but he will stand up against it, and it will wrench and shatter him. I am afraid, instead of making him better, it will only make him bitter and rebellious."

"He has a Father in heaven who knows how to care for him," said Mara. "I am persuaded—I feel certain that he will be blessed in the end; not perhaps in the time and way I should have chosen, but in the end. I have always felt that he was mine, ever since he came a little shipwrecked boy to me—a little girl. And now I have given him up to his Saviour and my Saviour—to his God and my God—and I am perfectly at peace. All will be well."

Mara spoke with a look of such solemn, bright assurance as made her, in the dusky, golden twilight, seem like some serene angel sent down to comfort, rather than a hapless mortal just wrenched from life and hope.

Sally rose up and kissed her silently. "Mara," she said, "I shall come to-morrow to see what I can do for you. I will not interrupt you now. Good-by, dear."

There are no doubt many, who have followed this history so long as it danced like a gay little boat over sunny waters, and who would have followed it gayly to the end, had it closed with ringing of marriage-bells, who turn from it indignantly, when they see that its course runs through the dark valley. This, they say, is an imposition, a trick upon our feelings. We want to read only stories which end in joy and prosperity.

But have we then settled it in our own mind that there is no such thing as a fortunate issue in a history which does not terminate in the way of earthly success and good fortune? Are we Christians or heathen? It is now eighteen centuries since, as we hold, the "highly favored among women" was pronounced to be one whose earthly hopes were all cut off in the blossom,—whose noblest and dearest in the morning of his days went down into the shadows of death.

Was Mary the highly-favored among women, and was Jesus indeed the blessed,—or was the angel mistaken? If they were these, if we are Christians, it ought to be a settled and established habit of our souls to regard something else as prosperity than worldly success and happy marriages. That life is a success which, like the life of Jesus, in its beginning, middle, and close, has borne a perfect witness to the truth and the highest form of truth. It is true that God has given to us, and inwoven in our nature a desire for a perfection and completeness made manifest to our senses in this mortal life. To see the daughter bloom into youth and womanhood, the son into manhood, to see them marry and become themselves parents, and gradually ripen and develop in the maturities of middle life, gradually wear into a sunny autumn, and so be gathered in fullness of time to their fathers,—such, one says, is the programme which God has made us to desire; such the ideal of happiness which he has interwoven with our nerves, and for which our heart and our flesh crieth out; to which every stroke of a knell is a violence, and every thought of an early death is an abhorrence.

But the life of Christ and his mother sets the foot on this lower ideal of happiness, and teaches us that there is something higher. His ministry began with declaring, "Blessed are they that mourn." It has been well said that prosperity was the blessing of the Old Testament, and adversity of the New. Christ came to show us a nobler style of living and bearing; and so far as he had a personal and earthly life, he buried it as a corner-stone on which to erect a new immortal style of architecture.

Of his own, he had nothing, neither houses, nor lands, nor family ties, nor human hopes, nor earthly sphere of success; and as a human life, it was all a sacrifice and a defeat. He was rejected by his countrymen, whom the passionate anguish of his love and the unwearied devotion of his life could not save from an awful doom. He was betrayed by weak friends, prevailed against by slanderers, overwhelmed with an ignominious death in the morning of youth, and his mother stood by his cross, and she was the only woman whom God ever called highly favored in this world.

This, then, is the great and perfect ideal of what God honors. Christ speaks of himself as bread to be eaten,—bread, simple, humble, unpretending, vitally necessary to human life, made by the bruising and grinding of the grain, unostentatiously having no life or worth of its own except as it is absorbed into the life of others and lives in them. We wished in this history to speak of a class of lives formed on the model of Christ, and like his, obscure and unpretending, like his, seeming to end in darkness and defeat, but which yet have this preciousness and value that the dear saints who live them come nearest in their mission to the mission of Jesus. They are made, not for a career and history of their own, but to be bread of life to others. In every household or house have been some of these, and if we look on their lives and deaths with the unbaptized eyes of nature, we shall see only most mournful and unaccountable failure, when, if we could look with the eye of faith, we should see that their living and dying has been bread of life to those they left behind. Fairest of these, and least developed, are the holy innocents who come into our households to smile with the smile of angels, who sleep in our bosoms, and win us with the softness of tender little hands, and pass away like the lamb that was slain before they have ever learned the speech of mortals. Not vain are even these silent lives of Christ's lambs, whom many an earth-bound heart has been roused to follow when the Shepherd bore them to the higher pastures. And so the daughter who died so early, whose wedding-bells were never rung except in heaven,—the son who had no career of ambition or a manly duty except among the angels,—the patient sufferers, whose only lot on earth seemed to be to endure, whose life bled away drop by drop in the shadows of the sick-room—all these are among those whose life was like Christ's in that they were made, not for themselves, but to become bread to us.

It is expedient for us that they go away. Like their Lord, they come to suffer, and to die; they take part in his sacrifice; their life is incomplete without their death, and not till they are gone away does the Comforter fully come to us.

It is a beautiful legend which one sees often represented in the churches of Europe, that when the grave of the mother of Jesus was opened, it was found full of blossoming lilies,—fit emblem of the thousand flowers of holy thought and purpose which spring up in our hearts from the memory of our sainted dead.

Cannot many, who read these lines, bethink them of such rooms that have been the most cheerful places in the family,—when the heart of the smitten one seemed the band that bound all the rest together,—and have there not been dying hours which shed such a joy and radiance on all around, that it was long before the mourners remembered to mourn? Is it not a misuse of words to call such a heavenly translation *death*? and to call most things that are lived out on this earth *life*?

CHAPTER XXXIX

THE LAND OF BEULAH

It is now about a month after the conversation which we have recorded, and during that time the process which was to loose from this present life had been going on in Mara with a soft, insensible, but steady power. When she ceased to make efforts beyond her strength, and allowed herself that languor and repose which nature claimed, all around her soon became aware how her strength was failing; and yet a cheerful repose seemed to hallow the atmosphere around her. The sight of her every day in family worship, sitting by in such tender tranquillity, with such a smile on her face, seemed like a present inspiration. And though the aged pair knew that she was no more for this world, yet she was comforting and inspiring to their view as the angel who of old rolled back the stone from the sepulchre and sat upon it. They saw in her eyes, not death, but the solemn victory which Christ gives over death.

Bunyan has no more lovely poem than the image he gives of that land of pleasant waiting which borders the river of death, where the chosen of the Lord repose, while shining messengers, constantly passing and repassing, bear tidings from the celestial shore, opening a way between earth and heaven. It was so, that through the very thought of Mara an influence of tenderness and tranquillity passed through the whole neighborhood, keeping hearts fresh with sympathy, and causing thought and conversation to rest on those bright mysteries of eternal joy which were reflected on her face.

Sally Kittridge was almost a constant inmate of the brown house, ever ready in watching and waiting; and one only needed to mark the expression of her face to feel that a holy charm was silently working upon her higher and spiritual nature. Those great, dark, sparkling eyes that once seemed to express only the brightness of animal vivacity, and glittered like a brook in unsympathetic gayety, had in them now mysterious depths, and tender, fleeting shadows, and the very tone of her voice had a subdued tremor. The capricious elf, the tricksy sprite, was melting away in the immortal soul, and the deep pathetic power of a noble heart was being born. Some influence sprung of sorrow is necessary always to perfect beauty in womanly nature. We feel its absence in many whose sparkling wit and high spirits give grace and vivacity to life, but in whom we vainly seek for some spot of quiet tenderness and sympathetic repose. Sally was, ignorantly to herself, changing in the expression of her face and the tone of her character, as she ministered in the daily wants which sickness brings in a simple household.

For the rest of the neighborhood, the shelves and larder of Mrs. Pennel were constantly crowded with the tributes which one or another sent in for the invalid. There was jelly of Iceland moss sent across by Miss Emily, and brought by Mr. Sewell, whose calls were almost daily. There were custards and preserves, and every form of cake and other confections in which the housekeeping talent of the neighbors delighted, and which were sent in under the old superstition that sick people must be kept eating at all hazards.

At church, Sunday after Sunday, the simple note requested the prayers of the church and congregation for Mara Lincoln, who was, as the note phrased it, drawing near her end, that she and all concerned might be prepared for the great and last change. One familiar with New England customs must have remembered with what a plaintive power the reading of such a note, from Sunday to Sunday, has drawn the thoughts and sympathies of a congregation to some chamber of sickness; and in a village church, where every individual is known from childhood to every other, the power of this simple custom is still greater.

Then the prayers of the minister would dwell on the case, and thanks would be rendered to God for the great light and peace with which he had deigned to visit his young handmaid; and then would follow a prayer that when these sad tidings should reach a distant friend who had gone down to do business on the great waters, they might be sanctified to his spiritual and everlasting good. Then on Sunday noons, as the people ate their dinners together in a room adjoining the church, all that she said and did was talked over and over,—how quickly she had gained the victory of submission, the peace of a will united with God's, mixed with harmless gossip of the sick chamber,—as to what she ate and how she slept, and who had sent her gruel with raisins in it, and who jelly with wine, and how she had praised this and eaten that twice with a relish, but how the other had seemed to disagree with her. Thereafter would come scraps of nursing information, recipes against coughing, specifics against short breath, speculations about watchers, how soon she would need them, and long legends of other deathbeds where the fear of death had been slain by the power of an endless life.

Yet through all the gossip, and through much that might have been called at other times commonplace cant of religion, there was spread a tender earnestness, and the whole air seemed to be enchanted with the fragrance of that fading rose. Each one spoke more gently, more lovingly to each, for the thought of her.

It was now a bright September morning, and the early frosts had changed the maples in the pine-woods to scarlet, and touched the white birches with gold, when one morning Miss Roxy presented herself at an early hour at Captain Kittridge's.

They were at breakfast, and Sally was dispensing the tea at the head of the table, Mrs. Kittridge having been prevailed on to abdicate in her favor.

"It is such a fine morning," she said, looking out at the window, which showed a waveless expanse of ocean. "I do hope Mara has had a good night."

"I'm a-goin' to make her some jelly this very forenoon," said Mrs. Kittridge. "Aunt Roxy was a-tellin' me yesterday that she was a-goin' down to stay at the house regular, for she needed so much done now."

"It's 'most an amazin' thing we don't hear from Moses Pennel," said Captain Kittridge. "If he don't make haste, he may never see her."

"There's Aunt Roxy at this minute," said Sally.

In truth, the door opened at this moment, and Aunt Roxy entered with a little blue bandbox and a bundle tied up in a checked handkerchief.

"Oh, Aunt Roxy," said Mrs. Kittridge, "you are on your way, are you? Do sit down, right here, and get a cup of strong tea."

"Thank you," said Aunt Roxy, "but Ruey gave me a humming cup before I came away."

"Aunt Roxy, have they heard anything from Moses?" said the Captain.

"No, father, I know they haven't," said Sally. "Mara has written to him, and so has Mr. Sewell, but it is very uncertain whether he ever got the letters."

"It's most time to be a-lookin' for him home," said the Captain. "I shouldn't be surprised to see him any day."

At this moment Sally, who sat where she could see from the window, gave a sudden start and a half scream, and rising from the table, darted first to the window and then to the door, whence she rushed out eagerly.

"Well, what now?" said the Captain.

"I am sure I don't know what's come over her," said Mrs. Kittridge, rising to look out.

"Why, Aunt Roxy, do look; I believe to my soul that ar's Moses Pennel!"

And so it was. He met Sally, as she ran out, with a gloomy brow and scarcely a look even of recognition; but he seized her hand and wrung it in the stress of his emotion so that she almost screamed with the pain.

"Tell me, Sally," he said, "tell me the truth. I dared not go home without I knew. Those gossiping, lying reports are always exaggerated. They are dreadful exaggerations,—they frighten a sick person into the grave; but you have good sense and a hopeful, cheerful temper,—you must see and know how things are. Mara is not so very—very"—He held Sally's hand and looked at her with a burning eagerness. "Say, what do you think of her?"

"We all think that we cannot long keep her with us," said Sally. "And oh, Moses, I am so glad you have come."

"It's false,—it must be false," he said, violently; "nothing is more deceptive than these ideas that doctors and nurses pile on when a sensitive person is going down a little. I know Mara; everything depends on the mind with her. I shall wake her up out of this dream. She is not to die. She shall not die,—I come to save her."

"Oh, if you could!" said Sally, mournfully.

CHAPTER XXXIX

"It cannot be; it is not to be," he said again, as if to convince himself. "No such thing is to be thought of. Tell me, Sally, have you tried to keep up the cheerful side of things to her,—have you?"

"Oh, you cannot tell, Moses, how it is, unless you see her. She is cheerful, happy; the only really joyous one among us."

"Cheerful! joyous! happy! She does not believe, then, these frightful things? I thought she would keep up; she is a brave little thing."

"No, Moses, she does believe. She has given up all hope of life,—all wish to live; and oh, she is so lovely,—so sweet,—so dear."

Sally covered her face with her hands and sobbed. Moses stood still, looking at her a moment in a confused way, and then he answered,—

"Come, get your bonnet, Sally, and go with me. You must go in and tell them; tell her that I am come, you know."

"Yes, I will," said Sally, as she ran quickly back to the house.

Moses stood listlessly looking after her. A moment after she came out of the door again, and Miss Roxy behind. Sally hurried up to Moses.

"Where's that black old raven going?" said Moses, in a low voice, looking back on Miss Roxy, who stood on the steps.

"What, Aunt Roxy?" said Sally; "why, she's going up to nurse Mara, and take care of her. Mrs. Pennel is so old and infirm she needs somebody to depend on."

"I can't bear her," said Moses. "I always think of sick-rooms and coffins and a stifling smell of camphor when I see her. I never could endure her. She's an old harpy going to carry off my dove."

"Now, Moses, you must *not* talk so. She loves Mara dearly, the poor old soul, and Mara loves her, and there is no earthly thing she would not do for her. And she knows what to do for sickness better than you or I. I have found out one thing, that it isn't mere love and good-will that is needed in a sick-room; it needs knowledge and experience."

Moses assented in gloomy silence, and they walked on together the way that they had so often taken laughing and chatting. When they came within sight of the house, Moses said,—

"Here she came running to meet us; do you remember?"

"Yes," said Sally.

"I was never half worthy of her. I never said half what I ought to," he added. "She *must* live! I must have one more chance."

When they came up to the house, Zephaniah Pennel was sitting in the door, with his gray head bent over the leaves of the great family Bible.

He rose up at their coming, and with that suppression of all external signs of feeling for which the New Englander is remarkable, simply shook the hand of Moses, saying,—

"Well, my boy, we are glad you have come."

Mrs. Pennel, who was busied in some domestic work in the back part of the kitchen, turned away and hid her face in her apron when she saw him. There fell a great silence among them, in the midst of which the old clock ticked loudly and importunately, like the inevitable approach of fate.

"I will go up and see her, and get her ready," said Sally, in a whisper to Moses. "I'll come and call you."

Moses sat down and looked around on the old familiar scene; there was the great fireplace where, in their childish days, they had sat together winter nights,—her fair, spiritual face enlivened by the blaze, while she knit and looked thoughtfully into the coals; there she had played checkers, or fox and geese, with him; or studied with him the Latin lessons; or sat by, grave and thoughtful, hemming his toyship sails, while he cut the moulds for his anchors, or tried experiments on pulleys; and in all these years he could not remember one selfish action,—one unlovely word,—and he thought to himself, "I hoped to possess this angel as a mortal wife! God forgive my presumption."

CHAPTER XL

THE MEETING

Sally found Mara sitting in an easy-chair that had been sent to her by the provident love of Miss Emily. It was wheeled in front of her room window, from whence she could look out upon the wide expanse of the ocean. It was a gloriously bright, calm morning, and the water lay clear and still, with scarce a ripple, to the far distant pearly horizon. She seemed to be looking at it in a kind of calm ecstasy, and murmuring the words of a hymn:—

"Nor wreck nor ruin there is seen,
There not a wave of trouble rolls,
But the bright rainbow round the throne
Peals endless peace to all their souls."

Sally came softly behind her on tiptoe to kiss her. "Good-morning, dear, how do you find yourself?"

"Quite well," was the answer.

"Mara, is not there anything you want?"

"There might be many things; but His will is mine."

"You want to see Moses?"

"Very much; but I shall see him as soon as it is best for us both."

"Mara,—he is come."

The quick blood flushed over the pale, transparent face as a virgin glacier flushes at sunrise, and she looked up eagerly. "Come!"

"Yes, he is below-stairs wanting to see you."

She seemed about to speak eagerly, and then checked herself and mused a moment. "Poor, poor boy!" she said. "Yes, Sally, let him come at once."

There were a few dazzling, dreamy minutes when Moses first held that frail form in his arms, which but for its tender, mortal warmth, might have seemed to him a spirit. It was no spirit, but a woman whose heart he could feel thrilling against his own; who seemed to him like some frail, fluttering bird; but somehow, as he looked into her clear, transparent face, and pressed her thin little hands in his, the conviction stole over him overpoweringly that she was indeed fading away and going from him,—drawn from him by that mysterious, irresistible power against which human strength, even in the strongest, has no chance.

It is dreadful to a strong man who has felt the influence of his strength,—who has always been ready with a resource for every emergency, and a weapon for every battle,—when first he meets that mighty invisible power by which a beloved life—a life he would give his own blood to save—melts and dissolves like smoke before his eyes.

"Oh, Mara, Mara," he groaned, "this is too dreadful, too cruel; it is cruel."

"You will think so at first, but not always," she said, soothingly. "You will live to see a joy come out of this sorrow."

"Never, Mara, never. I cannot believe that kind of talk. I see no love, no mercy in it. Of course, if there is any life after death you will be happy; if there is a heaven you will be there; but can this dim, unsubstantial, cloudy prospect make you happy in leaving me and giving up one's lover? Oh, Mara, you cannot love as I do, or you could not"—

"Moses, I have suffered,—oh, very, very much. It was many months ago when I first thought that I must give everything up,—when I thought that we must part; but Christ helped me; he showed me his wonderful love,—the love that surrounds us all our life, that follows us in all our wanderings, and sustains us in all our weaknesses,—and then I felt that whatever He wills for us is in love; oh, believe it,—believe it for my sake, for your own."

"Oh, I cannot, I cannot," said Moses; but as he looked at the bright, pale face, and felt how the tempest of his feelings shook the frail form, he checked himself. "I do wrong to agitate you so, Mara. I will try to be calm."

"And to pray?" she said, beseechingly.

He shut his lips in gloomy silence.

"Promise me," she said.

"I have prayed ever since I got your first letter, and I see it does no good," he answered. "Our prayers cannot alter fate."

"Fate! there is no fate," she answered; "there is a strong and loving Father who guides the way, though we know it not. We cannot resist His will; but it is all love,—pure, pure love."

At this moment Sally came softly into the room. A gentle air of womanly authority seemed to express itself in that once gay and giddy face, at which Moses, in the midst of his misery, marveled.

"You must not stay any longer now," she said; "it would be too much for her strength; this is enough for this morning."

Moses turned away, and silently left the room, and Sally said to Mara,—

"You must lie down now, and rest."

"Sally," said Mara, "promise me one thing."

"Well, Mara; of course I will."

"Promise to love him and care for him when I am gone; he will be so lonely."

"I will do all I can, Mara," said Sally, soothingly; "so now you must take a little wine and lie down. You know what you have so often said, that all will yet be well with him."

"Oh, I know it, I am sure," said Mara, "but oh, his sorrow shook my very heart."

"You must not talk another word about it," said Sally, peremptorily, "Do you know Aunt Roxy is coming to see you? I see her out of the window this very moment."

And Sally assisted to lay her friend on the bed, and then, administering a stimulant, she drew down the curtains, and, sitting beside her, began repeating, in a soft monotonous tone, the words of a favorite hymn:—

"The Lord my shepherd is,
 I shall be well supplied;
Since He is mine, and I am His,
 What can I want beside?"

Before she had finished, Mara was asleep.

CHAPTER XLI

CONSOLATION

Moses came down from the chamber of Mara in a tempest of contending emotions. He had all that constitutional horror of death and the spiritual world which is an attribute of some particularly strong and well-endowed physical natures, and he had all that instinctive resistance of the will which such natures offer to anything which strikes athwart their cherished hopes and plans. To be wrenched suddenly from the sphere of an earthly life and made to confront the unclosed doors of a spiritual world on the behalf of the one dearest to him, was to him a dreary horror uncheered by one filial belief in God. He felt, furthermore, that blind animal irritation which assails one under a sudden blow, whether of the body or of the soul,—an anguish of resistance, a vague blind anger.

Mr. Sewell was sitting in the kitchen,—he had called to see Mara, and waited for the close of the interview above. He rose and offered his hand to Moses, who took it in gloomy silence, without a smile or word.

"'My son, despise not thou the chastening of the Lord,'" said Mr. Sewell.

"I cannot bear that sort of thing," said Moses abruptly, and almost fiercely. "I beg your pardon, sir, but it irritates me."

"Do you not believe that afflictions are sent for our improvement?" said Mr. Sewell.

"No! how can I? What improvement will there be to me in taking from me the angel who guided me to all good, and kept me from all evil; the one pure motive and holy influence of my life? If you call this the chastening of a loving father, I must say it looks more to me like the caprice of an evil spirit."

"Had you ever thanked the God of your life for this gift, or felt your dependence on him to keep it? Have you not blindly idolized the creature and forgotten Him who gave it?" said Mr. Sewell.

Moses was silent a moment.

"I cannot believe there is a God," he said. "Since this fear came on me I have prayed,—yes, and humbled myself; for I know I have not always been what I ought. I promised if he would grant me this one thing, I would seek him in future;

but it did no good,—it's of no use to pray. I would have been good in this way, if she might be spared, and I cannot in any other."

"My son, our Lord and Master will have no such conditions from us," said Mr. Sewell. "We must submit unconditionally. *She* has done it, and her peace is as firm as the everlasting hills. God's will is a great current that flows in spite of us; if we go with it, it carries us to endless rest,—if we resist, we only wear our lives out in useless struggles."

Moses stood a moment in silence, and then, turning away without a word, hurried from the house. He strode along the high rocky bluff, through tangled junipers and pine thickets, till he came above the rocky cove which had been his favorite retreat on so many occasions. He swung himself down over the cliffs into the grotto, where, shut in by the high tide, he felt himself alone. There he had read Mr. Sewell's letter, and dreamed vain dreams of wealth and worldly success, now all to him so void. He felt to-day, as he sat there and watched the ships go by, how utterly nothing all the wealth in the world was, in the loss of that one heart. Unconsciously, even to himself, sorrow was doing her ennobling ministry within him, melting off in her fierce fires trivial ambitions and low desires, and making him feel the sole worth and value of love. That which in other days had seemed only as one good thing among many now seemed the *only* thing in life. And he who has learned the paramount value of love has taken one step from an earthly to a spiritual existence.

But as he lay there on the pebbly shore, hour after hour glided by, his whole past life lived itself over to his eye; he saw a thousand actions, he heard a thousand words, whose beauty and significance never came to him till now. And alas! he saw so many when, on his part, the responsive word that should have been spoken, and the deed that should have been done, was forever wanting. He had all his life carried within him a vague consciousness that he had not been to Mara what he should have been, but he had hoped to make amends for all in that future which lay before him,—that future now, alas! dissolving and fading away like the white cloud-islands which the wind was drifting from the sky. A voice seemed saying in his ears, "Ye know that when he would have inherited a blessing he was rejected; for he found no place for repentance, though he sought it carefully with tears." Something that he had never felt before struck him as appalling in the awful fixedness of all past deeds and words,—the unkind words once said, which no tears could unsay,—the kind ones suppressed, to which no agony of wishfulness could give a past reality. There were particular times in their past history that he remembered so vividly, when he saw her so clearly,—doing some little thing for him, and shyly watching for the word of acknowledgment, which he did not give. Some willful wayward demon withheld him at the moment, and the light on the little wishful face slowly faded. True, all had been a thousand times forgiven and forgotten between them, but it is the ministry of these great vital hours of sorrow to teach us that nothing in the soul's history ever dies or is forgotten, and when the beloved one lies stricken and ready to pass away, comes the judgment-day of love, and all the dead moments of the past arise and live again.

He lay there musing and dreaming till the sun grew low in the afternoon sky, and the tide that isolated the little grotto had gone far out into the ocean, leaving long, low reefs of sunken rocks, all matted and tangled with the yellow hair of the seaweed, with little crystal pools of salt water between. He heard the sound of approaching footsteps, and Captain Kittridge came slowly picking his way round among the shingle and pebbles.

"Wal', now, I thought I'd find ye here!" he said: "I kind o' thought I wanted to see ye,—ye see."

Moses looked up half moody, half astonished, while the Captain seated himself upon a fragment of rock and began brushing the knees of his trousers industriously, until soon the tears rained down from his eyes upon his dry withered hands.

"Wal', now ye see, I can't help it, darned if I can; knowed her ever since she's that high. She's done me good, she has. Mis' Kittridge has been pretty faithful. I've had folks here and there talk to me consid'able, but Lord bless you, I never had nothin' go to my heart like this 'ere—Why to look on her there couldn't nobody doubt but what there was somethin' in religion. You never knew half what she did for you, Moses Pennel, you didn't know that the night you was off down to the long cove with Skipper Atkinson, that 'ere blessed child was a-follerin' you, but she was, and she come to me next day to get me to do somethin' for you. That was how your grand'ther and I got ye off to sea so quick, and she such a little thing then; that ar child was the savin' of ye, Moses Pennel."

Moses hid his head in his hands with a sort of groan.

"Wal', wal'," said the Captain, "I don't wonder now ye feel so,—I don't see how ye can stan' it no ways—only by thinkin' o' where she's goin' to—Them ar bells in the Celestial City must all be a-ringin' for her,—there'll be joy that side o' the river I reckon, when she gets acrost. If she'd jest leave me a hem o' her garment to get in by, I'd be glad; but she was one o' the sort that was jest *made* to go to heaven. She only stopped a few days in our world, like the robins when they's goin' south; but there'll be a good many fust and last that'll get into the kingdom for love of her. She never said much to me, but she kind o' drew me. Ef ever I should get in there, it'll be *she* led me. But come, now, Moses, ye oughtn't fur to be a-settin' here catchin' cold—jest come round to our house and let Sally gin you a warm cup o' tea—do come, now."

"Thank you, Captain," said Moses, "but I will go home; I must see her again to-night."

"Wal', don't let her see you grieve too much, ye know; we must be a little sort o' manly, ye know, 'cause her body's weak, if her heart is strong."

Now Moses was in a mood of dry, proud, fierce, self-consuming sorrow, least likely to open his heart or seek sympathy from any one; and no friend or acquaintance would probably have dared to intrude on his grief. But there are moods of the mind which cannot be touched or handled by one on an equal level with us that yield at once to the sympathy of something below. A dog who comes with his great honest, sorrowful face and lays his mute paw of inquiry on your knee, will sometimes open floodgates of sober feeling, that have remained closed to every human touch;—the dumb simplicity and ignorance of his sympathy makes it irresistible. In like manner the downright grief of the good-natured old Captain, and the child-like ignorance with which he ventured upon a ministry of consolation from which a more cultivated person would have shrunk away, were irresistibly touching. Moses grasped the dry, withered hand and said, "Thank you, thank you, Captain Kittridge; you're a true friend."

"Wal', I be, that's a fact, Moses. Lord bless me, I ain't no great—I ain't nobody—I'm jest an old last-year's mullein-stalk in the Lord's vineyard; but that 'ere blessed little thing allers had a good word for me. She gave me a hymn-book and marked some hymns in it, and read 'em to me herself, and her voice was jest as sweet as the sea of a warm evening. Them hymns come to me kind o' powerful when I'm at my work planin' and sawin'. Mis' Kittridge, she allers talks to me as ef I was a terrible sinner; and I suppose I be, but this 'ere blessed child, she's so kind o' good and innocent, she thinks I'm good; kind o' takes it for granted I'm one o' the Lord's people, ye know. It kind o' makes me want to be, ye know."

The Captain here produced from his coat-pocket a much worn hymn-book, and showed Moses where leaves were folded down. "Now here's this 'ere," he said; "you get her to say it to you," he added, pointing to the well-known sacred idyl which has refreshed so many hearts:—

"There is a land of pure delight
Where saints immortal reign;
Eternal day excludes the night,
And pleasures banish pain.
"There everlasting spring abides,
And never-fading flowers;
Death like a narrow sea divides
This happy land from ours."

"Now that ar beats everything," said the Captain, "and we must kind o' think of it for her, 'cause she's goin' to see all that, and ef it's our loss it's her gain, ye know."

"I know," said Moses; "our grief is selfish."

"Jest so. Wal', we're selfish critters, we be," said the Captain; "but arter all, 't ain't as ef we was heathen and didn't know where they was a-goin' to. We jest ought to be a-lookin' about and tryin' to foller 'em, ye know."

"Yes, yes, I do know," said Moses; "it's easy to say, but hard to do."

"But law, man, she prays for you; she did years and years ago, when you was a boy and she a girl. You know it tells in the Revelations how the angels has golden vials full of odors which are the prayers of saints. I tell ye Moses, you ought to get into heaven, if no one else does. I expect you are pretty well known among the angels by this time. I tell ye what 'tis, Moses, fellers think it a mighty pretty thing to be a-steppin' high, and a-sayin' they don't believe the Bible, and all that ar, so long as the world goes well. This 'ere old Bible—why it's jest like yer mother,—ye rove and ramble, and cut up round the world without her a spell, and mebbe think the old woman ain't so fashionable as some; but when sickness and sorrow comes, why, there ain't nothin' else to go back to. Is there, now?"

Moses did not answer, but he shook the hand of the Captain and turned away.

CHAPTER XLII

LAST WORDS

The setting sun gleamed in at the window of Mara's chamber, tinted with rose and violet hues from a great cloud-castle that lay upon the smooth ocean over against the window. Mara was lying upon the bed, but she raised herself upon her elbow to look out.

"Dear Aunt Roxy," she said, "raise me up and put the pillows behind me, so that I can see out—it is splendid."

Aunt Roxy came and arranged the pillows, and lifted the girl with her long, strong arms, then stooping over her a moment she finished her arrangements by softly smoothing the hair from her forehead with a caressing movement most unlike her usual precise business-like proceedings.

"I love you, Aunt Roxy," said Mara, looking up with a smile.

Aunt Roxy made a strange wry face, which caused her to look harder than usual. She was choked with tenderness, and had only this uncomely way of showing it.

"Law now, Mara, I don't see how ye can; I ain't nothin' but an old burdock-bush; love ain't for me."

"Yes it is too," said Mara, drawing her down and kissing her withered cheek, "and you sha'n't call yourself an old burdock. God sees that you are beautiful, and in the resurrection everybody will see it."

"I was always homely as an owl," said Miss Roxy, unconsciously speaking out what had lain like a stone at the bottom of even her sensible heart. "I always had sense to know it, and knew my sphere. Homely folks would like to say pretty things, and to have pretty things said to them, but they never do. I made up my mind pretty early that my part in the vineyard was to have hard work and no posies."

"Well, you will have all the more in heaven; I love you dearly, and I like your looks, too. You look kind and true and good, and that's beauty in the country where we are going."

Miss Roxy sprang up quickly from the bed, and turning her back began to arrange the bottles on the table with great zeal.

"Has Moses come in yet?" said Mara.

"No, there ain't nobody seen a thing of him since he went out this morning."

"Poor boy!" said Mara, "it is too hard upon him. Aunt Roxy, please pick some roses off the bush from under the window and put in the vases; let's have the room as sweet and cheerful as we can. I hope God will let me live long enough to comfort him. It is not so very terrible, if one would only think so, to cross that river. All looks so bright to me now that I have forgotten how sorrow seemed. Poor Moses! he will have a hard struggle, but he will get the victory, too. I am very weak to-night, but to-morrow I shall feel better, and I shall sit up, and perhaps I can paint a little on that flower I was doing for him. We will not have things look sickly or deathly. There, Aunt Roxy, he has come in; I hear his step."

"I didn't hear it," said Miss Roxy, surprised at the acute senses which sickness had etherealized to an almost spirit-like intensity. "Shall I call him?"

"Yes, do," said Mara. "He can sit with me a little while to-night."

The light in the room was a strange dusky mingling of gold and gloom, when Moses stole softly in. The great cloud-castle that a little while since had glowed like living gold from turret and battlement, now dim, changed for the most part to a sombre gray, enlivened with a dull glow of crimson; but there was still a golden light where the sun had sunk into the sea. Moses saw the little thin hand stretched out to him.

"Sit down," she said; "it has been such a beautiful sunset. Did you notice it?"

He sat down by the bed, leaning his forehead on his hand, but saying nothing.

She drew her fingers through his dark hair. "I am so glad to see you," she said. "It is such a comfort to me that you have come; and I hope it will be to you. You know I shall be better to-morrow than I am to-night, and I hope we shall have some pleasant days together yet. We mustn't reject what little we may have, because it cannot be more."

"Oh, Mara," said Moses, "I would give my life, if I could take back the past. I have never been worthy of you; never knew your worth; never made you happy. You always lived for me, and I lived for myself. I deserve to lose you, but it is none the less bitter."

"Don't say lose. Why must you? I cannot think of losing you. I know I shall not. God has given you to me. You will come to me and be mine at last. I feel sure of it."

"You don't know me," said Moses.

"Christ does, though," she said; "and He has promised to care for you. Yes, you will live to see many flowers grow out of my grave. You cannot think so now; but it will be so—believe me."

"Mara," said Moses, "I never lived through such a day as this. It seems as if every moment of my life had been passing before me, and every moment of yours. I have seen how true and loving in thought and word and deed you have been, and I have been doing nothing but take. You have given love as the skies give rain, and I have drunk it up like the hot dusty earth."

CHAPTER XLII

Mara knew in her own heart that this was all true, and she was too real to use any of the terms of affected humiliation which many think a kind of spiritual court language. She looked at him and answered, "Moses, I always knew I loved most. It was my nature; God gave it to me, and it was a gift for which I give him thanks—not a merit. I knew you had a larger, wider nature than mine,—a wider sphere to live in, and that you could not live in your heart as I did. Mine was all thought and feeling, and the narrow little duties of this little home. Yours went all round the world."

"But, oh Mara—oh, my angel! to think I should lose you when I am just beginning to know your worth. I always had a sort of superstitious feeling,—a sacred presentiment about you,—that my spiritual life, if ever I had any, would come through you. It seemed if there ever was such a thing as God's providence, which some folks believe in, it was in leading me to you, and giving you to me. And now, to have all lashed—all destroyed—It makes me feel as if all was blind chance; no guiding God; for if he wanted me to be good, he would spare you."

Mara lay with her large eyes fixed on the now faded sky. The dusky shadows had dropped like a black crape veil around her pale face. In a few moments she repeated to herself, as if she were musing upon them, those mysterious words of Him who liveth and was dead, "Except a corn of wheat fall into the ground and die, it abideth alone; if it die, it bringeth forth much fruit."

"Moses," she said, "for all I know you have loved me dearly, yet I have felt that in all that was deepest and dearest to me, I was alone. You did not come near to me, nor touch me where I feel most deeply. If I had lived to be your wife, I cannot say but this distance in our spiritual nature might have widened. You know, what we live with we get used to; it grows an old story. Your love to me might have grown old and worn out. If we lived together in the commonplace toils of life, you would see only a poor threadbare wife. I might have lost what little charm I ever had for you; but I feel that if I die, this will not be. There is something sacred and beautiful in death; and I may have more power over you, when I seem to be gone, than I should have had living."

"Oh, Mara, Mara, don't say that."

"Dear Moses, it is so. Think how many lovers marry, and how few lovers are left in middle life; and how few love and reverence living friends as they do the dead. There are only a very few to whom it is given to do that."

Something in the heart of Moses told him that this was true. In this one day—the sacred revealing light of approaching death—he had seen more of the real spiritual beauty and significance of Mara's life than in years before, and felt upspringing in his heart, from the deep pathetic influence of the approaching spiritual world a new and stronger power of loving. It may be that it is not merely a perception of love that we were not aware of before, that wakes up when we approach the solemn shadows with a friend. It may be that the soul has compressed and unconscious powers which are stirred and wrought upon as it looks over the borders into its future home,—its loves and its longings so swell and beat, that they astonish itself. We are greater than we know, and dimly feel it with every approach to the great hereafter. "It doth not yet appear what we shall be."

"Now, I'll tell you what 'tis," said Aunt Roxy, opening the door, "all the strength this 'ere girl spends a-talkin' to-night, will be so much taken out o' the whole cloth to-morrow."

Moses started up. "I ought to have thought of that, Mara."

"Ye see," said Miss Roxy, "she's been through a good deal to-day, and she must be got to sleep at some rate or other to-night. 'Lord, if he sleep he shall do well,' the Bible says, and it's one of my best nussin' maxims."

"And a good one, too, Aunt Roxy," said Mara. "Good-night, dear boy; you see we must all mind Aunt Roxy."

Moses bent down and kissed her, and felt her arms around his neck.

"Let not your heart be troubled," she whispered. In spite of himself Moses felt the storm that had risen in his bosom that morning soothed by the gentle influences which Mara breathed upon it. There is a sympathetic power in all states of mind, and they who have reached the deep secret of eternal rest have a strange power of imparting calm to others.

It was in the very crisis of the battle that Christ said to his disciples, "*My peace I give unto you*," and they that are made one with him acquire like precious power of shedding round them repose, as evening flowers shed odors. Moses went to his pillow sorrowful and heart-stricken, but bitter or despairing he could not be with the consciousness of that present angel in the house.

CHAPTER XLIII

THE PEARL

The next morning rose calm and bright with that wonderful and mystical stillness and serenity which glorify autumn days. It was impossible that such skies could smile and such gentle airs blow the sea into one great waving floor of sparkling sapphires without bringing cheerfulness to human hearts. You must be very despairing indeed, when Nature is doing her best, to look her in the face sullen and defiant. So long as there is a drop of good in your cup, a penny in your exchequer of happiness, a bright day reminds you to look at it, and feel that all is not gone yet.

So felt Moses when he stood in the door of the brown house, while Mrs. Pennel was clinking plates and spoons as she set the breakfast-table, and Zephaniah Pennel in his shirt-sleeves was washing in the back-room, while Miss Roxy came downstairs in a business-like fashion, bringing sundry bowls, plates, dishes, and mysterious pitchers from the sick-room.

"Well, Aunt Roxy, you ain't one that lets the grass grow under your feet," said Mrs. Pennel. "How is the dear child, this morning?"

"Well, she had a better night than one could have expected," said Miss Roxy, "and by the time she's had her breakfast, she expects to sit up a little and see her friends." Miss Roxy said this in a cheerful tone, looking encouragingly at Moses, whom she began to pity and patronize, now she saw how real was his affliction.

After breakfast Moses went to see her; she was sitting up in her white dressing-gown, looking so thin and poorly, and everything in the room was fragrant with the spicy smell of the monthly roses, whose late buds and blossoms Miss Roxy had gathered for the vases. She seemed so natural, so calm and cheerful, so interested in all that went on around her, that one almost forgot that the time of her stay must be so short. She called Moses to come and look at her drawings, and paintings of flowers and birds,—full of reminders they were of old times,—and then she would have her pencils and colors, and work a little on a bunch of red rock-columbine, that she had begun to do for him; and she chatted of all the old familiar places where flowers grew, and of the old talks they had had there, till Moses quite forgot himself; forgot that he was in a sick room, till Aunt Roxy, warned by the deepening color on Mara's cheeks, interposed her "nussing" authority, that she must do no more that day.

Then Moses laid her down, and arranged her pillows so that she could look out on the sea, and sat and read to her till it was time for her afternoon nap; and when the evening shadows drew on, he marveled with himself how the day had gone.

Many such there were, all that pleasant month of September, and he was with her all the time, watching her wants and doing her bidding,—reading over and over with a softened modulation her favorite hymns and chapters, arranging her flowers, and bringing her home wild bouquets from all her favorite wood-haunts, which made her sick-room seem like some sylvan bower. Sally Kittridge was there too, almost every day, with always some friendly offering or some helpful deed of kindness, and sometimes they two together would keep guard over the invalid while Miss Roxy went home to attend to some of her own more peculiar concerns. Mara seemed to rule all around her with calm sweetness and wisdom, speaking unconsciously only the speech of heaven, talking of spiritual things, not in an excited rapture or wild ecstasy, but with the sober certainty of waking bliss. She seemed like one of the sweet friendly angels one reads of in the Old Testament, so lovingly companionable, walking and talking, eating and drinking, with mortals, yet ready at any unknown moment to ascend with the flame of some sacrifice and be gone. There are those (a few at least) whose blessing it has been to have kept for many days, in bonds of earthly fellowship, a perfected spirit in whom the work of purifying love was wholly done, who lived in calm victory over sin and sorrow and death, ready at any moment to be called to the final mystery of joy.

Yet it must come at last, the moment when heaven claims its own, and it came at last in the cottage on Orr's Island. There came a day when the room so sacredly cheerful was hushed to a breathless stillness; the bed was then all snowy white, and that soft still sealed face, the parted waves of golden hair, the little hands folded over the white robe, all had a sacred and wonderful calm, a rapture of repose that seemed to say "it is done."

They who looked on her wondered; it was a look that sunk deep into every heart; it hushed down the common cant of those who, according to country custom, went to stare blindly at the great mystery of death,—for all that came out of that chamber smote upon their breasts and went away in silence, revolving strangely whence might come that unearthly beauty, that celestial joy.

Once more, in that very room where James and Naomi Lincoln had lain side by side in their coffins, sleeping restfully, there was laid another form, shrouded and coffined, but with such a fairness and tender purity, such a mysterious fullness of joy in its expression, that it seemed more natural to speak of that rest as some higher form of life than of death.

Once more were gathered the neighborhood; all the faces known in this history shone out in one solemn picture, of which that sweet restful form was the centre. Zephaniah Pennel and Mary his wife, Moses and Sally, the dry form of Captain Kittridge and the solemn face of his wife, Aunt Roxy and Aunt Ruey, Miss Emily and Mr. Sewell; but their faces all wore a tender brightness, such as we see falling like a thin celestial veil over all the faces in an old Florentine painting. The room was full of sweet memories, of words of cheer, words of assurance, words of triumph, and the mysterious brightness of that young face forbade them to weep. Solemnly Mr. Sewell read,—

"He will swallow up death in victory; and the Lord God will wipe away tears from off all faces; and the rebuke of his people shall he take away from off all the earth; for the Lord hath spoken it. And it shall be said in that day, Lo this is our God; we have waited for him, and he will save us; this is the Lord; we have waited for him, we will be glad and rejoice in his salvation."

Then the prayer trembled up to heaven with thanksgiving, for the early entrance of that fair young saint into glory, and then the same old funeral hymn, with its mournful triumph:—

"Why should we mourn departed friends,
Or shake at death's alarms,
'Tis but the voice that Jesus sends
To call them to his arms."

Then in a few words Mr. Sewell reminded them how that hymn had been sung in this room so many years ago, when that frail, fluttering orphan soul had been baptized into the love and care of Jesus, and how her whole life, passing before them in its simplicity and beauty, had come to so holy and beautiful a close; and when, pointing to the calm sleeping face he asked, "Would we call her back?" there was not a heart at that moment that dared answer, Yes. Even he that should have been her bridegroom could not at that moment have unsealed the holy charm, and so they bore her away, and laid the calm smiling face beneath the soil, by the side of poor Dolores.

"I had a beautiful dream last night," said Zephaniah Pennel, the next morning after the funeral, as he opened his Bible to conduct family worship.

"What was it?" said Miss Roxy.

"Well, ye see, I thought I was out a-walkin' up and down, and lookin' and lookin' for something that I'd lost. What it was I couldn't quite make out, but my heart felt heavy as if it would break, and I was lookin' all up and down the sands by the seashore, and somebody said I was like the merchantman, seeking goodly pearls. I said I had lost my pearl—my pearl of great price—and then I looked up, and far off on the beach, shining softly on the wet sands, lay my pearl. I thought it was Mara, but it seemed a great pearl with a soft moonlight on it; and I was running for it when some one said 'hush,' and I looked and I saw *Him* a-coming—Jesus of Nazareth, jist as he walked by the sea of Galilee. It was all dark night around Him, but I could see Him by the light that came from his face, and the long hair was hanging down on his shoulders. He came and took up my pearl and put it on his forehead, and it shone out like a star, and shone into my heart, and I felt happy; and he looked at me steadily, and rose and rose in the air, and melted in the clouds, and I awoke so happy, and so calm!"

CHAPTER XLIV

FOUR YEARS AFTER

It was a splendid evening in July, and the sky was filled high with gorgeous tabernacles of purple and gold, the remains of a grand thunder-shower which had freshened the air and set a separate jewel on every needle leaf of the old pines.

Four years had passed since the fair Pearl of Orr's Island had been laid beneath the gentle soil, which every year sent monthly tributes of flowers to adorn her rest, great blue violets, and starry flocks of ethereal eye-brights in spring, and fringy asters, and goldenrod in autumn. In those days, the tender sentiment which now makes the burial-place a cultivated garden was excluded by the rigid spiritualism of the Puritan life, which, ever jealous of that which concerned the body, lest it should claim what belonged to the immortal alone, had frowned on all watching of graves, as an earthward tendency, and enjoined the flight of faith with the spirit, rather than the yearning for its cast-off garments.

But Sally Kittridge, being lonely, found something in her heart which could only be comforted by visits to that grave. So she had planted there roses and trailing myrtle, and tended and watered them; a proceeding which was much commented on Sunday noons, when people were eating their dinners and discussing their neighbors.

It is possible good Mrs. Kittridge might have been much scandalized by it, had she been in a condition to think on the matter at all; but a very short time after the funeral she was seized with a paralytic shock, which left her for a while as helpless as an infant; and then she sank away into the grave, leaving Sally the sole care of the old Captain.

A cheerful home she made, too, for his old age, adorning the house with many little tasteful fancies unknown in her mother's days; reading the Bible to him and singing Mara's favorite hymns, with a voice as sweet as the spring blue-bird. The spirit of the departed friend seemed to hallow the dwelling where these two worshiped her memory, in simple-hearted love. Her paintings, framed in quaint woodland frames of moss and pine-cones by Sally's own ingenuity, adorned the walls. Her books were on the table, and among them many that she had given to Moses.

"I am going to be a wanderer for many years," he said in parting, "keep these for me until I come back."

And so from time to time passed long letters between the two friends,—each telling to the other the same story,—that they were lonely, and that their hearts yearned for the communion of one who could no longer be manifest to the senses. And each spoke to the other of a world of hopes and memories buried with her, "Which," each so constantly said, "no one could understand but you." Each, too, was firm in the faith that buried love must have no earthly resurrection. Every letter strenuously insisted that they should call each other brother and sister, and under cover of those names the letters grew longer and more frequent, and with every chance opportunity came presents from the absent brother, which made the little old cottage quaintly suggestive with smell of spice and sandal-wood.

But, as we said, this is a glorious July evening,—and you may discern two figures picking their way over those low sunken rocks, yellowed with seaweed, of which we have often spoken. They are Moses and Sally going on an evening walk to that favorite grotto retreat, which has so often been spoken of in the course of this history.

Moses has come home from long wanderings. It is four years since they parted, and now they meet and have looked into each other's eyes, not as of old, when they met in the first giddy flush of youth, but as fully developed man and woman. Moses and Sally had just risen from the tea-table, where she had presided with a thoughtful housewifery gravity, just pleasantly dashed with quaint streaks of her old merry willfulness, while the old Captain, warmed up like a rheumatic grasshopper in a fine autumn day, chirruped feebly, and told some of his old stories, which now he told every day, forgetting that they had ever been heard before. Somehow all three had been very happy; the more so, from a shadowy sense of some sympathizing presence which was rejoicing to see them together again, and which, stealing soft-footed and noiseless everywhere, touched and lighted up every old familiar object with sweet memories.

And so they had gone out together to walk; to walk towards the grotto where Sally had caused a seat to be made, and where she declared she had passed hours and hours, knitting, sewing, or reading.

"Sally," said Moses, "do you know I am tired of wandering? I am coming home now. I begin to want a home of my own." This he said as they sat together on the rustic seat and looked off on the blue sea.

"Yes, you must," said Sally. "How lovely that ship looks, just coming in there."

"Yes, they are beautiful," said Moses abstractedly; and Sally rattled on about the difference between sloops and brigs; seeming determined that there should be no silence, such as often comes in ominous gaps between two friends who have long been separated, and have each many things to say with which the other is not familiar.

"Sally!" said Moses, breaking in with a deep voice on one of these monologues. "Do you remember some presumptuous things I once said to you, in this place?"

Sally did not answer, and there was a dead silence in which they could hear the tide gently dashing on the weedy rocks.

"You and I are neither of us what we were then, Sally," said Moses. "We are as different as if we were each another person. We have been trained in another life,—educated by a great sorrow,—is it not so?"

"I know it," said Sally.

"And why should we two, who have a world of thoughts and memories which no one can understand but the other,—why should we, each of us, go on alone? If we must, why then, Sally, I must leave you, and I must write and receive no more letters, for I have found that you are becoming so wholly necessary to me, that if any other should claim you, I could not feel as I ought. Must I go?"

Sally's answer is not on record; but one infers what it was from the fact that they sat there very late, and before they knew it, the tide rose up and shut them in, and the moon rose up in full glory out of the water, and still they sat and talked, leaning on each other, till a cracked, feeble voice called down through the pine-trees above, like a hoarse old cricket,—

"Children, be you there?"

"Yes, father," said Sally, blushing and conscious.

"Yes, all right," said the deep bass of Moses. "I'll bring her back when I've done with her, Captain."

"Wal',—wal'; I was gettin' consarned; but I see I don't need to. I hope you won't get no colds nor nothin'."

They did not; but in the course of a month there was a wedding at the brown house of the old Captain, which everybody in the parish was glad of, and was voted without dissent to be just the thing.

Miss Roxy, grimly approbative, presided over the preparations, and all the characters of our story appeared, and more, having on their wedding-garments. Nor was the wedding less joyful, that all felt the presence of a heavenly guest, silent and loving, seeing and blessing all, whose voice seemed to say in every heart,—

"He turneth the shadow of death into morning."

The Barsetshire Chronicles, Volume One, Including: The Warden, Barchester Towers, Doctor Thorne and Framley Parsonage
Anthony
Benediction Classics, 2013
1162 pages
ISBN: 978-1-78139-405-2

Available from www.amazon.com, www.amazon.co.uk

Anthony Trollope (1815 - 1882) was one of the most popular, productive and esteemed English novelists of the Victorian era. His best-loved works are the Chronicles of Barsetshire, which revolve around the imaginary county of Barsetshire. The novels focus on the dealings of the clergy and the gentry, and the political, romantic and social intrigues that go on among and between them. Enjoy these wry chronicles.

The Barsetshire Chronicles, Volume Two, Including: The Small House at Allington and the Last Chronicle of Barset
Anthony Trollope
Benediction Classics, 2013
1182 pages
ISBN: 978-1-78139-406-9

Available from www.amazon.com, www.amazon.co.uk

Anthony Trollope (1815 - 1882) was one of the most popular, productive and esteemed English novelists of the Victorian era. His best-loved works are the Chronicles of Barsetshire, which revolve around the imaginary county of Barsetshire. The novels focus on the dealings of the clergy and the gentry, and the political, romantic and social intrigues that go on among and between them. Enjoy these wry chronicles.

The novels in the series are:

The Warden (1855)
Barchester Towers (1857)
Doctor Thorne (1858)
Framley Parsonage (1861)
The Small House at Allington (1864)
The Last Chronicle of Barset (1867)

Five Novels by Thomas Hardy - Far From The Madding Crowd, The Return of the Native, The Mayor of Casterbridge, Tess of the d'Urbervilles, Jude the Obscure (complete and unabridged)
Thomas Hardy
Benediction Classics, 2013
1114 pages
ISBN: 978-1-78139-356-7

Available from www.amazon.com, www.amazon.co.uk

Thomas Hardy, (1840 - 1928) was an English novelist and poet. He was highly critical of Victorian society and focussed mainly on the declining rural communities.

Agatha Christie - Early Novels, The Mysterious Affair at Styles and Secret Adversary
Agatha Christie
Oxford City Press, 2012
392 pages
ISBN: 978-1-78139-292-8

Available from www.amazon.com, www.amazon.co.uk

These novels show Agatha Christie's detective writing genius began with her first Novel. The reviews of "The Mysterious Affair at Styles" at the time said this: The Times Literary Supplement of February 3, 1921 stated: "The only fault this story has is that it is almost too ingenious.... It is said to be the author's first book, and the result of a bet about the possibility of writing a detective story in which the reader would not be able to spot the criminal. Every reader must admit that the bet was won." And the reviews of "Secret Adversary" were equally enthusiastic. Enjoy these 1920 classics that are as compelling today as they were when they were written.

Also from Benediction Books ...

Wandering Between Two Worlds: Essays on Faith and Art
Anita Mathias
Benediction Books, 2007
152 pages
ISBN: 0955373700

Available from www.amazon.com, www.amazon.co.uk

In these wide-ranging lyrical essays, Anita Mathias writes, in lush, lovely prose, of her naughty Catholic childhood in Jamshedpur, India; her large, eccentric family in Mangalore, a sea-coast town converted by the Portuguese in the sixteenth century; her rebellion and atheism as a teenager in her Himalayan boarding school, run by German missionary nuns, St. Mary's Convent, Nainital; and her abrupt religious conversion after which she entered Mother Teresa's convent in Calcutta as a novice. Later rich, elegant essays explore the dualities of her life as a writer, mother, and Christian in the United States-- Domesticity and Art, Writing and Prayer, and the experience of being "an alien and stranger" as an immigrant in America, sensing the need for roots.

About the Author

Anita Mathias is the author of *Wandering Between Two Worlds: Essays on Faith and Art*. She has a B.A. and M.A. in English from Somerville College, Oxford University, and an M.A. in Creative Writing from the Ohio State University, USA. Anita won a National Endowment of the Arts fellowship in Creative Non-fiction in 1997. She lives in Oxford, England with her husband, Roy, and her daughters, Zoe and Irene.

Anita's website:
  http://www.anitamathias.com, and
Anita's blog Dreaming Beneath the Spires:
  http://dreamingbeneaththespires.blogspot.com

The Church That Had Too Much
Anita Mathias
Benediction Books, 2010
52 pages
ISBN: 9781849026567

Available from www.amazon.com, www.amazon.co.uk

The Church That Had Too Much was very well-intentioned. She wanted to love God, she wanted to love people, but she was both hampered by her muchness and the abundance of her possessions, and beset by ambition, power struggles and snobbery. Read about the surprising way The Church That Had Too Much began to resolve her problems in this deceptively simple and enchanting fable.

About the Author

Anita Mathias is the author of *Wandering Between Two Worlds: Essays on Faith and Art*. She has a B.A. and M.A. in English from Somerville College, Oxford University, and an M.A. in Creative Writing from the Ohio State University, USA. Anita won a National Endowment of the Arts fellowship in Creative Non-fiction in 1997. She lives in Oxford, England with her husband, Roy, and her daughters, Zoe and Irene.

Anita's website:
    http://www.anitamathias.com, and
Anita's blog Dreaming Beneath the Spires:
    http://dreamingbeneaththespires.blogspot.com

www.ingramcontent.com/pod-product-compliance
Lightning Source LLC
Chambersburg PA
CBHW081130300726
48982CB00005B/911

* 9 7 8 1 7 8 1 3 9 5 2 9 5 *